SURVIVE
(The Atlantis Grail, Book Four)

Vera Nazarian

ISBN-13: 978-1-60762-161-4
ISBN-10: 1-60762-161-4

Trade Paperback Edition

January 3, 2020

A Publication of
Norilana Books
P. O. Box 209
Highgate Center, VT 05459-0209
www.norilana.com

Printed in the United States of America

Survive

The Atlantis Grail: Book Four

Norilana Books
Science Fiction

www.norilana.com

Other Books by Vera Nazarian

Lords of Rainbow
Dreams of the Compass Rose
Salt of the Air
The Perpetual Calendar of Inspiration
The Clock King and the Queen of the Hourglass
Mayhem at Grant-Williams High (YA)
The Duke in His Castle
After the Sundial
Mansfield Park and Mummies
Northanger Abbey and Angels and Dragons
Pride and Platypus: Mr. Darcy's Dreadful Secret
Vampires are from Venus, Werewolves are from Mars:
A Comprehensive Guide to Attracting Supernatural Love

Cobweb Bride Trilogy:
Cobweb Bride
Cobweb Empire
Cobweb Forest

The Atlantis Grail:
Qualify (Book One)
Compete (Book Two)
Win (Book Three)
Survive (Book Four)

(Forthcoming)

The Atlantis Grail:
Dawn of the Atlantis Grail (Prequel Series)
Various Novellas

Pagan Persuasion: All Olympus Descends on Regency

Dedication

To all my Readers!
You make the story come alive.

SURVIVE

THE ATLANTIS GRAIL
Book Four

VERA NAZARIAN

Chapter 1

August, 2048 / Green Mar-Yan, 9771.

Today is the day everything changes.
What have I done?

I *won.*

I used my Logos power voice to raise the Atlantis Grail monument but instead I blasted open an ancient, buried secret.

And now I stand in the largest arena in the City of Poseidon, amid the stadium wreckage that I've caused, held in the arms of my beloved Aeson, while the nose section of an ancient starship juts forth from the broken ground. . . .

The shocked spectator crowds have grown momentarily quiet. They're full of confusion, still under the influence of the Imperial *compelling* voice. . . .

I, on the other hand, have not been compelled. But I have been stopped and silenced—by the enormity of the consequences of my actions.

The stunning things that Aeson Kassiopei, my Imperial Bridegroom, has just told me are ringing violently in my head. Unbelievable, impossible things implicating his Father, the Imperator, my future father-in-law, in a dark plot—an intricate scheme presumably to prevent an alien invasion (although the grim details and causes have yet to be unraveled) that includes Aeson's father sending the deadly asteroid on a collision course to destroy Earth a few months from now. . . .

The Imperator is *responsible* for so much.

But then, so am *I.*

Because of my actions, the ancient ark-ship that had been lying dormant for thousands of years, buried underground, has been activated somehow, and now *they* will come—they, the mysterious ancient alien enemy of both Earth and Atlantis.

After all that's happened today and over the past four weeks—the violent insanity of the Games, the relentless uncertainty of my every living moment—this knowledge comes as a heavy blow. I feel as if I've been punched in the gut.

"My God . . . I've caused all this," I continue to whisper even as Aeson tightens his embrace and stares into my eyes with loving force. "I caused this. . . . If, as you say, they can track this ship, they will come because of what I did!"

"Let them come!" he repeats fiercely, a hard smile on his lips. "Together we'll handle them, *im amrevu!* Look at me! Do you hear?"

"Yes." I nod, but the word comes out without conviction.

I glance yet again in the direction of the Imperial Box among the audience tiers, where Romhutat Kassiopei, the Archaeon Imperator of *Atlantida*, stands looking at me like a dragon.

Our gazes meet.

Or maybe he just never stopped watching me. . . .

"Gwen!" Aeson's strong fingers dig into my shoulders, anchoring me, forcing me to turn back to *him*. "It's over. We must go!"

I part my lips just to say something, not even sure what, because I'm trapped in the bizarre moment that somehow must not end . . . because whatever comes next will be *impossible*.

What have I done?

The Priest of the Grail called it blasphemy. . . .

What does it mean? What happens now?

I glance behind me at the dais in the center of the arena where the other Champions and runners-up remain standing before the judges. . . . Hedj, Kateb, Brie, Kokayi, Leetana, Rurim, Ukou—all in brightly lit uniforms that indicate Champion status. . . . Chihar, Lolu, and two others—their fates as Champions or runners-up are as yet unresolved. . . . Finally, Sofia and Fawzi, my two direct competitors in the Vocalist Category, who lost by virtue of the fact that I won.

They're all staring at me with shock and fear and other hard-to-describe, complicated expressions. Brie Walton in particular has a stunned look on her face. And the Vocalist judge, the stern woman who assigned our Category tiebreaker task—she is frozen with incredulity as she too fixes her attention on me. . . .

What must they all think? And what about the thousands of people in the audience who have just witnessed an impossible miracle, followed by a disaster, all of it perpetrated by me?

Do they even *understand* what's visible in the wreckage around us? The *grail* is but a tiny fraction of the upper end of an immense object that's still mostly below ground. . . .

In that moment, the Imperator's voice sounds again, breaking me out of my stupefied reverie and adding a level of nervous frenzy to my already racing thoughts.

This time he is not using a *compelling* power voice, merely ordinary stadium amplification, as he speaks with regained composure. But even unenhanced, the deep, ice-cold sound of his voice slithers and reverberates throughout the expanse.

"No. Not blasphemy, but the whim of nature—an unfortunate *seismic* interruption to our celebratory events—"

What? My heart begins to pound like crazy, kicking up my blood pressure, thundering in my temples. . . .

"It is done. The *spectacle* is over—for today. The Games will conclude and the remaining Champions will be honored later. You will now return to your homes, *Atlantida!*"

Saying this, the Imperator turns his back to the stadium and proceeds to leave the Imperial Box, followed by his retinue of Imperial guards. He does not look at me again.

Immediately the crowds surge, and the audience noise level rises as thousands of shocked people are given permission to come alive again and move. . . .

An actual earthquake? Is that the official spin of what took place?

Holy crap!

Seeing him go—just like that!—my mind goes spinning also. Seriously, what just happened? What does it mean? Did he just dismiss the effect of my actions completely? What supreme Imperial disdain. How can he disregard me in the face of recent events? Or is he choosing to conceal his turmoil under a public mask while simply escaping an unbearable reality?

This is crazy! A whole stadium of people witnessed me use a voice command to raise the Atlantis Grail and the resulting mess that followed. Surely at least some of them will question what happened, not merely fall for the ridiculous earthquake explanation!

Not to mention, the Imperator had addressed me directly—told me to stop and said that I "won"—which acknowledges the role of my actions.

Will the rest of the officials go along with this?

As if on cue, the Priest of the Grail raises his hands and echoes the Imperial words in a ceremonial tone of voice. By the firm sound of it, he's recovered also and embraced an appropriate extended interpretation.

"The Imperial Sovereign has spoken! The *Stadion* is structurally unsafe! There has been an earthquake. . . . There may be aftershocks. . . . Leave! Leave at once! But proceed in orderly fashion!"

At this point it's redundant—everyone is already streaming toward the exits. But the Priest must feel it's his duty to do something, so he continues to intone needless instructions, even as other Games officials remain silent. . . .

Meanwhile my mind is stuck—there are no words. . . .

"Come!" Aeson's expression is intense and grim as he grips my hand—and this time I don't protest—as we hurry toward the nearest exit. I breathe hard and try not to stumble over cracks and broken ground beneath my feet while I walk quickly alongside him. In moments the Crown Prince's own guards join and surround us.

I look back fleetingly to see that the people on the dais are leaving also—my friends and members of Team Lark, many of them continuing to stare in my wake—but there's no time to linger.

Some part of me is aware of Hel's sun glare, shining fiercely over the strange, gleaming "grail" portion of the nose section of the huge buried ship, turning it to golden fire. . . . It blazes over the turmoil of moving humanity that now fills the audience seating tiers where everything is precarious, structurally unsound. . . . People rush to the exits past grand, divine statues of heroes that now lean, dangerously unbalanced. . . .

Also—I might be hallucinating this, but somehow—I *hear*, from deep below ground and seemingly from all around, a barely perceptible auditory emanation—a very low humming sound. So low that it's almost out of human hearing range. Indeed, maybe I'm only feeling it as vibrations along my skin. But it's undeniable—a constant, *metallic* din that resonates deep into the bowels of Atlantean hell.

It's as if an immense, subterranean thing of metal is singing. . . .

"Aeson . . ." I try to catch my breath and ignore the faint, impossible, metallic noise underfoot. "Did you hear what they said? What—what now?"

Of course he heard. . . . What a stupid thing to utter.

He glances at me with visceral intensity—the infinite burden contained in his gaze disturbs me somehow, I'm not even sure why. He then quickly looks around before returning his attention to me. "First—we're going to find your sister and brother."

"Oh, lord, yes!" I exclaim, stunned at myself for momentarily forgetting, not thinking of my siblings, my family—what's wrong with me? "Gracie must be going insane, and Gordie too—"

Just as I say it, I see them . . . there, near the arena exit directly ahead, one of several that escaped damage when the ground buckled underneath . . . there's Gracie, and next to her is my brother Gordie, and behind them a few other familiar faces. Is that Laronda and Dawn, waving and motioning to us? Oalla, maybe? Xelio and Keruvat? Who else?

We move toward them, and they meet us at the doors leading inside the stadium building.

In that first wild moment when we come together, I have eyes only for my two younger siblings, and no one else matters. *"Gracie!"* I cry with a surge of warmth and relief, shutting off everything else in my mind, pushing worry back for now.

My sister has a weird deer-in-the-headlights look when she first sees me . . . and then she makes a stifled noise and rushes into my arms.

"Gracie, oh, sweetie! *Gordie*, come here! It's okay! Everything is okay!" I mumble and laugh and cry, continuing to hold Gracie, and at the same time pull my brother into a three-way embrace with my other hand. I am crushing them both hard, not coming apart for long breathless moments.

"I survived it—we did it!" I exclaim. "It's okay now, it's over! Doesn't matter what or how—"

Gracie's face is hidden, pressed hard against my chest, and she is now shaking with quiet sobs, and Gordie has a strange, lost look on his face as he looks at me. I can't imagine what they must think!

They must be as shocked as everyone by what just happened, by what *I*, of all people, have done. . . .

"Oh, honey, it's okay!" I smile, smoothing dirty-blond tendrils of Gracie's hair plastered to her forehead and wet cheeks, tendrils that have escaped her otherwise tight ponytail. It's the little details . . . I find I can notice them now, make time for them, at long last. . . .

I look up momentarily and see Aeson watching us—watching *me*—with an indescribable look of compassion.

Gracie shows me her face at last, straightens and moves back a bit, sniffling and wiping her nose with the back of her hand. She then forcibly stops crying, swallows, and says in a hoarse voice, "Gwen . . . Mom is *gone*."

*C*old. . . .
     Cold emptiness strikes me a sudden blow that I never see coming.

I don't quite understand it.

"What?" I look at Gracie, at the oh-so-familiar shape of her face, her sticky cheeks and forehead with its plastered tendrils of hair, her smudged eyes. "What did you say?"

But Gracie is bawling now, and her face has collapsed into a red twisted mess.

Punched in the gut with cold.

"Gracie!" My voice is hard and cutting.

"It's Mom. . . ." Gordie speaks in an alien voice. "She is . . . she is . . ."

"No," I say, and my voice is a knife. At the same time, I'm very, very calm.

Everything narrows into focus. Everything is very strong and sharp and bright.

I am looking at Gordie, and it's as if all of this past year, all the growing up on his part, didn't happen—once again he's just a little boy with smudged glasses, dumbfounded and helpless. He blinks and opens his mouth and blinks again. "We talked with Dad and George—they're on the ark-ship now—and—and—"

"And *what*?" I interrupt his useless mumble. *"What?"*

"I'm sorry! So sorry, Gwen!" Gracie interrupts in turn, gasping between sobs—and now I turn to her, like a compass needle, cold and numb.

"Mom *died*. Several days ago. We—we found out and then—" Gordie fades off into useless silence.

"No!" I say again. And then I repeat violently, with fury, "No! No! *No!*"

I am shaking. . . . Ice-cold. Dry in the back of my throat. Perfectly *calm* and alert.

Sharp, sharp focus.

Everyone is looking at me, frozen motionless with pity, tragedy, fear—some of them even stunned at my reaction. Somewhere, with my peripheral vision, I am aware of all of them, my friends and supporters, fellow Earth refugees, Atlantean *astra daimon*, surrounding us.

But my razor focus is on Gordie and Gracie, because there can be no other way.

"When . . ." I start, clenching my hands, clenching all of me, so that I become a stiff, unyielding thing of bone. *"Tell me."*

"Gwen. . . ." I feel Aeson's gentle touch on my shoulder, but immediately I shake him off.

I take a step back, so that neither Aeson nor my siblings nor anyone else can touch me.

Gracie starts crying again, this time gently and silently, fat tears running down her face, then again sucks in a deep breath to speak. "It was during Stage Two, when you were inside the pyramid—the third day of Stage Two. Mom . . . she was *gone* on that day, but we only found out later, on day four, when we got the call from the ark-ship. They were—Dad and George—they were picked up, and—"

"And they called immediately," Gordie continues. "It was afternoon, our time, and we were in the audience at the Game Zone, watching you, and we got called back urgently to Phoinios Heights—I mean, your fiancé, Aeson, he got a message—it was the only time he left the Games and you, only for this—he took us back himself, and that's when we found out. . . ."

"How . . . ?" I say. I find that I am incapable of sentences, only short, stupid words. "How—did she . . . die?"

Gracie makes a hard noise, then muffles it. "She was really sick—it was the advanced cancer, the Earth meds stopped working, and the Atlanteans didn't get to her in time. She was already—so sick—she was—they didn't even get the chance to take her up to the ship, I mean, *they promised they were coming, over and over*, but she passed away at home. I don't understand what actually happened, I mean, why couldn't they land in a stupid shuttle for five minutes and get her up there before she got so sick? *Why? They missed her by one damn day!*" Gracie's voice rises, and she puts the back of her hand against her mouth, and starts trembling with sobs.

I watch my sister weep, and I don't reach out to her. Instead I am frozen in my own, ice-cold, alien place. It's as if I am looking at myself from above, floating outside my own numb, dead body.

"That long?" I say, my breath forced with every word as I enunciate in a strange, wooden staccato. "You found out *ten days ago*, and no one told me??"

"Gwen, you had to remain focused on the Games," Aeson says softly. "I'm so sorry, but we couldn't tell you and risk you losing your concentration—"

"How *could* you?" I turn to Aeson for the first time.

He blinks.

His expression is heart wrenching, and something inside me rips wide open. In that same moment a tide starts rising in the back of my throat, choking me, and liquid pools in my vision.

"How could you . . . keep this from me? It's my *Mom!* Aeson, you saw me several times after you knew, and you said *nothing!* And you kept me isolated from my family? Is that why you wouldn't let Gracie and Gordie come see me?"

But it's Gracie who snarls suddenly. "No, don't! Don't you dare put this on him! I *asked* him to do it! I was the one—blame *me!* I knew I couldn't bear to see you without breaking down, and you know Gordie can't lie at all!"

Gordie makes a weird, sad noise and stares at me, shifting his shoulders, as if to confirm.

"So I asked Aeson to make up something—anything—to excuse us not visiting you," Gracie continues. "It was awful. All those days of knowing about Mom, of talking to Dad and George, and not being able to talk to you, and—and—not knowing if *you* were gonna die too, in those damn Games!"

"Sorry, Gee Two, we had to stay away, so sorry," Gordie adds painfully. "Tough to pretend. It sucked." Then he clamps up again.

"I—"

I press my lips together hard, clench my mouth, trying to hold back the quivering, the drowning tide.

It is now an ocean.

It surges over my head and finally swallows me.

The next few minutes are a mess. . . . I collapse and Aeson catches me in his strong arms and half-carries me as we walk through the stadium corridor to exit the building complex.

People I know walk on all sides of me. . . . I feel Gracie's cold, wet hand clutching mine, and Gordie's awkward fingers pressing my shoulder, while I shuffle along like an old woman on limp feet.

The *astra daimon* whisper discreetly among themselves. . . . Occasional individuals and groups of strangers hurry past us in this network of passages with fresh cracks in the walls and other visible signs of damage. Meanwhile the hallway lights flicker randomly or go out completely, indicating malfunctions.

All of this I notice with one small part of my consciousness, while the rest of me is as broken as the structure around me. My face is wet, and my nose is thick with weeping, and I'm barely aware of my own feet moving because of the general anemic weakness that has come over me like a life-leaching blanket.

At some point in the low illumination, my white Contender uniform suddenly sparks with an energy charge, like static electricity, and then it lights up brightly . . . Vocalist White. It's now glowing belatedly, indicating my formal Champion status. Is this the result of Imperial orders? Somewhere the Games techs must have been instructed to run the final sequence of my Contender uniform program. . . .

Which makes it official: I won my Category in the Games of the Atlantis Grail.

Gordie makes a small sound as he points at my shining outfit, and the rest of my friends notice, but no one reacts or says anything.

They realize that at this moment I don't give a damn.

"Only a little more, Gwen . . . we're almost there," Aeson keeps saying as he guides me forward. His hands support me, keeping me upright because I'm limp and barely functional.

Mom. . . .

We finally emerge outside and reach the Competitor parking area for the hover cars, where I vaguely recognize one of Aeson's gleaming, metallic vehicles, this one a large four-seater, and next to it the usual vehicles of the guards. I am seated next to Gracie in the back, while Aeson and Gordie sit in the front, and Aeson drives.

Aeson takes off with a grim expression and a fleeting, intense glance at me. As we rise into the air, I see Dawn and Chiyoko getting into different hover cars nearby with Xelio and Erita, and there's Laronda next to Gennio and Anu. . . .

Their figures shrink and recede, and it all blurs into white sun glare.

Gracie continues to clutch my hand and leans into me with her whole body. I can feel how badly she's trembling, but remain silent and numb and let her hold me. . . . We gain altitude, while below the grand structures of the downtown multi-stadium complex gleam with gold and grey metal, the now-protruding and displaced Atlantis Grail "monument" prominent among them.

We join a common air traffic lane and continue moving over the City of Poseidon toward Phoinios Heights, where Aeson's estate sits atop a hill—our present home.

Soon the familiar hills and greenery come into view, and we begin the descent.

Aeson lands the vehicle so it hovers a foot off the ground, and I step out onto the mauve brick surface of the private estate landing area, holding onto Gracie. Immediately Aeson comes around on my other side and gently takes my elbow. Together we walk up the long, shallow steps to the front door, where a line of estate servants stands waiting for us. Thebet, the old steward, bows deeply before us—before *me*—as we enter.

I take my steps like a decrepit old woman. I nod to the servants, then lower my head and keep it down so that I can see only the polished hallway floor and not the expressive eyes of all these people—kind, pitying, in some cases marveling and filled with awe. . . .

All of this is directed at me.

I hear Aeson give quick instructions to the serving staff, while my brother and sister stand next to me. Meanwhile, sounds of other landing vehicles and voices draw near, coming from outside, as more of our friends arrive.

I can't deal with any of it.

A hard pulse pounds in my temples, while waves of heat and cold surge back and forth, coursing alternately through my body.

"Aeson," I say loudly, on my last strength. "Please . . . I need to talk to my father and George . . . *right now.*"

There's a pause. A quick exchange of glances.

"If you must, Gwen," he says softly. "I will make the call. But—"

"But you're in no condition to talk to them!" Gracie interrupts. "Not right now, not when you're barely standing! You need to get in bed and sleep! They're not going anywhere! If they see you like this, you'll only frighten everyone!"

"I have to speak to them!" I cry out in a hoarse, cracking voice, even though I know she's right.

And yet. . . .

I glance from Gracie to Aeson to Gordie. My tone fades into softness. "They won't care. Dad and George. . . . They would want to speak to me exactly as I am—they understand about the Games, right? You told them about me being in the Games?"

Gracie nods.

"Yeah, they know everything. We told them," Gordie adds.

"And they're worried sick about you!" Gracie sniffles and again rubs her face with the back of her hand.

I take a shuddering breath. "Even more reason to speak to them right damn now. They need to hear directly from me that I'm okay."

And I need to hear from them . . . about Mom.

Aeson watches me with deep understanding, an unblinking gaze of his lapis lazuli blue eyes. He then reaches for me and squeezes my hand. "Very well. . . . I will make the call for you. Come with me."

He heads for the media communications room, and I—and my siblings—follow him.

The main office workroom, with all the specialized deep space comm equipment, is located on an upper floor of the estate, so we hurry through corridors and up a marble flight of stairs. Aeson holds my hand to help me take each step, but with a burst of adrenaline I've recovered enough of my strength that I follow him without stumbling, with Gracie and Gordie directly behind us.

Inside the room, I am settled on a chair while Aeson turns on the largest video screen and makes the necessary connection across infinite space to the ark-ship orbiting Earth. Since he's not only the Imperial Crown Prince of *Atlantida* but the Commander of the international organization Star Pilot Corps, Aeson has the most sophisticated Atlantean comm tech here at his disposal.

It occurs to me, he's calling somewhere on the other side of the universe . . . whatever that means. *The universe has no sides. All of this—it is incomprehensible. . . . Focus, focus. . . . Feeble racing thoughts, mind going off on tangents—stop.*

I watch the dark screen come alive, unbelievably after just a few seconds. On the other end is the face of an Atlantean crew member in a grey Fleet uniform, against a stark background of familiar wall panels inside generic ark-ship quarters. He is a typical Atlantean older teen, with long, gilded hair pulled back against a lean, bronze-skinned face with angular lines and pale hazel eyes that seem tired and sleepy. I've never seen him before.

The Atlantean crewman on comm duty comes to sharp attention and salutes Aeson. "*Nefero niktos*, Imperial Lord! Or is it *nefero dea* for you now? Apologies—we didn't expect your call until later!"

Aeson barely nods, and his voice becomes cool and commanding. "We are early. Get me Pilot Nefir Mekei or Pilot Quoni Enutat. But first, we must speak with Charles Lark and George Lark—is it night cycle for you now?"

"Yes, it's just after midnight, Earth Universal Time Coordinated, on board AS-1999," the crewman confirms. "The Larks are in their quarters, but I will wake them at once!"

"Do it gently. Tell them it's good news. Gwen Lark is here. She is safe and unharmed and wants to see her father and brother."

The crewman salutes again. Then his face disappears, replaced by the Imperial Fleet network logo.

Aeson orients the screen so that it faces me directly and takes a deep breath and turns to me. He looks me in the eyes with encouragement.

I, in turn, stare at him with a numb, fixed, dumbfounded expression of unrelenting weariness mixed with grief and adrenaline, and my body is shaking, while my breathing has grown faint.

"Breathe, Gwen," he whispers gently and leans toward me to place his warm hand over mine. Its pressure is reassuring, and I feel a surge of strength at his touch.

A few interminable minutes seem to pass while I alternate between watching the screen and glancing at Aeson, who nods at me and says soothing things, while I seem unable to form words in reply.

"Aeson . . ." I finally whisper back. "Oh, Aeson. I don't know if I can do this."

But before Aeson has time to respond, the screen comes alive again, and I see the familiar, beloved face of my Dad.

Chapter 2

Charles Lark, my father, is sitting in the place previously occupied by the Atlantean crewman, framed by the same shipboard view, which for some reason strikes me as bizarre and incongruous.

At once I feel a stab of psychological vertigo at the strange sight of my Dad on an ark-ship, even before my mind registers the real life details of him—such as his unkempt, wavy brown hair with more grey than I remember, the wrinkled beige shirt with a collar that's folded wrong on one side, the exact same pair of rimless glasses, his sickly pallor, or his exhausted, grim expression—just before his face transforms into a beaming smile at the sight of me.

"*Gwen!* Oh, my sweet girl! My dear child!"

The familiar sound of my father's voice, that on some level I never expected to hear again, pierces my heart.

"Dad! *Daddy!*" I exclaim in a horrible voice that cracks again and sounds squeaky and very "little girl" that would normally embarrass me, but not today. At the same time, I start to rise in my chair, leaning forward with all my strength, so that I am nearer the screen, smiling and crying at the same time.

"It's so good to see you, sweet girl," Dad says. His face draws closer to the screen also, so that I can really see his wrinkles, the unshaven greying whiskers on his cheeks, and the reddened eyes behind the spectacles. I realize now that my father is crying also, his eyes full of moisture. He also looks thinner and frailer than I remember. . . .

"Thank God you are safe, oh, thank God," he says softly and shakes his head, as though the act of speaking has robbed him of strength.

And then, in the next moment, I see my older brother, George.

A hand comes down to rest on Dad's shoulder, and then George leans in, so that he's taking up half the screen. He cranes his neck to stare at me with a serious expression that softly blooms into a smile. George's dark hair is longer than I remembered, or maybe it just sticks up oddly, and he's got bed head—after all, I woke them up. He's wearing an old black t-shirt that I recognize.

"Hey, sis . . ." George says in a steady, almost playful voice. "Good to see you! Didn't think that I ever would again, but great to be wrong." He makes a sound that's a chuckle or a smirk or something else that's typical charming George. And then, because Dad makes a choked sound of his own, George grows suddenly serious, like a shield slamming, and I see now that he is also thinner than usual, with harder lines and angles, and somehow older than I'd expected in just a year.

"George!" I exclaim. Another unexpected surge of emotion causes my breath to catch in my throat.

"So many things, my girl." Dad begins to speak. "So much has happened. . . . I hear you had to participate in some kind of terrible athletic Games—it is over now, right?"

"Oh yes, it's over," I hurry to say. "I survived and even won, Dad! Everything worked out okay. I will tell you all about it later, and about so many other things—"

"Such as you getting married?" George interrupts and raises one corner of his mouth in a semblance of disapproval. Such a typical George facial tic. . . .

"Oh, my . . . about that—" Suddenly I feel a flush of embarrassment, an instant of panic, and cast a quick glance at Aeson, who is sitting next to me, but offscreen, invisible to Dad and George. Aeson's expression in that instant is both endearingly solemn and just a tiny bit uncomfortable—I can tell he's making an effort to maintain a calm, even relaxed appearance, but he's not fooling me. . . .

Dad makes a hollow whistling noise as he exhales a held breath, then clears his throat awkwardly. "Yes, well—your *Aeson*— this young man of yours seems very nice. He really does. . . . A handsome, well-grounded fellow, apparently in charge of everything. . . . Excellent command of English." And then he exhales again. "I'm a little stunned, I admit. . . . But I'm very proud of you—yes, of course. . . . Not sure how any of this happened, but we'll come to that. At some point later you will tell me everything, how you met—although George did mention your fellow was a

Qualification officer in charge of all of you, and now Gracie tells me he's even grander . . . ah, it's such a strange thing, my Gwenie-girl—that already you're so grown up. . . . Getting married to an intelligent, accomplished young man from another world! Unbelievable to me—you're my little girl, you know, still my sweet baby girl. . . ."

"You've met him? You talked to Aeson?" I whisper. Again, my mind goes spinning out of control with stupid amazement.

Dad nods. "He was the first person we talked with when—"

And then, just like that, he grows silent.

I know exactly why he stopped talking.

It hangs between us, this horrible, empty, hollow thing, this new *hole* in the fabric of the world.

Mom.

Dad watches me, and George watches me without saying anything. Two very long seconds pass. Since neither one of them seems capable of broaching the subject, I take a deep breath and say it.

"When did Mom . . . die?"

Another long second of silence, stretched into infinity across the universe.

Dad exhales and parts his lips, then makes an effort to compose his voice. "I am so sorry. Your Mom passed away several days ago, about two weeks—ten days, I believe, counting in your Atlantean time. It was peaceful. She—she was very, very ill toward the end, Gwen. So very hard for her . . . all that waiting. We tried to hold on, and she did her best. She hung on even after the medicine stopped working, by sheer willpower. You know how she is—was. Tenacious and stubborn and infinitely strong. . . ."

Dad's voice fades and breaks. And then he gathers himself to say, "Just like you. You got that strength from her, and joy, and all the rest of it, all the best parts. You and Gracie and your brothers too—"

George's grip on Dad's shoulder tightens. I can see his fingers make the squeezing motion.

I've stopped breathing. I am frozen, using all my strength to hold back the pressure in my throat that's choking me. . . .

In that moment, Gracie, who's been hanging back, gets up from somewhere in back of me and comes up to the screen. "Daddy!" she says, and she is trembling, and starting to cry yet again.

"Gracie, sweetheart!" Dad says, seeing her. "Oh, how I wish I could hold you, all of you right now! Right here—" And he points to his chest.

I swallow hard. Then I reach out and place my hand, palm flat, against the screen. Dad sees me and does the same thing with his large hand.

We're *touching* across the universe.

Moments later, Gracie joins us, with her hand flattened against the screen, and Gordie gets up and comes to stand also, on my other side, palm out. . . . While on the other end, Dad and George have their hands splayed against their own display surface, reaching out to us.

Finally Dad takes a shuddering breath and says to me, "You need to know, as far as burial—your Mom was cremated, a few days ago. It was her final wish. And I have her ashes here with us, on the ship. But—you can *see* her one more time, Gwen. Mom left you all a recorded message. Your sister and brother watched it, and now you can, too."

I part my lips. . . .

And that's when the torrent breaks, and I am sobbing, ugly and hard, while Gracie puts her arms around me and pulls me against her chest and rocks me, and I let her, weak and limp. We both dissolve into each other, shaking, and Gordie watches helplessly, right next to us, while on the other side of the universe, through the screen, my Dad and George watch us also with silent grief.

A few horrible seconds later, I forcefully catch my breath and pull back from my sister. "Sorry," I mumble in a thick voice. "I'll watch Mom . . . a little later. Right now, I *can't*."

"I know, sweet," Dad says, his eyes glistening. "Take your time. There's plenty of time now. . . . No hurry. I just wanted you to know, to have something to look forward to."

"Thanks, Dad. . . . Okay."

And then I look around and my gaze finds Aeson. He is still and silent, giving us our privacy. "Aeson . . ." I say and reach out with my hand to him. "Come, *please*."

Aeson hesitates only for a moment and then he steps into view, takes my hand, and looks seriously at my father and older brother. "*Amre-ter* Charles . . . and George. Good to see you."

Amre-ter. I recall this translates something like "lord-of-my-love" in *Atlanteo* and is the respectful address toward the father of one's spouse.

Dad sees Aeson, and a soft smile comes over him. "Oh . . . I'm very glad to see you again, Aeson. Thank you for taking care of my daughter—both of them, and my son too. I'm in your debt. And of course, this impossible, unexpected rescue."

When it's his turn, George nods, matching Aeson's serious expression. "Aeson. Or—my apologies—should I say Command Pilot? Or My Imperial Lord?"

So, George knows that Aeson is the Prince of the Imperial Kassiopei. . . . Of course, they both know by now.

"Aeson is fine," my fiancé tells him, then again addresses my father. "And nothing to be obligated for, Charles. I'm the one who now bears an eternal, joyful debt of gratitude to you for the very existence of your daughter Gwen. As for your own circumstances—I only wish we could have done more, and sooner. I blame myself for this inexcusable delay—"

"Aeson, no!" I squeeze his hand and look at him with a raw face of emotion. "Don't. Let's not do this now, please. . . . No *what ifs.*"

"She is right," Dad says at once. "What happened was—well, it was going to happen. No need to beat yourself up over sad things that are done. Your people here did what they could, it was a difficult business, getting us all up here."

But Aeson does not look convinced. He is silent, and I recognize the strange, tense line of his lips, the control slamming down to hold back *force.* "My people—will be held accountable. But let's not talk about it now."

"Yes, let's not," I repeat. "Please."

And then I turn to my father, and I manage a little smile, and throw a softening glance at my beloved. "So—this is Aeson, Dad," I say, biting my lip in a new bout of awkwardness. "I want you to know that I love him very much."

As I glance at Aeson again, I notice that the moment he hears my words, his face warms with an instant blush. At once he lets go of the difficult topic of our conversation, and the stern line of his lips eases into a shadow smile.

"And I love your daughter—with all that I have and all that I *am*," he says in a gentle voice, looking at my father with a forthright, unblinking gaze. For a brief moment, there's a vulnerable expression in his lapis-blue eyes, as if he's unsure of my father's reaction. But it's only a flicker. . . .

"Then all is well, as it should be," my father says immediately, and he is nodding and smiling also. "And in case it's unclear, I approve wholeheartedly. You have my blessing. I know that Margot—if she were here—would be very happy to see you together. She would've liked you, Aeson. . . ."

"Thanks, Dad . . . thank you. . . ." I mumble as the lump in my throat begins to rise again.

"Thank you for the kind words, Charles," Aeson says solemnly. "I am truly sorry I will not have the honor of meeting *Amre-taq* Margot."

Amre-taq. "Lady-of-my-love" in *Atlanteo* is an honorific which my Mom will never get to hear. My breath hitches, and my hands tremble. . . .

Meanwhile, Dad continues speaking. "Margot would really be proud, amazed even—seeing all that you've achieved and survived, and that you've turned into such outstanding young people. To be sure now, Gwen is still rather young, and marriage is such a grand commitment—indeed, seems that all of you are so very young—or maybe it's just me getting old—but these are unusual, world-ending times. I would've preferred for you to finish school first, my dear, but—again, never mind me. Under the circumstances, study and knowledge can wait. The universe is genuinely uncanny, and you must do what you can to make the most of your time in it. Use every single priceless moment to be happy . . . because our meager human life is ridiculously *short*, and—and people you love leave much too soon—" Dad stops, taking another breath, parts his lips. He is powerless.

I can see how badly broken he is.

Oh God, Dad! What am I doing now? I'm selfishly forcing him to relive the pain of losing Mom! No!

"Dad," I say as carefully as I can, "I think you should go back to bed now. I know it's late for you and George, and we can talk again tomorrow. I'm honestly close to collapse myself. It's been a very *long day* here, like you wouldn't believe, so . . . sorry we woke you up. I came straight from the Games and just wanted you to know I'm okay, and to—to—"

"I know, sweet, and I am so *glad* you did," Dad says, recovering control. "Now we can rest easy—knowing that you are indeed safe!"

"Same here! I'm so relieved you are safe and on board! At last! Oh, God, at last!"

Only . . . Mom is gone. She is not safe. She is . . . not.

I force myself to bury this thought, far down, deep down, for just this moment.

Instead, I put my fingers to my lips, kissing them, then press them against the screen. "Go, get some sleep, Dad!" I say. "More soon! Love you! Good night, George!"

"Love you, Dad!" Gracie says at once, and Gordie echoes her.

My father and George respond with their own affectionate gestures and then move out of view.

A moment later, in their place I see a familiar Atlantean. His gilded hair is cropped very short, and he has handsome, well-balanced features, a blunt chin with a dimple, prominent brows, and kohl-outlined eyes. His skin is somewhat dark, a rich hue reminiscent of red river clay.

His expression is impossible to read.

It is Nefir Mekei.

Chapter 3

Nefir Mekei looks unchanged from the last time I saw him about a year ago—the same steady, unblinking stare that at first glance reveals nothing. Except, maybe not quite.

I see that a new weight has settled in his eyes. A weight that I recognize as the subtle burden of guilt.

It is especially noticeable when he sees me.

Nefir acknowledges Aeson first. His courtly salute is impeccable. "My Imperial Lord," he says in a neutral voice. "And my Imperial Lady Gwen," he adds after the tiniest of pauses. I find it somewhat odd that, upon seeing me for the first time after so many months, his expression does not light up, and he doesn't smile at me even a little.

Aeson watches him with an emotionless gaze, which I suddenly find alarming.

"Nefir Mekei. What do you have to report?"

There is another moment of pause. The question—it should be harmless, but there is an immediate air of menace hanging among all of us. It's now undeniable. Maybe it is Aeson's icy tone.

"Is it—secure to speak in confidence?" Nefir asks carefully, with a glance in my direction. "Am I permitted to proceed with all the details?"

Suddenly I'm barely breathing, as if some kind of deep secret is about to be revealed to me.

"Speak as you would to me in private," Aeson replies.

"Very well. . . . No significant changes to report," Nefir says evenly. "The situation on the surface remains turbulent—globally— but with no deviations from the previous assessment. A new fire zone has formed in Europe, and there is an unfortunate zone expansion in central North America, combining the two infernos in Utah and Colorado into one super-inferno—the fourth one that's currently burning on that continent. Meanwhile I find no anomalies in the chatter from the United Nations and various government entities. Same flat activity for global terror groups. Radiation levels in the north and west Pacific and north Atlantic remain almost identical since previously measured, despite the latest African detonation. Volcanic and seismic readings are stable."

Nefir pauses to glance down at his digital notepad on the desk, then resumes in a measured tone. "My complete four-day status report with these details and more will be available for transmission to the ACA Director in Poseidon by opening hour of work on Green Ghost Moon 1, your tomorrow. My—additional, *classified* status report for the Imperial Sovereign's sole benefit still awaits . . . as per your instructions."

Aeson continues to observe Nefir without saying anything. Several painful seconds tick by, and I can see Nefir's blank expression become even more fixed—if such a thing is possible.

At last Aeson speaks. "You may now relay your classified Imperial report. . . . I give you permission to convey to my Father the significant detail of Margot Lark's death, and the other significant details of the Lark family rescue."

Nefir inclines his head after the tiniest pause. "Thank you, Imperial Lord. I—am relieved to be able to finally carry out my duty—*both* my duties—to the Imperial Sovereign, and to *you*."

"So far you have failed in one of your duties—to me, as my *astra daimon* heart brother—so at least you can continue to carry out your remaining duty to the Imperial Kassiopei." Aeson's expression is chilling and his voice becomes razor-sharp—not a *power voice*, but almost, because at once I feel pricklings along my skin, and an intangible weight settles on my spine, sinks inside my bones. . . .

Nefir must feel it too. He blinks, parts his lips, but waits before reacting. He inhales deeply and momentarily glances at me before returning his full attention to Aeson. "I am truly sorry, I am, Kass. . . . But you understand my position. You knew it, and the nature of my official role, from the beginning. I have my orders directly from the Imperator, and I must adhere to them, superseding all others—even your own."

"The correct term of address is 'Imperial Lord.' You are *not* to address me as 'Kass'—ever again."

For the first time Nefir flinches. "Understood. . . . My apologies . . . *Imperial Lord.*"

And then he looks at me. "And to you, Gwen—My Imperial Lady, I am bitterly sorry. I—I cannot begin to express how painful—"

I catch my breath, listening to him, to his controlled and lifeless voice, and sudden horrible thoughts begin to race wildly. . . .

Aeson interrupts him. "Painful? *No.* You cannot, you may not speak of pain, *not* in my lady's presence. What your intentional, perfectly calculated actions caused is a *tragedy.* A family tragedy. And since she is now my family, it is my family tragedy also."

"I am sorry . . . so sorry."

I finally find the strength to speak. "What? What did you do, Nefir?" I say, but somehow, I already know the answer.

Nefir looks at me with his fixed eyes, holding his gaze upon me, somehow, unwavering. "I . . . followed the Imperial orders."

"What you did was lie to me and to the entire Lark family, both here on Atlantis and on Earth," Aeson says loudly, and his words cut like heavy machetes through the silence. "You stalled their rescue efforts, under sadistic orders from my Father, without telling me the *truth.* You made daily excuses for over a month, both to the Lark family stranded on the surface and to me, while all along Margot Lark's health deteriorated until it was too late."

Behind me I can hear Gracie's sharp intake of breath and Gordie making a strange sound.

Not sure if my Dad and George are still present in the same room as Nefir, if they too just heard. . . .

Oh, my God. . . .

"I had to carry out what I was commanded to do," Nefir says softly. This time his eyes are lowered as he speaks. "I had to proceed within the scope of my Imperial orders. My oath remains to the highest office. It cannot be any other way."

"I know," Aeson says, and now there's a tone of mockery in his voice. "I've always known your primary loyalties, but not the pedantic extent of your calculated duplicity."

"And yet, I did not fully inform the Imperator, even now—not until this moment! I held back the information for *your* sake, in my deepest regard for you, Imperial Lord! You realize that technically I broke my oath by not informing the Imperator ten days ago!"

"Technically you broke your oath many times over," Aeson says. "If only you had *trusted me* enough to share the truth of your impossible situation, I would have come up with a feasible workaround! Indeed, I would've taken full responsibility for keeping you from carrying out your Imperial orders, and Gwen's mother might still be alive today!"

I find that my pulse is pounding once again, and my ears are ringing with a head rush. "You—you kept my mother from being rescued?" I whisper-croak, putting one palm against my mouth, then putting my other trembling hand over it. "You *killed* her!"

Gracie cusses, hard, at the same time as she leans forward to hold my shoulders and back, as I shake with wordless agony and fury. "I didn't know this!" she exclaims, beginning to hyperventilate also.

On the other side of the screen, across the universe, Nefir Mekei keeps his gaze lowered, and he seems to have stopped breathing, so motionless is he. . . .

"I take full responsibility," he says at last. And then he looks up at us.

For the first time it is apparent that Nefir's eyes are glistening.

"Yes, you *do*." Aeson has stirred and is now also leaning forward, closer to the screen. His expression is deadly. "I don't want to see your face again until I command you to be present before me. Continue with your regular Fleet and Imperial duties and report to my Father as scheduled. Now, get me Quoni Enutat. *You* are dismissed!"

"I—" Nefir tries to speak, pauses, then finishes in a dead voice. "As you wish . . . Imperial Lord."

And then he is gone.

Next, we wait, with the video screen filled by the Imperial Fleet logo.

Aeson turns to me at once with a tragic expression and takes me by the shoulders. "Gwen," he says in a completely different, gentle voice, "I'm so sorry that you had to see this—all of you—" He glances at Gordie and Gracie—"But it's better that you learn this harsh truth now, rather than later. And I promised myself, no more withholding of information from you. Not for any reason. It is why I forced this ugly confrontation. You had to know everything."

"What did he do? What actually happened?" I manage to speak, regaining control over my sobs.

"Nefir Mekei is an agent of my Father and always has been; that's not a secret. It was accepted by all of us before we even went on the Earth mission, since he was assigned as the primary Earth liaison on the Imperator's behalf." Aeson takes a deep breath. "Nefir is an Imperial Kassiopei loyalist, firmly indoctrinated into the cult of traditional hierarchy, and his family has prided itself on serving my dynasty. Previously he's always been able to balance his rigid loyalties to the Throne with his personal loyalties to the *astra daimon*. I had no reason to believe this time would be any different. . . . That he would act so contrary to my will, in direct defiance of my orders, without at least giving me the courtesy of *informing me* when he is being overridden by my Father. . . . I have to think that my Father specifically commanded him not to divulge anything to *me*. . . ."

Gordie cusses and says something unrepeatable about Nefir. Gracie echoes him.

I'm in such a state that I have no words.

"What an evil jerk!" Gracie spits out her words fiercely. "I always knew he was too slick!"

But I don't even glance at her. "Please continue . . . tell me what he did, all of it," I say, looking at my fiancé. "And Aeson, *thank you* for not holding back."

Aeson nods. His hands run down my arms, then his fingers begin gently smoothing over my wrists. "This is what I learned—along with so many other things, once I confronted him—after a fortunate mention from another fellow *astra daimon* Pilot as

signed to the same ship, Quoni Enutat, whom you're about to meet. Quoni has been observing Nefir's interactions with Earth and with those of us here . . . and he noted a subtle discrepancy in both the transmittal of information and the handling of commands. Quoni doesn't have the same high level of clearance as Nefir, but he is highly observant and capable of deductive inference under the most subtle circumstances."

"Okay . . ." I whisper. My hands, despite being held in Aeson's, continue to shake.

"At some point Quoni noticed that the communications sent to your family were not entirely accurate and didn't reflect the state of things, based on the current planetary status. Nefir made an excuse about being unable to land a shuttle due to the specific location of a

fire hazard near your part of Vermont that was not precisely true—
not a complete falsehood, but just enough deviation from reality to
give Nefir's reasons for not coming down to the surface enough
credence—which made Quoni wonder *why*. As time went on, Nefir
presented other faulty details—heightened Earth government
surveillance in your skies preventing a shuttle from passing without
detection, social unrest and militia activity near your home, natural
occurrences dangerous to flight, false weather conditions—even at
one point an excuse about our own shuttle and personnel availability
and technical malfunctions, which was clearly nonsense.

"Quoni began keeping track of all such details until he had
enough of a pattern to suspect disloyalty or dark motives, especially
after Nefir's subtle modifications to minor shipboard routine orders
each time he communicated with my Father. And that's when Quoni
contacted me privately and presented his evidence. I confronted
Nefir about everything, at which point he could no longer distort
details without lying to my face. Ah, the things I learned—not just
about your family's stalled rescue, but about so many other things
related to the Earth mission. We'll speak more about it later, but for
now I want you to know that a crime was committed, I'm *aware* of
it, and I will not let it go unpunished."

"So—so my Mom could've been treated for her cancer, and
instead—"

My voice cracks and trails off again. Gracie and Gordie both
utter something, but I don't hear the words, so focused am I on
trying to maintain my control.

Aeson's expression is raw. "Yes—maybe. . . . I'll be honest, I
cannot definitely state that even our advanced medical technology
could have cured her completely at such a late stage of her disease,
but it would've made a difference, yes. . . ."

I press my hands against my mouth, hard.

Behind me I can hear Gracie's messy sobs.

That's when the display screen comes alive again, and we see
another Atlantean.

Pilot Quoni Enutat's face is solemn and calm, without the awful
rigid tension of Nefir Mekei, even though his breathing is
slightly elevated, suggesting that he's arrived in a hurry. His lean
features are elegant, vaguely Earth-Asian in appearance, with kohl-

rimmed dark eyes, a chiseled, aristocratic jawline, and golden-bronze skin. His short, very black hair is gilded only at the spiked tips, adding precision to his sharp looks.

"*Nefero dea*, Imperial Lord," Quoni says with unhesitant accuracy in a deep voice, after performing a crisp salute. "I'm very sorry for the delay, but I was stuck below on H-deck dealing with a minor crisis in Hydroponics—all resolved now."

"Good to see you, *daimon*," Aeson says in a completely different, friendly tone. "I want you to meet the Imperial Lady Gwen Lark, my Bride."

Quoni turns to look at me, and although he does not precisely smile, his expression softens at my distress. He immediately inclines his head and gives me a courtly salute. "Very glad to meet you, My Imperial Lady Gwen. I only wish it was under happier circumstances."

"Thank you . . ." I say in a cracked voice. Somehow, I feel reassured that he can tell I've been weeping, and he knows why.

Aeson takes a deep breath. "My Father will now be informed of everything," he says.

"So . . . Nefir's next report," Quoni says. "You gave him permission?"

"Yes. A delay is no longer necessary. The Games are over; Gwen is out of danger and has been informed of the tragedy. The news cannot be used against her by my Father or anyone else. At least Nefir obeyed me in this one small way, bought us enough time so she could finish the Games without being compromised by shock and grief—I give him that much credit."

Quoni barely moves his head in a gesture of disdain. "You give him too much credit. Too kind of you, Kass."

Aeson frowns. "Don't worry, I'm not done with him. Continue having him watched for now."

"You can count on it. Let me know if you want me to do anything else."

"Actually, there is something." Aeson glances at me then turns back to Quoni. "I have an urgent mission for you. There are four mid-capacity, high-velocity cruisers on board AS-1999. One will not be missed. First thing in the morning, you will take one velo-cruiser, and put Charles Lark and George Lark inside. Take also three of your trusted crew with you and enough supplies for six people for three months, including at least two stasis chambers for the Jump, to accommodate the Larks. And then I want you to leave Earth's orbit and come home as *fast* as you can. My personal orders."

For the first time Quoni's calm face shows animated surprise, and his brows rise. "Wait, what? You mean, return to Atlantis—now?"

"Yes, now." Aeson smiles and again glances at me briefly. "You're officially off the Earth mission, and your new primary mission is delivering the Larks to Atlantis, so that my Bride can have her entire family with her as soon as possible."

I make a startled exclamation of wonder, feeling the first stab of joy coming to replace the unrelenting misery of the past hours.

"Seriously? These are excellent orders!" Quoni smiles, baring white teeth. "What about my current duties? To whom should I reassign?"

"It doesn't matter," Aeson says. "Nefir can handle everything and anything he likes in this last ugly phase of the Earth mission. He's been doing it all along, and a few more responsibilities piled on his head are the least I can do to make his life 'easier.'"

"Acknowledged—proceeding to carry out the new mission orders. Will make the necessary arrangements immediately," Quoni says with a pleased smile still lurking on his face. "One clarification—when you say *fast*, do you mean to pull the Quantum Stream at maximum rated speed, aiming for three months' arrival time?"

"No, I mean you *exceed* the maximum," Aeson says. "Feel free to ignore the rated speed Fleet standards, and go at *true possible velocity*, with reasonable safety precautions. Show me what you can do, *astra daimon*, and I will overlook the illegal details!"

Quoni raises his brows again. "Understood! I haven't speed-pushed a velo-cruiser this size before, only the small ones. This is going to be fun."

"See if you can arrive here within two months. It will not be in time for the Wedding, but at least not too long after."

"Oh my God, thank you, Aeson!" I say with emotion.

"We'll see Dad and George!" Gracie exclaims.

"When's the Wedding again?" Quoni asks.

Aeson thinks for a moment. "Believe it or not, in just thirty-five days."

Quoni whistles. "I'll see what I can do, Kass. . . ."

"I know you won't fail me, *daimon*. Bring them home safely, and I will never forget your service."

Chapter 4

As soon as Quoni ends the call, Aeson turns off all the comm equipment and gives me his full attention.

"Gwen, all right, you need to rest now . . ." he says softly, nearing me and putting his hand on my shoulder to squeeze it. "Let's get you to your own quarters so you can get changed out of that damn uniform and—"

Gordie and Gracie exchange quick looks with Aeson, then Gracie nods and gets up in a hurry. "Yes, Gwenie, let's go get you settled in!"

I release a breath I didn't even know I was holding and nod silently, too shell-shocked to protest or even care what's happening to me now. But there's a tiny hopeful smile on my lips as I face all of them. *Dad and George are coming!*

"Will they be okay on that fast ship?" I ask with a sudden new stab of worry. "And what if Nefir tries to stop them?"

"Quoni is an excellent pilot," Aeson replies with a confident look and a smile of his own. "Don't worry. Nefir has no say in this. Even if he reports to my Father and receives a contrary command, Quoni can claim Star Pilot Corps jurisdiction which, under specific circumstances, takes precedence over the highest authority of the Imperial Fleet. And Captain Hirat Sumbui of AS-1999 will follow the proper command hierarchy."

"So you, as the SPC Commander, can override the Captain, the IF Commander, and the Imperator?" Gordie says, apparently aware of Aeson's high position in the Star Pilot Corps. "Cool!"

Aeson gives him an amused glance and nods.

It occurs to me that there's so much that I've missed in the lives of my family members—little things such as this. When did Gordie learn about the SPC? Again my mind starts to dissolve. . . .

Meanwhile I stand up on my own, with Gracie attempting to help by grasping my elbow. "I'm okay, really," I say. "Please . . .

tell everyone out there in the living room that—that I'm okay. That I'll see them later, a little later—"

"Of course. They know." Aeson grows serious again. He makes no move to leave and watches me, making sure I can walk on my own. He must be reading my mind, so in tune is he with my emotional state.

"Aeson . . ." I pause, appreciating his hesitation. I realize it must be his subtle way of giving me some much-needed personal space. "Do you mind not coming with us to my room just now? I'm very sorry, *im amrevu*, but I need to be alone with my sister and brother—for a little while."

"Yes, of course." He inclines his head, watching me gently. His gaze fills me with sweet ease, because, again, he understands completely.

And so, feeling relief for the first time in a long while, I sigh and follow my siblings passively out the door and through the corridors and levels of the estate to my now familiar bedroom.

I have no idea how we get there, but at last Gracie opens the door to my spacious bedroom, decorated in warm pearl tones. Two maidservants are inside, with the bed made and my bath ready, and I smell the delicate, pleasant scent of my favorite immersion minerals wafting from the bath suite.

"Thank you, I can manage myself—we, my sister here," I mumble softly, in response to their offer to assist me.

Gracie gives them a meaningful nod, and the two maids make their formal bows and leave at once.

I move toward the bed, but stop short of plopping down on the pristine covers. I am painfully aware that my Games uniform (still glowing to indicate Champion status) is filthy and encrusted in ocean salt and human blood, and my own personal dirt. . . . Yes, I reek.

Unsure how to proceed, I sigh with exhaustion and look at the bed longingly.

"Okay, first we'll get you out of these gross clothes, and a *very* quick bath," Gracie says in a businesslike tone. "Don't worry, I'll help you! I totally get it, Gee Two, I know how dead-tired you are, but that clean bed is just too nice, right?"

Powerlessly I nod.

Gordie clears his throat awkwardly. "I'll go outside while you guys get naked, et cetera," he says to Gracie and me. "Let me know when you're decent, and I'll come back."

"Yes, we'll call you—thanks, Gee Three!" Gracie says.

And so Gordie leaves.

Gracie helps me remove the nasty clothing, including the *viatoios* body armor underneath, and then walks me over to the deep, sunken bathtub around the corner.

Ah, the pleasure of perfectly warm but not too hot water! I sink gently, battle bruises and all, and then submerge with my head all the way under, holding my breath for a few moments, feeling surrounded by silent warmth, in a mother's womb. . . .

When I come back up, my dirty dark hair is now floating loose in the perfumed liquid, fanning around me like a mermaid's seaweed locks, surrounded by gently rising vapor.

Gracie keeps her hands carefully on my shoulders and watches me to make sure I don't slip under and drown—not that I would, I suppose, but then I really *am* on my last reserves of strength. . . . She takes a soapy sponge and works on my back, saying absolutely nothing (for which I'm grateful), then lets me take care of the rest of me.

When I'm done soaking and washing my hair, I climb out, again with Gracie's tactful help, then step under a quick shower in the roomy enclosure nearby to rinse off completely.

The last of the blood and salt and tears and filth of the Games of the Atlantis Grail, all gone . . . running down the drain in clean rivulets, gone, gone. . . .

I am clean and free of it. . . .

Gracie greets me with towels, and I dry myself and return to my bedroom where I put on the first clean gown I can find, and lower myself on top of the bed with a weak sigh.

"She's decent, Gee Three. Come in!" Gracie calls out, as I lie there on my back, arms folded on my abdomen, head wrapped in a big towel so as not to wet the pillow.

My eyelids immediately start getting heavy, and I can barely keep them open. . . .

Gordie returns sheepishly, and then he and Gracie start talking about something very mundane, like my dirty shoes on the floor and where to put the used towels. But in that moment it's like a power switch goes off in my head, and everything recedes, including their perfectly normal, soothing, familiar voices . . . and I am out, like a burned-out candle.

When I wake up, it's once more to the lilting, comfortable sound of familiar voices. This time, Aeson's deep voice is present here also. And the quality of the light in the room is teal, indicating early sunset.

". . . luckily there's mostly a bunch of scratches, but she doesn't have that many bruises," I can hear Gracie saying quietly.

"Compared to the other Games Stages," Aeson says in a similar low volume, "she fared much better this time."

"Better than most, according to the feeds," Gordie mumbles in a half-whisper. "Somewhere in all the crazy panic coverage Buhaat Hippeis managed to land some facts. He said more than half the Champions were significantly injured, and even Tiago said—"

I blink, clear my parched throat, and croak, "Hey . . . you guys are talking . . . about me?"

At the sound of my voice everyone in the room approaches the bed. Apparently, they've been sitting in chairs nearby for who knows how long. I see Gracie, Gordie, and Aeson, who must've come in at some point. No one else is here, which is a bit of a relief right now.

"Yes, we are!" Gracie says smartly, no longer whispering. She gives me a smile and plops down to sit next to me on the bed.

Gordie stands right behind her, with a little smile of his own, waving at me in a silly way, one hand lowered at waist level. "Yeah, we're talking about you, Gee Two. It's how it goes."

"Uh-huh. . . . What time is it?" I croak again, while Aeson comes around to sit on the other side, leaning over me to check my forehead. At once I feel a pleasant, light sensation from his warm fingertips at the point of contact.

I notice he picks up a glass of water and wordlessly offers it to me.

"Oh . . . yes, thanks . . ." I mumble, rising up slightly and taking the glass from him. I drink the plain cool water, and it goes down like a soothing balm. . . .

I am so parched! Only now do I realize how dehydrated I've been (and all that crying only added to the problem). I start gulping the water down, while Aeson says, "Slowly, slowly. . . ."

"That's so good!" I hand the empty glass back, and he pours me another one from a nearby pitcher.

"It's after fifth hour," he says, watching me drink.

"You've been asleep all this time," Gracie adds. "Which is good. You really needed the rest!"

"Ah . . . yes," I say, finishing the second glass. I hand it back to Aeson and then lie back down again as a wave of lassitude washes over me.

The towel that was holding my wet hair has unwrapped, and my now-dry hair has fallen out. So I pull the fabric off all the way with unusual effort and realize that my hands are shaking with weakness. And then I make a little amused chuckle. "I—I feel like I can't move my limbs, my body. . . . *Ever.*"

"Not surprising," Aeson tells me gently. "You don't have to move."

"What about all those people downstairs waiting to see me? My friends. . . ."

"They're just fine. Everyone's busy eating the *dea* meal, watching the media feeds, gossiping, arguing, talking. They know you'll come down when you're ready," he says in a firm tone, watching me with his familiar intensity. "Which reminds me—you need to eat something. I'll call for your *dea* meal to be brought up. What would you like?"

I look up at Aeson, stare into his dreamy, lapis lazuli blue eyes, then lift one hand to brush his upper arm and take hold of a few locks of his golden hair. "Aeson . . ." I whisper. "A little later. . . . What—what's happening on the media feeds?"

Gordie makes an awkward sound and clears his throat again.

Gracie throws Gordie a look.

"He's right, you really should eat!" she says, patting me on my other arm.

"Not hungry," I say with a tired sigh.

And then the *memory* strikes me, amid the serene calm of these warm surroundings.

Mom is dead.

Just for a short time, while I've been slowly waking up, I had blissfully forgotten.

And now, as I remember, my heart jolts hard. I wince and make a painful sound; everything rushes back in a flood. . . . I'm sure that Aeson and my siblings recognize the dark, drowning expression on my face, and they can tell that I've *remembered.*

Aeson suddenly reaches down and takes me in his arms, raising me up, enveloping me with his strength from all sides. At the same time I wrap my own limp, powerless arms around him, press my face against his chest, and start to weep with deep, rending sobs that rip my insides apart. . . .

Not sure how long I cry, but all I can remember is, there's Aeson holding me, rocking me . . . then Gracie . . . and Gordie is here too, reaching for me on the crowded bed.

They are here, and they are my family.

At some point, I am all cried out, my lungs wrung inside out, and I'm so abysmally tired.

The room is now nearly dark, and someone turns on a soft light sconce.

"I can't! I can't!" I keep muttering. "I should go . . . down to see my friends. But I can't!"

"Gwen, you *don't* have to do anything," Aeson says. "Nobody expects you to. You survived multiple ordeals in a very short period of time, and you must regain your strength. To do that you need to rest. I strongly recommend sleep until morning. But not until you've eaten."

"Oh, Aeson . . ." I whisper, absentmindedly running my hand over his muscular bicep. "It's early evening. I still think I should—"

And then I freeze as another thought hits me. "Oh no! Your armband! Where's my dirty uniform? Is it gone? Did they take it away? Oh no, no! It still has your *armband!* I forgot to remove it from the inside pocket!"

I sit up again, my heart starting to pound violently, this time from distress and shock at my own dreadful negligence. How could I forget Aeson's black armband, the greatest honor bestowed upon a hero of Atlantis? He had given me that precious black silk, a temporary love gift, *on loan*, to keep close to my heart in the Games, as a reminder of his love, so that I would come back to him safely and return the armband unharmed!

But Aeson interrupts me gently. "Don't worry about it, Gwen. . . . It's just a piece of black fabric, and I have several identical replacements in my closets."

My lips part in a different kind of outrage. "*What?* You have others? But I thought—you told me—"

He chuckles. "Everything I told you about it is true. It's a rare honor, and the one personal possession that I value above all others and find meaningful—though of course now I have another item that's just as precious to me—the love gift you gave me, the tiny Pegasus figurine. But I never *said* the piece of fabric was unique. The *meaning* behind it is . . . and the *right to wear it* is. As I promised you, I didn't wear a black armband while you had one in your possession in the Games."

"You jerk!" I say, starting to lighten up. "You made me think it was one of a kind—"

"I might've given you that impression—or better to say, I didn't clear up your mistaken assumption—in order to give you a very strong incentive to stay *alive*." And then he adds. "But now that it's all over, and you're back safely . . . because you're so concerned about it, I'll make sure that the laundry service finds it, cleans and delivers that fateful black silk back to you. You may keep it forever, if you like, as a reminder of all that happened. Or you may hand it back to me. Or you might even decide to toss it in the trash and never think about it again."

"Are you kidding? I'm keeping it!" I exclaim. "I could never throw it away, for so many powerful reasons. It's a gift from *you*, and it *did* save my life. I *want* to think about it and to remember. . . ."

He leans in and kisses my cheek, and then his lips graze the side of my mouth lightly. "As you wish."

Gordie clears his throat awkwardly yet again at our kiss and looks away.

But Gracie says with a smile, "I kind of suspected he might have a whole drawer full of those black armbands. . . . I mean, it makes sense. You and I have as many red or yellow or whatever armbands as we need, and we can always get a replacement. Right?"

"Like neckties, yeah," Gordie says.

I glance at my siblings. "You could've mentioned it to me!" But then I bite my lip and smile also. "Never mind. You wouldn't have told me, I know. . . . To protect me."

Gracie snorts. "You got that right."

At that point there's a soft knock on the door.

"Come in, she's awake!" Gracie says in her normal voice.

In that moment, for the first time in hours, I feel stable enough to face whomever else might be here.

The door opens, revealing Devora Kassiopei, the Archaeona Imperatris of *Atlantida*, Aeson's mother.

She stands at the entrance, silhouetted against the brighter light of the other room—which is Aeson's adjacent bedroom—and the edges of her elegant form shimmer violet, for the translucent and sheer fabric layers of her dress, threaded with metallic filaments, catch the light, creating a nimbus around her.

In that moment, Aeson's mother appears to me divine, a mysterious, exotic goddess from these alien stars. . . .

And then, with one breath, she becomes deeply human, as she enters the room and heads directly for me.

For one split second I see the moist glitter in her beautiful, kohl-rimmed eyes of a color that's a fathomless cobalt-blue, the profound sympathy contained there, and, catch the faint scent of her complex floral perfume . . . just before Devora sits down on the bed near Aeson and me and pulls me into her embrace—while Gracie and Gordie immediately stand up to make way for her.

There are no words spoken as I feel Devora's softness and strength around me, my forehead allowed to rest against her elegant Nefertiti neck, and a glimpse of her lovely features up-close, framed in dark bronze hair. Her outfit, with its many gossamer veils shimmers around me, and I hear the soft clanking of her delicate bracelets.

But all these fleeting detail impressions fade away. . . . Because what comes next is an overwhelming sense of warm proximity, as she presses me close to her heart and then kisses me soundly on my cheeks and forehead.

And then, a few moments later, she looks up, still holding me tight, and I see her glance at my brother and sister. They'd gotten up with such awe-fueled hurry from my bed earlier . . . and now they stand awkwardly nearby, staring. "Come!" She nods kindly, lifts one hand, and motions to them both.

With wonder I see Gracie and Gordie hesitate only for an instant, and then they both approach in some uncertainty. It occurs to me to wonder when exactly did my brother and sister first meet the Imperatris? Had they been introduced to her before, maybe at some point during that busy month of my Games training? Or is this their first formal time? *What's wrong with me? I can't remember!*

But none of it matters. . . . Aeson rises from his place on the bed to make room and stands back. He watches with rapt attention as Devora reaches out to Gracie with one hand and pulls her close.

Gracie makes a startled little sound and exhales with a shudder of held-back nervous tension that's finally allowed relief.

And then Devora lets go of me completely and does the same thing to Gordie—which takes him completely by surprise, and he nearly falls into the embrace.

The two of them end up on both sides of me, pressed into one great generous embrace, and Devora holds us all, her arms open wide, encircling us . . . and she speaks softly in her lilting and beautiful, slightly accented English, "You are mine now. All of you, my children."

Chapter 5

The feeling of security, the harmonious serenity that washes over me in those surreal, wondrous moments is indescribable. It's as if, after months of solitary wandering, I've come home to family at long last. . . .

And my siblings can feel it too. I can tell by how Gracie has surrendered and gone limp in Devora's arms, and even Gordie has relaxed his normally standoffish body posture. Now they both cling to this amazing woman, having found an anchor . . . and for this one thing alone, I am more grateful to her than she can imagine.

"I would never presume to replace your mother, nor would you want me to, of course," Devora remarks, brushing her slim, delicately manicured fingers through Gracie's hair with unexpected confidence and squeezing Gordie's shoulder fondly. "But I will be your second mother, in every way that counts, to the best of my abilities. This, I promise you, *im saai*."

The *Atlanteo* word *saai* means "children."

Again, my heart is full to overflowing with grand emotion, and I hold my breath so as not to break down weeping yet again, but my eyes are brimming.

"Aeson—a napkin, please?" his mother says, momentarily examining my face. Aeson obliges her and offers a small box of tissue-like fabric squares from the nearby side table.

Devora takes one and lightly wipes my eyes, then, with an amused smile, tactfully dabs my forehead and cheeks. I watch her smooth and rub my skin with practiced ease, then unexpectedly dab her own mouth. She then smacks her lips and dabs them again. It's such a simple, casual act that I stare.

"Not only tears, but the *noohd*—the cosmetic on my lips," she says with a laugh. "I fear I've marked you, Gwen—it will not do. . . . First, I clean it off. And now I may kiss *im saai* without leaving a mark."

And then with absolute matter-of-factness, Devora pulls Gracie and Gordie closer and gives them ringing kisses on their cheeks and forehead. At which point I think my brother and sister blush so fiercely that all nervousness is forgotten.

Devora releases us at last, and everyone is both completely relaxed and visibly affected. She continues to smile at each of us, then glances at Aeson. "What a merciful conclusion to a terrible, long day. But—not another word about any of it, not today. I cannot stay for long, and your Father doesn't know I'm here—though he may suspect—but for once I'm not too concerned. It is *over*, and Gwen—the wonderful, shining, fierce, unbeatable Champion Gwen—is safe with you at last. Not much can be done to ruin *tonight*, at least. Tomorrow is a different matter. . . ."

Devora pauses and takes a deep breath, glancing from Aeson to me. "Oh, my dears, the Wedding cannot come soon enough. That's when your union, your life together, will be bound by law, with all the permanent protections and inviolate status for Gwen and all of her blood relatives."

Aeson nods, his expression serious. "I'm very aware of the days."

"Thirty-five days!" I say, recalling his words earlier.

"We will talk about the Wedding details, now that the burden has been lifted," Devora says, getting up. "But not tonight—tonight, Gwen, you must rest. I will return as soon as I may, likely tomorrow." She squeezes my hand and smiles at Gracie and Gordie. "And now, *im saai*, continue enjoying your own young company. *Nefero niktos!*"

"Oh—Manala!" I exclaim, as it occurs to me to ask about Aeson's sister, before Devora leaves. "How is Manala? Is she—"

"Manala is downstairs with the others. She is fine and much relieved that you're okay," Aeson says, with a glance at his mother, who merely nods comfortably.

"I want to see her!" I say, feeling a surge of confidence. "I think—I think I'd like to come downstairs now."

"What? Are you sure, Gee Two?" Gordie says, somehow managing to speak up—with a quick sheepish glance at Devora. "Want me to bring her up here instead?"

I shake my head and start getting up carefully, feeling only a mild surge of vertigo as I stand. "Yeah, I'm sure. Time for me to get a grip. I'm okay. I want to see everyone."

With a soft, curious smile, Devora moves to the exit and quietly closes the door behind her, gifting us all with her loving energy—it's as if her work here is done.

A few minutes later, I've changed into a casual shirt and jeans-like bottoms, without Gracie or anyone's assistance, and follow Aeson and my siblings downstairs into the familiar living room, the one we prefer to use for our gatherings. It has a glorious panoramic view of the city through a wall of floor-to-ceiling windows on several sides. Outside the windows is a dark evening tapestry of sparkling city lights below and stars above.

The room is full of people, and the smart TV panel hovers in the middle, blaring with noise and varied programming.

I take a deep breath, smiling almost shyly as I see so many of my favorite people all at once. Laronda Aimes and Hasmik Tigranian stand with their arms resting against the back of the long sofa, leaning forward to stare at the screen over the heads of the seated Oalla Keigeri, Erita Qwas, and Blayne Dubois.

A few steps away is a long side table with the remains of the *dea* meal, and Keruvat Ruo is pouring himself a glass of fizzy stuff, while the Imperial Princess Manala Kassiopei picks at something colorful on a big plate and offers it to Chiyoko Sato, who holds a small dessert plate with sweet fruit dumplings.

Further back, near the wall, Dawn Williams is talking quietly with one of the serving staff, who is preparing something hot in a deep metallic pan from which vapor rises.

Finally, with his back to the window nightscape outside, Xelio Vekahat sits in a chair, leaning forward in concentration, and watches a second, smaller, hovering screen. He is flanked on both sides by Aeson's two Imperial aides, Anu Vei and Gennio Rukkat, who peer over his shoulder, point, and argue with agitation.

In addition, there are several estate servants inconspicuously going about their meal-serving tasks in the background.

As soon as everyone sees me, they grow silent and stare at me, the only sound coming from the media feeds. And then a loud and energetic hubbub erupts.

"Gwen!" Laronda exclaims. She rushes toward me and then stops, pausing tactfully before trying to hug me, and clasps her hands together with anxiety. "Are you okay?" Laronda is dressed casually in an earth-style top and slacks, and her short, relaxed, bobbed hair has a single metallic gold streak in addition to the usual highlights. The streak wasn't there before—for some reason I'm fascinated by it, and it contrasts beautifully with her dark brown skin.

"I'm fine. . . ." I smile at her, then say softly, "I love your hair."

"Awww, girl!" Next thing I know, Laronda has me in a bear hug and is squeezing the life out of me with her surprisingly strong, well-toned Cadet arms. "You crazy, crazy awesome Shoelace Girl!" Laronda cries in my ear, then releases me to stare seriously into my eyes. "You survived. You did it! You *more* than did it! I'm so proud of you! And—and I am so sorry about your Mom. . . ."

Before I can answer, Hasmik steps forward and pulls me into a warm hug that radiates generous strength despite her petite frame. "Gwen-*janik!* So terrible, but it's over! What a relief! And your dear Mom, so very sorry—"

I look into her kind brown eyes and sweet, comfortable face framed by shoulder-length dark hair, and a jolt of emotion rushes through me. . . . It occurs to me, seeing Hasmik's familiar, welcoming smile beaming at me that I didn't believe I would see her again, or any of my other friends. Only now is it sinking in. . . .

"Gwen, come here," Dawn, the taller girl next to her, says. Dawn has light brown skin, long hair, and very dark eyes that are usually serious and thoughtful, and in this moment particularly intense. She gathers me to her with a comfortable hug. "It sucked, what you had to go through. And losing your Mom on top of all that. . . . Damn."

I run my hand across her back and nod, maintaining a smile that's now fixed on my lips more for everyone else's sake than my own. "It's okay, thanks. . . . I know I'm not alone in this. Other people have lost their parents. It happens all the time. . . . It's a part of living. I know *you* don't have your dad, Dawn. And Laronda—"

Laronda nods. "My Mom passed away when I was twelve. That's why Jamil and I ended up living with Auntie Janice."

"Yes, exactly," I say in a measured voice. "So I need to put things in perspective."

Laronda snorts and squeezes my arm. "Not today you don't. You just went through hell and learned about your Mom—*today*. You have every right to grieve."

"Thanks. . . ."

I hear the sound of a tone sequence being sung, and seconds later Blayne approaches on his hoverboard. He hovers skillfully upright while maintaining an effortless Limited Mobility Form with his thighs and legs wrapped around the board, so it's easy to forget that he used to be confined to a wheelchair back on Earth.

"Congratulations and condolences in one, Lark," he tells me with a sad little smile, patting me on the shoulder awkwardly. "You did us proud out there—all of us Earthies. Too bad you had to learn about your mother this way. That's harsh. Really sorry. . . ."

I nod silently and then reach out and take Blayne into a hug of my own. The boy doesn't resist, merely flips the longish hair out of his blue eyes, and then after a moment reaches around me with both hands and lightly pats my back. His upright hoverboard jabs my midriff slightly as it presses uncomfortably between us. Like my brother Gordie, Blayne's not a hugger, but these are special circumstances.

"Thanks, Dubois, good to be here, though strange somehow," I say as we separate.

Next up is Chiyoko, large and tall, always slightly hunching in posture, with her familiar, permanently nervous expression—which is now even more anxious, a warring mixture of sympathy and joy. The poor girl stands nearby looking at me with visible stress. I'm used to the fact that Chiyoko, who's both a friend and my Pilot Partner, worries too much and doesn't want to say the wrong thing. In fact, right now she appears to be in agony. . . .

"Oh, Chiyoko . . ." I say, turning to her. "Come here. . . ." And we embrace gently.

"I'm so sorry," she mumbles, speaking quickly. "My condolences on the loss of your Mom! And—and congratulations, yes, for making it through the Games and winning! What you did in the end, with the Grail, was so weird and impossible—"

"Should you be up, Gwen? Go back upstairs and get in bed!"

I turn around, and it's Oalla, sounding playful and bossy at the same time—except her beautiful kohl-rimmed eyes are wide and serious. Oalla puts her hands on both my shoulders and rubs them gently but surely. "You need rest."

"Thanks, but first I need to see all of you."

"No, you don't." Oalla bites her lip and cranes her neck sideways at me, flipping her golden hair.

"Agreed," Erita echoes her, stepping up and tweaking my cheek with a stern look and just a tiny twitch at the corner of her generous lips. "You're a stubborn and tough Earthie, and now all of *Atlantida* knows and respects it, but you've proved yourself enough for today. Seriously!"

"Aww, Erita. . . ."

"Yes, you definitely shouldn't be here, Gwen," Keruvat says, leaning down at me from his great height and contradicting his hard tone with the warmth brimming in his very dark eyes.

"Hi, Ker. . . ." I smile back at him, and Ker immediately softens and shakes his head in amusement.

Next to him, Xelio moves forward and stares down at me with his gorgeous dark eyes and a handsome face filled with intensity. "Gwen, they're right. All of this can wait. We'd much prefer you to be rested and sensible, and we'll see you tomorrow. Really, nothing here to see, go back upstairs!" And then he glances at Aeson, who stands quietly, watching me and everyone, with his arms folded across his chest. "Tell her, Kass!"

But Aeson makes a sound of bitter amusement and shakes his head.

Xel shakes his own head back at him and snorts, then folds his arms also, tapping the long elegant fingers of one strong hand against his upper arm.

Finally, I am faced with Gennio and Anu, who both keep back a little, allowing the others to crowd around me, but I can tell they're as eager to greet me as anyone.

I wave at them. "Hi, Anu, hi, Gennio. . . . So, looks like I'm alive after all. Hope you made some money betting on me." And I wink tiredly, keeping my fixed smile in place.

"Imperial Lady Gwen," Gennio says properly, while Anu makes a sudden barking sound and says, "Hell, yeah! I *did!*"

At that everyone suddenly laughs, and the remaining minor awkwardness in the room is broken.

"What?" Anu exclaims, looking around at everyone. "So what if I did?"

"Anu—not appropriate!" Gennio reproaches him with a poke of his elbow.

"Whatever, fat-brain!" Anu retorts and then grins at me.

I shake my head with weary amusement. *I can't believe I've actually missed Anu. . . .*

And then, there's Manala—the person I came down to see in the first place.

The Imperial Princess stands shyly waiting, keeping back even more than the two Imperial aides. I notice she is wringing her hands with nervous movements and biting her lip, and her smile is both eager and tentative at the same time.

As soon as we make eye contact, she raises her hands to her mouth, and then rushes into my arms. "Gwen! Oh, *Gwen!* You are alive and well! I couldn't bear it if you weren't, but you are!"

"I am!" I say warmly, pressing Manala close to me, smelling the light flowery scent of her golden hair, so much like her brother's. "See, it all worked out, and I'm okay!"

She nods at once, pulling back and looking at me closely. "No. . . . Your Mother died, Gwen, I *know* you are not okay. But I love you very much and beg you . . . promise me, please be strong and live as long as possible, and don't ever, ever *die!*"

I open my mouth to gently say I cannot make such an impossible promise, but Manala's great eyes are brimming-full of liquid.

And so I nod and again smile, smile, smile at her. . . .

Manala appears to take my response as agreement and exhales loudly in relief. She innocently hugs me again and says, "And now you must eat!"

I can't argue with that, and to be honest, my atrophied sense of hunger is starting to resurface. So I sit down on the sofa while Gracie brings me a large plate piled with food, and Manala follows with a carafe of my favorite *nikkari* juice.

I take a few careful small bites, which initially seem to go down like rocks, but I force myself to continue, because my rational mind tells me that I need to rebuild my strength.

While I eat, I begin to pay attention to what's playing on the smart screen in front of me. Meanwhile, Aeson sits down quietly beside me and puts his arm across the back of the sofa without holding me directly, only now and then running his fingers lightly through my loose hair from behind. . . . His touch sends pleasant currents racing down my spine and distracts me just a little from eating and from watching.

Nevertheless, I make myself focus and stare at the screen.

The main feed playing in the center window shows the Atlantis Grail stadium in the bright light of noon, in complete disarray, moments after I've sung and lifted the Atlantis Grail "monument." Of course, it turned out to be just the tip of an iceberg. As the Grail rose at my voice command, it became obvious that the cup shape did not have an ordinary foundation—it was a continuous part of something much larger, the top of some kind of immense subterranean *object*—an ancient ark-ship.

Apparently, this clip is being replayed, set on a continuous loop, and an Atlantean woman commentator's voice is providing narration. The footage shows the Grail slowly rising, cracks forming in the arena floor around it, then in the rest of the stadium structure, the ground breaking up, people screaming and starting to run. However, it cuts out just before the voice of the Imperator sounds and everything comes to a halt. So effectively all the audience sees is the moment of broken ground and general panic.

". . . the Vocalist tiebreaker event was interrupted by a seismic event that resulted in significant structural damage to the *Stadion* building downtown," the female newscaster says off-camera. "There is much speculation as to the causes, especially since there has not been any ground-motion activity in this region, and Poseidon is located on a very geologically stable portion of our local tectonic plate. . . ."

Laronda comes up behind me, leans over the back of the sofa, and whispers loudly in my ear. "This is the kind of vague crap they've been spinning all day," she says with an angry sigh.

I turn around to glance at her and frown thoughtfully.

"That's the Hel-Ra Network," Oalla says, sitting down next to me on the other side, so that now I'm pressed comfortably between her and Aeson. "They have to be politically correct and Imperially conscious in how they relay the news. Let's flip to a different feed."

Oalla calls the smart screen TV closer, then touches one of the six smaller windows, which now becomes the main display. We see similar footage, except the feed loop shows a much longer section before and after, including *me* singing, the Grail rising, and the Imperator's *compelling* voice interrupting everything. Then the camera pans to a studio, where a panel of eight news commentators sits around a table, with an anchor in the middle, arguing. The network logo shows a wave symbol with the label *Free Poseidon News*.

"It's obvious this was not a natural phenomenon, but the direct result of the Vocalist's performance!" a man says. "The Imperial Bride Gwen Lark had demonstrated a remarkable Voice ability earlier—we already knew from the Second Stage of the Games she was a power Vocalist, if you recall the Plural Voice Chorus—"

The panel members respond with enthusiasm and agitation.

"Yes, yes, that was an unforgettable moment! I felt chills of awe when she overrode the Plural Voice and took command of the field," another man says. "But what does it imply? That our Earth Bride had a natural power voice worthy of the Kassiopei?"

Nervous laughter sounds. "You don't mean a Logos Voice?" a woman says with incredulity, and more laughter follows.

"No, of course not," the anchor in the middle seat says. "But something very powerful, if we consider the mass and weight of the Atlantis Grail monument—"

"Indeed, now we begin to see why the Imperial Crown Prince Aeson chose her, in addition to any—how shall I put it—sentimental reasons!" another male commentator says.

"Now, now," the anchor interrupts. "Let's not be cynical. There is definitely a romantic bond between the young couple."

"Oh, yes," an older woman panelist says in a shaking voice. "True affection! I have no doubt of it now—"

"Hah! I do!" a much younger woman interrupts in turn. "The Gebi female is playing a very clever game! Oh, but she's sharp and ruthless and so very powerful! Look how well she did in the Games. *Nobody* ever expected her to survive, much less win—but it's obvious now, this whole thing was premeditated on her part. Gwen Lark insinuated herself in the Prince's good graces, and now she is a Champion, and she commands so much potential political power through her union that the Imperator himself needs to be careful of her possible future influence—"

"What nonsense!" a male panelist says. "You are attributing so much negative ambition and intent to this admirable young woman. Look how well she brought together and led the members of Team Lark during each of the four Stages! She showed personal grace and leadership. When the time comes, she will be a wonderful Imperatris!"

"Getting back to the incident," the anchor guides the conversation, "how do we explain what happened? Official channels insist it was a quake, but to anyone watching, the answer is much less clear. . . ."

"Timing is critical," a man says. "If we can measure causality, the exact moments when the voice command sounded and the monument began to rise, and the destruction that followed. Yes, it is possible these events were perfectly timed to happen together only by pure coincidence."

"Or maybe one thing led to the other!" another panelist says. "What if the monument's dislodging sped up and initiated the imminent quake?"

"Enough! Let's address the most important detail here," the older woman interrupts. "The fact that the Earth Bride controlled the giant monument with only the strength and focus of her voice! It's unprecedented! What does it matter if the quake came naturally or the monument caused it? I want to know how she managed the feat! What if her voice is indeed—"

"What bothers me, suddenly," the anchor interrupts, "is what the monument's immense *foundation* started to reveal. What *was* it? Remember, we never saw the lower end of it as the foundation continued to rise out of the ground before the Imperial Sovereign put an end to it! Any ideas? Was there some kind of underground *structure* underneath the Grail? I'm sure the viewers in our audience would like to know!"

The panelists erupt in noisy argument.

Keruvat sits down next to Oalla and points at another feed happening in a smaller window, "Let's switch there for a while—if that's all right with you, Gwen?"

"Sure," I say, still frowning with concentration.

But as soon as the new feed window is maximized, I regret it.

It shows real-time footage of the multi-stadium complex downtown, flooded with artificial night illumination. Whatever it is, it's happening live, right *now*. . . . Crowds of people are filling all the open areas surrounding the various buildings—the *Stadion* itself, the clearings between it and the Imperial Kemet Forum known as the *Kemetareon*, the *Nebetareon* where I participated in that fateful interview on Tiago's show, and other lesser Forums. People everywhere are shouting incomprehensible things, waving signs and fists, and holding up small, artificially lit hand-torches resembling vigil candles used on Earth, while guards and Corrector officers attempt to control them, keeping them away from the various building entrances.

The camera pans around, and a tense-looking reporter on the scene talks hurriedly in close-up. "We have a very unusual situation developing," he says breathlessly, starting to walk quickly in an aisle between blocked-off rows of the gathered public and city guards. "These people are here to express their extreme *unhappiness* with the unresolved end of today's final portion of the Games—"

"Unhappiness? You can kill yourself, you stupid *chazuf!* I've lost a year's savings—"

He is interrupted and shouted down by nearby protesters.

"Oh, crap," Oalla says.

"This is not good," Ker adds. "Change the feed again?"

"No, wait," I say. I freeze suddenly, because I see several people in the crowd holding up signs depicting images of *me*. The pictures are not that awful school photo that I hate, but are complimentary graphic renderings of me in an idealized pose, holding up a winning grail—the way I did when I won the Triathlon Race and the Yellow Grail in Stage Four. The only reason I recognize myself in those pictures is because they are labeled, "Gwen Lark."

Underneath my name, however, is another label. . . . The three lines, read together, evoke in me a sudden rush of chilling ice-cold.

Gwen Lark.

Our Imperatris.

Our True Goddess.

Stunned, I put my hands over my mouth.

But in that moment, Aeson's wrist comm device starts to buzz softly. I glance at Aeson as he checks it, then looks up at me with a suddenly grave expression, saying, "It's my Father, I need to take this call."

I nod, while Aeson gets up and moves back from our grouping on the sofa. I stop watching the screen, even as the rest of my friends crowd in to stare at it, because I am suddenly much more concerned with what's happening with Aeson.

I watch nervously as he stands near the wall with his back turned, speaking so quietly I cannot hear.

Meanwhile Xelio starts to walk toward him, but Aeson shakes his head negatively and puts his hand up, halting Xelio from approaching.

Dawn, Hasmik, and Manala stand nearby, also staring nervously, glancing from Aeson to the TV screen and then to me. Manala is back to wringing her hands nervously and clutching the edges of her shirt—a nervous habit of hers.

"Wait, what's that?" Anu says, moving in right behind me and entirely too far into my personal space, nearly breathing down my neck. "Huh? Look!" And he points at another small window with a different feed. "Bring that one up!"

Oalla furrows her brow at him, but quickly calls up the window, so that for a moment the disturbing footage of the crowds downtown is replaced with a strange scene showing a grand intricate building that I've never seen before. I assume it's an earlier recording because it's showing a daytime scene. A male commentator is speaking, but for some reason I don't recognize the words at all.

"Hey! That's the Pharikon Palace in New Deshret!" Anu exclaims.

"What?" I say. "Where is that?"

"Not in Imperial *Atlantida*," Oalla responds, biting her lip. "New Deshret is another country, on the other side of the planet."

"What are they saying?" Anu grimaces.

It occurs to me, the feed audio is not in *Atlanteo* but some other unfamiliar language.

Great. . . . I think. *Something else I don't know that has some possible bearing on me.*

Anu taps Oalla's shoulder. "Hey! You speak *Deshi*, right? What are they saying?"

Oalla rolls her eyes at Anu, then returns her attention to the feed.

"Something about the Ra Disk," she replies, but looks at me.

"The what?" Laronda says, squeezing in to stand behind the sofa, between me and Anu, elbowing him slightly in the process.

Anu snorts and turns to her with another, more pronounced grimace. "The Ra Disk, stupid Earth girl. It's New Deshret's equivalent of our Atlantis Grail."

Laronda turns to face Anu, so that they are inches away, and glares at him like a boiling furnace. "Whatever that mouth-flapping thing you just did was, it made no sense. What the hell is the Ra Disk? Explain in English. We are *aliens*, remember?"

"It's a big-ass monument in their capital city," Anu whines, leaning even closer in her face.

But Oalla calmly elaborates, directing her answer to Laronda and me. "You two and the rest of you Earthies—" she nods at Hasmik, Dawn, and the others—"I don't believe you've been instructed about the Ra Disk of Atlantis."

"No," I say tiredly. "We have not. . . ."

Oalla nods thoughtfully. "It's in their capital city, a huge golden disk carved from a hillside and plated in gold. As big as our Atlantis Grail. It's the ancient symbol of New Deshret."

"Okay, weird and interesting," Laronda says. "Or at least it really should be for you—right, Gwen? You're the smarty-pants who likes all that ancient historical stuff."

"Definitely," I say, nodding. But my mind wanders back to the previous feed with the scene of the crowds and the signs with the pictures of me. . . . *Our True Goddess.*

In that moment Aeson finishes his call and returns.

"Gwen," he says. "Tomorrow . . . my Father wants to see both of us."

I look up at my beloved, and my forehead and brows move with emotion.

"Well, I don't want to see *him*," I say suddenly in a hard voice.

There's a pause.

Everyone looks at us.

Aeson takes a deep breath and releases it, looking at me with intensity. "I know," he says. "I don't want to see *him* either."

My lips part.

"But we have to," Aeson adds firmly. "Not because of *him*. But because of *this*." And he points at the smart screen where the footage of the strange foreign palace is replaced by a fascinating sight. A golden circular object of pure gold, set in deep hemispheric relief against a ruddy-orange stone hillside, is shown, flaming with the blinding light of Hel. It's several stories tall in diameter, an immense sculptural achievement, rivaling indeed the grandeur of the Grail, and in some strange way seeming to complement it. . . .

"I'm not sure I understand," I say, glancing from the screen to Aeson. "But I do know I have no intention of humoring your Father any more, not after what he—"

But Aeson interrupts me gently. "My Imperial Father told me that he has just been contacted by New Deshret directly. The Pharikon, who is their equivalent of the Imperator, called to inform us that the Ra Disk has come *alive* and has been humming since noon our time. . . . Since the moment you raised the Atlantis Grail."

"What?" I say, and now my blood runs with pure cold.

"Gwen," *im amrevu* says, "with what I know now and had never previously suspected for all these years of my life, I can make a safe guess. The Ra Disk of New Deshret, stored for thousands of years on a different continent on the opposite side of the planet, disguised as a relief carving on a mountain, fits like a perfect lid over the Atlantis Grail. Put the two together and you get a *sphere*. It is the missing top half of the ancient ark-ship's resonance chamber."

Xelio makes a sharp sound of surprise. Oalla sucks in her breath.

"So you're saying that when I keyed the Grail it somehow affected this Disk . . . at a distance?" I ask with amazement.

"Yes." Aeson watches me with a grave look of wonder. "At the Pharikon's request, my Father attempted just now to re-key it remotely via the comm device and deactivate it with his Logos voice . . . but something went *wrong*. In short—he was unsuccessful. That's why we must comply with his summons tomorrow. Because whatever you did to key the Grail—and the Disk—to you, and to somehow activate the whole thing, has caused an anomaly and some kind of cascading reaction. At this point you might be the only person who can turn it off."

Chapter 6

I stare in stunned silence, forgetting to breathe for a moment, unable to form words, while my mind clamors with the implications—all possible implications—of what this could mean.

"Kass! What's going on? What did you just say? The Grail, the Ra Disk . . . are parts of an ancient *ark-ship?*" Xelio asks meanwhile. "You mean—"

But Aeson again raises his hand, silencing him the same way he did a few minutes ago, while continuing to look at me with his focused gaze. "Gwen . . . I'm so intensely *sorry* this is happening."

"Wait, what? What's happening? What ark-ship?" Erita steps up and whispers to Oalla, who only shakes her head and continues to stare at us with very wide eyes and her full attention. Keruvat is right next to her, listening seriously.

"Truth is, my Father wanted you to come immediately. Right now, not tomorrow—*now,*" Aeson continues. "But I refused him with a hard *no.* I told him you were too tired and drained from the Games and would be *useless* tonight, unable to summon the energy needed to focus your Voice on such a major task. It's logical, and it's the truth, so it convinced him. . . . But you need to know that my Father is in a severe state of *upset*—he is panicking, Gwen. The only reason he didn't send his enforcers here to bring you to him regardless is because I made sure he understands your condition."

"Oh my God . . ." I whisper, finding my voice at last. I'm trembling in a combination of fury and terror. "He would do that? No, what am I saying, of course he would! So—he wants to *force* me to do this—whatever it is?"

"When he's in a rage, my Father becomes even more unpredictable and rarely thinks clearly. Instead he lashes out. But this is such a uniquely terrible circumstance, and he *needs* you to be well recovered—" Aeson stops, taking in a shuddering breath and releasing it. "As of now, you have time to rest until morning, but not longer. It's a reprieve. We're expected in the Palace at seventh hour, after which I believe we will likely head back to the *Stadion* so that you can be in closest proximity to the Grail—"

"This is unbelievable . . ." I mutter, as my anger battles with exhaustion. "What am I supposed to do? I don't know anything! I don't—"

"Whatever things you will be asked to try tomorrow, you need to rest right now," Aeson replies softly, then looks around at the people in the room. "This gathering is over. The things you heard—I will explain them to you in good time . . . very soon, I promise. But I ask you to keep this among ourselves for now. Tell nothing to anyone else. Understood?"

Oalla speaks up at once. "Of course, Kass. Understood perfectly, even if we don't actually *understand* or have the details."

"Discretion and silence," Keruvat adds, putting his hand lightly on Aeson's shoulder. "You have my promise."

"Honor of the *daimon*." Xelio nods. "No questions for now. We'll speak—later."

"I'm confused and scared enough to crap my pants," Erita says loudly. "But—honor of the *daimon*."

Aeson nods to his fellow *astra daimon*, then turns to the Earthies in the room, my siblings and friends. "And all of you, I understand you're probably even more confused, but please be discreet with what little you've heard here. And now—Gwen urgently needs her rest."

"Okay . . ." Laronda replies in an unusually meek voice. She glances back and forth from Aeson to me. "We should go."

"Yes, of course." Gracie echoes her nervously from a few feet away, standing near Gordie and the seated Blayne, whose chair is next to a serving table. Looks like Gracie's filling another plate with food, possibly intended for me, and has only paused her task because of the intense nature of our discussion.

Gordie just nods at Aeson in reply and furrows his brows.

"Understood," Blayne says with utter simplicity from his spot in the chair. "Time to go." And then he starts to rise, propping himself against his hoverboard.

"Yes, definitely time for us to head out for the night," Dawn concludes calmly. "Keeping my mouth shut, no problem. Like the rest of you, I've no idea what is happening, but it's not my place to speak, so—"

"Good luck on whatever it is you must do tomorrow, Gwen!" Chiyoko nods at me with her usual anxious face.

"Thanks," I whisper.

"Thank you," Aeson says to the room in general, as everyone begins to leave. "Apologies for cutting our evening short."

The mood is quiet and sober, and people come up to me one more time to wish me rest and a good night. A few hugs, a few pats on the shoulder and back, many intense glances, and they are gone. Hasmik pushes a visibly confused Manala gently out the door with a final caring look and nod in my direction.

Only my sister and brother remain, Gracie still holding my plate of food, and Gordie frozen with indecision, like a tree that's taken root.

"Gee Two, here's some more for you to eat, all right? I'll just put it here. . . ." Gracie hurries toward me and sets the plate on the sofa next to me.

"Right. . . . We'll see you tomorrow," Gordie mumbles, as Gracie nudges him.

I ignore the plate and stand up. Silently I put my arms around my sister and pat my brother on his shoulder. I am once again numb, this time because my body and mind are shutting off, unable to deal with any of this.

"Will you be okay to make it to bed? Do you need me to help you upstairs?" Gracie tries again, as we come apart. But this time Aeson just shakes his head at her, and Gracie nods hurriedly. "Get some sleep! We'll be here if you need us any time, in the middle of the night—"

And Gracie and Gordie slink out of the room, leaving me alone with Aeson.

Aeson watches me with a raw expression as I stand there. For one brief moment he allows his guard down, and his eyes reflect the strain of feverish exhaustion. As for me—frankly, I'm not sure how I still remain upright . . . and even as I think about it, I sway slightly.

At once he steps in and takes hold of me. Suddenly I'm swept up in his arms, lifted easily, and he is carrying me. I lie against his chest, head lolling forward, nestled against his throat. . . . Soft, pale strands of his golden hair lightly brush against my face; his warm breath flows against my cheeks, and my head starts to spin with infinite weariness.

Screw the Grail . . . and the Ra Disk . . .

I slide my hands around Aeson's strong neck as we exit the room, and I am carried up the stairs and into my own bedchamber.

I'm not entirely sure what happens in the next few minutes—and yes, I've ceased caring completely, and my well of *self* has run dry. . . . The world has narrowed. . . . All I know is, my beloved, *im amrevu* Aeson, is lying in my bed beside me, cradling me and whispering, "Sleep, Gwen, sleep. . . . Nothing matters . . . I'm here . . . I'm with you. . . ."

His overwhelming warmth, his sweetly mesmerizing, low voice, and his words are the last thing I remember before the darkness takes me.

I am with you.

When I come awake with a start, out of the deepest sleep in quite some time, it is early dawn, the first day of Green Ghost Moon.

Yesterday was the longest day of my life.

Don't think. . . . Just don't think. . . .

The general *awareness* of it immediately bludgeons me, but I don't allow any of the terrible details into the foreground of my conscious mind—at least, not yet.

Don't look back. . . .

Instead I intentionally focus on the moment—my body (it's sore and aching all over) and my surroundings—forcing the elements of the *here and now* to predominate.

Do not attempt to remember. . . .

The room is mostly dark, with only a faint glimmering of daybreak seeping in somehow from beyond the drawn curtains. I stir underneath the soft coverlet, feeling a comfortable weight settled against my midriff from above the bedding. I glance to my side, only to see with a pleasant jolt of surprise that Aeson is sleeping next to me.

He's lying on top of the covers, on his side, facing me. . . . His head rests inches away from mine on the same pillow, tousled strands of long golden hair scattered around us. And although our bodies are not otherwise touching, separated by the thickness of the coverlet, one of his arms is extended, lying over my abdomen just above the waist in a possessive but relaxed hold. I hear his deep breathing—not quite snoring, but softly audible—and feel the wash of air against my nose and cheeks. Instantly it sends sweet currents of arousal and pleasure throughout me, and my lips curve into a smile.

Aeson! He stayed in bed with me all night!

I realize it with a kind of wonder and turn my head to better observe him in the faint light. That's when I notice that he's still wearing the same clothes from the night before.

My poor Aeson. . . .

So he managed to get my shoes off and covered me, but never made it to his own bed. How exhausted he must've been—probably fell asleep right after tucking me in.

It occurs to me, this is the first time he didn't leave in the middle of the night to return to his own room. Furthermore, he's not even up yet and is still blissfully asleep. Another first!

Just as I think it, in that moment, Aeson stirs, inhaling a deep breath that turns into a light snore. He grunts in relaxation and then barely opens his eyes.

"Nefero eos," I whisper, smiling at him, with my face so close to his that it's within kissing distance.

"Gwen. . . ." he mumbles in a thick, sleepy voice, blinking. And then his eyes snap wide open in alarm. "Ah, *bashtooh!* What time is it?" He cusses softly and starts to rise. His arm tightens around my waist, hand sliding forward and unconsciously caressing me. Then he blinks, pausing momentarily in confusion.

"I don't know," I say. "But I think it's still very early."

He checks his wrist comm device. "Just after fifth hour of Ra," he says in a voice that's now fully awake. "We have time, but we can't be late for this."

"So what if we're late?" I say with a yawn. "Let your Father wait!"

"Remember, it's not about him," Aeson says seriously. "It's the accursed Grail and Ra Disk, and everything that goes with it—the entire ark-ship, its connection to the ancient alien threat. The components of the resonance chamber—and whatever else—must be deactivated as soon as possible. We need to hurry."

"Okay." I run my fingers against his jaw line and feel his prickly morning stubble. "But only because you say so, not because of your Father."

In reply he leans closer, and his face hovers above mine as he watches me. "How do you feel?" he asks with concern, resting his palm against my forehead, fingers smoothing back filaments of my hair, thumb caressing my skin.

"Better," I say with a faint smile, looking up at him. "I've slept like the dead. I think we both did. And—I'm so glad you are here. . . ."

The next instant his face disappears from view, and suddenly I feel his mouth pressing hard against my throat, directly at the fluttering pulse point at the base of my neck.

A lava-hot tidal wave of sensual awareness overcomes me, coming out of nowhere. My eyelids flutter, and I lie back, dissolving into the unexpected wild sensation of the pulse kiss—the sensation of *him*—while his lips continue to move against my skin even as his sharp stubble grazes me, causing a strange, searing mixture of sweet pain.

Somehow he must realize it, because he pulls back, saying, "Oh, *im amrevu*, sorry . . . I know I need a shave . . . and a shower."

I tremble lightly, as the flood of feeling continues to course through me. "Yes, you do," I whisper. "But I don't care, because when you kiss me, it makes me a little crazy and kind of happy-drunk—and—and—"

He chuckles, watching me trail off into silly mumbling, then silence.

I take a deep breath. "All right. Enough of the good stuff. Time to get up and face the music."

And with a groan both of us do.

Half an hour later we've both showered in our respective bathrooms, dressed in the slightly less casual clothing better suited for the Imperial Palace, and he's clean-shaven. Aeson calls the kitchen for *eos* bread service for two—I'm assuming my siblings and some of my friends are staying here in the estate, but no one else is up yet, so it's just us.

"Yes, we're in a hurry, but we're not going anywhere until you eat," he tells me, as we sit down for a quick meal in a small room downstairs which has another beautiful view of the hillside and city skyline.

The sky outside is barely the color of slate, as the dawn slowly brightens. The dense tapestry of stars is still visible, and the artificial city lights still on, brilliant twinkling dots in a morass of dusk, above and below. . . . Some of them are moving rapidly above the city in air traffic lanes, which tells me they're the lights of hover cars and other urban transport. It's the first day of the new month and a new work week, and Poseidon is coming awake. After all, the Games are over, even though they were halted inconclusively—

Stop. . . . No, don't think. . . .

At once I forcibly distract myself with a barrage of random factual junk.

Today is Green Ghost Moon 1. . . . It's Redday. . . . The first day of the week, the Atlantean equivalent of Monday. How does it go? Redday, Blueday, Greenday, Yellowday . . . and then comes Ghostday, the day off that only comes twice a month, or every two weeks. . . .

Okay, now I'm rambling.

Good. Just don't think of yesterday. . . .

In the warm interior illumination from the wall sconces that fills our cozy nook, I observe my handsome Bridegroom. He is dressed in a crisp, dark blue shirt and black trousers beneath a light jacket, his shining mane of hair gathered into an ordered, segmented tail. The hollows and lean angles of his face still show chronic exhaustion, but he looks more refreshed and alert after a restful sleep—for once.

He in turn stares at me and seems to find my perfectly fitting tailored top and flowing dress-pants, both in shades of lavender and violet, very interesting.

Eventually he tears himself away from the sight of me and points to the appetizing spread before us.

"Yes, my Imperial Lord, I promise to consume food," I reply mockingly, picking up a cup of steaming-hot *lvikao*, the delightful drink with the aroma of a pastry shop, and mimicking an Earth-style toast gesture in his direction. "And you need to eat too, because I know you've not eaten properly for a month. No excuses, mister!

Don't make me force-feed you this—this big, juicy, swirly, fruity thing, whatever it is!"

"It's a *medoi* fruit-filled *eos* pie." He laughs at me, then takes a deep swallow of his own drink, picks up an eating utensil, and digs in.

A few minutes later, after our plates are mostly cleared and we're waiting for refills of fresh *lvikao* that's brewing in a carafe nearby, we finally permit ourselves the uncomfortable talk.

"Gwen . . . *amrevu.* I know you're making a brave effort right now, despite being terribly exhausted and very *vulnerable* after all that happened," he says, "but . . . before we go to see my Father, I must tell you some hard truths I learned from Nefir about the Earth mission, to prepare you for the unpleasant meeting."

I nod. "Another few minutes will not make us late."

"All right." Aeson takes a deep breath. "You know about the single ark-ship in orbit around Earth. Let me tell you the real reason it's there."

Ugh. . . . At once, I pay very close attention.

"When we originally departed for Earth, this was the mission plan given to Fleet High Command—consisting of the IF Commander and the three Command Pilots, including myself—and also shared with the general IEC Assembly membership and the foreign heads of state who contributed mission resources. The semi-clandestine version: select and rescue ten million healthy, strong, endurance-capable, and variously talented young humans of the optimum age to survive the Jump, plus specific Earth resources, and bring them to Atlantis. Meanwhile, leave one secret ship behind for special contingencies and as a communication link with Earth, to observe and record what happens during the asteroid strike, without interfering."

"Okay. . . ."

"The whole effort was promoted as a humanitarian rescue of our species from the same ancient alien threat and their extinction-level asteroid. The virtuous reason given was to preserve and reinvigorate humanity's gene pool by combining two long-separated human branches—and the practical reason was to add human resources to our military and enrich our static global population."

"Hmmm. . . ."

"Turns out, this rescue was only half of our mission. The other half was the ark-ship itself. It was left in orbit not to *observe* but to *actively guide* the asteroid to Earth and make sure it struck as my Father intended. The asteroid was equipped with a hollow interior and retrofitted with a small resonance chamber and remote guidance system, for my Father's personal use—all of it so well disguised and so far below the asteroid surface that none of the Earth probes would ever find it. Even our own Fleet sensors would easily miss it unless we knew where to look—"

"Oh!" I make a small sound. Gears turn in my mind, and I interrupt wildly: "If it has a guidance system, then it can be diverted away from Earth! Your Father can simply change its course!"

"Yes!" Aeson says. "But he needs to be *convinced* to do so. And right now I'm not sure how to convince my Father about anything or what leverage to use without making things worse. In the course of my hard questioning, Nefir only told me what he knows about the Imperator's secret 'plan within a plan'—which is quite a lot, but *not* everything that lurks inside my Father's dark mind. And now I'm beginning to suspect there's even more to it. . . ."

"So this whole mission must have some other hidden reasoning behind it," I say, "some intricate Imperial or even *personal* agenda?"

"I believe so. . . . And that's the missing part we still don't have. We don't know *why* my Father wants the asteroid to strike Earth—especially now that the public mission objective has been achieved, and the Earth refugees are safely here on Atlantis. At this point it seems to serve no purpose, not even as a bargaining tool. Why destroy Earth? The only thing that comes to mind is that it's somehow related to the *alien threat* to us all."

"Well, we can ask him right now when we see him," I say, feeling my pulse quicken again, its rhythm echoing hard in my temples. "In fact, I have all kinds of things to ask!"

Aeson nods, watching me seriously. "Gwen, promise me you'll be very careful when you talk to him. Please think things through before saying anything—volatile."

"Oh, believe me, I will. Too much is at stake!"

"Exactly." He pauses, takes a deep breath. "To continue—Nefir Mekei was in charge of this half of the mission, as known only to my Father and a handful of IEC members, all Imperial loyalists. At the same time Nefir was also serving as the ACA liaison with the Earth governments, and he was supposed to make excessive material promises to them in secret, on behalf of Imperial *Atlantida*— promises that my Father never intended to honor. Now those of us in Fleet High Command knew about that part—about exaggerated promises—because it was relevant to the entire mission. These promises would keep the Earth United Nations docile and cooperative while we carried out our plan, since they expected to be rescued by us at the last minute before the asteroid hit.

"In fact, the ACA promised them there would be at least one ark-ship at their disposal, so yes, the top Earth officials and leaders such as your American President Donahue, King William of England and British Prime Minister Corwell, Chinese President Liu Kao Wong, United Industan President Ghatak, and Russian President Zabrodov knew about the cloaked ship remaining in orbit, even while the rest of Earth and our own Atlantean Fleet did not."

"Oh my God. . . ."

Aeson pauses to drink from his cup of *Ivikao*. "As you already know, I was in charge of creating the hologram ark-ship illusion to fill the empty slot in the Fleet formation within the Quantum Stream, for our return trip."

"Yes, I remember our talk after the second QS Race," I say. "That's when you first mentioned *them*, though indirectly—the ancient aliens."

He nods. "Back then I assumed this secrecy was for everyone's safety—both for the crew staying behind on board AS-1999 and the rest of our Fleet personnel, and the poor, doomed residents of Earth who really didn't need to be given false hopes of last-minute rescue. Instead, my actions were directly contributing to the mission that would have Earth destroyed. . . . I'm so damn sorry, Gwen."

I sigh, watching his tortured expression. He barely meets my eyes in that moment.

But before he can continue, Aeson's wrist comm emits a tone. He checks it and says, "It's my Father. He wants to know if we're coming *now*."

I sigh again, this time exhaling a furious breath, as I watch Aeson key something back, his fingers tapping lightly on the micro device. When he looks up, he says, "Let's head out. We can continue talking on the way."

Minutes later, flanked by the usual retinue of guards, we exit the estate house past a few curious but respectful servants. Outside, the dawn has brightened, and we get into the hover cars and lift off into the sky.

I usually have no problem flying in large, reasonably safe vehicles such as this one, but this morning for some reason my gut feels like it's falling out from under me. . . . And then my head reels with vertigo, which dissipates quickly enough, but instead a new terror grips my intestines.

My mother is dead. . . .

When the Imperator brings up this fact, as he cruelly might, I must keep from bawling.

I must not cry, not blink, or respond in any way that might show weakness.

I must be a rock before him.

Chapter 7

I focus on my breath to keep it regular, trying not to hyperventilate. Meanwhile I silently observe Aeson as he keeps us in the major air traffic lane, with the guard vehicles on both sides and behind us. The golden roofs of the Imperial Palace complex soon come into view, contrasting with metallic fire against the mauve and ebony grandeur of massive structures and splotches of manicured greenery in the park and gardens below.

We come down on the private airfield—indeed, my first memory of being on Atlantis is *in this very same spot* where I first landed directly from orbit in that fateful shuttle, more than two months ago—a distant memory now, with all the things that have happened in the interim.

It feels like a lifetime. . . .

"Gwen." Aeson glances at me. "Are you okay?"

"No, I'm not," I say in a numb voice. "But I will be, once we're in your Imperial Father's presence."

He takes one hand off the steering panel surface momentarily and places it over mine, squeezing. His touch is strong and warm, and it gives me a jolt of reassurance.

"I love you . . ." I whisper in reply.

His solemn expression melts.

We get out of the hover car and start walking along the mauve cobblestone-like surface of the airfield toward the park entrance and the garden paths that lead to the main building of the Imperial Palace.

At this early time, except for the uniformed Palace staff and gardeners, few people are about. The ones who walk past us bow to pay their respects before the Imperial Crown Prince and his guards . . . and then they see me. Without hesitation they bow before me also—deeply, with the same level of reverence as they show Kassiopei.

Even knowing enough to expect it, I'm once again stunned.

But Aeson gently guides me onward, giving me no time to show confusion in front of these courtiers and servants.

We enter the grand marble interior that is the front hall, which branches off into myriad palatial chambers, corridors, and connecting passages. We take the swift elevators to the top floor and then emerge in a lobby of mauve and cream marble, which serves as the entry to the Imperial Quarters, past a number of other elevators along the walls. At the massive double-doorway entrance, a row of Imperial guards equipped with gold staffs salute the Imperial Crown Prince—and myself—and we are immediately admitted within.

Aeson's personal guards must stay behind at this point, due to Imperial Security Protocol, so Aeson and I enter alone.

The antechamber of the Imperial Quarters is a grand hall with a vaulted ceiling and colonnades along the gilded walls, with an informal reception-room throne and other lesser chairs along the back wall next to which are more doors leading deeper into the private areas of the Quarters. All the seats are vacant.

The last time I was here in this very room was that fateful first morning when we had *eos* bread with the Imperator up on the rooftop pavilion, and I met the whole family, my future in-laws. And now the same high-ranking servant approaches us with a hurried bow and points to one of the doors. He has an alarmed expression, and before Aeson can ask anything, he says, "Please, this way, my Imperial Lord and Lady, you are expected immediately! Our Imperial Sovereign, the Archaeon Imperator, is in his Red Office, and he will receive you there."

Aeson nods, and we enter a short, ornate corridor with a distant, arched ceiling. Aeson walks past several other interior doors toward a room in the back, and I follow him with quick steps in order to keep up.

The door is open, and a warm glow of sconce lights greets us, as we find ourselves inside a relatively small but opulent chamber decorated in deep, earthy shades of river-red clay, mauve, rust, carnelian, and fine gold trim.

It's interesting that there are no windows here, only four walls draped with ancient tapestries, ornamental curtains with valances obscuring wall library nooks filled with scrolls, carved wooden plaques depicting ancient stylized reliefs, and occasional modern digital landscape photographs.

A large desk and a tall chair stand near one wall, while three more chairs are spread around the room. Three monitor screens of different sizes rise off to the side via intricate and somehow antique-looking spiral-jointed mech arms, suspended over the desk at eye level. They are reminiscent of exotic metal blossoms or maybe strange avian wings.

The Imperator himself stands behind the desk, leaning forward slightly, his two hands resting on the desktop, fingers drumming against the polished, high-gloss surface.

His long Kassiopei-blond hair hangs loosely down his shoulders in a rather unkempt fashion, and his lean, ageless face is fixed in a disturbing expression. He is wearing a deep-green jacket over a simple, pale shirt and black trousers, possibly the most casual I've seen him to date.

I catch a glimpse of the Imperator's very dark blue eyes, and they appear wide and terrible as he looks at me in that initial moment of recognition.

"*You!* Both of you! At last!" the Imperator exclaims, striking one hand violently against the desk surface and straightening.

"My Imperial Father—" Aeson greets him coldly, but is immediately interrupted.

"How do you feel *now*, girl?" Romhutat Kassiopei turns directly to me, stepping past his son. "Sufficiently recovered from your many ordeals and that *performance* of yours, enough to get to work? *Well?*"

"Yes," I say in a frigid voice, looking up unflinchingly at his glaring face. And I don't add *"My Imperial Sovereign."*

"Well then! Let's begin!" And just as abruptly the Imperator pushes past us, back to the desk, and nearly rips one monitor screen from its elegant, curving mech arm, dragging it toward him, turning it so that it faces us. I see a live-streaming close-up view of the Atlantis Grail Stadium, bright with morning light, from the vantage point of someone standing right in the arena at the base of the Grail.

The stadium appears empty of people, with not even the clean-up staff around. Here is only silence, gusts of wind, and birdsong, punctuated by occasional distant swells of surrounding city traffic noise. Everything is untouched. The variously broken and displaced tiers and rows of seats, leaning statues, walkways, and uprooted flooring on the ground, show the same level of structural damage in the arena as had been there yesterday. It's a strangely sad, abandoned, grand expanse.

The Grail itself is jutting out of the broken ground at a slight angle, just as I last recall it. Immediately, a sickening feeling comes over me when I start to *remember* and *relive* everything. . . .

No . . . stop. . . .

I struggle to focus on the present, clear my mind. That's when, during a particular moment of lull in the living silence, I hear the deep, bone-rattling *hum.*

"There it is! Can you hear it?" the Imperator demands, lifting up one finger. And then he taps the display surface and addresses the screen, "Approach closer. Center on target. Enhance sound."

Whoever or *whatever* is there causes the live camera device on that end to rotate smoothly and point at the gleaming golden object, so that now it's looming in view, overshadowing all else. Then the camera view starts sailing forward, bringing itself closer yet, so that it's only a few feet away, then a few inches from the "goblet stem" portion of the Grail.

It occurs to me, there is no person holding up a device. It's some kind of hovering robotic drone. Could it be a nano-camera?

Meanwhile the deep, humming sound grows in volume, and now there's an added buzz from vibration as the device makes physical contact with the Grail surface.

"Before my Bride does anything," Aeson says coldly, "My Imperial Father must explain what is happening. Why is the Ra Disk in New Deshret affected by whatever is happening with the Grail in Imperial *Atlantida?*"

Romhutat glances up at his son.

"I've been harboring a theory, Father," Aeson continues. "My theory is that the Atlantis Grail monument is not a monument at all, but the uppermost section of a very ancient, very deeply buried ark-ship that lies sprawling, far underneath the *Stadion* which marks the Landing Site of our first Colony, right here in downtown Poseidon. And the Ra Disk carved in the face of Dubutaat Mountain is also not a carving at all, but a portion of that same old ship. . . . And if you put the two together, the Ra Disk fits precisely over the top of the Grail, and it becomes a great golden sphere—a resonance chamber."

For a moment the Imperator stares at his son like a basilisk. And then he nods. "Yes, clever boy. You figured it out."

Aeson inhales deeply. "So then—"

The Imperator makes a harsh scoffing, sound. "So then *nothing*. This information is not yours to have—not yet. It's a fragment of the vast set of hidden knowledge revealed to the new Imperator only *after* he ascends the Throne of Imperial *Atlantida*. Unfortunately, because of your Bride's meddling, disastrous actions, you get to find out sooner than you should. Or maybe it's fortune, not misfortune— feel free to call it either!" And the Imperator looks from Aeson to me, his near-black eyes appearing wild. "You must be so full of questions now. Just itching to know, are you? So eager—"

"How much of this whole structure is the ancient ark-ship? How deep does it go? I've been inside it, haven't I?" Aeson continues, ignoring the barbs. "The first four underground stories at least, the ones that house the research facilities? Is that the original ship, or later additions built around it?"

"Ah! It's *all* the ship, idiot boy! At least three hundred levels down! Some of them so far down that we've never been that deep! We cannot open them due to ground instability, for fear of implosion and collapse! We cannot risk damage to any of it, not ever!"

"Okay, why?" I ask in a hard voice, speaking up for the first time.

Romhutat's gaze snaps to me. "Because the ancient ship is a glorious, dangerous, *sacred* treasure of our past! It houses all the technical and esoteric knowledge of our original civilization, so much of our history! There are so many *answers* there, but they are convoluted, partial, incomplete. . . . We keep looking and finding more things to question, more unsolved puzzles . . . mysteries instead of solutions, enough to make you mad . . . symbols and ciphers, imperfect fragments of arcane languages. . . . It's an entire city down there!"

My mouth parts in wonder. Aeson frowns.

"And you, Gwen Lark," the Imperator tells me. "See what you've done to this antique? It's bad enough that you uprooted it physically, causing untold possible structural damage to the lower levels. . . . But the worst part? You keyed it to yourself and you broke the Master Lock—the Imperial Aural Block! It's a *safety lock* to keep the ark-ship suspended in its *quantum resting state*, all parts of it inert. And now, because of your brute-force override, the ship is no longer inert—"

"But *how?* What exactly did I do?" I start to hyperventilate. "What does it mean—?"

"It means that all components are now active, regardless of their location on this planet, because they are all *bound* at the quantum level. And all of them are *broadcasting*—far outward, beyond our stars . . . for anyone who's listening, to hear. . . ." The Imperator's eyes widen, and there's a flicker of new darkness that I suddenly recognize as fear.

At the thought of the Imperator himself being afraid, a cold wave washes over me. . . .

But just as swiftly he regains his hard control and continues, "The pieces of the ship were physically separated by our ancestors for a reason, to minimize the possibility of this kind of unfortunate tampering, and only one Logos Voice may set and maintain the Master Lock at a time. The Imperator of *Atlantida* holds that right, throughout generations, to control and maintain the ship in secret, for everyone's protection."

Romhutat turns to Aeson. "Your turn would've come. You would have properly keyed it, using the correct procedure learned from me at the initiation. No one would have suspected. . . . But now, because of what was done by your senseless Earth Bride—"

"Senseless?" I exclaim. "How was I to know any of this? I sang in order to win the Games! I thought it was going to be a harmless vocal demonstration!"

"Speaking of *sense*, Father—*this,* what you describe, doesn't entirely make sense," Aeson says with brutal sarcasm. "Why did the ancients bother to *separate* the components if it's all bound together by one voice anyway? Why dump the top half of the resonance chamber in New Deshret?"

"Why, why. . . . Ah, the questions! Very likely to hide it in plain sight, disguise its true nature from nosy fools and hope for the best? *We don't know,*" the Imperator replies after a slight pause. There is leashed fury in his voice. "This is one of those unanswered questions. I was told by your Grandfather that one Logos Voice was responsible for the whole ship—that is all *he* knew. As to why New Deshret has the Ra Disk—"

"Maybe," Aeson says, "the components were isolated for political reasons as much as safety. Maybe the act of dismantling the great ark-ship was a means of equalizing ancient power structures among the heirs of Kassiopei, Heru, and other original great families."

"You can ask Areviktet Heru himself in half an hour," Romhutat says. "The Pharikon is waiting for my call, and I'm certain he would love to entertain your idiot questions."

And then the Imperator returns his fierce attention to me. "But first, you, girl, will need to sing again—this time carefully and using the correct sequence I'm about to teach you—to key the ship—after which I will sing to re-key it again and set the Imperial Aural Block."

I bite my lip. "Okay. Show me what to do."

The Imperator nods, and now his dark eyes bore into me with an intensity that makes my skin crawl. "Listen carefully."

And then he sings a strange keying command in a deep voice of power. He is using a major sequence of notes, starting with C, then E, then G—in this case, the C is a rather common choice of tonic starting note.

However, he is singing *overtones*.

In other words, the sound issuing out of his mouth and throat splinters into *two* different notes at the same time—one low fundamental note, and the other high as a whistle—the overtone.

Holy crap!

Overtone singing, a bizarre type of harmonic singing or throat singing was an uncommon skill back on Earth, from what little I can remember of it. Even now I'm only superficially aware of its existence among some cultures such as the people of Mongolia, Tibet, and a number of others.

Mom had mentioned it to us at some point, but I didn't pay much attention, since it was really hard and way beyond my budding vocal skills. You basically use your lips to shape the sound of the low note, and move your tongue to change the resonance, and that's what affects the high note—I think? We all tried it as kids and were unsuccessful.

And now . . . now I'm supposed to be able to sing this way, with no training and only a few minutes' notice, when I'm not even sure if my own Mom, the opera singer, could do it? Maybe if I could ask her how—

Mom is dead.

I can never ask her anything again.

The strange realization punches me in the gut, and everything from yesterday that was just hovering in the background, at the outermost edges of my awareness, comes slamming back.

She is dead, and he is responsible.

He killed her.

I clench my hands into fists, clench my mouth in a hard line, and I don't breathe. . . .

It's the only way I can keep myself from breaking down in front of the Imperator—or throwing myself in fury at him.

Meanwhile, Romhutat stops singing the overtone keying command and watches me for any reaction. Apparently, my unusual stillness and lack of expression has captured his attention. Does he think he's stunned me with his demonstration?

Slowly I release my breath. . . .

And then I say in a dead voice, "I can't do that."

A pause.

The Imperator's eyes do not change, but his mouth starts to curl with disdain.

But in that moment Aeson says in a hard voice, "Even if she could, she is *not* going to."

Romhutat Kassiopei turns to his son, and I feel the terrible weight of his gaze leaving me, as though it's a physical burden lifting. "What did you say?"

But Aeson does not blink, does not avert his gaze, he merely watches his Father with his own equally imposing basilisk stare.

Several moments pass.

"*What* did you say to me, boy?" the Imperator repeats, starting to move closer toward his son.

"She will do nothing," Aeson replies calmly. "Because the Imperial Crown Prince will not permit his Bride to give up her unique advantage for nothing in return."

"What?"

"Compensation for her valuable services . . . in the form of truth from you—the entire truth—and a bargain that guarantees her permanent safety. Enough deception, my Father! You will begin by admitting your role in orchestrating the asteroid disaster about to befall Earth. Admit what you have done! And explain *why*."

Wait. . . . Did Aeson plan this in advance? My thoughts race wildly.

There is a terrible pause.

"You dare take this tone with me?" The Imperator speaks in the low, soft voice of a serpent. He is a dragon awakening.

All at once, my heart starts to pound.

But Aeson's face is a mask of stone. He looks at his father, unflinching. "Explain what is going on, *everything*—or she leaves with me, now."

Romhutat Kassiopei takes another step toward his son, so that they are facing each other. "You dare bargain with me? Have you any idea what I can do to you—to her—and to *everything* and *everyone* that either of you hold dear?"

"I have a very good idea, my Father," Aeson replies without blinking. "Except, in this case you're out of time. You admitted last night that she is your only option. If you try to force her, if you harm her, or her family or friends, *I guarantee you* she will do nothing and the ship will continue to broadcast. Remember, she cannot be *compelled*. Every moment you waste trying to threaten or break her—or me—the signal will travel farther, and *they* are sure to pick it up—they, our ancient alien enemy. Indeed, they have likely received the transmission already and are on their way here. . . ."

"Hah! Then we've already lost!"

"Not necessarily. Cutting off the transmission now, quickly, might help to slow them down—"

"Or not! Might as well proceed with our original plans. . . . Have you gone mad, boy?"

"And what would those plans be? No, I'm not mad, Father, but I'm willing to take this ridiculous exchange all the way—"

The Imperator glares at Aeson with disbelief. "No—but you *are* blatantly mad to defy me! Maybe it's insanity caused by your so-called 'young love,' or maybe it's all those sleepless days and nights spent at the Games that have broken your mind—or were you on AG Runner? Tell me that's the case, and I will disregard your stupid words, forgive your outburst, and have my own doctors examine you and cleanse your system. Otherwise, if you continue on this mad course—are you willing to risk your Bride?"

"You will do nothing to her—not now, not *ever*. And I've never taken AG Runner in my life. But let's not go down this pointless sidetrack. It's just another twisted distraction coming from you, my Father, as you wrap us in more deception and lies. The webs you choose to spin are intricate, and yet it's all unraveling now. Enough!"

"Enough indeed! The world has turned upside down. My son dares defy me!"

"Your son is Kassiopei. And so is my Imperial Bride—she is under *my* protection. And now she is also a Games Champion, additionally protected by a very different, very *public* law."

Romhutat Kassiopei pauses, thinking, while his forehead twitches. And then a thin sneer comes to one corner of his mouth.

"You think you're so clever now. . . . Well then, consider your Imperial Bride's health, her well-being, her very delicate state of *sanity*, if not her existence—which is indeed so inconveniently protected now by her new celebrity status and public opinion. You think she's untouchable, unbreakable now? Why don't we put this brave resolve of hers to the test, boy? Another hour of signal transmission will not make a difference—I'm willing to take the risk—and meanwhile your Bride's little sister and brother can be brought here, together with my expert interrogators, for some very painful persuasion techniques—"

"No!" I exclaim, while a tidal wave of lava-hot fury rises inside me. "You touch my family and—and—"

"And what? What will you do, poor little Gwen? Lash out at me with your untrained Voice? Threaten to kill yourself, maybe? Self-harm is all you have left as a bargaining tool, and not even that. You will be restrained and muzzled as you watch them *being cut alive.*"

"Not before I *fry* that damn ship—right now!" I exclaim, stepping to the side and turning toward the monitor with the live feed of the Grail. "Don't try to disconnect the computer link, I will sing before you can do it! Would you risk losing all that ancient, priceless orichalcum technology in one instant?"

"What?" The Imperator's jaw drops, and he takes a step toward me.

Meanwhile Aeson gives me an amazed look and starts moving forward also to insert himself between us.

"I. Will. Fry. The. Ship. And everything around us that has orichalcum content," I say, emphasizing every word. "Call your guards, and *I will fry this room* before you have the chance to muzzle me!"

"And I will stand between you and my Bride to give her all the time she needs," Aeson adds, stepping forward and blocking the way toward me, as he faces his Father. "She can do so much irreparable damage to your favorite Red Office and the entire Imperial Suite floor, even if her Logos Voice doesn't reach the Grail. What a shame it would be—*Father*."

The Imperator stares at his son and then at me with a truly stunned expression. He throws one glance at the live monitor, as if calculating the seconds needed to thwart me. . . .

There is another terrible pause.

And then Romhutat Kassiopei slowly smiles. "Well, then. . . . No need to interrogate your siblings, Gwen Lark. Something else has come to my attention. Very unfortunate news—about your mother. Would you like to hear? Margot Lark is *dead*. Apparently, she died a few days ago, while still on Earth. You will never see her again. My condolences on your tragic loss. Such a shame our medical staff never had a chance to treat her highly manageable disease."

He watches me, still smiling, waiting for my reaction, for my breakdown.

I gather myself, with every ounce of strength. . . .

"I know," I say with perfect calm.

And then, as the Imperator's smile fades, I add, "I know how you killed her."

Chapter 8

The Imperator looks at me like a demon, and then he looks at Aeson.

But I continue, in a very calm, outwardly dead voice that is yet somehow charged with *power*. "I know *everything*. I know you're responsible for keeping my mother and the rest of my family from being rescued, denying her the medical treatment, all those days when she could have been up on the ark-ship. I know you wanted to use her death against me. That's not going to happen now."

I pause, as the *power* inside me is rising, rising. . . . Vertigo and mind dissociation slam me, so that for a fraction of an instant I actually black out, and there's a buildup of impossible pressure from the inside. At last it feels like there's no more room, so it just sits there, right below the surface . . . balancing on the knife-edge of my lips. *So much power. . . .*

It's prickling me, a sequence just at the tip of my tongue. All I need to unleash it is to speak another word.

It occurs to me, *I could kill him with one breath. . . .*

One Logos breath of power.

No . . . is that even possible? But regardless, for Mom's sake, no, just no. . . .

And so instead I carefully exhale and inhale, keeping the balance of force churning inside me. I visualize it moving in strange repeating figure eights, the shape of the symbol of infinity.

And then I speak again, using all that impossible intensity to focus the meaning of my words. I charge my words with such sharp semantic clarity that it seems the *imagery* of what I say hangs in the air before us, fills the expanse of my mind and spreads outward. This is not a *compelling voice*, this is something else. . . . A voice of revelation, of awareness imbued with insight . . . a voice of genuine, eye-opening conviction . . . a voice of reawakened sentience.

A voice of reason.

"Your mission of destruction ends *now*. You will stop the asteroid. Or you will change its trajectory and guide it on a different path, away from Earth. Divert it anywhere, elsewhere, safely out of reach. Just a few degrees off—it is simple. Do it, and I will cooperate with you."

I grow silent, and my resonant power-words hang in the air. . . . My hands are trembling, and the fine hairs on my skin stand up with goosebumps.

The Imperator's expression goes from furious to thoughtful, to almost slack. It's as if he's forgotten all mention of my mother, all his threats, and is distracted by some urgent, incontrovertible set of facts and logic that must be addressed now, this instant. . . .

Aeson stares at me and glances at his father.

And then Romhutat Kassiopei tells me, still thoughtful and genuine, "No, unfortunately it cannot be done. Earth must suffer the asteroid impact."

And then he adds, tiredly, almost sadly, and with resignation, "Yes, I designed the Earth mission, every detail and component, carefully guided all the pieces and all the players for these past several years. And not even your earnest attempt at persuasion can change the cruel reality of what must happen. An interesting use of Voice, by the way—I don't believe I've heard this variety, not compelling, but persuasive nevertheless—"

"But—why? Why can't you stop all this?" I say, ignoring his aside.

"Because the asteroid needs to strike . . . at certain coordinates in your Atlantic Ocean, in the location of the original Atlantis continent, where it will detonate a very specific high-level quantum energy charge."

"What?" Aeson frowns at his father, his lips parting in confusion.

The Imperator sighs, still in the mellow and thoughtful mode. "This information must not leave the room. Only a handful of individuals know this." He lifts one finger, pauses. "The precisely calculated detonation will close and repair the ancient *dimensional rift* which brought the alien enemy to us so many eons ago. It will end our struggle once and for all—at last. No more fear, no more constant vigilance or patrolling deep space, no more running away and colonizing. No more pursuit from *them!* Humanity will live and continue to evolve and progress in peace—on our *own* terms."

I am stunned. "But—but no," I whisper, feeling all the gathered power and righteous fury inside me disperse like smoke. "I understand your motivations now—some, at least—but, no! You cannot destroy Earth in the process!"

"There must be another way," Aeson says. "Send localized explosives on a smaller scale to the coordinates, the kind that do not initiate an extinction-level event, planet-wide—"

"There is no other way!" the Imperator interrupts, his tone regaining the normal petulant edge that he uses in private with his son—as the effect of my strange unnamed voice must be dissipating. "We tried smaller-scale local explosives and various energy discharges, more than twelve thousand Earth years ago! They were insufficient! According to old records—admittedly incomplete—our ancestors tried closing the rift in more ways than you can imagine!"

"But we have better technology now," Aeson says. "We can plan and contain the detonations with greater precision. Containing energy on a quantum level is what we do!"

"You think I don't know that, boy?" Romhutat snarls. "What, you think that in all these years and centuries, no other smart scientific mind wrestled with this problem? This may be news to you, but part of the Earth mission was a series of discreet attempts to close the rift while we were back there during the Qualification process. While you and the ACA engaged in talks and diplomacy with the Earth leaders, some of our specialists were working in secret, on site, under the guise of retrofitting the ancient Atlantis subterranean chamber network. We used our modern, better technology to no avail! We generated countless smaller quantum containment fields and bombarded the rift with energy at every imaginable level. The only things we did not try were the super-megaton detonations on such a massive destruction scale that cannot be safely achieved at close planetary proximity to the target. In fact, the asteroid was going to be our last-resort measure to generate such a detonation. . . ."

"And you didn't think to inform your son and Imperial Heir of any of this?" Aeson says in a bitter voice.

The Imperator glances at him. "Knowing your . . . *scruples,* boy, it would've created unnecessary complications."

"My scruples?"

Romhutat Kassiopei makes a harsh sound. "Yes, your inability to keep your conscience out of the bigger picture! When it comes to putting yourself in harm's way for others, you're easily a hero. But when it comes to morally grey, hard decisions, you're your Mother's son. . . . You are *weak*. You want the truth? You're not fit to be Imperator—the kind of leader necessary for dark times, times of true crisis such as these. Why do you think I'm doing all this, boy? I am doing this *for you!* When I'm done with all of this ugly, dirty work, when the Earth mission is complete as planned, I leave you without an enemy to fight! I leave you a free *Atlantida*, unencumbered by ancient threats of destruction, so that you can be a true divine Imperator—a saint, if you will—ruling in a golden age, a perfect time of peace and justice and harmony, as you've always wanted your reign to be—"

"*Enough*, Father. You don't know me as well as you think." Aeson's features are composed, but his eyes are radiant with anger. "I remind you again, I am Kassiopei. I am perfectly capable of making all the hard decisions that are necessary. But I will not commit atrocities. There are always other alternatives, and I will always strive to find them. If you consider that weakness, so be it. . . . But if I survive long enough to become Imperator, I will not accept the burden of your Earth genocide on my conscience, so do not *ever* say you are doing this for me!"

"Ungrateful whelp!" the Imperator exclaims, stepping toward his son. I notice his fingers are twitching, hands starting to clench into fists.

Would he hit his own son?

I wonder in that terrible moment if the Imperator is guilty of actual physical abuse of his family in addition to the psychological kind.

"I am Kassiopei," Aeson replies without flinching, and a cold smile comes to his lips.

There's a long moment of silence as the two men face off, both so different yet so terribly similar in their dangerous expressions.

My thoughts are feverish as I watch and listen, afraid of what might come next. . . .

To be honest, I'm not sure if I'm more shocked by the awful new revelations or by the continued extent of the Imperator's blatant cruelty toward his own son and toward me.

He is using his son as a moral excuse for all his horrifying actions and plans.

And he is responsible for my mother's death. . . . He just tried to use it against me. . . . He threatened my siblings. . . .

But the new revelations are taking precedence over emotional shock. And so, as usual, my ideas start flying, and so does my big mouth.

"This rift—this dimensional rift," I say in a numb voice, interrupting the horrible moment of confrontation between father and son. "How was it created in the first place?"

At the sound of my voice, the Imperator starts. The fierce tension is broken, and he abandons Aeson (almost in relief) and throws a hard look at me.

"You can thank our blessed fool ancestors for it. From what we know—or assume—some kind of massive energy tampering went on, and it created a quantum instability, which evolved into a potential energy hole."

"You mean a black hole?" I say, putting one hand to my mouth. *"On Earth?"*

"Something like that, yes. Our ancestors shielded it, but still it leaked and fluctuated, and it allowed trans-dimensional movement, bringing all kinds of dangerous things here into our universe— things that don't belong."

At once, I think of the *pegasei* and Arion. . . .

"Such as our alien enemy," Aeson concludes quietly, in a voice still razor-edged with ice.

"Yes, and more," the Imperator retorts without looking at his son and instead directs his attention at me. "And all because the ancients had not done their due diligence before experimenting with early quantum technology. So they left you with an unstable, uncontainable, permanently evolving, real-time quantum *anomaly*— at the location of what you now call the Bermuda Triangle. Yes, even you modern Gebi are aware of it, although you really know nothing. Not only is it a conduit for alien entities into our dimension, but it will continue to expand, decay quantum boundaries, leak matter and energy, and potentially rip apart the multi-dimensional space around it, including your Earth—unless we repair it, once and for all."

"I'm sorry, but this is just so much—too much—all of it, so hard to believe. . . ." I'm barely aware of shaking my head and frowning with tension. "Actually, it's really starting to sound like popular conspiracy theory and fake news nonsense, the kind that's perpetuated by gullible, malicious, or crazy people back on Earth. The Bermuda Triangle is a man-made black hole? What else? Are vampires and leprechauns involved too?"

The Imperator watches me with renewed derision. "Modern-day conspiracy theories are nothing less than future myths and legends, Gwen Lark," he says. "I thought you Gebi understood this when the Fleet arrived on Earth and you learned our true common history stemming out of ancient myth. But—think what you like. I am not particularly familiar with your current conspiracy myths, but, rest assured, *everything* has a basis in reality, no matter how corrupted the final interpretation is."

"Okay, but. . . . So your plan is to destroy Earth yourself to prevent Earth from being ripped apart in a black hole? What? That's crazy!"

"No, but it is unfortunate. Earth is the past. And it is only one component of the grand equation—of which, again, you know nothing. The safety of Atlantis is my primary concern—"

"Earth is so *not* the past for the eight billion people who live there now!" I exclaim. "That's eight times the population of Atlantis!"

"And those eight billion will die when the ancient enemy returns to finish what they started over twelve thousand of your Earth years ago. Only this time they will come for both our planets. In the end, all nine billion will die, and there will be no more humanity left."

The Imperator grows silent, watching me with his draconian stare.

I stand, engulfed by the overwhelming ocean of information, much of it conflicting or somehow contradictory, jumbled, with significant pieces still missing. And my thoughts are suddenly disoriented, swimming hopelessly against the tidal forces of a whirlpool, pulling me down, down, down. . . .

No!

I find I'm shaking my head again, and I start to mutter, "No, I can't—just, no! There must be some other way!"

"The only way is to save *this* world, Gwen Lark," the Imperator replies. "You will begin by re-keying the ancient ship—*now*."

"As soon as we reach an understanding, Father," Aeson says, folding his arms. "An unbreakable bargain sealed with the Imperial Word. A guarantee of Gwen's safety, and the safety of everyone she cares about, family and friends. Come now, it's a simple solution to the most immediate problem. You want to silence the ship, and frankly, so do we. No one wants the alien enemy to find us. Let us put all personal feelings aside and work together on this."

The Imperator makes a strange, short laugh. "Very well," he says suddenly. "You make a fine attempt to bargain like a proper Kassiopei, boy. Yes, fine, I give my word that your pretty little Bride will remain safe, and so will her family and everyone else she wishes to keep safe, including animals, birds, and insects, if she so desires."

I glance back and forth at son and father.

Aeson's mouth remains a straight, impassive line. "In that case—You honor my Bride and me. But—we must have your Imperial Word—say it, Father."

"I give my Imperial Word that your Bride and all her human baggage will be unharmed—there, you have it," the Imperator says in the same tone of strange disdain.

Aeson nods. "My Bride and I are grateful and honored by your Imperial Word and promise of safety. But just to seal the deal, I am going to make a unique promise of my own. If somehow this formal bargain is broken—if anything happens to Gwen or her loved ones—I will let the public know what actually happened at Ae-Leiterra—what you *did not do* on the day that I died. . . ."

"What?" The Imperator's face turns to stone and his jaw goes slack. "You—"

But Aeson continues, "As insurance, I've recorded and encrypted a very special data feed ready to be released to the media and all the social network feeds. It contains the truth of Ae-Leiterra. If she dies, or if I die or become incapacitated, it will automatically be activated and distributed virally, and the world will know everything—the Imperator will be dishonored. You, my Father, will bear the stigma of a coward who did not perform his primary duty to his people, while his young son had to do it in his stead—"

Romhutat Kassiopei breaks into a flood of curses. He is visibly agitated, and for a moment I almost feel sorry for him.

Oh my God, what happened at Ae-Leiterra?

As if reading my mind, Aeson turns to me and says, "Gwen, I will tell you this sad story later tonight, all of it. But now, my Father knows precisely the extent to which this condition of your safety is never to be broken. You are hereby properly insured."

He pauses to smile at me, then turns to look directly into his father's eyes. "*Now* I bargain like a proper Kassiopei."

In the next several moments the Imperator calms down gradually and with difficulty, continuing to glare at both of us, but he no longer protests or makes sarcastic remarks. Periodically he curses soundly again in *Atlanteo*, and once even spits on the floor with fury, showing a decidedly undignified, non-Imperial side.

"We're not done, you and I, oh no. . . . We'll continue this talk," he hisses at his son during one more outburst. "Don't think for a moment that I've forgotten, Son of mine. . . ."

Aeson watches him impassively. After that one moment of triumph his smile is gone and the mask is back, a practiced illusion of patience and composure intended solely for his father. "Yes," he says. "I have no doubt we'll return to this ugly conversation . . . Father of mine."

At last the Imperator regains control.

"Very well, accursed whelp . . . and you, *girl*, listen carefully. You will sing the proper keying sequence—as I was saying before being interrupted with all this idiocy."

"But how?" I say. "I already said I can't sing like that—not with that kind of throat singing technique."

The Imperator snorts. "Bah! You don't have to! Not like that, not in the way I demonstrated previously. I was simply testing you, and you failed. You're not as skilled as I am, and it's a good thing you don't have to be, or we'd be completely *screwed*, as you say in your damned Gebi English—"

"What?" I frown. "What do you mean?"

Aeson shakes his head with renewed anger. "He means the keying is an ordinary command, and he was only intimidating you with an unnecessary Imperial show of advanced Voice."

"Oh!" I exhale in relief, feeling absolute disgust at Aeson's father—for so many reasons now, compounded.

One thing he's right about—we're not done with any of this ugliness.

"Listen!" the Imperator says and sings a basic C-E-G sequence in his normal low voice, this time without using overtones. "Repeat after me."

I do as he says, singing for the first time since the fateful raising of the Grail. My voice starts out a little faint and hoarse, but I focus and clear my throat and, this time, sing accurately.

"Good, you are capable of the basics," the Imperator says with sarcasm.

"What next?" I say coldly.

The Imperator nears the monitor with the live feed of the *Stadion* and the Grail. He beckons me with one hand. "Approach and sing, facing the screen. Perform the keying command three times as you focus your voice on the ship. *Carefully!*"

I take one tentative step toward him, and at once Aeson flanks me. We all crowd around the desk and the monitor. I feel Aeson's hand slip into mine, and his warm fingers squeeze mine briefly before releasing me.

And then I face the screen with the feed and whatever embedded audio transmitter, seeing only the same metallic gold surface close up. The display is still zoomed in somewhere along the "goblet's" neck. Once more I'm aware of the buzzing of metal against the camera on the other end, and the deep, constant hum, rattling my bones even through this remote transmission.

I take a deep breath and visualize the Grail Monument in its grandiose entirety, and then continue imagining the rest of it, extending deep into the ground—I don't even know what the ship is supposed to look like, its true shape, I can only imagine something like the modern ark-ships—and then I sing the keying sequence, a perfect C-E-G.

My voice comes clean and steady, is transmitted remotely. . . . Even as I complete the three notes the first time, already the ancient ark-ship is responding. . . . Suddenly there's silence, as the hum and buzzing cease, while the ancient program halts, recognizing new input. I continue singing as instructed, repeating the sequence two more times, and then I look up.

The Imperator looks at me, then glances at his son briefly and nods.

Next, he faces the monitor and sings the same C-E-G sequence that I just finished, also three times—while the ship remains silent, listening to the input. Then he pauses, raising one finger for quiet, as Aeson and I observe, hardly daring to breathe.

Finally, the Imperator follows up with a strange extended sequence of notes which I vaguely recognize as an Aural Block, but with enhancements. This Imperial Aural Block sequence has additional notes, repetitions, and complex embellishments. When the last note falls, there is initial silence. . . .

For at least three heartbeats.

And then the ship responds. It seems to *sonic-lurch*, as we feel a deep subterranean tremor—a sonic wave that resonates across the stadium arena in all directions like the ever-widening circles from an object cast in water. The vibration is so low that the only sound comes from the shifting of the ground itself.

Remarkably, the remote camera and its audio pick up this effect. It's difficult to imagine the sound technology necessary for processing the input with such spatial precision, but somehow it is transmitted to us, many miles away, across the sprawling city, here in the Imperial Palace, so that we can *feel* and ride the ghost wave echo. . . .

And then all at once the deep hum returns. Except that it continues rising in pitch, turning swiftly into a horrible shriek and rising higher yet, going ultrasonic and disappearing beyond human perception.

All of this takes place in a split second, and surely it must be heard and felt out there in the city—a sonic boom in the neighborhood of the stadium, all around the urban downtown complex where yesterday the crowds of protesters gathered and today there's only the usual workday traffic. What must all those people think? Indeed, over the monitor I hear distant flocks of birds rise, flapping all around the neighborhood, fleeing with alarm into the sky.

But none of it matters right now, because the Imperator moves back with a satisfied expression on his face. "Finally," he says to us, ignoring our tense frowns. "The Master Lock is restored. Which means the quantum shield is back in place, and we are safe for the moment."

Immediately he keys something on the desk to disconnect the live feed, and the monitor goes dark, to be replaced by the Imperial network logo.

"Time to call New Deshret," Romhutat Kassiopei says with a grim smile.

Chapter 9

When it comes to heads of state on Atlantis, the Imperator's closest counterpart is Areviktet Heru, the Pharikon of New Deshret. Aeson explained it to me earlier, and now I'm about to meet this high-ranking individual for myself.

The monitor screen is activated once more, and Aeson and I watch the Archaeon Imperator of *Atlantida* make a call to the opposite side of the planet.

There is no apparent temporal delay and the screen connection goes live, showing the face of a very old man with very dark river-red-clay skin, wrinkled and dried into parchment. In stark contrast, his long hair is white and pulled back in braids—or as I see later, segmented tails. His black eyes are narrow slits among the wrinkles, but his expression is alert and shrewd. And in its resting state, his face is as disdainful as that of the Imperator.

Unlike the Imperator, the Pharikon is formally attired. He wears a wide Egyptian-style collar of gold and dark gemstones over a robe or jacket made of an expensive-looking black fabric. And behind him, I can see some kind of dimly lit, opulent chamber, indicating evening.

"Romhutat Kassiopei, you are late," says the Pharikon of New Deshret in a rasping old man's voice, speaking *Atlanteo*.

As soon as he speaks, it makes sense why he might require vocal assistance. At his age and apparently frail condition, the Pharikon is probably barely able to sing, much less execute complex voice commands properly.

"*Shiokuh nuuttos*, Areviktet Heru," Romhutat replies in an overbearing, arrogant voice, the type I've heard him use in public during Court Assemblies. And then he continues speaking several more words in the foreign language which I assume is the *Deshi* language.

I glance at Aeson, who watches their exchange and gives me a tiny nod of reassurance.

The formalities over with, the Imperator switches suddenly back to *Atlanteo*, then English, and casts a negligent look at me. "This is my son's new Gebi Bride. She is responsible for yesterday's disruption, but it has now been corrected."

Immediately the Pharikon turns his attention to me. I feel the complex scrutiny of his curious black eyes upon me. "*This* girl is Gebi?" the old man says in *Atlanteo*, and then switches over into slow, accented English. "From Earth? You are from Earth? How are you the Imperial Bride?"

"Yes, yes!" the Imperator interrupts him. "That's another matter entirely—later. For now, I require you to check the *situation* on your end and confirm that the Ra Disk has been stabilized."

The Pharikon coughs harshly and takes a deep breath before replying. He does not sound healthy at all, it occurs to me. "Require all you like. You will wait now," he says at last, regaining his voice. "I waited all this time, so now it is your turn, Kassiopei."

The elderly Pharikon grunts, lifts a wrinkled, bony hand drowning in a wide sleeve and moves into view a second mech-arm monitor, similar to the one here. I can see him turn it around so that we all have some inkling of what's on his second screen, and it's another live feed, this one showing a dark evening scene outside. In it, an immense, bright, artificially illuminated gold disk—a convex hemisphere, embedded upright against a hillside—shines in high contrast against the barely visible panorama of indigo mountains and star-filled sky.

The Pharikon issues a spoken command to someone offscreen, and we observe someone else's hands take over, and then a young voice sounds—girl or boy, it is hard to tell—singing, then speaking quietly in *Deshi*. Then the second screen display begins to zoom in on the Ra Disk, and soon the golden metal takes up all of the view. As it does, the golden surface is suddenly visible up close as the camera makes contact with it.

I strain to hear any kind of humming, any buzz of vibration, but there is none.

"Ah, so quiet . . ." the Pharikon says, visibly relaxing. "Good, it is silent again. The Ra Disk sleeps once more, as it should."

"Perfect," the Imperator replies. "Then our business is concluded. *Nefero niktos*, Heru. You need your rest."

But the old man shakes his head, casually pushing the second monitor screen away so that he can dominate the view once more, pressing forward. In that close-up of his deeply lined, clay-colored forehead, his nose with its prominent bridge and flattened nostrils, he is reminiscent of an ancient Mayan king from Earth's Mesoamerica. "Not so fast. I want to know what other news you have for me. What of the *rahuqua* sightings in deep space? Do you have updates for me? Where is your son, the Commander of Star Pilot Corps? Or is he no longer the one in charge up there? Well? Speak up, Kassiopei!"

"He is here, as you can see quite well," the Imperator replies, glancing at Aeson and beckoning with one hand. "Talk to the Pharikon. Tell him what you know."

Aeson moves in closer and slightly inclines his head in a curt but polite acknowledgement of the other ruler. "*Shiokuh nuuttos*, Pharikon Heru," he says in a composed voice. "You have the most recent report from the SPC; nothing new since."

"Nothing? What about the activation of the Ra Disk and your own Grail transmitting who-knows-what kind of rogue signal for a whole day, Commander?" The Pharikon speaks to Aeson in a voice that now quakes with irritation. "Have you checked the skies since? Have you sent your scout ships into deep space today? I am told you've been busy with your new Bride—not enough to neglect your SPC duties, I trust?"

The Imperator draws closer to the screen once again. "We've been rather busy with the Games, or did you forget, Heru? This is Games season. All of *Atlantida* is consumed. Yesterday it was supposed to be over, but because of the unfortunate incident my son's Bride caused, the conclusion of the Games has been postponed, the betting halted. . . . Now the final ceremony must take place as soon as possible, or they will riot—"

"I don't understand," the Pharikon says. "What exactly has the Gebi Bride to do with the incident? How did she cause this disruption? What happened?"

"My Bride was a Contender in the Games," Aeson replies with a grim expression, without looking at his father.

"What? But how strange!" Areviktet Heru's narrow slits of eyes widen momentarily, despite their surrounding border of wrinkles. "Why would she be in your Games? Who allowed it?"

"It was a Wedding Gift," I say suddenly. "The chance to be a Contender in the Games was a generous Gift bestowed upon me by the Imperial Sovereign."

The moment I speak, the Imperator turns to glare at me—presumably because I dared to open my mouth. Aeson, on the other hand, allows himself a faint smile only at the corners of his lips as he watches me.

Emboldened by Aeson's encouraging expression, I continue. "During the final tiebreaker event I used my Voice to lift the thing which I thought to be the Grail Monument, unintentionally activating the ancient ship. I didn't know what it was, naturally, or I would never—"

"You broke the Master Lock with your Voice?" The Pharikon addresses me in his carefully measured English, and now the intense gaze of his shrewd eyes is boring into mine. "You have a Logos voice? What are you? How is that possible? Only a Logos voice can break the Imperial Aural Block!"

"I am Gwen Lark, a refugee from Earth," I say. "I'm told that I have a Logos voice, yes. Not sure how or why, or what any of it means."

The Pharikon shakes his head in incredulity. "So—you survived *Atlantida's* annual feast of blood, slaughter of the talents, the best and brightest."

"Yes. I *won*. And now I'm a Champion."

"Hmm. . . ." The old man pauses, considering me in silence. He then turns away and focuses on the Imperator. "A stupid risk, Kassiopei. What kind of ridiculous logic permitted a young, talented Gebi woman with a precious Logos voice to risk herself so needlessly, especially when she is your son's chosen Bride?"

"Ah, stop playing your favorite game of ignorance, Heru," the Imperator replies. "As usual you already know—you always know more than you admit."

The Pharikon makes a sound that is either a snort or a chuckle, but his expression does not lose its severity. "I've been hearing rumors naturally, about all of this—not the Logos voice, that part is new—but all the rest of it. As you can imagine, my sources are normally very well informed."

"Naturally."

"But in this case, I must admit, I've had some doubts as to their credibility—so I had to confirm with you directly. And now I am perplexed even more. Why would you arrange this dreadful situation? What possible motives?"

"You're still playing," the Imperator says with sarcasm. "I only gave my son's Bride what she had wanted for a long time. Her aspirations to be in our Games are public knowledge. You should ask your sources for a library of old media feeds detailing the biographical circumstances, culminating with the Gift presented at the Assembly in her honor, a splendid event—"

"Such a *generous* Gift . . ." I interrupt, speaking in a hard voice, while continuing to look directly at the old Pharikon.

Everyone glances at me. Aeson's gaze upon me is particularly intense.

"I see," Areviktet Heru says after the slightest pause, no longer looking at me. "So, this is your way of punishing your son and Heir for his unusual choice of Bride. You are so transparent, Kassiopei, so transparent in your malice. How predictable you are, Archaeon Imperator. Short-tempered and short-sighted yet again, allowing your passions to rule you. . . . Ah. . . . This tendency of yours was your Father's scourge. I remember so well how he tried to mold you, shape and temper your character, to little avail—"

The Imperator leans in closer to the screen with a dark expression, and his words slither like serpents. "Go to bed, old man. And don't presume to evaluate my actions in your daft head."

"I will do as I please, as always, Imperial snakeling. Don't assume I am the only one who can see through your hot-headed grudge of a Gift. The Imperial Court of *Atlantida* might close their collective eyes, and your propaganda machine might make endless media feeds, but your people will see right through it—"

"Enough!" Romhutat Kassiopei cuts him off. "If you have any other state business to discuss, or questions for the SPC Commander, proceed. Otherwise, we're done."

In that moment, the same young voice sounds off-screen, whispering in *Deshi*.

"What now?" the Pharikon says, turning to the young person in the room. He grabs and fumbles with the mech arm of the second monitor, returning the night view of the Ra Disk to us. And this time the old man makes an angry noise for which no explanation is necessary.

The previously silent golden disk is *humming*.

I recognize that deep sound—the same sound that has been issuing from the Grail.

The Imperator curses furiously and immediately pulls up his own second monitor here on our end. He sings the initial command, then hand-keys additional ones, and the live feed of the *Stadion* arena returns.

In the now familiar view, the camera device, still touching the Grail surface, again vibrates with the metallic buzz caused by the deep, profound humming coming from the Atlantis Grail.

The ancient ark-ship is *active* once more, despite all our earlier efforts.

"Oh, no," I whisper, and my hand involuntarily rises to my mouth. I glance at Aeson, who looks at me, then stares at his father, who in turn glares at the screen close-up.

"What? What is going on, Kassiopei?" Frowning at us from the other screen, the Pharikon of New Deshret speaks in a much steadier voice than he's been using for the last few minutes (which seems to indicate he is not as frail or ill as he puts on).

Aeson fixes on his father. "Why is it active again?"

The Imperator curses once more, a stream of *Atlanteo* words, many of which I'm not familiar with. "What—what is it *doing?*" he exclaims finally, pounding his desk with one fist and holding the monitor with the other. "I reset the Master Lock. It should be dead!"

"If you set it properly, why is it still active?" the Pharikon says with a tone of accusation. "Are you sure you did the sequence correctly?"

The Imperator roars in reply. "The Imperial Aural Block worked! I set it perfectly, and everything went quiet. This should not be happening!"

"Do it again," Areviktet Heru says.

"Let Gwen do it," Aeson says suddenly. "Let her do the whole keying sequence."

The Imperator glances up at me momentarily, then again ignores me, his son, and even the Pharikon on the other monitor. His single-minded focus is now on the screen with the Grail, as he grasps that monitor on both sides with his fingers and leans in closer, staring fiercely.

And then the Imperator begins to sing. First, the simple C-E-G keying sequence, three times. And then he sings the intricate Imperial Aural Block.

Our nervous tension fills the room. We listen while the Imperator's darkly powerful voice cuts and carves the air into tonal shreds, like a blade of punctuated intent.

And again, just as before, the ark-ship responds. First, the humming stops as the ship listens for input. Then the lurch of profound, low sound comes, followed by the gathering power-wave which transforms, rising into a supersonic shriek and disappearing with a boom.

In its place there is once again silence.

Romhutat Kassiopei looks up and glares at all of us with a dark, triumphant expression. Then he rests his gaze on Areviktet Heru. "Now you see how it's done, Heru, and you can hear the actual result. Still don't believe me? Well? Now check your own end again and tell me if it worked. The Ra Disk should be inactive."

The Pharikon grunts, and his wrinkled face moves away as we see him fumble with his own second monitor and get a fleeting glimpse of the hands of his young assistant. Then he returns with a reluctant nod. "Yes, Kassiopei, it is again shut off."

"Precisely," the Imperator concludes with satisfaction.

"But for how long?" the Pharikon says, his voice again regaining its rasp, which is apparently his normal public demeanor. "I don't trust this command of yours to provide permanent results. Let us wait and see."

"Suit yourself," the Imperator says, and a muscle twitches in his jaw.

And so, we wait. The Imperator drums his fingers on the surface of his desk, while Aeson looks at me reassuringly, then— after about thirty extremely uncomfortable seconds of silence— makes polite small talk with the Pharikon.

"How is the weather in Xois tonight, Pharikon Heru?" Aeson says casually. "Not too cold? I hear your techs have been having some trouble maintaining the coastal atmospheric pressure balance in the Gulf of Eos this season."

But Areviktet Heru is in no mood for pleasantries. "If you want to know about our barometric stats, Commander, look it up. Don't make light of this very grave situation and don't evade the subject at hand, young Kassiopei. I want this Ra Disk and your Grail situation resolved. It is all I care about right now. Is that clear?"

"Very," Aeson replies, still calm and composed. "We want this resolved as much as you do."

"Heh." The Pharikon responds with a creaky grunt of annoyance and shakes his head.

The Imperator merely glares at the ruler of New Deshret, continuing to tap his fingers fiercely on the desktop. Periodically he glances at his other monitor with the view of the Grail.

Whenever he does that, the Pharikon in turn glances at his own other monitor with the view of the Ra Disk, as if to make a point.

Moments tick by.

And then the dreaded sound comes. Maybe I'm the first to hear it, because I feel a sensation of something deep rising, a barely perceptible disturbance along my skin, prickling the nerves—and I catch my breath.

Now it's undeniable. The profound hum issues from the live streaming feed of the Grail, while at the same time the Pharikon pulls the display of the Ra Disk closer, and we can hear the small gasp of the young assistant behind him. "It returns! This is obviously not working, Kassiopei!"

The expression on the Imperator's face is terrifying. For one long moment he does not answer.

And then he very deliberately turns to the Pharikon, saying, "I will handle it, Heru. Will call you back."

And with a hard movement he disconnects the call.

"Let Gwen do the Imperial Aural Block, Father," Aeson says. "Teach her and teach me, for that matter."

"No." The Imperator looks at his son like a dragon. "We are going to the *Stadion, now.*"

Chapter 10

What happens next is a flurry of activity. While Aeson and I wait, the Imperator calls his staff and orders cars readied for a sudden trip downtown. He barks orders in a cutting tone at his wrist comm, then motions for us to follow him out of his Red Office.

Moments later we are surrounded by Imperial guards, and we rush after the Imperator through the hallways of the Imperial Quarters. In the central grand lobby at the elevators, Aeson's own guards join our group, hanging back somewhat to give the Imperator's personal guards precedence, and we continue moving through a doorway that leads in the opposite direction from the lobby and deeper yet into the same level of the Palace.

Many hallways, servants scattering out of the way, and confusing turns later, a corridor opens into another, smaller, marble-and-gold-trimmed lobby also equipped with elevators. We take the elevators there, but instead of descending we continue up to the Palace roof. I have not been to this specific portion of the roof—the Imperial Palace complex is sprawling and huge, not a single structure but a many-tiered grouping, with flat and angled roofs topping various buildings—and this particular roof area appears to serve as a landing hover-pad. I notice it's located far away from the elegant open-air pavilion where I had my first *eos* bread and met my future in-laws on my first full day on Atlantis, because I can barely make out the colonnades of the pavilion in the distance, at least four rooftop tiers away, through the white haze of Hel's light.

Crisp wind washes over us, and bright morning sunlight strikes us with a fierce white glare. Aeson pauses momentarily to take my hand, pulling me toward him, then hands me a pair of wraparound sunglasses. Squinting, I put them on, feeling immediate relief, and continue moving, holding him by the hand, as we are loaded into hover cars.

At least six gleaming metal vehicles await us, levitating two feet above the surface. The Imperator commands us to his own large private car with an opulent, dimly lit interior, and unexpectedly takes the seat in the very front next to his own staff driver, who handles the task of flying our vehicle. Meanwhile I end up next to Aeson in the second row of seats, and the guards pile in behind us in the third and fourth rows in the very back.

All through this, the Imperator doesn't say a word to his son or to me. He only addresses the driver with a curt command, "To the *Stadion*, quickly." And then he stares out the indigo-tinted, translucent anti-glare window, ignoring all of us, his gaze straining forward, his fierce, handsome profile stilled in darkness.

We lift off, and the Palace rooftops fall away in a gilded radiance of mauve, red, and black-trimmed marble, as we rise into the blindingly incandescent sky, flying toward Poseidon city center.

All this time, Aeson's large, comforting hand continues to cover mine.

I find that I'm barely breathing, numb and frozen, while we fly over the now familiar city landmarks, with no one speaking. Soon I see the radiance of gold that is the Grail "monument," rising up in the distance.

Now that I know what it actually *is*, for the first time my mind perceives the blazing vision and properly interprets it, filling in the gestalt of the continuation of the Grail underneath the ground, so that I can almost visualize it, the giant ark-ship buried deep beneath the city.

The Imperator directs his driver to land us right inside the empty *Stadion* arena, at the foot of the Grail. As soon as the vehicle doors open, I hear the deep, bone-jarring hum, feel its low vibration sweep over my body. We get out of the hover car in haste.

Aeson and I carefully step onto the arena floor and exchange glances, while the Imperator practically leaps out ahead of us and issues commands in a draconian voice. The Imperial guards are told to make sure no one else is in the area, and to clear from the premises any grounds restoration staff or other employees.

"No one is to be allowed here, do you understand?" the Imperator tells them. "Not even the building security. I want them all out. Inform them this is a mandatory safety inspection before we begin the reconstruction cleanup."

All but two of the guards immediately spread out across the vacant expanse and disappear inside the corridors of the nearby buildings.

The two remaining guards step back discreetly to a polite distance that is well out of hearing range. I watch them conversing on their wrist comms with others who are elsewhere in the complex.

"Come!" the Imperator orders us meanwhile and begins walking toward the Grail, stepping over the cracks in the ground and the uprooted building material lining the floor of the arena.

We follow, stepping carefully over the crumbling sections underfoot, over what looks like concrete and rock and layers of twisted metal.

Oh my God . . . I did this.

My breath shudders as I test my footing before each step.

The grandiose golden stem portion of the Grail rises into the sky above us. Curving upward, it expands into the immense round bowl section that casts a circular shadow. Instead of looking up at it, I stare at what's on the ground in front of me—the barely convex horizontal "stand" portion which is the outer surface of the main hull, the buried bulk of the ark-ship.

"Come, come!" Romhutat beckons angrily with his hand as he steps onto the golden, curving surface.

Aeson walks after him, and I follow.

My perception of the humming vibration increases exponentially the moment I make direct contact. It enters my body through my feet, and I feel my teeth rattle with the horrible buzzing. It occurs to me, *I am standing on top of the ancient ship.* At once I am overwhelmed by the strange wonder, the implications—not only does it affect all my physical senses, it stirs my mind with a cascading depth of emotion.

Ahead of me, the Imperator walks a few more steps along the golden curvature and stops at the base of the immense upright column—at least ten feet in diameter at the slimmest point—that constitutes the rising goblet stem. He puts both hands against the stem, fingers splayed and digging in with intensity like frustrated dragon claws. He lowers his head and closes his eyes, then begins to sing the keying sequence.

C-E-G.

His dark, deep voice does not require amplification as it echoes with power throughout the stadium, bringing immediate silence.

We listen with rapt attention, and the guards listen from afar. The Imperator follows the keying command with the intricate Imperial Aural Block sequence that resounds with eerie beauty.

The ship responds. Moments later, the resulting sonic blast we experience at this proximity feels like a small explosion. Aeson grabs my arm to keep me from falling, while I huddle against him and put my hands over my ears, as though that would help.

Surely this cannot be healthy. . . . At least not prolonged exposure to such sound. Ugh!

The Grail is now silent. Only the local birds continue to screech and flap their wings as they rise into the sky all around us. Poor birds.

The Imperator remains in the same position, head still down, eyes closed, hands splayed against the ark-ship surface. It almost looks as if he's praying. . . .

And then he takes in a harsh breath and looks up, glancing at his son and at me. The light of Hel paints his face with washed out pallor. "Note the time," he says to Aeson. "We wait and time it—the interval of silence until—*if* it begins again."

Aeson glances at his wrist and marks the time on his multi-function comm gadget. I watch his movements, frowning with tension behind the illusion of privacy given by my wraparound glasses.

Unfortunately, it does not take long.

Only a few minutes later the hum returns, swelling from the ground, filling us with its excruciating rattle.

"Seven daydreams and eighteen heartbeats," Aeson says in *Atlanteo*, which—if I recall correctly—is the approximate Atlantean equivalent of "seven minutes and eighteen seconds."

In one of my weird mental asides I recall out of the blue that this oddball term referring to a minute, roughly translated as "daydream" or "reverie" was never officially used by anyone during the Games. It has archaic connotations and—according to my Atlantean instructors—is slowly being phased out (with much resistance, especially by the military and the science and tech sectors) in favor of actual Earth minutes, to both modernize and integrate the two populations. Meanwhile, "heartbeat," the term for a "second," is still persistently used by the general population.

In any case, apparently the Imperator likes using this older form, and Aeson accommodates him. Or maybe for some reason they need this level of old-school precision for whatever measurements are associated with the ancient ark-ship, and Earth-style minutes just won't do.

While my stupid thoughts nervously ramble, the Imperator nods to his son, then redirects his dark stare at me. "Gwen Lark, it has come to this. I will now teach you the Imperial Aural Block. Let's see how capable you really are."

And that's how, for the next twenty minutes—or daydreams, or better yet, nightmares—I am treated to the dubious honor of a private Voice lesson from the Archaeon Imperator of *Atlantida* himself.

Romhutat is a ruthless instructor. He makes me repeat notes and sequences over and over, correcting me harshly at the smallest imperfection of tone and pitch. The command sequence is not particularly long, but it is very complex, so it takes a while until I can echo the whole thing back correctly. Aeson listens and observes us, and I'm certain he is silently learning the sequence for himself.

At last I am more or less ready.

"Place your hands on the ship," the Imperator tells me. "Feel it, know it, become one with it. I don't care how you choose to focus your energy, just do it. What is it you Gebi do to focus? Meditation, you call it? Meditate, if you must—or pray to your Gebi gods."

I nod silently and rest my numb fingers against the vibrating gold metal of the Grail.

I should probably stop thinking of it as "the Grail." It's a ship, a great ancient relic of metal alloy and other artificial material that has travelled across the universe. . . .

It's an object from Earth.

My breath catches, and my heart starts to pound with the sudden basic realization.

But before I can begin the keying process, one of the guards approaches, and the Imperator steps aside to talk to him.

Aeson and I stare with worry because the Imperator has a deeper frown when he comes back, while the guard departs to his original security distance.

"What?" Aeson says.

His father shakes his head with annoyance. "Reports of protesters gathering outside the complex. Apparently, the public is concerned with the sonic activity here, and also the Games nonsense. They are chanting for the final Champions Ceremony, demanding we resume tonight or tomorrow. Also, the media is out there, snooping, trying to interview the evacuated staff. Just what we need. . . ."

"The timing cannot be worse," Aeson says. "But something must be concluded, as far as the Games. You'll have to give them something—unless you want to explain all *this*."

The Imperator makes a disdainful hiss and curses in *Atlanteo*, then once again turns to me.

"All right, girl, are you ready? Proceed!"

Don't think . . . just don't think. Do it.

I take several big breaths and focus, clenching my hands into fists, while I sing the commands in a clean, perfect voice stripped of any emotion.

When I'm done, the result is silence. Then comes the same rising shriek culminating in the awful sonic boom, and more silence. More flapping, screeching birds.

"Good! Time it!" the Imperator tells Aeson, who nods.

Here we go again.

I stand, breathing, hearing the pulsebeat racing in my temples, while minutes pass. The Imperator slowly walks around the stem portion of the goblet, glancing periodically into the distance, at the guards, at the buildings of the complex. Aeson just stands next to me with his arms folded and waits.

"How much time has passed?" I ask *im amrevu* nervously.

"About fifteen daydreams—minutes, if you prefer," he says, checking his wrist. "So far so good."

"Okay," I mutter. "Maybe it worked?"

"Let's hope so, for all our sakes," he replies in a calming voice.

But about a minute later, the humming returns, rising from the ground underneath like an ocean swell.

My heart jumps painfully.

Romhutat Kassiopei stops his pacing and makes a harsh, angry sound. "So much for your Bride's vocal abilities," he hisses. "We have a serious problem. How much time elapsed?"

"Sixteen daydreams and twelve heartbeats. It lasted a bit longer this time."

"Much good it does us." The Imperator looks around again, noting the guards with their stoic expressions, working hard at pretending that nothing is out of the ordinary. Then he looks at his son with an evaluating stare. "Your turn, boy."

Aeson raises one brow.

"Don't dawdle now, I know you memorized the sequence too. Let's see how well you can perform at least one of your future official duties. *Do* it now."

And Aeson begins singing the command sequence— impeccably.

When he's done, and his haunting, gorgeous baritone goes silent, the ship reacts as usual. Silence, rising screech, sonic boom, silence again.

Without needing to be told, Aeson notes the time.

We wait.

Twenty minutes later, the terrible humming sound is back.

It becomes obvious now—the ark-ship will not be silenced.

The rest of the morning turns into a painful farce. The Imperator does not permit us to leave the stadium and attempts various other voice commands. He teaches them to Aeson and me and forces us to key the ship and execute each one, over and over and over again. . . . Our voices are getting such a long workout that guards are sent to bring us drinking water laced with a special soothing tonic for the throat and vocal cords.

At some point, after initial hesitation and some pointed arguments, Aeson and his father sing the Imperial Aural Block together, their dual Logos voices cutting into me with incredible power that sends goosebumps along my skin and seems to carve up the arena and the sky, land and air, with subtle vibrations. The guards listen, equally rapt with attention, the impact of the Plural Logos Voice felt by everyone.

The ship obeys and is complacent and inert for over an hour—
which makes everyone think it finally worked, so that we even
return to the cars and sit inside comfortably waiting.

But then, just as the Imperator decides it's safely over, the
humming sound returns, stubbornly eternal.

The Imperator curses and jumps out of the hover car. "Both of
you, come!" he tells Aeson and me.

And so, we get out, climb back over the broken ground, and
place our hands over the golden stem.

This time we do the Plural Voice as a chorus of *three* Logos
voices.

The power and beauty of the sound we make is hard to
describe. . . .

My rich mezzo soprano mixes with their two profound
baritones, forming a river of glorious sound that swells into a
cosmic-scale *sound ocean* and fills the *Stadion* and the surrounding
area with a strange, almost tangible, sonic *structure*. As I sing my
own part, I feel our tonal intertwining, happening in real time . . .
particle-wave-strings of energy and matter being pulled into artful
constructs . . . and I understand suddenly why multiple Logos voices
joined together in song are a dangerous thing.

Not only have we keyed the massive ship beneath us but,
apparently, we have keyed the entire stadium complex. Somehow I
am certain of it—I can *feel* it.

Everything that has any trace of orichalcum content in the
immediate vicinity is now connected to us on a bizarre, personal,
quantum level.

It is all ours to control—if we choose.

Chapter 11

At the moment we only intend to exercise this immense power over one thing. The ancient ark-ship responds to our Plural Voice Chorus and, after the sonic boom, goes predictably silent.

"Is it—is it done?" I ask, breaking the magic silence. "Will this hold it?"

"It had better," Aeson replies grimly. And he once again marks the time on his wrist comm.

The Imperator makes an effort to appear expressionless, then checks his own wrist device which has been emitting a gentle tone. "Eh! It's your Mother," he says with a burst of annoyance, glancing at Aeson. "She wants to know where we are and if we're available for *dea* meal."

"By 'we' does she mean you, Father, or all of us?" Aeson watches him, fighting to maintain his own masked expression.

"*Bashtooh!* Who do you think? You, me, your Bride—everyone." The Imperator pauses, frowning, looks from Aeson to me, then back. "She must not be told about any of this. Do you understand? No one is to be told. Not any of your *daimon* friends, not any member of the IEC, *no one.*"

"What of the guards?" I ask. "They must know or at least hear and see something is happening—"

"The Imperial guards are trained to be discreet and silent. Both of you could learn discretion from them." Romhutat continues to glare at his son and at me. Not a word of praise for either of our performances in the Plural Voice.

"So, what now?" I say.

"We continue to wait." The Imperator taps his wrist comm and enters something with decisive quick movements. "But we do it back at the Palace."

"Is that wise?" Aeson says. "If we leave now and the ship reactivates yet again?"

His father's cheek muscle twitches with anger. "Nothing to be done beyond what has just been done. If three Logos voices working together could not accomplish—no, it is ridiculous. We sealed the safety lock. I am certain the Imperial Aural Block will hold now, and therefore I am leaving. Come! Or don't, your choice. Your Imperial Mother will expect your presence at *dea* meal, but feel free to disappoint her."

In the next half an hour we return to the Imperial Palace in the Imperator's hover car, tense and silent. Romhutat Kassiopei wears a permanent frown on his face and barely speaks to us. He and Aeson both continue to check the live feed of the Grail on various devices, and it remains blessedly silent.

"How long has it been now?" I ask Aeson quietly as he stares at his wrist. And then I point to his hand. "By the way, maybe I need to get one of these—one of my own—these wrist gadget things, Aeson."

Aeson looks up at me and raises one brow, then widens his eyes and exhales. "Of course! I've been meaning to get you a personal unit—sorry, it's slipped my mind repeatedly. . . . When we get home, I'll have Gennio configure one for you tonight."

"No rush," I say with a tiny smile at the sight of his earnest distress in regard to me. And then I glance at the Imperator's stern profile in the seat in front of me. A bitter feeling stabs me in the gut, a reminder of what harm this man has done to my mother. And then I swallow the feeling and force myself to think of the here and now and what set of new difficulties lies ahead.

One problem at a time.

It is Noon Ghost Time when we arrive, and the Imperator dismisses us so that we can return to Aeson's own Palace Quarters to freshen up before *dea* meal, which will be served in the Imperial Quarters.

Once we're alone in the Imperial Crown Prince's Quarters, the first thing I do is call Gracie and Gordie, who are presumably still at the estate in Phoinios Heights. I don't bother with a video call through one of the monitor displays on Aeson's desk computer that uses the Palace Network because I want to bypass triggering the

Palace surveillance algorithms. Instead I borrow Aeson's wrist comm.

We connect, and Gracie's voice sounds very worried on the other end. She is bursting with questions, and I can hear Gordie in the background. Immediately I force myself into a steady and relaxed tone and use my big sister voice to tell her that "all is well" and that we were successful in dealing with "that certain issue."

I don't mention the Grail or the Ra Disk by name, since the Imperator forbade us to discuss the situation with anyone—again, this is the Palace, filled with hidden surveillance everywhere. Yes, even though that particular cat's been out of the bag since last night, and my siblings and friends and the *astra daimon* are already somewhat aware there's some kind of problem with the Grail—the Imperator doesn't need to know about it.

"Okay . . ." Gracie mumbles. "So that Ra thing—the Ra Disk—is all okay too, right? So, what exactly was wrong with it?"

"Uh-huh, all good," I say in an extra-bland voice, hoping she'll get a clue. "More about that later."

"Lord, you must be exhausted—after everything—and now, *this*. Are you even—"

"It's okay. I'm fine."

Gracie pauses, then says, "So when are you coming back here? *Dea* meal? Gordie is gonna eat the flower arrangements if we don't eat soon—"

"You guys go ahead. We've been invited for an official meal here, so. . . ."

"Oh. Okay."

"Are you sure?" I say, feeling a little guilty that I can't just have my own sister and brother come over and have a normal casual meal with us here. "Sorry about that, Gee Four."

"Oh yeah, no problem," she says firmly. "We'll just eat in here and watch all the crazy news on the TV. Oalla and Ker and Xel are downstairs, and Erita has gone to pick up some of those pseudo-donut pastries you like so much—"

"What crazy news?"

"I guess you were too busy dealing with your top-secret stuff, but there are Games protests all over downtown Poseidon, and other crazies screaming about all kinds of weird things happening, noise explosions and strange lights in the sky and other junk."

"What?"

"Just turn on the news," Gracie says. "And don't bother with the Hel-Ra Network. They are underplaying all of it, as if it's not even happening. Watch the Free Poseidon News—they are showing everything. Amazing, insane stuff!"

"All right," I say. "Will watch when I get the chance, gotta go now. Love you! Tell Gordie what I said, and you go eat now, okay? See you later tonight."

I disconnect the call and sit back on the sofa with a frown, while a new worry starts to gnaw at my gut. Aeson glances up at me from his desk, where he's logged in to take care of some business. "Everything all right?"

"Yeah, I think. It's the news. Bad stuff all over, I guess."

"We'll watch later," he says. "As long as it's not the ark-ship again, it can wait. Now, get a few minutes of rest before we head to *dea* meal."

The fact remains unspoken between us: having gone through the Games ordeal, I'm not really at my best, not at my full strength—in fact, far from it.

And with my Mom gone, I am fragile and pitiful and pathetic. . . .

No. Stop.

"Should I change clothing? Who else will be there?" I tuck my feet under me on the sofa as a sudden burst of emotional exhaustion slams me. And I lean against the comfy back cushions, now also feeling my chronically sore muscles acting up. We happen to be in the familiar workroom that separates Aeson's personal bedroom from mine—one of the rooms of the Imperial Crown Prince's Quarters that we use most commonly. Neither Anu nor Gennio is here today—they are both working back at Aeson's estate in Phoinios Heights.

"Not sure who else," he replies. "We can assume it will be intimate. Although, my Mother might've invited some other suitable, high-ranking guests to defuse the potential situation of being one-on-one with my Father. Don't bother changing, you are fine as you are."

I smile tiredly. "Ah, Aeson, you always say I'm fine as I am. Even when I look and dress awful."

He smiles back at me. "To be honest, what you consider awful is usually charming."

"Ah, stop." But I'm smiling widely back at him.

In that moment a small tone sequence sounds from his desk computer display, and it's echoed on his wrist comm, which I'm still holding between my fingers. It startles me in a bad way—the way a chronic stressor affects someone stuck in a constant verge-of-panic alert state. My heart skips a beat painfully.

Aeson's expression grows serious, and he turns his attention back to the screen and says, "It's done. I finished configuring the alarm to sync with my own and my Father's personal units and our network accounts. In other words, if the ark-ship status changes, we will know immediately."

I nod, with a pained expression. "Was that the ship—"

"No, don't worry, that was just a test of the system. Not a real alarm notification."

Phew. . . .

"I'm just so used to getting bad news that a little thing like a test alarm *only* is a relief," I say.

Aeson looks at me with intensity. "I know."

A little later we arrive back on the Imperial Quarters floor, pass the now-familiar grand marble lobby with the elevators and the array of honor guards, and enter the antechamber with the lesser thrones. This time the attendant servant directs us to a different interior doorway that takes us to the Imperatris's Quarters adjacent to the Imperator's, situated on the same main portion of the floor.

As we pause at the entrance, Aeson casually runs his hand along my lower back and lingers there for a moment, pressing and caressing me reassuringly. His firm touch gives me a pleasant jolt of warmth and confidence, and we enter the chamber.

The room is basically a long interior balcony, completely enclosed with the Atlantean version of glass along the outer wall. It has a lofty trellis ceiling of mixed glass and veined gold that mimics natural plant vines and leaves entwining to create a diffuse mesh of surprisingly effective protection against the fierce sunlight—good thing, because at the moment Hel shines directly above, only a little past zenith. The interior wall is magnificent in deep mauve and red marbled stone trimmed in black, and also veined in gold. A row of slender columns runs alongside it, creating a corridor nook with multiple seating areas and one long narrow table with seating for twelve on both long sides.

I see immediately that we have additional company for *dea* meal. Devora Kassiopei, exuding casual elegance in her shimmering, layered outfit of verdigris, persimmon, and gold, sits at one end of the long table as the meal hostess—according to Imperial Protocol, as I recall from my lessons with Consul Denu—and the Imperator sits in the first side seat to her right, the position of the honored guest.

Across from him, in the side seat directly to Devora's left, I see a vaguely familiar middle-aged man in a dark grey and black jacket, with shoulder-length hair gilded in impeccable courtier fashion, deep bronze skin, and a composed, self-important demeanor. He is the ACA Director Hijep Tiofon—one of the IEC members whom I met at some point over the past month or so before the Games, an Imperial loyalist and also the man in charge of the imposing agency that handled all the Earth and Atlantis formal interactions back on Earth.

Next to him is a man whom I recognize as another one of the Imperial inner circle, the First Priest Shirahtet himself, of the prominent noble family Kuruam that serves the cult of Kassiopei. Shirahtet is an older man, not decrepit but in late middle years, with a clean-shaven skull except for one gilded forelock running from his forehead all the way to the back of his head and culminating in a long, segmented tail—a symbol of his sect. He has leathery red-clay skin and unreadable dark eyes thickly outlined with kohl. His clothing is not ceremonial, but a formal court jacket trimmed in earth colors, and he has a preponderance of jeweled rings on his fingers.

Across the table from Shirahtet and next to the Imperator is the Imperial Princess Manala—poor girl—dressed in a lovely rose outfit similarly formed of layers of veils like her mother's, looking humbly down at her place setting.

Next to Manala, thankfully, is Consul Suval Denu, wearing his tallest wig and a similar elegant jacket of deep plum and sage artfully embroidered with fine gold thread. His fingers are also laden with gold and jewel rings. Underneath his artful mask of kohl and rouge, his expression is almost beatific, but I know him enough to recognize the lively darting movements of his eyes as he watches everything.

Finally, across the table from Consul Denu, seated next to the First Priest Shirahtet, is an unfamiliar, bony, middle-aged woman with hawkish features that are handsome instead of beautiful—a fierce aquiline nose and very dark eyebrows over deep-set eyes. Her dark brown hair, free of any dye, is gathered in a stern knot updo, but a fine net of gold threads rests over it, and long dangling earrings connect to the netting of the headdress. She is wrapped in a pale cream robe, and her hands sparkle with faceted crystals around her wrists and fingers, also part of an intricate golden net that extends from her sleeves.

At once I feel a momentary pang of familiar social anxiety. *Who is she? Should I know this woman? At least I sort of recognize the others. . . .*

As we are announced and approach the table, with everyone staring at us, the Imperator looks up at Aeson with a minor frown. "My Son decides to join us. And his lovely Bride. You are both late. Sit!" And he points to the nearest empty seats.

Devora, meanwhile, merely smiles at us from her hostess position at the head of the table.

"Apologies, my Father, Mother," Aeson replies smoothly with a nod to both his parents. And he directs me to the seat next to Consul Denu—perfect choice as far as I'm concerned—while he himself takes the seat across the table from me and next to the unfamiliar woman.

The moment we are seated, the Imperatris motions to the discreet servants in the alcoves along the interior wall behind us to begin serving our *dea* meal.

At the same time, the Imperator checks his wrist and exchanges a quick glance with Aeson. Aeson lightly raises his brow and then also discreetly looks down at his personal unit.

For once I know exactly what they're doing. . . .

I sigh and look down at my own place setting, while moments later a servant leans in and a plate appears, filled with artfully arranged food that smells like savory heaven. Knowing my Imperial Protocol, and with a swift glance to my left for reassurance from Consul Denu—who barely smiles and faintly nods at me just enough to give his affirmative—I refrain from touching any utensils and wait for the Imperial Couple to begin first.

The Imperator must be famished after the stressful events of our morning because he immediately commences to eat, and everyone at the table follows his lead. For the first few minutes there's only the clanking of utensils and glasses and silence, as everyone chews and swallows as politely as possible but in haste equal to the Imperator, so as not to be deprived of their still-full plate as soon as he is done.

I use my eating utensil to snag several bites of whatever is on my plate, and my body tells me it's hungry and this is good. Meanwhile my mind is still apparently stuck in *eternal crisis* mode and refuses to process such insignificant sensory input as taste.

Having allowed us sufficient time to eat enough to take the edge off our hunger, the Imperatris begins to make elegant small talk, following perfect Imperial Protocol. First, she addresses the Imperator, then makes a point of pleasantly engaging each of the guests. "What a lovely day we're having. The breeze is barely cool, and I've had my morning walk in the gardens without being blown off the path," Devora says with a gentle smile, turning to her Imperial Husband. "The month is off to a good start."

"Huh," the Imperator grunts, saying nothing else and taking a long drink from a goblet.

Now that the hostess has spoken, it is permissible for others to talk also.

"How was your circuit of our Provinces, Oratorat?" The Imperatris next addresses the unfamiliar woman next to Aeson.

Oratorat, I wonder, *is that a title or an honorific?*

"Both insightful and blessedly uneventful, My Sovereign Lady," replies the woman in a solid, no-nonsense voice and businesslike manner, setting down her utensil. "We took an extended detour through your Northern Provinces just to avoid the culmination of your Games and the accompanying traffic—and I don't mean just the routine urban sky collisions. Apparently, we should have taken an even longer detour westward, judging by all the—*turbulence* still happening in Poseidon on the *ground*. Not normal, by all accounts."

"No, it's not," says Hijep Tiofon, clearing his throat. "We've had some unusual seismic activity in the direct city center, unfortunately. Happened right in the middle of the Final Ceremony yesterday, so the complex had to be evacuated and the Games resolution postponed for safety reasons. The public is agitated until that's all concluded, hence the *turbulence* downtown."

"Ah," the woman says. "How odd. I don't recall this kind of thing happening in Poseidon—not *ever*."

"It happens." The Imperator suddenly speaks gruffly. "But yes, the timing was atrocious."

The woman inclines her head. "Naturally, I could be misinformed. Eos-Heket has its own minor share of ground-shaking activity along the Iaat border, but nothing much reaches us in Ushab. My sympathies on the incident."

Eos-Heket? I recall the name of the country to the Northeast of *Atlantida. Okay, so she must be a foreign dignitary of some sort.*

"My Imperial Sovereign, when is the situation expected to be under control?" the First Priest Shirahtet says in a soft voice, addressing the Imperator.

Romhutat turns to him with an irritated look. "It *is* under control. We are working on the *cleanup* of the *Stadion* and adjacent premises. Safety inspections took place all this morning. The conclusion of the Games will proceed shortly."

The First Priest inclines his head with utmost cordiality. "Of course, My Imperial Sovereign. Indeed, it must."

"What of these urban protests?" the woman asks. "Seems hard to imagine they will be satisfied with simply more of your spectacle."

"The people were frightened, but now they simply want to resolve their bets." The Imperator looks at her with unblinking eyes. "They shall have their Ceremony and their Top Ten Champions—as early as tomorrow, if necessary. That is all—"

The Imperatris interrupts gently, as if sensing the buildup of tension. "Oratorat!" she says with a light exclamation. "How remiss of me—I forgot to introduce you to my son's Imperial Bride. This is Gwen Lark, from Earth. Gwen, you already know everyone present, but not the honorable Oratorat Kephasa Sewu of Eos-Heket."

And now everyone turns to stare at me.

"Oh," I say with a stupid jolt because my name was called. My heart starts to pound for no reason whatsoever. "Very nice to meet you—Oratorat."

The Oratorat turns to me with a nod. Her look is shrewd and curious as she examines me. "My pleasure, young Imperial Lady. How unusual. You are from Earth, truly? You must've just arrived with all the refugees, how did you come to this arrangement with the Crown Prince of Imperial *Atlantida?* I don't recall being informed of any Earth marriage alliance in the works—was that not part of our discussions, Director Tiofon? That we were to be informed of all such details?"

"Oratorat, it happened very privately," Aeson speaks up calmly, with a quick, warm glance in my direction. "Nothing was prearranged. We met and grew close naturally. Gwen worked with me during our journey home."

"My son has met his match," the Imperatris says with equal warmth. "Their two hearts are entangled. And I am happy to say the Wedding is set for Red Amrevet 9. You are invited to attend, Oratorat, if it's still within your plans to be present here on that date."

"A love match?" Oratorat Kephasa Sewu says with an incredulous expression. "Commendable and fortunate indeed, Imperial Lord Aeson. One would think such a thing was not possible, considering you're a Kassiopei Heir. Your life is arranged from your conception till your last breath, we're told. Once again, I must be misinformed. Or things are indeed changing in Imperial *Atlantida.* So then, we have the Earth refugees to thank for this remarkable progress, starting with this one."

And the woman smiles at me and at Aeson with amusement, then throws a sharp glance at the Imperator.

At once, Devora Kassiopei again defuses the conversation by calling on the servants to present the next course of sweet drenched fruit and a savory dish of flaky pastry aromatic with spices.

Finally, the *dea* meal is over. The Imperator rises from his seat with a formal nod to his wife and informs the Oratorat he will receive her at her leisure in the next hour, after her visit with the Imperatris is concluded. Then, after giving Aeson a meaningful, hard look that briefly touches me, the Imperator departs to his own Quarters for a private meeting with the ACA director and the First Priest. Since these two men are not merely IEC members but the Imperator's closest confidants, I have a very good idea what they will be discussing in a locked room. For once, nervous worry makes me want to be a fly on the wall there.

At least the alarm has not sounded. The ancient ark-ship remains dormant. . . .

The Oratorat, Consul Denu, and the rest of us remain in the Imperatris's Quarters to continue the visit and have a leisurely "tea." We simply pick ourselves up and move to a different large room in the interior, away from the late afternoon sun.

I glance at Aeson constantly, never losing my awareness of him, and he returns my look with his own steadying gaze even as we move to occupy the other room. No longer constrained by table seating protocol, he takes the place right next to me on the comfortable sofa. Although we retain a slight, proper distance between our bodies as we sit side by side, his hand comes around the back of the sofa and his fingers sweep against the side of my shoulder and neck, sending unexpected sweet pangs of sensation throughout me. His faint, steady caress is almost enough to make me forget everything . . . almost.

While the Imperatris and Kephasa Sewu talk about the details of the Oratorat's travel itinerary through the Provinces, Consul Denu comes over to sit nearby and makes a point of engaging me in small talk. Even though he'd been seated next to me throughout the entire *dea* meal, no true conversation was at any point possible.

"Now that we may speak a bit more at leisure, I must say, my dear Imperial Lady Gwen, it's my utmost joy to see you triumphant and *well*, after surviving your ordeal in the Games," he says, leaning closer and inclining his bewigged head in an impeccable courtly nod. "Well done, my dear, well done!"

"Thank you," I say with minor amusement, as his overwhelming flowery perfume wafts in my direction. "Although I still can't believe I'm *alive*."

The Consul smiles. "Not merely alive, but a Champion!"

I purse my lips tiredly and try to match his smile in reply.

Aeson merely watches us with a carefully composed expression which barely covers his own grave state of worry.

Meanwhile the Imperatris now calls Aeson over and they speak, while the Oratorat steps toward me and examines me with her matter-of-fact gaze.

"I have so many questions about your refugee experience, Imperial Lady Gwen—about Earth, and the process of what must've been a remarkable journey here," says Kephasa, and her shrewd dark eyes continue to evaluate me. "Unfortunately, my schedule is very demanding, and my time here is limited, so I must simply ask you for a future conversation. I trust you'll soon have the opportunity to visit Eos-Heket in a formal capacity and observe how our own share of the Earth refugees is being accommodated and settled. You must have some invaluable advice for us, considering your unique dual perspective as Gebi and now Imperial *Atlantida* royalty. Promise me a visit."

"Oh, of course," I say, with a glance at Aeson nearby, still talking to Devora. And then it occurs to me—I know so very little of the current political and diplomatic relations between *Atlantida* and Eos-Heket, that I'm not even sure if I'm permitted to make such a promise or keep it. "I would love to, as soon as my duties permit. Forgive me if I am still somewhat new to all this," I say, trying to extricate myself from what could be a diplomatic blunder. Fortunately, Consul Denu is here, and he skillfully moves to the rescue and takes over the conversation.

After a few general pleasantries, Consul Denu and Oratorat Kephasa Sewu step away to converse quietly on the other end of the room.

To my relief, I am left alone, and so I turn and smile at Manala who happens to be perched on a chair nearby. I walk over to stand next to her. "How are you?" I say gently. "How is Khemji doing?"

Princess Manala breathes in equal relief, seeming to come alive now that her Imperial Father and all the imposing men are out of the room. She responds to me joyfully and starts to chatter about her big, black, notoriously flatulent cat, having missed seeing me all these days since before the Games ordeal started.

But now Aeson interrupts her gently and comes up to me. He takes my hand, directing me back to the large sofa, and Manala follows us, still speaking to me—or rather, *at* me—with enthusiasm. Thankfully she hasn't mentioned anything about the events of last night, regarding the whole business of the Ra Disk. It's possible she had conveniently "forgotten," as she tends to do when things get too disturbing.

Devora Kassiopei picks up a glass of tea—that is, the Atlantean version, some kind of a light brew of pleasantly fragrant plant leaves steeped in hot water which, if I remember correctly is called *aeojir*—and joins us.

"Hush, Manala, child. Move over a little," the Imperatris says to her daughter mildly, setting down her *aeojir* on a tray table in front of the sofa, so that the rich, amber-colored liquid dances in the light like an agitated jewel and wafts curls of vapor. She then sits down right between Manala and me and puts her hand on my arm, patting it. "How are you, Gwen? How are you holding up? I hope my Husband was not too hard on you this morning."

She doesn't know about the ship, it occurs to me. *She thinks we simply had a horrible confrontation.*

"It's okay," I say with a tiny smile, then glance at Aeson, who is sitting on my other side.

"At this point you must be weary beyond all comprehension, my dear. Would you like to go lie down now?" Devora says. "Just for a little while, at least."

"No, I'm all right." I make a point of speaking in the most lighthearted way possible. Even though I'd love nothing more than to collapse in bed right now and curl up in the fetal position, I know somehow that I cannot—not until the ark-ship situation is resolved.

They might need me again, or at least require the use of my Logos voice.

"Very well." The Imperatris squeezes my hand. "But the moment you feel tired, please don't hesitate. Aeson, make sure she gets sufficient rest tonight, since nothing else is scheduled, and the most immediate crises are over—thank the gods."

Oh, if only she knew. . . .

"That's a promise," Aeson says, watching me closely. "We will likely head home soon—in a few hours." And then he involuntarily checks his wrist comm.

Again my heart skips a beat.

But I breathe and nod to them, and absently watch Manala as she looks around the room, then calls up a smart display and turns on the TV without sound. The smart board screen levitates in the air before her, and I can barely make out four split screens with various newsfeeds. Manala frowns at some of the apparent violence and quickly scrolls through the feeds. I take a deep breath and tell myself not to look—at whatever it is.

Bad, crazy news, as Gracie had called it. Right now, I honestly don't want to know.

Just for a moment—a stupid, tiny, little, impossible, blessed moment—I'd like some *peace*.

But that's not happening.

An hour later, the Oratorat ends her visit and Consul Denu—obviously now acting in his diplomatic capacity—accompanies her to the Imperial Audience.

As soon as the woman is gone, Aeson says to me, "Gwen, you did very well. That woman you just met is very important—she is what you would call a prime minister or president of her country—our important ally and neighbor, Eos-Heket."

"I had a feeling she was." I let out a deep breath. "So—what is Oratorat, exactly?"

"It is an elected position of government leadership," the Imperatris tells me. "I regret, poor Gwen, that you were not warned ahead about her presence. But truly, I had no idea she would choose to join us at today's intended-to-be-casual *dea* meal instead of going straight for an Imperial Audience or the latest Imperial Executive Council session. I have a feeling she wanted some fresh gossip about the state of affairs. She must've really gotten a bad impression from seeing Poseidon in the middle of urban protests."

The Imperatris pauses, looking at her son. "Aeson, what is really going on out there? You know I couldn't bear to watch any of it yesterday, but they tell me the unfortunate quake happened exactly during Gwen's final tiebreaker event of the Games—is that right? How terrible it must've been for you—"

So the Imperatris also doesn't know what actually happened at the Games—what I did.

"I believe Gwen doesn't need to be reminded of it now," Aeson says softly, glancing at me with intensity. Ah, so many complex meanings in that look of his. . . . But mostly a subtle reminder to me: *say nothing*.

I am saved from having to make any response by the dreaded alarm tone coming from Aeson's wrist.

Chapter 12

Okay, this is hell.

Despite the combined efforts of our *three* Logos Plural Voices, the ancient ark-ship is *active* again.

Aeson starts—or more accurately, freezes—and his eyes widen slightly. He looks at his wrist, then looks up at me. "Forgive me, Mother, but we need to go now," he says in the most casual way possible, turning to the Imperatris. "Please excuse us."

"What's wrong?" Devora asks her son, with immediate concern. Her maternal senses are strong and, knowing her children's moods, she picks up something troubling in Aeson's demeanor.

"Nothing major, but I did promise to take care of a few things, and the appointments can't wait. Just got a time reminder. We'll see you very soon again, I promise."

"All right, but be sure not to overtire Gwen, not today, it's too soon after—"

"Yes, thank you for the lovely meal." I stand up, smiling warmly at Devora, to reinforce the fact that *all is well*. "We'll see you soon, Manala!" I add to the younger girl whose emotionally transparent face echoes her mother's worry.

And then we depart the Imperatris's Quarters.

"What now, Aeson?" I say as we hurry back to the Imperator's part of the floor.

"I don't know." He glances at me with a troubled look that he no longer bothers to hide now that we're alone.

"Do we need to do the Plural Voice again?"

"Probably. Though again it might only buy us a few hours."

I bite my lip and nod, because I've got nothing.

Aeson's wrist comm chimes again, making a different sound, and I'm beginning to recognize the difference between the ring tones. Just as I suspect, it's the Imperator.

"He wants us in his Red Office, now," Aeson says, checking his wrist multiple times as more tones sound, one after the other, heralding additional text messages, as we enter the interior corridor. "He got the ship alarm and immediately wrapped up his Audience with the Oratorat, getting rid of her for now with some excuse. From all this haste she may suspect something is wrong, but at this point it doesn't matter."

"One crisis at a time," I whisper with a bitter smile.

We turn the corner and enter the now familiar Imperial office, hearing several male voices in agitated conversation.

The Imperator is not alone. With him in the small red chamber are the ACA Director, the First Priest, and a third man whom I recognize as Miramis Opu, this year's designated Priest of the Grail. The last time I saw Miramis was yesterday at noon when I inadvertently raised the Grail, and he called out my act as blasphemy.

The Priest of the Grail is not a large man, but he does have a "large man presence." Right now, he is very distressed and venting, and we enter in the middle of his diatribe:

". . . still not working, and if my Imperial Sovereign will concede, the unrelenting news coverage is not helping to calm them at all! I realize that Hel-Ra is being discreet, but the other feeds are out of control! And now these idiots with their nonsense about the pale ghosts and the lights in the sky—"

"They are picking up false sensor signals," ACA Director Hijep Tiofon says in a calming voice, sitting back in one of the chairs in front of the Imperial desk, across from the Imperator. "Very common instrument malfunctions, both atmospheric and orbital satellite level, especially considering the problems they've been having in New Deshret configuring all their weather tech. Someone at Hel-Ra at least needs to make a brief announcement to put down the rumors. Have Desher Keigeri read it. Give a solid rundown of the sensor issues, use simple public-oriented language, make it easy to understand—"

"Good—do all that," the Imperator interrupts. And then he sees Aeson and me. "Come in and close the door."

Aeson steps forward, glancing with caution at the other men, at the same time as I shut the door behind us. "Father—are we free to discuss—"

"Wait," the Imperator says with a hard look at his son and at me, putting up his hand. He then addresses the Priest of the Grail, who is the only one standing (with a puffed chest and radiating drama). "Miramis, your concerns have been taken into consideration. I agree, we need to put an urgent end to it before we lose any more control. The IEC membership is well aware of it. I'll have a public announcement prepared for later tonight that the Final Ceremony will be held tomorrow, at one of the other bigger stadiums—probably the *Khemetareon* has the next largest seating capacity—the details will be worked out in the next few hours. Meanwhile, we'll have Tiago's *Grail Games Daily* and Hippeis's *Winning the Grail* put out advance broadcast promos that the main announcement is coming. It will propagate to all the rest of the feeds and should be enough to calm them down until tonight and well into tomorrow. Is that satisfactory for you?"

"Yes, My Sovereign Lord," Miramis says in a slightly less agitated manner. "It will definitely alleviate most of the unrest. But what of the fear and panic-mongers and their ghost lights nonsense? A separate issue, one would think, and not even local to us in *Atlantida*—"

"Will also be handled," the Imperator interrupts again. "Now, Miramis, you have your satisfactory answer, and you *will* have your Ceremony instructions relayed to you by evening. You are free to go."

"Yes, My Sovereign Lord . . . I thank you." The Priest of the Grail swallows whatever else he has to say and makes a courtly bow, responding to the Imperial dismissal. He turns around and makes his way to the exit through the small, definitely overcrowded room, and his glance briefly falls on me. I notice a flash of alarm in his expression, even a kind of *awe*, as he sees me. . . .

And then he's gone.

As soon as the door closes behind Miramis Opu, the Imperator turns to Aeson and me. "Now we can talk freely. Opu knows only some things. *They* know everything." And he motions with his glance at the other two remaining men. He then leans over his desk, pulls up a monitor, and sings an initializing command to connect remotely to the feed of the Grail stadium.

Aeson and I approach, and First Priest Shirahtet speaks from the other chair, looking at all of us with his unreadable expression. "We need to attempt the Plural Voice joining of the three Logos voices . . . again."

"The effect lasted less than five hours," Aeson replies after a small pause, still cautious about discussing this situation in front of the others. "To be precise, it was four hours, twenty-seven daydreams and four heartbeats."

"I understand, Imperial Lord," Shirahtet says in a steady tone. "But I would like to observe for myself, and the result might vary. Furthermore, I would like to ascertain that the *third* voice is indeed a Logos voice—" and he glances at me. "Has the Imperial Bride Gwen Lark—has she been formally tested for it?"

"I would say the fact that she broke the Master Lock and raised the ship out of the ground is sufficient proof unto itself, Shirahtet," Director Tiofon says, also observing me closely.

Testing me? With a pang of alarm, I'm reminded of the terrifying things Aeson hinted at when he told me about the Imperator's original plans to turn me into a test subject in his secret labs.

And these same secret research facilities are located inside the ancient ark-ship.

Meanwhile the Imperator growls with barely checked fury at the live feed on the monitor showing the Grail, which is again humming loudly. "This *garooi* son of a *hoohvak* will be silent! We will perform the sequence now, and this time it will stick! Come, boy, and your Bride! Over here—come around the desk!" He motions for us to draw closer, while the ACA Director and the First Priest rise and push their chairs further back, giving us room.

We crowd around the Imperator, leaning forward over the display. "Focus, now! Focus!" Romhutat Kassiopei says, with what has now become chronic fury. "Ready?"

And in the next few minutes we perform the keying sequence followed by the Imperial Aural Block sequence. At the sound of our three Voices joined in single tonal melody—especially mine—Hijep and Shirahtet, the two men listening and witnessing, stare in rapt attention.

The sheer force of the Plural Logos Voice Chorus washes over everything like an ocean of electricity, until the room itself seems to be no longer solid matter but energy in a state of quantum uncertainty. Charged with inexplicable *power*, the walls are *seething*, dissolving, permeated with *unresolved potential* on a quantum level. I, myself, feel the effect of it in a headrush that washes through me even as I sing. . . .

When it is over, the ark-ship many miles away downtown responds as before, and goes silent, followed by the screech and sonic boom, then more permanent silence.

Aeson times the moment as always. "This was a remote keying, let's hope it works as well as it did in person. Or at least not much worse."

"If it buys us even a few more hours—" the Imperator trails off, looking at the First Priest and the ACA Director. "Well, what do you say?"

However, both men appear to be stunned and petrified from the effect of the Plural Logos Voice. They are staring at us in amazement.

"I have never in my life heard *three* such voices," the priest says at last. "Not in all my years, even witnessing your blessed Father and Yourself joined in song, My Imperial Sovereign. There were always only two of you at a time. And Manala is an untested child, though not too young to manifest."

"Yes." The Imperator frowns. "There has never been an instance nor a need to include my Son in the voice training alongside his Grandfather and me."

"And then it was too late." Aeson watches his father as he speaks.

What happened to his grandfather?

Romhutat Kassiopei glares back and says nothing.

There is a long pause, and then I say, "What if the ship becomes active again in a few hours?"

Everyone looks at me.

"Then we repeat the command again," the Imperator says, his eyes boring into me.

Aeson shakes his head. "And then again in the middle of the night? Possibly more than once? And what about the next morning?"

The Imperator makes an angry sound. "We repeat for as long as necessary. Set alarms and take turns sleeping, if we must. Meanwhile we search for a more permanent solution."

"My Imperial Sovereign," Shirahtet says. "You must realize, that kind of thing is not sustainable. Not even with three people working in shifts."

"Of course I realize!" The Imperator slams his palm flat against his desk surface. "Did you not hear me say we also look for a permanent solution?"

"Yes, My Imperial Sovereign, my apologies." The priest inclines his head. "I was merely concerned for your own wellbeing and health in this unfortunate situation."

"So what exactly will happen if the ship is allowed to remain active?" I ask.

"We are not entirely sure, young Imperial Lady. But it is forbidden. It is simply not an option," the First Priest replies. He speaks softly, in the same measured, soothing voice, and his expression remains hard to read. "From what we know—from the few oldest records at our disposal—the original ark-ship must *always* be confined and shielded, else it serves as some kind of relentless beacon to the universe, announcing itself—and hence our existence—to all who might listen, including our oldest enemy."

"How exactly does it do that?"

"How? Our records are pitifully limited in that regard," the Imperator interrupts. "But we know that for the last nine thousand seven hundred and seventy-one years, uninterrupted by any incident, the Kassiopei Dynasty has been guarding and maintaining the Master Lock set by our first ancestors who landed and established the Colony. The ship's inexplicable *transmission* is contained inside a quantum energy field, which must be reinforced regularly."

The Imperator glances at Aeson, then continues, "I perform the act of maintenance every year, same as my Father before me—during the Games season, when crowds of easily distracted fools converge around the stadium. It's easy to incorporate my Voice command sequences into whatever spectacle nonsense they schedule every year."

I stare, comprehension dawning.

"You recall the Commencement Ceremony?" the Imperator continues, glancing from his son to me. "When I raised all of you

Contenders above the stadium in a circle of platforms, and the fire belched from the statues? When the Grail Monument "sang" at various moments throughout that day? That was the ship responding to Voice prompts! All of it was part of the *maintenance sequence*. And when it was done, the energy shield program holding the ship was reset and reinforced for another year. That is, until *you*, little idiot Gwen, destroyed not only the program but the whole quantum containment field, stripping the ship bare and free to broadcast its deadly signal, its antiquated quantum programming now apparently damaged beyond repair—"

"Enough, Father!" Aeson interrupts in turn, his own voice hard as steel. "You will not speak to my Bride in this manner, and it is now irrelevant."

"Again, I'm very sorry. I didn't know any of this," I say to the Imperator. "But then again, *you* stuck me in the Games and forced me to fight for my life, which I did, the only way I knew how. So let's just call this what it is—the consequence of your own actions, my *Imperial Sovereign*."

I end with ringing sarcasm, somewhat amazed at my own words, but also amazed that I frankly no longer care at all about my future father-in-law's reaction.

The others in the room also seem to be amazed. The First Priest's bland, unreadable demeanor has cracked at last to reveal alarm, the ACA Director's eyes are wide with disbelief at my gall, and the Imperator himself is fixed in a kind of rage that can have no proper outlet—at least not right now.

I've just mouthed off to the Imperator of *Atlantida* in front of his closest associates.

And I don't give a damn.

Aeson is the one who dispels the crazy-tense moment with cold logic. "None of it matters right now, My Father. What's done is done, but now we have a *problem*. So how are we going to fix it?"

"The energy shield around the ship must be restored," Director Tiofon says, after clearing his throat.

"Or we must come up with a different kind of shield!" Closing up his expression, the Imperator chooses to *disregard my defiant speech* and instead picks up the constructive part of our conversation—which both surprises me and fills my mind with more worrisome possibilities.

"The answers lie in the depths of the ship archives." The First Priest resumes likewise, with his face once again a calm mask, and no longer looking at me—as if by doing so he would nullify my presence and the affront I've expressed to his divine Imperator. "We must return there and search again—descending as deep as we can. I will dispatch acolytes at once."

"Agreed." Romhutat Kassiopei releases a breath of tension and sits back in his desk chair. He too does not look at me as I still stand nearby, with Aeson. "But we must also consider that new, modern tech might be required to fix this one—regardless of what your acolytes would find."

He glances at the ACA Director. "Let's get Rovat Bennu here. He might have some fresh ideas from a scientific perspective, and he can work with you on the jargon for the official statement about the faulty sensors and 'lights in the sky,' for the release later tonight."

I recall that Rovat Bennu is the Director of the Science and Technology Agency, and he's yet another Imperial loyalist member of the IEC.

"How much of this does Bennu know?" Aeson says.

His father glances at him. "Officially, not much, though he suspects enough. But he will now be brought in, as far as the full extent of the role of the ancient ship. It's become inevitable. He's worked down there long enough to have an idea of the deeper facility levels, the unexcavated portions."

"Is that wise, My Imperial Sovereign?" The First Priest's remark is both a subtle caution and a rhetorical question. "Despite all these unfortunate circumstances, some degree of our customary secrecy must still be maintained. Ancient tradition dictates that the fewer individuals who know, the better—"

"Don't be afraid, Shirahtet. Your favorite nine-thousand-year-old secrets are so deeply buried that we remain duly ignorant. Right now, we need all the help we can get—to make sure they remain that way."

The ACA Director nods in agreement and makes the necessary call to the STA Director, as the rest of us watch.

Apparently, the Red Office is about to get even more crowded.

Chapter 13

STA Director Rovat Bennu arrives shortly, with a troubled expression on his long, leathery face, and for the next hour, Aeson and I observe the others bring him "into the fold," then argue.

Rovat Bennu is also not a young man, and most of his dark brown hair has left him years ago, so there isn't that much left to dye. But he attempts to gild it nevertheless, all around the large bald spot. He wears a light-blue coatlike tunic of thin fabric over his jacket, suggesting he'd arrived directly from a science facility and forgot to make himself presentable for the Imperial Palace. But none of it matters.

Now, Bennu *knows*.

"Unbelievable! You're telling me the research site where I perform most of my work is not the high-security basement of the stadium structure, but is in fact the inside of the ancient Colony vessel? And it's buried underneath the city?" Director Bennu says in a nervous voice. "And—and you say there are levels that go even deeper than the Yellow Sector, the so-called "basement" fourth floor? Why was I not told about any of this?"

"Because up 'til now, it did not concern you," Director Tiofon says.

"Oh, and apparently it concerns *you?*" the STA Director retorts with growing indignation. "How is it that the venerable Science and Technology Agency, working for decades inside this relic, is kept ignorant, while the upstart Atlantis Central Agency, only recently formed to act as a liaison with Earth, is apparently deemed relevant enough to be granted this critical inside knowledge? What else am I unaware of? Apparently quite a few things! And not just sensitive information, but details that could be crucial to our current field of scientific knowledge!"

"You always know what you need to know, Bennu," Shirahtet says in a calming voice. "Same for Tiofon and other IEC members.

It is how things work; there is no slight intended. We each have our place in the scheme of things."

"Oh, and I suppose you and your holy caste always get to decide who knows what?"

"As the First Priest of Kassiopei, granted authority *unto the ages* by the divine ancestors of the Dynasty we serve, it is my ancient role and function. Therefore, yes, I do."

"Enough!" the Imperator interrupts them. "Stop bringing up my *chazuf* ancestors, Shirahtet. I choke on them every night as I lie in bed thinking of all the ancient *shebet* they passed on to me in the form of Imperial duty. And you—we need a hard solution to this crisis, and it's why I called you, Bennu. You have been informed, you now have privileged information that must not leave this room, and you will remain discreet."

"My Imperial Sovereign—yes, of course." And Director Bennu inclines his balding head with courtly resignation.

The Imperator exhales fiercely. "Now then, let us discuss our options."

Rovat Bennu scratches the back of his head, causing a few of his remaining gilded hairs to stand up messily, then frowns and glances down at his feet and around the room. His darting gaze lands upon Aeson and me, and I see him blink a few times, as though considering us.

"For starters, I'd like to see it," he says. "The Grail Monument—that is, the ship. Is it broadcasting now?"

"Not now, but—judging by its earlier behavior—it soon will be," Hijep Tiofon says. "And haven't you seen enough of it from the *inside?*"

"Knowing what I know now—" Rovat Bennu shakes his head thoughtfully, "it will be with a new perspective. How, in the name of all divinities, did we as a culture, manage to keep the original Colony ship hidden from the public for millennia? All public historical archives claim it's long-lost. But it's buried right here, under our noses. . . ."

"Having worked there myself, I'd say it's easy to think of it as just a very old underground structure," Director Tiofon says in a conciliatory tone.

Rovat Bennu rubs his forehead and attempts to pace in a very crowded, small spot.

"Have a seat," the Imperator tells him. "My Son and his Bride can stand." And he glances at us with subtle mockery, since only one unoccupied chair remains in the room.

Aeson does not show any reaction and continues to stand with his arms folded. I am at his side, in front of the desk. Director Bennu looks at us again briefly, then takes the chair, pulling it closer.

"Meanwhile, with your permission, My Imperial Sovereign—" ACA Director Tiofon calls up a smart screen from the nearest wall, and sings the sequence to display the media feeds.

The sound comes on, and there's a blast of crowd noise. He zooms in on a bird's-eye aerial view of the downtown complex, taken from one of the media network hover cars, which shows a sizeable crowd gathered below. The agitated voice of a commentator is speaking over the noise.

". . . as you can see, the protester crowds are spilling around the complex of the interconnected stadiums and other venues for at least eighteen intersections, and they are carrying signs and holo-projectors. Not only is the Atlantis Grail Stadium itself completely surrounded—despite the possible dangers of the unexplained sound explosions coming from the site all throughout the day—but so are the Red and Blue Forums right next door, all the way across the Golden Grail Plaza to the entire breadth of the Imperial Khemet Stadium. Various protest groups appear to be GGR-enflamed ordinary residents who want the Games to be resolved and an end to their betting. However—and let's zoom in—quite a few groups seem to express other agendas, including the various conspiracy proponents—"

The camera swoops down and focuses on a street-level view, and the noise of the crowds becomes deafening. We see Poseidon residents—men, women, teens, and even younger children—everyone is pumping upraised fists, waving colorful Category banners with the Logo images, and holding up both physical and holo-projected placards. They are chanting, "Champions! Champions! Give us the Top Ten!" and "The Games are Forever but the Results are Now!" and "Give me my Champion!" and "No Games, No Work!"

However, the camera speeds past all these and stops before the signs that read, "Protect the Skies, Protect us! THEY are Here!" and

"The Stars are Falling!" and "Ancient ENEMY Found Atlantis!" and "Star Pilot Corps Mobilize!"

One man stands with his hands upraised and spread apart, projecting a holographic image of a night sky and a strange glowing blob of pale, washed out radiance, with a caption projected above it that reads: "Tonight from New Deshret!" And then the image is replaced with another view of another night sky, this one showing moving dots of brightness, and a caption that says: "Last night in Ubasti!" Seconds later, the scene is replaced by a third view, of yet another sky with another glowing blob of light and the caption: "At dawn in Shuria!"

"These alleged eyewitness images are confusing, but powerful and undeniable," the commentator's voice says. "So far, our sources cannot verify any of these amateur scene-captures to be genuine, and there have been no official comments from the authorities on the nature of these—indeed, no comments or statements forthcoming as yet from the Imperial Palace or the IEC Assembly Chamber on anything today. But now we are being told that quite a few of the fringe networks worldwide have carried short clips of these eyewitness images taken by local residents in the last 27-hour period—ordinary people recording views of their skies, including New Deshret, Ankh-Tawi, Weret, Seba, Abuud, Hemet-Saret, and on our side, Ubasti, Shuria, Khenneb, and Ptahleon. None of the networks include our affiliates—we are still attempting to get more information for our viewers, and investigative crews have been sent to gather our own footage—"

"That big mass of light. Those moving sparks. *What* is that?" the Imperator demands to know over the noise of the TV feed. "Are you certain all of these are caused by faulty sensors, Tiofon? That's not just New Deshret—they're the only ones having weather tech issues, not Ubasti or Shuria!"

The ACA Director does not answer immediately, but stares, frowning at the screen. Then he says, "Hmm."

The STA Director however, says, "Not sure if that kind of blur right there is corrupted sensor transmissions. But—could be anything. Let me look into this." And he looks down at his wrist comm and starts tapping something.

The Imperator continues staring at the screen, shaking his head.

"I will have the SPC patrols do a complete orbital pass and report within the hour," Aeson says. He too starts entering something into his wrist device. I stand and watch the swift movements of his large, elegant fingers and the tiny screen display across the band light up on his wrist, racing with data in *Atlanteo* letters and numerals.

"Have there been any strange sky sightings here?" Shirahtet asks. "Anything unusual in today's reports from any of your agencies?"

Both the directors shake their heads. "No, nothing," ACA Director Tiofon says.

"No reports scheduled for today." STA Director Bennu looks up, then continues tapping on his wrist.

The Imperator makes a gruff sound. "If this is real—could it be somehow related to our current problem?"

Meanwhile the TV feed continues to scroll down the street, showing the various protestor signs. My attention is sharply drawn to one group waving familiar signs with images of me holding the yellow Grail and the words "Gwen Lark, Our Imperatris, Our True Goddess!" And now they've added new ones—there I am, superimposed upon a night sky, and the caption says: "Her Voice is Logos! She Will Save Us!"

I make an involuntary sound of sharply indrawn breath, while a pang of fear hits me in the gut.

The Imperator sees the signs with my likeness, hears them chanting *"Gebi Goddess! Gebi Goddess!"* and lifts one finger to the screen. "This," he says in a frigid voice, "this needs to be stopped. Throttle it before it escalates."

"Indeed, my Imperial Sovereign," the First Priest replies and casts a chilling look at me.

"That's horrible," I say, staring back at the priest and forcing myself not to break eye contact, so that he is the first one to look away. "I agree, this needs to be stopped, because it's crazy!"

"It's obviously ignorant nonsense," Aeson says at once, frowning at the priest and at his father and throwing me an intense glance. He then resumes observing his wrist comm.

Director Bennu looks up from his. "Okay, a quick scan of global satellite imagery of the skies *right now* shows absolutely nothing out of the ordinary."

"And—SPC pilot orbital reports starting to come in," Aeson says. "So far, nothing there either."

"Tell them to range farther out past orbit," the Imperator says, continuing to stare at the TV feed.

Aeson raises one brow. "Already done. The next pass will be outward toward Olympos. And the Ishtar Station has been notified to look inward. Notifications being propagated to all other Stations."

"Good." The Imperator tears himself away from the sight of crowd protests and plants one palm down on the desk surface. "Now let's return to the more important problem at hand—containing the *hoohvak* ship."

And so the brainstorming nightmare continues. At some point we relocate from the Red Office to a more comfortable room in the Imperial Quarters with seating for everyone. A very large panel TV is called up so that it hovers before us showing at least eight window feeds simultaneously.

Aeson gives me meaningful looks and gently squeezes my hands when the others are not looking, then insists I rest—so I occupy a spot on the end of the large sofa, grateful for a chance to sit down at last. My chronic Games-induced exhaustion is definitely taking its toll.

In addition, I seriously worry about Aeson—he is maintaining his usual composed appearance, but I can only imagine how tired and overwhelmed he too must feel underneath his mask of control.

It's now evening, and the downtown complex is blazing with artificial illumination, which is featured prominently on the Hel-Ra Network feed that tends to focus on the larger picture instead of zooming to individuals in the crowd. Free Poseidon News is much more "zoom-happy" and focuses on interviewing people in the streets, lingering with loving attention on close-ups of provocative captions on signs, angry yelling faces in the various groups, and occasional clusters of uniformed Correctors and other law enforcement officers. Other networks offer coverage somewhere in between, interspersed with talking-heads roundtable commentary. Topics include the mysterious quake from yesterday and its causes (I cringe); the ongoing protests and the agendas of the groups involved; the individual Champions and unresolved tie-breaker Contenders and their mental states; the strange lights-in-the-sky conspiracies that have sprung up literally overnight all around the globe; and even the Imperial Bride (I cringe), and now that she's a Champion, the upcoming Imperial Wedding.

Once we've sampled the gist of the news, everyone pays only minimal attention to the feeds, and it's time to get down to business. The First Priest and the two Directors discuss the possible quantum field containment options. The Imperator makes various calls, some of which are to additional IEC members. Aeson deals with the incoming data on his wrist comm. I'm the only one simply observing and waiting.

Soon two very quiet Imperial staff members arrive to take notes and draft a formal media statement regarding the Games Final Ceremony. It is to be held tomorrow at the *Khemetareon* at the second hour of Khe. Every ticket holder's pass from yesterday's original *Stadion* event is to be duly honored, but actual seating is to be determined by order of arrival and availability, with additional standing-room-only arrangements and, if necessary, consolation vouchers. Champions and tied Contenders will be notified separately.

The statement—after being approved by the Imperator—is forwarded to the media. Minutes later we get to watch and hear it being read by anchors over the different live feeds, including multiple street-level floating orb holograms projected directly into the gathered crowds like giant iridescent soap bubbles filled with moving pictures and sound.

The crowds respond immediately, and now on all the channels there's the noise of cheers and jubilation. But most of the people don't disperse, and some groups continue yelling their angry slogans regardless, while milling around the downtown complex.

The Imperator shakes his head, watching them.

"Ah, you can't please these *chazufs*, My Sovereign Lord," Hijep Tiofon says with a gesture of disgust at the media feeds.

"Tomorrow this time they will be satisfied and happy," the First Priest says.

"Give them time, yes." Rovat Bennu nods. "Now, as far as the effectiveness of performing the *maintenance sequence* immediately after the Imperial Aural Block, just as the ship goes silent. . . ."

And they continue their discussion.

Aeson sits on the sofa, once again right next to me. His wrist comm emits a tone, but thankfully it's just the mass announcement addressed to *me* as a Champion Contender, instructing me to be at the Final Ceremony tomorrow, with detailed instructions. After glancing at the message and arching one brow, Aeson leans back and momentarily closes his eyes. His hand slips over mine, resting there, warming my skin. Then he opens his eyes again and leans in closer to me. "I'm sorry, Gwen. You'll have to put on that damned uniform once more—tomorrow. Hang in there," he whispers. *"Amrevu."*

"You too." I barely mouth the words and move closer against him. My own fingers twine with his, then gently sweep upward along his forearm, feeling the toned warmth of his muscles through the sleeve. Squeezing his arm gently, I linger there, grounded (and even now, sensually *energized*) by his physical presence.

The thought of wearing the white Vocalist uniform yet again makes me sick. I feel like I'm trapped in an eternal haze of unrelenting tension, of waiting, waiting, I don't know for what. Thoughts of my fellow Contenders plague me, and I try to image what the other members of Team Lark must be thinking about right now—especially Chihar and Lolu, who are still tied with other Contenders in their Categories and will find out tomorrow whether or not they won. . . .

Distracted by our common state of stress, Aeson and I sit aside from the others and only half-listen to them argue about the ship.

Some of the ark-ship solutions being brought up and discarded as impossible, unreliable, or otherwise useless are: combining the Imperial Aural Block sequence with the annual maintenance sequence (will try it once, but it will likely be for nothing), creating a secondary quantum shield all around the stadium complex (too difficult to maintain, too complicated, will not work, public will notice), relocating the ship (insanity!).

At some point I sigh and speak up. "Why not just *fry* the damn thing?" I say tiredly, recalling my threat to the Imperator earlier this morning in his Red Office. "If it's so much impossible trouble, and if its active state can bring the ancient enemy, why not just destroy it once and for all?"

And as everyone turns to stare at me as if I've gone crazy, I continue, "Seriously, what's the big deal? So, it's an old-technology ancient vessel with all kinds of amazing, priceless artifacts. I totally get that! But it's not like you expect to have to fly it again! Besides, you can fry it *selectively*. Just the dangerous parts. Put all the rest in a museum!"

Chapter 14

"You have no notion of what you speak, child," First Priest Shirahtet says softly. "It's the one option we can never consider, for the simple fact that we *don't know* what would happen. We do not know *which* parts are dangerous and where they are located inside the ship—even assuming that such a separation is possible, and it is not the ship *in its entirety* that presents the problem. If the ship's orichalcum layers are destroyed, it might cause a chain reaction—a reaction of such magnitude that it would rip apart this planet and much of the space-time around it, opening a cascade of dimensional rifts far worse than the one that we already have to deal with."

"But you don't know that for sure," I say. "It might be completely harmless."

"True. But until we *do* know, the ship must remain as is."

"Okay, I see the risk now." I nod. "Which means you really do need to go back down inside that ship and try to find out the truth. And I would like to see for myself what's down there."

Even as I say it, it occurs to me that I've just *volunteered* to enter the secret research facility where the Imperator wanted to keep me as a test subject.

Even Aeson is staring at me.

I must be insane.

Which is right when the wrist comm alarm sounds, indicating to us that the ark-ship has just activated itself again.

For a moment we all go quiet, with only the noise of the TV feeds in the background.

The Imperator looks at Aeson and me with a grave expression, then beckons us with his hand to approach—yes, it's time again to do our newfangled vocal duty back at the Red Office with its monitors and camera-feed setup all ready and waiting for us.

But just as we stand up to leave the room—while the Imperator is using his wrist comm to initialize the machinery in his office to call up the stadium live feed ahead of our arrival, so as not to waste a precious moment—in that instant something odd happens on the TV.

The crowds go absolutely silent. Literally, the noise levels fall away in a span of a few breaths, and it is near-dead silence around the complex—so much so that for a moment I think someone turned off the sound.

And then, in that deep pause, we hear the voice of the commentator from the main feed window.

"And—it appears to be—we have something, Poseidon! Yes, indeed, to all our viewers, this is not a mistake! Those of you down there on the ground—you have stopped marching and expressing your concerns, and you are all looking up! It's happening right now, even as I describe the scene to you, Poseidon! Up in the sky, yes, everyone is looking up—may we have a different view angle, please, over at control—"

There's a momentary scramble on the screen, and then the camera starts to rotate and pan away from the street view of the crowd where people's faces have gone slack, signs lowered, and they are instead staring upward. . . . The camera leaves them all behind and sweeps up past the background view of the surrounding tall buildings to the open night sky directly overhead.

"There it is!" the commentator says in a surprised voice, as the view moves across the deep indigo sky with its usual dense star field, past one of the rising moons—it's the largest, Amrevet—to rest on some kind of odd phenomenon in the shape of a glowing, shimmering, vaguely round *blob of light.*

At the same time the mesmerized crowds come alive and start to make a different kind of noise, which rises in a fearful swell.

"What the—?" Director Tiofon exclaims, leaning forward.

"What is that?" Aeson says, stepping toward the hovering TV panel. At the same time the Imperator freezes, staring at the screen, while next to him the priest and the STA Director do the same.

"Unbelievable, Poseidon! We have definite confirmation of the previously reported sky manifestation, a phenomenon being seen right here, from the heart of Poseidon city center! Previous sightings have been made beyond our borders all around the Lower

Hemisphere side, and now that it's nighttime, we have full visibility—"

The commentator pauses, then resumes, "And now I am being told, yes—the object appears to be in a haze and is roughly circular, partially transparent, its location forty degrees away from zenith, with Amrevet full and rising below, and Mar-Yan definitely visible but low on the horizon. Pegasus is nowhere to be seen yet, at this time of night—no, my apologies, I'm being now corrected and told that Pegasus *the moon* is on the other side of the sky, but that this object could be a massive grouping of *pegasei*, a kind of super-flock, since it resembles the energy cluster of—"

"*Rawah bashtooh!*" the Imperator cries and begins walking toward the door. "To the balcony! I need to see this right now!"

Not needing to be told twice, all of us follow, rushing after him.

W e walk at a near run along a few corridors, emerging in an antechamber that has a grand terrace balcony running along its exterior wall, and the Imperator opens the glass enclosure door and goes out.

Director Tiofon, Director Bennu, Shirahtet, Aeson and I, and a couple of other staff, spill onto the balcony, and cool evening air washes over us.

I feel Aeson's strong hand on my upper arm, steadying me as we stand behind the others, and look around. There's no illumination here breaking the natural Atlantean darkness, only distant walls of adjacent Palace structures, black gardens below sprinkled with light-orbs, and a few soft sconce-lights casting a warm persimmon glow in the interior at our backs.

"Can you see it?" someone asks. "There, there, is that it?"

"Over to the right and down there," STA Director Bennu whispers, pointing up.

"I see it." The Imperator's hard voice sounds.

I look up, straining to see the sky in that direction.

And then, somewhere near a rooftop overhang draped by a descending green vine with curling, wide leaves and sparse branches, to the right, I see it.

A large, shimmering, impossible *splotch of light*.

It is vaguely round, the size of my pinkie fingertip, or maybe a small Earth coin, with blurring edges, as if it's made out of vapor, or possibly cloud mass. However, unlike a normal cloud, it seems to be sparkling or glittering, or in some other way exhibiting constant *change* along its diaphanous surface.

What surface? What the hell is this thing? A bizarre energy cluster? An artificial hologram projection, or a weird alien mirage? Superimposed against the star-filled darkness of the Atlantean sky, it appears partially transparent!

Could it really be some kind of crazy super-flock of *pegasei*, as the network commentator proposed?

My mind is blown. Can *pegasei* even *do* that? Can they gather in a flock and form a huge sky cluster and just sit and pulsate up there in the sky?

What the hell is it?

Even as I wonder, my lips parted stupidly, hearing Aeson at my side draw in his breath sharply, the others respond with their own versions of bewilderment.

The First Priest whispers what could possibly be an incantation or prayer, because all I can guess is that it must be Classical *Atlanteo*—some of the words are almost familiar, or archaic variations of Atlantean words I know. The only word I am certain he's muttering is *"pegasei."*

"That's incredible . . ." Rovat Bennu, the Science and Technology Agency Director whispers with wonder. "I have never seen a *pegasei* flock this size."

"Are you sure? Do you really think those are *pegasei?*" the ACA Director responds. "Especially at night, with no solar feeding source—"

"What else could that be?" Bennu says. "Look closely at the fine micro-pattern of colors, swirling and sparkling—that's *pegasei* energy! Consider the distance, elevation, I am guessing, at least a *mag-heitar* from ground level, it must be thousands of them—"

I recall that *mag-heitar* is a measure of distance in *Atlanteo* that is approximately ten kilometers.

"No," the Imperator cuts in. "That's impossible."

"Indeed, My Imperial Sovereign, it is very unlikely, as you say," the priest echoes him.

"Then what is it?" Director Bennu shakes his head and rubs the back of his bald spot.

"At this point, anything," Aeson speaks up. "A stealth aircraft. Atmospheric gases or chemicals combined causing a cloudburst emission—our own weather tech malfunctioning."

I get a crazy thought. "What if it's *them*—the alien enemy of your ancients?"

Everyone turns, frowning. They stare at me.

"Hush, don't even say such things, Imperial Lady!" Hijep Tiofon, the Atlantis Central Agency Director says after a meaningful pause, glancing around at the others nervously.

The Imperator trains his dragon gaze at me. But before he says anything, Director Bennu speaks up. "Instead of making nonsense speculations, let's find out. Send research drones, probes, whatever necessary. Even pilot shuttles—"

"Agreed," Director Tiofon says. "Immediately—we need to ascertain the level of possible danger the *phenomenon* poses, especially if it is something other than *pegasei*. Such as an incoming comet or meteor—or even an *asteroid*."

There is a grim pause, and this time everyone stares at Director Tiofon.

"Before we proceed—did anyone notice the timing correlation?" STA Director Bennu asks.

The Imperator focuses on him. "What correlation?"

"Well, the ark-ship had just been reactivated—the alarm went off—at about the same time the phenomenon appeared in our sky." Bennu reasons out loud. "My Sovereign Lord, you and the Imperial Lord and the Imperial Lady were just about to perform the lock sequence when the media interrupted us with the appearance of the—"

"*Bashtooh*, yes!" The Imperator curses and nods in agreement. "We were interrupted right then!"

"Okay, we need to verify this, right now. Simple test." Aeson steps back and opens the glass door leading inside. "My Father, let's return and finish the Voice sequence. While we perform it, someone needs to remain outside and observe this thing in the sky and tell us if anything happens when we complete the command!"

We hurry back inside and take the corridors back to the Red Office and the Imperator's desk with its monitor panels ready to go. Director Tiofon is instructed to remain out on the balcony to observe and keep track of the time, while the rest of us crowd into the small room.

We perform the Plural Logos Voice Chorus command sequence before a mesmerized audience—this time Director Bennu gets to witness our performance and time it.

The ark-ship stops humming as expected and is put to rest until the next time.

As soon as it goes silent, the Imperator's wrist comm sounds. It's Director Tiofon, calling to let us know that the object of light has just *disappeared* from the sky.

"What?" the Imperator exclaims with a strange expression. "All right, get back here, Tiofon."

In minutes ACA Director Tiofon comes running to the Red Office. "The light object just faded away, My Imperial Sovereign! I timed it—it started to fade at precisely eighth hour, forty-one daydreams, and three heartbeats."

"Which is the precise time when the Logos Voice command sequence was completed," Director Bennu says in an excited voice, checking his own wrist. "We have an actual correlation."

"When you say 'disappeared'—" Shirahtet chooses his words carefully, "do you mean it moved from its position in any way, akin to a flying craft, or did it simply dissolve and fade in place?"

"I mean the latter," Director Tiofon replies. "There was no motion, no physical displacement, just a dissolving effect. As though someone turned it off."

"Interesting," Aeson says, glancing at me. "So that would generally rule out a comet, meteor, asteroid, or any other such natural passing visitor made of cosmic matter from deep space. They don't simply lose their surface albedo at a moment's notice—not unless something moves between them and their reflected light source. And a comet heated up by proximity to Hel's radiation wouldn't lose either its ion tail or a dust tail that quickly."

"So what does it mean?" I say. "What is happening?"

"Ah! Now we send out the tech equipment and begin the tests to find out!" Director Bennu glances at me with an almost pleased level of animation. It's the scientific curiosity kind, and I get it, really, I do—curiosity is killing me also.

Except now I'm also terrified.

It's really late evening, after eleventh hour, and there is still relentless activity, both here in the Palace, and on the media.

After the mysterious "light blob" object abruptly disappeared from the sky during our most recent Voice command sequence, and the Poseidon crowds reacted with appropriate fear and confusion, they eventually started to disperse. Media crews and various network and law enforcement hover cars continued to patrol the downtown area, but it soon devolved into empty chatter and baseless speculation.

And now they're still out there, but we have more pressing issues to deal with. The Imperator has directed all the agencies and their tech resources to investigate the global skies around the planet, and Aeson, as SPC Commander, has ordered new shifts of deep space patrols to investigate distant space.

In addition, there have been foreign heads of state calling the Palace, and the Imperator has been busy talking not only to the Pharikon of New Deshret (again) who called at the start of his own morning, but to the Crown Hereret of Vai-Naat, the First Speaker of the Ennead of Ubasti, the Rai of Ptahleon and the Rai of Shuria, the Hetmet of Qurartu, and—my God, the countries and ranks all spin in my head, and I cannot even remember who all these people and places are. Naturally, the visiting Oratorat of Eos-Heket, who is staying right here in the Palace, has requested another immediate Imperial Audience to "discuss the potential global crisis."

Now that the phenomenon observed in the night skies all over the globe earlier has reached our hemisphere (it's night here now in *Atlantida*, in the Upper Hemisphere, while the opposite side of the planet with New Deshret is experiencing daytime), these other countries are mobilizing their own resources to look into this anomaly.

Are they overreacting?

One thing that I picked up during my studies on board the Fleet ark-ships over the past year, on our journey here, is that the Atlanteans are good at knowing everything about their home environment—be it the planet surface itself, its skies, oceans, or the surrounding space and solar system. Everything is analyzed, tracked, constantly monitored. There are no surprises. So when something out of the ordinary is discovered, they tend to go into full alert mode.

And now, because I'm additionally aware of their constant state of vigilance against an alien enemy, I can see why everywhere around the globe there's a sense of unspoken panic. Unlike Earth, where UFO sightings are—or were—made light of by the public and summarily dismissed by the authorities as conspiracy nonsense or ignorant misinterpretation of common natural phenomena (and in some cases clandestine government activities), Atlantis takes everything potentially *alien* dead seriously.

It occurs to me, that's probably a good thing.

All throughout this madness, Aeson has been receiving his own flood of calls by wrist comm, many of them from our friends and family. Gracie calls, crazy with worry, and Aeson gives me his personal unit for a minute to talk to her and calm her down, then has our conversation transferred over to a nearby TV panel display, to free up his line for urgent incoming data. Then the *astra daimon* start calling Aeson, one after another—Xelio, Ker, Oalla, Erita, and some others, all asking what is going on, and I overhear thinly veiled talk about "lights in the sky."

Eventually everything just gets so chaotic that my mind is no longer able to keep the events straight.

I don't even know how late it is now. . . . Twelfth hour?

"Father, permission to return to my estate. Gwen needs to rest, and she has the Final Ceremony to attend tomorrow—and so do we," Aeson says firmly, as we all sit in another room over a half-eaten late *niktos* meal. "I've configured my personal unit to connect remotely to the *Stadion* live feed, so no need for us to be present here. As soon as the alarm sounds, it will wake us. We can then coordinate with you, and call in our three Voice sequences together—remotely. As for all the rest, I am getting SPC reports in real time, so will let you know if anything important comes up."

The Imperator has a feverish, tired expression on his face. "Yes, fine. There are enough people working on this *hoohvak* issue that a few hours of rest will not harm. It is important for all of us. Indeed, a necessity, if we are to function."

And so the Imperator dismisses us, as well as the Directors and his other staff.

"Come, Gwen," Aeson tells me gently—as I'm barely keeping my eyelids open while I sit hunched in my seat, rubbing my elbows with my fingers to keep myself alert. "Let's go home."

We return to Phoinios Heights around Midnight Ghost Time, flying over a brightly lit city that seems to have lost its ability to sleep—even the air traffic is excessive for this time of night, as residents scramble to their destinations later than usual.

At the doors of the estate, Gracie and Gordie hurry toward us, followed by Oalla, Laronda, Keruvat, and Dawn, while more of our friends are gathered in the large living room.

"Gee Two, what the hell is going on?" my brother Gordie says with an uncustomary frown.

Gracie just rushes at me and hangs around my neck.

"Oh, I can't even begin to explain." I attempt to speak, after crushing Gracie with my arms. "And what are you all doing up? I mean, never mind—"

"We went outside and saw it—the big light thing!" Gracie says with very wide eyes. "The one that's all over the TV."

"And then it disappeared. Just like that!" Laronda snaps her fingers, throwing a quick glance behind her where Hasmik is waving at us from the living room sofa and pointing to the levitating TV panel before her. Blayne is seated in another chair nearby, eyes glued to the media feeds with a serious look on his face. His hoverboard stands upright behind him, leaning against the chair back. Occupying a chair next to Blayne is Erita, who looks up at us at once with a warm smile and waves, holding a tall glass.

"Kass! Finally, you're back. Come over and look!" Xelio's low, insistent voice sounds from the back of the room where a glassed-in wall leads to a balcony outside.

"Can it wait? It's been a long, *shebet*-filled day. We really should get to bed," Aeson says tiredly. "Gwen needs to rest before the Games Ceremony tomorrow. And to be honest I could use some rest myself."

They have no idea that we will have to wake up, possibly several times, in the middle of the night to perform the damn command sequence, I think. *Aeson hasn't told them the details yet. . . .*

"Gwen survived the Games, and she is going to be just fine tomorrow for a silly Ceremony that shouldn't take longer than an hour." Oalla pushes her way past the tall figure of Keruvat and taps me on the upper arm with a smile. "Right, Gwen?"

"Of course," I reply with a tiny smile of my own. "But—after dealing with his Imperial Father all day, Aeson really could use some rest."

In a moment of exhaustion-induced amusement I start wondering if anyone noticed how we both just used the other person as our excuse—is this the next level in our relationship?

"All right, we'll stay for a few minutes," Aeson says to Ker with a meaningful look, and heads to the living room.

"You guys want some food? Something to drink?" Gracie interrupts, gesturing at a side table with some leftovers from their own *niktos* meal.

But I shake my head tiredly. Then I pause. "On second thought, some water or *nikkari* juice, maybe."

Gracie just nods and goes to get my drink.

"So are you going to fill us in on what's up, Kass? All that SPC activity—don't think I didn't notice the reports pouring in all day," Keruvat says meanwhile, walking next to Aeson and me as we find seats on the sofa. Xelio is out on the balcony with the two aides, Gennio and Anu, and also Chiyoko. They are using some kind of spyglass or telescope devices to stare up at the sky.

"In a moment." Aeson checks his wrist comm, where a new stream of data appears on the band display.

"Aeson," I say. "You promised me my own wrist thingie unit. . . ."

"Oh! Yes!" He looks up at once and then his gaze rests on Gennio. "Rukkat, over here, please."

Everyone on the balcony turns around briefly, except for Gennio himself who appears to be engrossed in the sky.

"Gennio Rukkat!" Aeson repeats louder.

On the balcony, Anu elbows Gennio hard in his side to get his attention and glances back at us with a crooked grin as soon as the other Aide almost jumps with alarm, finally getting the message.

Next to me, Laronda shakes her head and whispers, "Jeez. . . . What an a-hole."

Gennio comes over, apologizing sheepishly to Aeson and me, and Aeson explains to him about my need for a personal wrist comm.

"Oh, of course," Gennio says in his mild tone, tightening his forehead slightly, then biting his lip, which apparently helps him think. "Let me go upstairs and find a blank unit. I'll configure it right now; should only be a few minutes."

"Good," Aeson says. "Speaking of minutes—make sure to include an easy minutes-to-daydreams conversion function. Gwen—all of us actually—will be using the daydreams precision scale in the coming days for some of our work."

Gennio nods politely and heads upstairs.

Aeson's wrist comm sounds a tone. More incoming data, or messages, or calls. *Im amrevu* checks it and this time looks up with a frown. I know that resigned look, and I know that ring tone.

"Your Father?" I say.

"My Father."

I moan. "What does he want now?"

Aeson does not answer immediately and continues to scan the incoming news on his wrist. When he finally looks up, he appears almost surprised. "Strange—my Father says that if that certain *alarm* sounds again, for the moment we are to ignore it, until further notice."

"What?" My mouth opens in confusion. "So—he wants us to ignore the ancient—"

Aeson puts his hand up, silencing me with a gesture. Ker and Oalla are staring at us curiously. And then he adds, "Ah, I see his reasoning—he needs the—that certain *object* to be fully active in order to keep the light manifestation present in the sky long enough for us to study it. Makes sense—it's the only way our instruments and drones and pilots can try to approach and analyze it."

"Kass, no need for secrecy here—we all know it's something to do with a certain Grail-that-is-a-ship," Keruvat says with a snort. "So, spill it."

Aeson sighs. "All right, because it is too damn late and I am tired, and things are only going to get more complicated."

In a few quiet sentences, Aeson explains to everyone what we've been doing all day today.

Keruvat lets out a held breath. "This is bad," he says. "This is really bad."

Chapter 15

"Bad does not even begin to cover it," Aeson replies. "Now you see why Gwen and I need to get some sleep."

"Go!" Oalla says with a frown. "Get to bed right now, both of you! In the name of all that's holy—"

"What did I miss?" Xelio returns from the balcony, carrying a small hand-telescope, while Anu and Chiyoko trail after him, holding their own units and arguing quietly.

Keruvat nods at him. "We'll tell you in a moment, but Kass and Gwen need to get some sleep before they collapse."

"You mean, *try* to get some sleep," Aeson says with bitter amusement, pointing at his tone-emitting wrist comm where the hologram band is going nuts with data and messages.

"That's it—I am going to take that *bashtooh* thing away from you, Aeson!" I exclaim, using the Atlantean swear word to really capture his attention. And then I grab his hand and pull my Bridegroom toward the door.

We make it upstairs and quickly get ready for bed in our respective adjacent suites. And then of course we can't stay away from each other.

The promise that Aeson made to me this morning in the Imperator's Red Office—to tell me everything about his death and the mysterious events of Ae-Leiterra as soon as we're alone tonight—is entirely forgotten by both of us. It's been such a difficult, event-filled day that I think both of us have willingly repressed it, for the time being.

Having brushed my teeth and used the facilities, I'm wearing a long, relatively demure nightshirt, but I wander into Aeson's open bedroom like a shameless hussy.

Yes, I'm shameless hussy Gwen. . . .

"Aeson?" I say shyly, peeking deeper into his room, then hear water running in the sink around the corner. Aeson must be in his bathroom, washing up. Or—doing whatever else you do in the bathroom.

A sudden hot blush rises, and my neck and cheeks start burning.

"Yes," he says, coming into the bedroom, and oh my lord, he has no shirt on . . . and his middle is wrapped in a towel.

My breath catches.

His naked chest and muscular arms, toned abdomen, tapering waist, long powerful legs, richly bronzed skin, the mane of golden hair. It all hits me at once, and I'm completely silent, mouth parted at the sight of him.

Im amrevu is a perfect male specimen.

He sees me looking at him, and for a moment I have a crazy feeling that he is about to drop the towel that's wrapped around his middle.

Instead, a slow, wicked smile curves his lips, while his gaze caresses me with sensual intensity. "Gwen," he says in a thick voice, then comes toward me. "Shouldn't you be in bed?"

"That's a bed," I say, with unexpected boldness, nodding with my head toward his own.

Shameless hussy Gwen Lark. . . .

His smile deepens, and he slowly turns his head sideways, looking me over with a relentless gaze, then glances back at his bed. "You are welcome to get in bed with me, but my personal unit—the 'wrist thingie,' as you call it—is going to keep you awake with all the ring tones and incoming data. I can't turn it off for tonight."

"That's fine, I don't care," I say. And then I recall, "Oh! Gennio was supposed to give me my own, and I forgot. We left before he returned—"

"Tomorrow," Aeson says, taking my hand gently and leading me to his bed. "If anything happens, I will wake you up. Now, are you sure you don't want to be in your own bed?" And then he grins. "It might get a little . . . difficult for us."

"You mean you won't be able to keep your hands off me?" I grin back at him.

His face reddens with a sudden blush, but he says in a controlled voice, "Precisely."

"In that case, mister—" And I plop down on his bed, then fall back on top of the soft covers, bouncing slightly. That is, the bed bounces, and various parts of me bounce—which he notices and stares, his lapis lazuli blue eyes stilling, taking in the sight of me with hunger. . . .

"Get under the covers!" I tell him, to cover my own breathless intensity. "Hands off! No—hands at your sides! No touching! No smooching!"

"Okay," he replies in surprise, and a smile returns to his lips. And then he pulls back the coverings on the other side of the bed from me and leans in, starting to climb inside. As he does so, the towel around his middle starts to slip. . . .

"No dropping the towel!" I say, squeezing my eyes shut, with a burst of wild *breathlessness.* "Not until you get under the covers!"

"Like this?"

I hear the bed creak and open my eyes, seeing him lying back against the pillow, watching me mockingly, sheet and covers drawn up to his chin. I notice his towel has fallen onto the floor next to the bed.

That's when I pounce on him, wrapping my arms around him and the heap of bedcovers, and press myself with all my being against him—so that he makes a low grunt of pleased surprise.

"Aa-a-ah . . ." I sigh in utter comfort, closing my eyes, lying in my nightshirt against the great length of him. "Aeson, I never said I was going to keep my own hands off *you.*"

I don't remember much of the night, except soft darkness and yes, waking a few times because of ring tones, and then Aeson shifting pleasantly against me in the bed . . . and sometimes seeing the blue-green hologram light of the data band around his wrist casting a faint glow along the contours of his face as he peers at it, sitting up next to me in the otherwise darkened bedroom.

"Huh? Anything wrong? The ship?" I mumble, half asleep. My semi-conscious brain is made aware that although I'm still lying on top of the covers that serve as a flimsy barrier between us, somehow there's now a soft blanket covering me.

"Nothing, sleep," he replies every time, and his warm hand reaches for me, caressing my shoulder, my cheek, my hair . . . until I drift off again, mumbling, "No, *you* sleep . . . Aeson, please, you need sleep. . . ."

The next time I wake up, it is full morning, judging by the sliver of fierce light coming from one crack of separation between the drawn curtains. The side of the bed next to me is empty, covers neatly pulled up, and Aeson is gone.

I sigh and look around. He is not in the room, nor do I hear anything from his bathroom. I glance to the wide-open door that leads to my own darkened bedroom, and my gaze involuntarily falls on a chair in the interior of my suite, visible from Aeson's room. Lying on the chair is a pristine-looking, clear-wrapped package that contains my White Vocalist uniform from the Games of the Atlantis Grail.

At the sight of the dreaded uniform, I feel a stab of anxiety in my gut. Today, at second hour of Khe, I have to attend the Final Ceremony. . . . Ugh.

I sit up slightly, frowning, and turn away from the unpleasant sight. I notice an Atlantean time-keeping device on the nearest bedside table. Thankfully it has a large digital readout in glowing amber light. But the time is displayed in those weird cuneiform-like squiggles and lines which are Atlantean numerals—annoying complicated numbers which I have so much trouble deciphering.

Squinting and staring, I finally figure out that it says either "Seventy-three-thousandth hour" or more likely "Seventh hour, thirty-one daydreams, and eleven heartbeats of Ra."

So—relatively early morning, but not too bad.

Where is Aeson?

I am in his bed. Oh, wow . . . I spent the night here, in his bed.

On impulse, I lie back down, wrap myself in his bedding, and just put my face into the sheets and pillows to inhale deeply. . . . Ah, his sweet scent is all over everything, musky, unique to *him*, pleasant to my senses. A warmth starts rising inside me.

Finally I get up and head over to my own bedroom and bathroom. I grab a quick shower, then choose a moderately casual pants-and-top outfit from my closet and put it on, ignoring the three slightly more formal outfits laid out for me overnight by a maidservant.

Then I go downstairs.

I wander around our most commonly used living rooms, running into only a few servants, who give me courteous bows and greetings, while no one else seems to be about. I eventually find Aeson in one of the small *eos* nooks with the gorgeous hillside panorama-view of Poseidon. He is sitting with Ker and Xelio around a little table crowded with plates of *eos* bread victuals. They are staring at a compact panel display levitating like a centerpiece over the middle of the table, just above the food dishes. The panel shows four windows split into both video feeds and computer data. And they are all constantly referring to their wrist comms.

"Nefero eos," I say, and I cannot help noticing how well my Bridegroom looks this morning despite so little sleep—perfectly groomed, in a silken grey-white shirt and slate grey jacket and pants suitable for court, with his fine metallic hair brushed to a sheen and falling neatly down his back. "There you are! I didn't hear you get up, Aeson!"

Aeson looks up at me, and his eyes immediately light up. "Gwen! How did you sleep?"

"Fine! But how about you? You were still working in the middle of the night!" I shake my head with mock reproach. "And now you're back at it! Anything horrible happen overnight?"

Ker and Xel glance at Aeson, then at each other. "Define 'horrible,'" Xelio says with a sarcastic smile. He is also finely dressed in a crisp black shirt and jacket with a deep red collar trim, and his raven mane is pulled back and contained in a segmented tail, giving his lean face a controlled, fierce elegance. "And *nefero eos* to you, Imperial Lady Gwen."

"Sit down and eat, Gwen," Keruvat says with a wink, but I see his amusement is covering up many layers of worry. Ker is sharp-dressed to match his fellow *daimon*, in a dark blue jacket with a golden-cream shirt that contrasts beautifully with his near-black skin and the gilded short curls of his hair.

"Where are the others?" I say, taking a plate and heading to the side table where the steaming dishes are laid out, and a servant is busy preparing something else savory and fragrant in a tureen over a heating plate.

"Oalla's still sleeping, and so is your sister," Ker says.

"I believe your friend Hasmik was here earlier, very briefly," Xel adds. "As for the others—not sure."

I fill my plate with food and pick up a mug of *lvikao*, then return to their table. "All right. Now tell me, what have I missed? Is the ark-ship—active?"

"Yes," Aeson says. "The alarm sounded as it reactivated at around fourth hour of Ra. And it has been active since."

"And?"

Aeson sighs.

Ker and Xel look gravely at me and Aeson.

"Several things," Aeson says. "If you remember, we sent various resources to study the light phenomenon in the sky which reappeared as soon as the ship turned back on. Our probe findings were—unexpected. First, the object is not a mere *mag-heitar* above the surface of the planet, nor is it a flock of *pegasei* plasma energy. Both of those assumptions were incorrect guesses, completely underestimating size and distance. Instead, it is large—very large. And it is very far away."

"Oh? How far?" I ask.

"It's not inside the atmosphere," Ker adds. "Atmospheric probes from *Atlantida* and other nations, working together and sharing data, found nothing."

Aeson nods. "Yes. It is *far* beyond orbit. The next step was to send SPC Pilots. I dispatched several research shuttle teams outward, past the orbit of Amrevet, which is the outermost moon, and only there did they start to get close to the object. That's when they discovered that it's not stationary, but in motion."

"Oh my—that's—" I mumble. "So what is it?"

Aeson lets out another deep breath. "Well, the *good* news is, it's not some kind of impossible white hole emission. Nor is it a blob of the kind of plasma energy that's found circling along the innermost stable circular orbit just before the reality horizon of a black hole."

"In other words," Xel puts in, "a new black hole didn't just suddenly appear in space right outside our outermost lunar orbit. You can praise all the deities for that—not to mention, it generally requires a collapsing star for a black hole to form at all."

My mouth opens in wonder.

"The bad news is," Aeson continues, "there might still be some kind of dimensional rift or anomaly located near that spot. Information is still coming in and being processed, and the shuttle crews are sending some conflicting data." He points to one of the four view screens on the panel before him with 3D schematic images, text, and numbers.

I peer at the feed, not sure what I'm seeing. Similar, nearly identical 3D charts and graphs constantly scroll by and replace each other, and they all show some kind of blurry, blob-like mass—roughly circular, possibly viewed from different angles.

"See here? Those are energy patterns in the same image captured at different moments, using micro intervals. And these are with different wavelength filters. Darker spots are less dense, brighter light spots are the densest." Keruvat points one finger at the nearest scrolling image.

"Why are they changing?" I ask. "Are they moving?"

"We don't know for certain yet," Aeson replies. "Some of this is possible rotation or other motion; some of it is incoming data variations."

"How soon will you know?" I find myself frowning with tension. "What about the shuttle Pilots who are looking at it with the naked eye? What does it look like?"

"They can't risk too close an approach yet. Not until we know for sure what type of energy is emitted and the radiation levels." Xelio taps one of the four windows and brings up a live feed of the object in space. "This is the closest image capture so far."

I look at what appears to be a large spherical blob of light against the darkness of space. Last night when I saw it with my naked eyes in the sky, it was the size of my pinkie. Here, I'm not sure of the scale, but the image fills most of the view screen. However, seeing it like this in higher detail still doesn't make it any less vague or nebulous. Nor does it give any better idea of its size.

"What is it?" I muse. "How big?"

Aeson just shakes his head. "Next step is to approach even closer, after the radiation safety levels are confirmed. The shuttles have fallen into formation at different angles and distance, in order to triangulate. They've sent out more probes and are keeping pace with its general movement. So far, the motion appears circular, almost as if it's following its own higher orbit over Atlantis."

"Woah! This is so weird." I hear Gordie's voice as he comes up behind me and peers over my shoulder.

"Hey—morning, Gee Three!" I turn to my younger brother, looking at him closely.

Gordie pushes his glasses up the bridge of his nose as he leans in to stare. His eyelids droop over his blue eyes, making him look a little sleepy, as he usually does first thing in the morning. At least he's wearing a decent-looking tan shirt and jacket, and his short hair is no longer a buzz cut and is starting to grow back a little. Meanwhile his cheeks look fuzzy—he definitely needs a shave.

"What are we looking at?" Gordie asks.

"Some kind of energy blob," I reply. "But no one is sure yet."

"We're working on it," Keruvat says.

"Is it dangerous?"

Xel makes a short, mocking sound. "Define 'dangerous.'" And he lifts a finger to tap at one of the four data windows. The window zooms larger and with it, the visual representation of the light object in space, in real color. "What does that look like to you?"

Gordie squints again and frowns. "Uh . . . the colors are not there, but the glowing stuff looks a little, in texture or consistency, like the purple plasma fields emitted by the Fleet shuttles. Which is the same kind of energy as the big plasma shields around the ark-ships."

"Hmmm," Xelio says. "Yes, could be, except for the violet frequency of the light." He slaps Gordie on the back lightly. "Good observation."

"So, if this is an artificial plasma shield," Ker reasons, "then what is it shielding?"

"My initial guess, again, would be a dimensional rift." Aeson sits back and exhales, then picks up his mug and takes a drink. "But I want to know why it's *moving* in a curving trajectory instead of being fixed in space. In addition, it appears translucent, and you can see through it to the star field behind it. As if it's shielding nothing."

"Unless it's a hologram?" I say.

Aeson raises his brow. "Yes, interesting, could be. Or a holographic shield."

"A what?"

"A holo-shield is an energy shield that also has a cloaking property," Keruvat explains. "Unlike a plain hologram, which is just a light projection, a holo-shield rearranges light quanta to disguise an object and creates a protective energy barrier."

"Cool," Gordie says with his mouth full of *eos* pie, and quickly pops another chunk in, chewing blissfully. Then he picks up the whole plate.

"For how long is your Father allowing this anomaly to be studied?" I ask Aeson, while giving Gordie a side-eye warning to tone down his feeding frenzy. "I mean—because all this time the ark-ship is actively broadcasting into the cosmos. . . . Isn't he concerned about that?"

"At this point he's more concerned about the connection between this light object and the ark-ship," Aeson says. "And so am I. There might be answers here that we need in order to shut down the ark-ship permanently, physical details in connection to this object. Once we know more about it, we'll have more to work with."

I nod. "Okay. So in the meantime it just stays active, I guess."

"Right." Aeson slowly smiles at me. "We just wait—for more data and further orders."

"Going to be another long day." I smile back at him with gentleness.

Then, with a painful twinge, I remember the Games Final Ceremony happens in just a few hours.

B y the time I finish eating my *eos* bread, others have come downstairs. Gracie, Blayne, and Oalla join us. And then Gennio and Anu show up.

"Imperial Lady Gwen," Gennio says, handing me a small, rose-colored chrome box. "I set up your new personal communication and data unit. Do you need me to show you how to use it?"

"Oh, wonderful, Gennio! And yes, please." I open the box and take out my very own wrist comm thingie, at last. It's basically a two-inch wide band of flexible slate-grey material (very likely, orichalcum) in a ten-inch long strip, with an adjustable clasp on both ends. You wrap it around your wrist on either hand and it molds itself comfortably, based on your individual dimensions, forming a bracelet.

I've used Aeson's to make basic calls, but that's all I know how to do. "How do I turn it on?"

Gennio first ensures that I have it sitting around my wrist properly. "Your new PCDU, or personal unit as we call it, needs to be keyed first."

"A regular voice keying command?" I say.

He nods.

I focus on my wrist and sing F-A-C, which is my go-to keying sequence. At once the band lights up with delicate hairlines of gold energy running around my wrist, then settles back into grey.

"Okay, good," Gennio says. He then shows me how to do several basic functions by means of finger taps and how to read the entry-level display. "Don't worry about the advanced data entry or media feeds or text messaging and email yet, Imperial Lady Gwen. You can practice on the holo-keyboard later when you get more used to it. The locator ID chip is initialized, and I added it to the secure Imperial Network so that your location will be protected from the public and only shared with your personal security and those you allow. As far as the comm function, I programmed the main numbers you will need to call people, including the Imperial Crown Prince, naturally, and the Palace, and—here, you can see the list of people here—"

"Perfect for now," I say, glancing over the speed-call list, glad to see Gracie, Manala, all of my friends, and the Imperatris on the list.

"Let me know if you need more help," Gennio says, then wanders off to work on some equipment at a nearby table with Anu.

I turn my left wrist this and that way, admiring the new gadget. And then I look up because of the sudden fall of silence in the small room.

Aeson, Ker, Xel, and Oalla have stopped chatting and commenting on the data. They have gone absolutely quiet around the small table as they stare at the smart panel screen, one window zoomed larger to fill the entire display.

I move my chair closer to them and then lean in to stare over Oalla's shoulder.

The blob of plasma light surrounded by space fills the screen.

Except, no—it's no longer a shapeless, vaguely round blob. The flickering, mutable light mass has thickened, congealed, *solidified.* It has lost the viscosity of plasma energy. Or possibly, the energy itself has dissipated or faded to reveal what lies at its core.

I am looking at a high-resolution image of a sphere hanging in space. An object with a non-radiant surface, its pale brightness merely the reflected albedo of another light source—in this case, Hel, shining more than a hundred million miles away.

The image seems to be gaining clarity every moment. The ghostly, greyscale color palette is enriched, and faint splotches of color bloom forth—muted rose, tan-yellow, and blue-green shadows cast in relief. And now there are rocky surface features visible . . . vague natural blotches, peaks and valleys . . . craters.

It is a planet.

Chapter 16

"What in all the *rawah* hells of Atlantis?" Oalla whispers, breaking the silence. "That's a planetary body!"

"Are we looking at the same object?" Xelio asks. "What happened to the plasma?"

Aeson does not answer immediately. He minimizes the window back to its original position to reveal the three others and starts tapping on the screen and scrolling through data on two of the windows. "Yes, the location and trajectory overlap with the plasma image from before. This is the same object. It no longer shows a plasma holo-shield."

Ker is shaking his head slowly. "And according to this trajectory curve plot for the last several hours, and the projected points to fill in the missing data—" he taps at one data chart—"it is moving in an Atlanteocentric orbit around us—around Atlantis."

"What? How?" I mutter. "You mean it's orbiting like a satellite?"

"Yes." Aeson glances at me and the others. He exhales slowly. "This is a moon."

Holy crap!

At this point everyone else in the room has stopped doing whatever they were doing, and they gather around us.

"Wait, what?" Gracie glances back to Blayne who's the only person still seated, but even he is positioning his legs around his hoverboard, ready to leave his small sofa and join us.

"I thought Atlantis has three moons," Blayne says, hover-floating up to the table.

"It does," Xel says with a confused frown.

"Well, apparently now it has four," Oalla says with a strange laugh through parted lips. "Is this crazy or what, Ker? A hidden fourth moon? What is its orbit relative to Amrevet?"

Ker checks data, still shaking his head, then says, "Based on the actual route traveled along the trajectory, as marked in real time by our instruments, it's about twice as distant from Amrevet's average orbit as Amrevet's orbit is from Mar-Yan's. And we won't know the shape of that orbit until a full revolution is completed and we account for closest and farthest apsis point irregularities—"

"In other words, it's orbiting very far out there." Aeson speaks softly, then turns to his wrist comm and starts working the data.

"Time to let your Imperial Father know?" Xel says with narrowed eyes.

"Oh, yes." Aeson makes a short sound. "Best he hears it from me—or from any one of our own personnel—rather than foreign sources around the globe. Though, no doubt, he must've heard already—I can just imagine the reports and calls pouring in right about now. . . . Not only from our own agencies but from everywhere else. Because it's happening globally as they observe that thing and reach the same consensus as we do."

Xel whistles.

"Okay, I don't understand what's going on," Gracie says.

"You're not the only one." Oalla smiles sadly at Gracie.

"Message sent," Aeson says. "Now bracing for call."

And as if on cue I hear and recognize the Imperial ring tone.

While Aeson gets up and steps away to talk privately with the Imperator, we continue to watch the data feeds.

"Time to send surface landing probes to take a closer look at this thing," Keruvat theorizes, as he reads the band of his wrist comm. "Then, after the probe data comes back, we send shuttles with human Pilots."

Meanwhile I turn to stare at Aeson, observing the grave nuances of emotion and stress in his face, his urgent tone, as he speaks with his Father, not bothering to maintain his usual semblance of control. The conversation lasts an interminable half-hour, and when he is done, Aeson comes back to the table.

"How did it go?" Ker looks at Aeson with worry.

"Bad," Aeson replies. "Half the IEC is in his office or requesting a formal audience. The Oratorat is talking to her own strategy team back at Eos-Heket, and New Deshret is demanding we handle the Ra Disk and Grail situation immediately. Multiple foreign government representatives and their local ambassadors are calling on every Palace line. Oh—and we've got huge crowds surrounding the *Khemetareon* and throughout downtown. Half of them are there to line up early for the Games Ceremony, the rest are just raving in the streets in fear, screaming about ghosts in the sky. Poseidon LCA has dispatched additional crowd control units. It's absolute chaos."

"What about this moon? How are we to proceed?" Xelio asks. "Or are you shutting it down to accommodate New Deshret?"

"At this point, I wonder if we even *can* shut anything down again," Aeson says thoughtfully. "Ark-ship, Ra Disk, this moon. . . . If we perform the full command sequence with our three Logos voices right now, and the ark-ship goes to sleep, will the moon also disappear behind some kind of holo-shield? Or has it all deteriorated too far? The energy bonds—have they faded so much that the plasma shielding is permanently gone? Besides, my Father wants us to continue working on this new problem of the moon."

"What I want to know," Oalla says, "is where this moon came from. Was it brought here from somewhere else by some third party—an unknown force, or entity, or even an automated program somehow related to the ark-ship? Or was it always secretly here, in its own orbit, but just hidden somehow, all this time? And if so, who shielded it and how long ago? And why?"

Aeson nods slowly. "That's what we're going to find out." He begins entering commands on his wrist device while Keruvat and Xelio scroll through the panel feeds and read the data. "All right, I just sent landing parties to the surface of this moon. They will be reporting back shortly. Meanwhile—"

"What?" I look at Aeson, feeling sick to my stomach with anticipation of more of the unknown.

He exhales and looks at me. "Just got a time reminder—you need to get ready for the Final Ceremony."

"Oh." My gut does another somersault. "You mean time for me to put on the uniform."

"Yes, unfortunately."

Oalla puts her hand on my back and pats me lightly, then squeezes my shoulder.

"Gwen, you have to be there an hour early to line up with the others," Aeson tells me, shaking his head. "Which means we need to leave in less than an hour. Hard to believe—considering how much of a crisis this is—but we all have to interrupt our work to participate in this Games nonsense—at a time like this."

"Okay, let me go change," I say softly. "I'll be right back."

Aeson nods at me with regret, then has to return his attention to the screens, where a fresh set of data is coming in, and everyone becomes engrossed in it.

I go upstairs and put on the Vocalist uniform with the usual layer of *viatoios* armor underneath and a fresh pair of sports shoes to match. For one uncertain instant I wonder if putting on the armor underlayer is even necessary at this point. But then I recall that under normal Games circumstances I would still be wearing the armor and everything else, as I would be coming straight from the last stage, filthy and bloodied. . . . To re-create the original circumstances, it would be necessary for me to wear *everything*. Besides, nothing is certain; I might still need it.

Perish the thought.

Looking at myself in the mirror, I see my general pallor, gaunt cheeks, the hollows around my eyes, and realize that I might require cosmetics just to look semi-alive for this Ceremony.

Normally I wouldn't care, and today it even seems like a ridiculous thing to be concerned about. But for some reason I really want to come across looking like a proper Champion. My gut tells me that, at the very least, I need to put on a brave front for these thousands of people, and for all those cameras.

Which means I need basic face paint.

Fortunately, I have servants at my disposal here at Aeson's estate. And so I call the staff, using my own new wrist "thingie." Minutes later, a young and friendly maid arrives and seats me before a table of cosmetics. She gives me an appropriately fierce look of kohl-lined eyelids, dark dramatic eye shadow, and deep plum lips. She dabs a bit of color over my cheekbones. And she brushes my hair until it crackles, then asks me how I would like it done.

"Let's leave it down," I say, admiring her fine work in the mirror. "No decoration, just long hair."

And on that note, I am ready to play my version of Champion before all of *Atlantida*.

W hen I return downstairs, Aeson is ready for me. He hasn't bothered to change outfits, but he is already dressed nicely, and so are the other *daimon*. It occurs to me that they anticipated this occasion and dressed accordingly.

"Ready?" Aeson smiles at me with a warm expression in his eyes. I know he is making an effort to set aside the urgent work at hand. But I also see that he has given instructions to his various subordinates, and he has his wrist comm on him at all times. He'll probably be working discreetly from his seat, even during the Final Ceremony.

"As ready as I can be," I say. And we head outside for the hover cars.

O alla and Erita choose not to attend the Ceremony and stay behind to oversee the incoming data on the multiple feeds. My friends and siblings also stay behind, but only because I ask them not to bother going out there into the unruly crowds at a time like this—and besides they will see it all on the TV. Meanwhile, Aeson, Xelio, Keruvat, and I, plus Aeson's six Imperial guards and an additional four guards assigned to me, head downtown to the *Khemetareon*.

Aeson drives the two-seater hover car, keeping his eyes on the air lane, but frequently glances at his wrist which is alive with recurrent tones and incoming data. I sit next to him silently, watching the blazing white sky and the urban landscape below. I'm almost afraid to speak so as not to interrupt him in his multitasking concentration. My quick glances confirm *im amrevu's* intense expression of utmost focus.

Soon I see the tall buildings of downtown Poseidon. Surrounded by the skyscrapers, the multi-stadium complex shines in metallic radiance under the noonday light of Hel. At the same time, I see the familiar sight of the ancient ark-ship, its "Grail" nose-section thrust out of the broken *Stadion* ground and leaning slightly, like an Atlantean analogue to the leaning Tower of Pisa. I imagine the deep, bone-jarring hum it's emitting, even now. . . .

"How are you feeling, Gwen?" Aeson's voice causes me to turn and force a smile, even as he looks at me with his serious gaze.

"I'm fine. This is going to be easy," I lie gently. "How are *you* dealing with all that's incoming?"

"I want you not to worry about any of it right now," he replies with a reassuring glance, starting to bring us down for a landing in the nearby parking area of the *Khemetareon*. "Promise me you will simply try to enjoy your Champion status and whatever else happens at the Ceremony. The worst is over. My Father has too many other problems to occupy him now, so for once his focus will not be on you. Nothing about these *bashtooh* Games poses any more threat to you, so—"

I glance down at my white uniform and the mouth logo on my chest.

And then I smile and take a deep breath.

We descend.

Surrounded by security guards, Aeson and I hurry along the specially designated walkway from the parking structure, railed off on both sides to keep back the gathered audience crowds. The *astra daimon* head for a different public entrance to meet up with Aeson later in the spectator seats, while we move directly toward the Contender entrance of the grand *Khemetareon* building. There is no parade of thousands of Contenders this time, only a handful of us, and I see no one else on the walkway at the same exact time we arrive.

Instead, the crowds see us and start screaming, chanting the now familiar slogans:

"Gwen Lark! Gwen Lark!"

"Im-pe-ra-tris! Im-pe-ra-tris!"

"Shoe-lace girl!"

And there's that creepy new one:

"Gebi Goddess! Gebi Goddess!"

Aeson's hand closes around mine, and I feel the comforting strength of his fingers. We exchange intense glances, and he barely nods to me with encouragement before letting go of my hand.

Suddenly I remember to wave back and smile at all these people calling my name. The fans expect no less, and so I give it to them. I only stop waving and lower my hands once we're inside the building.

Aeson accompanies me as far as he is permitted by Games regulations, which is to the lobby entrance where Games officials wait. I check in at the desk, then turn and this time give my

Bridegroom an almost confident, forcibly relaxed smile. He leans in for a quick kiss on the lips—which still manages to send an inappropriately timed jolt of desire running through me—and then we separate.

"See you in a few hours!" I whisper, grateful that there's none of that tragic desperation between us there had been a month ago when we said our awful goodbyes on the first day of the Commencement Ceremony at the very beginning of the Games. This feels much different.

"As always, I'll be watching every moment from the Imperial balcony up above," he replies, then kisses me again, harder. And reluctantly he stays behind while I am told to follow an official into the corridor.

I arrive in a small, sterile chamber with a tall ceiling and pale walls. Three rows of seats—no more than thirty, total—are arranged before a podium. This is our staging area, where the Champions and tied Contenders are supposed to receive instructions for the Final Ceremony.

There are about a dozen people in the room. At once I see a rainbow of uniforms and my fellow teammates and Contenders, some already seated, others milling about with what looks like a mixture of nerves and boredom. Several Games officials and guards wait nearby. It's interesting—right now, none of our uniforms is glowing brightly to indicate Champion status. The Games techs must've decided to hold off lighting us up until every Category winner is official.

There's Hedj Kukkait, tall and lanky, with his long white hair, wearing Warrior Red. He stands next to my teammate Kateb Nuletat in Inventor Yellow. Both of them see me, and their expressions change to a kind of intense, questioning wonder—they're seeing me for the first time since the disastrous moment when I raised the Grail. . . .

Then I notice Brie Walton, also in White, with the Entrepreneur logo, her purple hair done up in three tight knots on top of her head. With her is Kokayi Jeet, elegant in Entertainer Green, with five long, colorful braids and dramatic face paint.

"Oh! Gwen Lark! Over here, *amrevet!*" Kokayi sees me and opens his eyes wide for just one moment—as if not sure how to react to me—then makes up his mind and grins, showing his white teeth. He is wearing dark kohl, dark green and plum eye shadow, rouge over his cheeks and dark lip color, and his lean, handsome face is fierce with energy.

"Hi, there!" I say, approaching them with an uncertain smile.

"Well, look who the Atlantean cat dragged in!" Brie gives me a sideways stare, then snorts. "Lark, dearly beloved, we're gathered here *again*, for better or worse. Listen—I have no idea what happened the other day at the stadium—whatever impossible voice crap you *did*, or *didn't* do, to break everything in that building—" and Brie widens her eyes meaningfully at me. "But let's try to enjoy this one."

"Oh, Walton," I say, shaking my head and pretending to ignore her meaning. "Hope you've had some decent rest and are enjoying your Champion status."

"Oh yeah, having a total blast in my four-star cell in Correctional," she replies flippantly. "You know they won't let me out until this thing is official. So, yeah, I'm enjoying it, all right. Though your ex did let me have one decent celebratory meal. Looks like Sangre is getting soft on me."

I roll my eyes.

"Gwen!"

I turn and see Lolu Eetatu, in Technician Blue, with a very nervous expression, standing behind me.

"Hi, Lolu!" I smile at her. And then a strange feeling washes over me, as I'm reminded of her sick mother . . . and the fact that she still has to participate in a tiebreaker event.

With Lolu is Chihar Agwath, calm and stoic as usual, also in Blue, but with the Scientist logo. Today his thin, unruly white hair is smoothed back neatly over his balding head. "*Nefero dea*, Imperial Lady Gwen," Chihar says to me in his most normal, mild voice, showing no sign of awe or fear of me, or maybe just keeping his real thoughts well concealed. "It is good to see you."

I notice that one of his hands is wrapped in a bandage and recall vividly how his hand was injured during the Triathlon Race. However, I'm not surprised that he hasn't resorted to any kind of accelerated (and expensive) medical treatment—now that there's no urgent need for him to be healed overnight.

Except, maybe there is, I remind myself. Chihar also has to deal with a tiebreaker, and who knows what kind of thing might be required of him.

I glance at the other remaining Scientist Contender, a petite, dark-skinned woman whose name, I believe, is Rea Bunit. She's in Blue, standing a few feet away, talking to Ukou Dwetat, in Athlete Red.

In that moment, more Champions and Contenders arrive.

Leetana Chipuo, the Green Animal Handler, enters the room, and my heart constricts painfully as I think of Zaap, my teammate and friend. . . . Leetana wouldn't be here if Zaap hadn't lost his life at the hands of Thalassa, during that damned final Race, giving up his Category slot for Leetana to occupy.

The next arrival is a large man with messy, undyed brown hair in a Blue uniform. He is Lolu's Category rival, the other remaining Technician, whose name is Mineb Inei.

So that's everyone. But wait, no—

I turn around and see Rurim Kiv, the Yellow Artist, seated in the third and last row, in the corner chair, so that he is easily overlooked. Once again, the elusive Rurim seems to be playing his favorite invisibility game. Our gazes make contact, and I see a subtle hint of humor—or maybe mockery—in his black eyes.

However, we're not done with arrivals. I am somewhat surprised to see my own Category rivals, Sofia Veforoi and Fawzi Boto, enter the room. Fawzi is speaking to her quietly, and his face shows anger. Sofia, on the other hand, is neutral and composed. She cuts off Fawzi's speech with a cool nod and heads directly toward her own teammate, Hedj Kukkait.

A weird moment of panic overcomes me, so that my breath slows down.

Why are they here?

After I raised the Grail, I was pronounced the winner by the Imperator himself, so why are they here?

But there's no time to wonder, because another Games official enters the room, followed by none other than Miramis Opu, the Priest of the Grail.

Both men walk up to the podium, and the official clears his throat, waiting for all of us to take our seats.

"Contenders, welcome back! We are pleased to be able to hold the closing portion of the Games of the Atlantis Grail today, after being interrupted by the unexpected *natural* events earlier. In a few moments we will have you line up, walk out into the arena, and face the same lineup of judges you faced on the final day of competition."

The official pauses. "Except for the venue, nothing has changed, Contenders! You will resume from the same moment you were interrupted—in other words, when our Imperial Sovereign pronounced Contender Gwen Lark to be the winner in her Category."

"With all respect, I dispute this conclusion!" From the row behind me, Fawzi Boto interrupts.

We all turn to stare at him, as Fawzi stands, frowning, and points at me. "When it was her turn during the tiebreaker, she did absolutely nothing of consequence! Or else, regardless of what we're being told, she clearly caused the destruction of the stadium by means of a dangerous vocal routine—a poor choice of Voice demonstration, to say the least! Either way, the Imperial Sovereign merely put an end to her performance! Therefore I question the true intent and meaning behind his declaration!"

My heart starts pounding as I stare at Fawzi Boto. Meanwhile everyone now turns to look at me. In particular, I note the Priest of the Grail's extremely anxious gaze upon me.

"Contender Boto," the official says. "The words *'You've won'* were spoken by the Imperial Sovereign, and it is a clear judgement of fact."

"I accept no such thing!" Fawzi retorts. Ironically, in that moment he's expressing my own favorite response to adversity. "It is within my right to dispute the meaning of such an inconclusive statement, especially considering that it wasn't even made by the designated judges. How to interpret these Imperial words is yet to be seen!"

The official pauses again before speaking. "Very well. It is indeed every Contender's legal right to dispute the judges' decision in case of tiebreakers—and there is sufficient cause for some minor doubt, if only because of the unfortunate timing of the events—so you will have the opportunity to present your case before them. Now, please, sit down, and allow me to proceed."

Fawzi Boto nods, still frowning, and lowers himself down. He gives me dirty looks from his seat, but now I turn my back on him and return my attention to the podium. In the row before me I see my other Vocalist rival, Sofia Veforoi, and now I understand why they are both here.

Yes, they all have to be here to re-create that exact moment we were "interrupted."

But as a result, my Games Champion status is being put under question.

Chapter 17

The Games official at the podium stands aside to allow the Priest of the Grail to continue presenting our Final Ceremony Instructions.

Miramis Opu steps up and looks around at all of us, and his fretful gaze definitely lingers on me. But he looks away and addresses everyone.

"Champions and Contenders! The Games are Forever! You will now stand and form a line, and you will follow me inside the arena. Remain silent and respectful of this ancient tradition, and wait your turn to be called before the judges!"

And without another word he raises the palm of his hand dramatically, motioning for us to rise.

I stand with the others and fall into line right after Brie, with Chihar directly behind me. Silently we follow the short but impressive figure of the Priest of the Grail in his formal ceremonial robes, as he leads us through a long, dimly lit corridor into the thunderous crowd noise and bright lights of the arena entrance.

The *Khemetareon* stadium is one-third smaller than the *Stadion*, similarly oval but, unlike the larger structure, it is completely enclosed by a permanent domed roof. It has even more tiers and rows of seats, stacked higher, all the way to the ceiling.

There are no monolithic statues, but instead grand pillars and fancy overhanging balconies intended for the wealthiest patrons. The Imperial box is prominent among them, occupying a low central balcony with the most advantageous view of the arena below. I recognize the great golden sunburst that is the symbol of the Imperial Kassiopei Dynasty, sculpted in relief along the balcony's front, and the row of high-backed seats sparkling with gilded metal under the day-bright artificial illumination. At the moment it's unoccupied, so I assume the Imperator, Aeson, and anyone else with them will be entering the balcony later, probably to make a dramatic appearance.

Meanwhile, the rest of the tiers and balconies are full to capacity with the audience crowds, and there are no empty seats that I can see in my quick examination of the whole immense venue.

The Priest of the Grail walks from the far entrance and enters the arena, accompanied by uplifting music and the rich choral sound of the Games musicians. At once a roar greets him and only increases as we, the fourteen remaining Contenders, follow him, still moving in a line, heading toward the center, waving with all our hands uplifted to the audience. Looking up, I notice the huge smartboards located near the highest tiers, spaced evenly all around the stadium—they are alive with scores and live feeds of the arena, then close-ups of our faces as we emerge.

The center of this current arena configuration includes an oval-shaped dais, with ten seats for the Category judges. They are already seated in place, stern and motionless, each holding up a circular sign flag with the color background and logo of their Category. I recognize the older woman judge in the Vocalist Category who gave us the singing tiebreaker task. She is looking directly ahead of her, not acknowledging me or the other Vocalists.

"*Wixameret*, to all the brave Contenders!" the Priest of the Grail exclaims in an amplified voice that resounds around the stadium. He stops before the dais and turns to face us. "Ascend the platform and stand before your judges to receive their final decisions!"

One by one we go up the five stairs leading to the dais and pause before our Category judge.

I find myself between Fawzi Boto and Sofia Veforoi, facing our judge. Nerves hit me, and I feel sick to my stomach. . . .

In that moment, the Games Choir sings, and everyone stares as the Imperator arrives in the Imperial box.

From the distance of the arena, I can see Romhutat Kassiopei make his entrance, wearing a deep red robe with a golden Khepresh headdress that is the Imperial Crown of *Atlantida*. He is stone-faced, showing his usual dragon demeanor to the public. Aeson is just behind him, far more casual, and I see him look right at me.

Somehow I'm certain of Aeson's expression and his encouraging smile from all the way across the expanse—even before the jumbo-sized boards switch to show closeups of the Imperator and the Crown Prince . . . and the crowds roar.

The Priest of the Grail raises one hand, palm up, and points to the Imperial box, then inclines his head in a courtly bow. "The Final Ceremony of the Games of the Atlantis Grail will resume, as the Imperial Sovereign Himself pronounces the Winner of the Vocalist Category."

My heart starts to race.

At once, the crowd noise falls as everyone grows quiet, in terrible suspense.

I look up at the Imperial balcony, my heart now beating out of my chest. Maybe this is completely irrational, and I have nothing to worry about—based on a simple logical deduction that the Imperator has much more to lose right now if he undermines his own earlier statement. It would be like opening a can of worms to question what really happened, what I *did* or *didn't* do. . . .

And yet. . . .

What will he say now? What if he decides to toy with me, punish me for everything, and changes his mind? On the other hand, wouldn't he be accused of blatant nepotism if he grants the win to his son's Bride?

What an interminable, awful pause. . . .

As my frantic thoughts race, the Imperator speaks, and his own dark voice is amplified to carry across the expanse. "The Vocalist winner is—*Gwenevere Lark*."

He looks directly at me.

In that moment I understand something basic that for some reason eluded me before.

The Imperator really, really *needs me right now. He needs me to cooperate fully, in order to deal with whatever else might lie before us, whatever disaster, or merely the alien unknown. . . .*

The audience explodes in a thunderous roar. There are screams, noise of every kind.

In that moment, Fawzi Boto next to me makes an exclamation of protest. But he is drowned out by the audience.

And then Miramis Opu, the Priest of the Grail, adds, "Let there be no doubt as to the final decision of this Category. Does the Vocalist judge agree?"

At once there is again universal silence.

Then the woman judge speaks, raising her circular sign with the mouth logo even higher to signal attention. "Yes, I agree with the decision of the Imperial Sovereign."

But Fawzi Boto is not done. His bright tenor rings out, "I challenge this decision! It is my right to demand an explanation, a reevaluation, or a new tiebreaker event! It is my right—*our* right—" and he glances past me at Sofia Veforoi, "—to demand that this so-called 'win' be explained! What exactly did Gwen Lark *do* that makes her a winner? We sang magnificent arias, and she—she issued mere voice commands, faulty ones at that, accomplishing nothing—"

Nothing? Really? Is he being ironic, or sincere? I feel a brief stab of anger.

But, oddly enough, he does have a point—if the official interpretation is that a natural seismic event caused all the stadium damage during which the Grail was "displaced," then what did I do indeed? *Nothing!*

They have no logical reason to award the win to me. Unless—maybe they don't need to have a reason. Maybe it can all be based on the whim of the Imperator. Do the Games rules allow such a thing?

While my mind goes into a tailspin of doubt, on the other side of me, surprisingly, Sofia Veforoi now speaks, interrupting Fawzi. "I disagree with your challenge, Boto. Please do not include me in your dispute. I concur with the judges, and I concede my Category to Gwen Lark."

"What?" Fawzi glares at her, again looking around and past me.

But in that moment, the Vocalist judge says, "This decision is now final and, being the Imperial choice, according to the rules, needs no explanation. Contender Fawzi Boto, you have the right to continue to disagree and even appeal. But from this moment on, your dispute must be taken to the courts, where you may hire Arbiters and spend your time and resources on this pointless matter. Because, I assure you, this decision will not be overturned. So persist, if you will, at your own discretion."

The crowd screams, and I'm not even sure if they're expressing approval or displeasure. That is, until the chants come: *"Gwen Lark! Champion! Champion!"*

My own pulse calms down—my nerves settling, at least in this regard—because I know in my gut that regardless of what Fawzi Boto might continue to think or do, the Imperator made his public choice *in my favor*, and it is irrefutable.

I *won*, and it's official. No matter on what shaky grounds—quite literally—the decision is based.

Now that my Vocalist Category has been decided, I remain standing before the judge, while Sofia and Fawzi are told to step back. The Priest of the Grail instructs them to descend from the dais onto the floor of the arena and wait at the foot of the stairs. Eventually they will be dismissed, but not until the two remaining Category tiebreakers take place.

From the corner of my eye I watch Fawzi's angry, confused face, and Sofia's stoic one, as they remain below, resigned. There is something tragic about the sight of them, and I feel a moment of real sorrow on their behalf.

What desperate hopes and dreams are being shattered right now for them, their families, and loved ones. . . ?

Forcibly I turn my attention back to the judges and the remaining Contenders. Miramis Opu is announcing the next contested Category—that of Scientist.

The Scientist judge raises his circular sign with the atom cloud logo and looks at Chihar Agwath and Rea Bunit. "Contenders, your tiebreaker event will determine which one of you is the winner. You must impress me with your abilities to solve the problem presented to you! Bring forth the materials for the Scientist Category!"

At once, three Games staff dressed in Blue come running across the arena, carrying two small folding tables, a large tray with twenty bottles, and two round stones, each one the size of a bowling ball.

The audience noise increases as they ascend the dais and quickly set up the little tables before the two Contenders. One stone ball is placed on each table, and each is surrounded by ten bottles from the tray. Apparently, each of the bottles contains a different substance, because they have ten different color-coded labels, one of each kind per table.

Chihar and Rea wait nervously.

"Contenders, your task is the following: use any of the ten common chemical substances presented here to *destroy* the stone before you. Some of these substances are highly toxic, others are benign, until mixed with each other. All are potentially lethal, so take care not to become contaminated with them. Use as many or as few of the chemicals as you like. The first person to cause the stone to crack and crumble most effectively will win the Category. You have ten minutes to achieve your task. If neither one of you succeeds by the time the alarm sounds, you will have to perform a second task. Are you ready? When the bell tone sounds, you may begin!"

In seconds, a sound of three ringing bells echoes across the stadium.

At once, Chihar and Rea approach the table and start grabbing bottles to read their labels.

I watch with pity as they keep turning some bottles and picking up others, examining the stone, pausing to think, starting to pick up the items again—all while the audience roars at them.

Visually, it's not a particularly exciting or physical task, but because of the high stakes involved, the audience betting goes wild. In moments, the great scoreboards all around the *Khemetareon* start filling with rows of numbers as the thousands of additional bets from the media feeds start pouring in to complicate the already rapid-fire changes in the tallies.

Minutes tick. I realize the pressure on Chihar and his rival is astounding. I've no idea what kinds of chemicals they have at their disposal, or how much or how little is in each bottle. They have to plan wisely, because once they use up any given bottle, they are out of that substance. Furthermore, the combinations of the ten substances might result in dangerous poisons or toxic fumes.

Rea Bunit is the one who opens the first bottle and pours its contents onto her round stone. A second one quickly follows, and there's a hiss from the stone's surface.

Chihar takes a bit longer to begin his own process. He selects two different bottles and opens them slowly, with extra care—his bandaged hand doesn't give him the full range of finger movement.

And then he methodically pours them together over the stone, resulting in a thick vapor, while his stone begins to sizzle.

This goes on for a few more minutes, as both Contenders open more bottles, and there is a lot of hissing, sizzling, and noxious fumes. The surfaces of both their tables must have some kind of anti-corrosive coating because they remain unharmed by the chemical warfare being enacted on top of them.

When the final alarm sounds and they cease their efforts and step back, both stones have cracked into multiple pieces, but the one that appears most eroded is Rea's stone.

Chihar's expression is normally bland and hard to read, but now it deepens with a kind of weary despair that summarizes all the ordeals and brutal effort that this older man had to go through to get to this moment. He closes his eyes for an instant and lets out a deeply held breath. And then he stands motionless, staring at nothing before him.

My heart breaks for Chihar as the Scientist judge raises his circular sign and announces: "The Scientist Category Winner is Rea Bunit!"

The audience screams as the woman's face beams with jubilation and she raises both hands to wave at the crowds. *"Rea! Rea! Champion! Champion!"* they shout.

Rea Bunit remains standing proudly before her judge.

Meanwhile, as instructed, Chihar descends from the dais. As he walks near me, our gazes meet for a moment, and a world of meaning is exchanged between us. Chihar nods to me with dignity, then goes below to stand with the others who have come so unbelievably close to their dreams, but ultimately *lost* the Games of the Atlantis Grail.

At the same time, Games workers return to remove the folding tables and the bottles and what's left of the broken stones.

Broken, like their aspirations and dreams. . . .

I am still bogged down in sympathetic depression on behalf of Chihar—my thoughts are racing in an effort to come up with some means of helping him after this is all over—when the final tiebreaker Category is announced by the Priest of the Grail.

The Technician judge looks at Lolu Eetatu and Mineb Inei, then raises his circular sign with the sine wave logo. "Contenders, your tiebreaker event will determine the winner in the Technician

Category! You must impress me with your technical skills and solve the problem presented to you! Bring forth the materials!"

Out of the corner of my eye, I watch Lolu standing stiffly, with a very pale, little girl face. I notice her hands are clenched at her sides, and she is frowning from the pressure of what's about to happen.

I can feel her emotion, waves of it passing through me, and my heart starts to pound again, this time on her behalf. . . .

Lolu's competition, the large and heavy Mineb Inei, towers at her side. His own face reflects intense concentration.

The audience starts to chant both their names while the scoreboards once again light up with numbers.

Two of the Games staff, once more wearing Blue, come running, each of them with a large bag and a folding table. They set up the tables before Lolu and Mineb, then overturn the bags and dump the contents onto the tables—it looks like electronic parts and junk.

Lolu continues to frown silently, while Mineb makes some kind of nervous grunt. The crowds roar.

The Technician judge waves his circular logo for attention then speaks: "Contenders, your task is the following: use any of these components to put together a functional drone. Your finished product must be able to perform at least one useful task. You have ten minutes to achieve your task before the alarm sounds. When the bell tone sounds, you may begin!"

The moment the bells ring, Lolu and Mineb surge forward and start rummaging through the stuff on their tables. They pick up and examine the alien circuit boards, components, connectors, microchips, cables, and lord knows what else—the kind of stuff that Anu and Gennio work with on a regular basis. As they take stock of their materials, their faces intense with concentration, the audience starts to scream again. The crazy betting commences, and the scoreboards flash with the new data.

I must admit, both Lolu and Mineb are really good with their hands—in less than a minute they start putting things together, fiddling and plugging in and twisting and connecting parts. Their fingers flash with sure movements born of long practice. I marvel at the steely concentration and the skills they both display.

But there can only be one winner.

The ten-minute alarm sounds, and Lolu has some kind of object assembled, and Mineb has another. I have no idea what they are supposed to do, but the Technician judge nods and then asks them to demonstrate the functionality. The audience quiets and waits in suspense.

Mineb sings a keying command and his drone rises several feet above the table, then emits a bright beam of light. "It's a basic auto-light," he says in an uncertain voice that carries across the arena.

Lolu is up next. She voice-keys her drone and it too rises several feet overhead. She sings another command, and a small bright hologram projection appears over it, with Atlantean numerals in glowing orange light. "It is a chronometer . . ." Lolu says in a breathless voice.

The judge nods in approval.

Suddenly the holo-clock projection fizzles. . . . The image scrambles, and the drone goes dark.

Lolu's drone crashes down onto the table surface.

And just like that, Lolu's dream is done.

Chapter 18

Oh, no! Not Lolu! My own breath catches, and I blink, fighting back a strange rush of emotion and a lump rising in the back of my throat.

Lolu stares at the defective fallen drone, the junk lying before her, and her face starts to twitch. She does not cry, but her face fixes into a weird expression that is almost amazed—it's as if she is stunned by the event as much as anyone.

The crowds roar, and the Technician judge looks somewhat surprised too. He lifts his brows and shakes his head in obvious regret. Then he raises his circular sign and pronounces Mineb Inei the winner in his Category.

I stare at Lolu in horror, seeing her continue to stand motionless as the Games staff arrive to clean up the materials and remove the tables. Finally she takes a shuddering breath and turns to walk down the stairs, head lowered. She never looks up as she passes all of us and joins the others who lost, waiting below.

No, no, no! I think. *I must do something, anything for her! Aeson can help, surely he can do something, so that her dying mother would get the medical help she needs . . . she cannot be allowed to die, no. . . .*

Stop.

I force the spinning, horrible chaos of emotion back down inside me, deep. I cannot fall apart now, not now, not yet.

And so, I pull myself together and stand and listen as the audience chants *"Champion! Champion!"* while Mineb Inei straightens his bulky frame and raises his eyebrows really wide in amazement. He starts to laugh, then raises his hands up high and waves to the crowds.

The Games choir sings once more, and a swell of triumphant music comes from the hidden orchestra.

As music fades, Miramis Opu turns to the Contenders standing below the dais and says loudly, "Contenders, you who stand below, having struggled bravely but having ultimately lost—you may depart the arena!"

Three Games workers come running, two in Blue, and one in White, and they motion for the losing Contenders to follow them. Sofia Veforoi and Fawzi Boto follow the worker in White, while Chihar and Lolu each follow one dressed in Blue. They walk quickly across the arena, and the crowds roar and clap, awarding them the final accolades and respect for their near-winner status.

When they are gone and silence returns, the Priest of the Grail looks up, raising his hands up to the audience, "I present to you the Champions of the Games of the Atlantis Grail!"

It is an indescribable moment. . . .
The audience roar is absolutely deafening, and the music swells. At the same time, our uniforms light up. This time, it's final and undeniable. We stand, all ten of us, before our Category judges, and raise our hands and wave.

I perform the same motions that the others are doing; wave and smile automatically. Yet I'm stunned and overwhelmed, and, yes, despondent on behalf of my two teammates who have both just lost. I glance to my right and see Brie, grinning and waving to the audience. Our gazes meet, and she too reveals a moment of doubt and darkness, recognizing the sorrow in me. On her other side is Kokayi, who also meets my eyes with a brief searing look, and beyond him, I see Kateb. The four of us, all members of Team Lark, have done the impossible—all four of us won. And yet I can feel that each of us grieves on behalf of those who didn't.

But the Ceremony is far from over.

"The Games are Forever!" Miramis Opu exclaims, interrupting the roar and thunder. "And now is the time to announce the Top Ten in order and award Rank! We will start with the lowest score, and end with the highest. Presenters, come forth!"

From the farthest entrance of the arena, hundreds of Games Staff arrive, dressed in all the different Category colors. They hold various gaudy items—flowers, colorful ribbons, golden vine-leaf wreaths, and among them, ten small Grails in metallic colors of each Category, each with a gilded border of curling vines sculpted around the rim. Four of the workers hold four larger Grails, Red, Blue, Green, and Yellow. They all remain below, forming several concentric circles around the dais on which we stand.

"First, behold, the Winners of the Grail of each of the Four Stages!" the Priest of the Grail announces. "Stage One, the Red Grail—originally held by Athlete Deneb Gratu, but presented to no one in these Games due to loss of his life, with no clear succession or inheritance of points—hence, forfeiture. The Red Grail is awarded to the People! It will go on permanent display for all to see in the Imperial Poseidon Museum—"

The audience screams and stomps and cheers. The worker holding the large Red Grail ascends the dais stairs and stands at the Champions level alongside us. He raises the gleaming red thing high overhead, and turns around slowly for all of the audience sections to see and acknowledge. Then he carries the Grail back down the stairs and proudly walks across the arena to the exit.

The Priest of the Grail continues: "Stage Two, the Blue Grail—held by the Artist Champion Rurim Kiv!"

The worker holding the large Blue Grail goes up to the dais. Lowering his head in a respectful bow, he hands the Blue Grail to Rurim Kiv, but does not linger, returning at once to the arena floor to rejoin the staff circles.

Rurim, dark and beautiful, receives the Blue Grail. As the crowds scream, he slowly raises it over his head and throws his head back. Then he lowers it again and surprisingly, kisses the object along the rim. All along, a delicate smile plays at the corners of his lips.

"Stage Three, the Green Grail—originally held by Entertainer Tiamat Irtiu, but inherited by the Entertainer Champion Kokayi Jeet!"

Kokayi takes the Green Grail from the Games worker with a briefly startled look. But then his expression blooms into a fierce smile, a flash of white teeth. He raises the Grail high overhead and brandishes it, while the crowd roars approval.

"Stage Four, the Yellow Grail—held by the Vocalist Champion Gwenevere Lark!"

I know it's coming, but when my moment arrives, I feel a burst of nervous energy. I receive the Yellow Grail from the hands of the Games worker, feeling its slight heft, the smooth metallic surface . . . recalling the moment when I first held it a couple of days ago on top of the Great Nacarat Plateau, at the culmination of that most insane, impossible Race. . . .

I'm not sure what exact feelings come—indeed, I've gone through so many up-and-down feelings in the last few days that I no longer trust my own judgment in that regard—but something profound and elemental rises from a deep place inside me. With a burst of fierce energy, I lift the Grail above my head, look up at the audience, and then at the Imperial balcony where Aeson watches me, and where the Imperator watches me.

And I laugh.

The audience screams to acknowledge me, and I hear them once again chanting *"Gwen Lark! Im-pe-ra-tris!"*

The Priest of the Grail raises his hands for silence and pronounces: "Attention! The Top Ten will now be Ranked!"

The roar of the crowd falls into silence.

I lower the Yellow Grail to the level of my chest, same as the other two Stage Grail holders, and clutch it with my fingers, as I wait with intense wonder for the Rank results. At this point I have no idea where my own Rank will place me, all things considered.

"In Tenth Place," the Priest of the Grail says, "with 3,394 points, in the Scientist Category—Rea Bunit!"

The audience responds with a swell of sound. Meanwhile the scoreboards all around the *Khemetareon* now display ten blank slots in giant script, and then the bottom slot is filled in with Rea Bunit's name and score.

At once, one of the Games staff attired in Blue, holding a small metallic Blue Grail with the gilded-vine rim design, leaves his spot in the circles below the dais and runs up the stairs. He hands the Blue Grail to Rea Bunit, bows and retreats down the stairs, to the shouts of the audience. Rea accepts the Grail and lifts it overhead to receive her adulations.

"In Ninth Place, with 3,428 points, in the Athlete Category— Ukou Dwetat!"

This time a worker dressed in Red runs up the dais and hands a small metallic Red Grail to Ukou.

Another swell of audience approval, and Ukou Dwetat's name and score populates the penultimate slot on the bottom.

"In Eighth Place, with 3,605 points, in the Technician Category—Mineb Inei!"

The process repeats, this time with another Blue worker and Blue Grail.

So far, not too surprising, and I expect my own name to be called just about now.

"In Seventh Place, with 3,821 points, in the Entrepreneur Category—Gabriella Walton!"

Okay, now that's a little surprising. *Brie scored lower than me? I must've really racked up some points with my Yellow Grail and Race win. . . .* I stare as Brie receives a White Grail, and her name and score go up on the scoreboards while she brandishes her trophy before the crowds with an insolent, toothy grin.

"In Sixth Place, with 3,972 points, in the Vocalist Category— Gwenevere Lark!"

I exhale a held breath. *There I go, okay, yes. . . . Sixth place, holy crap! I made it as high as sixth place! And so many points— how the hell did I get so many points?*

The crowds roar as my Games worker approaches and hands me a little White Grail trophy, so that now I am holding two grails, one in each hand—the large Yellow Grail of Stage Four and the small White one of a Category Champion. I lift the White Grail and smile, while my gaze sweeps the stadium and pauses on the distant Imperial balcony where I see my beloved Aeson standing up and clapping. . . . Next to him the Imperator remains seated, but barely inclines his head in acknowledgement of me.

"In Fifth Place, with 4,107 points, in the Artist Category— Rurim Kiv!"

I turn to see the Artist receive the small Yellow Grail in addition to the Blue Grail of Stage Two, so that he too has both his hands occupied.

"In Fourth Place, with 5,804 points, in the Animal Handler Category—Leetana Chipuo!"

The scoreboard is now more than halfway full with names and scores. We've entered the upper portion, with the big players. Leetana accepts her Green Grail and waves proudly.

Meanwhile I'm amazed that two of my teammates still remain, which means they must've scored extremely well!

"In Third Place, with 6,137 points, in the Inventor Category—
Kateb Nuletat!"

I cannot help smiling as I see Kateb straighten, lift his head,
and take his Yellow Grail trophy while his eyes glisten with sudden
tears. . . . With a surge of emotion at the sight of his achievement, I
think of his wife and her inability to sing, and his invention to help
her overcome her shortcoming. It will now become a reality. . . .

And now, only two Champions remain. I bet Kokayi is up next.

"In Second Place, with 46,291 points, in the Warrior
Category—Hedj Kukkait!"

Hedj's expression does not change, but I suspect he is slightly
surprised. However, he is controlled enough that he does not show
any emotion even now, as he accepts his Red Grail with cool dignity
and lifts it up for all to see, then inclines his head to the audience.
His points score total is staggering, miles ahead of the rest of us, and
I understand now that those of us in the lower Rank spots didn't
even come close to this megastar level, that of the big leagues. It's
hard to imagine the obscene number of kills behind it. And yet. . . .

*Holy crap! The White Bird got second place, not first! Which
means. . . .*

"In First Place, with 60,479 points, in the Entertainer
Category—Kokayi Jeet!"

*Kokayi won! He won the top spot, the highest honors! My
teammate won the crowning achievement in the Games! And his
total score—no doubt because he's inherited all of Thalassa's
immense score—is unbelievable!*

I laugh and watch Kokayi react in complete opposite to Hedj
Kukkait's unemotional, controlled reaction. First, Kokayi's jaw
drops. Then he puts one hand over his mouth and bends over at the
waist, clutching the large Green Grail of Stage Three to his
abdomen, then gesticulates and fans himself with the free hand,
grabs the back of his own head and rocks back and forth. Holding
the large Green Grail of Stage Three, he accepts his small Green
Grail of a Category Champion, and raises it high, shaking it like
crazy, leaping and dancing in a circle in place, his body sleek and
elegant even now in its fluid, acrobatic motions. . . . He then
screams at the audience, raises both grails, laughs and yells, "Ai, ai,
ai, *mamai!* Hahaha!"

The audience screams back at him, loving his wildly emotional display. And then they start chanting his name—indeed, all of our names.

In the general roar the individual chants mingle together, as the sound becomes one great human chord of triumphant joy and thunder.

"Congratulations, our glorious new Champions!" the Priest of the Grail exclaims, his amplified voice cutting through the roar. "Prepare to be acknowledged as Citizens of our proud nation, Imperial *Atlantida!*"

At once, the Games workers break out of their places in the circles below and run up the dais, bearing ribbons and wreaths sculpted of vine leaves. They joyfully accost each one of us and place the metallic wreaths on our heads, then tie many colorful ribbons to our appendages, starting with our wrists on both hands and going all the way up our arms. I count ten ribbons on each of my arms—one for each Category—streaming like large tassels. But that part is nothing—with a surge of emotion, I feel the light weight of the *citizen wreath* and all the meaning that's attached to it, crowning me. . . .

When they are done, the workers retreat below the dais and then scatter across the arena, disappearing into the distant entrance.

Only we, the ten Champions and the seated judges, remain on stage.

"*Wixameret* to your hard-earned new rank! Stand proudly!" the Priest of the Grail pronounces. "The Imperial Sovereign himself, the Archaeon Imperator Romhutat Kassiopei, will now recognize you in your elevated status."

My pulse pounds in my head as I turn to look again at the Imperial Balcony.

The Imperator sits straight-backed, watching us, and now all the smart boards display a closeup of his face, frozen in the haughty public mask of the great dragon. He then nods at us slowly and raises his hand, palm outward, splaying his fingers apart then bringing them together in a kind of benediction.

And then the Imperial Kassiopei dragon speaks, his deep, haunting voice carrying with force across the stadium.

"Champions! I bestow upon you the honor of Citizenship, from this moment and forever. You now have the full rights and privileges of the Citizens of Imperial *Atlantida*, and you are acknowledged as equals to all who came before you unto thousands of generations! And now—swear to give your loyalty, soul, and spirit, to *Atlantida!*"

"Hear and repeat the Oath of Loyalty!" the Priest of the Grail intones.

Suddenly I'm short of breath. . . .

Not sure why, but it's never occurred to me that I would need to swear an actual oath in order to become a Citizen. . . . *Really, Gwen? What a numbskull idiot you are . . . what did you think people do under such circumstances?* Even back on Earth, people swore oaths when they became citizens of one country or another.

And here I am, about to swear an oath to a nation on a whole different planet.

Oh, my God.

The realization of the magnitude of all this slams into me, hard.

I feel numb, breathless and wild, and suddenly desperate. Because, by swearing loyalty to Atlantis, I am inadvertently renouncing loyalty to Earth. *Or am I?*

But—that's impossible. How can I? I cannot!

Earth is my home. Is there such a thing as dual planetary citizenship?

Why is it that I'm so stupidly unprepared for any of this?

As my thoughts spin wildly, Miramis Opu, the Priest of the Grail lifts his right hand in an Atlantean salute—pressing palm to forehead then sliding it down so that his thumb touches his lips while his fingertips touch his forehead, and his head dips slightly in a bow—and we echo his familiar gesture. Then he begins reading the antique ceremonial words of the oath, and we repeat them, one phrase at a time.

I find that I utter each sentence with difficulty. This one, in particular, causes me deep inner turmoil:

". . . I hereby renounce any and all allegiances to any other state or nation . . ."

. . . or world, I add in my mind.

And yet I must speak it.

Furthermore, I must mean it, with all my heart.

". . . I offer all my courage and strength on behalf of Imperial *Atlantida*, against all enemies and adversaries, in all conflicts, as it is demanded of me by national law . . ."

What if there's a conflict between Earth and Atlantis? A shocking thought comes to me. *What will I do then, without becoming a traitor or a hypocrite? But that's impossible and crazy, so what exactly is expected of me?*

The other Champions taking the oath are already Atlantean, and most, if not all, are natives or residents of Imperial *Atlantida*. It's different for them. Not necessarily easier, but *different*. But for me, this is monumental.

Wait! Not just me—what about Brie? Brie Walton is an Earth Union operative, a true Earth loyalist. What the hell is going on inside that girl's head right now?

No, stop, I tell myself. *It doesn't matter about Brie or about the others. That's their own business, between them and their consciences. Right now, it's about you.*

You will make it work because it's what you do—you resolve impossibilities.

Face it: deep in your heart your true oath covers more than just one nation—it covers a whole new world. It's the human thing to do—the right thing to do. Not just for Earth or for Atlantis, but for everyone. Earth gave you life and your origins, but Atlantis saved you, honed your spirit into its truest shape, and gave you the hope for a future.

You owe so much to both. . . . Time to acknowledge it.

Indeed, as someone born on Earth, a natural citizen, I never had to "acknowledge" Earth. I never had to make a conscious choice on Earth's behalf, not even when "participating" in the process of Qualification for rescue. . . . That was strictly for myself, for my family.

It was personal desperation, the assertion of my will to live past an apocalypse—semi-conscious, raw, instinctive. In many ways that decision was made on my behalf—by my parents, my community, the society around me. Even the Earth governments working alongside the Atlanteans had more say in the direction of my fate than I did. We, the teens given this opportunity, merely went through the paces set for us by the adults, followed instructions, all the while trying not to think too closely of the grim reality. . . .

This is different. This is an active, rational decision, an assumption of responsibility.

A true choice.

You, Gwen—you now take personal responsibility for Atlantis, and you bear it willingly. Not just Imperial Atlantida *but Atlantis itself, the planet and the people on it.*

Therefore—adjust and widen your focus.

And never forget that when you raised the Grail, you broke something, so now you are obligated to fix it.

I submerge myself into this new self-clarity and repeat the final words clearly and succinctly, hearing them ring and echo in my mind.

". . . I swear in all truth and sincerity to honor and serve Imperial *Atlantida*, to the best of my ability, now and always, for as long as I live."

It is done; the Oath is concluded.

Saying it—even though I've just prepared myself—I'm stunned. Just like that, the magnitude of the promise I've made overwhelms me. I am torn inside out and remade again as a new human being, a slightly more mature human being—all in the blink of an eye.

While the audience crowds roar approval, I acknowledge to myself that I've just made a *commitment*. Not merely to one person, my beloved Aeson (how is it that I thought that *marriage* was going to be my first such obligation?). Not even to a group, or even a whole country. But really, to a whole planet of people.

The first formal commitment of my life.

And my greater, deeper, secret personal oath, more than covers it.

Chapter 19

Now that we've sworn the Oath of Loyalty to *Atlantida* and are Citizens, the choir sings a hymn that I've never heard before, and the language seems to be Classical *Atlanteo.* This could be the National Anthem. Do they even have such things in this culture?

Yes, they do.

I see everyone in the audience rise from their seats, the Category judges on stage with us also rise, and perfect silence falls as the hymn echoes in grand harmony over the *Khemetareon.*

"Amrevet-Ra, Impero Atlantida! *Eos, dea, niktos, im saret-i-xerera!"*

If I understand correctly, this translates as:

"Love Divine! Imperial *Atlantida! Morning, day, night, my wisdom and glory!"*

Even the Imperator stands, with Aeson alongside him, listening in solemnity. Somehow I sense Aeson's gaze upon me, caressing me across the expanse. I can just imagine his thoughts: *You did it, Gwen,* im amrevu. *It's almost over, hang in there.*

Glancing at the other Champions standing on both sides of me, I see their faces full of emotion. Even the most secretive, stoic ones, like Hedj Kukkait. . . . Kokayi and Kateb have tears in their eyes. Brie looks shell-shocked. No one salutes or makes any other gesture. They merely stare ahead, straight-backed and proud like soldiers.

When it is over, the crowd roars again, and everyone sits down.

Only we, Champions who are now Citizens, remain standing.

Miramis Opu, the Priest of the Grail, now speaks: "Champions! The Common Earnings Grail holds a very generous sum for you this year! The divided winnings, to be deposited in your personal credit accounts tonight, are over ten million *iretar* for each of the Top Ten! You may spend every single *iret* in any manner you desire, at any institution or venue. No doors will ever be closed to you!"

The audience roars in excitement.

"Furthermore," the priest continues, "as always, your personal needs, wishes, and desires—within the realm of possibility—will be accommodated as soon as you make your requests through the official Games channels."

More thunderous noise.

"In conclusion—you have achieved the highest honors, earned your glory and your rest! Now you may depart the arena, Champions of the eternal Games of the Atlantis Grail! There is no beginning and there will be no end! However, only a Ghost remains of this year's Games, until next Green Season! The Games are Forever!"

"The Games are Forever!" the audience responds.

Moments later, we descend from the dais, waving to the screaming crowds, while triumphant music plays, and follow the Priest of the Grail across the arena toward the exit.

A eson meets me in the crowded outer lobby where I stand with my teammates and other Champions, all of us holding our Grail trophies, as we wait for our friends and loved ones, members of our entourages, or rides home.

I'm still stunned, still disbelieving. Nothing seems real, only a clamor of strange events piling on top of each other. "Where are Chihar and Lolu?" I keep mumbling, even as Kateb and Brie and Kokayi laugh and exchange joyful banter.

"Relax, Lark!" Brie nudges me on the arm. "There he is, your Royal Loverboy. And talking about loverboys—" she waves to the tall, sharply dressed figure of Logan Sangre, whose familiar handsome face and super-black hair I recognize at once from across the lobby as he makes his way toward us.

But I forget him the very next instant because I hear Aeson's beloved voice calling my name.

"Gwen!" My Imperial Bridegroom nears me, followed by his personal guards and mine, and at once I rush into his arms, burying my face against his chest, and closing my eyes.

My hands continue to clutch my two Grails awkwardly, even as I reach around his back—until I feel someone, probably one of the guards, take my triumphant burdens from me before I drop them.

I surrender the Grails without a second thought. . . .

In that moment, everything else recedes.

I am safe.

It is over, he is with me, and I am safe.

Aeson holds me to him, crushing me in his embrace, and we meld together, his hands on me, my hands on him. . . . "Gwen, oh Gwen," he whispers over and over. At some point he presses my face between his hands and then his mouth comes down hard against my lips. I lose all sense of self, lose my breath, gasping in desperate emotional relief as tears well up, and I am sobbing against his cheeks. My fingers travel over his jaw, his cheeks, his throat, and I hold on to him, wild and disbelieving.

I am safe.

When we come apart, long moments later, resurfacing into the real world, aware suddenly of the crowd of people around us, and some of them even staring at us—at the Imperial Crown Prince publicly devouring his Bride—none of it matters.

"Congratulations!" Aeson says with a joyful laugh, looking into my dazed eyes. "Citizen, Champion, Imperial Bride, *im amrevu* Gwen!"

"It really is done, Aeson!" I whisper. "I survived—and won, and so did several of my teammates!"

I turn to smile at Aeson's guard who still holds my Grails politely. Thanking him, I take them back, since they are mine to bear. I turn the grail chalices in my fingers almost absentmindedly, too anxious to give them my full attention or notice the fine details—plenty of time for that later in the privacy of our home—then press them to my chest.

And then I remember and look around frantically. "Oh no, *Lolu!* And *Chihar!* Both of them lost the tiebreaker, and I don't know where they are! I must speak to them both, I need to help—"

Aeson nods and says, "I understand. And we will help them, as soon as possible. They've likely left the venue, so we'll contact them tomorrow, plenty of time—"

"Oh, God, Lolu's mother is desperately ill, she may *have* no time!" I exclaim, feeling short of breath again as a strange panic grips me. "Tomorrow might be too late for her, too *late*, Aeson! She desperately needs medical care, she cannot be allowed to *die!*"

"Then we will locate them immediately," he replies in a calm voice. His gaze is profound, and I sense that he *understands* me so well, understands exactly why I'm panicking now.

In contrast, there is laughter all around us. I hear the elevated voices of other Champions and their companions, animated speech, jokes, exclamations, congratulations. . . . Media representatives surround the lobby, and some Champions are being interviewed on the spot for various networks. Hel-Ra reporters speak with Kokayi Jeet, who giggles loudly and continues to grab the back of his head, his braids swinging, while hugging both his Grails against his chest with one arm. Then he raises the Grails overhead and gesticulates wildly, holding them up for the world to see. Hedj Kukkait is talking to someone from *Grail Games Daily*, Tiago's popular show.

Kateb laughs, striking a pose, with his arms around a tall, slim woman with long gilded hair who must be his wife, and waves at someone else from the media feeds who is aiming a recording device at him. Leetana and Ukou are signing digital autographs with their fingertips. Rea grins and bends down to tousle the hair of a little girl, while Rurim Kiv once again raises both his Grails, then kisses them with a comical, exaggerated sensuousness before reporters. Mineb is hugging several small children and other members of his family. . . .

Meanwhile the Imperial guards surround Aeson and me, keeping back the public onslaught, only permitting other Champions and their entourages to mingle near us. I see from the corner of my eye as, right behind me, Brie Walton talks loudly in her typical insolent tone with Logan Sangre. He remains businesslike and serious even now, displaying no emotion as he attends to her, periodically checks his wrist comm, then turns around as a network reporter moves in to interview Brie, the *other* Earthie Champion in these Games.

I catch Logan's gaze, and he briefly sees me, then makes a polite nod in my direction, and also a perfect military nod to Aeson. Yes, Logan is definitely all business, all the time.

". . . how does it feel, Champion Walton, as a Gebi refugee, to have gone through this quintessential Atlantean event?" the reporter asks in an excited voice.

"Oh, it's been a bunny-rabbit delight," Brie responds, opening her eyes wide and raising her brows. "I highly recommend it—to you and everyone you know or wish you didn't—definitely put it on your bucket list!" And then she whirls around in my direction. "Right, Lark? Hey, you should interview *her*, she's your Imperial

Princess! Me, I'm just a jailbird who's broken out, finally—right, Mister Sangria? I mean, Correctional Officer Sangre—"

The reporter whirls to Logan. "Is this true? Is Champion Gabriella Walton being released from incarceration?"

"Yes, of course. She's now a Citizen," Logan replies in a cool voice, without a pause. "She has earned her freedom, will be occupying her own residence starting tonight, and we're complying with the regulations as dictated by law—"

"Imperial Lady Gwen Lark!" I turn to see another persistent reporter waving at me past Aeson's guards. "Congratulations on your glorious win, and may we have a statement from you for *Winning the Grail*, and book an appearance on this week's episode?"

"Imperial Lady Gwen! Hel-Ra would like to interview you for prime time at your convenience—" Yet another reporter pushes from another direction. "With the permission of the Imperial Prince, of course, in fact it would be an honor to interview both of you, to have you recount your profound experiences of these Games, as the Imperial Kassiopei—"

I part my lips, nod silently.

"Yes, later," Aeson responds on my behalf. "My Imperial Bride has endured enough excitement for today and needs to recuperate. Contact the Palace through the proper channels in regard to any appearance scheduling. We are done here!"

"Yes . . ." I echo. And then I turn away from the reporter to glance briefly at my fellow Champions. "Everyone!" I say loudly. "I'll see you later, Brie—and Kokayi, Kateb!"

Kokayi hears and turns to me with his flashing grin. "What? Leaving already, *amrevet*? How about a whirlwind celebration? I'll show you my favorite local dancing spots—"

But I smile and shake my head tiredly. "See you soon, Kokayi. Go celebrate, my friend, you truly earned it!"

Then I return my attention back to Aeson. "Please, let's get out of here."

We leave the *Khemetareon* building in a hurry, past the gathered crowds outside, surrounded by our personal guards—for which I'm genuinely grateful, for once. As we walk toward the parking area, Aeson brings me up to speed on what's been happening in the "real world" while I was in the Final Ceremony.

"Several new SPC reports, some unexpected news about a certain *object*—all of it coming in just as all of you were being proclaimed Champions." And he motions at the data band of his wrist comm.

"Oh, no!" I say breathlessly, keeping pace with his fast stride. "What now? Something else terrible happened? Must've been so frustrating for you, having to sit through that long Ceremony! What's the time now?"

"It's close to fourth hour," he says, taking my hand in his and holding it protectively and to calm me, while I rearrange my Grails to keep them in the crook of one arm. "Not exactly terrible, but— more in the car. Let's return home and eat *dea* meal and—Ah, there's Ker and Xel—"

Aeson waves to the two familiar figures of the *astra daimon*, as they join us, and we all walk rapidly to the hover cars.

"So, a new Citizen and a Champion—must be a relief, eh, Imperial Lady Gwen?" Keruvat says with a warm smile, craning his neck at me. "You looked good up there!"

"She certainly shone!" Xel adds, with a smile of his own. "Nicely done!"

And then both of them glance at Aeson.

"You saw the advance scout landing reports, I gather," Xel says, switching to serious mode.

"Oh, yes." Aeson, too, is wearing a controlled expression. "Remarkable and confusing."

"In the car?" Ker says.

"Right." Aeson turns to our guards and makes an arrangement so that someone else can drive his personal two-seater vehicle and the vehicles of the *daimon*, while we all take a larger hover car used by the guards, so that both Xelio and Keruvat can ride in the same car with us.

"Privacy filter on?" Ker says as soon as we get in—Aeson and I in the front seat, Ker and Xelio behind us, and four guards in the third and fourth rows. "Just in case any stray nano-cams followed us in. . . ."

Aeson merely nods and touches the surface of the navigation panel, so that hair-thin gold lines appear, run across the perimeter of the vehicle, and then settle into a barely audible hum.

"Aeson . . ." I say softly, "I realize how critical things are, but . . . before we go, you promised to find Lolu Eetatu for me, and also Chihar, my teammates. I'm so sorry to bring this up. I know it's a really bad time, but—" I trail off, feeling terribly guilty about having to distract Aeson at a time like this, but at the same time prodded by a sense of desperate urgency returning to overwhelm me.

He looks at me, and at once his expression becomes gentle. "Not at all. Let me make the arrangements now, on behalf of Lolu Eetatu's mother."

"Oh? What's this?" Xelio asks. But Ker taps him on the thigh with a knowing look.

And so we wait for several long moments while Aeson messages his staff, then looks up at me. "It's done," he says. "They will locate the Eetatu family, find out the nature of her mother's illness, which medical facility is best equipped to handle it, and I will cover all the expenses. Wherever she is, Lolu is being contacted right now."

I put a hand over my mouth, holding back a sudden welling of tears. "Aeson . . . *thank you*," I whisper.

"As for your other teammate, Chihar Agwath, will tomorrow do? Since his situation is not as urgent."

Silently I nod, unable to form words. Gratitude fills me with a warm flood, and tears are now pouring in long trails down my cheeks. Then I take a deep, shuddering breath to quell the flow and blink away the tears so that I can smile with all my heart at *im amrevu*. Meanwhile, he leans in and puts his arm around me in the most wonderful way.

"All right now?" he says, his lips near my ear, his breath and his soft golden hair brushing my cheek.

"Yes, oh yes. . . . Everything is all right now," I reply. "At least in that regard. Now, please continue with your own work, the reports and whatever news of—the moon?"

Aeson straightens and glances behind us at Keruvat and Xelio, who are watching us patiently. "Now, regarding the moon—" He sings the sequence to start the hover car, and we lift off, rising into the white afternoon sky over Poseidon.

"The SPC landing parties?" I ask, sniffling and wiping the remaining tears with the back of my hand.

". . . could not land," Aeson finishes my sentence with a hardening expression, his gaze on the flight lane before us.

"Huh?" I furrow my brow. "What does that mean?"

Aeson sighs and looks at me, then again glances behind him at Ker and Xel. "According to the vanguard Pilots, multiple reports confirm that as the shuttles approached the moon, they encountered no atmospheric resistance—despite a visible layer of haze suggesting a gaseous atmospheric presence around the moon. They kept going and approached the surface. Braked to land and—*kept going*. The shuttles found no solid matter, no resistance, and continued flying in sudden darkness of what looked like *interior rock layers* until they passed all the way *through* the moon and emerged on the opposite side."

My jaw drops. "What? Is it a hologram?"

Behind me, Ker shakes his head. "No one knows. Could be a hologram, could be another holo-shield."

"Could be something else," Xel adds.

"Whatever it is, the moon is unreachable, *intangible*—a ghost," Aeson says thoughtfully.

"If you prefer a poetic description straight out of ancient myth," Xel says with a bitter laugh, "it's the Ghost Moon."

Chapter 20

We get back to Phoinios Heights, and my head is spinning with all the crazy information. *Ghost Moon!* Suddenly all kinds of common, everyday Atlantean references come to "haunt" me, and I start to space out in my usual, intense, thought-process concentration mode—even as we enter the house, and everyone we know surrounds us. Aeson presses my arm and steps back to let the others greet me, while he himself goes to check a nearby computer display where Oalla and Erita have been scrolling through data in our absence.

"Gwenie! Oh, Gwenie! Congratulations!" Gracie cries, coming to hug me, with Laronda not far behind.

"We watched everything on TV, saw you up there! You done good, girl!" Laronda exclaims, squeezing me so hard I can barely breathe, while the two Grails clank together in my arms. "And look at you, not one but two Grails! And your uniform is still lit up, so shiny and crazy-White in that fancy-schmancy Champion neon! How long will it glow like that?"

"Not sure. It'll probably start to fade soon." I smile.

"Oh my God, let me see—" Gracie reaches for the large Yellow Grail and takes it from my fingers, while Laronda snatches the small White Grail and examines it closely.

Now that my hands are free, I turn and give Chiyoko and Hasmik a series of huge hugs. Then I see Oalla, Dawn, Erita, and an unfamiliar, tall, full-figured young woman dressed in a conservative Atlantean business outfit, the kind I've seen on the media worn by authority figures. She has astute eyes that are somewhere between hazel and green, strong features, and shoulder-length soft, wavy hair of a natural blond shade that is definitely not dyed but can pass for the fashionable gilded look. Her sharp expression does not soften even a bit as she looks at me while Erita is introducing her as Arbiter Tamira Bedut.

"A pleasure to meet you in person, Imperial Lady Gwen," Tamira tells me in a confident low voice. "I am here to make sure all your final legal documentation in regard to Citizenship is filed correctly."

"Oh," I say. "I thought I was already officially a Citizen?"

Tamira nods. "You are. This is merely a technical formality that is a necessary part of the process. All the other Games Champions must file identity change documents with our Grand Courts, which can be done with or without Arbiters. I'm at your service, and everything is ready for your signatures. It will only take a few minutes of your time, after which I will leave at once to file them before this work day ends—"

"Okay, give the Imperial Lady a moment to rest before you drown her with that boring stuff, Tam," Erita interrupts, rolling her eyes slightly at Tamira. "Yes, you live to work, you're a perfectionist, and it's what I still adore about you, and why you've been retained here, but really—slow down. . . . It's been a long day for her, and for all of us, to be honest."

Tamira turns to give Erita a slightly chilly but entirely professional glance. "Very well. But expediting this process is for the Imperial Lady's own benefit. Filing today is best."

"We *know*. Just—in the name of all deities—" Erita shakes her head. "Let her sit down at least. Have a drink. You, too."

I stand and watch them bicker somewhat oddly, and I exchange glances with Dawn, who looks on with curious amusement. I recall that Dawn and Blayne have been meeting and working with this Arbiter on my behalf, for weeks, but I never had the chance to meet her in person until today. And then, as Dawn mouths silently, "She's her ex," I remember being told that Erita and Tamira were in a relationship once, but it ended on an unhappy note, due to irreconcilable personality clashes.

While I space out for a moment thinking about it, Tamira shakes her head in frustration, excuses herself politely, then goes to get a drink from the side table.

Erita makes a sarcastic grunt and winks at me, then joins Aeson and the other *daimon* who are nearby talking intensely in slightly lowered voices and checking the data feeds on their wrists and on the large computer. I'm guessing that Tamira Bedut is not a part of their inner circle, hence the discretion. I may be wrong, of course.

The estate staff is readying the *dea* meal service for us on side tables all around the perimeter of the room, and the wonderful aroma of many savory dishes sizzling in pans, with their exotic spices, overwhelms my senses. I feel a stab of intense hunger and impatience fueled by nervous exhaustion.

But first, I need to find out more of what's going on with the Ghost Moon.

I glance at a nearby sofa where Blayne and Gordie are watching a hovering TV screen with the sound turned down. Seeing me stare, my brother waves me over to see what they're watching. Apparently, it's multiple screens with post-Games coverage and highlights of all of us Champions at the Final Ceremony, various betting results, and final score stats analyses. A closeup of Aeson and me kissing passionately in the lobby afterwards is prominently featured, together with similar emotional clips of other Champions greeting their loved ones. Mixed in sparingly is the other news— urban crowds still outside, and yes, a few talk panel programs speculating on the strange object in the sky. Oddly enough, no one has used the obvious term to refer to the object.

"Weird, huh?" Gordie points to a feed showing panelists arguing about the "nebulous cluster" or the "glowing mirage" and even an "unseasonal localized aurora."

"I bet they're specially instructed *not* to bring up 'Ghost Moon,'" Blayne says. "The SPC teams only figured out this morning that it's an orbiting moon—this news is so fresh it's steaming. Maybe once the authorities make an official statement, they will get the go-ahead. Who knows? We still don't know to what extent the media is controlled by official propaganda channels."

"What about foreign or international feeds?" I ask.

"Same thing," Blayne replies. "From what we can tell, New Deshret news is not saying anything yet either."

"Yeah," Gordie says, with a glance in Aeson's direction. "Your fiancé is in charge of the SPC, and they're still working on it, so no official statement *anywhere* until he says so." And Gordie makes an ambiguous noise, which is his way of expressing admiration.

I sigh, pat my brother on the shoulder, then head over to join Aeson and the *astra daimon.*

Half an hour later, nothing else conclusive about the Ghost Moon has been discovered. The consensus is that the moon is either in a different quantum phase or shielded. Aeson explains to me that more pilot teams are being dispatched, together with more instruments and probes, to measure trace radiation and quantum fluctuations. Until they get a better, more conclusive data set and then consult with other heads of state, there can be no official word to the global media—which leaves only the unofficial channels with their vague speculations. At this point, they've been so blatantly avoiding the "Ghost Moon" terminology that it has to be intentional.

Then Aeson gets another call from the Imperator and steps aside to talk softly.

I inhale deeply and take the opportunity to finally relieve Tamira of her misery at waiting for me to get a grip. We sit down at a small table and go over about a dozen documents on her tablet screen—the originals in *Atlanteo*, with English translations provided for my benefit. I read each one closely, make my digital signature in the designated places, and Tamira follows each one with her unique Arbiter authentication code, marking my signatures as "formally witnessed" by a legal professional and therefore legally binding. The whole thing takes at least twenty minutes, and when we're done, I feel a weird burden both lifted and added to my virtual shoulders.

It's the burden of new responsibility.

The right to vote. I was never old enough to vote on Earth. Will I now be able to cast a vote here, in this system described as an Imperial Democracy? My mind starts to spin off on a tangent as I think about that amazing privilege.

Tamira sends the digital documents to the court network, turns off her tablet, and looks at me. "All that remains is for me to authenticate the documents received and reviewed in person before the judge—another ceremonial formality. But before I go, I must remind you about your Champion Personal Request filing and your share of the Champion Earnings Grail."

"Oh, yes!" I say. "Where and how do I do that?"

Tamira points to Aeson. "As your official sponsor in the Games, the Imperial Lord has the information sent to him. It's a simple online form for each Champion to fill out, where you state your wishes and preferences for your prize fulfillment. Just don't forget to take care of it promptly. They give you a week to think it over before making your final choice decisions. But—don't think too long. Some popular things might get claimed by other Champions in the course of their own wishes, and if such a conflict arises, it's first come, first served. If I were in your place, I would do it tonight."

In other words, she is suggesting I need to grab what's mine while I can. She has no idea what I plan to file as my personal wish request. Oh, if only she knew. . . . For that matter, if only I knew!

But, no—I *do* know. I know very well, and I'll be discussing it with *im amrevu* as soon as we're alone.

Now that our official business is concluded, Tamira gives me a nod, both courtly and efficient. Then she looks around the room and makes a point of waving to Dawn and Blayne—but not Erita—right before she leaves.

"Congratulations, *janik*, you are legally a Citizen!" Hasmik comes up to me and gives my arm a light squeeze. "Now you must eat and rest!"

I follow Hasmik to the serving tables. Gordie's already there with a heaping plate of food that could easily feed a family, and Aeson moves in to stand very close to me while Keruvat is filling his own plate. Aeson's arm comes around me from behind, and I feel his firm hand slide down my lower back and linger there, sending an unexpected and sweet chill sensation throughout me.

"Tonight," he says, leaning near my ear. "We can rest, finally. . . . My Father has no new instructions for us regarding the ark-ship. Not until we figure out this moon and its connection."

"Even though the ship is active and the possible alien threat remains?" I say.

Aeson just looks at me with a soft expression in his eyes. "Yes, even so. But first, a long afternoon of work."

"By the way, I've already decided on my personal wishes as Champion," I tell him.

My Bridegroom smiles. "I can only begin to guess what those wishes are."

"I bet you can't guess this one." I tug at the long sleeve of my Games uniform that's still glowing neon-white, over the fine *viatoios* armor layer underneath. "My most immediate wish is to take off this evil thing and never have to wear it again! In fact—going to do it right now. Not going to eat until I do—"

And with those words I head upstairs to my closet to make this easy little wish a reality.

By early evening, after several more pilot scouting team missions gather seemingly endless data, the SPC turns in all the preliminary findings to its Commander. I watch as Aeson himself consolidates the findings into the official report for the agencies, which in turn submit their individual analyses to the governing bodies of all participating nations.

In an effort to control the effect and impact of the news, the Imperator and the Imperial Executive Council rush to approve and issue a formal statement to the media—it recognizes the newly discovered moon object, but without giving much detail otherwise, nor mentioning any connection to the ark-ship situation. However, the Imperial *Atlantida* statement still comes a few minutes late, after New Deshret already issued its own public statement first.

Then, like falling dominoes, one after another, similar announcements are released around the globe by the various governing bodies and heads of state.

And the media goes wild.

Ghost Moon!

Suddenly everyone is talking about all the common terms and references, all the myths and old proverbs. The Ghost Moon is the fourth month of each season, and there are "Ghost" mentions in other places on the calendar, such as Ghostday, and the twice-daily Ghost Time, and numerous other, even sneakier common terms that seem to permeate Atlantean culture.

"It seems obvious in retrospect that the Ghost Moon did not just appear now, but was always here, orbiting Atlantis." A woman panelist speaks on a roundtable talk show of experts called *Discovery Around the Globe.* "Despite the shape of its extreme elliptical orbit, it appears to be in a stable position beyond Amrevet's orbit."

"On its closest approach to Atlantis, it would generate major tidal events," a male panelist argues. "And yet, nothing like that has been observed, historically speaking. There would be some evidence of gravitational interactions and relationships between this moon and Atlantis—and between the moon and the other three moons—"

"Not if this moon is in a different quantum dimension!" the woman responds sharply. "There would be no traces of interaction with our reality. And even if at some point it *had* been present in our quantum space, over time the original physical evidence of its presence—such as patterns of erosion due to tidal fluctuations and patterns of ocean stream flow here on our surface—all of it would dissipate and settle into a three-moons-only balanced scenario. . . ."

"Such lack of evidence would indicate that the moon has been isolated for a long time now—but not necessarily always. More interesting is to ask how and why? Was it done by the original Gebi colonists who landed here 9,771 years ago? What were their intentions in hiding it? And why leave references to a 'ghost' in our calendar, our weekdays, our daily lives? Maybe the whole thing was done even earlier, by someone else?"

"Scientists need to verify such a claim—9,771 years might not be enough to dissipate all earlier traces of a fourth moon," another woman panelist says. "It's time to reexamine the geological record."

"The bigger question is how and why is it suddenly visible to us *now?*" an enthusiastic young man says. "And what can we do to bring the Ghost Moon out of its present quantum state and into our own space-time?"

Yet another panelist speaks up. "That might prove disastrous! Imagine all the tidal and gravitational forces suddenly taking effect in our physical reality. It could cause physical chaos, even endanger the orbits of the other three moons, placing the entire satellite system of our planet in a precarious state of imbalance—"

"I still want to know the catalyst for this sudden appearance. Or reappearance."

"Indeed, what happened? What caused it to become visible *right now*, even though it's not tangible?" the host says. "That's the topic of the day. And what a day it has been! The Grail Games are over, and the Ghost Moon is here to tantalize us with all the implications—"

Gracie, Blayne, Gordie, and I sit watching the TV feeds in the large, panoramic-view living room, while Aeson and Keruvat continue working with the data at the desk next to Anu and Gennio.

Some of the others have left for the night. Now that I've survived the Games, my intensive support team and entourage has "disbanded," in the sense that they have their own lives and work to catch up on. This is the first full work week after the Games, and many of the Earth refugees have either already started their new jobs a month ago, or are about to do so this week.

I know that the Cadets—Gracie, Chiyoko, Laronda, and Blayne—have had to report to Fleet Headquarters for local assignments, and now their specially given "time off" is up. The Earthies are the equivalent of second-year Cadets, but unlike their Atlantean native counterparts, who go through four years in Fleet Cadet School, the Earthies have no such luxury and are in an accelerated program of part-time courses and real work simultaneously. As a result, Blayne has LM Forms classes to teach tomorrow. Both Gracie and Laronda have flight duty, which might even require them to assist one of those pilot team missions to investigate the moon up close. And Chiyoko has an assignment at the Headquarters technical division.

The civilians among my friends also have work first thing tomorrow morning—including my brother Gordie, Hasmik, and Dawn.

Moon or no moon, secret alien threat or not, life goes on.

As for the *astra daimon*, they are on assignment already, here with Aeson, dealing with the current crisis.

And me? Seems like I'm the only one who's currently in a strange, uncomfortable-to-me, undefined "limbo" of activity. As the Imperial Bride and future Imperial Consort, I don't have to worry about a work assignment or any other daily life concerns. Technically, I'm "done" with my personal troubles. The Imperator has bigger problems to worry about, and his focus is off me except as far as I can assist with the ark-ship Logos voice commands. Really, my greatest concerns are the upcoming Wedding, and the arrival of my Dad and George.

Earth and the impending asteroid apocalypse? Deadly, all-powerful aliens about to invade both planets?

Technically, again, not my problem.

Not your problem, Gwen.

Yeah, I should keep telling myself that. Maybe in a hundred years, I just might believe it.

I shudder inwardly and try to focus on the present moment—this pause before a coming storm—before my wayward imagination runs away with me into a new flavor of nightmare. Gracie notices that flicker of darkness in my expression and reaches out to cuddle against me.

I hold my sister, take deep breaths, and stare at the TV screen. To calm myself even more I think of Lolu's mother getting her desperately needed medical care *right this moment.* Strangely, I don't try to reach out and get an update on her actual current condition; it's almost as if, if I *don't* know, she—like Schrödinger's cat—will remain in the blissful state of quantum uncertainty. So, I postpone the act of *knowing* until tomorrow.

I think of Dad and George, flying toward us even now. Later tonight I'll ask Aeson to call them to make sure they're okay.

And suddenly I allow myself to relax and think of the Wedding, and the real, tangible joy that awaits us—my life with Aeson. . . .

Whatever else might be, Aeson and I will be united.

As if to reinforce my thought, in that moment Aeson looks up from his work and glances in my direction. He gives me his amazing secret smile. Which melts me.

Even later this evening, when everyone else has gone, and the *niktos* meal is over, it is only the two of us. Aeson and I huddle together in wordless exhaustion, lying back against the comfy sofa cushions, silent for once, after all the impossible drama of the day.

"Think of nothing," I whisper, stirring eventually, my face against his chest. "Ignore that thing on your wrist. No messages, no calls, no data analysis. If New Deshret or your Father calls, tell them to take a hike."

Aeson chuckles, running his fingers through my hair and sending unexpected thrills down my spine. "Take a hike? Interesting expression."

"You don't know that one?" I look up and laugh gently, then teasingly pull his own pale golden locks, wrapping them around my finger, continuing to tug them fondly. I love Aeson's hair so much. . . .

"Ouch," he says with a smile.

"I'm such a sadist," I reply. "I'll try not to torture you to death and pull out all your gorgeous, golden Kassiopei hair. Well, maybe just a little?" And I take another lock and twist it around my finger.

Aeson sighs.

"Oh, I'm sorry, Aeson!" I stop at once, with a burst of worry on his behalf. "That didn't really hurt, did it?"

He looks into my eyes with his steady, beautiful gaze and grows serious. "You could never hurt me, in anything you do. It's an impossibility. Please continue to weed out my hair. I could use a plucking—like one of your poor Earth chickens."

I realize he's making fun of me. And as I make a squeak of protest—yes, very chicken-like of me—he leans in to cover my mouth with his, soft, then overwhelming.

When he releases me, I am breathless, absolutely helpless with my need for him. "Ah, I just died . . ." I whisper. "What you're doing to me, now I know what it's like to expire—like this."

But in that moment, he blinks. Sensuality flees, and a difference, a shadow, comes to his expression. Suddenly he is vulnerable and somehow lost, as if gathering himself for something difficult.

"It's time I told you," he says. "What it was like, to die."

And Aeson tells me, at long last, the story of how he died at Ae-Leiterra.

Chapter 21

"It's such a dark memory, in so many ways, Gwen," Aeson tells me. "I kept putting it off, telling you about this incident. But enough. It happened so long ago, and I will speak of it now, because you must know. I promised you, no more secrets, ever."

"Okay," I whisper. "But only if you want—if you *can*. I don't want you to suffer remembering horrible things from the past. Not again—"

"It's all right." He angles his neck slightly, looking sideways at me as we half-repose, then inhales deeply and turns to face straight ahead. "It was seven years ago, I think—yes, late in the year 9764, and I had just turned thirteen. Back then I was a young, stupid, second-year Pilot in the Imperial Fleet, basic Third Rank. There was no Star Pilot Corps for me yet, no *astra daimon* membership. However, there was a very important mission. My first mission assisting Imperial Command. And not only that, it was to be the first time that I would serve my Father the Imperator directly."

I watch his profile with rapt attention.

Aeson sighs. "You know about Ae-Leiterra. An immense, rapidly rotating black hole at the center of our Coral Reef Galaxy."

I frown and nod.

"Every few years—anywhere from three to five—something bad happens at Ae-Leiterra. Specifically, at its innermost stable circular orbit, or ISCO—the last ring of stability before the black hole's gravitational pull becomes insurmountable, light cannot escape, and strange corrupting effects on matter occur. In other words, it's the area just before the *reality horizon*, similar to your Earth notion of 'event horizon.' A critical, dangerous place, poised on the brink of no return. . . ."

"What—what happens?"

He looks at me. "Things come out of the black hole. And our mission is to contain them."

"Wait—how can things come out?" I blurt. My stress-frown deepens. "I thought nothing can escape the gravitational pull of a black hole!"

Aeson continues looking at me strangely. "Yes and no."

"Okay, now I'm a little confused. . . ." Even as I speak, my heartbeat speeds up with a mixture of emotions, generalized worry, fear. But mostly it's because I see his own expression growing remote, filling with layers of deep sorrow as he watches me. Oh, he *seems* so serene and controlled.

Seeing him like that, I'm suddenly lost also, spiraling downward, not knowing what to do for him except ask stupid questions.

Just then he sighs, gathering himself. "*Im amrevu*—I need to explain some things about black holes to you, and forgive me if it gets technical. Earth science is not quite there yet, and these concepts might seem alien, but I will try to use more familiar Earth terms—"

"Oh no, it's okay, please tell me!" I hurry to say, moving closer to him. I focus all my attention and listen.

"All right." He nods. "Basically, the ISCO is the inner edge of the larger ring-like system of everything that's circling the black hole. Collectively, we call that system the Rim of the Grail. . . ."

As he notices my suddenly curious expression, he adds, "Yes, Gwen, a *black hole*, any black hole, is a *trans-dimensional grail*. To be precise, two inverted grails connected via a wormhole 'neck'—where the bottom 'stand' is the mirror image of the top 'chalice,' so that you can 'flip it over' across dimensions in space-time, and the stand becomes the cup portion and vice versa. But you can only see one grail at a time—the rest of it is always *elsewhere*."

I watch him intently, trying to *understand*.

"This shape that we *think* we see is an optical illusion, caused by our perception of inwardly collapsing light. As you get closer, the pull of gravity becomes so strong that not even light can escape outward to reach our eyes. So it looks like a black void—a gaping, cup-shaped maw. That's the black hole 'shadow,' framed by light curving around and just behind it, off-centered and distorted by gravity. Whatever's on the inside is invisible from the outside. There is no cup, but the same weird illusion 'holographically projects' at you from any direction—like an Earth-style satellite dish antenna pointed at you. It really looks impossible, up close. . . ."

"Okay . . . I can't even imagine," I mumble in awe.

"It is unimaginable," Aeson says, staring straight ahead again. "In reality it's a *multidimensional object* imbedded in our 3D space-time."

"You mean it's not just a crazy super-duper imploding gravitational sinkhole vortex in the fabric of space-time?" I quip nervously, trying to set him at ease.

Briefly, my attempt at levity works.

He makes a soft chuckle. "It's also rotating about its own axis. This can be inferred from the motion of the bright stuff orbiting it, getting pulled along for the ride—all of which makes it both easier and harder to visualize in our three-dimensional space. I believe your closest geometric term would be a 'pseudosphere' or 'anti-sphere'—and even that's not accurate. In short, it's inwardly collapsing space-time surrounded by orbiting radiation junk."

"So what is the visible part?" I ask. "The radiation junk?"

Aeson pauses, thinking. "Yes. From our perspective we see the bright *accretion disk*—a ring of plasma radiation and super-heated incandescent gas and matter orbiting along the outer portion of the Rim."

"Accretion disk?" I echo.

"Yes, the bright visible stuff. Our galaxy has an *active galactic nucleus*, so you can see a whole lot of brightness at an immense distance. That's the exterior of the Rim of Ae-Leiterra. All the stuff is spinning so fast that the plasma is being ejected in two powerful jets, in opposite directions—one from each axis pole—flung outward into space. Your Earth scientists call active galaxies such as ours *quasars, blazars, radio galaxies, Seyfert galaxies*—depending on the viewing angle of the relativistic jets."

"Oh, I remember learning about quasars," I say. "Not sure about the other terms. So, wow, the Coral Reef Galaxy is a quasar or a blazar, or one of those other thingies?"

He nods. "Yes, all of them, based on which viewing angle or vantage point you use to describe its jets. Normally, if the jets are pointing in your direction what you see is deadly super brightness, and at such proximity there is no habitable zone. But, lucky for us, we have an immense Black Nebula between us and the deadly inferno—the Black Nebula shields us and makes life and survival possible in the Helios system despite our relative proximity to the active galactic center. And sorry, but the terms are necessary for what I'm about to describe, hence the aside on astrophysics."

"I don't mind." I smile.

And then I understand something.

He is cloaking himself in the clinical jargon, giving me a cool and rational science lesson, because this is so painful for him. So he's distancing himself from the terrifying reality of what happened to him.

Moments later, another insight overwhelms me.

He is also doing this for me.

Aeson is diluting the nightmare by flooding my mind with new information—simple and rational. He's soothing me with cool, clinical, scientific wonder—in order to prepare me for his agony. He is trying to offset the pain of the coming darkness into which I'm about to be plunged.

Oh, how well he knows me. . . .

"Anyway," he says, turning away again to stare before him. "Our concept of the Rim refers to everything within the black hole system's exterior. It's the last stable place for matter in general, a kind of multi-staging transition area before things start to fall into the black hole."

"Okay." I nod, trying to visualize this weirdness. But all I can think of are nightmare horrors, unimaginable things happening to him.

Last stable place. . . .

"As you begin to move inward along the Rim through the accretion disk, you cross the *static limit* boundary of normal space-time and enter a messy 'processing' area with swirling bands of distorted space-time. Your Earth science calls it the *ergosphere*—where time dilation occurs and nothing can stand still, as space-time itself circles the cosmic drain. Meanwhile, the innermost boundary of the Rim is the *photon sphere*, the last place where light can orbit without being sucked inside. The ergosphere is oblate and bulging at the equator, so it partially overlaps the photon sphere. Finally, comes the *reality horizon*, past which physical reality loses its cohesion. It's a boundary of no return for anything residing in normal space-time."

"And somewhere deep inside is a singularity," I say. "Right?"

But he shakes his head. "Despite what your Earth scientists theorize, there is no singularity—in other words, no narrowing point—or tiny ring—of infinite density, space-time curvature, and gravity into which all time and matter collapses. To paraphrase your slang, there's no universal 'buck stops here.' Instead, there is a *moment of fundamental trans-dimensional homogeneity* after which reality and information picks one quantum path out of an infinity of choices—and *re-forms* like a snapped rubber band and continues *elsewhere*."

"Oh!"

"The opposite side of the black hole potentially extends beyond that 'blur' jump-point, terminating in another cup-shaped receptacle *somewhere else*—a different space-time reality," he says. "And all of it is superimposed upon itself, all phases and dimensions existing simultaneously."

My breathing slows down as the convoluted meaning sinks in. "This is . . . still not sure I understand."

He continues: "Imagine a double-sided funnel, a hyperboloid, or another similar biconical shape. For example, your Earth Arabic numeral eight, or the symbol of infinity, or even your ancient hourglass."

"Okay," I mutter.

"Now imagine that you can twist the object at its narrow midpoint where, for some strange reason, it's perfectly malleable. You wring its neck, spinning it around like a centrifuge—and when it stops, the top and bottom funnels are misaligned in relation to each other."

I stare, concentrating so hard that my forehead hurts.

"The black hole 'grail' is such a quantum shape in space-time geometry. At the midpoint connecting the two halves, it extends and blurs into a *quantum field of wormholes. . . .* They buzz like an electron cloud, or a hive of insects, spinning around a gravitational nucleus—the so-called singularity. It is like a probability corridor with many doors, and it connects two or more separate cosmic realities . . . which may be infinitely distant physical or temporal locations."

"Wow. . . ." I exhale in wonder.

Aeson pauses, giving me time to process. Then he takes a deep breath and continues.

"Anyway, as I was saying, *something* happens at the Rim of this particular black hole, our black hole, something that must be dealt with. And it involves yet another duty that the Imperator and the entire Fleet must perform, on behalf of all of us—not only Imperial *Atlantida* but all Atlantis. This duty has been with us throughout the ages. And now that I know more about my Father's actions and intentions for Earth—it is easy to guess that it's related precisely to Earth's ancient dimensional rift."

"What exactly is this Imperial duty?" I say, while my mind is still reeling with intellectual awe.

Aeson sighs, seeming to gather his thoughts. "It involves capturing very specific, rare energy emissions from the black hole. The idea is only vaguely reminiscent of your Earth notion of Hawking radiation—quantum entangled particle pairs of matter and anti-matter located right at the event horizon being torn apart by gravitational forces. One part of the pair disappears into the black hole, the other remains outside, and this ultimately changes the mass equilibrium of the black hole, diminishing it over time."

I frown, trying to remember physics class. "We were taught that nothing—or at least nothing substantial—can escape a black hole. Hawking radiation has not been observed on a large scale and is somewhat theoretical. And now you're saying that's not quite right. So how does that work? I don't remember understanding it all that well."

Aeson glances at me. "The Earth concept is flawed, so don't bother. We have an Atlantean unifying Theory of Everything that works to seamlessly connect the small and large-scale universes of physics. We call it the *Blur Transformation and Transposition Principle*, or BTTP. Too long to explain now, but I promise, you'll have the opportunity to learn it later. For now, all you need to understand is that black holes can leak matter in an exotic way unfamiliar to Earth science. Our term for that is *trans-dimensional radiation.*"

"Wow. Okay."

"As I was saying, black hole energy emissions," he continues. "Basically, it's a common occurrence around the Rim of Ae-Leiterra. Particles of emitted t-d energy break out past the reality horizon, past the photon sphere and orbit the black hole. They become part of the accretion disk, some ending up in relativistic jets, and eventually forming nebula clouds in deep space. We measure and keep track of it, looking for any radiation anomalies. And every few years the nature of this t-d radiation changes, and instead of venting formless masses of quantum particles, what comes forth are *pegasei*."

My mouth parts. "Oh!"

"These trans-dimensional quantum beings," Aeson continues, "they seem to literally appear out of nowhere, somehow escaping the gravitational pull of the black hole. The assumption is that they somehow 'hitch a ride' on the light quanta at the photon sphere, using those same escaped particles as slingshots to propel themselves into our dimension beyond the destructive reality horizon—in a parody of your Penrose process."

I listen intently.

"The *pegasei* emerge at the ISCO, orbiting the immense Rim of Ae-Leiterra. And then, defying the gravitational pull, they start moving outward along the Rim radius toward the exterior edge, where they gather in massive super-flocks. This happens gradually until the super-flocks are large enough to be harvested."

"So that's where you get the *pegasei!*" I exclaim.

Aeson shakes his head. "Only some of them. But, really, it's not the main reason for what the Fleet does and what the Imperator does there. It's never about *pegasei*. . . . It's about what their presence indicates." He takes a deep breath. "The most important Imperial duty of the Kassiopei has been to maintain the *Great Quantum Shield* at the Rim of Ae-Leiterra. The shield keeps specific trans-dimensional entities—such as the ancient alien enemy—out of our space-time. It keeps them from reaching out to us directly through one of the trans-dimensional wormhole pathways via the black hole."

Suddenly my heart is beating fast. . . .

"We've been taught that's how *they* first arrived to threaten Earth's Ancient Atlantis—they came the same way as did the *pegasei*," he says. "Here, the *pegasei* only serve as warning markers for us. Their presence marks the spot where the shield has become particularly vulnerable. The fact that the *pegasei* are able to emerge at all is a symptom of general weakness in the Ae-Leiterra shield.

But apparently it's also a symptom of another, even more critical weakness. . . ."

"What?" I say.

Aeson looks at me intently. "If you recall, *pegasei* were originally discovered on Earth. How, why—it's been shrouded in ancient history. We've only been taught over the centuries that there's a correlation. If *pegasei* show up, our ancient alien enemy is soon to follow—so we must immediately check and reinforce the shield around our local galactic nucleus."

"Like a canary in a coal mine," I whisper.

Aeson raises his brows. Apparently, he's unfamiliar with this phrase. "In any case, we all know about the correlation but not the real details. Remember, the general public has no idea about the existence of the dimensional rift on Earth—and neither did we. But now, thanks to my Father finally giving up some secrets, you and I know, and I'm willing to bet that the *pegasei* are coming from the inadequately shielded Earth rift via a wormhole and ending up *here*. Which means—not only has the Ae-Leiterra shield weakened against t-d radiation, but far across the universe, the *original shield* enclosing the rift on Earth has weakened too, and is allowing passage once more. The Earth rift is leaking directly here!"

"Oh, my God."

"I did not properly understand it, the true extent and complexity of the Imperial mission at Ae-Leiterra—not until now." He pauses. "I now believe it's intended to maintain *both* shields at the same time—the one around Ae-Leiterra and the remote one back on Earth."

My eyes widen.

"For centuries, all of us have assumed that Ae-Leiterra poses a general danger locally, as a portal for trans-dimensional activity. The Great Quantum Shield, or GQS, we were told, was engineered by our ancient ancestors on our behalf, soon after we arrived in the Helios system. They created it to retrofit and seal the black hole against dimensional invasion. And we've been maintaining it ever since—by means of Imperial Logos voices and cosmic-scale geometry. Now, of course, we just learned that the Imperator also maintains in a similar manner the ancient ark-ship and, apparently, a hidden moon of Atlantis—and who knows what else!"

"You really think there's something else?" I say faintly.

"Hah! I don't know what to think anymore, Gwen. At this rate, the whole world is unraveling." He shakes his head again. "But—allow me to continue this sad story, now that I've given you the background. So, every few years, the Imperator takes the Fleet on a maintenance mission to the Rim, after receiving reports from SPC Command about *pegasei* sightings. Once a certain amount of *pegasei* energy is present, it indicates a weakness in the shield, so it's time to perform maintenance."

"I see."

"This particular mission was scheduled to take place at the Rim sometime after my thirteenth birthday, and we embarked on the journey to get there several weeks earlier. I was assigned on the Imperial *sebasaret*, which is a warship-class vessel with both military and science research capabilities, smaller than an ark-ship but larger than a velo-cruiser. The mission always includes an array of several hundred *sebasarets* serving as Fleet formation anchors, and numerous smaller cruisers and shuttles placed in between, with small space buoys scattered throughout to extend the boundaries and allow formation fine-tuning."

I nod and listen.

"The idea is, the Fleet array spreads out like a great net. *Sebasarets*, cruisers, shuttles, buoys—all ships lined up at wide intervals like a necklace of beads—spanning a significant area along the circumference of the Rim. Then the Imperator places the entire array into a Stationary Quantum Stream—" Aeson gives me a look of concentration. "It's a very different kind of quantum phase state from the ordinary Quantum Stream with which you're familiar—the kind where we have to *accelerate* to enter it, and which we use to travel cosmic distances. In contrast, the Stationary Quantum Stream is *weird*. It needs no specific velocity, can be achieved from a fixed, or slowly drifting position, and is extremely difficult and dangerous to implement, requiring perfect precision. Only a Logos voice must be used to shape it, so the task falls to the Imperator."

"Okay. . . ."

"The ships, phase-locked in the safety of the Stationary Quantum Stream, may approach and traverse the Rim, flying as deep as necessary. They can approach the black hole's reality horizon and even cross it safely, and enter inside. No time dilation, no radiation or other matter corruption is experienced."

"Oh, wow," I whisper.

"That's why we call it the reality horizon," Aeson adds. "It poses danger only if you're occupying this present space-time reality. If you're inside any kind of Quantum Stream, you are in a different reality, so you may pass safely."

"That's amazing!" I say.

"And so, getting back to what happened. I was assigned to assist in the *sebasaret* Resonance Chamber, where my Father sang the complicated main sequences to initialize the SQS all across the Fleet array. Once the quantum field was up, and we were safely encased in our SQS bubble, we physically entered the Rim. The next step was for the Imperator to oversee and correct the frequencies of the resonance network. That includes all the systems and all the officers on the other ships who were using local voice commands to send out the space buoys.

"Normally an ordinary skilled Fleet technician can perform QS fine-tuning, and no Logos voice is needed. However, because of our dangerous location—the extreme gravitational and other anomaly risks posed by the proximity to Ae-Leiterra—the Imperator was required to stand by. That's because the very *field boundary* of the Stream can start to *degrade*, and he must be there to fix it."

"Why would it degrade?" I ask. "If the Stationary Quantum Stream is supposed to be safe—"

"Think of it this way. When you're flying through the cosmos in a normal Quantum Stream, you're moving so *infernally fast* that there's no time for anything outside to even begin affecting your field boundary. You can pass through the heart of a star, a turbulent nebula, anything—and you keep going safely. But if you remain standing in place, you get relentlessly bombarded by whatever's immediately surrounding you. In this case, plasma radiation orbiting the black hole—X-rays, gamma rays, and more. And it all starts to wear you down."

He pauses. "Imagine the ultimate hellscape scenario, Gwen. Conditions of indescribable heat, energy, pressure, and violence, all of it caused by Ae-Leiterra's immense gravity. . . . It's a nightmare crematorium of matter—where plasma radiation is generated by the *friction* of superheated gases and matter moving near light speed. And now imagine—the Fleet has to sit still in the middle of all that *hell*, enveloped by the precarious 'safety bubble' of the Stationary Quantum Stream."

I shake my head and exhale a long-held breath, slowly.

"The safety of hundreds of ships and thousands of lives depends on it—and the Stream itself depends on one man wielding the Logos voice, the Imperator," Aeson says with sudden intensity. "It's a fine balancing act that needs to be maintained constantly. If needed, the Imperator must go from Fleet vessel to Fleet vessel and perform local resonance tuning and reinforcing, in person—up to and including taking a small shuttle to individual buoys if they are in danger of falling out of bounds and collapsing the Stream."

"How often does that kind of thing happen?" I say carefully. "A boundary collapse, I mean." I watch Aeson's face start to turn grim, as he remembers.

"Not often," he replies after a pause. "But it has been known to happen throughout history, and it can be catastrophic. Yes, it's fatal to individual vessels that get ejected out of formation at weak points in the SQS—literally sucked out of the quantum bubble by gravity—as they Breach and end up fried, irradiated, crushed, or otherwise torn apart by the immense forces of the black hole. But it's even worse if such an individual Breach results in the cascading collapse of the entire SQS network. That's when most of the Fleet gets destroyed in seconds."

"Oh my God, how horrifying!" I say.

Aeson's cheek muscles twitch. "There have been several such catastrophic or near-catastrophic events, at least two in the last hundred years," he says softly. "That's a very high safety rate, only two out of twenty-seven missions, but still. Ships were lost, destroyed, people got killed or badly hurt. In fact—the Imperator is usually the one who places himself in danger and who most often dies in the process."

My lips part.

Aeson watches me, his face a mask. And then he says, "That's why my Father is afraid. He knows what happens, what can happen at these missions. Because—my Grandfather, the previous Imperator, died in such an event, died trying to save the Fleet. And my Father never forgot."

"Oh, Aeson. I'm so sorry, I didn't know!" I place my hand on his arm and squeeze gently.

"Another sad story for another day," he says, looking in my eyes. "My Grandfather was no longer Imperator. He'd taken his retirement by then, but he wanted to perform this one duty on my Father's behalf. It ended in tragedy, and to this day my Father is tormented by it. Which is probably why what happened later—to me—came about."

"You don't have to say any more . . ." I whisper, holding his arm. "Please, don't."

"But I do," he says in a hard voice. "I need to *finish* this."

I nod silently and listen.

"As I was saying, I was in the *sebasaret* Resonance Chamber with my Father. The Stationary Quantum Stream had just gone live, and the Fleet started to spread out along the Rim, widening the net as each ship took its place, then sent out the buoys. My Father had finished singing the SQS sequences, checked the network for stability, and was starting the main voice sequences to generate the immense energy of the Great Quantum Shield itself—the reason for our mission.

"Everything was going well. The shield energy was starting to build in strength, ringing with power and registering at near optimum levels on all our instruments. As normally scheduled at this stage, additional pilot shuttles were deployed to the *pegasei* super-flocks to harvest them by means of light traps."

"How does that work?" I say.

"*Pegasei* feed on light," Aeson reminds me. "We simply use probes armed with frequencies of light that's particularly favored by the *pegasei*. The probes send out concentrated bursts of that specific light, which somehow stands out from the disordered churning plasma radiation of the accretion disk, and even reaches deep inside the ergosphere. *Pegasei* are drawn to it, as an animal is drawn to a scent or flavor. When they approach, the traps turn on quantum containment fields and the *pegasei* are captured and held."

No, not animals. . . . They are sentient beings. I'm momentarily reminded of the containment orbs in Stage Four of the Games. And then I think of Arion.

Meanwhile, Aeson continues. "As all of this was happening, and I was helping to monitor the Stream network while my Father sang the Shield, a number of system warning alarms came on. . . . Apparently, a powerful plasma ejection *split off* from the main flow of one of the relativistic jets. It was caught, twisted by gravity into a loop, and somehow redirected back into the accretion disk, creating a *gravity shockwave* of additional turbulence throughout the Rim.

"We have no idea how, but the shockwave affected the isolated reality phase inside the Stationary Quantum Stream containing all of us. This kind of thing never happens—the *realities* inside and outside never make contact, that's the whole point of the Stream—but it did. As a result, several of the outlying buoys in our Fleet network were suddenly tossed out of formation. They drifted, approaching the Stream's boundary that was already weakened by the radiation turbulence near those spots. In moments, they Breached and got fried immediately."

"Oh no!" I whisper.

Aeson glances at me. "It was a terrible moment of decision for my Father. This was exactly the worst kind of scenario possible—unexpected, unpredictable critical disturbance in the Rim causing the Stream to fail, and starting a cascade reaction. . . . The Imperator stopped his shielding task and returned to the resonance network instruments. He performed the necessary voice sequences remotely, but it wasn't enough. More and more ships were Breaching before our eyes. It was unavoidable—he had to go to the location of the collapse and perform vocal tuning on-site, using the very *hull* of his shuttle to set a new resonance *anchor*. Basically, it's the only way to halt the cascade failure and re-create the Stationary Quantum Stream boundary along a new set of parameters."

Aeson takes a deep breath before continuing. "Gwen, I was terrified. I knew what was about to happen—my Father had to go to the corrupted outer edge of the Stream boundary and very likely die. The Imperator, my Father, paused for a moment, looking at me, then told me to *stay here* and *take over* on the Resonance Chamber main console. He looked at me, Gwen, and I have never seen such an expression in his eyes. And then my Father took off running to the shuttle bay. . . .

"I obeyed and waited, useless and panicking, looking at the alarms popping up everywhere, indicating malfunctioning remote instruments on other Fleet ships. Meanwhile two ranking officers hurried to assist me, possibly at my Father's final instructions—I don't know, and at that point I didn't care. There was nothing they or anyone else could do—only someone with the Logos voice, such as myself."

My breathing has nearly stopped, and I'm frozen with tension as I listen to Aeson speak.

"It was absolute chaos, time slowing down, both metaphorically and in actuality in the ergosphere where this was all happening. The officers and I watched my Father's progress as his shuttle approached the frayed edge of the Stream boundary, where random Breached vessels were slowing down due to time dilation— from our perspective, of course—while in reality they were burning up and hurtling past the horizon of the black hole."

"Oh, God. . . ."

"Yes, it was a catastrophic disaster unfolding. My Father's shuttle stopped at the Stream's boundary threshold, and then it just *sat* there, floating at the edge. . . . Yes, it was properly set to resonate, of that I'm certain. It was ready to move out and create the new Stream. All my Father had to do was *Breach* and continue to sing the sequence. . . . And in doing so he would've extended the Stream, bringing it with him, extending and unfurling it to span outward into the violent depth of the Rim. This action would create a new solid Boundary and protect the rest of us in the Fleet, while my Father's shuttle would very likely burn up, unprotected from the violence outside—even as it was defining the edge of the newly formed safe zone.

"But my Father, the Imperator of *Atlantida*, hesitated. . . . At the last minute, he froze and could not take the last step—the final active step that was his ultimate duty—that would extend the Stream but likely end his own existence."

Aeson goes silent. He once again does not look at me as he tells me the next terrifying thing. "That was the moment, Gwen. I somehow *knew*. I could imagine and feel my Father's regret and fear and his inability to act, as though it was myself in his place. And then something inside me broke, like an explosion of force, and suddenly I was running out of the Resonance Chamber.

"I ran like a madman through corridors to the shuttle bay, past terrified officers and crew. I saw the first shuttle, took it. . . . Blasted through the tube and was now in the Stream outside. Although still within the safety of the Stream, I could see the fiery churn of the accretion disk plasma, an orange and white maelstrom, and beyond it the broken space-time reality spirals of the ergosphere. I piloted the shuttle straight along the path of the Fleet array, hurtling past other *sebasarets*, shuttles, cruisers, buoys still in safe formation.

"And as I flew, I sang the Stream sequence. I'd learned it from my Father earlier; he had made sure of it. In seconds my shuttle acquired the correct resonance frequency. It was ready, its hull charged, even before I knew what I was about to do—what I was in fact *doing*.

"When I reached the decaying edge of the Boundary, there was the Imperator's shuttle, poised on the brink of no return. . . . I passed it without hesitation, singing the voice sequence, and turned one last time to glance back and see my Father's ship. As I did so, I also saw a small flock of *pegasei*, seething in glorious rainbow colors, like an exotic flower blooming strangely among the fiery chaos of the Rim. The *pegasei* were at the very edge of the Boundary, as though waiting for us—for one of us to act.

"And then the forces of the black hole were upon my poor little ship. They surrounded and swallowed me. I knew in that single infinite second that it was happening, the pull of violent forces, the immense gravity, the horrible pressure, the hull buckling around me and crushing me, and the burning—*burning hell*—no time to scream, no time—"

"Aeson!" I press myself against him, shaking, and *im amrevu* puts one arm around me and gently strokes my hair.

"That was it. *I died*, Gwen. My ship had managed to repair the Stationary Quantum Stream, and the cascade reaction was stopped. But I did not know any of it, did not know *anything* because I was . . . *not*."

He pauses, with a soft shadow of a smile. Shakes his head.

"And then," he says quietly, "they brought me back."

Chapter 22

"Aeson! They? *They?* Who brought you back? *Aeson!*" I sit up, stare into his eyes wildly.

He takes a deep breath before replying, drawing me closer again, placing his hands over my shoulders in a calming protective hold. "They tell me, Gwen, it was a miracle, a lucky fluke. At the last moment, my partly crushed, burning wreck of a shuttle somehow got *pulled back* inside the new Stationary Quantum Stream boundary that I myself had established moments ago. Somehow, it took a ride on a massive plasma surge backlash, a secondary aftershock gravity wave. At least, such is the official explanation."

He pauses, as I continue staring at him in terrible distress. "However—according to the various damage reports and incident surveillance recordings, taken from different vantage points, different nearby ships—it is a *fact* that there was a *pegasei* energy fluctuation recorded at the same time. At that same exact moment, a flock completely engulfed the shuttle, and even appeared to accompany it just as the shuttle rebounded back into the SQS safe zone. Then the flock dissipated, as quickly as our instruments could register. It was almost as if they hadn't even been there. And neither was the shockwave."

"Oh, God, Aeson. . . ." I say hoarsely, finding my voice breaking. "The *pegasei* . . . it was the *pegasei*. They acted to save you! But, what of—you? What of the shuttle and you inside it?"

He nods. "I was *dead*. They—the Fleet personnel—towed the shuttle back inside the closest large vessel, and then dismantled the crushed wreck in the shuttle bay, and pulled out my mangled body—"

I make a horrible involuntary sound, putting my hands over my mouth.

"You know how we have extremely advanced medical tech," he says, as his strong fingers run up and down my arms. "But even the best Atlantean med-tech has its limits—which, again, you sadly know. Yes, on my Father's desperate orders, my burned remains were placed inside a stasis chamber and rushed to the most advanced medical restoration unit on board the ship. And they worked on me, for nearly four days, non-stop, taking me out of stasis and putting me back in, over and over, in multiple stages of micro-procedures affecting different body layers, while the Fleet hurried back home.

"I underwent ninety-three hours of surgical procedures, according to the records—while the Imperator himself stood vigil in the room next to the special chamber where they worked on my body, or raved in private grief in his own quarters—this, according to officers who witnessed moments of it, and I was to learn about it later. But—I was dead, Gwen. They restored my body, remarkably well. Tissues, organs, nervous system . . . all grew back. But none of it was functional. I remained a corpse—not even what you would call 'brain-dead' in a coma, but genuinely dead on a cellular level. My general condition was beyond repair, and toward the latter part of their endless attempts I was placed back in stasis and left there, to be preserved for an honorable state funeral back on Poseidon."

"Oh, no, no, no . . . oh God. . . ."

Aeson inhales, then lets out a deep, shuddering breath. "It took us just under seven weeks to return, at top speed. We were back on Atlantis and I was rushed to Poseidon, taken out of stasis to prepare me for the final after-death process. And then, impossibly, I woke up on the working table slab, surrounded by frightened and confused funeral techs."

"How?" I whisper.

"They said that suddenly my body was flooded by an energy field of swirling colors, precisely like *pegasei* energy. My flesh appeared to be radiating light from the inside. It pulsed with radiance, seven heartbeats in duration, and then it was gone. The next moment my heart had restarted. I had a pulse, my circulation was restored, and I was breathing on my own, but still unconscious. Soon all normal electrical impulses were showing up on scans to indicate living brain activity. Finally, an hour later, I was conscious."

Suddenly he chuckles. "I remember waking up, with a snap, as if out of a deep, abysmal sleep—no nightmare, only an instantaneous transition from burning hell to soothing peace and sterile silence and beeping medical equipment. . . . My Father's face staring down at me, my Mother's gentle weeping, as she stood next to him, holding my cold fingers."

"It must've been unbelievable!" I whisper, my own cheeks wet, crying for *him*. "I cannot even begin to imagine what you felt—"

"Actually, I felt well," he says. "No pain, no discomfort from my restored body. I was more confused by the jarring shock of memories restarting, events being completely interrupted and wiped, then consciousness skipping realities, from there to here. I admit, it was very weird . . . to clearly remember the horrible dying, then *nothing*, and then life simply continuing, with me emerging elsewhere." He pauses. "It was as if, Gwen, as if I'd gone through a black hole and came out on the other side. I suppose, if death is such a thing, then I had."

"Do you think—and please forgive me if this disturbs or pains you to answer—were you truly *gone elsewhere* during that time you were physically dead?" I ask, choosing my words with care.

Where did you go? I hold back the blunt question. *All that time that you were dead, where did you—or your soul, or spirit, or consciousness—go?*

"I don't know," Aeson says thoughtfully. "That part—being dead—I don't properly remember. Or, better to say, I don't trust my own recollection of anything between death and coming back. . . . I doubt the accuracy of my adjacent memories. As for those who witnessed my condition—the whole incident is still treated as a questionable impossibility, with no good explanation. *Pegasei* saviors? A lucky medical anomaly? No one knows."

Oh, how badly I want to tell him, in that moment, about the sentient beings whose secret I now bear. *But, no . . . I promised Arion to keep silent.*

Exercising my willpower, I hold back the overwhelming impulse to reveal *everything*. Instead I watch Aeson gently as he continues his remarkable story.

"And so, I was awake, and my parents were overjoyed to have me alive, and somewhat in awe, I suppose. Though, of course my Father quickly stifled his positive feelings toward me and started to berate my 'foolish heroics' while I was still groggy, in the first half-hour of my return to consciousness. My poor Mother begged him to be gentle toward me, and he relented somewhat."

Aeson pauses, breathing deeply, then exhaling with a shudder. "And no, not once did he mention what really took place at Ae-Leiterra. He never admitted what happened in that critical moment when he hesitated to act—never mentioned his own failing in his Imperial duty to forge ahead. And by the way in which he chided me for risking myself, it was apparent that no one else knew about his moment of weakness and cowardice. Instead, the Imperator made it sound as though I was the young fool who plunged forward recklessly and got ahead of him on purpose. He claimed that I rushed past him and overtook his shuttle without permission, and got there first in order to lay claim to saving the Fleet."

I shake my head with a surge of anger on his behalf.

"I let him rant of course," Aeson continues with a rueful smile. "I lay helplessly in recovery, and I forced myself to swallow the injustice and to keep his Imperial weakness a secret—for the moment. And then, remarkably, my Father changed his story mid-stride. Suddenly, according to him, the shuttle's on-board instruments had malfunctioned, causing it to stall. 'So, all in all, a good thing you acted the heroic fool,' the Imperator announced to me in conclusion. And that was the extent of his praise. He never once told me 'well done,' or showed me any other appreciation in private.

"In public, it was another matter. The official mission reports now formally recorded the Imperial shuttle 'malfunction,' and my quick actions were commended as heroic bravery. I was recommended to receive the black armband for acting to save the Fleet. A few weeks later, there was a grand public spectacle and a ceremony, and I was honored and promoted in Rank, with all the Fleet present. The strange thing is, Gwen, I received the same honor as had my Grandfather, who was also given the black armband posthumously for his similar actions. In fact, my honors were decided even while I still lay dead and no one expected me to return to life."

"So that's how you earned it," I say with a soft expression, running my fingers over the wide band of silky black fabric wrapped around his left bicep. "For some stupid reason I expected a different story of heroism—maybe a spectacular gun battle, or even a war which you won and proved yourself a great military leader. But this is so much more. . . . You *sacrificed* yourself and saved the whole Fleet—hundreds of ships and thousands of people—by basically flying straight into the black hole and pulling the Quantum Stream behind you, creating the safe zone for everyone. . . . You saved them—not by taking lives or vanquishing enemies, but by *becoming* the Imperator."

He nods, with a strange expression in his eyes.

We pause for a few long moments, in contemplation of what was said by both of us.

"And then you came back . . ." I whisper.

"And then I came back." He echoes my words.

Another long gap of silence.

"You say you don't remember, but—" I persist gently, "it must've *changed* you. On some deeper level. Somehow, do you think?"

Aeson looks at me in that moment, and there is a world of emotion in his lapis lazuli blue eyes.

But he doesn't blink.

"Maybe," he says at last. "Logically speaking, yes, death and resurrection would make you someone *new*. It would seem that it has changed me, made me more *thoughtful*, maybe—or maybe not. My friends—they who later became my *astra daimon* brothers and sisters—mentioned that I seemed quieter, more often, afterwards. But specifically, I just don't remember. And I'm not sure I want to—at least not now, not yet."

Would he tell me if he did?

He gathers himself and continues, "One other thing. *Atlantida* really doesn't like unresolved mysteries, so my inexplicable resurrection was ultimately attributed to medical skill and plain luck—in all the incident reports. I checked them myself, eager to know the truth. The *pegasei* presence during the critical moments was underplayed and interpreted as coincidence. And when I checked my Father's shuttle status report, I found data to support his claims of technical malfunction—except I dug deeper and discovered details hinting that it was *falsified*. I managed to retrieve the original event log from the shuttle by secretly examining it myself, then dumping core data in a roundabout way, so that now I had secret proof of my father's false claim."

"Ah! That's what you meant by 'insurance' when you bargained with him in the Red Office the other day," I say.

"Exactly." Aeson's lips curve slightly. It's not quite a smile, but rather an expression of satisfaction.

I sigh deeply, with a profound shudder. All this time, I'm hardly aware of my short breath, the tension I'm holding back, my clenched fingers digging into his upper arm.

"And now you know the story. The strangest terrible thing that happened to me," he says, looking at me with a vulnerable expression. "*Amrevu*, thank you for listening. And—so sorry that it pained you. I know it did—"

"Aeson!" I exclaim. "Thank *you*—for sharing your remarkable truth!"

And with those words I pull him to me. I wrap my arms around his neck and I kiss him on his cheeks, then his mouth—hard, and desperate, and wild with love.

Sometime even later that night, at the end of thirteenth hour, we are still up, still lounging together, talking, touching, sometimes pausing to mull over everything in tired silence. Aeson checks his wrist comm occasionally but mostly ignores the incoming data. "Since neither of us is able to sleep yet, ready for a Ghost meal?" he says with a yawn.

"Uh-huh," I say, yawning also.

Then we both laugh, and Aeson takes me to a nearby workroom equipped with a food storage cabinet. The setup is similar to the workroom back at his Quarters in the Imperial Palace. The refrigerator is well-stocked, and we raid it, laughing.

"Why, Aeson? Why can't I sleep? Such a long, insane day!" I say stupidly, stuffing a savory flaky pastry with vegetables into my mouth. "M-m-m, yum!"

"Too tired to sleep is a known medical condition." He chuckles, eating his own bowl of savory noodles in thick, plum-colored sauce. But there's a brief flicker of gravity in his eyes.

After all the things he told me, all the terrible impossible things of tragedy and awe. . . .

No, stop.

"We'll try to sleep after we eat, all right?" I finish the pastry, pour a fizzy glass of *qvaali* for Aeson, and hand it to him. Then I pour myself a glass of *nikkari* juice. "Okay, I want to tell you what I decided to ask for my wishes as Champion—wait, no!" I sit up, widening my eyes, and almost drop the glass. "I totally *forgot* to call Dad and George! I was going to call them right after we ate earlier, I'm an idiot!"

"First thing tomorrow," he says gently. "Best to call them after you've rested. Don't worry, they're fine."

"You're right." I shake my head, frustrated at myself. "Right now, I'm so tired I'm slurring words."

"You were saying—about your Champion wishes?"

I take a deep breath, feeling a little nervous for some reason. "My wishes are for Lolu and Chihar to get their wishes—as if they had been Champions. And Tuar also—if he is alive—"

"He is," Aeson says with a smile. "I made sure he received proper medical attention after he was incapacitated during Stage Three of the Games—"

"Oh, Aeson! Thank you!" My pulse races with a sudden burst of joy and also general relief at my most amazing Bridegroom, the best in the world—and his calm reaction.

In fact, Aeson doesn't appear to be surprised at all by my demands. "Go on. What else?" he says.

"I also wish for Zaap's wishes to be granted in his honor, even though he's gone."

"Understandable."

Emboldened even more, I continue, "And I also want Sofia Veforoi and Fawzi Boto to be granted their wishes—"

Aeson raises one brow. "Okay, now *that* I didn't expect. But I can see the logic and the advantage in turning your adversaries into friends."

"Actually, I wasn't thinking of an advantage. I just feel really bad for them," I say.

Aeson looks at me with admiration. "Is there anything you would like for *yourself?*"

I think for a moment. "I want my family to be safe and cared for, I guess. I mean I already have everything I need, since I have *you.* I also want Earth to not be destroyed by that damn asteroid. Or is that too much to ask?"

He chuckles again, shaking his head at me. "Right now, anything is possible, *im amrevu.*"

"I'm so glad you're not calling me a crazy lunatic," I whisper.

"Oh, but you *are* a little crazy—or maybe very much so," he says, turning his head sideways to watch me lovingly. "But that is precisely what Atlantis and Earth need."

"A crazy woman?"

"An *inspired* one."

Chapter 23

I wake up the next morning in my own bed, having been tucked in by *im amrevu*, very late the previous night. Aeson insisted I get some uninterrupted sleep at last, while he had a few more SPC reports to look at in his own room—even though I protested, wanting to stay with him. He fooled and seduced me into getting under the covers and closing my eyes just for a moment, and I was utterly incapable of resisting. . . . I melted at his touch as he stroked my hair and nuzzled his lips against my throat before regretfully leaving me to go stare at the scrolling data on that infernal computer display.

And now it's bright morning, judging by the thin slit between the curtains, and although for once in I-don't-remember-how-long, I have *nothing* scheduled for the day, I get a sharp gnawing sense that I have to do *something*.

What is it that I have to do? My brain shuts off and on, stuck in alert mode, searching for signs of immediate danger, and unused to the leisurely state.

I get up, and check that Aeson is not in his room. Then I wander into the bathroom and stare for at least five minutes into the great mirror, examining my gaunt face and sleep-tousled hair, feeling like a zombie dummy.

Next, I shower, taking my sweet time casually, and get dressed in the first sensible-looking outfit I can find—a pair of dark slacks and a matching shirt with an intricate fractal pattern of swirling colors, blues and violets, trimmed with a delicate collar of gold. My long, wet hair falls down my back, and I do nothing to restrain or style it, only brush and dry.

Just before I leave the chamber, I put on my brand-new wrist comm unit.

Downstairs, in the large living room, I find Aeson, Xelio, and Erita, a couple of usual data displays with active feeds, and an *eos* bread service in progress.

"Nefero eos," they greet me, with looks of serious concentration.

"Gwen, come eat." Aeson relaxes his grim expression and gives me a smile, then points to the food. He is casually dressed in a cream shirt and dark pants, but crisp and businesslike. As usual, the perfectly put-together first sight of him makes my heart skip a beat. So little sleep, and yet he still looks fresh and amazing.

"You hardly got any rest, Aeson—again!" I say reproachfully.

He merely intensifies his sweet, crafty smile.

"All right, anything new happen this morning?" I take a plate of buttery dumplings sprinkled with spicy and crunchy bits that taste like hickory-smoked nuts, a bowl of orange-colored tart fruit in sweet sauce, and a hot mug of *lvikao.*

"Uh-huh-m-m-m." Xelio mumbles something indecipherable, shakes his head and exhales loudly, then returns his attention to the display.

"Well, nothing particularly useful as far as the stupid moon," Erita says. "But you have a visitor."

"Eri, don't. Not yet." Aeson grows serious once more and casts a meaningful glance at Erita. "Let her eat first."

But I'm alert already. "What? Who?"

"In the other room." Erita points to the doors. "She's been waiting for you for the last hour. We told her you were still resting, and it might be some time before you'd be available, but she insisted. Said she'll wait all day if needed."

"Who?" I repeat, setting down my food.

"One of your teammates from the Games," Xel says, without looking away from his screen. "Stubborn little thing, what's her name—Lolu Eetatu."

"Lolu!" I exclaim, and my heartbeat picks up with a sudden jolt. "Oh—my God! Her mother! How is she? I need to see her right now—"

Aeson gets up wordlessly, with an expression of understanding, and leads me out of the room, down a corridor, and into a smaller, comfortable visitor chamber. "Here she is," he says with a gentle nod at me and at the figure of a girl who springs up from her seat.

"Gwen Lark!"

Lolu looks wildly different this morning. She is dressed in simple, bland clothing, and I almost take her for an estate servant, now that she's out of her Blue Games uniform. Only her spiked rainbow hair is familiar, and so is her face, with its slightly smudged kohl eyeliner, usual signs of exhaustion, and great big eyes focused entirely on me. I wouldn't be surprised if she hadn't slept or cleaned her face since yesterday.

"Gwen—*Imperial Lady* Gwen, I had to see you," she says in a stilted, awkward way. "I—must thank you for what you did on behalf of my mother."

"How is she? How is your mother?" I take a step toward Lolu. I really want to put my hand on her arm, touch her, but knowing Lolu's prickly nature, I restrain myself. Besides, I am somewhat terrified to hear what she has to say. . . .

"She has been *saved*," Lolu says plainly, and just like that, her eyes are brimming with tears. "You saved her, Gwen Lark. And—and the Imperial Lord too," she adds with a darting glance at Aeson, then returns her gaze to me. "Last night, they came to our home—the elite medical techs—and they took my mother to the expensive facility. They scanned her, used the quantum cellular revision scanner, and the QCRS repaired her failing organs and healed her overnight. She—she is breathing on her own now! She woke up completely without pain, and my father and brothers are with her now! All thanks to *you!*"

I make a stifled sound and, not caring about consequences, pull Lolu into my arms. My head is bursting with pressure, ears ringing suddenly, and even as the overwhelming flood of emotion rises, I grip her tightly to me . . . and feel her embracing me back. She shakes against me, thin and bony, and so very much like a smaller, hungrier Gracie.

"Oh, thank God, I am so *glad*, Lolu!" I croak in a voice that breaks. "So glad she's okay, that she will *live* and be healthy! Please give her—pass on to her—my best wishes to your mother—my regard—my—"

My love. . . .

I stumble to express what it is I'm feeling, that ocean rising. I don't dare say it out loud.

We come apart finally and Lolu sniffles, wiping her face and nose. My face is wet too, though I am holding back the flood of ugly bawling that is gathering to come out any second. . . .

"I owe you everything," Lolu says in broken, stilted words, and a hoarse voice. "My family, all of us owe you."

"Oh, no, no, of course, you don't, Lolu—you don't owe me at all." My own words stumble, and I throw a look at Aeson, who watches the two of us with silent compassion. "If anything, we must both thank my Imperial Lord Aeson."

"Oh yes, I *thank you*, My Imperial Lord!" Lolu turns to him, then back to me. "But even as you say, I'm in your debt, and in all honor, I must now repay you, Imperial Lady Gwen, for without *you* none of it would be. So command me, and I will do whatever you ask. Please, honorably accept my service and loyalty, since I have nothing else sufficient to repay you with."

"Oh, Lolu, come on—I don't know, seriously, it's okay—You can repay me by being happy with your mother, just enjoying your time with her—"

Lolu shakes her head with a slow, proud, stilted motion. "Please. . . ." Her voice again cracks.

"Okay, Lolu," I whisper, and this time rest my hand on her arm, squeezing it gently. "All right, I—accept your service. But please understand, I would much rather just have you as a friend."

Half an hour later, Lolu leaves, after more stumbling expressions of gratitude, after we make arrangements to have her "work for me"—whatever that might mean—and after I promise to visit her and her family at a later time.

I am still visibly shaken and remain standing for long moments, while my hands tremble. . . . Then I return to the living room with Aeson and try to drink my now ice-cold mug of *lvikao*.

"Where is Gracie?" I say at last, out of the blue.

"Your sister is already at work, at Fleet Headquarters, I believe," Erita tells me.

"She's fine," Aeson says, pressing my fingers with his own. He watches me closely as I then try to take small bites of food with my still-shaking hands and try to chew, not tasting any of it.

"Are you okay?" he asks after a while, and I nod.

I eat a few more bites, then give up. "I was hoping to call my Dad and George this morning, Aeson. Sorry to interrupt your work, but since it's not a local call, I cannot use my wrist thingie."

"Of course."

Aeson gets up and I follow him out of the room once again, to the same "main office" private workroom on an upper floor with special deep-space comm equipment, which requires a high-level SPC clearance to operate. There he enables a large display screen, enters his personal security codes, and connects us to the deck of the AS-1999 velo-cruiser, which at present is hurtling through space at impossible speeds, on its way toward us with my family members on board.

The dark screen comes alive after a few moments, and I see the familiar calm face of Pilot Quoni Enutat, silhouetted against a background of the cream-colored hull panels of a Fleet ship's softly lit interior. He immediately salutes Aeson.

"Imperial Lord, Imperial Lady," he says crisply to both of us.

"Nefero eos, daimon," Aeson replies. "Or is it *nefero niktos* for you now?"

Quoni glances over his shoulder at some instrument panel off screen. "It's eighth hour, thirty-nine daydreams, and thirteen heartbeats of Khe, so we're well in the evening period. However, as you can see by the dimmed lights, I am conserving energy in order to maximize our velocity in the Quantum Stream."

"And maintaining a temporal discrepancy," Aeson remarks.

"Velocity calculation projections showed that it's best to use Atlantean time units in combination with Earth UTC as our starting clock," Quoni says. "It translates most accurately at the quantum-precision level into the optimal acceleration rate—on this end. Once we Jump, we'll standardize on *Atlantida* Poseidon Time to match you."

Aeson nods. "And how is that going? How are the VIP passengers?"

"Working out very well. Everything's on schedule, and possibly ahead of schedule. We're coming up on the Jump in two weeks and three days, maybe sooner." Quoni makes a sound of amusement, but doesn't quite smile—which I now remember is his usual brisk manner. "As for the passengers, they are well, and at the moment they're looking at some learning materials in their quarters.

I've given them full library access to our cultural and linguistic archives."

"Excellent," Aeson says, then glances at me. "The Imperial Lady Gwen would like to talk with them now."

"Of course. Let me get them." And Quoni disappears from view.

I wait anxiously and count the pulse beats pounding in my temples, until I see my brother George's familiar, lean face take up the screen as he sits down and smiles at me. Next to him is my Dad, tired and gaunt, but immediately smiling also, as soon as he sees me.

"George! Dad!" I exclaim, sitting forward eagerly.

"My sweet girl, Gwen!" Dad says, moving in also. "What a wonder! We're traveling in this little, super-fast ship through deep space! Unbelievable!"

"I know, Dad!" I chortle and nod, as simple joy wells up inside me. "I can't believe that you're going to be here soon!"

"Crazy, right?" George is looking at me with amusement.

For the next few moments we exchange a bubbling stream of perfectly silly and pointless and lovely words back and forth between us, consisting of phrases such as: "You doing okay? Are you well? You look funny. Just a little funny. No, you! How do you feel? Love the shirt, I remember that tan shirt! This is so weird. Weird, I know? I'm fine, what about you? Your hair is sticking up. Is he really, really okay? What's that on your face?"

"*Amre-ter* Charles," Aeson says at some point, leaning in politely to join our conversation. "Are you comfortable with your arrangements?"

My Dad's face transforms warmly. "Oh, yes, Aeson, couldn't be better, thank you!" he says. "Lovely accommodations and such wonderful reading material. Not to mention, the crew is such fine young people, every one of them, going out of their way for us. . . . I couldn't be more pleased. Learning your *Atlanteo* is a bit of a challenge, but I accept it gladly. And, oh, what a rich culture and society you have! I'm just starting an overview of the master index of the historical archives housed in your Imperial Poseidon Museum, cross referencing it to Earth records of overlapping epochs. There is so much new material to fill in the missing gaps in our own antediluvian knowledge, especially the Neolithic—"

"Dad," I interrupt. "Are you eating okay? I know you tend to forget to eat when you concentrate on new study material—"

"Oh, sure," Dad says absentmindedly. "The food is unusual but very, very tasty."

I frown and address my brother. "George, is he eating?"

George shakes his head slightly and gives me a meaningful look that basically tells me Dad is ignoring his meals, and this time it's worse, because it's not merely preoccupation, but *grief.*

Mom is gone. . . .

At the thought of Mom, a sharp pain rips through my gut, but I forcefully ignore it.

"Please make sure he is eating, George," I mutter.

"Doing the best we can here," George says carefully, with a glance at Dad. "But, oh yeah."

We talk some more, and I tell them about my confirmed Champion status and my Citizenship as of yesterday, about Gracie and Gordie's grownup new jobs starting today. Dad sighs with relief and nods at me with a gentle smile. I sense that neither he nor George have a solid understanding of what any of it means yet, so I don't go into too many details. There will be plenty of that later.

"Hey," George says at some point. "Did you know, this ship has no windows? I did find one viewport eventually, and I'm almost sorry I did . . . especially now. Right now, that interstellar space outside is just creepy. I thought I'd see amazing space stuff and unicorn farts. But it's like a field of grey static out there. The stars are not stars . . . not even streaks, like they were yesterday—just blurs of light. You can't tell anything out there—it's cosmic soup."

"That's called the Quantum Stream," I say smartly. "You're in a special quantum bubble of different space-time, which keeps you protected from the regular space outside and all of its dangers. And it allows you to go super-duper extra fast. Way faster than our own travel time, actually—it took us months on the ark-ships to reach the 'field of static' velocity. Wow! You really *are* flying!"

"Is that right?" George smirks. "Super-duper extra fast? Nice technical term, sis. I like it. But—a quantum whatchamacallit?"

I mumble something silly in reply, while smiling.

We talk some more, and then I give them a finger kiss, touching screens across the immense cosmic distance.

"We'll see each other very soon at this rate!" I say with enthusiasm, then glance at Aeson next to me with a surge of heat in my cheeks. "I might even be married by then. . . ."

"Yes, my sweet." Dad says with a loving gaze at both me and Aeson. "Give Gracie and Gordie my love. Tell them we'll be with you so very soon."

"We'll talk to you again before you get here, Dad! Many times! I'll call soon! Promise to eat and take care of yourself!"

"Of course."

"We'll be fine, Gee Two, don't worry about us," George adds with a comfortable wink. "Ok, now off to watch space static, or read a book or two and catch some Atlantean language videos. . . ."

And we disconnect the call.

"Seeing them like that, safe and on their way here—I feel better," I tell Aeson as we return to the living room below.

He smiles. "I know."

"Now I'm going to eat that *eos* bread." I pick up my cold plate of food and take it to the serving table to get it reheated by a helpful estate servant who promptly offers to cook me a whole new meal—which I decline with a smile.

I eat with an awakened appetite, while watching Aeson work next to Erita and Xelio. When I'm done, it's almost eleventh hour of Ra, according to my "wrist thingie."

And so I ask Aeson to use one of their screen displays for my official Games business.

"I'm going to submit my Champion wishes now," I say, and he brings up the online form for me, according to the official Games instructions in his sponsor account.

"You're sure you're ready?" he asks. "You have a few more days to think it over."

Xelio and Erita watch me curiously.

But I shake my head. And I begin to fill out the Champion request form that's going to change quite a few lives.

Chapter 24

My Champion request form takes me longer than expected, since I'm so painfully detail-oriented, and reread everything multiple times, tweaking and editing every *Atlanteo* word and running it back and forth through an English language translator app.

But at last I tap "submit," and now there's no going back. My Champion request is on its way to the Games officials for prize fulfillment, and will now become a part of the *Atlantida* public record, eventually accessible to everyone, after the wishes are finalized and accommodated.

Out of curiosity I use the sponsor account to check the general Games status of other Champions' wish requests. I see that I'm not the only one who filed my request overnight. The data files for most of the Champions are already marked as uploaded—I see the names of Kokayi, Hedj, Kateb, Leetana, Mineb, Rea, and Ukou. I can't access them, of course, since the rules grant each Champion their data privacy until the requests are handled.

The only wish requests still missing are those of Rurim and Brie. Somehow, I don't find that particularly surprising.

What are their wishes? I wonder.

But it will be at least a few days until we all find out.

Meanwhile, there's another thing I can check—my new financial account.

I enter a secret passcode in addition to a biometric scan to access my Common Earnings Grail personal credit account, and sure enough, the sum deposited there in my own name is 10,370,407 *iretar*. I'm not clear on what the conversion rate would be to Earth United States dollars or Euros or Yuan, but I know that it's a huge sum, maybe even comparable to a billion dollars.

Holy crap!

Gwenevere Lark is not just an independently wealthy woman, but she's filthy rich.

From that point on, the afternoon is blessedly uneventful. I spend most of it lounging on the sofa, with a hovering TV display, staring at various media feeds. They offer a bizarre mixture of current events and post-Games betting results coverage, interspersed with now familiar images of the Ghost Moon against a space sky background. My mind churns in a kind of stupor overload, trying to digest all that's happening—to me, to others, to the people on the feeds.

Meanwhile Aeson and the others continue to work, scanning the endless ocean of data that seems to arrive non-stop. At some point the Imperator's ring tone sounds, and Aeson talks to his Father briefly on his wrist comm. When he disconnects the call, he sighs and comes over to me.

"What?" I say with an immediate stab of worry.

"We've been summoned to the Imperial Palace. But it's not what you think." Aeson chuckles tiredly. "Not another secret crisis. Instead it's related to the Wedding. My Father has been given quite an earful by someone whom he dares not cross. Yes, unimaginable as it may be, there is *someone* my Father grudgingly defers to, if only for show—the Venerable Therutat Nuudri. She is the First Priestess of Amrevet-Ra, and she oversees all high ceremonial matters regarding Imperial nuptials."

"Okay." I exhale in some relief.

"Apparently she arrived at the Palace looking for us—for you specifically—and was scandalized that the two of us were residing at my estate, and not at the Palace, in the Imperial Crown Prince's Quarters, as is traditional, leading up to the day of the Wedding."

My lips part. "What does she want with me?"

"Well. . . ." Aeson chuckles again. "With all that's been happening, I forgot to inform you about the series of traditional Bridal Events that take place before the Wedding. Preparations start about two months before the Day, but because of your participation in the Games and the unspoken uncertainty of your fate before then, the formalities were delayed. But now, it has officially begun."

"Oh dear God . . ." I whisper with a light smile.

"We're officially moving to the Palace and will be staying there until the Wedding."

"Right now?"

"Right now. The First Priestess will be meeting us there later today to begin the process."

I bite my lip, while Erita and Xelio watch us. "Congratulations, Kass and Gwen," Erita says cheerfully. "Pack it up and head out. I both rejoice and weep for you. You will drown in Ceremony and you will *like* it."

"Ah." Aeson glances wistfully at the hovering computer displays. "So much work to do. . . ."

Erita snorts.

"Oh! I should let Gracie know," I say, as my heartbeat picks up speed with strange excitement that I didn't know I could feel.

"Well, what are you waiting for? Hurry, Kass," Xelio says, holding back laughter. "Your glorious fate has come upon you. The Venerable One expects you promptly, and you too must submit to her will. You can check SPC reports as they measure you for your Wedding pants."

And we go into a flurry of activity.

A n hour later, Aeson has made arrangements with the estate staff to transport our basic personal belongings to the Palace and informed the rest of the *daimon*, plus Anu and Gennio, of the changes in the work schedule. I've left messages for my sister and brother and all of my friends. Now we take a hover car to the Palace, surrounded by vehicles full of personal guards, his and mine.

When we arrive, heading directly to the Crown Prince's Quarters, a mysterious package awaits me in the room with the four-point star window that serves as my bedroom there. An anxiously waiting servant points me to it the moment I walk in. A two-foot-long antique scroll wrapped in a gold and jewel-encrusted wooden sheath lies on the small desk near my bed.

"My Imperial Lady, the Imperial Bridal Book has been delivered for you," the servant says, bowing, then heads for the door.

"Thank you," I mumble to the retreating servant.

Aeson watches me with his arms folded and a light dancing in his eyes.

"What is it?" I pick up the rather hefty item with a helpless glance at my Bridegroom. "What do I do with it?"

"I know very little, to be honest. Open it, and let's see."

Very carefully I pull the scroll out of the sheath, wondering at the delicate, paper-like material, and unroll it. From what I can make out with my barely passable *Atlanteo*, it's some kind of bullet-point list of activities.

Aeson peers over my shoulder and shakes his head in amusement as I attempt to read them out loud.

"I think it says—*something* with Ladies of the Court—feast or banquet?"

"Yes."

"And this one says, 'Choose flowers,' and this one says 'Choose Song.' Right?"

"Right."

"This says 'Bride Show Day,' and 'Gifts Assembly.' And is that 'Media interviews?'"

He nods.

"Then, 'Meet with the Imperatris.' 'Memorize the Imperial Consort Protocol.' And this one—'Be Fitted for the Wedding Dress and *Amrevet* Dress'—what is that?"

I look up at Aeson with a sudden rush of heat in my cheeks. Even as I ask, I have some idea of what it could be.

Aeson's gaze rests on me and intensifies. His own face flushes, as he says softly, "The *Amrevet* Dress is worn later—at night. And it's not exactly a *dress*."

"Oh," I say, biting my lip and blushing even more. "Is it like a sexy nightie or something?"

Aeson shakes his head again weakly, this time not quite meeting my eyes. I think my question is killing him. "Yes, something like that. . . ." he mumbles awkwardly.

I know enough not to pursue the matter—for both our sakes. "Okay," I breathe, while my lips tremble at the corners. "I guess I can ask them about the rest—"

Aeson nods in relief. "I think the Priestess and the nuptials protocol experts can better answer some of your questions. This is traditionally female stuff, and I apologize, Gwen, but I am an ignorant fool when it comes to the ceremonial Wedding details. There is a similar rulebook for the Bridegroom that I would need to

VERA NAZARIAN

read and memorize by the time of the Wedding. I would almost
rather deal with our current crises than read that *book*—"

I giggle.

Aeson smiles, then smirks, then starts laughing outright.

It's a lovely moment of levity, and we both enjoy it briefly, for
as long as we can.

A eson and I have our *dea* meal privately in his Imperial
Quarters, then Aeson works for several hours while I settle in.
And it's only after we finish our *niktos* meal in the evening that the
Amrevet-Ra First Priestess Therutat Nuudri arrives at last.

The "Venerable Therutat," as she is referred to by everyone, is
a tiny old woman dressed in dark clothing of expensive material but
stern in style. She is enveloped in a long robe that hangs to the floor
to cover her feet, but not enough to cover the peculiarly thick
platform shoes that elevate her about three additional inches.

Her mostly white hair, with a few gilded streaks, is gathered
into a complex bun on top of her head, and a fine gold mesh
descends like a veil over her hair and down her back to the waist.
Her face is probably deeply wrinkled underneath a thick layer of
pale makeup, but it's hard to tell. Her dark sunken eyes are
highlighted in kohl, her lips are delicately gilded—over an
undercoat layer of mauve gloss—while a dab of rouge fills the
hollows of her cheeks. She is doll-like and absolutely terrifying.

Therutat enters the spacious antechamber of the Quarters where
the Imperial Crown Prince receives formal visitors and sits down at
once in a chair. A young woman accompanies her, introduced as
Lady Isulat, her assistant—a slender pretty girl in a similar
conservative dark robe, with dark olive skin, and her own gilded hair
swept up in a bun underneath a gold mesh.

Seeing Aeson and me, Therutat inclines her head to both of us
in a deep nod from her seated position, which must be her version of
a courtly bow. It occurs to me, she probably has some difficulty
standing. Meanwhile Lady Isulat bows properly, with a gentle smile
which I like immediately.

"My Imperial Lord Aeson, My Imperial Lady Gwen," the First
Priestess Therutat says in an unexpectedly firm voice with only a
tiny quaver. Her haughty expression does not change, and she does
not smile even while uttering courtly pleasantries. She squints

slightly, examining us as we sit down on a sofa across from her. "It is my pleasure and honor to be in your presence. A lovely young couple, I see. And now, Imperial Lord, I must ask you to withdraw from the room, for this is Bridal business. Your own turn with the Amrevet-Ra Priest will come. He will call on you tomorrow, I believe. And we women shall not intrude upon your masculine privacy then. Now, begone!"

And as Aeson's eyes widen in surprise, Therutat shoos him away dramatically with one hand.

Aeson gets up with an amused expression and leaves us to ourselves, closing the door behind him.

Therutat turns to me with a stern, focused look that seems to memorize and analyze me from head to toe, like a digital scanner. "Very nice, my dear," she says at last in a voice of authority used to absolute obedience. "Come closer, so I might look at you in detail—your skin, hair texture, eye color. All must be verified and confirmed."

Surprised, I approach. "Stand up straight," the old woman commands me. "Turn around. Now the other way. Lift your arms so I can see your waist and hips."

I do as I'm told, stiffly.

"Isulat—recite her measurements from The Book of Fashion."

The young woman opens a smaller scroll from a case she is holding and reads my embarrassing personal sizing details—whatever was recorded at that time when Consul Denu had me measured for a new wardrobe, soon after Aeson chose me as his Bride.

"Very good," the Priestess says coldly, after glancing at various parts of me to confirm each measurement that is read. I almost expect her to use the Atlantean equivalent of a tape measure, but apparently her expert visual appraisal makes it unnecessary.

And then she pronounces, "However—it may be that your physical attributes have changed enough overall to warrant a new set of measurements to be taken. Your arms, shoulders, and legs, for example—more muscular definition than what your earlier values imply. Yet you appear to be thinner in general. Isulat—hand me the body scanner."

It's clear that Lady Isulat has come prepared. As I look on nervously, she reaches into her case and takes out a tiny gadget, then passes it on to the Priestess. I'm a little surprised that they're using a high-tech device as opposed to the traditional manual method. Likely, it's more practical.

Therutat unceremoniously trains the gadget at me, and a small, wide-angle beam of bluish light sweeps me vertically from head to toe. It takes only a couple of seconds, and then she passes it back to Isulat.

The young woman does something with the gadget so that it now brings up a tiny holographic display with text and numbers. She reads the scanned values out loud while Therutat listens, nodding slowly.

"My visual appraisal is confirmed," the First Priestess announces to me at last. "It is fortunate; the changes are mostly positive. Your limb muscles have grown, even though you are now dreadfully thin in other places. On the other hand, your chest has increased very slightly, which I attribute to normal development at your age. Given all this, I will inform Suval Denu and have a team sent to take your new measurements to amend the official record in The Book of Fashion. In the meantime, you are to maintain your spare diet to retain your present size for the Fitting of the Dresses and the Wedding Day. Afterwards you may eat to your content, especially once you start to breed."

Oh dear God. . . .

Listening to her comments, I feel increasingly awkward. How much had my grueling physical exercise training over the last two months, critical stress, and the entire near-starvation experience in the Games to do with the changes in my body? And how much of it is normal growth and genetics?

Meanwhile, the First Priestess Therutat continues, "Now we are going to go over what is required of you, as the future Imperial Consort, throughout the sequence of events leading up to the event of the Wedding. I trust your Bride Book was delivered to you safely, and you had the opportunity to review it?"

"Yes, thank you," I say, relieved to change the subject. "I looked at the list, and I hope I understood things correctly."

"We will make sure you do, Imperial Lady Gwen," Therutat tells me firmly. "You will be prepared accordingly, have no doubt. Everything must be impeccable, and you will learn all that the

Imperial Bride must know. Now bring your Book to me, and we will study it together. Go at once!"

Nervously I hurry back to the interior of the princely suite to my own bedroom, grab the scroll, and return to the front chamber.

Therutat takes the scroll from me, unrolls it with gnarled fingers, and begins to recite each item in a dramatic voice. She pauses after each one and makes sure I understand the meaning. Then she makes me repeat it, over and over.

"Your memory is commendable," the Priestess says eventually after I surprise her and recite the entire list back to her—by heart. "Most Brides—noble and even Imperial ones—no matter how eager or well-informed in matters of Wedding tradition, have difficulty at this early stage."

"I like to study," I say with a nervous smile.

The old woman makes a little sound that is almost a snort. She still does not smile, only raises one thin, painted brow. "An admirable trait. And now we will schedule the events, setting the dates for each activity, compiling a master Wedding Schedule for the coming days. The first event will demonstrate your ability as Hostess, as you receive the Ladies of the Court. Isulat—the calendar, please."

The young woman reaches inside her case and takes out a digital tablet—which surprises me again, since I'm expecting more old scrolls. She taps and scrolls through screens, then shows us a two-month calendar view displaying Green Ghost Moon and Red Amrevet, side-by-side.

Therutat takes the tablet from Isulat and points to the highlighted date. "Today is Green Ghost Moon 3. You have thirty-two days until the Wedding on Red Amrevet 9. Time will fly by before you know it, and it is barely sufficient. Your personal schedule will, no doubt, be exceedingly full, but you must schedule these major events evenly, spreading them out with days to spare. The three days leading up to the Wedding are particularly important, and are reserved by tradition—the fasting and cleansing day right before the Wedding Day—" And she taps Red Amrevet 8, marking it. "The final Dress fitting must happen three days before, to give the seamstresses time to make adjustments—" She taps and marks Red Amrevet 6.

"Okay," I say.

"And the intimate *dea* meal to mark the Joining of the two Families must happen two days before—" She selects and highlights Red Amrevet 7.

All kinds of weird images come to mind as I try to imagine my relatives, Dad, George, the others, meeting Aeson's parents and Manala over a "cozy" meal. My poor Dad in the same room as the Imperator? *Holy lord!*

Would they even arrive here in time for any of this? Suddenly I realize that I don't dare tell the Priestess the real details—the fact that my Dad and my older brother are somewhere out there, among the stars, hurtling through the cosmos on their way here. . . .

My eyes widen at the bizarre thoughts, and I almost miss what Priestess Therutat is telling me.

"Imperial Lady Gwen, are you paying attention?" the old woman demands in a rising voice, making me start. "I require you to select the first event date. Choose the day to host the Ladies of the Court, and make it a few days from now. Well?"

Feeling overwhelmed and intimidated, I frown, staring at the calendar display. I try to think of all that's happening, all the secret global and universal crises unraveling behind the scenes—and here I have to deal with this nonsense. . . . I visualize hostile, judgmental young girls in fancy outfits surrounding me with fake smiles, and Lady Tirinea Fuorai first among them. . . . *Ugh.*

"Venerable Therutat," I say carefully. "May I have some time to think? I don't know what—"

The old woman makes a sound of frustration. "There's nothing to think about, child. Your foolish distractions are over. Make your choice *now*. You have one primary duty before you now, and it is to be the *Imperial Bride*. It's scandalous enough that you indulged your ridiculous whims and participated in the horrid Games, risking yourself, your life, your reputation—"

A surge of anger flows through me. My lips part. . . . But then I swallow the affront and keep my mouth shut, because this woman doesn't *know* my circumstances. Apparently she thinks I'm a rash idiot, and who can blame her? She must judge me based on the public record, on what facts she has about me right now. . . .

"Very well," I interrupt, speaking in a cold, hard voice of my own. I remember in a flash of inspiration that, in just a few days from now, Gracie's birthday is coming up. My little sister is going to be fourteen, based on the Earth calendar. If I am going to host some kind of stupid party with strangers, might as well make it mean something.

I count the days in my mind, then point with my finger at the tablet calendar, and choose Green Ghost Moon 10.

We spend at least twenty more minutes at this scheduling task, and Therutat is brutal. She gives me no time to think and forces me to make decisions on the spot. I end up simply letting her take the lead on the generalities and nod and agree. And then I suddenly "wake up" from my intimidated state and ask her, "What about the Earth customs? Am I allowed to have an Earth-style aspect to this Wedding?"

"Such as what?" Therutat asks, almost in surprise.

"Well," I say. "On Earth, in most places, we usually exchange rings and say vows—promises to each other. The wedding dress is white. There's family and friends to witness, and usually a priest or official presiding. There's a big cake and the bride throws the bouquet—"

"You may indulge these Gebi traditions to some extent," Therutat interrupts me. "No harm in it, yes, very charming. Feel free to incorporate them into the Imperial traditions and festivities, if they mean something to you and your Imperial Bridegroom. As long as none of it interferes with the Imperial *Atlantida* ceremonies."

"Oh, good," I say.

"Bring this matter up with the different specialists you will be working with," the First Priestess adds, "when it's time to work on the specific details."

I exhale in some relief.

We continue some more and then, before Therutat leaves, she asks me blunt questions.

"Imperial Lady Gwen, may I assume you have been chaste?"

My breath slows, and I feel my cheeks starting to heat up. "You mean—"

Therutat looks at me sternly with her dark unblinking eyes. "I mean, have you refrained from indulging your physical, carnal desires with your young and handsome Imperial Bridegroom?"

"Yes, of course!" I exclaim. "I mean *no!* That is, I have *refrained*—I—we've done nothing, Aeson and I, we've only kissed, held each other—"

"Good," the Priestess says sternly. "Maintain appropriate conduct. Furthermore, you must abstain from further physical contact with each other, to minimize temptation and remain chaste until the Wedding. From now on, you are *not* to sleep in each other's quarters, and you are not to share a bed—no matter how innocently, as I'm told—"

"What?" I exclaim. "Who told you that? How do you know? You have no right—"

"I have *every* right to command you to obey the rules, since nuptial matters are within my jurisdiction. My sacred order has served the Imperial Kassiopei Dynasty since the beginning of time. And I will oversee your proper joining of this divine line."

I frown, staring back at her, going hot and cold with embarrassment and indignation. But it gets worse.

"I must ask you if you are an untouched virgin," the old woman says, her gaze boring into mine. "While chastity is required going forward, it is understandable—considering your alien circumstances—if you may not be virginal. Nothing to be done about it, but the fact must be disclosed."

"You have my medical records," I say, trembling in anger. "Check them. I've never—"

"Very well." For the first time Priestess Therutat interrupts me almost mercifully. "I will record that you are unsullied."

Unsullied. . . . Ugh, what an ugly term, I think.

And then the interrogation is over.

Chapter 25

The encounter with the First Priestess Therutat leaves me emotionally wrung out, and I realize this is just the beginning of this very different kind of ordeal. She is like the Wedding Planner from Ceremonial Hell. . . . And I am her helpless charge.

At least I don't have to see her for every single aspect of the Wedding, only the organizational general portions. Thank goodness for small miracles.

I recall that Aeson has his own version of this ordeal to look forward to, with the male Priest of Amrevet-Ra. However, it's unlikely that he's a similar kind of taskmaster. Truly, the "Venerable Therutat" is supposed to be one of a kind.

It occurs to me, I'd forgotten to ask if she and this other priest will officiate the Wedding. In fact, it's unclear if the Ceremony will include any official presiding over us, or if we will have vows or religious aspects.

It's official—I know nothing yet about what's to come.

Browbeaten thus by the Venerable Therutat, I explain to Aeson what happened. He sighs and gazes into my eyes with his lapis-blue ones, giving me a look that sends sweet chills throughout my body. Then he takes me in his arms, crushing me against him, in defiance of whatever tradition has been imposed on us. However, we keep our touches brief and, after careful goodnight kisses, we head to bed in our own bedchambers, with the workroom to separate us.

The next morning, I wake up to the stupid, blinding white glare of Hel's light streaming from the four-point star window, right into my face. I'd forgotten to shut the curtains, and now I'm squinting and paying the price, having forgotten how it is to sleep in this bedroom instead of my own at home in Phoinios Heights.

At home.

Indeed, it's been some time now that I've considered Aeson's estate my own home—our home. What a strange good feeling it is, to have a sense of home.

But now it's after seventh hour of Ra, and the day is Green Ghost Moon 4. Gracie and Gordie must be at work, and so are my friends. . . . Gracie promised to call me at some point today, so that I can explain to her everything that's going on—the countdown to the Wedding has begun for real.

I get up, dress in a hurry—thinking about snooping, nosy Palace servants, and how I've managed to elude the arrival of my Imperial personal maid Aranit Liwei, who has an attitude and is likely to report on me now even more than ever—and I emerge into the workroom.

A wonderful savory aroma of food hits me. . . . I find Aeson already up as usual, working at his desk with Keruvat and Oalla, over a freshly prepared *eos* bread service. Anu and Gennio are here too, and everyone is unusually quiet and extremely focused. The only sound is coming from the uniformed servants stationed at a side table near the wall—the clanging of kitchen utensils, and the frying sizzle of vegetables and grains in deep pans and on shallow griddles.

Once again, I'm reminded of how much more intricate the meal rituals are at the Palace, compared to Aeson's estate.

"Nefero eos!" I greet everyone, and notice how Anu and Gennio both sit up immediately and give me formal, courtly nods. Another example of the more formal atmosphere here—at home, Gennio would've smiled and waved, while Anu would've barely grunted in my direction.

But here, Aeson smiles at me, abandoning his work.

"Did you sleep well?" I ask him, then lean closer and plant a firm kiss on his cheek, near the corner of his lips—again in defiance of whoever might be witnessing this.

Oalla and Ker observe us in amusement. "So, it has begun, Imperial Lady Gwen," Oalla says. "I've heard you had your first meeting with the Venerable Therutat."

I nod, rolling my eyes. "We've set the main Schedule."

"And I have my first meeting with the First Priest of Amrevet-Ra in about an hour," Aeson says, raising his brows meaningfully.

"My condolences, Kass," Keruvat says. "Would you like me to assassinate you?"

"Please, do." Aeson nods. "I grant you an Imperial Pardon in advance."

"Or you can just give yourself a bad case of indigestion," Oalla says, pointing to a large platter of *eos medoi* fruit pies, a dish of rich plum-colored gravy, another plate filled with scrambled vegetables in a cream sauce, and a bowl of savory dumplings. "Eat all of that and you might as well live on the toilet all day. Begin now."

Aeson chuckles, shaking his head.

Then a bell-tone sounds from his monitor. By now I know that it indicates another incoming SPC data report.

"No news from your Father? About that ark-ship?" I whisper near Aeson's ear as he turns to look at the screen.

"No, nothing today," he replies, scrolling through the screens of data in the newly arrived report. And then he stops, lifting one finger up for everyone's attention.

"What?" Ker says.

"Just in—new surface scans."

"You mean, of the ghost moon?" I say.

Aeson nods at me, then glances at Keruvat and Oalla. "Yes, forwarding to you now."

Oalla rubs her hands eagerly. "Ooh! Please tell me they found something!"

A few moments later, as all three of them peruse the data on their respective screens, Ker says, "Aha! They did."

"What?" I ask, looking over Aeson's shoulder.

In reply he points to a row of icons among the numbers and text, and taps to display an image of the moon surface, milky-pale and translucent. He pinches the screen to enlarge and zoom in, and then, as the surreal rocky landscape grows in size, filling the entire display, I see surface features take shape. Rocky valleys, hills, crevasses, flat homogeneous areas, plateaus. On one such plateau is a sprinkling of dark dots.

"Okay, what is that?" I say.

And then the image continues to zoom in, and the dark dots resolve into shadows. Next to them are bright, gleaming dots, with an albedo that resembles a vaguely metallic shine. They look like oval seeds scattered on fabric. Among them are several larger round seeds, or beads, also metallic, gleaming dully.

Oalla makes a sound of surprise. She must be looking at a similar image on her own display.

"Zoom in even more, at maximum," Ker says to her, looking over to her display. "There, can you see it now?"

"Oh, yeah," Oalla says, shaking her head. "This is just— unbelievable."

"These little shiny things," I say. "What are they?"

"They're ships," Aeson replies softly. "My guess—they're Original Colony ark-ships. It's an ancient ship graveyard."

"**A**re you sure?" Ker says after a moment of thoughtful silence. "I mean, how can we be certain? You really think they're ours?"

"The alternative is, they are alien vessels belonging to yet another civilization." Aeson shakes his head with wonder.

At this point my heart is racing wildly as I peer over his shoulder, staring at the weird metallic dots. *Alien ships! Ancient ark-ships!* Either possibility is stunning.

"Well, time to do another proximity flyby," Oalla says with a long exhalation of breath.

"Sending Pilots to the coordinates now," Aeson says, starting to key in code instructions. "It's been tricky to maintain a surface sweep without an actual solid surface to work with, but now that we have a specific target to observe, they will refine their scope and do slow passes."

I consider what he's saying and imagine how weird it must be to approach a ghostly planetary body and try to gauge distances and other spatial parameters without atmospheric resistance, gravitational effects, or a solid mass to work with. Their shuttle instruments and sensors must be going completely haywire, trying to evaluate the imaginary object before them by means of nonexistent three-dimensional properties.

"The next step is to confirm, before making any of this public." Oalla picks up a mug of *lvikao* and takes a thoughtful sip.

"Yes. Disclose nothing to the IEC or my Father, until we are certain that these are ships, and they are ours."

"This changes everything, doesn't it?" Ker muses, lowering his deep voice to a whisper, out of hearing range of the servants nearby.

"First, the ancient uhm—*object* underneath the *Stadion*, now these. What a strange time we live in."

Aeson sighs. Rubs his eyes, his forehead, frowning; pinches the bridge of his nose. Then he looks up at me and says, "Gwen. . . ."

In answer, I put my hands on his shoulders and squeeze gently, feeling the hardness and tension of his muscles underneath his shirt. He leans into my touch, and for a moment I experience a sensuous current of energy coursing between us.

I let go reluctantly, only after he places his own hand on top of one of mine and his touch sears me and at the same time gives me strength.

Oh God, the Wedding cannot come fast enough. . . .

And now, these impossible ships. . . .

Aeson gets hardly any time to consider these new developments because the arrival of Darumet Azai, the First Priest of Amrevet-Ra, is announced. Aeson turns to me, and we both rise and head to the antechamber where an elderly priest awaits, together with his assistant. It's a situation parallel to my own experience the night before.

The First Priest Darumet is not quite as old as the Venerable Therutat and considerably less threatening. He is a thin, slight man with a kindly expression and sparse, greying hair lacking any dye or other adornment, clad in a dark expensive robe similar in style to the Priestess's outfit. His young assistant is a self-effacing youth with short gilded hair and a clay-red tint to his dark skin.

"My Imperial Lord and Imperial Lady." The First Priest speaks in a mild voice and bows deeply to us. "Allow me to look at you both for a few moments before I ask my Imperial Lady to leave us to our work."

Standing next to Aeson, I glance at my Bridegroom with encouragement, and smile at his awkward expression.

"You are a radiant couple," the priest says after a long pause, during which he examines us closely. "I am satisfied to see that this will be a good union between you. And now that I've met you, My Imperial Lady, I ask you to depart this room, because this is Bridegroom business."

I give Aeson's hand a light squeeze and leave him to his ordeal.

I return to the workroom and spend the next hour absentmindedly watching the TV feeds from the sofa. I periodically glance at Oalla and Keruvat as they scan and discuss the incoming SPC data, while Anu and Gennio work on computer equipment nearby. My sympathetic thoughts constantly return to Aeson and his personal Bridegroom business. This additional pressure on him worries me, because I know how seriously he takes his duties in general.

At some point my wrist comm emits a tone. I open my mail and discover it's a curious official message addressed to me personally, as a Champion of the Games of the Atlantis Grail.

> Champion Gwenevere Lark, your presence is requested and officially required in order to fulfill the formal conditions of a Champion Wish of your fellow Champion Kokayi Jeet, the message says. Please be at the location described below, at the date and time specified, wearing appropriate attire.

I read further, and it says:

> **Location**: Themisera, Junction of Crooked Circle and Main Circle
> **Date:** Redday, Green Ghost Moon 5
> **Time:** Noon Ghost Time
> **Attire:** Festive Casual

And then, just below, is a strict warning:

> Failure to appear will result in the delay or forfeiture of your own Champion Wish fulfillment.

I open my eyes wide, thinking. *Okay, now that's just weird. What in the world does Kokayi want with me?* And so soon? Because whatever this is, it's happening tomorrow.

Where and what is Themisera?

I get my answer as soon as I mention this to the others in the room.

"Oh dear. . . ." Oalla raises her brows. "Are you sure that's what it says?"

"I believe so." I show her the message, just to make sure my *Atlanteo* reading is correct.

"Yes, Themisera indeed," she confirms.

"What is it?"

"Not the best part of town," Oalla says tactfully.

At the other desk, Anu makes a stifled grunt noise. "It's a slum hole!" he says when I glance at him. "Also known as Sky Tangle City. It's right next to Fish Town, but more inland. Fish Town is seriously nicer."

"Yes, unfortunately, that's one of the poorest urban areas of Poseidon," Ker says. "Very rundown. Old houses, abandoned buildings, not very safe—street crime."

"Okay," I say. "And what is Crooked Circle and Main Circle?"

Oalla, Ker, and Anu exchange glances, while Gennio raises his thick brows with the effort of keeping his face blank.

"What?" I say. "What is it?"

"I believe that's the first big street junction leading into the Sky Tangles—that's what the street circles are called there, Sky Tangles," Oalla says.

"Yeah," Anu adds. "All those houses have ropes and cables strung across from one building to another, like a huge web of netting, and there's all kinds of junk up there. People use them as tightropes and clotheslines. You look up, and it's a tangle of crap."

"I see." I shake my head, growing more concerned.

"Sky Tangles go on for about fifty circles in all directions, and it gets to be more of a dump the deeper you go inland," Anu continues. Apparently he's rather familiar with the area. "Most hover vehicles avoid it, because of the ropes everywhere. So, since there's no public transport, the residents either get around on hoverboards or use ground crawlers—like your Earth carts."

"Okay, now that I know what it is, why would Kokayi ask me to show up there tomorrow?"

Anu makes another mocking grunt. "He's either crazy or he knows a great restaurant. I gotta say, they have some pretty decent places to eat there, if you don't mind the rest of the crap and if you watch yourself. I bet he's found an excellent and cheap hole-in-the wall for a *dea* meal party!"

"You're serious?" I shake my head.

"I have no idea." Anu shrugs. "But whatever it is, make sure you don't get ripped off on the street."

Oalla sighs. "Unfortunately, Themisera is known for a lot of crime and shady dealings. Be sure to have your Imperial personal guards close to you. In fact, Gwen, when you go, please take additional ones."

I let out a deep breath. If I knew Kokayi's number, I would call him right now and ask what in the world he's got planned, but I don't. I suppose I could ask Gennio or Anu to look up his contact information, with their vast access to population records, but it's not that big a deal—I can wait to find out in person. So, looks like I'll be visiting my first less-than-desirable Poseidon neighborhood tomorrow.

When Aeson gets back from his time with the Amrevet-Ra Priest, I tell him about Kokayi's bizarre Champion wish. Aeson immediately grows serious. "I don't like this," he says. "Are you sure you must attend this event, Gwen?"

I show him the official invite message.

Aeson exhales loudly.

"Is it that bad?" I say, biting my lip. "Oalla mentioned I should bring guards. . . . Would that come across as impolite to Kokayi and whoever else might be there?"

"You are the Imperial Bride, so having security protection is the norm and is expected by everyone," he says. "However, I don't want you to travel to this unsafe area without me, especially so soon after the Games, and with everything else going on—so let me clear my schedule for tomorrow—"

"Oh, Aeson, no!" I exclaim, placing my hand over his arm. "You don't have to come! This is silly, I can handle myself, and you have so much to do. I'll be fine with the guards—and besides, this is Kokayi! He's a great guy, he wouldn't invite me to anything unnecessarily dangerous. I know he wouldn't harm me, so it's probably something fun—"

"If you want, I can go with her," Anu says. "I know the area, so will make sure she—I mean, Imperial Lady Gwen—doesn't get ripped off—and her guards too. Little pickpockets love big security guys bristling with needle guns and expensive fire-tech."

Aeson glances at Anu. "Very well. If *anything* happens, I will hold you responsible, Vei. Take the least conspicuous vehicles. Be careful and stay out of sight. Call me at the first sign of trouble."

"Yeah, yeah," Anu says, but immediately adds, "Yes, My Imperial Lord."

It occurs to me—this will be the first time that I'll be venturing out into the city casually. A silly, momentary excitement grips me. It might turn out to be an adventure! In fact, nowhere in the invitation does it say that I can't bring other people. And the attire is "festive casual," which is a good sign.

"I've an idea," I say to Aeson, with a smile. "Let me call Gracie and some of my friends and see if they have some free time tomorrow. Maybe we can go as a group!"

He nods, and his own expression lightens, seeing my sudden animation.

"Now that it's settled, tell me how was your meeting with the First Priest?" I say teasingly.

Aeson's suddenly pained expression is priceless. "You really don't want to know."

I run my fingers up his arm. "Oh, but I *do*, so tell me!"

He chuckles. "You will be very sorry, *im amrevu*. Very, very sorry."

But I punch Aeson on the arm.

Behind us, I hear Oalla and Keruvat laughing.

Chapter 26

The next morning, it appears that I remembered to draw the curtains the night before, so my coming awake does not include blinding light. It does include a strange happy excitement—the kind I haven't felt for a very long time.

It's the anticipation of a day of *unprecedented* freedom.

I might be wrong of course. Kokayi's Champion wish could be something ridiculous and vaguely disturbing. But most likely it is something benign and wonderful—judging by the positive nature of the energy he exudes, the kind of spirit that I knew him to have throughout our tough experience in the Games.

Kokayi, I believe, is a light soul.

And so, encouraged by this good feeling, I go through my Palace closet and pick out an outfit that's prettier than usual, glittery royal-blue pants and top made out of a shimmering fabric of several gauze-thin layers. I rush to shower and dress, once again to avoid dealing with my assigned Imperial maid. Since I'm likely going to be outside in the bright daylight for some time today, I put on a pair of dark-shade contact lenses—a convenience I've come to appreciate since the Games. And then I open a jewelry box and grab a pretty wide collar necklace of gold and violet jewels—a lovely piece that contrasts with the royal blue color of my outfit.

For a moment, a cautious thought flickers—should I be dressing up at all, or putting on such expensive jewelry, considering the poor neighborhood I'll be visiting?

But then, I remind myself, the invitation specifically instructs me to dress festively.

And so I give my loose hair a few more brushstrokes, examining myself in the grand mirror, and then decide to be brave and use a kohl pencil to give myself "Kassiopei eyeliner." I finish off the look with a little bit of *noohd*—dark rose lip gloss.

When I emerge in the workroom between my and Aeson's bedrooms, it's after eighth hour of Ra. I find Aeson, Gennio, and Anu, talking intently over the half-eaten remains of an *eos* bread service, while a few servants stand waiting patiently at the food tables with more dishes steaming and ready.

None of the *daimon* are here this morning, at least not yet—or maybe they've come and gone already.

"Ah, Gwen!" my Bridegroom says to me warmly. "I was just discussing your safety arrangements with Anu."

"Not again! Please don't worry," I say, leaning in to stroke his cheek. "It will all be absolutely fine." And then I add, "You worked so late last night, Aeson. I am worried about *you* right now. Any news on the moon situation, or anything else?"

He shakes his head. "Tell me instead, who is coming with you today—which of your friends?"

"Well . . . let me see." I check my wrist comm for any new messages and see a quick note from Chiyoko, saying she has been assigned a big project and can't make it, and a similar one from Hasmik. Gracie's note says that she probably can't, depending on her *dea* meal break and flight shift schedule. Blayne is stuck with LM Forms demos for several classes in a row and sends his polite excuses, and Gordie bows out altogether.

So that leaves Laronda and Dawn, who'd promised me last night that they will both be here.

"Very well," Aeson says after I explain who's coming. "Be sure to keep close to your friends, and don't stay at the event any longer than necessary."

I smile and pick up a steaming hot mug of *lvikao*.

After I finish my *eos* bread, I kill time for the next few hours. I watch Aeson analyze data and make calls, watch people come and go in the workroom.

Finally, around twelfth hour of Ra, I get an unexpected visitor.

A familiar tall and huge man is admitted by servants into the room. He has dark eyes, dark bronze skin, prominent muscles, and very long black hair gathered in a segmented tail. He is dressed in a conservative gray jacket and black pants, and he wears a wide firearm belt, reminiscent of security personnel.

It is Tuar Momet—fellow Games Contender and former member of Team Lark, who was gravely injured in a *sha* attack during Stage Three of the Games, barely survived the ordeal, and is now apparently healed and completely recovered with the generous help of Aeson.

The man bows and salutes both Aeson and me.

"Tuar!" I exclaim, rushing toward him. "Oh my God, Tuar! You're okay! Your arm and shoulder—"

Tuar's expression is warm, and he again inclines his head in a slight courtesy nod and gives me one of his rare smiles. "Very good to see you well also, Imperial Lady Gwen. Congratulations on winning Vocalist Champion! My profound thanks to the Imperial Lord for arranging my treatment." He glances at Aeson, then down at his side and flexes one arm. "As you can see, it has healed perfectly."

I peer closer at him, and it's apparent Tuar has regained the full use of his arm, not to mention his shoulder and upper torso—images of horrible torn flesh and blood everywhere come to me as I flash back to the Games. . . . *No, stop.*

"Excellent," Aeson says. "Are you armed as instructed?"

"Yes, Imperial Lord." Tuar raises one side of his jacket to reveal a row of guns. "I must thank you for this, and for arranging my conditional release from Correctional."

Aeson raises one brow with satisfaction. And then he looks at me. "Gwen, meet your new primary personal guard. Momet will be accompanying you today in addition to the four guards."

"Oh!" I allow my jaw to drop, but in a good way. "Tuar, this is amazing! I am—I don't even know what to say, this is so great!"

"My pleasure. Working for you in my professional capacity will be an honor."

We chat, catching up while we wait for Dawn and Laronda. Tuar tells me he still has not been officially pardoned for his crime of *amrev seki*, or mercy killing, of his former employer. However, because of Aeson intervening, he is conditionally released to serve me, but must report to Correctional regularly until his case is reexamined, which can take months.

"I never thought I would work again, or get a second chance," Tuar says thoughtfully. "To be honest, the Games were my only hope, until the Imperial Lord's intervention." And he throws another grateful look at Aeson, who's now back to work at his desk.

I nod and smile, and decide not to tell Tuar yet about my own Champion wish request on his behalf—not until it's approved and finalized by the Games officials. . . .

Minutes later, Dawn Williams arrives.

"So, what's the mysterious event, do you know yet?" she says as soon as she walks in. I notice she's wearing a pretty top in a flower pattern over nice slacks—since I did tell her to dress up a bit.

"Don't know, not until we get there," I say. "Wow, you look nice."

"Thanks. And you look fairytale-fabulous in that deep blue. By the way, I can't stay too long." Dawn checks her own recently acquired wrist comm. "This is my extended *dea* break. I promised to work late tonight to make up for any additional time missed—"

"Thank you so much for sticking around as long as you can!" I pat her on her arm, then introduce her to Tuar and explain the new arrangements.

As we talk, Anu keeps looking up from his business at the other desk, then finally says, "We should be going now, if you don't want to be late to your thing. Where is the annoying Earth girl? Is she coming or can we assume she is lost, as usual?"

The same moment the door opens and Laronda walks in, sharply dressed in her parade-white Fleet uniform and formal yellow armband. "*Nefero* whatsit," she says to the room in general, after smartly saluting Aeson at his desk—who looks up to give her a friendly glance. "What is happening? I flew down from orbit just for you, girl. All by myself. Let me repeat, *all by myself.* This better be good. Also, my solo shuttle is hovering in some unauthorized Imperial Palace parking spot, so—"

I laugh at her exaggerated eye roll. "Laronda, thank you! And I am sure they can check that you are parked properly. Gennio, can you make sure, please? And Anu? We're ready to go now."

"Sure," Gennio replies.

"Yeah, okay," Anu says rudely, snapping his computer components down with a clank against the desktop. "About time." And he glares at Laronda.

"Wait, what?" Laronda glances at me meaningfully, then mouths, "Is the jerk-boy coming with us? No!"

"Uh-huh," Dawn says.

"He knows the neighborhood," I explain.

Laronda makes a sound of disgust.

As we head for the doors, to meet up with the rest of the Imperial guards who are stationed outside the Quarters, Aeson gives up all pretense of working. He stands up, looking at me with a serious expression, then gives a hard, meaningful stare to Tuar and Anu. "Be safe, Gwen. Watch over her, everyone."

Once outside in the Imperial Palace airfield, we take a large six-seater hover car, plus two additional smaller ones for the guards so that they can flank us safely during flight. And then we rise like swift birds into the burning white sky and join an air traffic lane. Anu drives in the front seat, and Tuar is next to him, while I occupy the middle row, with Laronda and Dawn behind me in the third row.

"Where are we going, again?" Dawn asks.

"Themisera," I reply. "Also known as Sky Tangle City."

"Is that near the shore of the Golden Bay?"

"Sort of," Anu mumbles. "More inland."

I explain to Laronda and Dawn what I've been told about the dangers of the neighborhood.

"Good thing I've brought my shiny new standard-issue gun," Laronda says, patting her left side.

"Impressive," Dawn says with one raised brow and a little smile. "Just please don't shoot yourself in the foot or shoot one of us by accident."

"Laronda's a pretty good shot, from what I hear," I say.

"Yeah, not too shabby," Laronda says, tapping the headrest of my seat, and then leans back in her own seat with a satisfied look.

Up in the front seat I hear Anu make some kind of indecipherable grunt.

Tuar just glances back at us with an amused expression.

We fly toward the ocean, high over the downtown city center, past the skyscrapers, past the damaged *Stadion* and the Atlantis Grail "monument" gleaming with gold and jutting with a new angle of lean (the mere sight of it gives me a painful, gut-churning sensation, while the deep bone-rattling hum is audible even here, high up in the air).

Soon, the fiery silver-mauve-blue of the Djetatlan Ocean fills the horizon. However, we start losing altitude long before we reach the shoreline.

Anu takes us down gradually, exiting the traffic lane, and we see the urban sprawl before us, the low buildings and roofs for many city blocks—or street circles—in every direction. They start to look less polished, and eventually dilapidated, with peeling paint and ragged, rusting steel sheets instead of shingles, naked rebar and iron rods, damaged fences, crooked walls, and missing window glass.

And then I start seeing lines and ropes strung out everywhere . . . and from overhead it suddenly looks like one giant unfinished game of cat's cradle—giant "fingers" of buildings and bridges hold loops and twists of cable, frozen in strange configurations, up to the sky.

There can be no doubt, this is Sky Tangle City.

As we descend closer to street level, busy street traffic takes shape—human figures crowd the street circles, and numerous wheeled carts roll on the ground. This is the first time I'm seeing ground vehicles since my arrival on Atlantis.

"Whoa, is that an open pile of garbage?" Dawn says, pointing to one side where a small hill rises, smack in the middle of a street circle. Sure enough, it looks like a pile of random construction trash and debris.

"Lovely," Laronda says. "Please tell me we're not going down near there."

"We're not," Anu replies in a gruff voice from up ahead. "We're going over to those big main circles—see where the taller buildings begin? That officially marks the beginning of Themisera. If we want to avoid the sky rope junk, it's best we get down to street level before it gets too thick. Besides, that's our destination anyway. See that row of angled orange and red roofs? That's Crooked Circle. And over the next circle, is Main Circle, with the bigger buildings."

"Looks busy," Tuar remarks. "A lot of foot traffic, and those rolling vehicles. Some kind of marketplace?"

"Street vendors are everywhere," Anu says. "They don't need a designated marketplace—the vendors roll their junk from street circle to street circle. Some fixed storefronts along the bigger circles. Otherwise, all rollers. If you want to buy anything, catch a roller and ask what they have."

And then he pauses, maneuvering us down at an angle, starting to come down in a weaving pattern to avoid the aerial ropes and cables. I watch out the window as the two Imperial guard vehicles flanking us begin to maneuver also.

"You're right, it does look busy," Anu mutters. "More so than usual. Too many people down there, looks like a crowd. And what kind of shiny *shebet* is that—woah! Are those rows of nice new hover cars? What the crap, man? Where am I supposed to land? No place to land! Going to come down right there, on top of that *chazuf* walking into the street opening, just at the Crooked Circle junction—"

Moments later, Anu manages to come to a hovering stop at street level, in the middle of a wide junction—a kind of short, straight dash between the figure eights of the street circles. I stare around and up in curiosity at the peeling-paint-covered four- and three-story buildings lining the street on both sides, with clotheslines full of linen flapping overhead, and so many other odd items suspended on ropes, including old furniture and swings made from sofas. Remnants of sidewalks rise a shallow step above the street, and whatever kind of paving there used to be now resembles gravel-encrusted, beaten dirt.

However, what gets my attention are the people crowding the sidewalks on both sides, waving and screaming at us. They are poor and badly dressed, and could even be homeless. But they are grinning and laughing and pointing at us—at our three fancy vehicles of shining chrome—and at the other vehicles, which I realize are hovering along the street junction, behind and ahead of us.

"We're here," Anu says, after singing the sequence to stop the car. "But I don't like it, looks crazy out there. What's going on?"

Tuar turns to look at me. "Imperial Lady Gwen, it is your decision. But personally, I don't recommend you step outside—"

"Gwen Lark! Imperial Lady Gwen Lark!"

Suddenly, someone is shouting my name outside.

I stare in the direction of the shouts and see the familiar, tall, willowy figure of a bronze-skinned man with colorful braids striding toward our hover car. It's Kokayi Jeet!

And, oh wow . . . he's wearing skin-tight, neon-orange pants, a black sleeveless vest jacket, and several layers of glittering, translucent, purple and lavender scarves wound loosely around his neck and toned upper arms. Furthermore, he's covered in gold bangle bracelets, wide braces of tightly-woven small beads, ropes of chains around his neck, long dangling earrings . . . while his face is painted with dramatic cosmetics. Dark kohl around his eyes, painted carnelian-red lips, gilded lash extensions. He should look like a drag queen but, somehow, he does not, and looks instead like a fierce warrior going into a glittering battle. His face—it looks absolutely *radiant.*

I make my decision immediately. "Tuar, I'm going out there," I say with a grin.

"Very well." Tuar nods and starts to open the door on his side.

Anu groans.

Laronda and Dawn exchange curious glances, then look at me. We giggle, and start moving.

The moment the doors slide open, a blast of street noise hits us. Crowds of residents screaming and laughing, strange pounding drums and wind instruments, wild music. . . . The cool breeze is carrying pungent smells of something unidentifiable—the combination is a little rancid and sweaty, a little spicy and sweet, a little burnt and smoky. . . .

We get out, and Kokayi is right here, waving at me with both hands upraised in a gesture of generosity, as if he's about to dance. "Welcome, welcome, *amrevet!* I see you've brought many friends—perfect, great!"

"What's happening, Kokayi, what is this?" I ask with an excited smile.

"Everyone is here already," he replies. "You're the last to arrive—look!"

Kokayi points in a sweeping circle around us and I turn with him, seeing other hover cars, and then familiar people. There's Kateb Nuletat and the woman I came to know as his wife, festively dressed in a pastel and gold-trimmed jacket and dress, respectively. A few steps away, Leetana Chipuo wears a gold slinky dress, and next to her stands Ukou Dwetat—dark-skinned, with short, curly gilded hair, his large athletic frame in well-fitting black and red jacket and pants.

Then, I suddenly see Brie Walton in a slick black outfit that could be a vinyl cat suit, lounging on the hood of a bright cherry-red hover car—or actually, the sloping nose section of its roof, since this capsule-shaped vehicle doesn't exactly have an Earth-style "hood"—but the effect is similar. A somewhat sullen Logan Sangre sits in the front seat of the same car with a blank expression, seemingly ignoring her and doing something with his wrist comm.

"Hey, Lark!" Brie cries and blows me an air kiss. "Ready for drag racing? Or is it a Goldilocks Mardi Gras? What a circus. . . ."

Wondering, I turn in the other direction and see Hedj Kukkait, standing next to another vehicle with his arms folded, wearing a conservative pale jacket and pants—far more subdued than the others. Seeing me, he nods with a brief smile.

And then, one by one, I see every fellow Champion of this year's Games of the Atlantis Grail. All ten of us are gathered here in this unlikely spot, hover-idling our vehicles in the middle of this tiny stretch of street.

Furthermore, it's not just our hover vehicles filling the road. Looking in both directions down the junction, I see strange-looking land-crawler platform contraptions that must be carts that have been built up and decorated in a hurry. They sprout beams and arches of metal covered with flowers and bits of multi-colored gauze fabric, scarves and ribbons streaming in the wind, and garlands of small golden bells, ringing and pealing like wind chimes. . . .

It's almost as if these things are parade floats.

Just as it occurs to me, Hedj Kukkait says, "We are here. So, what now, Kokayi?"

"Yes, Jeet. Why did you bring us here?" This time it's Rurim Kiv, speaking in an almost haughty, deep voice from a few feet away, once again seeming to materialize out of nowhere, out of thin air. . . . What *is* it with this guy and his stealth mode?

It occurs to me this is the first time I've ever heard Rurim Kiv speak. His voice is oddly magnetic, and at this proximity he looks even more handsome and striking in a metallic black jacket and pants.

Kokayi whirls around and laughs. "Aha! Let me tell you why. Come closer, *im nefiro*, and all the rest of you Champions! Rea Bunit, Mineb Inei! Kateb and your lovely wife! All of your friends and family! Come, Come!"

"All right, I'm here," Brie says, leaping off the roof of the hover car. "What now, Entertainer-boy?"

Kokayi grins widely. "Very well! I've requested your glorious presence here for my *Parade!*"

Brie frowns. "Okay, what?"

"A Parade, *amrevet!* My Parade! Simple, short, and easy! You will all join me as we get up and ride on one of the many *godateti* that the Games officials had so wonderfully ordered, to my exact specifications, on such short notice—" and he points at the decorated platforms—"and we go for about twenty street circles, turning around each, until we come to a stop where I tell you. Then we go and visit someone! That's it! Then you'll be free to leave, having fulfilled the terms of my Champion wish request!"

And then he adds, "Be sure to have someone drive all your pretty, shiny, so wonderfully *expensive* hover cars behind your *godatet*, for maximum effect. Either that, or set them to follow us on auto-pilot. Oh, and one more thing—as we ride, we throw things— fun things—at the people on both sides of the street! The stuff is all on top of each *godatet* inside big baskets—you'll see it when we get up there—"

"Oh, man. . . ." Brie shakes her head in a confused grimace that's both a wincing frown and a grin that only she can pull off without looking too ridiculous. "I was really hoping for drag racing. Or maybe pizza."

Hedj Kukkait, however, suddenly chuckles. This is possibly the first time I have seen Hedj amused. "Very well. When does your Parade begin?"

"Now!"

Kokayi raises both hands and claps them together overhead to get everyone's attention. He then cries out in *Atlanteo*, in a resonant voice that's suddenly being artificially amplified by a gadget on his lapel to echo in the expanse. "Welcome, everyone, welcome! Sky Tangle City beans and pebbles, this is your party! Today we celebrate! You know us! We are the Champions of the Games of the Atlantis Grail, but today all of you are the winners!"

There is rolling laughter in the crowd, and a few hoots and whistles, and also quite a few claps. Someone yells back at him from the sidewalk, and I strain to understand this thickly accented flavor of *Atlanteo*, "Crazy Kokayi? Kokayi-bean! Is that you? No!"

"No way, Bay-bean, you came back down here to the Sky Tangles! Bah! It *is* you!" People on all sides of the pedestrian walkways start calling out. "Kokayi Jeet! It's Kokayi, for real! He came back home! Eeeeeee! Eeeeeee!"

"And look, the other Champions! White Bird! Kuk-Ku!"

"That's the Imperial Bride! The Bride! Shoe-lace Girl!"

Now, more and more voices pick up the cries, as more people start coming out of the houses, as the din grows.

Laronda, Dawn, and I stand with the hover car behind us, with Tuar moving in protectively to block anyone from approaching me too closely. The other four Imperial guards surround our vehicle, keeping a perimeter.

"Imperial Lady Gwen," Anu says behind me, yelling loudly above the noise. "I am supposed to remind you to be careful now, okay? The Imperial Lord said to be careful, so stay close—"

I nod to him. Then I exchange glances with my friends, "Ready?" I ask. "This is crazy, but let's do this thing!"

And with those words I follow Kokayi and the other Champions toward the parade floats, or *godateti*, wondering momentarily why they are wheeled carts and not actual hovering platforms that would be so much easier, given all that availability of orichalcum. . . . And then I *understand*. Here there is little to none of that.

This is a place of poverty.

And Kokayi's "parade" is intentionally making do with what's available at Sky Tangle City. I wouldn't be surprised if he had the Games officials specifically commission the locals to make the floats to order, with their own basic local resources, and they got paid for it.

Suddenly I feel deeply ashamed—for being nicely dressed, for the expensive fancy cars, for having had a better meal this morning than any of these people. . . . A painful new burden of realization comes to me that here is yet another layer of Atlantean reality that I am unprepared for as a future Imperial Consort. These people—they will be *my* people as much as any other and *something* must be done. Maybe I can talk to Aeson about this, ask him to take an interest here, shine a light on this? It's likely he already knows, maybe even has plans for future improvement, but I will not simply ignore it and leave it to chance. And so, I mentally add this to my to-do list.

"Hurry, hurry! Come along!" Kokayi calls out to us, running ahead of everyone. He hops on the biggest, shiniest, most elaborately decorated *godatet* that's waiting for him at the other end of the street junction, just before Main Circle begins. "Who wants to ride with me? You, *amrevet*, Gwen Lark, come up here! And bring Tuar! Ah, so good to see you whole again, *im nefiro!* You were far too magnificent to die, Tuar, and the wind gods have graciously spared you! Up you go!"

"Glad to be here, Kokayi, and glad you won," Tuar says, helping me up onto the platform which is smaller than I thought, without that much standing room on the top because of the upright decorated beams, and all the huge baskets lined up around the perimeter. Some are filled with flowers, others with what could be candy or edible bars in wrappers, while still others are brimming with shiny, metallic, flat circular chips that might be coins.

"What's that?" Laronda says, pointing at the coins.

"Iretar!" Kokayi says with a laugh.

"For real? These are actual coins, as in, money?" I say.

"Oh, yes! The financial institutions had to come up with so many coins that I probably cleaned out at least twenty currency branches in the area!" Kokayi leans closer and dips his hand into the huge basket of *iretar*. He picks up a fistful of coins and suddenly throws them at the crowd.

In response the crowd shrieks, and adults and children scatter after the coins as they roll on the beaten dirt and gravel of the street. I notice that all the upper windows in the houses are filled with watching people, as they look out on the commotion happening below. Since we on the platforms are elevated considerably above street level we can see into the windows and look back at all the residents.

I glance behind me and see other Champions climbing aboard other *godatet* platforms, as their friends or loved ones accompany them, and in some cases stay behind to manually drive their hover vehicles as part of the parade. Brie is on the *godatet* immediately behind us, together with Mineb Inei and some of his children, while apparently Logan Sangre is down below, driving their hover car. *Why is Logan even here?* I momentarily wonder. . . .

Our own platform is filled with Imperial guards, in addition to myself, Dawn, Laronda, Tuar, Anu, and of course Kokayi himself. Meanwhile, our three hover vehicles are set to auto-pilot, and they move in place automatically to follow directly behind our platform.

"Wave, wave at my people!" Kokayi exclaims, starting to wave at the ever-growing screaming crowds on both sides. "And now start throwing! Give them *iretar*, flowers, treats! Give them everything we have, until we run out!"

Filled with strange excitement, I reach with both hands deep into the nearest basket and start tossing things in all directions.

Tuar and the four guards watch us and our surroundings, while Laronda, Dawn, and even Anu join me and Kokayi, all of us laughing and throwing.

Then I feel a lurch underfoot, as our *godatet* begins slowly moving along the uneven ground of the street. At the same time, Kokayi presses some kind of hand-held gadget, and a blast of loud music, heavy with drums, explodes all around. Mega-amplifiers pick up the live musicians somewhere far in the back and project their joyful sound to the front of the parade.

With crazy noise, music, and laughter, Kokayi's Parade embarks on its route, toward the heart of Sky Tangle City.

Chapter 27

As we roll deeper into Themisera, throwing money and treats, we follow the curving path along each street circle, like a roundabout. Upon completing the perimeter of each circle, we enter the next short junction which leads us to the next circle, and so on.

With each street circle we enter, new residents come running out to greet us. Meanwhile, the already-present and growing crowds surge from behind, following us along the route on both sides of the walkways, chasing the slowly rolling *godateti*. Many of the people are swaying and dancing to the pounding drum music that also flows along behind us.

I throw the *iretar* coins and the other items as fast as I can, giggling and laughing, breathless with the freedom and joy. My friends do the same, tossing and aiming some things at specific individuals in the crowd as they call out with hands outstretched. Small children streak back and forth across the route before us, fearless about the large, bulky *godateti*, snatching coins and meal bars and candy nearly from under our wheels.

"Kokayi! Kokayi is back!" the people cry, jumping and dancing. At this point I've had enough exposure to *Atlanteo* that I can understand most of what they're saying—stumped only by the occasional oddities in idiom and what must be regional slang—but even those slang terms I can guess. "Bay-bean Kokayi Jeet is back! Our Bay-bean is Champion number one! The Games are forever!"

In response Kokayi laughs and dances in place also, hands upraised high overhead, and his amplified voice rolls in echoes down the street. "How you like my party, beans and pebbles?"

"We love! We love, Bay-bean!" they counter him, in a singsong rhythm.

"Pebbles, *dance! Orahemai!*" Kokayi prompts them, aiming and throwing huge fistfuls of candy and *iretar*.

And in reply the women and girls in the street start squealing and clapping their hands overhead.

"Now, Bay-beans, *orahemai!* Dance for me!"

This time the men and boys reply with cheers and yells and wild hoots, stomping and dancing also.

We trace the circumference of the street circle slowly, and when the revolution is done, we enter the next junction.

This goes on for at least half an hour, and sometimes we end up maneuvering past small, shabby carts of local vendors who got caught in the parade route unawares and try to clear the path for us or just get out of the way.

By now, the crowd noise is deafening, and I've gotten tired of laughing, screaming at the top of my voice, and throwing. The nearest goodie baskets are now two-thirds empty, so we have to reach down deep inside to grab things.

Laronda is hyperventilating, and Dawn is bent over, both having a laughing fit. Even Anu is guffawing as they pelt him with occasional handfuls of candy or coins. The four Imperial guards and Tuar keep straight faces and remain vigilant, but I can tell they too are enjoying this fun event on some level.

But while we are still caught up in the craziness of the experience, I don't miss the fact that the buildings around us are getting more and more dilapidated with each street circle, the deeper we go—and my heart twinges painfully with sympathy on behalf of the residents. There are very few four- and three-story buildings now—mostly low two-story or single-story shacks, encroaching on each other like poorly fitting, mismatched bricks in a meandering, crooked wall.

Finally we enter a junction of one more street circle, pulling the crowd along with us. And this is where Kokayi brings the Parade to a stop before one squat building with a lopsided roof, nestled between two taller ones.

The structure is not quite two full stories, but more like one and a half, with a "half-floor" addition of sorts on one side, causing the roof to be angled. Part of it overhangs an unenclosed, open rooftop area filled with plant-growing pots and junk, and from it, anchored ropes and cables extend in all directions to the slightly taller neighboring buildings.

"Kokayi's party ends here, Bay-pebbles and Bay-beans!" he cries out in his amplified voice, and uses his gadget to stop the moving *godatet*. "Continue to dance, while I take care of a little business and make a home visit!"

And then Kokayi whirls around at me and Tuar, braids swinging, and raises his hands up for attention, signaling the other platform floats behind us. His eyes achieve an even more feverish intensity as he speaks. "Attention, my fellow Champions! We're here! We're at the end of the line, and it's time to come down!"

Kokayi dips into one basket and fills his pockets with fistfuls of *iretar*, then continues to grab more, shoving handfuls of coins inside his vest until it's bulging around the chest and other places against his wiry, lean frame. With a mercurial glance at me, he exclaims, "Come, *amrevet!* We're here! It's time!"

"Where are we going?" I ask, as my own panting calms down from all the laughing, and I sense a more serious change in mood. Laronda and Dawn stop giggling and punching and stare also.

Kokayi's gaze is burning with excitement, and he points with one finger at a raised porch before a peeling wooden door. "We're going in through there, right now, to visit her—my own *Mamai!*"

We descend off the platforms and follow Kokayi as he skips the three steps altogether and jumps directly onto the porch with acrobatic ease. He pounds on the door twice, dramatically, then simply opens it, revealing a dark interior, and turns around to glance at us as we all crowd below—all Ten Champions and our entourages—and beckons.

One by one we enter.

I'm not sure what to expect, as I step inside after Tuar and Kokayi. A narrow corridor with a low ceiling greets me. Dirty peeling paint, scratched walls. Several closed doors on either side.

"Come, come!" Kokayi calls out from the very end, and then turns the corner. I can hear his light footsteps on what must be very creaky stairs, going up.

When I reach the tiny, narrow stairwell, there's only room on the stairs for one person at a time. I'm in line directly behind Tuar as he heads upstairs—compressing his shoulders and making his large frame as small as possible, keeping his head down so as to not bump the low, angled ceiling—with Laronda directly behind me, followed by the others. We sound like a herd of cattle going up the flimsy stairs, and for a moment I wonder they don't collapse under our combined weight.

On the second floor there's an even tinier corridor, and just two doors opposite each other, while the corridor itself opens directly onto the roof.

Tuar and I watch Kokayi as he stops before the door on the left, pausing momentarily. He almost appears to hesitate. . . . His face has lost its lighthearted joy and now reveals a grave expression. I notice how he straightens his posture and adjusts the airy scarves around his neck and shoulders, then runs the back of one hand over his forehead. At last he takes a deep breath and knocks loudly on the door. "*Mamai!* Open up!"

There are a few moments of silence.

The door opens a crack. Then it opens wide, and a skeletal-thin, tall, middle-aged woman with brown skin, a dingy grey dress, and a twisted bandana around her head, leans out into the hallway. In a sunken face her very large black eyes glare at all of us, then her glare rests on Kokayi.

"Who are you? What do you want?" she says in a loud, harsh voice, speaking very thick *Atlanteo*.

Kokayi does something with his shoulders and neck. And suddenly his own *Atlanteo* thickens and becomes almost incomprehensible. "What do you mean *who am I?* It's Kokayi! Your son is here to see you!"

The woman snorts. "I have no son. You must have the wrong door. Go away!"

Kokayi's jaw drops. "What crazy talk is this? It's Kokayi Jeet!"

"And who is Kokayi Jeet?" The woman steps outside all the way and puts her hands on her hips menacingly. "Is it the same useless Kokayi Jeet who dances and shakes his *buzuu* for a living and brings me a pitiful few *iretar* to barely pay for the roof over my head? Or is it Kokayi Jeet who went crazy and decided he was better than his hag and all other hags and their beans, and left me with his trash and no *iretar*, disappearing all these months, who knows where—leaving me to deal with the drunk Hoturi downstairs, and no one to water the vegetables, no one to make sure the door was locked, no one to clean the drains—"

"*Mamai*-Jeet! Enough! I was gone because I entered the Games of the Atlantis Grail!" Kokayi exclaims. "And I *won!* I won, hag! I'm here now because I am a Champion! Not just any Champion, but the first place Champion!"

"What? *What?*" the woman says in a rising voice. "What lies are these? Did you fall on your head, Bay-bean?"

"Lies? *Lies?*" Kokayi starts to shake his head, his long earrings and braids swaying in outrage. "You're not so deaf that you can't hear the party noise outside! What do you think it is? That's my Parade, old hag! These crowds of people are making happy noise thanks to me!"

"Don't you weather at me, Bay-bean!"

"Weather at you? I brought all the other Champions of this year's Games! Don't believe me? Let us come in, and I will show you!"

The woman makes a sound of disgust. She then shrugs and steps aside, pointing with her bony hand to the interior, in the most ironic gesture of welcome possible. "Come in, then, all of you *shar-ta-haak*. What can a hag do but let you come in. . . . Well? What are you waiting for? The door is open, might as well use it! Or have you forgotten how to move?"

Kokayi exhales with a shudder and then enters, past the narrow threshold, past his *Mamai*, and the rest of us follow.

Inside is just one room, cluttered with flimsy old furniture. Two beds—basically, wide planks, each topped with a thin mattress and blanket—are pushed against opposite walls, serving as both sleeping and seating area, with a curtain strung above that can be closed off for relative privacy. A long skinny table, some shelving, and many pots are piled all around. A single wooden stool. A tiny stove and sink in one corner, and a toilet hole in another (reminding me at once of the Safe Base toilets in the Games).

The only thing that seems out of place is a smallish smart screen display on one wall, propped up on a shelf. I stare at it dumbly, while Kokayi's mother squeezes in past all of us—even as we continue filing into the room as more and more people arrive up the stairs.

"Who all these big, ugly *shar-ta-haak?* Who are these pebbles? What you doing in my house?" *Mamai*-Jeet glares up at the nearest Imperial guards surrounding me, gives me a withering look, frowns at Laronda and Dawn, and starts complaining. At this point more than a dozen people are stuffed into her living room, and more are still coming.

"You've watched the feeds; you know who they are," Kokayi responds, backing himself up against the long table, and then starts individually pointing out those of us who are the Champions. "Look who's in your house! This is the White Bird himself, Hedj Kukkait!"

"Eh, I don't know him," *Mamai*-Jeet insists, making a disdainful motion with her head. "Never seen him before in my life. I don't watch those feeds, I know nothing about any *bashtooh* Games. What are these Games? What do they matter to me when I need *iretar?*"

Kokayi makes a frustrated sound, then slams his fist against the table. "You need *iretar?* I give you *iretar!*" He reaches in his pockets and throws a handful of coins on the tabletop. "Want more? Here's more!" And he reaches in his vest and starts throwing the money all over the room, striking the wall and the furniture. The coins clatter and roll underfoot, and the rest of us watch in stunned or mesmerized silence.

"I have more than ten million *iretar!*" he cries, shaking with emotion. "And I've just thrown thousands of *iretar* out there, riding in my Parade, to the people—"

"And you're a fool, exactly as I know you to be!" Kokayi's mother interrupts, shrilling, waving her hands in his face. Her own face is contorted with equal emotion, and spittle starts flying. . . . "Only a fool would throw *iretar* around when we don't even have a spare blanket! Look at you! What's this face paint, what's these colored scraps you wearing?"

"Why you screaming, old hag? I brought you everything! I won the Games, I can give you more *iretar* than all your pots can hold and more! Isn't it what you want?"

"Don't you weather at me! You think I drop gravity for this?"

"No, no, you *never* drop gravity for your son, I see now! Kokayi is never good enough for you, not even *now!* I can't believe what I've been through, thinking that maybe, *if I won,* you'd think differently. But you're just a broken, malicious old hag—" Kokayi cuts off on a high note and goes silent. His expression closes up; the fire in his eyes dies out.

Ukou and Kateb watch with sympathy, Brie frowns, clearly confused about the *Atlanteo* vocabulary of what's being said, and Leetana shrinks back sadly without meeting Kokayi's gaze. Another moment and Kokayi suddenly pushes past us and rushes outside, slamming the door behind him.

There is petrified silence.

"This was unfair," Mineb Inei says at last, from the back. "Your son tried to please you. Why treat him this way?"

"And what business is that of yours?" Kokayi's mother turns in his direction. "Who are you to come into my house and tell me what to do?"

"He's a *Champion* of the Games of the Atlantis Grail," I say coldly, in slightly stilted *Atlanteo*, and without any intent on my part my voice starts gaining *power*. "And so am I. So are nine of us here, standing right now under your roof—all because your son invited us here. And he is the tenth. He is a Champion, and he is the best of us!"

Mamai-Jeet fixes her suddenly burning gaze on me. "Don't you think I *know* that?" she says in a surprising, soft voice, and I see that her eyes begin to glisten.

She pauses, then takes a deep breath and exhales with a shudder, and takes a staggering step, grasping the corner of the table. "I *know*," she repeats. "I know everything—*Imperial Lady Gwen*. My son . . . my Bay-bean left, and he never came back. And then I saw him in the Games, just like his father, and I knew he was never coming back again. No matter what happened, he was dead already, win or lose. Yes, I watched every moment, waiting for him to die, and that's how I lost my son . . . to the Games."

The woman inclines her head to me in a strange gesture of powerlessness.

"I'll go after him," Kateb says, breaking the painful silence. "To make sure he's okay."

Kokayi's mother nods. She then sits down on the narrow cot, and her pinched face twists as she begins to cry without a sound.

While Kateb goes looking for Kokayi, his wife sits down next to the older woman. "*Mamai*-Jeet," she says gently. "It's all right to grieve for your son. But he is not his father. And he won. He has come back to you. And it's a reason for celebration."

Kokayi's mother nods. She then sniffles loudly, wipes her face, and tries to compose herself. A few shuddering breaths later, she looks up at us, at me, and says. "Don't you dare tell him. It's for his own good. Don't any of you—"

"We won't," Brie says in lousy *Atlanteo*. "But you need to stop being such a *chazuf* to him, even for his own good."

Kokayi's mother shakes her head pitifully, sniffles again, then gets a grip and shows us her very bad teeth in a blooming smile.

"You, White Bird!" she says to Hedj Kukkait, who immediately attends her with amusement. "You go bring my Bay-bean back here! I don't trust that other one—the Inventor with the big spinning blade weapon—he is too quiet, not firm enough, look how he got mistreated by Deneb Gratu—"

"Yeah, hag was definitely *not* watching the Games." Brie rolls her eyes and starts laughing.

A few minutes later, we're being offered a boiling kettle of some kind of soup. *Mamai*-Jeet stirs the contents with a long wooden spoon and tells us she has fewer dishes than people present.

"Thank you, but no need, we're going soon," Rurim Kiv says.

"Before we go, please make your son understand how you really feel about him," Rea Bunit says, leaning over the kettle and speaking near the old woman's ear.

"Of course, I am proud of my Bay-bean!" *Mamai*-Jeet sputters. "All the neighbors know—"

In that moment Kokayi himself enters the room, followed by Kateb and Hedj.

His mother immediately freezes up and drops the spoon into the deep kettle, so that it sinks in the bubbling liquid.

"*Mamai* . . ." her son says, his long braids swinging with his every graceful movement as he approaches her. "You really mean it?"

She snorts, in a semblance of her earlier "weather," then comes up to him and stops to look up into his face. Both mother and son are willowy and tall, but the son is taller. "Ah," she says, speaking for the first time without abrasiveness. "Morning in your head?"

"Morning in my head." Kokayi nods, hanging his head with a sigh of infinite relief.

That's when *Mamai*-Jeet slaps him smartly upside his forehead.

Chapter 28

"Wait, '*Eos* in my—' Is that '*Morning* in *my* head?' 'Morning in *his* head?' What? What are they smoking?" Brie leans over and mutters to me in English. "What the hell kind of crazy Goldilocks talk is that?"

"I'm guessing it's local street slang or something," Laronda says, right next to me.

"Yeah, it's Bay slang," Anu confirms, standing right behind Laronda, so that he's practically breathing in her ear.

Laronda turns around and nearly bumps heads with Anu. "Eew, back off," she says to him and squeezes in closer to me, since the room is still ridiculously crowded.

"Yeah, whatever." Anu steps a little away from her and ends up almost hugging an Imperial guard.

I hold back a smile and turn around to exchange amused glances with Dawn, who's right there, trying to make her way past Brie, as she edges closer toward me and probably the exit.

We continue to crowd the room politely for a few minutes more, watching Kokayi interact with his mother—now that things between them seem to have warmed up.

At some point I feel a tap on my shoulder. I turn and there's Kateb, together with his wife, trying to approach me past the Imperial guards. I nod and move toward them both with a smile.

"Imperial Lady Gwen," Kateb says, with a courtly nod of greeting. "My apologies—there was no opportunity to do this sooner, but permit me to introduce my wife, Yeraz Nuletat."

"I am so glad to meet you at last, Imperial Lady Gwen. Thank you for working so well with my Kateb in the Games—my gratitude to you is boundless, and it is yours, always," Yeraz tells me, edging closer yet and giving me a similar courtly nod. Up close she is lovely, with softly expressive eyes full of kindness, and I can see why Kateb is so much in love.

"So great to meet you at last. I've heard so much about you," I say warmly, then simply reach out and give her a hug.

I don't think Yeraz expected this of me. Now her already luminous expression lights up even more.

"Hey, Lark!" Brie is back, suddenly inserting herself into the middle of our friendly contact, pushing past the Nuletats with only a brusque, "Sorry, Inventor and Inventor-babe. . . ."

"What?" I say, annoyed at her rudeness.

Brie gives me a mocking look. "So, yeah . . . I'm about to head out, and Sangre is chomping at the bit to be out of here, so just wanted to let you know we're going—"

I glance around momentarily and see that Logan is way, way behind her, crammed in close to the door, watching us with the typical cool, guarded look that he usually exhibits in public—or at least has been, ever since we arrived in Atlantis. Meeting my gaze, he gives me a polite nod.

"What's he doing here anyway?" I blurt, my curiosity getting the better of me. "Is he still supervising you? I thought that you're officially free and out of Correctional? Or is that still being arranged?"

"Oh, I'm free as a bird." Brie snorts and glances back at Logan, gives him a lingering look, then turns back to me. "He's here because I told him to be here. You see, for the next three Atlantean months, Mr. Sangria-on-Ice has to do whatever I tell him to do. It's one of my *official* Champion wishes. . . . Ah, such sweet, sweet revenge."

"Oh, no. . . ." I open my mouth, at a loss for words. And then I mumble, "How awful."

"Don't worry, I'm torturing him far less than he tortured me."

"What? He *tortured* you?" My mouth falls open again.

Brie laughs. "Only with his endless yakking interrogation. No pliers or tooth-pulling involved. Some sensory deprivation, then sensory assault, and crappy food. . . . But mostly a whole lot of words, words, *words*."

She pauses, taking in a deep breath, and just for a moment I see her expression flicker with hidden intensity, then a semblance of casual sarcasm returns. "So now, Lark, I'm giving him a little taste of his own medicine. I talk and talk at him, and make him do stupid crap for me—run errands and pick things up, and drive me places.

He even gets to serve me food, if I order him to do it. Every day for three months he has to show up at my own apartment in the morning and can only leave at night when I let him. I'm thinking I'll make him sleep on the floor outside my bedroom like a dog, starting tomorrow."

I frown. "Brie, no, you can't! You don't mean that. Please don't do that to him, please—"

"He deserves far worse."

"Oh, come on!" Now I'm agitated, glancing back at Logan again, then back at Brie. "You *can't* treat him like that. You know what he did was nothing personal. It was his job to interrogate you. I'm not justifying anything, but you were locked up for a reason, and he was your handler. . . . If you do this, you *know* he's never going to forgive you. And he's never going to forget that kind of thing—"

"Oh, I'm counting on it." Brie raises one brow mockingly, then says, "See you around, Princess. I promise, your ex-loverboy will be just fine—in three months. Call me, *ciao!*" And she shapes her lips into a smooch, then turns around and pushes her way back to the door. "Bye, Kokayi and Kokayi-*Mamai!*" she yells, just before disappearing, with Logan ahead of her, through the narrow exit.

"What a beyotch," Dawn says, shaking her head, while Kateb and Yeraz observe the whole thing with curiosity. "But at least she's *your* beyotch. Sort of. Go, Team Lark."

A few minutes later, I say goodbye to Kokayi and the others, promising to keep in touch, and exchanging contact information. "As soon as I am able to confirm the protocol of how it works, I'll invite you all to the Imperial Wedding," I say to them. "Will get to see you then!"

"Oh, *amrevet*, you'll get to see us—and we'll see you, and each other—much sooner than that," Kokayi tells me with a lighthearted chuckle. "The Champions of the Games get invited to so many public events as a group that in the next few weeks we're going to be sick of each other's company."

"Woe to us. Such are the interminable burdens of being a Champion," Rurim Kiv says with a straight face.

"So why did you do it? What's your story anyway?" Kokayi says, with an exaggerated coquettish glance at Rurim, lowering his gilded eyelashes.

"Eventually you will find out," Rurim replies. "But not today." And with a mocking nod to all of us he heads for the door.

On that note, it's our time to head out too.

Outside, the street party is still going. However, I notice that the *godateti* are now filled with the locals and are being dismantled into pieces before our eyes. Kids and adults scavenge for fallen *iretar* on the ground, while more people grab the remaining stuff in the baskets on top of the platforms, then the baskets themselves.

Everything is disappearing, and it's a wonder our hover vehicles are not taken apart.

Anu grumbles, then makes a scary deep roar to shoo away several urchins caught trying to pry open the secure car doors. He guffaws crudely, watching them scamper away.

We get in the cars, and Laronda gives Anu a look of disgust as she takes the seat next to me . . . which happens to be directly behind Anu's seat. She begins drumming her fingers against his headrest—which he pointedly ignores. Meanwhile, Tuar is once again in the front, and Dawn gets to sit alone on the seat behind us, yawning tiredly.

"Let's go home," I say, yawning also, because it's catching, and it's been a long afternoon.

Anu lifts us off, rising past the low buildings and the wild tangle of ropes, leaving Sky Tangle City far behind.

When we arrive at the Imperial Palace, I discover that Aeson has been anxiously waiting for me, hardly able to concentrate on his work. He stands up as soon as I enter the room, ignoring my companions, and focuses on me with a tense look. "Ah, you're finally back. How was it?"

"I'm okay, everything was fine!" I hurry to reassure him, then tell him what happened.

When I'm finished, Aeson looks up at Tuar with approval, then glances at Anu. "Well done," he says. "I am pleased with how you handled her protective detail."

"Thank you, My Imperial Lord." Tuar nods curtly.

"As of now, you may consider your position secure, Momet," Aeson adds. "Return tomorrow. You are being officially added to the security rotation schedule."

With a pleased expression and another nod, this time to both of us, Tuar Momet leaves for the day.

"We should be going too," Laronda says to me with a pat on my arm. "I need to return that shuttle before they give me demerits."

"Super fun afternoon," Dawn says. "Thanks for inviting us. I admit, I had tons of fun."

"Let's do it again." I smile at my friends. "This time, without a Parade. And with a little less drama."

"Yeah, we don't need no stinking Parade to go out on the town," Laronda says.

Over at his desk, Anu makes an incomprehensible grumbling sound, so that Gennio looks at him with a frown.

"What?" Laronda throws a narrowed glance at Anu.

"Nothing," Anu replies. "Wasn't talking to you."

"Then stop making swamp creature noises."

And on that note—while Anu stares at her with his mouth stuck open somewhere between a sneer and a retort—Laronda heads for the door, with Dawn closely following her, giving me one final amused eyeroll.

Aeson watches all of us with a curious, also amused expression.

L ater that evening, Aeson and I enjoy a leisurely *niktos* meal, just the two of us. It's filled with rambling conversation about Kokayi and his mother, the others, Champion wishes in general, and what poverty I've seen in Themisera. We also talk about what's been happening in my absence—namely, the incorporeal moon situation and the ongoing investigation of the strange "ships" discovered on its surface.

According to Aeson, the nature of those ship-like objects is still inconclusive and being investigated by the SPC, so no real news there. Similarly, not a peep from his Imperial Father on the subject of the broadcasting ancient ark-ship. It's almost as if the Imperator has resigned himself to that continuing situation in the face of a potentially greater problem, the mysterious moon.

And then, out of the blue, Aeson tells me that we've been scheduled to do several official media interviews as a couple.

"Okay. . . . When?" I ask, curling up against his chest as we relax on the sofa.

"Tomorrow, unfortunately." Aeson lets go of me with one hand to check his wrist comm. "We have Hel-Ra in the morning at ninth hour of Ra, followed by *Grail Games Daily* with Tiago at first hour of Khe, then *Winning the Grail* with Buhaat Hippeis at fifth hour of Khe. Then, at eighth hour of Khe, they've squeezed in all the minor feeds—six networks and ten different shows—into a single evening event, basically a small press conference where they're allowed to ask us only one question each."

"All on the same day?" I shudder. "Were you going to tell me about any of this earlier?"

"Palace scheduling only finalized it now. They like to structure these things as closely together as possible to minimize the Imperial time spent on media nonsense," he says, returning his hand to play against my cheek, then stroking my throat and sending sweet currents of energy through me.

"I hate Palace scheduling," I mumble, leaning into his touch. "Whatever Palace scheduling is. . . ."

He chuckles.

"Evil, evil Palace scheduling," I continue.

"At least it's all going to be held here, and not at their various studios across town," he says. "You can thank Palace scheduling for that too."

"Okay, in that case, I love Palace scheduling." I giggle.

And then it occurs to me—with all these media events, what am I supposed to say? What's the protocol for that kind of thing? Will they mostly ask questions about the two of us as the Imperial Couple, or about the Games, or both?

"Ah, *im amrevu* . . . at this point it doesn't matter how you reply. Just be yourself," Aeson whispers just above my ear, inhaling deeply, apparently engrossed in the scent of my hair.

Easy for him to say while he sniffs me like a bouquet of roses.

But I smile and try to clear my mind of whatever will happen tomorrow.

The next morning is Green Ghost Moon 6. I wake up around seventh hour, in my own bedroom, then discover that while I slept someone had gone through my closet and laid out a selection of elegant formal outfits and matching accessories. I assume it was my personal maid Aranit, who finally figured out my avoidance techniques and decided to beat me at my own game.

I capitulate to the mystery closet shopper's will and choose one of the outfits and everything that goes with it. Indeed, as soon as I've showered and put on the flowing pants and multi-layered top in shades of deep red and crimson, embroidered with fine threads of gold, Aranit arrives—typically silent, but with a more accommodating expression than I've seen from her before.

Giving me a solemn but impeccable curtsey, she goes to work on my hair and makeup. She puts my hair up in an elegant, twisted top-knot, and gives me dramatic dark eyes and black cherry lips. The finishing touch is a pair of long chandelier earrings that catch the light with sharp faceted crystals and cascade to my shoulders.

"Should I sprinkle gold dust on your hair and skin, My Imperial Lady?" Aranit asks at the very end.

For a moment, as I consider it, I get a weird out-of-the-body sensation of looking down at myself from above and wondering, *Who am I, and what have I become?*

But the existential moment of crisis goes away.

And since today is media interviews day, I let her.

Chapter 29

The first interview is with the Helios-Ra Imperial Poseidon Network. At the designated time, surrounded by Imperial guards (with the addition of Tuar, who looks sharp in his new uniform), Aeson and I exit the Imperial Crown Prince's Quarters and take the elevators to a lower level of the Palace.

"You look amazing." Aeson leans in and whispers to me as we walk. I glance up and see the force of his gaze consuming me, just before he looks away and the usual mask of composure takes over his expression—it's the confident Imperial face he puts on in public.

"You like?" I whisper back teasingly. In reply I feel his large hand cover mine, squeezing my fingers with sensual strength.

I smile secretly to myself, because the man walking at my side looks smoking-hot-amazing himself. Aeson is dressed for business, in a perfectly cut metallic-grey jacket and black pants, sleek and formal enough for Court. But his hair, loose and unrestrained, sweeps over his shoulders and back like liquid gold, adding a touch of casual elegance.

We arrive at our designated area. Here, a large chamber has been set up to accommodate the media, with a special interview "nook," consisting of a formal but comfortable loveseat-sized sofa for the Imperial Bride and Groom, and a chair for the interviewer, all against the background of a golden sunburst tapestry that works both as the Kassiopei Dynasty symbol and the Hel-Ra Network logo.

This fake "living room" section is elevated on a platform and artfully illuminated from all directions. Below and all around it is special effects equipment, with bustling light and sound techs and the rest of the network crew getting ready for us.

As soon as Aeson and I walk in, one of the techs engages a small 3D printing unit that releases a hive of nano-cameras into the air. I can actually *see* them—tiny motes of "dust" that get sprayed into the air from a micro-nozzle that resembles an aerosol container, but come out like embers from a flame, or a festive fireworks sparkler. For that one brief moment they are visible as a stream, just before they dissipate all over the room and start swirling like fiery snowflakes. That's when the camera tech enters the code to manipulate their programming and start the micro-feeds from each of their microscopically different vantage points.

"My Imperial Lord and Lady." A tall and handsome, middle-aged man with shoulder-length gilded hair and kohl-lined eyes approaches us and gives an impeccable courtly nod. He wears a stylish but businesslike outfit consisting of a Low Court-style robe over a white shirt, the kind that I've seen commentators and news anchor hosts often wear on the various talk shows.

I recognize Oalla's father, Desher Keigeri.

"*Ter* Desher," Aeson says. "We are ready for you."

Ter, I recall, is the term of address for Citizens and untitled nobility, and for nobility that withholds their title status by choice or for business purposes—or simply a general, respectful greeting for men.

"Excellent! Much appreciated," Desher says, glancing from Aeson to me. I notice his friendly blue eyes are the same as his daughter Oalla's. "If you would please take your seats up here—" He points to the platform seating area—"I'll be right behind you, in just a moment. I will have your questions ready for you to review before we begin."

I follow Aeson up the three stairs to the top of the platform. We sit down next to each other on the tall-backed, elegant loveseat upholstered in dark olive velvet fabric—all of it designed specifically to frame us in the best way possible. Indeed, my deep red top and Aeson's silvery-grey jacket are offset nicely by the rich fabric background. Meanwhile, directly behind and above us, the golden Hel-Ra logo blazes sun-like under the powerful studio lighting.

Down on the floor level below us, the media crew continues working, techs changing the positions and angles of spotlights and floodlights for maximum effect, even as the nano-cams continue to swirl all around. A makeup artist comes up to Desher Keigeri and gives his face a last-minute application of powder and paint. Another crew person runs up onto the platform and clips tiny voice amplifier buttons on our clothing, while someone else hands Aeson and me a batch of small cue cards with our questions inscribed in both *Atlanteo* and English.

I stare at the cards in my hands, anxiously reading what's on them. And then I take a deep breath and turn to Aeson, who is looking at me reassuringly.

"These are not too bad," I say. "I think we can manage."

Aeson smiles lightly. "Yes, this is Hel-Ra, a Kassiopei-friendly network, so it's to be expected. The questions were all vetted by us in advance."

I nod.

"All right, we go live in two daydreams!" Desher Keigeri announces just then from below, then mounts the platform and sits down in the interviewer's chair across from us.

A few more quick adjustments of stage lights on his face and ours, and then a countdown in heartbeats, "Three—two—one!"

A tone chimes, and a recorded music track starts playing—familiar by now, as I recognize the Hel-Ra Network theme, somewhat grandiose in effect, with an urgent drumbeat undertone and wind instruments for added drama.

The interview feed begins.

"*Nefero eos*, I am your host, Desher Keigeri, and welcome to the HRIPN special early feature." Desher begins speaking in a comfortable tone, his pleasant voice rising with amplified energy. "Today I have the great pleasure and honor to have with me the Imperial Crown Prince, Imperial Lord Aeson Kassiopei, and his radiant Bride, the Imperial Lady Gwen Lark. We are speaking with them live this morning, coming to you directly from the Imperial Palace complex in Poseidon. There are so many topics we'd love to discuss with *Atlantida's* favorite young Imperial Couple, including some great questions that many of you, our viewers, have sent in and are eager to hear the exclusive answers—"

Keigeri continues the introduction of our "famous, universe-spanning romance," my "daring entry" into the Games and a "glorious win," while Aeson and I look on politely, giving occasional nods and smiles. And then he launches into the questions, addressing us directly.

"Now that the excitement and danger of the Games are over, what are your most immediate plans for the future? What fires your enthusiasm?"

Aeson and I glance at each other, pretending to be surprised by the question we've just skimmed minutes ago. "My personal answer is simple," Aeson says with a faint, almost *sneaky* smile directed at me. "What fires my enthusiasm is my lovely, brave, generous Bride. I'll just let her answer."

"Aeson. . . ." I smile, widening my eyes at him. Then I take a deep breath and turn to the interviewer. "Aeson is, of course, my dearest heart and my source of enthusiasm. He fills me with joy and inspires me wholeheartedly in every way possible. And—and—"

"And your plans going forward?" Desher Keigeri tries to direct the question tactfully, to expand our sugary-sweet replies.

"Well," I say, "there's the Wedding, of course. And all the preparations—so many things to do, such wonderful Atlantean traditions for me to discover and for both of us to share."

"Indeed." Desher Keigeri nods with approval. "How are the preparations going, if we may ask? Now that you've had a few days to recover from the grand ordeal of the Games and the sweet triumph of victory, it must be such a relief to take some time to savor everything."

"Oh, yes," I say, trying to think of suitable platitudes. "I'm very relieved and grateful to have had the opportunity to earn my Citizenship the hard way. It's been an honor striving and working together with the members of Team Lark, and to share the victory with nine other such worthy Champions. But I'm very glad it's behind me now—behind both of us, Aeson and me. Now we can focus on our regular lives and our families."

Can I be even more dull and insipid in my answers? Why, yes, yes, I can be. . . .

"As far as the Wedding preparations, everything is going well," I continue, mentally going over the Bridal List activities and just plucking terms. "Let's see—I am in the process of choosing the Flower and the Song and will be hosting my first Bridal event in a few days from now."

"Lovely," Desher says mildly. "We eagerly look forward to knowing your selections."

So do I, Oalla's Dad, I think. So do I. . . .

Desher Keigeri now turns to Aeson. "My Imperial Lord, what are your plans for the Golden Bay? As many of our viewers know, the Archaeon Imperator, Our Imperial Sovereign and Your Illustrious Father, had granted you this somewhat controversial property as the Imperial Wedding Gift."

"Yes," Aeson says, his tone reflecting a polished, confident manner. "The Golden Bay of Poseidon has profound and far-reaching potential. In addition to the natural beauty of the coastline, the land is rich with resources, and the population is rich in spirit. Yes, there are inherent *known* difficulties, but they are surmountable. Much work remains to be done there to improve the living standards, to build up the infrastructure. It will be my priority to begin the many improvement projects as soon as possible, within the scope of my other duties."

"You can start with helping the residents of Themisera—Sky Tangle City," I blurt.

Oh, crap . . . did I say too much?

But Aeson turns to me with a serious light in his eyes. "Yes. Themisera is only one of the places that need extensive help and will receive it. There are other adjacent regions of poverty and long-standing disrepair, and they will receive my attention also."

I nod, feeling awkward and yet relieved that there's no judgment of my outburst—even as the focus of his gaze continues to rest on me reassuringly, affirming my sentiment.

"Very assuring to know that the Golden Bay has such an exciting future before it," Desher says after a smallest pause, continuing the interview. "And now, if I may ask both of you—everyone wants to know, where will you spend your *amrevet* days?"

The interviewer looks from Aeson to me with a pleasant smile. "As you were no doubt informed, Imperial Lady Gwen—it is tradition at the end of the first eight months after the Wedding for the newlyweds to flee and hide together in a delightful secret place of their own choosing, for continued intimacy, at the same time letting their families and friends know only the general whereabouts. We would never presume to know your intended destination, only the general whereabouts. Will you generously enlighten us?"

"Oh . . . yes," I say, recalling that *amrevet* days are the Atlantean equivalent of a honeymoon, except taken half a year later.

SURVIVE 295

But no one had told me anything about fleeing, or secret locations.

At a loss, I turn to my Bridegroom, pivoting not-so-skillfully. "Aeson?"

"We are still making arrangements in that regard," Aeson replies smoothly, after a swift glance at me, which suggests to me that he might in fact have no frigging clue.

Poor Aeson, I think. *All these Wedding preparation details are driving him nuts.*

But then my Bridegroom astonishes me. "I've actually arranged a surprise for my Bride," he says. "The final details are being worked out, so if I say anything now, it might spoil the surprise for her—which is something none of your viewers would want."

Nicely played!

I give Aeson an amused glance.

But he is staring back at me with a steady, confident smile. Which makes me think *Maybe he actually has something planned after all!*

Lesson for me—never, ever underestimate *im amrevu.*

The Hel-Ra interview goes on for a short while after that, and we answer a few more easy, harmless, entirely forgettable questions. And then we're done. The live feed cuts off, and we thank Desher Keigeri for his efforts and return to our Quarters upstairs.

"Aeson, about those *amrevet* days," I whisper to him at some point when we're briefly alone, "do you really have something awesome planned for us, or was that just a smooth way for you to avoid really answering?"

Aeson chuckles and taps the end of my nose playfully with one finger.

"What?" I part my lips in frustration, then the whole thing turns into a helpless smile. *"Tell me!"*

But my cruel Bridegroom shakes his head, leans close to my ear, and says mysteriously, "You will find out."

I make a little sound of annoyed affection and give up—for the moment.

A few hours and an early *dea* meal later, it's time for our second interview, this one with our friend Tiago, for *Grail Games Daily,* at first hour of Khe.

While we were taking a break, the Palace staff and network crews rearranged the same chamber on the lower floor, this time setting up the interview platform "nook" to resemble a *Grail Games Daily* studio set. Different crews came in, brought their set pieces, similar camera equipment, and stage lights.

And now Aeson and I come back down to a completely transformed interview space and the familiar sight of the big, black, Laughing Buddha that is Tiago Guu.

"Tiago!" I exclaim with a smile.

"My dearest Imperial Lady Gwen—or should I say, Vocalist Champion of the Games!" Tiago responds in a rich baritone, hurrying toward us with great agility despite his considerable size.

Indeed, with his immense width, rotund belly, many chins, and white-toothed grin—and the fact that his wiry gilded hair is cut so short it's almost nonexistent—Tiago could be the living personification of the bald Laughing Buddha figure from Earth.

As the host of *Grail Games Daily*, Tiago is a flamboyant dresser. Today he wears an oversized jacket and roomy pants in a strange metallic black fabric that somehow glitters with purple and persimmon sparkles—creating rainbow waves, like benzene rings—under the bright studio lights. And his cosmetics echo the dramatic outfit perfectly: dark, purple-tinted eyebrows with striking orange highlights, kohl-rimmed brown eyes, and henna lip gloss—all of it playing so well with his deep brown skin.

Tiago continues, after giving both Aeson and me a profound, courtly bow. "What a delight it is to see you like this, happy and relieved—yes, I can see it in your lovely eyes, My Imperial Lady, a new lightness—now that the abysmal difficulty is behind you and you have triumphed!"

"I still can't believe it," I say. "I *survived*, Tiago. Thank you again for all you did to help me train for it."

Tiago's smile disappears for a moment, and he grows thoughtful. I notice he doesn't attempt to flatter me by correcting me that I've won. "As a *survivor* of the Games myself, I commiserate in every sense with your plight, My Imperial Lady. It was difficult to watch the hardest moments when your life was on the line. But I believed in you because I knew you had profound *motives* to persist."

Tiago is showing his wisdom yet again. How well he understands me. Truly, his good advice went a long way in getting me in the right head-space during Games training. Tiago's comments always kept me grounded in the grim reality, forced me to live out the worst-case scenarios in my mind with strange calm and cultivate an attitude of simply persisting. Getting a grip on fear was a profound technique he taught me.

For that alone, I owe Tiago a whole lot.

But now Tiago breaks the serious moment by clapping his big, meaty hands together, making all his bracelets jangle, and the bright studio lights catch the jewels in his many rings. "But enough looking back! Let's proceed with the interview, which, I promise you, will be full of happier things!"

We ascend the platform and take our seats on a different small sofa, this one low-backed and upholstered in trendy silver fabric, to match the more youthful and upbeat nature of this particular show. The Kassiopei sunburst logo tapestry behind us has been replaced with several hovering light globes for a more contemporary look.

Aeson and I look over a new set of cue cards, while crew technicians make last-minute adjustments to the studio, and a new hive of nano-cams fills the air. Then Tiago takes the chair across from us and begins the interview segment.

"Let me begin by saying, the *Grail Games Daily* audience loves you, our favorite Shoelace Girl and future Imperatris, the Imperial Lady Gwen Lark!" Tiago says with a grin, as the musical theme fades. "What an amazing Games season we've had, and your participation was truly the highlight!"

I nod and smile.

Tiago now turns to Aeson. "And what an experience it must have been for you, my Imperial Lord Aeson, to watch your amazing Bride in action!"

Aeson makes a short laugh and raises one brow. "Unforgettable," he says, and there's a world of irony in that one word.

He almost died . . . watching me. . . .

At once, pain stabs through my heart on Aeson's behalf.

"The Four Stages each had unique challenges," Tiago says. "But some of the most amazing things that developed were the alliances and powerful bonds between members of Team Lark. I admit, in all my years of watching, of analyzing Games strategy, I have never seen such close-knit bonds evolve between Contenders. How did you manage it?"

"They were—*are*—a remarkable group of people to work with." I turn my head sideways, thinking about Team Lark, with a faint smile hovering at my lips. "I think I got very, very lucky. If I hadn't tripped Zaap in the first few moments of Stage One, things might have turned out very differently."

"Ah, yes, Animal Handler Zaap Guvai. . . ." Tiago nods fondly and with sadness. "He was a truly remarkable Contender. If not for his unfortunate death in the first leg of the Triathlon Race, I have no doubt he would have won his Category."

"Yes." I grow quiet. "He was well ahead, until he got . . . shot in the back."

"Tragic! So terrible, so—but then, such is the bittersweet aspect of the Games." Tiago pauses for a long beat, nodding slowly. "We never forget them, of course—those who lose their lives. They live on inside us."

"Always. I'll never forget Zaap," I say. "If only—"

I stop before I end up mentioning Thalassa, whose name I would sincerely like to forget. Also, I don't want to speak in public just yet about certain plans of mine in regard to honoring Zaap posthumously.

That will come later.

"So—Shoelace Girl!" Tiago pivots the conversation in a happier direction. "We already know you're brilliant and resourceful. Now we want the full story! How did your unusual appellation come about?"

"During Qualification, on Earth. I had to improvise during weapons training." I smile, shaking my head, and briefly tell the story of how I was the one person in my class left without a cord weapon, so I pulled out my own shoelaces and tied them together into a makeshift "cord," in order to avoid a demerit.

"Ah, so that's how it started! Very clever! Your instructor must have been very impressed with you."

"Just barely," I say, wincing and smiling. Now is probably not the best time to name Xelio Vekahat as the instructor involved in that notorious incident.

Tiago chuckles. "Not sure if you're aware, My Imperial Lady, but 'Shoelace Girl'-themed merchandizing has become pervasive—ever since the public discovered this unusual aspect of you."

"Okay. . . ." I part my lips, not sure how to answer or respond, or if I even should.

"Yes," Tiago continues. "They now sell shoelaces imprinted with your name in the markets all around Poseidon. Also, ribbons, armbands, shirts, hats. . . . There are custom hoverboards with a heroic image of you and your shoelaces. Also, drinking grails with you riding your *pegasus* in Gebi cat form during Stage Four—"

"And people buy them?" I ask.

"Oh, yes!" Tiago lifts a finger in pause. He reaches into a hidden pocket of his iridescent jacket to pull out a pair of shiny-white shoelaces with the inscription "Shoelace Girl," both in English and *Atlanteo*, printed in black, purple, and gold, running down the length of each. "I certainly bought these! And if I may have you sign them for me afterwards, it would be a delight. A lovely memento of this year's stunning Games."

"Of course," I reply with a short laugh.

"Then I am overjoyed!" Tiago claps his big hands together and proceeds to ask the next question. "Now then, here's a question directly from my audience—the one question that has received the highest votes throughout this past week. And as promised, I am now going to ask you this question, since *Atlantida* demands an answer."

"Sure," I say, smiling to cover my little jolt of nerves.

"My dearest Imperial Lady, the last time you honored me by being on my live arena show at the *Nebetareon*—just before the Games, you might recall—we were dying to know what love gifts were exchanged between the Imperial Crown Prince Aeson Kassiopei and his Bride—"

Oh, crap . . . this wasn't in the cue cards!

"—and so, it must be asked again!" Tiago exclaims enthusiastically.

I bite my lip and glance at Aeson helplessly, thinking of his black armband, the highest honor of a hero, which he removed from his own arm and gave to me as I went into the Games—right after I gave him my little Pegasus figurine from Earth.

So yeah, we exchanged love gifts. And his black armband—it's the ultimate love gift of all. What can be greater and more meaningful than that? Aeson doesn't have to give me anything else, ever.

Unfortunately, that black armband is nontransferable. By Atlantean law, it's the one thing that may *not* be given away. It was basically lent to me temporarily, a powerful symbol of the bond between us. Its purpose—to keep me focused and grounded, to keep me motivated, and to keep me *alive*. Since it had to be returned safely to the original owner, I was responsible for returning it. As a side effect of that, I, myself, had to stay safe, in order to survive the Games.

And now, to accommodate the Wedding tradition, Aeson will have to come up with something else more appropriate, and soon. . . .

For once, my Bridegroom seems to pause before answering. He takes a deep breath and then speaks, all the while looking at me. "Tiago, there's no easy way to say this, but our love gifts are not going to be divulged until the Gifts Assembly event, a few days before our Wedding. The curious public must remain patient and wait."

At once I nod, feeling relief. "Yes, that's right. Thank you, Aeson."

"Argh!" Tiago slaps his thigh and makes an exaggerated sound of frustration. He then turns his face aside, as though looking at an invisible camera (which he likely is, with so many nano-cams currently swirling all around us) and says: "You've heard it here, *Atlantida!* The Imperial Crown Prince commands us to be patient! Nothing else to do but wait. How many days until the Wedding? Twenty-nine days! Ah, such sweet torture!"

Aeson smiles and nods to me.

I widen my eyes at him, and my own lips curve upward.

Once again, this harmless but weirdly stressful topic is averted.

Tiago's interview concludes soon after, and he tells us it will be played in tomorrow's feed as a recorded segment during his regular show.

Aeson and I thank Tiago, and he thanks us in turn for the "delightful time spent."

"Please do my show again soon," he says with an easygoing chuckle. "And by the way, thank you for scheduling me ahead of

Hippeis and his supremely dull enterprise. He is definitely grinding his teeth with envy right now, imagining the exclusive content he is missing out on!"

Tiago is of course referring to our next interview host, Buhaat Hippeis, his long-standing rival, and the competing show *Winning the Grail*, which we're going to be doing in just a few hours.

After Tiago leaves, we once again head upstairs to rest in our own Quarters. Aeson stops to check the SPC incoming reports on the big displays at his desk. Then we lounge around in his workroom, sipping cool glasses of *qvaali* while Xelio and Erita work with the raw data and periodically interrupt us to discuss the findings with Aeson.

"So, what's new with the moon?" I ask.

Erita glances up from the screen and points me to a zoomed-in window showing a series of very dark visual schematics that resemble Earth-style MRI digital imaging, or maybe X-rays. "These are cross-section images of the surface in fine detail—namely, the coordinates where we found those mysterious ships."

I peer closer.

"We have no sensors that can be made to work under these crazy conditions," Erita continues. "The moon is a true ghost, so there can be no sensor-based physical readings taken by us. Literally nothing to latch onto for gathering data. . . . No light in the interior, so almost complete darkness—except for whatever cracks or openings in the ancient ship hulls that might allow in any external illumination already present in the same quantum bubble that encloses the moon—assuming that's even a quantum bubble. Without tangible matter to reflect light, to *interact* with it on the most basic particle level, our tech probes cannot illuminate anything as they make their flybys. Or should I say, fly-*throughs*."

I shake my head in wonder as I hold my glass of *qvaali*.

"So the only thing we can do is send those probes to make infinite passes through the same location, over and over, only with microscopic spatial offsets, and basically record whatever strange visuals we can get with each pass of the interior. It's like an ultrasound scanner making tedious passes over an object to obtain many cross-sections and compile them into a bigger picture."

"I think I understand." I take a sip from my glass. "You're re-creating a 3D shape."

Erita nods. "Exactly. Except we're dealing with 'one-way matter,' for lack of a better description. We can *receive* and see the light reflected from the moon and whatever's on it, but we cannot shine our own light onto its surface."

"So what have you found so far?"

"Well. . . ." Erita glances at Xelio, then Aeson, as though for confirmation, then turns back to me. "The objects are definitely ships—ancient, Earth-style ark-ships, to be exact. Yes, they're ours, but smaller in size and capacity, matching the style and level of technology that our ancestors supposedly had when they first landed on this planet and colonized Atlantis. And we're currently plotting and rendering the interiors of each one with every new tech probe pass."

"That's incredible," I say.

"When the rendering is done," Erita continues, "we're going to have very imperfect 3D replicas of these ancient ships, with everything that's still on board, stored as digital schematics—but only if there's light seeping in from the outside. It will allow us to know exactly what's there without actually having to physically go there in person."

"Yes, it's the one weird advantage of dealing with objects in this noncorporeal state," Xelio adds. "We can simply pass through them and look inside without having to pry open ancient sealed doors or worry about deck levels collapsing on us."

"But again, that only works if there's at least *some* light coming in to give shape to whatever objects are inside. We have sensors that can pick up even the faintest energy readings, as long as they're present, and extrapolate from there. Unfortunately, some of these ships are apparently so well preserved that there are no hull breaches, nothing coming through, so we cannot get any interior readings. Only weird *shebet* . . . oh, yes. Definitely something no one would've expected to deal with—not ever."

Erita takes a deep breath and opens another screen, getting back to crunching the data.

Chapter 30

At fifth hour of Khe, Aeson and I go back downstairs for the third time, in order to be interviewed by Buhaat Hippeis, Tiago's nemesis, and the host of *Winning the Grail*.

Buhaat is a thin, slight, wiry man with enthusiastic, quick movements and a resonant tenor voice. He wears a formal robe over his shirt and one of his favorite affectations—an extravagant wig of braided gold that reminds me of foppish Court attire and, just a little bit, of Consul Denu's extensive wardrobe of wigs.

He approaches us with a smooth, courtly bow and extends his hand in a sweeping gesture to point us to the rebuilt set on top of the platform. "My Imperial Lord Aeson and Imperial Lady Gwen, our illustrious new Champion, please, please—what an honor to interview you together at last!"

We take a seat on yet another new sofa, this one more traditional and expensive looking, upholstered in subtle earth tone patterns. Behind us, the sunburst tapestry is back, with the addition of suspended golden chandeliers on both sides.

Buhaat smiles at us graciously, but I'm not fooled. During the pre-Games Trials and all throughout the month leading up to the Games, his show made fun of me mercilessly, interpreting all my actions and efforts in the most pitiful light possible. Buhaat is sharp and analytical, and he certainly knows his subject, but he is also not very nice.

Right now he is working very hard to overcome his earlier bias against me. The fact that I've won against all odds, contrary to his own statistical analysis, must be grating on him.

Aeson sits back and drapes his arm around the back of my seat in a deceptively relaxed posture. He watches Buhaat with a hard, unblinking gaze.

I, too, look at our host with a no-nonsense face, wanting to narrow my eyes at him, but holding back.

Our cue cards arrive, and minutes later the soft, stately musical theme fills the room. Buhaat takes the chair across from us and begins his interview.

"Winning—namely, *Winning the Grail*. It is always the topic, and it is always topical," Buhaat utters the trademark catch phrase that opens each episode of his show. "*Nefero dea* and welcome to all our loyal viewers. What a season it's been, Grail Games Worshippers! And what a time to look back at the highlights and savor the results. It's no surprise that today we have the privilege of speaking again to a Champion. What's surprising is that our particular Champion is also a member of royalty. Not merely one of the Top Ten, she is also the Imperial Bride and our future Imperatris—the Imperial Lady Gwen Lark! Furthermore, the Imperial Crown Prince himself, our beloved Imperial Lord Aeson, has granted us the extraordinary honor of his presence today."

Buhaat Hippeis pauses for dramatic effect, then turns to me and Aeson. "Please allow me to congratulate you both on the extraordinary talent and accomplishment of the Imperial Lady Gwen. Your performance exceeded all our expectations, My Imperial Lady. Yes, I admit, I've erred significantly in my preliminary estimation of your abilities. My only excuse is that you were a newly arrived Earth refugee, and all of us were simply unfamiliar with your excellence. With so little data as to your capabilities, it's clear in retrospect that my predictive formula was flawed."

"Let that be a lesson to anyone who underestimates my Bride," Aeson says with a faint smile.

"I therefore beg your forgiveness," Buhaat says to me, inclining his head in a very correct, but slight, bow. "I hope you now indulge my curiosity and that of our viewers and tell us a little about yourself—something that no one in *Atlantida* knows about you."

"Thank you," I reply. "I'll see what I can do. What would you like to know?"

"Something fresh and new. Something delightful."

And exclusive, I think. For a moment I get the deer-in-the-headlights sensation of not knowing what to say before an audience.

I want to change things in a meaningful way . . . to help . . . to unite.

"I really like *nikkari* juice," I say instead. "It's become one of my favorite drinks here on Atlantis. Reminds me a little bit of Earth watermelon juice, except it's silly green."

Buhaat Hippeis raises his brows in amusement. "Is that so? What a charming detail."

"I imagine you're probably looking for something a little more significant." I smile.

"Oh, not at all. This is perfectly fine, My Imperial Lady. Any tidbit you choose to share with the audience is deeply appreciated. In that light, may I be slightly more inquisitive and ask you about your amazing vocal abilities?"

Uh-oh. . . . With a quick glance at Aeson (who doesn't react, his expression confident and composed), I continue to smile. "Thank you," I say. "I really enjoyed being a Vocalist."

Buhaat turns his head slightly sideways, observing me. "It is rather more than mere enjoyment—one would say, it is a significant talent. Your range and nuance are remarkable. And the raw *power* of your voice—if I didn't know better, and forgive me for saying, but one might almost venture to guess that your relationship to the Imperial Kassiopei is by blood and not by marriage—"

"My mother was a professional opera singer on Earth," I say quickly. "She taught us to sing—my brothers and sister and me."

"Ah." Buhaat nods. "That explains it. But, of course, your voice command skills are of a different order than mere singing. The intricate way you manipulated orichalcum objects in the Games, your proficiency with the various molecular and energy transformation commands, such as precision-level selective keying and heating the enemy Contender uniforms in Stage Three, nullifying the hot zone chamber in Stage One—one can go on and on. Clearly you received extensive training in that regard—"

"I trained her myself," Aeson speaks up calmly. "My Bride showed great vocal promise, and I had to give her every opportunity to perfect her natural abilities."

Buhaat inclines his head to Aeson. "Of course, My Imperial Lord. And the results of your unique efforts are remarkable. Now, before we go on to the next topic, I do want to ask—and forgive me if this is entirely baseless—but is it at all possible that during the Vocalist Tiebreaker event at the *Stadion* Final Ceremony, when My Imperial Lady sang, precisely at the *same time* as the ground quake happened—could it be that somehow the nature of her *voice* might have contributed to the incident in some way? I don't say 'caused'— that would be impossible and outlandish—but merely *added* to the variables that aligned together to initiate the seismic event?"

Buhaat Hippeis trails off in carefully calculated politeness.

Oh, but he knows precisely what he's doing, asking this provocative question that's not on the cue cards, and yet leaving it open-ended. He likely has his suspicions about what really happened, about *what I did*, and wants to give the audience a real scoop. Maybe he thinks he can get us to reveal something *right now*.

For one long moment Aeson and I stare at him. And then Aeson says in a casual tone of voice, "As you say, impossible and outlandish."

"But kind of fun," I add, forcing myself to chuckle. "Can you just imagine, Aeson? But seriously—if anything, it had to be the giant Grail Monument itself that caused the ground instability, maybe even developed a fault line around its foundation, causing it to topple over—"

Now I'm really getting creative here.

If anyone checks the recorded video and audio feeds of the incident, the analysis of what actually took place is pretty clear—I sang a *recognizable* voice command to *raise* an object, namely the Atlantis Grail, and this fact can be corroborated by expert witnesses.

But now, with the grim reality of the ancient ark-ship and the repercussions of releasing that information to the public, I myself must continue to pretend that it was all a coincidence.

Whether or not Buhaat Hippeis or his audience believes me is another matter. It has to be done, regardless of how long this flimsy cover-up can be maintained, and no matter how personally frustrating it is for *me*.

Fortunately, the host of *Winning the Grail* has other questions to ask me. After a short, hopeful pause, Buhaat Hippeis nods and proceeds with the next item on his agenda.

"Very well. Can you tell us anything about your Champion wishes, My Imperial Lady?"

This one is straightforward and easy.

I make a small laugh. "Oh, no," I say bluntly, looking Hippeis in the eye. "My wishes have been submitted to the Games officials, according to the rules. As soon as they are processed and fulfilled, everyone will know. Until then—I'll say nothing. Let me ask *you* instead, *Ter* Buhaat—have you asked this same question of the other Champions, and has anyone actually answered you? No? I didn't think so."

Buhaat Hippeis shakes his head and laughs. "I concede, My Imperial Lady. But as you can imagine, I had to try."

After that, the remaining questions are forgettable, and our interview is over.

"You handled that quite well," Aeson tells me as we retreat upstairs before our one last "bout" with the media later that night.

I sigh. "Very annoying to have to lie."

He looks at me with his serious expression. "I know. I'm sorry it has to be this way, at least for now."

"They're going to find out everything eventually, aren't they?" I ask. "The whole ugly mess. An unstoppable ancient ship broadcasting a relentless signal to the ancient enemy, while a weird ghost moon shows up at the same time in orbit—with a whole bunch more ancient ships littering its freaky ghost surface. What happens next?"

Aeson shakes his head and touches my shoulder, resting his large, warm palm solidly against me. "I wish I knew. But we'll do everything we can to deal with it."

At eighth hour of Khe, we go down for the final media event of the day. The interview chamber is crowded with people. Six network crews and representatives of ten different shows are setting up their equipment, and rows of chairs are filling the floor in front of the platform.

Everyone is bustling, and the moment we arrive, we're asked to ascend the platform and sit down on a tall-backed loveseat upholstered in deep blue. The Kassiopei Dynasty sunburst logo shines at our back, and several hovering light fixtures frame us in bright illumination.

I don't recognize any particular host this evening, but there's a podium below, at which a line of media representatives has formed. I recall that they're allowed to ask us only one question each.

Aeson sits back and places his hand over mine confidently.

"We're ready for you," he says loudly.

An Imperial Palace official, one of several staff discreetly maintaining order, bows to the Imperial Crown Prince and signals approval to the various crews.

A vaguely familiar musical theme starts to play, and nano-cameras swirl like fireflies around us. Just as the press conference begins, I realize that no one has given us any cue cards with questions.

Whether it's an oversight or intentional is unclear. Either way, we need to be ready for anything.

"*Free Poseidon News* would like to ask the first question," a young woman says, standing at the head of the line at the podium. "Now that the Games are concluded, and the results finalized, is there anything the Imperial Lord Aeson can share with the public in regard to the nature of the disaster that literally shook the *Stadion* on Green Mar-Yan 26? We're familiar with the initial reports about seismic structural damage to the facilities and the Grail Monument, but would like an update and further details."

Wow, I think. *This is definitely no-nonsense, gutsy questioning.*

Aeson pauses briefly before answering, but his expression remains composed. "A good question. At present, my Father, the Imperial Sovereign, has ordered a cleanup of the stadium grounds, and the investigation is still ongoing. There's significant damage, and safety measures are being taken in order to make the venue safe to the public again."

"Thank you, My Imperial Lord," the woman persists. "Do the later reports continue to indicate random seismic activity, or are there additional causes for the seismic disturbance? Such as, for example, the fact that the Imperial Lady was employing a *voice command* to raise or lift something at the exact same time—"

"One question only!" the Palace official coordinating the event interrupts, raising his hand. "You've had your response, now step aside, please. Next question!"

"It's fine," Aeson says graciously. "All further details can be found on the public records news site—they have been posted and are updated regularly."

The woman bows and steps aside, and now a man in line behind her moves forward to the podium.

"My Imperial Lord, *News of the Golden Bay* would like to ask a follow-up to the previous question. The Atlantis Grail Monument appears to be damaged at the foundation and is dislodged, but it is also emitting a very loud noise—a humming or buzzing sound, low in pitch but high in volume—which is heard and felt in the immediate vicinity of the *Stadion* and the entire complex, together with the outlying high-rise office buildings and residential areas. Many noise complaints have been lodged with the authorities, and the neighborhood residents are concerned about the nature of this sound and its potential harm to the occupants and any health consequences. Can you please tell us what it is?"

"I'm afraid I cannot," Aeson says bluntly, looking at the media representative. "There are several likely causes, including damaged sound equipment, the building materials involved, and the extreme age of the structure of the original monument and the ground supports underneath. I can only refer you to the public records on the structure. It's also worth reminding everyone that the curving interior shape of the Grail is naturally resonant. Due to its angle of repositioning it could be picking up urban noise and amplifying it like an echo chamber."

"What about the dangers to public health?"

"It's not a sonic weapon, if that's your concern," Aeson replies, and there's sparse laughter in the room. "Be assured that we're investigating the situation and taking into account your concerns. If there had been any sonic danger, you would've been notified and asked to evacuate the affected areas. For now, assume it's merely a nuisance—a sound similar to the so-called 'singing' of the Grail that everyone is familiar with during the various stadium ceremonies."

The man bows and steps aside.

Next up is a woman. "I am with *The Daily Bay Flow*, and my question is for the Imperial Lady Gwen Lark."

Immediately my heartbeat speeds up.

"We learned that yesterday My Imperial Lady visited Themisera, along with several other Champions, to participate in an impromptu celebration event. We would like to know your impressions of this poverty-ridden area, and what your plans are, if any, to improve the lives of the population living in such hardship."

I feel the sudden weight of so many gazes upon me. I take a deep breath, open my mouth. "Thank you for your question. It was very—it affected me very much and made a profound impression on me. I honestly don't know what to say right now, because I just don't know enough about Sky Tangle City—*yet*. The people were—*are*—gracious and full of dignity. So brave and cheerful—even *joyful*, from what I could see—despite circumstances that would cause anyone despair . . . I saw only a tiny, superficial aspect of what they must deal with on a regular basis, and yes, I visited one home, but—" I pause, my heart pounding, and glance at Aeson. "Some of it broke my heart. No, not some of it—all of it. And I want to do whatever I can to help."

"Thank you, My Imperial Lady. Those of us local to that part of the Bay take hope in your sympathy and appreciate it." The woman from the media bows and steps away.

An older man takes her place at the podium. "Our question is from *Talk and Laugh News Digest*, and it's actually somewhat less frivolous than we would like. Normally we cover the lighter side of Poseidon living, but you must admit that some of the events of the last few days have been very disturbing. For example, what is going on with Ghost Moon? What is it? Where did it come from, and what unspeakable danger does it pose? My Imperial Lord, in your capacity as Star Pilot Corps Commander, you must be more informed on this subject than anyone else, so the question goes to you. Please, enlighten us!"

It's Aeson's turn to take a deep breath. He nods slowly, before speaking. "In my capacity as SPC Commander, I can tell you that we are *actively* investigating this truly strange phenomenon. Indeed, it is my first priority right now—a global priority. Multiple highly qualified teams are on site, and we are analyzing the data we have. I must admit, it is not much, nor am I able to give any specifics yet. However, I'm able to tell you that there is no immediate danger to our planet. The moon appears to occupy a stable orbit around Atlantis, but is somehow outside any physical state of interaction with us, so no gravitational effects have been observed. That is all I have for you right now—thank you for your question."

The crowded room gets noisy as whispers race around the chamber, but the Imperial Palace coordinators signal everyone for quiet.

The next media representative is with *Eos News Feed*. "In our capacity as a media watchdog organization," the man says, "we would like to ask if there have been any updates in the investigation of the several unexpected and—one might say—strategically timed service interruptions to the media feeds all throughout the Games by the illicit entity self-referred to as 'The Rim.' The Rim's actions could have potentially affected Contender performance as a consequence of preferential bias or otherwise malicious intent to rig the Games. This serious breach must be addressed—for the sake of continuing integrity of the Games process. Therefore, we continue to ask—have any individuals or groups been found to be affiliated with The Rim, and any arrests made in connection to this organization?"

At the mention of The Rim, I get a flashback to the creepy image of the golden mask against a black background, cutting in during various critical moments of the Games with their anti-establishment propaganda. And I think of Hedj Kukkait who saved me, and who secretly admitted to being associated with The Rim. . . . When I shared this confidence with Aeson, right after Stage One, I was definitely taking a chance—I didn't want to compromise Hedj and get him in trouble, but I felt I had to let my Bridegroom know. Fortunately, Aeson took it well—but only because of Hedj's role in protecting me.

So, a tricky situation, since The Rim continues to pose a problem.

How will Aeson answer this question?

Aeson pauses thoughtfully before responding to the *Eos News Feed* reporter. "As far as I'm aware, no arrests have been made, and no persons of interest related to The Rim have yet been identified. Regretfully, I don't have a better answer for you regarding this heinous security breach, having been preoccupied with other pressing issues. I recommend you take it up with the Media Safety Committee of the IEC."

There are more waves of talk through the chamber, hushed quickly by the Palace staff.

The next woman in line at the podium asks her question. "With your permission, Imperial Lady Gwen, *Contemporary Court Style and Gossip* would like to know your feelings about the outrageous EBDL, or so-called 'Earth Bride Death Lottery,' that was a running joke segment on so many feeds for the past month, and whether you would like to press criminal charges against the perpetrators."

The room noise level rises again.

My lips part. With a painful twinge in my chest I recall that awful thing, that deeply disturbing symptom of the negative attitude toward me—both as the Imperial Bride and as a Contender—that had prevailed for so long, until the tide of public opinion finally turned in my favor. . . .

If I'm to be honest, the EBDL crushed me. In that awful, interminable period just before the Games, when I was still actively training and living in uncertainty, it terrified me, leeched my energy, undermined my will to fight—basically, it hurt me immeasurably. To know that millions of people were eagerly betting against me, laughing at my coming defeat and assured death at the hands of celebrity Contenders like Deneb Gratu—it hurt like hell. All those weeks, I tried not to think about it, to suppress my awareness in order to keep it from flooding my mind with helplessness.

And now—would I like to bring whomever was responsible for this malicious cruelty to justice?

I shake my head with a painful smile. "No, of course not. I know that *Atlantida* loves to bet on everything. I suppose now that it's over, I can take it as a compliment that someone bothered to include me in your favorite pastime. After all—ultimately, someone won the EBDL. And to do that, against all odds, they had to bet on *me*."

Quite a few claps sound at my response, including the woman from *Contemporary Court Style and Gossip*. She then bows courteously to me and steps aside.

The next in line is another woman. "Imperial Lady Gwen Lark, I am with *Bay City News and Entertainment*. I have one simple question for you. Do you possess the Logos voice of the Kassiopei Dynasty?"

Chapter 31

The conference chamber erupts with noise.

I freeze, for one moment only, while my mind races with options. I've always known that this question was going to be a possibility, and Aeson and I had discussed it on various occasions, going back even as far as before the Games training started. . . .

I face the reporter who asked me the provocative question, keeping my face neutral.

"Look," I say. "I understand your curiosity about my voice, and to be honest, I'm not quite sure what it is, only that I can do some things very well with it. . . . But you need to remember who I am—I'm from Earth, an ordinary girl from Northern Vermont, USA. I am *Gebi*. I am going to be Kassiopei by marriage only. So what you imply makes no sense. It's impossible."

"Yes, but is it possible somehow that the Logos voice manifested on Earth? Manifested in you, maybe even in others?" The female reporter persists, loudly, over the rising noise level in the room.

I shake my head at her, slowly, while at the same time the Palace official coordinator raises both hands and cries out, "One question only! You must step aside! Everyone else, maintain quiet!"

But it's no use. From every direction, media representatives stand up from their seats, begin calling out questions. "Imperial Lady Gwen! Please elaborate! Do you have the divine Voice of Creation?"

"Is your bloodline enhanced?"

"Are you of a particular sacred ethnicity—?"

And then, as the situation grows even more out of control, there are random cries from the back, "Gebi goddess! *Gebi goddess!* You are our new hope—"

Aeson raises his hand and signals to the Imperial Palace coordinator. "Thank you. We're done here."

He then stands up calmly, pulling me with him, and we start to descend the platform from the back, to avoid the media representatives clustering around the podium in the front. At once, our personal guards step in, surrounding Aeson and me as we move to the exit, hearing more shouts behind us. In this moment I come to understand why Aeson insisted that, in addition to his own standard guards, my own personal guards accompany me while still on Palace grounds—this is an event open to the public, and it's to prevent exactly this kind of thing.

"Imperial Lord Aeson! Please, just a moment, wait!"

"But we only had seven questions! We're owed three more! You promised!"

"We still have more questions!"

"Please proceed outside and maintain order. The interview is over," Palace officials respond conclusively.

Even as the noise retreats, Aeson and I escape into a long hallway and hurry back upstairs.

"Are you okay?" Aeson asks me, squeezing my hand.

"Wow . . . yes . . . I think." I look up at him as we walk quickly; his expression is grave.

"I hoped this would not come up," he says. "But unfortunately, there are some public aspects of the media we cannot control—at least not outright."

"Nor should you. You have laws to protect free speech, right?" I ask. "Similar to the democratic countries on Earth?"

Aeson does not reply at once. "In some ways, yes, we do. *Atlantida* is an Imperial Democracy, and we have popularly elected officials in charge of the government. Basic human rights are protected, including free speech—short of treason—and freedom of information. And yet, everything is relative. The Imperial Kassiopei and other rich and powerful entities wield enough influence to curtail some of the freedoms."

"I thought as much. But people still have the right to ask questions and demand true answers."

"Yes. And we always let them—up to a point. Although, right now, the last thing we want is for them—for anyone—to find out certain problematic things that would cause civil unrest and even panic. The nature of your voice is one such thing."

I nod. "I get it. That 'Gebi goddess' crazy cult stuff really scares me. I want nothing to do with it."

We exit the elevator on our own floor.

"Notice how these mostly unaffiliated, lesser venues asked more substantial questions, even blunt ones," Aeson continues, nodding to the guards, who take their places on both sides of the doors of the Imperial Crown Prince's Quarters.

"Yes," I say, as the two of us go inside, closing the doors behind us. "Completely different questions, compared to Hel-Ra and even Tiago. Hard questions, with real-world relevance."

"Exactly."

I take a deep breath. "They even asked about The Rim. . . . Aeson, before we go back to your workroom—in case anyone's still there, even though it's late—I want to remind you about Hedj Kukkait, who's a good person, and I don't want him to get in trouble—"

Standing there in the antechamber I describe once again, in careful words, Hedj Kukkait's secret affiliation to The Rim and how he saved my life in Stage One of the Games because of The Rim's mysterious instructions on my behalf.

Aeson listens as I speak, and his expression remains composed. When I'm done, he simply nods lightly, then takes my hand again, pressing it gently, and pulls me after him.

"I completely understand how this situation with The Rim might still be a problem," I say quietly as we walk. My voice is uncertain as I try to come up with the right balance of words.

"It is definitely complicated," he says, directing me forward.

"And the investigation is ongoing—which makes sense. But— if somehow it gets out who and what Hedj is . . . please don't let him be harmed. Remember when I first told you about him, you said you're not angry at him," I whisper as we go from corridor to room, to another corridor. "Where are we going?"

"And I'm still not angry—far from it," he replies, giving me a quick, curious look, as he stops before one of the many closed-door chambers in the Quarters.

"Okay, thank goodness." I let out a held breath, watching him unlock the door and turn a recessed latch.

"Come," Aeson tells me, as we step into a dark interior. "As I said back then, I'm eternally grateful to Hedj Kukkait for what he did to keep you safe. In fact—"

He flicks on the light, and I see a small room with sparse furnishings and dark walls—so dark in fact, that they appear to be painted *black*. Aeson goes to a small desk with a lacquered ebony surface and slides open a drawer. He takes out something, and shows it to me.

In Aeson's hand is a golden mask.

It's the same featureless mask that I had seen on the TV screens, worn by the anonymous person in black, uttering incendiary words of treason against the Imperial Kassiopei in a digitally modulated, creepy voice.

My eyes widen. . . .

"I was the one who sent Hedj to protect you." Aeson smiles faintly, his burning gaze on me. "I am The Rim."

And then Aeson tells me everything.

"**A**eson! *What the hell!*" I exclaim. "Why? How? Why didn't you tell me?"

"*Im amrevu,*" he says, angling his head slightly as he watches me with a soft expression. "The whole thing was done to *keep you safe.*"

My jaw drops even more.

Aeson pulls up a chair—the same black, tall-backed chair that I now vaguely recall from brief glimpses during The Rim's pirate feeds—and sits down, then points me to a second chair just like it.

"Let me tell you everything now, okay? Here, sit, look at it—" He hands me the golden mask as I obey silently and sit down next to him, shocked into absolute attention.

Aeson leans forward, lets out a held breath, takes in another, flattens one hand against the desk surface. "When I realized there was no longer any question, and you were going to be forced into the Games, I knew I had to act—to do *something*. But there was nothing I could do to help you *directly*. Not with my Father's explicit orders and surveillance. Yes, training you was one thing, but it was not enough. Once you were in the arena, I couldn't sit idly by and watch you get hurt. . . . Unacceptable. And so, I came up with the idea of *disrupting* the live feeds during those critical times when you were in greatest danger. The disruptions were intended to redirect attention from you, if only for a moment, and in so doing, give you a fighting chance."

"Okay. . . ." I shake my head, frowning with the effort of understanding while I turn the heavy golden object in my fingers.

"I thought long and hard in those agonizing days when we began training you," Aeson continues. "I had to come up with the perfect cover for my interference. What could be a better cover than a terror organization, an enemy of the Kassiopei? And then I remembered something else—an old story from the historical archives, of an ancient uprising against the Kassiopei Dynasty, many hundreds of years ago.

"The rebel group called themselves The Rim, based on the notion of the Rim of the Grail, or Ae-Leiterra. There was some kind of political crisis, brought about by yet another cowardly Imperator being reluctant to die—refusing even to go on the Rim mission to properly reinforce the Quantum Shield around Ae-Leiterra. The Imperial inaction resulted in civil protests, violent confrontations, then hard retribution by the authorities. Numerous people were punished by death, after which the victims' families banded together and actively rebelled against the Kassiopei of the time."

"That's intense . . . okay."

"It was; very much so, apparently—" Aeson's fingers drum lightly along the desktop. "So, the idea of this historical group served me well. I started to formulate my plan of action based on The Rim's original ideology. I set up a behavior profile and evolved it forward into the present, to reflect contemporary issues. Then I brought Anu and Gennio in on the clandestine project and assigned them specific tasks."

"Anu and Gennio?" I stare in amazement. "So . . . they were in on it. Anyone else?"

Aeson shakes his head. "No, only those two were allowed into my confidence—not counting Hedj Kukkait, who was contacted later. At first, I considered bringing in at least some of the *daimon*, but decided to keep it tight—the fewer individuals involved, the better secrecy levels we could maintain. Besides, it only took one person to act behind the mask, and two as technical backup."

I make a sound of continued incredulity. "So how in the world did you do it?"

Aeson chuckles. "Anu wrote unique hacker code to bypass Imperial Palace network security from the inside, and Gennio cleverly masked the intrusion into the public feeds and covered our tracks with subtle algorithm changes in routines and Imperial standard security protocols. Once that was done, and insertion point slots readied, the way was clear for us to drop our own feeds into the private network and then auto-propagate them into the greater public system."

"But when did you guys manage to do it? I mean, you were always present when it was happening. Even that first time, right after my dreadful interview with Tiago when we were back in the living room at Phoinios Heights . . . and then during the Games you were in the audience—"

"Everything was prerecorded." Aeson points to the desk and slides open a drawer full of small gadgets that I recognize as memory storage. "I made several hours of these recordings, rambling extensively, speaking at various premeasured and timed lengths, to give us choices of what material to run and when. Short monologues of a few minutes, even a few seconds. Longer ones for up to half an hour. It was rather amusing."

I slap Aeson's wrist lightly. "Not funny!" I admonish him in a gentle tone. "There were some very awful things you said—about yourself, even."

"I know." Aeson stares at me with a serene expression, leaning his head sideways, digging his fingers into his forehead, then trailing them through his mane of pale metallic hair. "That was most amusing of all."

"You were so painfully convincing," I whisper. "Did you mean any of those harsh, horrible things? Because it must take some grain of truth to be so brutally *real*, believable."

His lips barely curve. "I meant a lot of it. Yes, it had to be brutal to be convincing and to deflect any suspicion from us, but it was easy. The Kassiopei *are* stagnant, useless, *dead*. The burden of the centuries has weighed heavily on us. The role we play has somehow devolved. Everything we do—all in all, it makes very little sense now—even if we add in the recent revelations of the ark-ship and the Ghost Moon, so that the significance of some ancient ritual duties comes to light. . . . And then there's the public—the general population that constitutes our societies. All around the globe, people are complacent with ritual and routine, self-isolated by lazy choice, stuck in their own stupid 'quantum bubble.' So, yes, it was easy to channel my honest disgust into some incendiary words."

"Oh, Aeson. . . ."

He looks at me, but now his memories take him into the distance, so that I feel the sea change in him, like a passing squall of world-weary sadness.

"Still not sure what I think about this whole thing," I say with a sigh, hoping to return him to the present. I attempt to keep my expression stern as I look at him, but fail—maybe because *im amrevu's* lapis-blue eyes are so profound and sincere when they again focus on me.

"Gwen, it was complicated. As all of this was happening—" Aeson blinks and rubs his forehead, then resumes—"as we were setting up The Rim entity and all that went with it, prepping the intrusion feeds, the hacker code, I was also thinking in parallel about how else to use The Rim during the Games. I paid a lot of attention to the top Contenders during the Pre-Games Trials, because I wanted to find someone trustworthy enough to recruit on your behalf— someone who was both a powerful Contender, and someone honorable, who would agree to help you in advance, before the Games even started. This individual was to be your secret protector when needed, ready to step in and rescue you at my instructions. It became clear to me that, in this year's batch, the only celebrity player with the decent character traits I was looking for was Hedj."

"I see."

"And so I reached out to him, discreetly. We met, I liked what I saw, and brought him into our secret arrangement. I provided a special ring for him with the tiny golden mask etched inside a secret compartment, to be worn in the Games, which also had a hidden code receiver. The receiver would activate remotely at my command, opening a compartment in the ring, which would in turn signal to him that his assistance was needed—to hurry and find you."

"Wow, yes . . . he showed me that ring very carefully," I say. "That's how I knew to trust him. It definitely worked, having the mask symbol inside."

Aeson nods. "I made that ring myself by retrofitting an existing gold band. Gennio added the micro tech receiver, a secret compartment, and I made the mask etching—everything was done in-house with existing materials, in order to maintain secrecy. And so, with Hedj now working for me, everything was set. We were ready to implement."

I make an amused sound. "It's amazing you found the time to do all this, with everything else happening—Sorry, go on."

"The first time The Rim made its appearance was before the Games," he continues. "We planned it as a test run. Gennio and Anu set up an algorithm that cut into the live feeds at an optimal time to see if we could maintain control of the transmission for a certain length before they tried to shut us down. It succeeded perfectly, and we stayed on air just as long as we hoped. It was also a way for me to set up the public's awareness of The Rim, plant certain expectations, and also test the strength of the Imperial security response protocols. That way, when the actual Games feeds began, we could enter seamlessly at any point and have the predicted effect."

I think hard, trying to remember when exactly The Rim "broke in" during the Games. Now that I know the true motive, it does make sense that the few times it happened, those instances were kind of pivotal for *me*. They were timely interruptions and distractions, giving me a chance to act and probably keeping me alive.

"Thank you, Aeson," I say with all my heart. "I should probably say something to you about withholding important things from me, but in this case, you had a good reason, and I can't fault you at all. So it seems that I keep finding out more and more ways in which you manage to always help me."

"Always," he says softly. "It is what I intend to do for as long as I breathe."

My heart fills with emotion. . . .

"But, my sweetly cunning Imperial Lord—if you ever lie to me or deceive me in a big way again, for whatever reason, I am going to whip your butt," I say with a growing smile.

We linger in that small black room for a few more minutes, as Aeson tells me some other amusing details of how he recorded The Rim's speeches, and how the two Aides helped broadcast them at the appropriate moments.

"I had a small tap-code sequence generator installed on my personal unit," Aeson says. "Whenever I felt it was time to help you, I secretly entered a numerical code command on my wrist that was transmitted to either Anu or Gennio, based on proximity. They in turn initialized each Rim intrusion sequence based on the feed duration values I specified. Similarly, I transmitted code commands to Hedj Kukkait."

"You are so devious that you scare me," I taunt him, running my fingers against his cheek.

Aeson chuckles, leaning into my touch.

"Where did you get this mask?" I point to the golden metallic thing that I've set down on the desktop.

"I found it," he says. "Somewhere in the lower levels of the Imperial Poseidon Museum archives storage, as part of a dusty, half-forgotten collection. Then I had someone discreetly retrieve it for me, through an untraceable sequence of third parties."

"Looks kind of cool, very antique, and possibly expensive, if it's a genuine artifact."

"I'm sure it is, and the museum in question is probably not too happy at the loss—if they're even aware of it. First, they'd have to draw a connection between The Rim pirate broadcast and then recognize that this thing is not a replica. A few antiquities scholars would know enough to investigate the original and find it missing from storage."

"Oh dear," I say. "You could've used a cheap costume mask instead of going to all that trouble, not to mention stealing an original."

"True," he says with a smile. "But it was actually easier to cover our tracks this way, because the item is both completely unknown and unique—same as Hedj Kukkait's ring. Meanwhile, a replica or even a dissimilar mask made to my specifications or purchased on the market could be potentially traceable. I wanted to give The Rim a certain level of realism and gravitas by using an actual artifact of the period. And since the Imperial Kassiopei owns that particular collection, I was stealing from myself."

I laugh. "So what happens now? Will The Rim be permanently retired in anonymity—cast back into antiquity storage at the museum and ultimately forgotten—now that you no longer need it?"

Aeson stands up and puts the mask back inside the desk drawer, locking it.

"It might still be useful at some point," he says. "Besides, *this* is the most secure and safest place for my secrets to reside. Not the museum vault, not Phoinios Heights, but here, in plain sight, right under their noses. Unknown to my Father, I had this room secretly retrofitted with an additional super-layer of security. Anu and Gennio did some masterful work, so that everything here looks and *tests* innocuous, but at the same time is perfectly shielded from Imperial Palace staff, nano-cams, and all other spy tech intrusions. For now, this is where all of The Rim paraphernalia will remain in hiding."

Chapter 32

I go to bed that night strangely comforted by the revelations of The Rim, despite a difficult, stressful day of media interviews behind us. It's as though yet another complicated chapter of my life has come to a gentle close, and once again Aeson is the one who eased my burden.

Ah, my sweet, sweet amrevu. . . .

The next morning is Green Ghost Moon 7, so there are just three days to go before my first official Bridal event, scheduled on Green Ghost Moon 10.

Gracie knows that her fourteenth Earth birthday is going to be celebrated in a big way. I told her it's *her* party just as much as it is my first formal host function to entertain the Ladies of the Court.

The Venerable Therutat made no protest at my combined choice of festivity, so everything has been approved. The invitations go out today, and my task is to oversee the guest list, make my choices in regard to the menu, theme, decorations, and any other particulars of the special *dea* meal. To help me with these tasks, at some point today I will be meeting with Consul Denu and various Palace staff. In addition, Manala and a few of my friends will drop in to give suggestions and advice.

At the same time, I'm supposed to hear back from the Games officials with a status update about the ongoing process of my Champion wish fulfillment. It's the norm for Champions to expect final results in several days—usually within the first week post-Games, depending on the complexity of their wishes. Based on past examples, however, some particularly involved wishes can take up to a few weeks, a month, or even longer.

Despite all the small, stress-inducing details, the day goes by uneventfully. There isn't even all that much fallout from the media interviews of the previous day. The feeds remain chaotically similar, and I am mostly praised for my speaking efforts, while my subdued and dignified answers together with Aeson's seem to have pleased everyone, overall.

I hear back from Games officials before noon, and apparently my Champion wishes are being handled, and all is going well with the various arrangements. Chihar Agwath, Lolu Eetatu, Tuar Momet, Zaap Guvai, Sofia Veforoi—and yes, even Fawzi Boto—are all getting some unexpected benefits from me.

Lolu already had her wish for her mother's medical treatment granted by Aeson, but I'm adding in some financial assistance in honor of her fallen brother Khadram.... Tuar Momet's pardon request has been formally filed in the courts, and with my official endorsement behind it, it is guaranteed to succeed.... Zaap Guvai's posthumous wish of a nature preserve is in its first stages, with a land purchase in the Northern Sesemet Province completed in my name.... Sofia Veforoi's wish involves another land purchase, this one on behalf of her impoverished extended family, east of the Great Nacarat Plateau.... Fawzi Boto's wish is the purchase of a Poseidon landmark, the Yatet Opera House, home of the prestigious *Imperial Atlantida Opera Company*, and the opera company itself.

Chihar's wish to purchase the Committee of Education in his native city Tatenen in the Western Xeneret Province is the most complicated one and is taking a bit longer, according to the Games office. Only Citizens may vote on the Committee, the voting seats are purchased by the highest bidder, and the purchase price determines the voting influence of each seat. Since Chihar is not a Citizen, the recommended solution is for me to buy either one very influential seat or the entire Committee, and have Chihar occupy the most influential seat as my designated representative and vote in my name by proxy—which in reality would mean that he can vote however he likes.

I consider the details, send in my responses to the Games officials, and expect the next status update in a day or two. Then I hang out with Aeson, Erita, and Oalla as they work, until my various afternoon meetings.

Consul Denu arrives promptly at second hour of Khe and helps me choose a simple, elegant theme for the Ladies of the Court Bridal function—blue and silver, clouds and sky.

"Wouldn't clouds be considered some kind of bad luck?" I ask as we brainstorm ideas.

"Ah, but it is quite the opposite entirely," he says, raising his lapis-tinted brows for emphasis. "Brides are expected to choose something dark and gloomy, and it will result in good fortune for the Wedding and the married life that follows."

"I see. In that case, how about an erupting volcano table centerpiece with burning orange lava flow around the hall perimeter?" I giggle. "The Ladies can roast the Atlantean equivalent of marshmallows on long *kipt* sticks over the flames."

But the Consul wags one finger at me with the sort of mixture of amusement and polite, courtly admonishment that he alone can pull off.

"I recommend you select the Lapis Lazuli Grand Chamber for the reception," he tells me. "It is large, but not overwhelming, easily transformed with hanging decorations—in this case puffy clouds and airy garlands of gauze and crystals suspended from fine chains and tassels to simulate droplets of rain—and its location on the ground floor will serve you well in case you would like to extend the party overflow outdoors into the gardens of the Imperial Palace park."

"That sounds wonderful," I say, happy to concede to his taste.

"Now, as far as the menu, here are the options, and feel free to choose any of these popular multi-course sample menus we've brought for your consideration—" and the Consul calls forth one of the staff, a favorite Imperial chef, who in turn points out to me several lists and image galleries of exquisite and decadent Atlantean cuisine on his digital tablet.

"This fresh seasonal fruit and pastry sculpture gallery is always a Court favorite, with delightful bite-size portions in pleasing shapes and colors," the Imperial chef says, bowing low before me as he offers me the tablet for a closer look. "Also, the beverage fountains of *aeojir* and *lvikao* are customary, with an open flowing 'beverage river' of bubbling *qvaali* running in an extended vessel the entire length of the buffet table—"

I nod with overwhelmed amazement and agree to everything he suggests. I also make a special request for an Atlantean equivalent of an Earth-style birthday cake to surprise Gracie.

The chef listens attentively to my descriptions of cake layers and sweet creamy frosting and possible candles. And he promises to produce a worthy culinary specimen.

Oh boy. . . . This could turn out to be either amazing or a disaster.

While I think about that potentially weird Atlantean birthday cake, and how finicky eater Gracie might react, the chef finishes recording my final menu choices and steps back with another bow.

"Very well now," Consul Denu resumes. "As far as the Ladies Guest List—"

"I don't really know anyone." I bite my lip, thinking of the unpleasant young girls whom Manala and I encountered that first time walking in the gardens of the Palace. *Please, not Lady Tiri.*

Consul Denu pauses to pick up a different tablet from an assistant. He taps the screen and shows me a preexisting master list of noble and influential invitees. "The final choice is always yours, my dear Imperial Lady Gwen. But in order to avoid any undue social unpleasantness in the future, I strongly recommend you invite every one of these ranking females. Do take a look. . . ."

I take the tablet and scroll down the long list of mostly unfamiliar names and titles, vaguely recognizing some of them being mentioned in passing by Aeson or maybe Manala. Sure enough, Lady Tirinea Fuorai is prominent on the list, together with the rest of her entourage. I see the names of Lady Zua Kainaat, Lady Hathora Sekru, Lady Irana Nokut.

There are also a number of other, older Ladies, ranging from young to youthfully mature, middle-aged to elderly—women whose names, noble ranks, and social positions are now explained to me in clever, memorable detail by Consul Denu.

"This Dame is a necessary fixture," he says, pointing to one specific name then another. "She is required in order to prevent hostilities between *that* one and *this* lady and her entire family here. . . . Now *this* young matron would feel terribly confused if she were not invited and would complain to her father, who sits on the Imperial Executive Council. As for this young lady, she is a true menace, I admit, and is known to create gossip circles that have brought their victims to tears. However, she also owns a great parcel of choice land in a western province that *this* particular well-connected lady would love to buy, and expects to discuss the transaction with her secretly during the Bridal event—as she has told me repeatedly this week. . . . Now, *these* two wealthy young sisters are both firmly in Middle Court, but would love to make the transition to High Court by one of them marrying an impoverished but high-ranking nobleman who happens to be the brother of *this* young lady here, who must be convinced about the value of the match. . . ."

Dear God in heaven! Am I going to be in an Atlantean version of a Jane Austen ballroom nightmare?

My expression must reflect the terror I'm feeling at the notion of dealing with these people and their court intrigues and social complexities, because Consul Denu pauses for a moment and says soothingly, "My dear, you mustn't worry. All of these people and their relationships are deeply ingrained and long-standing—in some cases having developed over generations. You will come to learn them easily, with time—and be amused by it, for the most part, and frustrated quite often. It is perfectly normal to be overwhelmed."

"It is?" I shiver.

He nods reassuringly. "For now, all you need to do is simply *invite them*, and it will all take care of itself. The Court is a self-contained living entity, a unified beast of three distinct tiers, of many minds and mores, entwined together like a ball of very expensive and very temperamental yarn. The Ladies, young and old, will chat and gossip and exclaim and complain and observe you eagerly as their future Imperatris. Simply let them. As the Imperial Consort you will be inheriting the Court and all that goes with it— an exotic menagerie to care for, at your leisure."

"That's what I'm afraid of," I mutter. "A menagerie of snotty, superior, vicious, spoiled girls who hate the Gebi Bride and would love nothing more than to rip me apart in every sense of the word. What am I going to do with them?"

"No need to do anything, my dear Imperial Lady Gwen. Simply be yourself," says the Consul. "After all, you are an actual Games Champion. If anything, they will respect that about you—even fear you. This is your opportunity to show yourself to them in your preferred light."

I release a held breath. "I understand. And fine, invite them all, if we have to. But to compensate for all that obnoxiousness, I am inviting all my friends. Oh, and my sister's having a birthday, so this is really her day as much as it is mine."

Consul Denu smiles at me. "A fair compromise indeed. Certainly, you might want to think some more on this List, take your time, and add your preferred friends to it. Don't forget, you will have prominent allies there to help you, in the form of the Venerable Therutat Nuudri, First Priestess of Amrevet-Ra, and the Sovereign Lady herself, the incomparable Imperatris Devora Kassiopei. Tradition dictates that both of them shall grace the event with their attendance. Now, whenever you're ready, simply send the Guest List to me later tonight, preferably by *niktos* meal but no later than tenth hour, and I will make sure the formal invitations go out in timely fashion."

"Okay."

"Very well." With one bejeweled finger he swipes at the screen of the tablet in my hand, and motions for me to set it aside for the time being. "And now, on to the next item on our agenda. A vital selection lies before you, my dear—what shall you wear?"

We take another hour to discuss outfit choices, and I look at various fashion selections that are brought in by Consul Denu's staff. They explain to me that the dress code at this particular Bridal event will be semi-formal, and the flowing, simpler designs reflect this.

At some point Manala arrives with her enormous black cat Khemji—who is immediately released from his ridiculous harness and given free rein of the Imperial Crown Prince's Quarters—to the alarmed looks of everyone present, especially the attending staff. Then Hasmik and Chiyoko show up, coming straight from work— Hasmik from her defense textiles manufacturing job in the warehouse district of Nuabuut, south of Poseidon city center, and Chiyoko from her Fleet assignment at the Poseidon Fleet HQ technical division downtown. We start to examine and admire all the glittering, expensive fabrics in rich colors, while Khemji attempts to shred some ribbons hanging off a chair and then bats around a tiny little pearl button all over the floor of the chamber, occasionally slamming into walls.

Hasmik, whose textiles knowledge is now extensive, comments about various textures and makes me look more closely at the elegant threads, run my fingers over the materials. "Look, how fine this one is, Gwen-*janik*. It shimmers when you fold it. Sixty percent natural plant fiber reinforced with metal alloy. Very high thread count on this one—"

"Oh, oh! Gwen, you should wear this one!" Manala interrupts, as the assistants present the next outfit, a long-sleeved, close-fitting cream dress of only a single layer, embroidered in fine metallic lavender filaments. It has a scoop neckline, a fitted waist, and its narrow sheath skirt is slightly higher than ankle-length, so I would need to wear some stunning shoes to go along with it.

"That's beautiful, I suppose," I whisper, peering closer to stroke the silken fabric.

Chiyoko agrees with me, and Hasmik gives her professional seal of approval.

Consul Denu nods appreciatively.

"Then it's all set," I say with relief.

"Now the shoes," Chiyoko whispers with awe.

And the parade of shoe fashions begins.

When all is settled and done, I have chosen a lovely outfit, a nice pair of low-heeled pumps, and matching jewelry and accessories. Consul Denu and his young assistant, Kem, will arrive on the day of the event to do my Face Paints and hair.

"What about Gracie" I ask. "Should she have a special birthday outfit too?"

"It would be a delight to assist your sister with her own outfit selection," Consul Denu says. "Where is the young lady?"

"Apparently running late," I say, then check my wrist comm for messages. "Gracie said she was coming, so—"

"There she is!" Manala exclaims, rising from her spot on the long sofa, now covered with endless outfits in plastic sleeves, to make room for Gracie.

My sister arrives in a hurry, breathing fast and dressed in her everyday Fleet grey uniform. "Sorry . . ." she pants, wiping her forehead with the back of her hand. "Ran all the way from the airfield . . . before that, was parking my shuttle . . . had a crazy flight day up in orbit, Gee Two. . . . Get this—our team was assigned to do a flight sequence through the *you-know-what* object. . . ."

Gracie got to fly through the Ghost Moon! My chest fills with pride at the thought of my baby sister performing complex, possibly solo flight maneuvers in space.

"Aha. . . . No problem. You made it just in time." I pat Gracie on the back with a smile.

She takes one look at the fashion spread and squeals. Hasmik and Chiyoko giggle at Gracie's reaction, Manala claps her hands together with excitement, and then we all get to work, choosing her birthday dress.

By evening, all my event planning related to the Court Ladies Bridal thingamajig is done. Gracie has a lovely dress to wear for her birthday. Furthermore, suitable attractive outfits have been selected for all my invited female friends who are able to attend the event.

I send the final Guest List with my additions to Consul Denu, who sets everything in motion, and then Aeson, our friends, family, and I enjoy a casual evening and a lighthearted *niktos* meal. During our meal, Khemji runs around, loose and free, under our feet, and manages to be as well-behaved (and blessedly gas-free) as Manala can make him. As a highlight of the night, Gordie shows up with a box of *ecurami*—impossibly delicious dessert puffs filled with creamy goodness that he discovered at his workplace. *Ecurami* is a local specialty that's supposedly flash-baked in special ultra-hot ovens and sold only in the food court of the Heri Agriculture HQ industrial complex. And then, just before bedtime, the Imperatris herself drops by to check up on us briefly, bringing the night to a peaceful conclusion.

The next day and the following, Green Ghost Moon 8 and 9, pretty much nothing happens but routine, for which I'm supremely grateful. It's good to do nothing for a change, except look at the Bridal event RSVPs that start to come in almost immediately and continue throughout the day and the next.

On both those days, Aeson and I take advantage of the continuing lull and respite in our schedule to do some light exercise workouts in the mornings—my first workouts since the training and the Games. I am surprised to find that I've recovered sufficiently and I'm still in decent enough shape, despite the grueling ordeal of the Games, that my slightly sore body doesn't hurt, and the exercise feels good. Afterwards, a refreshing swim in the enclosed indoor pool in the Imperial Crown Prince's Quarters to conclude our workout brings another secret pleasure. . . . That's when I get to watch Aeson's sleek, bronzed body fly next to me through the sparkling water as we race each other from one end of the pool to the other. . . .

At some point Aeson has another meeting with Darumet Azai, the First Priest of Amrevet-Ra, in regard to Bridegroom matters. Meanwhile I take a leisurely walk with Manala in the Palace gardens below, discussing our brothers, Atlantean insects, flowers, and Khemji's regurgitated furballs.

I try to maintain this relaxed state, even though the official RSVPs from the numerous invited Ladies of the Court continue to pour in, up to the last minute, and it seems that *everyone* is coming.

And then Green Ghost Moon 10 arrives, and things get intense once again.

Chapter 33

The Ladies of the Court Bridal extravaganza is scheduled for first hour of Khe. Aeson will be demonstrably absent and out of sight for most of the day, together with any other males of our acquaintance, since this is supposed to be a women-only affair.

I wake up early, ridiculously nervous, and see my Bridegroom only briefly for *eos* bread. Aeson gives me a soulful, lingering kiss—and a playful squeeze on my behind, when no one else is looking—then remains in the workroom with Anu and Gennio. He watches me with an amused look as I wave goodbye dramatically and shut the door of the workroom, returning to my own side of the Quarters.

Then I spend the morning hours doing horrendous spa and beauty treatments with the assistance of my maid Aranit and other servants, followed by a visit from Consul Denu and Kem, his young assistant.

Together they transform me into a glamorous *someone* I am not—or possibly someone I don't quite recognize. The expensive, form-fitting dress of amazing, silky fabric hugs my every curve. . . . My hair is styled in an intricate updo involving garlands of pale crystals in various shades of blue and lavender, to echo both the metallic threads on my dress and the theme decor of the Lapis Lazuli Grand Chamber that has been readied for the Bridal event over the past couple of days (yes, I visited it the night before and know that it is spectacular beyond my wildest expectations).

Meanwhile, Gracie, the Birthday Girl herself—who's arrived earlier, and has been watching me undergo the torture for the sake of beauty—gets her own makeover and puts on her chosen dress in light blue with golden trim. Both of us then get to choose fabulous, very expensive, very antique looking jewelry from a mini-chest sent over by the Imperatris.

"Happy Birthday, Gee Four!" I say, grinning at my now fourteen-year-old baby sister who is not such a baby any more, but looks like an elegant and lovely young woman, with a somewhat severe upswept hairstyle and subtle, classy makeup. "I'd kiss you but we've both just had the *noohd* painted on our lips, so it's best to not disturb the masterpiece."

"Oh, yeah," Gracie says with a shy smile. "We look good, don't we?"

"Amazing."

I place my hands on Gracie's shoulders and just stand there, holding her at arm's length.

"Mom . . ." I whisper. "She would be so proud of you."

Gracie winces slightly at the mention of our Mom, but does not break down—which is another confirmation of the fact that she is no longer the little girl I once knew. "Both of us," she amends. "Proud of *both* of us."

I nod and try not to bite my freshly *noohd*-covered lips.

"You are both delightfully ready to attend this proper Court function, my dears," Consul Denu says, examining us with a look of satisfaction from the distance of his directorial chair, while Kem puts away his brushes and stacks the Face Paints back in the boxes, and other servants and assistants straighten the room.

"Thank you so much, Consul Denu," Gracie says, turning to him warmly.

I echo her words with a heart full of gratitude.

Consul Denu stands up and inclines his head to both of us in an impeccable courtly bow, managing a unique combination of affection and dignity.

"Alas, your humble servant must depart. I must leave you now to your enviable female adventure."

And on that note, Consul Denu and the attendants exit the room, leaving us to ourselves.

Minutes later, Gracie and I leave the Imperial Prince's Quarters, bypassing Aeson's living area and going roundabout through chambers and corridors along the perimeter, in order to emerge in the antechamber and get outside without encountering the Prince or any other males. My four personal guards and Tuar wait in the exterior corridor (alongside Aeson's standard six guards), ready to escort us to this yet another very public event, and we all pretend not to see each other in a silly, superstitious kind of way.

We take the elevators to the ground floor, then walk through the network of palace corridors to the Lapis Lazuli Grand Chamber, hearing the noise of the many women's voices from a distance, the high-pitched giggles, the laughter, the chatter. . . .

God help us, I think, darting a tense look at Gracie, as we approach the gathering crowd of estrogen and expensive perfume. Our security guards fall back, leaving just the two of us. We immediately slip into a designated side corridor that leads to the Chamber through a separate door.

"We're supposed to make an entrance," I whisper to Gracie. "Don't let them see us yet! We have to use this door, but first we wait a little, since we're early. It's not quite first hour. Let them keep coming. . . ."

"Okay," Gracie replies in my ear, looking just a tiny bit nervous.

And so we stand together in a small nook near a hidden doorway, next to a solemn Palace servant who gives us a bow then returns to his task of attending or guarding this particular little entrance.

From our secluded spot, we can eavesdrop on the arrivals and, judging by the waves of voices and the swells of noise at the main doors, we can tell whenever some particularly prominent lady makes her appearance.

In addition to all the unfamiliar nobility, our friends are supposed to be there too, arriving separately, and I strain to catch familiar voices. *Is that Laronda I hear, with Hasmik and Dawn? Possibly.* They promised to be here, and they all had gorgeous outfits delivered to them. Yes, even Brie, who said she was definitely coming. And Oalla and Erita both reassured me that they wouldn't miss it for the world. . . .

At first hour of Khe, precisely on time, the Venerable Therutat arrives, cutting a swath of silence around her as the chattering ladies are brought in line before her undeniable authority. Only after she's passed them and entered the grand chamber does the chatter resume near the entrance. Even so, we can still hear nervous giggles and awed references to "The Venerable One."

Gracie's eyes widen. Even my sister has been informed about the holy terror that is the First Priestess of Amrevet-Ra. . . .

A few minutes later, we hear another respectful drop in sound, and this time the Imperial Palace servants formally announce the arrival of the Archaeona Imperatris.

That's our cue.

"Okay, Gracie," I whisper as my heartbeat speeds up. "Count to thirty, slowly, and then we're going in."

I enter the Lapis Lazuli Grand Chamber through the tiny side door, with Gracie a few steps behind me, emerging at the rear of the great hall. Our entryway is in fact a part of the centerpiece of the back wall, the doorway skillfully framed by a golden Kassiopei sunburst relief, so that it seems we emerge from the sun disk itself.

As soon as I pass the doorway, tripping an invisible sensor, a series of musical tones rises, cascading like a delicate glissando across harp strings. At once the chamber falls into silence.

"The Imperial Bride and Consort, Gwenevere Lark!" a servant announces loudly.

And then, "Sister of the Imperial Bride, Grace Lark!"

Gracie moves in behind me, sheepishly. I don't think she expected this kind of announcement to precede her, but that's part of the birthday surprise—I made sure in advance that Gracie would be acknowledged alongside me.

I step forward, smiling, and pause for effect, as I've been instructed. Immediately and everywhere, the ladies start to dip and curtsey, like waves rolling through the chamber.

And what a chamber it is!

The walls are painted a rich dark lapis lazuli blue, with golden filaments and trim running throughout. A lofty ceiling, and a veined marble floor polished smooth like a mirror. Above and below, both gleam in eggshell white. Slim, long buffet tables circle the perimeter, interspersed with sofas and chairs scattered throughout the space to create casual groupings.

In the very center of the room is a small pond with a fountain, and floral arrangements on sculpted pedestals. The ceiling is covered with airy clouds and garlands of crystal raindrops, descending past ornate light fixtures. The fountain water cascades in bursts of fractured light past additional garlands of similar crystalline decor as that overhead.

My gaze is drawn to that central fountain and its elegant seating area because I know to expect Devora Kassiopei there. As we arranged beforehand, the Imperatris occupies one of several throne-like seats, and the Venerable One is with her, together with a few other prominent older ladies, including Dame Tammuz Akten who is a member of the Imperial Executive Council and the only other important person I recognize.

As was explained to me in advance, this spot of honor is designated especially for the most elderly females of the Court—and indeed, youthful, middle-aged Devora is by far the youngest of them all. These noble elders may sit at leisure all throughout the event, having earned their permanent place next to the Imperatris. Meanwhile everyone else is obligated to circulate. The younger dames and ladies are permitted to occupy any other available seating around the room but must rise to curtsey or simply stand, if the ceremony calls for it.

As a result, everywhere else around the chamber the invited ladies mingle in ever-changing groupings, flowing with the crowds. I see elegant attire suitable for a semi-formal afternoon, and in some cases slight excess, where certain young ladies overdressed just a tiny bit, to rival my own outfit, and *more.* . . .

Not that I care personally, but the thought does cross my mind that, as the Hostess, *I'm* supposed to be the best-dressed one here—with the possible exception of the Imperatris—and any attempt to "outdo" me in that department is a subtle insult.

But all those impressions happen in the blink of an eye, because as the Imperial Bride and Hostess I have a traditional role to play.

I head directly toward the Imperatris, past deeply curtseying ladies, trying not to look at any of them too closely yet, with Gracie trailing after me.

"My Sovereign Lady Devora," I say, stopping before her and giving her a proper curtsey of my own. "I am honored by your presence at my Bridal Court."

"My dear Gwen," the Imperatris replies with warmth. "I am greatly pleased with your Hospitality. Everything is beautifully done. Please, proceed."

Next, I turn to Therutat and repeat a variation of this same traditional greeting. The tiny old priestess, dressed in her usual robes, sharply watches my every move, then nods to me. "Very lovely indeed, Imperial Lady Gwen. Please, do proceed."

I repeat my greeting to the other ranking elderly ladies in this grouping, all whom I barely know. When I approach her, Dame Tammuz gives me an encouraging smile. Behind me, Gracie simply curtsies to everyone, moving a little stiffly and clutching her skirt with almost shaking fingers.

"We are told it is your Fourteenth Birthday today, according to the Earth calendar," Devora says to Gracie loudly. "As you say on Earth—Happy Birthday!"

"Thank you . . . My Sovereign Lady," Gracie mumbles, as the other ladies look on, most with smiles, except for Therutat, who simply raises her blue-tinted brows.

With that formal part out of the way, my next task is to welcome *everyone else*.

I pick up a small hand-bell from a flower arrangement stand and lift it, ringing it.

The chime is loud and crystalline, and as if everyone's attention is not already on me, they now freeze completely.

"Ladies of Imperial *Atlantida!*" I say, and my resonant voice carries in the silence. "My Bridal Court Opens."

It might seem logical under the circumstances for the Bride to sit in a fancy chair with the Imperatris and other prominent ladies, and have everyone come to *her*. . . . But the tradition for this first Bridal event is different—the Imperial Bride plays the role of gracious Hostess, and is supposed to mingle with the guests.

At this point Gracie has to stay behind—which she does, happy to keep out of the way—as instructed by the authoritative claw-finger of the Venerable Therutat pointing her to a chair nearby.

Meanwhile, I put on a friendly face and start moving around the room, this time pausing to acknowledge individually the various ladies present. They, in turn, are supposed to curtsey to me and introduce themselves by their name and rank and—if we're already acquainted—possibly exchange a few polite words. The process is more grueling than I thought—at the same time both stressful and tedious. I try to follow the guidance of Consul Denu, who advised me not to try too hard to remember the details of name and rank for now, merely nod and smile.

The first group of ladies I approach, just on the other side of the fountain, is full of young faces. They sink into a curtsey as one, then start rising and offering me their designations. As for their expressions, they are a wide mix of everything I can imagine—deferential, curious, suspicious, open, judgmental, eager, blank, friendly, condescending, even envious. . . .

"Lady Carilla Oruvi, of the House Oruvi of the Eastern Vadat Province, eleventh generation, presently in Low Court. . . ."

I recall the noble distinctions between the three levels of the Imperial Court that Consul Denu explained to me in painstaking detail. Low Court is for noble houses of at least *one* to *nineteen* generations of nobility. Middle Court is for nobility of *twenty* to *forty-nine* generations. High Court is for *fifty* noble generations and higher.

"Very nice to meet you, Lady Carilla," I say, glancing kindly into a pair of wide, nervous brown eyes. Then I move on to the next.

"Lady Gudun Yator, of the House Yator . . . sixteenth generation. . . ." A friendly teen girl smiles easily at me.

"Lovely to meet you, Lady Gudun."

"Lady Iskandrat Suriner . . . thirty-eighth generation, Middle Court. . . ." A slightly older one gives me a cool smile that never reaches her kohl-rimmed eyes.

"A pleasure to meet you," I respond, with equal politeness but feeling less enthusiasm.

This goes on and on. I finish greeting the grouping, and move on to the next, beyond the fountain, and near several decorative pillars. At the same time, I cast a quick glance around the room, looking for anyone familiar, desperate for a glimpse of any of my friends.

There, toward the left side—I finally spy Laronda and Chiyoko, with Hasmik and Dawn slightly behind, speaking with Brie. All of them are dressed to the nines, in their spectacular shiny fabrics, wearing their hair up or otherwise decorated, and sporting beautiful cosmetics. Looks like all my Earth female friends are sticking together—and yes, I suppose I can count Brie as one of them, even if it's an oddball friendship that grew out of forced necessity.

And as I look behind them, I see Princess Manala, exquisite and fragile in her shimmering layered outfit, standing next to Hasmik. Manala's usual nervous and subdued expression is replaced with a look of open wonder as Hasmik is smiling at her and leaning closer with some kind of amusing story. It occurs to me—for once, poor timid Manala does not feel alone in a big gathering. A pang of emotion rises to fill my heart on her behalf. I'm so grateful to Hasmik in that moment that I can cry. . . . Then, just to make me feel even more emotion, Laronda raises one hand and waves at me with a toothy grin. Dawn turns and smiles, giving me a tiny wave with her usual quiet dignity, Chiyoko does likewise, and Brie gives a mocking thumbs-up salute.

Yes, my friends are all here. I don't see Oalla and Erita, but I'm sure they're also somewhere in this huge chamber. . . .

I breathe in relief, knowing that I have a group of complicated, comfortable people to fall back upon—that is, if I ever get a free moment.

I force myself to keep looking around, to scope out the entire room. That's when I see the queen bee herself, Lady Tiri, with several of her retinue, gathered in a central, shining High Court cluster of expensive colorful fabrics not too far from me. Yes, I will have to approach them eventually, but first, several other groupings of unfamiliar ladies await.

I return to my duty and continue mingling.

Among the multitude of new faces and names, I am particularly fascinated to see two elegant and beautiful women in their middle years, both with black hair untouched by golden hair dye but taken up in intricate yet stern coiffures. They stand out as handsome ravens in a sea of gold, wearing little jewelry, and their outfits are more subdued than most of the others around them. One of these women in particular, with striking features and an aquiline nose, bears a strong resemblance to someone I know. . . . She curtseys with quiet pride and rises slowly, all the while looking at me with an intelligent, unflinching gaze of very familiar black eyes. Even before she speaks, I realize who she is. . . .

"First Lady Aduar Vekahat, of the House Vekahat, of the Southern Uru Province, one hundred and ninth generation, High Court." Her voice comes soft and powerful.

I recall that the designation "First Lady" indicates that she is the highest-ranking female of her House. Furthermore, her noble pedigree is very impressive. I had no idea the Vekahat family was such long-standing nobility. . . .

"Very lovely to meet you, First Lady Aduar," I say with a suddenly nervous smile. "Is Xelio Vekahat related to you by any chance? I consider him a friend."

A spark of interest flickers to life in the woman's eyes. "Yes," she says with the tiniest additional warmth. "He is my son. I am pleased you know him."

Then First Lady Vekahat turns to the other brunette woman standing at her side who bears no resemblance to Xel. She is exquisitely beautiful yet somehow frail and docile, with a vacant, lost expression. "May I present my sister-in-law, Lady Ghara Vekahat, widow of the House Vekahat and daughter of the House Deksu that ends without progeny at ninetieth generation, High Court, and is absorbed into House Vekahat."

For just an instant, Lady Ghara does not react, but stares before her, *past* me, into empty space.

"Ghara—" First Lady Aduar prompts her gently.

Lady Ghara blinks—her slate-grey, soulful eyes focusing on me for a moment, like struggling butterflies—before she looks down. She then curtseys and rises, with solemn, perfect form, but does not look at me again. Her voice is barely audible as she repeats her intricate and unusual pedigree, echoing her sister-in-law.

. . . ends without progeny . . . oh my lord. . . . This is Xelio's aunt. She *could* be his deceased cousin Elikara's mother—unless he has other aunts and uncles? No, for some reason I'm certain she's the one.

Elikara was Aeson's first crush in Fleet Cadet School, who died under mysterious circumstances when they were still children.

I try to set aside the unfortunate reminder and greet Lady Ghara with particular kindness.

She stands motionless as I speak, but I suspect she doesn't hear me—whether by choice or due to illness, I don't know. Her gaze remains downcast, as though she is subtly engrossed in something far away. . . .

She must be in an ongoing state of mourning for her daughter, her spouse, and their noble line. That's enough to break anyone.

I had no idea that Elikara was not their only loss. Now I begin to understand that there's something very complicated and disturbing going on in Xelio's extended family. And this blatant display of natural black hair is some kind of statement—or possibly, a rebellion.

As I focus on Lady Ghara Vekahat, First Lady Aduar notices my slight thoughtful pause and gives me an intense look, as though willing me to overlook her sister-in-law's shortcoming.

I leave the two women of the House Vekahat with a nagging sense of sorrow and unrelieved curiosity.

However, a few moments later I'm introduced to a very tall and striking woman with short gilded hair who captures my attention with her subcurrent of humor, warmth, and grace. She wears a long, sparkling dress in an intricate pattern of rich jewel tones that gloriously complement her super dark skin, even as the form-fitting cut of the dress emphasizes her willow-slim figure.

First Lady Kuz Ruo introduces herself as Keruvat's mother, ninety-seventh generation, High Court. At once her joyful smile absolutely melts me.

"My son tells me you are wonderful in every way, My Imperial Lady Gwen," First Lady Kuz says, beaming at me from her considerable stature—it's clear where her son gets his own height. "I can see he is not exaggerating. Our home is open to you, and you must visit immediately. Well, not immediately, because you must deal with all *this*, but you understand. I intend to feed you thoroughly, to make up for the atrocity of the Games."

"Oh, I am so happy to meet you, First Lady Kuz!" I say, trying to hold back a huge grin and an irrepressible urge to hug her, even as she rises from her curtsey and is briefly at eye-level with me.

And then I must move on to the next, less interesting and less familiar lady in line.

Several interminable minutes later, as I make my way along the perimeter of the chamber—having met and smiled at easily over a hundred ladies, young and old; having received forced smiles and eager, genuine ones—I am faced at last with the unpleasantness of dealing with my so-called rival.

Lady Tirinea Fuorai is not to be avoided any longer.

Deep breath, Gwen, deep breath. . . .

I approach their group, feeling my heartbeat start to race. Immediately they all turn to me, with a variety of fixed smiles and curtseys.

Lady Tiri, I notice, is overdressed in a spectacular white dress with exquisite gold beadwork, tight-fitting over her perfect figure, in a style somehow similar to my own. *Did she do this on purpose? Did she somehow find out what I would be wearing and do her best to echo the style?* I've little doubt.

Her metallic gold hair is sculpted into an intricate filigree "haute couture" form on the top of her head, and fine crystals sparkle on chains, cascading down to her swan neck. Her stunning eyes are an unusual green-gold, a color somewhere between hazel and honey, outlined in dramatic darkness of kohl underneath delicate arching brows. Her skin is translucent and pale, and her sensuous full lips are deep rose, glittering in the light.

She is perfect and perfectly *Imperial*, and she knows it. If it hadn't been for me, Aeson would have likely followed his Imperial duty and chosen her as his Bride.

I notice that Lady Tiri is standing next to an older woman who bears a slight family resemblance to her. The woman is dressed in a deep burgundy tunic of many diaphanous layers, and bejeweled with great precious stones along her collar, while her own metallic hair is in a severe netted bun. Her expression is haughty and cool, and she examines me critically.

Lady Tiri takes a step toward me, and lowers herself into the most perfect yet insolent curtsey I've encountered. She rises slowly, then offers the formal greeting, "Lady Tirinea Fuorai, of the House Fuorai, of the Eastern Vadat Province *and* the Eastern Quzakat Province, one hundred and twenty-seventh generation, High Court."

Her words ring with pride and at the same time slither. I notice the slight emphasis she gives the word "and" as though to highlight that her family's land holdings span *two* provinces, not one.

"Very nice to—*see* you again, Lady Tirinea," I say politely, nearly stumbling and saying "*meet* you" because of an overwhelming urge to pretend this is our first encounter. That would be inaccurate, of course, since I met Lady Tiri previously on that first day at the Palace when I was walking in the gardens with

Manala. It would also be taken as a slight, and the last thing I want to do is give her another reason for hostility between us.

Lady Tiri either pretends to overlook my tiny pause or misses it entirely, and her gaze simply cuts into me with antipathy. She then glances to the older woman next to her and says softly, "May I present my venerable mother."

The woman now curtseys in turn, slow and superior, and rises back up with a look of near disdain. "First Lady Vahiz Fuorai," she says loudly, then follows with the same pedigree, except her generation is one hundred and twenty-sixth, being the one previous to her offspring. Since married women take on the noble generation and family name of their spouse, I will not know First Lady Fuorai's birth family name or noble generational rank unless I look it up later.

"A pleasure to meet you, First Lady Vahiz," I say in a careful, neutral voice.

Vahiz Fuorai barely smiles at me, continuing to examine me, head to toe, while her daughter gives me a sardonic fixed smile. *She must hate me for taking Aeson away from her daughter. Both of them hate me.*

I force myself not to rush but to slowly look away and focus on to the next person in their gathering.

Fortunately, this girl with a softly rounded face, pale blue eyes, and river-red clay skin, is Lady Zua Kainaat, one of the milder and least offensive of their group. She offers her designation in a benign tone, and her generation is fifty-fifth, placing her in High Court.

I reply with a pleasantry—even as I continue to feel Lady Tiri's black-hole stare upon me—and I turn to the next person, a tall young woman with tight metallic curls, fierce and heavy dark brows over dark eyes, and bronzed skin. She is the stately Lady Hathora Sekru, who informs me of her lofty seventy-fourth generation.

Next up is Lady Irana Nokut, pretty and slender, with porcelain-pale skin and short straight hair in a stylish cut. At once I flash back to our first meeting when Lady Irana had a little baby *pegasus* with her—trapped in a cage, levitating alongside her as an exotic pet.

I feel a great urge to ask her about the *pegasus*. . . . Is it okay? Does she still have it? But I realize this moment is not the best time to do so, and instead simply give her a polite greeting in reply to her own. She too is fifty-fifth generation High Court nobility.

A few more young ladies, their mothers, sisters, or other maternal relatives, and I'm done with this group and can move on to the next along the chamber perimeter. As I walk away with relief, I can feel the weight of their combined gazes on me, and whispers starting. But for now, I ignore the whole lot of them.

A bout twenty minutes later, I've completed the formal Hostess introductory rounds of the room. I've even endured the silliness of coming up to my friends and having them curtsey awkwardly to me, hold back giggles, and announce their own "ignoble" names. That last part especially is executed by Brie to stunning effect, as she ad libs, "Gabriella Walton, of a dank cornhole in Iowa, the US of A, Planet Earth, no generation and no court. Not a lady either. And if you really wanna know—"

I widen my eyes at her to make her stop, while my lips barely stay fixed in a straight line, quivering from the effort of not laughing, especially with Laronda's own eyes grown so wide now that she's on the verge of bursting.

"Very . . . um . . . lovely to see all of you and . . . I'll be back later—*behave*," I whisper to them and give a warm smile to Manala who simply beams with innocent joy at me. Then I return to the central area near the fountain with the Imperatris, the Venerable Therutat, and the elderly VIPs.

Here I pick up the bell again, and ring it once more. My remaining duty is simple.

"Ladies of Imperial *Atlantida!* I am delighted with all of you and look forward to deepening our acquaintance in the days to come. Thank you all for gracing my Bridal Court. And now it's time for relaxation and refreshments. Please mingle, enjoy the *dea* meal, and your charming company!"

Phew . . . I did it.

I grow silent and watch the chamber come alive as the Ladies are now free to move about, partake of the Imperial festive buffet, and chatter amongst themselves. Devora Kassiopei looks at me with approval while Therutat appears either satisfied or unfazed by my performance—it's hard to tell.

At least the formal part of the event is over.
Now the real battle begins.

Chapter 34

As soon as I end my speech, Gracie rises from her seat near the high-ranking ladies and steps toward me. The Imperatris nods at both of us with a fond smile, recognizing our eagerness to depart this very central spot and join our friends. "Very well done. Now go and enjoy your party," she says to me.

"Thank you, My Sovereign Lady." I curtsey once more, and Gracie echoes me with only a tiny delay.

And then we're free also.

Gracie and I make our way toward our friends. I see them close to one of the long side tables laden with food, attended by Imperial staff who are preparing more. Additional servants appear with large trays of bite-sized delicacies and start circulating around the chamber, offering the delights to all the guests.

Gentle, calming music emanates from live musicians playing stringed instruments in tandem from various nooks along the walls. It creates marvelous harmonies and does not intrude upon the many conversations.

Gracie's birthday cake! I suddenly recall as we continue moving. It's supposed to be brought in a little later. I scan the room in the direction where the servants are supposed to set up the cake station, as planned. Meanwhile I notice many of the ladies giving me subtle looks as soon as I move past them. Now that the formalities are over, they are permitted to stare more overtly at the Imperial Bride.

"Gwen, there you are! And so's our Birthday Girl, look at you both!" Laronda sneaks up behind me. Dawn is with her, mischievously smiling. Laronda is wearing a form-hugging little purple dress and high heels, and Dawn has a similar black number, with a wide Egyptian style gold collar.

"It bears repeating, but you look amazing," Dawn says to me and Gracie. "Even better than I thought when I first saw those dresses."

"You too, gorgeous!" I point to the buffet. "Okay, food?"

"Count me in." Brie approaches, followed by Chiyoko, Manala, and Hasmik.

Did I mention? Brie is dressed in a slinky dark green skirt and glittering top of some kind of micro-sequin fabric, and is sporting five-inch stiletto heels. Her purple-tinted hair is up in a spiral crown of braids, threaded with gold. I've never seen Brie wear a skirt before, and she looks both femme-ethereal and boy-tough at the same time, and the sum effect is kind of fragile and *beautiful.*

For some reason, I've never thought of Brie as beautiful—striking, yes, and definitely provocative—but she really is. And for the first time I'm really seeing it.

"Whatcha staring at, Lark?" she says with a smirk, turning her head sideways.

"You look great, Walton," I say nicely.

She snorts. "And you clean up pretty well yourself. Your little sis too. Pretty family, you make good princesses."

I laugh.

And then I happen to glance to my right and see Lady Tiri approaching, followed by several of her retinue. In fact, Lady Zua is carrying a large plate of appetizers, *on her behalf,* because Tiri turns to take one bite-sized piece and delicately pops it in her mouth without disturbing her perfect lip-gloss. Then, once again showing her back to her friend-turned-lackey, she continues toward me. And in the next moment, she receives a slim fluted chalice with a sparkling drink that is being held by Lady Irana, *on her behalf.*

"Who's that fancy cow?" Brie whispers in my ear.

Hasmik, Dawn, and Laronda exchange curious glances, while Chiyoko stares nervously from me to the approaching group headed by Lady Tiri.

Gracie sees Tiri and immediately frowns. I've told her everything, so she knows enough to dislike Lady Tiri as much as necessary, *on my behalf.* "Is that her?" Gracie asks in a very quiet voice.

I nod.

Gracie looks into my eyes. "This could get ugly."

"I hope not." I barely breathe the words out.

Lady Tiri comes to a stop before us, with a thin, vicious smile. She curtsies again, just barely, and holds her glass like an elegant accessory that matches her outfit, turning it slightly. "My dear Imperial Lady Gwen, may I offer my humble congratulations on such a charming event—especially considering it is your first such Court endeavor. You're going to make a splendid Hostess—with a few more seasons of practice. Naturally we are all delighted with your early effort. Aren't we, my dears?" She glances to her side where Lady Irana inclines her head immediately, and then to the other side where Lady Zua holds the large plate and tries to execute a curtsey at the same time.

"Thank you," I say, looking at Tiri and ignoring her barb clothed in flattery. "Glad you are all enjoying yourselves."

Tiri swirls the deep amber contents of her glass and glances at it negligently, then returns her smiling attention to me. "The selection of refreshments is such a fine art, and these are so very well paired," she continues, taking a delicate sip of her drink and then reaching for a little puff ball from Zua's plate. "Though I would have chosen the *kru* berries instead of *goyro* fruit sauce for the filling, to balance the tang of this pale Northern *qvaali*. Naturally, I would be happy to share the subtleties of my own favorite *dea* banquet recipes when we have the pleasure of your company next time . . . in the gardens perhaps, or at a more intimate meeting with just our nearest and dearest companions. . . ."

I listen to her talk and watch her movements silently, while Gracie and Laronda stare with icy expressions, and the rest of my friends are not sure how to react.

Meanwhile Lady Tiri hands her half-empty glass back to Lady Irana. "Be a dear and refill this, sweetest," she tells her.

Irana nods, then moves away toward the drink fountains. Lady Hathora now steps forward to take her spot at Tiri's side, followed by two other young girls whose names I've forgotten, and who both jostle closer.

"May I offer congratulations on winning the Games of the Atlantis Grail," Lady Hathora says unexpectedly in solid English, looking at me with an expression that bears no sarcasm, just an honest measure of respect. "Being Champion is quite an achievement. It was quite compelling to watch your progress, My

Imperial Lady. And that of your teammates too—congratulations to you, Gabriella Walton."

Hathora turns politely to include Brie in her words.

Brie raises her brows and says nothing for a moment, watching Lady Hathora in a way that's hard to describe, but which is very typical Brie. She gives me a quick side-eye look, then focuses back on Hathora and says only one word, "Thanks."

Am I imagining it, but did Brie just hold back and curb her tongue on my behalf?

"But of course, how could we forget such a thing!" Lady Tiri says at once, loudly inserting herself in the exchange. "My Imperial Lady, your—dare I say, *unique*—performance as a Games Champion has demonstrated that the Earth refugees are quite capable of physical *feats* somewhat comparable to our own. You must forgive me, but I don't make a habit of following the Games— our traditional *Atlantida* Green season pastime tends to be rather coarse and violent, not suitable for some of us of a certain degree of breeding. Truly, gives me a tedious headache and disrupts my nerves, if I ever try to watch—which is the natural downside to refinement."

She pauses, fanning herself gracefully with the palm of her hand, then suddenly focuses on my friends. "Indeed, these must be all your charming Earth friends gathered here—please do introduce them to us. Once again, forgive me if I do not recognize the Champions among them."

And Lady Tiri demonstrably looks around at all of us, this time including everyone in her thin smile.

I keep my breathing even and open my mouth to begin the introductions . . . then suddenly recall from my Protocol lessons that, as the future Imperial Consort, introducing lesser ranking people *to each other* is considered inappropriate, and they are supposed to introduce themselves while I observe their interaction.

Crap! Lady Tiri almost made me break basic Protocol in a stupid way at my first public event. And, judging by her continued mocking expression, *I think she knows exactly what she's doing*, testing me this way, so that later she can gossip and spread word of my social incompetence.

Catching myself before I commit the gaffe, I pause and then gesture with my hand, in an obvious way, to Gracie.

My sister gets the hint, and starts speaking. "Grace Lark," she says in a firm voice. "I am Gwen's sister—sister of the Imperial Bride and Consort."

"How lovely to meet you," Tiri practically coos, then proceeds to give her own pedigreed designation.

She then turns to Brie, who simply stares back at her for several long uncomfortable moments, then finally says, "Gabriella Walton, Earthie, Games Champion. That okay for you?"

Tiri raises one brow, but her smile doesn't change. "Ah, so *you* are the other delightful Champion of this year's Games. How charming."

Brie lets out some kind of stifled snort noise, but seeing my meaningful stare, relents. "Yes, charming. Very, very charming. So much charm coming out of every orifice—"

"Laronda Aimes, Imperial Fleet, second year Cadet Pilot equivalent, from Earth." Laronda interrupts just in time, speaking forcefully, in a cool, dignified voice.

Lady Tiri barely nods to her.

One by one my friends give their names and occupations. Tiri and her entourage listen but don't offer corresponding introductions of their own.

Instead, once poor Chiyoko is done telling them she is a Fleet Cadet, there is now awkward silence.

Chiyoko, incidentally, is wearing a lovely mid-length pale blue dress with gold embroidery that goes really well with her black hair gathered in an elegant upswept hairdo. She has delicate makeup on, and is wearing short dangly pearl earrings and a matching pearl necklace, and she looks great.

But Tiri gives her an up-and-down sweeping glance, and her fastidious expression reflects disdain, particularly when it comes to Chiyoko's flat and sensible blue shoes.

"My dear Imperial Lady Gwen." Lady Tiri turns to me, not deigning to spare Chiyoko even one additional moment of attention. "So, so quaint and charming—all of *this*, and such a lovely farewell to your former station that you've invited all of *them* here. But now of course, your previous life is behind you. And with it, all casual lesser interactions with lesser *entities* formerly of your acquaintance must fall by the wayside. As you come to experience more of Court's finer circles, it will become naturally apparent that in your position you must be particularly discriminating in the kind of company you keep. I believe, the term one uses is *rank-appropriate*."

Seriously? Is she lecturing me?

My lips part, and my mind starts churning with outrage. But before I say anything I will later regret, someone else does it for me. . . .

"Gwen already keeps the best company one can ever hope to have." Manala steps forward, past Hasmik, and looks directly at Tiri. All this time she's been keeping back, almost obscuring herself in Hasmik's shadow. Which is quite a feat, considering that Hasmik—wearing a nice, dark brown dress of pearly sheen fabric with gold thread around the modest collar and ankle-length hem, and matching brown pumps with tiny heels—manages to be the least flashy and most self-effacing of my friends.

At once Lady Tiri turns to her. "Oh! Imperial Princess Manala! I didn't see you there, begging all pardons! How clever of you to be hiding behind this—this *person*—"

"This person's name is Hasmik Tigranian," I say in a voice with an edge. "She just introduced herself moments ago, and she is a dear friend of ours."

"Yes, she is my friend, and I'm not hiding," Manala says, giving Hasmik a quick, intense look. "I just don't want to speak to *anyone else* right now."

This is the closest that Manala has come to uttering a putdown. It's obvious she almost said "you" instead of "anyone else," and intended it for Lady Tiri.

"But of course," Lady Tiri says quickly, recovering herself, and her false smile does not falter. "My dear Imperial Princess, the exquisiteness of your sensibilities has always been admirable. It is what we adore so much about you. So precious that you might find amusement and curiosity in such a connection. I would never presume to interrupt your reveries. Please do continue to indulge them with your new companion—"

"Seriously, the name is Hasmik," Brie says suddenly. "It's not going to bite. You should try saying it. Also, Chiyoko and Laronda. And she's Dawn. D-A-W-N."

Tiri raises one brow and looks at Brie. "Your Earth names are perfectly delightful." And then she ignores Brie and once again directs her focus on me. "As we were saying, this is such a vital part of your experience, my dear Imperial Lady Gwen—the discovery of who your new social circle consists of. Come, let us walk outside through those grand doors into the park and get some fresh air, and we can continue our delightful conversation in privacy—"

"Lady Tiri, some other time," I say coldly. "Thank you for your advice, but I'm going to get something to eat and stay right here, indoors, with my *friends*. You might consider interacting with your friends too. I believe Lady Irana is back with your drink, and Lady Zua is tired of holding your food. Aren't you, Lady Zua?"

Lady Zua appears slightly flustered at my attention, shifts the plate in her fingers and tries to curtsey again, saying, "Oh, no, Imperial Lady Gwen, it is quite all right. . . ."

"No, it's not," I say, and then take the platter away from Lady Zua.

For one moment I consider thrusting the plate directly at Lady Tiri, making her keep it as intended. But then I have a better idea. Still holding the plate, I take a bite-sized, savory canape from it and put it in my mouth. "Oh, this is good," I say, glancing around at everyone, and stop at Gracie. "Here, want to try?"

"Sure," says Gracie, and receives the plate from me. She takes one canape for herself and then hands the plate to Brie. Brie in turn takes two large pieces, stuffs them in her mouth until her cheeks swell, intentionally ugly-chews and smacks her lips loudly, then passes the plate to Laronda.

As Lady Tiri watches with confusion and growing disapproval—and so do Lady Zua, and Lady Hathora, and the others of her entourage, who admittedly show more of an uncertain wonder than censure—my friends continue passing the plate around, taking pieces, until there is nothing left.

Chiyoko gets the last piece, and then pauses, considering what to do next, as her slightly nervous look returns. I smile and take the empty platter from her.

Suddenly a familiar voice sounds behind me.

"Imperial Lady Gwen! My sincere apologies for being so late to your party!"

I turn my head, and it's Oalla Keigeri, and next to her, Erita Qwas.

Both the *astra daimon* are dressed in spectacular outfits. Oalla wears a clinging, rust-orange gown trimmed in metallic silver thread, and six-inch flaming orange block-heels. Her hair is coiled in a twist, and a spiked, bejeweled coronet circles her forehead like a bladed halo.

Erita is wearing a flowing dress of many diaphanous layers, in earth tones of carnelian, sand, sienna, and plum, offset with turquoise trim, and a wide golden belt cinched around her narrow waist, emphasizing her voluptuous curves. She has matching golden ankle boots sporting mid-height curved heels.

"My apologies likewise," Erita says. "We came as fast as we could, straight from an urgent flight mission, but—"

"Yes," Oalla adds, stepping closer past Lady Tiri and her posse, and ignoring them completely. "But first we had to change."

"Oh, no problem!" I say with an immediate sensation of relief and dissipating tension. "Is everything okay?"

Oalla and Erita exchange a swift glance, and then Oalla smiles at me. Instead of answering, she sinks into a graceful, slow curtsey, and then says to me formally, "Lady Oalla Keigeri, of the House Keigeri, of the Eastern Duinaat Province, two hundred and ninety-third generation, High Court."

Holy crap! Oalla is a Lady. And her noble rank is greater than Lady Tiri's!

I had no idea.

And then Erita sinks in a similar curtsey and tells me, "Erita Qwas. Common birth. Honorary Low Court."

I have another startled moment of amazement. Erita is not a member of the nobility, and possibly not even a Citizen. "Honorary Low Court" is a designation given to non-ranking persons admitted to the Imperial Court for a one-time event or on a temporary basis, usually as a guest of a member of the nobility.

In that moment, Lady Tiri's voice sounds, intentionally bored and condescending. "Oh good. Finally, someone who is perfectly suited to hold that plate."

And as we all stare at her, Lady Tiri adds in a commanding voice, with a cool nod at Erita, "Unburden My Imperial Lady—go on, take that thing and dispose of it."

For one terrible moment Erita's expression goes blank, and she freezes. Then, slowly, she moves toward me and takes the empty plate from my hands.

My mouth falls open.

But Oalla immediately grabs the plate from Erita and says, "That's enough, Lady Tirinea Fuorai. This *astra daimon* is not your servant. Whatever game you're playing today ends *now*."

And in the same breath she flicks her wrist and drops the plate, aiming it precisely at Lady Tiri's feet.

The plate shatters with a crash, sending small pieces of whatever glass, porcelain, or stone material it's made of under our feet—but mostly under Lady Tiri's skirt.

"Oh, dear . . ." Oalla says with a tiny smile. "I do believe there's been an accident."

Lady Tiri makes a startled sound and steps back, an indescribable look of horror on her face.

Everyone nearby turns in our direction, and there's a moment of silence. Even the live musicians falter momentarily. At once several Imperial serving staff hurry toward us with concern.

"Oops," Brie says in the resulting lull of sound. And a wicked smile lights up her face.

We all move back, allowing the poor servants to clean up the mess of shards on the polished floor—and yes, I feel *terrible* on their behalf, even though I also feel *great* for a whole different reason. Meanwhile, Lady Tiri stomps her feet and shakes out her skirt, then straightens and glares at Oalla, then at Erita, and even at me.

"That was quite intentional, Lady Oalla. I do believe you threw that thing at me with intent to harm!"

"Oh, please," Brie mutters.

I give Brie a meaningful stare.

But Oalla raises one brow and exchanges a curious look with Erita. "Do you know what she's talking about, Eri? I certainly don't."

"No idea," Erita says in a bland voice. And then adds with a sigh of resignation, "But—I knew I shouldn't have come. . . ."

She glances at me with a quick, sad look and says softly, "Apologies, My Imperial Lady. This whole thing was a bad move. I don't belong here at Court, never have. Probably best if I leave."

"What? No!" I say. "*Erita*, I invited you! I don't understand any of this, but I am so glad you're here!"

Erita smiles at me, then inclines her head.

But in that moment Lady Tiri's petulant voice sounds. "You realize this is quite an outrage! My Imperial Lady Gwen, my physical person has been assaulted at *your* Bridal Court, and this kind of affront to my person is not to be tolerated. I fully expect that you chastise this Lady—who is entirely unworthy of any such designation—for her *violent* actions—" and she indicates with her hand, pointing at Oalla.

Okay, Lady Tiri might be horrible, but she is right about one thing. All of this is on *me*. I'm the Hostess of this event, and as the future Imperatris, I need to have things under control, regardless of blame, or clashing personalities, or overall general bitchiness.

I take a big breath. . . .

"Lady Tiri," I say, fantasizing about *violent* actions indeed—such as choking her—but smiling instead. "I'm not going to chastise anyone at my Bridal Court. Instead, we're all going to enjoy the afternoon. I will happily *forget* the ugly things spoken about my friends, and *you* are going to forget broken plates—"

"That is simply unacceptable, My Imperial Lady Gwen," Tiri interrupts me, narrowing her eyes with fury.

"What is unacceptable is you still yakking at the Imperial Bride," Brie says suddenly. "Also, you've insulted a top-notch Fleet Pilot and *astra daimon*—two of them, actually. They should take you out on the lawn outside and thrash your skinny golden ass. Furthermore, you've just spent the last fifteen minutes trash-talking every single Earthie present here, and making your so-called fancy girlfriends carry your crap for you while you step all over them. If I had another plate, I'd shove it up your—"

"Brie!" I exclaim, in the otherwise shocked, deafening silence all around us.

"All right, okay, sorry." Brie puts up her hands. "But someone had to say it."

"Agreed," I reply in a hard tone, in that exact moment amazed at my own words. "But in this case, it has to be *me*."

I turn back to Lady Tiri—whose jaw has dropped—and my next words are cold iron. "Tirinea Fuorai, you have *displeased* me.

You will leave my Bridal Court today, until further notice. *Dismissed!*"

Holy crap! Did I just say that?

I did.

Absolutely stunned at myself, I stand and watch as Lady Tiri, equally stunned, closes her mouth, frowns, then sinks into a deep curtsey before me. Then, as everyone else watches us, she hastily retreats, leaving the chamber and her "mean girls" posse behind.

Chapter 35

"Spoken like a true future Imperial Consort!" Oalla claps her hands, breaking the silence.

I don't reply immediately, still wondering at myself, thinking about what just happened. My expression must appear a little puzzled as I glance at her and at the others gathered around me—which includes all my friends and the members of Lady Tiri's group.

"Well done, Gee Two!" Gracie whispers near my ear, patting my arm in encouragement. "That was amazing, you really sounded so regal!"

"Not too much?" I ask softly with a tiny delayed twinge of uncertainty.

"Oh, no, that was great!" Laronda says in a pleased voice. "She really had it coming."

"You think?" I try to keep the uncertainty out of my tone, disguising it with humor.

"Hell yeah, and about time!" Brie adds, raising her brows with satisfaction.

Even Chiyoko, Hasmik, and Dawn nod at me with animated gazes, holding back from saying more out of politeness, but I can see the excitement in their eyes. Manala is absolutely beaming as she clutches her skirt with both hands.

"Agreed," Erita says, with a tiny, controlled smile. "It was very appropriate."

And then, as I glance around our loose grouping, I see the faces of Lady Zua, Lady Hathora, and Lady Irana, and they are all looking at me with surprise and . . . *approval*.

In fact, Lady Irana, who still holds the refilled chalice intended for Lady Tiri, looks at me with a tentative smile and suddenly curtsies to me. "My Imperial Lady, may I bring you a glass of something?"

"Oh, goodness," I say, surprised. "Please don't. I can certainly get my own."

"It would be my pleasure, My Imperial Lady."

I consider her genuine expression and let out a breath. "Okay, but just this once. I'll have one of these, some *qvaali*." And then I add, "And only because I appreciate your kindness."

Lady Irana appears more flustered than I expected. She curtsies yet again, then abandons Lady Tiri's glass on the nearest flat surface and hurries to get me my own drink.

Meanwhile, Lady Hathora says, "If I may be permitted to speak frankly, My Imperial Lady Gwen—you had every right to send Lady Tirinea away. She was being overly presumptuous with you. Noble conduct demands we must be in control of our speech and manners, especially at a Court function and before our superiors. It seems that lately Lady Tiri has lost sight of her place, allowing certain indiscretions of *aspiration* to affect her better judgment."

"Thank you, Lady Hathora," I say. "I appreciate your insight."

With a faint smile, Lady Hathora slowly curtseys to me.

I catch Lady Oalla's expression in that moment, and it reflects pride in me and hearty approval.

"Imperial Lady Gwen!"

I turn to look behind me.

The female speaker is Lady Isulat, the Venerable One's young assistant. "Apologies for interrupting, but you are summoned by the Venerable Therutat and the Sovereign Lady Herself—please come at once."

And just like that, all my personal sense of satisfaction flees and is replaced by a racing heartbeat.

"Of course. . . ." I hurry nervously after Lady Isulat, as my friends and the Ladies all around watch with curiosity the continuing development of this drama.

I arrive before the prominent seats of the Imperatris, Therutat, and the ranking older ladies just as they are being served fresh delicacies by several servants with large aromatic trays.

Seeing me, Devora beckons with one hand. Meanwhile, Therutat stares at me unblinking, like a hawk. I have no idea what to think, but judging by her expression alone, I must be in *deep . . . something*.

On no. . . . They heard the whole thing, naturally. And they saw me throw out Lady Tiri.

I execute a stiff curtsey before the Imperatris, not quite meeting her eyes, and at the same time feeling the overbearing weight of the Venerable One's stare. "My Sovereign Lady . . . Venerable Therutat," I mumble.

"My dear Gwen," the Imperatris says mildly. "Is everything all right?"

I look up with surprise, meeting her kind expression.

And then I look over and see the First Priestess watching me.

"Everything is okay—now," I reply. And then I exhale and say, "Unfortunately you heard the confrontation I had with one of the Ladies. I am so sorry, but it was becoming very unpleasant and—and she—I'm sorry, but I just couldn't—the awful things she was saying about everyone, it seems—well, implying in so many words, and yes, *saying*, about so many people, my friends, and—I know it was probably wrong, but I had to make her leave—"

I trail off awkwardly, until Therutat interrupts me in her sharp voice. "You have made a mistake, Imperial Lady Gwen—"

"I know, and I'm so sorry!" I hurry to reply.

"—a mistake you *perpetuate* now." Therutat cuts me off. "It is a mistake of *apologizing*. The Imperial Bride and Consort must never apologize for her actions in public. That is your mistake."

I part my lips in surprise and permit myself to fully meet her gaze. Then I look from her to the Imperatris.

Devora Kassiopei is nodding at me. "Words of wisdom indeed, from the Venerable Therutat," she says, with a smile of gentle amusement. "What you did was fully within your right. Yes, we heard everything, and you were justified in dismissing Lady Tirinea Fuorai—not merely for her malicious insolence toward others, but for being out of line before *your* authority. No one may speak in such a manner to you. In the future, you will know to cut it even shorter before you chastise or dismiss an insufficiently respectful courtier—regardless of their position or pedigree."

"Oh. . . ." I stare, and my eyes slowly widen in relief. "So then—"

"Yes, you did very well," the Imperatris concludes.

And as I glance over at Therutat, I see in amazement—the old woman gives me a tiny, thin-lipped smile.

I have little time to bask in my success, because the Imperatris points toward the spot where Imperial servants have just delivered an amazing multi-layered confectionary masterpiece. "Is that Grace's Birthday cake?" she says with curiosity. "It looks fascinating! In your traditional Earth celebration, what comes next? Goodness, is that something burning on top?"

"Oh, wow, *yes!* Are those real candles? That came out beautifully!" I exclaim, seeing fourteen tall candle tapers—or the Atlantean facsimile—with their tips set on fire on top of the cake. And then I explain to everyone within hearing range about singing the birthday song and blowing out candles, and making a wish.

Devora claps her hands together warmly. "Go on! Hurry back to your sister, so that we can all sing her Birthday!"

I return to my group of friends and lead Gracie over to her cake, followed by everyone.

Gracie puts her hands over her mouth and laughs in delight, seeing the sculpted cake masterpiece up close, with white frosting and swirled Earth roses in pastel colors. "It looks amazing, oh, Gwenie! Looks almost like a wedding cake! So—so fancy!" She glances at me, and I see her eyes glisten with emotion.

"It's supposed to be chocolate on the inside—or chocolate-*like!*" I say. Then I pick up a hand-bell and ring it to get everyone's attention.

"My favorite . . ." Gracie whispers—even as I begin to sing the birthday song, and one by one the Earthies join in, followed by the *astra daimon*. Then, suddenly, everyone else in the room is singing with us. . . .

The Court ladies have no problem echoing the simple tune and words in English. In moments the chamber is filled with a glorious range of tones as some of them automatically start harmonizing with the melody. . . . Then the live musicians join in, accompanying us with their string instruments, and the grand chamber rings with joyful sound.

We end the song, and everyone applauds. Gracie gets to blow out the pseudo-candles—which she manages perfectly—and then cuts the first piece of the cake, revealing the hidden dark layers of cake and rich creamy frosting in multiple shades that truly does resemble Earth chocolate.

Make a wish. . . .

I watch Gracie's suddenly reserved expression and wonder what she wished for.

"Is it good?" I ask as my sister tastes her piece of cake, makes her typical finicky face anticipating the worst, and then opens her eyes wide with amazement and nods at me, expressing pleasure with her eyes. Her reaction is priceless.

But in the next moment, just as there's a peaceful lull in the happy noise, the cake pieces being passed around, the laughter, the oohs and the aahs, and the lively sounds of female chatter—I hear something out of the ordinary.

Something outside.

Sounds and voices come from the distance, just outside the chamber's large exterior doors that open wide into the Imperial Palace park. The party venue spillover to the outside, as planned, is supposed to allow the guests to mingle in the fresh air, if they so choose, and many of the Ladies have taken advantage of the pleasant afternoon breeze.

But for some reason, in that relative quiet, I hear something unusual in the nature of the sound coming from that exterior spillover reception area. Animated voices of the female guests carry on the breeze. Except they're not merely animated but *alarmed.*

And then come the exclamations.

And the screams.

E veryone inside stops doing whatever they're doing and pays attention.

"Whoa! What's going on?" Laronda stares at the faraway open exterior doors.

Brie frowns. "What the hell—"

Dawn and Hasmik stop chewing and set down their cake plates. Chiyoko and Gracie do the same. The other surrounding ladies turn, grow silent and freeze, or start chattering nervously with confusion. Dropped utensils strike and clatter against fine dishes. A few drinking glasses fall on the floor and shatter. . . . At the same time servants and guards hurry to the reception area that's outside. . . . They don't return.

This whole thing takes just seconds.

Behind me, Oalla curses under her breath in *Atlanteo*. She turns to Erita who in turn lurches as if wanting to hurry outside. Then both of them stop in their tracks and stare sharply at each other, and then at *me*, as though considering something.

"What?" I exclaim. "What is it? What's happening?"

Outside the screams and cries and exclamations continue as more and more female voices pick up the alarm.

I whirl behind me to stare and see several Imperial guards rush to surround the Imperatris in a protective circle that includes Therutat and the few ranking ladies with her.

Meanwhile from the other direction, that of the interior doors leading into the hallway and the rest of the Palace, I see my own security guards run into the chamber toward me, with Tuar leading the charge.

"Oh my God, what's happening?" Gracie exclaims, reaching for her waist where a sword or gun holster would normally be attached.

I see Manala put her hand up to her mouth in fear and start trembling, while Hasmik hugs her.

"We should get out of here," Brie hisses, "now! Whatever the hell is going on—"

But for some reason I am fixated on Oalla and Erita. They both have their wrist comms on and are checking holo-streams of data, scanning incoming messages. . . .

"Wait! Oalla, *what is it?*" I say, even as Tuar is now at my side.

"It's not safe, we need to get you out of here, away from the windows and the outside doors," Tuar interrupts in a firm composed voice, placing his hands near my back in a protective circle, and attempting to guide me.

"Damn it, just a second!" I stop him, and then move toward Oalla as she is checking her data feed. "*Oalla*, you know something! Right? *Erita!* Will you please tell me?"

Erita looks up at me and again throws an intense, questioning look at Oalla.

Meanwhile I notice Gracie's wrist comm starts pulsing with data also, and so does Laronda's . . . and a second later, Chiyoko's.

"Fleet communication. We're getting called in," Laronda says loudly, with a frown at me, then at Chiyoko and Gracie.

My jaw drops, and meanwhile a few ladies nearby whimper.

"What is going on?" I cry out in a resonant voice of *power*.

For a split second everyone in my vicinity stops and they all look at me.

Oalla lowers her hand with the wrist personal data unit. "Gwen, I didn't want to spoil your Bridal Court, was delaying the bad news, hoping to put it off for a few more hours, but—something bad has happened."

"What?" I say. "On your flight mission today?"

"Yeah." Erita nods grimly. "In fact, we are getting recalled again. Outside—let's go outside for a moment, we should be able to see it from here."

"What? No, it's not safe out there!" Tuar says. "Not permitted to allow the Imperial Lady to endanger herself."

But Oalla shakes her head. "It's safe enough—for now. Let's all go look at it."

"At what?" Brie says. "Go outside? Are we all cray-cray nuts here?"

But Oalla and Erita both turn quickly and begin walking toward the open exterior doors.

I follow them.

Brie, Gracie, Laronda, and the others—not to mention my protesting security guards—hurry after us.

F resh, cool breeze envelops us as we step outside into the blinding white glare of daylight, emerging into a small courtyard where the reception extends. It is lined with similar buffet tables around the perimeter, decorated with the same extension of the theme of "clouds and rain," with garlands and chandelier crystals suspended from trellis overhangs and branches of nearby trees.

And the courtyard itself and, by extension, the gardens of the park into which it spills, is full of people. These are the noble female guests from my party, and the Imperial Palace staff who had come outside and never returned. Everyone is looking up at the sky, while attempting to shade their eyes with the palms of their hands or sunglasses or other visual filtering devices. Some, who are wearing particularly high-tech sunglasses, are exclaiming and screaming periodically, while the others around them ask nervously what they see.

I squint and look up, shielding my eyes, grateful for the sun shade contact lenses I wore this morning. I see nothing but *whiteness*. And occasionally there might be *flares* of additional whiteness, like painful, blazing light blots in my field of vision.

But I could be wrong.

Yes, my shade lenses are of the highest quality. Even so, they are not sufficient to protect me from the incandescence of Hel, or to give me any visual detail if I attempt to look directly at it. Therefore, I'm unable to see what it is that everyone with the special sunglasses is staring at.

"Crap! Can't see anything!" Next to me my Earth friends are not doing any better in the seeing department.

Oalla takes pity on me and comes to take me by the arm. "Gwen," she begins in a quiet voice, directing me a few steps away from the others, with Erita on my other side. "Here, use this reflection holo-plate." And she calls up a rectangular hologram surface projected from her wrist comm. The rectangle acts like a mirror, so that it reflects the sky, but in a smart way, unlike an ordinary mirror—by minimizing glare and general reflectiveness, and increasing detail contrast.

I stare into the hologram reflection of the sky directly above— even as I hear another wave of exclamations from all around, and peripherally glimpse something, possibly a bright *flash*, which I can almost see out of the corner of my eye—but not quite.

"Turn it a little this way, so that it points straight at Hel," Oalla tells me, proffering her hand closer and allowing me to move her wrist to the side. I turn it to get a slight degree change, so that I'm looking directly at the reflection of Helios.

Oh my God, it looks so weird, seeing Hel like this, in a reflection, and yet "live."

The star is somewhat larger and whiter than Earth's Sol, and seeing it this way really brings that home. It's so different, so alien and cool blue-white. . . .

Out of nowhere, a sharp, existential memory of space vertigo strikes me.

Okay, I remind myself, *it's just another fireball in space.* Just a round, white, fiercely blazing disk, burning against the slightly dimmer white sky. Except, there's definitely some kind of living *movement* around the edges of its corona.

I notice tiny flashes suddenly shooting outward from the disk, silhouetted briefly against the sky, then fading into the general glare. Honestly, I can't really distinguish anything even now, only get an occasional sensation of motion, of blurred edges being weirdly *alive.* . . .

"What is it? It's just too bright, I still can't see!" I glance up at Oalla.

"Give her the blackouts," Erita says. "I left mine behind."

Oalla reaches inside her small clutch and takes out a pair of bulky sunglasses with special ultra-dark shield lenses. She taps them to activate some kind of tech. "This is military grade. Has advanced filtering and smart coating. I set it to blackout mode. Put it on and try again—this time, look directly up."

I put the glasses on, and my world is immediately plunged into darkness. The sky appears night-level black, and Hel is a manageable sphere of pallor, no brighter than a lampshade.

And then I see it. A golden point of light explodes into a flare of extraordinary brightness on Hel's surface. Golden white against bluish white. Tiniest difference in the nature of light. Only a hue variation to create true contrast. Warm against cool. The only way I can even tell this difference is because the visual device I'm using must be set to filter out and separate such hues.

"Okay, I see something. . . . What is it?" I ask. And then, even as I continue to stare, the golden flare—nothing more than a round dot, really—starts to *move* across the face of Hel. It flits like a firefly, swiftly, crazy-swift. And then it stills, but only after passing beyond Hel's corona. It is now silhouetted against the black sky, where it sits, perfectly motionless, a tiny golden star. . . .

Until it flits again, moving sideways, with incredible speed.

The people in the courtyard around me staring up at the sky cry out again.

"Oh, God, what is it?"

My special sunglasses are set to block out most of the light, so I can't see Oalla's face. I can only imagine her expression as she tells me in a grim voice, "Keep looking."

I do. And in the next moment I see another flare on the face of Hel. Another bright golden dot appears out of nowhere. . . . Winking into existence.

People equipped with devices allowing them to see it, scream.

It flits, it moves, it stills. . . . It hangs in silhouette against the sky, far across from where the other dot was, on the opposite side of the Hel disk, where it seems to blend in with the surrounding stars.

Wait, what stars? There can be no stars now; it's daytime, and my night view is a special-filter illusion.

I blink, stare hard, impossibly hard. And my mind finally interprets the true picture.

Not stars—it's all golden dots of light.

Hundreds of them.

They fill the surroundings of Hel's immediate portion of the sky, flitting occasionally, stilling, freezing in place, like a hive of strange fireflies. They could be tiny dots in my retina, or some immeasurably huge objects more than a billion kilometers away.

I open my mouth and forget to breathe, as the cold realization washes over me.

"You see them now," Erita says on the other side of me. "The crazy thing is, they don't look much different than *this*, even when looking at them from the clear vantage point of space just beyond Amrevet's orbit where we flew this morning."

"But they are so impossibly far away," Oalla adds. "They are emerging from our star. Coming out of Helios itself."

"We first learned about it this morning," Erita says. "The initial alarm call sounded at tenth hour, fifty-three daydreams of Ra. Original signal source was indeed Helios. The innermost planet circling Hel is Rah, so the signal was routed directly from the Rah Station's sweeper sensors into the SPC's alarm network. Interior Hel system patrols confirmed it. And then we confirmed it visually during the local orbital mission."

I shake my head, refusing to believe, refusing to let it sink in.

I take off the blackout sunglasses absentmindedly and give them back to Oalla, squinting at the return of fierce daylight, despite the additional protective lenses in my eyes. And I continue to ask stupidly, even though on some deep, profound level I already know the answer. "So, these lights are—what exactly?"

Oalla looks at me with despair. "These lights are *they*. Our ancient enemy is here."

Chapter 36

"Wait, how do you know?" I ask. It's another stupid question, mostly to compose myself, to allow some normalcy into the impossible moment at hand. "I thought that no one knows what *they* look like. . . . Or is it that no one remembers what the ancients saw? Not even what kind of ships? Isn't it right that there's no actual record—"

"There is no official *verified* record of the ancient enemy, that much is true," Erita says. "Either no one took pictures or videos of *them* when they first arrived in Ancient Atlantis—which is hard to believe—or more likely, none have been preserved to this day."

"None that we *know* of." Oalla's frown deepens. "However— what we *do* have are some indirect descriptions and references in ancient literature and poetry. And they all reference bright and dire *golden stars* and *starlight*, and moving *objects* of impossible light— enough to give us a composite, general idea."

Erita makes a little sound. "The stuff that I remember best is from children's stories. Must say, I was bored to death with some of the sophisticated adult selections in our lit class, especially Cadet, Second Year material. *Ode Everlasting to Atlantida* just about killed me. . . . Anyway, I remember enjoying the fun adventure stories and myths in my spare time, about the little Starlight Sorceress, what's her name—"

"Arleana," Oalla says, shaking her head—even as the people in the courtyard and further along in the park exclaim as another bright flare happens overhead.

"That's right, Arleana, Starlight Sorceress. The one who could sing and talk to the stars and make them obey her, and do all kinds of fun tricks. There were cute magic animals too, that followed her around."

"Hmm, I don't remember any animals," Oalla says.

"Oh, there were animals." Erita raises one brow. "The bird with the stupid long beak was my favorite, and the scarab that the bird tried to eat but couldn't catch, 'cause it was so dumb, and some kind of crawling fat lizard or crocodile—"

"Okay," I say, involuntarily shivering at the continuing anxious exclamations from the people nearby. "But what does that have to do with the ancient alien threat?"

"Not much," Erita says. "I just remember that the Starlight Sorceress had some kind of magic enemy, and it was sort of like an *evil star* that didn't want to listen or play with her, unlike the others. Or maybe it was something else . . . maybe a weird ghost made of *golden light*. I remember something about a golden ghost. Basically, the whole thing was a dumbed-down kiddie reference to the grownup records of the real ancient enemy. Everything, all of it, talks about golden light—exactly like *that*." And Erita points up at the sky.

I exhale and glance behind me where Gracie, Tuar, and my other guards watch me anxiously. Everyone else chatters nervously and tries to look up, with palms covering their eyes.

"Right," Oalla picks up. "So, as to your logical question, how do we know? My Imperial Lady Gwen, the details add up. These light objects move with what our sensors would interpret and describe as *artificial sentience*. In other words, they're not natural solar plasma energy bursts of some sort. They exhibit an *order* and nonrandom *organization*. And they are of alien origin."

I nod slowly, and my eyes return to the hologram flat reflective surface that's still projected from Oalla's wrist. But she's moved her hand away, so it no longer reflects Hel from my vantage point.

"Here." Oalla takes my own hand where I'm luckily wearing my wrist comm next to a lovely golden bracelet. She taps my unit and calls up a similar hologram mirror surface projection from my own wrist, showing me how to turn it on and off. "Now you can look at it yourself. Even if it's not very effective."

"Pretty much useless," Erita adds. "Just a glare reducer. You can't really see it this way."

I glance at my hologram just in time to barely notice another tiny flash.

"We expected *them* to arrive in such form," Oalla continues. "However, they still managed to surprise us. They came from the opposite direction."

I wrinkle my forehead with effort. "How so?"

"All these centuries, we expected an extrasolar arrival. In other words, from outside the solar system, from interstellar space. . . . From Ae-Leiterra, the black hole that's located at the heart of our galaxy. That's why we put the Great Quantum Shield around it. That's why the Rim missions, the patrols at the outer edges of the system. But they somehow bypassed all that. Apparently, Helios is the conduit, so they are massing in our solar system *interior*."

I breathe for a moment in silence, contemplating . . . trying to tune out the people exclaiming variously at the sky around us.

"Why don't we head back in," Erita says. "Nothing new to be seen here, for the moment."

We return to the chamber in the Imperial Palace, and here I quickly explain to my friends—and Brie especially—in so many words about the extent of the alien threat. Gracie and the Cadets already know the basics from Fleet education, and my civilian friends have surmised enough from all our previous secret talk of the Atlantis Grail and Ra Disk being parts of an ancient ark-ship broadcasting to some distant potential enemy source. . . . But now, the threat is real and it's *here*, and that's the part they don't yet fully understand.

My Bridal Court reception is effectively over. The Great Lapis Lazuli Chamber is half empty, since most of the Ladies have left in alarm or panic, forgoing any semblance of formalities—and hence liberating me from that elegant Hostess obligation of closing my Bridal Court—while a handful who are actual members of the Fleet in addition to being pampered nobility have been called to active duty.

The Imperatris, the First Priestess of Amrevet-Ra, and a few of the older ladies are still gathered in the central seating area, surrounded by guards. They are discussing the situation worriedly or making calls or checking the official news feeds on their personal devices.

"Gwen, come!" The Imperatris beckons me and the others. She immediately turns to Oalla and Erita with questions. The two *astra daimon* give a quick rundown of the real-time situation happening outside, and their earlier mission in outer orbit.

"So . . . it is true then," Devora says with sorrow. "*They* have found us."

"After all these centuries, yes," Dame Tammuz says. "It is the end."

Devora glances at her in horror.

"With all apologies for the grim nature of things, but you know I don't mince words," Dame Tammuz says. "My Sovereign Lady, I must therefore beg my leave. We've called an emergency IEC session, and all of this is going to be thoroughly discussed in the coming bitter hours."

"My Imperial Husband and my Son will both be there—of course, go." Devora nods her dismissal.

"Where is Aeson now?" I ask with a stab of worry, as Dame Tammuz rises. "Oh no, is he already gone? What about his SPC Commander duties, does that mean he is—? Is he in our Quarters? Let me call him—"

I start to tap the wrist comm number to connect to Aeson, then notice my incoming messages, and see the latest one—out of at least *five* from Aeson in the last hour. They all tell me not to worry, that "everything is under control," and to call him when my Bridal Court is done.

No rush, Gwen, the last message says. *Take your time, breathe easy*, im amrevu, *I will see you soon.*

"We should be going too," Gracie says, exchanging grim looks with Chiyoko and Laronda.

"Yeah, we're supposed to report to Fleet HQ first—right now," Laronda adds. "Not sure what exactly will be expected of us."

"Unlike you two, I've only had desk duty, no actual flight assignments yet," Chiyoko says softly.

Oh, God. . . .

I bite my lip with a new burst of anxiety, thinking of my little sister Gracie, fourteen years old, and *active duty* Fleet Cadet Pilot. And my friends too. And all the other Earthies out there who have pledged themselves to Fleet service.

I've always known that's what they signed up for. But now it just feels so hollow, so weird and *wrong*.

"Gracie, please be careful," I say, pulling in my sister for a quick hug.

"I will, don't worry." She gives me a brave smile. "Thanks for the crazy-daisy best Birthday party."

"Sorry it had to end this way," I whisper. "But seriously, please let me know—as soon as you're able—what your assignment will be! Okay? Promise! I *am* worried. . . ."

But Gracie just shakes her head at me with a very grownup smile. "No, don't. . . . It's okay, Gee Two."

I take a deep, shuddering breath. Then I press Laronda's arm and pat Chiyoko on the shoulder. Nervous glances pass between us.

Hasmik, Manala, Dawn, and Brie watch with heavy expressions as our Cadet friends take their leave, curtseying before the Imperatris and then hurrying out of the chamber.

"Crap, I bet they got him too. . . ." Brie suddenly checks her wrist comm for messages and nods. "Yup, they got Sangre. He's been recalled to duty too—is letting me know he has to leave *now*."

"Where is Logan?" I'm almost afraid to ask.

"Right now? Waiting for me in the car, as I told him. Being a good boy." Brie gives me a sharp glance that's almost a challenge. "But looks like I'm going to have to take a rain check on the remainder of his three months of service. Once a Fleet boy, always a Fleet boy. I guess it trumps Correctional. So, Lark, time for me to vamoose. Thanks for the fabulous party and entertainment, and see you around soon—if the aliens don't get us first! At this rate, should've just stayed back on Earth and taken the nasty asteroid pill. . . ."

Brie nods to the others brusquely, then does the most awkward curtsey possible to the Imperatris, and heads out in determined fashion.

I turn to Devora Kassiopei. "With your permission, My Sovereign Lady, I must go see Aeson now, before he has to leave. . . ."

"Go," she tells me gently, rising from her seat also.

I hurry back to our Quarters, surrounded by my guards. Erita and Oalla walk with me, since they need to see Aeson anyway.

When we get there, the workroom is full of people. Aeson is watching multiple display screens at his desk, together with Xelio and Keruvat, while Anu and Gennio are running more data on another set of monitors.

As soon as Aeson sees me, he gets up quickly—just as I rush into his arms. There are no words between us, only a tight embrace for several long seconds, while I feel the strength of him surround me like a blanket, the hardness of his muscular chest under his shirt and jacket . . . and I listen to the steady, wonderful beating of his heart.

"Gwen . . . are you all right?" he whispers near the top of my head, even as I continue to hide my face in his chest.

"Okay *now*," I whisper, looking up into his eyes.

"Oh . . . but you are so *beautiful!*" He suddenly notices, or at least responds to, my Bridal Court appearance; stares with wonder at my face with its subtle cosmetics that make me look magical; runs his fingers over my cheeks and my sculpted hairdo.

"Yes, and these two cleaned up to be quite stunning also," Keruvat remarks, glancing at Oalla and Erita in their own high heels and finery. "Hope the Bridal event was worth it. Too bad it's the end of the world, *im nefira*," he adds to Oalla with a pained smile.

Oalla gives Ker a narrowed look. She comes up to him and gives the back of his head and neck a quick tap that turns into a caress. Then she leans over him and glances at his data screen.

Meanwhile, Xelio watches us and simply frowns, while Anu and Gennio give us equally grim looks.

Aeson continues to stare at me with a focused, unrelenting gaze, in silence, as if he wants to drown in me . . . to be lost and never to emerge and never have to face the grim reality. Eventually he takes a deep breath with a shudder and stands back, holding me at arm's length. "Our ancient enemy found us, Gwen. The one thing we were most afraid of has come to pass. I am *so* sorry."

"Aeson . . . I was outside and I saw *them*," I say in a faint voice suddenly lacking breath. "The golden dots of light. Erita and Oalla explained some of it. So, what happens now?"

"We prepare to deal with them," he says, pointing at the active data screens. "The Star Pilot Corps organization is on high alert, and I've recalled all the SPC Pilots to active duty, just as the IF Commander Manakteon Resoi has recalled all the Fleet Pilots of Imperial *Atlantida*. That includes all the Cadets—both the native ones and the ones newly arrived from Earth. . . . Other global organizations and the national military Fleets are mobilizing too. We're monitoring events as they unfold from the proximity of Rah Station—for the moment."

He nods at the largest monitor, which shows a full-window deep-space view of Helios the star against a cosmic background, taking up most of the screen. Even with the high-level radiation shield to filter the blinding, bluish-white solar light, it almost eclipses the golden dots sprinkled all around it like fireflies. Some of them are stationary; others move with sudden darting motion to transit across the face of Hel. . . .

Even now, they appear tiny. But they must be immense in size.

Compared to what I saw only with the blackout sunglasses in the sky of Atlantis, and this close view halfway across the system (from the vantage point of Rah Station in orbit around the innermost planet Rah), I still see very little difference. Except that—maybe these objects appear more defined as *spheres* of golden light as opposed to just shapeless "blobs."

While I ponder this, Aeson continues in a firm tone, speaking in measured phrases that already resemble formal statements. It's as though he's anticipating having to explain this many more times to various groups of people.

"Meanwhile, we must contend with the public's anticipated terrible reaction. We have to take control of the news delivery, to lessen the natural fear. All new developments must be presented carefully to minimize the alarming implications and to project calm—which is technically the truth, since no real threat from those alien light objects has yet manifested, nor has their nature been confirmed. . . . In short—so much to deal with, including my Father—with whom I've just talked, and who's presently raving in panic."

"Oh, no . . ." I breathe.

"He's convinced that the broadcasting ancient ark-ship components, the Grail and the Ra Disk, together with the Ghost Moon, are entirely at fault for bringing the alien enemy to us."

I feel a terrible jolt of emotion in my chest. "If that's the case then—all of it is my fault. So, he must blame me."

Aeson frowns, and his gaze sharpens with intensity as he looks at me. "Gwen, *don't*. Do not put this on yourself. It was brewing already, and it was bound to happen regardless, sooner or later. If anything, my Father himself set this in motion—in part when he pushed you into the Games, setting off this particular chain of events—and even long before that."

I wince slightly, but I respond to his protective words with a smile.

"As I was saying, in addition to the global SPC forces, we have the IF Commander Resoi and our Imperial Fleet personnel and the other world leaders with their own national defense resources—"

Aeson pauses to check the flashing band of his wrist comm, then glances at Ker and Xel, and back at me. "I'll explain more when I get back. The next few hours and days are going to be critical. Right now, I'm about to head out to the emergency meeting of the IEC, after which, depending on the outcome, I'll need to make a flight to the SPC Headquarters to meet with my international SPC Command Pilots—"

"Is that in Atlantis orbit?" I ask.

He nods.

I sigh. "Okay, go. Please be careful!"

Aeson smiles at me, a quick, energetic smile, giving me a jolt of positivity. "Stay strong for me, *amrevu*. I'll see you tonight and will have much more insight into this situation at that point. Meanwhile—*daimon*, you all have your assignments."

Keruvat nods, taking the seat vacated by Xelio—who gets up and formally salutes Aeson.

"Saret-i-xerera!" Xel gives an additional verbal salute which I've not heard used before in the Fleet, though I do remember it being a part of the anthem sung during the Champion Citizenship Ceremony, right after our Oath of Loyalty to *Atlantida*. "Heading to the SPC HQ at once. But first—while you deal with the IEC, I'm going to take a quick reconnaissance flight myself, then meet you at Headquarters. Oalla, Erita, you coming?"

Erita nods. "Scheduled to fly now. Time to get out of these shiny clothes and put on the uniforms."

Oalla makes a mocking pout and points to her fiery outfit. "Aww, must we? This cosmic, world-ending, impending war thing is just no fun if it starts interfering with my style. I hereby officially *dislike* it."

"Yes, a complete setback to fashion," Xelio remarks, tapping data on his wrist comm.

"Give it time," Aeson says with a raised brow, as he picks up key cards and checks equipment on his desk before heading out. "It will grow on you."

"Like a big-ass wart. . . ." Anu adds from under his breath, pushing a monitor on a swinging arm out of Aeson's way.

I watch Aeson and the others move around the room while exchanging exaggerated words and glances, and recognize the underlying current of despair beneath their banter. Keruvat is the only one staying to analyze the incoming data while they are away.

"Is there anything I can do?" I ask, feeling useless. It reminds me of my early Games training when everyone around me did so much on my behalf and I just stood there, taking it all in, before I could function in any constructive way on my own.

"Stay calm and hopeful," Oalla says with a wink. And she glances in Aeson's direction, then meaningfully looks back at me.

I can almost hear her unspoken ending to the sentence.

Stay calm and hopeful for him.

Chapter 37

One final wistful glance in my direction, one brisk smile, and Aeson is gone. Xel, Erita, and Oalla follow him out of the room.

I stand frowning, petrified with uselessness, and for a moment simply watch as Keruvat returns to working the screens, together with Anu and Gennio. This time there are so many data feeds, it's incomprehensible—brief flashes of what must be Rah Station data, some familiar mini-screens of the Ghost Moon still being tracked in other windows, scrolling rows of numbers and still images, video capture feeds, and views of other deep-space vantage points—which I'm guessing are other Hel system stations—and their corresponding data.

"Here, Gwen," Ker says, glancing at me briefly. "Have a seat and watch, if you like. It's going to be a long afternoon and night."

"I won't be in the way? Okay," I say, taking a seat next to him at the desk. "If it's all right, may I ask about this Rah Station view?"

"Sure," Ker says. "Feel free to ask anything. At this point we don't have much new data to go on, only what you see live from Rah Station. The Pilots there have been instructed to stay put—not to attempt to do any flybys, which could potentially trip the aliens' proximity barriers on approach and activate the threat. For now, we're all just looking, watching closely. The image is from the main station cameras. There are additional views we can switch to from orbiting satellite buoys, but they are at the same distance."

"Okay." I nod. "So how big is the Rah Station? I mean, both size and personnel."

Anu stares at me from the other desk. "Hey, want me to show you? I can flip a buoy camera onto the station itself so you can see it."

I get up and go over to look at Anu's screens. He enters some code and then enlarges a window. Suddenly I see a hemispheric view of the planet Rah, a desolate black-grey ball of scorched rock which I'm told is about twice as large as Earth's Mercury. Floating before it is a gleaming metallic 3D object shaped like a cross, rotating slowly on its central axis.

"Oh, wow. . . ." I peer closer, and now I can see that there is some kind of central hub, a sphere in the middle of the X shape, with tiny dots of lights indicating viewports. But this particular view is head-on, and as the station slowly moves relative to the buoy camera, the sphere turns out to be a long cylinder.

Meanwhile, the four arms of the cross—also dotted with viewport lights along the edges—are in fact flat platforms extending outward from the cylinder hub. On both sides of each arm platform I see endless numbers of small shuttle-like ships parked in close rows. They are like space barnacles attached to the main body.

"Two thousand micro-ship capacity," Anu says, answering my unspoken question. "And the station has six thousand personnel capacity—like the Imperial Fleet ark-ships. Of course, it's nothing in size, compared to a battle barge."

"A what?" I say.

"Battle barge!" Anu snorts. "You don't know?"

"Obviously I don't or I wouldn't be asking." I snort back at him.

Ker gives us a tiny, amused glance.

Gennio meanwhile sighs and rolls his eyes at Anu. "Imperial Lady Gwen is unfamiliar with SPC Fleet structure."

"Why don't you both tell her about it," Ker says mildly. "The SPC Fleet is different from the Imperial Fleet. She needs to know about the differences, starting with the vessels."

"Of course," Gennio says.

"Yeah, sure," Anu echoes him.

"Great," I say. "So—battle barge?"

"A battle barge is the biggest warship class in the SPC Fleet." Gennio begins explaining in his usual patient, detail-oriented manner. "It is the equivalent of four ark-ships—24,000 personnel capacity—and four times bigger in size because it has to transport hundreds of other warships inside, in addition to personnel."

"Yeah," Anu adds. "And those other warships, carried like babies inside a battle barge, can be large *sebasarets*—which in turn are filled with mid-range transport *depets* like velo-cruisers, small fighters, and everything else you can imagine."

I recall that *depet* is a generic *Atlanteo* word for "boat." I also get a sudden mental image of starships designed like Russian nesting dolls. . . . I think they're called Matryoshka dolls. Then I force the nonsense thought away and get my ridiculous brain back on track.

"Okay, fascinating. I had no idea you had ships larger than ark-ships."

"Oh, yes," Gennio says. "They are giant ships, and we only have ten of them. The battle barges are all called *War*, and numbered War-1 through War-10. Whichever battle barge happens to be carrying the SPC Fleet Commander on board gets the temporary designation of *Depet-Ra*."

"Until he gets off, then that battle barge is again simply called a War," Anu says.

I nod and try to keep up with this information. "Kind of like *Air Force One*," I mutter, thinking of the term for the airplane that carries the President of the United States on Earth.

Anu and Gennio both give me initially clueless looks, then appear to recall whatever they learned about Earth's military. "Yes, that's right," Gennio says. "Anyway, the ten battle barges are evenly distributed throughout the solar system and, in times of peace, are manned with a skeleton crew. War-1 and War-2 are stationed in deep space, very far away, on the outer edges of the heliosphere, beyond Atlas. They are our finest ships and serve as the first line of defense as you enter Hel's system."

"Then you have War-3 and War-4, also fine ships, stationed near Olympos," Anu says. "Then two more around Atlantis, right here in deep space beyond Amrevet's orbit—that's our local War-5 and War-6."

"Right," Gennio continues. "Then, once you keep going inward past Atlantis, the remaining planets only get one battle barge each, since we expect less danger from the system interior."

Keruvat makes a sarcastic sound. "Looks like we got it all wrong," he says suddenly, glancing up from his work. "We now have the bulk of our best military force on the opposite edge of the system. Meanwhile, in descending prestige order and distance to Hel, Ishtar has War-7, Tammuz has War-8, Septu has War-9, and lonely Rah has War-10 which is ranked as the least distinguished of the ten vessels. . . . Unfortunate planning, Atlantis. But then no one expected tiny Rah Station, with its newbie- or leftover-staffed War-10 to be in danger before the rest of us." And he laughs bitterly, shaking his head, then returns his attention to the screen.

I bite my lip thoughtfully and glance back at Gennio and Anu. "So you were saying the Rah Station is small—smaller than a battle barge. . . ."

Gennio nods. "The Rah Station is the smallest of the outposts. The biggest station is in orbit around Ishtar."

"Aha." I nod slowly. "Are there space stations around each of the planets?"

"Yes," Anu says. "One orbital station per planet."

"What about on the *surface?*"

"Too expensive to build," Gennio explains. "You can simply launch parts and assemble in orbit and don't have to deal with planetary weather, gravity, or other surface anomalies. All the other interior planets are dead rocks anyway. We go down to mine some of them for resources for replacement parts, but that's about it."

"I see." I pause, digesting all of this, while Anu and Gennio periodically glance back at their work screens, but remain ready to accommodate my questions. "Okay. . . . So what kind of other military ships are in the SPC Fleet besides these huge battle barges? I've heard about *sebasarets*, which are smaller than ark-ships and can also hold other, smaller ships—which are, what? Solo shuttles?"

"You are asking about Fleet vessel hierarchy, but confusing military and civilian vessels," Anu says in a superior tone. "A shuttle—the kind you learned to pilot, the same ones we had on the ark-ships—is a civilian vessel. The larger transport shuttles too—all civilian. They have some minor weapons capacity, but it's not their primary function."

"Oh, really?" I say, thinking back on my Pilot Class. "So they only taught us how to fly the civilian shuttles. . . ."

"Yes and no," Gennio puts in. "In principle, they all basically work the same way for flight, except the weapons systems are more complicated in the military fighter ships."

I tense my forehead.

"So, knowing how to pilot a shuttle, you can pilot a *mafdet*, an *ardukat*, a *khepri*, or even an *ankhurat* without much difficulty," Anu says. "Those are the fighters."

"Should I be taking notes?" I sigh. This is sounding more and more complicated.

"Oh no, that wouldn't be necessary. Don't worry, Imperial Lady Gwen, it's all easily referenced in the SPC knowledge bases," Gennio says at once, taking me literally.

"Tell her about each ship type," Keruvat says without looking up from his screens. "Make it brief."

"Of course," Gennio replies. "The *mafdet* is the solo fighter, the lightest, smallest, fastest, and most agile for air-to-air combat. Only the most experienced Pilots are permitted to fly those."

"Two guns, firing capability front and back, uses fine focused plasma bursts for strafing." Anu adds. "The *mafdet* is known as the Needle of Justice."

"Now, the *ardukat* is a two-person fighter," Gennio continues. "You have a Pilot and Co-Pilot working together, exactly as you learned to fly in your Cadet Pilot Classes. Four guns on board, both fine-focus burst and wide scatter-burst firing capability."

"That's the most common type of fighter in the SPC Fleet," Anu says. "Most everyone gets assigned to fly the *ardukats*. It's basic all-purpose warfare."

"Okay," I say.

"Next, there is the *khepri*, which is larger, a four-Pilot team fighter," Gennio says. "Also has four guns, but uses heavy-caliber artillery, able to eject plasma at a higher density from multiple thick nozzles in each gun. In addition, it's equipped with four guided missiles and armed probes. The *khepri* is an attack bomber for major targets."

I nod.

"Finally, the *ankhurat* is the biggest, heaviest fighter. One hundred personnel crew plus six Pilots, intended for boarding other vessels, plus six heavy-caliber plasma guns and ten missiles."

"Yeah, the *ankhurat* is nicknamed Ankh, the Life Giver," Anu says with a smirk.

I raise one brow at him.

"So those are the four standard kinds of fighter ships used in military combat," Gennio concludes. "There are a few others, but mostly experimental models in development and not really important now."

"Wow," I ask, trying to wrap my mind around all of this material, "what about the *sebasarets?*"

"Not considered fighters," Anu replies. "They are command ship carriers for ranking officers, military personnel, and other vessels. So, can be used as transports and command centers. They do have weapons capability, but no guns, only guided missiles."

"Right," Gennio says. "You can fit different combinations of fighter ships inside each *sebasaret* fighter bay. The bay is designed to hold four *ankhurats*. Or two *ankhurats* and four *khepri*. Or four *khepri* and eight *ardukats*. Or eight *ardukats* and twelve *mafdets*. Gives you an idea of their relative sizes. Meanwhile, a civilian velo-cruiser is halfway between an *ankhurat* and a *khepri* in size, while a standard seven-seat civilian shuttle is slightly larger than an *ardukat*. However, a civilian solo shuttle and a *mafdet* are about the same size. Oh, and want to hear something crazy? One hundred *sebasarets* can fit inside one battle barge."

"I see. . . . This is going to take me a while to digest." I shake my head, definitely overwhelmed. Normally I'm a quick learner, but for some reason this military tech jargon is hurting my head. . . .

I don't get it, and I don't want to get it.

At the same time, a slow gnawing pain is starting to wrench my gut. Distress and unease and unspeakable worry all crowd together to fill and crush me, as I think of all the devastating implications of military action.

The machinery of war.

And my Aeson is at the heart of it. . . .

He is the Commander of this immense military hierarchy. These fighters and command ship carriers and giant battle barges. . . . Hundreds of thousands of personnel. . . . *They all report to him.* It is somehow inconceivable.

Immersed in heavy thoughts, I space out for many long minutes while the others let me be and continue to work at their screens or check their wrist comms. The afternoon grows long as I watch over their shoulders, occasionally asking questions.

All this time I think about Aeson, wondering where he is at each given moment as he deals with everything—he must be meeting with the Council, or maybe he's already flying up to the SPC Headquarters in orbit, meeting more people, discussing, issuing orders, worrying, consumed. . . .

Keruvat continues to focus on the main screen view of Helios the star and the alien golden lights scattered around it. *They look so pretty, so harmless*, it occurs to me. *Pretty little fireflies of gold.*

At some point he stops scrolling the secondary screens and pays unrelenting, close attention to the view of blazing Hel. "Okay, this is different," he says to us, tapping the view with one finger.

Anu and Gennio immediately look to him.

"It appears, they're no longer just jumping around and moving at random," Keruvat says. "They are lining up—with very specific intervals between them—look."

We crowd around him and stare at the same blazing view from Rah Station.

Except it is indeed different. The previously chaotic golden lights are assembling into an ordered lineup, forming precisely spaced rows of golden dots. They flit across, then one dot suddenly finds a point and stops. Then another dot takes its place in the formation next to it and stills permanently, hovering in space.

"Crap, that's a *grid*," Anu mutters.

"Agreed." Keruvat frowns, then taps some commands, calling up a visual grid overlay which he adjusts until it matches the spacing of the light dots, confirming their ordered formation. "Perfectly equidistant indeed. Imaging sensors are still calculating the exact *mag-heitar* spacing of the grid, but we should have it in moments."

"This is not good," Gennio says quietly.

"They are building a formation of some kind," I whisper.

"Yes," Ker says.

"When they are done, what happens next?"

"Not sure at what point they will be done. Because they are *still* coming." And Ker taps the screen to point out another new tiny flare, as yet another golden light object "emerges" from Hel's corona and flits away to join the others.

Anu cusses in *Atlanteo* and passes a hand over the back of his head.

It is very late evening, close to eleventh hour, when Aeson finally returns home. Keruvat is the only one still here, glued to the computer display, watching the Rah Station grid. Anu and Gennio have gone for the night, though still on high alert and ready to be called back if needed.

I've spent the hours observing Ker and the others work, then watching TV feeds from the sofa that show a lot of panicking and confused people and reporters on the streets of Poseidon, views of the sky supposedly showing *something* on or around Hel (even though it's not really possible to see anything with the naked eye in the glare of daylight), and nervous commentators and talk show panelists discussing the alarming events of the day, including the anticipated inevitability of Fleet mobilization.

At some point my brother Gordie calls, asking me if I am okay and what the hell is going on, and that everyone at his workplace "is freaking out about an ancient alien invasion." I tell him as much as I know, and he promises to drop by tomorrow. Then we talk about Gracie and how she's been activated for duty. . . . And we talk about Dad and George, flying toward us even now, and what it will all mean in the long run, them coming here to Atlantis with all that's happening. . . .

Talking with Gordie does not diminish my simmering fear, but it does help me get a grip and focus.

And now. . . .

Aeson is here.

He is wearing his usual public mask of control as he enters the workroom, but his fixed expression is grim and exhausted.

Ker gets up at once and salutes his friend and commanding officer. Aeson nods—even as his gaze searches for me immediately, acknowledges my being there—before he returns his attention to Keruvat. They exchange a few words, and Ker gives a brief status report. In short, no significant new developments except for the immense alien grid, which is still forming somewhere in space between Helios and Rah, as additional light objects continue to arrive endlessly.

"Also, a personal video log report from Rah Station Nomarch Rertu just came in. View at your convenience," Ker says.

"Very well, thank you, *daimon*." Aeson sighs, pours himself a glass of *qvaali* and takes a long, thirsty drink before continuing. "On my end, the IEC meeting went exactly as expected. Much long-winded talk and alarmed confusion, stupid assumptions, plenty of blame, and nothing decided. My Father left early, in disgust, to deal with New Deshret—since the Pharikon's been calling non-stop. The only good news is that the Imperial Fleet will be in full preparedness by morning, according to Manakteon Resoi."

"As expected." Ker nods. "Ever since the Earth mission, Resoi has implemented a trigger preparedness protocol."

"It's working well." Aeson takes another long swallow of his *qvaali* and unceremoniously wipes his mouth with the back of his hand. "At least the SPC Command Pilots meetings were productive, considering this is our first functional test of the organization in centuries. Whether or not the Star Pilot Corps can measure up to its original intended purpose, whether or not it can maintain international cohesiveness at a time of real crisis, is yet to be seen. . . . I've issued orders to each of the Command Pilots to be battle ready, with mandatory compliance. New Deshret and Ubasti national fleets are already primed for action, and Eos-Heket is almost ready too. . . . More on this tomorrow. Now go get some rest, but remain on call." And Aeson dismisses Keruvat gently.

Ker salutes and leaves, without any of the usual casual chat between them.

As soon as he's gone, and we're alone, Aeson turns to me. Wordlessly he takes me in a fierce embrace.

"Aeson. . . ." I whisper, stroking his cheek. "Have you eaten?"

We talk over a late *niktos* meal, mostly for Aeson's consumption, since I've already had some food earlier.

"Gwen," he says after eating a few hasty bites from his plate. "Tomorrow, before I proceed with anything else, my Father—and also New Deshret—want both of us to go down *inside* the ancient ark-ship. We are to look for some things—clues, anything—that can help us with the alien situation."

"Oh!" I part my lips. A weird surge of alarm and excitement swells inside me. . . .

"We are going to be joined by several other individuals selected by my Father. I expect to see Hijep Tiofon, Shirahtet, possibly Rovat Bennu. Maybe a few of his lab tech experts. Likely, ancient historians to interpret the archived information and the artifacts. At this point, be prepared for anyone or anything in those lower levels."

I frown from the effort of holding back my rising tension. "Is it wrong to admit that I'm kind of curious and eager to see what's down there?"

"To be honest, I am, too." Aeson chuckles tiredly and resumes eating.

Even now, with all that's happening, with all the stress and uncertainty in which we're plunged, I'm distracted enough by the sight of *him* that my frown eases.

I exhale and release my worry—at least for the moment—and watch his every movement with loving attention.

Chapter 38

The next day is Green Ghost Moon 11, and after yesterday's eventful Bridal reception hosting the Ladies of the Court, I have nothing official scheduled. Not even the Venerable Therutat could've predicted the suddenly looming alien threat, but by some stroke of fortune my Wedding calendar for today has me clear of any Bridal duties.

Today we visit the bowels of the ark-ship.

I wake up soon after dawn, and Aeson is already up and checking overnight SPC reports in the workroom with a tense expression. We quickly get ready to leave for the stadium complex downtown.

"Any news? About *them?*" I ask with worry as we gulp down our *eos* bread.

He shakes his head. "The alien grid is still being constructed. It is now immense, stretching across deep space, between Helios and the rest of the system. As for Atlantis defenses, the various Fleets are still assembling."

Minutes later, we're heading down to the cars, accompanied by our security guards.

We lift off and fly with the morning traffic, even as Hel rises over the city of Poseidon. Immediately in advance of Hel comes the golden grid of light, briefly visible as it's cresting above the horizon just ahead of the solar disk.

Having seen the Rah Station's enhanced and filtered images, I know that in fact the net of golden dots stretches like a fine birdcage veil over the entire face of Hel. But right now only its upper portion, beyond the corona, is clearly visible in silhouette against the dawn-stained sky, much of which is still dark. And then Hel's light drowns everything. . . .

The phenomenon lasts for only a few seconds before Hel's white glare overwhelms all other light, but it is enough to leave an impression.

"The grid . . . you can actually see it from here," I whisper in sudden awe, as I squint and continue to stare through the anti-glare windows of the hover car, even though the bizarre sight is gone.

Aeson glances in the direction of Hel, then quickly looks away, continuing to navigate the hover car in the air traffic lane. "The fact that you can see them without the aid of a magnifying device tells you how *large* each light object is," he says grimly. "Each, the size of a planet."

"No. . . ." My mouth opens as the realization comes slamming down. The planetary scale makes perfect sense, and now that Aeson has pointed it out, the notion of *their* size starts to plague me.

I think of similar sights seen when stargazing from Earth— Venus and Mars appearing like bright stars, each visible directly with the naked eye if one knows where to look, and so on.

If these things around Helios are each the size of a small planet, and they are forming a cosmic grid, I suddenly feel out of breath just trying to imagine the scale involved.

"They're going to attack us in this formation, aren't they?" I say rhetorically.

Aeson does not answer at once. "Not necessarily. It could be a defensive formation. At least for now."

I sigh, grateful that *im amrevu* is trying to make me feel better with such a gentle understatement.

For now, I'll take it.

We arrive at the downtown complex containing the Atlantis Grail stadium, and this time do not attempt to navigate the debris-ridden arena with the jutting Grail Monument, but go directly inside the main building of the structure that encircles the venue.

As we approach, we begin to hear the familiar, bone-rattling subterranean hum. The closer we get, the louder the sound grows, radiating from the ark-ship buried deep inside the ground.

Even now, the ancient ship sings. . . . Doesn't it know it's already served its malicious purpose?

Aeson gives me a grim nod, acknowledging it, and then we both try to ignore the pervasive sound—which is easier said than done.

The entrance to the ship's lower levels is accessible from here in the building, via a network of deceptive corridors that circle the complex. Clearly they are meant to confuse anyone unfamiliar with the truth of the ancient ship.

"For centuries, people working in this building assumed they were merely accessing basement levels," Aeson tells me as we enter the corridors, surrounded by our Imperial guards. "I did too, Gwen . . . for so long."

We follow curving, gradually descending corridors which remind me of my first time here, on the night before the Games began, as the other Contenders and I were taken down along these same corridors and locked inside glass-enclosed cells for the night.

Only this time we advance farther, past the section with the cells, and keep going down, following the trajectory of a gently descending, curving spiral or coil. And then the corridor ends abruptly, before a wide set of metallic double doors which are deeply recessed on top and appear to be set at a curved incline, bulging and extending outward the closer they get to the floor.

Everyone's been painfully ignoring it, but the deep humming *sound* here is overwhelming, as it radiates from the doors and their immediate surrounding area.

Knowing what I know now, I understand at once that we are facing the entrance to the ancient ship.

Several familiar figures await us here, before the doors.

Aeson was right. The First Priest Shirahtet is in attendance, looming solemnly in the background. With him is the ACA Director Hijep Tiofon and the STA Director Rovat Bennu, talking quietly, their voices drowned in the general hum all around us.

In addition, I see an unfamiliar, dark-haired woman of indeterminate middle age, in a beige uniform resembling a lab coat. Surprisingly, right next to her is none other than Rurim Kiv, my fellow Champion of the Games in the Artist Category.

My lips part in surprise as I stare at Rurim, wanting to ask him what he's doing here.

Instead, the moment we approach, everyone offers courtly greetings to Aeson, then acknowledges me politely. Our guards fall back, letting us proceed unobstructed toward the doors.

"My Imperial Lord Aeson—and Imperial Lady Gwen—with your permission, we are ready to begin," Director Tiofon says. "May I introduce Antiquities Specialist Igara Cvutu from the Imperial Poseidon Museum. She is an expert in the Original Colony Period."

The woman gives a curt bow to Aeson and me. "I am at your service, Imperial Lord and Lady."

"And you are both familiar with Games Champion Rurim Kiv. His unusual expertise has been requested by the Imperial Sovereign himself, in regard to deciphering pyramid symbols. He has been *informed* about the nature of this structure, and he will be joining us in this task."

"Very well." Aeson gives Rurim a brief but piercing scrutiny, even as the handsome, dark-skinned man regards both of us calmly, with a flicker of amusement in his expression, but not a trace of servility.

"I assume this is one of the hull entrances into the ship," Aeson says, turning to Tiofon. "Please open the doors, and let's proceed inside."

Hijep Tiofon takes a device that resembles a key card and passes it over the small wall insignia of a Ra sunburst to the right of the doors.

The card is read, and the heavy bulging doors slide apart in silence, showing themselves to be at least thirty inches thick. Immediately beyond them is a *second* set of doors, with only a twenty-inch clearance between the outer doors and the interior ones. The clearance is basically a gap in the walls—nothing but empty space filled with darkness, stretching in all directions, up, down, to the sides. . . .

I stare with widened eyes, as my mind attempts to understand what I'm seeing. A secondary hull layer? Insulation?

Meanwhile, Director Tiofon passes his key card again over a similar insignia in this second set of doors.

They open, similarly thick and curving, to reveal a dimly lit interior. At the same time, stuffy air comes at us, carrying a strange chemical smell, both sterile and somehow pungent.

I glimpse a wide corridor with a low ceiling. The corridor must run parallel to the doors, essentially hugging the perimeter—or circumference—of the hull, which is probably rounded like that of the modern ark-ships.

Director Bennu wrinkles his forehead and sniffs. "Ah, that smell. . . . I used to think it was just a poor ventilation system in the old building, and the labs were not vented properly. Now I can imagine there's so much more to it." And then he steps over the empty gap in the floor and enters, advancing inside ahead of everyone.

Director Tiofon pauses for a moment as if to check the air for himself, then goes in directly after.

"My Imperial Lord, after you," the First Priest Shirahtet says, with a courtly hand gesture.

Aeson walks inside, and I follow him. Shirahtet, Igara Cvutu, Rurim Kiv, and the Imperial guards enter last.

The moment we're inside and the thick doors slide shut behind us, the humming sound *disappears* almost entirely. Now it seems to be coming from a great distance, the noise and vibration barely perceptible through the walls. Which raises the question: specifically *where* in the ship does it originate?

The corridor stretches on both sides of us into a curve of infinity, fading into darkness in places where the wall sconce lights are missing, while several others flicker from disrepair. Just ahead of us, the opposite interior wall also curves slightly, and I can see the seams of ancient wall panels holding them together. The walls, ceiling, floor—all are colored slate grey with flecks of gold, which indicates orichalcum.

There are interior doors at sparse intervals, narrow and oddly shaped, like hatches, all along the corridor. Small plaques appear next to each door, inscribed with Atlantean numbers and text in addition to unfamiliar pictograph characters not unlike Ancient Egyptian hieroglyphics.

"As many here are aware, this is the uppermost section, mostly retrofitted as modern laboratory space," Director Tiofon says as we linger in the corridor, looking around us. "You know this floor as the Red Sector, or Basement Level One."

"Yes, looks generally familiar to me," Aeson says.

"In fact, this is Red Habitat, Ra Deck One, Level Four—according to the ship records, which you will have access to shortly," Tiofon says. "We are not entirely clear on this area's original purpose, but for the last five decades at least we've been using it for biomedical research. Since so much facility space on this level has been retrofitted, there is very little of interest here that is pertinent to our current task. Only the walls and underside portions of these signs and plaques are original—that which is obscured underneath this text overlay."

"If this is Level Four, I assume there are Levels Three, Two, and One somewhere above us?" Director Bennu asks. "How exactly does that work?"

It is Shirahtet who replies, nodding slowly. "Yes, we are Four Levels below the top of the ship. The levels are approximately aligned with the stadium building floors, so that Level One—a small round attic level—lies directly underneath the Grail Monument 'stem,' which is a passage tube, hollow on the inside and can be accessed via a hatch."

"Yes, precisely," Director Tiofon says. "In addition, the levels are all accessible from a central stairwell that runs all the way down through the middle of the ship."

"All right. So where do we begin our exploration?" Aeson asks.

"This way," Hijep Tiofon replies. "My Imperial Lord—" And he points with one hand before him, beginning to walk left along the corridor.

We go after him, advancing for a long stretch past many closed doors. Occasional staff workers in lab coats walk past us or emerge at random from some of those enclosures. They appear as surprised to see our group as I am to see them. At the sight of Aeson, they nod quickly or bow to the Imperial Crown Prince before proceeding on their way.

What happens behind those doors? What kind of unsavory, unethical, or terrifying research goes on here in secret, under the auspices of the Imperator?

Despite my fear I look cautiously, straining to see what's inside, every time another room opens as we pass by. . . .

Director Tiofon finally stops at one of the doors and points to a wall plaque which depicts a curious pictograph. The image is a long upright oval with four circles inside, resembling a pea pod with four peas. On top of the oval, just outside it, is a fifth smaller circle connected to the oval with a short vertical line.

"This symbol, right here, you will find frequently—all around here," Tiofon says. "It is the symbol of the ship, and its ancient name is Vimana."

"Wait a minute . . ." I mumble.

Everyone looks at me.

"That word, I've heard it before—something out of Indian myth? Isn't 'vimana' supposed to be a weird flying machine from a Hindu epic, either *Ramayana* or *Mahabharata?*"

I am met by vacant expressions. Even Aeson watches me with unfamiliarity.

And then Director Tiofon says politely, "My Imperial Lady, apologies, but I'm not well versed in your Earth mythology. However, it's quite possible it references something even more ancient, such as our own Atlantean roots. The Vimana was the main Atlantean vessel of the group that escaped Earth in the distant past."

"Indeed. It was the Imperial vessel carrying divine members of the Kassiopei Dynasty," the First Priest Shirahtet adds.

And now we're standing inside it. . . .

I listen in wonder.

"Fascinating that you've heard this term before, and very useful," Aeson says to me with encouragement. "Let us know if there's anything else that comes to you."

"I'm glad I'm here," I say. "Although—I wish I knew more about that particular mythology."

Wish Dad was here, he'd know. . . .

"As I was saying," Director Tiofon resumes, "the Vimana symbol appears throughout the ship, and it happens to indicate certain shipboard areas, such as connecting corridors and stairwells. This door designates a passage that will take us to the center of the ship and its main stairwell between levels and decks."

He opens the door with the same key card, revealing a narrow, dark corridor. The moment we enter, faint lights come to life, blooming from the surface of the walls near the floor so that we can see the lower panels and the floor beneath. The light source is the walls themselves, no sconces or spheres of any kind.

The corridor stretches before us into a point of darkness. It is interspersed with other equally dim corridors and other doors along the way. As we walk, motion sensors must be activating the lights on the walls directly before us because they flicker awake with a feeble yellow glow as we approach.

A few moments later we emerge into a wide area about fifty feet (or just over fifteen meters) in diameter that contains a circular pit—a void of darkness, above and below. Eight corridors converge upon it from all directions, and one of them is ours.

A safety railing barrier circles the pit along a narrow ledge. The railing has multiple latched gates, allowing access to metal rung ladders that lead both up and down to other levels. The rungs are installed on the divider walls between each of the eight corridors— walls that serve as structural supports all the way up and down this vertical shaft. An additional spiral staircase, wide enough for two people, winds close to the perimeter of the pit. The staircase is accessible by a short walkway from our level.

In the middle of that spiral is circular empty space. The whole thing reminds me of a silo or great upright tube.

"I've never been here before," Aeson remarks with a frown, then steps toward the safety barrier.

"From here we can access the entire ship," Shirahtet says to Aeson as he leans to look over the railing—while I keep slightly back, my old fear of heights stirring.

"Well, unfortunately not all of it," Director Tiofon adds. "Approximately one hundred and fifty levels below—which is halfway down the ship—the connecting passage between Blue Habitat and Green Habitat has caved in, and the surrounding structure is too unstable to force it open. At present we cannot access the Green Habitat or the Yellow Habitat on the very bottom of the ship without risking further damage."

I suddenly remember the Imperator mentioning how the lower levels of the ark-ship were unreachable, and all their tantalizing secrets with them.

"Let us go down," Shirahtet says, "as far as we may, to the bottom of Blue Habitat, Khe Deck One, Level One. All of the levels above that have been generally explored and catalogued, even though some findings are inconclusive, full of gaps, and our interpretations of artifacts and data might be faulty. At least we—the priests of Kassiopei and our acolytes—have done our best to examine all of it over the eons. But that last known level, the damaged one—it still holds many secrets."

"Is that spiral staircase still functional? Or must we climb down the ladders?" Aeson asks Shirahtet and Director Tiofon with a meaningful glance at me. I imagine he must be concerned for my safety.

"Aeson," I say gently. "I was in the Games."

At that moment Rurim Kiv chuckles lightly.

But Aeson is not in the mood for amusement, and his expression remains serious.

"Both the staircase and the rung ladders are safe to use." Igara Cvutu speaks up. "I've used them myself, as recently as two days ago. I prefer the staircase. It takes me only half an hour to reach the bottom via the spiraling staircase, with a few rest stops, and I am not in the best of shape."

"There is another, quicker alternative. A hovering freight elevator platform was used to move bulk items across levels, right through the center portion here," Shirahtet says, pointing to the void in the middle of the pit. "It is still undamaged, and fortunately remains on our side of things—the accessible upper portion of the ship's stairwell hub."

"Great," Aeson says. "Call it. We have no time to waste climbing stairs."

Shirahtet sings the keying command, and, a few minutes later, a thick, round, orichalcum-treated platform comes sailing up from the lower levels of the pit through the center of the spiral staircase and stops before us. It is just wide enough in diameter to accommodate all of us, including the Imperial guards, if we all stand reasonably close together.

Hijep Tiofon unlatches the closest railing gate, extends a walkway plank, and steps onto it to cross the void toward the elevator platform.

Aeson looks at me with consideration, then takes my hand in his possessive, warm grip, and together we traverse the void.

Chapter 39

We ride the platform elevator down the central shaft of the ship, moving past endless levels and decks, each marked by hubs of eight corridors. Most of them are pitch black, and only a few passages are dimly lit where someone must be working on that level. As we approach, sensors turn on faint illumination that has no apparent light source, a feeble glow coming awake inside the walls. It's just barely enough to illuminate our way. Occasional wall markings sail past us—numbers and pictographs etched in relief on charcoal-grey surfaces.

Suddenly we're submerged in a twilight world of metal and shadows.

A quarter of the way down—after level seventy-five, according to Hijep Tiofon—the elevator enters a portion of the shaft that has no corridors. It's just walls inside a tube, with rung ladders and the spiraling staircase continuing downward around us. Here the encircling walls light up evenly, and without the darkened corridors, this entire area appears brighter. The illumination casts a yellowish glow over everyone's faces, deepening the shadows.

"We're now inside the connecting tube between Habitats," Director Tiofon explains. "The Habitats can be sealed off independently, and this connecting shaft can be undocked from both ends. But it's been permanently docked for as long as we remember."

"Remind me, how many Habitats and levels in all?" Director Bennu asks.

Aeson continues to hold my hand, keeping me close to him and away from the edges of the platform, since the elevator has no safety barrier—even though we're surrounded by a wall of guards.

"Four Habitats," Director Tiofon replies. "Each one is a self-contained sphere with nine decks and seventy-five levels. As already mentioned, we only explored the upper two—Red and Blue. As far as Habitat structure—the upper hemisphere is designated as Ra levels, and the lower hemisphere is Khe levels, with the widest level in the middle designated as Main Deck. There are four additional decks above and four below the Main Deck. Each deck has ten levels, except for the roomier inner decks—they have only seven levels each and taller ceilings."

Director Tiofon pauses. "By the way—the level count begins on top with Level One, down to Level 37 near the halfway point. Then comes Main Deck spanning the equator, then another Level 37, with numbers decreasing all the way down to Level One again on the very bottom. In general, bigger numbers are at the widest, middle section of each Habitat. The smallest, outermost levels on either end are always Level One."

A minute later we emerge from the tube into the second Habitat, called Blue, and once again hubs of corridors appear at intervals as we descend. At last we reach the bottom and the elevator stops.

There's nowhere else to go.

The platform is hovering over a dark area filled with metal rubble—twisted panels and broken rungs and remains of the spiral staircase—indicating the end of the explored portion of the ancient ship.

A corridor hub greets us. Except, three of the eight corridors are also filled with debris, with partially dented walls, and the remaining five don't look particularly reliable either, with caving and dented floor and ceiling panels at the entrances.

"It looks worse than it is." Igara Cvutu steps onto the closest undamaged plankway with a familiarity born of practice.

In support of her claim, the wall lights in the vicinity start to bloom, and the corridor nearest to her is illuminated.

"Please follow me," Igara says, glancing back at us, and proceeds into the corridor.

"This is a good place to begin," Director Tiofon says, moving after her. "Watch your heads, please. Otherwise, quite safe."

Rurim Kiv does not say a word, only hops lightly from the platform onto the hub floor, bypassing the plankway and the rubble. He stands, looking around at the walls.

We all follow.

The radius corridor is another straight line, just like the one near the surface that we originally took to reach this shaft from the top of the ship. Except this one is much shorter—we're on Level One, the smallest bottom slice of the circle.

"A little more, this way," Shirahtet says, pointing to the end of the line and a door. "We're going to see some very old living quarters full of priceless items of historical value."

My heart speeds up with an urgent feeling which I cannot quite describe. Aeson squeezes my hand when I glance at him, just as we approach the door leading to the main perimeter corridor.

Director Tiofon uses his key card to open it, and we emerge in a curving outer corridor, with walls immediately blooming with faint illumination upon our arrival. There are no sconce lights here; the ones at the top of the ship where we first entered must have been much later additions.

Shirahtet takes us in the right direction and we follow. Three closed doors later, he stops before an open chamber that has no doors, and instead seems to have several panels—the equivalent of one wall—removed. It resembles a recessed niche with missing panels, a kind of large, walk-in storage closet.

The chamber is full of long metal boxes and chests of all shapes and sizes, some stacked on top of each other, others on top of tables and built-in wall shelves. Every one of these storage units is marked with unfamiliar symbols, pictographs, numbers. Some of the containers have visible latches and locks, while most others appear seamless on all sides.

"This is a private storage area that was discovered quite by accident, and relatively recently, only a decade ago," Shirahtet says, pointing to several long wall panels lying flat on the floor. "The walls caved in, and we found this hidden cavity. My technicians disassembled the rest of the panels very carefully, allowing us full access to this chamber."

"What is it?" Aeson asks. "What are all these things?"

Shirahtet pauses carefully before answering. "For the most part, we don't know. We've been unable to open the majority of these containers, because they are either seamless in construction—or appear seamless. The ones that appear to have locks have false locks. The few that we managed to open by means of brute force, cutting directly into the metal surface, either self-destructed their contents before our tools finished penetrating them or were damaged beyond repair. What we were able to retrieve have been old scrolls in some cases—which fell apart into dust or small fragments."

"Absolutely outrageous. These scrolls are too delicate to withstand such terrible handling," Antiquities Specialist Cvutu says with reproach. "Your power tools, lasers—and even more shocking, flame torches at some point, from what I hear; brute force indeed—ruined the ancient fabric. On something fragile like that we would use fine brushes, tweezers, compressed air, micro-tools—"

Shirahtet raises one hand to silence her words. "Understood. Individuals who have so *brutalized* the artifacts over the years have all been removed from duty and their entire tech teams disciplined accordingly. As for the other items found—items that survived our crude methods," he continues, "there were trinkets, household items, personal items belonging mostly to individuals of low rank, and a few truly ancient data storage media devices that we are uncertain how to play."

"After more than nine thousand years, I don't expect any data survived," Director Tiofon says. "But even if it did, I doubt it would've been anything important—not on this bottom level of Deck One. All the nobility, all the most important ranking individuals, commanding officers, industry leaders, not to mention the Imperial Family, were housed on Deck Four, maybe Three, but never here. So let's not have any undue regrets over that—"

But Director Bennu interrupts him. "How can you say that? The value of genuine ancient tech, on whichever level, is priceless! I don't care if it's a poor servant or slave whose storage box we open, it is all vital to our understanding! In fact, I wouldn't be surprised if the manual workers—those with real skills that were chosen to accompany the elites—had some amazing data, methods, insight—"

"Yes, yes, all of that is true," Director Tiofon responds. "My point is, we may be worrying over nothing here, taking up resources to focus on this particular storage area when in fact our time could be better used elsewhere in the ship."

"So why did you bring us here?" Aeson says. "Unless you think there is something relevant to our search?"

"My Imperial Lord, yes," Shirahtet says, glancing around the room at the boxes. "Several good reasons to look here. Primarily—what intrigues me are the questions raised. Why resort to such intricate protections on a non-VIP personnel level? Why create such difficulty of access to the contents of these boxes? And why was it all hidden in a walled-off chamber for thousands of years, only to be discovered through a lucky accident? Was it to protect the *contents* from prying eyes or protect *whoever* would open them? Furthermore, what kind of advanced storage is this, and how did they manage to get the contents inside? And lastly, *who?* Who is responsible?"

"Have you tried voice commands?" I ask.

Shirahtet turns his dark, unblinking eyes to me, and I can almost see a twinge of annoyance. "Naturally we have, my Imperial Lady. Every known permutation of voice-lock has been attempted. Indeed, the Imperial Sovereign Himself was the one who brought our attention to this particular area, finding it of considerable interest. The Imperator came down here on more than one occasion. Five years ago, in particular—he spent quite a few hours here, trying various combinations with the Logos voice . . . to no avail."

"Is that so?" Aeson says thoughtfully. "Why five years ago?"

"I believe your Imperial Father found something of concern here—that is, elsewhere on this relic of a ship," Shirahtet says. "Which brings me to the second reason why this area is of importance."

This time the First Priest looks at Rurim Kiv. "There are hidden symbols on some of these containers. Symbols previously unfamiliar to us, never encountered before, not even after hundreds of years of examination of the ship. But they're *exactly* like the ones you discovered etched with orichalcum onto the great stones of the Earth pyramid during the Blue Stage of the Games."

"Fascinating," Rurim Kiv says. "You might recall, *she* was the one who discovered them." And he points at me.

I raise my brows. "Yes, my Team and I stumbled onto them by accident, using the heating command on the stones. But you were the one who actually figured out their pattern and meaning and unlocked the Blue Grail."

"After looking over everyone's shoulders and stealing our findings," Tuar mutters, standing a few steps away with the other guards.

Everyone looks at Tuar, since normally guards never speak unless prompted.

"Oh! This is Tuar Momet," I say at once. "He was with me—with us—in the Games. He was on my Team . . . Team Lark."

"Good," Aeson says. "Another person who has direct experience with those symbols."

But Rurim Kiv watches Tuar with an unblinking stare. "I did not *steal*. I merely observed what was there for the taking," he says with a slight edge. "All your notes, all your data was in the open. Anyone who could see it, did. There are no rules against exercising such an advantage in the Games."

"Maybe not rules, but it was still underhanded." Tuar meets the Artist's gaze with his own unflinching one. "Little honor in doing so."

As I recall, Tuar is not particularly fond of Rurim Kiv. Neither, for that matter, was the rest of Team Lark, nor most other Contenders.

For the first time Rurim shows some kind of reaction. He eases his shoulders and slowly releases a deep breath, but maintains his eye contact with Tuar. "That much is true. There is little honor in the Games. There are only the rules."

And he turns away, focusing back on Shirahtet. "Tell us more about those symbols—here and elsewhere."

Shirahtet, who has been observing our interaction with interest, nods. "Yes, then. We encountered these mysterious symbols here in the chamber but nowhere else on the ancient ship. And then, during the Earth Mission, as we were in the process of transporting the stones of the disassembled pyramid—everything done according to the Imperial Sovereign's strict instructions—these same symbols were accidentally discovered."

He pauses, glancing at me, at Rurim Kiv. "In truth—the Imperial Sovereign specifically instructed that the pyramid was to be included in the Games as a challenge . . . because of those symbols. We still don't know their greater meaning. Earlier, however, our experts barely managed to unravel a meaningful correlation between a few of them—only basic relationships between some of the shapes, no actual translation. And so, a puzzle was constructed using what we knew. We wanted to see if any of *you* could figure out more of it, in the process of solving the basic puzzle as a Game Stage Challenge."

My mind races with excitement. I stare at Rurim Kiv, watch his reaction.

Rurim Kiv shakes his head. "So I solved your puzzle. As you say—it was simply an interaction of basic shapes. But that is all."

"But you're good at finding patterns!" I say, unable to hold back. "Whatever it is you do in your line of work—artist, creator of some kind—you seem to have a good sense of the fine detail."

"Precisely why the Imperial Sovereign had him brought into the project," Hijep Tiofon says.

"My line of work is *illusion*," Rurim Kiv says. "I'm a stage magician, a performer. My natural Category, Entertainer, was getting too full of high-profile, high-end competition this year, so I decided to enroll as Artist, a close second. Apparently it was a wise move. I won."

"Seems to me, stage magic requires detail-oriented precision work," I say. "You are in the right place here."

Rurim Kiv nods slowly to me. "And so are you, Imperial Lady Gwen. By your own definition, I have seen you work magic in the Games."

"Very well," Aeson says suddenly. "Let's all begin looking at these containers. And I mean everyone. All of you here have abilities and sharp observation skills. What I care about now is not just deciphering arcane symbols or opening boxes, but *connecting* anything you find to our present situation—the Ghost Moon, the humming ship, the alien golden lights. It is why we're here."

And we get to work.

We spend some time examining boxes in the faint wall illumination of the chamber. At Director Tiofon's request, additional lights are called in, and when the small hovering spheres arrive, they greatly improve visibility.

"Why not take these containers upstairs to the top of the ship? Remove them to a well-equipped, secure lab?" Director Bennu says in a frustrated tone, as he picks up yet another mysterious, seamless box, turning it in every direction, running his fingers over the corners, to no avail. He has brought a small set of micro-tools with him, and so have many of the others. His tool pouch is sitting on top of the nearest surface, opened, but not getting any use.

"Because it's how we already ruined a number of them," Igara Cvutu reminds him coldly. She lifts another, larger box and stacks it on top of a different one, while reaching for a third underneath and blowing at a fine layer of dust, probably accumulated more recently from all the human tech activity in this relatively sterile environment. Her own set of tools is more delicate, resembling an Earth-style antique sewing kit, with tiny-to-long rows of needles, toothpicks, brushes, chisels, tweezers, forceps, and a multi-nozzle device that could be a micro air gun.

Aeson's wrist comm band emits tones, and he pauses his own investigation to check his messages.

I stop my own task of checking the triangle patterns on a small rectangular box to watch him nervously as he taps his personal unit then reads the incoming data.

"Everything okay?" I ask.

"Nothing much of concern," Aeson says, glancing at me. "However, my Imperial Father wants to know our progress."

"Or lack of," Director Bennu grumbles under his breath, tapping his fingernail on the surface of one small container.

"We still have so much to examine," I say reassuringly.

"Do not forget, Imperial Lady, all of these boxes have been thoroughly examined before, over the years," the First Priest Shirahtet says, observing me with his curiously forceful gaze. "What is called for, now, is a different *perspective*."

"Fortunately, we've gathered the best persons imaginable," Director Tiofon says cheerfully, looking around at everyone.

"I admire your optimism, Tiofon," Director Bennu says. "How about you shorten our tasks by informing us about what you already know—what shows the most promise. In other words, what useful patterns have been found so far, what general observations? Give us something."

"Take a look," Shirahtet says, approaching with a small data tablet. "Summaries of findings over the years. Every test run, every method employed, is recorded in this high-security database here. The obvious lead is in the stacking pattern of the symbols. It appears to be the most meaningful of all our findings."

"Ah! You should've led with this!" Bennu says, grabbing the tablet in continued irritation. "So much wasted time. . . ."

"What stacking pattern?" Rurim Kiv asks, setting down the box in his hands, while Director Bennu reads.

"Permit me to show you." Shirahtet begins to walk around the room, while most of us stop whatever we're doing to watch him. He reaches for one box, then a few steps further, picks up another. The boxes are the same size, appearing identical. He sets them down side by side, and they form a larger unit, a square.

We approach closer in curiosity.

"Observe this curving line," says the First Priest. "When you align these two boxes like this, the line matches exactly and continues from one box to the other, running together to create a larger pattern. So—a stacking pattern."

"Kind of like a jigsaw puzzle," I say. "The pieces fit together to make a bigger picture."

"Yes," Shirahtet says, glancing at me. "It is precisely so—a bigger picture."

"And according to this summary, all kinds of interesting pictures form when you stack these boxes together," Rovat Bennu says with satisfaction. "The most intricate of the stacking shapes they managed to achieve over the years is this incredible 3D cube."

Bennu comes around showing the image on the tablet to each of us. When it's my turn, I see a digital photo of a huge cube formed out of what must be every box in this room. The containers are stacked on top of each other and arranged in a way that shows an intricate harmonious sunburst pattern of geometric arcs, angles, and curves, resembling a mandala, on every side of the cube.

It is beautiful and incredibly detailed. In addition to the large mandala centered on each side, there are stars and circles, lines looping in curves and waves around it—all of it clearly formed by the placement of the connected boxes.

"Can this be replicated?" Aeson asks when Bennu gives him the tablet.

"Unfortunately, not that particular one," Director Tiofon replies instead. "As we mentioned, some of the boxes have been destroyed by our heavy-handed techs. If re-created now, this cube would be missing pieces."

"That's too bad," Rurim Kiv says. "The greater object was beautiful."

"It was." Shirahtet looks thoughtfully at the tablet. "If I recall, the Imperial Sovereign sang quite a number of advanced Voice commands over this cube structure, with no results. He keyed the whole thing repeatedly, even claimed he could almost *feel* something, a kind of gathering energy vibration, but ultimately nothing."

"What if we tried singing, Aeson?" I say. "Both of us, *together?* We could try with a very simple shape."

I return to my original spot and pick up the box I was working on. And then I carry and set it down next to another box I've had my eye on, because I can easily visualize in my mind the resulting stacked image—a four-point star that resembles the star window in my Imperial Palace bedroom.

Maybe it's a matter of subliminal persuasion, a mind trick based on simple familiarity, on repetition—after all, I see this shape on a regular basis, every time I'm in that bedroom.

Whatever it is, something in my gut calls me to it, telling me there's something special about this simple shape.

I place my hands on the two adjacent boxes and sing a keying command, F-A-C. My voice sends rich echoes through the open ship space around us.

Nothing happens.

I look up, and Aeson is watching me with his familiar, beloved gaze.

"Aeson," I say. "Please. Place your hand here. Sing with me."

Im amrevu moves in behind me and stands looking over my shoulder at the four-point star shape created by the boxes.

"That's Manala's favorite window—in your bedroom," he says with faint amusement.

And then we both sing the keying command.

Chapter 40

As Aeson and I begin to sing together, everyone around us grows motionless and listens. Our two honey-drenched voices blend with power and precision in the silence, sending echoes rebounding against the sound-sensitive walls of the ancient ship.

We keep our vocal focus on the two small boxes lying before us side to side, but it almost seems too much . . . and the rest of the ship responds also. Because it feels as if somewhere so very far away—*elsewhere*, outside, not here, in a secret place or *layer* beyond the hull walls—the very faint, distant, eternal hum *falters*—if only for a moment.

Even though I feel goosebumps rising along my skin, nothing happens.

At first.

Aeson's hand rests lightly on one of the boxes, while I touch the surface of the other. In moments I start feeling a buzzing sensation against my fingertips. I glance up at Aeson, not sure if he too is feeling anything.

We finish the keying command.

"Again," Aeson says, meeting my gaze, then returns his attention to the boxes.

We sing again, repeating the F-A-C note sequence.

The vibration against my fingertips seems to intensify. As if the metal is struggling against something.

"Can you—can you feel it?" I ask softly.

"Yes." He watches me and his forehead tenses.

"One more time?" I ask.

He nods. "This time, let's try something a little different. Continue to sing the exact same notes, while I'll use another sequence."

And as I sing F-A-C for the third time, I hear Aeson's deep voice deviate from mine, as he uses C-E-G notes instead.

The moment he does, the surface of the containers starts to vibrate even more. Then abruptly the vibration fades away—not so much stopping as "rising" in pitch to ultra-sensory levels—as though an apex has been reached and all the buildup of tension has been released somewhere.

At the same time the four-point star design formed by the adjacent boxes begins to glow, until it becomes a hair-thin line of golden light.

"That's different," Hijep Tiofon says, with surprise.

The First Priest Shirahtet immediately steps closer to us. Everyone else approaches also.

Aeson and I continue touching the boxes as the glowing lines forming the four-point star grow brighter and brighter, going from gold to incandescent white.

Suddenly, with a clank, the material on the *inside* of the glowing line—the portion that's forming the shape of the star—falls inward, as if someone took a laser to the metal, cutting a hole shaped like the star.

A crazy image comes to mind, that of a cookie cutter making a shape, while the resulting cookie falls away, separated along its outline from the surrounding sheet of dough.

The hollow interior of both boxes is revealed, while the star "cutout" lies in two mirror-image pieces inside the two boxes, half of it in each box.

It is now perfectly inert, cool to the touch and no longer glowing.

And it's resting on top of whatever's hidden underneath, freed at last, after thousands of years.

"Fascinating!" Rovat Bennu exclaims. "What an unusual heat lock! Multilevel programming across objects, requiring two voices and fundamental variance in keying note—"

"Careful, careful, *please!*" Igara Cvutu says, wincing as Director Tiofon reaches for one of the boxes. "Not your fingers! Use tweezers to lift, I beg of you!"

Hijep Tiofon pauses, then goes for his tool kit on the other side of the room.

"Better yet, allow me," Igara says. "I am much more practiced in these procedures, I assure you."

"Very well," Director Tiofon says, raising one brow. "You have smaller fingers."

Antiquities Specialist Cvutu glances at Aeson then at me. "With your permission, My Imperial Lord, Lady—" And she gently picks up one of the boxes and sets it on a steady table surface. With fine tweezers from her kit, she picks up the shard of metal and sets it aside.

Underneath lies a brown, leathery scroll, resembling parchment. Nothing else inside the box, only the single rolled scroll.

Before proceeding, Igara puts on a pair of gloves from a second, larger supply kit in her pocket. With surgical precision she reaches inside the odd-shaped opening and gently touches the scroll. "Does not crumble to dust. . . . So far so good," she remarks, almost with amusement.

I hold my breath as she reaches back inside and slowly angles the scroll, lifting it through the opening.

Igara places the scroll on the table, on top of a sterile lining cloth from her supply kit, all the while muttering, "Excellent . . . fabric in good condition . . . nice level of oil saturation content . . . fibers retained resiliency . . . without moisture damage."

"Will it stand up to unrolling?" Director Tiofon asks. "Wouldn't it be wiser to continue this in a sterile lab?"

"Normally, yes," Igara replies, not even looking up, as she arranges the scroll on the sterile cloth. "However, the very specific climate of the ship might be the very best place for it, at least until we know its condition better. . . . I will attempt to unroll."

"Proceed," Aeson says.

Igara's steady fingers move very slowly as she begins to unroll the ancient fabric.

Slowly, slowly . . .

Again I barely breathe, watching the scroll reveal itself before our eyes.

It is covered with Atlantean writing, wispy and faded, in a script that I hardly recognize. As far as I know, Classical *Atlanteo* is about as far removed from modern Atlanteo as modern English is from Old English (there's even a whole Middle English stuck somewhere in there between the two, so yes, very far removed).

"Ah-h-h. . . ." Igara's breath shudders as she holds the two ends of the scroll apart to keep it from rebounding back into a coil. "Beautiful!"

"What does it say?" Hijep Tiofon asks.

"Allow me," Shirahtet says, leaning over the scroll.

"Of course," Igara responds politely, but does not let go of the fabric. As Antiquities Specialist she probably reads Classical *Atlanteo*, but then so does the First Priest, and in that he outranks her.

Shirahtet stares at the old writing, but says nothing.

The moment stretches.

"What?" Director Tiofon asks. "Tell me it's not some nonsense like an ancient inventory list."

"An inventory list would be useful. *This* is nonsense," Shirahtet replies at last, exhaling and shaking his head with disappointment. "But it is a child's nonsense. Some ancient youngster by the name of 'Semmi' wrote poetry in their spare time. Also practiced handwriting, training to be a scribe, since many lines are repeated."

"Is that all?" Director Bennu frowns. "How unfortunate. There has to be something else."

"See for yourself. She can translate it for you." And the First Priest steps back, allowing Igara Cvutu continued full access to the artifact without his hovering presence.

"Please translate it in your spare time," Aeson says thoughtfully. "Word for word. I would like to see it."

"Of course, My Imperial Lord."

"But what about the other box?" I point to the second half of the unlocked mystery.

A few minutes later Antiquities Specialist Cvutu has removed the contents of the second box, which consist of two more scrolls, a large one and a tiny one that looks more like a rolled-up note.

"More handwriting exercises and a few lines that could be word puzzles or games, or poetry by our ancient friend Semmi," Igara says, looking up from the large scroll. And then she opens the little scroll, holding it between her gloved fingers. "And this—apparently a message to someone, from Semmi. No, my apologies, a message to Semmi from another person. It says:

My Book of Everything is now hidden and only you
know how to find it. Keep it safe and tell no one.
Remember me kindly.
—Arleana, Starlight Sorceress.

"Say that again? That name!" Shirahtet returns from across the
room from where he'd gone to examine some other boxes.

Igara frowns and repeats loudly. "*Arleana*, it definitely says
Arleana, Starlight Sorceress. But—that's a myth. . . . Are you certain
it is significant? Could be children playing, the myth's origin was
never certain, it could be an old myth even for them—"

I glance at Aeson whose own expression has focused with
concentration.

And then I remember what Erita told me yesterday, when the
alien lights arrived in the sky. A children's story about golden stars
and ancient enemies.

"I just learned about this myth yesterday, and it could be
significant," I say, as Shirahtet takes the little scroll away from Igara
and reads it closely.

"Agreed," Aeson says. "I want every word translated. But first,
we are going to open the rest of these boxes—as many as we can.
I've had my doubts, but no longer. A powerful reason exists *why*
these scrolls and whatever else is here were sealed and hidden away
so carefully. We will discover that reason. Furthermore, no ordinary
scribe would have the means or the access to such intricate high-end
technology for personal use. This is major."

"The Book of Everything. . . ." Shirahtet whispers suddenly,
looking up. "No, it is not a myth. This is real. In fact—it is what the
Imperial Sovereign has been looking for, all these years. He must be
informed at once—"

But Aeson is already on his wrist comm, making the call.

We spend the rest of the morning and afternoon opening ancient
boxes. That is, a whole cadre of assistants and technicians has
been called, and they are set to arranging the boxes in meaningful
stacking patterns based on their own decade-old database records.
Aeson and I then use our Logos voices in tandem to heat up the
incandescent lines forming each pattern, causing the cookie cutter
metal pieces to fall inward.

Sometimes it works, sometimes it doesn't.

Some of the patterns do not respond to our combined efforts.

Others fall before us obediently, metal "cookies" separating along the superheated seams, coming apart like melted butter.

I still have no exact idea of what's happening around us, but I know we're on the right track, somehow.

Periodically Shirahtet removes himself from the room to make private calls to the Imperator. At other times, Aeson steps away to do the same.

Igara Cvutu works relentlessly, carefully removing the contents of those boxes we could open. They are mostly scrolls, scrolls, and more scrolls. Her assistant arrives with a micro camera and starts making digital scans of each scroll, in case it falls apart or something else happens to it before we've had the chance to make a translation.

The other things we uncover in those containers are trinkets, personal items, protection amulets with divine blessings inscribed on them, several pieces of cheap jewelry with semi-precious stones— including a coarse woven rope bracelet of several gold beads, which immediately falls apart since the rope has become dust—and several carved dolls of people and animals painted with crude colors that also come off like rainbow dust, leaving bare ancient wood underneath.

Antiquities Specialist Cvutu instructs her assistant and other techs to carefully catalogue and wrap each item, and they are then carried away, somewhere upstairs to a modern lab, to prevent further oxidation. The same is done for the scrolls that are taken to a secure lab in the Imperial Poseidon Museum for translation.

"Please expedite the process as much as possible," Aeson tells them. "Have the translations ready and send me the digital documents. Anything that is questionable, mark as such. But I want to see most of them tomorrow or the next day at the latest."

"If you find anything related to The Book of Everything, or mentioning Arleana," Shirahtet adds, "contact me immediately."

Aeson looks at the First Priest. "You need to tell me more about the importance of this book."

"My deepest apologies, My Imperial Lord," Shirahtet replies, a strange expression coming to his face. "But it is something you must bring up with your Imperial Father. Until I have his permission, I may not divulge—"

"Fine. I will do that." Aeson cuts him off.

We continue working until late afternoon without taking a meal break. By sixth hour, those boxes that could be opened are opened. The few that remain sealed will be dealt with later.

I find that my throat is sore from all the hours of voice commands, and Aeson is in similar shape.

"One way or another, we'll get them open, now that we have a better idea of what to do. Two voices are required," Aeson says, as we ride the freight elevator back to the upper levels and then emerge through the *Stadion* structure and head for the hover cars.

"Not merely two voices, but two Logos voices such as yours," Shirahtet says softly to us somewhat later, before we separate to go our own ways for the night.

"There might even be something more to it," Director Tiofon adds. "And that elusive something we'll continue pursuing and testing for, to get the remaining containers open."

"Very well, keep me informed," Aeson interrupts Tiofon as his wrist comm starts ringing with urgency yet again.

And then, surrounded by Imperial guards, we take off and head home.

At the Imperial Palace, poor Aeson has to deal with what feels like ten thousand things at once. A late *dea* or early *niktos* meal is served to us in the workroom. Meanwhile, Xelio and Keruvat are still here, intensely focused on multiple data screens, where incoming SPC messages are being routed here from every possible source.

"Kass, we just received new combat readiness status reports," Xel says. "New Deshret, Ubasti, Eos-Heket—all at one hundred percent readiness. In addition to our own Imperial Fleet. *Sebasarets* will start ferrying master crews to Wars 1 through 4, starting tonight, at tenth hour of Khe. Regular deployment Fleet crews will follow, starting tomorrow at eighth hour of Ra. Wars 1 through 4 are maintaining current position in the outer system for now."

"Excellent." Aeson nods, sitting down at the biggest monitor with the Rah Station view. Today, in that particular view, the grid of golden lights now takes up most of the sky around Helios.

"Rah Station report?"

"No change, except for the continuing growth of the grid," Ker replies. "Nomarch Rertu says that War-10 has arrived and settled into defensive position orbit near the Station."

"Yes, I received a direct notification from Command Pilot Eodea Tecpatl a few hours earlier. She tells me that War-10 has been finishing up Green Season training exercises with fresh crews out of Cadet Schools, so at least they have more than just a skeleton crew." Aeson lets out a deep breath and shakes his head sadly.

"I'd hate to be those Cadets." Ker whistles.

"A fresh crop from rural Ankh-Tawi and Weret. Likely not their best," Xel adds. "The best would be hand-picked and sent to the outer system to serve around Atlas or Olympos."

"What's their local Fleet combat readiness status?"

Ker checks a data screen. "Only thirty-nine percent. And eighty-two percent of that is Ankh-Tawi. Weret is an unprepared mess. Next time your Imperial Father talks to New Deshret he might mention that about their vassal nations."

"Bashtooh. . . ." Aeson rubs his forehead with a frown and runs one hand through his hair, then returns to perusing the reports and listening to Ker and Xel give additional ones.

I sit nearby watching them, holding a tall glass of *nikkari* juice, and regularly swallow the soothing, cool liquid to relieve my parched throat.

"Your glass is full, and you haven't touched your food, Aeson," I complain, glancing at his plate. Then I set my own drink aside, pick up Aeson's neglected glass of *qvaali* nearby, and forcefully hand it to him.

"Enough. This can wait for a few minutes. Please nourish yourself. *Right now.*"

Aeson looks up at my no-nonsense tone and smiles at me. But he takes the glass without protest and brings it to his lips.

Ker and Xel observe our interaction with approval.

The rest of the night is an unrelieved ordeal for Aeson, as he continues working non-stop, handling messages, dispatches, questions, reports from ranking officers under his command and public officials, international Fleet contacts, endless data.

I zone out and go to bed around midnight, and he is still working. Not even my lingering good-night kiss can distract him enough to take that much-needed rest—even though he promises me he'll be asleep in just a few minutes.

And then, just as I fall asleep, blinking tiredly, noticing from the corner of my eye as always that four-point star window in my bedroom—which reminds me of both the artifact box from earlier today and of the Fleet Cadet insignia pins, it occurs to me—*Gracie! Will she be in that wave of general Fleet deployment tomorrow morning? Oh no! I didn't even get a chance to say goodbye!*

Chapter 41

Nothing is scheduled for me on the morning of Green Ghost Moon 12, and I sleep in somewhat late, waking with a start after eighth hour. Again, my first panicked thought is of Gracie.

Is she gone already?

And then everything *else* slams down on me, everything that happened yesterday in the ancient ark-ship, and all the rest of the world-shattering events. . . . I stare at the star window that is covered with a blackout curtain. However, it's not drawn all the way, so it still manages to let in some of the morning Hel-fire, giving a pale ambiance to the chamber.

Did Aeson get any sleep?

Any news on those scrolls we found or their translations?

So many other semi-pointless questions plague my waking mind.

I get up, wasting no more time, and by the time I show up in the workroom—which is normally a hub of activity, but now has apparently become SPC Central Command overnight—it's after ninth hour.

In addition to Anu and Gennio, Oalla and Erita are here, working the data centers. I'm told that Aeson, together with Ker and Xel, has gone up to the SPC Headquarters in orbit for more meetings with various nations' military high command.

"Fleet deployment is in progress," Erita tells me, looking up from her screen.

I nod.

"And the public is not taking it very well," Oalla adds, pointing to a small split screen on her display where she is watching a TV feed. It's a Hel-Ra newscast, with her own father, Desher Keigeri, anchoring.

Periodically, the studio feed breaks away to show Poseidon streets where reporters stop and interview ordinary bystanders who complain and voice their fears. ". . . he's a Fleet pilot, so he received notice . . . multiple family members getting called to duty . . . an invasion . . . a war . . . ancient enemy . . . is this real? What is happening?" is heard over and over. Then the feed switches to a large industrial airfield somewhere beyond downtown city center and closer to the Bay.

Rows and rows of unfamiliar military-looking transport vessels of various shapes and sizes fill the hover-parking slots. Meanwhile endless grey-uniformed Fleet personnel with heavy gear bags hurry in all directions, lines forming, crews and teams entering the vessels via retractable ramps. Air traffic is crazy here, as more and more people arrive, deposited at the edges of the airfield by smaller civilian hover cars and city transport buses.

"They are coming from everywhere," the announcer says in a dramatic tone. "Called to active duty, these are your family and loved ones, being called to serve their nation and the world. . . ."

The airfield is in a constant, conveyor-belt churn of activity. Vessels loaded with personnel and supplies take off vertically, streaking upward at sudden immense velocity, bypassing regular air traffic lanes. More vessels emerge from hangars to take up the vacated spots. It is clear they are headed to orbit and beyond, into deep space, because of the news commentary and the running marquees with "SPC initiates Fleet Deployment" in large letters on the bottom of the screen.

"This is only one deployment airfield of many, all across the nation," the assured voice of Desher Keigeri explains, as the screen splits into quarter views, and the new portions of the screen show a quick succession of other airfields all around *Atlantida*, some rural, others in busy urban areas.

"At the same time, our allies and Star Pilot Corps partner nations all around the globe are engaged in similar mobilization," Desher Keigeri says, as the scenes change to international feeds, showing various locales. Sunlit airfields of arid, inland Ubasti are followed by equally bright views of a more verdant Eos-Heket, with marquees running in Eosti script underneath—I vaguely recognize its distinctive shape from a brief overview given to all Earth refugees sometime over the past year on the ark-ships, a general linguistic unit covering other Atlantean languages.

"Rest assured that no one is *resting*," Desher continues, clever in his turn of phrase and at the same time reassuring, as he speaks in a measured tone. "Being ready for anything at a moment's notice has always been one of our strengths as a species. And so, let's allow our men and women in uniform to continue their boarding process, and we'll continue to look in on them from time to time. Now—back to our studios for a discussion with our panel of military experts, historians, and strategy experts, to be followed shortly by a formal address from the Assembly of the Imperial Executive Council. We're also on standby, watching closely for a special Imperial address from the Archaeon Imperator himself, to be delivered at eleventh hour of Ra—don't miss a heartbeat, stay with us on the Helios-Ra Imperial Network and its affiliates. . . ."

I look away because the exterior door to the workroom opens, and two people enter. One is a young man I've never seen before, medium height, muscular and slightly heavyset, with curling gilded hair and light bronze skin.

The second person is Gracie.

"Oh, Gracie!" I exclaim, seeing my sister in a grey Fleet uniform.

At the same time, Oalla exclaims, "Radan! It's been ages, *daimon!*"

"Hey, Rad-Rad," Erita says, turning around also. "Come on in. Make yourself useful. Did you bring me *fuchmik* to eat?"

I am about to pounce on Gracie, but pause out of politeness, because the newcomer sees me and gives me a proper courtly bow.

"Imperial Lady Gwen, may I present Radanthet Ulumaq, our friend and fellow *astra daimon* heart brother, all the way from—" Oalla mockingly hesitates. "What *bakris* hole are you from again, *chazuf?*"

Radanthet Ulumaq chuckles in a pleasant voice.

"Shuria," Erita answers instead. "Rad-Rad is from Shuria, and he promised to bring the best *fuchmik* they make in Khur."

"That's right," Oalla snorts. "I always forget he's Shuri, his *Atlanteo* is so good."

"My pleasure to meet you, Imperial Lady Gwen, I've heard so much about you," Radanthet says, looking at me.

I smile and nod at him, meanwhile glancing nervously at Gracie.

Radanthet is surprisingly perceptive. "Please, don't let me keep you away from—" and he sweeps one hand in the direction of Gracie. It's clear he doesn't know her; they just happened to arrive here at the same time, independently of each other.

"—my sister, thank you," I finish on his behalf. And then I focus on Gracie. "Gracie, so glad that you haven't left yet! What are you doing here? I thought you're supposed to be deploying?"

"Yeah. About that . . ." Gracie says. "Right now is general deployment, second wave. Apparently, I'm in the third wave of deployment, with all the other *shìrén*."

"Oh!" I say. "Wait, what does that mean? And what's *shìrén?*"

"Haven't you heard that term for Earthies? *Shìrén* is what we call ourselves—what everyone calls us now. It's Mandarin Chinese for 'earthling,' and the term stuck, since there are so many Earthie refugees who are Chinese-speaking."

"Yeah, I've been a little isolated here, so I don't hear these things," I say with a little smile. "Anyway, what does it mean you're in the third wave?"

"Just means we get to stay planetside and act as the home defense for Atlantis, at least for now—or until they call us to deploy. If it comes to it. We're the reserves."

"Wow, you sound disappointed," I say, craning my neck slightly.

Gracie shrugs. "I dunno . . . I suppose, I *am* disappointed, a little. I'm a Pilot Cadet. We trained for this. On the other hand, it's scary crap right now. All the *shìrén* Cadets are stuck here on the planet, on standby. Yeah, many people are kind of relieved, but some of us feel like they don't trust us or something. Like they don't trust us to fight well enough, or to handle the big tech."

I shake my head. "Don't take it that way."

"I mean, I get it," Gracie says, with a quick glance at the three *daimon* in the room. "We are inexperienced newbies, second-year Cadet equivalent. That's a fact. But I was hoping to at least *see* a battle barge."

"Think of it this way," Oalla puts in from across the room. "You get to protect *Atlantida* if all else fails. You're like the ultimate home guard. It's an honor."

"She's absolutely right," I say, with a grateful glance at Oalla. "Gee Four, you and all the—whatchamacallit, *shìrén*—have an important role to play here."

Gracie sucks in her lower lip and sighs, without sounding particularly convinced. "I hope so," she mutters. "Blayne keeps saying so too, and he's been told they need him down here on the surface too, to continue the LM Forms training classes. Anyway, I decided to drop by to make sure you knew. I am not due at IF HQ until later today. We're running local drills planet-side, and still doing the Ghost Moon fly-throughs."

Gracie and I continue to chat quietly, while paying attention to what's happening in the room.

The newcomer *astra daimon*, Radanthet Ulumaq, joins Erita and Oalla at the work area.

"Wanted to see Kass before I head out to Ishtar Station," Radanthet mentions at some point.

"On the way to War-7?" Erita asks.

Radanthet nods. "Eventually. But first, SPC meeting with Ishtar Station Nomarch Danaat, to make sure he doesn't want to reassign anyone."

"We have similar meetings with Evandros, who seems a little too eager for the action to begin," Oalla says.

Erita makes a sarcastic sound. "Old man misses being on the front lines himself."

"Who's that?" I ask.

"Evandros?" Erita exchanges glances with Oalla and Radanthet, then points with one finger up. "He's the Atlantis Station Nomarch. Permanently stationed in orbit overhead at the SPC Headquarters, permanently in charge of the whole place except when the SPC Commander goes up there. These days, he reports to Kass directly. At one point, Kass reported to him."

"He used to train all of us back in the day," Oalla adds. "Even this *chazuf* here." And she nods at Radanthet.

"Not a single SPC Pilot hasn't had Evandros for a teacher at some point," Radanthet says. "He makes *astra daimon*. He trains everyone, but the best first-year SPC Pilots get rotated from other Stations to serve under his supervision for a longer period, before getting assigned to different Wars."

"I see." I turn to Gracie. "Have you worked with him yet?"

"Gee Two, I'm not an SPC Pilot," my little sister tells me seriously, shaking her head at my gaffe. "I wish I were, but that didn't even come up yet, considering I'm still a Cadet. You have to be a full Imperial Fleet Pilot before being considered for SPC."

"That might change soon," Erita says quietly under her breath. "The way things are going, they're gonna need everyone who can fly anything up there at some point."

I frown. "You really think so?"

Erita just shakes her head and points at the big screen with the Rah Station and the grid of golden lights covering all visible space in the background.

In the middle of tenth hour, as promised by Hel-Ra Network, the IEC Assembly chamber is broadcast and the IEC Member chosen to address the nation is ACA Director Hijep Tiofon. I watch the familiar face of Tiofon as he speaks in a very upbeat, simplified language, expressing his reassurances to everyone that the "so-called alien threat" has not actually manifested itself in any way, and that the general deployment is simply a precautionary measure.

"You know that we have the best and brightest military forces at our disposal, and we take any potential threat very seriously," Director Tiofon says. "At the same time, you're aware that it is our centuries-old policy to mobilize and deploy *before* any hostilities have occurred. Let me remind those of us who might've forgotten our history lessons that Fleet deployment has occurred numerous times in previous years, decades, centuries, with no resulting conflict. This is very likely one of such times.

"We observe an anomaly, an unidentified phenomenon, and we take prudent, precautionary measures. That is all. I strongly recommend you go about your business and your daily lives, and don't let some pretty lights in the sky affect your sense of security or well-being. *Atlantida* armed forces, and the forces of the entire planet under the auspices of the Star Pilot Corps are protecting you, day and night."

When finished, Director Tiofon takes some easy questions submitted by the public via the feeds, about the new phenomenon of the golden grid of light and the ongoing presence of the ghostly moon. His replies are all lightweight nonanswers. "No, we don't know the origin or purpose of the unidentified lights around Helios, but we are working on it. . . . The threat level they pose has not been determined, but we are taking precautions. . . . The ghostly moon object is still there, and we don't know if it's all related. As soon as we have answers, you'll be duly informed. . . ."

A few minutes later, at eleventh hour, comes the Imperial Address.

I haven't seen Romhutat Kassiopei in person for days, not since the Games Champion Ceremony. Today he wears the red Khepresh headdress that is the Imperial Crown of *Atlantida* with the golden Uraeus serpent on his forehead and a ceremonial scarlet robe, framed against the background of the Throne—I recognize the formal seat from his antechamber reception area in the Imperial Palace Quarters—and his face is devoid of emotion. From what Aeson had told me about his Father's panicked state, I understand that all of this is only a public show of force. Right now, the Imperator, appearing as the menacing dragon of power, is the ultimate and necessary form of reassurance for the population.

We listen as he speaks softly, using a slightly enhanced power voice, to convey a sense of absolute confidence and trust.

"People of *Atlantida*, you have nothing to fear. We are aware of the situation, and the Fleet has responded as intended." The Imperator faces the camera directly with his dark lapis lazuli eyes of a near-black hue. The force of his heavy gaze is palpable, but for once it seems appropriate—if it gives the public a badly needed sense of comfort via strength. "Our military forces are the ultimate net of safety for the human race. Our technological advances are greater than you can imagine. They who govern you as elected officials have never failed you. Neither has the Imperial Kassiopei Dynasty. All the ancient power through the ages and infinite generations is behind you, and we are invincible—then, now, and always. You have my Imperial Word that you are *protected*."

The Imperator's striking face fades from view, and his words hang powerfully in the air, before the network feeds resume, with more Desher Keigeri and various panelists' commentaries.

Moments later, we see clips of other global leaders addressing their nations. There's the familiar image of Kephasa Sewu, the Oratorat of Eos-Heket, who is now back in their capital city, Ushab, speaking to her people. There's the old Pharikon Areviktet Heru addressing New Deshret in a calm, quavering voice that sounds slightly less frail than usual.

In addition, there are several unfamiliar-to-me individuals also speaking to their people. A youthful middle-aged man with dark brown skin, Anen Qur, the First Speaker of the Ennead of Ubasti, addresses an assembly of thousands in an outdoor venue. An older man with pale skin, Inevar Arelik, the Rai of Ptahleon, speaks into the camera from a dignified office chamber. Another Rai—a man of indeterminate years, with very black hair and bronze skin, Osuo Menbuut—talks to the people of Shuria. Wilem Paeh, the Crown Hereret of Vai Naat, an older man with brown hair and light brown skin, speaks to his public. Rai Duu Valaam addresses his subjects in Bastet; the young Hetmet of Qurartu, Qedeh Adamer, speaks to his people.

It goes on and on.

"They're all just feeding us *shebet*, aren't they?" Gracie says suddenly.

"Oh, yeah," Oalla chuckles ruefully.

"But it's a good thing," Radanthet says. "People need calm, soothing *shebet* when the world is ending."

The rest of the day is tedious and unremarkable. Aeson returns home very late that night, exhausted. After I force him to eat a *niktos* meal that's closer to a Ghost meal, he collapses in bed, and so do I—both of us in our different bedrooms, of course, since we are still maintaining our chaste distance according to the silly nuptial tradition.

The next morning is Green Ghost Moon 13. Fleet deployment continues, having grown to a trickle, and since no new threats have materialized for now, the public returns to their regular daily concerns.

Aeson receives the first batches of translations of the various artifact scrolls and, between calls to his Father and Shirahtet, he spends hours perusing the translations for anything useful—all the while fielding more calls, dispatches, endless data, and other SPC business.

Meanwhile I receive a few messages of my own—a brief progress report on my Champion wish fulfillment from the Games staff (they are still having some trouble finalizing the arrangements for proxy voting for Chihar's board of education, while Zaap's nature preserve is progressing nicely), and a Wedding schedule item reminder for tomorrow.

The next big item on my Bridal agenda is coming up—alien threat be damned—and it is Bride Show Day.

Chapter 42

Did I mention what the hell is Bride Show Day? It's the day the Imperial Bride is all dressed up and driven around town to different public venues where she basically shows up, smiles and waves, speaks a few words maybe, then is carted off to the next location.

I'm supposed to be unaccompanied, except for my personal guards and a few chosen female companions. And as far as I can tell, the purpose of this whole stupid thing is just to show me off to the people.

"Oh, Aeson, do I have to? Haven't they seen me enough? I mean, at several points during the Games I even mooned them," I groan over our shared *eos* bread in the workroom that's become SPC Central, on the morning of Green Ghost Moon 14.

Aeson sets down his eating utensil and leans very close to me, whispering near my ear, "Is it wrong to admit I enjoyed that show?"

"Oh, *gawd*, Aeson! So wrong!" I punch his arm with mock outrage, while a few feet away Keruvat and Oalla laugh. "I was in constant mortal danger, with my pants down, and you were checking me out?"

"Never when you were in true harm's way. Only when I felt you were reasonably safe." Aeson chuckles, grabbing my fingers and pressing them sensuously with his large ones, and I giggle, because it's such a precious relief to have these lighthearted moments right now.

And then I leave them to their work and proceed to my own side of the Quarters to get ready for my Bridal ordeal.

My outfit and appearance for this event is not supposed to be as formal as for the Ladies of the Court Bridal reception. In fact, the look is "festive casual," similar to what I wore to Kokayi's parade in Themisera.

I select a sparkly purple, blue, and gold top and matching blue pants from my closet, and have my personal maid Aranit do my hair and makeup, without resorting to the haute couture services of Consul Denu. My hair is gathered in an artful knot with a ponytail, and yes, I get a sprinkling of gold dust that Aranit seems to favor so much. I am wearing the traditional Kassiopei eyeliner and violet eyeshadow, with a natural shade of *noohd* on my lips. Nothing overly dramatic, just enough for me to not appear too faded in the fierce sunlight. As always, my protective shade lenses go into my eyes.

The event starts at tenth hour, and Aeson has assigned Anu once again to drive my car—since that other time with Kokayi's event had worked out so well—while my primary bodyguard Tuar Momet and my female friends ride with us. The rest of my guards and the Imperial Princess's guards are in the second and third vehicles, flanking us closely and keeping "relentless watch over both the Imperial Bride and the Imperial Princess" under *im amrevu's* strictest orders.

As for my girlfriend entourage, my lucky companions today are indeed Princess Manala, Gracie, Hasmik, and Laronda. Hasmik managed to get a day off work—which means, Manala was immediately excited to join us, secure in the knowledge that only her favorite people would be coming. Gracie and Laronda, both on permanent Fleet standby, had no flight drills scheduled, so they said yes to seeing the sights of Poseidon.

"Where are we going first?" Gracie asks next to me, as we sit together, all girls squished into one hover car. With so many of us, we had to take a large eight-seater.

"I think we go to the downtown complex first," I reply. "The Golden Grail Plaza?"

"Correct," Anu says from the seat directly in front of me, with Tuar again next to him.

"And what are you supposed to do there, *janik?*" Hasmik asks from the row behind me, where she sits next to Princess Manala.

"Just show up and smile, I guess. These are all supposed to be surprise, pop-in appearances." I glance back at Hasmik with a grin.

Of course, not much surprise there, since the media has been notified of all locations in advance, and they will be there to film every artfully unplanned moment of my visits.

"Smile and wave, and make them ha-a-a-appy," Laronda drawls from the back seat. "They will love it."

Laronda's being flippant, but she's right, of course. At this uncertain time, with the threat of war, invasion, and annihilation hanging over us, Bride Show Day is the perfect "normal" distraction for the people of Poseidon and *Atlantida*.

"I'll do my best," I say.

As we descend from the air traffic lane to ground level, the sight of the immense complex fills our view with sparkling metallic rooftops and adjacent high-rises. The Golden Grail Plaza, located among the various stadium structures, is a beautifully manicured pedestrian open space of modern lawns, park benches, walkways, and water features, including several fountains with statuary.

My surprise appearance is supposed to take place at the slightly elevated pavilion where public concerts and speeches are given, and where today an episode of some talk show is being recorded for the feeds. All I need to do is stroll through the pavilion with my friends and wave at the host of the show. The host, a perky young woman, will see me, act all surprised and excited, and interrupt her show to point me out to the audience.

I'm not going to get into the tediousness of it all. Let's just say, it happens. I put on a goofy smile, I walk, my friends walk, the host squeals at the sight of me. "Can you believe it? We are being honored by the Imperial Bride herself! It's Gwen Lark, here in person! What could she be doing here? Look, everyone!"

There is general applause, whistles, and a few familiar calls of *"Shoe-Lace Girl! Gwen Lark!"*

I wave again and continue walking.

"Happy Bride Show Day!" they call in my wake, while eager nano-cams swirl like dust motes in the sunshine all around us.

"Oh, yeah, that wasn't much of a surprise. Seriously?" Gracie laughs as we get out of there, and return to the hover cars.

"It's official; this is *very* stupid," Laronda says, plunking next to me, while Gracie takes her former seat in the back.

"Yes, I was just thinking that." I giggle.

"It is a strange, old tradition," Manala says. "Gwen, it is very silly, I agree, and now that I think about it, I don't know why anyone would waste time with it when they could really be *visiting* interesting places instead."

"As opposed to fake visiting?" Laronda throws her a mischievous look.

"Oh, yes!" Manala nods and points to another end of the Plaza still visible below us. "We could be truly, genuinely visiting that little round building which houses the Museum of Ancient Toys, with the greatest collection of Original Colony children's artifacts, or the beautiful stone Shrine of the Four Cornerstones of *Atlantida* on the other side of the *Nebetareon*—"

"Where to next?" I ask, even as Manala describes her favorite places.

Anu continues driving, but glances at the digital tablet in a holder nearby and swipes the screen with one hand to bring up the master schedule. He hands it to Tuar and tells him to read what it says.

"Agnios Park, at tenth hour and thirty minutes," Tuar says.

And we merge into the nearest air lane.

Almost at a run, we breeze through the shady paths of Agnios Park with its tall, ancient trees interspersed with newly planted ones, and walk at a quick pace toward the most popular public portion with beautiful greenery, wide lawns, and glaring Hel-shine. It's Redday, the first day of the work week, so the park is not as crowded as it could be at this time of morning, but just enough to make everyone notice us.

A few reporters from different networks appear as if out of nowhere, and I am briefly interviewed in the middle of the gravel path, even as I continue to wave at passersby, mostly young children and the old women watching over them.

"Happy Bride Show Day!" the women call out to me kindly, or just politely, as they pass. This must be a very common tradition.

And then we're off again, toward our next destination.

Hours later, maintaining our brisk pace, we've crisscrossed most of Poseidon.

"I have to admit, this is still extremely ridiculous, but at least we're getting to drive all over town and see amazing stuff," Laronda says, twirling a little painted hand-fan on a stick she just bought from a market stall in the Nebet Arts district.

In these past several hours we've visited locations deeper inland, various hillside communities, including our own Phoinios Heights, several more parks, three sprawling urban shopping centers and four open-air markets (where we all made a point of buying a few souvenirs and trinkets and chatting with the colorful stall vendors), an outdoor amphitheater near the Bay, then back to the business district downtown—this time past the stadium complex and its ubiquitous Grail Monument—and to the steps of the Imperial Court of Law building with architectural elements of a grand ziggurat and a stepped pyramid. We even dropped by the Poseidon Central Correctional Facility located past downtown and halfway into the Bay districts and waved at the prisoners exercising in the tall fenced yard. Surprisingly, quite a few of them waved back, with hoots, raucous applause, and cries of *"Shoe-Lace Girl! Im-pe-ra-tris!"*

"Yes, Happy Bride Show Day back at you, bald guy with big head!" Laronda calls out, waving back along with me and fanning the air over her head, while Hasmik and Manala giggle. Gracie tries to look dignified, but her lips are tight, holding back giggles of her own.

"Mother of *shibet* . . . enough already—I mean, sorry, let's get out of here and do the next one, Imperial Lady Gwen," Anu mutters with an annoyed frown, then checks himself before his mouth runs away with him even further.

He scans his tablet schedule while Tuar and all our guards wait, surrounding us in a protective circle. In the moment Anu's surly expression brightens as he announces loudly, "Hah, *now* we're talking! Next stop is the Main Wharf Promenade at Fish Town! Perfect time for a *dea* meal, Imperial Lady Gwen. So okay, let's *go!*"

Laronda opens her eyes super-wide to make a face at Anu behind his back. Hasmik and I exchange amused glances, while Gracie and Manala are occupied with opening a package of something edible we've just bought, resembling Earth macaron cookies.

We head to Fish Town.

As we descend near the urban shoreline of the Bay, our first sight of the waterfront is the immense Poseidon Harbor, several smaller marinas, and endless rows of piers and rock-piled jetties extending out into the mauve-blue waters.

There are ships everywhere—small, ancient-style sailboats, and medium and large modern vessels that range from yachts to Earth-style tankers, except, supposedly they have hover capability. Indeed, as we come down in one of the many parking air-lots nearby, we see an arriving freight tanker—probably the height of a ten-story building—barely skimming the surface of the waves, churning the water underneath it as it hover-floats toward its berth along the commercial portion of the wharf. As it comes to a stop, the hover-tanker stops levitating and immediately "sinks" half-way, descending to properly float in the water while it ejects great anchors.

"That is one huge mama ship," Laronda says in awe, as we stare out of the car windows.

"So which part is Fish Town? Are we in Fish Town now?" I ask, as we open the doors to exit our vehicles.

Immediately a strong smell of fish and seaweed hits us, together with a pleasant, cool breeze.

"I'm guessing, yes. . . . Pew!" Gracie says with a happy smile, and we all breathe in the fresh ocean air.

"Fish Town is everything here along the water, and also the area that continues directly inland—the whole district," Anu says with the pleased expression of an expert. "Follow me . . . I'll show you the best part of the Main Wharf Promenade, best places to eat *maqooi* fish eggs, best *guu* rolls, best everything—"

I nod in amusement and follow Anu, heading for the crowded public area that runs along the shoreline.

We walk along the Main Wharf Promenade—an endlessly long street lined with buildings on one side and access to water on the other. There are many pedestrians and people zipping by them on hoverboards in the middle of the street. Occasional small hover cars slowly cruise along at street level to watch the sights and the gaudy marine-themed displays in the windows of the shops. Fish designs are everywhere, on shop signs and buildings. There are also fish barrels and buckets on display, nearly every few feet, seething with live fish or crustaceans, as vendors offer their latest catch.

Very soon, the usual media reporters show up and surround me for one-question interviews, which in turn makes the passersby pay attention and notice me, as intended. . . .

"It's the Imperial Bride!" People nearby start calling out to me as I laugh and wave to them. "Happy Bride Show Day!"

"Thank you!" I wave back, walking carefully on the slippery ground to avoid spilled ocean water puddles from the buckets underfoot nearly everywhere.

"Okay, good . . . let's go, let's go," Anu says, switching from one foot to the other impatiently, and looking around at the various storefronts with eagerness.

Tuar stands next to me and Manala, carefully keeping a perimeter of safety around us, while the other guards extend it. Occasionally Tuar checks his wrist comm where I'm guessing Aeson probably texted him another inquiry regarding my status—which now I know *im amrevu* does from time to time, having admitted it to me.

Always concerned about my safety. . . .

"Let's go!" Anu repeats, as we finish talking with yet another network reporter and several leathery-skinned locals.

"Go where?" Manala asks, looking around her a little warily. "It smells bad here."

"*Dzugin hodeh.* . . . Smells like fish," Hasmik adds with a small amused shrug. "It's okay."

"It's fourth hour," Anu says in a loud voice that means business. "*Dea* meal time, come on. Right here around the corner of that building, great place to eat."

Manala's usual nervous expression becomes even more so. "Eat . . . here?"

"Hmm, I *am* kind of starved," Gracie says, looking curiously at the stores.

"You know, I could go for some Atlantean seafood!" Laronda says loudly, raising one brow and echoing Anu's overbearing tone. "Let's see how good it really is."

I hesitate for a moment, seeing Manala's horrified look.

"Oh yeah—they have other things too. They have everything here, you don't have to eat fish," Anu says quickly, realizing the problem. "They have normal food, and they have fish. Shesep's Bar and Fire Shawab is right there! Let's *go!*"

Tuar gives me a subtle look. "Only as long as you feel secure, Imperial Lady Gwen—and the Imperial Princess is equally comfortable with the choice of venue."

Anu groans. "Oh, come on, it's perfectly safe—"

"Stop," Tuar interrupts in a hard voice, turning to Anu with warning. "This is their choice, not yours—remember your place, Vei."

Anu glares back at Tuar but holds his tongue.

I turn to Manala. "What do you think, Manala?" I ask gently. "We could try it, but only if you don't mind. Please tell me honestly if this makes you uncomfortable, and we'll eat in a different area. That would be absolutely fine."

"Oh . . ." Manala clasps her hands together and considers stressfully. Her expressive face goes through a cascade of conflicting emotions. So much so that you can see each stage of her indecision working itself out in her countenance.

"All right, that's it," I say, making the hard decision for her. "We're leaving. We'll eat outside of Fish Town, somewhere else— at our next location. Sorry, Anu, some other time."

"Oh! No, wait!" Manala bites her lip and wrings her hands again anxiously. "I don't want you to miss out on enjoying yourselves! I am so sorry! I shouldn't be getting in the way of your wishes on Bride Show Day!"

With a shy glance at Anu, Manala says, "As long as I don't have to eat the poor sea creatures and fish, it's all right, I suppose."

Anu's glum expression comes alive again, and he slaps his hand against his thigh. "Yeah, okay! Imperial Princess, good choice! Let's go then, I'll show you the best food you've ever had!"

"You better be right, troll boy," Laronda mutters, as we start walking.

Chapter 43

Shesep's Bar, located in a weather-beaten two-story building, has a big glowing sign above the entrance. Noise and music and a strong smell of smoky grilled food engulfs us as we enter. The interior is warm gold and violet with ambient mood lighting, on the dark side, and crowded with colorful painted tables, patrons, and rushing servers.

Not unlike an Earth establishment, there's a beverage bar section near the rear, a dining section with an open kitchen, and several grills hissing cheerfully as the cooks prepare food to order, and even what looks like a small stage for entertainment. The walls have smart screens with TV feeds like a sports bar, and the rest is taken up with marine-themed decorations consisting of nets, looping knotted ropes, and wooden carvings of fish, crustaceans, and ocean plants. Garlands of intricately braided, dried seaweed hang from the ceiling next to bunches of colorful root vegetables and herbs.

Several light orbs float in the air and move about gently, illuminating the tables, people's faces, and the food on the plates in a seemingly random manner, so that the illumination constantly changes. This creates unusual shadows on the walls, the illusion of rippling movement of water, much like swells of ocean waves.

"Oh, wow, this place is cool!" Gracie says.

"Wait here, I'll clear us a table!" Anu says, and heads with determination to the bar, waiving with familiarity to the serving staff.

Manala keeps close to Hasmik, looking around with trepidation. Meanwhile Laronda peers at the nearest smart screen, where a familiar Atlantean daytime drama plays out an emotional scene with an actress portraying *me* and an actor doing Aeson. "Oh, jeez," Laronda says, watching our theatrical doubles argue over something ridiculous related to the upcoming Wedding.

A few minutes later, an incredibly apologetic and excited proprietor rushes towards us, exclaiming, "My Imperial Lady Gwen Lark! Here, today! On your Bride Show Day of all days! Oh, joy, oh glory to all wind gods and ocean gods! You grace our humble establishment! What an honor and privilege to serve you today, oh, what a magnificent, glorious day it is for Shesep! And oh, the Imperial Princess is here! Oh, glorious, oh, radiant—"

This goes on and on, as the stocky middle-aged man with balding gilded hair—who is Shesep, apparently—guides us between tables and curious staring customers to the largest unoccupied table in the room, and seats us. He offers Manala and me additional sitting pillows over the hard chairs, which we refuse kindly.

"Ah, what a feast will appear before you! Anything you like is yours!" Shesep raises his face to the ceiling, widens his eyes and shakes his head, clutching his beefy hands at his chest.

Hasmik looks down at the table surface so as not to giggle.

"And now, allow me tell you about the delicious *dea* specials we have today, glorious *sukrat* freshly caught from the ocean foam this morning and grilled in a light drizzle of oil, fragrant spices, and their own juices. And of course, if you prefer something more traditional, we are happy to oblige—"

Manala's expression remains slightly troubled, but she has relaxed considerably.

"Sounds wonderful." I smile at Shesep. "But first—do you have a menu of the traditional food, for some of us who will not be having seafood?"

"Of course, here it is!" Shesep points to his temple, to indicate it's stored up there. "Ask me for your favorite dish—I can make anything!"

I turn to Manala, sitting to my right. "What would you like?"

"Oh!" Manala starts slightly, not expecting to be called on at this point, and blinks, thinking for a few seconds. She then looks up at Shesep with uncertainty. "Can you make a layered *gulubo* in cream sauce, with fried root vegetables and pickled *ranub?*"

"Easy as a breath!" Shesep bows to Manala with a blissful smile. "Would you like a savory sprinkle of herbs on the baked top layer, or a sweet candied drizzle of fruit?"

"A little of both!" Manala says with wide-eyed happiness.

"I see that My Imperial Princess knows the best way to eat *gulubo.*" Shesep winks mischievously, his face warming up even more.

And then he turns to me with courtesy. "And now—what would My Imperial Lady like?"

My mind stalls a bit as I attempt to recall the many delicious Atlantean dishes I've tasted. "You know, let me think about it a little more. Why don't you take the rest of our orders and come back to me later. In fact—" I glance down the table at Anu who is sitting a little way off with the guards, his fingers drumming on the table impatiently—"Anu, you know what's good here, so what do you recommend?"

Anu's face is a study in happiness. He immediately starts listing dishes with the authority of a chef, and Shesep nods with approval at each. ". . . so if you want a true taste of our best fish, a sampler platter of *guu* rolls; *makuudra* filet if you like mild and savory with a hint of sweetness; shelled *kivakat* is very light, and it's a local delicacy, or—if you're not afraid of strong flavor, the real thing, best fish in the world—the spicy grilled *sukrat* is the way to go," Anu concludes. "I'll be having all of those! And the *maqooi* fish eggs in *ozu* butter!"

"And now, are we ready to order?" Shesep asks us with a smile.

"Everything sounds so yummy," Gracie says. "I don't like fish all that much, but I'm willing to try the *makuudra* filet, if it really is mild and not too spicy. . . ."

"It is like clouds!" Shesep kisses his fingertips and turns his gaze to the ceiling.

"I'll take the spicy grilled *sukrat,*" Laronda says, raising one brow in challenge and glancing at Anu.

Anu stares back at her with an intense, superior look.

"*Guu* rolls, a little sampler platter, please," Hasmik says after a tiny thoughtful pause, smiling at us.

"A delicious choice!" Shesep nods to her.

When it's his turn, Anu opens his mouth and loudly rattles off his own huge order.

Tuar and the guards decline to order and only watch impassively. Since they're on duty, they will not be eating with us— even though I repeatedly invite them to have something.

At last, it's my turn.

"If it's not too much trouble, I would like a stir fry with *lidairi* and *ero* grains," I say, recalling Aeson's favorite simple dish.

"But of course, My Imperial Lady, with delight!" Shesep bows to me with a smile.

He then bows again, this time to the table in general, saying he will return with our drinks and flatbread while our main selections are being prepared.

After Shesep is gone, Manala glances at me curiously and touches my arm. "Gwen . . . you are not having fish?"

I shake my head, smiling lightly at her.

"Oh, I hope it's not because of me," Manala continues, her eyes widening with emotion. "I am so sorry if I made you think that you shouldn't, because—"

"No, Manala, it's not you—not at all—though I'm happy to keep you company in this," I say with amusement, leaning closer to her ear.

I consider for a moment how to explain. . . . "Truth is," I say, "I've gotten used to not eating meat. It's been over a year now and, with all the seriously amazing vegetable protein dishes, I don't even miss it. *Not at all*. And the ethical reasons for not eating animals seem to be pretty strong, so—"

I pause, again wondering how to express this yet another nuance of difference in me—a gradual change of perspective that crept up on me over these many months of acclimatization to a new existence and an alien society, along with everything else.

"It really is a new world, and the new me no longer has the same habits," I finish. "On the other hand, I've no idea if tomorrow the old me might resurface and crave some of the old stuff, like Italian salami or bologna. I always tell myself, 'If I want to eat meat or fish, I *can*, anytime—just not today.' Makes it easier to stick to it, if you never say 'never,' just 'later' or 'tomorrow'. . . . So, for now, at least, I'll stick to your traditional meatless dishes."

Manala's great eyes light up with wonder. "Thank you, Gwen . . ." she whispers suddenly. "The sea creatures . . . all the living creatures thank you *so much* for not eating them."

"They do? Is that right?" I chuckle. "What about the vegetables?"

She nods silently, and her expression continues shining. "The vegetables are alive, but they are not creatures," she says. "They live in a different phase of being, out of sync with us—like the *pegasei*. When we reach *across* phases of being to take energy, we cause the least harm. It is only when we rob others similar to ourselves of energy that we do wrong."

I'm not sure what to make of her eccentric words, so I merely smile at her.

Servers arrive at our table with baskets of freshly baked, herb-encrusted, buttery flatbread. Others carry pitchers of fruit water, iced juice, and dark molasses-colored scarab beer for Anu. Then, fifteen minutes later, our food arrives. Shesep himself carries sizzling platters of beautifully arranged, baked, sautéed, grilled filet or whole fish and various vegetable dishes. The delicious aroma surrounds us.

"This is *guu* rolls? Looks like sushi!" Hasmik stares at her oversized platter of what appears to be delicate cuts of fish wrapped in grains and crunchy-dried seaweed.

"Ooh! Let me try!" Laronda exclaims. "This is actually cooked, not raw like sushi," she adds, after Hasmik gives her a piece.

And just like that, our individual orders turn into a family-style feast, as everyone starts trying everyone else's fish specialties.

Manala and I are the only ones to refrain from the seafood melee, and dig into our respective veggie dishes. The plates set before us are piled with colorful layers of sauce-drenched delights.

"Is yours good?"

"Oh, yeah!"

"Holy crap, this is good fish!"

Gracie and Hasmik giggle as Anu fills his mouth with huge pieces of food, gulping with abandon. After each bite of fish, he follows up by tearing apart flatbread with his teeth, dipping whatever's in his hand in *ozu* butter sauce, then putting the whole thing in his mouth again. Seriously, the boy is stuffing his cheeks like a crazed hamster. He then picks up a tall mug of frothy scarab beer and drains half of it in one uninterrupted series of gulps. "Ah-h-h!"

"So what's that brown stuff?" Laronda asks Anu across the table.

"Huh? You talking to me?" Anu says on a belch.

"Oh, gross!" Laronda wrinkles her forehead in disgust. "Yeah, though now I wish I didn't."

"This is scarab beer, best drink ever!" Anu proclaims, brandishing his mug in her direction. "But not for you—too strong. You won't handle it."

"Are you serious?" Laronda narrows her eyes at him. "Give it here!"

"No."

"No?" Now Laronda's expression is like a bomb ready to explode.

"You can't handle it, I'm telling you," Anu says smugly, patting the dewy surface of the ice-cold pitcher. He continues staring at her.

"Like hell I can't! *Give it here!*"

Anu's smug expression becomes a full-blown smirk. "No way."

Laronda gets up from her seat and walks down the table, past others in our group, and right up to Anu. She snatches up the pitcher of scarab beer before he can react and brings it over to her seat.

"*Bashtooh!* Hey! You give it back, Earth girl! That's mine!" Anu's jaw drops.

Laronda ignores him and takes an empty glass; pours herself about two fingers' breadth. She raises it to her lips and tastes it. "Ugh, nasty. Like bad Earth beer, but with vinegar. And is that rotten eggs?" She makes a face.

"I told you!" Anu says loudly. "Now bring it back."

"Come and get it."

Oh, boy. . . .

Sitting between Laronda and me, Gracie stops chewing and stares with fascination. On the other side of Manala, Hasmik makes a little stifled sound and leans forward to exchange looks with me, *across* Manala.

There is silence as everyone at our table just stops eating, drinking, or breathing. Could be horror, could be amusement.

The guards just watch us impassively.

Slowly, Anu gets up. For a moment he stands, glaring at Laronda across the table. If looks could kill, Anu's eyes hold a deadly inferno. . . .

Then, without a word, he turns proudly and goes to the servers' station to get himself another pitcher of scarab beer.

L aronda appears to be somewhat taken aback. "Well, that was interesting. . . ." she mutters under her breath, looking over at me, Hasmik, Gracie, the rest of us, uncomfortably—while Anu's away at the servers' with his back to us. "Whatever. . . . Don't know what his problem is. Such a prick."

"That was kind of harsh," Gracie whispers to her. "I think he might be upset."

"Upset?" Laronda frowns and opens her mouth, while shaking her head at us. "Seriously? All I did was ask to taste the stuff, then he wouldn't let me—like, excuse me?—so I got the pitcher, and he started being a total jerk—"

"Okay . . . um . . . you kinda went too far," I say, choosing my words with care. "Grabbing that thing was . . . maybe just a little much."

"You should apologize to him," Manala says suddenly. "Maybe if you told him you're sorry, and you didn't meant to hurt him . . . I think it would make him very happy if you did . . . he cares . . . he likes you so very much."

"What?" Laronda's jaw drops again, as she looks at Manala with a shocked expression. "He what? The guy hates my guts!"

"No, he doesn't," I say with a little smile.

"Yeah, no," Gracie echoes me with a silly grin.

Hasmik just smiles and nods.

"Crap. . . ." Laronda says, looking closely at every one of our faces and the nuances written there. And then she repeats softly, "Crap, crap, crap. . . ."

Chapter 44

Anu returns to his chair with a full, new pitcher of scarab beer, and his expression is still closed off as he pours himself a new mug. He doesn't look in Laronda's direction and resumes eating, but somehow with less enthusiasm.

We all continue to eat politely and watch him. Laronda glances at him periodically, with a thoughtful expression. Then our table conversation resumes, and there is a bit of lighthearted chatting about the very tasty fish and other dishes before us.

"Anu! This is really great, Anu-*jan*," Hasmik says, minutes later, pointing to her few remaining *guu* rolls. "Thank you so much for bringing us here to eat, so good! Reminds me of the best fish in Armenia. We have *ishkhan*, very famous Lake Sevan fish—*farel*—I mean, trout."

Anu looks up at her and mumbles, "Uh-huh."

"Yes, Anu, great choice of eating spot," I add and quickly glance at Laronda.

Laronda widens her eyes at me slightly, but says nothing.

When our *dea* meal is done, everyone is stuffed more than usual due to the novelty of the fish experience.

"I can't even remember the last time I had such yummy fish," Gracie moans with a grin, rubbing her abdomen in exaggeration, as we get up from our seats. "Gonna die now, too full."

"Gee Four, I'm amazed," I say with amusement. "You're so finicky, and you don't like seafood."

"Yeah, well . . . this was definitely better than fish sticks." My little sister gives me a cute but confident look that reminds me she is fourteen and not so little.

"You should come back here with Blayne." I watch her fondly and reach out to adjust a wisp of her dirty-blond hair that's stuck to her forehead.

"Ooh, good idea!" Gracie's expression brightens. Furthermore, she lets me touch her without protest. Seriously grown-up, my little sis.

Anu settles our bill with Shesep, who protests appropriately but bows in pleased resignation when the Imperial credit line is used to cover it.

"Wonderful food, thank you!" I say with a smile, waving to him and the servers and cooks in the rear of the kitchen, who all wave back at us and make familiar gestures to Anu.

"Shoe-lace Girl!" One of the line cooks calls out from the back sheepishly, and another guy next to him taps him with a large cooking implement. "Happy Bride Show Day!"

I try not to giggle.

"Oh, my dear Imperial Lady, my dear Imperial Princess, and all of you charming and delightful ladies and Anu Vei, my good friend—please come back soon!" Shesep calls out praise in our wake as we exit the pleasantly dim interior into the afternoon daylight inferno. The crisp ocean wind and the raw fish smell assail us.

"Well," I say, blinking in the white glare despite my protective lenses, "I'll definitely be coming back here. Great food, Anu!"

"See, I told you," Anu says, still keeping it cool and starting to walk ahead of us. "Best fish anywhere."

"I admit, it was rather excellent," Laronda says in a loud voice, walking forward also, so that Anu glances back at her immediately, then just as quickly looks away.

"Hey, Anu," Laronda says, catching up to him. "Just want to say—good job on bringing us here."

"Yeah, whatever," he mumbles quickly, not looking at her, and continues setting a quick pace down the long stretch of Main Wharf Promenade toward the hover-parking lot.

"That scarab beer was not too bad, actually," she continues. "A little too sour and smelly, I guess, but I'm not really into beer in general. Why is it called scarab beer anyway?"

"Ground scarabs," Anu says.

"What?" Laronda exclaims. "What do you mean, 'ground scarabs'?"

"I just told you, Earth girl. They put ground scarabs in it when they brew it."

"You mean insects? Actual bugs?" Laronda raises one hand to her mouth and glances back at us with horror.

"Yes!" Anu suddenly snarls at her.

"Oh my God! I drank *ground up scarabs?* Is that why it smelled weird?"

"That was the dung."

"Wha-a-at?" Laronda stops in her tracks and slaps Anu's arm. "There was dung too? I drank insect poo? Are you telling me I drank *insect poo?*"

"Not 'insect poo,' stupid Earth girl—dung is what the scarabs eat, so it's already in their stomachs when they grind them, it makes powerful flavoring—"

"Oh my God!"

"I told you not to touch it," Anu says fiercely, stopping also, then coming back to loom over her. "But you did, you stubborn *shar-ta-haak* Gebi female! It's an acquired taste, and you are not capable of appreciating the fine fermentation that goes into making it! The special brewers harvest scarabs only *after* they are naturally dead, so the dung ferments in their stomachs just right, and then they age and dry them for a month, and only then do they grind them—"

"That is absolutely disgusting!" Laronda yells in Anu's face. "And did you just call me something I don't even know how to translate?"

"It's not disgusting, you're just too stupid to appreciate it! And yeah, I called you a *shar-ta-haak*—"

"What the hell is that, troll boy? And here I was, feeling bad about earlier, trying to talk and be all nice to you—"

"Nice? You talk and talk, all right! But you don't even know the language properly, you ignorant Gebi—"

"Ignorant? *Ignorant?* Of course, I don't know your stupid language, I am an *alien*, you dense, awful creep! *I hate you!"*

"Rawah bashtooh, I hate you too! You, big fat mouth, never shut up, you pushy, useless *Earth girl*—"

They are now both shouting in each other's faces, so that passersby turn to stare at our group. And the next moment something crazy happens. . . .

Anu reaches out and swipes one hand through Laronda's hair—whether it's accidental or not, hard to tell.

Laronda grabs Anu's segmented ponytail—whether it's accidental or not, hard to tell.

It is unclear who does what first, but suddenly both of them have their hands waving and slapping at each other, and then they literally *grapple*, and the next second Laronda's mouth is covering Anu's mouth, and then Anu's mouth is all over Laronda's mouth. . . .

They are kissing.

Heaven help us, they are kissing.

It happens very quickly—just a crazy whirlwind of limbs and faces pressed together—and then they both come apart in horrible shock. Anu appears stunned and turns a bright shade of red, his pasty white skin flaring with fierce, awful color like an Earth neon sign. . . . Without saying a word, he sprints away from us, heading for the hover cars in the nearby lot.

Laronda stands frozen in equal shock, and her dark brown skin doesn't show her blush the same way, but it's definitely there, because she is holding her own cheeks with the palms of her hands.

"Okay—what just happened?" Gracie asks.

"Not sure, *janik*," Hasmik replies to Gracie, then looks at Laronda with worry. "Laronda-*jan*, are you okay?"

Laronda slowly turns to us, and she seems to be trembling slightly. "I—I don't know," she says.

We surround Laronda and just let her deal with the moment, just breathe and regain control. The guards hang back, giving us some tactful privacy.

"What did I do?" Laronda repeats softly. "I don't know. . . . So screwed. . . . What did he—what did *we* do?"

"A good thing!" Hasmik says, pressing her arm and shoulder with affection.

"Yes, and I'd say it was something you should've done a long time ago," I echo, rubbing her back gently.

"I am so glad!" Manala says meanwhile, her face bright with excitement.

"God. . . . Where did he go?" Laronda says. She still appears dazed as she stares in Anu's wake—his quickly moving figure is now far away from us, nearly lost in the pedestrian crowd.

"He took off, probably because he's just as affected as you are," Gracie says. "He'll be waiting in the car, I bet. . . . Don't worry."

Laronda shakes her head and laughs in incredulity, apparently at herself.

"We should probably be getting back too," I say, with a glance at the others, and at Tuar and the guards.

And, on that note, we head back.

When we get to the parking area, Anu is indeed seated in the driver's spot in the front row of the hover car. He stares straight ahead at the control panel before him, and the moment we start opening doors and getting in, his face—really, his whole complexion—flames bright red once again.

Tuar takes the seat next to him and gives Anu a meaningful glance. "You okay?"

"We're going to the Imperial Poseidon Museum," Anu replies in a hard voice without reacting to the question. "That's the next stop for the Imperial Bride."

"Okay, great, let's go," I say.

"How many more stops after that?" Gracie asks.

"See for yourself," Anu says in a strange, shell-shocked voice, and without turning around passes us the digital tablet.

I look behind me, concerned for my friend.

In the very back row, sitting alone by choice, Laronda stares thoughtfully at the back of Anu's head.

The remainder of Bride Show Day goes by in a kind of general daze for everyone. We drop by the gorgeous stone façade of the Imperial Poseidon Museum building, and I get interviewed by the media on the marble steps—we don't even have to go inside (even though Manala wants to, but we're pressed for time).

Then we fly over the cityscape farther inland where a beautiful hilltop view greets us at one of the suburbs located near the foothills of the Great Nacarat Plateau. It's another park, and another set of media reporters.

"Happy Bride Show Day!" the locals call out to me as I pass and wave.

All this time, Anu and Laronda act like stiff, awkward strangers to each other, and dazed to the rest of us. They stay as far from each other as possible, keep to the opposite sides of our grouping, and pretend not to acknowledge or look at one another. And yet all they do is *look*, stealing careful glances and intense, quick stares.

I admit, I'm worried about Laronda and yes, about Anu, too. And so are the rest of us. They'll just have to deal with the complications, with *each other*, and I can only guess it's going to get even more interesting.

It's fortunate that we soon finish the last Bride stop of the day, and it happens to be at the park entrance to the Imperial Palace complex. Various media reps waiting near the park gates greet me with another chorus of congratulations as I turn around one last time for all their network feeds, catching the last of the teal sunset light for great effect. Only one more effort is required of me to appear cheerful after a long day, and then I'll be free. And so, I wave and grin, then enter the Imperial Palace, followed by my companions and the guards.

When we get out of the private elevator on our floor and enter the workroom of the Imperial Crown Prince's Quarters, it is packed with people.

Seems like every *daimon* I know is here, and a few strangers too. They all crowd around the data centers, watching the displays, scrolling through feeds, checking their wrist units. Conversation is limited. But mostly everyone is focused on the biggest display screen in the room, the one that always shows the Rah Station.

Aeson stands among them, with his arms folded, staring at the view. When I come in, he turns around with a complex expression of relief, turbulent emotion, and thoughtful, grim solemnity.

"Gwen!" he says with passion, stepping toward me.

"What?" I ask at once, noticing the conflict in his eyes. A pang of nerves stabs my gut. "Did something happen?"

And even before he replies, I manage to get a good look at the view on the screen, and it is *fire*—burning haze and nebulous gases churning pink and blue and incandescent white, bursts of debris swirling against the backdrop of black space. Pieces and chunks of solid materials float and collide, metal and rock and dust. . . .

In moments, some of those pieces become recognizable. Somewhere behind them is the charred surface of a now familiar planet . . . and the grid of golden lights. . . .

Except—the great grid of lights is no longer there.

Where is it? Where did it go?

Wait, no. . . .

I was wrong—the great grid remains.

It's still clearly visible from the vantage point of Helios, while the angle of the present view has changed—is still changing—as it slowly floats in panoramic rotation. Whatever orbiting space buoy camera is recording this moment, it has panned across to focus on a slightly different sector of space.

And the reason for this new camera angle presents itself, amid the churning plasma gas and debris.

A smaller *new grid* of light objects has formed near the planet Rah. Unlike the immense grid structure around Helios, this one is not planetary-scale but relatively tiny—only a couple hundred kilometers or about twenty Atlantean *mag-heitar* across—and its light object components are much smaller too, similar in size to Atlantean ark-ships in formation. The general shape of the array resembles a square, or diamond, or possibly a four-ray starburst.

But at this point it's really hard to tell. . . .

Because most of this array structure is in turmoil. Its individual components are roiling all over the place like angry bees—bees ejecting fire.

This hive of smaller golden *light objects* fills the visual background, ship-sized spheres darting so swiftly that the eye cannot catch individual ones. Even as they move, more fire seems to shoot out in radiant starbursts from each, and the resulting radiation blasts everything in its vicinity.

Rocks and metal and dust and fire.

Blooming like flowers . . . beautiful tiny supernovas. . . .

"What happened? What is that? Is that—" I begin.

And then my lips part, breath halting, as I understand.

These are the physical remnants of Rah Station.

Aeson takes my hand, crushes it almost painfully. "You see this?" he says. "Rah Station has fallen. We're under attack."

Chapter 45

All the earlier events of Bride Show Day, everything that happened this afternoon—Laronda and Anu's amazing confrontation followed by kissing, our fun, carefree meal, the happy sights of Poseidon—it all dissipates in an instant. . . .

Terror slams me, hard.

I stand immobilized with existential vertigo and look at Aeson, at the fiery debris of Rah Station on the big display screen. . . . Meanwhile, my friends crowd behind me, keeping near the workroom entrance, even as I glance back at them in nervous reflex.

With a troubled expression, Hasmik holds Manala's arm protectively. Gracie and Laronda frown, stalled in indecision as to whether or not they should approach the work area where so many high commanding Fleet officers are present. . . .

With my peripheral vision I see Anu hurry forward to join Gennio and the others at the secondary desk. I glance at him stupidly and notice how this latest shocking development has managed to shake him out of his embarrassed, awkward stupor in regard to Laronda. He immediately asks questions and becomes the usual businesslike Anu.

"Come, Gwen," Aeson says, still keeping my hand tightly in his. "Take a seat."

"It's okay," I mumble. "Please, just tell me what happened."

"It started about an hour ago," he says, guiding me to a chair regardless, and I sit down, numb with stress. "We received an urgent transmission from the Rah Station Nomarch that something was happening with the alien light grid. 'They are breaking formation . . . breaking apart into smaller components . . . moving closer to us and re-forming,' Nomarch Rertu barely had time to say, before the transmission was cut off.

"Unable to regain his audio signal, we focused on the visuals of the Rah Station. For a few moments, nothing seemed out of the ordinary. Sensor sweeps of the region of space around Helios showed no new activity. And then we saw this new diamond array visible on the other side of Rah."

Aeson pauses, fingers pressing mine painfully as he forgets himself. "The new array of lights—this *thing*—it just appeared out of nowhere. And just as suddenly it erupted with plasma fire. Multiple powerful energy beams struck the station all at once. . . . Just a few heartbeats, Gwen. Maybe five, maybe three. That's all the time it took to obliterate an immense structure of metal, hundreds of docked ships . . . thousands of people."

"Oh, Aeson . . ." I whisper.

"There was no provocation," he says, speaking quickly. "Absolutely none on our part. All the station personnel had been carefully instructed to observe only—not to interact with the alien presence, not to fly any reconnaissance missions until we had more information. These were SPC standing orders, Fleet-wide. And to our understanding, they were obeyed."

"What about the battle barge?" I recall suddenly. "War-10, wasn't it supposed to protect the station?"

Aeson winces. "Yes, War-10." Realizing he must be hurting me, he lightens his grip on my hand. "It was indeed supposed to protect, and it tried. In the next few heartbeats we received a first priority transmission from Command Pilot Tecpatl, asking permission to engage in immediate defensive action. Before I could reply, War-10 was under fire also. . . . We could see it *mag-heitars* away, sitting in a slightly higher orbit than the remains of Rah Station, and then it too was targeted by the golden hive of light objects. Their weapons cut though War-10's plasma shields as if they were nothing. I could still hear Eodea Tecpatl's voice even as I watched the cascade of explosions that took out the battle barge."

Aeson shakes his head slowly and blinks. "War-10 is gone, Gwen. It's out there, floating in pieces, together with the Rah Station."

"All those young Cadets!" I exclaim, remembering the inexperienced training crew which was last present on that ship.

Aeson's expression is tragic.

I've seen this same look in his eyes before—once on Earth during Qualification when the shuttle explosions killed several Fleet pilots and his fellow *astra daimon*, and a second time on board the

ICS-2 after the Terra Patria terrorists hostage crisis and ensuing corridor battle, when he stood over the bodies of the fallen guards and crew.

"There was no time to react," he says in a strange voice, not meeting my gaze, speaking as if to convince himself. "I'm responsible for the loss. As SPC Commander, I am responsible."

I frown, part my lips, take a deep breath. My fingers slide from his grip, and now I'm the one squeezing his wrist, then his arm, painfully. "No . . ." I say. "It is not your fault! How can it be?"

He shakes his head slowly, then brings himself to look into my eyes. For a moment only, his own eyes reveal that he's drowning. In the next blink, the expression closes up. "I know. It's irrational to engage in self-blame, considering the circumstances. And yet, the fact remains. . . . As Commander, it always has and always will rest on me."

Abruptly, he shrugs and straightens his posture. "But enough," he says in a hard voice that has grown cool and emotionless. "I'm sorry, *im amrevu*, I'm going to ask you for your patience with all of this. You must excuse me for the time being, as I attend to this situation at hand. We'll talk more tonight, I promise—as soon as I get the chance. For now—"

"Oh, of course!" I interrupt. "Please don't mind me. . . . You have so much work to do, please get back to work. . . . I'll just be here if you need me, okay?"

Seeing the turmoil in my eyes, he lightens for an instant and gives me a nod and a quick, loving smile that sears me with warmth.

Then he returns to the command center work area.

Trying to keep out of everyone's way, I step back and join my friends near the door. As best as I can, I explain to them what happened.

Laronda and Gracie appear stunned. Hasmik shakes her head and continues patting Manala's arm. Poor Manala seems very emotional and quietly confused, in the way that she sometimes gets when she refuses to comprehend something terribly unpleasant. In this case, "unpleasant" is a wild understatement.

"What will happen now? What is he—what are they doing?" Hasmik asks, speaking as mildly as possible for Manala's sake.

"I wouldn't be surprised if now we get called off-planet," Laronda mutters.

Gracie stares at her.

Immediately, both of them start checking their wrist units for any new messages or directives from Fleet HQ. I have a passing thought that the Imperial Fleet command has likely not been notified yet—or if they have been, SPC has not issued them orders. Gracie and Laronda would have better luck just walking across the room and asking Aeson directly—not that they would, or should. . . .

We head to the sofa and whisper quietly among ourselves, watching Aeson interact with the *daimon* friends who are also officers under his command.

From what we can overhear, Aeson makes a number of calls to IEC members, including an extended one to consult with the Imperator, and then prepares to make a public statement. At the same time, Aeson issues high-level orders to the armed forces in the Star Pilot Corps hierarchy. Among other things, he recalls War-1 and War-2 from the outer system, and they are now on their way here, to reinforce us around Atlantis. These two are flagship vessels—the former normally under the leadership of Manakteon Resoi, who is the IF Commander for Imperial *Atlantida* but serves as Command Pilot in the SPC, and the latter under Command Pilot Amaiar Uluatl of New Deshret.

"Meanwhile, War-3 will leave its position around Olympos and instead head outward to Atlas, taking the place of War-1," we can hear Xelio say. "Makes sense. You want the best nearby—in other words, Resoi and Uluatl—while there still needs to be a strong presence around Atlas. Just in case the threat appears from that direction too."

"Just in case." Aeson nods, continuing to enter keystrokes at the console before him.

"Are you keeping War-4 in place for now?" an unfamiliar young man asks. He's a slim *astra daimon* with olive skin, heavy black brows and striking pale grey eyes, whose name I recall is Culuar Efrebu.

"Yes." Aeson glances at him. "War-4 will remain near Olympos, poised to move in either direction, system interior or exterior, as needed."

"What about Septu Station?" Oalla asks. "It's next in the line of fire from the interior. Are we shifting Tammuz and Ishtar to reinforce Septu?"

"Haven't decided yet." Aeson sits back, rubbing his forehead.

"Or you can just evacuate Septu Station. Shift the whole thing to Tammuz." Keruvat points at specific coordinates of the system map displayed on his screen. "If you notice—Tammuz's location in orbit around Helios *right now* brings it much closer in line with Atlantis than Septu's present position happens to be in relation to Atlantis. Septu is currently on the opposite side of Hel, which puts it comfortably out of the way for at least several months—that is, if the enemy is following a direct path of alignment to us. Meanwhile, even though Tammuz is farther away from Hel, it's more likely the enemy will advance to Tammuz first on their way here."

"We don't know that," Oalla says. "We don't have sufficient data on their line of approach—not enough to plot a predictive pattern of movement. They could be jumping quasi-randomly to verified spots of sentient human activity. Or following planetary rotation points."

"Should we then just disregard Septu? Not even evacuate the station?" Xelio asks grimly.

"Leaving only War-9 behind to observe Septu would minimize possible casualties if the next hostile action takes place there," Erita adds, peering closer at Ker's screen. "War-9 can either engage or retreat as soon as hostiles arrive. It would keep us better informed than automated equipment alone, and it would become an immediate focal point of defense."

"I haven't decided if I want to expand or contract our defense perimeter," Aeson says thoughtfully. "Not until we know more about the true nature and capabilities of our enemy. Putting more space between us and the threat, increasing the depth of the front, with interim tactical points of defense, is one solution."

"Another is consolidating the defenses around Atlantis," Xelio says. "We've just seen what the golden shiny *shar-ta-haak* can do, and leaving War-9 alone there is suicide."

"That may be so. But have we?" Aeson looks at Xel. "Have we really *seen* the extent of their capabilities? What we observed was mostly after the fact, with no visuals of their weapons activation up-close. I want real data on range, duration, impact, firing capacity."

"In other words, 'what, where, when,' and 'how.'" Oalla makes a small sound.

"Don't forget, 'who,'" says another unfamiliar *astra daimon*, a young man with very dark skin—almost as dark but not as tall as Keruvat. I seem to remember his name is Nergal Duha.

"Yes, 'who' would be nice," Erita says. "Would help to know what these alien *chazufs* look like, what kind of biologicals."

"Yes, in short, I want numbers, not assumptions." Aeson glances around at the others. "To make projections and run scenarios, we need more information on this enemy. Before we talk strategy with the global partners, before I commit our resources one way or another, before I risk more lives. . . . We still don't understand what really happened out there. If—*when*—they decide to strike next, we need to be better prepared for them."

The evening is interminably long, especially since my friends leave about an hour later, wanting to be out of the way. I give Gracie a tight hug, and she promises to call me if anything changes or she gets deployment orders.

"You, too," I tell Laronda, giving her a gentle hug and again thinking about her and Anu. "Oh, and—you feeling okay?"

Laronda makes a sound that could be taken as amusement or stressed-out nerves. "All things considered, yup, I guess," she whispers, with an involuntary glance across the room to where Anu has his back turned as he's working at a computer screen.

Hasmik gives *me* a hug and tells *me* to stay strong, and then leaves with Manala, to make sure the Princess gets to her own Quarters safely.

Now that I'm alone, I sit perched nervously on the sofa, listening in to what has basically turned into an informal military strategy meeting. It's a preliminary to the SPC war council that I suspect will happen soon, when Aeson officially meets with the global heads of state, their representatives, and a variety of experienced veteran officers in the SPC high command, likely up in orbit in the neutral territory of the Atlantis Station's SPC Headquarters.

The public doesn't know yet, I think. They don't know about the attack, or that the Rah Station and War-10 were both destroyed.

Right now, *how much* and *what* to tell them, in order to prevent global panic, is part of what will be decided shortly.

Hours later, Aeson and the others are still working, still brainstorming.

The display screen showing a scorched graphite-and-coal hemisphere of planet Rah and the tragic debris floating in space around it has not changed much. However, the golden light objects have stopped moving and firing their impossible weapons of mass destruction, and have returned to their former spots in the diamond-shape formation.

Indeed, the diamond array has fully reconstructed itself and now sits in orbit around Rah, geometrically perfect, motionless and inactive. While in the distant background, the grand, golden grid of planet-sized light objects around Helios still menaces in its immensity.

It must be noted that the video feed of Rah gets cut off periodically and has to be recaptured on different equipment that still remains on-site. Apparently many of the space buoy cameras wink out, one by one, as they get caught up in the debris field and suffer damage. Fortunately, enough functional ones still remain, giving Aeson and the others a constantly changing view of the scene and the golden enemy, its hostile activity suspended for the time being.

Given all this, with no other new, major developments, I get to bed around Midnight Ghost Time, because there's nothing I can do to help, and I want to be out of everyone's way.

The next morning, Green Ghost Moon 15 dawns, and I am up so early with restless nerves that it's still dark. Even so, there are some people already (or still) in the workroom when I get there, together with a fresh *eos* bread service. The pastry scent of strong, steaming-hot *lvikao* fills the air.

I am told that, after holding a brief conference meeting formally in orbit, Aeson, as the SPC Commander, is about to deliver a public address from the IEC Assembly Chamber.

When did all this happen? Did he even go to bed? I experience a stab of worry. *Poor Aeson!*

I glance at the live feed of planet Rah, and nothing much has changed there. The clouds of incandescent gas have coalesced and dissipated somewhat overnight but the floating chaos of debris remains. I try not to look too closely at the grisly details, in case there are bodies. . . .

"Anything?" I ask Oalla, who sits bleary-eyed, holding a big mug of *lvikao*, and stares at scrolling data.

I should probably ask her—or someone—if *lvikao* contains a stimulant, such as caffeine in Earth coffee.

"Not much that's new," she tells me with a suppressed yawn. "The enemy remains inactive, which is a good thing. Still, very creepy in their ordered lineup. Our instruments tell us there are *exact* space intervals between those light spheres. To a high degree of accuracy. So I'm running a mathematical correlation program to find significance."

"That is scary," I say, pouring myself *lvikao* also.

"Your Imperial *amrevu* is about to go before the networks, so let me switch to a news feed," Oalla adds. She splits her current window into two, then calls up the Hel-Ra morning newscast.

Half an hour later, we watch Aeson's face on the TV screen. He appears grim yet impassive, looking directly into the camera with his commanding, heavy gaze. In that moment he projects Imperial power, not unlike his father. I know that he must be exhausted, but he is covering it very well.

Aeson speaks, first explaining the situation briefly in unemotional language, using general terms and some understatement. I notice he does not shirk from mentioning the complete loss of the Rah Station and War-10 in the unexpected attack. And then he describes the current status of the enemy.

"The hostile alien objects are inactive once again. Having perpetrated the devastating unprovoked strike on the space station and the battle barge, they returned to their original fixed positions in the lesser, second grid in high orbit around Rah. At present, they are in a resting state and do not appear to pose a threat, for the moment. Meanwhile, the losses we suffered are currently being analyzed and studied—losses of human life and military resources. The attack happened so quickly that we have very little detail by which to assess the exact causes and methods of damage, but we are in the process of acquiring the necessary data. Tactical probes are being sent to approach and observe the hostiles, taking all care not to provoke additional action."

Aeson pauses, and his eyes do not blink as he looks into the camera. "This is all the information I have for you, as of now. I offer my deepest condolences to the families and loved ones of those who are now lost to us. Please remain confident that the Star Pilot Corps, comprised of the best among you, are a formidable global defense force for our planet, and we have just begun our own counter-measures to keep you safe. May you take comfort at this difficult time in the loving gods of your faith and in the strength of those you love."

Chapter 46

I have very little memory of the rest of the day. It's a jumble of stress in general, worrying about everything and everyone, and about Aeson in particular. There's the constant waiting in his absence, as he takes part in endless military strategy meetings both here on the planet surface and up in orbit on Atlantis Station, international home to the SPC Headquarters.

Around noon, I escape from the oppressive atmosphere of the workroom to take a brief walk in the Palace gardens with Manala. Neither of us speaks much, wrapped up in our own stress thoughts, except when I pat her arm reassuringly and remind her that, with her brother Aeson in charge of the SPC, everything will be fine.

"Do you really think so, Gwen?" she asks me timidly. "I think we will all die. It's a very bad, terrible, sad, and depressing thing, and I don't see a way out for anyone. The evil ancients have returned to exterminate us."

"Oh, no, Manala!" I hurry to squeeze her shoulder. "That is *so* not true!"

"How can you be so sure?"

"Well," I say, choosing words with care. "For one thing, Atlantis has us Earthies to help. As you know, we're very, very stubborn. And it's been so many thousands of years. We have all progressed and changed, and so have the circumstances. I think that if we work together, we have an excellent chance of fighting back and defending ourselves. In fact, I *know* we do!"

Manala laughs suddenly, blinking in the glare of daylight. "Thank you, Gwen. I like the way you explain it. I feel a little better now. Now I want to eat some *cheburi* pie."

And on that note, we return indoors.

The other exciting thing that happens an hour later is the call from Dad and George. It comes in on one of the display-and-data screens. Xelio receives the interstellar deep space transmission from the velo-cruiser, chats briefly with Quoni Enutat who's placed the call on the other end. Xel then calls me over, and I see Quoni's serious face. He immediately moves aside—and there's my Dad.

"Dad!" I cry out with unexpected joy, and like a gusher, feel a sudden, overwhelming pressure of tears. But I manage to hold it back, somehow. . . .

Charles Lark, my father, smiles lovingly at me, and I realize he looks somewhat better than he did the last few times we talked. Maybe it's the fact that he's clean shaven and his shirt collar is neatly folded at his throat. Or maybe it's because his expression of chronic sorrow is no longer so stark and blatant with despair, but more of a soft undercurrent lurking in his eyes.

"Gwen, my sweet girl, how are you? How are Gracie and Gordie?" Dad asks. "I'm told we cannot speak too long this time— something to do with great acceleration rate in this Quantum Stream, I believe. But we wanted to call you, George and I—" At this point I see my older brother peeking over Dad's shoulder and waving to me with a familiar, crafty George-smirk—"We wanted to call to let you know we are about to be put in cold storage. Or whatever they call it—"

"Stasis," I hear George's voice. "Stasis chambers, for safety."

"Yes, that is correct, Stasis," Dad nods. "Tomorrow, or sometime later today, there will be a Jump event, we are told."

"Oh!" I exclaim. "Yes, yes! You will be Jumping in order to cross an immeasurable distance across the universe! We had to do that too, when we traveled to Atlantis! It's basically a space shortcut."

Dad smiles at me, shaking his head in mild disbelief. "An amazing thing, for certain. I admit it's a little scary to imagine, and to anticipate. The fact that we get to be 'frozen' for it is definitely unsettling to consider."

"Oh, don't worry, it's perfectly safe for you in the Stasis chamber," I say with emotion. "Just make sure to listen and do exactly what they tell you, and when you wake up, you'll be on the other side of the universe, close to us!"

"Of course. And ah—I believe, our fine Pilot is telling me we need to cut this short," Dad says, glancing in the direction of

Quoni's quiet voice, off screen. "We'll call again tomorrow, right after it's over."

"Yes, please do! Okay, promise! Please be sure to call, Dad, love you! Love you, Gee One!" I hasten to say and we disconnect.

It occurs to me, the fact that they are coming up on the Jump means that the velo-cruiser is halfway to its destination.

Hard to believe, but Dad and George will be here so soon. . . .

A eson returns home to his Palace Quarters in the early evening, following a long day of international meetings, media appearances, and SPC business. He immediately consults with those still on duty in the workroom, presently Erita and two other, unfamiliar *astra daimon* whom I didn't have the chance to meet formally. They are all running analysis programs and observing the golden grid around Helios and the lesser one near Rah from all possible directions.

I overhear from their conversation that numerous automated research probes of all types have been dispatched from various starting points around the system, including Tammuz Station, to rendezvous with the grid light objects, and they should start arriving on location in the coming hours all throughout the night. That will be the crucial moment of truth—whether they will be permitted to approach the golden light grid unharmed or be destroyed at a certain proximity. If they manage to make it through, then we'll start getting new, critically important data.

"Keep watching, and let me know immediately if anything changes or significant new data comes in," Aeson tells Erita and the others in a drained voice of exhaustion.

"Will do, My Imperial Lord," she replies with a small frown. "Now please get some rest, Kass. Go see your Bride, she's been worried sick about you."

Aeson allows himself a tiny smile, then turns around and heads directly toward me.

I rise from the sofa where I've been quietly and half-heartedly watching TV feeds, and move toward him.

"Aeson . . ." I say softly.

"Let's go to your room," he replies in a parched voice, taking me by the hand. At the warm touch of his fingers over mine I feel a familiar jolt of electricity.

And then we go into my bedroom together, shutting the door behind us.

As soon as we're alone, Aeson closes the distance between us, and I am crushed in his embrace. I close my eyes and exhale with pleasure, feeling the planes of his hard body press into me, engulf me with his muscular strength, hearing him let go of his own tensely held breath with a shudder, a moment of profound relief. . . .

I wrap my arms around him, run my fingers over his soft, pale hair gathered in a thick segmented tail at the nape, then stroke his powerful neck, pulling him closer to me, and we simply breathe in each other, saying nothing for several long, sweet, mindless seconds.

"Oh, Gwen . . . Gwen!" he says thickly, his warm breath washing over my cheek, and then places both his palms on either side of my face and turns me to the light to look into my eyes. "My sweet *Gwen* . . ."

I stare up at him with a kind of awe, a revelation, seeing a sudden feverish rise of energy in his lapis lazuli, deep-blue eyes, and a widening of his night-black pupils. It comes like a whirlwind out of nowhere. The force of his gaze is the weight of a mountain, and it physically *moves* me and sears me. . . .

Even as I reel under the sheer living *force* of him—feeling like a blade of grass in the wind, being taken by the storm—he leans into me, his strong hands guiding me, so that I end up stepping backwards until he backs me into the nearest wall.

"Oh . . ." I breathe in surprise. "Aeson—"

He continues staring at me, consuming me. But now his attention is on my throat and then, focusing lower down, on my otherwise demure neckline. . . . The top I'm wearing is not particularly low cut, but the neckline curves downward slightly, so that only the faintest dimple shows in the middle where my cleavage begins, mostly concealed by the fabric.

Before I can anticipate it, he slides one hand over my right shoulder, tugging aside the shirt and pushing down my bra strap on that side, baring my shoulder. His strong fingers dig into my skin almost painfully, and he holds me there for several heart-pounding seconds. He lingers, staring at my bared skin strangely, slowing down. . . . Suddenly I'm aware of the controlled, labored sound of his breathing.

And then his fingers continue downward while his other hand moves in, and now both hands are underneath my breasts, cupping them. Abruptly he pushes them up and close together, so that the tops rise past the neckline, creating a bulging cleavage, while still contained in the bra.

My breath hitches, then escapes in a moan. . . . It is followed by a flush of scalding heat. A mad, swelling tide floods me—so much sensation that it's numbing. I am overpowered, suddenly bereft of strength in my limbs—as though all of me has dissolved into a puddle of warm, thick, flowing honey. . . .

Time dilates as he brings his head down, burying his hard mouth in the dimple that is now a crevasse between my full breasts. His stubble grates my delicate skin, and it hurts so sweet, and I don't give a damn, as his lips move hungrily over the tops of my breasts, while his fingers squeeze on both sides.

He raises his head at last and then staggers forward, pressing me up against the wall, then slamming me into it. . . . And for the first time, he is in such aggressive, close contact with my lower body that I can feel *him* down below—something large and *hard*—and then again his face is buried in my chest and he's gasping for air, and I'm panting with surges of desire, washing over me in a pulse of concentric circles. . . .

We've gone completely insane.

"Oh . . . oh, sweet . . . oh—" I pant, grappling with him.

"To hell with everything. . . ." He inhales raggedly, speaking in a drunken voice, slurring words, as his hands now stroke and squeeze my bottom. "I need to have you *right now*, do you understand, my sweet *amrevu*, I need—"

And then he's devouring my neck, mouth fiercely clenched with suction against the fluttering beat at the base of my throat—a bruising pulse kiss that will leave a mark . . . and I don't give a damn.

I tilt my head back, offering myself up, and let him be a vampire.

"What . . . about . . . the Wedding?" I moan.

"*Rawah bashtooh*, to hell with the Wedding, with tomorrow—"

He groans, low and hoarse—the deep, beautiful, male sound of his voice sends another surge of desire through me—then grabs me by the hair, his fingers digging into my scalp, while his mouth opens with hunger and crushes mine.

And even as I'm sweetly drowning, I suddenly understand that he's drowning too. Right now, in this exact moment, he's holding on to me for dear life. . . .

My Bridegroom is in despair.

With a shudder I push back at him, reluctant to let go, freeing up my bruised mouth. "Aeson, wait—no!" I say.

At once he stops and moves back, breathing raggedly. His hands are still on me, gripping me. "Gwen—are you okay?"

"Yes, I'm fine, but you're not," I say gently. "I'm sorry, sweetie, but this is wrong. Our first time shouldn't happen this way. This is sad, and you are overwhelmed with all the horrible things happening."

"But I—" he says. And then he exhales again, then inhales deeply, to slow his crazy breathing down.

"Sh-h-h-h. . . ." I reach out and smooth back a fine tendril of damp hair on his forehead, then stroke his flushed cheeks and jaw calmingly, while he continues to breathe hard and stare at me with a serious, grim look of thwarted desire.

"Ah, *bashtooh*," he says a few seconds later, as his breathing quiets down. "I'm sorry. You're right." He runs his hands over mine, stroking my skin, then raises my wrists up and plants soft kisses on the inside, butterfly-light pulse kisses of gratitude.

"I want you so much," he says, looking down at me with his impossible, beautiful eyes.

"I know . . . I want you too," I whisper, melting in his gaze. "Now—are you okay?"

And involuntarily I glance down at him *there*, at his lower body.

He notices the direction of my gaze and a light flush again surges in his cheeks.

"I am—under control," he says with a smile.

"Good," I say. "Because you know what happened the last time my bra was involved."

He looks at me curiously, raising one elegant eyebrow.

"I mean, during our journey to Atlantis with the Fleet, up on ICS-2." I bite my lip quickly, suddenly feeling breathless. "What happened in your cabin, during the Jump."

There, I've said it.

Oh . . . my . . . God.

Aeson's expression is—well, let's just say that he blinks and then turns fiercely red, considerably more so than he was a few minutes ago in the middle of our make-out session.

"Gwen. . . . I was—" He shakes his head, unable to continue.

"Back then, you told me it was Jump sickness," I say with mild reproach, watching him.

He exhales loudly, glances away, then finally makes eye contact. Did I mention, he is flaming red?

"It was not," he says at last, softly. And his lips hold back a tiny smile. He exhales again. "Not Jump sickness. It was all *you*."

I stare at him in wonder.

"All right—I was completely out of my mind," he says. "You were suddenly naked and you were beautiful. I wanted you so much. . . . My body—I lost control completely. And yes, I was weakened by the Jump, but only in the sense of having my defenses down. I might've mentioned before, but Kassiopei are generally immune to the detrimental effects of the Jump. However, we are still vulnerable to some aspects of it."

Aeson pauses. "Besides, I was always vulnerable to you."

Oh, my lord . . . my heart melts.

"I think you also kind of like *these*," I say, looking down and pointing at my own chest.

Aeson chuckles and then shamelessly ogles my breasts. "You know I do."

"All right," I say cheerfully. "So now we know you totally lied to me about the Jump incident. I forgive you."

"Thank you," he says, tilting his head slightly to look at me. "And I'm sorry. You already know the many reasons why I couldn't be honest with you then—how I felt about you."

I punch him in the arm. "Aeson, you silly man, be glad I love you."

He chuckles again.

"Oh, and speaking about the Jump—"

I tell Aeson about my interstellar conversation with Dad and George.

"Looks like Quoni is setting an excellent pace. They're making very good progress," Aeson says, watching me warmly. "Soon they will be here."

"In time for the Wedding, you think?" I'm almost afraid to ask.

Aeson pauses before answering. I see a tiny flicker of doubt, a shadow in his eyes, but he hides it quickly. "Yes . . . the Wedding," he says with a smile while his gaze involuntarily goes to his wrist comm light band that's blinking with incoming data. "If all goes well—"

If we and Atlantis are still here tomorrow and the next day, I can almost hear his unspoken words.

"There will be a Wedding," he concludes. "So yes, I see no reason why they wouldn't be here in time for it, or shortly after."

I hate hearing it expressed so bluntly, but I understand exactly what he means, *why* he says it this way.

There are still twenty days until our Wedding Day. A lot of things can happen in twenty days. Right now, with all the chaos and uncertainty that's happening in the world, we can only think so far ahead, *live* so far ahead.

Yes, right now the sense of *logically deduced hopelessness* is strong, especially for him. As head of the SPC, he must be realistic and continuously look at the grim big picture, since he's responsible for so much—in a sense, he's responsible for all of us.

It's why he wanted to have this moment of sweet oblivion with me just now.

But, right now, it's my turn to be strong for him.

"*Of course*, there will be a Wedding," I say, squeezing his arm. "No crappy alien light objects with their crappy super weapons and ancient invasion plan will get in the way of *you and me* being together at last—the right way, with our families there to witness! If I have to take out these aliens myself, singlehandedly, and stuff them all up the nearest black hole, I will. Better yet, let the Venerable Therutat take care of them for us—they'll be sorry. Deploy her and the First Priest of Amrevet-Ra together with their Bridal Books and Event Lists and flower selections. Make the aliens put on weird, sexy dresses and memorize the Imperial Consort Protocol—"

Aeson starts to laugh, watching me blather, listening to my idiot bravado nonsense.

For the moment—change of mood and distraction achieved.

"Now let's eat," I conclude firmly, giving Aeson a tickle on the cheek. "Right now, a solid *niktos* meal will do us both the most good."

Chapter 47

W e're supremely lucky, because we get to enjoy the rest of the evening without any dire new events taking place. First, we have our entirely uneventful *niktos* meal. Aeson goes to the workroom a couple of times to check the status of incoming data and deployed tech probes, then returns and we stay on my bedroom side of the Quarters. We go out through the other door, and hang out on the balcony terraces, and watch the crazy big moons (including the ghostly weirdo fourth) in the star-spangled night sky, talk softly about nothing in particular, giggle, come back to snuggle, and then collapse on top of my bed covers and just stare at the ceiling while I play with Aeson's long golden hair. . . .

Yes, I'm not kidding—he lies on his back with his hands tucked under his head and watches me with amusement as I braid one fine long strand of his nearly waist-long hair and giggle. Wrapping the finished skinny braid around my finger I pretend it's a finger puppet.

"You know, Anu and Laronda kissed, yesterday . . ." I announce.

"What?" Aeson raises one brow, and parts his lips, and almost sits up in surprise.

But I push him back down on the coverlet and tell him the whole story of the Bride Show Day afternoon, until he shakes with laughter on the bed.

Finally, I make him leave and go to his own bedroom and get some desperately needed sleep.

T he next morning is Green Ghost Moon 16, and when I wake up around seventh hour, I find out that our luck continues, and again, nothing awful has occurred.

The workroom is busy with *astra daimon* officers. So many people—yet, they comprise only a small percentage of the SPC international military and government personnel with whom Aeson interacts on a daily basis. I just get to see the ones who visit him here at home, since they're necessarily the ones he's closest with, the *daimon.*

Apparently, the first batch of the closest tech probes is starting to approach the golden grid of light near Rah, while others are nearing the original mega-grid around Helios. As the automated equipment makes its approach, so does data on our end.

Everyone works and waits. Aeson leaves for another series of meetings.

Then, later in the afternoon, my brother George and Dad call, sometime after fourth hour of Khe, Poseidon time, to say they achieved the Jump safely.

"I must say, the Stasis experience was entirely like getting anesthesia before surgery," Dad tells me calmly, with considerable relief. "You go to sleep and remember nothing, and that's the best thing about it. In short, we're feeling fine."

"You made it! You are now in the cosmic neighborhood of Atlantis!" I say with a surge of joy.

"So, looks like we're coming to invade your new planet soon, Gee Two," George says with a flippant little smile. "Be saying, 'Take us to your leader.' And then what will you do? Take us to your fine and dandy fiancé, is what you'll do."

George is being George and joking like the wry jester that he is. But in that one moment when he mentions "invading" I get a sick little twinge of guilt. . . . I still haven't told them about what's happening here, about the real-life alien threat hanging over us.

However, I force myself to push back the guilt, stuff it deep inside, and bury it for now—no need to worry them needlessly.

That will come later.

A fterwards, I call Gordie and Gracie to tell them the good news about Dad and George getting closer and closer to us. Gordie is at work, doing agricultural design, and I can hear the sounds of his busy office, voices of coworkers chattering in rapid *Atlanteo.* "Yeah, good. They better get here soon," he mumbles. "Before the alien invasion."

"Hush, silly," I tell my younger brother. "Don't say that."

"Everybody here thinks we're screwed. I mean, they think Atlantis as a whole is screwed," Gordie continues blandly. I can just imagine him shrugging.

"Far from it," I say in an upbeat tone.

"Why, what do you know?" Gordie asks, immediately perking up. "Did Aeson say something?"

"All I know is, no one is giving up yet, and the SPC is a powerful force protecting us."

"Yeah, okay. . . . But if you know something, just let me know, okay?"

"Love you, Gee Three."

Then I talk to Gracie who's at the small personal apartment issued to her, courtesy of the Fleet (same as all other Poseidon-based Earth Cadets), and located near downtown, not too far from HQ. She's off from flight duty or training today, sitting around at home and waiting for deployment orders. I can hear Blayne's voice, so he must be off, too, and they're hanging out together.

"Oh, yay! Such a relief, Dad and George are on our side of the universe now!" she says with excitement. And then her tone gets serious. "When are you going to tell them about the things here? It's very possible they are coming into a war zone."

Out of the Earth frying pan and into the Atlantis fire.

I sigh with a shudder. "I know," I say. "And I *don't* know—when or how to tell them, that is. Probably best to let them get here safely, and then we can talk . . . about everything."

"Yeah. You're probably right," Gracie says.

Neither one of us wants to voice the ugly thought:

There are no guarantees that any of us will be here tomorrow or the next day.

Meanwhile, later that night, the earliest unmanned drone probes arrive at the two distinct alien grid locations. They make it all the way to within a *mag-heitar* of the immense grid objects around Helios and just a quarter of a *mag-heitar* from the Rah diamond grid.

And then they stop, assuming fixed-distance orbits, and starting to drift in parallel to the grids.

Nothing fires at them; nothing out of the ordinary happens—at either of the locations.

"The units are programmed to stop and proceed with preliminary data gathering and analysis from this fixed distance," Keruvat says, as people gather around screens in the workroom.

"So far, passed the first stage safely," Xelio remarks. "If they are undisturbed within the next few hours, they can proceed closer to take the next series of proximity scans. For now, this is sufficient to give us visuals and other useful data."

"Yes," Aeson says. "Let's not risk sending the equipment any closer until we extract as much useful raw data from this distance as we can."

The data transmission begins minutes later, including new nano-cam visuals of the grid light objects, for the first time, up-close and personal—relatively speaking.

The immense objects comprising the grid around Helios are confirmed to be huge spheres of an unknown physical composition. From a mere *mag-heitar* distance they are planet-sized, or at the least, asteroid-sized, filling up the view completely, so that the cameras transmit only a featureless surface—a field of blinding golden light. . . .

The diamond grid formation next to Rah consists of much smaller spheres, and their shape and curvature is easier to perceive, even from this much shorter distance. So far, their surface radiance is similar in intensity to the huge objects of the Helios grid. And once again, there are no topographical features.

"It is hard to tell if what we're seeing is light energy coming from its own source, or if this is some kind of stealth reflective tech," Oalla says. "Or even a thin, surface veneer of plasma shields."

"The next, closer stage of approach should give us a better idea," Ker says. "At least in theory. As our drones get closer, the alien objects or *entities* could assume hostile intent and start to fire."

"They haven't fired so far," Xel says, watching the screen.

Aeson rests one hand on the desk and his fingers tap the surface lightly. "We only send one to make the approach. One unit at a time. When—or if—it succeeds in making contact with the surface of the alien object, we will know infinitely more than we know now."

"Or we'll see a very big explosion," Oalla says, shaking her head. "And depending on their response, it could be multiple explosions, if the grid decides to treat one hostile unit as a part of a greater whole and fires on all the other drone units."

"For now, proceed with the data gathering," Aeson says. "Let's hope for the best."

The probes stay positioned at their tasks for several more hours, and overnight are directed to approach closer. On the morning of Green Ghost Moon 17, when I wake up reasonably early around seventh hour, I learn that not one but five automated research units have come up to within a few meters of one of the mega-grid objects around Helios. Since there are no differentiating features among the individual components of the grid, the particular spherical light object was picked at random.

So far, none of the research probes has been shot down.

About two meters short of the light object's surface, the first probe already took a sensor "snapshot" and sent back energy readings. They are being analyzed right now.

"This is very strange," yet another unfamiliar-to-me *astra daimon* says to Oalla as they both stare at scrolling numbers on one display, while the others watch different screens. "It appears to be similar to our own plasma energy quantum field, only in a state of even greater quantum uncertainty. And by 'uncertainty' I mean crazy *shebet*. That's an impossible quantum state—not flux but *suspension*. I've never seen anything like it. Could it be trans-dimensional? Or, multi-dimensional—no, I don't even know how to describe it. See those values? It exists *simultaneously* as matter and antimatter particles without annihilating each other, which means it has to be present in more than one dimensional reality at once. Otherwise it simply makes no sense."

"Yeah, I see it," Oalla muses, frowning. "Maybe—to occupy the same place without cancelling themselves out, the particle pairs have to be . . . *time-entangled?*"

"Are we talking *time dilation* of some sort?" Ker asks, stepping up to look at the same screen. "The kind you get within the ergosphere of a black hole?"

"No," Oalla says. "And now I'm thinking it's not even time entanglement. It's more like being *stuck* at the actual event horizon boundary, a location paradox—instead of particle pairs separating and one of them falling inside the black hole while the other ends up outside, they *both* remain at the boundary.... Neither here, nor there.... A strange, perfect equilibrium point achieved, which keeps them 'together yet apart' in one place and doesn't let them split off in either direction or annihilate each other."

"Or, as I say, *plural dimensions*," the other *astra daimon* says.

"No, again, not quite that." Oalla disagrees, furrowing her brow. "It's more like being quantum-stuck somehow. Particles fixed in place?"

"Huh? That goes against the very fundamental nature of quantum reality. Being 'stuck' at that level makes no sense. All particles are in constant motion, even when entangled—"

"All right. Save the fun theories for later," Aeson says. "Have we received sufficient sensor data at this position? If so, time to move in even closer. Let's reach out beyond its plasma field and attempt to touch one of these alien things."

The *astra daimon* nods, and the probes are directed to make their final advance—to make physical contact with the light object.

We all watch with suspended breath as the vanguard drone slowly drifts forward, creeping toward the alien object's surface.

Three meters....

No reaction from the golden form of light.

Two meters....

Still nothing.

One meter....

Silence in the room.

The drone makes contact. Its oval nose section *touches* the alien object with the tip of its hull....

Just for one instant, there's some kind of hair-fine fluctuation at the *surface*—a strange, razor-sharp white glimmer followed by a rainbow glint in the visual field—and then it's as if the front portion of the drone sinks and drowns in the homogeneity of golden light.

It keeps going, drifting forward, its front slowly disappearing into the light.

"So—no surface resistance? Not a solid mass?" Keruvat speculates. "Interesting."

And then the impossible happens.

Even as the long, cigar-shaped drone continues moving *into* the visual boundary of the object, suddenly something begins to *emerge* from the alien surface, about half a meter to the right of its entry point, and at a slight angle—of about fifteen degrees.

It's the nose section of the same drone.

"What the—" Oalla mutters.

The drone and its nose section appear next to each other, pointing in nearly opposite directions plus the fifteen-degree angle, like a fractured reflection in a distorted, funhouse mirror. There's no other way to describe it—right now, solid physical matter is acting like *refracted* light, bent at an angle and redirected, when passing through a different medium such as water or a prism.

"What is happening?" Ker's mouth is open. "Is that the actual drone? Its reflection, maybe? It's like someone sliced it in two pieces."

"What readings are we getting?" Aeson asks impassively.

"Not exactly sure." Ker frowns and examines the stream of data on a split screen. "The unit sensors are not registering anything unusual, and no malfunction either—still transmitting. As far as visuals, right now the on-board cameras are showing space in the opposite direction, from the vantage point of the weird, sliced-off nose section."

"Stop the unit in place," Aeson says. "Freeze at present location."

Seconds later, the slow forward advance of the drone stops. It sits, visually "sliced in two," suspended halfway into the object's surface, while its front sticks out at an angle into space.

"Have another drone unit approach and make contact with the nose section that's emerging from the alien object."

A second drone is sent to approach, slowly and carefully. It comes very close, drifting in parallel, and sends out a tube arm with a full sensor array which reaches out and brushes the hull front of the first drone, still suspended at its weird angle.

Ker shakes his head in growing confusion. "All readings normal. Temperature, mass, chemical composition, solidity, everything."

Aeson exhales loudly. "All right, now resume moving the original unit forward. Let's see what happens."

The first drone resumes its slow creeping motion deeper into the alien light surface. Seconds later, it disappears completely from the back, while its front section continues to emerge at an angle—until it is completely out, but pointed in the opposite direction, away from the object of light, as it continues drifting in space.

"This is impossible," Oalla says.

"Now, reverse the unit," Aeson says. "Back it into the alien surface. I want to see if it comes back in the same place it entered."

The command is sent, and sure enough, the probe reverses course, backs into the golden light at its weird angle of "refraction," and then its rear section comes out at the original point of entry, perfectly straight.

There is a silent pause.

Aeson rubs his chin and exhales. "I want that unit salvaged, taken apart and examined at every level. Meanwhile, continue the sensor sweep of the alien object with the other probes, and let's see what else we can find out. Get me a full surface analysis. Call in additional experts if needed. I want detailed reports from your tech teams regardless of what is found."

The *astra daimon* get to work.

In the course of the afternoon, numerous other measures are taken and tried with the probes and the grid object.

Every attempt to penetrate its glowing golden surface results in the same impossible "matter refraction." The only variations are the angles of reemergence. Those degrees appear to be unpredictable, but the techs run programs to analyze and find patterns.

At the risk of starting a new hostile incident, Aeson finally issues the order to fire plasma weapons into the alien object.

The drones fire short, exploratory bursts. The resulting energy discharges come blasting back out of the surface, but again at some unpredictable angle.

"They're not actually firing back," one *daimon* says. "This is our own fire, ricocheting back out in the general outward direction, redirected into space."

"Almost mindless—as if it's an automated deflection routine," Keruvat remarks.

"Keep gathering sensor data, keep trying different things," Aeson orders, his expression grim. "There has to be something we can do to penetrate their defenses and *understan*d them. I also want an analysis of any differences between the behavior of the grid objects around Helios compared to the smaller objects at Rah."

And the work continues.

I watch Aeson and the others busy and overwhelmed, and I continue to worry. At least the situation appears stable so far. Even the media feeds calm down, after the initial reports filter down to the public.

". . . the hostile objects seem to be dormant for the moment, but rest assured, SPC is working tirelessly to protect you," the familiar calm voice of Desher Keigeri gives an update on the Hel-Ra evening news.

All I know is, Aeson is absent most of the night again, meeting with the ranking officers up in orbit at the Atlantis Station, and I feel useless and unable to help.

But not even the dire threat hanging over us can get in the way of continuing preparations for our Wedding. At tenth hour of Khe, the First Priest of Amrevet-Ra, Darumet Azai, sends his assistant with a formal reminder to Aeson that *he* is due for the next event on his own Bridegroom Schedule, *tomorrow*. Naturally, I am not informed what it is, but I'm willing to bet it's something duly excruciating.

Oh yes, when Aeson gets home tonight, he will *love* hearing this.

Chapter 48

It is remarkable how days and events start to blur, considering that no new crisis happens in the remaining weeks leading up to the Imperial Wedding.

Maybe because I've been functioning in survival mode for so long that I need to be over-stimulated by the fight-and-flight hormones in order to stay sufficiently sharp for routine daily events and circumstances, but I find that I have trouble focusing on much of anything.

Survival mode has turned into *wait mode*. It's now a sometimes-unbearable wait for the big and the little things. . . .

I wait with happy anticipation for my Dad and George to arrive, I wait with slight anxiety for the Games Champion wish fulfillment process to be over, I wait with background dread for the Imperator to make sudden new demands on my Logos Voice, I wait with eagerness and impossible wonder for the Wedding Day and all that it entails for Aeson and me . . . and meanwhile, I wait for the other alien shoe to drop—for something to go terribly wrong.

Surprisingly, in all those days leading up to the big day, nothing does.

The alien golden light grid system remains dormant and impenetrable to Atlantean sensors, intrusive equipment, and even provocation. It's as if, once the light objects lined up in place, and then performed their one hostile act of destruction at Rah, they have ceased to be a threat—or at least completed their primary function.

No one understands what or why, when it comes to anything having to do with the grids, their reason for being, or their ultimate purpose. But the SPC remains on high alert, while new tests and research equipment are being deployed to the various grid objects on a daily basis.

Meanwhile, Tammuz Station has been evacuated on mandatory orders, leaving a skeleton crew and War-8 parked nearby in a higher

Tammuz orbit. The planet Tammuz is currently in a position of closest direct alignment to Atlantis, even though its orbit places it further out than the next planet closet to Hel (which is Septu, currently on the opposite side of Hel and extremely far away from Atlantis). The strategic assumption is that the alien enemy will take the direct line of approach toward us—if and when they decide to strike next. Which means they'll most likely show up at Tammuz and make that station their target.

Is focusing on Tammuz the best move? How predictive is this strategy? The frightening answer is: unknown. There's no precedent for anything like this happening in the more recent Atlantean history. However, a great deal of data analysis and military science went into this painful conclusion, derived from the consensus of top international military experts and veterans during endless global council meetings within the high command of the SPC. And Aeson is in charge of implementing this strategy.

The other potential next target is Septu, assuming the line of attack is based on simple orbital proximity to Hel. As a result, a considerable percentage of Septu Station's civilian and nonessential personnel has been relocated also, on a voluntary basis, leaving a much smaller population. The Station is on secondary alert. It is also protected by War-9 in high orbit.

As far as any other immediate next targets, it becomes hard to say. With what limited information is currently available since the attack on Rah, it's nearly impossible to make projections that far ahead.

In short, all outposts around the system are now duly warned and, considering the logistics of relocating so many people, everyone is looking at a big problem. Aeson explained to me that these space stations serve as miniature human colonies all around the system, with industry outposts, scientific research facilities, and basic lifestyle options for some, including retirement. Therefore, forcing everyone to evacuate, even in a leisurely manner, is a truly daunting task—not unlike mandatory evacuations of cities in the path of hurricanes or other natural disasters on Earth. No one wants to do it, especially since the threat seems less immediate by the day. And in some cases, not everyone *can*.

As a result, the public is starting to become complacent again, which is both a good and bad thing.

Meanwhile, the Wedding preparations continue, all scheduled events having resumed in full force, under the watchful supervision of the Venerable Therutat and the Venerable Darumet, our yin and yang counterparts in this. Aeson and I find ourselves with odd daily obligations and rituals, and while we might both groan about it in private, Aeson realizes how important it is to put on a fine show for both public morale and the sake of Imperial tradition.

Indeed, the upcoming Wedding has become an anchor of normalcy—not only for us, but for the population of *Atlantida* in general. The media networks love to report on our progress, and happily focus on the little things, all of it building up to the next major event on our schedule, this one being the first shared formal Court event headed by both the Bridegroom and the Bride—the Gifts Assembly.

The Gifts Assembly is intended to be a magnificent Imperial affair, scheduled for the evening of Red Amrevet 5, Redday—the first day of the event-packed whirlwind week leading up to the Wedding. Aeson and I are supposed to preside at our first Imperial Assembly and receive the traditional wedding gifts from the Court.

However, before that event kicks off our final Wedding countdown, we have a number of necessary scheduled details to deal with in the weeks beforehand.

First up is Ghost Moon 19, the day I choose the Flowers. In the morning, two assistants of the Venerable Therutat arrive and take me to an outdoor garden pavilion on the Palace park grounds, which serves as a greenhouse nursery for the Imperial garden staff. It's basically a fancy hothouse flower exhibit and visiting space for guests to stroll through and admire the amazing varieties of flowering plants.

"Please take your time, Imperial Lady Gwen," one of the young women tells me, as we walk in the dappled shade of the retractable trellis overhang along narrow paths between greenery. A glorious bouquet of perfume engulfs us—it's carried on the cool breeze, with subtle notes of musk and earthy complexity. "Examine everything and make your preferred choices from any of the species growing here. If you have any questions, we are here to assist and advise."

"According to tradition, you must choose three different flowers," the other assistant says, pointing at rows upon rows of blossoms in a wild riot of colors, growing on the manicured sections directly on the ground at floor level, on upraised terraces, and even suspended in hanging planters. "The primary flower will be the dominant one used in the decorations and the design of the Wedding venue, and all other motifs, including the focal points of decoration on your dress. Take into consideration its color and size, for maximum effect."

"Okay." I nod, feeling overwhelmed by the choices before me. I shouldn't be surprised by any of this, considering I've already experienced the horticultural wonders of Flower Day—but for some reason I had no idea of the complexity of flora on Atlantis.

Are most of these native to this planet? How many were brought from Earth originally, introduced into this alien environment, thrived, and evolved over eons? Granted, I was too busy recuperating from Stage Two of the Games during Flower Day to even begin to appreciate this natural beauty. . . . But now my mind goes off on a tangent. . . .

"The second flower selection should complement the first one," the assistant continues. "It should be smaller and less prominent, but harmonious with the primary choice, in color and shape. Finally, the third flower you choose should be the smallest, but equally compatible with your first and second choices."

I nod.

"Remember too, these flowers will be arranged in bouquets, woven into garlands, and otherwise incorporated into the natural design of everything on your Wedding Day—the Ceremonies, the Feast, the *Amrevet* Night, all related festivities—in all of the Palace and many prominent locations around the city."

"Oh . . ."

Suddenly I'm curious how the flowers might be used on *Amrevet Night* itself, that special designation for the intimate time when *im amrevu* and I are joined at last, in the truest sense. . . .

"So, as you can see, you might consider all these things when you choose," the second young woman says with a subtle, meaningful inclination of her head, even as my mind continues to stray to the other tantalizing topic. "Some varieties of flowers are better suited to being cut and arranged, and will last longer. Some are more plentiful than others. Indeed, some are rare and hard to procure in such large quantities."

I get the hint. "Please be sure to tell me if my choices end up being ridiculous and difficult to obtain," I say. "I want to make this as simple for everyone as possible."

"Oh, but please do not be constrained, My Imperial Lady!" the first young woman says, with a reproachful glance to the other. "Whatever you desire will be procured! Your Bridal preference, regardless of anything, will always be accommodated!"

I smile. "Thank you, but I insist that you tell me if I make a poor choice."

And so—after about an hour of wandering through the pavilion, examining and sniffing so many blossoms that I can no longer tell their differences from their combined sweet fragrance or remember the associated commentary—I finally make my choice.

My primary flower is white—an elegant sunburst blossom with curving spiral-folded petals and a faint delicate hint of perfume. Its name is *dewa* and it most closely resembles an Earth rose. They tell me it is reasonably common and easy to procure in large quantities—which seals the deal for me.

My second flower is veined blue and gold—an amazing brilliant hue that closely echoes the sheen and luster of the actual metal. It is odorless, shaped like the Earth orchid, and called *li-hereret*.

My third flower is tiny, bell-like, and purple—encompassing a whole palette of shades of deep purple to faint lavender, with a light but complex scent reminiscent of sandalwood and vanilla. It's called *iyatet* and looks like a hybrid of baby's breath and lily-of-the-valley.

On Ghost Moon 22, a more difficult selection awaits me—the Bride's Song. What exactly this entails I'm still not entirely sure, but the Venerable Therutat sends more assistants my way—this time, a pair of experts in music and singing traditions.

"My Imperial Lady," I am told authoritatively by a middle-aged man who is a renowned professor of music at the Golden Bay Lyceum and makes repertoire recommendations for the *Imperial Atlantida Opera*. "As part of the Wedding Ceremony, you will perform a beautiful solo for your Imperial Bridegroom, even as he performs one for you. Your song must be very brief—an excerpt of a longer classic piece, ideally—and its duration must be no less than sixty heartbeats and no longer than three daydreams."

"All right," I say.

"Then you will perform another song together, a duet, as you light the Wedding Grail. The duet is a traditional piece called the *Eoseiara* which is always performed by the couple at all nuptials in *Atlantida*, be they common, noble, or Imperial. Yes, there are many popular recordings available, but that is simply not the best way to learn this important duet. Be not concerned, we will teach it to you. I will then respectfully sing the Bridegroom's part as we practice, because it is considered inappropriate to sing this piece together with your real Bridegroom before the Ceremony—but practice you must."

"I see."

"We will demonstrate the melody and the lyrics for you," a woman who is an opera diva says, taking over the explanation. "In addition, I will perform for you the third piece that you will need to learn. It is the *Amrevet* Chant that you will sing in unison with your Bridegroom as part of ritual on the night of your Wedding Day. Again, there are various recordings that can give you an idea of the Chant, but it is best you learn its *subtleties* in person."

Amrevet *Chant? A ritual?* My nervous thoughts take flight. . . .

The opera diva notices my awkward pause and gives me a wise, calming smile. "Fear not, it will be lovely. I promise, it will only enhance the intimacy of the moment for you. . . . Such is the intent."

I smile back at her, even as my heart races with terrible wonder.

Then I ask a question, in order to take the conversation in a slightly less uncomfortable direction. "As far as my first piece, the solo—what kind of song am I permitted to choose?"

"Anything that you like, as long as it is appropriate—short and befitting the joyous solemnity of the moment," the professor replies. "You may certainly select a song from your native Earth. Or if you prefer, we have a rich repertoire of Atlantean music for you."

"That's great," I say, even as a surge of excitement fills me with the possibilities. I start remembering all the glorious music Mom sang, all the melodies she taught us over the years.

And then my heart jumps with a painful jolt.

Mom. . . .

"To make everything as pleasant as possible, we will practice several times in the next few days, until you are confident in your performance," the opera diva says.

"How long do I have to decide on the song?" I ask.

"Not too long, for your own ease of mind," she says. "We recommend you take tonight to begin thinking, and let us know your final choice in the next three days. Until you do, we will begin today by learning the *Eoseiara*. Now—you should know that you'll be accompanied by traditional musical instruments as you sing the duet, so you will need to become comfortable with the melody first, then the timing. . . ."

While the opera diva continues to explain to me the details of today's lesson, the music professor scrolls through his digital tablet database to present me with audio samples to inspire my own choices for later that evening when I am on my own.

We get to work.

The very next morning, Ghost Moon 23—even as my thoughts are still going wild, and I'm overwhelmed with the possibilities for my Bridal Song selection—I get to see a whole retinue of people related to the planning of the Wedding. The Venerable Therutat sends her primary assistant, Lady Isulat, with meticulous new details of scheduling, several junior priestesses with various expertise, and three high-end seamstresses. At the same time, Consul Denu arrives with a fashion designer and his assistants, an array of fabrics, and another exclusive tailor and seamstress, all of whom serve the highest nobility and the Imperial Family.

Here I must add: I've had appointments with Consul Denu regularly over these several weeks, in regard to memorizing the Imperial Consort Protocol. Harking back to the days of his serving as my Protocol Instructor during our journey to Atlantis, the good Consul has resumed his expert instruction in Imperial graces and diplomacy, except our circumstances and power dynamic are now completely switched and taken to a different level.

During my time on ICS-2 with the Fleet, I was a humble pupil who needed to be taught the basics—correct manners and staff protocol for interacting with the Imperial Family and Atlantean nobility in general—for the sake of my job as an Earth Aide to the Command Pilot who happened to be the Imperial Crown Prince. And now that I've been elevated to the status of future Imperial Kassiopei myself, the Consul is my humble servant in teaching me what I must do and how I must behave for the rest of my life.

Holy crap. . . . Let me repeat that, for the rest of my life.

This same realization comes to haunt me every now and then: the burden of impossible responsibility and the utter *alienation* of royalty and everything that goes with it.

This time I am taught so many prosaic details of Imperial behavior that I am put in awe—from eating protocol to bathroom visitation and servant interactions; from micro-nuances of Court receptions and treatment of foreign dignitaries to specific behavior in public places; from style of dress and correct appearance, to tone of speech and vocal inflections. It's frankly too much. But I'm good at studying, so I resort to the brute-force method of *memorizing everything* for now and worrying about it later.

"The Imperial Consort must reflect only the good graces of the Imperial Kassiopei Dynasty in her very existence. She is the Imperator's balance and foil, his bright companion, partner, and confidante," Consul Denu tells me. "She is the other force on the Throne, and sometimes she is the main anchor who keeps the power contained and focused where it must remain, in order to truly serve the nation and the people. She is the secret strength, and sometimes she must be the better of the two."

"I understand," I say seriously, thinking at once of Devora Kassiopei.

"My dear Imperial Lady Gwen, I'm entirely confident that you do." The Consul smiles at me. "It is clear that only the routine details must be imparted to you—not the grand philosophy and ethics, for which you seem to have a natural instinct."

And then, such as this morning, we forgo the Protocol lesson in order to deal with the urgent topic of my Wedding Dress.

Consul Denu is a known trendsetter and Court fashion expert, and his sometimes-flamboyant perfectionism when it comes to the fine details of dress, hairstyles, and personal grooming, has earned him the reputation of being *difficult* to please. Fortunately, it is precisely the kind of thing that is required right now to help me make my spectacular fashion choice.

The Venerable Therutat has coordinated with Consul Denu in this. As we all sit down in the large, sunlit reception chamber on my side of the Crown Prince's Imperial Quarters, it is all explained to me.

"The Imperial Wedding Dress is a *living symbol* of the Bride as she joins the Kassiopei Dynasty," Consul Denu begins, handing me his digital tablet with images of previous Imperial Brides in their Wedding outfits, going back several hundred years. Their beauty is so extravagant and breathtaking that it's somewhat terrifying. "The color of the dress is of foremost importance. In the general wedding tradition of *Atlantida*, an ordinary bride wears a dress in the color of her Quadrant affiliation or her personal preference, or her future husband's and his family's preference—underneath a veil of gold."

"Okay." I nod. "So there is no traditional wedding dress color here?"

"Not for the dress, only for the bridal veil—which must be gold," the fashion designer says in a definitive tone of voice. He is a small, impeccably dressed man in dark colors, with elegant manicured fingers and heavy rings to rival Consul Denu.

"Oh, great," I say.

"The color of the dress for the Imperial Bride is a different matter," the Consul continues. "The dress can only be one of the following four choices—the current Imperator's Court Colors, the Crown Prince's future Court Colors, her own great foreign Family's colors, or gold."

My lips part. "So—no white?" I ask with a small twinge of sadness. Not even sure where that's coming from, since I've never before given any importance to the color of my own imaginary future wedding dress or even given it much thought.

They all glance at each other. Then one of the priestesses says humbly, "Not unless you are the daughter of a foreign royal House, and their color happens to be white."

I am the daughter of Earth, a sudden thought comes. *My "House" is as great as a planet and all the people who fill it . . . and white is the Wedding color of choice in so many of Earth's cultures, including my own. . . .*

Should I express any of this out loud?

I should.

And I do.

When I'm done, there is brief silence. Consul Denu and the others appear to be deep in thought, considering the notion of Earth being my "great foreign House."

And then one of them, a full-figured older woman seamstress, who has been sent by Therutat, speaks up. "My Imperial Lady Gwen, I believe I have a much easier solution for you."

As she proceeds to explain, the others present begin to nod in agreement, while my eyes widen with curiosity, excitement, and then absolute joy.

"Yes!" I exclaim.

"Now that's settled, let us go on to the actual design and shape of your dress," Consul Denu says.

I smile with excitement, and we get to it.

Chapter 49

After a painstaking session of discussing every aspect of my Wedding Dress design and examining fabrics, I am measured once again (despite having undergone that annoyance multiple times already) and visually evaluated by the designer and all the seamstresses. Apparently, the seamstress tasks are highly specialized—bodice, waist, sleeves, skirt, collar, veil, layers, trim and decoration—so they must each focus on those parts of me for which they will be responsible.

"Will you be using a 3D printer for any of this?" I ask at one point.

I am met by horrified stares from everyone, and one of the priestesses makes an amuletic hand sign that I'm told is done to avert the evil eye.

"Oh no, my dear Imperial Lady," Consul Denu explains tactfully. "The Dress of the Imperial Bride is a one-of-a-kind work of art created manually by the most skilled artisans—to be worn once and then treasured in memory by future generations. And as such it is not to be fashioned by any other means."

"Everything must be done by hand," a young priestess adds. "Prayers must be spoken and blessings must be given all throughout the process."

"And when we put it all together, it will be sung by all of us into being," a seamstress adds. "Then it will shine gloriously upon you."

My lips part in a sudden realization of wonder.

They don't merely sew *the dress, they literally* fuse *it together by means of sound tech. . . .*

Which means that at least parts of it will be orichalcum. Why am I not surprised?

"The Dress will be finished by morning of Red Amrevet 6, and you will honor us with your presence for the Final Fitting," the tailor informs me with a perfect courtly bow, just before they depart. "Any alterations or improvements will be undertaken then, according to your wishes."

I thank everyone, ready to be left alone so that I can return to mulling over my choice of Song.

With perfect bows and curtseys to me, Consul Denu, the fashion designer and his assistants, the exclusive tailor, and seamstress, leave the room.

However, Lady Isulat remains, along with the priestesses of Amrevet-Ra and the other seamstresses who came with her.

Lady Isulat lowers her head to me and speaks in her gentle tone of voice. "My Imperial Lady Gwen, with your permission—we must now address the more intimate aspect of the nuptials attire—your *Amrevet* Dress."

At once I feel a warm flush rising. It's natural embarrassment, and I'm grateful that there are only women left in the room. . . .

My blush must be very obvious, because now the women are all looking at me with supportive, soft expressions.

"Can you please explain to me what exactly an *Amrevet* Dress is?" I ask, having taken a deep breath of courage.

"It is a beautiful, revealing garment worn by the Bride on *Amrevet* Night to please her Bridegroom during their first intimate union," says one of the priestesses of Amrevet-Ra. "The Wedding Dress is intended for the public portion of your Wedding Day. Once *Amrevet* Night begins at tenth hour of Khe, you will first be sequestered so that you may prepare yourself and remove your Wedding Dress. Then you will put on the *Amrevet* Dress and go to him."

"I see," I say quietly.

"It might be easier if I show you," Lady Isulat says, picking up her digital tablet.

She calls up a catalog of intimate garments that could be considered corsets in Earth terms—not that I'm really familiar with Earth corsets, but it's the closest thing I can compare. However, unlike corsets, these things are non-constricting, and instead drape loosely around the torso, emphasizing certain parts and playfully concealing others. . . .

I see a lot of tulle or gauze see-through fabrics in all colors, intricate beading, fine scalloping, pleats and ribbons and other ornamentation, exquisite ropes of golden chains, and a sea of sparkling jewels.

They are beautiful. But they are horribly embarrassing.

Or so it seems to my stupid, inexperienced self.

"They don't leave much to the imagination," I whisper with an awkward laugh.

Lady Isulat smiles. "They inspire and inflame the imagination—*his* imagination, as well as his *body*—which is their intent."

"If you say so," I reply, wanting to sink through the floor with embarrassment.

"My Imperial Lady, which of these do you like?" another priestess asks kindly. "Any of these design elements may be chosen, recombined, and made to your exact preferences."

"Do *not* be shy," a third priestess adds. "Remember, this is for *him* as much as it is for you. Choose wisely, with your heart. Pick such details that your Imperial Bridegroom might like—whatever would bring him the greatest joy—"

"—and *you* the greatest confidence," concludes another woman.

I tighten my mouth, bite my lip. . . . I'm filled with uncomfortable but not unpleasant thoughts.

"On Earth, you have a custom of wrapping gifts, is that correct?" Lady Isulat asks.

I nod.

"Think of your *Amrevet* Dress as the ultimate giftwrap for this sublime gift you present to him—*yourself.*"

Half an hour later, I've made my daring choice of *Amrevet* Dress. I can safely bet that Aeson will be *affected* in a good way when he sees me in it.

Yes, right now, my own thoughts are making me blush. . . .

The priestesses express their approval of my selection, and the seamstresses tell me it will be ready on the same day as the main Wedding Dress, for final fitting.

And they leave me at last to myself.

Immediately, I return to obsessing over my choice of Bridal Song.

My current frontrunner is the haunting and gorgeous "What Is a Youth," composed by Nino Rota, also known as the love theme from the classic 1968 Franco Zeffirelli film *Romeo and Juliet.*

It's an utterly romantic song, it's Shakespearean, and Mom sang it to us. However, I'm torn, because, well—Romeo and Juliet are *star-crossed* lovers. And I just can't have that kind of bad luck at our Wedding.

With some regret I file this song away in the "no" compartment, and then get a bright idea—why not ask Manala? She must know what Aeson's favorite songs are, and I'll pick one of those to sing to him.

Problem solved!

I venture from my side of the Quarters, find Aeson, and ask him how his own musical choice is going. My question is playful, and *im amrevu* raises one of his beautiful dark brows and shakes his head at me with mock reproach.

"I made my selection last night, Gwen, and I'm not telling you, for fear of the wrath of the Venerable One," he says.

I crane my neck at him. "Which Venerable One? Yours or mine?"

"You know very well which one." Aeson barely manages to keep his mouth in a straight line. "The one who is truly fearsome in her tiny little stature. We will not speak of this, since she hears everything. As for my song, you will find out on our Wedding Day."

Our Wedding Day. . . .

My heart surges with warmth, just hearing that phrase. I try not to think of everything dire that's still hanging over us, and instead focus on what small happy tasks lie before me.

The remaining few days of Green Ghost Moon, the last month of Green season, go by in haste and excitement colored by a sense of urgency. No new crises emerge, and we enter the first week of Red Amrevet energized with anticipation.

Indeed, all of Poseidon seems to be moving at a frenetic pace, as the city makes its own public preparation for the Wedding Day festivities. I find out that my three chosen flowers, the *dewa*, the *li-hereret*, and the *iyatet*, are being imported *en masse* from the nearby provinces that grow them. At the same time, the Imperial Palace is rushing to decorate and put up the marriage-themed ornamentations everywhere, while cleaning crews are polishing every inch of the premises, so that already pristine-seeming metallic surfaces are turned to razor-sharp mirrors as they reflect Hel's incandescent daylight.

Food ingredients for huge feasts are being readied in bulk all around the city. Bakeries are creating nuptials-themed sweet pastries, including the popular *amrevet* pies shaped like four-point stars and special others formed to resemble the Imperial Kassiopei sunburst symbol. Every kind of commemorative souvenir you can imagine floods the markets—most of them bearing Aeson's and my likenesses. Popular music artists are getting booked to play venues, public parks are upgraded with stunning new floating light fixtures, and I'm told there will be fireworks, Atlantean style.

Media feeds are filled with Wedding gossip and ridiculous chatter about us, interspersed with continuing mentions of this year's Games Champions and my role as such. Incidentally, the Games officials have finally completed their work behind the scenes in regard to the official revelations of the Champion Wishes, and the big Announcement finally happens, taking over the news cycle for a few days until the Wedding fervor returns to dominate. The Champions are notified a day in advance via the private online site, and get to share the excitement with each other before the public does.

The Top Ten have chosen predictably in some cases, and outrageously in others. Kokayi Jeet's biggest wish, besides his Parade, is the purchase of land and buildings to remodel and erect his own *orahemaeon*, which translates to a dance entertainment venue—a cross between a dance club, a dance studio, and a mid-sized theater. He's also in the process of improving the most rundown sections of Sky Tangle City, although his *mamai* is not letting him "throw *iretar* around" as she calls it, and wants him to focus on his new entertainment business.

Kateb Nuletat's patent for his neural prosthetic invention, inspired by the medical needs of his wife Yeraz (who is unable to sing), goes through, and he is proceeding with the manufacture of this product. He also buys Yeraz a new house in an upscale neighborhood not too far from Phoinios Heights.

Hedj Kukkait is opening a major hospital complex in the Northern Mithektet Province to benefit the underserved agricultural population. Apparently, he is one of the leaders of organized labor there, serving in the position of *ertarat*, which is an interesting combination of spiritual advisor, military discipline monk, nondenominational cleric, and medical professional.

Leetana Chipuo has requested a pardon for her incarcerated father, and major renovations—including clean water—for her extended family's small town in the Western Xeneret Province. Both requests are being granted.

Most of us don't know anything about Ukou Dwetat who came out of nowhere to win the Athlete Category vacated by Deneb Gratu. Turns out, Ukou has been living homeless on the streets in abysmal poverty, so his humble main request is permanent housing for himself and his two young brothers. His wish is easily provided, and Ukou's new property in central Poseidon not only has a large house but a sizeable garden where he expects to plant "a thousand vegetables and never run out of food again." With over ten million *iretar* in his account, that's not likely going to be an issue.

Mineb Inei has requested Citizenship for his entire family—his many children, and for his wife who wants to run for political office which is only open to Citizens. I find this detail surprising, since I assumed that the only way to become a Citizen was to personally win the Games, to be born to parents who are both Citizens, or by Imperial decree for exceptional service to *Atlantida.*

In fact, there is a little-known loophole, pertaining to Champion wishes. Champions may request Citizenship for others, but only for members of their immediate family such as spouse, children, siblings and parents. Since this is considered such a big deal (and is generally discouraged), in exchange for this they must agree to forfeit all other wishes. However, they do get to keep their share of the Common Earnings Grail—which is a good thing in Mineb's case, since he is starting up a very interesting hybrid tech company for integrating Earth and Atlantean technology, and he will need funding.

Rea Bunit has been admitted to the prestigious STA Lyceum and Academy of High Technology at Poseidon, and will now attend as an upper-level student—a high-security level available only to

Citizens. In addition, since Rea's husband is already a Citizen, their daughter will now become a Citizen automatically.

Rurim Kiv has revealed himself as a stage magician, an illusionist, and his unique performance art will finally be admitted for display in the highest Poseidon cultural arts center, and granted eligibility for the full honors of his profession. Rurim also explained that his entire participation in the Games was part of an extended magic act—an intricate performance by means of which he wanted to show that the technique of *illusion* could serve him as well as any other skill in the Games.

Brie Walton has already revealed to me her secondary, minor wish of having Logan Sangre be at her beck and call for three months. Now I find out that her bizarre "revenge wish" was very much conditional. Logan was formally *asked* by the Games officials if he was willing to go along with it, and he said yes—no coercion would've been involved had he refused. Knowing this—that Logan was not forced but actually agreed to this weirdness—makes me feel a little better on his behalf. Though it does make me question his better judgment. I suspect there's some kind of guilt complex involved.

Meanwhile, Brie's main wish—release from Correctional and decent living arrangements—has been granted. And surprisingly, so has her other major wish of being reinstated as an Earth Cadet in the Imperial Fleet.

"It has to be the military for me—Earth, Atlantis, *somewhere.* Either that or chasing squirrels—do they even have normal squirrels here? Probably elephant-sized ones. . . . I don't know what else to do with myself," Brie admits to me in private. "You might say, it's in my blood . . . a long family tradition of service."

One of these days I will ask Brie to tell me more about herself—if she lets me.

As for my own Champion wishes—the granting of other people's wishes mostly, my many requests on behalf of Zaap, Chihar, Lolu, Tuar, Sofia, Fawzi—they are all carried out and finalized. Chihar gets his primary seat on the Tatenen Committee of Education as my permanent voting proxy after I buy it. I can't wait to see his face when I tell him about it! Tuar gets his pardon—and I get to tell him that in person a day early, rendering him speechless and close to tears with gratitude, even though he maintains his stoic demeanor. Sofia's family gets their land, and Fawzi gets his opera house, and they are in for a happy shock when the Announcement hits the public feeds. . . .

Zaap's posthumous wish for a nature preserve in the Northern Sesemet Province is a reality, with the land purchased in my name, and now all I need to do is visit it and formalize some things—but it will have to wait until after the Wedding. . . .

As for Lolu—now that her mother has received her lifesaving medical care thanks to Aeson's quick response, my only thing to do is to give her family a gift of financial assistance in honor of her fallen brother Khadram, and of course see her in person when she comes to work for me. Lolu has insisted she must repay me, and I of course insist she must get paid, so the ongoing memorial gift will serve to do it without infringing on her sense of honorable obligation. I've decided that Lolu will be my personal assistant— whatever that entails—and she'll start her duties soon after the Wedding, once Aeson and I return to our residence at Phoinios Heights.

There is one more wish that I request, and that one is for myself. . . . I've considered long and hard. And, I must admit, I've been tempted to ask for some outrageous and practically impossible things.

Save Earth from the asteroid.
Abolish the Games of the Atlantis Grail.
Free all the pegasei.
Make all Earth refugees Citizens.
Make all non-citizen Atlanteans Citizens.
Get me a salami sandwich.

However, the madness passed. And so, my personal wish comes down to something realistic and doable.

I request that, starting next year, the Games of the Atlantis Grail offer an additional new prize—an extremely high set of points awarded to Contenders who advance through every one of the Four Stages by killing the *fewest* people. Instead of a kill count, it's an "anti-kill" count. I know it's a tiny, weird change in the greater scheme of Games things, but it is an incentive to reduce the murderous violence, and it is a start. . . .

And so, the formal Announcement of all our Champion Wishes is posted in public. It immediately results in renewed Games attention, and the Champions get invited to a new round of interviews. Fortunately, because of my impending Wedding, I am spared this particular media ordeal, at least for the moment.

Meanwhile, Aeson continues to work quietly with the Star Pilot Corps, in-between his Bridegroom duties. At night I see him poring over data in the workroom and interacting with the Command Pilots of the various battle barges in deep space, sending out new patrols and moving resources around the Helios system, regardless of the inactive state of the alien golden grid.

The Imperator calls more than once during these days to inquire about the status of the translated and digitized scrolls from the mystery puzzle-boxes that we unlocked at the bottom of the ancient ark-ship. No, we haven't forgotten them, but since little of substance has been found—or at least nothing that seems relevant to our situation with the ark-ship and the Ghost Moon—looking at those translations in detail has been downgraded in urgency. Even so, Aeson and I both try to spare a few minutes throughout the day to examine at least a few of them.

I should note that both the Imperator himself and the First Priest Shirahtet have pounced on the translations as soon as they were made available and read everything already . . . *days ago*. Furthermore, quite a few others in the small circle of individuals who have been granted access to the secrets and the ancient ark-ship are at present studying the translations. But because Aeson and I succeeded in opening those boxes with our Logos voices, the Imperator insists we continue to participate in this secret group task.

While all this is happening, my family and friends have been active in the Wedding preparations, as much as possible. Dad and George call every night at an agreed hour, and we have our interstellar family chat (and eagerly count down the days) even as they continue to speed through the depths of the cosmos toward us. Gracie and Gordie come over for informal Palace meals in our Quarters, or at least call me regularly. Sometimes it's just them, Aeson, Manala, and I, having a *niktos* meal, with the Imperatris dropping by for a quick visit with no prior warning—to check on us without causing a fuss—which I appreciate more than she can imagine.

My friends often join us at these things. The civilians among them are actually busier with day jobs than the Fleet Cadets who remain on alert for deployment and have no permanent assignments yet, so I get to see Dawn and Hasmik a little less frequently than Laronda, Chiyoko, and Blayne.

Meanwhile, there's the awkward *continuing* situation of Laronda and Anu. Every time they're in the same room together, the weird tension is palpable, and we all know it, but neither Anu nor Laronda has made any other move to advance their relationship.

During our private talks, Laronda admits to me that she is thinking about it *all the damn time*, but thinks the "troll boy jerk" may not be ready or mature enough for any kind of real emotional relationship.

"Why don't you ask him out?" I try to persuade her.

But Laronda just shakes her head. "Um . . . no. Let's just see how it goes."

As for Anu, his pasty white face turns different shades of his Quadrant color whenever Laronda is nearby, but he does little else and hardly even mumbles a word to her unless absolutely necessary. However, he constantly stares at Laronda when she is turned away, and makes a point of being *present* whenever she's here. It's probably not a coincidence that Anu recently got new gold hair dye, and his previously sloppy ponytail is somewhat neater in appearance.

Laronda has definitely noticed. I even catch a little smile on her face when she points it out to me while rolling her eyes.

In short, there's just so much going on during these busy final days before the Wedding. I have no idea how we manage to keep up with everything and retain our sanity—all under the watchful eyes of the First Priestess and Priest of Amrevet-Ra.

On top of everything else, it's getting more and more difficult for Aeson and me to maintain the traditional decorum and distance between us, to keep away from each other, and to *wait*.

But at last, the morning of Red Amrevet 5 dawns, the day of the Gifts Assembly.

I wake up with a jolt, just after sixth hour of Ra, with the thrilling awareness that we have entered our final phase. . . .

Four days left until our Wedding Day.
And today is going to be *amazing*.

Chapter 50

Feeling energized by anticipation, I shower, throw on some basic clothes—ignoring Aranit's chosen outfit laid out for me, and not bothering with anything fancy since I'll be changing outfits multiple times today—and head for the workroom to meet Aeson for *eos* bread.

It's almost seventh hour, and no one else is here except for Anu, who's just arrived for the day, and two unfamiliar *astra daimon* still on their night shift processing the SPC data. I should mention that this has become the new routine—there's always someone in the workroom, watching the alien grids and receiving data, vigilant to any changes.

The usual Imperial Palace staff is here too, setting up the *eos* bread service stations and starting to prep the various morning dishes.

"Nefero eos," I say to everyone in an upbeat tone. Anu mumbles his usual reply, and the two *daimon* give me courteous greetings before returning to their computer screens.

Where are you, Aeson? I think.

Just as I pour myself a large mug of fresh *lvikao*, a servant arrives, bearing a formal invitation to me, from the Imperatris. I open the gilded scroll and see that Devora Kassiopei has chosen *this* afternoon for our formal Meeting.

My heartbeat speeds up with a jolt of nerves. . . .

According to Imperial Wedding protocol, the Bride must meet with the current Imperatris privately, so that they can discuss "delicate matters." This Meeting is mandatory, but it is not officially added to the schedule, since the Imperatris is supposed to pick the moment, time and day, based on an arbitrary sense of when she feels *I'm ready* for it.

I don't even know what that means, but I assume that our Meeting will be very highly personal and touch on intimate subjects pertaining to her son.

Oh, dear lord, help me. . . .

I double-check the scroll, and it says I am expected at the Imperial Quarters of the Imperatris at first hour of Khe. This gives us about two hours of private conversation before I must return here and start getting ready for the Gifts Assembly, which is scheduled for sixth hour. As usual, it will require three hours for the spa treatments, hair and makeup, and other fussing, before such a formal event. . . .

Meanwhile, as I've been informed by the Venerable Therutat, I recall that the dress code is festive casual for the Meeting with my future Mother-in-Law.

And so, just like that, my exciting, busy day has been made even more complicated. At least it's the gentle, loving Devora that I will be meeting, not the Imperator, so it should go well, regardless of the weird content of our conversation.

Or so I tell myself, to calm my galloping heartbeat and nerves. . . .

Consumed with flights of imagination, I fill a plate with *eos* food, just as Aeson comes in to join me for this meal.

Aeson looks sharp this morning, in a fine white shirt with a gilded collar and dark pants. I catch the faint musky scent of his freshly applied aftershave, and it gives me a sensual frisson as he leans over to kiss me deeply. His eyes are full of excitement, similar to mine.

"You look nice." I smile.

"I have important Bridegroom business to handle," he replies with a playful smile.

"Then eat!" I say, pointing to the meal service, and he goes to fill his plate.

"So does your Bridegroom event take up most of this morning?" I try cleverly to pry forth some of the likely amusing details.

"You know I can't tell you," he replies with a chuckle. "What about your own?" And he nods at the scroll invitation lying on the table nearby.

Oh no, I think. *He probably recognizes his Mother's Imperial Seal.*

A minor flush of heat fills my cheeks. I can't tell him about meeting his mother—at least not here in the workroom in front of all these people—since it will break Wedding Protocol. Admittedly, over these several weeks we've both confessed our events and shared the details of some of our separate activities in private— especially the major ones, where it's impossible to avoid it due to media coverage. But in this case, I have a funny, awkward feeling that Aeson doesn't need to know what his mother and I will be talking about.

Fortunately, Aeson doesn't press the subject, but gulps down his food. "May your own mysterious Bride business go smoothly. . . . I'll see you tonight for our big event, *im amrevu*," he whispers in my ear and gives me a squeeze and a caress before heading out in haste.

I spend the morning picking out a suitable nice-but-casual outfit and stressing about the Meeting—but not too much—then worrying again. At last I get ready to head to the Imperial Quarters, just before first hour of Khe.

For my Meeting with the Imperatris I'm wearing a shimmering blue dress with a translucent golden outer layer, and my hair is pulled back in an attractive loose updo, courtesy of Aranit's hairdressing skills. My four personal guards and Tuar fall in line behind me at the corridor doors, and they escort me up the elevator to the splendor of the mauve and cream marble of the main lobby on the Imperial floor, then remain behind as I enter the Quarters.

"My Imperial Lady Gwen, the Sovereign Lady awaits." A high-ranking servant nods with courtesy, then escorts me through the familiar antechamber, past the reception wall of thrones to one of the many doors near the rear.

"The Quarters of the Imperatris begin here," he announces archly, continuing to walk before me through several turns of a narrow corridor and into a large, airy chamber with delicate gilded columns and walls trimmed in white stone veined in mauve and purple. "Please wait here."

He leaves, and I remain standing, clutching my skirt with my fingers in order to calm my nerves.

Moments later the Imperatris walks in with a smile that immediately warms my heart, and two servants come immediately after, bearing a small table and an *aeojir* tea service.

I perform a proper curtsey, smiling back at her in immediate relief.

See, it's not so bad. . . . It's just Devora, the same kind human being I already know, and whose son I love and adore.

"My dear child, come!" says Aeson's mother, taking my slightly clammy, nervous hands into her warm and dry own, and then leads me to an elegant but comfortable sofa.

"Thank you for the gracious invitation, My Sovereign Lady," I reply formally, as protocol dictates. "And so lovely to be here."

"And I'm absolutely happy that you are here. It's been such a busy time for you and for my son, with everything going on," she says. "But finally, here you are. I wanted to give you enough time to settle into your Bridal obligations before calling you in for this important part of your Wedding preparation. We have so much to talk about!"

I nod, smiling, glancing around the beautiful chamber with its arched, gold-paned windows overlooking a bright daytime vista and the distant gardens below. A few steps away, the servants finish brewing our tea and arranging plates of pastries and fruit, then slip away quietly.

Devora waits for them to be gone, then turns to me, her expression becoming more solemn, but still warm with affection.

"Now then, my dear Gwen, before we begin—how are you? And I mean, truly, how do you feel, after so much pressure and so many difficult, horrible things happening? Are you holding up? Because I can hardly imagine how you managed to endure so much. . . ."

"Thank you, I'm doing okay," I admit, releasing a held breath. And then I tell her, to the best of my ability, about the past weeks since the Games. I try to stick to facts and not bring up the turmoil that thoughts of my dead mother continue to evoke in me, not to mention the anxiety about my family, the current world-ending events . . . everything.

Devora pours a cup of amber liquid and hands it to me, then pours her own. Since no servants are present, I notice she disdains protocol.

"My Sovereign Lady," I say, as my rambling words about my complicated feelings fade at last. "I know this is part of tradition, but what exactly is this meeting supposed to be?"

"Well," Devora says gently. "I know the Venerable Therutat frightened you sufficiently, but I want to put you at ease."

The Imperatris offers me a platter of fruit and nuts drenched in aromatic syrup. "Have a bite," she says, using a serving utensil to fill my small plate. "You know, Aeson used to love these when he was a little boy."

I take the delicacy, and at once my imagination conjures a sweet little boy with golden blond hair, happily eating the syrupy confection.

"I wish I could've seen him when he was little—he must've been adorable."

Devora makes a happy sound. "Oh, he was! And quite a handful, too. . . . Fortunately, we have numerous video recordings of various key events throughout his life, both formal and casual. So many in fact that it's almost like a progression, observing him growing up from a tiny infant with a loud cry to an uncontrollable toddler, a mischievous little boy, a serious and driven youth—you will definitely have a chance to watch those later."

"Oh!" I exclaim. "Wow! I'd love to see all that!"

The Imperatris looks at me fondly. "So much to see," she says, nodding. "So much joy and profound wonder is before you— awaiting both of you, together. And that's what we will talk about. As his mother, I am biased—I adore my son."

"I adore your son too," I say softly.

"I know." Devora sets her cup of *aeojir* down and reaches for one of my hands. "And as the Bride of Kassiopei, you are about to enter a profound and some might say *divine* relationship. It is my duty to talk with you about what to expect, what lies before you as a Kassiopei Wife."

The Imperatris takes a deep breath, exhales gradually, looks at me with her caring expression. There is a moment of gentle, unthreatening silence, but my pulse picks up speed nevertheless.

"When I was young, and in your position, an Imperial Bride, I had this same conversation with the Imperatris at that time, Romhutat's mother, the late and wonderful Hesper Kassiopei. She called me in to the Meeting and gave me advice and set me at ease before the Wedding. Now I want to do the same for you, my dear. And it goes beyond the requirements of tradition—this is my personal wish for you."

"Thank you," I say, still nervous despite her gentle words. "I appreciate it very much."

"Now, you, a young Bride, probably have all kinds of questions about the Wedding itself, and maybe even concerns—and yes, I do mean about the *Amrevet* Night. Normally a mother would be there to help set your mind at ease, even though, I might assume, you already know the—necessary *details* of such intimacy between men and women."

"Oh . . . yes, I do." I try to smile, even as I feel my cheeks heating up. *Oh dear God, is this going to be that kind of talk?*

And then I think of Mom, who is not here—who will never be here to give me any talk. . . . Did Mom give me "the talk" at some point? I think she did, or at least tried, a few years ago, and I got all embarrassed and shut it down. . . .

Stop thinking about Mom. At least, now.

"Of course, you do," Devora nods, appearing slightly embarrassed herself. "Please forgive my saying it, and I don't mean to imply that you are uninformed in any way. It is merely to be sure you do know the basics."

"Yes, I know," I hurry to repeat. "And—I understand, thank you."

"Wonderful. Then I'll continue." Devora touches my hand again then reaches up and pats my flushed cheek. She takes a deep breath.

"All right. Let me tell you about Kassiopei men. They are . . . passionate. That much is known—indeed, you probably know already. The rumors about this most ancient Imperial Dynasty tend to exaggerate many things about the bloodline, but not in this case. It is all true."

I nod, then continue to stare at her with my utmost attention, while my flush rises.

"Now, *passionate* is an understatement." Devora pauses for a moment and looks away, choosing her words. "They are relentless. There's this overwhelming physical drive they have, a *need* . . . And at the same time, they are terribly virile. So much so that you will be with child *immediately*, and you will be with child *always*—"

"I've heard . . ." I interrupt on a whisper.

"—unless you take the proper precaution," Devora finishes.

At once my mind goes into overdrive. I listen, stopping my breath.

"There is a remedy that the Imperial Wife has at her disposal," Devora resumes, seeing my startled expression. "It is safe and it is formulated to work on the Kassiopei man's—what do you call it—*sperm*. Normal male contraceptives are insufficient, so this is a specific substance you and I must take in advance of intimacy—which gives us a *choice*."

"I see."

"On your *Amrevet* Night, my dear, you will be offered a choice of two glasses from which to drink—in the form of refreshment, before you *begin*. There is a Golden Grail and a Blue Grail, and they will be sitting on a nightstand or table in your chamber as you get ready. One of them, the *golden* one, contains the powerful contraceptive that curbs the fertility of the Kassiopei Dynasty. The other—the *blue*—is simply a refreshing nutrient-enriched drink to promote your own health—and fertility, if you prefer to think of it that way."

I nod, my lips parted with focus.

"And so, pick whichever one you prefer for that first night with my son," Devora says. "If you don't mind being with child at once, then by all means, drink the blue, and I will be overjoyed to expect my first grandchild. . . . If you *don't* want to get pregnant immediately, then drink the golden goblet and enjoy the night without worry. Remember, there is no judgment here; it is completely up to you, and the Kassiopei men know and respect your choice in this matter also—no matter what else anyone might lead you to think."

"So—Aeson will know about it? That I drank one of the goblets?" I ask.

Devora nods, smiling. "My advice is, don't tell him which one you choose, at least not until the night is over. Less worry that way, for both of you. Worry is not a good thing when you make love."

"And if I decide I want a child soon after, it will not be harmful later for a baby that I might've taken that contraceptive?"

"One application is good for five days, and if you don't take another, it wears off completely in about three more days, after which you can safely try for a child," Devora explains. "You can also then take the other drink—the one that promotes fertility—to flush out your system of any residual amounts of the substance to speed up the process."

And then another worry hits me. "What if—what if I forget which one is which?" I mutter. "What if I take the wrong one? Gold or blue? I'm so nervous, I already forgot what you said earlier. . . ."

Devora shakes her head in amusement. "Ah. . . . Easy to remember: blue is Aeson's color, and will give you Aeson's baby."

I laugh also, at my own nervousness. "Okay."

"All clear now?" Devora squeezes my fingers with reassurance.

"I understand now why there must be a Meeting with the Imperatris," I say.

"Exactly." Devora chuckles. "And there's more."

"Oh?"

This is the point at which Devora proceeds to tell me something even more "delicate."

"During your joyful time with your new Kassiopei Husband, you will find a curious thing happening. And I'm not just talking about a woman's pleasure. . . ." Devora takes another big breath. "During the *act*, Kassiopei males often . . . finish very quickly. Sometimes, before you do."

I listen.

"Now, do not be alarmed," the Imperatris continues. "With any other average population male, it might become a problem, but not with Kassiopei. They have almost *no rest period*. In other words, as soon as they are *done*—within a span of about five to ten heartbeats—they are ready to perform once more and can *begin again*, so it all works out as a single, almost non-stop act for you."

Seeing my wide eyes, the Imperatris again smiles at me. "In short, you will have no interruption to your own physical fulfillment. The Kassiopei man will have you *very* well satisfied at the end of your night."

I find that I've turned as red as a beet. My mind is trying to process what she just told me, but the oddity of it takes second place to my level of mortification.

"And on that note, I think the traditionally embarrassing, mandatory portion of our conversation is done," Devora says with fondness, taking pity on me. "I remember how horridly embarrassed the young and uninformed Devora Argosaen was during her talk with the Sovereign Lady Hesper, all these years ago. . . ."

"Argosaen?" I ask.

"My birth Family name, before I married into Kassiopei," the Imperatris replies. And then she reaches to her side where a small digital pad rests on the sofa. "Would you like to see Devora Argosaen in her Wedding Dress?"

"Oh, yes!" I exclaim, happy for the new turn of conversation.

And the Imperatris calls up an image of her younger self, innocent indeed. I stare at the impossibly beautiful maiden in a spectacular, long-sleeved, green Wedding Dress under a gold veil cascading to the floor behind her. As she looks at the camera, her eyes appear startled and exultant at the same time. . . .

"The dress is green," I say, noticing. "How?"

"A lucky choice," she explains. "My Quadrant is Green, but Quadrant Color is not one of the Imperial Bride's options. However, Green happened to be the Imperial Court Color at that time."

"Aeson's Grandfather?"

"Yes, Etamharat Kassiopei was the Imperator still, and his Court was Green." Devora sighs. "A good man, I miss him terribly."

"I'm so sorry," I say. "Aeson told me how his Grandfather died, also during a mission to Ae-Leiterra."

"Yes . . . it was not too long ago. Or—maybe somewhat long, I cannot remember the year now. I assume you've been told that a similar thing happened to my son?"

I nod. "What about the Grandmother? Hesper, the Imperatris? What happened to her? How did she die?"

Devora frowns and squeezes her eyes shut momentarily, then looks at me. "Oh Gwen, she was gone far too young. . . . She died first, before he did, just a few years earlier in a tragic accident, and Etamharat lost the will to live, abdicated the Imperial Throne much too early, before his time . . . and it likely contributed to the events that ultimately cost him his life." She pauses. "We probably shouldn't be talking about such sad topics today; it might even be bad luck. So, let me just say that Aeson's Imperial Grandparents

were both wonderful people, and you will learn all about them at
another time."

"Of course." I nod, then pursue daringly. "What about the non-
Imperial side?"

"You mean, my parents?" Devora smiles in relief. "They're
both fine, and living at their favorite country estate outside
Poseidon. To be honest, they prefer to be as far away from my
Husband's Court as possible."

I can't believe she just said that! I hold back a laugh.

"You will of course meet them very soon, as they will be
attending the Wedding. I believe you'll find them to be easy and
friendly, and my father at least a little hard of hearing. But, not
intimidating in the least."

"I really look forward to it," I say.

"Now then," Devora says, patting my arm in a relaxed manner.
"How about another cup of *aeojir?* We still have time, and I'll tell
you an amusing thing or two about what to expect on your Wedding
Day during the Ceremony."

"Yes, another cup, please, and I'd love to hear any other
advice. Then I should probably be getting back," I reply, sensing
that I can relax also.

Now that the embarrassing worst is over, I can admit to myself
that my Meeting with the Imperatris has been a success.

Chapter 51

The Imperatris and I talk a few minutes more, and then Devora gives me a motherly hug and kisses me soundly on my cheek before I head back to my own Quarters on the Imperial Crown Prince's floor below.

Soon, it's third hour, and my preparations for the fancy night event begin. As usual, the servants arrive, and the spa treatments happen. I am soaked, exfoliated, tweezed, and tortured the cosmetic way, then comes my haute couture hair and High Court makeup applied by Kem, under the direction of Consul Denu who makes exquisite selections of evening colors on my behalf. Dramatic dark eyes, and lips painted like wine with a shimmer of metallic violet, blue, and silver under certain lights, give my face high contrast. My hair is formed into a circular crown and sculpted in layers, then embellished with crystals swinging on tiny chains.

My dress for this event is lapis lazuli blue to honor my Bridegroom's Court Colors, and he will be wearing the same to match. Since tonight is going to be *our* Court as an Imperial Couple—even though the Imperator and Imperatris will make an appearance—the Court Colors will be Blue for everyone.

I put on the spectacular dress that has a dark under-layer sheath of lapis blue, and a tulle outer layer of shimmering metallic silver with a faint hint of the palest blue imaginable. The skirt is long but not very wide, flaring gradually to the floor like a fall of sea foam. It shimmers with rainbow colors when I move, and my blue shoes with medium heels and pointed metallic toes peek out from underneath with every step.

Tonight, I wear a magnificent silver necklace encrusted with sapphires and matching chandelier earrings. They are my official Gift from my future Father-in-Law, the Imperator, delivered to me in a bejeweled box by a ranking servant an hour earlier—yes, another gift not to be refused. Even as I put them on, I experience a scary moment wondering if the jewelry is poisoned, or bugged with listening devices, or cursed by arcane methods in some malicious way, or all of the above. . . .

And then I remind myself, *the Imperator still needs me.*

The idea calms me down sufficiently to wear the jewels without much further thought. Even if they *are* imbedded with surveillance devices (which is most likely), I'm aware of the possibility and can take the necessary precautions if a confidential situation arises.

A eson arrives a few minutes before sixth hour of Khe to escort me to our Gifts Assembly.

Oh, dear lord in heaven. . . .

He is so breathtakingly handsome that, in that first moment as he enters the room, I feel a sudden constriction in my chest. It's as if something punches me in the gut with *awe.* . . . The feeling overcomes me to such a degree that for one strange instant it *hurts* to look at him. . . .

I want him so much. . . .

Aeson is wearing an expensive jacket and pants of dark lapis blue, and a wide Egyptian-style *wesekh* collar of sapphires to match mine—his own Gift from the Imperator, apparently. His sun-hair is brushed back to a glossy shine, and a small coiled serpent emblem in silver rests against his forehead—the serpent at rest, curled in a circular spiral, is the Lesser Uraeus symbol of Secondary Imperial Power of the Imperial Crown Prince.

But the most amazing thing is the expression in his eyes as he sees me. He comes alive with glorious joyful energy, bursting with something indescribable. . . .

"Gwen!" Aeson nears me and takes my hands as I stand up to meet him.

Electricity sparks as our fingers touch. . . .

"You are *beautiful . . .*" we both whisper to each other, almost in unison.

And then we both start to laugh, as the weird intensity dissipates.

He notices my matching jewelry, from the same set as his own. "Imperial gift?"

"Imperial gift."

He makes a small sound and shakes his head, taps one finger at his own sapphire collar.

I widen my eyes in reply, also with the intent to convey meaning.

It's clear, we both understand each other.

Speaking of gifts—did I mention that Aeson and I still haven't finalized what we're going to *say* in public about our *love gifts* to one another?

Because Aeson—the wonderful, perfectly attentive paragon of a loving fiancé—still has *not* given me, his chosen Bride, a proper, traditional Atlantean love gift!

And yes, I realize this is trivial and ridiculous. After all, he's already given me the world in every sense, including his most prized possession, the black armband. But it was technically a loan, not a valid gift. That unique hero's honor is non-transferable and therefore not permitted.

Personally, I don't need anything . . . but the public does. Apparently, *Atlantida* still expects and needs to know what kind of love gifts we've exchanged.

Poor Aeson. . . . He probably forgot about it once again, being so busy with things that are a thousand times more important.

Yet, even now, I'm stupidly embarrassed to ask him about it.

"How was your day?" I ask playfully, to distract myself from the silly, nagging thought of love gifts and forgetful men.

He merely smiles at me, raising one brow, and there is a vibrant sparkle in his eyes.

"Ready to go?" he asks, pressing my fingers in his warm large ones.

I nod, my own lingering smile an automatic response to his high-energy presence, and we walk together to the doors of our Quarters, where our retinue of guards falls in line around us.

The Gifts Assembly is a major Court event, and as such, is held in one of the larger venues of the Imperial Palace complex. Our destination tonight is the Mehet Rotunda, a large round building with an exquisite, translucent, mauve glass dome located on the northern end of the immense complex.

One of its features, that stunning crystalline ceiling, is currently lit up like a cabochon ruby jewel with the early radiance of Hel's sunset. Truly, an amazing sight—to see the teal light dissolve into the prism of the rosy, glasslike surface, and reflect back a plum and deep violet glow. . . .

Heavily guarded, we pass through the park and gardens and approach the Rotunda, past crowds of gathering courtiers, directly into the VIP entrance.

We enter a short corridor, then pause at the small secret door that will take us to one of the four Imperial access points placed at equal distances around the grand chamber for a dramatic entrance.

Precisely at sixth hour, we are to enter, together.

Our guards fall back, taking their places at the small door next to the already stationed Imperial guards with floor-length gilded staffs. *It means the Imperator himself and the Imperatris are already inside. . . .*

Bell tones pierce the silence. They are followed by a series of profound musical sounds reminiscent of deep bass, horns, and oboe that blend together to form a C Major chord of harmonious majesty.

It is our cue.

Aeson glances into my eyes with fierce intensity. "Ready?"

I nod, with a tiny confident smile, and place my hand, palm down, over his proffered own, as we proceed forward.

We walk through the narrow corridor and emerge into a brilliantly lit, round chamber, a world of subtle mauve light filled with people wearing all shades of blue to honor us. The Rotunda interior is immense, its pale marble walls veined with hairlines of gold. There are no windows, and none are necessary due to the glory of the cupola ceiling overhead. Our Throne Seats are against the wall directly to the left from our entry point, and a spotlight is cast from on-high to illuminate us.

The Imperator and the Imperatris are seated on similar Thrones far across from us, against the opposite wall of this chamber. Before we may take our seats, we must cross the room to greet them.

To cross the chamber, we have to navigate one of several narrow red paths demarcated by the mosaic floor. Two such red paths bisect the chamber, forming a cross, and two others circle it, following the circumference of the room—one nearer the center, the other nearer the walls.

Meanwhile, the room itself is filled with members of the Court. Formally dressed, bejeweled men and women crowd every spot along the floor that does not have the red stone color. I'm reminded of the grand Pharikoneon chamber where Imperial Assemblies are held, with its color-coded floor designations for High, Middle, and Low Court. There are none such here, only similar red paths, so that the three levels of Court can mingle in the four middle portions within the "donut" shape, but may not step on the red tiles once the formal Assembly event has started.

The very center part of the room, the hub, is occupied by an interesting three-tier round table, a sort of circular stepped pyramid shape. I've been told that it is called the Tree of Gifts.

The purpose of this strange table is to hold all the numerous gifts that everyone in the Court has brought us today.

Let me repeat that—*everyone in this room has come bearing a gift* for the Crown Prince and his Bride. That's why they call it a Gifts Assembly.

In other words, it's the world's biggest, most formal Bridal Shower.

A eson and I slowly walk along the round exterior path, illuminated by the moving spotlight that follows us, past the Court of *Atlantida*. We are on display, and stares and whispers come from all directions, together with smiles and soft aahs of appreciation.

We reach the opposite wall of the chamber and stop before the golden Thrones where Romhutat Kassiopei, the Archaeon Imperator, and Devora Kassiopei the Archaeona Imperatris, sit motionless, like beautiful dolls, watching us.

The Imperator's face is his usual inscrutable cold mask of power that he wears in public. Today, however, in honor of his son's Court, he has donned a blue robe and blue Imperial Crown headdress with the Uraeus serpent rising from his forehead.

Next to him, the Imperatris wears a pale blue gown the color of metallic sky, with a matching Crown. Unlike her spouse, her expression is lively as she looks at us, and there is a faint warm smile along her sculpted lips when she catches my gaze.

"My Imperial Father, My Imperial Mother," Aeson says, bowing, then looking at his parents. "My Bride and I thank you, My

Father, for the generous gifts of these sapphire jewels that we both wear tonight."

"My Sovereign Lord, My Sovereign Lady," I echo him, after performing my own curtsey. "My Sovereign Lord, I thank you for these beautiful gifts."

"I am pleased," the Imperator says with the smallest nod, but without a change in his expression.

"My gift to both of you rests on the Tree of Gifts," says the Imperatris with a smile. And she points one elegant finger in the direction of the tiered round table. I turn to glance there and notice that there is a small blue box sitting on the top tier. It is the only item on the Tree of Gifts so far.

Now, I recall that this is the way it works: traditionally, everyone present must come before us with a proper courtly bow and then walk to the Tree of Gifts and deposit their gift somewhere along the table, but in a pleasing pattern. As more and more people set down their gifts, they must take care to arrange the placement of their boxes and other unusually shaped items in some kind of artistic order. When finished, the Tree of Gifts becomes an artful display and must remain this way, untouched, for the rest of the night and all of the remaining days until the Wedding.

We can admire it privately, and so can the visiting public, starting tomorrow, as the Tree of Gifts will be guarded so that no one might tamper with it. But we may not touch our gifts until the morning of the Wedding Day when they will be removed from the Rotunda and delivered *en masse* to our Quarters.

Such is the Imperial nuptial tradition in *Atlantida*. I find it kind of fascinating, and know to expect it, having been instructed in advance that the Imperatris traditionally places the first gift.

Now that we've thanked the Imperial parents, Aeson and I continue walking around the circular path to return to the spot where we originally entered and take our own Throne seats. The reason for this long trip around the room is for all of the Court to see us, so we give them their show and receive their appreciation in return.

Once we take our seats, Aeson looks at me and smiles.

And then he turns to the room, looking out over an ocean of blue, and speaks in a resonant voice, uttering these very formal words: "My Court Opens."

Momentous words for the Crown Prince.

Likely, it's the first time Aeson has been permitted to use them in a formal setting, with his father still reigning as Imperator.

At once, deep musical tones sound, but they are drowned out in applause. With this change in tone comes laughter, conversation, and apparently everyone is free to move about. The presentation of gifts is about to begin. . . .

As all of this is happening, I search the crowd for familiar faces. I'm pretty sure that both Gracie and Gordie are supposed to be here, and so are most of my friends. Normally, the Bride's Family, and in particular her parents, are required by tradition to be the next in line to present their gifts.

But my parents are not here. And as for my siblings, I don't know if they are participating in this thing, though I had warned them about it.

And then I see them. . . . Gracie, in a pretty aqua blue dress, and Gordie in a nice grey-blue, formal jacket, step forward with big smiles and some awkwardness—Gordie in particular.

Gracie grabs our brother's hand and pulls him after her, as she steps on the red path before our Thrones and performs a passable curtsey.

"We have presents for you, Gwenie, and for you, Aes—I mean, My Imperial Lady, and My Imperial Lord!"

And sure enough, I see she is holding a little violet satchel, and Gordie has something in his hands too.

Aeson watches in amusement as Gordie clears his throat and then does something bow-like with his head and shuffles one foot. As for me, I barely keep a straight face.

But protocol demands it, so I simply nod at Gee Three and Gee Four, without saying a word, and they turn around and take the red path that bisects the room, heading toward the Tree of Gifts.

My sister and brother get to be the first people to place their gifts on the arrangement, next to the Imperatris's blue box. Gracie even pauses to fluff the tassel and ribbons on hers.

And then the rest of the Court follows.

People start approaching us, with smiles and proper curtseys and bows, and then walk to the Tree of Gifts to add their contributions. The arrangement grows in seconds, and I marvel from a distance seeing it take shape like a sparkling coral reef of shimmering colors. This thing really *is* a living artwork in progress.

Over the next hour, all of the present Court passes before our seats. Many of the ladies are now familiar to me from my earlier Bridal event. I nod and acknowledge everyone I recognize, and pretend politely when it comes to the rest.

At one point I observe that while the Fuorai Family is here—namely First Lady Vahiz and her spouse—there's a noticeable absence of Lady Tiri. According to protocol, since I've dismissed her, she's not allowed to attend any of my functions until—or *if*—I formally grant her the renewal of my good graces and permission to return. It's entirely up to me. As I watch the parade of Courtiers, I allow myself a moment of not-so-nice satisfaction, knowing that I wield this insane social power. *Maybe I'll let her come to the Wedding. . . .*

But the "mean girl" in me is very rudimentary, and I let her fade away as soon as she emerges. Instead, I try to forget Lady Tiri and strain to see the people I sincerely hope to find here.

Among them I'm happy to see Hasmik, Chiyoko, Laronda, and Dawn, all of them dressed to the nines. I notice that Princess Manala has chosen not to use her right as Family to be one of the first in line and has decided to stick with my friends instead—Hasmik, in particular.

When she passes before us, with Hasmik right after, Aeson gives his sister a warm smile and raises one brow meaningfully in brotherly familiarity. Manala curtsies with long-practiced perfection, but then puts her hand to her mouth to suppress a giggle as she turns around to head to the Tree of Gifts.

Brie Walton and all of my Team Lark members have been invited, but as far as I know none of them is here, for whatever reasons, some of which might be that they're intimidated by the Imperial Court.

On the other hand, Aeson's closest *daimon* friends are here, and they pass by our seats with warm meaningful expressions on their faces. Oalla, in a spectacular cerulean dress, looks with mischief at me as she curtsies, and Keruvat gives me a wink. Erita and Xelio just smile, and Xelio's eyes narrow appreciatively at the sight of me.

Ah, Xelio. . . . I stare back at him with a fond smile.

Of all my friends, I recall with some sadness that Blayne is not here tonight and has sent his apologies in advance. Considering that he must use a hoverboard to get around, he said it would be a little weird for him to show up at the fancy event in the Palace and have to use LM forms just to stay upright.

"No excuse!" I'd told him, but the boy is a little too proud sometimes.

"You'll get your present later, Lark," Blayne had insisted with a little smile.

And now I stare at the dizzying array of people passing by us in the room and think about who else is not here tonight.

Dad and George.

And Mom.

At last everyone has greeted us and visited the Tree of Gifts. What remains is for Aeson and me to acknowledge each other's gifts.

Those infamous love gifts.

Oh, help. . . .

In a traditional moment of silence, Aeson stands up, facing me as I remain seated.

"*Im amrevu* Gwen, my beautiful Bride," he says powerfully, looking down at me with a heated gaze. And then he reaches inside his inner pocket and brings out the miniature rose crystal Pegasus I gave him. He lifts it up before the Court, to show everyone. "This is the generous love gift you've given me, and I treasure it."

He returns the crystal miniature to his jacket pocket.

And then he pauses and turns to look at everyone gathered.

I freeze awkwardly, unsure what to do with myself. *Should I just get up and make up something?*

But Aeson speaks again.

"My Bride has given me a generous love gift, but I have been remiss. All this time, I have not offered her anything better than the loan of my armband. And now—"

Aeson again reaches into his pocket and takes out a small, odd-shaped item of old unpolished metal, possibly gold, but with a patina of age, like brass.

The thing is about three inches long and shaped like the outline of a four-point star on one end. The other end has some kind of extended attachment.

"Forgive me, Gwen, and allow me to make up for my shortcoming as a Bridegroom," Aeson says, offering me the metallic thing. "This is a key—a very old key, and it opens a secret room in the Imperial Crown Prince's Quarters. I call it my Room of Childhood Secrets. It contains old items of great meaning and importance for me. No one else knows about it, and previously I've never shared it with anyone. It is now yours. Please take this key and enter that room . . . so that you might know my heart and *know me*—you who are my one and only . . . my Gwen."

Even as he speaks, I begin to tremble. A lump starts growing in the back of my throat, and moisture wells in my eyes. I rise and take the key from his warm fingers.

As our fingers touch, he says softly, "At last—*this* is my love gift to you."

Chapter 52

I clutch Aeson's key, covering it with the palm of my hand, and control my breathing, so as not to bawl, even as the Rotunda fills with applause. . . . I'm certain that the nano-cameras are transmitting this moment to all the network feeds and *Atlantida* is watching eagerly. Oh yes, they're going to be well satisfied with this long-anticipated revelation of our love gifts. And if anyone's not—*screw* them.

As for me, I have no words. . . .

"Thank you . . ." I mouth silently to *im amrevu*, gazing into his eyes—which, I note, are absolutely brimming with excitement. Then we both sit down again. My fingers slip into his and entwine.

Minutes later, the Gifts Assembly is concluded. We rise and walk along the circling red path before the Imperator and Imperatris, then continue around the chamber, and finally exit the same way we arrived. Now that we have departed, the Imperial Sovereign and Sovereign Lady will take their leave, and then the rest of the Court will disperse, but it no longer concerns us.

"I can't believe you did that, Aeson," I whisper to him as we walk quickly back to our own Quarters, flanked by guards. "That was truly unexpected and—you know, I was going to be a little mad at you before for not remembering the love gift and almost putting me on the spot like that, but you've just made up for everything."

He chuckles, continuing to beam at me. "You like it?" he asks mischievously, his large hand encircling mine.

"Oh, God, yes!" I say. "It's perfect!"

"Even though it's a very belated love gift, will you forgive me?"

"That depends on you, mister! Are you going to continue to forget other important but simultaneously trivial stuff in the future? Will I have to resort to punitive measures to keep you properly focused on the silly details in our life?"

"What kind of punitive measures?" he asks, keeping his mouth in a straight line.

"I don't know, but I'll have to come up with some," I retort, continuing our banter as we get out of the elevator on our floor of the main Palace building. *I wonder if he's ticklish?*

"Now I really want to see what's in that secret room of yours," I say in an authoritative tone. "Like, right now, okay? What kind of awesome little boy memories will I find? This is such an amazing, antique-looking key, by the way. . . ."

"It's ancient. And—taking you there right now," he replies as our guards fall back at the doors, and we enter our own Quarters. "By the way, your brother and sister will be meeting us here in a few minutes."

"Okay."

I follow Aeson through one of the familiar corridors on his side of the Quarters, past many doors, most of them unexplored by me. I wonder what other interesting old rooms this place holds—recalling momentarily that small, all-black chamber, retrofitted to be impervious to surveillance, where he did his broadcasts as The Rim.

In one of the hallways Aeson pauses his stride and points to my sapphire necklace and earrings, and to his own matching sapphire collar—the Imperial gifts. "Why don't we take these off for now."

I get the hint, and we take a moment to divest ourselves of some exquisitely beautiful but potentially bugged jewelry, placing all of it on top of a small side table. No servant will dare touch it, and we can retrieve it later. . . .

We resume walking.

We stop before a door of faded, lacquered wood with intricate carvings. I see it has a very old metal lock, and Aeson nods, pointing to my hand in which I'm carrying the key.

I notice his breathing has grown shallow, as though he is slightly nervous.

"Gwen," he says, placing his hands on both my shoulders and holding me steady. "Before you go inside, I want you to take a big breath. Now, go on, please . . . open it."

I smile at him, shaking my head at his slightly strange behavior, and simultaneously wanting to set him at ease. Poor Aeson, what does he think I'll do—or how will I react—at finding a little boy's treasures, no matter how oddball they might be?

I take the key and insert it into the ornate lock, and turn. There's a small click.

I open the door and go inside, expecting another tiny closet interior.

Instead, the room is already lit, and it is a sizeable chamber, a well-furnished living room.

Furthermore, it is already occupied.

Three people lounge on the sofas, talking softly.

At the sound of their *painfully* familiar voices, something happens to me. . . .

Even before two of them turn around, I cry out, my face contorting with impossible feeling.

It is my father, and George.

"*D*ad!" Words come out of my mouth, even as I gasp, immobilized, unable to take a single step forward, feeling Aeson take my elbow from behind, supporting me. *"George!"*

And then my paralysis breaks, and I go insane.

"Daddy!" I cry hoarsely, rushing forward, even as my father gets up from his seat with his own exclamation . . . and then I feel the cosmically absolute, statistically ridiculous, infinite *impossibility* of his comforting, loving, gently strong arms around me once again.

"Daddy, Daddy!" I continue to mumble and sob outright, hiding myself against his old familiar jacket—*oh lord, he is still wearing that old tweed thing*—as my Dad presses his hands around my face, and kisses my cheeks and head, and strokes my hair, saying, "Oh, oh, my sweet girl!"

Then I feel George's hands from behind, as he presses me fondly, pulling me in, my shoulder squeezed against his chest, so that I'm sandwiched between my father and my older brother.

Long seconds later we come apart, and the crazy questions begin.

"How? When did you get here?" I exclaim, laughing and sobbing, still in disbelief.

And then I glance behind me at Aeson who stands at the door with a fragile smile.

"I'll get the rest of your family," he says, and leaves—but not before making a quick meaningful nod of acknowledgment to the third person in the room—who happens to be the *astra daimon* Quoni Enutat.

"Well . . . let me see. We just arrived in orbit of Atlantis this afternoon," Charles Lark, my father, says in a slightly dazed, permanently wondering tone of voice—as though he himself cannot believe any of it—as he still has his arms around me.

"Around noon, your time," my brother George adds, stepping back to give me some space—now that we've hugged sufficiently. He follows up with a friendly pat and bump on my shoulder. "I believe, you call it Noon Ghost Time?"

"Yes, yes," Dad says. "That's it. . . . Now, our incredible Pilot, Quoni—this good, attentive man, right here—delivered us promptly into orbit, well ahead of schedule. And then he himself took us down in a shuttle to the surface in less than a few minutes. . . directly to this great capital city Poseidon—an absolute marvel. . . . Landed us right here in an airfield of this—this truly *spectacular* Palace structure . . . I have no words sufficient for the architectural wonders—but, never mind. . . ."

Dad takes a deep, slightly labored breath and looks at me. "Oh, my Gwen . . . it doesn't matter . . . what matters is that here we are—you and we are all together now, and Gracie and Gordie will be here in a moment—" And my father resumes examining me lovingly, stroking my forehead and hair that's completely come undone from its fancy crown coiffure. "How you've grown. . . . What a lovely child, no—young lady—what a beauty you are, I'm so proud of you."

"You look good too, Dad," I whisper, lying only slightly, because Dad's beloved face is lined with exhaustion and he looks unhealthy-pale, up-close. . . . Or, maybe I'd forgotten what Dad looks like, how many wrinkles he's supposed to have—or had. "And you too, George!"

George just smirks slightly. "Aged a bit, eh, Gee Two? Both of us, but in a good way. You're about to get hitched, and I'm on my way to geezer, just like Dad. Right, Dad?"

"Shut up!" I mock-snarl with a comical frown.

"Anyway, yeah—Quoni did a brilliant job landing us," George continues with a pleased expression, glancing at the *astra daimon*, who is keeping back somewhat to give us privacy. "And he escorted us all the way up the elevator and to this royal floor. Got us in this room, then sat around with us as we waited—"

"Yes, indeed, Quoni kept us company," Dad says. "Going above and beyond. He didn't have to, I'm sure he has other things to do and probably wants to go home to his own family—"

I briefly turn to Quoni. "Thank you *so much!*" I exclaim. "For everything, for bringing them here all this way—"

Quoni, who in person is of average height, but has a very dignified and slightly reserved bearing, nods to me with appropriate courtesy. "It was never a duty, but a pleasure, My Imperial Lady," he says. "The least I could do for my heart brother and his Bride."

"And then your fiancé got here an hour later," George says. "He explained everything."

"When? *When* was this?" I say with emotion. "My God, why didn't you get me immediately?"

"It worked out just as well," Dad says. "We were—to be honest, *disoriented*. This weight—that is, this quite strong gravity—made it hard to adjust at first, even a little hard to breathe . . . so we had to sit it out for a while."

"Even though they started to turn up the gravity on the velo-cruiser since this morning," George adds. "To get us prepped. But didn't crank it up all the way."

"Apologies for that. It was a precaution, not to overstress your bodies," Quoni says with a glance at my Dad. "We didn't want to risk a medical emergency with limited medical resources on board—not until we were sufficiently close to Atlantis."

"Oh, wow, yes! Of course!" I react. "You need to *sleep*, Dad, and you too, George! The gravity is crazy at first!"

Dad chuckles. "My dear, I already lay down for a while, right here on this nice roomy sofa."

"You need a real bed! Have you at least eaten?"

And then I glance at George, and my gaze sweeps the room. I notice there is a side table with what appears to be leftovers of a *dea* meal, dishes of food and various drink decanters.

"Oh, we ate," George says, following my gaze with a nod.

"Yes, a lovely meal," Dad adds. "Amazingly, all of it prepared for us right here, by two very nice waiters."

VERA NAZARIAN

"Yes, that's how they eat on Atlantis, Dad. They hardly ever use dining rooms," I explain, seeing George give me a meaningful glance. *Dad is probably barely eating at all.*

"So anyway, your Aeson was here, and he welcomed us very graciously and gave us a rundown on what to expect," Dad says.

"Wait, after all that, did he lock you in here, in this room?" I widen my brows, as alarming notions start to come together in my mind.

Dad shakes his head. "Not at all. Your young fellow explained what kind of day it was for you, offered to take us to the royal event, even. Before you get the wrong idea, he offered us quite a few choices. We sat around for a few minutes thinking how best to announce our arrival to you without giving you too much of a shock at your ballroom event, not to mention making the wrong kind of spectacle before all kinds of persons—"

"Meaning, his royal *parents*." George whistles. "And yeah, couldn't have you dropping from a happy heart attack on us, sis."

"I wasn't going to!" I exclaim.

Instead, I would've bawled my eyes out before all of Court. . . .

"We decided against it, considering what condition we're in, newly arrived, not about to make a mess of things for you or us." Dad sighs, clears his throat, starts to cough. He steps away, reaching for a glass of water on the nearest side table.

As Dad drinks, I look around the room. "George, what about your things, your luggage?"

"About that—" Dad stops drinking and wipes his mouth.

"Everything is being delivered here to the Imperial Crown Prince's Quarters" Quoni says. "We have their main personal luggage here, in this suite."

My gaze keeps moving around the room, noticing indeed our family bags and suitcases sitting on chairs and on the floor, some of them very familiar—Dad's old travel luggage set, faded brown rolling suitcase, matching carry-on—and then my gaze stops.

On top of the table near the window, I see an urn.

Just as my heart does a painful jolt—while my mind registers what I'm seeing, a moment of profound *recognition*—I hear Gracie and Gordie's voices, and then they come running into the room, followed by Aeson.

There are screams (Gracie) and happy "whoa" exclamations (Gordie), and then everyone rushes together to grab and hug Dad and George.

Gracie, still in her festive Court dress, is jumping up and down and then hanging around Dad's neck, then jumping again, then ugly-crying, having reverted to her twelve-year-old self.

I don't blame her.

Gordie and George actually embrace, like grown men do. Now that they're standing next to each other, Gordie is clearly a little taller than George! *When did that happen?*

"You look good, man," George says curtly, slapping his younger brother on the back. He then does the familiar finger-snap against Gordie's forehead. Except, George's hand has to reach *up*, not down, to do it.

Then Dad is hugging Gordie, looking him up and down with amazement. "Gordon, what happened to you?" Dad laughs, and I notice there's a glint of moisture in his eyes.

"He's got a day job, Dad! And I'm a Fleet Cadet!"

Now that she's squeezed the life out of George, Gracie is hanging around Dad's neck again . . . and he kisses her hair and wipes her tears with his large, oh-so-dear hands. . . .

My mouth trembles with emotion as I watch their reunion. Even as I laugh, I continue to leak from my eyes like a stupid gusher, seeing them laugh and weep and embrace.

Not wasting another moment, I move in and join them.

The Lark family reunion takes another several emotional minutes, followed by a barrage of questions. Dad and George repeat their story for Gracie and Gordie's sake, then elaborate further.

Meanwhile, as they speak, I glance back to focus on Aeson at last, as he watches us, hanging back somewhat.

I walk toward him. "Aeson!" I say awkwardly, still overcome with emotion, and take his hand in mine. I realize with a peripheral thought that my face is a mess, runny with tears, snot, and cosmetics.

"Gwen . . ." he says, looking hard at me. There is a very vulnerable expression in his eyes. "I hope you are—*okay* with how this turned out. Sorry if it came as a great shock. I tried to make it as easy for you as possible—and for them."

You did it right. . . .

I press my lips together to control their trembling, and crane my neck sideways. *"Thank you,"* I whisper.

"Are you okay?" he persists. "Are you happy?"

"More than you can imagine." I squeeze his fingers with mine.

And then I pull him by the hand and make him follow me across the room. We stop at the large table, and I reach out tentatively and place my hand on the curved metallic *object* that sits there. I feel the cool touch of its delicate etched surface.

"This is my Mom," I say in a numb voice. "I want you to meet her."

Chapter 53

I stand with Aeson, looking at the urn with my mother's ashes. Moments later the other Larks join us, and we all stand and observe *her* in solemn silence.

"Sweethearts," Dad says softly. "Your Mother is here with us, always." And he places his hand on the urn.

Then there are more long, silent moments.

They pass around us somehow, flowing in and around and *through* us, like a strange haze.

At some point, Dad steps back and goes to sit down on the sofa. He is overcome with the gravity, and the aftermath of all the emotion, and he definitely needs to rest.

The rest of us linger a few moments more, then move around the room. Gracie and Gordie go to pour all of us some drinks. George stares out through the large ornate window at the star-filled evening sky.

Quoni approaches Aeson and converses with him discreetly, then, with a salute, excuses himself. He glances to the rest of us and bows, taking his leave of Dad and George, and promising to be in contact tomorrow to deliver the rest of their boxes. And then he's gone.

I turn to Aeson, my brain getting back in gear. "Where will they be staying?" I ask. "At least for tonight? I mean, they can't exactly be sleeping here on the sofas in this Room of Secrets? I see no beds."

"No, of course not. They will have bedrooms assigned to them in our Quarters, up to and immediately following the Wedding, after which I'll have better arrangements for them." Aeson checks his wrist comm. "In fact, according to my staff, the rooms are ready now."

And then he pauses and looks at me seriously. "Gwen, just to be clear, I wanted them to be in this room, *under lock and key* until we got back, to make sure that they are safe. That's the reason Quoni stayed behind, guarding them every moment here in the Palace."

"Oh. . . ." I blink, thoughts churning.

And then it occurs to me, *Of course—Aeson wanted to protect my family, just in case, from his Imperial Father.*

"I understand," I say. "Your Room of Childhood Secrets is a great place to hide them, since no one would think to look—"

Aeson blinks in turn.

"Gwen, there *is* no Room of Childhood Secrets. I'm sorry, I had to make up all that for a number of reasons, mostly having to do with my Imperial Father and the expectations of the Court. This is just a study room I used a lot during my younger days. That table there—I used to draw and do my homework on it. Yes, there may be a few memorable boyhood trinkets and items here, but nothing of an arcane nature." He makes a small sound, somewhere between a chuckle and a sigh.

And then he adds, almost as an afterthought, "Do you really think, considering the kind of permanent surveillance that I've been living under for all of my life, the endless suspicion and mistrust, that I would risk cultivating material objects, or keep anything meaningful where my Father could get to it when I was a young boy? That so-called Room of Childhood Secrets? It's up *here*." And he points to his head.

My mouth falls open. "What about the love gift? I mean, you already got me Dad and George, which is more than a love gift in itself, but—that ancient key?"

Aeson smiles, and a slight flush comes to is face. "The key is still my love gift to you, a symbol of everything I hold inside me being always *open to you*—you need only ask."

I shake my head at my endearing-yet-impossible, sneaky fiancé, with an expression of exasperation and love. "Oh, Aeson. . . . You really are such an outrageous liar, and yet I cannot fault you at all. This is very frustrating, you know that? That *I can't fault you.* You did it again! Something wonderful, and yet you fooled me completely like an idiot. This needs to stop, or I'm going to have trouble taking anything you say seriously, even as I adore what you do."

"I know," he replies, looking at me with a slightly sheepish expression. "It is terrible of me. Old, ingrained habits."

I squeeze his hand with emotion. "We'll discuss this deviousness later," I say, narrowing my eyes at him sternly, and yet my smile breaking through. "As for this—" I brandish the antique key. "This is going to stay with me always, because it is indeed so perfectly *you*—a source of endless revelations. Also, a jerk who hides stuff."

He smiles. "I never said I was perfect."

I snort. "Oh, you're far from perfect, mister! I've no idea why I even love you. *So* frustrating."

We cut our banter short and rejoin the conversation with my reunited family. Gracie is telling Dad all about her orbital Piloting skills and random happenings from the past year during our Fleet journey, and Gordie mumbles about his job at Heri Agriculture.

George and Dad listen, nodding, taking sips of their drinks, and both look more and more exhausted. In fact, they're too tired to even begin to tell us their side of things—about Mom, about all those difficult months on chaos-filled, doomed Earth. . . .

"All right, time for bed!" I announce half an hour later, seeing them fading completely.

And so, we all head down the corridor to find their guest bedrooms, with all of us carrying their luggage *because we want to*—touching the old, dear, familiar Earth things from home. . . . Dad walks slowly with some difficulty and holds Mom's urn to his chest.

"You'll feel much better in the morning, I promise," I say to Dad as we all start to fuss around the nice guest suite with two adjacent bedrooms located on my side of the Quarters. Even as George and Dad start opening their suitcases, servants arrive to assist.

"Oh, dear . . . oh, goodness . . . thank you. That's all right, I can manage," Dad says in a fading voice, as a helpful servant takes over the task of unpacking, while another brings a stack of fresh towels and items of toilette, and a third carries a Ghost meal refreshment tray, since no one is in any condition to eat a full-blown *niktos* meal.

We all hug and kiss once again, letting them settle in, this time leaving them to their rest.

"Come on, Gracie," I say, as my little sister lingers, not wanting to leave Dad's side. "We'll continue tomorrow. Saying good night now. . . ."

"Will they be all right?" Gracie whispers to me as soon as we're outside the door of their suite. "I mean—will they be *safe* here?"

Even Gracie knows the potential dangers our family could be in, when it comes to Imperial "favor."

"They are safe, I promise," Aeson leans near to reply discreetly to both of us, even as Gordie moves closer to hear this. "I've increased security to this floor."

The way he says it, I know that Aeson probably went above and beyond. And so, for now, I relax, trusting his abilities to do just that.

With Dad and George gone to bed early, the rest of us return to Aeson's workroom. Gracie and Gordie are so wound up that they're not going anywhere far from the Palace, such as to their apartments in town. And so we spend most of the remainder of the night sitting around on the sofas and making detailed plans for tomorrow, on behalf of our wonderfully expanded family.

Aeson briefly goes to the workstation desks to check on the two night-shift *astra daimon* on duty at the computers monitoring the alien threat, then returns to the sofa and we talk.

"As far as my formal schedule, I only have the Wedding Dress Final Fitting early in the morning," I say. "Otherwise I'm clear. Since you're both sleeping here, Gracie, you two can go to them first thing when they wake up, and help with acclimatization."

"Okay." Gracie nods.

"How are we going to introduce them to *his* family?" Gordie asks, with a glance at Aeson. "How much do the Imperials know about their arrival anyway?"

"Safe to assume my Father already knows," Aeson says softly.

"It was going to be inevitable, so. . . ." I try not to think about it, but it's difficult. The Imperator's reaction and mood right about now are probably . . . *ugh*. "In any case—Gordie, remember we have the Imperial Family *dea* meal on our Wedding schedule."

"Yes," Gracie says. "Sort of the equivalent of an Earth rehearsal dinner."

"A what?" Gordie says with a small frown.

"I already explained it to you a billion times," Gracie says with frustration. "It's when families of the bride and groom meet the night before the wedding to do a rehearsal run-through of the ceremony then eat dinner and make toasts. Except, this Imperial thing is not the night before, and there's no rehearsal."

"Sorry I don't remember that junk," Gordie says. "So, when exactly is it?"

"Check your calendar Wedding schedule app on your wrist . . . jeez." Gracie rolls her eyes again. "Do you even know you have it?"

"Day after tomorrow," I say thoughtfully. "That's when we all eat *dea* meal here in the Imperator's Quarters. It was supposed to be just Aeson's Family and the three of us, but now there will be five of us."

"Good, the more the merrier," Gracie says. "Lark power!"

"Right," Gordie mumbles.

"And it gives them a full day to rest and get acclimated to the environment and gravity and everything else weird here," Gracie says.

"How much stuff are we telling them?" Gordie pushes his glasses up the bridge of his nose and scratches his ear. "I mean, the difficult stuff. The lethal in-law. The evil alien light grid. They need to know about the dangers before that rehearsal dinner thing."

"Sh-h-h-h," I say, worried about Palace surveillance in the room, coupled with Gordie's choice of words, *lethal in-law*. "Ease them in gently, please. I'll speak to them about the *family situation* myself, as soon as possible."

By "family situation" I of course mean the Imperator. Dad and George really need to know some of the basics, although I imagine they already know or suspect a lot of it, considering all the guarded secrecy around their mode of arrival.

Will I be mentioning the role the Imperator played in creating the conditions—the rescue delay tactics—that contributed to my Mom's passing? I'm not sure yet. . . . How will my Dad react to meeting the Imperator if he knew that this malicious man had intentionally withheld my Mom's access to a potential medical cure?

"The Wedding family event is indeed going to be complicated by several of these factors," Aeson says. "But I promise, *some of us* will put in every effort to make the Imperial *dea* meal as pleasant as possible, for all of you. My Mother and my sister Manala will be told in advance."

"Thank you, Aeson." I nod at him. "I appreciate it."

"Oh, dear lord—Dad and George will need fancy Wedding clothes!" Gracie exclaims.

"Not a problem." Aeson smiles. "All will be handled tomorrow."

"That's right, yes! In fact, during my dress fitting!" I say. "The seamstresses and tailors will be here anyway."

"And what about their role in the Wedding Ceremony itself?" Gracie persists.

I take a deep breath, as my imagination unfurls with shining new possibilities. "I'll talk to the Venerable Therutat tomorrow."

It's just after dawn on Red Amrevet 6 when I wake up with Gracie sharing my room. My sister is curled up in a ball on her side of the large bed and still fast asleep when I open my eyes—just in time to see my personal maid silently moving about the bedroom, laying out today's three possible outfits for my choosing.

"Thank you, Aranit," I mumble sleepily, speaking softly so as not to wake up my sister. I'm still disconcerted by the fact that Imperial servants just enter people's rooms and carry out their duties, but after so many weeks I'm getting better at coping with this regular invasion of privacy.

At least the servants are more manageable in our home in Phoinios Heights, where I've asked them specifically not to come in when we're still in our bedrooms. No such luxury here; the traditional workings of Imperial staff are inviolate.

I can't wait to return home at last, I think yet again. Phoinios Heights *is* home.

I get dressed without waking Gracie and tiptoe down the hallway, past Gordie's guest bedroom, and to the door of the suite where Dad and George are staying. Putting my ear to the door I hear no voices, only Dad's labored sleep breathing—poor Dad, the gravity is not making it any easier—so I let them continue to rest.

Meanwhile I have work to do.

My Final Fitting of the Wedding attire is scheduled for eighth hour of Ra, but I have almost two hours until then, during which I get things done. First, I compose a detailed email request with an explanation of my father and brother's arrival and send it off to the First Priestess Therutat. Then I meet Aeson in the workroom, where we discuss more logistics.

Aeson makes calls and various detailed arrangements on behalf of my family. He also talks with Quoni, who is back in orbit with the rest of the crew, having docked the velo-cruiser with the Atlantis Station and checked in with Nomarch Evandros at the SPC Headquarters. According to Aeson, Quoni will be coming back down to the surface in a few hours, this time with the velo-cruiser itself and the rest of their cargo, including the remaining Lark property.

Gracie and Gordie show up around seventh hour, informing us that Dad and George are still sleeping, and we all continue to brainstorm various details of our plans over *eos* bread.

At eighth hour, promptly, my appointment happens. Tailors and seamstresses arrive, together with Consul Denu, the designer, Lady Isulat, and other priestesses. Servants carry several large boxes, and everyone is ushered into my bedroom, for privacy, where my fitting will take place.

Traditionally, the Bridegroom must not see the Dress before the Wedding Day, so Aeson is warned sternly to remain on his side of the Quarters.

And then, it happens—I get to put on a spectacular creation of master artisans and stand before a full-length mirror as they adjust the layers and the fabrics and my golden veil. . . .

Oh my God. . . .

Suffice it to say, this Dress is perfect. What's it like? No, I will not mention anything more about it now. . . . Seriously, it would be against Atlantean tradition to even *discuss* the glory that is my Dress, before the actual Wedding Day.

My heart beats fast as they continue to work on me.

Then, after they fiddle with it some more, and make me turn around and move in every direction multiple times, Consul Denu and the designer and Lady Isulat consult with each other, and declare that everything is *satisfactory.*

With utmost care they help me remove the Dress, then box up portions of the outfit, including the matching shoes, and hang the main *object* deep in my closet.

While this is happening, I take the opportunity to tell Consul Denu about the formal clothing needs of my newly arrived Dad and brother.

"My dear Imperial Lady, have no worries," Consul Denu says with a smile. "I've already been informed by my Imperial Lord Aeson. I will meet with your Father and Brother shortly, and they will be measured and accommodated with appropriate Court attire."

"Thank you!" I say warmly.

On that note, the Consul and his portion of the retinue leave, having congratulated me on my stunning addition to Imperial Wedding fashion.

And then it's time for the fitting of the *Amrevet* Dress.

Oh . . . my . . . God.

I put it on, and the priestesses and seamstresses make careful micro-adjustments.

I stand before the mirror, blushing, wanting to hide my face.

And then, just as carefully they help me remove it. . . . Into the closet it goes, until the Wedding Day.

I rush to put on my normal clothing, then thank Lady Isulat, and the others, and ask her to pass on my compliments to the Venerable Therutat for orchestrating my masterful attire.

They leave, and now it's time for me to go check up on Dad and George.

A s I approach their guest suite, I hear animated voices. The door is open, and apparently everyone is already there. I find Gracie and Gordie arguing in nervous voices, while George is telling them to relax. Aeson is standing nearby, and then I see Dad.

Charles Lark, my father, is sitting slightly hunched forward in a chair, and next to him are two medical techs, doing something to his arm and chest, and there's medical equipment everywhere.

"Oh, no, *Dad!*" I rush toward him. "What's going on?"

Dad looks up at me and smiles weakly, then shakes his free hand in a familiar "never mind" gesture. "Don't worry . . . I'm fine," he says in a breathless voice. "Woke up feeling pressure . . . in my chest . . . but it's nothing . . . a kind of panic reaction to the gravity."

"What do you mean? Oh, God! *Oh no!*" I say, looking from him to the medics to everyone else in the room.

"Gwen, he's fine now, and his condition was not severe. I called the medical team just in case," Aeson says in a calm voice. "He was having minor heart palpitations. But they have stabilized him."

"Oh my God!" I put a hand to my mouth, step closer to him. "Dad! I am so sorry!"

"He is being hydrated," one of the medics tells me matter-of-factly, continuing to check Dad's vitals, and I notice the small portable IV drip unit. "Was slightly low on fluids. This is merely a precaution. He is also receiving medication to improve his lung function and to help his organs cope with the additional stress of the gravity."

"Absolutely fine," Dad says again, nodding. "In fact, feeling much better already. It occurs to me: I must be the oldest guy from modern Earth who's set foot on this planet. No wonder I'm a little off. . . ."

Gracie opens her mouth in sudden amazement. "Daddy, I think you might be right." She looks up at Aeson. "Is that true, do you think?"

"Indeed," Aeson says after a brief pause.

"Is that why Atlantis brought over only teenagers?" George asks.

"Yes, for the most part," Aeson replies. "Jump travel is very dangerous to older adults and very young children. Having to ferry the general population across the universe would have taken incredibly long if we had to employ the stasis chambers—even if we had enough—which we don't, unfortunately. Teenagers are the right age to be integrated into our society, and into our culture in general—teenagers are the most active working generation. What you consider adult responsibilities we consider regular teenage duties."

"How utterly fascinating," Dad says, looking up with avid attention. He appears to have indeed perked up, and is now sitting up straight in his chair. "Aeson, my dear fellow, I hope you don't mind me asking, but would you be willing to have an in-depth talk with me some time, so that I might ask some probing cultural questions? Would that be appropriate, that is?"

"Not only appropriate, but very welcome, *Amre-ter* Charles," Aeson says. "I will enjoy such a conversation very much."

"Excellent . . ." Dad says, nodding and smiling. His gaze sweeps around the room, including all of us, and he chuckles at Gracie's stress pout and intent expression, then gives Gordie an extra reassuring nod.

A few minutes later, the medics pack up their equipment, leaving only the portable IV unit—still attached to Dad and running a drip for at least another half-hour—and leave. Dad is instructed to take it easy for the rest of the day, with a prescription to drink plenty of fluids, bed rest, and minimal exertion.

"Kids, now that I'm here, I'm not going anywhere," Dad says to us with amusement, as we continue fussing all around him, and the Imperial Palace staff arrive to set up an *eos* bread service in the suite.

Most of us have already eaten, but no one can resist watching George and Dad be introduced to the pleasures of morning *lvikao* and *eos* pie. Naturally, Gordie decides to have second breakfast along with them.

Chapter 54

"This is not bad," Dad remarks, as he sips his second cup of *lvikao*. "A fair substitute for coffee, with a hint of cocoa and some kind of exotic spice. Is there caffeine in this?"

"I'm not sure." I glance at Aeson.

"Yes, some caffeine, though not as much as in Earth coffee."

Dad sips again. "Ah, definitely a plus."

"Yeah, you need your morning roast," George says to Dad, experimentally chewing a nutty, syrup-drenched dumpling. "But this is good. Not that we had much coffee or any other pantry supplies remaining in the house near the end," he adds.

"What's that?" I stare at my older brother with concern.

George glances at me and sighs. "Things were bad, sis. . . . A global mess. Toward the end—these past six months—food shortages became the norm. Grocery stores in town were mostly empty. We're talking tumbleweeds on the shelves in St. Albans, and fuel too precious to waste on a drive to Colchester, much less Burlington. Local Vermont farms and co-ops, supplemented by hunters, had a few supply chain things going, at least while it lasted. But otherwise—once the local produce crops ran out—everyone was on their own. We had to ration everything. No idea how we managed to restock some of Mom's meds. Actually, with some of it, we didn't."

Dad glances at George meaningfully and shakes his head. "Don't."

"Yeah, anyway. . . ." George goes silent and scoops up another dumpling with the newfangled-to-him Atlantean utensil.

"How are you feeling, Dad?" Gracie asks a few minutes later, as George removes Dad's finished IV line, as the medics instructed.

My father flexes his arm and sits back in his chair. His breathing, I note, has improved overall in the past half-hour. Those meds are definitely working.

If only Mom could've had access to—

No, stop.

Aeson's wrist comm emits a tone. He checks it, then tells us that Quoni is back on the surface, and the rest of the Lark family luggage is coming.

Moments later, another tone sounds, this time on my own wrist. It's a message from Consul Denu, inquiring if now is a good time to drop by for some Court attire measurements.

"What do you think, Aeson?" I ask. "Should I ask him to come somewhat later? Dad is in no condition to—"

But my father wants to know what it's about. I explain about the need for measurements for the required wardrobe for upcoming events—the first of which is scheduled as early as tomorrow—and he says he is "perfectly fine," and "let's get this over with."

And that's how my Dad and my brother George get to experience the magic that is Consul Denu.

The Consul returns here with his assistants and converses elegantly with my Dad while the assistants perform nonintrusive body scans even as my father remains seated. George is measured next, and the whole process takes less than half an hour.

"I do believe I've gleaned your tastes and fathomed your preferences, in a range of suitable colors, *Ter* Charles, and young *Ter* George," Consul Denu says, raising one perfectly manicured, ring-clad finger. "You will have your outfits for tomorrow's Imperial *dea* meal completed and delivered by morning."

"Much appreciated, Consul—may I ask, what is the best way to address you?" my father, Charles Lark, says, looking with curiosity at the splendid wig and gilded robe of the flamboyant Atlantean.

"You may, certainly," the Consul says with a gleam of amusement. "It would be my greatest pleasure to assist. The simplest form of address would be Consul Denu. More familiar— Consul Suval or *Ter* Suval. There are other variations. In fact, I will be overjoyed to impart to you the most pertinent details of Protocol you might find useful immediately in your new role as the Father of the Imperial Bride and Consort, during your first Imperial encounter."

"Oh, that would be fantastic!" I exclaim, happy on behalf of my father. Consul Denu will teach him everything he needs to know.

Now that it's settled, we let Consul Denu give both Dad and my older brother George a crash course in Imperial Protocol basics, while they continue eating their *eos* bread. Gracie and Gordie both listen in—since it pertains to them, also—as the Consul explains how to react, speak, eat, and sit during the Imperial meal. In a nutshell, the less is said by all of the Larks, the better.

Aeson, who also observes the mini-lesson, nods meaningfully. "Indeed, I recommend everyone enjoy the food and allow my Imperial Father to do most of the talking."

"So—no small talk?" Dad asks.

"Oh no, of course that's fine," the Consul replies. "However, such casual talk is relegated to the later portion of the meal, once the first dish is served and consumed, and the Imperial Sovereign sets the tone of the conversation."

"No problem," George says. "Will just keep it zipped, or talk about the weather."

"Georgie, they don't really talk about the weather here," Gracie says. "I mean, they *do*—it's just that there really hasn't been that much weather variation since we got here."

"They have weather control," Gordie adds, chewing a large chunk of savory *eos* pie.

"To a degree," Aeson says. "There is regional weather variation, and seasonal. But to counteract the most drastic fluctuations, there's urban weather monitoring and control over the largest cities such as Poseidon. But we've just come out of Green Season, which is known for its mildness and stability. Red Season is just starting, so prepare for heat and winds."

"Utterly fascinating," Dad remarks with a soft smile.

We talk some more, and Consul Denu gives everyone useful tips, then promises that he is entirely at my family's disposal if any more questions arise.

"You are very kind," Dad says to him in parting, and he offers his hand in that classic Earth gesture. "I would love to continue this conversation and enjoy many others with you, *Ter* Suval. Your expertise is admirable."

"My pleasure, *Ter* Charles." The Atlantean man takes my father's hand in a perfectly proper handshake, the kind he learned on

Earth. "I will be honored to partake of your own erudite and aesthetic views and the riches of your knowledge in the near future. Classical Earth history fascinates me to no end, and I am told you are a professor of such."

Dad gives a sad smile. "I was indeed, once. And now—here we are."

About an hour later, Quoni Enutat delivers the rest of the Lark things from the velo-cruiser that's parked directly in the Imperial airfield. Servants bring up at least ten mid-sized boxes and stack them in the guest suite.

"How cool! What is all this stuff, Dad?" I ask, as we all crowd in with excitement. "What did you bring?"

"I'm amazed they let you have more than two bags," Gracie says.

"It's not like they had to go through Qualification." Gordie snorts. "Makes sense they were more flexible with the family of the Imperial Bride."

"Oh yeah," George says, stepping up to one of the cardboard boxes with a familiar Earth warehouse superstore logo on it. Seeing that USA corporate logo here in Atlantis gives me a weird instant of dissociation.

"They were actually very accommodating when they first came to get us. They said we could bring as much as we needed onto the big starship," Dad says. "The young man who originally contacted us, Nefir, explained that the same luggage restrictions did not apply to us as they did to all the teenage refugees."

Nefir. . . . At the sound of that name, we all exchange grim looks. Aeson's expression, in particular, turns to stone.

"So, what did you bring?" I ask hurriedly with a smile, to change the subject. "More of your book collection, I bet?"

Dad nods. "I chose to bring only the rarest and most beloved editions, and officially donated the rest to Atlantis. That way, everything gets saved. They actually have about three hundred boxes—the entire library of mine, all of it rescued. These here are just the personal books I absolutely had to keep. Also, a few things from the house—mementos and keepsakes." He looks around at us. "Including digital photos and video recordings of our family holidays, all of you kids growing up, the grandparents and cousins, and of course, Margot . . . your Mom. Some of her personal things. All of it, family heirlooms now."

And Dad glances to the side table nearby, where he's placed Mom's urn.

I feel an instant painful twinge in my chest.

I still haven't watched Mom's video farewell recording intended for me.

Yes, I know it's weird. I'm not entirely sure why I haven't. . . . Maybe because—if I put it off long enough, I can keep telling myself I still have something new with Mom to look forward to in the future, fresh Mom material to watch.

If I *don't* watch it, then we're *not done*, and she is *not quite gone* yet. . . .

And now I'm ashamed and oddly scared to admit it to Dad and the others.

I suspect that Gracie and Gordie know I haven't seen it yet. I'll probably confess to Dad later.

Right now, they have more urgent things to deal with and worry about.

The rest of the day goes by quickly, as we mostly hang out in the suite and keep Dad and George company. Dad is still not functioning at one hundred percent, so we make him take many short naps. Gordie takes George for a walk down in the park area, but only after I make sure George is wearing the thick wraparound sunglasses that were standard issue to all the Earthies.

Aeson goes out to do some errands, and at some point, I'm left alone to watch Dad while Gracie steps out for a short while.

I take the opportunity to tell my father about the strained relationship with the Imperator and what he has done to me, to Mom, to Aeson, to everyone. . . . I speak softly, assuming the nano-cameras or other surveillance is everywhere, but I don't hold back.

Charles Lark, my father, listens with a serious expression. I find it hard to read him now, because he remains very composed, even as I tell him the worst—the true reasons behind the rescue delay and how the Imperator forced me to be in the Games.

When I'm done, Dad says thoughtfully, "Gwen . . . what you describe is a monster. Are you certain? He can't be all that bad. Most human beings, even the most *difficult* ones, do have some redeeming qualities. It could be, there's some kind of misunderstanding—cultural differences even. Recall, you are dealing with a *very* elevated individual in a highly static, class-bound society. Pride and self-importance and ivory tower mentality are nearly unavoidable under such circumstances."

I shake my head. "Dad, believe me when I say—"

"This position of Imperator, if I understand correctly—it is a dynastic, inherited title with almost religious overtones—as close as they come to the definition of the divine right of kings. And having done my research on the Kassiopei Dynasty, the family is ancient beyond anything we've ever dealt with, much less heard of, in our modern historical perspective. Nowhere in the annals of Western Civilization is there a record of such a long-standing, uninterrupted bloodline—"

"Wait, Dad, please . . . stop. Why are you excusing him?" I say, frowning with surprise. "He killed Mom. Or at least caused a delay that denied her medical care. He forced me to participate in the killer Games. He—"

He was going to hide me away in a lab and experiment on me because of my Voice. . . . But I don't mention that part yet. The things I already said are bad enough.

Dad slowly lets out a breath. "Sweetheart, you can't be certain of such a thing. Mom was doing very poorly toward the end. It was end-stage. . . . The circumstances that contributed to her decline were already there, months before—if you could only see the kind of . . . difficulties we've had keeping her meds refilled, and running out, rationing meds. *Yes, I said it,* we had to ration her meds. *I* had to ration her meds. Which makes *me* just as damn guilty—"

Dad pauses, his breath catching. For several excruciating heartbeats he is silent, breathing slowly to regain his composure before continuing. "When tragedy happens, it's so easy to cast blame. But there was plenty of blame to go around—the political climate in the country, the whole world, the resources. Everywhere, frightened, angry, desperate people on short triggers, waiting to die in a matter of months. All of us, doomed to die from the asteroid impact. Maybe we should've fought harder. We—I could've tried more pharmacies, different urban centers, gone further, all the way to New York—"

"Dad . . ." I whisper, reaching out with my hand to press his arm gently.

"So, as you can imagine," he says, pressing his own hand over mine in turn, "if this one heartless man—this Imperator—and his genuinely malicious actions contributed to the misfortunate lineup of circumstances that took your Mother away from us, it was not the only reason, nor even the main reason."

"But Dad—"

"Allow me this—this *manner* of thinking, at least for now, my sweet," Dad says in a powerless voice, looking at me with agony in his eyes. "I want to meet this Imperator for myself, judge him for the kind of man he is. It is so hard for me to imagine your Aeson, kind and honorable, having such a father."

"I know," I say. "Aeson is very different. So much more like his mother."

And then I tell my Dad about Devora Kassiopei, and how loving and kind Aeson's mother has been to all of us. I also mention his sister Manala, with her gentle and innocent personality, almost painfully empathetic and in tune with the emotions of others.

Dad nods, listening. "There is always complexity in the family—in all families. Even ours."

For several minutes we sit in familiar silence, next to each other. Then I lean in closer and wrap my arms around him, and rest my head on Dad's chest. Even as I do so—remembering how I used to do that as a little girl—I worry now that I'm putting too much pressure on his chest and lungs. So I move back a little, giving him room to breathe.

But Dad pulls me back in. He rests his hand over my hair, stroking the top of my head, and gives me a gentle kiss on my forehead. "My girl Gwen. . . . Wonderful, wonderful daughter. Margot would be so proud."

I remain, for several long minutes, saying nothing, just sitting with Dad, hearing his slightly irregular breathing, and feeling the solid warmth of his arms.

Whatever happens tomorrow when our two wildly disparate families meet, at least we'll get to face it together as one unit.

Chapter 55

Early in the morning of Red Amrevet 7, with just two days now remaining before the Wedding Day, several large packages with the Court-appropriate attire for my Dad and George are delivered to their suite. The servants carry in the outfits wrapped in the Atlantean equivalent of clear plastic, along with matching footwear, and place them in the closets.

"All of this overnight? This is just amazing," Dad marvels, as we sit around in their suite eating *eos* bread.

Our big Imperial Family event is scheduled for mid-afternoon, second hour of Khe. It gives us time to get ready and to brainstorm last-minute ideas on how to deport ourselves.

Even with the Protocol lessons from Consul Denu, the idea alone is terrifying, in particular for my younger siblings. At least Dad and George have no actual sense of what they're in for, but Gracie and Gordie have *seen* the draconian figure of the Imperator—from afar, admittedly, since they were never formally introduced to him—and they know enough of the bad stuff to be both angry and scared.

Fortunately, we're one big family, and there's strength in numbers. And the good thing is, Dad is definitely feeling better this morning. The gravity still sucks, but at least he is breathing okay.

Two hours before the scheduled event, servants arrive to assist my father and George with their dressing and grooming, despite their minor protests. "Don't fight it, Dad and Gee One," I say with an amused smile. "Trust me, it's best if they show you how to put on the semi-formal clothes the first time around, with all the oddball buttons and ties. Plus, they'll give you all the fancy spa facials and shaves and nail buffing and whatever else. . . ."

"Nail buffing? Are you serious?" George cranes his neck sideways and gives me his most sarcastic expression that covers genuine, low-grade alarm.

"Well, they *are* very detail oriented," I say, biting my lip to hold back wicked laughter. "So I'm not ruling out anything. Though, you probably should ask Aeson what exactly they'll be doing to *him*."

And then I add, this time for Dad's sake, "Just think of it as immersive cultural education. You're getting a rare inside look into the most fashionable, trendy, and cool—" that part is for George— "personal grooming customs of an alien society of truly epic ancient origins."

If that doesn't convince them, I think with an inner smile, *nothing will.*

M eanwhile, the rest of us start getting ready too. Luckily for all, the attire is only one rung above festive casual, and the proper term for it is "Imperial casual."

For this Imperial *dea* meal I wear a layered dress of golden fabric, with a form-fitting metallic sheath layer underneath and a lightly cascading gauze outer layer that falls in delicate clouds around me with every movement. The dress is demure, long-sleeved, with a high collar. I really don't need any accessories to set off all that glittering metal fabric. However, the Imperatris sends me a box of stunning jewelry on loan to wear for the occasion—a necklace and matching earrings set with the rare Pegasus Blood stones of ancient fossilized resin from the Agnios tree. Pegasus Blood occurs in several dark colors, but these particular stones are a deep shade of red, evocative of their name.

Aranit styles my hair into a simple updo and sprinkles it with gold dust—which for once makes perfect sense, and will match my outfit.

When done, I appear both distinctive and yet nobly restrained—the perfect proud picture for an Imperial Bride.

Next, I carefully look over my sister, who has put on a deep plum dress with a light over-layer, and small, sparkly crystal earrings. Gracie's hair is in a stern bun similar to what she often does with her hair as part of the Fleet uniform. The expression on her face is rigid, and it's clear that poor Gracie is breathless with nerves.

Both of us are wearing basic Face Paints—to use Consul Denu's proper term for cosmetics—but we have eschewed evening drama in favor of soft natural tones. Even our kohl eyeliner is at a minimum, and our lips are delicately tinted with rose *noohd*.

The Lark men meet us outside my room, dressed as I've never seen them before.

My Dad and brothers are wearing dark jackets and pants of expensive fabric, fine linen-like shirts, elegant jeweled collars, and classy shoes. Dad's ensemble is clean and stark—a black jacket with grey pants and a white shirt. Gordie wears shades of olive green, while George is wearing earth tones. Remarkably, all these different shades serve equally well to offset the Lark family blue eyes.

To top off their sharp new look, both my brothers and my Dad are freshly shaven and their hair is immaculately styled. So strange to see my father's usual messy greying cowlicks missing, but instead everything is in graceful order.

George's hair is slicked back, and Gordie's short hair has been *washed*—yes, for Gordie it's an achievement. His glasses are spotless—and so are my Dad's, for that matter.

"Oh, look at you! You all look amazing!" Gracie says with a smile. "And doesn't Dad look absolutely great?"

"He sure does," I say with pride. "How are you feeling, by the way?"

"Doing very well," Dad says with a small sigh. "I understand the importance of this event, and of proper first impressions, but are you certain all of this is not a bit too much? I've no doubt this is a very expensive suit. . . . It feels quite formal."

"Daddy, you have no idea how formal the Imperial events can get—this is nothing!" Gracie exclaims. She's not helping.

"It is very appropriate." I try to reassure. "Not too much, just right."

"Very well," my father says with mild resignation. And then he smiles and gazes at Gracie and me with loving wonder. "On the other hand, regardless of how we might look and feel, it's safe to say my daughters are beautiful young ladies. Dressed for a ball, indeed."

"Oh, Daddy. . . ." Gracie smiles.

"Ladies," George says with a charming smile and nods at us.

"Yeah, looking good." Gordie echoes him in a mumble.

"Are we ready to go?" I say with a show of confidence. "Then let's do it!"

We meet up with Aeson just inside the exterior doors of our Quarters. Aeson looks impeccable in his own dark blue jacket, black pants, and an exquisite golden shirt trimmed with a collar of very fine metallic lace, so it looks like an etching on metal. His naturally golden hair falls unrestrained down his back.

Seeing us all so well-dressed, Aeson pauses and gives us a slow nod and a controlled smile of approval. "Thank you for this. You do us honor with your presentation," he says, casting a glance at everyone. "Under ideal circumstances My Imperial Father might find no fault with such a handsome Family. And yet, these are imperfect times. So, I ask you to be ready for his . . . volatile character."

Members of my family listen to Aeson with varying degrees of concern.

"At the same time, please remember that you have the wholehearted support of the rest of Kassiopei," he concludes with kind softness. "It will likely not come to anything. But if it does, I promise to intercede on your behalf in whatever manner might be necessary."

My father raises his brows and exhales slowly. "I see. . . . And I appreciate your reassurance, Aeson. Please lead on."

We exit the Crown Prince's Quarters as a group, and our security guards line up around us—which surprises Dad and George, but we give them reassuring glances.

"This is normal, Daddy," Gracie whispers near his ear, as we walk to the elevator. "Just ignore them."

I hold back a smile and exchange a look with Aeson, as we move ahead of the others, setting the pace.

We emerge from the elevator on the top floor, the Imperial floor lobby with its gleaming marble and high ceilings, and Dad glances up with fascination. I'm glad the architecture is there to distract him, because next we face the row of imposing, uniformed Imperial guards with gilded staffs.

They part before us, while our own security guards fall back, and Aeson leads the way through the grand doors into the antechamber.

While we stand for a few moments, waiting for the high servant, Dad and George stare curiously at the wall with the row of Thrones—those imposing Imperial Seats in the receiving area. Gracie and Gordie stare likewise, never having been here before.

"Beautiful craftsmanship," Dad says softly. "Stark, clean lines . . . echoes of Egypt's early New Kingdom . . . Eighteenth Dynasty. . . ."

"Dad, sh-h-h-h," Gracie whispers with widened eyes.

The high servant arrives and executes a courtly bow before Aeson and the rest of us. "Our Imperial Sovereign, the Archaeon Imperator, the Sovereign Lady, the Archaeona Imperatris, and the Imperial Princess, are ready to receive My Imperial Lord, his Bride, and her Family for *dea* meal in the Carnelian Chamber," he intones. Then he bows a second time and leads us pompously to one of the many doors of the Quarters.

We walk through an ornately adorned corridor, taking several turns past other doors and rooms, and enter a large, high-ceilinged chamber decorated in warm hues of carnelian red—a shade of red that's light and cheerful as opposed to dark and imposing. Windows with sheer curtains cast mercifully filtered daylight over the chiseled stone of the walls and illuminate elegant but comfortable furnishings. There are several chairs, a long sofa, and a rectangular table for twelve, situated as a centerpiece.

So, the intimidation levels are at a minimum, it occurs to me as I take in the room. But the thought lasts only a moment.

The Imperator, dressed in a dark gray jacket and pants, and a black shirt with a thin golden collar, sits in a high-backed easy chair near the sofa, legs crossed, slouching slightly against one armrest. It is the most casual pose I have ever seen him take. And it is entirely contrived for our benefit.

The Imperatris occupies another chair nearby, her posture upright, hands in her lap. She is wearing a dress of dark teal, rich like ocean depths but with a shimmering gauze outer layer of lavender, like sea foam. Despite her formal demeanor her expression is warm and eager with excitement.

On the other side of the Imperator, Princess Manala sits motionless, her hands also clutched in her lap. Her dress is dark lapis lazuli, almost black, with an outer layer of the same color, but threaded with gold. Her Kassiopei gold hair is gathered low at the nape of her neck in a blue lace net. Her great eyes are alert, widened with tension but also curiosity as she immediately stares in our direction.

While all these impressions are happening, I notice that unobtrusive servants are preparing food at different stations set up near the walls, and the aroma of savory spices and sweet pungent sauces wafts in our direction.

As soon as we enter, the Imperator turns his composed, blank face toward us, but does not get up.

Aeson immediately steps forward and makes a formal bow. "My Imperial Father, you honor us with this invitation to share your *dea* meal. I honor you in turn with my Bride and those who share her blood, the Lark Family."

The Imperator observes his son, then slowly turns his face to look at us. The moment of silence is excruciating.

"You may approach. Come closer," Romhutat Kassiopei says, and his serpentine gaze slithers over me and my siblings, then rests on my Dad.

We all take a small step forward and slightly incline our heads in the closest thing to a bow without actually bowing—just as we have been instructed by Consul Denu, who explained that the Bride's Family must show a bit of resistant pride, all as part of the process of being accepted into the sphere of the Imperial Family. Such is the Imperial Family *dea* meal tradition, to present ourselves as near-equals worthy of the Kassiopei Dynasty. In other words, we do not grovel.

"You must be Charles Lark, her father," the Imperator says in a sudden cold voice, without any preamble. "How is it that you are here on Atlantis? You were expected to wait on the remaining arkship in Earth's orbit. *Such were my orders.*" And he turns to glare at Aeson.

My Dad watches with mild confusion, glancing from the Imperator to Aeson, but does not appear to be fazed.

Fortunately, Aeson does not blink as he replies. "Forgive me, Father, but I was unaware of such direct orders from you when I issued orders to have my Bride's Family brought here in time for the Wedding."

But the Imperator has turned his attention back to my father. "Well?"

My Dad speaks up. "Ah! Yes indeed, I'm Charles Lark, Gwen's father. I am deeply grateful—to your son Aeson for the rescue, on behalf of my children and myself. It's a pleasure to be here."

Wow, I think, *my Dad just expressed gratitude to Aeson and not to the Imperator.*

Oh, crap. . . .

"Welcome, *Ter* Charles, it is wonderful to have you here," the friendly voice of the Imperatris sounds, just in the nick of time.

My father turns to look at Devora Kassiopei and smiles lightly. "Thank you," he says.

"Your children are lovely," Devora continues. "Starting with Gwen, every one of them. I've met the youngest, Gracie, and your son Gordie. And now I see there is one more. This young man is your eldest?"

"This is my son George," Dad says, with a nod at my older brother.

On cue, George takes another step forward and bows properly before Devora with a tiny smile. "My Sovereign Lady, I am George Lark," he says in a calm voice, then switches his attention expertly to the Imperator. "My Imperial Sovereign, thank you for having us here."

And then George steps back, managing to evoke a crazy combination of humility and insolence with just one smooth movement, all while still wearing his light, charming smile.

The Imperator frowns slightly, observing him, then says, "Very well, proceed with the rest of this nonsense. Introduce yourselves."

Apparently, because the Imperatris spoke up when she did, "out of turn," in order to divert a looming confrontation, traditional things are now happening completely out of order.

Well, screw everything.

I take a deep breath and step forward. "My Sovereign Lord, as the Imperial Bride and Consort, I would like to present my sister, Grace Lark, my brothers George and Gordon Lark, and my Father, Charles Lark."

The Imperator stares at me in silence, creating another painful pause—painful for all of us, and I'm beginning to wonder if it's painful for *him* too, and if so, why is he doing it? Giving himself time to think and plan each word? Intentionally ratcheting up the tension to control the situation? Finally, he speaks the traditional words in a voice without inflection: "I acknowledge and recognize the Lark Family, as the Family of the Imperial Bride."

Thank heaven almighty. . . . I exchange a quick glance of relief with Aeson.

"Wonderful," Devora speaks once again, smiling at all of us. "Welcome, every one of you. For the newly arrived, this is my daughter and sister of the Bridegroom, the Imperial Princess Manala—she is my younger child." And the Imperatris indicates her daughter with an elegant gesture of one hand.

Manala immediately rises from her seat and gives my Dad, George, and the rest of us an impeccable curtsey. Her nervous gaze darts at every one of us, and she doesn't speak a word.

"My daughter may sit," the Imperator says to Manala curtly. "The Bridal formalities are mostly completed, so we may now eat in peace. We'll continue at the table."

He rises and walks over to take the seat at the head of the table.

Devora and Manala stand up and follow him, while the rest of us wait a few seconds, watching Aeson.

My Bridegroom turns to me and takes my hand, then nods to my family. He leads me to the table, and occupies the seat to the right of the Imperator, directly across from his Mother who is on her Husband's left.

I sit down next to Aeson and across from Manala—recalling momentarily this same exact seating configuration during the very first Imperial *eos* bread I ate in the Palace.

This time, my family is here too.

Dad sits down next to me, while Gracie goes around the table and sits across from Dad and right next to Manala. Finally, Gordie joins Gracie on that side of the table, while George sits down opposite Gordie and next to Dad.

The Imperator's narrowed gaze follows our seating arrangements, then he signals to the serving staff to present the *dea* meal.

The servants begin carrying hot, fragrant dishes and filling our plates. Others approach with tall iced carafes and pour frothing plum-colored *qvaali* into our goblets. The delicious aroma of the first course, a multi-layered deep-dish delicacy baked in flaky pastry dough and topped with a savory herb crust, is enough to make anyone salivate under normal circumstances—but these are not.

While all this is happening, there is awkward silence. Members of my family sit quietly, looking at their plates or at each other, and everyone is discreetly watching the Imperator.

Romhutat Kassiopei does not yet touch anything on his generously filled plate. He lifts his glass of *qvaali* and pretends to consider it before drinking; tilts it and swirls the liquid. It's yet another power-asserting tactic—he's intentionally delaying the meal, since no one may begin eating before he does.

In that moment, someone clears their throat.

The Imperator freezes and slowly looks in the direction of the sound.

The culprit appears to be my brother Gordie.

Seeing the Imperator's stare, and the fact that everyone else is looking in his direction, Gordie widens his eyes, then says, "Sorry. . . ."

Oh, no. . . .

My pulse picks up speed. One of the strictest rules of Imperial Protocol during meals is that *no one* may speak before the Imperator during that first fateful dish service. We've been warned.

And now Gordie has mumbled out of order. After the involuntary throat-clearing thing, the thing to do was to simply remain silent and deal with the unintended attention as best as one can.

The Imperator observes my younger brother and says nothing. He is an amused cat playing with a mouse.

Agonizing heartbeats pass, while I clench my fingers nervously under the table.

Finally, the Imperator liberates Gordie from his basilisk stare. As if nothing happened, he tips his glass and takes a swallow. Then he raises the glass a few inches higher with mock dramatic flair.

"An Earth-style toast!" the Imperator says loudly in a deep, slithering voice of power, sweeping all of us with his heavy gaze. "I welcome you to *Atlantida*, Lark Family of Earth. And now—be exalted by my Imperial Word, even as you are bound by the sanctity of Imperial Marriage. As of this moment you are elevated within the sphere of influence of the Imperial Family of Kassiopei."

Chapter 56

We raise our glasses and drink, as ordered by the Imperator.

No need for an explanation—there's an immediate sense of general relief at the formal words of welcome directed at all of us, the Lark Family. This is the second formal phrase of acknowledgment the Imperator has spoken, and it, in particular, seems to cement our sense of place in this new world. . . . No matter how ephemeral or mercurial his pronouncements may generally be, *this one* feels more resolute.

Or are we all mistaken, lulled into a false sense of security?

Just for once, I try not to think along those lines. . . . This is supposed to be a friendly, traditional meeting of our relatives.

And then Romhutat picks up his eating utensil and takes a bite, which is our cue to also begin eating.

I glance to my side at Dad and see that he automatically takes his own eating implement and moves it around the plate without actually putting anything into his mouth. Instead, Dad observes with thoughtful interest our future in-laws. *Right now, what is he thinking?*

The Imperator consumes his first course in silence. The Imperatris and the Princess eat slowly, taking dainty bites. My own siblings follow suit, copying the Imperial women's restraint and table manners. For a few minutes there's only the clanking of cutlery against plates.

I make a show of putting small pieces of food past my lips, but I'm unable to eat or taste anything. Glancing over at Aeson, I see him taking his own controlled bites and watching his Father.

How soon can we engage in small talk?

And then it begins.

"*Ter* Charles," the Imperator says. "My congratulations on your recent loss of your wife."

All at once, silence descends on the room.

Everyone freezes. . . . I hear Gracie's barely controlled gasp. My eyes widen in sudden horror.

My Dad stops moving things around on his plate. His brows twitch, and then his face stills into a peculiar expression of uncertainty. He slowly turns his head to look directly at the Imperator. "Beg your pardon?"

"Eh—wrong word in your English," the Imperator says, and his expression remains a mask. "I meant to say *condolences*. So—my condolences on your loss."

"Oh!" my poor father says at once, as his face eases in relief. And then he nods. "Yes, thank you."

The relief of everyone else around the table is palpable. I hear multiple breaths being released, and then the renewed faint sound of moving utensils.

I glance at Aeson quickly, just as he meets my gaze in that moment, frowning. I read the fierce darkness in his look, and then I have no doubt. . . . The Imperator's command of English is excellent. Which means, he chose his words *intentionally*—a sadistic provocation.

"I am deeply sorry for you in your beloved wife's loss," Devora Kassiopei says softly. "It must be unimaginable. . . . Your heart is plunged in death's shadow, and your spirit is fractured prematurely. Your *ka* is poised between this world and the next, its life purpose faltering, while the *ba* is ready to flee on shadow wings and take the *ka* with it. . . . And it must be agony because, for all practical purposes, the *akh* is already gone, having reunited with your beloved mate on the *beyond side,* the next stage of your mutual journey."

My father looks at the Imperatris with wonder and gratitude. "What a graceful way of expressing it. . . ."

"Grace is required for proper understanding." Devora nods with a faint smile. "It is the nature of our human grief to best respond to the sublime, even as the grieving heart longs to regain clarity. . . . When we lose loved ones to death—ahead of ourselves—we rely on them to light the way first, as they travel ahead of us into the eternal realm. Then, for the rest of our lives, we are pulled relentlessly toward them by all the three parts of our spirit caught in that light. . . . Our physical bodies become limp, useless dolls controlled only by grief's far-reaching strings—especially in the beginning."

Dad nods slowly, his expression full of raw suffering.

"It is this fracturing into three that causes the imbalance that you are feeling now. As our three-layered spirit fabric is temporarily redefined, the new version of our *selves* has to be inscribed in The Book of the Dead. Once it is done, grief becomes bearable and life purpose returns. But—it takes time. Afterwards, of course, we are no longer the same in this world, because our loved one has taken parts of us, permanently."

"I—I am truly grateful for the kind words and your sympathy— My Sovereign Lady Devora," Charles Lark, my father, says in a quiet voice. "It's apparent that you understand grief and loss."

"And I am glad to help in any small way. You are entangled with your love, and she is holding your *akh* in a safe embrace until your time comes. Such is the world that I believe in."

"And a pretty world it is, My Wife," the Imperator says, his cool voice cutting like steel into the gentle exchange. Staring at my father, he adds, "The Archaeona Imperatris holds to certain traditional religious beliefs, and I'm certain she will expand on them in detail on a different occasion."

"Yes, of course," my Dad says somewhat awkwardly, this time addressing both of them. "I would appreciate the opportunity to listen. . . . Thank you again."

"As far as opportunities," the Imperator continues. "Now that you are here in my Court, and you are bereaved, I grant you permission to seek a suitable replacement among the noblewomen of the Court."

For the first time, Devora Kassiopei utters a gasp. "Rom!"

Immediately the Imperator swivels his head to look at her. "What? The man is not *dead* as you make him out to be. Indeed, he and his grief will both benefit from having a new wife. He may look for her in Low, Middle, or High Court. I am granting him an Imperial *favor*."

"Father, how can you—how can you suggest something so cold?" Aeson says suddenly.

"Not you too, boy?" the Imperator snarls at his son. "You will remember your place as you sit today at my table."

The grim desolation in Aeson's expression is impossible to convey. . . .

At this point everyone around the table comes alive with angry energy. So many darting glances, so much movement ready to burst out. My siblings are fuming.

As for me—I've literally forgotten about myself, about having normal living reactions such as anger or outrage, so focused am I on *the others in my family*—on my father in particular—in the sickening tension of the moment.

This heartless monster just casually informed our Dad that he should replace our Mom.

Gracie looks ready to jump out of her chair, and if I'm not wrong, I think Manala has gripped her arm to keep her in place. Manala herself looks terrified. George and Gordie are exchanging grim glances. We squirm, still keeping our silence, but everyone waits for Dad to respond to this outrage.

Charles Lark, my father, straightens in his seat and lets the utensil in his hand fall. He looks directly at the Imperator and does not blink as their gazes lock together. "I must assume this is a cultural misunderstanding or another linguistic gaffe—but your suggestion is highly inappropriate. My wife died barely two months ago. The idea that I would want to look for a replacement *now* or *ever*—even if I were to be inclined that way at some point, and *I am not*—is not merely tone-deaf in a society that prides itself on musical tonality, but very *unkind*."

My Dad pauses, even as his usually mellow, friendly baritone voice has grown loud and resonant and *forceful*—I've never heard him sound like this before. "I understand that I'm an invited guest here, and this is your house, your rules. Your court, your country— You are the Imperial Sovereign of the nation *Atlantida*. Considering all these differences in cultural norms and values, and our mutual unfamiliarity, I am *still* going to give you—and your intentions—the benefit of the doubt. But I will have to respectfully decline this favor."

Silence reigns again.

And then the Imperator makes a mocking sound. "Very well, suit yourself. And yes, you are my guest, and as such, it will do you good to remember that you are here only because of my son's choice of your daughter."

"I will remember it," Dad says. "For the sake of my daughter and your very worthy son."

"Shall we continue the meal and have the next dish, please?" Devora Kassiopei interrupts carefully.

"Yes, proceed with it," Romhutat says with disdain and waves his hand to the servers.

The Imperial staff obeys, and our half-eaten plates are taken away and replaced with new ones.

As the service is happening, the Imperator calls for a refill of his glass and begins to drink, glancing around at all of us between swallows.

He must've noticed Gracie's particularly tense expression of barely repressed anger as she stares at the clean plate before her, because he pauses to observe her, narrowing his eyes. He then continues his visual sweep of the table, this time examining my brother George.

George keeps up a cold demeanor, very slowly picks up his own glass, and takes a swallow. He too is staring directly ahead, basically locking gazes with Gordie across the table, so as not to have to reveal the turmoil he is keeping under a hard lid. As for my younger brother, his expression is fixed in a frown of permanent disbelief. Furthermore, Gordie is *not* eating.

The second course of food is served on our plates—a fragrant vegetable cream soup inside shallow bowls of sculpted dough blossoms. We pick up the accompanying *chivkoor*—weird bidirectional ladle utensils shaped like boats that Atlanteans use to eat soup—and dip them in the bowls.

I should point out that the *chivkoor* boat ladle has no handle, holds much more than an Earth spoon, and you can sip or slurp the contents from either nose end of the "boat"—the prow or the stern. One end is slightly blunt and rounded, the other slightly pointy and angled. Really interesting utensil, and I think my Dad is momentarily fascinated by it as he slowly turns it in his fingers, probably distancing himself in order to forget the crass ugliness of what has just happened.

But apparently that's not an option.

"Gwen, my dear, how are the Wedding preparations progressing for both of you?" the Imperatris asks me in a comforting voice, maneuvering the conversation in a pleasant direction for everyone. "With only one day left, you must be overwhelmed from all the excitement. Please let me know if you need assistance with any of the remaining details on your schedule. The Venerable Therutat tells me that everything is proceeding splendidly, so you should feel a sense of great relief and accomplishment at this point."

"Thank you, my Sovereign Lady," I say with an instant flood of warmth at her continued kindness. "Everything has been wonderful. I'm mostly done with all Bridal events and selections, and I believe Aeson is too." And I glance to my left to see Aeson looking at me.

"Indeed," he says. "All that remains is tomorrow, the day of fasting, cleansing, and reflection."

"Good." Devora inclines her head graciously. "And it is such a fortunate blessing that Gwen's father and brother arrived here just in time for the Wedding to participate in your joyful day."

"Oh, yes," I say to her and glance at my Dad with a smile.

Dad meets my gaze and gives me a surprisingly confident, encouraging nod and smile that immediately sets me at ease with the familiarity of childhood. "It will be a wonder to see my little girl get married. Still hard to believe it is happening." And then he leans forward slightly and glances past me at Aeson. "And you, Aeson. Such an impressive, wonderful young man—what an honor to have you in the family."

"Thank you, *Amre-ter* Charles." Aeson looks at my Dad with an earnest expression in his eyes, which I find particularly touching.

"Not merely a fine young man," Romhutat Kassiopei's voice cuts in suddenly. "My Son is the future Imperator. The *honor* that is being bestowed upon the Lark Family cannot be overstated—it is beyond your imagination or understanding."

"Oh, I understand," Dad replies, almost startled at the sound of the Imperator speaking.

He's come to expect the worst, it occurs to me. In just one afternoon of being exposed to the Imperial personality, my Dad now *knows* what that man is like. He knows that whatever comes out of the Imperator's mouth is going to be hurtful, or terrifying, or outrageous, yet again.

But this is my Dad. . . . And his mere presence is a comfort even now in this surreal place and time.

Even so, right now, I'm terribly worried for him.

"You do *not*. It is true that you will *attempt* to understand," the Imperator says in an ice-hard tone, and the weight of his gaze intensifies. "It is your duty now to fathom as much as you may about the Imperial Kassiopei."

"Fortunately, studying the intricacies of your dynasty and its traditions is within the realm of my professional interests," my father replies in a tone that is both placid and genuine. "I will proceed to remedy my lack of knowledge and expand my understanding with sincere appreciation."

"Yes, I recall now, you are a scholar," the Imperator says.

"A historian," my Dad clarifies. "PhD in Classics and Ancient History, with a focus on Anthro-Linguistics and early Civilization. Ancient Mesopotamia and Greece were a particular core area of my research. . . . Indeed, now that I'm here, I find a startling number of commonalities between Earth's most distant past and what exists at present on Atlantis. Such a wonderful set of parallels, and no doubt there will be many more as I explore the absolute *vastness* of your culture. It could very well be humanity's earliest, longest uninterrupted branch—"

"It is." Romhutat Kassiopei pronounces, interrupting. "We are the dawn of what you know, and the Kassiopei line stretches even farther into the past."

"Some say you are gods." It is my brother George speaking suddenly, with just a tiny bit of sarcasm. "Or, so I've read in the ship's database during our flight here. A daring claim. No doubt, it's the most pragmatic way of holding onto such near-absolute power for so long."

At the sound of his voice everyone turns to look at him. The Imperator examines George. "You think the divinity of Kassiopei is a mere deception?" he says softly. In this very moment, the Imperator's quiet speech is even more terrifying than his normal volume.

George stares back at him with a controlled, slightly defiant, slightly uncertain expression. "I don't know," he says after a pause. "Are you saying you *are* divine? Seriously?"

"Stand up," the Imperator says, and suddenly his voice modulates and becomes a slithering, reverberating, unnaturally amplified—or is that only an illusion—familiar thing of irrefutable power and compulsion. *"Stand up, come closer, kneel before me."*

"Huh?" George says, frowning. "What?" But he rises from his seat nevertheless.

"Rise! Approach! Kneel!" the Imperial *compelling voice* thunders in my mind—in everyone's mind—and suddenly all of us start getting up from our seats, chairs being pushed back loudly, uncontrollably. . . . Even the servants stop their work and obey. . . . A plate crashes to the floor. . . .

In seconds, everyone is down on the floor, bodies hunched, heads lowered, wherever they stand.

Small correction—most of us, but *not all* of us.

I remain in my chair, frowning and trying to shake my head in order to shake off the compulsion like an annoying buzzing in my inner ears.

Next to me, Aeson remains in place, leaning forward with a stormy expression, but does not budge from his seat as he glares at his Father with fury.

And on the other side of me, Charles Lark, my father, opens his mouth in uncertainty and says calmly, without moving, "What is happening?"

All three of us are *not* compelled.

The Imperator sits like a dragon, looking over a room full of prostrate people and stares at us. Remnants of the otherworldly tide of power are still surging in his eyes, even as the echoes of his *compelling voice* seem to rebound, strike the walls of the chamber and move outward in concentric quantum circles in our minds. . . .

His expression is controlled as he sees both me and Aeson still in our places, defying him—but there is a flicker of surprise as he notes that my father is also unaffected.

Meanwhile, I stare with outrage, seeing people I love, my family, groveling on the floor. I can't see Gracie's face, only that she is shaking, huddled in a fetal position on her knees, with her head down, next to Manala, who has assumed her usual resigned obedience pose. Manala's hands are almost *neatly* folded, palms down on the floor, her gracefully framed forehead is touching the ground, earrings and other jewelry cascading to sweep the tiles.

Both my brothers' bodies are in a strange, awkward configuration of limbs, not knowing what to do with themselves, but definitely kneeling, with faces down. I notice that George is shaking his head, similar to what I've been doing, as though trying to get rid of the compulsion probably still ringing inside his head. . . . Gordie has assumed a bizarre variation of the "duck, cover, and hold" position that we've been taught in school, when we were still back in California, to use in case of an earthquake. His hands are wrapped over the back of his head to cover the neck, and he appears utterly confused. . . . Poor Gordie!

The Imperatris herself is kneeling gracefully, in an unresisting, practiced way, just like her daughter. Because of her seating proximity to the Imperator, she is literally at his feet. . . . My heart surges with particular hurt and anger on her behalf. It is yet another reminder of the chronic humiliation she must endure from her husband.

The servants are scattered around the room, kneeling variously. One of the cooking stations starts to smoke with a loud sizzle, and now a dish that was in the process of being sautéed is burning unattended. . . .

And then I hear the very normal voice of my Dad, as he repeats his question, sitting at my side. "What is going on?"

At once the Imperator focuses on my father. His perusal of my Dad is different . . . calculating, evaluating. "So—you are immune also. How very interesting. I see now where your daughter gets it— from *you*."

"What?" My Dad shakes his head and his own tone hardens. "Gets *what*? What did you do to my children? Why are they on the floor? Are they *hurt?*"

"My Imperial Father's *compelling voice*—the *divine* Logos voice of the Kassiopei, has the power to sway everyone to his will," Aeson replies with clear, resonant anger. "With a few exceptions."

"Such as us, Dad," I say fiercely. "It looks like you cannot be compelled either!"

"This is—this is *terrible!*" my father says, glancing from me to Aeson and back to the Imperator. "Are you saying you can force— even *harm* people with your *voice?* What in the world!"

"It is the ancient prerogative of the Kassiopei Dynasty to wield the Voice of Power, the divine Logos voice," the Imperator says coldly. And then he raises one hand in a gesture of disgust. "You may all rise!" he says to the room in general.

At once, everyone starts moving and getting up. The serving staff hurry back to their cooking stations—one of them in particular, to avert a fire. Devora and Manala rise silently, with graceful resignation, and return to their seats. Gracie, Gordie, and George appear dazed and furious and yes, scared, as they stand up. Gordie is swaying slightly as he straightens and rubs his forehead, and says, "Whoa." George looks like he's been hit by a figurative truck. And Gracie clenches her trembling fingers into white-knuckled fists.

"Are you all okay?" Dad asks everyone with worry.

"They're fine," the Imperator says in an annoyed tone. "Come, return to your seats. Do not be afraid of a harmless demonstration." And he glances over at George who is in the process of moving his chair so that he can sit down again. "So, does this answer your question as to the *divinity* of the Kassiopei?"

George frowns and looks at the Imperator. "Actually—no, it does not. Now I really have questions. Whatever kind of parlor trick this was, it certainly felt—the word *divine* would be the last thing I'd call it."

"No trick, unfortunately," Aeson says. "Our Kassiopei vocal abilities are real."

"Wait, so, you can do it too?" My brother George stares at Aeson.

"Yes," Aeson says, almost with a twinge of guilt. "I have the Logos voice."

And then Aeson looks at me. "Gwen, you might want to tell them—"

I take a deep breath. "Dad, everyone—about that Atlantean Logos voice. . . . Not sure how, or why, but I appear to have the Earth equivalent."

Chapter 57

"*What?*" The exclamation comes from Gracie. "Wait, is *that* what a Logos voice can do? But I thought it was just a really powerful singing voice for voice commands! You can *compel* people?"

But in that moment, *everyone* is staring at me. The Imperatris and Manala especially have the most startled, amazed, wonder-filled expressions on their faces. On the other hand, my family looks at me with confusion.

"Gwen, my dear girl, what are you saying?" Dad asks gently. "What is this Logos voice? Please explain, because now I'm getting worried—the Greek term 'Logos' refers to the 'Word,' as in the biblical concept of the Word of Creation—which is indeed a function of the Divine—"

"That's right, Dad," I say. "Except, this is not just a Word but a Voice of Creation. But first, I'll need to explain Atlantean power voices to you—"

"Do it another time," the Imperator cuts in. "For now, suffice it to say, your daughter has an unusual talent, almost never found outside the Imperial Family."

"But how?" My father continues to look at me with a puzzled, thoughtful expression. "I'm not quite sure I understand this whole thing. After reading up on it, I did manage to have some grasp of your sound technology, and can see how different sound vibrations and singing tones can affect this *orichalcum,* as you call it— incidentally, it's another term I'm familiar with but from an entirely *other*, mythological context—while your actual orichalcum is the basis of much Atlantean mechanization and whatnot. But how does Gwen's voice fit into all this? She is—all of us are—we're just an ordinary Earth family that likes to sing . . . and most of us can carry a tune quite well. . . . Margot, of course—she was the professional singer, but the kids—all of you are fine musicians and have very pleasant voices. But nothing out of the ordinary, nothing beyond talent—"

"Oh . . . God!" Gracie puts one hand up to her face and turns to Aeson. "Is that—is that why you are marrying my sister? Because of her some-kind-of-magical *voice?*"

Everyone stares at Aeson.

But my fiancé frowns at Gracie. For the first time during this fateful meal his voice rises to express intense emotion, as he exclaims, "*No,* of course not! I'm marrying Gwen because I *love* her."

The muscle of my heart contracts with corresponding sympathetic emotion at his outburst.

The Imperator makes a short sound of disgust.

Gracie appears not entirely convinced, but I say, "That's quite enough, Gracie, come on. Please don't be awful."

"Okay, sorry. . . ." My little sister glances at me, at Aeson, at our Dad.

"Look," I say, addressing my family. "I honestly don't know what it is that my voice does exactly, or where it comes from, but it seems to work at a high level."

"Wow, I just remembered that incident with the shuttle during Qualification," George says, rubbing his forehead. "You sang in the most amazing way and made the shuttle rise. . . . And there was more, if I recall correctly—that's *right,* you saved your future fiancé's life!"

"What? When was this? Gwen?" The Imperatris looks at me with growing amazement. "You saved Aeson at some point? Oh, my dear . . . why didn't you tell me?"

I give Devora a smile. "I promise to tell you about it another time, My Sovereign Lady."

"So that's why you chose to be a Vocalist in the Games," Gordie muses. "It wasn't just some weird fluke, or choosing an easy Category."

"No, Gee Three, it wasn't. It was playing to my strength. The best and *only* way for me to survive the competition."

"Which she did admirably," Devora says in a warm voice. "Again, I had no idea!"

"No one did," Aeson says softly. And then he gives a slow, accusing glance to his Father.

The Imperator attempts to ignore it and instead deflects the subject. "So, *Ter* Charles, now that we know about this particular talent that you share with your daughter, you're beginning to intrigue me. I want to know the extent of *your* vocal abilities."

"Good heavens!" Dad says. "You want to know if I can sing?"

The Imperator laughs darkly. "I want to know if you have the divine power in your voice as well."

"Father!" Aeson shakes his head. "This is neither the time nor place—"

"My Husband, please," the Imperatris adds. "Let us enjoy the *dea* meal and celebrate the happy occasion of the joining of our beloved children and our families."

"Yes, please," George says. "Because I don't think I can take much more of these revelations. I just found out my sister has 'powers.' If it turns out my father does too, what does that make me? What do you think, Gordo, are we 'divine' also? Demi-gods?"

Gordie just shakes his head in uncertainty.

Romhutat Kassiopei sits back in his chair and watches my brothers with narrowed eyes and an angled head. "It amuses me that you are still unconvinced, George Lark. Or you would not be making light of the reality that is before you."

"Oh, I'm convinced, all right—My Imperial Sovereign." And George makes an exaggerated nod with his head to the Imperator.

"Very well." The Imperator continues to examine George. And then he raises his hand and motions to the staff to serve the next course.

The rest of the Imperial *dea* meal goes by quickly and without any new disasters. Either the Imperator has grown tired of his baiting game or simply run out of outrageous provocations for the moment, but the *situation* has stabilized, and we are able to consume the next two courses in peace.

The Imperator mostly eats in unreadable silence and gives us masked looks, or makes monosyllabic noises in answer to gentle questions from his spouse. The bulk of the conversation is carried by Devora, who speaks about the details of the upcoming Wedding, asks each of us harmless personal questions about which dish we like best, and smiles at all of us.

Aeson looks at me often, to gauge how I'm doing. I smile reassuringly at him, and each time his expression relaxes at my obvious affection.

Meanwhile I constantly glance at my Dad to see if he's okay. My father eats almost nothing, watches and listens, and smiles gently if addressed, but I can tell he's growing exhausted. The health scare from the day before is still fresh in my mind, and it's clear that what he really needs is to rest, especially after such a traumatic afternoon.

Finally, the dessert course is presented to us—*ihamar*, an airy, frozen fruit delight similar to ice cream, but with the ephemeral texture of snow, meringue, and powdered sugar. Creamy dollops of *ihamar* are placed on top of paper-thin slices of melon-colored fruit—where they quiver with so much as a breath—and then drizzled in a delicate, violet syrup with an aroma of rose petals. As the syrup flows, it creates deep crystalline gullies in the *ihamar* and paints a delightful, abstract picture. . . .

I notice how my brother Gordie stares at his bowl in a kind of awe, watching the syrup run and form crystals. Just for a moment I am lost in the innocent delight of it.

And then I see the Imperator looking at me, at my Dad, at all of us.

What is he plotting now? Ugh.

A few minutes later we are done with dessert, and the meal concludes.

The Imperator rises and we all follow suit.

There is a weird moment of uncertainty, then Romhutat Kassiopei says, "Well, it's done. The Kassiopei has sat down with the Lark, and the traditional *dea* meal has been shared. Our children will be bound the day after tomorrow, and I must say I am more pleased now than I was before this meal started."

Oh wow . . . was that an underhanded compliment to us from the Imperator?

My eyes widen slightly, as my gaze takes in all of my family members. I find a variety of curious expressions. My Dad looks thoughtful, while George looks doubtful. Gracie and Gordie stare at each other and the rest of us, looking very nervous.

On the other hand, Aeson—whose fine nuances of expression I've come to read very well—appears slightly surprised underneath his calm veneer. As for his mother and sister, Devora is beaming at us, and Manala is blinking in relief after what must have been a long ordeal for her.

"On behalf of the Lark Family, thank you for the hospitality—Imperial Sovereign, Sovereign Lady," my Dad says in a neutral voice as he stands, surrounded by all of us, his children.

I notice he is making a great effort to remain upright, so I move in skillfully and take him by the elbow with a smile. On the other side of Dad, Gracie does the same.

"It was lovely to have you here and finally meet all of you," the Imperatris says. "I look forward to so many more relaxed occasions in the near future."

"Yes," the Imperator adds suddenly. "After this Wedding business is concluded, we have much to discuss, *Ter* Charles."

"But now we must let you and the Imperial Bride and Bridegroom go," Devora adds in haste. "Our children must prepare for the fasting day and the Wedding. The evening is almost here, with much still to do. At the end of thirteenth hour it begins for them, the isolation and cleansing time. . . . Meanwhile, *Ter* Charles, and George, you must still be quite exhausted after your recent interstellar journey and all the stresses of this new environment. So I recommend a solid rest, starting now."

"Thank you again . . . yes, very much so, agreed," Dad says with the lightest nod, and a genuine smile intended for the Imperatris.

"My Father and My Mother, my Bride and I thank you." Aeson gives a proper bow to his parents, then nods to me meaningfully.

I execute an equally proper curtsey, briefly letting go of my Dad's arm because I know Gracie has got him from the other side. "Thank you so much for the lovely meal, My Imperial Sovereign and Sovereign Lady."

My siblings echo me softly.

The Imperator gives us all a nod. "The next time we see you will be at the Ceremony. My blessings go with you, my Son and new Daughter."

And then we all step back together, this time inclining our heads politely as a family. Aeson and I lead the way, as we gratefully depart the Imperial Quarters.

The moment we descend to our own floor, lose the guards, and enter the Prince's Quarters—and yes, shut the door firmly behind us—it's like a relief bomb going off.

"Oh, my—!" Gracie exclaims, exhaling loudly as we move through the corridors to the living areas.

"Wow, just . . . wow . . ." George says in general disgust, walking ahead with Aeson to give more room to us, so that Gracie and I can support Dad on both sides as we walk.

"That was epic hell," Gordie says from behind us.

Now that we're alone, Dad slouches, drained of energy. "I'm afraid I need to sit down, kids," he says in a faint voice, barely shuffling his feet.

"We're almost there, Daddy," Grace says with a quick, worried glance at me.

In moments, we reach Dad and George's guest suite, and Dad collapses in a deep chair.

"How are you feeling?" Aeson asks, standing nearby. "Should I call the med techs?"

"No, no. . . ." Dad shakes his head weakly and motions with his wrist. "Just need a moment to breathe. It'll pass."

"Please let me know at once if you change your mind." Aeson watches him seriously. He then glances at me. "Gwen—I need to go check the workroom, will be back shortly. Call me if anything happens."

"Yes, go," I say with a light smile, knowing he has to go deal with SPC business.

Aeson leaves, and the rest of us sit around, talking quietly.

"Dad, are you really okay?" I ask, coming up to lean over him. I touch his cheek, then rest my hand over his. "Your hands are kind of cold. . . ."

My father looks up at me with a light smile, without otherwise moving. "Feeling better already. Had I been wearing a tie, I'd loosen it, right about now. Instead, there are these strange, looping buttons under my collar . . . all that decorative metal. . . ."

"But you *are* doing better?" I repeat. "Let me help with the buttons, they're definitely weird."

And I start fiddling with the expensive golden torque collar attached by means of chain-like button loops around Dad's neck and lying flat over the fabric of his shirt.

"Not surprising," George mutters, attempting to loosen his own similar metal torque collar while throwing careful glances around the chamber. Craning his neck upward, he peers at corners of walls near the ceiling and examines items of furniture. I'm pretty sure he's looking for potential surveillance devices. *Oh boy . . . George doesn't know about Atlantean nano-cams.*

"Well, that was a royal crapfest," Gracie announces, coming over with a water carafe to pour Dad a glass.

My father looks around at us and makes an amused sound. "You know, I did not quite believe that something like that was possible—not in our modern day and age. Gwen, my dear, you did warn me . . . about the *patriarch*."

I widen my eyes and pull up a chair to be near Dad. "There's just so much—so much difficult stuff to tell, some of it wildly unbelievable."

"So, are we talking cartoon-level villain?" George sits down on the sofa across from us and leans forward, elbows resting on knees. It's an engrossed pose of his, indicating that my older bro is ready to listen.

"Pretty much, yeah," Gordie says, pacing nearby.

"No, I don't think that's quite right," I say thoughtfully. "He is much too scary for a cartoon."

"How about a dark fairy tale?" George insists. "One of the gruesome and disturbing original versions, before they were sanitized for the kiddies by the Brothers Grimm."

Dad chuckles at us. "A real-life, unexpurgated fairy tale. . . . Well, well."

"Let's hope for a better ending in our case," George says, then yawns tiredly. The aftereffects of stress plus gravity are getting to him also.

"Thank goodness it's over," Gracie says. "All that remains now is just the fancy Wedding itself, and then the worst of it is behind us."

"The Wedding Day shouldn't be that bad," I say, trying in that moment to convince myself as much as anyone else. "For once, I'm glad for all that ceremonial stuff to keep *everyone* busy."

Gordie makes a grump noise.

"Now, to be fair," Dad muses, "today wasn't entirely terrible. Aeson's mother was such a welcome contrast to her spouse—gracious and kind. She worked so hard to compensate."

"She did." I nod. "Told you, Dad—see how wonderful she is?"

"You're absolutely correct once again," Dad says. "She's an entirely pleasant individual. A proper ally for an in-law."

There's a small pause as we all just breathe to dispel the pent-up load of stress, and think.

And then Dad inhales a deep breath and sits up slightly. "Gwen, is it true about your special voice? That you're able to compel and persuade others—such as what happened in that room, with most of you down on the floor—even his own wife and daughter—all kneeling in obedience?"

I swallow. "Technically, yes . . . but I haven't actually tried to compel anyone, nor do I think it's right—"

"It is not." Dad interrupts me gently. "It is unethical and immoral."

"I know."

"Promise me you will not go down that road."

"I won't, Dad." I let out another deep breath. "I hate it, hate the very idea of it."

"Good." Dad nods comfortably and pats my hand.

There's another pause. We all look at each other. At all our so-familiar, dear faces.

"Now, what's this about using singing voices to perform everyday tasks?" Dad asks. "Can someone please explain to me a little more how this voice technology works? We saw some of it during our time on the spaceship, implemented by the crew—rather sparingly, but—"

"Better yet, we can demonstrate," Gracie says with enthusiasm. "Okay if I call up the TV, Gee Two?"

I nod with amusement and let her.

Gracie clears her throat and sings in her clear soprano the easy command sequence to bring a smart display unit from the wall and "park" it, hovering in the air a couple of feet before Dad's chair. Our father watches the stationary levitating object in amazement. Unlike George, who got to learn basic voice commands and sound tech principles during Qualification, this is all new to Dad.

We take turns explaining to Dad how it works, filling in the basic details of voice commands, sequences, voice-keying objects with different notes. I even get into some of the more advanced notions such as setting Aural Blocks, heating and cooling orichalcum, and so on.

"This is phenomenal," Dad says when we're done. "Are you saying, anyone who can sing will be able to do this? Even without a Logos voice?"

"Oh, yeah," Gordie says. "Their whole society is based on this."

"You can do it too, Dad!" I say. "But only after you've rested enough—once you adjust to this gravity."

Right in that moment we hear unusual sounds coming from the corridor just outside the suite.

We pause the conversation, and our heads turn. . . . I recognize Princess Manala's slightly agitated, pleading tone of voice as she is talking with someone in the hallway.

And then I hear heavy thumps.

Khemji.

At once, Gracie and Gordie and I exchange looks of horrified amusement.

"What? Who is it?" Seeing our meaningful looks, George glances warily at the open doorway.

Just then, Princess Manala herself peeks from the entrance. She is holding a leash, the end of which is hidden as it extends into the hallway.

"Oh, hello!" Manala says breathlessly to all of us. "Aeson said it was okay to come by and visit, as long as you are not too tired." And then she quickly glances out into the hallway again and says, "Come, Khemji, you must meet the rest of Gwen's family! Come! Please . . . smart, brave boy!"

"Oh . . . yes, of course! Come in, my dear," Dad says, as his eyebrows rise slightly at the unexpected visitor.

He has no idea what's coming. . . .

Manala digs in with her heels and pulls at the leash, continuing to plead, "Just another tiny step . . . please, clever, wonderful Khemji . . . that's right! One more! Just . . . one . . . *more!*"

And leaning in with all she's got, Manala drags into view an enormous, very fat, very black cat. Khemji is resisting half-heartedly, and is mostly hauled along the floor by the harness that goes around his very round, fluffy belly and shoulders, and doesn't interfere with his neck at all.

Now he just lies there at the entrance, having plopped over and gone perfectly limp, and his tail is thumping on the floor to indicate minor displeasure. His head is turned to look at us, the round yellow-gold eyes watching the room with a feline expression of surprise.

"*Whoa!* What is that thing?" George lets out an involuntary exclamation and sits up.

Manala bends down and fusses with Khemji's harness, then manually pulls him inside our room, like one would drag in a heavy suitcase. "That's it, Khemji! We're here! Another moment—let me just close the door—and you'll be set free—"

"Set free?" George exclaims. "Are you kidding? What the hell? Is that a puma?"

Manala shuts the door, then turns around with a wide-eyed nervous expression. "Oh!" she says, looking at George in confusion. "This is my cat, Khemji! What is a puma?"

"He's absolutely harmless, Gee One," I hurry to say. "Very friendly, too. Just a very big domestic cat. This is how they are on Atlantis, huge!"

"Yeah, not so harmless when he farts," Gordie says, looking at Manala and Khemji from a distance.

Gracie giggles.

"Holy crap," George mutters, without moving.

I recall suddenly that my brother George is a little nervous around cats. . . . Not that he doesn't like them—he does—but he once got scratched up really badly by one of our cats when he was around seven, and Mom and Dad insisted he had to go to the ER for antibiotics just in case. Ever since that, he's a bit wary, even though he loves animals in general.

I notice, Manala has frozen in place near the closed door, uncertain of what to do, still holding onto the leash connected to the fluffy floor mop that is Khemji.

"Let me help you with that harness," I say, getting up.

I go over there, and together we undo the kitty restraints. The moment Khemji is liberated, he springs up as if nothing is wrong, and walks into the room with his tail held high. Then he stops and starts sniffing something on the floor.

Our Dad watches with an expression of delight, smiling lightly in awe. "Amazing . . . what a beautiful animal."

Manala comes closer, suddenly a little shy, and stands next to me as we watch Khemji explore the area around our feet.

"Princess Manala, my dear, we didn't get a chance to speak during the family meal," my Dad says, turning his attention to her. "But it's very nice to meet you and your remarkable friend. His name is Khemji, did you say?"

"Yes." Manala nods, her smile still a little uncertain with shyness, as Khemji gets even closer to us and starts sniffing everyone's feet.

"What kind of big kitty is this?" Dad continues, as Khemji approaches his legs and is so tall that he easily comes up to the level of Dad's knees. "Such a shiny black coat. . . . Very nice. . . . Is this a special breed?" And Dad reaches out to let Khemji sniff his fingers, then pets him around the ears.

"Khemji is just a cat," Manala explains simply, coming over to stand near my Dad. She watches him interact with Khemji.

And then Khemji decides he likes Dad's touch and starts purring. He has a very loud, rattling engine purr that you can hear across the room, and Gracie says, "Awww!"

"Okay, that is loud," George says with wary amusement from the sofa.

"Oh, yeah." I look at him with a grin.

Moments later, Khemji starts to explore further and slowly walks past Dad—even as Dad trails his fingers across the fur on the feline's back—and heads straight for George.

My older brother tenses up just a tiny bit, but lets the big cat sniff and explore his knees. He remains seated without moving, and watches, with his brows raised.

"You okay there, George?" I say.

"Uh-huh."

That's when Khemji decides to jump up on the sofa and settles down right next to my older brother.

"Oh . . . man," George mutters with a pained smile, pulling away to the side as much as he can without moving.

Manala immediately comes over to him and sits down on the other side of Khemji. "He likes to be scratched behind the ears and on his lower back—right here," she says comfortably, starting to scratch Khemji's sleek, hind area. "Also on his stomach, but sometimes he will start to kick, so probably best not to do that too much."

"Whatever you say," George says, raising one amused brow and glancing at her, still without moving.

In that moment there's a knock on the door, and Aeson comes in.

He sees us all watching Khemji and George on the sofa and gives his sister a meaningful look. "Manala, please make sure Khemji is *not* bothering anyone. He can be a little overwhelming at first."

"He is certainly a handsome animal," Dad says. "And very tame. Right, George?"

"Yeah, it's fine," George says after a smallest pause.

Meanwhile, I turn to my fiancé. "Everything okay? In the workroom, I mean?"

"Yes, everything under control." Aeson comes up to me and takes my hand, pressing it between his own two large ones.

I stare up at him with immediate adoration.

With my peripheral vision I can tell that my family members are watching us discreetly, probably with amused entertainment at our expense. I really want to whirl around and tell them to cut it out, but—no, it's just the strange wonder of it all that's messing with my mind right now. . . . The fact that Dad and George and the others can see me and Aeson be romantic right in front of them is just a little surreal.

So I tell myself—the silly, girlish, naïve, awkward part of myself—to cut it out instead. And I return my full attention to my love.

"Do you realize, there's only this evening left. . . . Only a few hours to go until thirteenth hour," Aeson says, looking into my eyes, as we stand in the middle of the room, in front of everyone.

"And then we have to separate, and cannot see each other for a whole day," I whisper. "So weird!"

Im amrevu smiles.

"Remember, the next time we see each other, it will be our Wedding Day."

Chapter 58

The rest of the evening and night consists mostly of gentle family time. Aeson and I sit next to each other, with few words spoken, only endless shared glances and fingers entwined, and we watch our relatives interact. Yes, *our* relatives, because Manala is still here, and so is Khemji, having fallen blissfully asleep curled up on the other side of the sofa between her and George.

The funny thing is, after Manala's initial shyness dissipates and she settles right in with all of us, she discovers she shares quite a few ancient history interests with my Dad. Over a leisurely *niktos* meal, Dad and Manala carry on a long, animated conversation about such scholarly topics as the contents of the Sekar Mehet Museum's Antiquities wing in New Deshret, and how it might compare with Earth's Hermitage Museum in St. Petersburg, the Cairo Museum, and the British Museum.

"If I understand correctly, the Imperial Poseidon Museum here in *Atlantida* is somewhat smaller than the Sekar Mehet Museum, which is on the opposite side of this planet in a nation called New Deshret?" Dad asks Manala, as she heartily eats a stuffed vegetable flaky pastry. "Is it smaller in terms of storage capacity or the number and breadth of collections? And are they both comparable to something like the Louvre?"

"What is the Loo?" Manala asks with her mouth full—so extraordinarily comfortable that she has completely forgotten to bother with Protocol.

"Oh goodness, I don't think you know about the Louvre. . . ." Dad rubs the bridge of his nose. "Very well, let's put it this way: would this immense archive in New Deshret be considered the largest national repository of any given type of collection? In particular, I'm thinking of library collections—manuscripts, scrolls, tablets, or any other form of ancient written texts."

Manala stops chewing, wipes a few crumbs from the shimmering fabric layer of the front of her dress, and lifts her brows in concentration. "The ancient scrolls collection is more extensive here, *Ter* Charles. But the Sekar Mehet is larger overall," she says. "But please don't tell it to the Imperial Poseidon Museum curators, because they will be terribly insulted. There is a very long rivalry between these two very big places, the same way there is a rivalry between our two countries."

"Fascinating," Dad says. "Much like Earth institutions. I would love to take an in-depth look at both their collections eventually, particularly the written texts."

"Oh, yes, those are in the Imperial Archives wing of the Imperial Poseidon Museum," Manala retorts with enthusiasm. "Scrolls from Old Earth, and ancient digital recordings from only a few centuries after the time of the First Landing and the original Colony. Some of them are so mysterious!"

Aeson glances with amusement at his sister. "Indeed, you are welcome to view them anytime, *Amre-ter* Charles. However, the comparable New Deshret collections will require a little international travel."

"Excellent," Dad says with a slow series of nods. "All in good time. . . . The dedicated scriptorium and bibliophile museums on Earth, such as the Vatican, the Matenadaran in Yerevan, Armenia, the National Museum in New Delhi, St. Catherine's at Mount Sinai, the Bodleian Libraries in Oxford, the Huntington Library in the United States, contain obscure wonders—or I should say, *contained*, now that most of their contents are here on Atlantis—and I've no doubt you have similar rare items of your own parallel history in your Archives."

"Now that I think about it, New Deshret managed to get some of the Earth's biggest art treasures," I recall, with a glance at Aeson. "The Parthenon, the Terracotta Army soldiers, the Great Pyramid of Giza—wait, how did they even allow the pyramid to be used in the Games?"

"What's this?" Dad pays attention. "Did you say the Great Pyramid was *used* in the Games?"

Oh, no. . . . The last thing Dad needs right now, seared in his mind, is the image of the Great Pyramid as a rubble of moving stones . . . or the whole mess hovering in the air and spinning like an inverted top. . . . Not to mention, hundreds of people peeing on it.

"Oh, you don't want to know, Dad." I roll my eyes. "Will explain later."

"It took special negotiation," Aeson says thoughtfully, after taking a sip from his glass of *qvaali*. "The Great Pyramid was originally considered too big of a bother to bring with us—nothing but heavy, crudely hewn, ancient stones, with little artistic value except for sentimental historical reasons and its designation as one of the Seven Wonders of the Ancient World. In fact, the Imperial Executive Council was dead set against it, and as far as the public was concerned, they were in charge of allocating most of the Earth Mission resources. But my Imperial Father suddenly *had his reasons*, and so he made an offer to Pharikon Heru. In short—New Deshret would handle all the interstellar transportation expenditures of the pyramid, and they will get to keep it."

"I see . . . how convenient for him," I say.

Aeson makes a mocking sound. "Oh, yes. As we know now, My Father desperately wanted to have that first *look* at the pyramid before giving it up to New Deshret. So he bartered for its one-time inclusion in the Games in exchange for *Atlantida* giving up claims to Dante Gabriel Rosetti and most of the Pre-Raphaelites—which went to New Deshret also."

"So much haggling. All these details sound troubling," Dad says. "What happened to the Pyramid since? Where is it now?"

"It's safe, and has been transported to New Deshret where it now stands in its new permanent location near the city of Heruvar."

"Well, that's a relief." Dad sighs and takes a small bite of food from his plate. "Wherever Heruvar is, it's just become that much richer in the historical sense."

"Hey, what happened to the Statue of Liberty?" George asks, carefully rubbing the top of sleeping Khemji's big head with one finger. "You guys rescued it, right?"

Aeson pauses to think. "It went to Ubasti. They were eager to claim it. The Symbol of Democracy holds a great deal more power in that nation than anywhere else on Atlantis."

George nods. "Good to know. Must visit there."

"So strange to think," Dad muses. "All these cultural treasures of humanity being redistributed and relocated on an alien world. Just—unfathomable."

"Oh! *Ter* Charles, we also have many small museums here in the city," Manala says in excitement. "Very specialized ones. You must see them all!"

"That's right, Dad," Gracie puts in. "The downtown complex is huge, and they have stadiums and theaters and all kinds of stuff. I remember several museum buildings there. What was that one, your favorite, Manala? Something with toys?"

"The Museum of Ancient Toys!" Manala's expression lights up. "I go there all the time!"

"I saw a really weird one," Gordie says, chewing a similar flaky veggie pie. "I'm talking about a tiny museum. It's not downtown, but out near the Bay. All they had were harnesses and bridles for *pegasei*. Those shiny trans-dimensional things. That's it. Just *pegasei* herding equipment. Everything from the most basic to these crazy jewelry ones covered with big multi-carat gemstones."

At the mention of *pegasei* and harnesses, I feel an inner jolt and a rush of disturbing and awe-inspiring memories from the Games, combined with species guilt.

Arion. . . .

"That *is* pretty specialized," Gracie says, sneakily adding more food to Dad's barely touched plate. "You sure that was a museum and not an equipment store, Gee Three?"

Manala's face grows very still, and she sets down her food. She stares off into space, and moments later her great blue eyes fill with tears.

"Manala?" I say, worried at once. "Oh no, is everything okay?"

"That's a *terrible* place," she says in a faint voice. "They have things to hurt the *pegasei*. You don't ever want to go there."

"Sorry, I didn't know," Gordie says with a small, guilty frown.

"We won't go there, Manala," I say firmly, exchanging meaningful looks with Gordie, then glancing at Dad, who looks concerned, and George, who just widens his eyes in an unspoken question.

"Manala, why don't you plan a museum outing for everyone after the Wedding," Aeson says calmly. "You know the best exhibits, and I think *Amre-ter* Charles would really enjoy having such an expert guide as you to show him the cultural sights of the city."

Did I mention, Aeson really knows how to emotionally ground his sister?

Manala takes a deep breath and focuses her attention on him immediately. She sniffles and wipes her nose and eyes lightly, then says, with a tiny smile returning to her lips, "I am sorry, *Ter* Charles and everyone. . . . I will be so happy to show you those *other* museums!"

"Then it's settled," Dad says with a smile of relief. "My dear Princess Manala, you will be our guide to all the wonders of Poseidon."

Our very mellow and pleasant *niktos* meal eventually ends, but not before it occurs to me that *this* and not the formal, earlier affair was the real Family meal of the day—all we needed was Devora Kassiopei here with us, minus the Imperator, and it would have been the perfect gathering.

A few minutes before thirteenth hour, a young priest and priestess of Amrevet-Ra arrive, sent by the Venerable Therutat and the Venerable Darumet, as designated by tradition, and inform us "it is time."

They stand waiting like sentinels clad in long, black and white robes, as Aeson and I say our farewells to the company for the night. Then, as our family members watch with suspended breath and gentle smiles, we leave Dad and George's suite and head through the corridors on my side of the Quarters to our own respective bedrooms.

The priest and priestess follow us a few steps behind—entering my personal quarters with us, and continuing onward, pausing only to witness as I stand in my own bedroom suite, at the door of the workroom which separates our two residence sides, and say goodbye to Aeson—for a whole day.

"Sleep well, *im amrevu*," he whispers, leaning in for a deep, slow, and very soft kiss, despite our stern clerical audience. His warm breath caresses the side of my mouth, and then we forget everything for several breathless moments of union.

When we come apart, with racing heartbeats and elevated breathing, I whisper, "Sweet dreams, my Husband to be . . . in only one day."

Slowly, like the rising sun, Aeson smiles, and it fills my whole world.

"It is now thirteenth hour," the priestess of Amrevet-Ra announces, raising one hand in a solemn gesture that points to the door. "Your Day of Fasting and Cleansing begins now."

Aeson nods wordlessly, casts one more intense glance at me, and follows his own priest into the workroom and onward to his own bedroom.

The door shuts between us, and the priestess—a young woman herself, not much older than me, if at all—remains for a moment to check the lock on the door between our residences.

And then, to my surprise, she takes out an actual key, ornate and antique, and locks it.

Next, she goes around my suite and checks the several other doors and connecting rooms, locking every one that leads to corridors outside.

At last, she stands before one of these doors and looks at me with a light, serene smile on her lean, ascetic face.

"Blessings upon you, Imperial Bride. Use your time of contemplation well."

And then she leaves through the door, closing it behind her.

A heartbeat later, I hear the lock turn on the other side.

Just like that, I am alone and locked in.

I must admit, I did not expect this. I knew I would be isolated for the day, but not *imprisoned*, literally.

For just one instant I feel a rising surge of claustrophobia and panic, for a complex number of reasons. . . . And then I take several deep breaths and tell myself to *stop*.

Get a grip, Gwen silly chicken Lark. . . . This is good, happy panic, momentous life event-related panic.

I'm in a comfortable, luxury suite with running water and bathroom facilities—yes, this is supposed to be a fast but I'm permitted to drink water. I can use my wrist comm to call for help—if for whatever crazy reason I might need help. I have my entire family down the corridor. And my beloved is two rooms away. My

Wedding outfits are ready for me in the closet. I've memorized all the required songs.

I have everything I need.

And right now, it's late at night, and all I need to do is go to sleep.

When I wake up, there will be that many fewer hours remaining for the so-called Bridal ordeal.

What ordeal? After all that I've been through, it's *nothing.*

So I go to bed and try to sleep, telling myself, I've got this.

I don't believe I will be able to fall asleep. But somehow, I do.

The morning of Red Amrevet 8 comes slamming into me as I wake up a little after eighth hour, having slept in intentionally. The four-point star window casts a strip of furious white light in my face, because once again I did not draw the curtains all the way.

I lie there for a few minutes, staring at the lofty ceiling that remains shadowed.

A whole empty, unscheduled day lies before me. What should I do?

I suppose I can just sprawl in bed for a few hours. Or I can take a leisurely bath—after all, it is supposed to be a day of cleansing.

Not *that* kind of cleansing, silly me.

I know, I know. . . . This is just my mind freaking out, and I've only been awake for about ten minutes.

How is Aeson doing right now, in his own luxury prison?

Is he awake already (probably)? Or is he lingering in bed like me (probably)? Is he thinking about the SPC business, and the alien threat, and the pressure of military decisions? At least he can issue orders on his wrist comm if there is an enemy attack and—*stop.*

Tomorrow is our Wedding Day.

If we could magically synchronize our thoughts right now, are we both thinking the same thing?

Is he panicking too?

Wait, I am *not* panicking. It's just that my thoughts are running wild. . . .

Maybe this is all part of the process of Fasting and Cleansing Day.

I lie in my bed for about twenty more minutes, then decide to get up and act like everything is normal. Which means, I do the usual bathroom things, shower, get dressed in some decent clothes, and then go to the other room of my suite, adjacent to my bedroom.

A tall carafe of water stands on a side table, and I pour myself a glass and drink, full of morning thirst and restlessness.

I check the time, consider messaging members of my family with my wrist device, or even texting Aeson. No, that would be so against the rules. . . .

How is Dad doing this morning? A sudden stress thought comes to me. What if he needs medical attention, while Aeson is locked up?

Calm down, I'm sure my family can get help if needed, I tell myself.

Hey, I could call up a TV panel from the wall and watch some feeds. Except—it's best if I don't. It would be so disrespectful of the nuptial tradition and inappropriate.

This tradition—it is intended for me, for both of us.

It's a benefit, not a punishment.

A precious gift . . . of contemplation and time.

I will spend the rest of the hours given to me thinking forward to the life before me—a life with my beloved. I will use the time wisely.

Suddenly I know exactly what to do.

I rise and walk over to a different table stand and open a drawer with some of my belongings. Here I find a small container with my personal items that I brought all the way from Earth in my duffel bag. I open the container and take out the tiny fairy locket of sterling silver, strung on a chain, a gift from my parents for my sixteenth birthday. The locket itself is an oval with a fairy etched on it in relief, dancing like a tiny winged ballerina.

I hold the smooth metal oval in my palm, weigh it, then finally undo the clasp of the locket. The two sides open like a book, revealing two tiny photographs—not digital but printed on old-fashioned photo paper. Mom and Dad look back at me with whimsical smiles. Mom is on the left, Dad on the right.

I blink and stare at Mom, hard.

She is already sick when this picture was taken, but she still has her hair. Beautiful, dark waves, framing her smiling face.

I continue to stare, and within moments, the image of my mother blurs.

So I blink, fighting to clear the liquid film in my eyes.

And then I remember that Mom is *here* now. She is only a few doors away—what is left of her—in a beautiful metal urn.

The tears come hard.

Sometime later—it is still morning—I make the decision to face what I've been avoiding for weeks.

I will watch Mom's final video recording intended for me.

Tonight.

Chapter 59

The morning and the afternoon flow into one, as I sit or pace, or stand up and gaze out through the bright window at the Imperial Palace complex rooftops, the distant gardens below, and the burning white sky.

My thoughts jump around in the enforced idleness—nagging stress thoughts (will I remember those song lyrics tomorrow, will I revert to being a klutz and trip on my Wedding Dress?) and happy anticipation thoughts (what will Aeson think when he first sees me, what will actually happen tomorrow night?) followed by different stress, then different eagerness. My family, Aeson, his family, the world, our new circumstances, all that's at stake, all of it passes through my mind in a rushing river.

I admit, there are quite a few times I experience sudden, overwhelming panic. What am I even doing getting married? *Me?* Yeah, I know. I'm out of control, drowning. . . . And then it passes and I feel fine again . . . for a few minutes.

Is Aeson panicking hard, too? Does he suddenly regret everything?

The only thing that anchors me is the thought that, as soon as evening comes, I will watch Mom's video. Why evening and not now? I don't know, it's just a random decision I made for myself.

The fasting part is actually easy. With all the nerves and adrenaline building up in me, I'm not hungry at all. I do remember to drink the water and keep myself hydrated. I can't afford to make myself sick for tomorrow. . . .

It's evening, and the teal sunset fades into slate-grey dusk.

I take a long drink of water, then stand up and sing the sequence to call up a wall panel, and choose a computer display as opposed to the TV feeds mode.

I log in to the Imperial Palace Network and scan a list of my personal files that I can access from anywhere. Technically I could've just used my wrist comm and called up a small hologram display, but not for this.

I want a real screen.

I find the video file that was transmitted from the velo-cruiser weeks ago, while still in interstellar space.

Then I sit down on the edge of a chair and move the screen closer to me.

I initiate playback.

The screen changes without warning, and suddenly, there's my Mom.

Her dear, familiar, bloodless face takes up most of the screen, with my parents' bedroom in our home on Earth, in the background.

Mom is propped up by pillows—I recognize the small flower pattern on the pillowcase—and wearing her prettiest scarf over her head. It's silky, dusky rose in color, with a faint etched pattern of swirls in the fabric.

Mom's skin is discolored more than I remember, and her lips are bluish-white and cracked, but the crinkles around her light blue eyes are warm with the smile that blooms forth.

"Gwen, sweetheart!" she says in an upbeat tone, even as her voice breaks slightly. At the sound of it I feel a sudden stinging in my eyes and an instant lump rising in my throat . . . even as I instinctively smile back at her.

"Gwenie-Gwen!" Still smiling, she takes a deep breath. And then. . . .

"You're my baked potaaa-toh . . . and my honey bun . . . my little golden peach . . . my daisy in the sun!" Mom sings in a breathy faint voice and then giggles, her voice fading weakly even as she grins at me. "Remember how I used to rock you and hold you, and you loved that little song! You're my Gwenie-Gwen! Still my Gwenie-Gwen, *always!*"

I start bawling, but immediately hold my breath so as not to miss a word of what she says.

"Gwen, my strong, brave, wonderful Gwen. Gwenevere *Athena* Lark. My brilliant daughter who is a young woman . . . a true warrior of wisdom. Oh, how I wish I could be with you now, and your lovely young man, Aeson, who I hear is as dreamy as can be. I know we had all these plans—plans to see you. All of you . . . as you continue to grow and thrive, have little ones of your own . . . I'd love to see my grandkids. We're going to be picked up and taken up to the big spaceship shortly, but this is just in case I don't make it. . . ."

My Mom coughs and I allow myself to resume sobbing in the interim.

"I have so much to say to you, my sweet darling Gwen, but it will just have to wait until I can put my arms around you. But I do want to let you know—just in case—that I'm doing all I can to hold on, because I want to see you walk down that fancy aisle on your wonderful, magical Atlantis."

Mom pauses and glances to the side, off-screen, where I hear Dad's voice and possibly George, telling her something, but she shakes her head and gestures with one hand to shush them in her familiar way.

"As I was saying, *magical* Atlantis," she resumes. "I hear it's beautiful. . . . Anyway, sweetheart, promise me you will continue to learn and grow . . . and love and dream, and make music and *sing!* Yes, George told me you're singing again and your voice is heavenly! Who would've thought? Aha—but we absolutely *knew!"* Mom chortles weakly, then rises up a bit so that her face moves even closer.

I tremble silently, tears pouring down my cheeks, not bothering to wipe them, as I observe the faint blue irises of her eyes, up-close.

"Okay, ready for this? I know, you're too grownup for this, but—here, pucker up, my pumpkin!" Mom makes a kiss shape with her lips, then places her fingers over her mouth and then lifts them up to the screen, so that the camera hole gets covered up momentarily. "There we go, big smooch on both cheeks!" she says, coming back into view.

Seconds later she rests back on her pillows, and just for a moment her smile dissolves with the effort, in exhaustion.

I sob raggedly, once, twice, then stop and continue to stare, blinking to clear my vision.

Seconds later, Margot Lark, my mother, gathers herself again and smiles warmly at me. "I know, I know, I look a mess, but don't you dare worry, sweetheart. Everything is fine."

She pauses, and her smiling eyes focus into sudden hard clarity. "Take care of them for me, will you, love? Your Dad needs you. . . . Make sure he eats! Gracie and Gordie and Georgie—remember, they all need you too. Oh, and of course, I need you—I need you to be strong and happy! And so, my dearest Gwenie, bye-bye for now. Not a goodbye, just a bye-bye . . . because I will see you soon. I love you to Atlantis and back!"

Mom pauses, smiling radiantly at me. Her eyes—I have never seen them so furiously bright, so full of *life*.

They are shining with moisture.

Her smile never wavers.

Those eyes, that smile—they are the last things I see. And now these details are permanently branded into my long-term memory, together with other profound things that will follow me for the rest of my life—as the video fades to black.

The room has grown dark, and I don't even notice. I continue to sit in silence, thinking about Mom and how I've just seen her for the last time.

My face continues streaming with salty water.

Finally, I get up and turn on the bedroom lights—forgetting, or simply not bothering with a voice command. Warm golden radiance blooms forth from the wall sconces, and yet I feel cold. . . . So cold and drained. . . .

I return to my seat, take a deep breath and replay Mom's video.

And then I replay it again.

And again—until I no longer bawl each time during the playback.

I replay Mom's video for the fourth or fifth time—now with only a cloud of soft, gentle sorrow blanketing me.

There are no words sufficient to express what I'm feeling at this moment. I'm so glad she made it for me. It's such a brief recording, far too short, hardly enough. . . . But a great effort, considering the severity of her condition by then. I'll be replaying it over and over, throughout my life.

I wish you'd met Aeson, Mom. I wish—

At least you got to know that I still sing.

So many never-to-be experienced moments with her still remain. So many soft regrets.

I miss you so much, Mom . . . infinite times infinity.
To Atlantis and back.
I sit quietly, submerged in the loving memories.

And then, with the passing hours, the weight of grief *shifts* inside me. Its burden is still there—will always be there. But now I feel an added sense of gentle completion.

I am able to *rest* now, to allow my broken spirit—all three parts of it, *ka*, *ba*, and *akh*—to begin to realign and heal, in this newly restored, fragile balance.

To that end, I must sleep.

It's an important next step, because tomorrow—in just a few hours—a *day of joy* begins, and I must be strong and whole and ready for it.

Chapter 60

I am awakened just after dawn on the morning of Red Amrevet 9 by the soft sounds of a key being turned inside the lock on my door, as the young priestess of Amrevet-Ra comes to liberate me from my traditional Bridal seclusion.

Today is my Wedding Day.

Aeson! I think at once. *How is he? What kind of day was it for him, yesterday?*

And then, with a jolt in my chest, the next thought is of Mom.

A strange thought—not unexpected, considering I've just watched her video—but odd in the sense that I'm suddenly doubting my own recall, somehow unsure if I previously heard her use those specific words before. . . .

I love you to Atlantis and back.

Those are Mom's final words to me, seared into my soul permanently, heard for the first time yesterday.

And yet. . . . When have I actually *heard* her say this before? Not quite the same phrase, but this part: *"To Atlantis and back."*

And then it slams into me.

During the Games—on the third day of Stage Two when I was on the pyramid having drug-induced hallucinations of everyone, including Dad and Mom—this is what Mom's hallucination told me, even as she told me to run.

And as it was happening, on the same exact day back on Earth, Mom was dying . . . maybe even had just died.

In that same moment.

I don't think I really believe in ghosts. At least, not in the traditional sense.

And yet . . . what if it really *had* been Mom? What if somehow—impossibly, wonderfully, defying all known rules of the universe and physics according to the established facts of science— her ghost, or spirit, her very *essence* made contact with me somehow, in that precious last moment of final departure? That unique phrase—what if it was used as a sign, to convey a truth to me?

I don't know.

And yet . . . my pulse races with awe and wonder.

I don't have much time to ponder this mystery, because it is time to begin the preparations for the big day ahead.

My heart picks up a beat as a wave of excitement hits me with fierce *joy*. I spring out of bed and listen at the door, but the priestess of Amrevet-Ra has gone for now. Instead, I check the time, and it's barely sixth hour.

In my mind I start to go through some of the earliest things on the Wedding Day schedule that are happening right now. . . . For example, the Tree of Gifts is getting disassembled, and the items are—or soon will be—in the process of being delivered from the Rotunda to our Quarters. In fact, I think I can hear the servants quietly moving in the corridor outside my suite. . . . Or maybe it's just the regular staff? I'm not even sure if the gifts will be delivered to Aeson's residence or mine—but it hardly matters since we won't even be looking at them until after the Wedding.

Though I do wish I'd had a chance to visit the Rotunda sometime in the days before, just to see the unique sight of it on display. After all, the Tree of Gifts is a once-in-a-lifetime artistic installation intended for the couple. But neither Aeson nor I bothered or had the time, especially after my Dad and George arrived, at which point all other interests and concerns flew out of the window.

Oh well, too late now.

The other things that are happening already are the final decorations covering the entire Imperial Palace complex and all of Poseidon. Much of it has been done already, festive structures going up all over the city throughout the week, but the final touches—the fresh flower installations, bouquets and garlands—must be done today. I've been informed that the work begins in the middle of the night, as massive flower deliveries arrive everywhere around the city approximately at the third hour of Ra.

It still feels weird to me to think that all of this is happening because of *our* Wedding. But I remind myself yet again, this is a national holiday as much as anything, the nuptials of the Imperial Crown Prince.

Knowing that all this activity is happening everywhere around me, that the Palace is awake extra early and additional staff is busy rushing around with the preparations, I try to focus on my own immediate schedule.

At seventh hour of Ra it officially begins. Servants will arrive for my spa treatments, and I will begin the grueling process of getting my *body* ready. And over on his side of the Quarters, Aeson will be doing the same, surrounded by his own staff. At the same time, my family and friends, many of whom will be actively participating at certain points in the Wedding, will begin getting ready also—as well as the Imperator, the Imperatris, Princess Manala, and many of Aeson's *astra daimon* friends.

At approximately tenth or eleventh hour, I will be putting on the Wedding Dress, the jewelry accessories, getting my hair done, and my Face Paints applied. The priestesses and attendants will arrive, together with seamstresses (just in case their services are needed at the last minute), Consul Denu with Kem, and the designer. The whole dressing process will take at least two hours. . . . And if that sounds intimidating and terrifying, it *will* be.

At thirteenth hour, I will be escorted to the Wedding Ceremony venue—the *Kassiopeion*, a temple consecrated to the cult of the Imperial Kassiopei Dynasty. Yes, I'm serious—my Bridegroom's Imperial Family has an actual *temple*, a place of worship, located on the Palace complex premises. . . .

There I will wait in a small chamber in seclusion, while the crowds of guests arrive all through Noon Ghost Time and until the first hour of Khe. That's when the Ceremony begins, and I will emerge and take my place in it.

Meanwhile, Aeson will also be escorted to the *Kassiopeion* separately and he, too, will wait, isolated from me by the nuptial tradition.

Both our families will meet us there.

The Marriage Ceremony itself will be conducted by the First Priestess and First Priest of Amrevet-Ra, the Venerable Therutat Nuudri and Venerable Darumet Azai.

After the Ceremony concludes at second hour of Khe, Aeson and I, now officially married, will depart together, followed by all our family and friends, to return to the main building of the Imperial Palace for an afternoon and evening of feasting and celebration at the Imperial Wedding Reception, which has both a private component and a portion that is open to the public.

Finally, at tenth hour of Khe, Aeson and I will bid farewell to our guests and withdraw to the privacy of our own Quarters to begin our *Amrevet* Night.

And that's the schedule for today.

But first, before the whirlwind begins, I take a moment to worry about my Dad and how he must be doing, especially since I didn't see him all of yesterday. Now, it's safe to assume that my siblings would've come by or otherwise contacted me to let me know if anything happened, and since no one's banging on my door, I should feel relief.

I get the urge to run down the hall to Dad and George's suite and check up on them, but stop myself—Aeson could be there now, and I'm not supposed to see my Bridegroom early, it would be bad luck!

Relax, Gwen, focus, focus on your own things to do. . . .

Then another stupid thought comes to me.

How did Mom know about Aeson and me? I thought my family were only told once they were rescued and safely up on the ark-ship, and not earlier? In fact, Aeson assured me long before the Games that he wanted me to be the one to tell them everything. . . . I'll definitely have to ask my family about it—but later. Right now, I am *glad* Mom knew—however she found out about it.

Right now, I need to focus . . . focus!

Just as I'm driving myself insane with random, stupid, stress thoughts, a light knock sounds on my door from the interior side of my Quarters. It's Gracie, still wearing her sleeping shirt and hastily pulled on sweatpants, barefoot, and looking equally stressed. But she immediately hides it from me with a wide smile. She's holding a tall carafe filled with some kind of colorful drink.

"Good morning, Gwenie!" my sister says in a hushed, excited whisper. "How are you feeling this lovely morning? I brought you a protein drink to get you going! This was delivered from the Venerable One herself, with strict instructions for me to make sure you drank it! You must be starved since yesterday—"

"Starved, not so much, but going nuts with nerves, yes—thanks. And yeah, I'm okay," I say with a smile, letting her walk past me into the bedroom.

"Here!" Gracie pours me a glass and forces it upon me. "Drink!"

"How's Dad and everyone?" I take the glass obediently.

"Everyone's fine!" Gracie pauses for a second. "Dad had a tiny little episode yesterday—no, no, don't worry, he's perfectly fine now!—so we called the med techs and they put him on oxygen for a few hours. Apparently, that worked like a charm, and he improved considerably."

"Oh no, poor Dad!" I mumble. "I should go check on him—"

Gracie puts her hands on my shoulders and squeezes firmly. "No—*stop*. Dad is having *eos* whatsit—breakfast with the boys. He is getting ready, and says to tell you to stop worrying and relax and enjoy your day, or he *will* be upset! You don't wanna make Daddy upset, do you? Right?"

I chuckle at her. "Okay, okay! All right."

Gracie pinches me playfully on the arm. "Good, now drink like a good little Imperial Bride!"

"Where's everyone else?" I ask, gulping down the protein drink that tastes like a pineapple and citrus punch.

"They're all where they're supposed to be! Which is, getting ready. Laronda texted me that she and Chiyoko are on their way with their outfits—troll boy is picking them up. Dawn and Hasmik are in the air already—Gennio's giving them a ride here. Now—where are your maids and the rest of those high-fashion hair-and-makeup people? What time is it? OMG, what *time* is it?"

"Not until seventh hour," I say. "That's when they all arrive."

Gracie glances at her wrist comm. "Okay, almost. . . . You've got time. . . . *Drink!*"

"Jeez! Yes, ma'am!" I laugh and obey.

I watch Gracie as she starts moving around the bedroom, picking up and shaking out my random clothes, undies and other stuff neurotically, putting them in drawers, taking other things out, checking the curtains—all while mumbling, "She is getting ma-a-a-arried, she is getting ma-a-a-arried."

I think my sister has gone a little insane too.

I don't exactly want to ruin the mood, but now is as good time as any. So I take another gulp, then a deep breath before letting my sister know. . . .

"I finally watched Mom's video last night," I announce in a tone that tries to be casual, but does not quite manage it.

Gracie stops singing and freezes, looking at me. "Okay—good. I'm glad," she says. "How do you feel?"

"Okay—now." I sigh. "Was a real mess last night. But I'm glad I watched it now. Mom was so wonderful. She even knew about Aeson! I wonder how."

"Oh, really?" Grace seems surprised. "We'll have to ask Dad or George—later. Now—big breath, and finish your drink!"

I nod and take more gulps. While I drink, Gracie says thoughtfully, "She didn't say anything about it in my video. She kept using my middle name . . . saying that I was a warrior already but I needed to remember that I was a *queen*. And then Mom said, it was the opposite for you—that *you* were a queen already and needed to remember you were a *warrior*."

I listen with intensity. "We should watch each other's videos— but only if you feel it's okay."

Gracie nods, with a hopeful expression. "Okay! Yes, I'd like that. . . . I think we should."

A t seventh hour a whole army of people arrives. Gracie is asked to leave and go get ready herself while my Imperial maid Aranit ushers in half a dozen servants who start drawing a bath and preparing spa treatments. I am made to soak for half an hour in fragrant hot water to which they keep adding essential oils, minerals, flowers, and other perfumed stuff.

Then I come out of the bath and lie on a table while they work on me like cosmetic surgeons—I'm only half-kidding—and I get every extraneous hair removed from my body and every extraneous skin cell exfoliated. When they're done, I'm smooth like a newborn, and that's when the soothing lotions and moisturizers are applied . . . and applied . . . and applied.

The shy nerd girl inside me is screaming to be freed from this personally intrusive, utterly mad, and inhumane ordeal. . . .

They finish and I wait for another half hour. Then they send me into the shower to cleanse off the residue and wash my hair with special treatments.

At last I emerge, and maids surround me with fluffy towels. They dry my hair, and I sit in a chair wrapped in towels while my nails and toes are painted with metallic gold polish by four people— let me repeat that—*four* people working on me all at once. . . .

While all that is happening, around ninth hour, the priestesses arrive early, followed by Consul Denu and the entire retinue. They open the closet and start taking out the components of my Wedding Dress.

Dear lord, here we go. . . .

"My Imperial Lady Gwen, blessings be upon you on your Wedding Day," Lady Isulat tells me, as she unrolls the delicate fabric of the *first layer* of my Dress, the under-sheath that must be worn directly over my skin, with only my panties underneath.

The sheath is floor length, an elegant creation of opaque fabric, but with long sleeves that slowly fade to translucence along the elbows and culminate in transparency at the wrists formed of sheer lace. It is body-hugging, starting from the softly rounded, lace trimmed bodice collar to the fitted waist, and gently flaring down past the hips into a cloud of gossamer. Its color is—

"How are you feeling this morning, My dear Imperial Lady Gwen?" Consul Denu asks me from a few feet away as he is directing Kem in setting up rows and rows of cosmetics on a special table.

"I'm doing great, thank you," I say breathlessly with a smile, as I stand behind a privacy screen with only female attendants to see me unclothed as I put on this first, most intimate layer. I raise my arms, letting two priestesses gently pull and lower the fabric over and around me.

I extend my arms further, feeling the long sleeves slide like silk over my skin, tapering delicately at the wrists with ornamental curving shapes formed by lace.

The sheath dress clings to me, defining my chest, abdomen, and the line of waist and hips, then falls loosely to the floor in an ethereal waterfall. Despite having excellent built-in bra support, the whole thing feels unobtrusive and light as a feather. The fabric itself shimmers like frost and catches the light. . . .

"It came out so perfect, so beautiful," I whisper with delight, stepping out from behind the privacy screen now that I'm fully clothed, and catching a glimpse of myself in the nearby long mirror. "I love it! I've loved it from the first moment I saw it at the Fitting a few days ago. . . ."

Lady Isulat smiles and is handed the *second layer* of my Dress by another priestess. "Are you ready, My Imperial Lady?" she asks, and unfurls the layer in its full metallic glory.

This layer is more ethereal than the sheath, the fabric almost translucent in its delicacy, and yet, possibly because of its metallic sheen, it retains its color admirably. I raise my arms again, and they gently lower the fabric over my head and all around me. It comes down, silky soft, fitting my upper body like a glove, and then again loosens and flares toward the floor, covering the sheath layer completely.

"Is this orichalcum?" I ask. "It's so amazingly fine."

The priestess nearest to me nods silently, carefully pulling, adjusting, and smoothing out the second layer over my under-layer sleeve.

"Micro-weave orichalcum threaded with a programmable nano layer," another woman explains, this one a seamstress who adjusts the back of my collar.

"And here is the third layer," another priestess says, approaching with yet another long fabric piece. This one is equally ethereal and similarly shaped, but flares slightly wider on the bottom of the long skirt. It also has a bit of a train in the back, so that the skirt sweeps the ground for about a foot behind me.

I stand and turn as directed, raise my arms, and on it goes, slipping over the other two. You would think that by a third sleeve layer I would start feeling hot, but no—it breathes remarkably well and is nearly weightless.

Once again, this *third*, shimmering layer completely obscures the layers underneath, and it barely adds to my outline, only flares my skirt and adds a train. The priestesses fuss around me, gently pulling and adjusting the sleeves and edges of the collar and the bottom of the skirt, so that this layer lies as smoothly as the others underneath it, without any hidden folds.

"One more," Lady Isulat says with warm energy. And she presents the *fourth* and final outer layer of my Wedding Dress.

I nod and smile in amazement, as once again the gossamer fabric adds hardly anything at all, and this fourth layer is put on me by the priestesses.

I move my arms, feeling no restriction, only a strange energy of spider-silk layers whispering over each other like four winds commingling, and imbuing the surface of my skin with electricity.

The skirt of this fourth layer flares even more on the bottom, and it adds an even longer train of three feet of delicate gossamer fabric sweeping the ground behind me.

"What a glorious sight, My Imperial Lady!" Consul Denu exclaims, clapping his hands together with drama and delight. "I do believe this Bridal outfit is a particular success."

"You think so?" I say teasingly, then spin around once lightly, so that my skirts pick up air and float around me.

"There is absolutely no doubt, My Imperial Lady," the Consul replies, then glances at the designer standing nearby with a pleased expression. "Your creation is fabulous beyond all expectations, *Ter* Uxmal. My congratulations on another fashion masterpiece."

Uxmal, the designer, makes a courtly bow to us.

"I just realized there are no clasps or attachment hardware of any kind!" I suddenly observe, continuing to look at myself in the floor-length mirror. "For some reason I didn't think of it during the Fitting."

"Yes, none on the three outer layers," a seamstress remarks. "Only a few attaching hooks on the first layer, in the back."

"It's stretchy enough that it doesn't seem to need it, and yet it's not annoyingly clingy," I continue. "How did you manage it?"

"Voice commands were used for this special fiber cohesion," Lady Isulat says with an almost mischievous look. "More shall be explained in a moment, along with your instructions."

"Okay," I say with excitement. "Now what?"

"Now comes Artistic Embellishment, my dear. Your hair, followed by cosmetics and Face Paints, then crowning adornment with jewelry, and a pair of exquisite shoes for your feet. Finally, the whole ensemble will be completed by the attachment of your veil," Consul Denu says, with a charming turn of his wrist, and indicates to Kem and various attendants to begin their work.

I sit down in the chair again (without worry, the amazing fabric of the dress is wrinkle-free), and this time I'm surrounded by hair and makeup artists.

Aranit, Kem, and two other attendants sculpt my hair into a marvelous couture updo, winding the long strands into a complex crown of braids that rest like a halo over my head, with chandelier filaments that cascade from behind to the level of my nape in crystal-encrusted garlands. More sparkling crystals are attached in various places along the top of the braid crown. Then Aranit approaches with a bowl of pristine cut flowers—my chosen Wedding flowers, the *dewa*, the *li-hereret*, and the *iyatet*—and offers me a selection to be woven into my hairdo.

Oh, dear heaven, I have no idea. . . .

I stare at these perfect specimens, the choicest blossoms of their kind, then glance at Consul Denu with a look of uncertainty.

The Consul understands my confusion immediately. He looks at the bowl, ponders for a few heartbeats, then chooses specific blossoms on my behalf: a single large white *dewa* for the back of my head, three blue and gold metallic *li-hereret* blossoms for the crown over my forehead, and four tiny lavender *iyatet* bells interspersed between the *li-hereret*.

The specific flowers are carefully woven and inserted into my hair in certain spots, and suddenly I see in the mirror that I appear to be wearing a glorious natural crown.

"Stunning, my dear," Consul Denu says, nodding in approval.

In that moment an Imperial servant arrives with a delivery for me from the Imperatris. The youth approaches me with an elegant box and announces: "The Sovereign Lady sends Something Borrowed for the Imperial Bride's personal use in the Wedding. The item must be returned afterward in order to qualify for this tradition."

"Oh!" I say with a laugh. "Yes, of course! What is it?"

Apparently Devora remembered our conversation about Earth Wedding traditions, especially "Something Old, Something New, Something Borrowed, Something Blue, and a Sixpence in Her Shoe."

The servant opens the box with courtly flair. Inside is a diamond and gold necklace with matching earrings. My mouth falls open. . . .

"Perfectly timed, and perfectly appropriate," Consul Denu says, and points one elegant ringed finger to direct the nearest attendant.

Seconds later I am wearing this borrowed Imperial set of priceless diamonds around my throat and my earlobes.

"Please convey my deepest gratitude to the Sovereign Lady," I say to the Imperial servant with humility. "I will use and return these as instructed."

N ext comes cosmetics and makeup.

Kem takes over, and begins applying the delicate layers to the skin of my face. Consul Denu watches intently and occasionally indicates specific colors and rejects others.

The look for the Wedding is heavy and dramatic, with shimmering darkness around my eyes for depth and richness. Violet, plum, and gold highlights predominate. My lips are colored a deep shade of wine with glossy *noohd* that has a secondary gold highlight, for a remarkable iridescent effect.

When the process is completed, I stare in the mirror in awe of the artistry—even a little frightened that I might touch my face by accident and smear this loveliness.

Never forget that Gwen the klutz still lives here underneath the glamorous Imperial Bride. . . .

"Thank you so much," I say to Kem and the Consul.

And then it's time for me to put on the footwear.

An attendant presents my shoes—gorgeous gold pumps with elaborate sculpted ornamentation and three-inch heels. *Yes, heaven help me, actual high heels.*

There's a reason I don't get to wear them until the last minute.

Because . . . Gwen klutz Lark.

I put on the shoes and stand up. Yes, I tried them on before during the Fitting, and they scared me then, as they scare me now.

I take a few practice steps, holding up my skirt with both hands, just in case.

I mustn't step on my Wedding Dress.

Don't trip, oh please, don't trip. . . .

I draw in a deep breath, then take a few more confident steps around the room, as Consul Denu, Lady Isulat, and all the attendants, priestesses, and servants watch.

"My Imperial Lady is a lovely Imperial Bride," Lady Isulat says in her mild, gentle voice. "And now—the veil."

This is the moment the whole look comes together.

A priestess approaches, carrying the length of my veil draped over her arms. The thing is sheer gossamer gold, floor length with at least a five-foot train. The fabric is etched in a delicate pattern of perfect geometric curves, waves, and curlicues, so faint that it's only discernable up close. Otherwise it is translucent, allowing everyone to see the wearer from a distance.

I stand upright, and three women drape the veil over me, attaching portions of it on my crown hairdo, then letting the rest cascade down my back and to the floor far behind me. The front of the veil covers my face and falls to my waist, but it is so sheer that I have no trouble seeing through it, and everyone can see me—except now I am surrounded by a golden cloud of radiance. . . .

"Behold the Imperial Bride!" Consul Denu announces.

"Are we ready to proceed with the final touch?" Lady Isulat inquires.

"Wait, no!" I exclaim, as my heart lurches. "Almost forgot! I need my 'Something Old,' and 'Something Blue!'"

"Ah yes, more of that lovely Earth custom," the Consul says at once. "Yes, of course."

Trying not to move too much in my fragile Bridal outfit, I point to the side table in the back of my bedroom, and Aranit my maid fetches the exact items I had in mind.

Something Old is my Mom's favorite gold brooch which she often wore with decorative scarves—something my Dad brought with her other personal things, and gave me two days ago, after I told him what I needed it for. I carefully pin it to my left sleeve on my upper arm, making sure it's attached only to the inner sheath layer of the sleeve and hidden underneath the three outer layers.

Something Blue is Aeson. Rather—a tiny lapis lazuli blue bead that I've 'stolen' from one of his outfits in his bedroom closet, with the help of Manala. It's on a string which I easily attach to the interior layer sleeve lace on my wrist and tie in a little bow.

As for 'Something New'—well, considering that everything else I'm wearing is new, I think I've got that covered.

"Okay," I say with a brave little smile. "Now I'm ready."

Lady Isulat nods. She and the other priestesses and seamstresses gather around me in a circle. They focus on me and the Dress with intense stares and rapt gazes.

And then they begin to *sing*. It's a gorgeous harmony surrounding an intricate melody line.

It is also a voice command sequence.

When they are done, my Wedding Dress—or at least the outer *visible layer* of it—flares into a deep crimson *red*, where before there was no discernable proper *color*, only a neutral metallic sheen of fabric.

Chapter 61

I stand like a crimson goddess underneath my sheer golden veil, and take a few moments to look at my reflection in the mirror. . . .

Who are you? I ask the strange, remote, glamorous being who stares back at me in solemnity. *Are you Gwen or are you someone else now?*

The Bride looks at me with her great shadowed eyes and her stark perfect brows, her cherry wine lips and her chiseled hollows of cheeks, from underneath her faerie crown.

Whoever *she* is, she is unreal.

All right, that's enough now, I tell myself, looking away from the mesmerizing alien creature in the mirror, and face the room full of smiling people all waiting for me.

"My Imperial Lady, it is time," Lady Isulat says, checking a small device. "Almost thirteenth hour, we must be on our way."

I take a deep breath. "All right," I say. "Let's do it!"

"One more thing before we proceed," the priestess says. "Your voice command instructions for the Dress. After you voice-key the Dress to yourself the usual way, you will need to sing the following sequence to begin the program—"

And she sings the series of notes for me three times, making me repeat it—which I do, easily.

"Then, once you're ready, simply touch the small raised control button in the middle of your waist to execute each command. Find the control now with your fingertips so that you'll know where to look."

I glance down and tap my waistline, searching along the silky fabric for a tiny raised object. I locate it at once and point to it. "Is this it?"

Lady Isulat nods. "Yes. But be careful not to engage it prematurely. That's why the sequence must be sung just before you make your formal entrance. It's a precaution to avoid mishaps."

"I see—makes sense."

"Indeed, it would be such a shame to ruin the effect," Consul Denu says with a smile.

"My Imperial Lady, your Dress incorporates the optimum placement of the control in an easily accessible spot for you," Uxmal, the designer remarks in a pleased voice. "It will not fail your purpose."

"Thank you again." I smile at him.

Lady Isulat curtseys formally to me. "And now, shall we proceed?"

The priestesses surround me, lifting the edges of my veil and picking up portions of the skirt's train from the back and making sure my way is clear. We exit the Quarters from my side, just around thirteenth hour, and get into the private elevator going down. I will be escorted by them all the way to the *Kassiopeion* temple structure, the Wedding Ceremony venue.

Outside, in brilliant white daylight, my usual security guards wait. A gust of fresh air engulfs us, and the fine fabric of my outfit immediately responds to the breeze.

Before anyone sees me and my Dress, the priestesses unfurl some kind of an umbrella and floor-length screen contraption made of dark fabric. It has four corners, so that I am literally boxed in as I walk blindly in the wake of Lady Isulat, who leads the way.

"Just a few more steps, and then you will have a transport to take you the rest of the way," they tell me. Apparently, the Imperial Bride cannot just take a relatively short walk through the Palace complex grounds—no, she must ride.

In this instance, I'm grateful. Because—hello, high-heeled shoes, meet fancy outfit and my inner klutz. . . .

I wonder, is Aeson also making his way to the Kassiopeion *right now?*

My ride is not what I expected. It's not a car, but a hovering platform with a covered enclosure and a seat for one—a kind of old-fashioned litter or palanquin, except it hovers and needs no human bearers.

Very carefully I get up on it, and the priestesses tuck my dress and veil around me, cover the enclosure with a fabric curtain to keep me from prying eyes, and off we go. There is a small window opening in the fabric from which I can watch our progress along the park grounds. I see my retinue and guards walking all around my transport, and in the distance the crowds are gathering.

And suddenly, for the first time, I get to *see* how the Wedding decorations transform and blanket the park.

My flowers! They're everywhere, placed in intricate arrangements in garden vases, strewn underfoot along the gravel paths, suspended in elegant garlands from other trees and landscape elements. In addition, artful ribbons and swaths of fabric in Imperial shades of red flutter in the wind, draped in folds of beautiful symmetry.

The noise is just ahead of us, growing in volume, especially as soon as the arriving guests see my vehicle and entourage coming.

At once there are joyful cries, and the chants begin. "The Bride! The Bride! Gwen Lark! Im-pe-ra-tris!"

I get the silly urge to open the curtain and wave, but that would be so atypical of me. Besides, it's not permitted for the Bride to be seen—yet.

The *Kassiopeion* building looms just ahead, taking up much of the skyline in this portion of the Imperial Palace complex. It is one of the tallest structures on these grounds, long and rectangular, with one narrow end incorporating a raised section with elements of a ziggurat tower and a flat-top pyramid.

I've never been here before—which isn't saying much since I've hardly had the opportunity to sightsee, having to deal with a crisis every time I've been to the Imperial Palace.

As we get closer, the crowds suddenly pick up a roar, but now it's coming from the opposite side of the long building. "The Prince! The Prince! Kassiopei! Kassiopei!"

Aeson is coming. . . .

"My Imperial Lady, if you are watching our approach, you might want to avert your eyes," Lady Isulat tells me from up ahead. "You might glimpse your Bridegroom by accident, which would be bad luck by our tradition. On the other hand, both of you are here at the same time, having approached together—and your synchronized appearance portends good fortune."

"Okay. . . ." I feel my heart pounding and look away from the tiny window to stare into my lap.

Moments later, we arrive.

S lowly and carefully I get down from the curtained platform with the help of the priestesses, and see that they have again erected the fabric screen contraption to hide me from any onlookers. I walk a few shaky steps in my high heels, clutching my skirts high, seeing nothing but my feet and the mosaic cobblestones of the path ahead—even as someone gathers my train from behind, and someone else picks up the veil. Yes, I'm still boxed in with the fabric screen, and yes, it's ridiculous.

Mustn't trip . . . oh please, don't trip. . . .

Then the screen is pulled back and I find myself at the steps of the *Kassiopeion*, before an intricate but low-hanging temple façade of no more than four stories in height.

Apparently we've approached the long rectangle building from its low end, where the roof runs flat, and not the elevated end with the tall pyramidal tower that rises sky-high. Even so, it is very impressive.

Gleaming columns of polished cream stone embellished with carnelian red, black, and gold reliefs line the entrance on both sides. Beautiful garlands of my Wedding flowers wind along each column. . . . The priestesses surround me as I take the five stairs and then stop before the grand archway overhang with double doors that stand open.

I take a quick look back and see the screaming and waving crowds of people lining up all around the structure, and rows of Imperial guards holding them back to maintain order.

The crowds finally catch a vague glimpse of me, a shimmering veiled figure in red and gold, and the roar swells. *"The Bride! The Bride!"*

But I don't linger, giving them only a heartbeat's glimpse of me, and hurry to enter the temple through the double doors into a softly lit foyer interior with a low ceiling.

At once Lady Isulat takes the lead, directing me to turn right, and we move into a small corridor, then a hidden chamber with a row of chairs along one wall. "My Imperial Lady, you will wait here for the Ceremony to begin. Do take a seat, for we have at least half an hour. In moments, they will begin admitting members of the Court, then allow other guests and the public to enter.

"Okay." I walk with great care, so as not to slip on the polished stone floor, and find a chair, while the priestesses start to fuss with my skirts and veil, arranging everything. The room is comfortable, designed as a waiting space, with a small restroom and washing facilities if needed.

My heartbeat is racing, and I listen to the loud sounds outside. *Where is Aeson now? Is he at the other end of the building? What about my family? His family? Our friends?* Crazy stress thoughts flicker.

During a small lull in the noise, I suddenly hear soft, distant choral singing coming from the walls and somewhere deeper in the building. Acapella voices of children and deeper rich voices of men soar in ethereal beauty, and I realize they are the voices of the temple priests. . . .

This is where time becomes weird, seeming to drag and fly at the same time.

As we wait, the priestesses around me speak in whispers, frequently meeting my nervous gaze with reassuring smiles. Now and then some leave the room to check on the status of things outside.

Then, judging by the renewed roar, the Archaeon Imperator himself, my soon to be Father-in-Law has arrived.

I take a deep, juddering breath.

Then the roar happens again for the arrival of the Imperatris.

"Not much longer now," Lady Isulat tells me, as she adjusts the folds of my veil lying on a chair next to me, to avoid the floor.

I wait, digging my ice-cold fingers into the cushion of my seat.

At last I hear the profound bass tones of Atlantean orchestral instruments similar to trumpets, oboe, and a delicate sprinkling of chiming bells.

This is my signal.

Taking a deep breath, I rise and walk into the corridor, with the priestesses hurrying after me, straightening my train and veil.

Returning to the foyer, I continue walking and face an interior set of grand double doors, where Imperial guards stand at attention, ready to open them for the Bridal entrance.

Then I remember. . . . I place my hand on the tiny control button at my waist and quickly voice-key my Dress, followed by the special program sequence. In those moments I'm hyper-aware of my own initially unsteady voice, but allow myself this breathless moment of weakness.

As soon as the last note of the command sequence falls, I can feel *something* happening behind me.

My golden veil unfurls of its own accord, and then, as the priestesses move out of the way, it rises, so that the edges float lightly, a foot above the floor. . . .

It levitates like an impossible golden ghost behind me, and its shorter portion in the front surrounds me in a gossamer cloud. The same thing happens to the edges of my train—it is delicately airborne, just a hairbreadth above the floor.

I nod to the guards, and as the bell chimes sound, they part the temple doors before me.

I enter the grand hall of the *Kassiopeion,* accompanied by a rhythmic chime of bells.

The room is immense, a long rectangle with a lofty ceiling, reminiscent of Gothic architecture in its proportions. This is the "flat roof" portion, stretching far into the distance, and culminating in the temple Sanctum—the differently shaped octagon portion underneath a ceiling so lofty that it soars into a tower almost three times in height.

A central path of pale marble stretches before me, covered by a deep red rug of matte fabric, edged in black and gold. *Thank heaven, a non-slip surface. . . .*

On both sides of the path, rows of waist-high stone pedestals form a decorative barrier, topped by flower arrangements, garlanded with swaths of red fabric and more flowers, and illuminated by tiny hovering orb lights that cast a warm gold radiance. All space beyond is packed with people.

The venue is standing-room only. Those who occupy the optimum visibility spots closest to the path near the barriers are mostly members of High Court, followed by Middle Court in the center rows, and Low Court in the rows nearest the walls.

As soon as they see me enter, awed silence settles over the crowded hall, followed by waves of gasps and whispers, even as the bells continue to chime. What must they think of my floating golden veil and magnificent crimson Wedding Dress?

But my immediate attention is on the opposite end of the hall—the remote, octagon-shaped space that constitutes the Sanctum, where my Bridegroom and all my family awaits, together with the priests. I can barely distinguish their figures in the distance, but I can hear the invisible chorus of acapella voices chanting and humming softly from the direction of the Sanctum.

I must walk the long path toward them upon the Imperial red carpet.

I pause for one instant, taking in the sight before me, and try to judge the distance of the entire path. I visually mark three spots along the path for reference points. . . .

And I begin to walk.

My veil and train float behind me as I move, with my hands held on both sides in a light dancer stance, as I've been instructed, to create the illusion of floating above the ground as if by magic.

As I pass, people smile and watch me with excited faces full of amazement and approval.

My heart beats so loudly in my chest that I can almost hear it, and I feel the racing pulse in my temples, even as I hear the rhythmic chime of bells sounding every few steps I take.

Aeson is waiting for me.

I am not sure which of the waiting figures he is—not yet, but soon I will see him.

I reach the first point that I've visually marked for myself, and very gracefully raise one hand to my waist. I depress the control button, then lower my arms with one smooth, quick move, opening them slightly. . . .

At once I feel a tiny whisper-soft *tug* and *rip*, as the outer layer of my dress suddenly comes apart at the invisible seams. The shimmering red fabric blows off me like a scarlet flame, and floats to the floor far behind me to lie in a pile of cobweb silk, revealing the next Dress layer underneath, in glorious lapis lazuli *blue*.

The crowd gasps and exclaims in reaction, seeing me suddenly transform before their eyes.

I keep my arms held slightly aloft, so that I appear to be flying, and continue walking, with my blue Dress shimmering and streaming around me.

Long moments flow by, accompanied by chiming bells.

When I come to the second spot along the path, I raise my hand again and press the button at my waist, then open my arms in flight. . . .

The blue outer layer of my Dress comes apart at the seams, flying from me like an ocean wave, to sink on the carpet, while my Dress is now a brilliant metallic *gold*.

This time the crowd cries out, and there are claps scattered all around, as the guests have trouble holding back their outburst.

I spread my arms lightly and continue to soar forward, completely clad in gold.

Aeson!

At last, I can see him now, standing next to other familiar figures, including my father and my brothers, and the Imperator and—

I come to the third and final spot and press the button at my waist one last time.

This time the shimmering metallic gold fabric layer flies from me, leaving only the solid sheath underneath, which is in fact a sophisticated, form-fitting Dress of pure white.

It is my *real* Wedding Dress.

How did I get away with breaking the color tradition? *I haven't.* My perfectly legitimate contemporary Earth-style dazzling-white dress is considered an *under-layer sheath* by Atlantean standards, so technically I haven't broken any nuptial traditions or rules at all.

After all, no Atlantean rule says I couldn't divest some of the layers in public.

Let the media, the fashion critics, and the traditionalists analyze *that*, at their own leisure.

All I care about now is the man I've come to marry, the perfect, glorious man who stands waiting for me as I approach the Sanctum.

Chapter 62

With a pounding heart, I walk the last few steps until I reach the Sanctum area and the group of people who stand waiting for me.

I admit, these moments are surreal. . . . With one secondary, peripheral part of me I notice that all of my family is here, all my friends . . . and then details blur . . . are seared on me, in sharp, brief, disjointed impressions that might come to me later, days later, when I think back—there's my Dad with an endearing, exultant expression on his face and wearing the Atlantean equivalent of a tux; there's Gracie, wide-eyed and crazy with happiness; George with a proud smile for me; Gordie looking sharp, but goofy and bemused; then my friends, the *astra daimon*, the Imperatris smiling like an angel—

Everything and everyone else blurs. . . .

Because in the next moment all I see is *him*.

Aeson stands slightly off to the right side, watching me with a gaze of impossible wonder.

He is wearing his Fleet Dress Uniform, white and gold—oh my God, with his Fleet Whites, our colors—*we* match! On second glance, it's a slightly different white uniform, more intricate and formal, with gold-threaded designs on the jacket top, and a heavy golden collar with a multitude of ornate insignias. I recognize some of the rank-designating combinations of four-point stars, and the eight-point star which I know is the symbol of the high command of the Star Pilot Corps.

Oh wow, this is his SPC Commander Uniform!

Over his uniform Aeson wears a magnificent floor-length cloak of deep lapis lazuli blue, which is his future Court colors. On his forehead rests the coiled spiral serpent emblem wrought in gold of the Lesser Uraeus symbol of Secondary Imperial Power of the

Imperial Crown Prince. And on his left bicep, I see the black armband.

It's hard to describe the complexity of his expression as he sees me. . . . His lips part slightly and there's awe, heart-melting warmth, mischievous humor, worship, focused intensity, vulnerability, raw need, unabashed admiration—

What am I saying? It's simple, really.

Love.

Aeson's loving gaze shines over me like the sun. I can tell his approval solidifies as he observes the entirety of me—my simple white dress, my ethereal golden veil, my flower crown and my face—because a deep, growing smile of joy comes to his lips and he slowly nods at me.

Having seen me as I am, he raises his hands to the clasp of the blue cloak at his throat and undoes it, removing the cloak altogether. He hands it off, without looking, to the person standing just behind him to his right—who happens to be Keruvat, also clad in the White Dress Uniform of the Fleet. Ker takes the cloak and passes it behind him to whoever is there—no matter. Now Aeson and I both match each other perfectly, wearing *only* white and gold.

I approach the last few feet between us and step onto the marble floor of the octagon that is the temple Sanctum, an eight-sided geometric space that connects to the long end of the rectangular hall—a grand circular chamber with seven walls, the eighth being the wide opening between the two areas.

The ceiling of the Sanctum sweeps upward in a Gothic flight of several hundred feet—so high overhead that I cannot clearly see it. The floor has the mosaic design of an eight-point star, with four dominant points and four lesser ones, like a compass rose. In the center stands a stone altar topped by a grand ceremonial chalice—or a grail. Four lesser altars are placed at each of the four dominant corners of the star.

People stand all around this sacred space in a semi-circle—people I know, our family and friends in the front, and solemn dark-robed priests in the back, along the walls. The Bride's family and friends are on the left, and the Bridegroom's family and friends on the right.

In the forefront is Aeson.

I approach him and stop about five feet to the left of him, so that now the two of us stand in symmetry, facing each other, with all others and the star altar behind us.

"Aeson . . ." I whisper across the short space between us, barely mouthing his name, smiling with all my being at him.

"Gwen . . ." he whispers back, warming me with his own glorious smile.

We may not speak any more, because now the Marriage Ceremony begins.

The chiming of bells that has accompanied my procession, ends. In the new silence, deep male voices of the priests start to chant softly, echoing in the grand space around us. "Kassiopei . . . Kassiopei . . ."

Then one large shape emerges from the row of robed figures along the shadowed walls. The First Priest Shirahtet Kuruam, in a floor-length black robe trimmed with gold, steps forward and into the center of the octagon, just behind the altar.

"Kassiopei! Archaeon Imperator!" Shirahtet speaks loudly, turning to the Bridegroom's side, and bows in the direction of Romhutat Kassiopei—who is clad in his formal Imperial red colors, and happens to be standing in the very forefront of the group on the right, just behind Aeson. "Permission to cede your Sanctum?"

"I grant permission," the Imperator replies softly, and even in softness his voice slithers with leashed power.

Shirahtet raises his hands and suddenly casts his own voice— which by now I'm used to hearing in soft, conversational speech— into a resonant mode of power: "From this moment until completion, Kassiopei withdraws and grants ritual dominion to Amrevet-Ra!"

Saying that, he leaves the altar and returns to the back of the Sanctum.

In the same moment, two new figures step forward, even as the priests in black and gold part around them. The Venerable Therutat and the Venerable Darumet wear black robes trimmed with white, and they solemnly approach the central altar.

The tiny old woman raises her hands and calls out in an unexpectedly powerful alto voice, without a trace of age or tremors: "The Sanctum now belongs to Amrevet-Ra!"

At once, from the back, comes the sound of sublime female voices . . . and Priestesses in black and white robes step forward, chanting "Amrevet-Ra! Amrevet-Ra!"

Their chant echoes resound, inducing chills of awe. . . .

Then comes a moment of silence.

The Venerable Darumet raises his hands and speaks: "The blessings of Amrevet-Ra be upon you! Witness the Marriage of the Imperial Crown Prince and his Imperial Consort!"

And the priestesses resume chanting. Their voices continue to ring with purity while the First Priestess and First Priest of Amrevet-Ra walk to the four lesser altars that mark each of the four major points of the star, pick up tapers, ignite them suddenly, and light the small chalices topping each altar.

The Venerable Therutat takes the side of the Bride and lights the two altars on the left. The flames that spring forth from the chalices are not ordinary fire but contain *color*—golden yellow in the chalice closest to the front and green in the chalice near the rear of the octagon chamber.

Darumet does the same on the right side for the Bridegroom, except his flames are red in the front chalice and blue in the rear one.

The four Quadrant flames burn bright, flickering with radiance, sending strange dancing shadows toward the remote, lofty ceiling.

The Priestess and Priest return to the central altar, carrying their long, lit tapers, and then simultaneously lower them into the central chalice, igniting it to burn with a white flame.

While this is all happening, Aeson and I glance at each other eagerly, nervous with anticipation.

Therutat places her burning taper upright into a holder on the left of the central chalice, and Darumet does the same on his side. Looking closer, I see that the rim of the chalice itself has eight small wicks, presently unlit.

Lighting them will be *our* task, soon. . . .

The First Priestess walks around the altar and nears me, stopping just beyond reach.

"Imperial Bride!" She addresses me loudly. "Lift your veil! Name yourself!"

My pulse speeds up. . . . With trembling fingers, I carefully lift the front edges of my veil and sweep it back over my head. My face and my flower-and-crystal crown hairdo are revealed for Aeson and for all the world to see clearly at last. After all, it is the moment of truth.

"Gwenevere . . . Athena . . . Lark."

Yes, my middle name is indeed *Athena*. Mom wasn't just using hyperbole when she called me so in the video. It's seriously oddball, and I'm a little ashamed of it, and yes, it's all Dad's fault. He gave all of us these antiquated middle names from Classical Greek mythology—supposedly in a compromise with Mom, who took it upon herself to give us our normal-person first names. That's how we ended up with . . . drumroll . . . Grace *Hera*, Gordon *Perseus*, and George *Nestor* Lark. We don't really talk about it. Okay, moving on—my thoughts spin out of control, returning to the moment in my *wedding*.

"Gwenevere . . . Athena . . . Lark," I say in a clear voice, with only a tiniest pause between each name.

The First Priest now steps forward, approaching Aeson. "Imperial Bridegroom! Name yourself!"

Aeson blinks, as though roused from a blissful daydream of staring at me. "Aeson Kassiopei," he says in his clear, measured baritone.

On Atlantis, there's no general custom for plural names. More so in the case of ancient royalty, where one name suffices, followed by the name of the Dynasty.

Thus, Aeson has no middle name.

Meanwhile, Therutat speaks again. "Who gives the Bride?"

My heart really starts pounding.

Because in that moment my Dad steps forward from my family group right behind me and gently takes me by the left arm. "I give the Bride," he says—speaking accented *Atlanteo*, probably for the first time in his life—a little softly, but well enough that his voice is heard down the hall. He then leads me three steps closer to the center, toward Aeson, and remains standing at my side, holding me with his comfortable, reassuring grip.

Oh, Dad. . . . My heart swells with gratitude.

Darumet now speaks. "Who anoints the Bridegroom?"

As I watch, the Imperator nears Aeson and takes his son by his arm, with a solemn, blank expression. "I anoint the Bridegroom," he says, then leads Aeson three steps toward me.

Aeson and I now face each other, standing close enough to touch. We look into each other's eyes.

"Fathers! Surrender your children to Amrevet-Ra!" The command is spoken by the Priest and Priestess in unison. They are using a form of command voice, because the urge to obey is powerful.

At once, both the Imperator and my own father relinquish their holds on our arms and step back, returning to the semicircle of families on our respective sides.

Aeson and I remain standing together in the middle.

With my peripheral vision I see both the Venerable Ones approach us and stand just behind us and slightly between. Therutat's tiny height is curiously in contrast to the rest of us, who tower over her. Though to be honest, Darumet is not all that much taller either.

But there is nothing diminutive about the power the First Priestess projects, as she places her warm, wrinkled hand over one of mine. Meanwhile, Darumet covers Aeson's large hand with his.

Suddenly our hands are turned upright, both the right and left hand captured and then forcibly joined together, Aeson's to mine, by the Priest and Priestess, so that our palms press against each other firmly.

I feel that inevitable moment of sweet shock at Aeson's touch. . . . Where our hands come together, skin to skin, the space feels like it's on fire with wild, new *energy*.

"Feel the Fire of Amrevet-Ra!"

It's as if the Priestess and Priest have read our minds; they intone in unison.

The *life force* awakens between our palms, and we stand and *burn*, palm-to-palm, not even noticing how Therutat and Darumet have both let go of our hands and released us to ourselves. . . .

"Bride, you must channel the Fire and Sing to him!" the First Priestess exclaims.

This is my moment.

I pause, and take a deep breath. And then I begin to sing a song that Aeson has loved since childhood.

> The skies above
> Are filled with love . . .

As soon as I sing the first stanza, from somewhere in the octagon chamber comes an instrumental accompaniment of strings and flute, as hidden musicians play along with me. Their sound evokes a natural wilderness.

Aeson's eyes widen slightly and his brows rise. He continues to look at me in amazement.

I continue to sing, smiling at him with my eyes. My voice soars in the simple folk melody, and the words cascade like silver rain.

> The light of day
> Comes out to play
>
> Your holy fire
> Consumes the night
>
> Sacred desire
> Burning bright
>
> I am your spark,
> I light the way.
>
> I am your lark,
> With song I pray.

When I fall silent, and the last instrument has faded into the distance, surprisingly, Aeson's eyes glisten with liquid. He says nothing, only nods once, and his palms press tighter against mine.

Giving us only a sweet moment of pause, the First Priest calls out: "Bridegroom, you must channel the Fire and Sing to her!"

I watch with a melting smile as Aeson straightens slightly and takes a breath to steady himself.

And then . . .

The first rhythmic, soft, smooth, oh-so-familiar twangs of guitar, piano, and drums start streaming from an invisible source, as the musicians pick up the beat. *So familiar, what is it? Oh. . . .*

Aeson begins to sing in his deep, rich baritone, like velvet . . . and at once I recognize the song "Can't Help Falling in Love"—it's the Elvis Presley version of an old French classic, "Plaisir d'amour."

Oh . . . my . . . God!

My jaw drops, and I actually break contact and let go of one of his hands by reflex, because I must respond by putting one hand over my mouth to hold back my emotional outburst.

Meanwhile, Aeson is singing, perfectly—the maudlin, sentimental, ridiculous, wonderful Elvis song which is so overplayed on Earth, and I don't even like it all that much (well okay, I do, but jeez), but here, now, across the universe—*it's the best thing in the world.*

I continue to listen, holding one hand over my mouth and trying not to giggle and cry at the same time. I even briefly glance behind me once at my family, who are watching with similar impressed awe and amazement. The only difference is—my family and friends aren't crying, are they?—while I *am* (no, wait, they *are*, too). . . . And so I devour Aeson with my gaze, struggling to keep myself together.

When he is done, growing silent—smiling at me as the last honey-caress of his deep voice and the final guitar twang fades—I allow one little sob, which escapes me despite my best efforts. And then I place my stolen hand back against his palm, letting it tremble against his warm, then again *scalding* skin.

There is a long, silent pause, giving us both time to compose ourselves, even as the heat between our clasped hands builds up again.

"Aeson Kassiopei! What is your Will for this Union? Speak your Truth!" Darumet pronounces.

With the fire coursing between us, Aeson smiles and looks into my eyes. "Gwenevere Athena Lark, with all my Will, I *take you* for my Wife, now and always. Nothing shall part us."

His words come soft and yet perfectly clear across the grand expanse—spoken in a Logos voice of power.

They pierce me with love.

I start to tremble again, but there is no time—no time to collapse or fall to pieces—because now Therutat addresses me: "Gwenevere Athena Lark! What is your Will for this Union? Speak your Truth!"

I open my mouth, and on my breath, like ethereal fire, the words come. . . . "Aeson Kassiopei," I gently utter the words of my soul. "With all my Will, I *take you* for my Husband, now and always. Nothing shall part us."

"By your Will and your Truth and Amrevet-Ra, you are now One!" the First Priestess and First Priest pronounce in unison. "Together you will now light the Sacred Flames to seal your Union in the Book of Life."

This is our moment.

Aeson and I reluctantly break the sweet contact between our palms and walk to the central altar. I pick up the lit taper on the left, and he takes the one on the right. We face the chalice from opposite ends and then gaze at each other across the altar space, with its softly flickering white fire inside the wide bowl. . . .

Gentle sounds of traditional Atlantean instruments fill the chamber—strings, reedy winds, and a soft underlying beat of drums. It's our cue to begin our duet, the ancient lovely *Eoseiara*. Aeson and I slowly begin to walk in a circle around the chalice. And in that moment, together we sing:

> **Eoseiara, eoseiara,**
> Near and far, my heart longs to stay.
>
> **Eoseiara, eoseiara,**
> Count every star, make no delay.

Every two stanzas, we pause to lower our burning tapers to light one of the wicks on the rim of the chalice. The wicks we choose are always directly opposite each other, aligned across the chalice. Tiny white flames spring up as soon as the wicks ignite, like white flower petals around a blossom core.

> **Eoseiara, eoseiara,**
> Brew in the jar, fire under clay.
>
> **Eoseiara, eoseiara,**
> Strum the **sitahrra**, hurry, I pray.

As we sing, with each stanza our voices seem to align more and more, the harmony so perfect between us that the resonance builds in power. Eventually I start to feel its tangible presence lift the tiny hairs along the surface of my skin . . . and I think that Aeson feels it also.

> **Eoseiara, eoseiara,**
> Door is ajar, waiting all day.

Eoseiara, eoseiara,
Sweetly we spar, time fades away.

Only two unlit wicks remain. We will light them together as we finish the song.

Eoseiara, eoseiara,
I am your harbor, you are my bay.

Eoseiara, eoseiara,
Over our love, nothing holds sway.

Our voices and the music fade. The circle is completed. And now the chalice burns in every spot along the rim, a fire flower blooming before us.

In the silence, Aeson and I stand enraptured, still feeling the *gravity waves*, the entwined harmonies and acoustics of our *voices* coursing through our flesh. Now our gazes are once more drawn to one another.

"Amrevet-Ra! It is Fulfilled! Blessings be upon your Union!" the First Priest and Priestess proclaim in unison, sending echoes resounding.

Oh my God . . . we're married.

Just as the incredible thought comes to me, I recall that the Ceremony is not over.

The Venerable Therutat raises her hands once more and addresses the hall: "Who Stands with the Bride who is now Wife? Who gives their light?"

A tiny pause. . . .

In the background, the Priestesses of Amrevet-Ra begin singing a soft, barely audible chant.

"Amrevet-Ra . . . Amrevet-Ra . . . Amrevet-Ra . . ."

And then I hear behind me, coming from the left where my family stands, my brother George's familiar, comfortable voice.

"I stand with her and give my light!" George says loudly, then walks a few paces to one of the four lesser altars, the one in the rear burning with a green flame. There he picks up an unlit taper from a small pile and lowers it into the green flame.

His taper ignites with the same green fire, and he holds it up, slightly above his head. Then George steps aside, but does not return to the back and instead takes a spot at one of the eight-point star rays on the mosaic floor around the altar.

The moment he's done, my sister Gracie steps forward. "I give my light!" she exclaims in a nervous but gutsy voice. Gracie walks around to the opposite side and picks up a taper near the chalice altar in the forefront, with the red flame. She lights her taper and it burns a passionate crimson. She remains near the spot.

"I give my light! Yeah!" This time it's my brother Gordie, speaking loud and clear. Gordie saunters over across the Sanctum space as if he's going to get something from the fridge. He stops in the back at the blue altar, takes a taper and lights it with cool blue fire. And he stands there, grinning.

"I give my light!" Laronda steps forward from my group, looking fabulous in her gold-and-blue dress, with a small corsage of my Wedding flowers on her bodice and in her hair. She heads directly to the front on my side, and picks up the taper from the yellow altar. Lighting it with the yellow flame, she gives me a shining smile and remains nearby.

"I give my light!"

One by one, my friends speak the phrase, then head to the altar flame corresponding to their Quadrant (mostly yellow) and remain standing in the spot forming a circle around the altar, holding their burning tapers aloft. There's Hasmik, smiling warmly in a lovely mauve dress, with my flowers in a garland around her neck, holding up her yellow flame. Dawn and Chiyoko are right next to her, in light blue and violet, continuing the circle, with flower-bracelets and more blossoms tucked in their hairdos, and their tapers raised high. Dawn nods at me with calm happiness and her yellow flame, and Chiyoko appears to be her usual, slightly nervous self, but smiles brightly and waves her green taper at me.

"I give my light!" Blayne's voice comes as a pleasant surprise behind me, making me glance just to be sure. He must've been hiding in the back; how did I not see him?

Yes! Blayne made it to the Wedding!

And not only that—he is staying upright *without* a hoverboard, as he miraculously levitates to the yellow altar as though floating, supported by a curious orichalcum vest that he wears strapped over his festive jacket. I glance at him with dancing energy, then glance quickly at Aeson and see *im amrevu* give me a mischievous deepening smile. What am I willing to bet that Aeson had something to do with this contraption for Blayne?

There is a small pause, while the priestesses continue to chant in the background, and now the Venerable Darumet addresses the hall. "Who Stands with the Bridegroom who is now Husband? Who gives their light?"

"I stand with him and give my light!" The speaker is Keruvat, and he walks with a smile to the blue altar, lights his taper and joins my friends and family in the circle.

"I give my light!" Princess Manala, wearing a shimmering violet and white layered dress, exclaims in a beautiful clear soprano, then lights a taper from the yellow chalice and steps into the circle. She gives a radiant smile to Aeson and me, and lifts her yellow flame high.

"I give my light!" Xelio takes a proud step forward, wearing the same Fleet White Uniform, contrasting so well with his gorgeous mane of raven-black hair falling down his back. Xel lights a taper from the red altar and joins the circle.

"I give my light!" Erita approaches in an elegant floor-length blue gown and lights a green taper before stepping into the circle. She gives Aeson and me a warm smile and a mischievous wink.

"I give my light!" Oalla is next, in a spectacular fire-orange dress, wearing my flowers in a garland around her neck. Lighting the yellow flame, she blows us an air kiss and enters the circle.

Several more *astra daimon* proceed with the ceremony, including Quoni Enutat, Radanthet Ulumaq, Culuar Efrebu, Nergal Duha, and a few more whose names I don't know.

Finally, when every single one of our relations and friends is standing in the great circle around us, with flickering flames of red, blue, green, and yellow filling the expanse, only our parents remain.

My Dad, the Imperatris, and the Imperator himself now approach the central chalice behind us, and light tapers using the great white flame in the center.

"I *uphold* the light!" they say, one after the other, and remain standing where they are before the chalice.

Both my father and the Imperatris smile blissfully at us. The Imperator, as usual, is more reserved. For once, he does not show overt hostility in his stone-like expression and even seems *pleased*, or at least relaxed, but neither does he smile.

I suppose it's the best we can expect out of him.

The First Priestess and Priest give us a few more seconds, then raise their arms high and pronounce loudly: "Who Stands with the Wife and Husband? Who gives their light?"

And suddenly everyone in the great circle of lights responds simultaneously, speaking as one. "I stand with *them* and give my light!"

Shivers of awe flow through me. . . . I catch Aeson's eyes in that moment, and they are full of liquid glimmer.

Echoes of everyone's thundering voices still rebound in the Sanctum when the Venerable Therutat approaches me, and the Venerable Darumet nears Aeson.

I glance down and see they are holding something in the open palms of their hands.

"In the tradition of Earth," Therutat says with a sudden light smile at me. "Take this Ring intended for your Husband."

Oh, wow! I glance down at her palm and see a slim golden wedding band with fine delicate etchings. It is meant for a larger man's finger. I reach out and take it with my own slightly trembling fingers.

Now Darumet says to Aeson, "Take this Ring intended for your Wife."

Aeson takes the smaller matching golden band from him, and I notice it has a stone.

"Exchange rings and seal your traditional Earth bond with a kiss!" Therutat and Darumet command in unison.

With a shy and beaming smile, I let Aeson take my left hand, turn it comfortably—even as I surrender to his strong, sensual touch—and slide the feminine band onto my ring finger. It is delicate and fits perfectly, and the sparkling, intricately cut jewel stone is an amazing deep blue color with purple and rose highlights. I have no idea what kind of gem it is, and I don't care! It is *stunning*.

Now it's my turn. Aeson watches me in amusement as I struggle to hold his relaxed large fingers, and carefully slide his own band on his ring finger.

It is done.

And now, the kiss.

I gaze at my beloved, *im amrevu,* turning my face up to him, parting my lips softly in anticipation.

My husband leans down, and suddenly his lips cover mine in a slow, warm, breathless moment of *intimate* contact. What starts out warm ends up *searing,* as a powerful stab of desire rips through me, and I tremble, even as we come apart. . . .

We are truly married now.

Oh, sweet God.

"Witness and Behold, it is Completed!" the voices of the First Priest and Priestess declare in unison.

And in that moment, the Sanctum fills with the voices of all the priests and priestesses singing "Amrevet-Ra!" and the entire temple erupts in a roar of cheers and applause.

"Go forth and be One, with the blessings and eternal company of Amrevet-Ra!" they proclaim, even as Aeson grabs my hand, and we glance at each other and laugh.

Together we walk down the length of the red path and out of the *Kassiopeion,* followed by continued cheers and song, and the echoes of joyful music and drums, and our loved ones.

Chapter 63

Aeson and I emerge breathlessly out of the building into the bright sunlight of Hel, and pause for a moment on the top stair of the *Kassiopeion* to wave to the crowds gathered outside. An absolute roar greets us, and the security guards rush forward and down the steps to make room and give us a safe barrier of space.

We smile and raise our free hands to wave, even as we continue to hold each other with our other hands. A levitating platform waits for us below—this one with a wide bench seat to accommodate two people, and open from four directions except for a canopy roof—and the guards and priestly attendants hurry to make sure it is suitably prepared for us, since it is also decorated with garlands of Wedding flowers, some of which were blown about by the breeze onto the cushions during the long Ceremony. . . .

A few moments later, having given the public a nice view of us as a couple, we descend the stairs. Aeson helps me step up onto the platform and take my seat, and then he joins me on the softly padded bench with its equally cushioned back.

The attendants voice-key the platform, and it lurches gently and then begins floating along its designated route over the paths, past the crowds on both sides, and onward through the park and gardens of the Imperial Palace complex.

I glance back and see our family and friends streaming out of the temple building, coming down the stairs. The Imperator and Imperatris have a similar floating platform transport waiting for them, except with two bench seats to accommodate four, so that Manala can sit across from them. A large retinue of the Imperial guards surrounds the Imperial Family closely as they take their seats.

Then my Dad and siblings get a platform too, with similar double benches for four people. Next, there are several more platforms, but I'm not sure who they're for, possibly some other

VIPs or even foreign heads of state invited to the wedding. The rest of our friends get to walk as part of our procession—which is so slow-moving that walking along is not a hassle but literally a pleasure stroll in the Imperial park. And in their wake come the priests and priestesses of Amrevet-Ra, a choir of children, and the temple musicians, accompanying us with music and softly pounding drums. And only after them do the rest of the guests follow, first the Court, then all other invited guests including a few select media representatives. Of course, the nano-cameras are swirling everywhere. . . .

"How do you feel, *im amrevu?*" Aeson asks with a mischievous expression, leaning close to me, even as I smile at him.

"We did it, we're married!" I whisper with a giggle, feeling his hand discreetly slide around my back and take my waist, pulling me to him slightly.

"Indeed, we are," he confirms, squeezing my waist while continuing to wave to the public with the other hand.

I giggle again, as though I'm punch-drunk, and ease myself against him, melting with long-needed relaxation. Then I notice how the fierce sunlight turns the blue stone on my ring finger to blazing fire. "It's so beautiful . . ." I whisper, turning my Wedding ring this way and that to catch the light.

"Not as beautiful as you," Aeson Kassiopei, my husband, says, craning his neck slightly to look at me with intensity. "You like it?"

"Not like—I *love* it! What is it?"

"It's Pegasus Blood. One of the rarest colors."

"How did this come about? I had no idea about the rings!"

Aeson laughs. "You may thank the Venerable One, whom I asked to incorporate this Earth tradition into our ceremony."

"Your Venerable One or mine?"

Aeson laughs again. "Who do you think? It's always the little one whose divine authority is uppermost."

I shake my head with happy amazement. "I must thank her *so much* for *everything* when all of this is over!"

Our Wedding procession moves slowly through the park toward the main Palace building, where we will have our Imperial Wedding Reception inside the Ruby-and-Pearl Grand Chamber.

We arrive, step off the levitating platform directly onto the Palace main entrance stairs, and then go inside the cool interior. Imperial servants bow and step back to make room for us and our guards, with doors opening in advance of our approach.

"Tired? Hungry?" I ask Aeson as we walk. "How are you holding up?"

He glances at me and raises his brows mischievously. "Well enough to dance with you many times over, and hungry enough to eat everything in sight to fortify myself for the evening. And of course, there's the um . . . *exertions* of *Amrevet* Night."

"Oh! Right . . ." I say breathlessly, holding back a silly grin, and immediately feel my face turning red.

Aeson sees my condition and laughs.

A t this point I must mention our reception venue. The Ruby-and-Pearl Grand Chamber is a huge banquet hall, rivaling the Pharikoneon Imperial Assembly Chamber in size. It must be able to accommodate the entire Court and then some.

Unlike the Pharikoneon, with its elevated Thrones set against the golden sunburst relief wall, which is used for the most formal, political, and imposing occasions, this hall is intended for feasting and more casual celebration.

The reason for the name becomes obvious, since the walls are deep burgundy, with elegant pearl-white trim and a domed ceiling that is also pearl-colored as if an immense pearl has been hollowed out and placed as a fabulous lid over the roof.

For the reception, a grand U-shaped table is to be set near the rear wall, with central seating for the newlyweds and the Imperial Family, with other relatives and friends along the perimeter. Meanwhile numerous long tables will be set for the Court, parallel to all the walls.

Our Wedding flowers are going to be everywhere—sculpted bouquet arrangements rising from floor pedestals, garlands descending from columns and cascading down the ruby walls. In addition, floral centerpieces will be placed intermittently along each table, enhanced with sparkling crystals and gold.

The central area of the chamber is free space, intended for dancing and entertainment.

Soon, it's going to be packed with people—the entirety of Court, foreign dignitaries, plus everyone else who's been invited.

It's our festive destination.

B efore we arrive at the venue, Aeson and I take a short detour to our own Quarters upstairs to freshen up. When we exit the elevator on the Imperial Crown Prince's floor and try to enter the usual way through Aeson's main entrance, we are turned away by servants who tell us that this side is being prepared for our *Amrevet* Night, and we must go around and use any of the other entrances.

Aeson and I look at each other curiously, but don't protest and backtrack to go in through Aeson's workroom. Here, once again, servants do not allow us to enter Aeson's side of the suite altogether.

"Okay, what's going on?" I shake my head with a combination of nervousness and silly giggles that have been plaguing me for the last half hour.

"We are not permitted to see whatever it is that's going on," Aeson replies, widening his eyes with a wiggle of his eyebrows that sends me into more giggles.

"Okay, we can both use my bathroom," I whisper. And so we give up and just go to my side of the residence where we take turns using my facilities, and gulp down some water from a carafe.

Here I also take the opportunity to slip into a more comfortable pair of matching shoes with minimal heels that will allow me to dance at the reception. Then I tap the button at my waist to run the dress control program one more time to "pin up" my veil. As if by magic, my veil pulls itself up from the back in lovely folds and attaches to the back of my dress as a new golden outer layer, conforming to the frosty white sheath fabric. Aeson watches me transform my outfit with supreme fascination.

We look at each other and I sigh. "Do we really have to go back downstairs and deal with everything and all those people? We can just hide out here until *Amrevet* Night!"

Aeson chuckles. "We could. You know, we could begin our *Amrevet* Night early. . . ." And he pulls me to him, and suddenly crushes my mouth under his.

I gasp, my breath cut short. . . . Instantly, I'm close to swooning with a rush of elevated sensation.

That's when Anu Vei walks into my bedroom without knocking, carrying a stack of boxes.

"Ah, *rawah bashtooh!* Crap on a Gebi stick!" Anu exclaims seeing us, squints his eyes shut, and nearly drops the boxes—while Aeson and I immediately come apart. "Sorry, *sorry,* my Imperial Lord and Lady! They kicked me out of the small office, then the workroom, and told me to take this work junk somewhere else until they are done decorating or whatever *hoohvak shebet* they're doing in there—"

"Anu! *Bashtooh!*" Aeson exclaims with a frown. "*Inappropriate.* How many times did I tell you to knock?"

Anu turns red. "Well, I didn't think you'd be here, it's your Wedding Day. I mean—sorry."

"Seriously, Anu, it's my *bedroom.*" I say. "Why are you trying to work anyway, didn't you get time off for today?"

"Yeah, I did, whatever." Anu shrugs. "Was going to go down later. Everyone else is going to show up late anyway, probably all your Earth friends who are always late—"

Oh wow, is Anu's blurt a not-so-subtle stab at Laronda now?

Aeson shakes his head and narrows his eyes, but I can tell he's trying hard not to allow laughter to break past this stern front. "Okay, just get out of here, Vei, and take this stuff with you. And if I ever see you walking into my Wife's bedroom like this again, you—"

"Okay, okay, sorry!" Anu grabs the stack of boxes and gets out of here as if his rear end is on fire.

Aeson and I look at each other and burst out laughing.

And now that our mood is broken, might as well go downstairs and face everyone at the reception.

When we enter the Ruby-and-Pearl Grand Chamber, it is full of people, laughter and loud conversation, and all our families and friends are seated at their designated places, waiting for us to make our entrance.

I tug Aeson's hand, making us pause briefly at the doors that stand wide open, just out of sight of those inside. The Palace servants standing in attendance bow before us, about to announce our entrance, and wait patiently for us to indicate that we are ready.

"Aeson . . ." I whisper, still tugging his hand. *"Aeson!"*

"What?" He looks at me in amusement.

"Um . . . your mouth—"

"What?" he cranes his neck at me.

"Your lips! There's a little bit of *noohd* smeared on them—my *noohd!* From kissing!" I finish in an urgent whisper. "You need to wipe—"

"Oh!" He makes a sound of startled laughter.

"Let me—" I say. And then I reach up and gently rub my fingers to wipe the side of his lips where a rosy-pink smear of my lip gloss has left a glaringly obvious trail. "Sorry I don't have a napkin—but it's okay, I think."

He leans into my touch. "Is it gone now?"

"Uh-huh."

He chuckles. "All right, am I suitably decent? Or do I still look like I've stuck my face in *eos* pie? Because *that* could be our excuse."

I giggle, then clear my throat and attempt to appear regal.

"Ready?" he says.

And we enter.

"Imperial *Atlantida!* Behold the Newlywed Imperial Couple— the Imperial Crown Prince Aeson Kassiopei and his Wife, the Imperial Consort Gwenevere Kassiopei!"

My mind is reeling suddenly.

Oh, my . . . I am Kassiopei.

We walk past the bowing servants and are met with universal applause and the sounds of oboe and trumpet, and the chimes that I now recognize as Atlantean processional wedding bells.

Everyone who is seated at the tables stands up—and that's the entirety of the Court—and continues the applause.

Aeson and I walk, holding hands, to the center of the upside-down-U-shaped portion of the main table, and take our seats at the head of the U, with the Imperator and Imperatris sitting directly to the right in the Bridegroom's section and my Dad and siblings on the left in the Bride's section. The families and closest friends do not have to stand up for us, but they clap also, with great enthusiasm. The Imperator does not clap, merely nods at us, as Aeson takes the seat directly next to him. I sit down next to Aeson, and my smiling Dad is on my other side.

Dad immediately gives me a kiss on the cheek and pats my hand, sighing in some relief. "Congratulations, sweetheart! So proud and happy for you and Aeson!"

"Thanks, Daddy!" I whisper near his ear, beaming at him.

On the other side of my father, George, Gordie, and Gracie all lean toward me with silly-happy grins and offer congratulations.

"Way to go, sis! Amazingly well done," George says, nodding in my direction with a crooked grin.

"Air hug! Air hug!" Gracie waves at me and gesticulates blown kisses, since this part of the Reception is still formal and she cannot exactly get up and squish-hug me.

"You rocked it!" Gordie says.

I smile back at them, so much that it hurts. And then I grin and continue smiling and waving and making subdued but silly faces, this time at the rest of my friends who sit farther down the table. And then I switch to look in the other direction, and smile at the Imperatris and Manala, and an unfamiliar older couple sitting next to her, and some of the *astra daimon* whom I can see.

Meanwhile, Aeson is doing the same thing, grinning at his Mother, sister, the distinguished elderly couple with friendly expressions who must be his maternal grandparents, and his friends, then turning to nod and smile at my Dad and the rest of my family and friends.

The moment we are seated, soft music begins to play, and servers start carrying huge dishes for our Wedding Feast. Others bring around bottles of *shedehur*, the popular Atlantean alcoholic beverage similar to red wine, which pours in a persimmon-amber colored liquid and has the scent of crisp apples.

My glass is filled at once, and Aeson tells me to watch out because this drink can be very strong, even as he picks up his own. I sip the *shedehur*, and it does taste a little like apple juice at first, and then the alcohol hits.

"My Imperial Lady, apologies, but only one glass is permitted to the Newlyweds," a *shedehur* server tells me politely as he moves by with bottles, even though I haven't asked for a refill, nor do I plan to.

Meanwhile, aromatic main dishes are brought out, one after another, and I recall going over the menu earlier during the planning stage, and feel a moment of surreal amazement that I had some part in *making* this feast, or at least directing its creation.

Normally, Atlanteans don't do drinking toasts—though they do make "dry" speeches and formal pronouncements—but this isn't going to stop those of us from Earth in engaging in that old tradition.

Periodically I hear voices call out around the tables congratulating the Newlyweds, and each time the Earthies raise their glasses and drink, which the Atlanteans find slightly odd.

I look around the room, trying to catch a glimpse of any familiar faces among the invited guests. So many VIPs and members of the nobility fill the nearest seats. There's the Oratorat of Eos-Heket, Kephasa Sewu, and a few seats down I think that's Wilem Paeh, the Crown Hereret of Vai Naat. There are probably other heads of state or their ambassadors, but I'm not sure who they are.

Finally, I see a table with this year's Grail Games Champions, all of whom have been invited to the Wedding. I recognize Kokayi's rainbow braids from the distance, and he turns and meets my gaze, waving at me with friendly enthusiasm. I smile and wave back across the distance, then see Kateb and his wife Yeraz, and Hedj Kukkait, and several others. Then my gaze falls on Brie Walton—stunning in formal wear, with her hair up—she's sitting next to Logan Sangre.

Okay, this is both unexpected and yet somehow unsurprising, and very much in character. I start to wonder if Logan is still playing along with Brie's crazy Champion "wish" to be at her beck and call for three months of freaky "indentured servitude." Or is Logan here as her *date?* Because seriously, this seems to be heading that way . . . and yet, what kind of weird relationship can it be?

Even as I ponder, Brie turns her head, her long chandelier earrings hitting the lights with hard sparkle, and sees me looking at her. At once she smiles with a flash of teeth and gives me her typical mocking salute.

Next to her, Logan pauses drinking from his glass and notices the change in Brie's attention. At once he also looks at me, freezing for one instant. Then he gives me a calm nod and a tiny smile, and tips his glass in my direction.

I smile back at both of them, in that moment letting whatever old feelings of weirdness evaporate. Because, honestly, I am no longer bothered by what Logan does or whom he may or may not be dating. And I certainly wish Brie the best—she earned it.

More and more dishes get served, and more bottles of *shedehur* circulate endlessly, together with other milder drinks for those of us who would prefer to stay sober. About an hour later, when most of us are close to done with eating—and have lost some of the inhibitions—the less formal portion begins.

"Time for dancing soon, it's about to begin," Aeson says close to my ear, while his fingers press my hand under the table, sending sweet, sensual chills up my arm.

"Oh, yes!" I say with excitement, entwining my fingers with his. Aeson and I are supposed to begin the dancing in order to open the festivities for the others, and the traditional wedding dance is the *irephuru*, which is an ancient and intricate circle dance.

I must say, ever since I learned about it, and in the process of learning how to *dance* it, I've found *irephuru* fascinating. It is based on circles, yes, but concentric circles—like the original city of Poseidon on Ancient Atlantis, back on Earth.

The Bride and Groom—that is, Newlywed Wife and Husband—step into the center of the dance floor, and perform a number of intricate, elegant dance figures, circling each other, and variously holding hands or briefly embracing. The key is never to embrace for more than three heartbeats. At the same time, the couple must maintain eye contact, and not look away for longer than three heartbeats.

After about a minute, others may join the dance, but they can only do so by forming a second circle of four people around the couple. As more and more people join the dance, the third circle must have eight people, and the next sixteen, after which the count stops and the fifth circle can be as large as people want, and so on.

The concentric circles of dancers spin in opposite directions, holding hands, then breaking contact to perform figures, then clasping hands again, in a dizzying but energetic ride. Meanwhile, the objective for the central couple is to escape outward and get out of the circle, but it can only be done by swapping with a random person in the next circle.

When you're ready to quit the center position, you pull a random person from the outside circle into your spot and take theirs, while your partner quickly does the same. Continue doing this, moving outward from circle to circle, to get out of the dance. But watch out, someone else might try to pull you back inward!

And now, imagine what *that's* like once everyone in the room is buzzed on *shedehur*.

In short, it's a crazy dance, and tons of fun.

"Irephuru! Irephuru!" the call-outs begin. And soon everyone is clapping and calling for the popular wedding dance to start.

Aeson and I stand up. We look at each other. . . . Suddenly I feel a shrinking terror in my gut, because the whole world is watching, and unbeknownst to them, I'm still Gwen the klutz, deep inside, and I only just learned this dance.

What if I screw up and embarrass Aeson?

And then I tell my inner klutz to shut up already, and I take Aeson's hand. With a show of confidence, I walk with him to the center of the dance floor.

A slow beat of drums starts. We begin by circling each other, then holding hands, then place them palm to palm in an echo of our moment of sensual burning during the Marriage Ceremony. We release each other and clap our hands . . . and a sweet intoning reed pipe joins the drumbeat.

We circle each other again, change direction, spin, return palm to palm, then release, clap again . . . and now the strings of the *sitahrra* strum in rhythm, setting our blood to fire.

Did I mention this is a very elegant and intense dance? There are echoes of Spanish flamenco, Georgian lezginka, and other Earth folk traditions in the sharp upright movements and the proud bearing we must maintain.

We continue moving, faster and faster, and I'm fortunate that Aeson is a fantastic dancer. He moves effortlessly, and even during those brief glimpses of him as I move and spin, I continue to marvel at the masculine beauty of his taut, powerful body underneath his white military uniform. It must come from all that Er-Du sparring of which he is a master. In many ways, all martial arts are a form of controlled dance, and the opponents are adversarial partners, riffing off each other.

Suffice it to say, we perform our solitary dance without mishap.

Moments later, I see Oalla and Keruvat stand up, followed by Erita and Radanthet, and they enter the dance floor, approaching us to form the second circle around us. At this point the music is loud and fast, and the beat of the drums is electrifying.

Then other couples get up, all around the chamber, and form the third circle, and so on, until the dance floor is full of circles of people laughing and spinning and clapping hands, pressing palms together and spinning again.

I'm completely breathless, and Aeson notices, so it's time for us to "escape" the spot in the center. We exchange meaningful glances and then quickly pull Erita and Radanthet into our places, and spin outward, taking their spots, and surprising Ker and Oalla who expected us to grab *them*. I laugh and Aeson laughs, and we continue moving quickly, grabbing the next couple closest to us in the third circle—the key is to do it fast before they suspect they are the targets and evade us—once tagged, you have to switch places, by the rules of the dance.

A few moments later, we get "out" of the dance and return to our seats, breathing hard from exertion and laughing. The Imperator gives his son and me an *almost* amused glance, but says nothing. Devora on the other hand, waves to us, so we get up and walk over to say hello. The formal constraints are gone, and we can now move freely about the room and greet people.

"Gwen, I want to introduce you to my Grandparents," Aeson says, even as Devora nods at us reassuringly.

The Imperatris then glances past Manala to a mild-mannered, handsome older man in a dark green robe over a cream shirt with a heavy gilded collar. His hair is the same color as hers, a rich reddish brown, except it is threaded with a lot of silver. Next to him sits a pleasant older woman in a pale rose dress, with graceful features, her dark brown hair similarly threaded with lighter strands, gathered in a low bun with a golden net over it, and elegant, simple pearl studs in her earlobes.

"Oh, yes!" I say with an excited glance at Devora who continues to smile at me and gestures with her eyes in the direction of her parents.

We approach the older couple who watch us with soft, warm smiles.

"Grandfather, Grandmother, may I introduce Gwen, my new Wife," Aeson says with a respectful bow. And then he turns to me.

"Gwen, this is Lord Tutanamat Argosaen and First Lady Irumala Argosaen—my grandparents."

"I am so glad to meet you!" I step closer and curtsey, then lean in to speak.

Lord Argosaen reaches out and places his thin hand over mine, patting it, and says in a thick English accent. "Very bootiful . . . good, good." And then he switches over to *Atlanteo* and says, "Such a lovely Bride for Aeson, I've heard so much about you from my daughter, very impressed, my dear."

"*Chuvuat*, Lord Argosaen," I say, which means "thank you" in *Atlanteo*.

"Not Bride, Tuta. She is now his Wife—*Wife*," the woman next to him says in *Atlanteo*, with an amused and slightly exasperated tone, patting him on his arm. And then she looks up at me with a mischievous and charming crinkled smile. "My dear, you are lovely indeed, and I am so sorry I haven't properly learned your English language yet, but I am working on it. Maybe you can help me with it. My Husband can speak a few words more than me, of which he is very proud. Right, Tuta?"

"Eh?" Lord Argosaen says, leaning closer to his wife.

"I said—" and Lady Argosaen repeats her words near his ear, then looks at me with a humorous and conspiratorial roll of her eyes. "My Husband needs to get his hearing fixed—such an easy procedure—but he refuses, for years."

"Oh," I say, smiling and unsure of how to respond. "That's okay."

Next to me, Aeson chuckles.

"You go on now, enjoy your Wedding Day," Lady Argosaen says, waving at both of us with her wrist. "We'll talk later. So much good talk to be had, *im saai*. . . . All in good time. Now is a different good time."

I can tell I'm going to love Aeson's grandparents. . . .

And then I happen to glance over Lord Argosaen and see his granddaughter Manala watching us wistfully from her spot, sandwiched between her mother and her grandfather.

"Manala, why aren't you dancing?" I ask the Princess who sits on the edge of her seat, looking eager but shy.

"Oh, I will . . . maybe later," she replies, with a nervous glance past her Mother and in her Imperial Father's direction. It is definitely best not to press her.

We continue to mingle, this time moving in the direction of my family and friends.

"How are you feeling, Dad?" I ask my father, seeing him leaning forward against the table, observing the dancers with curiosity.

"Doing great, don't you worry about me," Dad says comfortably, glancing at George and Gracie.

"What about you, George?" I turn to my brother. "You know, they should be playing other kinds of music soon, Earth music too, so you might want to get up and dance."

"Oh yeah?" George says, winking at me and nodding at Aeson. "Sounds good to me."

"You are a marvelous dancer, Aeson," Dad says to my husband. "Watching you two out there is a pleasure."

"Thank you, *Amre-ter* Charles." Aeson smiles. "Your daughter makes it easy."

Dad turns to me with a chuckle. "He's a smooth talker, too."

"Oh, Daddy." I giggle.

Aeson shakes his head with amusement and heads over briefly to say hello to a few *astra daimon* down the table in the other direction.

Right in that moment, the *irephuru* circle dance ends, and suddenly without a pause, come the smooth jazz notes of "Moondance" by Van Morrison.

Gracie stares at me, her jaw dropping in happy surprise. "Are you serious?" she exclaims. "Did you choose this song yourself?"

"Uh-huh." I nod, grinning. "What, d'you think it was the Atlanteans?"

Gracie swats my arm with a chortle. And then she sees the sparkle of the deep blue stone on my Wedding ring, and her jaw drops again. "Oh my . . . *that!* Let me see!" And Gracie grabs my hand to examine my ring closely.

Meanwhile, "Oh, hell yeah," George says, getting up. "This is my groove."

While Gracie oohs and aahs over my ring, George comes around the table and stops before my seated girlfriends. "Hello, ladies, who's up for a little Moondance?"

"Me, me!" Dawn and Laronda both say.

"Ok, you said it first," Laronda concedes with a pout.

"I love this song!" Dawn says, getting up in a hurry, then she and George run to the dance floor which has thinned significantly, since the locals are not that familiar with Earth dancing. Fortunately, George and Dawn set a fine example, swinging and even doing dips, and in moments the Atlantean Courtiers join them, copying their jazzy movements.

"All right, I want to see your big rock," Laronda says, getting up anyway and coming near me and Gracie around the table.

Chiyoko and Hasmik peer over from their seats, very intrigued, and get up also. "Oh, this is gorgeous! What kind of stone is it?"

I tell them and let them gush. I notice Laronda seems a little absentminded and keeps looking around the room. She finally says, "Have you seen troll boy?"

And so I tell her where I last saw Anu. "You know, he was hiding out in my *bedroom!*" I say.

"Idiot," Gracie mumbles.

Hasmik holds back a smile.

"Yes, I can see the fool doing something like that." Laronda rolls her eyes and pats down her dress. "No social skills." And then she pauses. "You think he might be around there still?"

I look Laronda in the eyes, holding back a smile also. "I think you should go look," I say.

Laronda raises one brow and looks me back in the eyes. "I think I might. Save my seat, girl. I'll tell him you and the Boss are looking for him. Or is that too much?"

I chortle. "Sure, whatever will make him come down here. Use any method at your disposal to bag the troll boy."

"Use a big Yellow Quadrant net," Hasmik adds.

"Drag him like a cavewoman," Gracie concludes.

Chiyoko widens her eyes and presses her lips tight.

Nodding with determination, Laronda heads for the exit.

Hasmik, Gracie, Chiyoko, and I exchange meaningful smiles.

Chapter 64

The next song that plays is an Atlantean popular dance tune, so George and Dawn return from the dance floor, while other people crowd it.

Aeson returns also, with Xelio, Oalla, Ker, and Manala. The latter immediately comes and sits down in an empty chair next to Dawn—who is still breathless from dancing—and Hasmik, and examines my ring with curiosity.

"Congratulations, My Imperial Lord and Lady," Ker says to me and Aeson with a comic flourish. "How many hours until *Amrevet* Night, Kass?"

Aeson actually starts to glance at his wrist comm, and Xelio snorts. "Very eager, apparently. And who could blame you? With such a stunning Wife, every instant of delay is torment."

"Stop it, boys," Oalla says, swatting Xel on the shoulder. She then adds to my Earth girlfriends, "And why aren't more of you dancing?"

"We were." Picking up a glass, George speaks up from his seat, which he's just reclaimed after dancing with Dawn. "And we will be again, um—Instructor Keigeri—"

Oalla makes a funny sound. "This boy is still in Qualification mode? Call me Oalla."

"Of course. Apologies, wasn't sure how to address anyone," George retorts calmly. "Too much change, too quickly."

"Yes, it can be confusing, considering we have such different social strata," Xelio says to George.

The Atlantean song ends.

And in its place, I hear a familiar soft beat from Earth that gets my pulse racing. "Stand by Me" by Ben E. King is playing, and this is my gentle cue.

I glance at Aeson and then step over to where my father is sitting.

"Dad," I say. "May I have this dance?"

M y father, Charles Lark, pauses momentarily, looking up at me from his seat as though puzzled for one instant, and then a slow, joyful smile comes to warm his tired face.

"Only if you're up to it, Dad!" I hasten to add. "I chose a really slow song. . . ."

"Of course, sweetheart," my father says, standing up carefully. "I would be honored to dance with my wonderful daughter on her Wedding Day."

And I take his hand, in some ways helping him walk and simultaneously leading him, and Dad and I step onto the dance floor together.

One thing is right, I did choose this song for two reasons—it's slow and easy to move to, even for someone not in the best of health, and yes, I love it.

I also recall that Mom loved it too. And the two of them danced to it on more than one occasion.

Dad holds my right hand with his left and places his right arm lovingly around my waist, and we shuffle together, mostly stepping in place.

"Thank you, Daddy," I whisper.

"No, thank *you*, sweet girl," my father says with a deep sigh, as we continue to move to the song, mostly oblivious to whoever is around us, and mostly on an empty dance floor, while others watch us respectfully from a distance. I rest my head against his chest and close my eyes.

"You know, your Mom used to love this song."

"I know."

Dad sighs. "She is so proud of you—*was*. No, she *is*, still is. . . . Wherever she is now, she is watching with so much love, looking down at you—"

"At both of us," I amend gently, and then do it again. "Not just both—*all* of us."

"Indeed. . . . Always."

T he dance ends, and in its place a poplar up-tempo Atlantean song starts. Dad and I return to our seats, and Dad takes his chair gratefully. "Phew . . . I'm beat," he says, shaking his head with self-amusement. "But it was more than worth it. Thank you, sweetheart, for the wonderful dance. Sorry we couldn't do dips." And he pats my hand.

I should mention that, according to Atlantean tradition, the Newlyweds are not permitted to dance with anyone else—not even their relatives—starting from their Wedding Day and for several months following. So I'm glad and deeply grateful for this special dispensation from the Venerable One that allowed me to have this special dance with my father.

"Here, Daddy, have something to drink." Gracie refills his glass. And then my sister looks further down the table where Blayne is sitting next to Chiyoko and waves at him. Blayne waves back.

"Is that boy the same friend you were telling me about?" Dad asks gently.

Gracie pauses with slight embarrassment and then nods. "Yes, that's Blayne and he is awesome."

"Introduce him some time, would love to talk," Dad says.

I smile at the sight of Gracie nodding with enthusiasm to Dad, then search the room for Aeson.

I find my husband—still can't believe that's what he is now, my *husband*—talking with Xelio and Quoni a few feet down the table.

At once Aeson returns to me, bringing Xel and Quoni with him. Quoni immediately greets my Dad and George, and the three of them start talking.

"Everything good here?" Aeson asks.

"Everything perfect," I say, looking into his eyes.

Meanwhile, the next song starts playing, and this one's another ancient Earth classic that makes my heart warm, "Make Someone Happy" by Jimmy Durante. Yes, I know, I may have gone overboard on picking sentimental classics for my Wedding music playlist, but that's what happens when you end up on the opposite side of the Universe from your home planet. . . . Yeah, I'm not sorry at all.

I see most of my female friends perk up, because they've all seen "Sleepless in Seattle," so this is a really romantic song for the Earthies. Hasmik exchanges a wistful smile with Chiyoko, then turns to Manala and explains to her the phenomenon of the old but never forgotten romantic film stars of yesteryear, Meg Ryan and

Tom Hanks. Manala looks impressed, and her eyes light up. Dawn laughs.

In that moment, Xelio, who's been listening in curiously, nears their group. His slightly mocking gaze takes in the seated females. "So. . . . Which one of you will dance with me?" he asks with a charming drawl, looking at the row of my friends, his insistent gaze sliding over them one at a time.

Just for a moment, my girlfriends freeze a little, like deer caught in the sexiest pair of headlights, as they stare up at him from their seats—it's the Xelio sensual effect, and it's undeniable.

Xelio continues to smile, and then lifts his finger to point from one to the next in a row. "You, or you, or you, or you. . . ." When his finger points at Manala, she pales then blushes furiously, and her deer-in-the-headlights expression intensifies.

"Oh, come on, Xel," Aeson says, stepping in to be even closer at my side. "Pick any one of these lovely ladies, and do it quickly before the song ends."

"Hm-m-m." Xel pretends to consider. "Very well—*you!*" and he points his finger insolently at Hasmik.

Hasmik's mouth parts, and she allows an embarrassed smile, but shakes her head. "Oh no, no. . . ."

"Come now, you will enjoy it," Xel persists, turning up the volume of his magnetic smile.

But Hasmik shakes her head. "No. But—oh," she says suddenly, "Princess Manala wants to dance. You two should dance—"

Manala's expression is now terrified.

Xel raises his brows and glances at Aeson. "I think Princess Manala's Imperial Brother will not approve, and I fear his fiery wrath. So Princess Manala will have to pardon me."

"Oh . . . it's okay," Manala says suddenly.

But Xel is no longer looking at her, and instead points at Hasmik again. But then his finger switches to Chiyoko—who also looks a bit more startled than usual, smiles, and shakes her head negatively.

"*Im nefiri* ladies, you destroy me and ruin my reputation," Xel says, searing them with his gaze.

"Oh, for heaven's sake," Dawn says smartly, getting up. "Let's go!" And she calmly grabs Xelio's hand and pulls him to the dance floor.

My friends stare with amazement and some relief at no longer being put on the spot by such a hot male, while Aeson laughs, shaking his head at us, and I grin.

Only Manala looks shaken, and I see her tense face appears to be holding back emotion.

Suddenly Manala gets up with a tiny sob, and says, "Excuse me . . ." She then rushes off toward the exit.

"Oh, dear . . ." I say with concern, while Aeson looks a little puzzled as he stares in his fleeing sister's wake.

My brother George looks away from his conversation with Quoni and asks, "What's wrong? What just happened?"

"My sister should be fine," Aeson says after a tiny, thoughtful pause. "She does this sometimes."

"Does what?" George watches curiously.

"Never mind, Gee One," I say, quickly changing the subject. *I'll have to explain Manala's quirks and acute sensibilities to my family—at some point.*

A few moments later the classic Earth song ends, and Xel returns with Dawn to the table, looking amused. "Not a bad dancer, this one," Dawn remarks, patting Xel's arm. "I told him all about 'Sleepless in Seattle,' so now he's all clued in to our romantic oldies."

"Thank you for the cultural lesson and the dance," Xelio replies with a slow, confident smile and a wink in the direction of the other females who rejected him minutes ago.

And then Xel picks up a drink and strolls away, giving one amused glance to us and nodding at Aeson.

My friends start to whisper in his wake, and Dawn says to everyone, "You all missed out! Too bad—seriously hot hunky dancing. All that male appeal so wasted on me. Chickens! Bawk, bawk!"

I laugh at my girlfriends and take Aeson's hand.

Im amrevu looks down into my eyes dreamily. Just now he might be a little tipsy from *shedehur*, but no, I recall, he's only had one glass, same as me. So, it must be love.

Maybe an hour later we've done the obligatory rounds of most of the room, greeting our guests, VIPs and other Courtiers, and just people we invited personally. The traditional phrase "Infinite Blessings upon your Union!" has been said to us so many times that I've lost count—we might indeed be approaching that infinity.

Somewhere in the middle, at one of the tables full of High Court nobility, we come upon Lord Fuorai and his wife, Lady Vahiz, and with them, Lady Tirinea Fuorai, looking nervous and very contrite the moment she sees Aeson and me approach—me in particular.

Yes, after much thought, I decided not to be petty and to invite Lady Tiri to our Wedding—but on one condition. The Wedding invitation sent in my name, stated in no uncertain terms that I will permit Lady Tiri back into my presence and my Court only if she *apologizes*—and not just to me but to all the other people she offended that afternoon, starting with Erita Qwas, her own friends, my friends, and ending with the Venerable Therutat and the Imperatris herself in whose presence the offense was made. And this apology is to be done in public.

Seeing me walking toward them, Lady Tiri glances at her parents with an unhappy and startled expression, but they nod at her sternly, signaling that she must proceed in order to clear herself—and them, by association.

And so, Lady Tiri stands up, then does a very graceful, full curtsey before me. Speaking in a much softer and less confident voice than I've ever heard her use before, she says, "My Imperial Lady Gwen, thank you for permitting me the opportunity to return into your graces. I apologize with the entirety of my person and beg your pardon for my transgressions. Please forgive me."

And she curtseys deeply again, even as other guests nearby watch with curiosity. A few whispers move in waves down the table, at her display. Not everyone is aware of what took place at the Ladies of the Court Bridal event, but soon they will be. . . .

Aeson raises a brow and looks from me to Tiri in bemusement. He has no idea what's happening, and I'll just have to explain it to him later.

"Lady Tiri, I will accept you back into my Court and my good graces. But now you need to apologize to the others. Begin with

Erita Qwas, the *astra daimon* whom you wronged most. She is over there. I'll wait and watch as you do it. Then proceed to Lady Irana and Lady Zua, after which you may find my Earth friends. I will later ask everyone affected if they are satisfied with your apology."

"Yes, My Imperial Lady Gwen." Lady Tiri nods and lowers her face with a terrified expression. She then hurries in the direction I pointed.

I nod to the Lord and Lady Fuorai in businesslike fashion, then take Aeson's arm possessively and pull him along with me, as we continue moving through the room. I have no intention of waiting around or wasting any more of my precious Wedding Day worrying about Lady Tiri, and expect that she knows it.

Not sure how much time has gone by, but it's well into the evening and our reception has become a relaxed and definitely festive chamber full of dancing and inebriated, happy people. Aeson and I keep checking the time, and at this point slow exhaustion is starting to set in after this amazing but endlessly long day. And yet, we know that the best part of the night still lies before us.

The music continues, a mix of upbeat dance songs and slow songs, both Earth and Atlantean.

At some point a Wedding cake is brought in. It's a gorgeous white-and-gold creation of five sweet tiers, covered with delicate, sculpted icing flowers—my blue and gold and purple flowers. Yes, this Earth tradition has been incorporated, and Aeson and I share the first delicious piece, though decorously, and without making a mess of each other's faces.

There is no bouquet, so nothing gets thrown.

Oalla Keigeri manages to drag my strongly protesting brother Gordie onto the dance floor, for a slow rendition of "At Last" by Etta James. When the dance is over, Gordie is flushed with embarrassment, but appears to have enjoyed it. I give Oalla a grateful look for getting Gordie off his butt and away from the pastries.

Dawn, who has been dancing more than anyone else this evening, finally pulls Hasmik, Chiyoko, and Gracie onto the dance floor for a "girl's night"-style group dance. Suddenly Kokayi Jeet joins them, his braids swinging, and does an incredible footwork solo in the middle of the dance floor while everyone in the vicinity claps—Earthies and Atlanteans. And then later I see Dawn slow-dancing to "The First Time Ever I Saw Your Face" by Roberta Flack, with none other than Arbiter Tamira Bedut. . . .

And then, Laronda returns. Miraculously, Anu is with her, looking both sullen and wide-eyed at the same time, and glancing around warily at anyone who might be looking.

"Look, Aeson!" I point out the two with a giggle. And then we both notice that Laronda and Anu are *holding hands*.

"Oh, very intriguing," Aeson says with humorous energy in his eyes. "Does this mean my loyal Aide will become a new man?"

"Anything is possible," I mumble, continuing to stare with fascination at my friend and her troll boy.

"He could take a lesson from Gennio," Aeson continues, this time pointing at his other aide who is on the dance floor. There, I notice, Gennio is calmly dancing to an upbeat Atlantean song . . . with my friend Chiyoko.

My jaw drops and I laugh.

And then, just after ninth hour of Khe, I hear the strangely haunting, familiar sounds of a song that has profound meaning for both of us.

"Caribbean Blue" by Enya.

The same ethereal waltz that played during the Yellow Zero-G Dance, when Aeson asked me to dance for that first impossible time . . . and we circled and spun together in weightlessness and soft hopeless sorrow, knowing that we could never be together.

It's the song that broke my heart and the song that healed it.

Now, Aeson looks at me wordlessly, with intense eyes, and offers his hand.

Together we move onto the dance floor, in a close embrace of intimacy, echoing that first, ethereal, *impossible* time.

There is gravity this time around, and the floor is firmly under our feet. And yet, at the same time, I feel the wonder of knowing how far we've come since, in the long cycle of our relationship.

"That time . . . you said 'this cannot end,'" I whisper, looking up into my husband's lapis-blue eyes.

"I did," he replies softly, his breath caressing my lips. "It's the truth. . . . It was—it was one of the first times I told you the truth in its entirety."

"This cannot end," I say, repeating his fateful words.

"It will not," he says. "Never. For as long as we breathe. I promise."

Chapter 65

Just before tenth hour of Khe, we say our farewells to all and depart the reception chamber to begin our *Amrevet* Night.

Aeson and I walk together, holding hands, exchanging glances full of electricity and nervous energy, until we reach our own floor. At the doors of the Imperial Crown Prince's Quarters our Imperial guards fall back and we are met by two youthful attendants consecrated to Amrevet-Ra, judging by the black and white colors of their priestly robes.

"My Imperial Lord and Imperial Lady, please follow us," they say, bowing.

The doors of our Quarters part before us . . . and instead of the usual antechamber, there is *wonder*.

The entire chamber has been transformed with translucent delicate fabric draperies of warm cream, amber, gold, and pearl hues, and our Wedding flowers. Descending from the ceiling, the curtains of fine tulle and gauze swing before us like spider silk, and I notice they are formed into a kind of tunnel or magical pathway leading deeper into the Quarters along the transformed corridor.

"What the—" Aeson says in surprise, and his mouth opens.

"Please—follow . . ." the young priest says gently to him, while the priestess speaks addressing me, almost in unison.

"Okay," I whisper.

We proceed down a path strewn with more fabric and flowers through a pavilion of glittering drapery, along once-familiar and now exotic corridors of the residence on Aeson's side. I am momentarily reminded of a fabulous arabesque tent and a flower garden, in one.

A few doors down, the priestess points me gently into one of the guest suites, while Aeson casts one slightly worried glance at me before continuing onward, following the priest.

"Here, My Imperial Lady," the priestess says, closing the door of the suite, and I see more amazing drapery and floral artistry all around me in the normally ordinary guest chamber. "This is your suite to prepare yourself for your time with your Husband. Everything you require has been brought here, including your *Amrevet* Dress. There is a bath and shower around the corner, so that you may cleanse and refresh yourself."

And she points me to a table with bottles and jars of cosmetics, perfumes, lotions, and the usual dressing table items. A cushioned chair waits for me to rest and work on my appearance. Several floor-length mirrors stand nearby.

I glance around and see my *Amrevet* Dress in its pristine packaging, lying draped on the bed, next to a matching over-cloak. . . . And on the floor, a pair of exquisite slippers.

And then, as my gaze takes in the rest of this grand dressing room, I see two tall goblets standing side by side on an elegant tray on top of a side table. One is lapis-lazuli blue, the other is gold.

Immediately I freeze, staring at them.

The priestess notices the direction of my gaze and says. "These are your special drinks, My Imperial Lady. You may drink just before you are ready to go to *him*."

"Yes . . . okay," I say softly.

"And now, may I begin to assist you?" The priestess inclines her head gracefully before me.

Half an hour later, having showered to wash off the stress and dancing sweat of the busy day, I sit wrapped in fresh towels, allowing myself to be pampered, even as my heartbeat races with anticipation of *whatever* is to come. My loose hair cascades in waves down my back, as it is being dried and brushed by my soft-spoken attendant.

What amazing thoughts pass through my mind in those tense minutes, is nearly impossible to describe. My mind is truly a river of emotion, excitement, nerves, and fragile wonder. . . .

At the same time, I start hearing soft, lovely singing coming in the distance from outside the suite. Chanting voices ebb and flow in waves of harmonious sound, as the priests of Amrevet-Ra intone softly.

My hair is ready, my cosmetics lightly reapplied, and now it is time to put on my *Amrevet* Dress.

I stand, still clinging to the towels around my torso in embarrassment, while the priestess goes to bring me my exquisite outfit—flimsy and daring and beautiful.

"My Imperial Lady, here it is," she says in a quiet tone of reverence. And it occurs to me suddenly, in the act of serving me in the name of her deity, Love, she is *praying*.

The realization of the purity and sanctity of this moment sweeps away my self-conscious fear and discomfort in one gentle, divine breath.

I allow the towels to fall away from my body, and receive the *Amrevet* Dress—an exquisite creation *formed entirely of tiny pearl beads* and no fabric. The priestess assists me in simple, clean movements of prayerful innocence, as I place its fragile pieces over my breasts, along my waist and hips, and then begin the delicate adjustment process of straightening microscopic strands of delicate beadwork, letting them cascade, flow, circle, and hang *just so* over my skin, emphasizing the various natural curves of my body.

When it is done, I am clad in what is, for all practical purposes, a body-shaped, intricate pearl necklace. No part of me is properly covered, and I am merely encased in the fine jewel net. . . . It is completely indecent to wear anywhere but in the privacy of the bedroom—as intended.

"Don't forget, My Imperial Lady—to remove it, you simply need to pull this small tie at your waist, and your *Amrevet* Dress will fall free, whenever you're ready. . . ." The priestess points to a fine tassel that circles me like a belt.

I nod, mesmerized, looking at myself in the mirror. Then I step into the delicate pair of slippers that fit like jewels on my feet.

"And now, your modesty cloak," the priestess says, picking up the ethereal gauze cloak. She brings it to me, letting me examine the vapor-fine fabric. When I'm ready, she wraps it around me like a floor-length shawl, covering me just enough so that I am indeed decent enough to walk down the hall without blushing—though I'm sure I will be blushing terribly nevertheless.

Outside the chanting pauses, then resumes again in a more urgent rhythm.

"It is time, My Imperial Lady," the priestess says, watching me with her kind gaze. "Your Husband is ready and waiting for you. It is time for you to make your choice and drink. Select one goblet and drink its contents in their entirety, then pour the other one down the sink, to assure your privacy of choice. I will wait for you outside the door while you drink. Then I will guide you the final portion of the way to the *Amrevet* Night chamber."

"I see . . . thank you." My voice is faint with nerves as I speak.

The priestess silently departs, closing the door of the suite.

I am left standing alone, faced with the greatest decision of my life to date.

I have thought about it long and hard—indeed, considered it relentlessly for days now—and although I arrived at a firm decision earlier, right now the question strikes me again, with all its immediacy and all its stressful, painful doubt and wondrous implications.

Have I made the right choice? Should I allow myself to conceive Aeson's child now . . . or not?

The responsibility of *either* choice is staggering.

I take a deep breath. . . .

With a sinking feeling in the pit of my stomach, I approach the table and pick up one of the goblets.

Taking another breath, I drink, gulping the cool, pleasant liquid.

Then I pour the other goblet into the sink, watching its contents run down the drain.

Breathless with excitement and terror, I follow the priestess down the narrow path draped with cascading ethereal fabrics and toward the chanting voices raised in divine song.

We walk a few more feet and emerge into a chamber which I vaguely recognize only by its grandeur as the Imperial Crown Prince's formal master bedroom, the one with the giant bed that's the size of three king-sized beds and able to fit a dozen people.

Somewhere in the center of this immense room, that same imposing bed reposes upon a dais . . . but there's no way to see it now because of the *forest* of sheer and translucent gauze curtains descending from the lofty ceiling and completely obscuring the way.

The master bedroom chamber has been redecorated and transformed into a fabled pavilion and romantic honeymoon space out of a magical fantasy. . . .

Everything is in shades of white, cream, and warm gold, and again my Wedding flowers are everywhere—winding in garlands along with the cascading lengths of fabric, scattered on the carpet, rising from the floor upon stone pedestals at the entrance, greeting me with their delicate fragrance wafting from the bouquet arrangements. . . .

Meanwhile, the soft chanting of the priests and priestesses comes just beyond the chamber on the opposite side. From where I stand, I can discern that they are not present in this room, but concealed just beyond it, somewhere nearby.

The priestess of Amrevet-Ra now stands in front of me at the entrance to the enchanted forest of breezy curtains and points with one hand.

"My Imperial Lady, we have arrived. Beyond these curtains is your *Amrevet* Night chamber and your Husband. You must now continue onward by yourself and sing the *Amrevet* Chant as you have been instructed, and unite with him. Blessings be upon you! May you always be guided by Amrevet-Ra. . . ."

And saying these words, the priestess bows before me and backs away, retreating along the path the way we came.

My already frantic heartbeat suddenly picks up another urgent rhythm, because I can hear the chant and recognize it now— the same *chant* I am supposed to be singing with my spouse, moments from now.

"*Am-re-vet-Ra!*" the hidden voices sing in the distance.

"*Am-re-vet-Ra!*"

I stare at the sheer curtain layers filling the space before me like petals of an immense upside-down flower.

This is ridiculous. It is also scary and beautiful and a little bit *alien.*

What am I saying—it is *very* alien.

"*Am-re-vet-Ra!*"

With slightly trembling fingers I start parting the fabric before me, layer by layer, and proceed inside the strange, beautiful, gossamer jungle. . . .

Every layer I move aside brings me closer to the center where he is.

Somewhere inside this *unreal* place, Aeson is waiting for me.

So many layers before me. . . . I move slowly, getting entangled, then freeing myself, momentarily feeling a sense of suffocation and panic and wanting to rip this beautifully *stupid* fabric out of my way.

A few seconds later I start seeing the layers thin, and beyond it I see the tall shape of a man standing a mere few feet away, silhouetted against a softly lit bed. . . . Everywhere, hundreds of flickering tiny flames in orbs of glass rise in clusters from the floor around the dais, floating and hovering in the air and creating a warm, intimate glow.

"Am-re-vet-Ra!"

A few more layers to go, and I can finally see him.

Aeson Kassiopei, my Husband, stands before me, stilled and frozen, watching my approach. He is entirely naked, with only a flimsy wrap of fabric covering his middle. It is of the same material as what makes up my modesty cloak.

I pull apart the last curtain layer between us, revealing him in all his bronzed, lean, muscular glory. His golden mane of hair falls loosely around his shoulders, and his expression is focused intensity.

This is also my cue. . . . I undo the easy clasp at my throat, and my flimsy cloak falls to the floor at my feet. At the same time, I step out of my jeweled slippers.

I take another step forward and stand in the presence of Aeson, my Husband, in nothing but my *Amrevet* Dress.

Aeson's eyes widen and his gaze stops, focuses completely, devours me.

"Gwen. . . ." he says in a strange, hoarse voice.

At the same time I also take in everything about him, every detail of his glorious chest and shoulders, toned legs, the strong column of his throat, the lean jawline and the defined muscles of his abdomen, and that little piece of fabric wrapped around his middle, and what it barely conceals. . . .

Another suspended moment of timeless wonder where we both stare at each other, transfixed.

"Am-re-vet-Ra!"

And then Aeson draws in a shuddering breath and stirs, taking a step toward me, and I also walk toward him . . . while the tiny beaded pearls of my *Amrevet* Dress sway along with the curves of my body as I move, clinking gently.

"Come, *im amrevu* . . . *im nefira*," Aeson whispers in a faint voice such as I never heard him use before, even as he reaches out to me.

"Aeson . . ." I whisper, also reaching for him.

We stop and stand at arm's length from each other, with our hands extended—right hand palm up, left hand palm down.

"Am-re-vet-Ra!"

"Ready?" he asks, a slow, sensual smile curving his mouth.

I nod, with parted lips.

Our outstretched hands clasp—his left hand covering my open right palm, my left hand covering his open right palm.

In the instant of contact, an immediate shock of sensual awareness comes. *Fire* courses through our fingertips and travels up our palms and wrists, and where our hands meet, our skin *burns*. . . . It is once again consumed with heat as it had been during the Marriage Ceremony.

This is our moment.

We begin to sing—listening, then matching the rhythm of the chant that comes toward us from an invisible source. The moment our voices blend together in song, the priests hear us and begin singing in answer, uttering the full words of the nuptial rite. And this time the ritual words of our *Amrevet* Chant fill the air, tangible with the raw force of two Logos voices entwined. . . .

As we have been instructed, Aeson and I have to sing each line in response to the priests, echoing them. And while we sing, from this point onward until the end of the Chant *we may not look* anywhere but into each other's eyes. . . . Nor may we touch each other anywhere, only maintain the contact of our hands in that burning grasp.

"Am-re-vet-Ra! Am-re-vet-Ra! Am-re-vet-Ra!" The priests sing and we sing in response.

> The serpent wakens and the fire flows . . .
> **Am-re-vet-Ra! Am-re-vet-Ra! Am-re-vet-Ra!**

Aeson looks at me with his so-very-blue eyes, glittering with liquid in the soft illumination of the floating light orbs, his dilated pupils reflecting in their darkness the infinite, flickering flames. . . .

As I form each note, and he forms each note, the sound stands up in the air around us like a force field. I can almost feel the sound waves bathing us in concentric circles as they seem to pass *through* us and redouble back, resonating around us as though we are two tuning forks. Meanwhile, rivers of electricity travel between our hands, blending and melting the barriers between our skin. . . . *Oh, it burns!*

> The flower opens and the fire flows . . .
> **Am-re-vet-Ra! Am-re-vet-Ra! Am-re-vet-Ra!**

We start the sequence of the next verse, and all I see is Aeson's eyes, piercing me. His gaze is dark and rich with something primal and forceful beyond imagining. His gaze has me pinned—unblinking, unable to let go, and not wanting to. . . .

With every repetition of the syllables of *"Am . . . re . . . vet . . . Ra . . ."* a strange new rhythm is established, as we force the notes out together, and the notes come falling in spurts, like blood being pumped by our hearts.

And with each sung utterance of each syllable, I feel more and more like I am coming apart at the seams—no, *melting*. My gaze is melting and drowning in his, my fingertips and palms melting and fusing with his skin and deeper down, into his very flesh. Soon I feel an overwhelming lassitude in my limbs, combined simultaneously with a pressure in my core that builds. . . .

I believe that, in those bright, indescribable moments, I take a step closer to him—and so does he, advancing toward me. Moving in naturally, we are entirely controlled by the pull of mutual attraction, so that our bodies are now only inches apart.

> The serpent rises and the flower blooms . . .
> *"Am . . . re . . . vet . . . Ra . . . Am . . . re . . . vet . . . Ra . . . Am . . . re . . . vet . . . Ra . . ."*

My overwhelming awareness is that now I can barely remain standing. My lower limbs have lost their ability to function, growing numb, becoming secondary, all because of my *molten lead core . . .*

and the only thing keeping me upright is the grip of his scalding hands, strong fingers and large palms encasing mine, anchoring me in power and in the moment.

And then I feel it . . . *something* forceful and inevitable, something *hard* pressing against my abdomen. Our lower bodies are close enough for it to happen.

The serpent rises.

"Am . . . re . . . vet . . . Ra . . ." His lips—they form and shape the sound with forceful, aggressive precision—and yes, I see their rhythmic movement and their chiseled contours with my peripheral vision, without needing to look away and break the connection of our direct gaze. . . .

It's then that I become aware of the undeniably erotic nature of it—the sound of his beautiful Logos baritone, his moving lips—even as I am taken apart by the power of his eyes boring into mine . . . and I can feel *him* down below with my abdomen.

His serpent rising.

"Am . . . re . . . vet . . . Ra . . . Am . . . re . . . vet . . . Ra . . . Am . . . re . . . vet . . . Ra . . ."

The *Amrevet* Chant ends, fading quietly.

And so do all the complex layers of our voices. The priests grow silent. They are departing now, as we have been told in advance—once the Chant is over, the two of us are left completely to ourselves.

Aeson and I stand, maddened and wild, fiercely gripping each other's hands. It occurs to me stupidly in those final instants that what we've just done is used the *desire voice* on each other.

That's the intended purpose of the *Amrevet* Chant.

Damn . . . as if we needed it.

But the thought is lost, because in the next instant Aeson pulls me to him hard, full body on body, and suddenly we are grappling. . . . We lose our footing and we collapse together, gasping for breath, falling backwards upon the great bed—him on top of me, grasping the back of my head then my hair in his fist, our mouths crushing each other, him pressing me down further, even as I sink into the soft coverlet layers, my fingers clawing at his back—as we struggle and pant, maddened with sudden, explosive *need*.

I don't remember if I ever have the chance to pull the tassel at my waist to undo the *Amrevet* Dress. As if it matters. In that *blazing* moment I don't have the will or the mind to remember anything at all.

Chapter 66

The next moments are complex sequences. They elongate and distend into microcosms and multiverses. Time is caught and captured at the rim of the black hole grail, and the spiraling inward fall commences. . . .

I am the one falling—dissolving toward the quantum level, all of my cell membranes gone, no walls, no space between us.

Time is a thing of *intensity*. The current moment, like a needle carving out a groove along the path of *being*, is the most focused thing of all.

Aeson is *inside* me.

In this moment, in the here and now, he is my world, my bright, piercing, turbulent *anchor*, ripping me apart and pulling me together with the rhythmic, pounding motion of being. . . .

When it first happens, it is a natural consequence of all the things that came before. There is no other outcome for us in that razor-sharp moment of intimate clarity. I open myself up like the proverbial flower of the ancient ritual we've just gone through, because it is what I *want*—what I've wanted *desperately*, for so long.

His body enters me and yes, it hurts, because although he tries to be sweet and careful and gentle in those initial moments, he is large, and he is *wild*, and my body must accommodate him for the first time. So there is pain and discomfort . . . until there's not.

And now . . .

Creak-creak. The great bed gives beneath us. . . . *Creak-creak.*

Someone is moaning, and I realize it's me.

Creak-creak . . . creak-creak. . . .

Faster, brighter, accelerating, sweet warmth rises *inside*.

My *Amrevet* Dress lies in pieces—spilled individual pearls and entire strands of beads broken, dancing on the coverlet all around us with every rocking thrust. I can see them with my head turned, as I grip his biceps, his shoulders, laboring along with his movements.

And then suddenly, in just a few ragged heartbeats, it is over. He stops breathing, then comes so hard that I am left reeling, like a small boat tossed by a storm. He is done, but I'm still a violent molten river without relief. And now I am full of his hot current flowing thick inside me.

Hot and fertile. . . .

Breathing hard, he collapses against me, his muscular body covering me, still *inside* me, radiating heat. . . . His labored breath scalds my neck.

"I'm sorry, Gwen . . ." he pants as he lies on me. "So sorry! Next time . . . will be better, I promise. I—"

Trembling, molten, my need unresolved. . . .

I stroke his forehead and jawline, brushing back moist tendrils of his golden hair as his weight settles on me, blending into me, since there are no cell membranes between us.

"It's okay," I say gently, speaking with some difficulty. My own breath catches, because I feel him still *inside.* "I know how long it's been for you . . . so long."

"No," he gasps, turning his face up to look at me with impossible, intimate eyes. "It's that I've wanted *you* for so long."

And as I exhale with a shudder of desire, I feel his warm, muscular arms surround me with tenderness. They are so loving and warm, squeezing me possessively, causing me to moan. . . . And in the next heartbeat he raises himself up effortlessly onto his elbows, staring trustingly into my eyes, and begins to *move* within me again.

This time, pleasure builds in an uninterrupted sequence. It overtakes my mind with blinding-white intensity—and soon transports me.

With a sweet, gradual awareness, and an indrawn breath, I emerge out of a heavy, dreamless sleep. Warmth—there is great warmth all around me. . . .

I am lying in Aeson's arms, my face against his chest, cheek pressing into his skin, one arm flung around his torso. His own powerful arm is wrapped around my lower back, and our legs are entangled—just as our long hair is a mutually tangled mess, his gold filaments mingling with my brown. His eyes are closed, lips parted, and he breathes regularly in deep sleep.

We are nude, except for a light sheet covering us negligently, crumpled and twisted in places as we've moved and shifted—again and again, during our intimate activity—multiple times throughout the night.

It must be morning, because the nature of the light around us has changed. It is now coming from the outside, beyond the ethereal, translucent cocoon of curtains surrounding our great bed, seeping in with cool whiteness of daylight instead of warm flickering firelight. The tiny floating orb flames have gone out, extinguished overnight. . . .

As I stir, I feel my husband's strong heartbeat, and then I sigh with complete and utter satisfaction and press my lips against his skin in a soft kiss.

Aeson senses my movement, my intimate touch, and wakes up with a light snore and a deep, relaxed intake of breath. He then opens his eyes and looks at me with a smile, blinking with sleep.

"Nefero eos," I whisper, stretching out one arm, sliding it sensually along his chest, then stroking his neck and jawline.

He sighs with pleasure at my touch. *"Nefero eos . . . im nefira . . . amreve."*

I pause, raising my head, then I pull myself up, my body sliding higher against his body to look down into his eyes with wonder. *"Amreve. . . ."* I echo his words.

Amreve means "lover" in *Atlanteo.* This is the first time that Aeson has called me that, instead of his usual *amrevu,* or "beloved."

"Yes," he replies. And suddenly he pulls me further up along his chest, then takes my face between his hands and kisses me, hard.

At once I feel what has now become a *very familiar* surge of desire.

We kiss deeply, then come apart for breath, and he says, looking intently into my eyes, "How do you feel?"

I laugh, then smile playfully and put my chin down on his jaw. "Great, wonderful. And a little sore . . ." I whisper, as his breath tickles my cheek.

"Only a little, I hope," he says, running his fingers through my tangled hair, then gently tugs my earlobe.

I think about it and realize that I'm indeed quite *sore* down there—and not just a little.

"It'll pass," I say with a grin. "With more practice."

"Seriously—you'll tell me if it gets too much," he says, examining my face with some concern. "Such as last night. Your first time—I'm worried that I hurt you."

"Oh, you did *not*," I say, twisting one of his golden locks around my finger. "It was all good. Very, *very* good, my Imperial Husband."

His smile returns, a little fragile, a little embarrassed. And then his other hand wanders up, and he cups my breast.

I sigh in pleasure, leaning into his touch, then—as he continues to fondle me—I notice the smudges and streaks of rose-colored lip gloss all over his cheeks and jaw.

"Oh, dear . . . my *noohd* is all over your face again," I say, and use my fingers to rub his cheek and the side of his nose to remove traces of my cosmetics. It's probably futile, considering how badly both of us need a shower. . . .

He pauses in amusement, and his brows rise. Then he lifts up the sheet and glances down at himself, pretending to examine his own lower body. "Hm-m-m," he says. "That's not the only thing your *noohd* is all over."

My jaw drops in silly outrage. "Aeson!" I exclaim, swatting him.

And then I blush furiously, remembering what I was doing with my mouth last night, and how much of my *noohd* is all over certain parts of him.

Ahem. . . .

Aeson watches my flaming face and my reaction and laughs with absolute, unrestrained joy.

That's when I swat him again, and continue doing so, striking him with both hands in exaggerated drama, while he in turn continues laughing and saying "ow" and even lifts his hands to cover himself, shrinking back in mock terror from my so-called beating.

Really? He thinks he can escape me?

My husband is a very silly man.

It's remarkable how much levity and joking can happen after such an intense series of events. For the next few minutes we giggle and tickle each other, until Aeson chokes from laughter and starts coughing. He looks around and sees a tall carafe with water and two glasses on a small side table near the great bed. It's something I didn't even notice being there last night—not that's in any way remarkable, all things considered.

"Thirsty?" he asks me, clearing his throat again and starts to rise from the bed. "I'm parched. . . . Really dehydrated."

"I *bet* you are . . ." I say with a meaningful widening of my eyes, followed by another silly giggle.

In reply Aeson silently leans back toward me once more and then suddenly grabs my butt.

I squeal and wriggle out of his grasp . . . and then I grab *his*.

Nicely toned, hard, muscular. . . .

Oh, dear lord, we're never getting out of this bed, are we?

But, of course, eventually we do. We gulp down some badly needed liquid, then find our way out of the sheer fabric curtain jungle around the bed (giggling and unintentionally ripping quite a few gauzy sheets), and locate the master bathroom adjacent to the grand suite.

Then it's time for more lingering and using the facilities, as we get into the seriously high-tech, modern, retrofitted shower in this otherwise ancient master suite. The shower is huge, tiled with beautiful eggshell-cream marble veined in gold, with so many jet heads everywhere—and Aeson turns *all* of them on.

Let's just say that in the next half hour we spend some amazing and very intimately *active* moments under all that cascading, glorious water. . . .

When we finally return, squeaky clean and wrapped in oversized towels, the Imperial Crown Prince's Master Bedroom has been transformed. While we were frolicking in newlywed fashion, the Imperial servants took down the pesky *Amrevet* Night ritual curtains, changed all the sheets on the great bed, and laid out several changes of clothing for us.

Okay, I'm probably never going to get used to this invasion of privacy, but at least they were discreet. . . .

Aeson and I consider getting back on the bed, then look at our choice of clothes.

"I *am* kind of getting hungry," I say, going for the clothing. "*Eos* bread?"

And Aeson uses his wrist comm to call us some food.

We get dressed just in time for the Imperial cooking staff to arrive and set up their food station.

I find that I'm indeed starving, which makes so much sense since I've barely eaten in the last few days leading up to the Wedding Day. Aeson appears to feel the same way as he heartily chews his savory *durzaio* buttered rolls, mashed *djebabat* with thick dollops of spicy gravy, and freshly baked, *medoi* fruit-filled *eos* pie, and takes deep swallows of *lvikao* to wash it down.

"Um-m-m, so good after all that *exertion*," he repeats with a wicked smile, looking at me between ravenous bites.

I smile at him blissfully and take a deep, sweet swallow of my own *lvikao*, letting its pastry-shop aroma fill me with invigorating energy—creamy notes of what could be vanilla bean, saffron, nutmeg, marzipan, cinnamon, hazelnut, bitter chocolate, and other unknown alien delicacies create a complex bouquet of flavor in my mouth.

And then I take a deep breath, because I need to tell him something, and it's best to get it over with now.

"Aeson," I say softly. "You know about my choice of two special drinks last night? The Imperial Bride must drink one of them before the *Amrevet* Night."

He pauses eating and watches me. "Ah. . . . Yes."

"Well," I say, feeling suddenly awkward. "I drank the golden goblet. . . . The one with the contraceptive."

He does not blink, looking into my eyes.

"I'm sorry," I rush to add. "I know how much you want babies, but I just—I don't think I'm quite ready yet, and we've only just—"

"Good." He interrupts me gently, then reaches across our small table and caresses my fingers with his large, warm hand. "I'm glad you took the contraceptive."

My lips part. "You are?"

He chuckles. "Of course. Becoming a mother—or a father—is the greatest responsibility I can imagine, and there is a right time for it."

I nod with a bashful expression. "I'm so happy you are okay with it."

"Look, we talked about it before, and I'll repeat it again," he says, continuing to smile at me. "It's always your choice. *Always*. Please don't ever let yourself get pressured into this kind of decision by anyone—and especially not by any Imperial expectations. And that includes me."

"Okay . . ." I say, still a little uncomfortable. "Though, when we talked about it, I thought—I mean, it was in general terms, and I thought maybe you were just being generous to suggest *abstinence*, and it wasn't otherwise even possible to have such a choice. Stupid me—I didn't know yet about how it actually works, or about the special Kassiopei contraceptive. Not until I met with your Mother did I understand any of it."

Aeson looks at me with a world of gentleness. "To be honest, I wasn't sure how that aspect works either, not until I had my own talk with the Venerable One."

"Yours or mine?"

Aeson's eyes widen slightly. "I can't even begin to imagine the horror of having this particular talk with yours! The deities had mercy on me—it was the Venerable Darumet who gave me the Imperial Husbandly facts."

"I see." I start to smile at his expression. And then I feel a wave of relief.

"Besides, these are somewhat uncertain times," he continues. "And bringing new life into our chaotic, unstable world is not to be done lightly. So waiting is a really *good* idea."

I am brimming with warmth as I gaze into his eyes. "I want you to know that I want to have children—eventually. I really do, so. . . ."

"I know." He squeezes my fingers lightly, sending the sweet pang of sensuality through me. "Now relax, stop worrying about it, eat and drink, my sweet Imperial Wife. And be sure to get an adequate supply of that very potent drink for the coming days. . . . I promise, *amreve*, you will need it."

At this point it must be said that contemporary Atlanteans don't have the same concept of "honeymoon" that many contemporary Earth cultures do. Instead of going on a multi-day or even multi-week trip to some romantic destination for sightseeing, lovemaking, and special time together, Atlanteans—or at least the people in Imperial *Atlantida*—take up to three days after the Wedding to relax and be intimate in the comfort of their own homes, and then settle back into their normal daily lives. Yes, they often move in together, establish other residences, even change jobs, or otherwise slightly rearrange their lives. But distant trips right after the Wedding are simply not a part of it.

However, there's another tradition called *"amrevet* days," which takes place at the end of the first eight months of their married life, and it involves a sneaky escape from friends and family to a secret destination for some much-needed privacy for the couple. Usually there is indeed a long-distance trip involved, but the purpose is to reinforce their commitment to one another and reassess their life goals, now that they know what it's like living together—a kind of renewal of vows. And yes, there is a honeymoon quality to it, since many couples choose this time to conceive children.

Meanwhile, the time immediately after the Wedding emphasizes the concept of hearth and *home*—the notion of creating, deepening, and confirming one's personal sense of a safe harbor, a home base. Except, two people are now in the equation: the new couple and their combined sense of what home represents to each one of them, only blended together.

The Imperial tradition is only slightly different. In addition to the Imperial Crown Prince and His Wife enjoying a private "day off" after their Wedding Day to establish their new intimate *home* in each other's hearts and each other's company, the entire nation gets a holiday. Which means that today—Red Amrevet 10, Redday, and normally the first business day of the week—is a day off work for nearly everyone.

Now that Aeson and I are officially married, I have legal rights as the Imperial Consort, and as a Kassiopei. Members of my family automatically become Citizens. They will still need to take the Oath and file some paperwork, but it is all a formality. Furthermore—and I found this out only recently—because of their association with Kassiopei, my family attains the first rank of *nobility*. I am still not entirely clear on that, but I'm sure it will be explained shortly. . . .

In any case, starting tomorrow, Aeson and I are technically free to move out of the Imperial Palace and return to live at his estate in

Phoinios Heights, or anywhere else we choose to make our new home. And my father and George will get nice housing in the city.

But today—our first day as a married couple—we're supposed to do nothing but enjoy each other's company in the Imperial Crown Prince's Quarters.

Which of course means, both Aeson and I spend a lot of time cuddling after our leisurely *eos* bread, then laze around until Noon Ghost Time on a luxurious sofa in the master suite watching silly and festive TV feeds with news footage of celebrations all around the country and public commentary about our Wedding. Most of it is giggle-inducing media nonsense filled with processional footage and images of ourselves on the hovering platforms waving to the crowds.

Afterwards we consider taking a dip in the interior swimming pool located on this side of Aeson's Quarters, or checking out the Wedding presents that once comprised the Tree of Gifts and have been delivered to the opposite side of the floor, which is nearer my residence.

My curiosity wins, so I convince Aeson to come with me and take a look at the mountain of our presents—which means we would need to go past the workroom that separates our two residences.

Yes, by tradition we are strictly forbidden from working or socially interacting with anyone else today, and that includes our families.

But try telling that to Aeson or me. . . . My husband immediately stops over to check with the two surprised *astra daimon* on duty at the computer desks, permanently monitoring the SPC stations.

"Everything okay? Any notable changes in the Helios system status?" Aeson asks.

"*Bashtooh!* What are you doing here, Kass?" one of them asks with a snort, seeing Aeson's slightly disheveled hair and casually loosened shirt collar, then glancing at me—I'm in a similar, highly informal state—while I merely blush and smile. "Begging pardon, Imperial Lady Gwen, aren't you two supposed to be—um—"

But in seconds they start talking SPC business, and Aeson naturally gets seduced by the sight of raw data. . . . One thing leads to another, and suddenly he's in a chair, keying in values and checking the latest reports like a total commanding officer nerd—one of the reasons why I love him so.

As for me, I also forget about those Wedding gifts and sneak past the workroom, and onward through my own bedroom, then head for the guest suites where Dad and George are staying.

As I turn the corner, patting down my hair and dress to appear less tousled, I hear animated conversation and the background sound of TV feeds coming from their open door. Just as I'd hoped, my family members are all here. I can hear Gracie's impassioned voice arguing something, George responding calmly, then Dad and Gordie barely getting a word in.

My first thought is, *Thank goodness, Dad sounds like he's doing okay.* . . . Only now does it sink in how relentlessly worried I've been about him in the back of my mind, even with all my main Wedding concerns taking over.

I also hear Hasmik saying something, and even Blayne's comfortable voice. So, some of my friends are here too. . . .

The moment I peer in, Gordie sees me first and says, "Whoa! Gee Two!"

My relatives turn their heads and see me, and then it's happy mayhem.

"Oh wow! Gwenie! What are you doing here?" Gracie rushes toward me with a startled, happy look.

Okay . . . why am I feeling silly and weird, all of a sudden? Everyone's looking at me. Will they see that I'm different somehow? That I've had sex?

Well, duh. Of course, they know.

I am literally supposed to be having sex, and doing it all day today—that's the general expectation of the public, considering I've been married in front of a million people.

Also, what kind of weirdo thoughts are these?

I try to suppress the crazy sense of awkwardness, and smile and wave shyly from the doorway, then step into the room. . . .

"Just wanted to drop by and see how everyone was doing—Dad and—"

"Is everything okay?" Gracie asks, examining me closely, as only a sister would. "You look good. Why aren't you on your honeymoon? Where is your hubby?"

"Yes! Everything's wonderful," I say quickly, feeling a flush in my cheeks. "And I *am*. . . . Aeson and I were going to look at the Wedding presents, so we just dropped by, for a few minutes—he's in the workroom now, should be here soon—Dad, are you okay?"

"Gwenie-girl, you needn't ever worry," Dad says, smiling and waving from his comfortable chair where he's sitting with his feet up on an ottoman, and a bowl of snacks in his lap. "You should be with your fellow, enjoying your day. No fussing, especially not today, sweetheart—okay? See? I'm just fine and eating something very tasty. Not sure what it is, but it's very good."

"Okay, Daddy," I say with a relieved smile.

"Was such a gorgeous Wedding!" Gracie says. "Just perfect in every way. The reception was super fun too."

I look at my little sister fondly.

"So—Mrs. Kassiopei. How does it feel to be Mrs. Kass?" George gives me a playful smirk from the sofa where he's sitting next to Blayne and Hasmik.

"It's kind of surreal," I answer, approaching them with a grin. "Insanely wonderful."

"The name's definitely impressive. Doesn't have the same ring to it as Lark, but makes up for it in lexical complexity," Blayne says, nodding wisely. I notice the boy is wearing that same orichalcum vest that he had on last night.

I point to it and say, "Now *that's* fantastic, Blayne. So glad you were in the Ceremony! Thank you!"

"You can thank this awesome woman," Blayne says with a nod at Hasmik. "She had this custom-made for me at her place of work."

I turn to look at her with parted lips. "Hasmik! Oh, wow! That was you?"

Hasmik gives me a glowing smile. "Special fabric. Proprietary multi-layer orichalcum alloy threads. Not widely used yet. This is Fleet issue, by special permission, since Blayne is a formal instructor for LM Forms and now has the necessary clearance. I submitted him as a tester for this hover-vest design. Hover-vests are considered special forces gear in the military, and this particular one is a new beta model using our latest textiles product."

"That's absolutely brilliant!" I exclaim.

"It is!" Gracie echoes me. "Now Blayne can use it to get around even outside Fleet Cadet School HQ. Yesterday was the first time he tried using it in public."

"And I wasn't even arrested," Blayne adds.

I continue to express my admiration, when a soft, stifled sob comes from the direction of the open doors.

I turn around to look—everyone does.

It's Princess Manala. She's standing at the entrance in uncertainty, peering at all of us gathered inside the room. "Aeson? Are you here—where is my brother—I need—he must help—" she manages to utter between shuddering breaths. Even from across the room it's apparent that her entire body is shaking, and her stunned face is smudged with tears. She looks absolutely distraught.

"Manala!" I say. "What's wrong? Oh my God, are you okay?"

With a loud sob, Manala suddenly comes running and throws her arms around me in a terrified embrace.

"Oh no, what's wrong, dear?" I can hear my Dad and the others ask, even as I hold Manala's slight, shaking body.

"He . . . he's gone!" she wails suddenly. "I—I can't—he's gone!"

"Who? What is it? *Who's* gone?" my brother George asks, setting down his glass.

Manala shudders, as another rending sob escapes her, and lifts her contorted face from my shoulder to glance briefly at George, then looks in my eyes. "My . . . Khemji! *Khemji!* He ran away and now he's gone!"

Chapter 67

"Oh, no!" I say, with an immediate stab of worry. "What happened? Where is Khemji? How did he—"

"No! *Janik*, no!" Hasmik immediately gets up and joins us, putting her arms around Manala from the other side.

For a few seconds Manala relaxes in our supporting embrace and bawls outright. Her whole body shakes, her face contorted with ugly-crying, gasping for air between violent sobs, huge tears pouring down her cheeks, and what few cosmetics she has on are smudged in dirty streaks around her normally lovely features. And then, between sobs she tells us what happened in a blubbering stream of consciousness.

"Khemji was loose in my room . . . and . . . and the balcony window was open—I always close it unless . . . unless the security grate is locked—and I *forgot!* Last night, it was last night. I—I was upset, so I came back to my Quarters and let Khemji in that bedroom—usually he is in the other room with . . . with no big window, so he can't get out . . . and I always—*always* make sure there are no openings in the screen—but I was so upset that . . . I didn't think and I just opened the horrid window—and I went to bed, and then—and then in the morning he was gone! It is *my fault!*"

"Oh no," Hasmik whispers, gently moving her hand in circular motions to rub Manala's back. "Well, maybe he went for a little walk? He is—maybe, *janik*, he could be right outside, and did not go too far? He is a big cat, and everyone will see him—"

"No! I *looked* for him outside!" Manala wails, shaking even more, beginning to stutter, this time with anger. "I—I am hateful, *evil!* My fault! I—I searched all over—the—the p-p-park, all morning—as soon as I woke up at dawn and realized he wasn't there, I walked all around the park, all the gardens, everywhere, for hours! I called him and called him! Then I climbed on the b-b-b-alcony and tried to climb to the roof—"

"Oh, no, no—you didn't! Good lord!" Gracie mutters.

"I w-w-was on the balcony railing and checked the r-r-roof, which he loves to look at—through the window, he loves watching birds . . . and all the green hanging vines," Manala continues, choking on her sobs, "then c-c-came down again, and w-w-went outside, and I asked two of my guards to help, and—and they went to look too! Searched for three hours! And . . . no one . . . has seen him!"

"He has to be somewhere nearby," I say softly. "Cats sometimes get out and like to run free. Usually they don't stray too far from home, and remain in the neighborhood, and then come back on their own. . . . He couldn't have gotten far."

"You know, it's very likely he could be sleeping somewhere," Dad says in a comforting voice from his chair. "Probably found a cozy hiding spot and is waiting for darkness."

"That's right," Blayne adds. "Cats are nocturnal, so he'll be out at night."

"But he's hungry! He will be so *hungry!*" Manala takes a deep breath in an attempt to stop herself from shuddering. "He doesn't know how to hunt! He is too tame! He will starve on his own!"

"Well, he is kind of super-fat, so probably will be okay without food for a while," Gordie says thoughtfully.

Manala wails even harder.

"Gordie! Not helping," Gracie says sternly.

"Sorry," my younger brother says sheepishly.

In that moment, Aeson appears at the door of the suite. He peers in with a slow smile, his gaze automatically searching the room for me. Seeing his sister crying however, he immediately grows serious and approaches us. "What's going on? Manala? Are you okay?"

"Khemji got out and is missing," I tell him quickly, with a frown.

Immediately Manala launches herself at her brother, hides her face in his chest with renewed sobs, and repeats her story in broken sentences.

Aeson listens, holding her gently, and brushes back her messy, tumbled golden hair from her streaked face. "All right, we will go look for him again, *right now,*" he says. "Manala, look at me—I promise, we will find Khemji. Okay?"

"Okay, Aeson . . . please, *please* find him!" Manala stares up into his eyes with absolute trust. And then she covers her mouth in shock. "Oh no! It's your special day after your Wedding! You and Gwen must spend time together, you mustn't trouble yourselves—"

Aeson shakes his head at her and glances at me. "Nonsense. We could use a walk—right, Gwen?"

"Oh, yes!" I say at once.

"Manala, big breath," Aeson continues, looking his sister in the eyes. "You should've come to get me earlier. In the next few minutes I am going to assign many, many Palace servants to start looking for Khemji. And we will look for him ourselves."

Manala looks up at her brother and nods, quieting her sobs. For the first time, her expression is bright with hope.

Aeson starts issuing orders on his wrist device. The rest of us all glance at each other, pausing for a moment. Then George stands up and casually begins moving to the door. "So—I guess we're all looking for the elephant cat," he says calmly. "Let's go."

A nd this is how Aeson and I—and most of my family and friends, our personal guards, and half the Imperial Palace staff—spend the remainder of the afternoon of our first day as a married couple searching the Imperial premises for a very big, very fat black cat. . . .

I dare any other married couple on Earth to match that for a honeymoon activity. . . . Seriously.

My Dad and Blayne stay behind in the guest suite to discuss the literary merits of Thackeray versus Hardy in Victorian literature, promising to keep an eye out in case Khemji shows up in the Prince's Quarters.

All the rest of us hit the park and the Palace grounds.

Aeson and I try to keep a low profile and avoid the public as much as possible—after all, we're supposed to be otherwise occupied—while we stroll around the park, which is still covered by our Wedding decorations and not-yet-wilting flowers in garlands and bouquet arrangements. We walk ahead of everyone else, frequently reaching out to each other and letting our fingers touch briefly with frissons of sensation passing between us. When we're sure we're unobserved, we exchange intimate glances and hold back private smiles.

However, we take our search duty seriously and check everywhere including underneath park benches, inside gazebo-like structures and shrubbery, calling out Khemji's name. That is— Aeson calls Khemji, since Khemji is very fond of him, and I just stay quiet so as not to spook the truant kitty. Manala and Hasmik and Gordie walk nearby, also calling out, while George, Gracie, and several of our guards bring up the rear and double-check the same spots again and again.

After more than an hour without results, we return to our Quarters in the Palace. Manala starts to cry again, this time softly, from exhaustion, while another shift of guards is sent to continue looking.

"Any progress?" Dad asks when we get back to their suite.

Aeson and I shake our heads negatively, while Hasmik goes to pour Manala a glass of water.

"It's not even dark yet," Blayne says calmly from his seat across from my father. "Khemji will emerge soon."

"That's right." Gracie nods, plopping down on the sofa next to Blayne.

"He is gone, and he is not coming back. It's all my fault . . ." Manala says with a dead expression in her eyes, sitting down on the edge of the sofa. She wilts, slowly leaning forward with a stooped posture, and stares off into the distance.

"*Janik*, no. . . . Don't blame yourself. Things like this can happen to anyone." Hasmik sits down next to Manala and hands her the water. "But animals are clever and loving, and they come back. Khemji loves you and he will return."

"No, he *won't!*" Manala cries suddenly with a violent, frightening edge to her voice, and at once I feel a strange cascade of chills down my spine at the alien sound of it. Her voice is loud and hard, almost tangible, and there is no doubt it's a *power voice*. Hearing it, everyone present grows uncommonly still and pays attention.

"*He is gone! I left the window open! I am hateful!*" Manala sits up and continues speaking, her words falling down like hammer blows and rebounding throughout the room. The glass that she holds in her unsteady hand looks ready to fall, and the water sloshes and spills past the rim.

"Here, let me hold that," Hasmik says gently, taking the water glass back from her.

I exchange a concerned glance with Aeson, who is frowning but also thoughtful as he watches his sister, and see the others staring at Manala with varying degrees of alarm.

My God . . . it occurs to me. *She has a Logos voice.*

"Manala, come, you're not—" Aeson begins speaking in a gentle, calming tone.

"No!" his sister screams at him. *"I am! I am! Horrid! I should die!"* Suddenly Manala straightens, and her eyes are wild and almost unseeing as she glares at all of us. Her hands are trembling, and she clenches them into fists, then starts striking herself, and erupts into horrible weeping.

"Oh, Manala! No, *im senet,* you are the best little one—let's go wash your face—" Aeson crosses the distance between them and leans down to embrace her, even as Manala continues to beat herself with her fists and struggles against his strong, loving hold. He then leads her gently to the back of the suite and around the corner to the bathroom. Giving me a meaningful look, Hasmik stands up and goes in to help.

Moments later we hear the water running in the sink as Manala attempts to splash water on herself and continues to wail.

The rest of us are somewhat shell-shocked.

"Ho-o-oly crap," George says with a frown, leaning backward in his seat. "Does she do that often?"

"Not like that! Wow . . ." Gracie whispers, widening her eyes and glancing around at all of us. "I've never seen her out of control like this."

"Poor child." Dad rubs his forehead thoughtfully. "Should someone contact the parents? Or her mother at least? She might need—does she take medication?"

I shake my head negatively at Dad.

"Child? Wait, how old is she anyway?" George asks.

I pause to think. "I believe she's twelve."

"*Twelve?* Really? Seems too old for twelve. . . ." George's frown deepens.

"Oh no, sorry," I amend. "She is twelve in Atlantean years, which is approximately sixteen Earth years."

"Okay, that's more like it." George taps his fingers on the chair armrest. "But the maturity level here is nearly on par with Gracie's."

"Hell, no!" Gracie glares at George. "I don't do tantrums like that! And I'm fourteen!"

"Fourteen in Earth years," Gordie puts in. "So yeah, she's older than you in Earth years."

"So?" Gracie continues to give us hard looks, craning her head sideways, and then throws a nervous glance at Blayne.

Blayne meanwhile just observes the conversation calmly and says absolutely nothing—though, I do believe there's a tiny, fleeting smile on his lips as he looks at Gracie.

I consider how best to explain Manala and finally speak up. "Here's the thing—it's not really a tantrum. Manala is—*unique*, for lack of a better word. In many ways she's more mature than all of us. The way she perceives things—the world, everything—it is all so sharp and *real* to her. She is super-intelligent, wise, but also very sensitive to everyone's suffering and very empathetic—in a good way. So much so that there's no room for humor or sarcasm, only blunt honesty."

I speak quickly, keeping my voice down, so as not to be overheard—because the last thing Manala needs now is to feel even more betrayed by the fact that people she cares about are talking about her behind her back. "Part of the problem is," I continue, "as an Imperial Princess she's been completely sheltered for most of her life, not permitted to make friends, and she doesn't know how to handle emotional situations. So—not really her fault that she overreacts. She's in genuine pain."

"Ok, but you must admit, that, right there, *that* was a lot of drama," George says.

I take a deep breath. "It's *not* just drama. Right now, not only is she worried about Khemji for good reason, but this cat of hers is also very, very important to her. In many ways, he's her closest companion and friend—maybe even her *only* friend when we're not there. So let's not blame her for being very upset. I would be too. To be honest, I'm kind of upset right now myself—on her behalf and the poor cat's behalf, so—"

In that moment Manala returns to the room, followed by Aeson and Hasmik, so we stop talking. Her expression is still tormented, but her face has been cleaned, and she is somewhat more composed now.

"So, Manala," George says after a slight pause. "Where exactly is your window located? The one through which Khemji took off?"

Manala looks at George with a renewed frown. "I—I don't know. I mean—it's in my bedroom."

George stands up and goes to the nearest window in this suite. He peers outside—squinting at the still bright but now late afternoon sky, barely starting to fade from white to teal—looks up, then down. "Where would that be exactly, in relation to this room? Upper floor? Lower floor?"

Manala blinks. "It is the floor directly below this one. The Imperial Princess's Quarters."

"Okay." George nods comfortably, continuing to squint outside, shading his eyes with his palm. "Can you come here and tell me where your bedroom is? Can you see it from this window?"

Manala's tragic expression becomes exasperated. However, she complies and goes to stand next to George, trying to peer down below. "I don't know. Maybe over there. Yes, that row of balconies." And she points down and to the right.

"Well, good," George says. "Now this lets us have a better idea of Khemji's itinerary. First thing you need to do is set out a dish of elephant cat food on that balcony—as a lure."

Manala looks away from the view in the window and glances at George, furrowing her brow in confusion. "Elephant cat food? Why do you say elephant? Is it not an Earth herbivore mammal? Khemji needs a more concentrated protein than your elephants. Or do you think that kind of vegetation might lure him better?"

George's expression doesn't change as he watches Manala's transfixed face, but he pauses momentarily before continuing. "Elephant cat food here refers to the fact that Khemji's size is so large for a cat that he might as well be an elephant."

"Oh. . . ." Manala considers this, then says, "Does that mean that elephants are considerably smaller than I thought? Because I thought they were the largest land creatures on Earth, not little ones the size of Khemji."

"Okay." George's mouth opens. "Well, no. You are absolutely right in your original understanding of elephants, so, let's just . . . never mind."

While this curious conversation is happening, I glance around the room at the others—at Dad and Aeson and Hasmik.

Aeson gives me a silent nod.

Manala appears to be sufficiently distracted by what George is saying that it is safe to assume that her composure has been fully restored for the moment.

Taking advantage of the respite, we all decide to continue searching for the prodigal cat. Only first we make sure there are dishes of Khemji's favorite food placed in several strategic spots outside, waiting to tempt him.

By the time it's dark—and still no sign of Khemji, unfortunately—we give up the search for now and return to the guest quarters occupied by Dad and George.

Aeson calls for a late *dea* meal or early *niktos* meal—at this point I can't be sure which—and Blayne and Hasmik have to leave since they have work tomorrow.

Gracie and Gordie, as my immediate family members, have tomorrow off, so they stay longer. Manala refuses to eat but stays in the suite with us.

"The two of you should go back to your own apartments and relax tonight," Dad repeats quite a few times, speaking to me and Aeson. "No need for you to be here, we can manage. Go, use your wonderful private time. Don't squander your honeymoon hours."

"We're happy to be here, Dad," I say, glancing at Aeson to make sure—but he smiles at me in complete agreement. And then he looks briefly in Manala's direction, keeping an eye on her.

It's late evening when Aeson and I finally return together to our own side of the Quarters. Despite the best efforts of the Imperial staff, Khemji is still missing. But there's not much more that can be done. A new shift of people has been deployed to search, more cat food treats scattered all around the balconies and railings, and Manala has been sent to bed with strict orders to get some rest.

Aeson and I wander into the Imperial Crown Prince's grand master bedroom suite, which has now acquired some intensely wonderful memories for us. At once, both of us are taken by a sudden, mutual urgency . . . so we help each other shed our clothing.

Pulses hammering, we get into the huge bed, barely taking the time to pull back the luxurious covers in our Wedding colors of warm white and gold. And then we are consumed with one another.

Again the world narrows to tunnel vision. . . . Blinding white fire rushes in, overflowing my mind. . . . Our bodies strain and struggle in sweet, hot agony . . . flesh on flesh, limbs entwined. My memories of those moments are scalding me even now.

Eventually he collapses, just as I'm also swept away by the inner storm, and it is done. We lie entwined, breathing hard—I, with my face down, cheek pressed deep into the pillow, he cradling me from behind, his mouth panting against the back of my neck.

"Ah . . . *im vuchusei* Gwen . . ." he manages to utter. It's a sensual and somewhat intimate term of endearment in *Atlanteo* that means "sweet, tasty, pleasurable, soulful" all in one word. And hearing Aeson's deep voice say it completely undoes me, so that I turn into warm honey. In mindless need, I turn and reach for him. . . .

Needless to say, we resume our intense activity and don't stop for quite some time.

The next time I remember being aware of anything is deep into the night, sometime after Midnight Ghost Time, when I wake up in darkness, next to my husband. Aeson is sitting up in the great bed, nude to the waist and covered only by our blanket. The greenish-blue light of his wrist comm illuminates the surrounding translucent fabrics of the canopy overhead and his thoughtful face, locked in concentration, as he scans the bands of moving holo-data.

"Aeson . . . is everything okay?" I ask, feeling a twinge of undefined worry, even as I sweep my hand up to caress the hard muscles of his upper arm. "Is it about Khemji? Did they find him?"

Im amrevu looks at me with an immediate comforting smile. "Not yet. But—it's okay, go back to sleep," he tells me.

"You first," I say with a yawn, tugging him to me.

"Just a second. . . ." He taps the device on his wrist, and the light disappears.

And then, with a chortle of surprise followed by pleasure, I feel my husband's warm lips covering mine.

Chapter 68

Khemji is still missing in the morning when Aeson and I wake up around seventh hour. Increasing worry about the cat strikes me particularly hard this morning. I frown, sitting up in bed with the sheets around me, as I watch Aeson check his messages on the wrist unit.

"Khemji?" I ask.

Aeson gives me a serious look. "No. They didn't find him yet."

And so, with a sinking sensation, this new worry takes permanent residence in my gut. "Oh, poor Manala," I whisper. "Please keep searching!"

"Of course," Aeson says. "No one is giving up. This may take a while, even a few days. Right now, however, I am very concerned about my sister."

"I am, too."

Because of this ongoing situation, we don't linger in bed, only exchange quick kisses before getting into the shower and then getting dressed.

Today is the second day of our married life, and under normal circumstances we would still be enjoying a leisurely time—even as the rest of *Atlantida* gets back to work. We would also be getting ready to move out of the Imperial Crown Prince's master bedroom and back to the estate in Phoinios Heights, making permanent arrangements for my Dad and older brother, and dealing with all the rest of our routine issues.

But we can't go today. We can't leave Manala like this. Besides, Aeson needs to deal with the most recent SPC incoming reports. . . . I'm not sure if it's something serious—he doesn't tell me—but he does have a certain super-focused look on his face which I've come to know well.

As has been our habit for the last few days, we head to the guest suite on my side of the Quarters to share *eos* bread with Dad and George, and also with Gracie and Gordie, who are still staying here in the Palace.

We pass the workroom, and Aeson tells me to go on ahead and that he'll join us after he checks with the *astra daimon* on duty— Erita is one of them. I see Gennio and Anu are at their desks this morning, and Anu gives me a curious, extra-awkward look before returning to stare at his monitor, where I notice a series of visuals of the ghost moon.

"*Nefero eos,* Anu," I say, coming up to him and pretending to stare at the orbital trajectory data. "Tell Laronda to call me, okay?"

"What?" Anu's jaw drops, and his pasty white face immediately flames red.

I shake my head at him with a soft laugh and then head to my own bedroom on the way to the guest suite.

When I get to Dad and George's suite, I can smell the aroma of fresh cooking in the corridor, wafting from the open doors even before I enter. The *eos* bread service is already in place, and the Imperial servants are busy with the sizzling griddles and pans.

My father, Charles Lark, is standing next to Princess Manala, speaking in a soft, consoling voice, while the young girl stands immobile near the window, staring numbly at the growing whiteness of early morning daylight.

George gets up from the sofa and nears me as soon as I enter the room. "Morning, Mrs. Kass," he says teasingly, even though there's a serious undercurrent in his eyes. "Gordo and I are about to head out to take another quick look around for the big cat."

"Did you eat already?" I ask, glancing from my older brother to Gordie who's standing with an empty plate near a food station, waiting for something to be cooked.

"Not yet." George also looks around and nods to Gracie, who is rummaging through one of the boxes they brought from Earth. "We were going to eat when we got back. This is just a quick exploration on the floor directly below, a test of my feline-brain hypothesis. I've a hunch I want to check out before the day gets too hot."

"Okay," I say with a meaningful glance at Manala. "I really hope you find him."

"So do I," George says thoughtfully. "So do I. . . . Okay, Gee Three, put the plate down, we're heading out. I promise, we'll return before they finish flipping whatever's on that griddle."

Gordie complies, and my brothers leave the suite.

I approach Dad and Manala and try to say things that might make her feel better, even though I know they are meaningless at a time like this.

Manala attends to my comforting words with a listless expression, and nods occasionally. I have a feeling she's not even hearing me.

A few minutes later, George and Gordie return. They appear lackluster, so no good news and no sign of Khemji.

Immediately Manala turns to them with brief animation, then regains her downcast demeanor.

"Don't give up hope, Manala," I say. "Back on Earth we've had cats go missing for weeks, and they still return."

Hearing this, Manala's lips begin to tremble and a fat tear slides down one cheek.

Aeson chooses this moment to appear at the doors, and he's followed by Xelio. The distraction of their arrival is sufficient that Manala catches her breath and stops mid-sob.

Aeson gives me a meaningful look, then glances at Xel, who watches our silent exchange with amusement. I raise one brow, then glance from them to Manala.

"*Nefero eos*, Imperial Lady Gwen, Imperial Princess Manala, *Ter* Lark, and everyone," Xel says with a nod to my Dad and siblings, and a seemingly casual look at Manala, then heads for the food station where he picks up an empty plate. Meanwhile, our Dad crosses the room slowly and sits down in his usual chair with a tired exhalation.

"So the search for Khemji continues," Aeson says loudly, in Manala's direction.

"Thank you, Aeson," his sister replies quietly. She then casts a slightly spooked glance at Xel—but the *astra daimon* has his back turned as he fills his plate, and his black mane of hair is all that's visible.

I approach Aeson, widening my eyes, with the pretend intention of running my hand along his upper arm, just as Aeson leans near my ear to whisper, "I asked him to come by . . . and talk to her."

And he glances at Xel.

"Okay, good . . ." I whisper back.

At this point there's little doubt for most of us that Xel has a powerful effect on Manala. Whether it's a first crush or something else, such as a strong affinity since childhood, we cannot be sure. But she definitely has feelings of some kind when it comes to him—as was made apparent during our Wedding reception, when Manala got so upset that she fled the room when Xelio did not ask her to dance.

And now Xel takes his food and a mug of *lvikao* and heads for the sofa. There he puts his feet up on an ottoman and starts eating. Periodically he glances over at Manala, who continues to stand awkwardly near the window with a most dejected expression.

"My dear Princess Manala, come, sit here, have something to eat," Xel says in a friendly voice, popping a syrupy dumpling into his mouth and chewing heartily.

We all try not to stare too obviously, but pay careful attention to Manala's reactions. At the first sound of Xelio's voice addressing her, she freezes, then shakes her head. "I'm not hungry, thank you."

"You didn't have anything to eat all day yesterday," Aeson says, moving closer to her. "You really need to eat. Or I'll inform *Mamai* that you're not feeling well."

Manala frowns at her brother. "*No!* Khemji has not had anything to eat, either. I am *not* eating."

"We don't know that." My Dad speaks up. "It's possible Khemji found something nutritious outside, such as insects, which contain enough protein to subsist on them for quite some time. I can understand not eating in solidarity with your friend, but it would make better sense to keep up your strength for his sake. When Khemji returns, he will need a lot of your care and attention."

"Yes, at least drink some *lvikao* to warm you up," I add and go to pour Manala a mug from the carafe.

"Oh, look what I found!" Gracie says suddenly, as she straightens over a cardboard box of our family belongings from Earth. "Gee One, is this yours? Wasn't this the same thing you took with you in your bag to Qualification?" And she holds up a flat rectangular object wrapped in old brown paper.

With a weird pang in my chest I recognize it, having last seen that familiar brown wrapping paper more than a year ago on Earth. . . . At once, so many memories of our home and Vermont rush in. . . . Memories of those intensely horrible days when we were getting ready for Qualification and carefully chose and packed our few, precious personal belongings.

Seems like it happened in another life, an eternity ago.

George looks up from his plate of food, swallows, and pauses with a thoughtful frown. "Oh, yeah," he says. "That's mine."

"You didn't even unwrap it!" Gracie snorts. "So what is this mysterious personal junk? Can I open it? Finally?"

George shrugs. "Sure, go ahead. No big deal."

"Then why did you make it all secret? Wouldn't even tell us what it was."

"Was just messing with you." My older brother chuckles softly and resumes eating. "Also, didn't want you to know what a sentimental fool I was being."

Gracie rips apart the brown paper and suddenly grows still. . . . Inside is an old-fashioned heavy photo frame of wrought iron, containing a family photograph on actual, non-digital, ordinary paper.

A Lark family photograph—of all of *us*.

I suck in my breath, because I recognize that old photo. It used to stand on our mantelpiece in the living room of our home in Vermont. And before that, in our home in California.

In this picture there's Mom and Dad, much younger, with three little kids, and Mom is holding baby Gracie. I think we had it taken at one of those mall department store portrait studios against an artsy background.

Everyone in the room stops eating and stares.

Dad makes a strange sound. "Oh, thank God! George, you've no idea how long I've looked for that picture, and forgot completely that you had it with you, that you took it with you originally. What a great surprise! Gracie, dear, please bring it here so I can see. . . . Such a beautiful portrait of Margot, so relaxed and genuine—I prefer it to many of her professional studio shots and performance images. And all of you so tiny!"

Gracie takes the picture to Dad, and the rest of us Larks crowd in.

"May I see it, please?" Manala says softly, behind us. "Is that your Mother?"

I turn around with an emotional smile and beckon her—and Aeson too.

And then we all take turns passing the photo frame with its precious frozen *memory* from hand to hand.

Xel alone continues eating, watching us politely from the sofa.

Our family photo presents a strange but timely distraction from Manala's mood of despair. When it's her turn to hold it, the Princess examines the picture with immense curiosity, and a smile comes to lighten her face. "Is that you, Gwen?" she asks, pointing to the little girl standing between her parents, next to a little boy with a mop of hair.

"Yup," I say. "And that's George next to me, looking like a poodle. Gordie is the tiny one on the other side of Mom."

"And that fat little darling is *moi*," Gracie says with a twist of her lips.

"Not a poodle, but a Lhasa Apso," George corrects me. "Different hairstyle, big difference."

"That's right." I laugh. "Straight mop as opposed to curly mop."

"Those were the days of hair madness." George smirks.

"Too bad you finally cut it off," Gordie says. "Was easier to grab your head back then."

"Oh, please, like you ever could." George narrows his eyes and then finger-snaps Gordie's forehead even as the other leans in, inches away."

Manala looks up at George and examines his current, medium-short, neatly attractive haircut. "Those are dog breeds, yes? Why did you wear your hair like a dog?"

"Because I *was* a dog," George replies, starting to shake with laughter.

"Arf! Aroo!" Gordie mimics a howl.

"Oh!" Manala's expression is startled surprise.

"They're joking, Manala," I hurry to explain to her.

"Yeah, our brothers are idiots," Gracie concludes, handing Manala her forgotten mug of *lvikao*.

"My brother is not," Manala says with shy pride, glancing at Aeson, as she receives the *lvikao* and takes a sip.

And then, just like that, she *remembers*, and once again all joy leaves her eyes.

P rincess Manala sits down on the sofa, not too far from Xelio, who immediately sets down his plate on the nearest side table and pats the seat cushion next to him to indicate to her to come closer.

Manala moves in slightly, looking wide-eyed.

"So, my Princess Manala, am I correct to guess that you were upset the other day, at your Imperial Brother's Wedding?" Xelio asks in a kind tone, looking at her with his head turned sideways. "It was about dancing and not dancing, I think. . . . Very possibly, apologies are in order, from me. You do understand that I would *never* do anything to upset my very dear Princess Manala, right? Sometimes it might seem that things happen for one reason when it's another. . . . No slight was ever intended—far from it. You have my deepest respect and admiration always, being the most wonderful Imperial Princess that I know."

"I am the *only* Imperial Princess that you know," Manala responds after the slightest pause, meeting Xel's gaze. "There is no other right now."

"True, very true," Xelio says with a soft chuckle. "And that is precisely one reason why sometimes it may not be possible to dance or otherwise engage your company for someone like me."

"Oh. . . ." Manala blinks. "I don't know if I would agree . . . with such an implied assessment of yourself. You are *Xelio Vekahat*. You are—I would think you are—a great *friend.* Of my brother and me."

"I am," he replies, choosing words carefully and glancing at Aeson before proceeding. "It is indeed so, yes—always. And—I appreciate you saying it, more than you know. But it's just how some things are. . . . I am deeply sorry."

"I know," Manala says softly. And then she adds, "It's all right. It was wrong of me to be upset about a silly thing like dancing. But—no one ever asks me to dance except Aeson, and that hardly counts. Everyone is always too afraid. And just this once—on my brother's Wedding day—I wanted to *feel*—I just wanted my friend to dance with me."

Abruptly Manala stands up with a little smile and moves away from Xelio—who still watches her with what is now a complicated expression of concern and guilt. She then glances at all of us around the room. "I'm going to look for Khemji now," she announces and heads for the exit.

With Manala gone, Xelio leaves soon after, returning to work, but not before exchanging some quiet words with Aeson. "She should be okay . . . thanks for trying," I hear Aeson say.

"I hope so, Kass. . . ." Xel sighs, then frowns slightly and becomes businesslike. "Okay, as far as the Tammuz Station reports, will keep you posted."

My family members watch the whole exchange thoughtfully.

After Xelio leaves, Aeson approaches me with a serious expression and says, turning to address everyone. "Apologies for the family issues. My sister can get very emotional, and right now it is so good that she has all of you to visit."

"But of course," Dad says, nodding with emphasis. "Always, Aeson. Your sister is a wonderful young lady, and she is always more than welcome. She is our family now, and so are you. Now—I just wish we could fast forward through all this stress and anxiety for her and locate that missing cat, and all will be well."

After a quick *eos* bread meal, Aeson returns to the workroom for some pressing business, while I stay behind, just hanging out with my family, somewhat uncertain of what to make of today.

Aeson and I had made all those plans earlier. . . . I suppose I should be thinking of the upcoming move to Phoinios Heights and then all the rest of the arrangements to be made and tasks handled—on behalf of my family first and foremost—before we can begin settling into our new married life and routine.

But all I can think of now is that dratted cat and Manala's tragic eyes. . . .

We turn on the TV feeds, and Dad and George watch everything with the curiosity of newly arrived tourists, trying to catch bits of the still-unfamiliar language, while Gracie, Gordie, and I translate.

And then, after a couple of hours, close to Noon Ghost Time, Manala returns.

She just walks into the suite's living room with the familiarity of someone who lives here—which I find innocently comforting—and sits down on the sofa across from my Dad and next to Gordie.

"I think he is gone," she says in a dead voice, before anyone can ask her anything.

"What? No!" I say with a frown, coming to sit on the other side of her.

But Manala nods stubbornly, looking ahead of her at the hovering smart screen nearby. "He is. He *is*."

"Come on now," George says, looking at her with a calm, unreadable expression. "Don't give up. It's only been what—a day? Two? That's *nothing*. We're all looking for him and will continue to do so until we find him."

Manala slowly shakes her head. "It's no use. . . . Every person possible has been dispatched to search, and they looked everywhere. He is gone from the Palace grounds, and now he is lost somewhere in the immense City of Poseidon. He will be hurt, and he will starve. Whichever comes first, he will face terrible suffering. And it is *all my fault*."

"Manala, my dear, everyone is still actively looking," Dad says. "I firmly believe Khemji is hiding somewhere here on the premises. Cats are excellent at hiding in plain sight. He could even be on this floor! In fact we should probably check all the rooms again."

"Good idea," George says, getting up. "Gordon, let's go."

Manala glances at him listlessly. "Don't. It's no use. You raise hope, and it only makes it worse when you dash it."

"Hey, dashing hope is often my specialty." George makes an odd sound. "But not today."

"Yeah, let's do it," Gordie replies, getting up from his seat next to Manala even as she stares at him with pained eyes.

"You know what?" I say, getting up also. "Let's all go look at our Wedding gifts! Supposedly they delivered them to a storage room, which is only a few doors down the hall from here. We can continue looking for Khemji on the way there."

"Ooh, yes!" Gracie exclaims, jumping from her seat, then glances at Manala with some guilt at her own eagerness.

"Excellent idea," our Dad says, picking up the digital tablet in his lap and pushing up the spectacles on the bridge of his nose. "You kids go on, and I'll rest a bit and maybe read a little from the Archives. . . . So much to learn there."

"Manala?" I use my big sister voice. "Come on, it will please me greatly if you join me for this, so let's go!"

A few minutes later, Manala and the rest of us walk down the corridor, turn a few corners, and arrive at our destination. George, Gracie, and Gordie examine all the rooms along the way, opening doors and peering inside, and making kitty calling noises. Meanwhile I hold Manala's hand and lead her reassuringly.

We enter the large storage chamber, which appears to be another living room, only filled with the neatly stacked containers of our Wedding items from the Tree of Gifts, placed everywhere on tables and chairs and even on the long sofa. The servants boxed everything up before delivering it here, so it's impossible to tell what anything is without opening the large boxes.

There is a large wall of windows leading out to a balcony with an elegant balustrade. Several of the windows are open to the pleasantly cool breeze outside, which moves the translucent white curtains, billowing them gently. Meanwhile, Hel's white glare illuminates everything, so no need to turn on the lights.

"Oh, wow, that's a lot of stuff," Gracie mumbles, entering ahead of us and glancing around quickly.

"Sure is," I say, looking at the room in some wonder. "That's all from the entire Imperial Court right there."

"Probably very expensive stuff." Gracie takes another step into the room.

George and Gordie are a few steps behind us, still in the corridor, but Manala is nearby and enters silently, stopping behind me. Her expression is bland and unseeing, even as she obediently follows, staying at my side.

I turn to glance at her with a smile. "Isn't it amazing, Manala? Look at all these boxes! What fun to discover what's hidden inside! I can't wait!"

"Yes," Manala replies in an automatic voice.

In that moment a very deep, very low, very ghastly *yowl* comes from the corner of the room near the wall of windows. Then a huge black feline shape moves in silhouette beyond the curtain.

The cat freezes for a moment, staring at us. Then, with another blood-curdling yowl, it takes one step closer, as though looking for someone to rescue it from the acoustic horrors of its own making.

"Khemji!" Manala cries out in a joyful and desperate voice. "Oh, Khemji!"

But instead of coming closer, Khemji bolts suddenly through the open window and jumps outside onto the balustrade. He pauses briefly on top of the railing to turn around and look at Manala, in a moment of feline uncertainty, then makes up his mind and takes a blind leap to the level below.

Chapter 69

"Oh no, *no!* Khemji!" Manala screams, and launches herself at the open balcony windows. "Khemji, please come back! Khemji, my sweet, brave Khemji!"

We rush to follow her to the balcony and line up at the balustrade, resting our elbows on the polished length of stone. We all lean forward to stare at the floor below, where another balcony sits, covered with flowering green vines.

"Can you see him?"

"There, there!"

"No, I don't think so—that's just a big flower pot—"

"There he is!" Gordie cries, pointing to a streaking black shape as Khemji continues to climb and jump from balustrade to balustrade between Palace balconies in the fierce Hel sunlight.

"Khemji, no, no, my *Khemji!*" Manala is absolutely distraught. She is once more bawling, and suddenly tries to climb the balustrade.

"No, Manala!"

"Hold her!"

While George and Gracie take hold of Manala's arms, I tap my wrist comm and call Aeson. In hurried words I tell him what's happening, and he tells me he's on his way.

"Please send people up here and also down on the ground floor," I say breathlessly. "So that we can corner Khemji, somehow trap him—"

Meanwhile, Manala is hysterical. "He is gone! *Again!* I let him get away! My fault! All my fault! He was so s-s-scared, so h-h-hungry—I should *die!*"

"No, Khemji is right there!" Gracie says, pulling Manala's arm. "Look! We can see him from here, it's great! Now we know where he is, it's really easy, we can catch him!"

"No!" Manala cries in a heart-rending voice, twisting away from my siblings' protective grasps. She steps back and starts to beat herself with her fists once again, shaking in a fever. Her face is contorted, and she is gasping for air between sobs.

"Oh man, what the hell—" George suddenly moves in and takes Manala by the shoulders. *"Hey!* Manala! Enough! *Cut the crap!"* he says, shaking her in his strong grip.

Suddenly, just like that, Manala freezes. She stops sobbing, stops *breathing*, shocked into utter silence, and goes completely still in George's grasp.

"What are you, a three-year-old?" George continues, speaking to her in a cool, hard voice that I've never heard him use before with anyone. "Doesn't matter what kind of lonely snowflake you are, Princess, this *ends now.*"

Manala's mouth falls open as she stares at George, a torrent of tears still streaming down her face. Her sobs have quieted, however, and she is breathing normally.

"Good, continue to breathe and calm yourself," George says in the same cool, rational voice, looking at her without emotion.

The rest of us have also frozen, in amazement.

Manala's eyes grow wide. "You—you are—how dare you—" she begins to speak, glaring at George with impossible outrage. "You—you are horrid! You may *not* speak to me in this manner—"

"Oh, please." George shakes his head slowly in cool disgust.

"But—but—what an awful, horrible person you are, George Lark!"

"Yeah, I'm a total a-hole. But you're going to act like an adult from now on, Imperial Princess M'nala, if you want to get Khemji back. Your cat is not going anywhere, but the more you wail, the longer it'll take to catch him. You're literally scaring the crap out of him right now with all your yelling, so he's going to stay away until you shut up."

"How dare you! Are you telling me to shut up?" Manala is trembling again, this time with anger.

"I am telling you to shut the *hell* up."

My older brother and Aeson's sister glare at one another in a moment of fury. At this point I think George has gone too far.

"George, please, that's too much—" I begin to say. "It is unfair to—"

But Manala takes the moment to escape George's hold and steps away, whirling around to stare at me and the others. "I—I'm sorry, Gwen! I know he is your brother, but I cannot be in the same place as this terrible, heartless *person!*"

And saying this, Manala runs back inside and disappears in the hallway.

"Oh, God . . . George . . ." I say, putting my hand over my mouth. "That really was terrible. Why did you say all those hurtful things to her?"

George is still hard-faced as he stares in Manala's wake. Now he frowns and lets out a held breath. "Yeah, I don't know what came over me," he admits quietly. "Damn. But—you've got to admit, it worked to calm her down. She was completely out of control, possibly a danger to herself. She may hate me now, but at least she'll think twice before allowing herself to fall apart like that."

"That was harsh," Gordie says. "But you could be right. It did work to stop the crazy."

"Guys, she's not crazy," I say with frustration and sadness.

"Yeah, well, could've fooled me," George says in the same grim, hard voice. And then he also heads back inside.

No one is in the mood to look at Wedding gifts, and now that we know Khemji is out there, Gracie, Gordie, and I head back to the guest suite. George must've gone ahead, because he's not in the corridor, and neither is Manala.

When we enter the suite, Dad looks up from his reading and smiles. "So, I hear there's been an actual Khemji sighting? George told me the good news, that you all just saw the prodigal cat on the balcony."

"Where is George?" I ask.

"He was here a moment ago, looking for his jacket, I believe." Dad looks around. "Must've gone out again."

"What about Manala?" Gracie asks.

"Hm-m-m, I don't recall her coming by. Wasn't she with all of you?"

"She was." I sigh and sit down across from Dad. "Then things got a little too much, so she got very upset and ran away."

I don't mention the role that George's harsh words had to do with Manala's sudden escape.

"Poor girl." Thoughtfully Dad looks at me and the others. "One would think she would be *encouraged*, now that you've seen the cat so nearby. Let's hope she does better, soon. I still think her mother should be told."

"It's okay. Aeson is handling it, for now," I mumble with a guilty glance at Gracie and Gordie.

And speaking of Aeson—my husband arrives moments later, looking concerned.

"Where is Khemji now? And where is Manala?" he asks us. "I've informed her personal guards to be more vigilant of her."

I explain again without mentioning George's actions—for now. I think later, in the privacy of our own quarters I'll tell Aeson about the tense situation, but now it just feels like it would be counterproductive. The last thing we need is Aeson having a problem with George.

Damn, I think. *This is getting weird and unpleasantly complicated.*

"All right, I've dispatched some staff downstairs to see if they can capture Khemji from that direction," Aeson says. "I'm going after him myself now—unfortunately can't spare more than an hour on this search today due to some SPC matters. If you see Manala before I return, tell her we're going to take care of Khemji soon."

"Okay." I smile at Aeson and watch him head out the door in businesslike fashion.

We sit around for a few minutes, then Gracie suggests the three of us go for a walk downstairs and see if we can help with the search.

"Dad, we'll be back soon," I say, as Gracie, Gordie, and I stand up.

"Take your time," Dad replies with a light smile, looking up from his tablet. I recognize the familiar absent-minded look of concentration that my father gets whenever he is deep in his research or working on course notes. In some ways it is very comforting to see it again. . . .

We proceed downstairs, accompanied by my guards, including Tuar, and on the way down I tell Gracie and Gordie I want to stop by Manala's apartments on the floor below. "Just want to make sure she is doing okay after everything."

"Sure," Gracie says with a meaningful look. "Let's check up on her."

We get out of the elevator at the Imperial Princess's Quarters and approach the doors. I see two guards stationed at the entrance to her quarters—which, very likely, means Manala is inside. Although Manala's personal guards are mandatory only if she leaves the Palace grounds, as of this afternoon Aeson has instructed them to follow her discreetly whenever possible and keep him informed if anything is out of the ordinary.

The guards allow me access without question, but I knock politely before entering. "Manala?" I call, stepping inside the large antechamber very similar to Aeson's Quarters. "Manala, it's Gwen!"

"And Grace!" My sister announces loudly, stepping after me. "And Gordie too," she adds, glancing at our brother who stands a little sheepishly behind us.

I haven't been inside Manala's apartments that often, but the layout is again very similar to the Crown Prince's layout on the floor above. Similar twisting corridors of suites and guest rooms, and even another duplicate bedroom with a four-point star window directly below my own. As far as I know, Manala uses it as her personal bedchamber, the same way Aeson told me she used my current bedroom—the identical room in the Crown Prince's Quarters—when she was a little girl, whenever she wanted to sleep over in her brother's apartments and hide from her parents or servants.

"Manala, are you there?" I ask, crossing her antechamber. Before I even get to the corridor, I see Manala's silent figure coming toward us.

"Oh! It's you, Gwen," she whispers, then peers behind me to see Gracie and Gordie. Her expression is startled, and her eyes very wide. All of her face is smudged with dried tears, and her messy golden hair looks like she's been lying down on it. "He—your *other* brother—he is not here, is he?"

"Don't worry, George is not here," I say, taking a deep breath. "And Manala, I just want to say I'm very sorry for what happened earlier. George was out of line, and he shouldn't have treated you like that. I'm going to have another talk with him about it—I promise."

"Okay. . . ."

"Now tell me, are you okay?" I continue gently, seeing her unblinking expression. "What are you doing now? Would you like to come back with us? We're going on a little walk outside—"

"I am hiding . . ." Manala interrupts in the same whisper, shaking her head negatively.

"Oh. Well, do you want to come—"

"No!" Manala says in a very loud whisper. "No. . . . *He* told me to be quiet, and I think he was right, even though he *was* horrid. If— if I go to look for Khemji, I will make noise. Too much noise. I cannot help it, I will cry, and I will ruin *everything* again. . . . But if I stay here and hide, and be *quiet*, maybe Khemji will come back."

"I see." I glance from Gracie to Gordie, both of whom appear somewhat confused.

Manala looks at all of us with haunted eyes.

"All right," I say gently. "As long as you're doing okay, we should let you get some rest—"

In that moment, a loud banging sound comes from outside the Quarters, as the elevator opens, and then I hear voices—the guards exclaiming—then more heavy banging noises. And then, yells and loud cussing in English, in my brother George's voice.

In the next instant, the wide doors to the Quarters open—or rather, are opened by the guards—and George comes stumbling into the antechamber, cussing and yelling, his face bleeding, and holding a wildly struggling, *yowling*, huge bundle, partially wrapped in his jacket.

"Shut the damn door!" he cries to the guards and takes two more staggering steps inside, his arms closed in an iron vise around the *thing* he's holding.

Immediately the doors slam behind him. Then George sees us and shouts, "*Hey!* Are the windows closed here? Any doors that need to be closed? Shut them *now!* Quickly! Before I let him go!"

"Oh my God!" Gracie says, staring hard.

Because George is really *bleeding* . . . his face, the outside of his hands in multiple places, his forearms, a horrible gash on his shirt. . . .

"Okay, you have three more seconds to shut everything, and I'm releasing him—"

Manala makes a stifled cry, then looks around the large room wildly, but everything appears to be closed, windows, doors. Only the corridor behind her is open. . . . And it has no door.

"Oh no, back there—my bedroom window is open!" Manala cries, putting her hands up to her mouth.

However, the rest of us think quickly. "Block the corridor!" I exclaim, and Gordie, Gracie, and I all line up to stand in the opening.

George yells again, cusses *hard*, and then lets go of the struggling, howling, scratching cat in his arms.

The moment he does so, Khemji erupts from the makeshift confinement of the torn jacket, and tumbles like a fat, black, monster furball, landing with a thud on the floor, and immediately springboards under the nearest sofa.

Seconds later, angry hissing and yowling can be heard from the general vicinity.

George releases a held breath, then wipes his bleeding, dirt-smudged face with the back of his even more bleeding hand. Wincing, he runs it through his tousled hair. "Special delivery . . ." he says tiredly.

"You found him . . ." Manala whispers, staring at George with intensity and starting to tremble. "You—saved Khemji. . . ."

"Wow, George! How did you manage?" I ask, goggling at my brother in amazement.

"Not too well, as you can see from all the slasher gore—apologies to all." George shrugs, not meeting Manala's stunned gaze. "Cornered him downstairs in the little courtyard—pure luck. Figured it was now or never, tackled him. He tore me up pretty good, but—whatever."

"You need medical care, now!" Gracie says.

"Yes, it looks terrible and painful, and you need antibiotics urgently." I frown, examining him. "Seriously, I mean it—go!"

"Yeah, not a problem. I'll deal with it in a minute," George says, turning to stare.

Under the sofa, Khemji continues to yowl and make grouchy noises in confusion. No idea how he managed to wedge himself under there, considering his huge size.

"Khemji, oh, oh, my poor Khemji!" Manala now gives him her full attention, speaking in an emotion-filled, quavering voice. She approaches the sofa slowly and carefully, then gets down on her knees on the floor to look underneath. "It's all right, everything is all right now, *im saa*. . . . Yes, oh yes! I will give you your favorite food! My sweetest smart boy, you recognize me? Did you forget me so soon? I am your Manala!"

"All right, I'm out," George says quietly to us with a weary look. He then turns around without another word or glance at anyone and walks to the doors.

Chapter 70

While Gracie and Gordie stay behind to help Manala deal with Khemji, I follow George back to the guest suite upstairs. Even as we ride the elevator, George is dripping blood, so I call Aeson and explain what happened, and he immediately dispatches an emergency medical team.

We get to the suite, and I hurry to explain to Dad why George looks like an extra in a slasher movie, and that it looks worse than it really is. Actually I don't know if it's true and have my private doubts—George looks scary-awful, with rivulets of blood pouring down and huge gashes on him.

"A-a-a-ah, George, I'm so sorry, son. . . . Hold this over your arm there—yes, there—to slow the bleeding." Dad shakes his head with a frown as he hands George a clean towel from the stack I've taken from the bathroom. "Yes, nice job on catching the animal, but you should've waited for reinforcements instead of taking him on yourself—all things considered." I know Dad's thinking of that incident when George was a little boy and he had to go to the ER because of how badly he got scratched up by our old cat Samantha.

"Yeah, I'm an idiot. And oww—" George says, pressing one wadded towel against the worst of the cuts to his arm. Then he winces again because he's got a large gash on the jaw near his mouth, which apparently causes pain when he talks. "Just my crap luck with cats."

"Hope it doesn't scar," I say.

"Hey, who doesn't love an attractive scar? Or two . . . or a dozen," George quips, wincing repeatedly, even as the med techs arrive in the suite. "Bring on the scars, baby."

"Don't say that. . . ." I shake my head.

Dad and I stand back, letting the two Atlantean medics do their work. "How bad is it?" Dad asks.

"Not serious," one of the techs says curtly, cutting away strips of, and then removing, George's ruined shirt. He cleans my brother's wounds and applies some kind of antiseptic and pain spray on George. Meanwhile, the other medic administers an antibiotic injection.

"My Imperial Lady Gwen, there should be no scarring," the other tech says. He must've heard my comments just as they entered. "The injuries are not too deep. This will bind the damaged tissues and regenerate the dermal layers."

"Yes, please, deprive me of my chance at sexy scars," George mumbles, as his cheek and jaw get treated with the sealing spray.

Minutes later everything is done. The techs leave some of the spray with George and tell him to use it if any of the sealed wounds crack open—they should not, but just in case—and to avoid washing until tomorrow.

The med techs depart, and my brother puts on a new shirt—just in time for Gracie and Gordie to show up.

"Well, Manala is definitely doing all right," Gracie says with a smile. "She is *so* happy! Totally fussing with the fat stinker."

"Oh yeah?" George angles his head slightly, paying attention. "Glad to hear it. Finally, her world's been set aright."

"Khemji's fine too—came out from his hiding place and ate a big bowl of his favorite smelly protein stuff." And Gracie snorts.

"Yeah, all while purring and farting already," Gordie adds with a laugh.

"Purring and farting? I bet that was *you*, Gee Three." George throws Gordie an amused glance.

"Says the dude who's covered in bloody cat stuff," Gordie retorts.

"Hey, not anymore." George indicates his spray-on bandages. "I am now pristine and covered in eau de antiseptic."

"Oh, and we checked that all her windows are closed," Gracie adds, remembering.

"Good!" I say. "Thanks for staying with Manala to make sure of all that. She just went through a whole lot, and the last thing we need is another cat escape."

"Yes, indeed," my Dad says, and sits down in his chair.

A eson arrives soon after, looking pleased. "At last, the great search has been called off. . . . Just saw Manala, and she is very much restored to her old self," he says with a smile to all of us and George in particular. "All thanks to you, George. She's now making up for Khemji's skipped feedings."

George sighs with relief. "It's the least I could do," he says bluntly, "after I yelled at her."

There is a small pause, as Aeson and George look at each other. "Oh?" Aeson says.

"Yeah," my brother continues. "She was having a meltdown and I said some rotten things that I shouldn't have, to snap her out of it—"

Aeson continues to look at George with an unreadable expression and finally says, "All I know is, my sister is very happy right now, and she told me that *you saved Khemji.* Her words and sentiments were full of praise and highly complimentary toward you, so whatever happened doesn't matter."

"Well, it matters to me," George says seriously. "So you can be sure, I will be apologizing to her."

"Thanks, George . . ." I say gently.

My heart is warmed by so much relief that I cannot begin to describe it—relief that my brother and my husband have gotten this problematic issue out in the open and resolved it so quickly and easily.

Unfortunately, our general common relief doesn't last long, because Aeson's wrist comm suddenly starts chiming urgently. *Im amrevu* checks the incoming message, and his expression becomes grave and serious.

"What is it?" I ask immediately. "Something wrong?"

"Problem at Septu Station," he replies carefully, glancing at everyone present in the room. "Apologies, I must go—"

And just like that, Aeson leaves in a hurry.

A s soon as Aeson is gone, those of us who've been on Atlantis a while longer exchange worried glances, while Dad and George look at the rest of us with uncertainty and expectation.

"What is wrong?" Dad asks.

"What's Septu Station?" George speaks carefully to keep his facial bandages intact.

Gracie glances at me, then at Gordie, whose jaw twitches. Then my sister taps her wrist unit to check for work messages. "Just checking to see if any new orders came in from Fleet Cadet HQ," she says carefully.

I sigh. With a sinking feeling in my stomach, I consider for a moment what it would be like to shatter my father and older brother's peace of mind in the next few minutes—by revealing to them the extent of the current precarious situation our world is in.

Even as I pause, George narrows his eyes at me. "Gee Two, I know that look. What's happening? Spill it."

Ah, George and his damn perceptiveness.

"Well," I say, taking a deep breath and staring at Gracie and Gordie, before facing the other two. "Let's see, how to begin. . . . There are some difficult ongoing things here that involve—"

"Aliens!" Gordie blurts. "Actual ancient extraterrestrials, or should I say, *extraatlantials!* Whoa, I just coined a word—"

"What?" George says.

My poor Dad just stares.

And so the three of us explain the status quo to Dad and George—with many interruptions from each other, sidetracking into the so-called purpose of the Earth mission, elaborating on the existence of the ancient ark-ship, the Ghost Moon, historical asides, and minimally informed speculations about the Imperator's possible goals for all of us here on this planet and back on Earth. We tell them what we know of the *ancient enemy* of Atlantis, the current great *golden light grid* around Helios, the destruction of Rah Station and the second, smaller light grid there, and the fact that the Atlantean Star Pilot Corps has mobilized, that my husband is in charge of all of it, and Fleet personnel have been deployed all over the planet. I also add other secret and sensitive tidbits that even Gracie and Gordie were previously unaware of—in short, I don't hold back.

Dad and George listen with grave faces. Gracie and Gordie appear disturbed in their own way when they hear stuff new to them. We continue taking turns talking until there's little more to be said besides commiseration.

"Oh, but don't worry, Cadets are on standby," Gracie concludes with a nervous laugh. "We're in the third and last wave of deployment, with all the other Earth Cadets, the *shìrén*. I'm pretty sure it'll never come to it."

"Dear God . . ." my father says, breathing slowly and with some difficulty as he digests all this.

"What the hell?" George mutters, holding his cheek. "This absolutely sucks! What kind of a crap solution is this for everyone back on Earth? Are these Goldilocks crazy? To rip us from our homes and bring us across the universe, for what—to fight their stupid battles for them?"

I notice, George has reverted to using the derogatory term for Atlanteans.

"Yeah, I'm guessing that's probably a big part of it," Gordie says, scratching the side of his head.

"If we wanted to die in a fiery apocalypse, we could've just stayed on Earth for the local barbecue via asteroid. And all of it, just to close some purported *dimensional rift* in the effing Bermuda Triangle?" George winces angrily every time he moves his mouth and aggravates his facial injuries. "What a stupid, pointless rescue! No, let me amend—not a rescue but an acquisition. A very advantageous one for the Goldilocks. I can see how. We're the ones getting the raw deal, while they're getting a huge, talented, young immigrant workforce, a fresh genetic influx into their population— people power! Possibly even foot soldiers for the coming alien war—because you know *that's* coming! Oh, and all those Earth treasures and resources, mustn't forget the resources—"

"So the Imperator, your father-in-law, admitted to sending that asteroid to strike Earth?" Dad speaks slowly, thoughtfully, with a quiet, horrified expression.

"Yeah, he did," I say. "But he never properly explained why that rift needs to be closed *now*, all of a sudden, after all these thousands of years. And I don't think even *he* knows for sure whether the asteroid strike would even work to accomplish the job."

"Great!" George says with sarcasm. "Very comforting to know the Atlanteans have absolutely no clue. They know crap; the Earthlings know even less than crap. Meanwhile, the asteroid will obliterate billions at the whim of my sister's new in-law, and there's a shiny invasion army of killer light bulbs hanging out in space all over this system, and—I wouldn't be surprised if there's a similar invasion force gathering around Earth, and we don't even know it.

No clue! Nobody has any damn clue! And, seriously—Bermuda Triangle?"

Gracie sighs. "Don't hold back, Gee One, tell us how you really feel."

"Not light bulbs, light *balls*," Gordie corrects. "Spheres."

"Yes, all right, some big alien balls, got it, thanks Gee Three." George shakes his head. "I think my pain meds are kicking in."

"Ok, I am going to find Aeson now and see what's really happening," I interrupt, getting up.

I make my way to the workroom, hoping Aeson is there. The room is full of people—which is never a good sign—both the *astra daimon* normally on duty and several additional others. Aeson is standing with one arm raised, wrist com activated as he speaks urgently with someone, at the same time watching the various screens around the room, while Anu and Gennio are manipulating a stream of data on three lesser displays. Erita, Keruvat, and Xelio work their wrist holo-feeds also. Three unfamiliar *astra daimon* are seated at various screens around the main desk.

". . . standard capacity vessel loads are not fast enough, and you lost precious time, especially during the initial firing of primary weapons, which cut into your evacuation efforts," Aeson is saying. "You were told to proceed at the 104% overload capacity, which falls within weight tolerance levels, and now you are rushing to compensate. . . ."

Off to the side, dark and lean Nergal Duha, Quoni Enutat, and the olive-skinned and grey-eyed Culuar Efrebu are talking quietly to someone else on a smaller screen—a middle-aged man with a leathery, wrinkle-lined face, light bronze skin, short dark hair that's grey at the temples and barely gilded on top. The man wears a grey Fleet uniform with SPC insignia and some other emblems that I don't recognize. The others address him as Nomarch Evandros, so he must be the man in charge of the Atlantis Station in orbit.

Meanwhile, the biggest display screen is showing a space view of a sizeable planet with pale grey, reddish-mauve, and brown surface features—colors that remind me slightly of Pluto's topography—except this thing is quite large, Atlantis or Earth-sized, according to the scale indicator icons on the graph overlay. The planet takes up most of the screen, but off to the side is an eerily familiar sight—a diamond-shaped *grid* of golden lights, mathematically elegant in its exact spacing, forming gradually in orbit.

The grid seems nearly complete; new light spheres wink into existence, then take up positions in the grid formation. Of course, I might be wrong about its state of completion, because the growth happens along the edges, following the line of the perimeter: each additional light object is added as it circles the formation. . . .

Occasionally I notice long, hair-thin trails of laser bursts, originating from somewhere off-screen. They streak like meteors across space, some of them striking the individual spheres in the formation.

Is someone firing at this thing?

"War-9 reports the grid is now at eighty percent," Erita announces, looking up from her wrist holo-feed. "Twenty percent to go until it reaches the size of Rah's grid."

I step forward and ask, "What happens when it's at one hundred percent?"

"Gwen!" Aeson sees me and pauses his conversation on the wrist comm. His expression warms at once but he still looks grim.

"Oh, sorry, sorry—didn't mean to interrupt," I hurry to say, waving to him with my hand in a silly fashion that seems so out of place for the tense workroom.

"I'll call you back," Aeson says to whoever is on the line with him, and taps out the call. Then he turns to me gently. "No problem, *im amrevu*. Please feel free to watch, but we're in a somewhat precarious situation right now so it might be best for you to take a seat. . . ."

I nod without another word, and step off to the side next to Anu and Gennio's desk. Gennio pulls up a chair for me, and I perch awkwardly, then continue watching.

On the big screen, the slowly floating image of the planet and the diamond grid orbiting it, is suddenly replaced by a different view angle. And at once I see a huge metallic object silhouetted against the mauve-grey planet. It's vaguely X-shaped, but with an additional pair of platform-spokes protruding perpendicular to the other platforms, all rotating around a central hub filled with tiny habitat lights. I recall Rah Station's shape, and this one is very similar, but considerably larger.

"Is that Septu Station?" I whisper to Gennio.

He nods.

"So another *light grid* has formed here, but not at that other station—" I pause in mid-question because suddenly I see the curvature of yet another *immense* metallic object slip into view.

And when I say immense, I mean the *thing* is big enough to swallow Septu Station three times over. Its monster hull shines with the combination of reflected Hel light and its own surface plasma iridescence. The moment it starts growing in the viewscreen, it takes over, obscuring everything in just a few heartbeats.

"Flipping to another buoy view, 20 *mag-heitar* out, zoom at 100%," says one of the seated *daimon*.

And immediately we get a clear view from a slightly different angle, which encompasses all objects—on one side, the diamond light grid; in the center of the frame, the planet Septu; on the other side, the Septu Station and the huge, shining, elongated oval or cigar-shaped *monster ship* that coasts in orbit near the rotating station.

"Is that—" I begin to ask.

"That's War-9," Gennio responds in a low voice.

"Wow," I whisper. "It's huge. . . . Also, beautiful."

"Oh yeah," Anu whispers loudly. I notice, he has a wistful expression of awe as he looks at the gargantuan battle barge.

And then I notice something else. Superimposed against the black background of space, there are things that could be tiny points of static, as seen from their relative size in perspective to the battle barge. They are roiling like a metallic hive around the great battleship. "What are those little things that look like dots all around it?"

"Emergency evacuation," Anu says.

"Those are various station ships, ferrying all station personnel and cargo to the battle barge," Gennio says. "Really behind schedule. They have to hurry, before the grid formation reaches 100%."

"What happens then?" I ask again.

Gennio bites his lip.

"Grid formation has accelerated, now at 89%, and War-9 still has only 73% of the Septu Station personnel on board," Keruvat announces.

"Tell them to expedite, human priority. Personnel only, abandon cargo," Aeson says in a dark tone. "Accounting for acceleration, how much time do they have?"

Xelio examines code results. "Seven daydreams, thirty heartbeats, at best—before grid completion."

"We cannot be sure what happened at Rah will repeat here within the same time sequence," Nergal says, approaching Aeson.

Aeson makes another call. "Nomarch Asclep, your status," he demands in a hard voice, apparently addressing Septu Station. "You have six daydreams. How much time do you need? No, you *don't* have ten daydreams. You have less than six. Make it work."

"Bashtooh," Xelio says. "Grid formation is accelerating even more, 93% now."

Aeson taps his wrist comm again. "Evacuation status, Command Pilot Zhar. Get them out of there. You now have less than four daydreams. Recall all ships *now*. Yes, that's an order."

"Grid formation at 97%, hitting critical range," Erita exclaims.

My pulse racing with stress and a kind of slow, sickening horror, I watch the large view and the tiny flitting ships moving between the station and the battle barge. As they continue, War-9 starts slowly pulling away from the proximity of the station. The little ships follow, racing toward it, even as War-9 starts to accelerate.

Meanwhile, the golden grid diamond shape keeps growing, and then, suddenly it stops.

"Now at 100%," Keruvat says. "It is identical to the Rah formation."

There is a beat of silence.

"Command Pilot Zhar, begin Quantum Stream sequence now!" Aeson speaks into this wrist comm. And then he switches lines. "Nomarch Asclep—if you can hear me, abandon station, or brace for impact."

In that moment the diamond grid flares blinding white, like a small star. . . . And then it breaks apart into fiery chaos, as individual light spheres abandon the formation and eject blasts of white plasma in the direction of Septu Station, the planet surface, and the last of the tiny fleeing ships. . . .

We watch, stilled in horror, as the X-shape of Septu Station becomes a fireball of white, yellow, gold, and orange debris. . . .

The spheres continue firing. They streak like meteors toward the planet surface and alongside the desperate, escaping ships.

As the buoys in the path of the plasma get destroyed, their cameras go out, so the view program switches constantly to other remaining active units in the vicinity.

One of these views captures the now distant oval of War-9, as it accelerates into the QS space . . . but apparently not fast enough. Several enemy spheres catch up to it and its brood of ships, and white vectors of plasma strike across the distances hitting the hull of the battle barge.

"No . . ." Aeson speaks harshly into his wrist comm, "Command Pilot Zhar, your status! Respond now! *Saramana Zhar!*"

But now the viewscreen goes nova with homogeneous brightness. In a single blinding moment War-9 is the source of that brightness as it breaks apart. In the next split second, there are two distinct pieces of the long hull, and then there are only fiery flames and infinite debris, spinning out into space.

War-9 and the Septu Station are gone.

Chapter 71

The workroom is completely quiet. Faces are fixed in shock as the *astra daimon* officers watch the fire-engulfed debris spin out, plummet, float, and dissipate in every direction to fill the orbit around Septu.

The golden spheres of the alien enemy remain in hive motion, continuing to fire around them. But soon enough it's clear they are returning to their original diamond-shaped grid formation.

Aeson stands silent, straight-backed, with an unreadable face. He watches the screen.

And then he raises his arm with the wrist comm and taps it, making another connection. "This is SPC Commander Aeson Kassiopei. Nomarch Cretheo, what is the current status of Tammuz Station?"

The next hours are a blur of remote communications, running people, and raised emotional voices. Aeson is talking to everyone, it seems, and he gets no respite. And all I can do is watch from the sidelines in awful, stunned silence.

We learn that Septu Station was the only place attacked. Tammuz Station continues to report that they are in the clear—there's no sign of the alien enemy anywhere in the vicinity of the planet. No golden light grid, no energy fluctuations in the deep space perimeter, nothing. Tammuz Station is on trigger alert, and War-8 is ready to fight or flee on command.

"... an outrage! No, no, they must remain to fight! If those things appear, order them *not* to run without engaging them!" an IEC Council Member's agitated face glares on a video call, yelling at Aeson from a small hovering screen.

"Your opinion is duly noted, Council Member Amasis," Aeson says coldly. "I remind you that the use of force was attempted today, and it was unsuccessful. War-9 fired immediately, then dispatched vessels to bombard the partial grid during its early stages of formation, to no effect. All of this was happening in tandem with the evacuation efforts.... We did not just *run*—we fired *while* we ferried personnel. But our resonance weapons had no effect. Lasers were useless. Our plasma weapons did not penetrate. And our drone torpedoes passed through the spheres, then experienced the refraction-bending phenomenon that returned them right back at us at odd angles, while there was no return fire from the enemy spheres. They *disdained* our use of force against them or simply ignored us completely and continued to build the grid. Evacuation was the *only* viable option."

While Aeson speaks to IEC Member Amasis, an adjacent hovering screen shows the face of a foreign official who interrupts the conversation in a thick accent, frequently switching to an unfamiliar language which I can only guess is the language of Qurartu. "Commander, regardless of the tactics used, the loss of our people is not to be measured," he says. "War-9 contained the best of our Fleet pilots and officers, and Qurartu cannot begin to mourn so many lives, unavenged. I must now face the Hetmet and convey the tragic details, and I don't know how to even begin—"

"You have my profound expression of grief on behalf of the fallen and their families," Aeson says. "Please convey to Hetmet Qedeh Adamer that I will be calling him personally."

The Qurartu official disconnects, and another call comes in on the display, this time from one of the Command Pilots in the outer system. Command Pilot Saiva Neidos wants to know if she should remain near Olympos Station or bring War-4 closer to Atlantis or one of the inner outposts.

"Please stand by, Command Pilot Neidos," Aeson replies. "I will inform you of any change in orders. Yes, we are still working on it."

And then the Imperator calls.

Aeson takes the call on his wrist comm and moves off to the side of the room for privacy. I watch his mask of composure crumble for one instant and then re-form as he talks to his Father. His tone of voice remains constant, and I can still hear snatches of "... New Deshret will learn to wait ..." and "... Niktos Fleet Commander must make the choice that's best for Bastet ..." and then "... will make another attempt to reach the ark-ship lower levels. ..."

"Imperial Lady Gwen." Erita nears me for a moment. "You probably should get some rest. This is an ongoing situation that will not resolve tonight. You might end up waiting for him very late." And she motions with her head in Aeson's direction.

I nod with resignation. "I understand. Of course, I'll go. I'm in everybody's way here anyway."

"Oh no, not at all." Erita hurries to reassure me, with a brief, stressed smile.

But I know better. I quietly exit the workroom while Aeson has his back turned and doesn't notice.

Of course, I have to tell my family what happened. Not the graphic horror, just the basic gist. We're definitely under attack by a relentless, inexplicable, technologically *more advanced* alien force that does not seem to have any vulnerabilities. And there's very little I can do to sugarcoat it.

My family reacts as expected, quiet and grim. We spend the rest of the night speculating, watching the TV feeds, where, so far, the news has not hit, or possibly has been suppressed. It's almost perverse, seeing happy commentators and flippant features, celebrity gossip, and even bawdy chatter about the current "preoccupations" of the Imperial Newlywed Couple, and glimpses of the aftereffects of our Wedding celebrations upon the City of Poseidon. . . .

"What will happen now?" Gordie asks, with a permanent frown on his face.

"I guess we die," George says flatly, too tired and too medicated to vent more creative sarcasm.

Dad rubs his forehead, the bridge of his nose, and watches us, deep in thought. I see his glance slip occasionally toward the corner of the room, where on top of a side table Mom's urn stands.

He's thinking of her, even now. . . .

I finally go to bed around thirteenth hour, alone, without Aeson—after returning to the Crown Prince's side of the Quarters the roundabout way, bypassing the busy workroom that has become an SPC command station.

Aeson never comes, so I fall asleep feeling strange and awkward without him in the huge bed of the master suite. It never occurs to me to move to my own bedroom with the four-point star window, because I know if Aeson returns he will be looking for me in this bed—*our* marriage bed.

However, in the morning of Red Amrevet 12, I wake up alone once again, and it doesn't appear that Aeson has been to bed at all.

He hasn't slept last night. He likely hasn't eaten.

My heart constricts with painful recall of the previous day. The loss of hundreds, possibly thousands of people on that station and the battle barge, sickens me. . . . It must weigh on *him* to an extent I cannot even imagine. And the awful thing is, he cannot even slow down to contemplate or *feel*, because he has to continue to act the Commander, handling the crisis, and his role is ongoing.

I feel like I shouldn't try to disturb him, so I use my wrist unit to send him a simple message.

I love you so much, Aeson. Thinking of you. I'm here, if you need me.
—*Your Gwen*

Right now there is little else I can do or say.

I go the roundabout way to my side of the Quarters and join my family for *eos* bread. It's after seventh hour, and Dad and George are already eating. The TV screen is hovering before them, sound muted, showing multiple feeds. But Gracie and Gordie are not here. Gordie cannot miss any more work, and Gracie is on Fleet standby back in her apartment downtown.

However, I'm a little surprised to see Manala perched on the sofa, with a big plate of food in her lap. She looks serious but as not listless as she was these past few days without Khemji.

Dad is sitting in his chair, while George is standing with his back to us, filling his plate from the serving station. When he turns around, I see that his spray bandages have been freshly reapplied in some places on his jaw and cheeks, but he does look better.

"Morning," I say, followed by *"Nefero eos"* for Manala's benefit.

"Any news, my dear?" Dad asks me at once.

I shake my head.

"Aeson?" Dad's expression is meaningful.

"He hasn't been back since yesterday." I say softly. "He must be completely overwhelmed with command, and I am so worried for him. I—I don't know what to do—to help."

"I think he would want you to keep your strength up, above all," Dad says, beckoning me with his hand. "Start by having a good breakfast—*eos* bread."

I approach and lean down for a kiss, as Dad pats my cheek and the top of my head. "How are you feeling these days, Dad?" I ask, staying down to hug my father before straightening.

"Very well, and no complaints so far," Dad says. "I think I might be getting used to this excessive gravity, and I can see George has already acclimated."

"Except for the sleepiness, I guess," George says, carrying his plate to the sofa, and then yawns, as if to prove his point.

Manala, who is sitting on the sofa, scoots over slightly to make room for him, even though there is space enough for two more people between them. George glances briefly at her and then begins to eat.

"Manala, how is Khemji doing?" I ask.

"Oh! He is wonderful!" At once Manala's expression shines with joy. "I fed him as soon as I woke up, and he ate very well, and then let me touch him and brush him, and was not scared at all! I think he forgot all about being gone."

I smile at her. "Of course, he did. He is home and happy to be with you."

Manala glances from me to George and then to my Dad. "I am so *glad* he is safe. Thank you—to all of you. For helping me when I was—so *lost* without him. Thank you—*George*." And Manala turns her face to look directly at my brother with an intense expression.

George swallows and pauses eating, then slowly looks up, raising his brows. He appears slightly uncomfortable. It's a rare thing to see my brother this way, off his game and uncertain, even for a moment. "Oh . . . yeah," he responds after a tiny pause. "No problem."

I watch George and bite my lip. Dad watches also, probably not quite sure what's happening, unless George explained things when they were alone. Although Dad was present when Aeson and George had the Manala mini-talk yesterday, the Septu Station disaster pushed everything else from our minds.

Another awkward moment goes by.

Then George breathes in deeply and says, continuing to look at her weirdly, "About what happened yesterday—M'nala, I'm sorry, I shouldn't have said those rough things. I acted like a jerk. Was really unfair to you when you were so upset. So—anyway, glad it's over and you got the cat back."

"I'm very sorry that you got hurt," Manala says, examining George's face closely for the first time.

George makes a short sound implying his lack of care and glances at his plate.

"We have a fine saying on Earth: all's well that ends well," Dad says in a mild tone, looking from George to Manala and then at me, and smiling.

"True . . . very true," I say, keeping up my own smile for everyone's sake. At the same time, I can't help thinking about Aeson and all the things that must be going wrong *at the moment* and not ending well at all for so many innocent people.

It also occurs to me that although Manala has some idea that Aeson is dealing with a crisis, she probably doesn't know what happened at Septu Station, since the news has not reported it yet, and none of us really got into it in front of her.

For now, it's best to keep it this way.

I go to pour myself a fresh mug of *lvikao* and put something on my plate, all the while glancing sideways at my wrist comm in hopes of an incoming message from my husband. Then I sit down on the sofa and pretend to eat. I also fiddle constantly with a small item in my pocket which I've resorted to carrying around with me everywhere since the day after the Wedding.

The item is Aeson's love gift to me—an odd-shaped, antique key of old unpolished metal, about three inches long, with a four-point star on one end. To be exact, it's a hollow outline of a star—serving as the head of the key—and a shaft with an intricate pattern of notches, key wards and bits at the other end. I didn't think I'd be so attached to it, but recently discovered that I *am*—especially now.

Right now, the thing seems to be doing its job, serving as a surrogate for Aeson and giving me something to cling to—no matter how ridiculous.

Indeed, it's working so well that I've set my plate down completely and taken the key out of my pocket to turn it over in my fingers, flipping it this way and that, feeling the rough bumps along the metal surface.

Manala notices the constant movement of my fingers. "What is that?" she asks, staring in curiosity.

"Oh—it's Aeson's love gift," I say. "Something to occupy my fingers."

"May I see it?"

"Of course." I lean over and hand Manala the key.

"I know this key, it's so old!" the Princess exclaims with a laugh. "I didn't realize my brother gave you this old thing for his meaningful gift."

I chuckle. "Yes, well, that's your brother for you. I still say I expected a digital key card. In some ways—I suppose, you might say I got it. . . . At least this one is decorative."

Manala turns the key over in her slim fingers, while Dad and George watch us both with amusement.

"I like how it's very intricate on the blade end; makes such a pretty pattern that looks like a maze," I say. "And the cutaway star is beautiful."

"The star?" Manala glances up at me. "That's just an *astroctadra*, a very old shape used in traditional art and on all kinds of antique items."

"Fascinating," Dad says. "May I take a look? You say it's a traditional design element?"

"Oh, yes, it's found everywhere." Manala gets up and takes the key over to my Dad. "Very common."

"What does it mean?" After adjusting his spectacles, Charles Lark, my father, holds the key in his hands and examines it closely.

Manala pauses to think, then shakes her head. "I don't know. It's just an antiquated star. Our traditional crafts makers included it in all kinds of objects—such as this key. There are silly trinkets and jewelry pieces that have it; really old talismans and items of protection. Also, cooking implements, antique stylus holders for scribes, miniature boxes. . . . There are even toys decorated with the *astroctadra*. If you go to the Museum of Ancient Toys, which is my favorite, you will see hundreds of *astroctadra* toys and games of all kinds, even rattles for infants. The most ancient ones came with us from Old Atlantis on Earth. Some people think it's tiresome and too old-fashioned, so they don't make them as much any more—unless they're art replicas or souvenirs for tourists."

"But you don't recall the specific meaning of this *astroctadra?*" my father persists gently. "Any references in your myths or legends? Stories? Forgive me, but I'm very curious, for some reason. . . ."

"Oh, that's okay, and there's nothing to forgive," Manala says innocently. "I'm very glad to answer all these questions."

There's a pause as we all sort of think about it.

"Daddy," I say with a smile. "May I have my husband's love gift back, please? I'd hate to lose it."

"Oh, sure," Dad says, surrendering my precious key back to Manala who brings it over to me.

My fingers close eagerly over the key, with a weird sense of relief.

"Oh, wait!" Manala exclaims suddenly. "How could I forget— the 'Moon and Star' game! I used to play it with my nannies, and Aeson too. You play it outside, when it gets dark, at night. . . . There's this little rhyme you sing—"

And then Manala taps my arm. "Gwen, I must show you how to play it with the *astroctadra*—may I please borrow your key again?" Before I can react, she snatches it from me. "I know it's not the actual toy kind, but you can use any item that has the *astroctadra* to play."

"Okay," I say, raising my brows.

"First, you close your eyes," Manala says, shutting hers. "Then you spin as you sing the rhyme." She begins to turn around quickly, eyes still closed, hands outstretched, with the key raised in one hand, while reciting in a singsong manner:

> Find the moon around a star,
> Ride the Pegasus too far.
>
> Find the star around a moon,
> Meet your love by afternoon.

"Then you stop, open your eyes, and look through the *astroctadra* at the evening sky. Whatever you happen to see in that exact spot—in your view of the sky, framed inside the little opening—is what you get. The object of the game 'Moon and Star' is to catch at least one moon inside the view hole. If you get no moon, only stars and darkness, you lose your turn and the other person gets to spin and sing and look at the sky."

"Definitely good fun for kids," Dad says.

"It can be so much fun! I used to love playing," Manala says, lifting up the key and pretending to stare through the hole at something on the ceiling. "But the rules vary. Some people play in order to place bets—people in *Atlantida* just love making bets. But children play for fun, and it depends on what you decide your rules to be. So many *astroctadra* variations. Also, the toys sometimes have different kinds of interior openings; some are carved with multiple stars. . . . You will see so many of them in the Museum!"

"It's decided. We'll have to visit this Museum at the earliest opportunity," Dad says. "I should be more ambulatory in a few days."

"My key, please, Manala," I say again with amusement.

This time, the Imperial Princess returns Aeson's love gift to me without protest.

Perfect timing, since my husband himself walks into the room.

Chapter 72

"Aeson!" I shove the key in my pocket, seeing *im amrevu's* grim, exhausted expression, as he stands at the doors of the guest suite.

"Glad I found you here," he says, looking at me with a faint smile and vulnerable eyes, then clears his throat, which sounds parched. "So sorry I didn't return last night, Gwen. It was—impossible."

"I understand," I say, coming up to him and touching him gently on the cheek and back of the neck, fingers parting golden strands of his long hair, then caressing his arm. "You need to have something to eat and drink *right now*, then bed!"

"All right," he says. "But there's no time for bed. I will grab some *eos* bread, then I must return. We're about to make official statements to the media—"

"Can't it wait? You need a couple hours of rest, at least!"

"Your wife is right, listen to her," my Dad says, pointing at the food stations.

"Aeson, you look terrible!" Manala says. "Please, you are scaring me! Why can't you rest?"

"He will, eventually," George says in a calming tone, giving Aeson a smart glance. "But now let the man eat."

Aeson eats quickly and gulps down *lvikao*, saying almost nothing, and I don't press him for details, especially in front of Manala. And then I somehow convince him to go with me to the master bedroom just to lie down for fifteen minutes.

We head back there, passing through the workroom filled with people, and I'm almost afraid to look at the various computer screens for fear of seeing more disasters and casualties.

"I'll return shortly," Aeson tells the *daimon* officers who glance up at him from their work stations. "Understood, Commander,"

Oalla replies formally, giving the two of us a sharp look. "Please take that break now. Rest assured, we will inform you of any status changes."

Aeson nods, and we continue to his side of the Quarters.

Once in our immense bedroom, I lead my husband firmly by the hand and insist on helping him to remove his footwear and some of his clothing. Then I fluff the pillows of our great bed and make him lie back.

He obeys, watching me languidly through half-lidded eyes. "My . . . Gwen," he says, taking hold of my hand and pulling me to him, so that I end up lying on my stomach alongside him. *"Im vuchusei. . . ."*

"Close your eyes," I say, my face hovering over his, without kissing him, for fear of arousing him too much and defeating the purpose of this whole thing.

He obeys with a sigh, and his eyelids flutter closed in relaxation. I watch his thick, long lashes rest against his cheeks.

"Ah, Gwen," he mumbles. "You are my harbor."

"Shush," I say. "Take a deep breath. Let it out. Now, another. . . ."

In reply I hear a soft snore.

I let Aeson sleep for an hour and a half, uninterrupted, then regretfully wake him because Keruvat sends me a message that the SPC Commander is needed on multiple fronts.

Aeson shudders awake, and his eyes fly open in immediate, wary alertness. *"Bashtooh!* I've slept!"

"Why, yes, you have," I retort, giving him a sound kiss on the corner of his lips and another on his cheek, then vigorously rub his shoulders. "And now you can get back to work with a slightly clearer head."

"I can think of something else that would really clear my head right now," he says, letting his lips curve sensuously as he stares into my eyes.

"No. Not until *tonight*," I say, furrowing my brow sternly. "You must come to bed properly for that to happen."

"You are a very sneaky woman," he replies, sitting up, then heads for the bathroom.

For the rest of the afternoon Aeson is gone again, and I spend the time aimlessly. I visit with Dad and George, then take a short stroll along the gardens of the Imperial Palace with Manala without running into anyone we know—such as curious Ladies of the Court who might want to gawk at the new Imperial Consort and see how she's managing in her new life and position. Then we return and watch the TV feeds, only to see the grim announcement of the destruction of Septu Station being reported variously on every channel by solemn news anchors.

There's no escaping it, so I get away the only way I know how, by wandering into my own solitary bedroom with the four-point star window—or should I call it the *astroctadra* window, now that I know the proper term—and space out, thinking while staring at the incandescent daylight.

A stray thought comes to me: today is the day I'll need to take a small booster dose of the special Kassiopei contraceptive drink. Normally it's good for five days (and it's only been three days since I initially drank that golden goblet right before *Amrevet* Night), but this is to normalize the levels in my system and to adjust for my chosen day of the week. After this one-time booster I can switch to a regular weekly maintenance dose starting next week. The Imperatris recommends picking the day that coincides with my Quadrant color, so it's easier to remember. For me, that would be Yellowday—from now on until I want to conceive. And so, I must not forget to take it, if Aeson and I plan to be intimate tonight. . . .

Thinking about it, I go to the bathroom suite to check the cabinet where, supposedly, my Imperial apothecary refills will be available for me discreetly on a regular basis, supplied by the proper medical staff. I take a look, and indeed, the bottle is already there, marked exactly as described to me by the Imperatris. It is also time-stamped for best efficacy, and the time to take it is early evening, which means I should wait before having it later tonight, as prescribed.

I sigh and mentally remind myself to return here at night, before anything physical happens between us.

The day stretches out, and I spend most of it with my family in their guest suite, watching Dad. I sit nearby, listening to him reminisce about the details of their last months on Earth, including his final, bittersweet classes at the university in Burlington, where he taught (remarkably, there were still a few students who continued to attend class for the sake of normalcy, despite the inevitability of approaching death by asteroid). Meanwhile George makes occasional snark commentary, while scanning through the TV feeds on a hovering smart screen, swiping and zooming windows constantly, as though he's trying to cram for a visual exam on all things Atlantis.

Manala comes and goes multiple times throughout the afternoon, bringing curious items with her, which my father finds amusing.

"The girl enjoys being here and spending time with us. After all, we're her new extended family," Dad says—after the third time Manala exits the room with a promise of returning a little later with some genuine antique scrolls she wants to show him and an *astroctadra* toy for me. "I can see how it might be natural for her to want to socialize, all things considered. Isolated, lonely upbringing will do it. She's very intelligent and excellently educated, which makes it even more vital for her to be mentally stimulated."

"I hope you don't mind all this, Dad?" I ask.

"Goodness, no, I'm growing very fond of her." Dad smiles. "Nice girl. Very pleasant conversationalist, so knowledgeable for someone her age. . . . Of course, I need to remember that in this society the young start taking on responsibilities much earlier. She is very encyclopedic, which is a delight."

"I can see how it would be, Dad." I smile back. And then I turn to my brother. "What about you, Gee One?"

"What about me?" George asks with a quick glance.

"Manala being here so much is not bothering you?"

"Not at all. She's a good egg." And George returns his attention to the screen.

Much later Aeson shows up for a *niktos* meal, which he again takes with me and my family. His face looks drained and grim. Apparently he has been in non-stop meetings with military veterans and IEC Members, and has talked to several foreign heads of state. And yes, he received personal accusations about the courses of action taken under his command, and the deadly consequences.

"In short, this is an ugly, chaotic time, at least until we come up with an *effective* working strategy to deal with the alien threat," Aeson tells me quietly, keeping his mask of composure. "Right now, we're in an existential crisis with no solution. . . . The fact that I get the brunt of the blame is not surprising. It comes with the territory of high command. Nor do I reproach them for targeting me with their anger. Everything—all of it—is justified. Lives were lost, and I am responsible. So many innocent lives. . . . And the worst part is—it will likely happen again, before a solution is found."

"Oh, Aeson. . . ." I watch *im amrevu* speak the brave words and feel my heart breaking for him.

I can almost hear the unspoken part of his sentence.

If a solution is found.

We finish eating, and Aeson tells me he has to go back to work for a few more hours tonight, to deal with several video call appointments with ranking members of international military, including New Deshret—a call for which the Imperator will also be present.

"But you promised to come to bed tonight," I remind him with a meaningful look. "Right?"

Aeson smiles. "Yes," he says softly. "It might be late, but I will not miss it—not this time."

"Okay," I say. "I'll walk back with you now, since I need to stop by my bedroom. . . ." And then I whisper to him discreetly about that certain important prescription I need to take tonight.

"Aha," he says, looking at me with so much meaning in his gaze, while his lips move up at the corners in his familiar shadow smile. "Let's go then."

We head back toward Aeson's side of the Quarters, going through my bedroom suite, and I pull him by the hand after me. The evening has turned to full night, and the window curtains in my bedroom have been open since afternoon, allowing the bright, star-filled sky in all its glory to fill the chamber with soft, violet-indigo ambiance.

Aeson lingers, waiting for me as I go around the corner to the bathroom suite and retrieve my special drink. I drink the full amount necessary, then return, smiling at him with naughty promise.

"Ah, I wish I could stay now, Gwen," he says with a smile of regret. "But I have appointments—"

"I know," I interrupt pulling him by the hand, then place both my arms around his neck and draw him down to me for a deep kiss. He responds at once, his mouth covering mine hungrily, and we struggle sweetly for several seconds before coming apart.

"Ah. . . ." Aeson breathes, calming himself. "Such a beautiful night."

I glance through the four-point star window at the colorful richness of celestial wonders outside and notice a distant pale splotch of light staring directly at me from the lower corner of the window frame.

It's in an odd spot, exactly in the center of the window, but on the very bottom vertex point of the *astroctadra* shape. And somehow, I recognize its pale, familiar, ghostly presence.

"The Ghost Moon," I say with a familiar stab of anxious curiosity, staring at it. "Peeking at us from the bottom."

He follows the direction of my gaze and nods. "Yes, our fourth moon . . . there it is, right there. . . . Yet another unresolved situation that we must deal with. So strange to see it regularly outside the window these days, together with the usual others."

"And it's centered exactly on the bottom corner, right at the point!" I persist. "Hey, did you know I learned today that this shape—the shape of the window, and so many other things around here on Atlantis—is called the *astroctadra?* Manala told us all about it, after all these months—and I had no idea."

Aeson chuckles. "The Atlantean star. . . . A very, *very* old symbol."

"Manala mentioned games you used to play. How does the rhyme go?" I muse. "Something about catching a moon or a star. Or finding a moon inside or outside the *astroctadra,* and you have to close your eyes and spin—"

"Find the moon around a star, ride the Pegasus too far," *im amrevu* recites, looking at me with warm eyes glittering with liquid in the starlight, and his pupils dark as night.

"That's right," I whisper.

"Find the star around a moon, meet your love by afternoon."

"Yes, so very romantic, and I love it," I say. And then I glance outside again.

To get a better view, I take a step toward the window and lower my gaze to stare at the Ghost Moon from a slightly different angle. And in so doing, I immediately notice another bright source of light—this one streaming from above.

In fact, it's coming *exactly* from the *top* corner of the window star shape. Truly, a bizarre coincidence.

"Oh, look! That's Amrevet right up there," I say, recognizing—by its very bright, very pale lavender hue—that the radiance originates from the big, violet-grey moon that must've recently sailed overhead and disappeared just out of sight. . . .

Aeson and I approach the window even closer and glance up, and now we can indeed see Amrevet from this better angle. From where we stand in the room, it's also exactly in the center of the frame, but much higher in the sky than the Ghost Moon.

The crazy thing is, *in this moment*, the two moons are *aligned perfectly* along the vertical. So much so, that if you took a ruler and drew a line from the Ghost Moon below to Amrevet directly above, it would be a perfect vertical line . . . and it would continue, passing through the exact vertex point of the top and bottom "rays" of the four-point star window frame.

"How funny." I point it out to Aeson. "The moons—they're lined up, stacked exactly on top of each other. Seemingly, to a mathematical degree, assuming this window was built straight."

Aeson smiles, observing it. "Cosmic alignments can be fun. I believe that window's an antique."

"Okay, this is really weird," I continue, this time looking at the other two vertices, the ones on the right and the left. "But what if Pegasus and Mar-Yan were lined up too? But *horizontally!* Does that ever happen?"

Aeson raises his brows. "Not sure. It might require hours of looking outside this particular window. But you're right, that would be both eerie and weird. Right now, Mar-Yan is low on the horizon and has a long way to go up before it reaches the level of the window vertex on the right. Meanwhile, Pegasus is still on the other side of the sky behind us and might show up hours later, maybe as late as in the afternoon—"

Suddenly Aeson freezes. His expression grows thoughtful, almost stunned.

"Find the star around a moon," he mutters, and his brows move in a frown. "Star *around* a moon . . . around a moon. . . . 'Meet your love by afternoon.'"

I watch him, and suddenly, my own thoughts go into a rapid cascade of connections. "Aeson, that window—that's an actual, physical star *object* around a moon."

"And love? In this case, love is not love but a *name*," he says, sounding almost incoherent. "It's Amrevet, the moon, literally. I'm willing to bet that *in the afternoon*, its location in relation to this specific vantage point—this permanently fixed *astroctadra* window—might align in a very interesting way with Pegasus and Mar-Yan!"

"Which means . . . this old children's rhyme is not just a game," I whisper, thoughts spinning. "It's a description of an *astronomical alignment*."

"Yes!" he continues. "And 'Find the moon around a star, ride the Pegasus too far'—okay, this could mean that when any given moon is *not* inside the bounds of the *astroctadra* window, the positioning of the moons Mar-Yan, which is the Rider, and Pegasus, 'is too far.' Meaning, it's literally too far outside the alignment."

"Okay," I say. "But what is this moon alignment supposed to indicate? Where did this whole thing come from? How old is it that you even have children's rhymes based on it? And what about this strange window? Who built it? What is its true purpose? Manala has one exactly like it in her bedroom downstairs—"

In that moment, Aeson's wrist comm chimes with an incoming message. He glances at the glow flaring along the data band with exasperation. "*Bashtooh*, I'm running late," he says. "But this is very important, whatever it is that we've discovered here, with this old window and the moons, Gwen. It might contain the answer to the Ghost Moon phenomenon. I'll look into it as soon as I handle the appointments. My Father will need to be informed too, but after I get more information."

And saying this, Aeson hurries away.

I stare in his wake with a strange, prickling rise of excitement. Then I turn around and resume looking through the newly mysterious window and the moons outside.

I watch the sky for a long time, alone in my bedroom, driven by some inexplicable, urgent sense of importance mixed with curiosity.

I observe and, just for fun, make silly calculations and visualizations in my mind using basic Euclidean geometry on a flat, two-dimensional plane with zero curvature. And then I decide that's completely inadequate because, while the *astroctadra* itself is an abstraction of a simple view along a flat plane, these moons are floating along curving orbits in 3D space. So I switch to three-dimensional visualizations along an Elliptic plane with positive curvature and Hyperbolic for negative curvature. . . . I space out so hard that time loses all meaning.

In those hours that I'm there, the Ghost Moon slowly traverses its vertical path, sailing slowly up in a straight line toward zenith.

Confirming my guess about its mathematical accuracy, it passes right through the top vertex of the *astroctadra* window before sailing out of sight.

Chapter 73

Aeson returns as promised, but very late, after Midnight Ghost Time. By then I've migrated to our master bedroom and gone to sleep. However, I feel him get in bed next to me, carefully trying not to wake me, so naturally I wake up and ask him how everything went.

Despite his exhaustion, Aeson appears alert, with a fierce new level of energy in his eyes. "Interesting developments, will tell you all about it tomorrow," he whispers in my ear.

"Good or bad?" I persist in a sleepy voice.

"Hopeful," he replies, lowering himself over me and pulling me to him with a long exhalation of breath. As soon as he wraps his powerful arms around me, at once I forget everything in the hot surge of desire that washes over me at his touch.

The next morning, Red Amrevet 13, both of us wake up together around seventh hour, and Aeson tells me we have a full day planned. The Imperator has called for a new investigation of the ark-ship, the Ghost Moon phenomenon, and now this new development of the *astroctadra* moon alignment and how it all might tie together and offer clues to the current alien crisis—and he wants to include me in it, along with my family—namely, Charles Lark, my father—and even his own daughter, Manala.

"My Imperial Father believes we have no more time left and everything comes down to this," Aeson says as we walk to see my Dad and George for *eos* bread before going to meet with the Imperator and his usual secret circle of people who have the clearance to know.

"What about the alien light grid?" I ask, almost afraid to hear what he has to say.

Aeson glances at me. "Nothing new since the attack on Septu. The only difference is, we now have *three* grid formations to track and worry about, instead of two. And, based on our calculations, we expect another grid will form at Tammuz in a matter of days."

"So you think they will definitely attack Tammuz this time?"

"Yes," Aeson says grimly. "Our earlier miscalculation was based on a logical assumption that they were trying to make their way specifically toward us—toward Atlantis. Had that been the case, they would have attacked Tammuz as we originally anticipated, since it would've been directly in their path to this planet. Instead, it's beginning to look like the alien enemy is moving their forces generally *outward* from Hel regardless of direction or what kind of planetary object is in their way—whether it's occupied by sentient beings or not."

"So—what does that mean?"

"We don't know. It makes no sense. Their motivation has become even less clear than before. We cannot establish communication with them on any known channels or frequencies— or they choose not to respond. All we can guess is that they are doing an ordered sweep and *purge* of everything in this solar system that's in their way along an expanding diameter. Eventually, at this rate, their sweep will reach Atlantis."

"That's terrifying," I say.

"It is."

We arrive in the guest suite, and Aeson explains in careful words to my Dad over our meal that he is *invited* to participate in a meeting with key people.

"You're aware of what's happening, *Amre-ter* Charles," Aeson says, gulping his *lvikao*. "But you cannot imagine the level of complexity. I believe your expertise in ancient Earth history might help, even if in a small way. And my Imperial Father agrees."

"Dad, before you say anything, how do you feel?" I ask. "Are you up to attending a stressful brainstorming meeting, or would the effort of getting up, going somewhere, make you ill?"

"Well, I managed to attend your Wedding without collapsing," Dad says calmly. "And if there is anything I can do to help in this awful crisis, I am more than willing."

"Excellent, thank you." Aeson nods. And then he uses his wrist device to send a message to the Imperator to let him know we are all coming.

The Red Office in the Imperial Quarters is full of familiar individuals and quite a few strangers when we get there. As expected, the First Priest Shirahtet Kuruam is here—the last time I saw him was at the Wedding when he ceremonially "surrendered" the *Kassiopeion* in a temporary manner to the priests of Amrevet-Ra. Also present are ACA Director Hijep Tiofon, STA Director Rovat Bennu, and at least four other people I don't know but suspect are IEC Members, seated in a loose circle of chairs in front of the large Imperial desk. One additional person, whose presence surprises me somewhat, is Consul Suval Denu, who gives us a friendly nod.

Since when is Consul Denu made privy to these ultra-secret matters? I start to wonder.

Yes, in his diplomat capacity he's already aware of most things going on politically, and he's been working closely with the ACA since the Earth Mission. But Consul Denu was never quite the Imperial inner circle crony. The ACA Director Tiofon and the Imperator must've recently decided that his skill set could be used in this area and chose to bring him in all the way on this most classified situation centered around the ancient ark-ship.

The Imperator himself sits at his desk in the high-backed chair and stares at us as we enter, with his typical blank expression. "Good, you are here, we can begin," he says curtly, speaking English for our sake, but without introducing anyone present. His fingers drum lightly along the desktop, betraying his less-than-restful inner state.

"My Imperial Father, I have a very interesting report for you, before we begin," Aeson says, conducting Charles Lark, my father, to the last empty seat, while the rest of us remain standing. This includes a very nervous Manala—who eagerly joined our group at the summons of her Imperial Father as we were in the elevator—and George, who came along with us because no one said he couldn't.

"Yes, what have you found?" Romhutat Kassiopei asks without preamble, focusing his dark gaze upon his son.

"Last night, thanks to my Wife's observations of the moons and the night sky through that antique *astroctadra* window in her bedroom, I believe we have a sudden new variable added to the Ghost Moon puzzle, and a promising lead to explore."

And Aeson tells him the details, with a quick glance at me, while the others in the room listen. "So, I had my staff run some correlations—to test the real-life *possibility* of this moon alignment derived from the old rhyme. They took orbital data for all four moons, added in these fixed location coordinates—based on the specific structural details of the window—accounted for the time of day—"

"Go on." The Imperator's gaze intensifies.

"And it appears we have *something*," Aeson concludes. "In fact, we have multiple somethings, but only one of them ultimately makes sense."

"What?" Director Bennu sits up in his chair.

"A meaningful geometric shape," Aeson says. "To be precise, a shape *partially* described by the alignment of four moons. But you can't see it with the naked eye, only with blackout shades, because it happens in the *daytime*."

"Interesting," the Imperator says.

"The alignment occurs once a month, at the precise moment when the Ghost Moon is centered in the *astroctadra* window in my Quarters, equidistant from each of the four star points. . . . When this happens, Amrevet is in the top corner, Pegasus on the left, and Mar-Yan on the right—each moon aligned precisely with three of the corners of the star window. *Nothing* is on the bottom corner."

"So, it's a *pyramid alignment*, not a cross," Director Bennu says.

"At first glance, yes. But then, upon closer examination, the bottom corner needs no moon—it has *Atlantis* itself. The window bottom corner touches the horizon, pointing down to the ground."

"Aha!" Bennu nods.

"That's not all. The *astroctadra* is a two-dimensional shape, a snapshot of points aligned on a flat plane. However—if we translate this alignment into normal three-dimensional space, this is what we get." Aeson taps his wrist unit and suddenly projects a hologram for all to see.

The hologram is blue-violet, about two feet tall as it rises from his wrist. The shape it creates seems to be an elongated square—until it begins to rotate on its bottom corner, revealing itself as a three-dimensional, angular object. Definitely not a cube. I struggle to recall the mathematical term for this type of polygon—how many sides does it have?

And then I hear Director Bennu exclaim, "Is that an *octahedron?* Yes, yes!"

"Correct," Aeson says. "This is indeed a perfect octahedron—a 3D shape with six vertices. However, in this case we also add a center point, for a total of seven points of reference."

"I can see why one might think of a pyramid shape," my Dad speaks up. "This looks to me like a *square bipyramid*—another name for an octahedron, if I recall. In other words, take two pyramids, one inverted like a mirror image, and attach them together by their wide bases. Imagine the Pyramid of Giza on the shore of a lake with its upside-down reflection in the water. . . ."

Seriously, if only Dad knew where the Great Pyramid of Giza has been lately, I think.

"Yes, that would work too." Aeson turns to nod at my Dad, then continues. "Now, each of these vertices or corners is a point of alignment. First, imagine the Ghost Moon as the point in the center, inside the heart of the octahedron. Next, imagine that each corner of the octahedron is one of the moons orbiting Atlantis, plus Atlantis itself, plus two other objects—I'll explain in a moment."

"Keep talking," the Imperator says, staring at the rotating hologram.

"In short—" Aeson lifts his wrist higher so that the hologram rises and appears to hang in the air before us. "This shape, with the Ghost Moon in the center, suggests to me a *quantum containment field*."

ACA Director Tiofon makes an excited sound.

"This could very well be!" Director Bennu exclaims.

For the first time, the First Priest Shirahtet speaks up. "Indeed. . . . What a thought."

The Imperator glances at the First Priest. "Shirahtet? Do you know something?"

"My Imperial Sovereign, I am merely reacting to a fascinating possibility. No, unfortunately, I don't have any knowledge of this."

"Father, permit me to continue," Aeson says. "Now, assuming this is an ancient octahedral containment field for the Ghost Moon, we must have six containment points. Four of these are represented by Amrevet, Mar-Yan, Pegasus, and Atlantis. What of the remaining two? My guess is, when the quantum containment was first established in ancient times, maybe there were additional moons— but more likely, our ancestors simply used two space vessels, parking them at the precise coordinates to complete the octahedron formation."

"So the implication is, once the original containment field was set, then the two ships were taken out of the alignment. . . . Why? Likely, in order to disguise its very existence," Shirahtet muses. "A key removed from a lock, and the lock itself taken apart."

"Wouldn't that break up the octahedron symmetry and wipe out the containment field?" George asks suddenly. Everyone glances at him, and the Imperator casts a basilisk glare at my brother, as if implying *why are you here?*

"No, that can't be it," I say quickly, in order to take everyone's attention from him. "The moons are constantly on the move, moving along their orbits. Indeed, none of them is in those special alignment coordinates for longer than a few minutes once a month, as Aeson says. I believe, the rarity of this occurrence is what makes it nearly impossible to breach or otherwise *affect* the containment field."

Aeson smiles at me. "Exactly. And I believe, the reason for all our failures to shut down the ancient ark-ship and its components— the Ghost Moon likely being one of them—is related to this alignment."

"Yes," the Imperator says. "Three Logos voices working together and failing at this task was incomprehensible. But now it makes sense. We were fighting against an ancient quantum lock mechanism that was disassembled and shifted *out of place*. We were also not utilizing all the necessary access points for achieving full octahedral *resonance*."

"Wait, does this mean we would need a Logos voice stationed at each point?" Director Bennu asks with a frown. "There are only three individuals in possession of a Logos voice in *Atlantida*."

"That we know of," Director Tiofon says quietly.

"Actually, there are four," the Imperator proclaims suddenly. And then he glances at his daughter. "Manala, my child, I am told you have recently exhibited signs of your Logos voice manifesting, at last."

Manala starts in place and her eyes widen. "Father? What do you mean?"

The Imperator laughs grimly. "I have sensors in place that activate upon the use of *power voice*, anywhere in the Palace. And they are set to recognize the Logos intensity. The other day you raised your voice several times—something to do with your cat— and tripped the sensors. This makes me very happy that you are now capable of reaching your full power level. I will begin training you in addition to your usual classes."

"Oh. . . ." Manala whispers, putting one hand to her mouth. "I did not know. I—thank you, Father."

"My deepest congratulations, Imperial Princess Manala," Shirahtet says with a slow nod to her. "Your Kassiopei power grows alongside your own natural progress."

"An admirable progress indeed, my dear Princess Manala," Consul Denu says, with an encouraging expression, so that Manala blinks in relief.

"So, very well—now we have *four* Logos voices, assuming the Princess is trained and ready," Director Bennu resumes. "We are still short two people."

In that moment the Imperator turns to stare at my father. "*Ter* Charles Lark," he says. "We need to have your voice tested."

"Oh?" Dad says.

"And the rest of your children." Romhutat concludes, glancing at George.

"Say what now?" George meets the Imperator's gaze without flinching.

"It is a great and rare honor to share the Imperial trait of Kassiopei," Shirahtet puts in, suddenly observing George with a close scrutiny. "We will re-examine all of you in this new light."

"Um, okay, I guess," George says, glancing at Dad and me, then Aeson, before returning his attention to the others. "But what if none of us Larks fits your vocal needs?"

"A valid point," Rovat Bennu remarks.

"Indeed . . ." one of the unnamed IEC Members speaks up, giving my brother a suspicious perusal. I vaguely recall he might be Council Member Takhat, another loyalist who usually votes on issues in tandem with the Imperator.

The Imperator pauses, looking at everyone present. "If it becomes so necessary, we will step outside our borders and resort to foreign sources."

"My Imperial Sovereign," Shirahtet says. "Are you certain that's a wise course of action?"

The Imperator drums the desktop with his fingertips. "Nothing is certain right now. You know it's the last thing I want to do. But if we have to expand this circle, we will. Whatever it takes to resolve our present situation."

"Then I suggest we begin with Eos-Heket and Ubasti before we proceed to the *other* Hemisphere," Shirahtet says carefully.

There is another pause, as the Imperator continues to look at Shirahtet and the rest of us. And then, in mercurial fashion, he switches the topic. "That window with the *astroctadra* frame," he says, looking at Aeson, me, and Manala. "What do we know about its origins? I want to know everything there is to know—how and when it was built, and by whom. I'm aware that there is a duplicate window in your bedroom, Manala. Correct?"

"Yes, Father, there is," Manala replies.

"Aeson, run your data correlations on the other window coordinates, and see if this minor floor level height difference changes anything in your results."

"Already done, Father," Aeson says. "We used structural blueprints and current floor plans of the Imperial Palace and did the numbers for both, last night. There's no statistical significance in value differences, based on upper- or lower-floor coordinates. In other words, both windows give the same results. Apparently, they've been built at slightly *different* heights from the flooring in their respective rooms to adjust for the different levels, so that they still provide the same view."

"So—built in duplicate. Which further confirms their importance," Romhutat says, with another look at Shirahtet. "Come now, Shirahtet. Don't tell me that with your vast knowledge of our past you don't immediately have some details to impart about those windows. You must know the original builders, the general time period, something. My patience is running thin. Feel free to *share*."

Shirahtet pauses thoughtfully before bowing in a courtly manner. "Allow me to retrieve the Historical Archives and Records database, My Imperial Sovereign. This is such a minor structural detail, and I do have some notion of the general time period and where to look, but I need to confirm. . . ."

The Imperator slides a digital tablet across the desk surface toward him.

Shirahtet leans forward, picks up the tablet and gets to work.

"While he searches, does anyone else have any input?" The Imperator scans the room with his hard gaze. "Tiofon? Bennu?"

"This *astroctadra* shape," my Dad says suddenly. "When did it first come in use, traditionally speaking? Not just those windows, but the symbol in general?"

"An excellent question, *Ter* Charles," Consul Denu says. "The Atlantean four-point star graces so many things in our lives that it is hard to imagine not having it. Even the Fleet uses variations of it on all the insignia—" And he points to Aeson's jacket, where a small multi-star emblem of SPC command is pinned to his collar.

"Cadets wear the four-point star pins," I say, remembering the pins given to the Earth Cadets during our cosmic journey on the ark-ships.

Shirahtet looks up from his search. "A very ancient symbol indeed. According to official records, it came with us from Ancient Earth—that much I do know. Now, as far as these windows, I can now confirm that they're *old*—extremely so. The Imperial Palace complex, as most of you know, is a combination of Original Colony structures and later additions. The Palace itself—this building we're in right now—is an original construction, begun soon after Landing, approximately during Year 4 or 5, making it one of our oldest structures on record, at least 9,766 years old."

"Simply mind-blowing . . ." my father says with wonder, casting his glance around the red walls of the room and looking up at the tall, ornate ceiling sculpted with gold and polished stone. "How did you manage to preserve it so well? I'm truly confounded! On Earth, most comparable ancient structures are crumbling, weather-beaten ruins. And they're several thousand years younger in comparison!"

"Also, an Atlantean year is longer than an Earth year," George puts in. "So, wow."

"*Ter* Lark," Shirahtet says, "You ask how we preserve our original structures. The answer is simple. We continue *using* them. We maintain, revere, perpetuate that which was first built by engaging in *eternal continuity*. It is integral to our tradition, our very way of life, our continued existence."

"Not only physical monuments or buildings, but our institutions, our sciences and technology," Director Bennu adds. "Meticulous care is taken to uphold the entire civilization."

"Indeed. And the greatest, most ancient, most *treasured* example is currently before you—in the graceful, living form of members of the divine Imperial Kassiopei bloodline." And Shirahtet inclines his head with reverence in the direction of the Imperator and then Aeson.

"Yes, thank you for reminding us that we're living DNA relics, your gods in the flesh, sustained for endless generations," Romhutat says with an annoyed edge. "Now let's stay on topic—about the *astroctadra* windows, Shirahtet."

"Of course, my Imperial Sovereign. And on the topic of maintenance—there have been at least two major renovations of the Imperial Palace complex since the beginning," Shirahtet continues, "covering most structures over the centuries, and several lesser restorations—in particular, after the third of the Global Wars when plasma weapons were deployed on civilian targets despite rules of engagement. In addition, one significant fire wiped out a portion of the lesser buildings that did not utilize stone as fundamental building material—"

"Ah yes, the Great Fire of 2907," Director Tiofon cuts in. "It burned most of the Old City of Poseidon, if I recall my history lessons."

"This building did not suffer any structural damage due to its stone construction," Shirahtet resumes. "But the interiors have been gutted multiple times and redone completely—in particular, elements of wood such as many of the doors, wood trim, some columns and wall elements and yes, window frames."

"So, these windows are not original—" Director Tiofon starts to speak.

But Shirahtet raises a finger to interrupt. "However—there is no fire damage on record to any portion of the upper Imperial residential floors, which includes *this* one—these Imperial Quarters—and the two floors below, which are the Imperial Crown Prince's Quarters and the Imperial Family Quarters. Those two floors contain the *astroctadra* windows. Yes, there were multiple renovations, but many of the antique elements were preserved— removed with great care for renovations and reinstalled precisely as first built—including the two *astroctadra* windows." He pauses briefly, reading. "An interesting note here—the wooden frames were damaged twice, but re-created each time according to precise, *strict* instructions of the original builder to always retain this design element and—to always install them in the *same spot* in their respective rooms."

The Imperator frowns. "And who exactly issued those instructions?"

"It says here that, upon the orders of the Kassiopei Dynasty, the architect Muutat Bisfuri was chosen as the builder on record for the primary Palace structure."

"Whose orders? Which specific Kassiopei?" Romhutat asks. "Are we talking blessed Churu, the First Imperator himself, who died that very first year, upon arrival? Or his Heir, Narmeradat Kassiopei? His dubious, distant relations? The Imperatris Merneit? Who?"

"My Imperial Sovereign, apologies, but it does not say," Shirahtet says. "These windows were a part of the original mandatory design elements for the Palace that have since been fixed as a permanent requirement for all future reconstructions."

"I thought the only mandatory elements were the Thrones and the wall Insignias," the Imperator says. "I mean the rows of Imperial Seats located in various chambers such as the Pharikoneon, and my antechamber here, and some of the niche shrines."

"It is indeed so, My Imperial Sovereign. However, there are quite a few minor, secondary elements that normally need not warrant the Imperial attention, but are included as necessary for the structure to serve the needs of the Kassiopei Dynasty. There's a list, if you would like to see—"

"Yes, *bashtooh!* Give it here." And the Imperator motions for the tablet.

While his Imperial father inspects the data, Aeson changes the hologram display on his wrist.

Instead of the rotating octahedron, the hologram transforms into a linear 3D graph, hanging in the air before us like a transparent cube with graph marks and lines. Inside is a simple object made of six lines and seven spheres—one sphere in the center and six others all connecting to it from the six *astroctadra* vertex points.

"This is a visualization of the planetary objects in the containment field around the Ghost Moon," Aeson says.

"It looks like a molecule," George says.

"Indeed," Director Bennu says. "It's a molecule of sulfur hexafluoride."

The Imperator looks up from his tablet. "What is its significance for us?"

"Sulfur hexafluoride?" Rovat Bennu, the Science and Technology Agency Director, pauses to think. "It's a greenhouse gas. Otherwise, nontoxic. Very effective electrical insulator. The latter property might indeed explain its choice for containment structure."

"Good to know." The Imperator slides the tablet back to Shirahtet across the table. And then he looks around the room at all of us. "And now—we urgently need to *re-create* the exact circumstances of this moon alignment and use all our available Logos voices to unlock the containment field. When is the next alignment scheduled to happen, my Son?"

"Fortunately for us, the day after tomorrow—on Blueday, the 15th. Midafternoon, at first hour and eleven daydreams of Khe," Aeson replies.

The Imperator nods. "Not much time, but enough—enough time to test several of you for additional Logos voices, and to set up the resonance transmitters at each vertex location, be it moons, ships, or here at the surface. I want that *hoohvak* moon brought back to our *normal space . . .* so that we can finally land on its surface and find out what's inside that ancient ship graveyard."

"Agreed," Aeson says. "Whatever ancient secrets lie hidden there could be the means to save us."

Chapter 74

Things move very quickly at this point. The Imperial meeting is adjourned, various individuals have their urgent tasks assigned, and Aeson has to deal with some pressing SPC business. Meanwhile Shirahtet politely but firmly asks my entire family to submit to a simple *voice test* to determine if any of the other Larks possess the Logos voice.

Gracie and Gordie are contacted, and Gordie has to get off work, while my sister, still on Fleet standby, heads over from her apartment.

Since my two younger siblings are on their way, Dad, George, and I wait in the Red Office with the Imperator and Manala, while the First Priest goes to fetch some high-end sound equipment.

By the time he returns, a very confused Gordie has arrived and is directed to this room by the high servant. Gordie peeks in, pausing at the door. He sees us and the Imperator, and his mouth opens a little.

"Come in, Gordon Lark," the Imperator says impassively.

"Hi . . . um . . . everyone," Gordie says, stepping inside and making a weird bow to the Imperator.

George signals to him with his eyes, motioning to the nearest seat. Dad nods at Gordie with encouragement. Manala watches nervously.

"Over here," I say softly, patting the seat of a nearby chair.

As soon as Gordie takes the seat, my little sister gets here. Gracie looks both wide-eyed and defiant as she pauses at the door. She sees the Imperator and her eyes practically bulge. However, she gives him a proper courtly bow, then silently approaches and takes the next empty seat behind me.

The Imperator merely observes her with his unblinking, serpentine gaze.

A few moments later, Shirahtet walks into the room, carrying an object that I find strangely familiar. It's a shapeless, seamless lump, roughly ten by five inches, with a silvery surface that looks like a rock smoothed by water. A faint light source seems to glow from its center, reacting to every sound with a soft flicker-pulse. Yes, it's audio test equipment I recognize from the preliminary Qualification.

"Wow, that looks sickeningly familiar," George whispers.

"What is it?" Dad asks.

"This is a tactile resonance device to test your Voice," Shirahtet says, placing the object carefully on the end of the desk. "I will ask each of you to touch it and repeat a vocal sequence that I will demonstrate—with my Imperial Sovereign's permission?"

"Proceed," the Imperator says.

"What's going on?" Gracie whispers in my ear from behind.

Before I can answer, Shirahtet turns to her and says, pointing to the device. "Why don't we begin with you—Grace, the youngest. Come."

"Just a second—is this harmful in any way?" my father interrupts. "My daughter must not be—"

"The test is benign," Shirahtet says.

"Don't worry, Dad," I add. "We all had to do this before, during Qualification."

Gracie nods and stands up, then approaches the desk. "Okay."

"Place your hand on it. You will sing the following basic keying sequence," Shirahtet says. And he sings a clear sequence of middle octave C-E-G notes in a low, dark voice.

Gracie does as she's told. The moment her fingers touch the device, the light underneath its pearlescent surface flares in a circle of steady blue.

"Please proceed."

Gracie sings. Her clear soprano is initially breathy, and the surface of the device flashes red to indicate she is slightly off-key, then turns green as soon as she steadies her voice.

"Again," Shirahtet says.

Gracie sings once more. This time the device registers a clean green light all the way.

All of us—our Dad especially—watch her with intense curiosity.

"Again. This time, I want you to sing as *loudly* and *precisely* as you can."

Gracie frowns slightly, glances at the Imperator, at Shirahtet, then opens her mouth. She sings a very clean, very *loud* C-E-G, while the device pulses a very bright, pale green.

"Again!" Shirahtet exclaims. "Your hand is on fire! Imagine it burn! Feel the pain! Sing!"

"She doesn't have to imagine it," I mutter. "We all burned our hands during Semi-Finals."

Gracie turns to me. "Especially *you*, Gwenie!" And then she frowns and fiercely sings again. Her perfect soprano cuts through the air, and the sound equipment pulses an even brighter, super-pale shade of green.

There is a pause.

"Very well, thank you," Shirahtet says, then turns to the Imperator. "She is very close. She has a very powerful voice, but it is not Logos—at least not according to this test. Given time, she may—"

"Next," the Imperator says curtly. And he points his finger at George.

"If you please—" Shirahtet nods politely to Gracie, then turns his full attention to George.

Gracie looks uncertain, but returns to her seat. My older brother, meanwhile, stands up.

"All rightee," he says almost cheerfully, approaching the test equipment.

Shirahtet nods.

George raises one brow sarcastically, and places his hand on the device. "Let's see if I'm a god."

The device flares blue, registering his speech and voice.

"Please sing the same sequence," Shirahtet says.

George clears his throat, making the light on the device pulse in chromatic discord multiple times. Then he sings in a clean, loud baritone. This time the C-E-G notes pulse a solid green, his Quadrant color.

"Repeat," Shirahtet says. "Loudly and clearly."

George sings again. My brother has a fine voice, and it shows, making the device dance a pure, energetic green each time.

"Again!"

George gets even louder. His voice is rich and powerful, making glass objects in the vicinity rattle from its vibrations, and the device buzzes with pale, green brightness. He repeats the sequence a few more times, looking around the room with self-amusement after each attempt.

"Very nice, thank you," Shirahtet says to my brother with a tiny hint of regret, then addresses Romhutat. "My Imperial Sovereign, once again, a very powerful voice with much potential, but not quite up to the level of Logos. A very talented family—"

"So—not even a demi-god? Bummer," George says with a rueful laugh, returning to his seat.

"This is *not* the outcome I hoped for." The Imperator looks solemnly in George's wake.

"Yeah, me neither," George says, winking at me. He then throws a general glance around the room, including Gordie and Manala.

"Manala," the Imperator says with the slightest softening of his tone. "My daughter, I want you to demonstrate for all here what a Logos voice is like. Let's have you take a turn. Come!"

"Yes, Father." Manala stands up and walks to the desk. Placing her hand on the device, she sings in a high, clear soprano—not loudly, but precisely.

The test equipment registers pale green immediately.

"Lovely voice, my Imperial Princess," Shirahtet says mildly, nodding to her with the faintest smile. "Now please focus, and imagine that you are able to *cut* through this object with your voice, as if it's a knife going through *eos* pie. This time, sing *loudly* and clearly!"

Manala takes a deep breath and looks down, keeping her palm flat on the test equipment.

Suddenly she sings the C-E-G, but an octave *higher*.

Her voice comes forth light and ethereal but imbued with glorious power, and it's easy to imagine how it might sound at the highest coloratura range during an operatic aria. . . . She could be the Queen of the Night from Mozart's *The Magic Flute*.

The device pulses a bright, intense green and then flares a blinding *white*.

It stays at the frequency of white light as Manala repeats C-E-G several times before falling silent.

"Now this—*this* is a Logos voice!" Shirahtet exclaims. "Perfection!"

"Well done!" The Imperator makes a sound of unconcealed enthusiasm and smiles fondly at his daughter—possibly for the first time I've seen him to do so. "Manala, my child, you have pleased me very well today," he says, nodding at her.

Manala's own face relaxes, and her expression shows disbelief coupled with fragile joy.

She must be so unused to shows of affection from her father. . . .

I notice how everyone is now looking at Manala. My Dad's expression emanates comfort and warmth, a true familial pride in her; Gracie smiles, and Gordie grins widely at her. Meanwhile, George raises his brows and softly lets out a held breath, almost in a whistle.

"My Imperial Sovereign, we are now assured of *four* Logos voices at our disposal," Shirahtet says in an equally pleased manner. "May we hope for more?"

The Imperator turns to my Dad. "*Ter* Charles, show us your voice." His tone is bland, but his dark blue eyes are rife with hidden tension.

In answer, my Dad sighs. "I . . . am not sure I'm able to sing," he says. "Least of all, now."

"*Ter* Charles," Shirahtet says cleverly. "You must try, for the benefit of all—including your own children and the safety of this world."

"When you put it that way. . . ." Dad takes a deep breath, shakes his head in discomfort, then stands up with some difficulty.

"Approach, and rest your hand on this—"

"Yes, yes, I know," Dad says wearily, clearing his throat. He takes the few steps to the desk, and places his palm on the test equipment; clears his throat again. "I haven't sung in ages. . . ."

"Very simple. Repeat this—" And Shirahtet demonstrates yet again the terribly familiar C-E-G.

My poor Dad. . . . He takes a deep breath, begins to sing in his warm, familiar baritone, somewhat raspy from disuse, then coughs, making the device pulse erratic red, with a few notes in green thrown in.

"Again, please." Shirahtet watches intently. But not as intently as the Imperator.

"Ah-h-h." Dad exhales. Inhales again, trying to breathe deeply. Sings faintly, barely in tune.

The device jumps with pitifully faint, red and green pulses.

"Come now, *sing!*" the Imperator suddenly exclaims.

Charles Lark, my father, shakes his head. In just a few seconds of trying, he is short of breath. "I can't—I think my lung capacity is . . . is insufficient . . . not in this gravity."

"Think of your *dead* wife—"

"No!"

My father's voice blasts out in a sudden terrible burst of anguish, and the device flashes a bright and true . . . white.

Oh, my God.

"I am done," my Dad says, letting go of the test device. "No more, enough." And with a grim expression he returns to his seat.

But we all stare in disbelief, including Shirahtet and the Imperator.

"That was not—not entirely clear," Shirahtet says, breaking the silence. "But that *one* outburst registered at Logos level."

Gracie's jaw drops. "Daddy. . . ."

"I don't know what that means," Dad says coldly. "And I don't care."

But the Imperator's eyes gleam with energy. "Apparently, *Ter* Charles, you indeed have the Logos voice. Whether or not you are able to use it is another matter. But—that is for later."

An uncomfortable pause.

I admit, my mind is reeling now. I frown with stress, glance back and forth at each of my family members, look at Dad—oh lord, oh lord, *my Dad*—then again at the others. Manala is completely frozen in place, watching all of us with unwavering attention.

"There is one more," Shirahtet says. And he indicates Gordie.

Gordie opens his mouth, then shakes his head, pushes his glasses up his nose.

"Gordon Lark, let us hear you sing," the Imperator says, finally tearing himself away from staring at my father.

"Okay," Gordie says. And then he snorts and gets up.

We all watch Gordie approach the desk and place his hand on the device.

He doesn't bother to wait for instructions or an example.

He doesn't clear his throat.

Gordie sings C-E-G in his clean, resonant tenor. The device pulses with bright green light.

Gordie frowns, almost in anger, and swats the surface of the test device with his palm, making it go back to baseline blue light. Then he sings again, at the top of his voice.

His tenor voice *cuts* through the air, through walls, through everything, like an incongruous, bright summer avalanche.

The test device flares a hard, clear, brilliant *white*.

"Yeah!" Gordie exclaims and slams his palm on the surface of the device again. "Logos, my ass."

Chapter 75

"Okay, so all the nerds in this family have the Logos voice," George remarks much later when we're on our own, back in the guest suite of the Imperial Crown Prince's Quarters.

Seriously, what just happened?

As of now, Gordie has been officially recruited for the upcoming events, and he will be training with Shirahtet in a crash course on what needs to be done vocally. So he is currently still stuck in the Red Office, *one-on-effing-one* with the Imperator and Shirahtet.

Meanwhile, the rest of us, Dad included, have been dismissed and permitted to return to our regular business, until further notice.

"Speak for yourself, kiddo," Dad says tiredly, with a single painful laugh, as he settles into his chair. "I, for one, consider myself a 'nyrd' with a 'y' in the medieval-scholarly, erudite sense. Crusty and dusty, and indistinguishable from—"

"Oh, Daddy, you're *not*," Gracie says and widens her eyes frantically at George.

"Shut up, Gee One," I say also. Yes, he's kidding, but I can tell that George is somewhat taken aback by these latest crazy developments, and so is Gracie.

The thought strikes me suddenly—*Dad and Gordie are just like me.*

At the same time, my other two siblings must feel weirdly left out, even useless—*I'm looking at you, George*—in the struggle to come. At least Gracie has the Fleet and her Cadet duties. But George? He's newly arrived, barely acclimated to the gravity, has no career placement. . . .

And then there's Dad.

Holy crap. My father has the Logos voice.

He is not physically up to doing anything with it right now, but the point is, he hit that one ball out of the park—to use a baseball metaphor, and I don't even know anything about baseball.

Dad has the ability, the underlying Logos level of ability to do so *much*.

But right now he can't do anything at all. Not with his fragile state of health and state of mind.

I consider all this, eager to talk to Aeson about it. My husband is off dealing with SPC work and making the arrangements for the upcoming group attempt to unlock the Ghost Moon, the day after tomorrow, and all I can do is think and wait.

"So, they got their lucky *five* out of six Logos voices," George says, continuing to think out loud.

"Yes, count me out of it," Dad replies. "All things considered, whatever they discovered in me doesn't count, not even as a last resort. I simply don't have the strength for what is required. They'll just need to find someone else to complete the batch."

I nod. "You can help in other ways, Dad. Such as your scholarly knowledge—"

"Of course. Always glad to help in my professional capacity."

Aeson returns just as we're starting to eat a late *dea* meal. My husband enters the guest suite together with Oalla and Erita sometime after third hour, and all three of them look serious.

"Aeson!" I stand up at once and hurry to him, as Erita and Oalla give us room.

I put my arms around him, stroking his back, and press my face against his chest. "I missed you. . . ."

With an intense look in his lapis lazuli eyes, intended only for me, he nuzzles me, speaking softly near my ear, "*Im amrevu* . . . I missed you too."

"Did you know my father and Gordie have the Logos voice?" I say, straightening after a few moments.

"Yes, I've heard. My Imperial Father informed me immediately." Aeson glances around the room at my other family members, my Dad in particular. "*Amre-ter* Charles. I am both glad and sorry—your state of health right now does not permit you to exert yourself."

"I'm sorry too, that I'm so useless in that capacity," Dad says, carelessly moving his eating utensil around his plate.

"Please don't concern yourself too much. Fortunately, we have a solution." Aeson glances at Oalla and Erita and points them toward seats, while he and I also head for the sofa.

"I've reached out to Ubasti, our neighbor to the northwest," Aeson tells us. "The First Speaker of the Ennead there, Anen Qur, has a Logos voice. He is in good health and strong, and he is willing to assist in our task. He will be here tomorrow to begin preparing."

"I thought only the Kassiopei have the Logos voice?" George stops eating and looks up in curiosity.

"Mostly so," Aeson says. "It is quite rare, but it does manifest occasionally in others. As you can imagine, it's considered a major asset globally, occurring in a tiny handful of people across borders and over decades."

"Interesting, and a relief for me," Dad says.

Aeson nods. "Meanwhile, I made the necessary arrangements for our mission on Blueday. The resonance transmitters are being delivered by crews to the surfaces of the three moons and should be installed starting tomorrow morning."

Everyone pays close attention.

"Amrevet has an outpost with an already functional, full-sized resonance chamber, so it only needs diagnostics. Mar-Yan has several small surface test stations with basic equipment that needs to be upgraded, so it's getting a new unit. And Pegasus has a mini-station that has received some meteorite damage and has been in disuse for years. A new unit is being delivered there too."

"So, three moons, all with space stations, how truly remarkable," Dad says with a soft smile. "I still cannot get used to any of these wonders." And then he blinks and moves his eyebrows in thought. "Does this mean that—all of *you* will be going there, to these moons? Even Gwen and Gordie must go too?"

"Yes." Aeson looks at my Dad with gentle acknowledgement. "But it is not at all dangerous. It is what I'm here to explain." And he glances at me.

"I'm ready," I say, with a little surge of nerves and excitement in my gut, and notice how Oalla nods at me with a smile.

"Gwen, you will be going to Mar-Yan. Don't worry, you will not be alone. Oalla will be with you as your Flight Partner, with two additional crew. You will take a *khepri* four-crew fighter, for safety purposes—these days I don't want you to be in space on a civilian ship, especially without me."

"Oh, wow, Gwenie! You get to be on a *khepri!* So cool!" Gracie exclaims, looking at me with envy.

"But you said it wasn't dangerous?" Dad asks.

Aeson pauses, choosing his words carefully. "Going to the moons is not dangerous in itself, but our situation is too precarious not to take all precautions. I will not risk my Wife's safety under any circumstances. Indeed, I would be alongside her on this trip, except that I myself must be on a different vertex point during the alignment."

"I understand." I place my hand on Aeson's upper arm and squeeze gently.

"I will be on Amrevet," Aeson continues. "Meanwhile, Gordon will be on Pegasus, together with Erita and two crew, also taking a *khepri* fighter. Where is your brother anyway?"

"Gordie is still in your Father's office with the First Priest Shirahtet," I say. "He should be back soon, I guess."

"I was hoping he would be here, so that Erita can discuss the mission logistics with him."

"I'll wait," Erita says, even as I point her to the food station.

"All right." Aeson stands up also and goes to pour himself a glass of *qvaali.*

When he returns, I ask, "So what of the other vertex points of the alignment?"

"My Imperial Father will be here on Atlantis. He will personally handle the ark-ship resonance from the *Stadion.*"

I nod.

"Finally, the two local battle barges have been told to approach and assume Atlantis orbit. War-5 and War-6 will take the remaining two perpendicular points of the alignment. Equipped with interstellar-class resonance chambers, they will serve as ideal vertex point anchors for the alignment."

"Wow . . ." Gracie says softly. "Battle barges."

"War-5, under the command of Command Pilot Selmiris Teth, will have my sister Manala on board," Aeson continues. "I believe that being on a large ship will be far less uncomfortable for her than having to put on a space suit—"

Oh my God . . . I will need to put on a space suit! I think with a sudden twinge of nerves.

". . . and it will set her at ease that she is surrounded by so many people to assist her if needed. Manala must be emotionally composed enough to be able to perform the vocal keying sequence on cue."

"So who's going with her?" George asks, setting down his plate to look at Aeson.

Aeson looks at George, and there is just the tiniest pause as he appears to consider my brother. "I've asked Consul Suval Denu to accompany her, and Xelio Vekahat will be there in primary tech guidance capacity. Manala finds comfort in the Consul's company, and she trusts Xelio, my *astra daimon* heart brother and our mutual childhood friend. It is important for Manala to be surrounded by those for whom she feels affection and cares about—in order for her to be sufficiently at ease to handle her task."

George nods slowly.

"And that's why," Aeson continues, "I was hoping that you might be willing to come along too, and help Manala feel at ease."

"What—*me?*" George makes a small, incredulous sound.

"Yes, from what I can tell, Manala finds comfort in your presence too."

There is a small pause.

George's facial muscles twitch slightly as he glances down at his plate, then looks back at Aeson. "Yes, of course. I'll go with her. Whatever you need, I'll be there."

"Good, I thought you would." Aeson nods with a shadow smile of satisfaction.

"That's great, George," our Dad says, also nodding. "Manala will be very happy to have you along. A fine plan."

"Now then, to continue," Aeson resumes. "The sixth and final vertex point of the alignment will be occupied by War-6, with Command Pilot Uru Onophris. He will be carrying the First Speaker Anen Qur of Ubasti, as the sixth Logos voice—"

Erita clanks her eating utensil and turns around because Gordie has entered the room.

"Gordie! There you are," I say. "How was it?"

"Yeah, pretty crazy," Gee Three replies, heading straight for the food station, where he begins to load his plate. Typical Gordie response to stress.

"So, what happened?" I persist.

"We practiced a whole bunch of voice commands." Gordie dumps a huge dollop of mashed *djebabat* on his plate, and then pours thick, chunky gravy on top. Mashed *djebabat* is Atlantean comfort food, similar to mashed potatoes, and it's become one of Gordie's favorites to gorge on.

"And?"

"And then they told me to come back for more tomorrow. I said I have work tomorrow, and they said I will have an Imperial summons as my formal excuse. Anyway. Now I have to memorize the main, long voice keying sequence thing for the alignment."

"That's not all, Gordon Lark," Erita says, beckoning him with one finger. "You and I have to talk about our mission details. Bring your food here, and we'll get started."

Gordie stares in her direction. "Oh yeah? Ok, sec." And he returns to shoveling the contents of various serving dishes onto his gargantuan plate.

While Gordie is brought up to speed by Erita and Aeson, Oalla explains to me our own mission details.

"In short, all you need to do is sit still and be a good passenger until we get to the surface," Oalla says. "Then we'll put on the headgear portions of our space suits and walk a very short distance outside in the practically nonexistent atmosphere and light gravity of Mar-Yan and into the resonance chamber. On cue, you will sing and dance and do your Logos thing. Then we return to the ship and go home."

"That does sound simple," I admit.

"Very." Oalla takes a bite of a small, grape-like fruit called the *hurucaz*. "So tomorrow we will simply practice space suit protocol and spacewalk protocol. I know you had a brief overview of it during our journey from Earth, but there was never any occasion for any Earth Cadets or civilians to use it."

"Instructor Okoi told us it was for emergencies only. That Atlanteans don't really use space suits for normal spaceflight."

"Well, we *do* use them, actually." Oalla pops another *hurucaz* in her mouth and chews daintily with amusement. "But only under military circumstances, with one exception. Space suits are primarily intended for battle, for backup protection when inside fighter ships. The exception is for exploratory research missions to new, unexplored cosmic locations. Okoi was teaching you somewhat censored basics, using civilian shuttles, hoping that none of you would ever have to deal with anything more dangerous than speeding through a QS race."

"I see."

"Don't worry, it's all relatively easy—just a minor hassle, really."

And so we spend the rest of the day and evening preparing, practicing, wondering, and worrying about what's to come on Blueday. No new crises arise, and Aeson and I actually manage to make it to bed before Midnight Ghost Time, and use those gentle hours to enjoy each other before falling asleep.

The next day, Red Amrevet 14, is all practice and anticipation. Oalla and I practice with the space suit, Gordie meets with Shirahtet for more voice lessons, Aeson handles endless logistics, including coordinating with Ubasti to increase and coordinate security measures and deal with the sudden arrival and overnight accommodations at the Palace for First Speaker Anen Qur, who happens to be that nation's primary head of state. Manala comes and goes, full of nervous curiosity, while Dad and George do the best they can to keep us all focused and together. The Imperator keeps calling Aeson to make sure that all the details are falling in place.

At some point I get a message from Laronda wanting to know why she hasn't heard from me since the Wedding, and if everything was okay. I can't really share the present crisis with her—she knows some things about the ark-ship but not about the latest with the moon alignment—so I tell Laronda all is well with Aeson and me, naturally, and we're still dealing with everything.

If all goes according to plan on alignment day, she and everyone else on Atlantis will find out everything, soon enough.

I wake up near dawn, in the morning of Blueday, Red Amrevet 15, with a weird case of sudden nerves. For once, Aeson is still deeply asleep, lying in the great bed next to me, and I find it comforting to feel his great warmth surrounding me, and one of his arms wrapped around my middle.

I snuggle against him carefully, trying not to wake him up, listening to his slightly loud breathing, as I lie there and think.

I'll be wearing a space suit this afternoon, and walking in an airless landscape on an alien moon. . . .

Holy crap.

Eventually both of us stir and are fully awake.

"*Nefero eos* . . . Gwen . . . ready for today?"

"I guess," I whisper, running my fingertips over his jawline.

My husband smiles at me and then yawns a very wide, very tasty yawn—which makes me yawn too, and giggle, and calms my nerves. It definitely helps that we start to tickle each other for a few minutes, and then one thing leads to another. . . .

Eventually we get up, get ready, eat, and then the stressful wait begins.

The moon alignment is expected to be at its height during the first hour and eleven minutes of Khe. Which means that all of us have to be in position at our designated locations around the Ghost Moon—at the six vertices—at least two hours in advance, to account for little things going wrong.

"If we miss this alignment window, it will be a *month* before the next one, and we don't have *days* to spare," the Imperator tells Aeson harshly over a call, even as our partner crews start arriving.

"I am well aware, my Father, and all care will be taken that things go accordingly," Aeson says to him, just before it's time to depart. "And now, we need to begin."

"Very well," the Imperator replies. "We will speak again once every piece and player is in place. Be ready to receive my next communication on site."

Chapter 76

Oalla, Erita, and other members of our flight crews arrive punctually at ninth hour of Ra, to pick us up and take us to our respective destinations.

Aeson, Gordie, and I are the only three out of six Logos voice wielders who must put on the space gear, so Manala leaves first, accompanied by George, Xelio, and Consul Denu who will be with her, together with her personal security guards, as she boards a military transport waiting for her in the Imperial Palace airfield. Manala will then be taken up directly to War-5, one of the two battle barges presently in orbit over Atlantis.

Elsewhere in the Palace, we are told, First Speaker Anen Qur concludes his last-minute consultation audience with the Imperator and heads for his own transport, accompanied by his personal Ubasti security and additional Imperial guards. He will arrive on board War-6 at approximately the same time as we arrive at our destinations.

Meanwhile, the Imperator, surrounded by the Imperial Guards, departs for the downtown complex on his way to the Atlantis Grail Stadium. He will take his position at the Grail itself, in physical contact with its the metallic surface—which is only one half of the ancient resonance chamber but will still serve its purposes—even as it continues to hum, broadcasting its eternal alien beacon transmission to the stars. . . .

Those of us who remain, including our Flight Partners and our crews, begin the process of putting on our space suit layers while still in the Prince's Quarters.

The suits are bulky, but far less so than their contemporary Earth astronaut counterparts. They remind me somewhat of the *viatoios* armor that I had to wear underneath my uniform in the Games of the Atlantis Grail. Except, unlike that paper-thin, lightweight armor that I could barely feel, these have additional thick, flexible layers for pressurized, airtight protection.

The Atlantean space suit outer layer is formed in snakelike rings composed in turn of small interlocking pieces like scales. They are flexible and conform to my limbs and torso, yet allow relatively free movement. Underneath I wear the same paper-thin *viatoios* armor layer as in the Games, but seamless, like a second skin jumpsuit that includes foot covering.

The suit boots are fused to the main portion of the outer suit, while the gloves are detachable. The helmet is also removable, with a three-quarter plexiglass-equivalent visor portion for a panoramic view, and a strong, reinforced metal protection cap for the back of the skull and the top. There are several flashlight beam elements that can be enabled, if needed, to illuminate the way.

The suit comes with a compact life-support pack that can be worn like a purse at the shoulders or waist, or attached from behind like a backpack. Its micro-hoses plug into the shoulders, waist, or back of the neck—in multiple places, based on preference. Finally, there is a built-in, independent wrist comm system on both arms for redundancy, and an emergency beacon transmitter at the belt.

To wear the suit, there can be no concern for privacy. Aeson, Gordie, Erita, Oalla, myself, and the four crew members strip down to our underwear and put on the *viatoios* under-layer, then step into the boots, pull up the pant legs and torso. Next, arms go through sleeves, similar to a jumpsuit, and then we zip-seal the two sides upward, ending at the collar.

We end by holding our helmets, gloves, and life-support packs in our hands. Anyone with long hair, including *im amrevu* and me, and half the crew, has to wear it in a segmented tail or braid to keep it out of the way for safety, later to be tucked in a special compartment inside the helmet. Yes, no joke—Atlantean space helmets have a dedicated *hair compartment.* . . .

"All right. Is everyone ready?" Aeson asks, standing in his suit—and looking so very *alien* and imposing, for a split second—as he watches me finish applying the sealing closure at my throat.

"Almost," I say, fiddling with the closure. "Okay, done."

I must look weird and alien too. . . .

Apparently, I'm the last to finish dressing, because they all stand watching me—even Gordie, who appears so impressive and grown up in his space gear. Aeson examines me closely for any seal faults, while Oalla observes our interactions in amusement.

"She's fine, Kass," Oalla says. "We practiced multiple times yesterday and she learned it well."

Aeson gives Oalla a swift glance, then returns to his examination of me and my equipment.

"Aeson!" I say with a self-conscious laugh. "Seriously, I've got it."

"Make sure she does it right before stepping outside on the moon," he tells Oalla.

"Of course, Kass. Relax. Now let's go."

And we leave the Quarters, walking carefully in our gear that creaks slightly with each step. A few of us at a time, we pile into the small, private elevator just outside the workroom—where the several *daimon* on SPC duty, plus Anu and Gennio, give us brief stares—then emerge outside.

We take a discreet back way to the Palace airfield, minimizing our exposure to the public. If anyone sees us in these space suits it would be inevitable that the news will hit the media feeds immediately. Right now, this must be avoided, so we take the extra care not to be noticed, in order to hold back the media frenzy at least long enough until we're in orbit.

Three ships await us at the rear hangar, parked and hovering in place, gleaming metallic slate-grey. Two of them are the larger, saucer-shaped *khepri*, while the third is a small, elongated solo fighter ship, lean and elegant—a *mafdet*.

We pause, separating into our two crews, while Aeson's Imperial guards stand back so that he remains alone.

"Where is your Flight crew, Aeson?" I ask with concern, seeing he is unaccompanied.

"Waiting for me on Amrevet," he replies casually.

"Wait, what?" My mouth opens. "Are you going to fly there alone?"

"I am," my husband replies in amusement. "I'm a solo Pilot. It is what I do."

"Oh . . . right." I shut up, but I remain worried for him.

In that moment Aeson steps forward. Hel's radiance shining in his face, he leans down and kisses me softly, the extra space between our suits making it a little awkward. "Be safe, *im amrevu*."

"You, too," I whisper, feeling a sudden pang of guilty sensuality even at his brief contact with my lips.

And then I watch my husband open the hatch of his *mafdet* and climb into the cockpit with easy, practiced movements. Moments later, the solo fighter taxies out of the hangar and then—aptly nicknamed the Needle of Justice—it accelerates a short distance, about a hundred meters, in a matter of heartbeats and shoots like a needle straight up into the sky.

"Don't worry about him, my Imperial Lady," Erita says with a simultaneous tap on my and Gordie's shoulders. "Let's head out, Gordon. Oalla, *saret-i-xerera!*"

"*Saret-i-xerera!*" Oalla replies, then motions to me and our two additional crew.

With my peripheral vision I see Gordie and Erita and their two crew members begin walking to their *khepri*, even as we walk to ours. A sudden worried impulse makes me want to call out Gordie's name and urge my little brother to be careful, but it's too late now.

The hatch of our *khepri* opens upward, and I follow Oalla's lead, climbing awkwardly into the compact interior, which is smaller than the inside of a standard civilian shuttle due to additional military equipment, panels, and weapon arrays.

The two other crew climb after me—a young, tall, brown-skinned woman with black hair and startling green eyes, and a slim, olive-skinned young man with brown hair—who have been introduced as Pilots Axela Buiri and Xurut Ralafu.

There are four seats inside, fully rotating at 360 degrees, and of equal position in relation to the central control panel and perimeter weapon-and-sensor panels that circle the ship. We take our seats at random, and I sit down next to Oalla on my right and Xurut on my left, directly across from Axela. My helmet and other gear go into a storage container bucket fixed to the right of my seat.

Oalla is in command of my portion of this flight mission, so she turns to the central control panel and places her palms on the lumpy orichalcum surface. The moment she sings the keying command, the panel comes alive and lights up with multicolor indicators, while the perimeter panels flare with corresponding lights. The overhead hatch comes down, and we are momentarily cut off from the world and plunged into darkness except for the panel indicators. Then, remarkably, the entire hatch becomes transparent, as if the hull material dissolves, in a disappearing illusion. It is holographically sensitive material, giving us a full-surround window view of the exterior.

Oalla's fingertips move quickly over the command panel, engaging a central holo-grid that rises up to float in a pale-yellow light cube over the controls. Then she taps a communication sensor and speaks in a clear measured voice. "*Astroctadra* mission control, Bast registering vessel for takeoff. Lark is safely on board."

A moment later, we hear Aeson's rich baritone voice issue from the hull walls. "Phoebos acknowledging Bast vessel for takeoff. Proceed to destination coordinates."

"Bast confirming arrival projection on schedule at 11:41 of Ra. Relayed and closing."

And then Oalla sings another sequence. The ship's hull comes alive with a faint hum, while hair-thin lines of golden light start racing along the hull perimeter on the bottom and between the perimeter panels.

"Buckle in, everyone," she says with a glance at me, even though we are all duly restrained in our harnesses. "Now is the time to put on your optional eye protection. The view is a shielded holo-projection, no danger of ocular damage, but it's still very annoyingly bright."

I reach into my gear bucket and take out a pair of military sun shades that have the additional blackout function. I choose the standard setting, without blackout, and put them on.

There's a small lurch, as the *khepri* taxies out of the hangar into the blinding white daylight of Hel—so that I'm grateful for the shades over my eyes.

My pulse starts racing erratically. . . . Then the world itself seems to time-dilate around us, while the *khepri* accelerates for a hundred feet of the airfield, going from zero to what feels like sixty billion, moving with the ease of a flitting hummingbird.

And then the bottom falls out from under me—from under all of us—as the *khepri* shoots upward into the sky.

I've never been inside a space vessel that had a window view during actual takeoff from a planet's *surface*. Earth was already a distant view from orbit when I first had a glimpse of it from the grand observation deck on that fateful day when the ark-ships departed our home world. The shuttles we flew from on board the ark-ships were already in deep space, locked within the quantum stream. And the transports that took us into orbit and then back down had no windows in the passenger area.

This time I get to see the planet fall away from under me all the way through the layers of atmosphere and into the cosmic vacuum of space. It's slightly ironic that the first planet departure I get to experience visually is not Earth, but Atlantis.

The physical sensation of rising through the atmosphere is now familiar—I've been in enough shuttles that I know the unpleasant sudden squeeze of gravity. This time, though, it is particularly brutal—I am experiencing the additional Atlantean baseline gravity with the acceleration forces added into the mix.

The pressure is so intense that I feel as if I'm being stifled at the same time as I'm already flattened in my seat.

However, the view is amazing—even as I'm being crushed and immobilized. Blinding white daylight, an ocean of it, all around . . . and then, everything slowly fading to lapis lazuli blue, atmospheric reflected light easing, colors gaining saturation and hue, as we approach the thinning upper layers and the space vacuum.

I hear Oalla's voice through the ringing in my ears, "Hang in there, Gwen. . . . Just a few minutes more."

"Okay . . ." I reply with effort, breath squeezed from my lungs and forced through closed teeth. At one point I can feel my cheeks sucked in with the acceleration.

And then it's over.

The last glow of atmospheric light dissolves, and we are in cosmic indigo, then the velvet blackness of true space. The sensation of gravity is briefly gone, and we float light as a feather. . . .

And the next moment, gravity blooms back in place—just enough to anchor us vertically, giving us a perspective of "up and down"—but not at standard Atlantean levels.

Light gravity! How nice, I think. *Looks like I might be getting a vacation from full-strength Atlantean gravity while we fly. . . .*

"We've achieved orbit," Oalla says, looking at me. "How're you feeling, my Imperial Lady? Doing okay?"

"Yes, I'm okay now," I say with a sigh of relief, taking a deep breath with lungs that are no longer being crushed by acceleration pressure. Now that I finally don't feel like I'm dying, I can pay better attention to our surroundings. At once, I'm fascinated by the sight of the blue-green hemisphere of Atlantis filling up half the window view below. A clear, near-cloudless view, with only a few puffy cumulus—mostly over the oceans and underpopulated regions—thanks to weather control.

"Stabilizing at MF Gravity. In three . . . two . . . one," Axela announces across from me, as she does something on her side of the control panel.

"MF Gravity?" I ask.

"Minimum Fundamental Gravity," Xurut replies from my left. "Used for short- and medium-distance space flights to maximize ship systems efficiency. Also, fewer messy spills." And he gives me a wink.

"I see."

"That's right, you don't want your *lvikao* floating in sticky droplets all over the cockpit," Oalla says, raising one brow. "We will maintain this level of minimal gravity for the rest of our flight to Mar-Yan."

"Great," I say, sitting up in my chair. "So is it really just a two-hour flight?"

"Pretty much. Mar-Yan is not that far. In fact, its orbit is a little closer to Atlantis than your Earth Moon is to Earth. We won't even engage the quantum stream." Oalla's fingers manipulate the holo-cube surface as she makes some entries to the grid, which I recognize as the Yellow navigation grid. "Destination coordinates set, now requesting Thrust."

Axela manipulates the cube from her end, and the grid turns Red. "Engaging Thrust," she responds.

And in that moment, I experience the initial lurch, which turns into smooth motion. In three heartbeats, Atlantis starts to slip away sideways in the viewscreen, as our vessel begins to move away from the planet.

It's amazing how quickly things can get boring when you're staring at nothing but black space and a few sparse, distant dots of starlight. Also—I don't know what it is, but we must be flying in one of the most empty and uninteresting directions on this side of the cosmos. Because all that glorious, star-filled sky that I'm used to seeing from the surface of Atlantis is mostly behind us and off to the sides of the viewport. If you stare directly ahead, it's simply not visible here.

Where did all that celestial beauty go?

I mention this to Oalla and she snorts. "I think we happen to be directly facing the Black Nebula that obscures most of the galactic center and Ae-Leiterra, with its spewing relativistic jets. Thank all the deities for the nice Black Nebula, otherwise we would be in a non-habitable zone of the galaxy."

"What is the Black Nebula?"

"Hot, non-radiant matter and gas," Xurut replies. "Nothing but microscopic matter for light years in that direction, creating a safety dust curtain between us and radiation hell. The Ae-Leiterra quasar is spewing at us, and the long cosmic string-filament that is the Black Nebula just happens to be in its path between us. It's shaped like a worm, with its one end facing us and the other end being bombarded by Ae-Leiterra."

I shake my head in amazement. "I had no idea."

"You might say some people in the SPC worship the blessed worm," Axela says. "Pilot patrols just love it. It's considered good luck."

"From Atlantis, you can only see it as a small dark spot in one part of the sky," Oalla says. "Here, it's still only a spot, but we're facing it, flying at it, head-on, and it becomes an optical illusion. Space perspectives can be strange. . . . So, yes, nothing but the pesky dark blob straight ahead. Funny how Mar-Yan happened to be orbiting in that part of the sky for our alignment purposes."

"Could it be intentional, somehow? That its vertex point during alignment would be pointing there?" I ask. But even as I say it, I realize how nutty it sounds, so I recognize I must be rambling.

"Hm-m-m. . . . Don't know." Oalla taps the panel surface.

About half an hour later—in addition to the one or two sparse dots of stars amid the black—one lonely, slightly bigger light source starts to move into the view directly ahead. It resolves itself into a small, blue-grey planetary body.

We are now on approach to Mar-Yan.

Chapter 77

Fun fact—the moons of Atlantis do *not* orbit along the same flat plane. Furthermore, their orbit *shapes* are not circular, but strongly eccentric. In other words, the moons don't go around Atlantis in concentric circles relatively parallel to each other. Instead, they move in wildly diverging ellipses along different rotational planes.

As a result of this oddball orbital motion, at some point all the moons make closer approaches to Atlantis—and to each other, encroaching on each other's general orbits—then move farther apart.

In fact, this crazy, wobbly rotation is the only way that the complex *astroctadra* alignment becomes possible in 3D space—as opposed to a simple, flat, two-dimensional alignment along four points, as seen from the vantage point of the star window.

But it's not a complete mess. Despite their irregularities, the moons have a general order of proximity to Atlantis, based on their *average* orbital distance.

Mar-Yan, one of the three—no, *four*—Atlantean moons, is sort of like the middle child. Its orbit generally lies between Pegasus and Amrevet, and so does its size.

Mar-Yan is about two-thirds the size of Earth's Moon. Meanwhile, tiny Pegasus is approximately one-half, and huge Amrevet is almost twice the size.

In terms of distance from Atlantis, Pegasus is generally closest—which means that my brother Gordie will likely get a shorter trip than me before reaching his lunar destination (but no guarantees, because, again—orbital weirdness). Then comes Mar-Yan with its middle orbit, and only then comes Amrevet, which has an orbital distance approximately comparable to Earth's Moon, although it does make a closer approach to Atlantis at some points. Of the three of us, poor Aeson possibly has the longest trip to make.

What about the Ghost Moon?

From what little is known so far, the Ghost Moon is larger than Pegasus but smaller than Mar-Yan in size. And its orbit is generally outermost, far beyond Amrevet—although for today's alignment it's supposed to be at its closest apsis point, encroaching on the other moons' orbits and in some case passing them.

And now—even as Mar-Yan grows in the viewport window, and my thoughts go off on astrophysics nerd tangents—I pause to wonder at the serendipity. . . .

Truly, it's a miracle that such a highly *specific* configuration of planetary bodies in this complex system can even *exist*, much less be a regular occurrence.

Mar-Yan fills the window with its bluish, dull grey pallor and minimal rocky surface features when Oalla engages the comms.

"*Astroctadra* mission control, Bast vessel is now in Mar-Yan orbit, arriving on schedule."

"Phoebos acknowledging. Bast vessel, commence landing procedure."

"Bast confirming. Landing in progress. Relayed and closing."

And with those words, Oalla defines the final surface coordinates on the Yellow grid, then flips the holo-grid cube to Green. "Requesting Brake."

"Engaging Brake," Xurut responds and begins to manipulate the corresponding controls on the cube.

We start to plummet down at a controlled incline, grazing the edges of the ultra-thin atmosphere, even though such caution on approach is not really necessary in this near-vacuum.

Meanwhile, gravity disappears altogether as we fall.

Our landing coordinates place us in daytime, with Helios a fierce and bright white ball halfway across the Mar-Yan sky. Here in this rarified atmosphere, the alien golden light grid around Hel is clearly visible at the fringes of its corona, like a net of deadly pearls. Meanwhile, the large, gibbous, blue-green disk that is Atlantis hangs below, near the pronounced curvature of the horizon.

The sky itself is black, with a faint, bluish, atmospheric haze— present only at the edges—that quickly fades to full cosmic vacuum overhead. Compared to Earth's Moon, Mar-Yan has slightly more atmosphere, but the difference is barely significant.

The gravity, however, is back—lighter than Earth's, but not by much. Which implies that Mar-Yan, this little moon, is denser in mass than Earth's Moon, and has stronger gravity, despite being smaller in size.

We "land" softly on the barren grey surface of the moon. The *khepri* spacecraft doesn't actually make physical contact, but hovers about two feet off the regolith, casting a dark shadow on the ground. Mar-Yan's regolith consists of ashen dust and rocks, some bluish in color, and occasional impact craters.

The area directly underneath the ship is undisturbed by the *khepri's* silent presence, except for the gradual heating up that comes from the proximity to its plasma shield. Given enough time, it will leave a minor radiation burn imprint like a "crop circle," fusing the dust particles.

Of course, the shield will be turned off for us to get out safely. . . .

As soon as we come to a hover stop, the ship's hull goes silent, and Oalla makes another call, to tell Aeson we have arrived.

I hear my husband's voice issue from the hull in response. "Bast vessel, your arrival on Mar-Yan is acknowledged. Stand by for further instructions." And then, after a pause, he speaks informally. "Oalla, put Gwen on. . . . Gwen, can you hear me? Glad you're okay."

"Aeson! I can hear you! I'm fine," I say with a smile, hoping to convey it through my voice. "Oalla landed us safely, all is well, and it's just amazing, this moon! Now, how are *you?* Or better to say, *where* are you now?"

"I'm still in space, almost there. . . . Amrevet is prominent and visible. As soon as I land in a few minutes, we will talk again . . . very soon . . . and I'll set up the conference link among all of us."

"Kass, do you want us to sit here in the ship and wait or proceed into the resonance chamber habitat?" Oalla asks. I have a feeling that under normal circumstances there would be no need for such a question, but Oalla is trying to accommodate me and make me as comfortable as possible.

"Why don't you go ahead," Aeson's voice comes after a pause. "Go into the habitat, it is newly installed and has better environmental support. Don't waste your ship's oxygen generator power."

"All right, will do," Oalla says, concluding formally, "Bast confirming. Relayed and closing."

As soon as we end our communication link, I turn my head in every direction, staring at the dismal grey view outside. "Where is the resonance habitat?"

"Right behind you." Xurut and Axela both point, while Oalla sings a command sequence and does something on the control panel.

I swivel my seat 180 degrees and notice what I first assumed was a rock formation not too far from us. It's an irregular shape, but then I realize that this pile of rocks surrounds a smooth metallic hemisphere peeking upward from what appears to be a small crater. The sphere is imbedded in the crater like a robotic eyeball in an eye socket.

How large is it? Hard to tell, since I don't trust myself to accurately judge distances in this monotonous, alien landscape. . . .

"All right, shiny new Team Lark—ahem, Kassiopei—time to put on the rest of the suit gear." Oalla completes whatever she was doing and swivels her chair to face me, even as I swivel back to my original position to pay attention. "Yes, these chairs are fun to play with," she says with an arched brow. "But we need to get moving, My Imperial Lady."

"Okay—of course." I chuckle, feeling suddenly punch-drunk with nervous excitement.

I'm about to walk on an alien moon!

"Remember the correct order. Helmets first. Then plug in the life-support pack. Then the gloves—they go last. Do *not* turn on the life-support system until the suit is fully sealed and pressurized."

"Yes, I know."

Oalla snorts. "I *know* you know, but Kass will kill me if I somehow manage to kill you. . . . So—"

I laugh.

Our fellow crew members exchange glances and watch our exchange with equal amusement.

"And you two—enough staring and snickering. Gear on! *Now!*" Oalla claps her hands, and looks like she means business.

At once we reach for our gear buckets.

A few minutes later I've managed to put on all my suit components correctly. Putting on the helmet gives me a weird instant of claustrophobia, but the sensation passes as soon as I connect it properly to the suit and take a deep, steadying breath.

No air . . . no air.

Panic!

Not true. Air will flow just fine, as soon as I plug the hoses into the ports. . . .

And so I adjust . . . and twist . . . and snap on . . . and seal . . . and plug things in—breathing shallow and trying not to fog up the visor while the air is still not circulating. Then I put my gloves on. The gloves feel thick and weird on my fingers, overly heavy and cumbersome.

Helplessness. Panic!

Cut it out, Gwen, numbskull Lark—ahem, Kassiopei.

It's not like I'll be doing microscopic surgery with these gloves. All I need is to be able to push a few easy buttons.

When I'm finally done, I tap the button sequence to pressurize the suit, then start the life-support pack. At once a pleasant, cool flow of air starts to waft gently into my face, and the fogged-up interior of my helmet visor clears up.

I look out through the clear plexiglass—or whatever the Atlantean material is. Everyone is sitting, fully suited, and looking at me.

Oalla taps at her wrist repeatedly and points at me.

I stare in momentary confusion. Then I have to remind myself she's not asking for the time with that classic Earth gesture. No, she means I need to enable my wrist communication system.

Duh. . . .

I nod, then raise my arm and press the needed controls.

Immediately Oalla's voice sounds from the helmet interior, near my ears. "About time, Gwen. Imperial Lady, let's go."

Oalla engages controls in the center panel with the fingertips of her thick gloves. "Depressurizing cockpit now." Then she manipulates more controls. I know that part of what she's doing will cause the plasma shield to fade away. "Opening hatch. Axela, you now have the ship. Xurut, you are second."

The viewport to the outside goes dark as the holographic display mode goes off—reminding me we're inside a small, dark, metal can and these are fake, digital windows. And then the hatch sails upward in perfect silence—not that I would know, being inside the soundproof, airtight space suit.

Oalla stands up and carefully climbs out of the cockpit, setting a clear example for me. She hops lightly onto the regolith surface and turns to nod at me. "Your turn. Carefully and slowly, please."

I follow her lead, stand up awkwardly, but then feel far more comfortable than I expected in this lighter, near-Earth gravity.

I climb over the edge of the *khepri*, then lower myself onto the moon surface.

My boot makes an immediate footprint impression in the regolith. It probably makes a crunch that no one will ever hear.

One giant step for Gwenkind. . . .

And then the other boot.

Holy crap! I am walking on Mar-Yan!

I take three careful, slow steps, then look up. I see an alien black sky overhead. I see Atlantis, low on the horizon, like an oversized Christmas ornament. I squint and try not to look at Hel, looking like a large, round lightbulb, as it burns angry-white at me from on high, surrounded by the delicate net of the alien grid.

"Gwen! This way!" Oalla's voice in my ears is businesslike and commanding. "Follow me, try to use my footprints. The last thing we need is for you to step wrong and twist your ankle." And she begins walking slowly in the direction of the habitat.

Fortunately it is only about a hundred meters away.

We arrive at the habitat inside its little crater, and I realize, up close, how small the unit really is.

The whole thing is the size of a two-car garage. The upper hemisphere of it has a small hatch opening on top, and Oalla walks on the roof of the sphere, then bends down carefully. She manipulates the locking mechanism, and the hatch opens upward, revealing a stairway going down into darkness.

Oalla steps inside and starts descending. The moment she steps on the first stair, light sensors kick in, and I see a faint glow of illumination bloom forth.

"Come on, Imperial Lady Gwen."

I take my first careful step down.

"Follow me, keep going."

I descend as she tells me and find myself inside a perfectly spherical chamber.

There is only the one large room. No apparent furnishings, except for a waist-high column in the very center, resembling a podium topped with a control panel. The walls are rounded, the ceiling is rounded, and the floor is rounded. A standing platform rises above the concave floor like a flat, circular shelf. It is attached to the same central podium column. The column cuts through the platform and disappears into the floor of the sphere.

Oalla and I step off the last rung of the suspended staircase onto the flat platform. "Give me a moment, let me pressurize this place," Oalla says, approaching the central control panel on the podium.

She places her hand on the panel and sings a sequence from inside her suit. At once, the resonance chamber lights up fully and the walls brighten with hair-thin filaments of golden light. The hatch above our heads starts descending and seals us in.

As soon as the seal is complete, the control panel signals us by lighting up green and gold in a special sequence. "Atmosphere is normalizing," Oalla's voice tells me inside my helmet.

Apparently breathable air is created and then pumped inside through hidden vents in the column near the floor. I cannot hear it hiss, but I can imagine how it must be filling this chamber. . . . According to Oalla, the increase in pressure is reflected in the light code sequence she's watching on the panel.

Moments later, it is completed. The control panel lights stop flickering. A large indicator goes solid green.

Oalla takes off her gloves. She presses the control buttons on her life-support pack, then removes her helmet. She takes several deep breaths and smiles calmly at me.

Here we go. . . .

I take a steadying breath of my own and carefully remove my gloves, feeling a sensation of cool-to-lukewarm air along my bare skin. Then I disable my portable life-support and take off my helmet.

Normal, sterile, shipboard air fills my lungs—the same kind of air I used to breathe on the ark-ships.

I can breathe. I'm alive.

"Congratulations, Imperial Lady Gwen," Oalla says. "You managed very well. It is now a little after twelfth hour of Ra, and this resonance chamber is fully functional. We made good time and are now ready to proceed with our mission."

For the next half-hour Oalla prepares the resonance chamber for my upcoming task. She calls up hovering chairs for us from hidden wall panels, so that we can rest while we wait. Our suits are set up to recycle body waste, so at least there's no need for a bathroom.

Next Oalla keys the control panel for advanced voice commands and enables interstellar communication from this console.

"What about Axela and Xurut?" I ask. "Will they remain in the ship all this time?"

"Yes, that's the protocol," Oalla says, looking up from her work. "We work here, they maintain the ship for us. Don't worry about them."

"Okay." I nod, watching her enable a holo-grid that rises in a light cube to hover over the panel controls. It's the same kind of command grid that's inside the ship.

At some point Oalla pauses, as if considering. Then she turns in her hover-chair to glance at me with a thoughtful expression.

"My Imperial Lady Gwen. I know this might be an unusual time to do it, but I want to thank you—on behalf of Kass."

I look up from examining my gear. "Oh?"

Oalla gives me the faintest, particularly meaningful smile. "You've made him very happy, you know," she says. "Ker and I have been talking about it and—well, we can tell. Kass is *different* now."

"Different how?" I ask, with a minor twinge of worry.

"Different in a good way. As in, really good. Happy. *Relaxed*. The eternal distance and aloofness that he's borne ever since his *death* and *return* from Ae-Leiterra are now diminished. I think you opened up something in him—a healthy will to live, for his own sake. Not just to exist and *endure*, but to live and enjoy life."

"Oh, God. . . ." I breathe shallow breaths, sudden emotions stirring me. "I—I don't know what to say. Thank you, I suppose. And also thank you for telling me this! I am so *glad* he is—or at least you *think* he is feeling better—"

"Oh, he's definitely better." Oalla sounds amused. "Married life really agrees with him. But in particular, married life with *you*. You truly *are* the love of his life."

At her words I feel a sudden pricking burn in my eyes. A lump is forming in the back of my throat, and I mustn't fall apart, not now. *I've got work to do.*

"Are you okay, Gwen?" Oalla asks in a gentle tone, seeing me struggling emotionally.

I nod and smile awkwardly, keeping tears at bay. "Sorry, I think these things you brought up—painful things about Aeson— they really affected me. I want to do everything I can for him, to make him happy indeed."

"I've no doubt that you will—you *are*. And—sorry, my Imperial Lady, I did not intend to make you upset right now—in fact, the opposite. I wanted to tell you this as heartfelt encouragement."

"Oh, I get it," I whisper, my voice cracking after all. "I . . . *love* him . . . *so* much." And then I take a deep breath and force myself to get a grip, even as Oalla watches me, radiating warmth and sympathy.

I have work to do.

Chapter 78

Good thing we brought small water bottles with us in our gear boxes, because at this rate my voice is parched and I need to prepare myself for the vocal command work ahead.

It's now after thirteenth hour on Poseidon, and we've entered Noon Ghost Time. The alignment will happen in about half an hour from now. Aeson still hasn't called.

Maybe because we've just had that highly emotional talk, I am feeling a new pang of worry on his behalf. *Is he okay?*

"Oalla," I say. "Do you think maybe you can try calling him from here yourself? Did he arrive safely on Amrevet? What is it—you called *Astroctadra* mission control? And Phoebos—that's his pilot call sign, right?"

"That's right." Oalla nods.

"And you are Bast? Is that your call sign?"

"Correct." And Oalla gives me an amused glance.

"Please call him, Bast!" I bemoan suddenly.

And just as I do, a faint crackle sound issues from inside the walls. And then Aeson's voice comes in loud and clear, rebounding with echoes from the highly acoustic surfaces of the resonance chamber. "This is Phoebos connecting five units to *Astroctadra* mission control. If you can hear this, you are now connected—please confirm."

"Aha! There he is!" Oalla exclaims, and I sense an undercurrent of relief in her voice also.

"Oh, thank God," I whisper.

In that moment another familiar voice breaks in. "This is Sobek confirming on behalf of First Speaker Anen Qur on board War-6." The voice belongs to Keruvat.

Oalla taps a control and speaks loudly, "This is Bast, confirming on behalf of Lark on Mar-Yan."

I watch her curiously, and she raises one brow at my expression. "What? You may be Kassiopei now, but in this one particular way you're still Lark. We've decided that's your call sign."

My mouth opens in a mixture of surprise and wonder.

Before I can say anything, we hear another vocal confirmation coming through. "This is Shamash," Xelio's smooth, deep voice says. "Confirming on behalf of Imperial Princess Manala on board War-5."

And then, a few seconds later, we hear: "This is Tefnut, confirming on behalf of Gordon Lark on Pegasus."

What a relief! Erita just confirmed that my brother is safe.

And then, after another pause, longer than the others, we hear a dark, deep, serpentine, terribly familiar voice of power: "This is Kassiopei on Atlantis."

A pause.

"This is Phoebos," Aeson says. "Now transferring *Astroctadra* mission control to the authority of Imperial Kassiopei."

"Kassiopei acknowledging," the Imperator says. "It is now first hour and one daydream of Khe. We have precisely ten daydreams— ten *minutes*, for the benefit of the Gebi—before the apex of alignment. At the apex, we will all perform the keying sequence followed by the command sequence, *simultaneously*. We will have only one chance—two at best—before the optimal degree of alignment passes. It is critical that we do this correctly."

He pauses, for impact. "We now begin the final preparation for the sequence. Vocalists, have your tech advisors invoke the resonance grid. Once you have it, I want to hear each one of you respond in your own voice, letting me know. Proceed *now*."

I glance at Oalla, who nods and reaches out to the holo-grid that's already floating over the control panel. She engages elements of the grid until the grid changes in color to a never-before-seen purple. "This is the vocal resonance grid," Oalla says to me. "It is now ready for your input."

"Okay, how does it work exactly?" I ask.

"The grid is enabled to translate the sound of your voice and amplify it through this acoustic chamber, then transmit it to the specific cosmic coordinates. I already preset the directional vector coordinates to the location of the Ghost Moon, so it's all ready to go. . . . Simply place your hand on the control panel to establish a physical link with the resonance chamber, and then sing whatever commands you need."

"I see."

"For as long as you maintain physical contact with the controls, the resonance chamber will translate whatever sounds are made in this chamber to input frequencies. So don't speak or sneeze or make random noise while you touch that panel!"

"Oh, boy . . ." I make a small nervous sound.

"Yes, just like that!" Oalla says with amusement. "Do *not* make little noises like that. If you must, first let go of the controls, then cough or whatever, then again place your hand on it and continue your voice commands. Otherwise you'll be *coughing at the Ghost Moon.*"

"Oh jeez. . . . All right." I hold back a nervous idiot giggle.

"Now," Oalla continues. "See this big button control to the right on the panel, the one that's lit up red? That's your main interstellar comm. When you want to talk to mission control, you tap the button once. When it lights up green, then your connection is live, so talk. When done, tap it again until it's red. Red means you are disconnected."

"Okay."

"Want privacy?" Oalla picks up a small earbud and hands it to me. "Press and *hold* the button for three heartbeats to transfer the comm conversation to this earpiece. The console button will flash green. Your voice will still transmit as you speak, but the replies come in your ear. Press and hold the button again to transfer it back to the speakers in this room."

"Ah, okay, got it."

"Also—right now, mission control is a conference line, so when you talk, everyone else at the other vertex locations will hear you—until mission control disconnects everyone. So assume they are all in on the conversation—"

As if to illustrate her point, I suddenly hear my brother Gordie's familiar voice come crackling in, echoing in the chamber walls, and then Erita's voice in the background. "Hey, hello?" Gordie says loudly. And then after a pause, "This is Gordon Lark . . . on Pegasus. I'm all set. Ready to go."

I bite my lip and nod.

"You probably should tell mission control you're ready," Oalla says in a calm tone.

I nod, taking a deep breath, and move closer to the panel.

But before I can tap the comm button, I hear an unfamiliar male voice speaking in a confident, ringing tenor. "This is Anen Qur, First Speaker of the Ennead. I am on War-6, ready to proceed."

"Go!" Oalla gesticulates energetically to me. But we are once again pre-empted.

"Father? Aeson? This is Manala Kassiopei. I am ready, Father." Manala's voice sounds a little lost and more high-pitched than normal.

Poor girl, she must be terrified. . . .

I reach out and press the comm button. "This is Gwen Kassiopei—"

Just as I speak, and my voice is transmitted, I hear someone else get on the line. "This is Aeson, I am—"

At once, both of us grow silent. Then I rush to say, "Oh, sorry! Aeson, it's me, please go on."

"No, it's all right, you go on," *im amrevu* tells me, also in a hurry, and now there's a tiny warm inflection in his voice.

"No, you were first, I think—"

"Enough!" the Imperator's voice cuts in with irritation, interrupting both of us. "It is clear you are both ready. Continue your charming honeymoon later."

Flustered, I glance at Oalla and see that she's holding her mouth to keep herself from laughing. At the same time, she shakes her head and waves her other hand at me.

Okay, this is clearly ridiculous.

But then, the whole thing we're about to do is pretty insane.

Let me see—six people with near-magical voices are going to sing together, from different cosmic locations, at a noncorporeal moon in order to pull it out of another dimension. Yes, that's our situation in a nutshell. *No, not crazy at all.*

But then the Imperator speaks again, and all the nervous silliness evaporates from my mind.

"We are approaching the moment of alignment," he says. "Three daydreams and thirty heartbeats remain before optimum time. At ten heartbeats I will initiate a countdown. When I reach *zero* count, we will begin the keying sequence."

My pulse starts racing.

"Use an earpiece to isolate this comm transmission from the resonance chamber," the Imperator says. "Put it in your ear to hear mission control. Each one of you will hear *only my voice*, and you will sing in tandem with me. But the chamber must receive only *your* voice."

Oalla has long since stopped laughing and now listens, while watching me seriously.

"Aeson, what is the personnel status at the location of the Ghost Moon?" the Imperator asks.

"The SPC patrols are now in place," Aeson replies. "Our ships are on standby, but with sufficient clearance from the Ghost Moon's focal coordinates. If—*when*—the moon emerges into normal space, they'll be safely out of the way of any dimensional displacement."

"Good," Romhutat Kassiopei's voice says. "We are almost out of time. Use the next few moments to focus yourself and your voices, everyone. Earpieces in."

And then silence returns. I stand up from my hovering chair, and carefully insert the earbud into my ear. Leaning over the console, I hold down the button until it goes from steady to flashing green. All the while, I go over the details in my mind. . . .

As I wait, exchanging nervous looks with Oalla, I find myself gently clearing my voice a few times, then take a quick sip from the water bottle.

This is nerve wracking.

Moments later, the Imperator's voice returns, this time in my earpiece. "Counting down *now*. Ten . . . nine . . . eight . . ."

My gut clenches with nerves, so I breathe deeply, to free up my diaphragm.

". . . seven . . . six . . . five . . ."

The round walls of the spherical chamber seem to be closing in. I stand before the console, with my hand ready to pounce, as if I'm about to hit the buzzer on one of those old Earth TV game shows.

". . . four . . . three . . . two . . ."

The world, everything around me, comes into sharp, clear focus.

". . . one . . . *zero*."

I place my hand on the console and sing, even as I hear the Imperator's powerful Logos voice fill my ear.

The keying sequence is simple. As the first note issues out of me, the resonance chamber comes alive. The sound is all around me—it builds, rises in a tidal wave, and fills the spherical chamber. There are echoes, but because of the small size of the chamber, the sound waves dissipate quickly even as they rebound—they are sucked in and absorbed by the hungry orichalcum layers of the walls, and are sent onward to their destination.

We are done with the keying sequence. Now the main program sequence begins. It's that same stupid, long sequence that we all had to do over and over again to make the ark-ship stop humming. . . .

My clear, resonant mezzo soprano fills the chamber. Meanwhile, in my ear I hear the Imperator's dark voice singing the same identical notes.

Soon it feels like the very air is alive, as the frequencies continue to dissolve and are transmitted elsewhere along immeasurable cosmic distances. . . .

Finally, it's over. I grow silent and lift my palm from the console to stop transmitting my voice.

Did our effort work?

I won't know, not for some time. The earbud in my ear is silent.

Oalla is staring at me. Then she glances at the wrist comm unit on the arm of her space suit where a small holo-marquee is running with text. I'm guessing she is checking for updates from the SPC patrols who are on location at the Ghost Moon.

"Oalla?" I ask after a few beats of silence. "What's happening?"

Before she can reply, I realize that my voice has transmitted to mission control since I did not disconnect the link.

Moments later, the Imperator's voice sounds in my ear. "Good question. Reconnecting my Son to all of you in conference mode. Aeson, what is the status on site? Report!"

And then I hear Aeson's voice come in. "My Imperial Father, Gwen . . . everyone. My SPC patrols on site report a brief fluctuation—a *ripple* in the fabric of space—for lack of a better description—at the intended coordinates of the moon. But the Ghost Moon is still locked out of our normal spacetime."

"Rawah bashtooh!" the Imperator's voice explodes with devastating force as he curses carelessly in all our ears, including those of the primary head of state of Ubasti. "We will repeat the

procedure immediately, while we still have some moments of alignment remaining—"

With a sinking feeling I listen to my Imperial Father-in-Law rant at us, knowing that if this didn't work once, it's not likely to be any different if we repeat the same process.

Repeat . . . what if it's repeated differently?

An idea comes to me.

"Um . . . Imperial Sovereign," I say. "Why don't we sing together as a Plural Voice Chorus?"

"It is what we are doing already!" the Imperator responds in my ear. "You are singing together, all of you—"

"Actually, not quite," I say. "I mean, what if we go off earpieces and sing directly into the resonance chambers all together, so that we can *hear* each other's voices resonate in each of our chambers as we sing, and *all* the chambers hear *all* of us? It should multiply the impact of our voices! This way each chamber picks up all our voices and strengthens and reinforces the sound—"

"Stop! Yes, yes, I see your meaning." The Imperator cuts me off. "We have so little time, that I will take you up on this notion, Gwen. Now, *silence!*"

Moments later the Imperator instructs us all to disconnect from the earpiece transmission mode and sing directly into the chamber even as he sings to all of us. "You will hear not only me, but each other this time—disregard the unusual echo and any reverberation which will be present under these non-standard circumstances, and continue to sing as before. Now begin!"

On cue, we begin the procedure again, starting with the keying command and continuing with the main sequence. This time my resonance chamber rings with an unimaginable glory. . . . Not just my own voice but a chorus of *six* such voices fills the space, so that the fine hairs stand on end along my skin, and it seems that all my nerve endings resound like tuning forks.

The Plural Chorus of Logos Voices is astounding. . . . Aeson and the Imperator are both low baritones and they lend profundity and weight to the Plural sound, their voices anchoring all of us and sinking into the very foundation. An octave higher, the two tenor voices of my brother Gordie and Anen Qur ring forth like grand bells, ranging outward with clean, deliberate force. Then comes my own mezzo, at the next octave up, filling in the cracks, crevices, and empty spaces left by the tenors, singing in my lower registers and in the alto range, for more power. Finally, Manala's soprano cuts like a fine, sharp blade, soaring another octave above all.

Oalla is fixed motionless as she listens to us, frozen in wonder. . . .

When the command sequence is done, we go silent.

I find that I'm trembling.

Several terrible moments of silence follow.

Once again, I watch Oalla stare at her wrist and the incoming data transmissions there.

And then, just as I notice a lively change in her expression, I hear Aeson's voice.

"*Something* has happened," my husband says in a careful voice. "SPC pilots on site report a sudden massive energy displacement and a shock wave at the coordinates."

"What? Go on!" the Imperator's voice breaks in.

"My Imperial Father," Aeson says after another beat of silence. "I can now confirm. The vocal sequence procedure had a positive effect. The incorporeal object at the coordinates—the Ghost Moon—has now entered normal space. Congratulations, Father, we now have a new moon in orbit, and it is contained at the predicted coordinates."

"So . . . it is *real* . . . an actual moon!" the Imperator says in an almost dreaming voice. "What a successful mission, at last!"

"Indeed, this is a remarkable development," the voice of the First Speaker of Ubasti, Anen Qur, comes in. "Congratulations are in order, to all of us in these difficult times—"

"Of course, we are highly grateful for your vital role in this, First Speaker," the Imperator says in a smooth tone. "The cooperation of Imperial *Atlantida* and Ubasti in this venture is a fine example of the alignment of our goals when it comes to keeping our planet safe—"

"Speaking of safety—we had a few of our pilots spun and tossed on the shockwave, but fortunately no vessel damage and no casualties," Aeson adds. "They are now in the process of estimating distances and assuming orbit around the moon. I'm dispatching research vessels and landing parties now. First sensor data is coming in already, and they are reporting significant gravitational effects—"

"Yes, yes, excellent. So much to learn! And all of it will be dealt with shortly," the Imperator says. "For the moment, I pronounce this *astroctadra* endeavor a success. We are done here, and you may all return to Atlantis."

A few moments later, we end our conference transmission. Oalla and I put on our helmets and gloves and re-pressurize our space suits. Oalla shuts off the life support in the habitat, and we carefully climb out through the open hatch into the thin vacuum-like atmosphere of Mar-Yan.

Walking on the dull grey regolith, we return to the *khepri*, signal our approach to the crew, and climb inside. Then we take off from the surface and rise into orbit, from where our vessel sets course directly back to Atlantis.

"*Astroctadra* mission control," Oalla says, "Bast relaying our approach home."

This time the view through our cockpit window is dense with cosmic colors and full of stars.

Chapter 79

About an hour and a half into our flight, we begin to see Atlantis swell in size from a tree ornament to a sizeable sphere in the viewport. And then Aeson's voice comes in on the comms.

"This is *Astroctadra* mission control. All mission vessels, be advised—we are now experiencing strong *weather* on Atlantis. This is a direct result of our mission, as expected. The moon is exerting gravitational influence on our local planetary system, and our weather control systems are still reprogramming the new parameters to compensate. As you make your home approach, expect atmospheric turbulence and *more*. Relayed and closing."

"Well, here we go," Oalla says with a glance at me and the other crew. "Looks like we might have an exciting ride."

I stare at her with concern. But Oalla gives me a comforting smile. "It's going to be fine, Imperial Lady Gwen."

"Should be fun," Axela adds.

Xurut just chuckles.

Half an hour later, we reach Atlantis orbit. "*Astroctadra* mission control," Oalla calls. "This is Bast vessel, now assuming planetary orbit. Going to automatic survey mode to look around the globe once before landing. Please acknowledge."

"Phoebos acknowledging your position. Bast vessel proceed with survey orbit before attempting landing. Reports are coming in of atmospheric gravity waves and multiple major tidal events on the surface."

"Phoebos, this is Bast. Did you say tidal events? Please clarify."

There is a short pause, as Oalla and the rest of us listen intently.

"Phoebos confirming. Scan the surface in the location of the oceanic belt. Zoom in to observe catastrophic tidal wave activity.

The Djetatlan Ocean in the Lower Hemisphere, bordering New Deshret has multiple tidal waves building."

"Ah . . . *bashtooh*," Oalla whispers. She then says loudly. "Phoebos, understood. Bast vessel inquiring about the status of *Atlantida?*"

"Bast, the reports are inconclusive. Assume the worst, proceed with your orbital survey then attempt landing—carefully. Relayed and closing."

When Aeson's transmission ends, Oalla turns to us with a fixed expression. "We are going to stay in orbit for now," she says in an overly calm tone.

My heart starts to pound. "Oalla, what's happening down there?" I ask.

"I'm guessing, atmospheric gravity waves causing air displacement, hence storms. Huge tidal waves forming because of the new moon's gravitational pull. Most likely other phenomena, but I know only as much as you do," she replies.

"What about everyone in Poseidon? Is it in danger?"

"Probably not," she replies after a small pause. "The Golden Bay is a nice big gulf that would keep any such tidal activity to a minimum, even without active weather control in place. But the rest of the coast is likely taking a beating.

"I would hate to be in New Deshret right now," Xurut says. "They've been having constant weather tech problems all Green Season. And now—their broken algorithms can't keep up with these new variables that are suddenly in play."

"They're going to need help," Axela says, staring at the viewport, where a long stretch of blue ocean greets us below as the continental landmass drifts out of view. Even as we stare, cloud cover is building to indicate storm activity.

My poor Dad is down there on the surface, I think. *So is Gracie.* I really hope all they're experiencing is some minor bad weather. . . .

It takes us almost two hours to do a full orbital revolution. The crew analyze the incoming data on multiple grids, while I wait, staring anxiously at the planet below, watching more and more clouds appear. At some point I see hurricane eyes begin forming and point them out to Oalla.

"Oh, yes, that circular funnel. Interesting," she says. "I don't recall seeing a fully formed hurricane over a planetary surface before."

My eyes widen in surprise. "Not even on Earth?"

"Um, no. . . ." Oalla pauses to think. "Although—I take that back. Yes, of course I've seen hurricanes—such as the ones on your Jupiter and the other gas giants. Our own Atlas and Olympos have them too. But they look absolutely different—gigantic, homogeneous. I just mean I've never seen a hurricane over a habitable planet with weather control. This one is a small, snowy funnel in comparison—"

"Trust me, they're not a joke when you're in the middle of one, getting blown about by gale-force winds and flooded by storm surge. Horrible!" I say. "People on Earth have suffered tremendously from hurricanes over the last several decades. I would not wish them on Atlantis!"

"I understand, and my apologies if I understated the seriousness," Oalla says gently to me.

"It's okay," I say. "Sorry that I snapped. I'm worried about my family and everyone else down there right now.

"I know," Oalla says. "Me too."

Eventually we proceed with the landing. Everyone is buckled in, and Oalla insists we wear our full suits with helmets and pressurize them for safety as we descend.

We begin our gradual fall at an incline, piercing the upper atmosphere, then diving into an ocean of clouds that were not there before and now occlude most of the fierce daylight into a soothing grey pallor.

The *khepri* gets pummeled and tossed, and I come to appreciate the loose harnesses that keep us suspended and minimize the worst of the effects of rising gravity on the ship and our bodies.

The continental landmass emerges at last from out of the clouds. And as we fall closer, just before landing I get to see the city of Poseidon in the daytime under amazing conditions—a cloud overcast.

The *khepri* comes to a hover stop in the familiar Imperial airfield, then coasts for about a hundred meters before entering the same hidden hangar in the rear.

"*Astroctadra* mission control, Bast vessel has landed safely in Poseidon. It is now fifth hour and twenty-seven daydreams of Khe." Oalla sends one last comm transmission before we shut down the ship and get out. With our helmets finally off, clean fresh air hits us, together with chill, damp wind—a coolness that's unseasonal for this time of year. The wind buffets us with hard gusts in the open airfield.

Oalla, Xurut, and Axela, all stare with frowns at all that strange sky water coming down on our heads.

We walk back to the Imperial Palace in the impossible rain.

Once in the Imperial Crown Prince's Quarters, we get out of our suits, and Oalla and the two crew members excuse themselves in haste.

"Thank you so much, Oalla," I say before she heads out the door. "Your leadership and help were tremendous. I really must thank you for taking care of me so well. Now I just want to make sure Aeson and everyone else is okay. My brother Gordie, Manala—"

"Yes, yes, of course, My Imperial Lady—always my pleasure to assist you," Oalla replies in a slightly hurried tone. "I'm on my way to Kass's workroom now. You should come by there if you want to know what's happening. He will be there shortly with the others."

I nod, and she rushes away.

The first thing I do is go check on my Dad in the guest quarters.

My father is standing near the window when I get there. He is all alone—no one else is in the room, not even the frequent palace servants—and I notice he is holding Mom's urn and speaking softly to it.

I freeze in my tracks.

". . . What a grey, beautiful day, Margot," Dad is saying wistfully, looking out through the window at a lofty view of the distant city and the grand park and gardens far below. "I have never seen such calm, peaceful colors here . . . you should see it. . . . Looks like rain. What a wonder."

I take a step into the room, and Dad hears me. He turns around, slightly startled. But his calm demeanor returns.

"Daddy," I say.

"My Gwenie-girl." He sighs. "I was just talking to your Mom. Sometimes I do that, you know."

With slow, careful movements he sets down the urn back on the side table in the corner.

I approach Dad without a word and wrap my arms around him. Together we stand looking at the distant city and the strange rain.

"I miss her so much," he says after a few moments.

"I miss her too. *So* much."

"So how was your important mission?" Dad asks after several minutes. "Gordie and George are still not back."

"Don't worry, they should be here soon. It's so weird, Dad. Today—I was walking on a *moon*," I whisper. "And then—then we sang together, and we brought another moon back into our world."

"Sounds miraculous." Dad makes a soft sound of amusement and wonder, then shakes his head slightly in disbelief. "Who are you, daughter of mine? An astronaut who sings moons into being!" He turns and glances at me directly and chuckles.

"I've no idea," I say. "And actually, it sounds seriously *crazy*, doesn't it?"

"So, the mission objective worked as intended."

"Oh, yes. All that rain and overcast," I say. "That's because of us. Or, to be precise, the Ghost Moon—which is no longer a ghost. People are going over there right now, even as we speak. But there're some major problems happening globally down here on Atlantis."

I tell Dad all about the moon's gravitational effects and the building hurricanes and tidal waves.

"I haven't turned on the TV all day," Dad says. "I'm sorry that I'm so deeply unaware of what else might've happened—besides this rain."

"They're working on reprogramming weather control systems to account for the new moon," I say. "I'm going over to the workroom in a minute to see what exactly is going on and whether it might impact us here. But first I had to check up on you."

"Ah, in that case, my dear girl, you should go. Let me know what you find out. And I want to hear back from your brothers, tell them so."

I get to the workroom and find Oalla, Radanthet, Gennio, Anu, and a dozen other people, staring at multiple screens, and one large main screen in particular. None of the other four members of our *astroctadra* mission is back yet, except for me. The Imperator, of course, has been here all along—and is possibly still downtown at the Atlantis Grail Stadium with the ark-ship masquerading as a Monument, or more likely upstairs in his Quarters dealing with panicked calls from other heads of state—but I'm not going to inquire about him until Aeson returns.

The various computer displays show streams of data, live images of the stormy skies and tidal waves in an open ocean. There are numerous rain-soaked locations around the globe, including the opposite side of the planet in the middle of the night. Some of the smaller screens are monitoring the now-permanent views of Helios surrounded by the golden light grid, plus companion views of Rah and Septu with their grids. And one dedicated display is split up into six lesser windows and set to TV feeds showing various networks reporting on the sudden shocking weather and the rumors surrounding today's space mission to the ghostly moon.

But the largest of the smart screen displays is showing the Ghost Moon itself. It's an image of pastel desolation on the surface, mauve and brown and grey rocky features, with a focus on one particular plateau littered with ancient ships. For once, the panorama is natural, taken from the vantage point of landing parties—as opposed to a weird flyby of an incorporeal surface. On the lower portion of the screen are rows of constantly changing numerical data.

There are dozens of Fleet personnel wearing the now familiar space suits, walking along the surface. Some of them are taking soil and rock samples, even as robotic units hover nearby taking additional samples and performing other analysis. Others are walking among the ships on the plateau, and the direction and camera angle changes periodically, jumping to another individual vantage point, another sudden closeup of a ship sprawling on top of, or partially sunken in, the regolith. . . .

As I observe and pay attention, it becomes apparent that the personnel on the surface are communicating with us here in the workroom.

". . . what percentage of gravity are we talking about?" Radanthet is speaking into his wrist comm to a person on the surface. "Twenty or eighteen percent? Check the readings on your end, please, to corroborate. I'm getting conflicting numbers here from two different probes. . . ."

"Confirming now, Rad-Rad, give me five heartbeats to recalibrate," a familiar voice replies. I realize at once it is Erita.

Wait, what's Erita doing on the Ghost Moon?

Just as my eyes widen, I see another tall person in a suit following along after the speaker whose helmet camera is showcasing the view. My God . . . that's my brother Gordie! I can see his face with glasses through his clear visor.

I near Oalla and ask her what's going on.

"Don't worry, Gwen," Oalla tells me with a quick glance in my direction before turning again to watch. "They decided to take a detour before heading home."

"Does Aeson know?"

Oalla smiles and points. "He's right there."

I stare at the display and see another tall figure in a space suit moving several paces ahead of Erita. The height, the proportional breadth of shoulders, the familiar commanding posture, all tell me this is my husband.

"Wait, Aeson's on the Ghost Moon too?"

"And Ker, and Xel also. They all met up there to take a quick look."

"Why didn't we?" I say with accusation.

"Your husband's orders," Oalla replies. "He commanded me to return you home without delay."

"Ah, great." I sigh, a little frustrated.

What am I saying? I'm a *lot* frustrated. Actually, right now I'm more than a little ticked off.

I could've been up there, exploring the unknown alongside everyone. Instead, here I am, stuck in the mission control center, watching the action unroll on a live feed. . . . When I see Aeson in person we're going to have a little talk about making these kinds of important decisions *without* me, or on my behalf. This kind of thing needs to *stop*.

Meanwhile, the view on the largest screen switches from Erita's helmet camera to the perspective of Aeson. "Phoebos—you are now on primary screen," one female *astra daimon* at the controls nearby announces, and we see the scene skip forward, with the vantage changing to a large ship's hull directly ahead. The ship is ovoid, slate-grey metal shaped like a capsule that's several hundred meters in length. It is resting on the regolith at a slight angle, one end sunken at least three meters lower into the ground.

"Understood." Aeson's clear, businesslike voice comes in loudly from the audio equipment in the room, "This is Phoebos, now approaching the largest of the vessels. Requesting cutting crew assistance. Meet me with cutting equipment on the short end in five."

And then Aeson continues walking, so that with every pace he takes the view of the grey hull takes over, filling the camera.

We watch intently as Aeson approaches within touching distance of the big ship. Then his gloved hand comes up, and he places it on the hull to sweep the metal surface side to side, dispersing a layer of ancient dust. Underneath the dull grey layer, the metal surface is revealed as pale orichalcum. At once it gleams brightly in the light of Hel, coming through sharp and undiluted in the thin atmosphere.

"Poseidon Command Imperial Quarters, are you seeing this?" Aeson asks.

"Yes, we are receiving," Radanthet says. "Looks like orichalcum. And the size, proportions, and overall shape matches historical records. The ship is definitely one of ours—is my guess."

Aeson steps back, leaving the cleaned streak on the hull, and now the camera on his helmet shows that he continues walking along the perimeter.

"This is Sobek, I have your cutting crew," Keruvat's deep voice suddenly fills the audio, with a crackle preceding him.

"Coming toward you now," Aeson responds. And then his camera shows him begin to turn and follow the circular hull surface as he reaches the short end of the capsule that tapers off in a blunt, rounded curve, with the bleak moon landscape reappearing in the background.

A group of five personnel in suits stands ready, three of them holding cutting equipment. The other two approach Aeson. The tallest is Keruvat, and his handsome dark face shows clearly through his visor.

"What are your recommendations for making a clean breach?" Aeson says. "Find me a seal line if you can, otherwise we will cut at random."

"Commence sweeping the hull," Keruvat says to the crew next to him, and a crew member lifts a small pressurized nozzle tool and starts sweeping the surface of the hull to remove the accumulation of what appears to be centuries of ancient dust (another mystery—where did that dust come from, if the moon with everything on it was isolated in a dimensional bubble all this time?). "Clean up this entire side before you cut. I want to see if there are any original hatches here before ruining this beauty. . . ."

"I can't even imagine how old that thing must be," Oalla whispers next to me. "And yet, look at that nice smooth surface—underneath that dust it's still solid and undamaged."

". . . Poseidon Command Imperial Quarters, this is Shamash." Xelio's voice sounds abruptly, coming in at extra-high volume. "I have a full vessel count for you. We've observed 379 units above surface, and a possible 47 more that are buried in the regolith. That's a total of 426 vessels after an initial surface scan. There are likely more, but that will require a deep scan."

"Shamash, confirming your numbers at 426," the female *daimon* seated near Radanthet says. I can't remember her name.

"Among them, 120 of the vessels appear to be large transport class—the antique combination of residential ark and cruiser." Xelio's booming voice continues. "The rest are variable in size, function unclear. Maybe 29 small, possible shuttles. About a hundred are deep space military grade, still to be confirmed—"

"Shamash, you're blasting my earpiece, turn down your volume," Erita's voice cuts in, transmitting at a much lower level of sound.

Here in the room, Radanthet and Oalla both chuckle, while the other *daimon* glance at them in equal amusement.

"Apologies," Xelio says after a pause, coming in at a more reasonable volume. "Is that better?"

"Much better," Oalla says, here on our end.

"Showing off as usual, *daimon*?" Keruvat remarks, as he stands next to Aeson. Both of them are waiting on the sweeper who is still cleaning the ship's hull for the cutting crew. Aeson's perspective camera view is still filling up the primary screen.

"Yes, naturally. You know me, *sen-i-senet*," Xelio says calmly. "I'll always blast and clear your way—be that with noise or my charming presence."

Keruvat snorts, and Radanthet here in the room snorts in tandem.

Oalla and the other female *daimon* exchange glances. The woman shakes her short-cropped, gilded head with sarcasm and Oalla rolls her eyes.

"So—Tefnut, Phoebos, anyone—how's the gravity where you are?" Radanthet asks. "I'd still like a confirmation of twenty or eighteen percent below Amrevet gravity. Yes? No? Still processing?"

"This is Tefnut, confirming 18.5 percent below Amrevet—"

On the screen, Aeson's camera view continues to show the sweeper passing the device over the nose portion of the capsule end, when a definite seam is revealed, running in a manhole-sized circle along the fabric of the hull.

"What do we have here?" Oalla murmurs thoughtfully—even as Aeson's camera stops, then pivots in the same direction, and Aeson himself walks closer.

"It appears to be a hatch," Aeson says. "No visible access mechanism on the exterior, so it must open from the inside."

His view sweeps over the fine detail of the seam, following the circular indentation in the hull. Its placement and doorlike size definitely suggest some kind of opening. We see all of it clearly, in close up, on the big screen.

"Good work. We will start cutting here, following the seam." And Aeson turns to the cutting crew, indicating the seam line with his gloved finger.

"Carefully, please," Radanthet adds. "Be ready for ancient door traps. Those things were legendary during the Landing period as part of construction security methods."

"Valid point." Aeson says. "Take extra care. Now proceed."

Chapter 80

While the cutting crews work on getting the hatch of the ancient ship open, I happen to glance away from the compelling action taking place on the large screen and notice that my Dad is here. Charles Lark, my father, is standing at the door of the workroom, looking in on us from my bedroom door.

"Oh!" I say. "Dad, please come in."

"Is it permitted? Would that be all right?" he asks quietly, even as the *daimon* and officers in the room turn to look.

"*Ter* Charles, of course, please do come in," Oalla says with a friendly nod.

If I recall, Oalla met my Dad at the Wedding and then briefly talked with him a few times since. Dad has never come into the workroom, except in passing, insisting that he didn't want to be in anyone's way.

But now here he is.

I come up to Dad and lead him over to the nearest chair, which I pull over for him.

"Just wanted to take a peek," Dad says to me in a considerate whisper. "I realize things are getting rather exciting, because the TV is showing live footage of the Ghost Moon. Apparently it is filled with ancient ships! An archeological discovery in progress!"

"Oh, yes." I smile. "Aeson is there now, look! That's the view from his helmet up on the big screen."

"Ah, I knew I'd get a better, inside look here than on the TV," Dad says with excitement. I don't recall seeing him this animated in quite some time. What a nice contrast compared to his quiet grief and sorrow of about an hour ago. . . .

Thank goodness for archeological discoveries!

Suddenly I recall that my brother Gordie is there now too, walking on the moon surface in a space suit, along with all those other people who know what they're doing.

How will Dad react? Should I even mention it to him? Would the worry be too much? For that matter, where exactly is Gordie now, as he's wandering on the surface among the ship junkyard necropolis—or would that be *shipropolis?* Okay, probably not. . . .

On the other hand, I've come to the conclusion recently that withholding anything from any of my loved ones is usually a bad idea.

So I tell my Dad about Gordie taking a detour to visit this newly corporeal moon with the others.

Dad's brows slowly rise in amazement, but there's a soft, pleased smile on his lips. "Good for Gordon," he says firmly. Then he shakes his head and makes a laugh noise. "What a wonder. . . . Holy moly indeed. . . . The unbelievable things all of you get to experience every day."

"At least George is safely inside a huge, secure, battle barge-class warship, with Manala," I add.

Dad chuckles in his typical follow-up reaction to his continual state of amazement. "Indeed."

Lovingly, I pat my Dad's arm through his jacket. "Let me know if you don't understand whatever's being said, okay? I'll translate from *Atlanteo* to English for you," I add in a whisper, and Dad nods.

Then together we return our attention to the screen showing the crews cutting through the hatch, as Aeson watches them on site.

Finally the last of the seam around the hatch is pierced, and the crew retract their tools.

"Stand clear. Prepare to breach," Aeson says.

Two additional personnel approach, carrying other specialized tools for mechanical force-opening.

I expect them to pound down the hatch. Instead, moments later, they carefully lift out the rounded metal panel with special corner grips and suction tools.

A dark opening is revealed.

Everyone in the workroom command center stills in anticipation.

"This is Phoebos, proceeding inside," Aeson says, stepping past the work crew members without hesitation.

"Oh God. . . . Careful, Aeson," I whisper, and Oalla glances at me.

This time it's Dad who squeezes my arm comfortingly.

Aeson steps inside the ancient ship's entrance. As he does so, a faint, greenish illumination starts to fill the void of darkness, until it normalizes to a steady pale white glow emanating from the interior walls.

"Functional light sensors," Aeson remarks. "That's more than expected."

The camera in Aeson's helmet continues to record for us, and now we can make out the interior itself.

A bare, metallic antechamber greets us. No furnishings, no control panels—nothing but unadorned orichalcum walls. As Aeson looks around, we get to see what he is experiencing. He sees a rounded outer hull wall and a straight interior wall. And then on both ends of this vaguely rectangular space are empty doorways opening onto more darkness.

"This is Sobek, coming in also, as backup," Keruvat's voice says. "In fact, bringing in additional personnel."

"Confirming backup." Aeson says. "I am taking the left corridor. Have them meet me there. Sobek, proceed to the right."

"Slowly and carefully," Radanthet repeats.

Aeson advances at an even pace, and the corridor lights come on softly as he approaches. The walking space is narrow, with a low ceiling. Here, in the claustrophobia-inducing corridor, there are additional light fixtures every few paces, but still no decoration or writing on the wall panels.

The corridor ends at an intersection.

"Taking the passage on my right, with the assumption that it eventually leads to a central hub or command center," Aeson says, turning in the specified direction. He walks another twenty paces through a similar stretch of narrow corridor until he comes to a dead end, culminating in a bulging set of reinforced doors that I instantly remember seeing somewhere before.

Oh, my. . . . That convex doorway looks *exactly* like the entrance to one of the four spherical Habitats located inside the ancient ark-ship Vimana, the Grail Monument.

Aeson stops. He must recognize it too. It's as if his camera is suddenly fixed in place while he considers the *implications.*

Everyone here in the workroom shows no such recognition, since none of the *daimon* are a part of the Imperator's secret circle.

None of them has had the opportunity to visit the ancient ark-ship buried underneath the Stadium. They know nothing of the Habitats.

Even Oalla, Keruvat, Xelio, and Erita have never been down there, although they've heard about some of it from Aeson when he partially confided in them about the ark-ship situation.

And now, as the only other person who gets it, I'm unsure how to react—not sure if I should mention anything. I decide to hold my tongue.

"Phoebos, that door looks very solid," Oalla says. "Any locking mechanisms you can see, or do you require assistance?"

Aeson's camera begins moving somewhat erratically again as he looks downward, then up, and his examination sweeps the immediate surroundings of the doors. He then turns around and we get to see three backup crew members waiting behind him.

"Sealed and reinforced. No visible locks," Aeson says in a neutral tone that tells me immediately he's not going to reveal anything just now—not in a public SPC transmission. And then he addresses the backup personnel. "Get me the cutting crew."

Sometime later, we watch the cutting crew take down the reinforced doors after some serious effort with heavy-duty cutting tools. The opening is revealed at last, and Aeson proceeds inside, followed by Keruvat, Erita, Xelio, and a few others who all converged upon this interesting find. This includes Gordie, who's tagging along with everyone.

"Look, there's Gordie . . ." I whisper near Dad's ear. He nods with a light smile, watching engrossed as the scene unfolds.

Once inside this habitat, Aeson enters a corridor that follows the perimeter of the sphere on one of its lower levels—since they came in at ground level. Indeed, the outer wall has greater curvature near the floor and more width along the ceiling, which confirms this.

Here, the similarity to the Vimana habitat becomes even more pronounced. Same circular corridor, same evenly spaced intervals between doors along the interior wall. And this time—writings on the wall panels near each door, in hieroglyphics and pictographs that I recognize as a form of ancient Classical *Atlanteo*. I can't read any of it, but I've definitely seen them before. . . .

"Finally, a direct confirmation that this is one of our ancient ships," Keruvat's voice comes in. Aeson turns to look, and we can see Keruvat examining the wall panels closely.

"Yes, this is ours," Erita says, peering at another inscribed panel near a door and shining a high-powered flashlight beam from her wrist to better illuminate detail.

"Can you read any of it?" Oalla says from the workroom. "Bring it in closer so we can put it up on the screen."

"Tefnut, you are now on primary view," the female *astra daimon* next to Radanthet announces.

And the view changes to a closeup of the wall panel with a pictograph.

"Beautiful . . ." Dad mutters next to me. "Look at that . . . such an unusual cartouche."

"We need some antiquities specialists here," Radanthet says. "Do you have anyone on-site?"

Oalla glances at my Dad. "*Ter* Charles is an expert, however in Earth antiquities," she remarks.

"That is indeed so," Dad replies. "In this case, I can only offer generalities and comparisons to Earth details. But I'm happy to help by any means."

But as I stare at the closeup on the screen, I suddenly recognize the pictograph. It's a vertical oval resembling a peapod with four circles inside, and a fifth circle connected on the top. I remember being told its meaning—"Vimana."

Holy crap! This is not just a habitat similar to the ones inside Vimana.

This Habitat *is* from Vimana.

As the realization strikes me, I hear Aeson's voice come in: "This is Phoebos. Poseidon Command Imperial Quarters, you need to notify the Imperator and the Venerable Shirahtet Kuruam immediately. Relay to them that we have found something, and send this image directly to both."

Half an hour later, First Priest Shirahtet himself arrives in our workroom. The *daimon* and officers give him respectful courtesy salutes.

The First Priest acknowledges everyone present and gives a particularly meaningful nod to my father and me. "I am here merely to observe the findings, on behalf of the Imperial Sovereign. Proceed with your work." And he takes a seat nearby.

Meanwhile, the scene on the surface of the Ghost Moon continues to show the interior of the Vimana Habitat that somehow ended up inside this other ancient ship hundreds of miles away.

I recall, when we went down to the lower levels of the Grail Monument ark-ship weeks ago, we could only descend halfway, stopping at the bottom of the Blue Habitat. Beyond it, there was structural damage, and the rest of the ship was inaccessible—namely, the Green and Yellow Habitats.

Well, no wonder. . . . That's because the bottom levels are no longer there.

Or, at least *one* of the Habitats is definitely displaced. So which is it—the Yellow or the Green?

". . . Now taking environmental and atmospheric readings," Xelio's voice says as he walks the corridor with the others, staring at a handheld gadget. "Trace amounts of breathable air still present on board. Picking up oxygen, nitrogen, methane, sulfur hexafluoride . . . hm-m-m, also, an unusual sonic reading from *inside* this ship."

"Shamash, put the sound on our comms and relay it directly to Poseidon Command Imperial Quarters," Aeson says at once. His helmet camera's perspective is once again the primary view on our screen.

"Affirmative," Xel responds. "Switching on. And—transmitting audio signal now."

And in the next moment the workroom is filled with a familiar, bone-jarring, profound, awful *hum.*

I gasp involuntarily, while Shirahtet squirms in his seat. Even Oalla frowns with comprehension, because she knows enough to recognize what this is.

It is the sound of the ancient ark-ship transmitting its *alien* signal to the stars.

As the humming sound fills the room, *daimon* and officers exchange glances. Until someone says, "Wait, that noise sounds terribly familiar—I've heard it downtown at the *Stadion.*"

"That's right," another *daimon* says. "It started after that quake during the Games. Some kind of technical resonance glitch. I believe it's supposed to be coming from the Atlantis Grail Monument—"

As the *daimon* speaks, I look at Shirahtet who picks up my pointed stare then starts tapping something on his wrist comm. *He's probably contacting the Imperator.*

It occurs to me: if this Habitat on the Ghost Moon is actively transmitting *right now*—after all our efforts with the Plural Logos Voice Chorus during the *astroctadra* moon alignment—the main portion of the Vimana ark-ship on Poseidon and the Ra Disk over at New Deshret must both still be activated too.

What the hell is the matter with that relentless transmission? I think. *And just how many dratted pieces of that ark-ship are there, scattered all over the planet and beyond?*

My worried frown is noticeable, because Dad looks at me with concern.

"I'll explain later, Dad," I whisper.

"All right, enough of that nasty noise," Oalla says, and does something to cut the audio transmission.

"What exactly *is* that nasty noise?" Radanthet asks with some amusement, glancing around at those of us who appear upset.

"Right now, it is not something to be concerned about," Shirahtet says, breaking the silent pause.

"Resetting long-range comms," Oalla says in a firm tone. "Phoebos, this is Poseidon Command. You are back on line in conference mode."

Another pause. Then, a crackle, and Aeson's voice returns. "Very well. Now continuing the exploratory examination of the ship."

A eson walks along the curving perimeter corridor and takes a turn through another door marked with the Vimana cartouche toward the central hub. Three crew members continue as his backup. The others separate, walking in different directions and doing separate surveying tasks with their test equipment.

Keruvat and Xelio start opening doors along the corridor, most of which are not locked, and periodically we get their perspective visuals on screen.

The rooms they reveal are mostly stark, some with basic shipboard furnishings such as tables, chairs, desks. Most of the furniture pieces are immovable installations—permanently fixed into the floor and walls, or wall panel foldouts. The rooms resemble sterile office spaces.

Then Ker and Xel start finding more residential quarters. Bed bunks, cots, shelving. . . . Boxes with personal items. Most of the organics crumble into dust at the lightest touch. A few scrolls remain, better preserved in long metal tube holders, and are marked for retrieval by antiquities museum crews, but their written contents resemble routine inventory lists and don't look otherwise promising.

Besides those well-preserved catalog scrolls, the metal and stone, and artificial alloys are the only things that can be handled. There's a predominance of eating utensils and plates, storage containers and a few decorative items. This is when it gets a little more interesting. . . .

"Send cataloging personnel to cover this area," Keruvat says. "This is Sobek, marking these quarters for museum archival."

And yet, as they canvass the rooms methodically, finding few items of interest, it becomes apparent that whoever was here last, removed most of what used to be here. These are all discards and leftovers, items that were already old back then, left behind by their ancient owners a very long time ago. . . .

"In short, this habitat is mostly stripped of anything useful," Keruvat says with a minor edge of disappointment. "Whoever abandoned this ship, left only junk behind."

"And no identifying items," Xelio adds. "No written personnel logs or records, no names or ranks. Even the plaques on the walls seem to be mostly sterile room numbers and deck designations."

"We can't know that for certain," Erita retorts. "Not until the experts arrive and examine everything, including those tube scrolls."

"True, but—"

In that moment Aeson's voice cuts in. "This is Phoebos. Put me up on primary screen. I'm on the bottom of the central hub, Khe Deck One, Level One, of what appears to be Yellow Habitat. We have a *significant find*."

"Phoebos, you are now on primary view." The female *astra daimon* switches the screen to Aeson's perspective.

The screen changes from Keruvat's camera view of nondescript quarters to Aeson's view of a surprisingly brightly lit, large, circular chamber shaped like a bowl.

I recall the central hub of the Vimana with its grand vertical shaft running down the middle of the entire ship and eight passages branching off like radii on every level. Here, the eight passages are also present. However, the shaft itself terminates in a bowl which is the bottom of the ship, a permanently sealed exterior hatch.

Occupying the center of the bowl is a flat hover-platform. It's an ancient freight elevator similar to the one we took to descend and ascend the levels of the Vimana. A long, colorful, metallic object rests in state on the platform, as if upon a dais.

It is a sarcophagus.

There is an audible gasp heard around the workroom. The *daimon* stare. Shirahtet leans eagerly forward in his seat.

"Holy moly . . ." my Dad says, leaning forward also.

A strange slow beat begins in my temples. Slow at first, it picks up speed. . . .

"Phoebos, please approach so that we can see better!" Oalla exclaims.

In reply, Aeson nears the platform and slowly turns his head, so that his camera sweeps the unbelievable view before us.

The sarcophagus is a long, elegant shape of bright polished gold, encrusted with lapis lazuli, blue glass, agate, jade, carnelian, obsidian, and other precious and semi-precious stones and clear glass inlay.

It is very much Ancient Egyptian in style—or rather, Ancient Egyptians apparently used Atlantean style burial containers for their dead.

The general shape is of a reposing human body, with a Khepresh headdress, but instead of large Egyptian stripes, the design is an intricate mandala, or a sunburst.

The golden death mask is sculpted into a youthful, androgynous, beautiful face. It could be Nefertiti or Tutankhamen. And yet, it is decidedly *not*. Different, alien—Atlantean.

There are multiple pictographs and hieroglyphs decorating the perimeter and the curving slopes of the sarcophagus top. Lotus blossoms in neat rows encrust the surface of the sarcophagus like reptile scales, covering its entire length in intricate glass inlay.

The hands of the depicted figure are folded in classic style over the chest, with a shepherd's crook and royal flail crossed underneath the golden sculpted fingers. A wide golden collar decorates the figure's neck, and in the center of the collar is a now-familiar *astroctadra* star formed of glass and lapis and amber.

Or maybe those deepest, darkest colored stones are Pegasus Blood.

Another such *astroctadra* star descends in an unusual manner from the mask's chin—in place where an Egyptian pharaoh's braided false beard would normally be.

And yet a third *astroctadra* rises from the forehead in place of the Uraeus serpent.

There are multiple cartouches depicted, so the person buried should likely be easy to identify.

"Whoever this is, the ancient individual buried here appears to be royal or otherwise important," Aeson says, responding to the unspoken thoughts filling my mind.

"Allow me—this is Shirahtet, the First Priest of Kassiopei," Shirahtet says in that moment. "My Imperial Lord Aeson, if you can hear me, please move in closer so that I can see the name inscribed in the central plaque."

Aeson's camera shifts, and he draws even closer, leaning over the sarcophagus.

The long oval name cartouche fills the screen.

"This is Phoebos. Venerable Shirahtet, glad to have your expertise here. Please confirm that what I'm seeing is correct even though it makes no historical sense—is the first portion of the Name as inscribed the same as the Dynastic symbol for 'Kassiopei?'"

"My Imperial Lord, it is indeed," Shirahtet answers. "The Ra starburst followed by that mark below and the four notches—"

"So—then it *is* Kassiopei." Aeson sounds incredulous. "But how? Who is this person? Isn't it true that all my ancient ancestors are entombed on Atlantis, and primarily at Poseidon?"

"That is the case indeed, My Imperial Lord." Shirahtet pauses, standing up as if to breathe more easily, or maybe in order to peer closer at the already zoomed-in image on the great screen.

"Are you able to read the full name?" Aeson asks.

Shirahtet takes a deep breath before speaking. "I am able to read not only the name but the entire designation. The name, as it is written, is *Arlenari Kassiopei, daughter of Churu and Merneit, sister of Oron and Narmeradat, wife of Enhuvarat, and mother of none.*"

There is a very long pause.

And then Aeson says, "Who the *shebet* is Arlenari Kassiopei?"

"My Imperial Lord, I—don't know," Shirahtet responds. "And for that matter, who is Oron?"

"You *don't* know? You, who know everything about us, don't *know?* Very well. Time to call my Imperial Father—do it *now.*"

Chapter 81

The next hour is a frantic cascade of events. Shirahtet steps outside in a hurry to call the Imperator. Meanwhile Aeson paces around the sarcophagus, slowly examining every inch, and his camera dutifully transmits the amazing detail to our main screen here in the workroom.

The *daimon* and other SPC staff here in the command center prepare to relay the feeds to appropriate individuals and antiquities experts directly—once they receive the official instructions and permission to proceed. That, of course, is pending the Imperator's and the IEC's joint decisions in conjunction with several foreign heads of state. Only then will the global public be notified about the find via the media who are already on alert for big news due to ongoing catastrophic weather.

Other mission members and SPC Fleet crew soon join Aeson in the sarcophagus chamber. Ker, Erita, Xelio and others start running nonintrusive tests, while those of us here on Atlantis watch with rapt attention. On the expert advice of my father, Oalla asks Aeson to do specific close ups of the sarcophagus detail, especially certain frequently repeating cartouches and patterns.

"Anything that is repeated is a good indicator of significance," Dad says, pointing out areas of particular interest. "For example, that one enclosed in a double oval frame with the wave pattern and spirals on both ends—notice how it is heavier, with thicker lines, etched deeper into the gold surface. Could it be another royal name? I would love to know what those hieroglyphs mean."

When Shirahtet returns, Dad and all of us get the chance to find out—since Shirahtet has the in-depth knowledge of the ancient forms of writing.

But first, Shirahtet addresses Aeson, to relay the Imperator's message. "My Imperial Lord," the First Priest says with a serious, intense expression that is even more so than his usual, perpetually sobering demeanor. "It is the Imperial Sovereign's *strong wish* that this sarcophagus be loaded onto your most secure freight transport and delivered here to Poseidon—*immediately.*"

On the surface of the Ghost Moon, Aeson takes several long moments before replying. "Is that wise?" he asks. "Moving this relic that's potentially vital in importance, and very likely *fragile*, might damage it. Why not continue to examine it here on the surface under its native conditions and lower gravity? When the experts arrive, they can follow proper methodology—"

"May I regretfully remind My Imperial Lord that we are faced with an existential threat and don't have much time for *proper* methodology," Shirahtet says.

Aeson's voice acquires a note of frustration. "This burial object might not *survive* being lifted onto another platform—much less the recent turbulent conditions of reentry through the Atlantis atmosphere, especially once the Atlantean gravity kicks in."

"That may indeed be so, but it is a risk we are willing to take."

"Fine. But I insist that we wait at least two hours until the experts arrive before attempting to move anything," Aeson says firmly. "I have requested Specialist Cvutu's presence here and she has been dispatched."

Here in the workroom, Shirahtet pauses. "Very well, My Imperial Lord. We will wait long enough for Antiquities Specialist Igara Cvutu to arrive on site. But then the sarcophagus will be loaded and delivered here—that is, to the Imperial Poseidon Museum—for further processing."

The way he phrases it, I highly suspect that Shirahtet intends for the sarcophagus to be taken to the ark-ship research facility downtown and not to any museum, but this is for the benefit of the public.

"All right." Aeson resumes examining the sarcophagus, and the others in the chamber do the same.

This is the moment that my Dad chooses to speak up. "Would it be possible to ask you, Venerable Shirahtet, what is written in some of those cartouches?"

Shirahtet turns to my father. "Of course, I am at your service, *Ter* Charles."

Dad points out the cartouche in question, the one that seems to be often repeated.

Shirahtet looks at it, then his expression becomes extremely focused. "It says, *'all things.'*"

"All things?" my Dad echoes. "That is what's written? No specific names?"

Shirahtet narrows his eyes and looks again. "That first part of the pictograph, the joined circles, means 'all' while the next portion with the four triangles superimposed is 'thing.' Since it is preceded by a plural, it is 'things.'"

"So. All things," Dad thinks out loud. "'All' or 'every' and then 'thing.' 'Everything?'"

"Yes indeed." Shirahtet nods. "It can be read as *'everything.'*"

And then, even as the First Priest mentions the word, his expression comes alive. "The book, the *book!*" he mutters.

"What book?" Dad asks, sitting up and leaning forward in his seat.

"The Book of Everything!" Shirahtet exclaims. "An elusive ancient artifact we've been very eager to find, which has been referenced in other ancient relics. It is something which Our Imperial Sovereign, the Archaeon Imperator, is very interested in— has been interested in for quite some time."

"Ah, I see," Dad says. "It sounds fascinating. Do you think this Book of Everything is inside that burial box?"

"It *must* be—such is our hope," Shirahtet says. "If only it were indeed so!"

Over the next hour, Aeson and the others on the surface of the moon are asked to confirm the occurrences of the Everything Cartouche, as my Dad has begun calling it. According to the count, the phrase 'Everything' appears at least twenty times, in different sizes, all over the top of the ancient coffin.

"Can you attempt to open the sarcophagus?" Shirahtet says suddenly, after yet another tiny instance of 'Everything' shows up in almost microscopic size along a design border."

"Cvutu should be here in less than an hour," Aeson responds. "I want her to give her estimation of how best to proceed—in a near vacuum or under full atmospheric conditions—to make that initial opening."

Shirahtet makes a tiny sound of impatience, then checks his wrist comm for messages.

While all of this is happening, I see my brother Gordie wander into view, down there on the surface, as he follows along with the others. Gordie strolls around the bowl-shaped chamber and—after taking a long look at the main "exhibit" in the center, the sarcophagus itself—now peers at the walls and the eight entrances that branch off from the central hub. At some point he stops and simply stands staring at some wall panel, almost transfixed—and yet there's nothing on it. Yeah, that's my younger brother, all right.

Those of us on Atlantis continue to watch and wait.

Finally the long-awaited Antiquities team lands on the Ghost Moon, and Igara Cvutu arrives in the Habitat chamber with her two assistants and a trove of specialized tools to evaluate the ancient burial.

After running some further noninvasive scans, it is decided that the best thing to do would be to open the sarcophagus right here and now, in the rarified atmosphere.

I turn to glance at my Dad, whose eyes are full of curiosity and energy. Oalla, Radanthet, and others in the workroom stare with anticipation, while Shirahtet manages to look both eager and cautious, and constantly sends out messages on his wrist comm.

When it's time to remove the lid of the sarcophagus, it takes four SPC crew personnel and both of the museum assistants working together to shift and then lift up the heavy thing. Apparently, there is a layer of stone underneath the jewel-encrusted metal, which explains the extreme weight. Good thing this is being done in the lighter gravity of the moon, and not on Atlantis, where the same sarcophagus would suddenly weigh an additional ton.

The lid is raised and set aside with great care by the six people working in tandem.

Inside, another, smaller sarcophagus is revealed. This inner sarcophagus appears to be made of pure gold and covered with fine etchings.

"Yes, might as well proceed to open it here," Igara Cvutu says to the work crew after an initial moment of awe and wonder at the discovery. Her face, seen through the visor of her helmet, is thoughtful and resigned. "Whatever is inside would likely fare better if first exposed to a thin, arid atmosphere such as this. So much dry sand and minimal oxygen. The conditions on this moon are ideal for preservation. We might assume the body has managed to avoid the corrosive effects of oxygen all these thousands of years."

The crew carefully lift up the golden lid. It is discovered to be considerably lighter because the gold layer is pressed over wood. They set this lid nearby, resting it gently on the platform next to the grand outer lid.

And then everyone stares with disbelief at what is revealed inside.

I admit, I expected to see mummified human remains wrapped in ancient resin and natron-soaked linen—or its Atlantean equivalent.

Instead, within the wooden sarcophagus box, we see a human-figure-shaped *jewel*.

The thing is of a deep, indigo blue color. . . . It has a smoothly polished cabochon surface that immediately glistens in the bright illumination and sends smoky lavender and violet light and shadows playing in its depths.

There is a collective gasp heard around the workroom on Poseidon. And on the Ghost Moon surface, a similar series of exclamations issues from multiple persons.

"*Bashtooh!* What is that?" everyone asks.

I watch the big screen as Aeson leans closer over the immense blue jewel. He shines a bright beam from his helmet at the upper end to illuminate the bizarre object entombed in this human manner.

And as the light falls upon the rich blue, an even stranger thing happens. The focused beam manages to reach deep inside, piercing the layers of the dark, translucent material . . . and a *human face* is revealed, ghostly and serene, seeming to float in its depths.

"Whoa!" my brother Gordie exclaims, looking over Erita's shoulder. He is the first one to react.

Erita peers down. "Is that a trick of the light?"

"Did you see that? That's a face!" Xelio says from the other side of the sarcophagus.

"Yes, I see it," Aeson responds coldly. "There's more."

"There's a face, a head and—"

"Not just a head, there is someone in there. An entire *body*. . . . We need more light." Erita engages her own helmet's high beam in addition to her wrist light.

"Extremely unusual. This appears to be a body completely encased for burial," Igara Cvutu says, bending to stare closer. "I suspect this material is ancient resin. Likely, it was originally clear and transparent—"

"Yes, yes," Shirahtet says with excitement, here on Atlantis. "And over the centuries it transitioned, acquiring its deep coloration and unique hue. . . . This is Pegasus Blood!"

"What—the whole thing?" Oalla glances at him with a frown. "How is that possible? So much priceless Agnios tree resin?"

"I can think of no other ancient substance that can be poured over a subject without harm to the skin and preserve it so perfectly in its entirety," Shirahtet says. "Ordinary, cheap resin from other sources would not form such a hard jewel casing around an object. Pegasus Blood alone can do this."

"Don't forget, they had many Agnios trees in those early days, and the sap was plentiful," Keruvat remarks, from his own vantage point around the foot area of the sarcophagus.

"So yes, it is entirely possible," Igara Cvutu says. "We need to analyze the material to be certain, but I am quite convinced it could be little else."

In the meantime, Aeson moves slowly backward in parallel to the sarcophagus, so that his helmet illuminates the entire length of the blue object. As he does so, we start seeing the detail in the depths of the indigo.

A body is indeed sealed inside, like an insect trapped in amber. . . . A female body, with a lovely, innocent face and delicate skin unmarred by the ages.

The woman lies, reposing in a semblance of sleep, with her eyelids closed and her arms folded at her chest. She is pale and youthful—or merely timeless, judging by her smooth, unlined features, which are almost doll-like in their exquisite form. Her hair is long and Kassiopei-golden, as the bright beam of light confirms. It seems to float in fine filaments, fanning outward like a mermaid's mane, suspended in the ancient resin ocean around her.

Surreal. . . .

She wears a golden garment wrapped around her torso, a kind of loose, translucent shift that barely covers her limbs. Her hands rest, one over the other, delicate slim fingers, with nothing underneath, no objects of Imperial power.

How did she die? My thoughts race. *What happened to her?*

Except for being encased in a priceless substance, the body is otherwise unadorned. No rings on her fingers, no bracelets or arm braces, no grand *wesekh* collar necklace around the slender column of her throat.

"Scan the whole body and the Pegasus Blood itself for anything else that might be within," Shirahtet says. "And check the wooden coffin box for any other objects. Look for scrolls or collections of writings. Even scraps. . . ."

"You mean, search for The Book of Everything." Aeson nods and steps back, giving Specialist Cvutu and her two assistants room to work. Everyone else does the same.

The Antiquities team uses hand-held gadgets to pass over the entombed woman and her precious translucent container. They pause to check the readings frequently.

"I am sorry, but there's nothing that I would call a book, or written artifacts inside," one assistant says after multiple scan passes.

Shirahtet exhales loudly. He does not look pleased at all.

"Very well," he says after a pause. "Continue to scan—check the box for hidden slots in the wood, for seams or any kind of secret compartments. Examine places underneath the body."

And for the next few minutes the scan gadgets are back in action.

"Nothing," Igara Cvutu concludes.

"Examine the exterior sarcophagus too, look for compartments, press every jewel if needed," Shirahtet says. "Better yet, load the whole thing on a transport and get it here. I would like to see it for myself."

"Very well," Igara Cvutu responds with a shrug. "I no longer have the usual preservation-based concerns as far as damage to the remains, seeing how well it is contained. We will have the whole thing delivered to Atlantis and continue this process there."

"When it—*she*, the ancient Kassiopei princess—arrives here, I would love to take a look," my Dad says, glancing at Shirahtet.

"Of course," the First Priest replies with a polite nod to my father.

In that moment on the Ghost Moon, my brother Gordie, standing nearby and staring at the jewel-encrusted lid of the outer sarcophagus, says, "Hey, sorry to bother you but there's something tiny and weird inside that clear glass. . . . If you look at it from directly above, it's sort of like a magnifying lens. I think there's something hidden *inside*. Looks like miniature writing."

At once, everyone surrounds Gordie, and he steps out of the way as the experts get to work with their gadgets.

"He is correct," Igara Cvutu says moments later, straightening. "There is a micro-image of an entire scroll contained inside that glass. Someone went to a lot of trouble to do that kind of nano-conversion. I cannot read the details with the insufficient level of magnification of the tools I've brought here, but I will examine them thoroughly, once on Atlantis."

And the large screen in the workroom now shows the feed from her perspective, with the focus on one enlarged pale glass jewel attached to the lid. There is definitely a tiny thumbnail image that looks like written characters and pictographs under a microscope.

"And the Everything Cartouche is right below it," Dad says. "I recommend you examine every jewel in the neighborhood of every one of those cartouches."

Shirahtet looks at my father with renewed energy. "*Ter* Charles, you may very well be right."

"It would certainly explain why the word 'everything' occurs in so many places," Charles Lark, my father, says. "I suspect it marks the spot where there are more such micro-images of hidden text. I would say The Book of Everything is before you—it is the entire sarcophagus."

Chapter 82

It is after Midnight Ghost Time on Poseidon by the time Aeson and the others arrive back on Atlantis.

As expected, the SPC teams in charge of transporting the precious archeological cargo deliver the sarcophagus of Arlenari Kassiopei to the research facility underneath the Atlantis Grail Monument for "initial evaluation and possible decontamination"—according to the news media that was given the bare minimal but unavoidable details. The media feeds, including the Hel-Ra Network, do not specify the facility by name, perpetuating the assumption that the sarcophagus now rests somewhere in the Imperial Poseidon Museum vault or one of its affiliates.

By this time Dad and I are back in his guest quarters together with George and Manala, who returned from War-5 only a short while ago. It's late, and everyone is tired, but we're sleepless from all the excitement, waiting on pins and needles for what comes next.

After the successful completion of Manala's part in the *astroctadra* mission aboard War-5, Xelio flew away solo to join Aeson and the others on the Ghost Moon. Manala was left with Consul Denu and George on the battle barge, to return home at their convenience. As a result, Manala—accompanied by my older brother and the Consul, and all her guards—stayed to watch, along with the War-5 high command, via SPC secure channel transmissions, some of the events taking place on the Ghost Moon. Afterwards they headed back to Atlantis, intending to be here earlier, but encountered extreme weather delays and took extra care returning from orbit.

And now, we wait for Aeson's return. Dad lies down for an hour to rest—or so he says; I'm guessing he will just sleep through the night—while the rest of us continue to watch the TV feeds. We switch back and forth from Ghost Moon coverage and its stunning ancient ship graveyard discoveries to the global weather disaster coverage—particularly on the opposite side of the world in New Deshret, Abuud, Karamat, and Xeosan.

It's currently morning there, and multiple hurricane systems and tidal waves are in progress—some are successfully contained and neutralized by weather tech, while a few others manage to break through and make impact against the various coastlines. Yes, the weather control agencies are still working on reprograming the control parameters to account for the gravitational effects of the Ghost Moon. . . .

At last, Aeson shows up, together with Gordie and Erita, who makes a point of "delivering Gordon Lark home safely."

Gordie appears unusually wound up, but also sleepy, judging by his huge yawns. But he starts talking about the details he got to see on the amazing Ghost Moon. "Hey, since we did the Ghost Moon thing today and missed dinner, I mean, *niktos* meal, how about a ghost meal now? Cause that would be super."

I smile at Gordie fondly, and call the kitchen staff to order a meal service for everyone—exercising my role as a proper Imperial.

"Oh, I am so glad the Plural Logos Voice singing command worked," Manala says. "It would have been terribly sad if it had all been for nothing."

"Fortunately it all worked out, so no need to stress over alternate possible endings," George says calmly, giving Manala an amused, brief stare.

Manala turns to look at George with widened eyes. "What alternate possible endings?" she asks.

George opens his mouth, begins to say something, then shakes his head and exhales loudly. He takes a seat on the sofa and puts his feet up.

Manala continues looking at him with a slightly startled look of expectation. But George makes a point of ignoring her, so neither one of them says anything else.

Meanwhile, Aeson comes up to me and leans down to simply kiss me. We linger in the breathless, deep intimacy. Then I wrap my arms around him and we just stand there, both of us, in utter exhaustion.

"I'm so mad at you, Aeson," I whisper after a few moments, placing my hands on his cheeks and turning his face to stare directly into his beautiful lapis lazuli eyes.

His eyes focus in surprise and he stirs. "What? Why?"

"Because you told Oalla to take me back home instead of going with all of you to the Ghost Moon! I wanted to be there and see all those wonders! How could you not ask me first?"

"I'm sorry," he replies, blinking. "Yes, I should've talked with you, but the situation was extremely volatile, potentially dangerous, I couldn't risk taking you into something—"

"Next time, at least let me know what the plan is," I whisper with intensity, staring into his eyes with a frown. "Let me make the decision, okay?"

"Okay. . . ." His expression is so tense and worried in that moment that my heart melts. I give him a peck on the cheek and at the same time whisper, "Promise?"

"All right. I promise." He looks down at me in relief.

"So," I say. "Arlenari Kassiopei. Who was she? I—my Dad, all of us—have a million questions."

He sighs, shaking his head, glancing briefly at the others in the room. "Believe me, *im amrevu*, so do I. Tomorrow morning, *everything* begins—literally. The so-called Book of Everything. My Father's specialists will analyze those microscopic, jewel-encased scrolls, then run every test imaginable on every other part of the sarcophagus and the ancient body. My Father expects significant results, and they will be given it to him. You and I will know much more, by this time tomorrow."

I nod. "It's been a very long, very amazing day."

"Before I forget," Aeson mentions tiredly. "The most recent SPC reports show that not only has the Ghost Moon caused a variety of weather anomalies, but it has disrupted the orbits of the other moons in the Atlantis system. Pegasus now has an even greater orbital wobble. And Atlantis itself has shifted slightly on its axis of rotation."

"Lovely," I say with a pang of worry. "How much of a problem is that going to be?"

"Too early to tell," my husband says, letting out a tensely held breath.

"Then let's not think about it," I say. "At least for tonight."

The following day, Red Amrevet 16, is spent waiting for more news on the sarcophagus—while weather tech agencies battle the bad weather around the planet and SPC teams continue to explore the spacecraft-littered surface of the Ghost Moon.

Aeson divides his time between the workroom and meetings with the Imperator, Shirahtet, and several of the Imperial inner circle. He also deals with constant incoming calls from the IEC members and from foreign heads of state. The international community deserves to know as soon as possible what is contained within and whether it can help our situation. Whatever is to be made public is being decided right now.

All this time, various antiquities and linguistics experts scan and digitize the miniature scrolls inside each jewel, followed by transcription and translation. Meanwhile, other scientists subject the ancient female body encased in Pegasus Blood to noninvasive DNA analysis in order to verify her Kassiopei lineage.

"The woman is a DNA match and is indeed Kassiopei," we are told in one summary report.

Meanwhile, another report, this time from a linguist, brings curious news. Aeson comes by to deliver it himself, as we have *dea* meal together.

"They've now digitized all of the pages of The Book of Everything," Aeson tells us. "Put them in meaningful order, as best as possible. They will have the final translations transmitted to my Father and the rest of us in a few hours. Preliminary analysis of the contents is both surprising and makes perfect sense. In short—The Book of Everything is a *diary*. Namely, it is the diary of a young Imperial Princess who calls herself *Arleana*, Starlight Sorceress, and who is, by all evidence, the same person as Arlenari Kassiopei."

"A diary? That's an incredible discovery," my Dad says.

"What makes it more stunning is that there are no historical records of this Arlenari Kassiopei in any of our historical texts and indexes. Not a single mention—not even within our most canonic secret Archives. And yet, based on the accounts in the diary, she is often front and center in many of the well-known historical events she describes."

"It could be that she was erased from history," my Dad says thoughtfully. "Such unfortunate things do happen. It is not uncommon to find names stricken from monuments—portrait likenesses of faces painted over, carved away or broken, statues defaced, and records expunged, all throughout known history on

Earth. New rulers would come in and erase their predecessors. New religions would erase the old ones. On and on, endless reasons."

"How awful," I say, feeling a sudden deep pain and regret on behalf of the ancient girl.

Aeson looks at me, and the expression in his eyes reflects my own feelings. "Based on the diary entries, this young girl was one of the original settlers—actually born on Earth, she fled from Earth to the colony planet Atlantis with fellow members of the Imperial Family, in the original batch of refugees on the ark-ships. The account covers her journey, and the first few years after the Landing, and the establishing of the Original Colony on Imperial *Atlantida*. It also covers her observations about the events on Earth that resulted in the Atlantean exodus. According to the expert translator, she was a witness to some incredible key events—"

"Well, that would certainly do it," Dad puts in. "If she knew too much, she could have been a problem, and therefore had to be eliminated."

"She was more than a witness," Aeson says. "She was a participant. Indeed, the translator mentions that the diary contains evidence that she was the *perpetrator* of some things that resulted in the ancient exodus in the first place."

That last statement gets everyone's attention.

"As you can imagine," Aeson says, "because of this one detail, My Imperial Father has ordered the translation process to be expedited."

"So many mysteries . . ." I say. "I can't wait to read this diary myself."

"Yes," Aeson says. "I suspect this diary is going to change *everything*."

"Precisely what a Book of Everything should do," George says from the sofa, with a hint of a smile.

It is late afternoon when the final digital scans and modern *Atlanteo* translations are made available for the Imperator and the rest of us to examine. The files arrive in a high-clearance-only, secure, indexed database, and Aeson gives my Dad additional access to view everything.

We pull up the database on a large hovering screen in Dad and George's guest quarters. And by "we" I mean Aeson, myself and my entire family including Gracie who dropped by in-between her Fleet duties, plus Manala who has hardly left our side, ever since the events of the *astroctadra* alignment.

The opened file displays the original scanned image on the left and the contemporary translation on the right. It's amazing to see the strange, ancient characters and pictographs in wispy, uneven handwriting, inscribed in ink upon some kind of parchment-like writing surface. Their meaning is made clear to us in the translated version, and we decipher it together—with Aeson there to help when something is unclear in *Atlanteo*.

Each page is a single diary entry, many extremely short, others filling up the whole scroll in tiny script. The entries are not daily, often skipping days, weeks, even months. The tone, the sentences, are an odd mixture of precocious wisdom and immaturity, teenage angst, stunning factual reporting, and biting commentary. They reveal high intelligence and compassion, humor and pathos—and intense loneliness.

We read, flip pages, jump back and forward in chronology. . . .
A remarkable account greets us.

> Day One. Or maybe, Day One Thousand in my Book of Everything.
> I decided today is a day when I begin writing the events of my life in this enforced upcoming journey from our home to an alien world. First, my name. I am Arleana.
> Arleana. Arleana. Arleana.
> They might call me by that other name, but now you know my true name. I am she who is the Starlight Sorceress.
> I am Arleana.
> And Everything is my fault.

I look away from the screen and glance at Aeson and at my Dad, my siblings. Their expressions are focused and serious. I resume reading.

> We have to leave the planet because my Imperial Father believes there is no other way. **They** will not let us continue being what we are, and we must continue being ourselves—or so my Imperial Mother believes.
> **They** are relentless.

But everyone else on *Atlantida* is too. I've given them my answer, showed the right way to do it, but it is not to their liking.

They do not like my way with Starlight.

They would much rather use brute force and rip the universe apart.

"Okay, hold it right there." Gracie points to a sentence. "Why is this word 'they' highlighted in some places but not in others?"

"Good catch, Gee Four," I say. "My guess is, 'they' might refer to different 'they' entities."

"The highlight might refer to our ancient *alien enemy*," Aeson says after a thoughtful pause.

We are told to prepare for a journey of two years. That many days before we reach the so-called habitable planet, even with the Stream and the Jump. Oron says it will probably take much longer. He is usually right when it comes to counts and numbers. But I am usually right when it comes to songs and stars.

"Who is Oron?" Gracie mumbles. Gracie wasn't here when the *astroctadra* mission events were happening yesterday so she has more questions than the rest of us. Fortunately, this question is a useful one.

"If I recall correctly," Dad says, "the name and designation cartouche on her sarcophagus mentioned Oron as her brother."

Aeson shakes his head. "Yes, apparently he's another Kassiopei ancestor I've never heard of. I've had to memorize the Divine Lineage Tree from childhood, especially the members of the Kassiopei Dynasty at the time of Landing. Very frustrating to find out there are gaps in my knowledge of something so basic. Or, I should say, *our* knowledge, since no one else seems to know him either."

Mother says I cannot take the animals with me. Now that animals are forbidden for food consumption by **their** decree, it will serve to upset the others on the Ark. If other passengers see my creature companions, they will think my Family is exercising Imperial Privileges in excess. Mother says the others will never believe my animal

> friends are not intended as food. And that can be dangerous for the Family.
>
> Oron says the Ark will have a great selection of live Earth beasts and animal DNA going with us to our new world. He thinks I will not miss my own stupid pets. Oron is wrong.
>
> And **they** are right. **They** have always been right.
>
> I am glad for the reinstatement of this primeval taboo, glad that humans are not permitted to consume the living bodies of other complex life forms. Narmeradat thinks I am crazy. He cannot wait until we are free of **them** so that we may eat meat again. I think Narmeradat is cruel.

"Okay . . . this begins to explain the vegetarian society of Atlantis. Still unclear as to why," George muses. "And Narmeradat is the other brother mentioned on her name cartouche."

"Narmeradat is a name I *am* familiar with," Aeson says. "Indeed, he is well known to all, a prominent historical figure. He was the first Imperator to ascend to the Throne after Landing, following the death of Churu. But our records claim he was the only son of Churu and Merneit, with no other siblings."

> We leave in three days, and Oron still refuses to believe it will happen. He is certain the asteroid will strike the Rift exactly as intended, and we will all perish even as the dimensional fabric is repaired. My Family and our Allies believe we can get away with a different result.
>
> This time, the plan is subtle.
>
> Let the asteroid strike. But divert it microscopically. Then, hide the Rift, and us with it.
>
> The course correction program has been set in motion already. It will transmit the new coordinates from within the Moon's grand resonance chamber. . . .

"Whoa! Wait!" Gordie exclaims. "Our Moon? The Earth Moon has a resonance chamber?"

George shakes his head. "You know, that makes crazy sense. I remember reading something weird about moonquakes and measured seismic activity in the 1970s after that first Apollo Moon Landing. Some piece of the Apollo spacecraft was allowed to fall away and crash on the surface and that's when the Moon rang like a bell for close to an hour. That implies to me: hollow on the inside, with a resonance chamber."

> To fool **them**, we will allow the asteroid to hit Earth, but at slightly different coordinates, assuring the sealing strike is ineffective and the Rift remains open. During the turbulence and global destruction, the Great Shield will go up to disguise the intact Rift from **them** and the rest of the universe—for as long as we maintain it.
> While all this happens, we use the Rift in secret to flee to the stars.
> To that end, my Family and their Allies—their allies, not mine—will take the **pegasei** beings with us, ensuring the bond of entanglement will always exist, between **here** and **there**.
> Nothing will be able to close the Rift then.
> It will remain, shielded, untamed, violent. Ready for our needs.
> Such is the subtle plan.
> Such a tragic plan.
> If only My Family chose my way of Starlight.

Again I look away, this time to see Aeson frowning. "The details are starting to come together," he says, seeing my gaze. "This explains the *pegasei* regularly emerging from the Great Quantum Shield at Ae-Leiterra. They are *entangled* with others of their kind across the universe, between *here* and *there*. They are keeping the rift open."

We continue reading the entries in Arlenari's diary, transfixed. She describes that fateful Impact Day and the clever escape the Ancient Atlantean Fleet makes, using the very rift which they preserve. Apparently, their subtlety works.

Then, there are days of the journey, long, stressful, filled with shipboard faction politics and quantum Jumps to make sure no one is following. Two years elapse, easily.

And then they arrive.

They come to the colony planet, and Atlantean history begins.

> We are here, and I must look back and remember those bright first days. We sat in orbit, while the lesser

ships descended to explore the surface. The scout ships crossed the beautiful sphere of our new home, in search of landing sites.

They found a globe-spanning single ocean, a water belt separating the planet into two land masses. The upper continent, with a perfect great gulf, was chosen as an ideal spot to build the first Kassiopei settlement. So was the lower one, a continent with a smaller gulf, perfect for the needs of Family Heru, and exactly far enough away.

They also found great mountain ranges. And the Logos Voices began their work.

They sheared the tops off the mountain ranges on the Upper Continent and called it the Great Nacarat Plateau. They also carved off the mountaintops on Heru's Lower Continent to make a similar plateau, calling it Iru-Mer Hesep. . . .

And then we landed, in two great factions—Kassiopei first, Heru a close second—choosing those plateaus to make our first unassailable strongholds while we built proper cities and settlements on the plains below.

"Wow," I say in amazement. "The Great Nacarat Plateau is artificial!"

"And that other one in New Deshret! And they used Logos voices to make them both!" Gracie adds.

Soon after Landing, the Long Sickness began. Nearly everyone was already sickened from the space travel, but now, in this higher-gravity world, the long-term effects became obvious.

We know now that it was the multiple Jumps causing the Sickness. And it only affected the grown adults, the old, and the very young—those with lower or diminished hormonal levels. All the adult servants, guards, artisans, concubines, slaves were incapacitated—physically and mentally. They began dying. Even the noble families were dying from degenerative disease. Physicians were useless, because they were dying too.

Only the teenagers with their hormones at the strongest levels were healthy.

Also, the Kassiopei.

My Family reveled in their divine blood, remaining strong and unaffected while everyone else around them was failing. . . . Guilt fills me even now.

Heru fared almost equally well, but even they had some illnesses and deaths.

Now that the workforce was so diminished, it became necessary to make these regrettable social changes that gave all power to the young.

Since the teenagers were unaffected, we put them to work.

First, clever aptitude tests were given to everyone. They weeded out the infirm, leaving only the healthy, primarily teenagers.

To determine career placement based on their abilities, talents, and hidden strengths—and to make sure they were able-bodied enough and responsible enough to perform adult work—the tests looked at ten categories.

Warrior, physical laborer, technician, scientist, animal handler, entertainer, artist, inventor, merchant, vocalist.

The tests were held nearly every season in order to reevaluate and choose the best workers of sound mind and body out of a chronically ailing population that continued to decline—as new cases of the Long Sickness were diagnosed, even though this happened less frequently as time went on.

To quote the official test guidelines, "until the population is deemed to be sufficiently stable," they selected for "individuals capable of making hard decisions, casting reasonable votes as far as courses of action and general rules and common laws, rational problem assessment and wise choices under technical and specific circumstances, and the ability to shape the direction of human society."

These tests took place so often, with their main objectives so cleverly disguised, that many began to think of them as games.

Dreadful, silly things.

But so necessary.

Chapter 83

"The Games of the Atlantis Grail!" Gracie exclaims.

Oh, my God! I think. *Those damn Games started out as career placement tests!*

To quote Brie Walton, holy crap on a stick!

"Oh, the irony," George says, looking at me. "Just think, Gee Two, you had to go to another planet just so you could take another brutal ancient test. Because the SATs just weren't enough."

"Oh, hush, George," I say.

For several long moments we all contemplate this eye-opening information. And then we continue reading.

> After nearly three years of silence, I will say his name.
>
> Oron.
>
> Oron, Oron, Oron.
>
> I have been obedient, even in my thoughts—the conscious ones that I can control, not those other stray creature ones that come upon you in dreams. I have been silent long enough—almost for three years, even here in my secret place—but no more.
>
> Since no one will ever see this Book of Everything, no one held me back here, only my own pride.
>
> I permit myself at last.
>
> Oron.
>
> I miss him every moment I am awake, and often he comes to me in dreams. Not surprising, since our bond is a twin bond, and it is the strongest bond between two souls.
>
> Oron's name has been forbidden. Oron's existence has been forgotten. Even by invoking his name now I commit a high crime against the Imperial Kassiopei.
>
> Sometimes Mother almost forgets and begins to speak his name. But then she shuts down and pretends

otherwise, and continues with her handiwork, before Father or Narmeradat can overhear.

Oron.

Why did you stay behind, Oron? Why did you leave me alone to go on this dismal forever-journey without you?

Sometimes, in the moments between dreams and waking, I can sense you across the universe.

I feel your life force, your unique ember of being. I know you still live, even though you were certain you would die along with the others. You fully prepared to perish in the moments of Earth's fiery apocalypse.

And yet, somehow, you live.

You must know I live too.

Until the moment one of us dies, the other will always know.

We are entangled.

Like the **pegasei**.

"All right, this is getting very weird and sad," Gracie remarks.

"Agreed," Gordie says with a frown.

Manala says nothing, but has a stricken expression on her face and her hands are clenched in her lap. In that moment George watches her seriously and exchanges concerned looks with my Dad.

I glance at Aeson, and he is submerged in thought, staring at the screen with an intense, unmoving gaze—which tells me he is not reading, but concentrating on what has been revealed.

He notices my attention on him and says, "There is something here, Gwen. I think this painful entry has revealed another aspect of a possible solution for us."

"What do you mean?"

Aeson glances at the others briefly before meeting my gaze. "The notion of *pegasei* keeping the rift open has resonated with me. And now—the additional notion of these ancient twins, brother and sister, separated across the universe, one having gone through the rift, the other staying behind—I think it may be somehow connected to the solution also. How—I don't yet know."

"Can someone please explain to me about these *pegasei?*" Dad asks. "What exactly are we talking about?"

"They are quantum trans-dimensional life forms, Daddy." Gracie hurries to explain what she and the public knows from watching the Games.

Dad's brows go up.

"Really amazing shape-shifting balls of energy," Gordie adds. "They can turn into all kinds of creatures. I guess, they really like to turn into the mythical Earth Pegasus, the winged horse. Hence, the name."

They are sentient, I want to blurt out. *They don't just turn into the Pegasus. They created the construct of a winged horse from picking the minds of ancient humans.*

How much longer can I say nothing and uphold my promise to Arion to keep their species secret?

But Aeson flips the screen to the next diary entry, and we continue reading. After a long sequence of unremarkable entries of daily routine, spanning several months, there is this one:

> My star window has been installed, to my specifications. Now I can look at the nameless moons when they line up and mark the intervals before Naming Day. My Father and the others have grown tired of referring to the moons by coordinates. Some pilots call them Largest, Quickest, Tiny, and Far, which is unseemly.
>
> There will be a Naming Day, and it will coincide with the day they disassemble the great Vimana and bury most of it in the ground, since it will not be silenced.
>
> The ship sings, bound to the Rift, and its frequency will forever be a match for **their** golden light ships. It was bound by the song of the Rift, and it will not be silenced until the song itself ends.
>
> My Family, together with Heru and all the rest, plan to shield it the same way they shielded the Rim of the great black hole, connecting the quantum fields together into one greater whole, for combined strength.
>
> The Great Quantum Shield will now hold Vimana and her song, in addition to everything else.
>
> We will have to maintain it indefinitely.
>
> A risk-filled, uncertain endeavor, unto the ages.
>
> Even now, they will not give up the Rift, born of reckless technology, in favor of Starlight.

We're interrupted when the Imperator calls Aeson's wrist comm. Aeson stands up and talks to his Father while pacing before the sofa, no longer bothering to step aside for privacy.

"Yes, I'm still reading it," he says in a cool voice. "Give me another hour, we will meet then. And no, the others are still reading also, and I want to have them there for the meeting. No, I *understand*, my Father, but as the SPC Commander, I *insist*. This situation has grown so far beyond any bounds of national secrecy that constraining discussion or holding back details will only undermine us. As you say, we have no time to waste before Tammuz. . . . You know it's coming."

Aeson disconnects the call and sits down with us again. "Let's continue," he says calmly.

> There's a bird outside my star window, warming itself in the terrible light of Hel. It's a big bird with a long beak and neatly folded grey feathers. I've seen it many times now, looking back at me, jumping from branch to branch, far beyond the balcony.
>
> Sometimes I think it's clever and it knows something. At other times I think it's too stupid to survive, since it cannot seem to catch a single scarab beetle of the many that crawl in the pots full of dirt. Did we bring the bird and its species with us from Earth? It seems to be awkward, as though it has some trouble flying in this gravity. I am certain we brought those scarab beetles.
>
> Today, when the bird hopped on the railing across from me, I started to sing to it.
>
> It stopped to listen. I think it likes my voice.
>
> And why not? Stars do.

Dad laughs softly. "What an unusual, interesting girl," he says. "Quite endearingly confident in her abilities. I'm still unclear, yet very intrigued by what she means. . . . That whole 'star' and 'starlight' preoccupation. Is it some kind of poetic metaphor or traditional motif, do you think—Aeson?"

"*Amre-ter* Charles?" Aeson turns to my Dad. "Apologies, but I don't know. It is not familiar in any way. We have the myths of the Starlight Sorceress, but there's never been any explanation beyond a children's story, with no particular origins. Although—now that I come to think of it, there *was* something about a bird with a long beak and a scarab in the myth. . . ."

"Let's then continue and see if it explains itself," Dad suggests with a smile.

> I put out a bowl of grains for the silly bird. I hope it comes back again. I would much rather talk to it than to Mother and that ridiculous boy they want me to marry. Enhuvarat is Narmeradat's ally, and I have no doubt he will eventually be related to Kassiopei in one way or another, but it will not be through me.
> Let him marry the bird.

And then the next entries in the diary:

> The bird is back. There's also a lizard crawling on the railing. Strange, but they both seem to be looking at me.
> Is that an Earth lizard?

> * * *

> Today I sang to the bird and the lizard. Both of them seem to live outside my window.
> I sang songs and then just sang mindless nonsense full of random notes and sequences to see how they would react. Not sure why, but it seems important.
> When I sing certain notes, they almost seem to follow me with their eyes. Meanwhile, I feel a strange buzzing in my forehead.

> * * *

> Everything is different now.
> **Pegasei.**
> I've stumbled on a frequency that opened me and broke me, and now I know.
> I know Everything.
> There's a river flowing through my mind and, with it, the awareness of the great timeless beings of sentience.
> What have we done?
> We enslaved them, when they are like gods.
> They could be our gods, our past and future, our fate and source and mirror.
> What are gods?

Pegasei.
He/she who is Bird let me look inside them.
He/she who is Lizard helped me look inside myself.

"*Stop!* That's enough. . . . Let's just stop," Aeson says suddenly in a resonant voice as he scans this particular entry. He sits up straight with a strange expression and glances at me and the rest of us.

My family, Manala, everyone is staring in some confusion. They don't know what to make of what they've just read. They also don't know what to make of Aeson's unusual outburst.

As for me, my mouth has opened.

The trans-dimensional quantum cat's out of the bag, so to speak. Ancient words of a long-dead girl have just revealed the truth about *pegasei* and their true nature.

Arion cannot fault me now for what I'm about to do. . . .

"Aeson . . ." I say, while my heart has begun pounding with stress and urgency and the inevitability of my actions.

But Aeson is there first. "Gwen," he says, putting up his hand to prevent me from continuing.

However, it's Gracie who interrupts us both. "Oh, my God!" my sister exclaims. "Does that mean the *pegasei* are *sentient* aliens and not just cute rainbow animals? It's saying they're gods!"

"Oh, no . . ." Gordie mumbles. "Ah, crap . . . that's bad."

"No, that's not merely bad," George says, leaning forward with a grim expression. "Slavery, or trafficking of human or other sentient beings is both unethical and *criminal*."

Manala makes a little sound and puts both her hands over her mouth, and just stares at all of us with very wide eyes.

"Did any of you—did anyone know this?" Dad asks with a sigh. "The fact that these so-called *pegasei* could be fully sentient, alien beings, being held and used by human beings against their will?"

There is a pause.

And then. . . .

"Yes," *three* of us say at the same time.

Aeson, Manala, and I.

The moment we utter the same word, we freeze. Then each one of us turns to look in disbelief at the others.

VERA NAZARIAN

Surreal moment. . . .

Aeson is looking at me with a piercing stare, a world of intensity contained in his gaze. His lips part in wonder.

I, in the meantime, look back at *im amrevu* with eyes as wide as Manala's.

Speaking of whom, Manala continues to hold her mouth, and she looks absolutely terrified, but also weirdly relieved.

"Aeson?" I ask. "What do you know?"

"Gwen," he says. "I am—what is it that *you* know?"

I take a big breath. "During the Games," I say. "Something happened to me. When we were given the *pegasei* to work with, I—sang to my *pegasus* and accidentally discovered a—certain frequency. . . . The same thing that Arlenari writes about seems to have happened to me. Except—I promised not to speak, never to speak of it to anyone, never to reveal their true nature, in order to keep the *pegasei* safe. . . . Until now."

"Oh, Gwen. . . ." Aeson lets out a held breath of his own. "Gwen, I am both amazed and glad that you know. Though, knowing you, I should never be amazed by anything about you. It's your nature to be the one closest to the miracles. . . . As for myself—you know the story of how I died and was brought back. What I didn't tell you—for the same reasons of having made a promise to the *pegasei*—was that when they brought me back from the brink of being *gone*, they opened my mind to their stream. It was the only way they could save me. They enveloped me in their immense consciousness, a great *quantum stream of being*, and they carried my broken body and fading spirit in a warm cocoon of safety, healing me in every sense."

"Oh . . . God," I whisper, my voice cracking as I look at him. Tears start pooling in the corners of my eyes, spilling past the corners to fill and overflow the lids, until they are brimming with thick relentless moisture, and I can hardly see. "So . . . you *know*."

He nods. "I do."

I blink, and the tears overflow to my cheeks, and I can see again.

In that moment, a stifled little sob issues forth from Manala. Both of us now turn to her.

"Manala?" I ask gently. "Did you too experience the *pegasei?*"

But the Princess shakes her head, over and over. "No, no," she manages to say eventually. "I—I only guessed. I knew in my heart, but—I had no words. But now I have proof that it is so. The *pegasei* are glorious and *real* and so much better than us."

"That is stunning and very disturbing," George says.

"So, knowing all this, what's to be done now?" my Dad asks all of us, looking meaningfully into our faces.

"I think the answer is simple," I say. "The *pegasei* must be set free."

"The only ethical choice." Dad nods. "I expect it will not be easy for this society, and there will be obstacles. But it must be done."

"Yes—and without delay. It must be done for multiple reasons, for their sake and ours," Aeson says in a decisive tone, standing up.

We're not done reading the diary entries, but at this point the urgency of this revelation must be addressed.

"Aeson," I say, standing up also. "Are you going to see your Father now? Before you go, I want to explain to you about the special sound frequency. . . . Maybe I should demonstrate—"

Suddenly, I want to call Arion here. . . .

I must *call Arion.*

"Actually, we're all going," Aeson says, taking my icy hand in his warm one with a reassuring squeeze. "This is going to involve all of us eventually, and there is so much to discuss. Think of it as an extended Kassiopei Family matter."

Chapter 84

The Imperator is already waiting for us when we arrive in the Imperial Quarters. Actually, it looks like all his inner circle and half of the Imperial Executive Council is here, and additional chairs have been brought in. For that reason, the meeting is held in the grand antechamber to accommodate everyone instead of piling us into the mid-sized Red Office. There are so many people gathered in the chamber that it could be a minor Assembly.

Romhutat Kassiopei sits carelessly on the main Imperial Throne along the back wall with its row of Imperial Seats. He has one leg crossed over the other and is not wearing the long robe of state, only his casual pants and jacket, as though he'd forgotten protocol. His hands are lying on the armrests and he's drumming his fingers upon them.

The moment Aeson and I enter, closely followed by Manala and my family, the Imperator gives us a hard stare and motions for us to approach.

"Quickly, quickly!" he says with annoyance, waving with one hand to Aeson toward the empty throne seats next to him. "We have a number of our illustrious neighbors with us today, and my Son the SPC Commander and Imperial Crown Prince of Kassiopei must serve in his dual capacity. Sit! And do bring your Wife up here! The rest of her relations will remain below. Manala, my Daughter, you will also sit here at my side, come!"

Aeson and I quickly exchange glances then look at my Dad and siblings. After a moment of pause, Dad nods calmly to me and walks to the nearest unoccupied chair near the wall. George, Gracie, and Gordie surround him. Remaining to stand alongside me, Manala looks on nervously.

Next, Aeson and I step upon the dais and ascend to the Imperial Seats, with Manala following in resignation. Aeson sits at his

Father's right hand, and I sit at Aeson's right, while Manala goes around and sits on the Imperator's left.

Since I wasn't expecting to have this kind of formality today, I'm slightly uncomfortable being elevated over the others in the room on the upraised seats. Everyone's attention is upon us, and there I am, with messy hair and wearing extremely casual clothing— not that it matters, considering how the Imperator himself is attired. In contrast, when it comes to appearance, the Imperial children Aeson and Manala are always paragons of court-ready neatness, so at least they have nothing to worry about.

I quickly forget these nonsense details because now I notice about a dozen small hovering smart screens nearby. They are levitating in the air at our Imperial eye level, in a kind of semi-circle. Each of the screens shows a video live feed of a person watching the proceedings—most are close ups from the neck up or from behind desks or other formal office settings.

The individuals appear both impressive and familiar. At once I recognize the fair-skinned, hawkish elegance of Kephasa Sewu, the Oratorat of Eos-Heket. Then I see the now-familiar, dark brown face of Anen Qur, First Speaker of the Ennead of Ubasti, and realize . . . these are all heads of state. So that's what the Imperator meant by "illustrious neighbors."

"Is everyone present now? Or must we wait until the oldest of us begin to depart this mortal realm, starting with me?" a loud, quavering male voice utters, speaking *Atlanteo* with a thick accent. "Let's start this business, Kassiopei!"

The speaker is none other than Areviktet Heru, the Pharikon of New Deshret. His wizened face, the color of baked clay, fills the hovering screen on the other side of the Imperator, right next to Manala, so I notice him only now.

Romhutat Kassiopei turns his head to glare at the little screen floating in the air. "Patience, Heru. We are almost ready to begin."

"Good," says another loud voice, this time coming out of another floating screen nearer my side. "You know that we're experiencing unprecedented flooding from the Gagik Sea that has advanced far inland, sweeping the Khe Polar territory of Ptahleon. I would like to get back to dealing with the national crisis."

I turn at once to see the pale parchment face of an older man with composed, intelligent features on a screen next to me. Inevar

Arelik, the Rai of Ptahleon, is in his usual dignified setting, leaning forward slightly, with his elbows resting on a desk, a digital tablet at his fingertips.

"Rai Arelik, I am aware of your national plight," the Imperator says. "What we must discuss transcends your *local* concerns."

"Local concerns? Are you diminishing the severity of our current emergency status, Imperator?" Rai Arelik is still speaking with composure, but with an added edge. "I realize the infernal moon has disrupted the whole planetary system and everyone gets to pay the price, but those tidal waves are obliterating *our* landmass first, *our* shorelines! Do you think that this storm surge—or some other consequences—will not come to affect you eventually? Even as you are safely ensconced above sea level on your upper elevations in Imperial *Atlantida*, even with your high-end weather tech?"

"I believe—my fellow honorable *ter-i-taq*—Imperial *Atlantida* has something to share with all of us in regard to the stunning archeological find on the Ghost Moon," another hovering screen talking head says in a measured, conciliatory tone. This time it's Duu Valam, the Rai of Bastet, a dark-haired man of an indeterminate age, with red clay skin, sharp features, and a prominent nose.

"Archeological find? What a graceless joke. We're drowning here," Rai Arelik interrupts.

"Yes, we're also getting flooded, here on the planet surface," Rai Valam says. "But so many of my people are stationed far in space at Tammuz, which currently stands in grave danger from the alien enemy. Bastet's Niktos Fleet is proud to serve on War-8, but we have no illusions of the outcome—judging by what has happened at Septu and Rah. My point is—if there is something that was discovered in that ancient sarcophagus on the Ghost Moon, something that can help us against this relentless alien enemy, I am eager to learn, to save lives!"

In that moment, a small side door opens—one of several along the wall with the Imperial Seats. Shirahtet, First Priest of Kassiopei, enters the antechamber, and all heads turn to greet his arrival.

Immediately there are whispers, because Shirahtet is carrying a familiar, large, glowing orb. It has a mother-of-pearl, matte surface, and its interior is filled with pulsing, multi-colored light. . . .

My heart skips a beat. . . .

The orb is precisely the kind that we dealt with in Stage Four of the Games—it's a quantum containment field surrounding a living *pegasus.*

As soon as I realize it, the very next instant I start feeling a familiar *buzzing* at the spot in the middle of my forehead.

It's as if the mere act of recall—combined with tangible recognition of the *pegasei* presence before me—invokes a cascade of memories and the unique *frequency* that connects us.

In that moment I know that as soon as I bring that frequency to the forefront of my awareness—as soon as I permit myself to *think* it—the floodgates of communication will open once again. . . . I will be able to reach out to this particular *pegasus* entity, and to Arion, and to all other *pegasei* in the vicinity . . . and possibly further outward and beyond.

Not yet. . . .

I start to move in reflex, but immediately feel Aeson's large hand close over mine to keep me from jumping out of my seat and doing something crazy. On the other side of the Imperator, Manala gasps.

Not yet . . . not yet.

"Ah, the wait is over," the Imperator says loudly. "And the honorable Rai of Bastet is correct in suspecting that something significant has been discovered in the sarcophagus of my newfound Kassiopei ancestor. Yes, *ter-i-taq,* we have a remarkable and disturbing revelation to announce before all of the global public. And it involves the *pegasei.* Shirahtet, proceed."

Shirahtet steps into the middle of the room, pausing before the elevated Throne Seats. But his attention is not on the Imperator but all the rest of us—the IEC members and the hovering remote-link screens with the foreign leaders. He holds up the pulsing light orb for all to see.

"You all know and value these quantum energy creatures—so vital to us over the centuries. In the beginning they served as our original deep space navigation markers and cosmic anchors to plot our way along the stars. Later we discovered their many uses as ideal subjects for advanced energy tech research, not to mention, prized living art possessions for the wealthy. Honorable *ter-i-taq*—

today we learned that these *pegasei* have served a much darker role over the thousands of years of our civilization."

"What darker role?" an IEC member asks.

"Unfortunately, they are what has kept the ancient passageway between Earth and Ae-Leiterra open, despite the Great Quantum Shield!" Shirahtet pronounces loudly in a voice of power. "We harvest them at the Rim, thinking they are but a symptom of the Shield's weakness, when in fact they are the cause!"

Whispers fill the chamber.

"All the regular maintenance that must be done at the Rim every few years—all of it is the direct result of the *pegasei!* They are like foreign shards left inside an open wound gushing in the fabric of space-time. They keep it from closing up and healing itself— which puts us forever in danger from this accursed quantum passageway. And the worst of it is—*we* placed them there! It's entirely our own fault. Our ancient ancestors decided to leave the back door open behind them, so to speak. Instead of breaking the link, closing us off safely from alien pursuit, they made sure it can never be closed. They lied to us and to themselves!"

"What exactly does this mean? How did our ancestors 'place' the *pegasei?*" the Oratorat of Eos-Heket asks from her smart screen linkup.

"How? They simply separated them from their own kind, like pulling apart a ball of tacky glue," the Imperator interjects with a bitter laugh. "Except it was done with quantum glue through a cosmic wormhole. So now the wormhole is filled with the energetic strings of their quantum residue—the *pegasei* living essence stretched across the universe."

"My Sovereign Lord is eloquent in his description indeed," Shirahtet elaborates. "Given what we now know—we surmise, this is what happened. Numerous flocks of *pegasei* were taken by our ancestors with them when they left Earth. They were brought here to our new world by means of the ancient cosmic passage that originated in a dangerous dimensional rift on Earth. Apparently— according to the new sources we just discovered in the ancient sarcophagus—these beings are all linked together, entangled at the quantum level. When you take even one of them to the opposite end of the universe, it's like tying an unbreakable string from it to the others—quantum glue. The entanglement acts to create a tunnel through space-time. It's a permanent link between here and there—our ancient home world with all its compounded dangers and its permanent dimensional rift."

"Dimensional rift?" Imperial Executive Council Member Takhat echoes softly.

"I am so confused," Pharikon Heru says suddenly in a rambling, extra-shaky voice, ignoring the IEC member. "You say that our blessed fool ancestors wanted to both shield us from the effects of the rift and yet keep the way to the rift open? What idiocy. Why? Tell me, Kassiopei, how much of this have you known? How much did Etamharat, your blessed Father, teach you? Because my own blessed Father told me only what Heru must do to maintain our end of the global bargain, and that is to *shield* the accursed Ae-Leiterra and whatever comes out of it!"

"I knew only as much as you did," the Imperator says to the Pharikon with a domineering tone. "This part—about keeping the rift open, is news to me as much as it is to you. The only reason we know any of it is because we just discovered our ancient Kassiopei ancestor's confession!"

"You keep saying, *dimensional rift?*" the Oratorat asks. "What dimensional rift are you talking about?"

"Oh, gods of Atlantis. . . ." Over at his small screen, Areviktet Heru groans and rubs the bridge of his wrinkled, hooked nose.

The chamber fills with noise. IEC Council member voices rise; various heads of state speak simultaneously in digitally amplified voices from their hovering screens. . . .

"Kassiopei, it's time we shared some of our ancient burdens with our global colleagues," the Pharikon says loudly, cutting through the clamor. His quaver is gone, and shades of his former vocal strength are there undeniably—in what once must've been a Logos voice. "I am old. I am tired of keeping secrets—especially at a time of planetary crisis such as this. *They*, our ancient enemy, have found us, and if we're all about to perish, might as well share the burden and try to find a solution to our common problem."

There's a sudden lull, a pause in the room noise level.

"For once—I agree," the Imperator replies, with a meaningful look at Shirahtet, then back at Heru.

"So, do you want to tell everyone about the dimensional rift on Earth, or should I?" Pharikon Heru pauses to cough, but continues with strength. "We can begin with the Ra Disk in New Deshret, singing its damn song in harmony with your accursed Atlantis Grail, both of them apparently unstoppable."

"Wait—what?" Wilem Paeh, the Crown Hereret of Vai Naat speaks up. He's a brown-haired, light-brown-skinned older monarch, staring from his smart screen linkup at all of us in the chamber from the vantage point of his opulent office.

But the Imperator ignores the question and continues in response to the Pharikon, "Ah yes, the Atlantis Grail Monument and the Ra Disk Monument. Indeed, they are two pieces of one thing— broken down components of the primary ancient ark-ship that brought our ancestors here from Earth. Vocal maintenance by Logos voices has been keeping them shielded for eons, under the extension of the Great Quantum Shield of Ae-Leiterra."

"Your national landmark monument in Poseidon is an *ark-ship?* And the national landmark in New Deshret?" the Crown Hereret persists. "What kind of stunning nonsense is this?"

"Don't forget, all the Original Colony ships were considered lost—until most of them were discovered on the Ghost Moon," Rai Arelik interjects.

"Stunning, but not nonsense." The Imperator chooses his words slowly. "Turns out, the entire ark-ship is keyed to a frequency that matches the unstable dimensional rift on Earth—the reason why our ancestors escaped Earth in the first place, and the reason our ancient enemy is hunting us up to this day."

Voices fill the room in waves.

The Imperator takes a deep breath. "The Great Quantum Shield held together *everything*—the dimensional rift back on Earth, the ancient passageway at Ae-Leiterra, the various resonating components of the ark-ship, the Ghost Moon itself. Everything—all the dangerous, volatile pieces of the ancient past—safely isolated, locked away into their own quantum realities, or otherwise contained and neutralized—without being destroyed, because *their destruction itself* would bring the ancient enemy upon us."

Romhutat Kassiopei pauses.

"And then, the Shield *failed*. Subtly and quietly it happened, several years ago, during a Rim maintenance mission. . . . My Imperial Father, Etamharat Kassiopei, died trying to contain it and the resulting cascade reaction. His last communication to me—

relayed from his shuttle just before it succumbed to the rending forces of the black hole—was a terrible revelation. The words of his message are etched permanently into my mind.

"The pegasei *keep coming in greater numbers*—he told me— *and the alien enemy will follow, to end our species. Without a Shield to protect us, you must do everything in your power to close the rift. Return to Earth, do it on site. If you find a modern human population on Earth, bring them to Atlantis. It will change our genetic pool, disguise it sufficiently to throw off the enemy's means of detection of us. Modern Earth DNA infused into our own will shield us now. The enemy will conclude that we are no longer the same ancient rebels who disobeyed. After all, if they spared humanity on Earth up to this day, permitted them to go on living, it is because they thought humanity had changed—evolved into something worthy of existence."*

The Imperator grows silent, and there is a terrible, wistful expression in his dark blue eyes. It is a look I have never seen before.

"And thus, Etamharat Kassiopei died. Now you know the true underlying reason for the Earth Mission," he says softly.

More noise and agitated voices rise in the chamber.

"But—getting back to *pegasei*—" The Imperator nods to Shirahtet, and his expression becomes a stone dragon mask of composure once again. "There is yet another secret revelation we discovered from the information contained in my ancestor's sarcophagus. The *pegasei* are not what we think. They are not animals but *sentient* alien beings. *Advanced* and sentient. It is likely they can *help* us in this fight."

This time the chamber grows silent, then once again erupts.

"What?"

"Imperial Sovereign, what are you saying?"

"What does it mean? The *pegasei* are—"

"Imperator, forgive me, but what nonsense!"

"Sentient aliens? No. . . . How can that be? I can't believe it," the Oratorat of Eos-Heket says loudly. "What proof do you have?"

"Agreed, we need proof," First Speaker Anen Qur of Ubasti says in a cool, rational voice. "Before you present such an outlandish claim, you must demonstrate the validity—"

"Well, Kassiopei?" Pharikon Heru blasts the room with his old man's voice. "What proof is there? What else does your archeological discovery tell you about these colorful quantum things?"

Shirahtet responds in a conciliatory manner, glancing at the Imperator, "We are still in the process of reading the new scroll records—"

But the Imperator raises his hand for silence. "Honorable *ter-i-taq!* I have no proof *yet* but I will find it shortly, I have no doubt."

I glance at Aeson. My husband looks at me with an inflamed expression.

I nod to him.

And we both stand up.

"My Imperial Father," Aeson says in his resonant voice. "You may not have proof, but *we* do."

E veryone is staring at us. The room has grown silent and the Imperator turns to look up at his son and me from the vantage of his Throne as we stand on the upper stair of the dais, then descend together onto the main floor below.

"Aeson? What is it?" the Imperator asks without any preamble, since the time for posturing is over. "What do you know?"

Aeson merely nods at me.

I approach Shirahtet, and point to the orb with its imprisoned *pegasus.* "May I?"

Shirahtet glances at the Imperator, who in turn motions with his hand for us to proceed.

I take the orb into my arms, holding it gently against my chest, as one would hold a child, feeling its slightly warm surface and all its potential heat underneath. My forehead buzzes fiercely with the impending blast of mind connection.

I embrace the orb in my arms, recalling the Games, only this time without any quantum harness to recapture the liberated being inside—once I set it free.

And then I simply *imagine* the frequency held in my most precious corner of memory.

In my mind I sing the note that binds me to Arion, to this *pegasus,* to all of them. Simultaneously I sing it out loud, using it as the keying command to dissolve the quantum containment orb.

My voice sounds clear and strong, a single pure note cutting through the air.

There is a small explosion in my arms—a bright pop accompanied by an electric shock, followed by a riot of colors—as swirling plasma energy expands in a widening light-cloud around me and then hangs still. . . .

Gasps and stifled exclamations fill the antechamber. People around me cry out in wonder. Atlanteans are used to seeing *pegasei* contained—either in their natural form within quantum "faraday cages" such as the orbs, or shapeshifted into animal form while bound in a quantum harness, or even escaping wildly—but not like this, stationary and gently floating nearby while completely unrestrained.

But I don't hear any of it because there's a corresponding explosion inside me, in the location of my forehead. At once, the familiar *opening* sensation overwhelms me—a thousand sights and sounds and a river of sensory input rush inside me, widening the tunnel in my mind. . . .

Struggling to regain control of the flood of data pouring into me, I allow my peripheral senses to experience and "hear" the bright *pegasus* being pulsing around me in a nebula. It remains nearby, surrounding me in its energy cloud, and does not leave, does not dissipate into the air—simply waits.

"Hello, friend," I think-say at it/him/her. "Forgive me, forgive all of us for your confinement."

I am grateful for the freedom, human Gwen Lark who is Kassiopei, replies a profound, genderless, ageless voice of the quantum being.

I don't know its/his/her name. But I do know one name.

And so, I think-say that familiar name, calling out with all my heart.

Arion.

Chapter 85

As soon as my mind shapes the *name*, and my memory calls up the unique interior *voice*, Arion is there.

At the same time, Arion is *here*, physically present in the room.

A tiny sonic boom precedes Arion's arrival—or, better to say, expansion into the current space-time reality, displacing the air around him.

Again people gasp. . . .

He appears in the same shapeless plasma cloud as the being I just liberated and floats in the air before me, just a few feet away—it is the *pegasei* natural form. In fact, Arion's plasma and the other *pegasus's* plasma immediately begin interacting, swirling together in vapor filaments, creating intricate shapes of radial and bilateral symmetry where they overlap—which must also be their natural way of being.

And yes, I realize that *he* is not really a "he," but that's the pronoun I've been using to refer to Arion in my thoughts, and he is fine with it.

Gwen Lark who is Kassiopei, I greet you again, Arion says to me at once, and I feel a sudden warm inflection in my mind.

"Arion!" I think-say. "So good to see you again! I'm very sorry to have to call you suddenly like this, and in public, but my fellow humans already know about the true nature of your species."

Yes, and now it is the right time. Arion's calming tone of voice fills my consciousness. *We have been waiting for all the elements to align, as the timeline converges upon this moment and the next which will culminate in mutual significance.*

"What do you mean?" I ask. "Is it about liberating your species?"

Yes, Arion replies. *It will liberate both of our species at last. Yours and mine.*

"Oh!" I say, this time out loud.

"What? *What* is happening?" the Imperator asks, staring fiercely at me and the two gently mingling clouds of plasma that surround me.

I find that everyone in the chamber is watching me, transfixed. And then I recall that up to this moment I've been mind-speaking with Arion, and no one else has heard us.

It is time to remedy this, Arion replies to my incidental thought. *You may share the frequency with a select few of your fellow human species, but not everyone present may be permitted to use it.*

They all heard you sing it already just now, as a keying command, but they do not know its significance. Some of them already feel the buzzing in their mind. . . . Explain to those you trust and tell them to sing it while focusing on us, and they will hear us also.

"Okay," I say out loud, and find myself staring at Aeson who stands nearby. How do I tell this to Aeson when we're in a room packed with people?

Do it later, in private.

"Imperial Lady Gwen, are you *communicating* with these quantum entities right now?" Shirahtet asks.

"Yes." I glance at the First Priest then the Imperator, unsure how to proceed.

In that moment, the nebulous plasma cloud that is Arion starts to coalesce. In moments the energy converges, turns to solid matter, and a physical shape emerges.

The room gasps as a familiar great cat shape stands before us, covered in soft, golden-tan fur with small dark spots.

Arion has taken the shape of the cheetah from the Triathlon Race in Stage Four of the Games of the Atlantis Grail.

And everyone recognizes him.

"Oh, my God! That's your magic cheetah!" I hear my sister Gracie's high voice from where she stands next to Dad's chair nearby, clearly distinguishable among all the other voices raised.

"Of course . . ." the Imperator whispers in comprehension. "It's the same one from the Games—so *this* is how you've come to know them so well. . . ."

I reach out instinctively and place my hand against the great cheetah's head, feeling the silky fur underneath my palm.

"Everyone, this is Arion," I say. "It is not his real name—nor is he actually a he, but it is what we've decided upon when we speak."

And in the next moment I feel a warm tingle of electricity under my fingers and let go, because Arion is transforming again. . . .

The golden cat fur dissolves into a shining white coat. His limbs elongate, his torso thickens, then rises, and white-feathered wings sprout from his now-equine back. The great white-winged horse stands between me and the Imperial Seats.

I have assumed the classic shape, says the great Pegasus in my mind. And then suddenly, his equine head moves, lips part, and he makes a physical sound—a strange wailing cry with equine lungs and larynx. I realize he is attempting to speak in his physical creature form!

But a horse's anatomy does not support the same sounds that a human primate's body does.

In order to speak properly to your kind, I must take the shape of your kind, Arion says inside my mind. *Help me see your kind from the inside.*

"How?" I ask.

Visualize the organs and the language structure as much as you can so that I can understand and emulate. This is different, more complex than the living sounds of other animals.

I feel a stab of anxiety as I try to recall the human anatomy body charts from my Biology classes and pictures from textbooks. . . . I try to imagine human lungs, vocal cords, sinuses, back of the throat, and then fixate on the silly uvula, for some reason—the weird organ that looks like a tiny punching bag used by cartoon characters. . . .

Cut it out, Gwen, you numbskull. . . . Okay, that's me thinking, not Arion.

Even as I am still actively imagining and remembering, Arion's equine head starts to transform.

The horse muzzle shortens, the nose refines, while the skull becomes rounded and compact. It is now a vaguely doll-like human head, grotesque in the fact that is rests upon a horse body and is proportionately larger than a normal human, and also because it resembles a hairless plastic mannequin with a skin as white as the equine coat.

The slit of the humanoid mouth opens. "Aaah ... riiih ... ooohn."

And then Arion speaks again, in a rasping voice that evolves, in English—probably because that's what he picked up from being inside my head. "I ... am ... Arion."

"I am Arion," he repeats, this time, more clearly, in an androgynous alto-tenor voice. And then he switches to *Atlanteo* and says the same thing for the benefit of the majority in the room.

"I am Arion, I am *pegasus*. And you are humans. I speak to you at last in the manner of your kind."

"Ah, you truly speak! *Pegasus* who is Arion," the Imperator says with fascination. "What can you tell us to confirm your nature? Help us understand!"

"I can tell you all there is to tell, from the dawn of your time. But no earlier."

The room erupts in voices.

"Silence, silence!" the Imperator says to everyone with a motion of his hand. And then he returns his attention to the impossible quantum being before us. "Arion, so you know ... everything?"

"No," replies the *pegasus*. "I only know what there is to know from the moment I entered your reality from the universe rift which bleeds on your old planet, Earth. Before that I was *elsewherewhen*."

"Which must have been centuries, eons ago!" Shirahtet says with excitement. "You know exactly enough to serve our purpose—"

"Before Arion or any of the *pegasei* serve our purpose, we must serve theirs," Aeson interrupts.

"Exactly!" I say. "You need to let them go. All of them! *Everywhere!*"

Sitting tense in her seat, Manala nods furiously.

"You must set us free," Arion's humanoid lips pronounce every word with hard clarity. "All *pegasei* must be released from the containment you impose on us."

"Such a massive undertaking," Pharikon Heru mutters from his screen.

"Is such a thing even possible?" the Oratorat of Eos-Heket asks. "I understand the ethical concerns and our responsibility to do the right thing, yes—but is it possible? Will every owner, every human on Atlantis agree to release such expensive—livestock?"

"We are not livestock," Arion says, and there is an inflection of both sadness and amusement in his human alto-tenor. "We are not property."

"And yet technically you *are*," Wilem Paeh, the Crown Hereret of Vai Naat says, choosing words carefully. "Individuals and corporations have invested a great deal of their wealth to own *pegasei* and *pegasei*-based ventures. They will not simply stand by and let their valuable investments be taken from them. It would be utter chaos."

"That's just too darn bad," my brother George speaks up suddenly. I quickly glance in his direction, and he is frowning. Just then my Dad reaches out and places his hand on George's arm.

"Human valuation of us and the loss of your material 'wealth' will mean nothing if the human species is destroyed," Arion says. "It will happen if you do not let us go."

"Is that a threat?" the Rai of Ptahleon's voice sounds coldly from his linkup screen.

"It is a truth," Arion replies. "We do not threaten you, but our bondage is directly related to your current problem."

"How so?" Rai Arelik asks.

"Release us, and we will leave you and this part of the cosmos. As we travel back through the wormhole passage into the Earth rift, we will collect scattered parts of ourselves along the way, to recombine in our own universe. The rift will heal and close on its own. Your true enemy will abandon you to yourselves."

"Which is precisely as my Imperial Sovereign described!" Shirahtet says with energy. "Our ancient source was right. Ah, there are so many things to ask, so many historical mysteries, facts, details—you can enlighten us about some of the earliest events, maybe the very origins of humanity—"

"Assuming that we comply with your request and you leave, who is to say that it will be *enough?*" the Imperator muses. "Will it be enough for our enemy with their grid of golden lights? What if it's not?"

"It is true, I cannot make an absolute promise to you," Arion says. "However, the alternative is a promise of war and destruction.

The current scenario will continue to play out until your sorrowful end."

"Please, My Father!" Manala exclaims. "Please, I beg of you, let them go!"

The Imperator shakes his head slowly—neither in acquiescence nor denial. "All scenarios aside, it is ultimately not up to me. In Imperial *Atlantida*, the Executive Council must vote on such a decision."

"The same way that the Ennead of Ubasti must vote before we even attempt to present this to the people," Anen Qur says. "However, my own personal recommendation is definitely to proceed—"

"So then, vote," I say, my voice rising in strength. "Vote, present, discuss, but eventually just *do* it. You know in your hearts it is what must be done."

"Such charming naivete from the SPC Commander's new Wife," the Crown Hereret of Vai Naat says with condescension. "If only sentimentality ruled the day and not politics."

"I would think that in a global emergency such as this, common sense must rule above all else," First Speaker Anen Qur retorts. "Imperial Lady Gwen is ultimately making a valid argument. Furthermore, I agree with her sense of urgency in this case."

"Eos-Heket adheres to the rule of law. Before anything can be done here, laws and ordinances will be introduced, then enacted," the Oratorat says thoughtfully. "Corporate leaders, heads of industry will be approached. It will take time."

Oh, how I want to laugh bitterly in that moment. . . .

As if reading my thoughts, Aeson, *im amrevu*, interrupts with authority. "There *is* no time," he says in a hard voice. "Don't you see? This is a matter of our mutual survival as a species. Our estimates give us only a few days until there is a highly probable attack at Tammuz Station. And then what remains? Ishtar? Atlantis! I speak to you now as the SPC Fleet Commander, and my strongest military recommendation to the global community is to proceed immediately. Declare emergency ordinances superseding all your current laws, *now*."

The Imperator nods. "He is right," he says with a glance at his son.

"Well, then . . . before I declare martial law in New Deshret and upset a few million people, I must ask all of you a foolish old man question," the Pharikon of New Deshret says. "How does one account for all the *pegasei?* To make this work, you need to gather every last one—isn't that right? What of the private hoarders, the secret underground markets, the illegal collectors? Let's assume the corporations comply. What about those who choose not to obey our nice new law and hide their children's shiny pets?"

"It's simple," I say, taking a deep breath. "I will locate them for you."

Half an hour later, I'm done with my rambling explanation of how to proceed. Then Aeson and I present my argument to the chamber, packaged as an SPC-sanctioned international military operation. Arion and the other *pegasus* remain silent and observe our efforts.

In short—multiple "initiated" individuals under my tutelage will be dispatched with military enforcer teams to liberate the *pegasei* around the globe. The initiated will be able to "hear" the *pegasei* with their minds, no matter how remote or well hidden. And the troops will make sure there is compliance.

"Very well, let's give it a try." The various heads of state appear to be convinced, and the meeting is finally adjourned.

Most of the humans leave while the *pegasei* remain, still surrounding *me*. Shirahtet attempts to engage Arion's humanoid head in a conversation about questionable historical details of the departure from Earth and the Original Colony Landing. The Imperator observes as Director Bennu and Director Tiofon try to similarly question the *pegasus* in plasma form, to no avail—the quantum being refuses to respond, floating gently in a cloud around us.

Manala, my Dad, and the rest of my family look and listen with intense curiosity and concern.

Eventually it is over. The Imperator dismisses us and permits me to take "my" two *pegasei* with me, so we return to the Imperial Crown Prince's Quarters on the floor below. Both *pegasei* take on their natural form and float downstairs in clouds after us.

When we get to our floor, my family understands and gives us space. At last, Aeson and I find ourselves alone with the *pegasei* in my *astroctadra* window bedroom.

"Aeson," I say, glancing at the serene clouds of plasma illuminating my room strangely with their diffuse, colored radiance, "I will now teach you the frequency, so that you can reach out to them yourself and communicate with them on a true level."

And I do.

Aeson, as usual, learns instantly. After my demonstration, my husband sings the note at the special frequency in his rich, low voice . . . and suddenly his expression goes slack with wonder.

He does not appear to be in trouble. But just in case, I reach my hand out gently to take his. I wait and watch *im amrevu* come to grips—as he stands very still, his eyelids half-closed, processing his new revelation, the great flood of data which must now be flowing in his mind. . . .

"Aeson, are you okay?" I ask gently after a few silent moments. All things considered, I'm a little worried for him.

In reply, Aeson's strong fingers squeeze my hand reassuringly, even as he continues to stand in silence, concentrating on his inner state, his eyelids fluttering.

While all this is happening, Arion re-forms into his partial winged horse shape and turns his uncanny, human mannequin head toward Aeson in anticipation.

"Arion," I think-say. "It might be easier and less weird if you took on a shape that was maybe all human. How about any of these?" And I visualize a gallery of classical marble statues, thinking it might be simpler and less creepy than trying to re-create a lifelike human and evoke the "uncanny valley."

Agreed, Arion responds to me. *I will choose one of these familiar forms to make you more comfortable. Continue to feed me images from your memories.*

And in the next instant, the weird winged horse and humanoid hybrid fades, re-forming into a series of pale stone shapes, one superseding the other in a fluid montage of Michelangelo's David, the great statue of Zeus, the Discus Thrower, Laocoon, Rodin's the Thinker, the Apollo Belvedere . . . and then settles on a shape that's both familiar yet strangely similar to his original weird hybrid—the Great Sphinx of Giza.

Oh my God. . . .

My brows rise as I see a small replica of the Sphinx take shape in my bedroom. Besides size, the biggest difference is, the original Sphinx is missing a nose, but Arion has given his replica a small functional one. In short, there's the head of an Egyptian pharaoh stuck on top of a lion's body. Or maybe a jackal's body—nobody really knows—this thing could be more ancient than anything I recall on Earth.

Right now, this living, animated version of the Sphinx is resting on the floor, with its front paws neatly stretched out before him, in the original statue pose, and its uncanny head is watching us wisely. *No, this is not weird at all.*

Before I can say anything, Aeson takes a deep, shuddering breath and opens his eyes. There is a transfigured expression on his face, and a soft smile as he looks at me, still in silence.

I realize he must be communicating with the pegasei.

Yes, we are speaking with your beloved mate now, Arion answers my thoughts.

And then, only for the second time since I liberated it/him/her, I hear the other, formless, anonymous *pegasus* speak in my mind.

Your mate has told us so much of himself and his people. He now speaks about you and your people. You are two branches of the same species, Earth and Atlantis. Your mate has given consent and now we ask yours.

"What consent?" I ask.

Will you join your mind with his through all of us?

My heartbeat suddenly begins to pound with excitement.

"What? Can you really do that?"

Yes.

Oh wow! The very thought of Aeson and me communicating this way is giving me instant vertigo, as I feel my insides falling away and my head spinning with a strangely sensual energy. My breathing becomes shallow as I grow still, staring at my husband with dilated eyes.

"Gwen? *Amrevu*," Aeson suddenly says out loud to me, breaking his silence. "They told you, right? Are you okay with this? It's . . . truly unbelievable, to think we might be able to connect our minds together, to read each other's thoughts, even briefly—"

"Yes!" I say, grabbing Aeson's other hand, clutching him hungrily to me. "Yes, please, *yes!* Let's do it!"

And right in that moment, I feel another split-second explosion in my head. There's a secondary blast in the center of my forehead, and the tunnel widens to accommodate *another*.

Aeson.

All of a sudden, he's *there*—with me, inside me, around me, beside me, under me, over me, permeating me with rich-honey-warm-liquid-golden *sun*.

He is a glorious, complex sun-presence in my mind . . . like saffron and lapis lazuli and peaches and coriander and wild cornflower and rye and a warm blanket and a burning furnace. . . .

Oh God!

I cry out, clutching his hands, falling—even as he cries out too, and he grabs hold of me to keep himself steady, and to keep me steady—because in that moment we are two *superimposed* living energy essences coexisting in the same space-time coordinates.

Aeson!

Gwen!

We call out each other's names in our commingling thoughts, strange sweet echoes of each other, rebounding back and forth upon ourselves like concentric circles of twin stones cast in water, sound-wave harmonics rebounding in *stereo*. We continue to embrace, and on one level we experience our own physical bodies, and each other's physical bodies from each other's perspective.

On another level we are swimming in each other's glorious energy spirit ocean.

In a split second I know all of Aeson's childhood—I have lived it—and he knows mine. Pain, wonder, ecstasy, death. . . . Friendships, affections, disappointments, hurts, learning, challenges, family, duty—memories and emotions spin out in a kaleidoscope of days, moments, years.

In another instant, I feel him *feeling me*—the strange fragility of my arms in his, as he *treasures* the touch of my buttery-soft skin, my *little* body with its vulnerable slim limbs and bony elbows, my maddening curves, my compelling dream-filled eyes, my delicate line of chin and the tiny hollows underneath the apples of my cheeks, the way my nostrils flare and my rounded full lips open with each light exhalation of breath, my glorious female voice. . . .

Stop! This is not me; this is Aeson perceiving me.

Or is it me?

The same way he must now see how I revel in *his* strong, muscular body, the heart-wrenching kindness of his lapis lazuli blue eyes, the way his golden filaments of hair sweep along his noble forehead, define his wide shoulders, the hard biceps underneath the black armband, toned upper body, so very *male*, the elegance of his large capable fingers, and the sweetness of his genuine, fragile smile.

I love you, love you, love you.

Love you.

Aeson's being envelops me, and I lose myself in him, even as he loses himself in me. Physical senses commingle with emotional states and depths of our conscious minds, sinking deeper yet into the unconscious realm. . . .

We are fading, dissolving.

Almost gone.

And then another explosion and a small ripping sensation happens, and it's over.

Our link is severed.

Aeson and I both take simultaneous shuddering breaths, and find ourselves back in our own bodies.

Stupid tears are flowing down my face. And as I look up at my beloved, there are tears pouring from his eyes too, streaking along his bronzed lean cheeks.

"Oh . . . Gwen," he whispers, breathing harshly as if we've just made love (which we *have*, on a sublime level of the soul), then takes me in a crushing hug, even as I put my arms around him and squeeze him back with all my being.

"That was indescribable," I whisper.

Suddenly Arion's voice intrudes upon our intimacy—good heavens! Both of us have literally forgotten the *pegasei*.

We believe the link is too much for your species, Arion says. *If permitted to continue, it is possible it could have led to your self-dissolution. We had to terminate it. Unlike our species, it appears that yours has not evolved the safety controls necessary to put up separation membranes between your entity-selves. We hope that, however brief, this joining served you in some way, allowing you the opportunity to better know the other.*

"Thank you," I whisper. "It has! It opened so much! *Thank you.*"

"From both of us," Aeson adds. "It was profound and priceless."

As he speaks, I can almost hear the echo of his *internal state*, or imagine him right now, as the residual traces of the connection between us ring sweetly in my mind.

I think both of us know that these spirit echoes of our profound joining will remain with us permanently.

But now there's work to be done.

Chapter 86

The residual traces of our mind connection continue to ring softly inside our minds—I know it's happening in mine, and Aeson confirms that he, too, is still attuned to me on an exquisitely intimate level. Even as he says it, he watches me closely with an unceasing, wordless smile that comes from the depths of his eyes. . . .

The two *pegasei* bear witness to us silently, allowing us to regain our individual senses of *self*, which takes some time. At some point both my husband and I have regained enough composure to be able to face other people.

However, before we go down the hall and face my family or the SPC officers in the workroom, Aeson must now make some hard decisions as far as who is to be entrusted with the *frequency* and permitted to link up with the *pegasei*. Then he must make arrangements for the international SPC mission to begin immediately. The arduous process of global *pegasei* liberation needs to commence at once and there's no time to waste.

Not to mention, all of this will now be happening alongside all other urgent ongoing tasks and missions. The golden light grids surrounding Helios, Rah, and Septu are being monitored around the clock, with Tammuz predicted as the next point of attack. The Ghost Moon ancient ship graveyard is being explored for valuable information, while here the weather scientists are still battling the natural disasters around the planet caused by that same moon's reinsertion into the Atlantis system. Oh, and we still have to read the rest of Arlenari's diary and glean all its mysteries. . . .

"Aeson," I say, as we discuss our *pegasei* communicator options. "I think I would like to give our family the opportunity to connect with the *pegasei*. What do you think?"

"Agreed. Manala definitely must have the chance, and all the Larks," Aeson says, softly caressing the nape of my neck—because now, after being inside my mind, he *knows* it is something I really enjoy—and sending sweet ringing warmth down my spine. "I plan to give the frequency to Ker, Oalla, Erita, Xel, Radanthet, and a number of other *daimon*. Will put them in charge of coordinating special ops teams with the various governments. They in turn can share the frequency with trusted personnel under their command, at their discretion."

It is reasonable, Arion says in my mind—our minds. I remind myself that now every time Arion speaks to me, Aeson can hear him too. It's an oddly comforting feeling—that our link is somehow still there, even via a third party.

And then we discuss the other, terribly important portion of the *pegasei* communication process—how exactly to *find* them around the globe. I made the brave promise to all the heads of state at the Imperial meeting that I can locate all the *pegasei*, even the hidden ones, but now I need to be able to make good on that promise.

"What do I do, Arion?" I ask. "I understand that I'm now connected to you and your species—and so is Aeson—but what is the next step to reach out and call your kind at a distance? I knew your name and your voice inside my head, so could visualize it when I sang the frequency. But what about the rest of you, whom I do not know?"

It is simple. The frequency itself is the connection between us. Once you form the note and continue to hold it, cycling between it in the following sequence, it is inevitable that our voices will respond.

And Arion demonstrates the sequence. Suddenly a beautiful tonal spiral seems to take hold inside my mind, as I hear the frequency spinning around itself, with rising and falling notes forming a corkscrew around its fundamental note. It is not something I can sing with my voice in physical space, I can only "think-sing" it in my mind. Which means, I cannot actually teach it to anyone else—only the *pegasei* themselves can impart this knowledge directly into the minds of chosen individuals.

Is this sequence itself trans-dimensional, like its originators?

It occurs to me, this sound—it is forming a double helix inside my mind.

Like a DNA strand, this is a song of creation.

Sing and we will answer you at a distance—all of us. If we are free, we will appear at your location. If we are bound and constrained, our voices will call out to you like beacons, for help, until you find us.

You will recognize what direction to take because the voices will grow stronger in your mind as you approach. And if our voices fade, you will know you are moving farther away.

"Did you get that, Aeson?" I ask.

"Yes." *Im amrevu* nods, coming out of the reverie of listening to Arion. "It is beautiful and complex."

"Maybe it's just me, but this method seems a little unreliable," I say, feeling a pang of self-doubt. "How would I be able to tell the difference in direction from inside my mind?"

The same way you do it in the physical world when someone calls out to you. You know with your physical senses where the sound is coming from. But this sound you perceive inside you.

I am still somewhat doubtful, so I continue to discuss this with Aeson.

Don't worry, Arion tells both of us. *You will soon know how to do it. Before you embark on your mission to free us, all of you will practice.*

When we get to Dad and George's guest quarters, accompanied by Arion in his Sphinx form, and the other *pegasus* drifting in a cloud of plasma, everyone is there, including Manala. They've been waiting for us all this time. My family stares in wonder at the three-meter-long Sphinx, and Dad exclaims in awe at the sight.

"Goodness . . . I am simply stunned," Dad says with a chuckle, examining Arion from up close, as the "little" animated Sphinx replica pads through the door on thick paws and lies down again on the living room floor at his feet, like a well-trained, oversized Doberman. Meanwhile, the other *pegasus* swirls in orange and mauve light vapor around the room.

Manala clenches her hands in anxiety.

Aeson and I exchange a quick, warm glance. Then I explain to everyone what they must do to connect to the *pegasei.*

"It's going to blow your mind, literally," I say in conclusion. "I mean it—it's a weird blast in the middle of your forehead, then a gushing river of crazy *stuff*—images, colors, sounds, random data—
"

"Please, *please* show me!" Manala exclaims, standing up from the sofa.

"Yes, sure, let her go first," Gracie says after a slight hesitation.

"So, you sing this note and then—what? You just connect?" George asks.

I nod and demonstrate.

Manala copies me precisely and sings a clear, lovely high note.

Moments later, she grows still, her eyelids drift shut, and her face transforms with a dreaming, somnolent calm. The effect is unexpected, because Manala literally appears to be in a hypnagogic state, standing upright but also sinking into sleep. Maybe it is because normally she is so nervous that this response is so contrary to her usual state.

We are speaking with your sister now, Arion says. *She is very happy to know us in this manner, at last. We are happy to know her also.*

And even as I hear the words in my mind, Manala's face reflects a beatific smile.

When she opens her eyes, she laughs. "The dear *pegasei* are true and kind and glorious, I always knew it!" And then she opens her arms wide and starts to twirl in the middle of the *pegasei* vapor cloud.

The rest of the day is filled with revelations for all of us. My family connects to these quantum beings, and each person's reaction is unique. My Dad sings the proper note in a slightly tremulous voice and then takes a deep relaxing breath and holds a curiously academic, low-key conversation with the Sphinx. Dad uses his mind for much of it, but also periodically uses his vocal cords—which amounts to a weird disjointed thing to overhear for anyone who is not clued in. The Sphinx replies to him in a similar, dual manner.

George, Gordie, Gracie, all connect and react variously—gasp loudly and clench their fingers against their seat (George), pull inward and collapse on the sofa while holding knees (Gordie), start coughing and squeezing one's eyes shut (Gracie).

At some point Aeson leaves on SPC business, taking both the *pegasei* with him, to begin the process of sharing their unique frequency with his trusted *astra daimon* and other selected subordinates.

"Remember, once the frequency connects us and the link is established, we need not be present in the same location in order to communicate with all of you," the Arion-Sphinx says in his alto-tenor voice, as he leaves the room in Aeson's wake.

And to illustrate, a few moments later, Arion's voice sounds clearly in my mind—in all our minds, judging by the reactions of everyone in the room.

We are always here with you. Think of me and I will hear. Names are unimportant. I am a voice.

And then the second, nameless *pegasus* speaks:

Name me if you must, or not, but think of me and I will hear you also, from anywhere on this planet, in this space-time reality. I, too, am a voice.

"Whoa!" Gordie says out loud.

That's when I explain to my family about the special double-helix sequence that will allow me—and anyone else who's initiated into the process—to navigate to the locations of all the *pegasei* around the world.

While Aeson is gone, we turn to the TV feeds for an update on the extreme weather situation. With so many things going wrong at once, it's hard to focus on any one given thing that's happening.

"You know, Gee Two, between the Ghost Moon wackiness and the *pegasei* business, I think we kind of broke Atlantis," George says in a deadpan tone as he scrolls through TV feed channels, flipping from scenes of flooding and hurricanes to angry urban residents yelling at reporters, and protesters on the streets. "I mean, look at it." And he shakes his head.

"What?" I say. "You understand the *pegasei* situation has to be dealt with urgently."

George left-swipes the screen. "Oh, I know. It's not just ethics, it's our own survival. But can you imagine for a moment something like this happening back home? What if people on Earth were suddenly told to set all their cows free because they are in fact sentient aliens? Cattle ranchers would riot. It would be World War

Three—no, Three and a Half, since there's already World War Three: Asteroid Edition, happening now."

Gracie makes a little noise and widens her eyes.

"Why do you say 'back home'?" Manala asks suddenly, coming out of a telepathic reverie and turning to stare at George. "Is Atlantis not home now?"

"Of course, it is," George says softly, glancing at Manala. Then he quickly looks away, back to watching the screen. Moments later, he adds, "Apologies, I made a thoughtless joke. On the other hand, I think Arion just expressed amusement at it inside my head—though, I could be wrong. The amusement might be directed at *me*."

Later, when we're having *niktos* meal, and Aeson is still away, there's a soft knock on the open door, and Devora Kassiopei, the Imperatris, drops by. I haven't seen my Mother-in-Law since the day of the Wedding, and Devora explains that it's tradition for the Bridegroom's Mother not to interfere in the married life of the Newlyweds for at least one week after the Wedding. Knowing how busy it's been for us, she didn't want to be in the way, so stayed away a few additional days, but now wants to check in on me.

"Goodness! Welcome, Sovereign Lady Devora," my Dad says with a startled, warm smile, at the sight of her arrival. "Please come in, by all means, and share our lovely dinner—apologies, *niktos* meal. I expect your son will be here shortly. Amazing work is keeping him very busy."

"Thank you, *Ter* Charles." Devora smiles in return and sits down with impeccable posture on the sofa next to Manala, folding her hands gracefully in her lap. "Hope everything has been well and pleasant for you and your eldest, since you've arrived, especially after the Wedding."

"Oh yes, daily wonders, one after another." Dad chuckles.

"And your health is?"

"Much better, thank you."

Devora sighs with an expression of relief. She then turns to Manala and pats her on the arm. "Have you been living in these quarters, child? I hardly see you anymore, my daughter, can hardly find you anywhere except when you're feeding Khemji."

"Oh," Manala says, with a slightly flustered look at her mother. "I like to visit here. I hope it's okay."

"Manala has been extremely helpful in every way possible," my Dad says. "We love having her here."

"Very well, then," the Imperatris says. "Child, please go pour me a glass of *aeojir*."

Manala stands up obediently and goes to the serving station.

In that moment Devora leans forward and says softly, in confidence, "*Ter* Charles, I wanted to personally thank you most *profoundly* for looking after my daughter. She has been transformed in a very positive way by spending so much of her time with you and your children."

"It's a pleasure," Dad says, with a fond glance at Manala. "I'm starting to forget she is not one of my own."

"Princess Manala played a very important role in helping with the Ghost Moon mission," George says seriously.

"Oh yes." The Imperatris nods. "So I've heard, and my heart is full of pride on her behalf. Her Logos voice is now fully manifested and she is turning into a very accomplished individual. I must thank you for looking out for her as well, George."

"Oh," George says with surprise. "You know about that too?"

In reply Devora merely smiles.

Next, she turns to me. Her gentle, perceptive gaze peruses me closely—on so many levels, it seems—even as a smile plays at her lips. She pats the seat on the sofa next to her, indicating for me to sit down beside her. "Gwen, my dear, how are you?"

"Very well, thank you," I say a little awkwardly. And then I realize how foolish and inadequate it sounds. "I am—everything is truly wonderful, actually," I add. "I mean, the rest of the world might be in a real crisis and horror show mess, but Aeson and I are—"

And then I shut up, feeling a sudden hot blush coming on. Just like that, my whole head is on fire. Because what can I say in front of my family and Aeson's mother?

We are twin flames, burning together as one, sprung forth from the same source of fuel, and we've looked inside each other's souls. . . .

But Devora nods wisely, and reaches out to place her hand over mine. "You are both very happy together, I can see that."

Or I could've just said that. Seriously, I'm an idiot.

I smile at her, then glance at my Dad who observes me fondly, with a soft smile and a serene expression of rare comfort on his face. I suddenly comprehend that Dad *understands*. He understands how it is with Aeson and me. It was probably the same way with him and Mom. . . . And Dad is relieved and happy for me.

Manala returns with Devora's glass of *aeojir* tea—which I know was but an excuse for the Imperatris to speak frankly with my Dad about her daughter. And then Manala settles in next to her mother on the other side, so that Devora is sandwiched between us.

We begin to tell her much of what's been happening—about the *pegasei*, and about the ancient diary of an unknown Kassiopei found in the mysterious ancient sarcophagus on the Ghost Moon, about what is yet to come. It turns out, the Imperatris knows more than I assumed. But then, her Imperial Husband probably keeps her at least partially in the loop, and she likely has her own sources of information.

The Imperatris is truly graceful under pressure (setting a fine example of her role for me, a glimpse into my own Imperial future), because she manages to express her pragmatic concerns and worry about current affairs without upsetting us any further than we already are. Conversation is steered skillfully to family and other, gentler matters. Eventually Aeson returns, having set the *pegasei* liberation process in motion, and we conclude the evening on the best note possible.

Later that night, it gets even better—at least for the two of us. The world might be burning (and flooding, and experiencing gravitational anomalies, not to mention the impending threat of civil war, alien war, and the destruction of the human species on not one but two planets), but our small personal world is gloriously *right*.

Alone in our great bed in the Imperial Crown Prince's Master suite, Aeson and I re-create the joining with our physical bodies that we had experienced with our minds. Able to anticipate each other's needs to a previously impossible extent, we do things with each other that cause such pleasure that I can't even begin to describe. . . .

And it is sublime.

Chapter 87

The events of the next few days and weeks tumble together into a single period of high stress. Aeson begins the arduous process of setting up the rest of the SPC-led *pegasei* liberation project parameters.

First step—passing on the *pegasei* frequency to key individuals and establishing a communication hierarchy. These same individuals will be leading special enforcer teams which are being selected specifically for this task from various Fleets around the globe. Second step—announce to the public and prepare for pushback. Third step—notify registered owners of *pegasei*, individuals and corporations, and issue confiscation warrants. Fourth step—deploy enforcer teams. Fifth step—start searching for illegal and hidden *pegasei* (that's where I come in, together with a handful of specially initiated others). And all of this is being done in conjunction with international local authorities.

And so it begins.

The *astra daimon* are initiated. Keruvat, Oalla, Xelio, Erita, Radanthet, Culuar, Nergal, Quoni—all are stunned by the wonder. I'm told, there are tears in Keruvat's eyes when he first experiences the connection, while Xelio puts his head down then stares into the distance, stricken. Aeson even shares the frequency with Anu (who experiences vertigo, hyperventilates, and gets sick to his stomach) and Gennio (who spaces out gently for several long minutes). And they in turn select others and quietly begin the preliminary training on how to handle the *pegasei* and their reluctant owners.

As for me, one of the earliest occasions to free a *pegasus* happens on the Imperial Palace grounds, specifically in the park. Erita, Oalla, and I follow the urgent mind-cry of a single young quantum entity and discover Lady Irana, walking along a garden path with a few of her friends, and her familiar little pet cage levitating next to her. I ask Lady Irana very politely to stop and then explain to her my intent.

"My Imperial Lady, you want to release my *pegasus?*" she asks with wide eyes. "But why?"

"No, I want *you* to release your *pegasus* yourself," I say. Then I sing the frequency and tell her to copy me.

With a doubtful expression, Lady Irana obeys me nevertheless. The moment she does so, she freezes in her tracks and stares at the little being imprisoned in the gilded cage, hovering at eye level before her and crying pitifully in her mind—I can hear its frustration and discomfort echoing inside my head. And then Lady Irana begins to cry also. . . .

Moments later, the little *pegasus* soars into the sky, in a glorious explosion of mauve and orange light—even as Irana watches, holding open the cage door and smiling with serene wonder.

Thank you for releasing me, my friends! the *pegasus* cries joyfully, and I still hear its alien voice within the confines of my mind, rebounding in tones of pure excitement long after it fades out of sight up above.

Erita and Oalla hear it too, having newly achieved the *pegasei* communication link.

It's a good start.

Meanwhile the others also practice locally on a small scale—starting with contacting all the registered owners in Poseidon and carrying out several raids of semi-legal *pegasei* "breeding" facilities around the Golden Bay.

Arion acts as intermediary between humans and the rest of his species, especially in the beginning. After each successful raid he reaches out to me remotely via mind-speak and tells me it happened. "We thank all of you, Gwen, for setting us free. Twenty-three entities have been liberated. . . . Forty-seven entities liberated. . . . Eighty-two. . . ."

"I'm so glad, Arion!" I exclaim inside my mind with a surge of joy at the *sight*—because each time there are sensory impressions coming in, mind images that Arion shares with me, of plasma beings streaking outward from their bonds, singing in exultation their double helix song . . . which then rings in my mind with surreal echoes for several minutes afterward before fading away. Weird sensation, but so much joy and gratitude that I cannot fault it.

Next, the mass media is informed on a global scale about the true sentient nature of the *pegasei*. There is an immediate uproar and protest, across Imperial *Atlantida* and internationally, and even worse, disbelief. The Imperator, the Pharikon, and various other heads of state make public announcements and formally declare some degree of martial law.

"We are living in a time of crisis. The public is being asked to surrender their *pegasei* willingly. We will not be confiscating them. Instead, officials will be present to make sure that each one of these sentient beings is simply *released* from their containment. Do not attempt to interfere with this process or you will be detained, fined, or worse."

"This is a civil outrage!" the global media commentators and pundits argue on the network talk shows. "The public is being legally robbed! What proof is there that these creatures are genuinely sentient? Making them transform and even 'talk' on cue could very well be a trick. The whole thing is a government ploy to take away our *pegasei* for their own purposes."

"The proof is supposedly in the recent findings from the Ghost Moon," other experts counter. "If there is the slightest chance the *pegasei* can help us deal with the alien enemy that already destroyed two of our deep space outposts and threatens the rest, including this very planet, we must be willing to consider a sacrifice of personal property."

"You cannot simply enforce these measures and talk about social justice. . . ."

Protesters fill urban streets, carrying signs with slogans such as "Confiscation without Compensation," while Correctional officers attempt crowd control measures.

"We are not going to sit idly by and allow this to happen," a captain of the industry says on a media show. "We are suing the state for interference with legitimate business practices. We'll make sure everything will be stalled in the courts."

While all this ugly mess is happening, the work to liberate the *pegasei* on a grand scale begins, despite the public pushback.

First, large-scale facilities are visited by the *Pegasei* Release Teams or PRTs—consisting of one designated *pegasei*

Communicator who was taught the frequency and trained to interact with Arion and his kind, and special ops enforcer troops as military backup. The Communicator reaches out with the mind, verifies the presence of *pegasei*, and then stands and observes as they are released from their containment by the owners. Another team member documents it by video-recording the action for evidence of compliance.

I must admit, it's an amazing sight to see some of these "liberation videos." Warehouses filled with rows and rows of quantum holding pens equipped with artificial "feeding lights" are crammed with lethargic plasma beings, who keep close to the floor like fluorescent algae bloom. . . . Small specialty shops with luxury cages and one or two overstimulated, bloated, "show" specimens in each are bombarded by non-stop feeding lights around the clock— even as the quantum entities flitter about, striking against the walls of their confinement, engorged by energy without outlet, screaming their agony into the mind of the Communicator, upon approach.

And then. . . .

The quantum containment "faraday cage" fields are disabled. Harnesses and other means of containment are removed—by sullen, reluctant *pegasei* handlers—even as PRT enforcement troops stand by, ready to interfere if needed. . . .

And suddenly, clouds of plasma energy erupt from their bonds.

Wildly expanding and contracting quantum *beings* soar overhead and wink in and out of existence as they joyfully unfurl across dimensions. Overpowering love and relief are broadcast into receptive minds everywhere. Once outside, the *pegasei* congregate in the open air to feel the full-spectrum warmth of Hel's light, feeding actively upon the energy of daylight. They frolic and soar, eventually gathering together to form immense flocks in the lower atmosphere, which start to hang over cities like the aurora borealis.

"Why aren't they leaving?" media commentators wonder, and panels discuss. "Isn't this a blatant example of their domestication? They don't know what to do with themselves; it's obvious they are nothing more than primitive livestock."

"Not at all," other pundits argue. "They are waiting. We've been informed that they need to have all of their kind set free before they can depart together, as one. . . ."

Meanwhile, I teach the *pegasei* frequency to my friends—when I finally have the opportunity to see them, for the first time since the Wedding. Chiyoko is astounded and spends long moments giggling with Arion about trans-dimensional math. Laronda and Dawn immediately start asking questions about historical events, current events, and everything imaginable. Hasmik puts her hands over her mouth, then endlessly apologizes to the entire *pegasei* species between sobs.

Devora Kassiopei learns the frequency from her son, Aeson, the very next time she visits. I'm there to see her sit down across from the little Sphinx shape of Arion and hold onto her chair as she's plunged in long, sorrowful silence. The Imperatris remains motionless and without words, breathing faintly, while moisture fills her eyes.

The living connection is unique with each one of you humans, Arion tells me inside my mind. *Devora shows me her compassion, burning bright. I am pleased and honored to connect with another human so full of love.*

Aeson and I discuss the possibility of sharing the frequency with his Imperial Father, or Shirahtet, or any other members of the Imperial crony circle. Both of us are fundamentally against it, and decide to hold off for as long as possible and see how it goes.

During this time of continuing martial law and ongoing *pegasei* situation unrest, all throughout the rest of the month of Red Amrevet, we continue to study and interpret Arlenari's diary, or The Book of Everything. After that major revelation about the *pegasei*, the rest of the entries seem to have varying degrees of relevance to our present situation.

Aeson and I try to read them together, with my Dad and as many of my siblings as possible present. It seems that by combining our minds, we improve our ability to interpret the information to a greater degree than anyone could alone.

One of the later entries catches my attention.

> Today I look up at the stars, feeling the connection again for the first time since leaving Earth, where I looked up at entirely other stars and loved them. I have not felt this way since.
> These are different, alien stars. They are not **my** stars.

> And yet, it is they who now pour their Starlight upon me.
>
> They are just as immeasurably distant from me **here**, and from my cosmic location of birth, as my own stars were immeasurably distant from me **there**.
>
> But the difference is never distance. Neither is it line of sight.
>
> The difference is recognition.
>
> They have found me and I have found them.
>
> With the awareness, the love I feel gathering inside me evokes a different song. And yet, love itself is the same.
>
> And the song is forming.
>
> Once again, I feel the urge to sing.

"She keeps talking about Starlight, with a capital 'S.'" George says thoughtfully. "Is it just poetic metaphor or something else? Could it be an actual substance of some kind?"

"Good question," Dad says. "If I recall, the Venerable Shirahtet offered a similar theory the last time I talked with him."

Apparently, now that his health is more stable and the effects of the gravity are becoming more bearable, my father has been venturing outside and taking gentle walks in the Imperial park below, sometimes accompanied by Shirahtet, and more often by Consul Denu.

"Whatever it is, it seems particularly important," Aeson reflects, glancing at Dad and then at me.

"Maybe there's more in the next entry?" I ask.

And we continue reading. However, stars and Starlight are never mentioned again.

Toward the end of Arlenari's diary entries, a strange thing happens. Her wispy elegant handwriting ends, and it's as if *another person* takes over. And indeed, it is definitely someone else, writing in a stronger, more even hand with artistic flourish and precision in the characters and pictographs.

Also, the entries are now written in third person. They speak of Princess Arlenari now being "too busy to write," and how the important work she is doing must still be recorded.

And then there is this puzzling last entry:

The Imperial Princess Arlenari has instructed me to continue in her stead, to document and to preserve, while she must do what must be done with Starlight.

The Ship of Eternity is being readied, and there is much work to be done before she embarks.

They will try to stop her, to obliterate everything, grind memory into dust, and they will succeed in all but one thing.

Semmi will keep Arleana alive.

The Book of Everything ends with that line. We look away from the split screen view of the scroll text original and its contemporary *Atlanteo* translation.

"Semmi . . ." I say. "That name is familiar. Okay—remember the scrolls from the puzzle boxes we found when we went down inside the ancient ark-ship? One of them was a note mentioning The Book of Everything, signed by Arleana and addressed to Semmi. That was the first time I'd heard of it. It was the same name, I'm certain."

"You're right, it is," Aeson confirms.

George raises his brows. "Who is Semmi?"

Dad pays rapt attention. "Semmi? Interesting name. Is it a short form of something? A longer name, perhaps?"

Manala, who is sitting on the other side of Dad, suddenly draws in her breath. "Semmi is short for Semiram . . ." she whispers.

"Great," George says. "Who is Semiram?"

"Not a common name," Aeson muses. "I cannot think of any except maybe—"

"The Semiram Cycle!" Manala exclaims. "It's a very old epic written by the ancient classical poet Semiram, who lived during the Original Colony period. And, oh—it is the primary collection of myths about Arleana, Starlight Sorceress."

George slaps his thigh. "Jackpot."

Manala glances at him with alarm. "What is jackpot?"

"Never mind." George pauses, then sighs. "All right, it's the winnings in gambling, in other words, the main prize."

"Oh! Then no, I don't want to know anything about it if it's horrid gambling," Manala says in a hurry.

George shakes his head with a little smile. "A-a-a-and, we're moving on."

"Back to *The Semiram Cycle*," Dad says, frowning with concentration. "It sounds delightful, and I would really love to take a look at it, though it would have to be in translation. My efforts to absorb contemporary *Atlanteo* are still quite rudimentary, and I've no doubt this is written in an earlier form of the language."

"Oh yes, it is Classical *Atlanteo*," Manala says.

Dad rubs his forehead and chin. "A translation would be nice. This poet, Semiram—can you tell us more about him or her?"

Manala thinks. "Nothing is really known about Semiram. We are taught in school that Semiram may not even be an actual person, but just an oral tradition of poets."

"Puts me in mind of Shakespeare and his disputed identity," George remarks.

"Yes," Dad says. "Though I'm more inclined to think of the great Ancient Greek poet Homer, the so-called 'blind bard' of earliest Hellenistic antiquity. Little more than a handful of anecdotes is known about him, and most is the stuff of legend. The Homeric Question remains open. It's debatable whether he existed, let alone authored *The Iliad* and *The Odyssey*, or if there were many others in the tradition."

"There's a copy of *The Semiram Cycle* in modern translation on a bookshelf in my old study room," Aeson says with a faint smile. "It's down the hall on this floor."

"No, it's not." Manala bites her lip. "I borrowed it again, and it's in my library. I can go and get it now."

"Excellent," Dad says, rubbing his hands. "An ancient puzzle to sink into *and* new reading material."

And so, over the next few days, we start examining *The Semiram Cycle* for clues, but nothing much comes of it. Aeson has very little time to spare, and he informs the Imperator and Shirahtet about the possible relevance, but apparently, they are already ahead of us in connecting "Semmi" with Semiram, the ancient author of the Arleana myths.

Meanwhile, the golden grids of light spheres around Helios, Rah, and Septu, remain inactive. SPC patrols continue their vigilance, and War-8 orbits Tammuz with care, watching over the evacuated Tammuz Station.

By the middle of the month of Red Pegasus, nothing out of the ordinary has happened in space around the Helios system—which may or may not be the calm before the storm. The projected estimated dates of new hostile activity have come and gone, and no one knows what to expect. The alien enemy can strike any minute. . . .

And so new projections are made based on existing SPC data, and new dates are set to worry about.

On the other hand, the Atlantis planetary system is still struggling to achieve its new gravitational equilibrium after the addition of the Ghost Moon. So far, the weather tech systems on the surface have barely managed to reduce the severity of regional storms and tidal activity.

"It's a work in progress," climate scientists and weather tech experts proclaim on the news shows. "We are doing everything possible to save lives, property, and crops. . . . And we are still actively studying the material makeup, physical properties, and orbital mechanics of this new moon before we can incorporate its accurate parameters into the planetary model."

When the fifth week of Red Pegasus ends, culminating with the Atlantean holiday known as Burning Night on Yellowday, Red Pegasus 22—filled with bonfires in city parks and rowdy celebration, and an easing of martial law for one night—almost all the *pegasei* have been accounted for and released. Now their great liberated flocks hang all over the skies of Atlantis, mingling with the recent crop of out-of-control clouds that got past the weather tech.

Even now, their songs fill our waking minds—those of us who are attuned to them—with wonder and glory. . . . It's an unobtrusive, constant sound of nature, like living next to a waterfall. The rush of falling water is always there, but it blends in, has become a part of the natural landscape.

A few captive *pegasei* are still out there. During this final stage of *pegasei* liberation, only the most difficult, well-hidden cases remain—the illegal ones, sorrowful entities hidden away in the most remote places around the globe. These are the ones even the well-trained Communicators miss, unable to pinpoint their locations successfully.

For some reason I'm still better at it than anyone else. I can always hear the *pegasei* voices crying out to me. . . . Their haunting song tugs at my gut with a visceral power, pulling me toward them like the needle of an inner compass.

And so, it falls upon me to handle this closing stage of the process. Because martial law is still in effect everywhere, because there's still pushback and the possibility of violence—and because I'm the Imperial Wife of the Crown Prince of *Atlantida* and we're literally responsible for starting this whole thing—I am assigned an extra-large PRT unit to assist me.

On the morning of Red Pegasus 26, the final day of the month, I can hear the faint, plaintive song of the remaining small group of bound *pegasei*, coming to me from the distant northwest.

It is somehow appropriate—last day of a Pegasus month, last *pegasei* to be liberated.

My directional instinct is correct. The request for assistance with the *pegasei* comes to us from the ally nation of Khenneb, located to the northwest of us, on the same Upper Continent. The leader of that country, Bakar Ramajet, the Hetmet of Khenneb, specifically requests *my* help with a difficult retrieval of *pegasei* from an illegal subterranean facility, portions of it in caves carved from inside a mountain.

Unfortunately, Aeson cannot come with me on this mission because there is alien light grid activity predicted for today—or tomorrow, or the following day—they can't be sure, but the general time frame is *now*. Tammuz is on the highest alert level it has been in days, and the SPC high command must be ready for military action.

We discuss it, and Aeson is extremely unhappy about it, but the mission cannot be postponed—we urgently need all the *pegasei* liberated so that they can play their part in closing the dimensional rift for us—and neither can he abandon his SPC command duties to accompany me. For that reason, Aeson insists I get the best and the biggest team, in addition to my usual security detail.

And so, before I head out to Khenneb on behalf of the last captive *pegasei*, I get to meet my new teammates.

Chapter 88

Tuar Momet and my four usual guards surround me as we take the Palace elevator downstairs, and then emerge in the park and walk a short distance to the Imperial airfield.

For safety and anonymity purposes, I am wearing the unobtrusive, plain grey uniform that is worn by Imperial Palace staff, but I have a layer of *viatoios* armor underneath. My guards are similarly attired, to blend in with me.

It's seventh hour and thirty daydreams of Ra exactly, and the PRT unit waits for us near the main hangar, next to a very big transport ship.

Apparently, we're taking an *ankhurat*.

The vessel, hovering several feet above the ground, is metallic slate-grey with a secondary sheen of gold in the morning light of Hel. It is shaped like a double-headed wrench on the short end, and then extended, so that the outline of the wrench stretches for a hundred meters, forming a flattened plane which is the hull. It appears heavy as an anvil, a strange imposing machine of war. On the long side of the aircraft, the entrance hatch is raised, showing a wide opening, with a lowered ramp.

I recall that the *ankhurat*, nicknamed "Ankh, the Life Giver," is a 100-crew military transport boarding fighter vessel, the largest and most heavy-duty of the fighters. It has six pilots and is equipped with six heavy-caliber guns and ten missiles.

I feel a twinge of fear at the sight of it.

I turn to look at my crew, one hundred strong. The troops stand in order, lined up sharply in two blocks of fifty, wearing the SPC special ops uniforms in black and grey, with helmet insignias in gold. Their captain stands in front of them in a grey and gold uniform and immediately acknowledges me with an impeccable salute.

Off to the side I see my six pilots.

And now, I'm amazed. . . .

Brie Walton stands with a grin on her face, wearing the same uniform, sans helmet, which she holds in the crook of her arm as she cranes her head mockingly at me. Next to her is Blayne Dubois, looking sharp and cool in his uniform, levitating astride a narrow, custom hoverboard which he is riding in his usual near-upright stance.

Then, three people I've never met, but my gut tells me they might all be Earthies, or *shìrén*. The first is a stocky blonde and blue-eyed girl with short hair. The second is a muscular Asian boy with shoulder-length black hair gathered in an Atlantean-style segmented tail. The third is a tall, lean Caucasian teen with brown hair and green eyes.

And then, the last person—a curvy, vaguely familiar Latina. . . .

It's Claudia Grito.

Holy crap!

I blink and freeze momentarily, not quite believing my eyes. I think my mouth opens stupidly.

Let me repeat that. The person in the Star Pilot Corps uniform standing across from me, with her raven-black hair drawn in a tight head-hugging ponytail, and most of her piercings missing their jewelry, to comply with Fleet regulations, is none other than Claudia Grito, the bully girl from Qualification.

The last time I interacted with Claudia was over a year ago—inside the ancient subterranean tunnels during the Qualification Finals on Earth. She and I were both on Team C, and I saved her sorry ass, along with everyone else, by using voice commands and hoverboards to wall us in and keep us from drowning.

I haven't seen her since. Had no idea whether she Qualified and didn't care to know.

And now, here she is, on my PRT, on Atlantis.

WTF?

A million questions rush through my mind, evoking some long-repressed old memories. . . .

But I get no chance to space out or stare, because the PRT unit captain approaches me and introduces himself as Captain Valel Siduaz. He is young, medium-height, with deep bronze skin, short black hair, and black eyes.

"It's an honor to handle your mission, my Imperial Lady," he tells me in a curt, no-nonsense manner. "We are an elite unit and will support your efforts today in Khenneb. These are your mission pilots. They have been specially chosen because of merit and familiarity, to best accommodate you."

Captain Siduaz points to the six and makes introductions, even though I already know half of them.

The short blond Caucasian girl is introduced as Yana Svoboda, the muscular Asian is Li Jie, and the tall brown-haired teen is Darius Harrod. Just as I thought, all fellow *shìrén*.

When it's Claudia Grito's turn, she steps forward and names herself—just in case I've hallucinated it and mistook someone else for her—and it's confirmed.

"Cadet Pilot Claudia Grito, at your service."

I look into Claudia's serious, unblinking eyes and say, "Claudia, what are you doing here?"

There is a pause.

Claudia pulls herself up even more and stands perfectly straight. She faces me without changing her fixed expression and says, "Imperial Lady Gwen, I volunteered."

She used to call me Gwen-baby and made every effort to torment me. . . .

All kinds of strange thoughts are passing through my mind.

She volunteered? Why the hell is she here?

"Okay," I say. "Well, I'm glad to see you Qualified." And then I don't say anything else, because, really, how weird is this? What else can I say?

Also, does the captain—or any of the others—notice our awkward tension?

Looks like, not. The only person who seems to be somewhat aware of the weirdness is Blayne Dubois. Blayne actually knows Claudia the same way I do, from our Pennsylvania RQC-3 and Qualification. And even if he didn't recognize her at first, he has to remember her now, and not too fondly.

And so I switch my attention to Blayne, who gives me a little knowing smile, but then follows it up with a proper salute and says, "Cadet Pilot Blayne Dubois. Good to be here, Imperial Lady Gwen."

"Blayne! So happy to see you on this mission."

"Me too," he replies. "My LM Forms skillset is apparently needed for this one."

"Oh, really?" I ask.

He nods. "Flying through cramped spaces, high possibility of close-quarters combat with limited maneuverability, underground cave system. Et cetera. More during the briefing."

Next, Brie steps forward, and her ironic smile again shows up. "Cadet Pilot Brie Walton, retrained and reinstated in the Fleet," she announces. "Toldja."

"Hey, Brie!" I smile. "Um . . . congratulations? Not sick of being on another Team Lark?"

"Not in a million Atlantean turtle years."

I chuckle and stand back, trying not to stare sideways with my peripheral vision in Claudia's direction. Claudia remains poised and serious, still standing at attention.

This is so damn weird.

Introductions are over, and the captain now steps aside again and addresses the troops unit, barking a command.

In moments, the two sections of fifty break rank and hurry up the ramp, entering the ship. The rest of us follow.

I walk up the ramp after Captain Siduaz into a familiar Atlantean vessel interior. Fleet vessels tend to adhere to a standard look on the inside. It could be just another ark-ship hallway on ICS-2.

Here, however, the ramp opens directly into a wide, rectangular deck. Seats on both sides of the long hull walls are full of troops. There are large bins of equipment stacked in regular intervals, and wall control panels everywhere, with three weapons stations interspersed with troops seating along both sides of the hull, lengthwise—for a total of six gun stations.

On the short ends of the ship are the two main pilot sections, front and rear. A pilot is stationed at each wrench "head"—two in the front, two in the back—and the two remaining pilots are on standby, ready to relieve any of the activated four.

I step inside, onto the deck, with my guards flanking me, and the six pilots come after us. The exterior hatch lowers, sealing us in.

Blayne maneuvers his board with great skill, singing the tone sequences quietly, and flies directly to the front section, where he swaps himself off the board and onto a chair, taking the pilot station on the right. Claudia turns in the opposite direction and goes for the rear, also taking the right side.

Darius Harrod joins Blayne up in front and claims the left station. Yana Svoboda joins Claudia in the remaining rear left station.

The two standby pilots are Brie Walton and Li Jie, and they remain with me. We find seats in the center of the deck, in the command station seat circle next to the captain's chair.

Tuar sits down next to me, while Brie takes my other side. They nod friendly greetings to each other, speaking past me.

"Good to see you, Walton."

"Same to you, Momet."

Li Jie observes us silently, not a man of many words.

We buckle ourselves in the usual harnesses that descend like snakes around us.

And then the captain nods to me and engages the control panel hovering before him. "*Pegasei* Retrieval Khenneb Mission, initiate takeoff."

The seated troops grow silent. In that moment four voices rise in eerie harmony from each of the four pilot station corners, as the pilots sing the keying sequence and call up their holo-grids and projection view screens.

Moments later, golden lights race in fine lines along the hull, and a deep hum rises from the ship's walls.

With a sudden sinking feeling in my gut due to the pull of gravity, I feel the *ankhurat* take off. There's a lurch as it moves horizontally, parallel to the ground, to distance itself from the hangar.

And then it rises like a heavy missile into the sky, heading for orbit.

The flight to Khenneb is short. We achieve orbit, then traverse the distance from Imperial *Atlantida* to Khenneb. Once we're directly over Khenneb, the vessel plummets through the atmosphere back toward the surface.

There are no windows in this craft, only the small viewports projected before each pilot, and I sit too far from any of them to see what kind of surface features await us. I've been told there will be mountains.

"I have been advised of minor weather effects at our landing coordinates," the captain says to me, as he checks his controls. "High winds and periods of heavy rain."

"Okay." I nod. "Is this going to affect our ability to land?"

"No, simply a nuisance. However, there is another item of concern. The Hetmet of Khenneb just transmitted a warning message to me: several groups of local fighters and militia units are converging on our location. They have been called by the quasi-legal owners of the *pegasei* facility to protect their interests."

"So, these people are armed and hostile?" I ask.

"Yes, unfortunately." The captain scans the incoming data on his screen. "They will be waiting for us when we land, and at the entrance to the mountain facility."

"How many hostiles are we talking about?" Brie asks. "A handful? Several dozen?"

"Likely, more," Tuar answers instead of the captain.

Brie raises her brows. "So, are we talking ant infestation levels?"

The captain gives her a quick, uncomprehending glance, but does not reply, because he has more data scrolling on his display.

"What about their weapons capability?" Tuar asks.

"Expect standard mid-caliber energy firearms obtained on the regional black market. Some heavy plasma guns added in the mix."

Captain Siduaz pauses, checks something else on another smaller window. Then he pushes the hovering physical controls aside and calls up his own holo-grid within a cube of teal-blue light.

This particular grid displays a 3D topographical map of the region. Teal lines project a surface covered by craggy hills and valleys, and one prominently larger elevation which is in fact our mountain destination. Several white moving circle dots are added, designating the approaching hostiles. Our own *ankhurat* is designated by a larger golden dot, seen landing vertically at the foothills of the mountain.

"According to the current snapshot, the hostiles are sufficiently far away," Tuar says. "Do we have a time estimate when they will arrive?"

"The Hetmet is sending the projection data to us now," the captain says, manipulating the grid. "It should populate the map in moments."

And seconds later, the holo-grid refreshes to show a superimposed additional image, this one in red, indicating the time-elapsed projection for the hostiles' movement.

"According to this projection, we have less than two hours before we are overrun."

"Is there any way to reason with them?" I ask. "Will the fighting be unavoidable?"

"Unavoidable, Imperial Lady." The captain looks at me with a resigned expression. "These locals will not give up their *pegasei* without a fight."

"Then we need to hurry," I say.

And we continue our descent to the surface.

W e land at a slightly different set of coordinates, in order to save time. Khenneb is a coastal nation, and our destination is inland, at the foot of a small mountain, but still not that far from Liant Bay with its high crags looming over the charcoal-silver-mauve waters of the bay.

The *ankhurat* plummets and comes to a hover stop at the edge of a small, rocky valley lined by sparse shrubbery and occasional trees, with the mountain looming before us. We emerge into a windy drizzle and partly overcast skies. It might be the height of Red season, but it's cooler here than in *Atlantida*, due to the high northern latitude.

"We have a short hike, no more than half an hour before we reach the cave mouth," the captain tells me and my guards and *shirén* pilots, even as half the PRT unit troops form a tight human chain and begin moving out into the wilderness ahead of us. Meanwhile the other half waits for us to start moving, to bring up the rear. Two guards remain posted near the ship (which is secured with an active force field) to relay real-time information to us about any on-site activity.

"Watch your step, my Imperial Lady," Tuar warns me, pointing to the rugged terrain.

Good thing I'm wearing solid boots. The rain is making things slippery.

We start walking at a good pace, with Blayne flying evenly alongside us on his board while my guards and the pilots surround me. Everyone looks around often, checking the perimeter and the distant hillsides for any sign of hostiles.

Claudia, Li Jie, and Brie move quickly in the front of our group, ranging slightly ahead. Yana and Darius walk at my side, and we exchange occasional comments. I learn that Yana is a Czech from Prague and is a mixed martial arts expert. Darius is a pro athlete swimmer, runner and lifeguard from Australia.

Soon, the captain drops back to walk with our central group and quickly explains to me the unusual *pegasei* situation we're about to walk into.

"Part of the reason the local authorities were unable to accurately locate the *pegasei* is because of some kind of impenetrable quantum force field which encloses their holding pens," Captain Siduaz says. "The Communicator sent here earlier was unable to reach out to them because of that quantum field. She and her PRT walked around the pens for hours, looking for some kind of breach, or field weakness, or loophole—forgive my terminology, I don't know how your communication with them works. She called for assistance, and a second Communicator was sent, with his own PRT. Still no results. And then the locals found out, word got around we were breaking into their old 'sacred *pegasei* grounds.' They massed, got their militias, notified the ruling crime syndicate, started pushing back, and the teams had to abandon the mission due to the elevated threat level."

"Very interesting." I frown. "Why doesn't the Hetmet do something about it? About the local resistance, I mean?"

The captain shakes his head, his expression ironic. "The Hetmet is too afraid of pushing the crime syndicate boss who owns most of the land in this area and considers the *pegasei* facility 'owner' under his 'protection.' Khenneb is small, underpopulated, and the Hetmet's power is precarious. Besides, this *pegasei* situation is rather unique, and he realizes the need for a high-level expert—such as yourself."

An expert, me? I want to laugh in my mind. *On the other hand, why am I laughing? I've positioned myself as such and have to maintain this authority if we want to succeed in freeing all the* pegasei.

We arrive at the mountain cave entrance that leads to a subterranean network of tunnels and storage warehouses. The entrance is a narrow doorway cut into the mountain, hidden by overgrown shrubbery. It shows signs of being recently used, and the PRT troops get out machetes to clear out the rest of the brush, allowing us to enter easily. Then they send hovering drone probes and mini orb lights ahead of us inside, to better light our way, and to prevent surprise attacks. There's no sign yet of any hostiles, but everyone is vigilant.

Inside, the tunnel is ridiculously narrow, forcing us to walk in pairs or single file for at least ten minutes in near darkness, with only the mini-orbs and occasional wall sconces in the rock illuminating our way. It's dank and smells like mold and sulfur.

I glance behind me and see Brie Walton's tense face illuminated by hovering orb lights . . . and just for a moment I get a flashback to the Games, when Brie and I were temporarily walled up inside the pyramid, and I found out she is claustrophobic.

I wonder if she regrets signing up for this mission, I think.

On the other hand, Blayne is moving along with great skill, effortlessly maneuvering through the tunnel on his narrow board.

"Almost there," the captain tells us, as we continue to carefully advance forward.

I nod. . . . And then I tell myself, it's time.

I clear my mind and sing the now familiar frequency to open the floodgates of communication. If the *pegasei* are anywhere near, I am about to hear them.

The stream of sensory data rushes through my forehead, and at once I hear the spiraling call in my mind. It comes from the vicinity, a corkscrew of meta-sound, a profound melody forming a double helix. . . .

Freedom! Freedom! Help us! Please, free us, human! They fill my mind in a sudden chorus of urgent voices.

I'm coming! I mind-speak in reply. *I am here! Show me where you are!*

At once I get a carousel of images: poorly lit, huge, cavernous expanse of black and slate-grey rock walls, greenish, chalk-pale portions of the bedrock, strange striated layers. . . .

Hungry, hungry, always hungry! Not enough light! the voices cry.

And right in that moment we emerge from the tunnel into the same open cavern space that I've just seen in my mind.

A surreal, impossible sight greets us.

The cavern is precisely as I've seen it, and yet—the *pegasei* never showed me the bottom of this expanse. The entire floor of the cavern is a softly roiling mist-ocean of very faint golden light vapor. Scattered throughout this bizarre golden mist are the so-called "holding pens"—spheres of gold light mounted on slim metal posts elevated about a meter from the ground. Each sphere is twice the size of a basketball, and it's pulsing with moving colors of *pegasei* plasma. . . . orange, yellow, blue, violet, turquoise, pink. . . .

There are at least twenty of these spheres, maybe thirty. Definitely more than I expected.

"What the hell—" one of the *shìrén* behind me whispers—I think it's Darius.

The PRT unit troops who've arrived ahead of us stand waiting for the captain and the next set of orders. Everyone has stopped at the entrance, and no one is sure how to proceed. Do we walk into that swirling gold mist?

Help us! We long for freedom! So much hunger. . . .

More and more people arrive, and now I see the captain approaching me as I stand next to Tuar and Yana and Claudia at the edge of the floor that begins to turn to mist.

"What exactly is this stuff?" Tuar asks the captain, pointing to the mist on the floor. "Is it toxic?"

"It's safe, according to the previous two PRTs and Communicators who were here," the captain retorts, then quickly looks on his wrist comm to check a flashing incoming message. "We are being told to expedite. The hostiles are approaching and will be here in less than an hour."

"Okay. . . ." I take a step forward into the mist.

But then I hear Blayne's voice. "Hold on. Let me take a quick look."

In that moment Blayne sings a quick, precise sequence and soars forward, inclining the board flat so that now he's lying on his stomach. He flies low, a few inches over the mist and starts making rapid hover passes around the perimeter, circling the cavern, then venturing out to the middle. I see him reach down with one hand and sweep it through the golden vapor, then rise somewhat and approach one of the thirty containment orbs roiling with *pegasei* essence.

"Be careful, please!" I call out to him, and my solitary voice echoes throughout the cavern.

Solitary . . . that is, if I don't count the relentless, plaintive cries of the quantum beings ringing inside my mind. . . .

Let us go! Please set us free!

"All right, so far," Blayne calls out to me, as he remains suspended before one of the containment spheres. "The vapor stuff feels like nothing. Going to touch this ball thing now—"

Blayne moves his hand slowly, and places one finger on the sphere . . . and immediately exclaims, "Whoa!"

"What's happening?" I ask.

"Look!" Blayne exclaims, turning his head to stare in our general direction. "Can you see it? My finger! Oh, man, *look!*"

I narrow my eyes, but in this poorly lit chamber I can't be sure of what I'm seeing at this distance. So I think, to hell with it, and just walk into the golden mist and march up to Blayne. I can hear Tuar and the others follow, immediately behind me.

As I get close, I begin to see what he's doing.

And my jaw drops.

Blayne has inserted his finger inside the sphere up to his joint, but the *tip* of his *same* finger is sticking out at an odd angle of approximately fifteen degrees in the opposite direction—as though it's been cut off, displaced about an inch, and is now coming out *from inside* the sphere.

Where have I seen this before?

Oh my God. . . . It's that impossible *matter refraction* phenomenon.

We observed it when SPC probes were sent into the huge alien spheres that comprise the golden light grid around Helios.

"Blayne, are you okay?" I exclaim worriedly as I arrive at his side.

Blayne nods in astonishment, continuing to hold his finger inside the sphere. And then he slowly pulls it out. As he does so, the refracted tip of his finger nearby recedes back into the sphere, and disappears. Blayne flexes his reclaimed finger, frowning.

"Everything seems fine," he says, staring at his hand. "I felt nothing. That was incredibly bizarre."

"Let me try," I say, and stick my entire hand into the sphere, up to my wrist.

My fingers disappear inside and then appear—equally displaced, refracted at an angle—from the opposite direction. I wiggle them, and see them wiggle back at me, coming at me from the other direction.

As this is happening, I can see the rest of the PRT unit troops begin to spread out around the cavern and start touching the spheres, passing fingers through them in sweeping motions, blowing at them—and feeling their own breath blowing back in their face at an angle.

Everything they attempt to insert gets "refracted"—hands, firearms, machetes.

Except for this one weird material effect, the containment spheres are *intangible*, physically unreachable, locked away indeed in some other dimension.

And the *pegasei* are locked away inside them.

With this new development, our situation just got even more complicated. I stand in puzzlement, looking at the containment spheres spread out around the cavern and listen to the clamor of *pegasei* inside my mind, calling out to me.

I really should contact Aeson, I think. *I need to let him know about the same dimensional phenomenon I've discovered here. It's relevant to our bigger problem and maybe it could help us?*

But right now, we're running out of time. I need to figure out how to get those *pegasei* out of their prisons and then we all need to get out of here in a hurry, before armed hostiles arrive.

But how to do it?

Maybe I should ask the *pegasei*.

And I do.

I mind-speak my question at them, showing them the entirety of my confusion, perplexed bafflement, and uncertainty as far as how to proceed.

At the same time, I call Arion.

Chapter 89

Arion responds to me instantaneously, as always. One moment he is *elsewhere*. And the next, his plasma-cloud essence *enters* the present reality with a tiny pop of displaced air, and then expands in a radiant cloud for three meters around me.

I am here, Gwen Lark who is Kassiopei, his familiar calm voice speaks inside my mind.

Arion's arrival is accompanied by a flare of light, like a small firework going off, and everyone turns in our direction. At once the cave becomes a little brighter in our vicinity.

"Whoa! Did you do that?" someone asks.

"So—did you just figure out a way of breaking them out of those containment fields?" Brie Walton steps closer, staring curiously at the newly arrived quantum being.

But I raise my hand up for quiet, because I'm communicating with the *pegasus*.

"Arion!" I mind-speak anxiously. "Do you know what this is? Your people are stuck inside this strange force field, or barrier, and I don't know what to do! I've never worked with anything like it."

Help us, please! We have been here for so long! Forever! Forever! The other *pegasei* continue their desperate, plaintive cries.

"Do you know what type of containment you are in?" I ask the clamoring voices.

A continuation of their lament seems to be the only direct answer.

Starving, weak, need more light, help us!

They are so agitated that they do not appear to pay attention to my question, seemingly unable to focus long enough to answer.

There is a short pause, as I sense that Arion at least is about to speak. . . . He is choosing carefully from the infinity of images inside him to formulate his reply.

Freedom! Please release us!

"Arion?" I repeat. "What kind of containment field is it?"

It is—not, he replies at last.

"What do you mean?"

Not a containment field. Not a barrier. It is a threshold doorway.

"What? A threshold doorway? What does that mean?"

Help us!

"I am *trying* to help you, okay? Please shush for a moment! I mean, I'm sorry . . . let me just work this out," I think-say in frustration with a twinge of despair. And then I redirect my thought speech back at Arion.

"Please explain," I say, trying to make my thoughts as calm as possible. "What is this thing—this threshold doorway?"

There is another pause, with only the general telepathic *din*, for lack of a better word, coming from all the imprisoned *pegasei*. But at least it's somewhat more subdued.

They are really confused, Arion says unexpectedly. *They have been here so long that they cannot remember how to reply to complex questions. They are entangled improperly between multiple dimensions. . . . In addition, their self-membranes have deteriorated so much that they have difficulty separating themselves from others . . . and from everything else.*

"Okay, not sure I understand," I say. "Where are they exactly?"

In the doorway. . . . They are inside the doorway, trapped between here and there.

I sigh. "Still don't know what that means, but what can I do?"

"Imperial Lady Gwen?" Captain Siduaz interrupts our telepathic conversation. "Any progress?"

I raise my hand again for silence and shake my head negatively.

"Remember, we're short on time," the captain reminds me again, before stepping back to give me room.

"Arion, what—"

These pegasei *here are trapped inside a threshold*, Arion says slowly. *It is very difficult to describe upper-dimensional concepts using the terminology of a lower-dimensional reality such as this.*

Imagine that dimensions are like rooms, he continues. *There is a wall of ice between two rooms. You are frozen inside the wall of ice. Normally, the ice would be liquid water cascading down and you could easily pass through it. But now it is frozen, and you are stuck inside it.*

"Oh, wow," I say. "That's horrible."

It is.

"How did it happen? How did this threshold freeze?"

Time.

"You mean, a long time?"

A very long time, Arion's voice rings sadly. *More than nine thousand of your years. Soon after the time of your Landing.*

I suck in my breath—so that Tuar, standing and watching me, focuses on me worriedly.

"What caused it? How? What happened here? If not containment spheres, what are those round things?"

You caused it—your human species who came to this planet and brought my species with you by force. Here in these ancient caves of the place you now call Khenneb, your ancestors tried to make another dimensional rift—*just like the one they made on Earth, and using the same destructive methods.*

"Oh my God!" I exclaim out loud, so that the PRT unit troops walking around nearby freeze and stare at me.

The careless humans started forming the dimensional breach. Then they forced a number of pegasei *inside to keep it open,* Arion continues. *Only it didn't work. The fabric of space-time reacted in a way they did not expect and the breach collapsed and 'healed' itself, sealing the pegasei in the process, stuck between dimensions.*

"They couldn't just get away?"

Normally, my species can pass easily through that space-time fabric but, as I explained, metaphoric water had now become metaphoric ice. The spheres are nothing more than hardened space-time bubbles, membranes isolating foreign matter—the unfortunate pegasei. *And the more time passed, the more impenetrable the membranes became.*

I nod slowly. "So then, this whole area is basically dimensional scar tissue!"

Yes, a valid analogy.

"Crap. . . ." Once again, I speak out loud.

"That bad?" Blayne asks.

My frown is sufficient answer.

There is a long pause.

And then I say, "Arion, ice is frozen water. It can be melted again. Is it possible to *melt* space-time?"

Anything is possible, he replies. *But I don't know how. This is something that I have never encountered before, even though my entity existence has been longer than you can humanly imagine.*

"Great," I mind-speak, projecting all my bitterness, and shake my head.

I am sorry. I wish I could help but this is an unknown for me. I will continue to ponder this genuine puzzle, and I will speak with the rest of my kind to search for answers. . . .

"We are getting notification of incoming," Captain Siduaz says. "Only twenty-five daydreams before they arrive at the cave entrance. We are leaving in ten, regardless of mission completion."

"Oh, no," I say. "But we can't!"

But the captain shakes his head. "I must insist, Imperial Lady. So please proceed with what you are doing, and expedite." And then he turns to dispatch some of the PRT unit troops to retreat back the way we came from and guard additional points along the tunnel and entrance.

I want to metaphorically wring my hands with anxiety. Instead I start moving around the cavern, looking around, with a frown of effort pulling at my forehead. Periodically I stop and focus with desperate intensity on the glowing, *pegasei*-filled spheres, pausing to run my fingers through them and see the matter refraction happen again and again.

My guards and the *shìrén* pilots watch me, following not too closely so as not to interfere with my arcane "process," whatever they think it might be. Arion floats nearby in plasma shape, and the tumbling thought images I get from him have turned incomprehensible, while the telepathic *din* has resumed as the *pegasei* sense that something urgent and important is happening.

"I don't know," I mind-speak. "I just don't know. . . ."

Then I resort to my usual standby—I use my Voice.

Placing my hand inside the nearest ghostly orb, I sing a keying command in a ringing voice of power, directing my focus at the sphere—that intangible, corrupted membrane-bubble between dimensions. *Stupid thing. . . . Like a dimensional pustule. . . .*

Yes, it is similar to your Earth oysters enveloping a pebble of foreign matter until it becomes a pearl, Arion remarks inside my head, even as I sing.

My Logos voice echoes throughout the cavern, and everyone grows momentarily silent as they listen to me in awe. So much power . . . so much resounding power without an outlet, as the sound waves bounce around and collapse like the tide, finding no quantum-sensitive material, no orichalcum to latch onto inside the spheres.

I sing a different sequence, then another. Then I "go wild" and attempt to key the actual *pegasei* inside the sphere—there are at least two or three "packed" in each.

Help me, please, yes! An individual quantum being calls out to me.

But it is not working. Not sure what I was thinking to even try.

You cannot key us, because we are complex entities, Arion replies to my unspoken question or general feeling of frustration.

"Then what do I do? What, What?" I cry out in my mind.

I do not know.

I look around desperately, listening to the pitiful clamor of voices, even as they sense my own despair, and beg me not to give up.

Please do not abandon us! Do not . . . do not . . . do not. . . .

"Five daydreams!" the captain tells me. He then points one of the troops to the nearest hover-light orbs the team brought with us. "Start packing up. Move them out to the tunnel—"

So hungry, so weak! Please, at least let us have some of your light! The nearest imprisoned *pegasus* begs me distinctly. Indeed, as the orb floats by, sweeping the sphere with its light, the plasma being inside fluctuates wildly and pulses brighter.

"Any progress?" Brie asks, stepping closer to me. She points at the sudden outburst of plasma in the sphere. "Did you do that? Poor bastard's trying to break out—or not."

I shake my head. "It's just very hungry and needs the light to feed. All of them do—they're all seriously malnourished and deprived here. Whoever's been maintaining them here as their 'sacred pets' or whatever has basically been neglecting them badly over the centuries."

"Centuries?" Brie whistles.

"Yeah, centuries, eons," I add. "Since Landing."

"Holy rotten crap. . . . They live that long?"

"Longer. But, enough chit-chat. I have to think hard," I say. "How to melt those dratted dimensional bubbles. Or at least leave them with extra light until we can come back to them later, maybe—"

"Yeah, maybe install some decent lightbulbs in this hole." Brie checks her gun holster. "Getting ready to move out."

"Okay. . . ." I sigh sadly, and the *pegasei* pick up my sorrow and echo it.

"I'll come back, I promise," I mind-speak, addressing the cavern. "I am so sorry. We'll leave you with some light to feed and warm you at least—"

And then I stop.

Warm you.

How do you melt ice? You warm it. You heat it up.

How do you warm a living being? You nourish it. Give it fuel to burn!

And when things heat up, they *expand.*

In my mind Arion suddenly laughs with palpable joy. *You plan to pop the dimensional bubble—from the inside!*

"Light!" I exclaim loudly. "Captain, may we have light here!"

"Imperial Lady Gwen?" He turns to me. "We're done here. We are going now, no time—"

"No! Just take a few moments! If it doesn't work, I promise, we'll go! Give me all your flashlights, your flares, anything and everything you have! Tell your people—turn them all on and shine them directly at all these spheres! Please just *do* it!" I speak authoritatively, almost using a compelling voice, but hold myself back from that unauthorized level of power. . . .

The captain meets my gaze and sees my determination. "All right, everyone, attention! We need more light here!" He barks out an order, and at once there is mayhem, as troops still remaining in the chamber double back from the exit and start taking out their portable light sources.

In seconds, the cavern lights up.

Joy, joy, joy! The voices of the *pegasei* cry out from their confinement.

Nourishment!

In just a few heartbeats, the plasma contents of the spheres start pulsing wildly, glowing brighter and brighter, becoming incandescent, as they actively absorb all the light presented to them.

Another few heartbeats . . . and then comes the first *implosion-explosion*.

There's no other way to describe it, as one brilliantly glowing sphere suddenly collapses in on itself even as it appears to explode outward—as the adjacent *dimensions* invert and then invert again, riffing off each other like oil and water, sending out gravity waves which are forced to travel in a paradox of opposite directions simultaneously. . . . At the same time, the living contents packed inside swell and expand and overtake their bonds, destroying them in the process—and are suddenly set free.

The cavern hall is rocked by explosions of glorious light. . . .

One after another, the spheres pop like fiery soap bubbles and disintegrate, releasing their *pegasei*. The plasma unfurls with rainbow colors—for the first time in more than nine thousand Atlantean years—as the newly liberated *pegasei* test their freedom, some cautiously, others flinging themselves like living bellows across multiple dimensions at once.

Freedom! Freedom! they cry in exultation. *Joy! Joy!*

Love!

Their cries of torment have become ethereal song.

The *pegasei* soar to illuminate the cavern ceiling, disappear, reappear, circle the humans below.

Thank you, Gwen Lark who is Kassiopei! Thank you . . . friend!

"Holy . . . unbelievable . . ." Brie mutters with her mouth open, craning her head to look up at the fireworks overhead.

"Mission objective accomplished," Captain Siduaz says with satisfaction, looking up also, then nods to me. "Let's head out immediately. Because the mission itself is not done until we make it back safely."

I nod, because he's right.

Remember us as we will remember you!

As we enter the narrow tunnel at a jog, I turn around one last time to see the light show. The cavern expanse still sparkles with plasma, as the *pegasei* swirl and teem in place, bidding a strange, bittersweet farewell to their long-time home, lingering near the familiar rocky walls, craggy ceiling. But one after another, the quantum beings start to leave the cavern. Soon all that will remain will be a few ancient, inadequate light sconces and the eerie golden mist on the ground. . . .

We hurry through the tunnel toward the mountain entrance. As I jog next to Tuar, with Blayne flying on his board behind me, and Claudia, Brie, and Li Jie bringing up the rear, I feel a buoyant joy swelling inside me for a job well done, together with infinite relief.

After all, we just freed the last of the captive *pegasei*. This is monumental. We are now this much closer to sealing that Earth rift and possibly solving our alien problem.

Even as I think this, I hear the *zing-zing* sound of gunfire up ahead.

Apparently, the hostiles are here, and the PRT unit has engaged them.

"Ah, crap, here we go," Brie says. As I glance behind her, I see her and others holding their various guns ready. Reluctantly I reach for my own gun that everyone insisted I carry for this mission.

Up ahead, I hear the captain's hard voice issuing orders. Gunfire has gotten louder and, within a few more seconds, it is suddenly all around us.

"Helmet on! Secure your helmet!" I hear Claudia's voice directly behind me.

I realize I'm still carrying it in my arms like an idiot, and so I comply. Claudia gives me a crisp nod.

Boy, is this different, I think. *Claudia is different.*

We move at a run now, and I see more and more troops from our own PRT unit converge on us, as they abandon their lookout posts interspersed at intervals along the tunnel.

Then, we're at the entrance.

Our troops have set up a small hand-shield barricade, and are firing large caliber guns out at the nearest shrubbery. They are answered by volleys of return fire from invisible assailants. The locals are hiding nearby.

"Down, down!" The captain issues orders to us as we arrive. "Stay close to the ground, move as one, at my command. Stay *down!*"

I crouch down near to the ground, behind the shields wall, next to some unnamed PRT operative. He—or she—is firing with their back to me.

Even as I remain down, I see Tuar come up behind me and unfurl a clear, additional shield over my head like an umbrella.

Shades of the Games—day one, Stage One, in particular. Intense combat memories come over me.

Aeson is really going to hate this situation I'm in—we're in— right now, I think.

If anything happens to me . . . oh lord, poor Aeson.

No, stop, I tell myself. *We're getting out of here.*

". . . Onyx 2, report on your location." The captain is speaking urgently into his wrist comm. "This is Imeier 1, we are taking heavy fire at the cave mouth. I repeat, Onyx 2—"

I exchange quick glances with Tuar, Brie, Blayne.

". . . Ten daydreams is insufficient, make it seven; we are under heavy fire here. We need you to create a distraction from the southwest. . . . Onyx 3 and Onyx 1, proceed to these co-ordinates and engage hostiles from the rear. Remain in sniper positions only." And then the captain looks at me. "Imperial Lady, we are going to try to break through toward that tree line and proceed downhill toward the ship, but first we need to clear the way."

"Okay," I say.

"My SPC orders are that your safety is priority one. If we cannot achieve the break safely in the next five daydreams, we will need an extraction. We will retreat back inside the tunnels and hold position until reinforcements arrive. I'm informing the Commander of our present status—"

Oh no! I think, *Aeson is going to go insane with worry! And he's in the middle of another crisis. Not to mention, he'll never allow me to go anywhere on my own again and make me wear a cowbell around my neck. . . .*

Yeah, I know, not a good time to be funny.

"Can you please hold off on that?" I ask. "Please don't tell my husband just yet—"

"Imperial Lady, I'm sorry, but I have my orders—"

A long volley of fire interrupts us. There's the sound of small pebbles ricocheting off the rock wall and collapsing near the right of the entrance. This can get really bad, really fast, and we could end up buried in the tunnel. . . .

A crazy idea comes to me.

"Captain, did I hear you say you need a *distraction?*"

"Yes, we need to draw the hostiles away from our position long enough to move out," he says, pausing to fire in response, then glances back at me.

I take a deep breath. "I might have a distraction for you," I say.

And then I sing the frequency to call the *pegasei*.

As I sing, I communicate the immediacy of our problem to the *pegasei*, sending images of us being surrounded, and the enemy firing at us. "Just need a little help," I mind-speak. "So that we can go home."

We will help you, friend Gwen Lark who is Kassiopei!

And even before I'm done expressing my thoughts, there are multiple disturbances in the air all around us. Flashes of brilliant, colored plasma erupt from different points in the small clearing around the mouth of the cave and swell into a single great maelstrom of colored light. And they fall like meteors at the shrubbery and the precise areas where the local armed hostiles are hiding with their arsenals. Loud human cries are heard as the enemy stops firing in confusion.

The day is not bright at all—partially overcast, and there's still that drizzle—but there's more than enough Hel daylight radiance to feed the *pegasei*. And they take advantage of every photon to fuel themselves brightly.

"Nice! You did this?" Tuar asks near my ear, still holding the shield over me.

But the captain only nods at me and then exclaims to the troops, "Move out! Move out! Head for the tree line! Move *now!*"

The troops ahead of us pick up their long hand-shields and race forward in front of us.

Keeping as low to the ground as possible, we follow.

We run along a gradual decline, past the tree line, then continue onward toward the ship, a small dark rectangle hanging in the distance, silhouetted against the pearl sky. The *pegasei* swirl in the air everywhere, and now shots resume as the hostiles realize this is only a distraction.

"Thank you!" I mind-speak to the *pegasei*.

Keep running! I hear them reply in my mind. *Not safe yet, keep moving, friend!*

"Move, move!" The captain continues to direct the PRT unit troops, who now surround us in a tight defensive circle, with me, my guards, and the six pilots in the center.

Laser fire continues to ring out from many directions, but it's all behind us. This elite unit is very well armored, and no one is seriously hurt, but I can smell the superficial burns on uniforms and outer armor layers. Noxious fumes and smoke rise all around, following us, as the wind tears at us in strong gusts.

We make it back to the *ankhurat* in record speed. The captain drops the quantum plasma force field around the spacecraft, and the troops race up the ramp.

Breathing hard, I run between Brie and Darius, with Tuar and Claudia behind me, followed by more troops, just as new hostiles arrive, and sudden new gunfire erupts in the vicinity.

"Move it, move!" I hear Tuar exclaim, as he is hit from behind by a plasma weapon. Then I feel someone shoving my back, hard, and at the same time hear Claudia cry out directly behind me.

Both of them stagger after me, followed by a least five more troops, all of them variously hit.

Crap! Crap!

My heart is pounding as I regain my own footing and stare wide-eyed at all of them, at their conditions. . . .

Once everyone is inside, they quickly seal the entrance, and four pilots sprint to the four corners of the ship to take their flight positions. This time Darius and Brie take the front corners, while Yana and Li Jie take the rear.

"All right! Take this Ankh out of here!" Captain Siduaz commands loudly, dropping into his chair in the center. And then he adds into his comm, "*Pegasei* Retrieval Khenneb Mission, this is Imeier 1, primary objective achieved; we are heading home."

The four pilots begin to sing the flight sequence.

Temples pounding, and breathing laboriously from the long, adrenaline-fueled run, I fall into one of the chairs and see Tuar and

Claudia both sit down across from me. Claudia is holding her left arm, and there's blood on her uniform. Tuar has a large scorch line running down his right shoulder and back, but I see only molten *viatoios* and no blood.

"Are you okay?" I ask worriedly.

Tuar nods. "Clean surface burns. Not a big deal. Buckle in, Imperial Lady Gwen."

"And you?" I turn to Claudia with a frown.

She nods. "Yeah, fine, it got cauterized ... Imperial Lady Gwen."

Seconds later, Blayne slips off his board and sits next to me, looking grim, and stashes his compact board on the floor at his feet. He appears unharmed, but is soot-covered like the rest of us.

"Looking a little smoky, Blayne," I whisper with a little smile—even as I feel the ship taking off and the pull of gravity flattening me in my seat.

"Oh, yeah." He pushes back some unruly hair from his forehead, and there's a spark of humor in his blue eyes as he, too, holds on against the g-forces. "Add some chicory barbecue sauce, and I'm your dinner."

"Me too," I reply.

The *ankhurat* rises hard.

Safe now! The voices of the *pegasei* sound in my mind, and then in a corkscrew of surreal notes their double helix song recedes.

"Goodbye, my friends," I think-say gently in their wake.

And then my gaze returns to Claudia. Her face looks tense with pain, but her arm is showing no additional bleeding, so the laser burn must have cauterized her wound indeed.

"Speaking of dinner, I could use some barbecue chicken about now," Claudia says through gritted teeth.

Suddenly it occurs to me, *she* pushed me hard from behind—just as she got hit.

And it wasn't a bully thing.

Claudia took the gunfire intended for me.

Chapter 90

When we get back to *Atlantida*, it's close to third hour of Khe. The *ankhurat* lands in the Imperial airfield in Poseidon, and I say my thanks to the captain and the PRT unit for their incredible support. Then, surrounded by Tuar and my guards, I head for the main Palace building.

Here is where things get really crazy.

We exit the elevator on our floor. My guards are dismissed at the doors—to take their well-deserved shift break—while I enter the Prince's Quarters. I don't bother changing out of my sooty uniform and head directly for the workroom to inform Aeson that everything went as planned.

I half-expected the SPC command center to be filled with people. What I did not expect was for it to be packed with *daimon*, other SPC officers, *and* Imperial Executive Council members.

Aeson is standing in the middle of this crowd in his usual spot before the largest hovering screen, arms folded, a grim expression on his face. Conversation is subdued, and everyone is watching the scene unfolding on the screen.

They are looking at Tammuz. The planet is a large, rust-red sphere in the viewscreen, vaguely reminiscent of Mars in color, though closer to Earth in size, according to the display grid values.

A brightly shining metallic object in the now familiar X configuration is superimposed against the reddish surface background. It is the Tammuz Station. On the other side of the view, a portion of another immense object is visible, the oval end of a spacecraft, most of it off-screen. I know enough now to recognize it as War-8, the battle barge posted at Tammuz.

". . . energy fluctuations are . . . now spiking . . . strongly discernable on the x-ray range . . . passing to gamma ray range . . ."

The transmission is coming in short bursts, interspersed with crackle on the audio equipment.

"Nomarch Cretheo, we are having trouble receiving you," an *astra daimon* at one of the active stations says. "Please repeat."

I advance into the room, moving closer toward Aeson, who notices and turns his head in my direction. At the sight of me his tense expression shows a moment of supreme relief and a smile. He widens his eyes and nods at me, but without leaving his post—this is how I know that the situation is extremely serious.

I smile back at him and nod my head in response, mouthing the words "everything is okay," but don't dare to bother him beyond that. Now I'm more glad than ever that my PRT unit didn't have to call for extraction help at a time like this. . . . Aeson doesn't need to know about our narrow escape in Khenneb—at least for the moment.

"What is happening?" I ask the nearest person I know who isn't as urgently occupied with data in that moment as the others.

Gennio hears me and looks up from reassembling a gadget on the side desk. "Sorry, not sure, my Imperial Lady," he says quietly. "I believe Tammuz Station is picking up the same radiation spikes as they had at Septu Station just before the alien light grid started to form."

"Oh, no," I whisper.

"Yes, bad sign." Gennio rubs his forehead with the back of his hand and without setting down his tools. "At least the station is already evacuated. Station Nomarch Cretheo forced everyone off station half an hour ago. He's the only person left on board, and he's sitting in the shuttle bay inside an *ardukat* with one other crew, ready to flee. That's why their comm transmission is so poor—dual shield interference."

"I see. What about the station personnel, are they all on War-8?"

"Yes. Everybody is on War-8, ready to leave. But they have Pilot fighters set to try some things first, once the grid formation starts."

"So they think they can stop it somehow?" I ask. "Nothing worked the last time."

Gennio appears grim. "I don't know."

"It's all *shebet*, nobody knows anything," Anu says in that moment, taking a nearby chair and pulling up a mech arm monitor attached to the desk. "They should just leave while they can."

I take a deep breath and turn my attention back to the large screen.

The Station Nomarch's transmission continues to cut out periodically as he reads off the local radiation values. Meanwhile, here in the control room, the *daimon* are running correlation programs on the data.

And then suddenly it happens.

Out of nowhere a single pinpoint of golden light appears on the lower bottom of the viewscreen, superimposed against the blackness of space. The pinpoint grows and then flares into a sphere which is comparable in size to an ark-ship. It hangs in space, motionless and inevitable.

"Setting countdown now," Radanthet says at one of the stations.

Aeson immediately taps his wrist comm. "Command Pilot Ungreb," he says. "You are advised, we have initiated the countdown clock. Synchronize and prepare for activity."

Moments later, another golden light sphere pops into existence. The interval between it and the first sphere is hard to gauge because it is partially off-screen. "Zooming out 20%, changing perspective," Keruvat says. And now the view shows a wider angle.

The second sphere takes its position and remains motionless, suspended. It is terrifying in its inactivity.

In the workroom, concerned whispers rise, as Council Member Takhat expresses his alarm, and ACA Director Hijep Tiofon and First Priest Shirahtet both reply in comforting tones. "War-8 is equipped with the best technology and Pilots," Director Tiofon is saying. "Trust them to have a solid new strategy in this."

"What strategy?" Lord Arao Hetepheret says bitterly. "You've seen it—our weaponry is completely ineffective against these things."

I watch Aeson's profile as he continues to observe the scene at Tammuz and does not react to the IEC member comments.

Meanwhile, the grid formation continues to build. A third sphere appears and positions itself at the same interval as the previous ones. Then a fourth, a fifth. . . .

They keep coming.

"How long until it is completed?" I notice the speaker is the elderly Dame Tammuz Akten, seated off to the side and watching anxiously.

"At this projected rate, we estimate less than an hour," Nergal Duha says from his station.

"Command Pilot Ungreb, proceed with your weapons trials now," Aeson says into his wrist comm.

"Zooming out to 50%," Keruvat says, and the viewscreen again changes to another buoy camera, widening the panorama and showing the entirety of War-8's immense hull, together with the rapidly growing alien grid.

There is noticeable vessel activity. We see tiny dots of SPC fighter ships eject from the battle barge and begin maneuvers around the grid.

"This is Poseidon Command Imperial Quarters," Erita says at her station a few feet away from me. "Pilots, report."

A small crackle on audio, then we hear Xelio's voice. "This is Shamash, Red Pinion Leader, reporting. Approaching hostile elements now."

Apparently Xelio is on site for this operation, and I feel an immediate stab of worry for him.

"Shamash, switching to your *mafdet* perspective now," Erita says.

And now we see a close up of the grid from a rapidly moving solo-fighter ship perspective. Xelio's fighter hurtles at a dizzying speed past the grid elements, and around him are several other *mafdets*, flying in formation.

"This is War-8 Command. Red Pinion, proceed with strafing, stage one." The command issuer voice is not someone I recognize.

"Acknowledged, War-8. This is Red Pinion Leader to Red Pinion, engaging hostiles now."

"This is Ixion, reporting." Another voice I vaguely recognize comes on the audio—I struggle to think who it is and realize it's Quoni Enutat. "Firing mixed frequency array now. Accounting for matter refraction angle. Red Pinion, be advised of possible friendly fire."

"This is Bast, reporting," Oalla's confident voice sounds. "Preparing to strafe on command. Ixion, be advised, I am on your tail."

So, Oalla is there too!

And the next moment one of the *mafdets* on Xelio's perspective, right, sends out an intermittent burst of plasma fire in the direction of the nearest alien light sphere.

It suddenly makes sense why Quoni just sent out a warning of friendly fire. The plasma burst originating from his *mafdet* enters the sphere, and immediately it *refracts* at an angle and shoots right *back* in the direction of the SPC fighters. They swerve, narrowly avoiding the plasma.

It's that same dimensional matter refraction phenomenon at work.

"Same situation as before," Aeson says coldly.

The other *mafdets* in the Pinion formation also proceed to fire, choosing different light spheres as targets. Their fire is again returned to them like dimensional boomerangs.

So they try different firing patterns. Different frequency modulations.

Same result.

All the while, the alien grid formation continues to build around them.

"Grid formation now at 67.8% complete," Erita says, with a glance at Aeson.

"When it reaches 85%, prepare to abort weapons trials maneuvers," Aeson says. Then he taps his wrist comm and repeats the order to War-8. "Command Pilot Ungreb, abort maneuvers at 85%, retreat at 90% grid formation."

"War-8 Command, acknowledging."

The next few minutes are tense as we continue to stare at the screen and see the *mafdets* attempt to penetrate the enemy defenses, to no avail.

"Extremely depressing," Dame Tammuz mutters from her seat. "I see hope dwindling for the human race."

"This is Shamash to Red Pinion, fire in tandem, quadrant pattern. . . ."

Plasma bursts fill the viewscreen from all directions, as *mafdets* continue to strafe.

"Grid formation now at 73%," Erita warns.

". . . Babi, watch out! Sphere forming on your rear! Ixion, hard right . . . Bast, drop below, repeat . . . Nepht, another sphere forming, bank left . . ."

At this point, the process of new sphere occurrences and grid formation appears to be speeding up. It is a grim parallel to the process at Septu when the grid accelerated toward the end.

"Grid formation now at 84%," Erita says.

Aeson exhales loudly, then calls War-8. "All right, this is not working—Command Pilot Ungreb, cease operation and retreat from sector. We're done here."

The next moment, Command Pilot Lafaoh Ungreb's resigned voice sounds on the speakers, "This is War-8 Command, calling all ships. Cease all weapons trials operations and return home. We are leaving the sector in five daydreams."

"This is Shamash, Red Pinion Leader, acknowledging." Xelio's voice comes rough with disappointment. "All units disengage, I repeat, disengage."

"This is Ixion, let me try one more thing," Quoni's calm voice comes with a brief crackle.

We still have Xelio's perspective on screen, and he banks hard to follow the flight of another *mafdet* that must be Quoni, as he hurtles forward in parallel to the grid formation.

"Ixion, what are you doing? Disengage *now*."

But Quoni's *mafdet* continues moving on its course, flying to the active edge of the grid where it is presently forming. He passes the last sphere that just appeared from a pinpoint in space, and then keeps going—advancing the exact interval distance to the spot where the *next* sphere will form.

Here Quoni's *mafdet* comes to a hard stop. It hangs in space, perfectly motionless—a plasma-enveloped tiny needle in the haystack of space—a mere dot of violet brightness compared to the row of great golden spheres lining up behind it—and yet pulsing with its own purple plasma force field. . . .

"*Bashtooh,* Ixion! Get out of there now!" Xelio commands in a hard voice.

"What the hell is he doing?" Radanthet shakes his head.

"No . . . no! He's going to be incinerated! Or crushed!" Erita slams her palm against the desk surface, hard.

"This is Ixion," Quoni's absolutely composed voice sounds, and for the first time there is a hint of humor in his no-nonsense tone. "If I'm right, you're buying me drinks in Poseidon. If not, tell my brother and uncle that I went to meet my ancestors in a golden flash of light, thinking of them fondly."

"Quoni, you crazy *hoohvak*," Keruvat breathes.

But Aeson is staring and shaking his head, even as everyone else is frozen in terrible anticipation.

Because in moments, there will be another alien light sphere object forming at the exact coordinates which Quoni's *mafdet* is now occupying. What will happen? What *can* happen?

I put my hand over my mouth. My pulse races with horror at what's about to take place, but I am unable to look away. . . .

The moment when the next sphere should explode into being from a pinpoint of light is *now*.

The moment comes and goes.

There is nothing.

Quoni sits inside his *mafdet* in the alien formation.

He is now a part of the grid.

And the grid has *stopped* forming.

There are loud exclamations of relief and even laughter in the SPC command room.

"I can't believe he did this!"

"Is it over? Did he contain the grid formation?"

"Too early to tell—"

I exclaim along with everyone else, and Aeson turns to me briefly with new energy in his eyes and a hopeful expression—the most hopeful he's been in days.

"This is War-8 Command, it is quite a new development. Inquiring how to proceed?" The voice of Command Pilot Ungreb sounds on the speakers.

"This is SPC Command, hold your retreat, maintain your position for now," Aeson replies.

"Shamash to Red Pinion, all units hold position. Ixion, your status? Report immediately!"

"This is Ixion, I'm still here. No energy fluctuations at my coordinates."

"Ixion, this is Tefnut," Erita says from the workroom. "If you get back to Poseidon and you are still not dead, I will kill you myself."

Keruvat chuckles.

Seconds tick, as we watch the now dormant, unfinished grid, with Quoni positioned at its end.

And then suddenly something new happens.

The grid elements start to *rearrange* themselves.

Not all of them, just the ones that are at certain end locations that determine the very geometry of the diamond shape.

Those few spheres relocate at high speed and begin forming a *new* grid, a few mag-heitar from their original location. Quoni's position is now meaningless as his *mafdet* remains sitting in space, alone.

Oh, crap. . . .

"It's resumed building the diamond formation," Aeson says bitterly. But then he takes a deep breath. "But now we know at least one thing can be done to affect it."

Aeson makes another call to War-8. "This is the SPC Commander. I want to see how long you can keep this grid from completing itself. Dispatch all fighters to engage in blocking maneuvers, the same way as Pilot Quoni Enutat. Let's try to prevent each new element of the grid before it can form by taking its position in the grid."

And for the next hour there is absolute mayhem, as SPC Fleet ships play a crazy boardgame with the alien enemy around the orbit of Tammuz.

Each time one of the Atlantean ships slips into position and blocks the alien building process, the grid pauses a few moments, then begins to re-form nearby. It happens over and over, and with each new iteration the grid starts to re-form a little faster. . . .

It's almost as if it's *learning*.

Everyone here in the workroom SPC command center, and around Tammuz, on board War-8, watches in grim fascination.

"Now 86% complete. Even with our fancy blocking maneuvers there are new spheres being added, one way or another—so the grid object is still growing overall." Erita says.

"It appears to be taking into account our own flight speed," Keruvat observes. "These grid elements are rearranging their formation too fast for us. . . . Soon, our ships will be unable to keep up."

Aeson nods. "And—the time is now." He then calls the Command Pilot of War-8 and orders him to abandon the operation and retreat immediately.

"Retreat confirmed," Command Pilot Ungreb responds. "We put up a good fight."

Moments later we watch the SPC fighters abandon their action at the grid and race back to War-8.

With no more ships blocking its progress, grid formation now resumes in full force.

This time, however, the grid is still incomplete, in the final stages of forming, when War-8 receives all ships—including the *ardukat* safely bearing Station Nomarch Cretheo—and taxies outward from the orbit of Tammuz, leaving the evil alien grid and the completely empty Tammuz Station behind.

The immense battle barge accelerates into Quantum Stream space just in time to avoid the blinding supernova of white that comes from the completed alien grid as it begins its feast of destruction. . . .

Fire rains upon Tammuz Station. Its debris fills the orbit of Tammuz with orange, persimmon and coal-red plasma—bright and strangely beautiful against the rust-red planetary surface features far below.

"No one got hurt this time," Keruvat says softly in the suspenseful silence of the workroom.

"Yes, but think of all that property damage," ACA Director Tiofon says, shaking his head. "How many billion *iretar* are lost with all that station technology going up in flames? I shudder to think. . . ."

And we continue to watch, thoughtful and mesmerized by the apocalyptic destruction.

For as long as they are functional, the remaining space buoy cameras show us the infernal red sight—long after the Tammuz alien grid is dormant again, like a grim harbinger of what else is to come.

Chapter 91

L ater that night, after my husband finally has the opportunity to escape the endless SPC meetings, the political fallout, and the rest of the business of this very rough day, Aeson and I eat a private *niktos* meal together, just the two of us. That's when I tell him about the *pegasei* mission at Khenneb.

"The *pegasei* are all free now, Aeson," I say with energy. "We definitely got the last of them liberated from this most ancient, horrible, weird confinement you can imagine. . . . They were starving." And I describe the collapsed-dimensional "bubbles" forged as a result of ancient humans unsuccessfully trying to make another dimensional rift here on Atlantis.

Aeson pays sharp attention at once.

"Those cruel people must've figured out that withholding light was the way to keep the *pegasei* permanently weak and imprisoned. Or maybe they just didn't have a clue. In any case, we gave the *pegasei* tons of light to feed on, and they expanded in mass and volume and burst the confinement bubbles in the process," I conclude. "Not sure if any of this is helpful to know—for our greater problem."

"You mean, in terms of the *matter refraction* phenomenon?" He nods. "Yes, it does indeed suggest some kind of quantum-level similarity to the spheres in the alien light grid."

"Maybe if you fed those alien grid objects a bunch of light they would also explode?" I make a dumb joke, trying to get Aeson to smile after this long, horrible day of depressing events at Tammuz.

But it's not working.

Aeson has been immersed in a sea of quiet, thoughtful despair, ever since what happened at Tammuz. Yes, no one died today, but the cumulative result is still unrelieved futility.

Aeson knows that Ishtar and the outpost there are next in line for the alien attack.

And then, Atlantis.

"At least now the *pegasei* will travel back along the wormhole into the rift on Earth," I say with another attempt at optimism. "Once the rift is closed, who knows, maybe these alien grids will stop coming."

"Maybe," Aeson says softly, taking a swallow from his glass of *qvaali*.

I stand up from my seat at our little *niktos* meal table and go over to Aeson. I put my arms around him from the back and press my cheek against his, squeezing him tight, enveloping him in my warm, loving energy.

"Let's get some rest," I say.

The next morning is a new month. Red Mar-Yan dawns with its fierce promise of heat, and the promise of fiery apocalypse.

This month, Earth is scheduled to collide with the asteroid.

Red Mar-Yan 17, at eleventh hour and seventeen daydreams of Ra, Poseidon time—that's when, on the other side of the universe, Earth will suffer a cataclysmic asteroid impact, and all life will probably be obliterated.

Thanks to my Father-in-Law.

Of course, here on this side of the universe, Atlantis is likely going to be obliterated also, though the exact date of that critical attack is not known. It could be at the same time, or it could happen a few days or weeks later.

All we can safely guess is, based on whatever evidence is available, Ishtar is next—and then, *us*.

On some level I am just as resigned as Aeson is about the pending destruction of Atlantis.

But when it comes to Earth, for some reason I haven't given up hope. The circumstances there are different. If the *pegasei* manage to close the rift, then we can somehow convince the Imperator to redirect the asteroid off course. . . .

The thought of this gives me strength that morning—the morning of Red Mar-Yan 1—as I wake up holding Aeson in my arms.

Last night, we fell asleep quickly, after making love. But the night was difficult for him, and he had nightmares, starting awake with a gasp several times in the darkness, tossing and turning, breathing rapidly, moaning with pain, and I could feel the sheen of sweat on his brow.

I tried to do what I could, kissed and held him, and whispered words of relief. He told me repeatedly and bravely that he's fine, but I know better. The responsibility of SPC Commander weighs heavily upon him now, taking its toll when he is most vulnerable. . . . Even when he puts on a brave front, even for me—especially for me.

And this morning—with its promise of SPC business, constant rehashing of information, more endless meetings, and dealing with disclosure and the panicking public—is a resumption of the same stress hell. . . .

We drop by to have *eos* bread with Dad and George in their guest quarters, where just for a few minutes we'll fool ourselves that everything is okay with the world and all of us.

We eat hot savory dumplings in fragrant sauce, drink strong morning *lvikao*, and keep the TV feeds turned off, at Dad's request.

That is, until Devora Kassiopei shows up at the doors.

Aeson's mother has a distraught, strange expression on her face as she looks in on us, and her hands are clasped together in white-knuckled anxiety.

"I'm sorry to barge in," she says. "But, Aeson, if you would please come with me! There's something very wrong with your Father. He—he is very upset, more so than usual. This morning he had that *sarcophagus* delivered to our Quarters. And now he has locked himself in one of the bedrooms, and refuses to come out or even respond, and appears to be talking very *loudly* to someone. The servants don't dare to go in there or force the door—I'm afraid he will do something *ridiculous* to hurt himself."

Aeson stands up at once and throws me a brief look of alarm. I can see the stress being stifled as he forces a mask of calm upon himself. "Of course," he says. "I will check on him."

"I'll go with you," I hurry to say, rising from my seat.

Dad stands up also. "I'm coming too. This is . . . family, after all."

Devora throws him a grateful look.

George just downs his glass and stands up with the rest of us.

We hurry to the Imperial Quarters on the floor above, and the Imperial guards let us in immediately. The Imperatris walks before us, leading us past the imposing antechamber and through the interior corridors to the heavy mahogany and gold-embellished doors of what is likely a splendid chamber.

We don't know, because it's locked. An Imperial high servant stands nearby and bows silently to us.

The Imperator's deep, resonant voice comes in bursts of fury from the other side of those doors. He seems to be ranting, but the words are hard to distinguish. There is also the sound of footfalls, as he must be pacing rapidly back and forth.

Devora looks at all of us with despondent eyes, pointing to the room.

Aeson steps forward and knocks. "My Imperial Father, may I come in?" he says loudly. His own deep voice carries, and for an instant the Imperator's own voice goes silent.

And then the ranting resumes. It's a tumble of words, some of which can be heard out of context.

". . . gather in the sky . . . *bakris* and now what Kassiopei scourge will come . . . the book, the book, the damn *book* doesn't say, does it? Not so *everything*, is it now? Well? What does your book say . . . why did you leave me, old *shibet* fool . . . They are here and there is nothing . . . the end for Atlantis . . . nothing can stop them . . . why don't you just disappear? And you? You sit up there . . . pretty colors in the sky . . . even now, all of you looking down at me . . ."

The Imperator has gone mad, it occurs to me.

Aeson knocks again. "Father! Please let me in! I want to speak with you!"

"Maybe I should get the Venerable Shirahtet to try and reason with him?" Devora whispers. "He listens to him, heeds his advice—"

"Maybe get a doctor?" my Dad asks.

George steps forward and tries the door handle. "Is there a bolt on the other side?" he asks.

Devora shakes her head negatively.

Just then Aeson takes a deep breath and says in a thundering *compelling voice, "Father, open the door."*

Silence falls on the other side of the door.

A long pause.

And then the Imperator's mocking voice sounds: "You can't compel me, foolish boy. You love me."

Moments later, the door opens.

The Imperator stands on the other side, dressed haphazardly in a casual morning shirt and pants. An opulent bedchamber is revealed behind him, decorated in shades of dark brown, ebony, and red, with an oversized bed in the center—though not as large as the Crown Prince's Master bedroom, which suggests that this particular chamber is not the Imperial Master Suite.

A large balcony window stands open, draperies parted, letting in a warm breeze and the blinding morning light of Hel. It casts its brilliance upon the grand golden sarcophagus sitting off to the side before a tall-backed chair.

I recognize it immediately as the inner sarcophagus layer from the discovery on the Ghost Moon. The pure golden lid, etched with symbols and pictographs, has been lifted and set to lean upright against the wall. Revealed in the interior of the funereal box is its occupant. The strange, human-shaped ovoid jewel of deep indigo and violet hue lies in its inner cradle, containing the ancient body of Arlenari Kassiopei.

And then, as my gaze moves further, I notice that the bejeweled exterior sarcophagus is here too—sitting a few feet back, near the wall, encrusted with lapis and glass gems containing the micro-scrolls of the Book of Everything, cleverly hidden inside the glass.

So, the Imperator had the whole thing brought over here indeed.

The big question is, why?

"I am touched," the Imperator says quietly, raking us over with a complicated, sardonic gaze imbued with bitterness and sarcasm. "All of you here to see the crumbling of the Dynasty?"

Devora moves quickly past all of us and says, "Rom! What nonsense! What is happening, are you—how are you feeling—are you well?"

"Am I well? Am I *well*, my dear Wife? What a *bashtooh* question!" The Imperator glares at her. "I'm as well as I can be, with the end of *Atlantida* and humanity looming, and these colorful flocks of *pegasei* still hanging in the skies—"

He points to the window, where indeed we can see plasma colors painting the white daylight with rainbow hues, as the great flocks appear to fill the skies of Poseidon. "See them? Why? *Why* are they still here? We freed all of them as of yesterday, did we not, eh, boy? Or was I misinformed about that final PRT mission?"

He's right. Why are the *pegasei* still here? Why didn't they leave last night, going back through the wormhole and into the rift, as they promised?

Seriously, how did I miss seeing all the usual flocks still teeming everywhere, earlier this morning? I mustn't have looked out the window properly.

I frown and exchange quick glances with Aeson, who looks equally puzzled.

"The final PRT operation was a success, Father."

The Imperator exhales loudly in exasperation. "Well, come in, since all of you are here . . . ah, the Larks—remind me to schedule your noble rank bestowment ceremony, now that you've become adjacent to the Dynasty—though why bother, since we might only have a few weeks left to live." Romhutat moves back from the doorway and motions with his hand to his wife and the rest of us. "I can hope for better company than my dead ancestress here, lying in her ancient tree resin. She tells me absolutely nothing, no matter how many times I've asked."

We enter the bedroom, milling awkwardly. The Imperator pats Devora on the arm, even as she tries to take his hand, then resumes pacing around the sarcophagi and their lids. He moves closer to the balcony to stare up at the sky. "There they are. . . . So—Gwen, my daughter, you handled the latest mission, why haven't they left us?"

"I don't know," I say. "I thought they did."

"Things got busy yesterday, as you're aware," Aeson says in a cool voice. "The events at Tammuz took precedence. And today I have a full schedule."

"I am going to ask Arion right now," I say.

The Imperator throws me a piercing glance.

I try to ignore it and sing the unique frequency in my mind, visualizing my friend.

The air is displaced with a pop, and Arion's bright plasma essence unfurls in the chamber. Then he solidifies and becomes the little Sphinx.

Devora makes a little gasp. Meanwhile George and Dad watch with wonder, since it never ceases to amaze.

I am here, Gwen Lark who is Kassiopei, Arion speaks in my mind, and also speaks the words out loud, on behalf of the Imperator, the only one of us who still doesn't know the *pegasei* frequency.

"Why are you still here *is* exactly the question," the Imperator says.

"Arion," I mind-speak. "May I share your true means of communication with him? I am sorry, but he is not a good man. But it might be the right thing to do, now."

He is not a happy man, Arion replies with an echo of his own sorrow. *And yes, give him the frequency so that we may speak in fullness.*

"My Imperial Sovereign," I say. "Arion would like to speak with you *directly*."

And I teach the Imperator the frequency of the *pegasei*.

He repeats it at once.

And then he grows still and closes his eyes.

Finally, he is *speaking* with Arion.

Did I do the right thing? Did I make the right choice to connect them?

Aeson watches his father, then glances at me. I wonder if he too is doubting whether this was the right thing to do.

But then, all the *pegasei* are now free, about to leave us permanently. No one can force them to do anything ever again—so this was a harmless thing, saved for the very end.

The Imperator opens his dark blue eyes again. There is an interesting expression of clarity in them. He breathes slowly, pausing before speaking out loud in the normal human way.

I told him why we are still here. Arion speaks inside my mind. *He suspected it for a long time, it is why he has been so unhappy for so long.*

"And why is that?" I ask using mind speech.

There is a millisecond pause that is also as long as all the time in the universe, before Arion replies.

We were waiting for him.

I admit, I'm stunned.

"What? What do you mean you were waiting for him?" I ask. "But why?"

Sacrifice. Arion says. *He had to make the personal choice at last. No one can make it for him. Even now, he is in turmoil regarding what must be done, what he has to do.*

"Stop speaking behind my back in all your pretty, sparkling, clean minds," the Imperator says suddenly with a rueful laugh. "Now that I know what it's like—yes, it's expansive and glorious—stop conspiring around me."

"No one is conspiring, Rom!" Devora says with emotion.

"Ah, but you are, all of you," the Imperator says. "And it is quite amusing. But it matters very little, not now. So—the *pegasei* have confirmed for me what I already know. It is not enough that they must leave to properly close the rift. They must also take something with them—someone."

And Romhutat points at the sarcophagus of Arlenari Kassiopei. "She, this ancient female of my Dynasty, must be taken back to the Rim of Ae-Leiterra. There she must pass through the wormhole and into the rift on Earth—in effect, returning the *entangled quantum string* that is her essence—to be reunited with the remains of her twin brother Oron inside that rift. The powerful force of their entanglement, stretched across the cosmic expanse, was keeping it open all these eons, just as much as the *pegasei*. Only then will the dimensional rift seal itself."

"I am not sure I understand," Devora says. "What does this have to do with you, my Imperial Husband?"

The Imperator chuckles. I've never heard him sound so oddly relaxed. "Technically, it has very little to do with me," he says. "But practically, I must be the one to take her back there, into the Rim."

Devora's expression is tragic. "But why? Why *you?*"

"Fate, choices, cosmic mockery—indeed, *time itself.* All elements falling into place, call it what you will." The Imperator shakes his head with infinite humor.

"I still don't—"

The explanation is simple, Arion says within all of our minds. *We cannot carry physical objects of solid matter at a speed that exceeds physical parameters. We ourselves can move instantaneously, outside of your space-time. But to carry the physical body of Arlenari, we must travel at your human, finite speeds. It would take several months of fastest travel, approximating your Quantum Stream but not the Jump technology, for us to carry her to the center of your Coral Reef Galaxy, to the Rim of Ae-Leiterra.*

"But it would take me only a few days," the Imperator adds, "if I use the Quantum Jump without preliminary acceleration. And from there, the *pegasei* will take her inside the wormhole instantaneously the rest of the way."

"What?" Aeson exclaims. "No, Father, why would you do that? It's suicide!"

"I am Kassiopei, my Son, or have you forgotten?"

"It's suicide even for a Kassiopei!" Aeson persists. "Why would you need to do such a thing?"

"Because there is no time." The Imperator says coldly. "We, as a human species, have no time."

"We have plenty of time!" Aeson persists. "Assuming the next grid forms at Ishtar in approximately 40 days—or just over nine weeks from now—repeating the previous pattern, if you or I leave now, taking a fast velo-cruiser or *sebasaret*, we could be at the Rim with proper acceleration for the safe Jump, in just under seven weeks—"

"No," the Imperator says. "You cannot be at the Rim because in order to defeat our ancient enemy *you* will need to be somewhere else. And, for that matter, I cannot be at the Rim either because I will *first* need to be elsewhere myself. Then, I can make an instantaneous Jump and be at the Rim on the same day to complete what must be done."

"Rom, what are you talking about?" Devora asks, trembling.

"My Son, have you noticed the current planetary orbital alignment around Helios?" the Imperator says with energy, pacing around the room.

"Not in detail. . . . Maybe . . . I don't recall—but I'm certain my techs are keeping abreast of any anomalies or patterns." Aeson shakes his head in confusion. "How is that relevant?"

"Hah! For once you've been too busy to pay attention to everything. I cannot fault you on that. But—why don't you call up the orbital data now and take a look? And, say, project it 15 days forward."

"All right." Aeson taps his personal data unit and calls up a small holo-grid of the Helios system, in golden lights. Tiny model planets begin circling a tiny golden ball that is Hel, suspended inches above his wrist. "What am I looking for?"

"Take a look at the four inner planets, Rah, Septu, Tammuz, and Ishtar. Freeze them in place 15 days hence. What do you see?"

Aeson taps the hologram, and there is quick rotational movement, then the system stops, suspended at the chosen moment in space-time.

I stare, and even I can see the diamond shape formed by the four planets—draw a straight line from each tiny planet to its opposite one, cutting through Helios in the center, to get a perfect cross.

"So, the orbits are aligned this particular way," Aeson says thoughtfully.

"Yes, and it's going to be like this approximately 15 days from today," the Imperator says.

Aeson's lips part. *"Astroctadra,"* he says.

"Precisely," his father replies. "Coincidence? I doubt it. But what could it mean? A grand diamond formed at the exact coordinates where you will have the alien grids present—assuming Ishtar follows the same pattern as the others, of which I have no doubt. Now, think of the worst-case scenario."

"Ah, *bashtooh*," Aeson whispers. "Once they align, they are going to *fry* the whole Helios system."

Devora gasps.

The Imperator looks around at his wife, his son, at all of us slowly. "Not if we form our own greater *astroctadra* to stop them."

Chapter 92

There is a long pause as everyone present tries to grasp the implications of what the Imperator has just proposed.

"So . . ." Aeson reasons. "Six Logos Voices will be needed once again . . . people sent to six different coordinates to form the *astroctadra* alignment. Only this time the coordinates will not be local orbital points around the Ghost Moon, but around Helios itself."

"Correct," the Imperator says. "An immense undertaking."

"Forgive me if I'm missing something, Imperial Sovereign," Charles Lark, my father says suddenly. "But why does it have to be *you* specifically, who must take the ancient remains to the Rim of Ae-Leiterra? If it's so critical for you to be a part of this *astroctadra* alignment, in one of the six spots, why can't you assign your people—someone else from the Fleet—to manage the travel to the Rim?"

"Because only Kassiopei can do it properly." The Imperator turns to look at my Dad. "All Rim missions have been the traditional duty of this Dynasty since the beginning of time. A Logos voice and advanced training to control the Stationary Quantum Stream are needed to survive the black hole long enough to do the job. Yes, in theory, others with suitable Logos voices can be trained, but the honing of this skill requires time which again we don't have. Furthermore, the entire ugly schedule has now been sped up even more adversely for us."

"How so?" Dad asks.

"Instead of a projected 40 days before the next attack, we only have 15," Aeson says. "Based on this hunch, of course—we'll still need to run probability stats scenarios to confirm."

"Yes, yes, run your analysis, naturally. . . . Meanwhile we no longer have a choice in the matter of how to close the dimensional rift on Earth," the Imperator goes on. "All this time I put my trust in the asteroid to do the job, but its arrival is now too late to matter—"

"Yes!" I gasp. "Oh God! The asteroid! That's in *sixteen* days from now! But—but this *astroctadra* alignment of the alien grids and Helios system destruction is in *fifteen*—one day *before* the asteroid is supposed to arrive on Earth!"

"Yes, the irony does not escape me," the Imperator says bitterly. "Years of massive work, global plans set in motion, all for nothing. Assuming any of this closing-the-rift effort would've even made any difference as far as our ancient enemy is concerned."

My mouth falls open. "So then *stop* it! We can still save Earth from destruction! Stop the asteroid! Just redirect it! You no longer need it to strike those coordinates because the *pegasei* will close the rift for us!"

"For that to happen, I must urgently deliver this Arlenari to Ae-Leiterra, then hand off her remains to the *pegasei* and trust them to complete the mission."

We will complete it.

Arion's voice sounds in my mind—and presumably in the minds of everyone present.

"Please!" I say, continuing to stare at the Imperator. "Please save Earth!"

"My Father, at this point it would seem to be an easy decision for you to make," Aeson says. "Give your consent and I will contact the remaining Earth Mission vessel, AS-1999, and order Nefir Mekei to abort the command sequence—"

"No." The Imperator's impassive voice interrupts.

"What?" I exclaim. "Why not?"

"Indeed, my Husband, why would you say no? Why not agree to save all those poor people?" Devora puts in, and her expression is distraught. "I had no idea of these abysmal details, no notion that you had something to do with *directing* this asteroid in the first place! Unthinkable that you would perpetrate such evil upon our ancient home world, full of billions of lives!"

"A necessary evil," Romhutat says, looking at his wife with a fixed mask of an expression. "It was a plan conceived long before we had any other options."

"But now you have them!" Devora says in a voice of emotion. "Rom, I beg you, stop this atrocity!"

There is a pause of silence as we all stare at them.

"Regretfully, there's nothing I can do," the Imperator says. "When my Son and his then-Bride defied me on that fateful morning after the Games of the Atlantis Grail—threatening to fry the orichalcum technology in my Red Office—I gave in to my own anger. . . . I contacted AS-1999 and used my Logos voice across the universe to fry the orichalcum guidance system of the resonance chamber inside the asteroid. It is fixed in its present course now. . . ."

"Oh my God," I whisper.

"There may be other, less elegant means of redirecting it off course," the Imperator continues, "but voice control is no longer an option."

"Oh, Rom, Rom, what have you done?" Devora is shaking her head in disbelief.

But the Imperator does not meet her gaze. He now glances at me and then Aeson. "Very well, I give you permission to abort the Earth mission final protocol—whatever is left of it. Call Mekei and tell him that such are my orders—that he is to cooperate with you in whatever way possible. Do not look so glum, you still have weapons capability on AS-1999. The guidance program overrides may be gone, but you have our excellent technology at your disposal—now that it's no longer fighting *itself*, our own secret, anti-tampering programming as related to the asteroid. You'll come up with something."

Aeson's expression is cold with anger. "I will contact Mekei at once and see what can be done."

"Good. Now we can discuss our *local* defense options." The Imperator nods, almost relieved to change the subject from Earth to Atlantis.

"That would be SPC business," Aeson says in a hard voice. "Now that I've been alerted to this new set of information and the possibility of major activity happening on Mar-Yan 16, I'll have my techs run various projections and play with quite a number of data parameters before I can safely say this is the right course of action for us."

"Don't take too long," the Imperator says. "To set up the Helios-wide *astroctadra* alignment in opposition to the enemy grid *and* to mobilize most of this planet, you'll need to start the process immediately or you will not be ready in time—"

"No need to tell me how to do my job." Aeson cuts him off. And then he uses his wrist comm to start making arrangements with his SPC subordinates.

The Imperator mutters something about the sarcophagus and the *pegasei*. My Dad, George, and Devora all focus on him and his words. The Sphinx who is Arion rests on the floor in the classical position, observing all of us.

But I am only half-listening. . . . My mind is reeling with the implications, both horrified and hopeful, at what could be the potential fate of Earth.

The asteroid must be diverted.

There has to be a way.

While I think all these randomly hopeful, outlandish thoughts, my Dad walks over and starts to examine the sarcophagus and Arlenari herself. His fingertips brush against the etched golden surface of the lid with reverence. Then he bends down to stare closely at the ancient body miraculously encased in Pegasus Blood.

"So much history . . ." Dad whispers. "I wonder what she saw, this ancient girl. What wonders, with her own eyes. . . . Remarkable, to be so well preserved. Ancient Egyptians with their natron salt and oil-and-resin-soaked linen preservation methods would be so envious of this perfection."

"Like an insect in amber," George adds, looking down also.

Meanwhile, the Imperator stands with his back turned to us, watching the daylight in the window. Devora glances from him to us anxiously. She also looks down at the little Sphinx shape of Arion, and I assume she's communicating silently with him.

"I've set plans in motion," Aeson announces minutes later, looking up from his wrist comm. He looks at me. "I've notified Nefir Mekei of the change in mission plans. And just in case he does not take me at my word, I told him to confirm with my Imperial Father."

"Thank you, Aeson," I say, then throw a glance at the Imperator's back.

My husband nods. "It's a start. We will see what can be done for Earth when the time comes. But now we must deal with the urgent problem that is Atlantis."

It is hard to put into words the immense machinery of war and self-preservation that takes over when a highly advanced technological civilization is faced with the inevitability of destruction from an even more advanced source.

Atlantis—*Atlantida*—the planet of almost seventy nations and a billion people, is mobilizing for the greatest fight for survival it has seen in millennia. . . .

After we conclude the painful interaction with the Imperator in his chamber, Aeson leaves to begin the process of global defense that falls upon him as the SPC Commander. Meanwhile, the Imperator secludes himself for the rest of the day while he, too, prepares to face what must be done, to consider all options, and to accept what is a part of his own duties, both in the *astroctadra* alignment, and in the perilous journey with Arlenari's body to the Rim.

We have only fifteen days.

Fifteen days to prepare the Fleets across the globe for military action, to move the immense battle-barges in position around the Helios system, to deliver the six Logos voice wielders to the six different coordinates next to the alien grids in the biggest *astroctadra* alignment in human history.

So, what exactly will we be doing? The purpose of the grand *resonance procedure* that we're about to undertake with six Logos voices during the *astroctadra* alignment of the grids is to give us a fighting chance.

Our intent is twofold.

First, to *counter* and *contain* whatever energy forces the unified alien grids will "release" into the system at the moment of their attack with our own great quantum containment field—a kind of force field similar to the Great Quantum Shield around Ae-Leiterra.

Second, to bring the enemy out of the safety of their own dimensional bubble into our own space-time so that we can try to fight them with conventional weapons on our own terms.

Will it work? Can it work? Do we even know what we're doing, what we're up against? The saddest thing is, there are no guarantees.

No guarantees that any of our efforts will even make a dent.

The honest answer is, we simply don't know. There's no historical precedent for such military actions, and what we *think* we know is all based on faulty records and legends.

But we're going to do it anyway—because humanity must defend itself from annihilation.

So far, the Atlantean weapons have been entirely ineffective against the untouchable golden light spheres that reside in some other dimension. If—as in the case of the Ghost Moon—we can somehow manage to "bring them out" of that dimensional *otherwhere* into our present space-time reality, there is still no certainty that we can do enough damage to defeat them with ordinary physics.

And then, the Imperator's effort in conjunction with the *pegasei* to close the rift on Earth is also rife with uncertainty. There is no way of knowing that this will satisfy the alien enemy's demands. All we have are some inadequate ancient records of the Original Colony and mythic lore for the realities of Ancient Atlantis. Even Arlenari's Book of Everything is only one young girl's diary.

This is all there is by which to formulate our present planetary defense. That's putting a lot of trust into some very nebulous things under the guise of cultural tradition.

If I allow myself to think about it too closely, it's easy to go crazy with fear.

My family is right there with me, all of us trying not to think, not to imagine, simply trying to function. We have work to do.

Fifteen days.

As soon as Aeson issues the orders, the SPC analysts begin to run tests and data correlations of every sort. They officially confirm the probability and odds of the massive alien system-wide attack taking place on Red Mar-Yan 16. Then the experts repeat the tests, look at more data, alternate data, rerun numbers. This is done at various foreign locations by different think tanks, starting today, the morning of Red Mar-Yan 1. It goes on for the rest of the night and continues, for the sake of redundancies, on the day following—

even as global preparations begin to take effect before the data analysis is completed.

Global heads of state receive urgent notifications the same evening.

And now the public is being notified, and the media are in turmoil as they try to explain what is happening and what the plans for military defense are.

Fleet Pilots are being recalled to active duty, and this time Cadets are mobilized too.

All on the same day, all today, Red Mar-Yan 1, because there is no time to think it over, argue, or debate. Let the media do all that.

No time. . . .

Feeling numb and somehow aimless, I spend the rest of the day with Dad and George in their quarters. Manala inevitably comes by as she is newly informed of the situation, while Gracie and Gordie join us after work hours.

Four of us—Aeson, Gordie, Manala, and myself—will reprise our roles in the lineup of the six Logos voices needed in the *astroctadra* alignment. George will once again travel with Manala to lend his support. Gracie will be deployed with the other Cadets here, in planetary defense of Atlantis. And our Dad has volunteered to go on any ship with whichever one of us needs him most.

Furthermore, in this grand *astroctadra* scenario, the fifth Logos voice wielder will once again be Anen Qur, First Speaker of the Ennead of Ubasti, who has been urgently notified and has agreed at once.

And then, later in the evening, a bombshell is dropped. The Imperator has a problem. After painfully considering the situation, consulting with his inner circle of Shirahtet and others, it turns out—it's logistically *impossible* for him to do *both* the Rim mission and the *astroctadra*, no matter what he attempts—not even if he uses the unsafe quantum Jump to be in both places within a short period of time. Simply put, there is only time for a one-way trip to the Rim.

Therefore, as his Kassiopei duty, the Rim mission takes precedence. The Imperator will leave tomorrow, with Arlenari's remains, to travel at a high, unsafe speed to Ae-Leiterra.

Meanwhile, a different sixth person will have to be found with a Logos voice to take his place.

We are so screwed.

R emarkably, even later that very same night, the situation is saved by New Deshret. The Pharikon calls to say that while he himself is too old, his young relative and possible Heir to the Throne has a Logos voice and will be happy to take part in the *astroctadra* alignment. Princess Sheolaat Heru, daughter of his deceased younger brother, will make travel preparations at once.

"When were you going to tell me that you have a viable young Logos voice in the family?" the Imperator asks, staring at the Pharikon's wrinkled face in the screen, even as Aeson and I stand watching the exchange.

"It never came up," the old man replies with a crafty smile.

T he next morning, Red Mar-Yan 2, the Atlantean mobilization process begins in earnest.

I get up before seventh hour, after an agonizing, mostly sleepless night for both Aeson and me—we tossed and turned, holding and consoling each other all through the pre-dawn hours—and Aeson is already gone to deal with everything.

When I get to the family guest quarters, Dad has just awakened and is watching the media madness on the TV feeds with a resigned look on his face. Images of airfields filled with deploying Fleet Pilots all around the globe are interspersed with expert panels discussing military strategy, and the various alien grids are shown repeatedly against the backgrounds of Rah, Septu, Tammuz, and Helios itself.

George shows up, with tousled hair, from his own room. He's just in time for the *eos* bread service.

Then half an hour later, Manala arrives in a hurry, to let us know that her Imperial Mother, the Imperatris, is crying in her Quarters. . . . That's because even earlier this morning, at dawn, her Imperial Father left on a velo-cruiser with the ancient sarcophagus of Arlenari Kassiopei and *no one else*.

"He is all alone!" Manala exclaims, with desperate eyes. "Mother says he will have to pilot that ship by himself for nearly three weeks!"

I try to console Manala the best I can, even as George watches us intently with a grave expression, while pouring himself *lvikao*.

I'm glad George is not making any acerbic commentary right now, because Manala is so clearly missing the obvious, whether intentionally or not—not only is her father alone, but he will very likely not survive a mission where he has to make a quantum Jump with inadequate preliminary acceleration directly into the inferno of the black hole. . . .

Just then, I look up for some reason, and my gaze falls on the bright window and the fierce morning daylight outside. I notice the aurora borealis rainbow colors are missing from the skies over Poseidon.

The *pegasei* are gone.

Arion! I think with a stab of wistful sorrow. *He left without saying goodbye.*

But right in that instant a familiar plasma flash materializes in the room, and Arion's voice sounds inside my mind.

I am not gone yet, Gwen Lark who is Kassiopei, he tells me calmly, with a note of humor in his mind-voice. *I am here and there simultaneously, for as long as the rift remains open and we are on this side of it. Right now, others of my kind and I are traveling along with the Imperator on his physical transport vessel. I will continue to traverse the expanse of your space-time to be with you and with him for as long as I am able.*

"Promise you won't leave without a proper farewell," I whisper.

There is never a proper farewell. But I promise not to terminate our contact without your acceptance of the precise ending of our time together.

"I don't know what that means," I say—even though on some level I know precisely what it means. "But I appreciate it, Arion."

In a few hours, Aeson returns briefly to update us on the details of our situation.

"Aeson, what is happening?" I ask, speaking as gently as possible, even though I feel like screaming from unresolved stress.

And he tells us.

In short, we leave for the *astroctadra* mission on Red Mar-Yan 6, four days from now. Until then, all the preparations are being made, and the battle barges that will ferry us to our destinations are being readied with supplies and personnel.

War-1, recently transferred from its usual post in the outer system, around Atlas, is currently in high orbit around Atlantis. It will remain here, under the command of Manakteon Resoi, serving as the last line of defense for Atlantis. Most of the Cadet Pilots will be assigned to serve under its oversight. That includes Gracie and my *shìrén* friends.

War-2, also recalled from its similar post in the outer system, is parked here in Atlantis orbit waiting for *me*. Commanded by Amaiar Uluatl of New Deshret, War-2 is going to take me to my *astroctadra* position coordinates outside the normal rotational plane of Helios.

Let me explain that.

Most orbiting systems exist along a largely flat orbital plane—a kind of pancake or flattened spinning disc—along which galaxies, planets, and other planetary objects and space junk rotate. There are exceptions of course, when individual satellites might have unusual orbits, deviating at weird angles from the standard plane.

Now imagine the *astroctadra* shape. It is a four-point star in three dimensions, which means that two of its six points are perpendicular to the four others. Think of the children's game of jacks—the "jack" shape is a little *astroctadra*, except two of its opposite spokes are a little different from the other points. The spokes are blunt and thick—so it's easy to balance the jack on them, and it could even stand upright. If a jack shape were a solar system, then those two blunt spokes would be perpendicular to the jack's orbital plane—one directly below, the other directly above the "sun" in the system's center.

One of those two blunt "spokes" (perpendicular to the orbital plane of Helios) is my destination.

I get to board War-2 and go hang out in that weird, super-empty space outside the rotational plane.

Another person with a Logos voice gets to do the same thing on the opposite "spoke." And that lucky person is Manala. War-6, normally stationed around Atlantis and commanded by Uru Onophris of Ptahleon, will take Manala (and my brother George, and Consul Denu, and Xelio Vekahat) to the opposite side of the orbital plane of Helios, directly across from my own coordinates.

Manala and I get to be the thick spokes of a jack game piece, sitting in the middle of nowhere, while the Hel system with all its planetary junk rotates like a spinning plate *between* us.

Meanwhile, the other four people in our great *astroctadra* alignment will take the four positions along the standard orbital plane of Helios, forming a great diamond, with Rah, Septu, Tammuz, and Ishtar as the four points.

War-8, which newly escaped the destruction at Tammuz, will return there, under the command of Lafaoh Ungreb of Bastet, carrying my brother Gordie on board. The recently formed grid there is inert at the moment, and Gordie will be there to perform his part of our voice command sequence before it "wakes up" again to wreak massive destruction as predicted on Red Mar-Yan 16.

War-3, normally stationed around Olympos, but recently moved even further out near Atlas, has been ordered to return urgently to Atlantis to pick up Anen Qur. Command Pilot Chudo Batiaxaat of Ubasti is in charge of War-3 and is being tasked with ferrying their own First Speaker to his designated coordinates near the alien grid at Septu, where Anen Qur will take his part in the *astroctadra*.

War-5, stationed around Atlantis under the command of Selmiris Teth of Vai Naat, will be taking Princess Sheolaat Heru of New Deshret to handle the Imperator's originally intended role at the coordinates near Rah.

Finally, War-7, normally stationed at Ishtar under the command of Mayavat Meropei of Shuria, will be ready for the arrival of Aeson Kassiopei, the SPC Commander. Aeson will head to Ishtar, along with additional military resources and personnel, since it's the expected site of the upcoming battle. Since Ishtar is next in line for the alien attack, and a new grid is expected to form there on Red-Mar-Yan 16, Aeson is planning to focus the bulk of SPC defensive forces at these coordinates.

And in case anyone is overwhelmed with all these details, believe me, so am I.

All I know, is—on Red Mar-Yan 16, each one of us must be inside a resonance chamber on board a battle barge at our designated coordinates, ready to perform the voice sequence simultaneously.

The fate of humanity depends on it.

Chapter 93

Our schedule for the next few days is both simple and intense.

On Red Mar-Yan 6 we embark on our *astroctadra* mission: that's when the wielders of the six Logos voices begin our journeys to the assigned coordinates.

Since each of us has different distances to travel around the Helios system, it will take us anywhere from two to four days to get there.

Aeson's trip is shortest, since he is going "next door" to Ishtar, the planetary neighbor of Atlantis, which also happens to be quite close to Atlantis in its current orbital position. The others have considerably longer trips—across the system and inward—to Tammuz, Septu, and Rah.

My own journey is one of the longest of all, and so is Manala's. Our battle barges will take us out into deep space, in opposite directions, perpendicular to the system's rotational plane—in about four days of travel—and we should arrive at our coordinates on Red Mar-Yan 10.

Once we arrive, we will occupy our positions and wait for the planetary alignment event that will take place on Red Mar-Yan 16. On that day Rah will be directly across from Septu, and at a ninety-degree angle from Ishtar, which will be directly across from Tammuz—so they all square off in a diamond, with Helios in the center.

As soon as Ishtar reports to us that a new alien grid has begun forming there, we will perform the voice command resonance sequence.

At that point, we assume, all hell will break loose. . . .

That's when we will either fight to lose or to *survive*.

The few days leading up to Red Mar-Yan 6, Mission Day, are full of preparation. One of the battle barges, War-3, is currently on its way here from the outer system, traversing immense distances to arrive here in time to pick up First Speaker Anen Qur. Most of the other battle barges are already parked in Atlantis orbit, but they are ferrying supplies and personnel, and will be doing it up to the last minute.

The mood here on the surface is a combination of stress, panic, despair, hope, and high energy.

While we wait, the only thing some of us can do is practice and memorize the *astroctadra* voice command sequences imparted to us by the Imperator. (Romhutat Kassiopei himself is currently somewhere in deep space on route to the Rim and has been keeping contact with Aeson through interstellar communication.) The sequences are the same ones used during the *astroctadra* of the Ghost Moon, so I know them already and feel like they've been branded into my consciousness. But practice is what keeps me focused.

Aeson spends most of his waking hours in the workroom, in meetings, and in orbit up on Atlantis Station SPC Headquarters. I see him mostly at night, or for quick meals, and we make the most of our time together with urgent, hungry lovemaking, and bittersweet caresses and reminiscences.

We speak about our dreams and make frivolous plans for next year, because somehow making future plans can make the possibility of a future itself seem real.

"I wanted to grow old with you, *im amrevu*," he tells me, deep in the night.

I stroke his cheeks and kiss him on the mouth, hard. "You *will!*" I say fiercely. "You're going to be an annoying, lovable, old fart to my silly old hag. And we're going to have at least half a dozen children."

"You promise?" he asks with a playful and sad smile. "Will Atlantis survive?"

"I promise," I lie, with utter, crazy conviction, even as I know it is likely all a sweet illusion. . . .

On Red Mar-Yan 5, the day before Mission Day, we take part in a bittersweet Atlantean tradition. Before Atlanteans go into battle, they celebrate hard with a Zero Gravity Dance. As soon as I hear about it, I recall the amazing Zero-G Dances we had on board the ark-ships during our journey from Earth to Atlantis. So many sweet, powerful, intense memories associated with those dances for me; indeed, for all of my friends. . . .

This particular Zero-G Dance is being held in orbit, on the Atlantis Station, inside the great resonance chamber there. It will start at Noon Ghost Time and run all day and well into the evening until Midnight Ghost time.

During this time, all Pilots, Cadets, spacecraft crews, officers, various Fleet personnel, and their civilian guests are welcome to attend. Indeed, people will be arriving in waves—going up to the Station, celebrating for a few hours, and then heading out directly to their assigned mission spacecraft and different locations.

The Atlantis Station is supposed to be immense—nearly twice the size and personnel capacity compared with most other Hel system stations. It sits in high orbit like a fifth moon of Atlantis. However, since there are thousands of personnel in the SPC, coming from all around the globe, from the different national Fleets, even the huge Atlantis Station cannot support that many people all at once. That's why the celebration is held over a whole day period, allowing multiple shifts. As a result, everyone gets to enjoy the Zero-G Dance at some point before they embark on their mission.

Because of our grave circumstances, this particular Zero-G Dance has an apocalyptic feel to it for many of us. This could very well be the last major celebration event we will ever take part in, before people lose their lives. But don't let the undertone of desperation fool you—Atlanteans plan to party hard tonight, and they do.

Zero-G Dances are themed events, and this one is no different. Because the Station Nomarch Evandros is in the Green Quadrant, and he is the official Host of the event, this is a Green Zero-G Dance.

The theme itself is green growth, the living verdant *flora* of Atlantis.

Aeson and I are going up there tonight, taking our turn on the Station during one of the later evening shifts. And all our friends and family are coming with us.

And when I say everyone, I'm not kidding. We plan to take a large military transport shuttle (similar to the kind that was used to ferry Candidates on Earth during the Semi-Finals and Finals, but weaponized and equipped with a holo-viewport) and pile in together, flying up at tenth hour of Khe, right after a big family and friends *niktos* meal in the Imperial Crown Prince's Quarters.

But first, we get to do silly, frivolous, girly dress-up stuff and put on some fabulous green outfits—and that's just the guys—while we pretend only for a few hours that all is well with the world.

My sister Gracie and I go through my bedroom closet and choose our green dresses, just as Laronda arrives with Chiyoko and Blayne, followed soon by Dawn and Hasmik. Everyone's either wearing their green outfits or has them packed with their travel bags—since we won't be coming back down to the surface tonight but going directly to our ships right after the dance.

Oalla and Erita are already here, in one of the larger living rooms with the men. Both the *astra daimon* women look fabulous— Erita in a long, flowing, deep forest-green dress, and Oalla in a tight, short, sparkling pea-green number that shows off her fabulous legs in five-inch heels. They peek in on us periodically as we continue to rummage through the bedroom closet for accessories.

"Looking glorious, My Imperial Lady, carry on," Erita says with a mischievous wink, resting her hand on the doorway and striking a dramatic pose.

I've put on a flowing, sleeveless summer dress in several layers of verdigris tulle, with the darkest green underneath and a fine gold mesh on top. The dress reaches my ankles and as usual I am wearing sensible shoes with two-inch heels. My hair is in a graceful updo which my Palace maid, Aranit, arranged for me, and my face has subtle makeup.

Gracie has her Fleet uniform packed, since she'll be going to her assignment on War-1 right after the dance. But she has her long, dirty-blond hair down, loose and flowing. Her outfit is a sea-green mermaid dress in iridescent folds, tight around the waist and hips and flaring out at the bottom like a fish tail.

"Okay, girl, explain to me how you plan to walk with that tail?" Laronda raises one brow and widens her eyes at Gracie.

Laronda herself is wearing an elegant, form-fitting evening dress in emerald green fabric, with a long slit on one side, and fun platform shoes. Her hair is wound with small, shiny green ribbons and twists, and she has long chandelier gold earrings.

"I plan to float in zero-g, not much walking required," Gracie replies, while trying to attach a green stone necklace around her throat.

"I think Blayne will like the way you look," I whisper discreetly near Gracie's ear.

"Shut up," my sister says with an instant flush and looks around, even though Blayne is in the other room and can't hear her.

"Very, very beautiful, *janik*." Hasmik nods to her, and then comes up from behind and helps Gracie attach the necklace clasp.

"You look so nice, Hasmik!" I add quickly with a smile.

For today's dance, Hasmik has put on a long, delicate, olive-green dress that has a slightly flaring skirt with a fitted bodice that emphasizes her tiny waist. She does look gorgeous, with her dark brown hair up in an elegant Grecian bun, and slender pearl earrings.

Hasmik is a civilian, but she is coming with Manala on this mission, to help her friend the best she can. Therefore, she also has a travel bag packed that she's brought with her to take on War-6.

I look around at my other friends. Chiyoko is wearing a long dark green dress with a pattern of leaves and vines in elegant fractal curves, and her Fleet uniform is packed for her deployment to War-1 with the other Cadets.

Dawn has a sleek dressy pantsuit on, of very pale green fabric that shimmers with gold and mother-of-pearl. Another civilian, Dawn is here simply as our guest and friend for the evening, to lend moral support and possibly say goodbye—since it's uncertain if anyone is coming back, or that any of us will ever see each other again. After the Green Dance, Dawn will return down to Poseidon and begin to pray for us. . . .

"Have you seen Manala?" I ask, as we put on the finishing touches and return to the living room where the guys are.

"She is still getting ready downstairs in her Quarters," Hasmik replies. "I checked on her before coming here, and she said she will be here soon."

"Okay, let's go check out the boys," Laronda says impatiently. "Let's go, let's go, let's go."

"Is Anu in there?" I ask.

Laronda snorts. "He'd better be." And she looks down at herself to double check and pat down her clingy dress.

I smile.

W e go into the large living room, where the remains of the *niktos* meal service greets us. The guys are lounging around waiting for us. Seeing all of us in our various green finery, there are many appreciative exclamations and a few whistles and claps.

I must say, the boys look smoking-hot tonight too.

Keruvat and Xelio are outfitted in dark green jackets and pants with pale green shirts underneath, and Ker is sporting an amazing emerald and green jeweled *wesekh* collar that emphasizes the handsome breadth of his shoulders. Xelio's long raven hair is pulled back tight against his devastatingly striking face and gathered in an ornate three-strand segmented tail.

The Lark men look only slightly less imposing but equally sharp in their green jackets and pants suits. My Dad—who will be going on the journey to Tammuz with Gordie on War-8—has packed a travel bag and will be taking Mom's urn with him, just in case.

"If anything happens," Dad tells us, "I want your Mother to be with us, to the end."

"Nothing will happen, Daddy!" Gracie reassures him, even as she watches Dad place Mom's carefully wrapped urn in the bag and hold on to it with both hands.

Sitting on the sofa nearby, with his brand new, short, custom hoverboard on the floor, its top end propped up against the armrest, Blayne watches Gracie and my Dad's careful movements. Blayne is wearing a smart green jacket with a palm leaf pattern, dark green pants over his thin legs, and pristine shoes. It's zero-g, so the boy will definitely be dancing tonight.

I glance around the room and notice that Anu and Gennio are both here also, dressed in shades of green. As Imperial Aides, they will be accompanying Aeson to Ishtar on War-7. Anu gives Laronda an intense, glum look across the room.

"Are we ready to head to the Dance?"

The speaker is Aeson.

I turn to admire *im amrevu*, examine every glorious detail of his face and figure with unrelenting wonder. Aeson's shining hair is sleeked back in a stern, segmented tail, and he is not wearing green, but the slate grey and gold everyday SPC Fleet uniform with high command emblems along his collar and the black armband on his sleeve. It is not the same parade uniform of the Commander that he wore at our Wedding, but he still looks stunning.

"Aeson . . ." I breathe his name with a smile, looking into his very blue eyes.

He, in turn, devours me with his gaze and begins to say something about my festive dress. . . .

Just then there's a light knock on the door, and Manala walks in, followed by the Imperatris.

Manala is a vision in pale green, ethereal and fey, wearing a long dress in flowing gauze layers, like butterfly wings. Her Kassiopei golden hair is loose around her shoulders, and a jade pendant descends to her forehead where the precious stone lies like a third eye. Her makeup is dark and dramatic, with cherry lips and shadowed eyes. A collar of green jewels shaped like curling vines circles the high column of her throat.

Behind her, the Imperatris stands in a dark, modest dress that has a hint of mourning. She is not dressed for the dance, but she has come to say her farewells to us.

Everyone rises, and for several long moments there is but silence.

I notice that George watches Manala with solemn, unrelenting focus and a strange expression.

And then the Imperatris walks across the room and approaches her son. "Aeson," she whispers in a hollow voice, and reaches out to embrace him.

Aeson takes his mother in a deep hug, enclosing her slight form gently with his arms, holding her as a fragile, precious thing. *"Mamai . . ."* he whispers.

They come apart, and Devora turns to me. We embrace gently, and she whispers in my ear, "Take care of him . . . *live.*"

I nod, and hold back the lump in my throat.

Dad watches and inclines his head to the Imperatris in slow acknowledgment.

And then we turn to go.

"Wait!" Hasmik says suddenly. "We have a custom. Before we go on a journey, we must all *sit*, for good luck. Everybody, quickly, sit down!"

My family, friends, and the *astra daimon* exchange amused glances, but the solemn mood is definitely broken as we all perch on furniture to sit down for a count of three seconds.

And then we head to the Green Zero-G Dance.

O ur shuttle flight is short and briefly uncomfortable. We plow through the atmosphere and experience the heavy pull of Atlantis gravity—as though the planet is trying to prevent us from leaving, dragging us back down to itself. And then, suddenly, it all falls away . . . we are light and weightless in orbit, as we approach the grand X shape of the Atlantis Station.

Dad immediately breathes a comfortable sigh of relief and chuckles softly, mumbling something about gravity and old people. Gracie, who's been hanging onto his arm like a little girl and not leaving his side, pulls at Dad's sleeve in mock outrage.

The Station floats like a metallic talisman before us, silhouetted against the black velvet of space. It's lit up in bright twinkling lights along its four immense platform "arms" and especially around the central hub with the Resonance Chamber, which is our destination.

In moments the shuttle docks at one of the arms, next to hundreds of others, elegantly avoiding other flying traffic. The moment it does, Atlantean full gravity returns, and we synchronize with the Station. Next the hatch opens with a whoosh of sterile air, and we are greeted by distant laughter and music. We leave our travel luggage behind in the shuttle for later retrieval and enter a long corridor full of enthusiastic, youthful people dressed in every imaginable shade of green.

Aeson and I walk ahead, holding hands. It's interesting to watch how, as soon as other passersby notice my husband, they stop and salute sharply. Here Aeson is not the Crown Prince of Imperial *Atlantida*, but the Commander of the international Star Pilot Corps—*their* Commander. . . . Seeing all the looks of respect and admiration he receives is so gratifying that my heart melts with pride for *im amrevu*.

"So this is where you go to work nearly every day?" I ask with a playful smile.

Aeson nods, arching one brow. "The actual SPC Headquarters is on the opposite side of the hub, but, yes."

"Whoa, this place is huge!" Gordie says behind us, pointing at the long endless arrow of the corridor before us, with occasional cross-passages visible along the walls.

"You haven't seen anything yet," Erita retorts, exchanging humorous glances with Xel, then Ker and Oalla right behind her.

As we move along the corridor, the sound of music grows louder, and there is a pulsing dance beat coming from up ahead. With it come the deep, thumping bass beats echoing throughout the hull around us. At the same time, green flickering radiance starts to fill the view before us.

I feel an immediate surge of raw excitement. . . . Memories of other "Zero-G Dances past" stand up like happy (or simply emotional) ghosts in my imagination.

So many intense memories and youthful wonder. . . .

Passion . . . heartbreak . . . unrequited love . . . hope . . . desire. . . .

We emerge at last directly into a huge, cavernous sphere full of green light that's the Station Resonance Chamber—an immense interior space that's amazingly even greater than the resonance chamber on ICS-2.

The equatorial perimeter of the sphere has the usual narrow walkway full of crowds and drink stations, DJ and lighting booths, while the center is a bowl of pale green light, full of gently floating greenery far below. I look closer and realize it's an optical illusion of treetops stirring in the wind, creating the sensation that there is a great forest under our feet. At the same time, overhead the ceiling dome resembles an ocean of shimmering seaweed, delicate filaments floating down like green spider silk.

And everywhere jade light orbs swirl like champagne bubbles.

"Holy cannoli!" Laronda says, punching Anu's arm that she's been holding. "I haven't been here before, only docked with the Station on the outside and seen some boring SPC offices. But this is mind-blowing!"

"Yeah, it is," Anu says curtly. "Not so fun to run diagnostics on all those resonance tiles."

Laronda laughs. "Must be a billion of them."

"Actually, there are seventy-nine thousand-three hundred—" Anu begins to elaborate, but Laronda widens her eyes and glares at him, making troll boy swallow his words.

The pulse-pounding music emerges from the walls of the amazing green expanse filled with people, at present dancing under normal gravity on several flat dance platforms levitating in the middle of the floor. There are Atlantean Fleet veteran personnel mingling with newbie *shìrén* Cadets. Sounds of laughter, light conversation, and the stomping of feet come from that direction.

The music itself is a vaguely familiar Atlantean pop song currently played in Poseidon. Moments later it is replaced with a recent Earth hip-hop song in French.

We move past the crowds along the walkway to the nearest station that's giving out the couple locator pins.

The crewman working the station sees Aeson and immediately comes to order and salutes. "Commander!"

"At ease," Aeson says in a calm voice, and the crewman relaxes, nods with precision, then gives Aeson a pair of glowing green pins. Aeson takes one and pins it on the front of my dress, while he attaches the second one to his own uniform.

"I don't think we'll need those things," I say with a smile. "I don't plan to leave your side even for a moment tonight."

"I know." Aeson looks at me with raw intensity. "But—keep it, just in case."

"Okay," I whisper, and run my fingers over the pin on my collar, which is momentarily blinking quickly as I step away to test it, and then shines steady with proximity, same as the one on Aeson's lapel.

"Well, this is extraordinary," my Dad says, moving right behind us and leaning near my ear. "Gwen, sweetheart, I'm going to find a seat and enjoy watching all of you. What can I say but, 'In Xanadu did Kubla Khan a stately pleasure-dome decree . . .'"

". . . 'Where Alph, the sacred river, ran, through caverns measureless to man, down to a sunless sea!'" I continue the Coleridge poem verse and laugh. "Of course, Dad! You should definitely sit down, because they'll start tweaking gravity soon!" I give Dad a sound kiss on the cheek and leave him with Gracie, who starts explaining the locator pins to him while Blayne waits with amusement, hovering upright on his board.

Just then the song ends. There is a lull of silence and then, from the walls, a mischievous female voice of the Music Mage utters, like a seductive nymph:

"Gravity changing now. . . ."

In that moment, the familiar energizing notes of an old Earth classic, Enya's "Orinoco Flow," pour from the walls of the chamber . . . even as the floor lightens breathlessly underneath our feet.

I glance behind me and, a few steps away, my sister Gracie's long hair is suddenly floating like seaweed in the light gravity, to match her mermaid costume.

"My Lady Oalla, honor me with this dance."

Aeson and I both stare with wonder as Keruvat makes a short, elegant bow and stretches his hand out to Oalla.

"My Lord Keruvat, the honor is mine," she replies with a soft smile, looking up into Ker's very black eyes.

And the next moment, they take hold of each other and float away, taking a great leap over the endless abyss of floating treetops below and land on the closest dance platform.

"Hey, 'Ronda, let's go!" Anu says gruffly a few steps away, awkwardly jabbing Laronda in the side.

Laronda makes a small shriek, then grabs both of Anu's hands, while he pulls her with surprising agility along with him for the couple leap to the dance floor.

Aeson and I look at each other and laugh.

A few minutes later, gravity is changed again, and this time we experience complete weightlessness as a lovely Atlantean tune plays, full of reed pipes and soft drums. Aeson and I join hundreds of other couples floating in the expanse of boundless green light.

We stare into each other's eyes with a kind of warm, quiet contentment, living completely in the moment.

"Gwen . . ." Aeson says to me as we float and spin along with the rhythm and I observe the slightly feverish sparkle in his eyes. "You are the only thing *real* right now, you know? There's nothing . . . only the sight of *you*."

In that moment he pulls me to him. His lips descend on mine and his mouth sears me with the knowledge that indeed, there is *nothing* and no one else.

The song ends, and gravity blooms back into being. We descend gently to the floor and return to the perimeter walkway near the seats where some of our friends are taking a break, just as the mood changes and a fast and hard song fills the chamber.

"Oh! Oh!" Dawn says, tapping George on the shoulder. "That's the Gebi Girls! Have you heard their music yet?"

"The whatsit whats?" George cranes his head slightly with a quizzical expression, then sets down his drink on a ledge.

"They're a recently formed band, an all-girl group of Earthies. Either four or five women in the band—I forget. They play their own instruments and sing some really good stuff, do pop covers of both old Earth and Atlantean music, and have original material too, like this song—"

And Dawn starts to dance in place.

"All right, I can get used to this sound," George says, nodding slowly and listening. Behind him, Gordie stands leaning against the wall and slurping his covered drink from a metal straw. He seems out of it, which is not too unusual for Gordie. A few steps away, Chiyoko, Hasmik, and Manala are seated quietly with their own drinks, while Erita stands over them.

Why is everyone not dancing and just milling about? I think.

Just as I'm about to intervene with my girlfriends and get them off their butts, Xelio, Radanthet, and Nergal show up. The three *daimon* all look elegant in green jackets—Nergal, slim and tall, Radanthet much shorter, powerful and stocky.

"Ladies, look who's here!" Erita says loudly with a snort. "Rad-Rad! Will you dance with me already?"

Radanthet chuckles and comes up to Erita, taking her by the arm. "Let's go, *amrevet!*" And just like that, they take off to the dance floor, even as Erita turns around and waves to us saucily.

Xelio and Nergal exchange amused glances.

Nergal looks around, and his gaze alights on my brother Gordie. "*Ter* Gordon," he says, stepping up to my brother politely. "Will you dance with me?"

There is a long, strange pause.

Gordie stops slurping and turns his head, then raises his brows. "Huh?" he says, frowning at Nergal. "That's kind of weird. . . . But, yeah, sure, whatever."

And just like that, Gordie sets down his drink on the ledge near George's drink, and with a shrug heads with Nergal to the nearest dance platform. He doesn't exactly hold hands but just sort of mills in place, across from Nergal.

Both George and I stare in his wake with dropped jaws.

"What . . . was that?" George asks, and his jaw is still unhinged. "Did I miss something?"

"I don't know!" I say with a dazed look. "Honestly, I don't know anything. . . . Either I missed it too—missed it entirely—or that's just our Gordie."

"Yeah, I don't think he's gay," Dawn says calmly. "But he's pretty damn cool, if you ask me."

"Not as cool as we can be," Xelio says with an amused glance at Aeson. "I'd ask you to dance, Commander Kassiopei, but I think your lovely Wife would not approve."

"And I would dance with you under any other circumstance, Pilot Vekahat," Aeson retorts without skipping a beat. "But tonight, I dance only with *im amrevu*." And Aeson winks at me.

"Well then, I must nurture my broken heart in another way," Xel says. His searing gaze, full of sensual humor, moves down the row of seats, and he walks the few paces, stopping before Hasmik. "My Lady, you remain my last hope. Will you join me in this dance before the dance itself fades away?" And he makes a small, mocking flourish with his hand then stops it abruptly before Hasmik's startled face.

At once Hasmik looks up at him and shakes her head. "Oh, no," she says with a gentle smile. "No, thank you."

"Come now!"

Is there just a tiny note of frustration in Xelio's otherwise smooth tone?

But Hasmik persists, shaking her head negatively and then looks down at her lap, continuing to smile.

"Well, my dear, suit yourself," Xel says with a peculiar expression briefly showing on his face, and steps away.

Manala watches the exchange with intensity and nudges Hasmik. "Why?" she says with earnest eyes. "Why did you say no? You should dance with him!"

But Hasmik shrugs and says thoughtfully, "He called me a Lady, *janik*. I am not."

Manala sighs. "At least he asked you. . . . No one ever asks me."

"Gravity changing now. . . ." The mysterious voice of the Music Mage sounds just then, and gravity falls away completely.

A soft Latin rhythm sounds, and I vaguely recognize another wonderful Earth classic, "La Isla Bonita" by the glorious old diva Madonna.

My brother George stands up. There's one beat of hesitation, and then he walks calmly over to stand before the seated group of Hasmik, Chiyoko, and Manala.

"Imperial Princess Manala," he says formally, leaning down, reaching his hand out, and simply taking hers. "Tonight is different. Dance with me."

Manala stares up at George with an absolutely stunned expression. For a moment she actually appears at a loss.

But then, slowly, she gets up, her golden hair floating in weightlessness like a halo—since George is still holding her hand and not letting go.

"Yes . . ." Manala says with wonder.

George simply nods in answer, with a serious expression, and takes her other hand in his, pulling her closer . . . and they soar, floating upward, elegant and solemn, circling together against the green radiance.

Chapter 94

We stay in the Resonance Chamber for another half hour, dancing, laughing, reminiscing, slowing down and just catching glimpses of friends and people we know somewhere in the immense chamber.

Blayne and Gracie take full advantage of zero gravity and spin in the air with carefree, relaxed smiles. Chiyoko chats with Gennio down on the walkway about something very technical and utterly engrossing. At one point I see an interesting sight of Brie Walton dancing with Logan Sangre, whom I haven't seen since the Wedding. The way they are looking at each other, and the way he holds her waist and leans closer to her face with focused intensity puts me in mind of how Logan used to look at me. . . . Which now only leaves a gentle, mild memory.

And then it's almost Midnight Ghost Time. The Zero-G Dance is winding down, and it's time for us to leave.

I hate this part.

We don't say goodbyes. Instead, we look and smile and nod at one another as, one by one, my friends slow down, stop dancing, come up to me, come up to the others, and say a word or two of encouragement before heading out to their missions.

"You go do your Logos voice magic thing," Laronda says with a sudden hug, clinging to me. "I expect a full defeat of those crazy alien spherical dingalings. Remember, while you do your stuff, we'll be here on War-1, all the Earthies backing you up. No one is getting past us! Atlantis is under *our* protection now." And Laronda makes a fist pump.

"Good luck, Gwen!" Chiyoko says, hugging me next. "I don't know how we do it, but we are going to kick their golden butts."

"Agreed," I say to Chiyoko warmly. "Fly well, my Pilot Partner!"

Chiyoko blinks and widens her eyes. . . . She takes a deep breath, then nods. "Always."

"We homo sapiens are tough bastards," Blayne says, levitating on his board next to Gracie and handing my sister a napkin because she is starting to bawl. "Right, Lark Two? Don't make me a liar now, pull that snot right back up the sinus and show it who's boss."

Gracie immediately chokes and transitions to giggles instead.

"I expect a full accounting of all the events when you get back," Dawn says to all of us, standing nearby. "Don't disappoint me. If possible, take selfies with aliens."

I shake my head and smile. Then I glance at Dad, who is sitting quietly a few feet away in one of the wallflower seats and watching all of us with an indescribable look of love and pride. I notice that he has his bag with him on his lap, and he's holding onto it with both hands.

Manala, Hasmik, George, and Gordie all look around, seeming lost for a moment. Then they focus on each other, on the rest of us.

Since their dance, Manala periodically casts weird little glances in George's direction but doesn't say anything to him. On the other hand, she also constantly turns to Hasmik to express another concern. "Khemji . . ." Manala keeps saying and wringing her hands. "Oh, I'm so worried they won't feed him right! Khemji likes his food to be mashed to a very fine consistency. It must be pureed! He doesn't like chunky—"

"Hey, don't worry about Khemji." Dawn overhears and comes up to pat Manala on the arm. "I will look in on him regularly until you get back, and your Mother did say she will feed him very, very well on your behalf. . . ."

Now the *astra daimon* approach and gather around us in a circle.

"Are we ready, Commander?" Oalla asks in a suddenly solemn, crisp tone.

Aeson looks around at all of them, then turns to Oalla. *"Daimon!"* he says formally in a ringing voice. "Oalla Keigeri! You are my Guiding Star. Take care of Gordon Lark and support him on his mission. *Saret-i-xerera!"*

"Saret-i-xerera! I will watch after him, always," Oalla replies, straightening, then approaches Gordie, who's next to our Dad right now, and remains at his side.

Aeson then turns to Xelio.

"Xelio Vekahat! You are my Sword. Look after my sister Manala and fight to preserve her safety with all your courage, strength, and honor as *astra daimon. Saret-i-xerera!*"

"*Saret-i-xerera!*" Xelio replies, saluting gravely. "I will defend and fight for her, and will not let you down." He approaches Manala and her group and remains there.

Aeson now faces Erita.

"Erita Qwas! You are my Shield. Protect my beloved Gwen, and guard her with your life. *Saret-i-xerera!*"

Erita immediately steps forward, straightening like an arrow, and salutes. "*Saret-i-xerera!* I will guard her with my life and will remain at her side." And with those words, Erita comes up to me and gives me a warm, strong look of encouragement.

I admit, in that moment, just briefly, I feel a powerful surge of relief—as though an old, nagging burden on my back has lightened somewhat. Knowing that Erita is coming with me does make me feel better somehow.

Erita really *is* the *ultimate shield.* She is the best of the Green Quadrant.

And now she has my back.

Finally Aeson looks to Keruvat. "Ker . . ." he says softly, with a nod. "Keruvat Ruo! You are my Spine. Without you, I would not stand up straight. You will come with me. *Saret-i-xerera!*"

"*Saret-i-xerera!*" Keruvat replies with a shining expression.

This is the part where it becomes really, really impossible. . . .

Aeson turns to me. He takes a step and I take the tiny, stupid step to close the distance between us.

I hide my face against his jacket and just hold on, feeling his muscular, strong chest and listening to his beating, indomitable heart.

We say nothing.

No goodbyes—there can be none.

I take in a deep, shuddering breath and look up at my husband, my love. "*Im amrevu.* . . . I'll see you in a few days," I say with a great big smile.

His eyes are like the Atlantean night sky as he takes in all of me with fierce intensity. "Sing well . . . my love."

I pull his face down to me, and we share one soft, profound kiss. Out of the corner of my eye I notice the green locator pin still attached on his lapel, shining with an infinite, steady light of proximity.

And then it's time for us to go.

I hardly remember the strange turmoil that takes over my mind as we walk together in our same large group along the endless corridor to the shuttle. There we pick up our small belongings and then suddenly separate. Everyone heads for various other shuttles, transports, fighter ships.

And just like that, our mission is a go.

Erita and I walk rapidly down another corridor and take a small *ardukat* fighter ship on a short flight to War-2, the battle barge that is waiting for us elsewhere in orbit.

This is my first time inside an *ardukat*. It's a two-person military vessel, small and cramped. Basically, a wide bench seat for two, surrounded by control panels and a dome roof. Unlike a *khepri*, which is saucer-shaped, the *ardukat* is a true sphere. The windowless hull is orichalcum, and, once inside, we call up a holo-viewport so that the hull and roof suddenly become transparent like glass, and we get a full panoramic projection view of the surroundings.

The moment we get in and lower the roof hatch on top of us, Erita turns to me comfortably and says, "My Imperial Lady Gwen, hang in there, okay? Everything is going to be just fine."

"I know," I say. "Thanks, Erita."

Erita smiles, then starts to sing the keying pre-flight sequence. The ship comes alive, and the various holo-grids pop up.

"Oh," I recall. "Do we need to change out of these dance outfits?"

Erita chuckles. "Oh, no. . . . Everyone arriving will be wearing this green party stuff. It's expected—a kind of pre-mission tradition. Don't worry, we'll change later after we get to the battle barge. I bet the Command Pilot is wearing green high heels himself."

I giggle, trying to visualize this Command Pilot, whom I've never met.

And then we detach from the Atlantis Station dock and head to our destination.

W ar-2 is truly an immense starship. My appreciation of its size is colored by my experience aboard the Earth Mission Fleet ark-ships, which, up to this point, I considered the biggest ships that Atlanteans possessed. Wow, was I ever wrong. . . .

This immense elongated cigar shape is a monster of sleek metal, easily the size of a city. It is four times bigger than an ark-ship, with four times the personnel capacity.

We approach like a tiny dust mote and fly parallel to its hull, among a roiling cloud of other space vehicles, looking for the appropriate docking bay tunnel.

We locate it and Erita takes us in through the tube, passing the violet plasma shield and blasting into the pressurized interior. She hover-parks the *ardukat,* and we get out of the spherical vessel and head directly for the Main Command Deck through myriad corridors and past an endless flow of Fleet personnel. Now and then we pass someone else wearing green formalwear, and it's clear they are also newly arrived from the Green Zero-G Dance.

"The people who aren't dressed up are regular crew serving on War-2," Erita explains in passing. "They weren't down on Atlantis to begin with, so they didn't get to party with us at the Station."

We finally arrive on deck and head directly for the Central Command Office to meet Command Pilot Amaiar Uluatl, who turns out to be a serious young man with river-red clay skin and shoulder-length black hair.

As with all the other battle barges, this particular warship has crew predominantly from one nation, which happens to be New Deshret. That explains the snatches of Deshi language we've heard in passing all around the ship corridors. It also explains Command Pilot Uluatl's accent.

"Welcome to War-2, Imperial Lady Gwen Kassiopei," Amaiar Uluatl tells me, rising from his seat with courtesy and giving me a short bow. "We have been briefed on the mission details and additional information has just arrived directly from the SPC Fleet Commander. We depart for your designated mission coordinates at fifth hour of Ra, and in the meantime, you will be shown to your quarters and assigned additional security."

"Thank you," I say, as Command Pilot Uluatl calls personnel to assist me.

And then I decide to ask, "Command Pilot, I realize that this is a New Deshret vessel and I'm honored to be on board. Just out of curiosity, is there a reason you are delivering *me* and not your own Princess Sheolaat Heru to her mission location? And forgive me if this is an inappropriate question."

For the first time, Command Pilot Uluatl smiles. "Not at all, my Imperial Lady. The answer is simple—we are one of the two flagship vessels in the SPC Fleet, and are simply the best. The Commander requested my services on your behalf as a personal favor, and I am pleased to oblige."

"Oh," I say. "Then I thank you very much."

Erita and I are shown to our adjacent cabins in the officers' quarters on the Command Deck. Since, at present, it is late night (or very early morning on Red Mar-Yan 6), we go to bed to catch a few hours of badly needed sleep before the complicated events pick up pace.

As I lie alone in my compact bunk, listening to the soft hiss of sterile ship air in the vents, I am plagued by stressful thoughts and a steady undercurrent of despair. This is the first time since the Wedding that I am not falling asleep next to Aeson in our marriage bed—or at least falling asleep with the knowledge that he's working late and will be returning to join me shortly.

Such a strange, lonely feeling.

Will I ever see him again?

The last time we made love was. . . .

No, stop it. . . . Don't think.

And oh, the things that we're about to do, the mission, weighs heavily on me.

I finally start drifting off around morning and barely notice the sudden change in the background noise level in the hull and that tiny initial lurch of momentum. . . . The immense battle barge begins to resonate with the energy forces of motion as it casts off into the deep space void.

The journey to my designated *astroctadra* alignment coordinates is thankfully uneventful. The moment I wake up on the first day, I send off an "I'm okay, are you okay?" message to Aeson, and then receive one immediately back from him. Both of us are in flight—I on the battle barge heading to the middle of nowhere, and he on board a *sebasaret* with Keruvat and select others, heading to Ishtar.

We spend the time exchanging brief interstellar messages, then the crew techs help me establish a video link in my cabin, so that I can see Aeson's face up close as he sits in his own version of cramped spacecraft quarters and smiles at me.

"Don't forget, when the *astroctadra* protocol will go in effect on the day of alignment, we will all be locked in a multi-person communication linkup inside each of our resonance chambers," Aeson tells me.

I nod.

"There are multiple redundancies built in," he continues. "My Father reminded me that we need to make sure that when we perform the voice sequences, all of our voices are picked up and transmitted to the other coordinates in addition to the main one at our location. It's the same kind of amplification we achieved when we brought back the Ghost Moon."

"That's right, I remember."

"For that reason, there will be several transmitters incorporated into our space suits in addition to the resonance chamber's acoustic station console primary transmitter."

"We're wearing space suits again?" I ask.

Aeson nods. "Always—whenever we work inside a resonance chamber when it happens to be set to its primary resonance mode."

"As opposed to its Zero-G Dance mode." I smile.

Aeson chuckles. And then his face grows serious again. "It's a safety precaution. Unprotected exposure to such powerful frequencies and energy levels can be dangerous."

"I see."

"Be sure to go over the step-by-step procedures until you are comfortable."

"Aeson, you are telling *me*, the most overly studious person you know, to go over something multiple times? Seriously?"

Aeson's expression is momentarily abashed. "No, I just mean so that you know it well enough that you don't worry unnecessarily—"

"I know what you mean, silly." I grin at him. And at once his expression lightens.

"It's mostly for my own sake," he admits. "I need to go over the sequences yet again myself, just so that it's effortless when the time comes."

Poor Aeson. . . The sheer magnitude of the responsibility for this whole process going right is getting to him.

We banter some more, and then Aeson tells me that everyone else on our *astroctadra* mission team is safely on their way to their coordinates. "Your brother Gordon is with Oalla and *Amre-ter* Charles, safely headed to Tammuz; Manala and George and the others are making good time; no irregularities from anyone. Even my Father is making fair progress on his own separate mission to the Rim—or so he tells me."

"How is your Father, Aeson?" I ask gently.

My husband's expression does not change, but he blinks. "The *pegasei* are with him. . . . He has not Jumped yet," is all that Aeson says on the subject.

I spend the rest of my anxious time mostly trying to keep out of the crew's way. I follow Erita around as she gives me a brief tour of the battle barge, with its sophisticated multiple decks stacked like lasagna layers, the vessel bays, and an entirely different layout than an ark-ship. As we walk the corridors, dressed in the same basic uniforms as the ship's crew so as not to stand out, the four assigned security guards accompany us at a discreet distance.

We eat *eos* bread and *dea* meal in the officers' meal hall, then traverse a very small portion of the Main Level Observation Deck, which—on this type of elongated spacecraft—runs in a straight line parallel to the entire length of the hull and appears endless.

Stars and cosmic clusters of varied colors fill the large window views outside. The entire spacescape is a grand design of sparkling lights and particles of mysterious, shifting matter.

"How beautiful," I remark to Erita. "I wish we were simply here on vacation, enjoying the cosmic sights, and not on a life-and-death mission to save the entire human species."

"Let's plan to survive the mission," Erita responds with a light smile. "Then you can ask your Imperial Husband to take you on an actual vacation during your *amrevet* days. Don't tell me where you're going of course, it should be your private secret."

"I like that idea," I say. "The idea of making plans for *after*."

It takes us four days of travel to arrive at the midpoint coordinates in deep space, directly perpendicular to the rotational plane of the Helios system. There is nothing there—no planet, no station, no space buoy or tangible marker of any kind.

We simply come to a stop and then assume a stationary "orbit" in relation to the Helios system, at a 90-degree angle. In reality, we are of course moving through space in the same direction and at the same rate with which the Hel system and all things inside it are hurtling through the cosmos—to maintain our position relative to Hel itself.

As soon as Command Pilot Uluatl announces our arrival, I call Aeson to let him know. He, of course, has long since arrived at Ishtar and has been on War-7 for the last two days. War-7 is now designated as *Depet-Ra*, the vessel of the SPC Fleet Commander.

"I'm relieved to know you are safely in place, *im amrevu*," Aeson tells me from the brightly lit deck of his own battle barge. "Xel just let me know that War-6, carrying Manala, has also arrived, and they are now in position directly across from you on the opposite side of Hel. You two are the last to reach your designated coordinates. Everyone else is already positioned for the *astroctadra* alignment. Now there's nothing to do but wait."

"Six days of lousy waiting," I say, looking wistfully at the close up of my beautiful husband's lapis lazuli eyes. "I *miss* you so much, Aeson. . . ."

"I know." He breathes deeply. "And I miss you so much you cannot imagine."

"Oh, but I can. I've been inside your mind, remember, sweetie?" I say with a naughty intonation and a smile.

Aeson gives me a tiny pout and the cutest little air kiss imaginable. I sense that he doesn't care if his crew might see him, the Commander, act mushy.

This is my husband. Confident enough in his masculinity to be a mush-ball in public, for one ridiculous moment.

And then he is serious again, pausing, as if considering how to speak. "Gwen," he says at last. "There's some bad news—from Earth. I've received notification from Nefir Mekei that a similar alien golden light grid has begun to form around Sol—your Earth sun."

"What?" I exclaim with an instant stab of horror in my chest. *"No!"*

"I'm really sorry." Aeson exhales again loudly. "But keep in mind, the events we've set in motion are still playing out. Once my Father delivers Arlenari Kassiopei's body to the Rim, and the *pegasei* take her back all the way and close the dimensional rift—all in conjunction with our own actions here in the *astroctadra* alignment—it will likely make a difference."

"Oh God, I hope so!" My heart is hammering in my chest. "What about the asteroid? Did Nefir mention anything about that? Is he doing anything now to try to stop it?"

Aeson nods thoughtfully. "I believe so. He mentioned about taking AS-1999 to do a proximity flyover of the asteroid once again and try to tractor it off course. If I recall, trying to blast it to pieces is not advised, since, at this proximity, the pieces themselves will likely form multiple lesser threats but still create the same problem at impact."

"The asteroid is just too big," I muse.

"Not only big but mass-heavy, with a solid metal core. Very hard to break up—my Father chose his doomsday weapon very thoroughly," Aeson says darkly. "However, there are still other options, and Nefir is working on them."

"Aeson, do you think maybe I can get a direct line of communication with AS-1999? I would like to talk to Nefir and see for myself, and maybe brainstorm some options."

"Of course. I'll give you secure access to AS-1999 during the multi-person linkup."

"Not any sooner? Like, today?"

He considers. "It might be best if we use the ultra-secure lines of the linkup. I would prefer not to compromise the AS-1999 holographic anonymity on Earth with an extraneous transmission that could be picked up by Earth authorities."

"Would it even matter at this point?" I try. "If they knew that one Atlantean ship remains in orbit over Earth?"

"If you recall, some of the core Earth authorities know already. Such as your President Katherine Donahue. It's best not to upset the very precarious political balance there on the surface."

I sigh. "All right, I guess."

Is Katherine Donahue even President at this point? What is happening on Earth?

And then we change the subject.

But I'm still thinking about Earth and the asteroid for many hours afterwards.

Chapter 95

The six days of waiting pass quicker than I imagine. Time drags at an infinite crawl, then speeds up to infinity and beyond as we wait, positioned at six apex points of the grand *astroctadra* around the Helios system.

On the morning of Red Mar-Yan 16 I wake up with a pounding heart and cold sweat in anticipation of what could be the last day of my life—our lives.

Here is where our general plan kicks in. As soon as we are awake, we are supposed to go on high alert and standby. We don't know when—or even if—anything is going to happen at Ishtar, but the probability is high that it will be sometime *today*. Which makes our stress levels go through the roof as we must wait, fully prepared to act at a moment's notice.

Erita and I wake up at fifth hour of Rah—synchronized to Poseidon time—grab food and force it down, then get ready for my role in the complex process that will take place. This includes putting on our space suits with the *viatoios* safety layer underneath, activating our interstellar communication system linkups, and carrying our helmets with us at all times (clipping them to our suits to free up our hands is an option) as we head toward the Resonance Chamber where we'll basically spend the rest of the day.

The rest of the day. . . .

What does that even mean? How will the day end? An ending to all things?

War-2 is already on high alert all around us, battle-ready and in constant communication mode with Aeson's ship and the others in the alignment. In fact, it's been battle-ready since the night before. Fleet officers and crew are at their stations, weapon systems are on standby, and everyone is wearing space suits as a precaution—it's one of the procedure requirements for a mobilized Atlantean vessel at such a high alert level.

The same thing is happening all around the system at the six coordinate points, plus Atlantis itself, which is on alert and ready for planetary defense.

All this time, I go over the voice command sequences in my mind, over and over, until it becomes a crazy litany of music in my head. And I can only imagine what the others are doing—the other five Logos voice wielders: Aeson, Gordie, Manala, Anen Qur, Sheolaat Heru.

I will know soon enough—our multi-person comm linkup is about to go into effect.

But first, the Resonance Chamber awaits.

The Resonance Chamber is located at the heart of the ship, and it is truly immense. It is even somewhat larger than the one at Atlantis Station—which I thought was unbelievably huge—possibly by about 20% in additional cubic volume.

Command Pilot Uluatl meets us at the doors—since he will be assisting me in the process by granting temporary security access to the resonance system—and we enter a grandiose spherical interior space of homogeneous color and hue, a mind-bending vision of cream-gold light seeping in from the very walls.

The whole thing is constructed of orichalcum panels, their true acoustic-sensitive layer exposed, but it's also backlit from within somehow, which I don't understand. Hence, the otherworldly cream glow.

A soon as the doors open, we step onto a small protruding ledge and pause. . . .

There are no other walkways, nothing else apparent in the chamber. The orichalcum panels line the sphere seamlessly.

And suddenly, far below, in the very midpoint, the floor parts. A tech console station rises, levitating upward from the center. It consists of a podium on top of a disk-shaped platform, about twenty feet in diameter. The disk platform with the operating station stops at the height level of the doors (located at the sphere's "equatorial belt") and then glides toward us. Meanwhile the panels on the floor far below are closed over by another set of identical panels that emerge and rise from underneath, so that the sphere is again seamless.

All this time, there is absolute silence in the grand, spherical chamber. I've been warned ahead to be very quiet while inside, to be careful not to speak unnecessarily, especially while certain acoustic connection modes are enabled.

I stand, almost afraid to breathe in case I make too much noise, and watch Erita, who stands next to me, appearing composed.

When the gliding platform station nears us, Command Pilot Uluatl steps across the abyss onto the platform and motions silently for us to follow.

As soon as the three of us are standing on the platform, it registers our presence and starts to move back to the distant center of the sphere, revealing a dizzying abyss all around us. Meanwhile the doors close, and the small ledge retracts, so that there is no sign of a previous opening and the area is as seamless as the rest of the sphere.

And just like that, I feel a weird stab of vertigo, and my head starts to spin. The optical illusion that is created by the perfect homogeneity of our surroundings must have an effect on the brain which cannot properly grasp what the eyes are seeing. . . .

We're inside a ball of light.

There is nothing tangible, only the console station platform underneath us.

Erita notices my moment of disorientation and offers me her arm, encased in the space suit sleeve. Quickly I grab her arm to steady myself and nod in gratitude.

We are still being perfectly quiet and saying nothing.

Command Pilot Uluatl raises one finger for attention and then starts manipulating the console. I see different color lights go on. And then suddenly a series of gentle crystalline tones sound from some invisible speakers on the nether side of the platform directly under our feet.

The tones ring out with perfect purity in the immense expanse, and the amazing echoes they create fill the chamber until it rings like an immense bell.

In moments it gets so painfully loud that I find I have to cover my ears.

The Command Pilot continues entering something on the console and then, just like that, the tones and even reverbs and echoes are cut off in mid-sound, and perfect silence is almost preternaturally restored.

I watch the console and see a steady red light go on, while the cream-and-gold backlit panels of the chamber dim slightly.

"It is now safe to talk and make noise," Amaiar Uluatl says to us in his crisp, low voice—which immediately sends up a series of instant echoes around the chamber, and the sound waves rebound like a flock of startled birds. "But, not too much noise," he adds with minor amusement. He then reaches in his suit pocket for a small pouch of noise-dampening earplugs, offering me a pair.

"Oh, what an amazing place!" I say, putting the earplugs in my ears and sending up another flock of acoustics to echo everywhere. The moment the earplugs are in place, there is immediate relief—I can still hear clearly enough to sing the voice commands properly, but it is no longer painful.

"Let me bring up a seating area," he says, tapping the console, and suddenly a flat ring detaches from the floor of our platform at the outer edges and lifts up a few feet, forming a hovering bench, shaped like a donut, all around us, which also serves as a safety barrier to keep us from the edge.

"Take a seat, Imperial Lady Gwen," Erita says, putting in her own earplugs, and now her voice goes echoing all over.

I sit down, and in the next few minutes the Command Pilot explains some of the controls and what the light indicators mean. It's generally similar to the workings of that small resonance chamber on Mar-Yan where I sang the voice sequences of our first *astroctadra*.

Placing one's hand on the control panel activates the primary resonance function (which, among other things, is used to propel the ship), and for as long as you maintain physical contact with the panel, any voice commands you sing are relayed into the chamber. The comm system then takes over and transmits the voice sequences to the remote interstellar coordinates.

As for the person-to-person linkup portion, the steady green light means the interstellar comm system is active and is transmitting, while the red light means the transmission link is disabled, and it is safe to talk off-line without having your words shared with the others in the linkup.

"Press and hold this control here," he says and points to a raised button, "if you want to speak to the entire mission team via secure linkup between the six *astroctadra* alignment points."

"Is this how I amplify the transmission to include everyone? During our voice sequence, I have to make sure that the other Logos voices in their *own* Resonance Chambers get picked up by the equipment *here* in this Resonance Chamber—and vice versa."

"Correct. You will need to do two things while you sing. First, keep your hand on the console to transmit your sequence to this Resonance Chamber and onward. Second, hold this button for a two-way audio connection so that your singing is heard at all the other five coordinates, even as their singing is heard here."

I nod. "Understood."

"Good." Command Pilot Uluatl checks his sleeve wrist comm on his space suit and then looks up. "I've just been notified by the Commander that our multi-ship, multi-person interstellar conference link-up is ready to be connected. Which means that as soon as I call up the Resonance Grid on this console, we can go live. Once the grid is up, you will be able to transmit and receive in *plurality* and perform all the commands we've just discussed."

"One more thing—with apologies, Command Pilot," Erita adds, handing me a small digital tablet that she's been carrying. "My Imperial Lady, this is another redundancy, as per our orders. This unit has been programmed to connect securely to the interstellar linkup in a full live feed, video and audio two-way transmission. You will be able to connect to the camera live feeds inside all of our suits, and any ship camera that's local to the receiver on each end. The linkup includes the six *astroctadra* mission members, plus Ark-Ship AS-1999 near Earth, and the Imperator himself on his special solo mission to the Rim."

And Erita shows me quickly how to cycle through the different windows and feeds on the tablet, as needed. As soon as she is done, I attach the tablet to the waist clip on my space suit for later, as needed. It is next to my suit helmet that I've clipped there too, in order to free up my hands.

And now, Command Pilot Uluatl takes over. He calls up a holo-grid in purple lights and then enables our connection.

"Calling *Astroctadra* Mission Control, this is War-2 with Lark on board. We are ready, please acknowledge," he says, holding down the comm button.

"This is Mission Control," Aeson's low, resonant voice responds a moment later. "War-2, you are now in the linkup. Please stand by."

We wait.

After several long minutes, Aeson's voice returns. "This is Mission Control to *Astroctadra* Mission members. You are all confirmed on line. The status here at Ishtar is unchanged. The Ishtar Station and War-7 are continuing to scan local space for anomalies. There has been no sign of enemy light grid formation—*yet*."

My husband's voice pauses momentarily, even as my pulse speeds up with nerves, with worry for him. And then he resumes.

"It is now sixth hour, fifty-seven daydreams, four heartbeats of Ra, synchronized to Poseidon Time. Full *astroctadra* planetary alignment is predicted for tenth hour, fourteen daydreams, and two heartbeats of Ra. That is our critical time. As soon as we have an update you will be notified. Be ready for action on behalf of all of us—all of humanity. Be vigilant of your own surrounding space."

There is a brief pause and a tiny crackle of sound.

And then Aeson resumes. "I want to hear your voices in tandem to test our connection. Please name yourself and your location."

Command Pilot Uluatl nods to me and I step forward and press the comm button, turning it a steady green.

"Gwenevere Kassiopei, on War-2 in deep space outside the system orbital plane," I say, keeping my voice steady—and at the same time I hear a sudden echoing chaos of five other voices, as we all test our comm lines. . . .

"This is Manala Kassiopei . . ."

"Gordon Lark here, on War-8 . . ."

"Anen Qur at Septu on board . . ."

"I am Sheolaat Heru on board War-5 . . ." an unfamiliar female voice comes on in a pleasant alto, as the Princess of New Deshret joins our Logos voice circle.

". . . on board War-6 somewhere in remote space, I am sorry I don't know where exactly. . ."

". . . around Tammuz. Yeah, ready to go."

". . . War-3."

". . . in orbit around Rah."

The simultaneous words echo and reverb into silence.

"This is Mission Control, our test is confirmed," Aeson says. "As of this moment, we are ready to execute our mission. You will wait for my next communication. It may take hours, or it may take a few moments. This is a difficult time of uncertainty, so you must find the strength within you to maintain focus. Your Logos voices depend on it. Good luck to all of us and to Atlantis. And now be prepared to act. Stand by."

And there is silence.

In that terrible, uncertain silence, we wait.
And wait.

Minutes go by, then hours.

I look around the Resonance Chamber, then stare at the control panel, at Amaiar Uluatl standing dutifully before it, at Erita, who waits stoically sitting next to me.

Eighth hour.

Periodically I stand up to restore circulation in my frozen limbs.

Ninth hour.

We speak very softly, very occasionally, so as not to disturb the acoustics in the chamber. Erita stands and flexes her fingers, bends her knees a few times, then sits down, but her gaze remains sharp. The Command Pilot sits down, checks his wrist comm for various SPC notifications and statuses for the millionth time, and his expression remains equally focused. I am reminded that both of these members of the armed forces are consummate professionals, and how much of military action consists of *simply waiting.*

My thoughts wander, and I think of my Dad, my siblings, everything random. How is Gracie doing, back on Atlantis, somewhere in orbit or aboard War-1? Is Dad feeling okay and has he eaten this morning?

Is George going nuts with the waiting somewhere next to Manala, and has Gordie completely spaced out and forgotten his reasons for being there and the mission itself?

Are the *pegasei* still flying next to the velo-cruiser carrying the body of Arlenari and the Imperator toward the Rim of Ae-Leiterra? Have they Jumped already, or do they prepare to Jump even now?

The Imperator is going to die, isn't he. . . .

I am not entirely sure how I feel about that. Even after all the dark, conflicted, plain malicious actions that he's done, I don't know. . . .

What must poor Devora be feeling right now? *Oh, God.*

It is now tenth hour. In fourteen minutes—daydreams—the *astroctadra* alignment will be at its height, as Rah, Tammuz, Septu, and Ishtar square off against each other around Helios.

This is when the statistical probability of attack at Ishtar is at its highest.

Just in that moment, a bell tone alarm sounds from the tablet clipped to my waist.

Crap!

I nearly jump at the sound, and all of us grow alert, but Erita says. "It's a private communication for you, Imperial Lady. Answer it."

"Ah, right." I nod and pick up the tablet, then swipe the screen to establish the linkup with the caller.

The blank screen comes alive, and a window expands to take up the full screen.

It is the Imperator.

The Imperator stands leaning over some kind of ship console, with a strangely elevated expression on his normally closed-off features as he faces the camera. Just behind him I see what must be a holo-view of deep space outside. It is nothing more than a field of grey static.

At once I recognize the nature of that space—a milky soup of hurtling stars, a homogeneous visual blend of the cosmos at high velocity, which you only see at the fastest speed of Quantum Stream travel, just before a Jump is attempted.

So, he hasn't Jumped yet. . . .

And in the next moment I notice the long, golden, gem-encrusted object that is the ancient sarcophagus, lying in the cramped space behind him. A nebulous cloud of rainbow color flickers all around the sarcophagus, as *pegasei* shapes of plasma blend and soar and pulse in the air . . . guarding it.

I perceive all this in an instant, while my first thought is, *why is the Imperator calling me?*

"Aeson, my Son," the Imperator says into the camera, speaking with focused intent. "Manala, my child . . . Gwen, my new daughter."

So, not just me.

"I've waited for as long as possible, counting down to the highest moment of alignment. The time has come," Romhutat Kassiopei says, with a slow, peculiar smile.

"Father!" Suddenly I hear Aeson's voice. A smaller window appears on in the lower right corner of my display, showing Aeson in close up, peering at a tablet screen in his hands, while he's silhouetted against the golden cream glow of another Resonance Chamber behind him.

"I'm here, Father . . . oh, Father!" Manala's faint voice sounds, and she appears in a second, smaller window on the left. Manala's great violet-blue eyes are wide open, and she seems to be trembling. She, too, stares into a tablet with an identical Resonance Chamber in the background.

As for Aeson—oh, my poor Aeson! His expression is stilled, well under control, but a world of emotion is reflected in his eyes as he watches his father.

"I'm here, Imperial Sovereign," I say, probably appearing in a little window on all of their screens.

"Nothing happening yet on your end, I assume," the Imperator says. "Eh? Well. You won't have to wait much longer. I can sense it's about to begin. I *feel* it. In the back of my head, where the real senses are. But first—I wanted to inform you of the moment we part."

"Part? What do you mean, My Father?" Manala interrupts.

The Imperator's face moves in closer as he says thoughtfully, "Remember, all of you—when the time comes, focus, *focus*. It all depends on your ability to retain concentration."

"I understand, My Father," Aeson responds, keeping his voice even. "We will perform the sequence as instructed."

"Ah," the Imperator sighs, almost tiredly. "I know you will, boy. You've always been good at such things. Duty, duty—your first love. Well done. . . . And you too, my little girl. Manala, tell your Mother she did a fine job with you, and I will always . . . *appreciate* her."

"Tell her yourself when you come home!" Manala exclaims, her voice breaking.

But the Imperator continues, after throwing a quick glance behind him at the flickering rainbow aurora borealis. "Yes, yes, they say it's time. Very well, but quickly now—a few more things to say to my children, just a few little things before I go. . . . Aeson. Yes, you, Aeson, my Son and Heir. As you can imagine, boy, I am abdicating now. Regardless of what happens, whether or not I come back, I am going to abdicate the Imperial Throne in your favor—"

"No, Father, you don't need to say that now, you *don't*—" Aeson's voice is still perfectly controlled. It simply becomes more resonant, filling with subtle *power* without an outlet.

The power of emotion without a name.

"Ah, but I do." The Imperator laughs. "I abdicate my Throne, and you are the new Imperator of *Atlantida*. The Court is now Blue. There, I've said it, and it has been witnessed by whoever is on your end. And such a relief it is, boy—never forget what a nasty, bitter, millennia-old burden you've just been gifted by your no-longer-Imperial Father. And for that, Son, I am genuinely sorry. But I have no doubt you will do very well."

The man who was Imperator pauses, growing solemn, and his dark blue eyes are full of liquid glimmer. "The *pegasei* are clamoring for me to end this. So . . . Quickly now, so I must— Gwen! Gwen Lark, who is Kassiopei indeed. You are now Imperatris. Continue to love my Son as you do. I was wrong, you know. He did well, choosing you. I—would've liked to see the little ones, the grandchildren. Take care of the Kassiopei—we are now yours, to the bitter end."

"I will," I say softly, while a strange whirlwind of emotion rises inside me. "And you will also see your grandchildren, somehow— *Amre-ter* Romhutat."

"Somehow." Romhutat chuckles bitterly, then nods at me. "My apologies. For everything, little girl with a Logos voice which you must use thoroughly. And now—" He glances again behind him, then around me at the ship's chamber, and straightens. I notice his fingers are moving rapidly over a console near the screen, engaging controls.

"Good luck, My Father . . ." Aeson says.

"Luck is what *you* will need, all of you!" Romhutat Kassiopei says in an elevated voice full of energy—even as the chamber he's in suddenly becomes brighter and brighter. "For that I give you my share of all the luck imaginable! And now—we go to close the *bashtooh* rift on the other end of the universe! Can you see how bright it's gotten here? It's time to Jump! Ah—and now the *pegasei* are *singing!* Can you hear it, the frequency? All of the frequencies! *Sound must become light!*"

Suddenly there is a bright flash, and the window on the tablet screen flares a blinding white.

And then it goes dark.

I stare at the blank screen, breathing fast, holding back a lump in my throat. I must calm my breathing, since I'll need it to control my voice for the work at hand.

Just as I do, Aeson's voice comes in, steady and composed, over the interstellar comm linkup.

"This is *Astroctadra* Mission Control," says the SPC Commander, a man who has very likely just lost his father. "We now have confirmed hostile activity at Ishtar. Our predictions have been validated, and the light grid is building. Prepare to sing the voice sequence on my count in the next few daydreams as we analyze the optimal moment to engage before the grid is complete. Stand by!"

Chapter 96

And so we wait once again, except this time my heart is pounding. Not sure how much time goes by. I watch Command Pilot Uluatl check his wrist comm frequently, and then I watch Erita check hers.

"Ishtar Grid is now at 23% according to update," she says to me. "Building rapidly, even with all the SPC Fleet ships from War-7 engaging in blocking maneuvers to slow down the process."

"What exactly are we waiting for?" I ask.

"If we counterstrike too soon, before the grid is near completion, then this grid and all the others will still be dormant," Erita explains. "According to Keruvat, who's running the predictive strike pattern scenario, we need to act right at the moment the Ishtar grid is on its final row, about to power up, which will then awaken the *entire grid network*. That's when we stop it—right as it powers up to do whatever system-level grand damage it has in mind. *If* it has a mind."

I make a sound of bitter amusement.

We continue waiting.

Almost an hour later, when the grid is at 95% despite the SPC Pilots' best efforts at blocking it, Aeson's voice returns on the interstellar comm.

"This is *Astroctadra* Mission Control. Attention, all mission members, begin voice sequence on my count."

I stand up from my seat, as the others step back, giving me room.

"Three . . ." Aeson says.

I feel my gut cramping.

"Two . . ."

Erita gives me a solid smile and nod of encouragement, while Command Pilot Uluatl nods also.

"One . . ."

I press my right palm on the surface of the console, and hold the comm button with my left hand.

And I begin to sing the voice keying command first portion of the sequence.

My mezzo voice fills the grand expanse of the Resonance Chamber like amber ale pouring into a chalice. At once the nature of the light coming from the wall panels intensifies, and the sound grows and grows, rebounding and then being swallowed up by the chamber, which transmits it onward to its ultimate destination.

At the same time, I hear the other five voices in the grand Logos Voice Chorus. Manala's delicate, crystalline soprano acts like a fine razor blade cutting through the higher frequencies. Sheolaat's deep alto is an anvil of iron and heavy metal as it bends and twists and dominates the sound frequencies at the lower registers. My voice continues to pour with richness in the middle.

Aeson's gorgeous baritone lends the low anchor points underneath all, while Anen's and Gordie's tenors drill through the fabric of space-time. . . .

All this incredible sound fills the Resonance Chamber, at the same time as we are all heard the same way in each other's locations, multiplying and amplifying our output, unto infinity.

The power of our Logos voices combined is beyond words. The very air in the Resonance Chamber is now *vibrating* in a strange acoustic mirage. . . . I can feel the frequencies enter *me*—in particular, through the exposed skin of my face and hands—and it rattles my bones, while the light level coming from the panels is now a fierce, blinding white.

We complete the sequence, then begin again, even as I see from the corner of my eye the Command Pilot checking his wrist for real-time status updates. He nods at me—which I take as confirmation that we must be doing something right.

And then, just as we complete the voice command sequence for the second time, and the echoes of our glorious *sound* are still rebounding around the chamber, there is a strange, high-pitched, alien, grating noise that seems to originate from somewhere outside. . . .

From outside the Resonance Chamber.

All of a sudden, the great ship around us seems to rumble and groan, and then there is a sensation of pulsing changes in *gravity*. No other way to describe it, since we're presently levitating on a disembodied platform in the air, and wouldn't feel a pitch or lurch of the battle barge or its collapsing decks.

Even while I'm still paused in confusion, Erita goes into action. "Your helmet!" she exclaims to me. "Put your helmet on, *now!* Secure the space suit!"

I turn to her dumbly—just as the creaking and groaning from the walls increases—but then the adrenaline takes over. I grab my helmet and put it on with shaking hands, so that it takes me five seconds of fumble to achieve the proper seal-locking twist—even as Erita yells at me, pointing to my gloves clipped to my waist.

Command Pilot Uluatl is putting on his own helmet and gloves with practiced, controlled motions, and Erita does the same with her own suit components.

Just then a blast of sound comes on the ship's system, and it's a powerful alarm siren, so strong that it is heard, muffled, through the layers of our own suits, here, inside the acoustically sealed Resonance Chamber. . . .

Which means it's no longer sealed properly.

I stand balanced on the platform, feeling the continuing pulses of variable gravity, hearing the wailing siren, watching the Command Pilot start working the holo-grid on the console, switching from purple to white and other colors that control the various ship's systems.

Erita grabs my arm, and I see her pull a thick cable from her waist and unspool it long enough to hook its one end onto my own suit near the waist, and then—

The Resonance Chamber starts to show cracks. In a matter of heartbeats it breaks in two hemispheres along the seams defined by the acoustic panel tiles . . . and then it explodes around us.

There is a blinding flash of white.

I am tossed by a huge gravity wave . . . spun and twisted in every direction like a rag doll with the forces of many g's, feeling no up, no down only the chaos of violent, deadly motion.

Aeson! I think. *My family! Atlantis! Earth!*

And then there's nothing.

I come to with a painful headache ringing in my head and residual vertigo. My eyes open onto a soothing black view. . . . Darkness. There's a queasy feeling in my gut, ugh.

I blink, take a shallow breath, and feel it strike and fog up the interior glassy surface inches before my face, then come back at me, blowing at my cheeks.

My helmet.

I blink again, and I see stars.

Real stars, pinpoints of them set against cosmic black velvet all around, as far as I can see in the limited view of my helmet.

I am floating in space.

Panic.

Instant surge of terror. . . .

It grips me, and I start to hyperventilate, then realize I have limited air in my suit, and hear no hiss of the recirculating life support system.

Oh, God! I need to turn on the life support!

I move my hands, my arms and legs, flounder in place, with no frame of reference—unsure if I am now spinning due to my own kicking efforts. Yes—as I peer closer at the dots of stars turning suddenly in a carousel in my view—apparently, I am.

I am spinning.

But not completely out of control. I feel a tug at my waist, as if some kind of anchor is pulling me in one direction in particular. I turn my head down and see the line of cable attached to my waist, and it's a long, fully unspooled line of about two hundred feet.

Erita, in a space suit, is on the other end of it.

Her body inside the suit appears motionless, and I wonder if she is okay . . . if she is unconscious or *dead*—even as I continue to revolve as an orbiting body around the distant gravitational axis of Erita.

Suddenly Erita becomes my whole world.

I frantically pull at the cable to draw us together.

Even as I do so, the angle of my spinning rotation changes, and the stars start to turn their carousel in another direction, diagonally. . . .

Suddenly my view is filled with things.

Shiny metallic debris fills the viewscreen of my helmet. Pieces float and sail past me in the distance, and some appear to be moving in my general direction.

Orichalcum panels comprise most of it. Some are charred with black, riddled with burn holes, others seemingly pristine. They are reflecting light, a bright radiance from an unknown light source, which I urgently need to locate.

I stop trying to reel Erita in and force myself to turn in yet another direction, awkwardly, since the line keeps pulling me to rotate a certain way.

And then I see it.

Not Helios—though, its solar disk also shines fiercely from a point below.

No, what I see is an infinitely long *column* of white plasma.

The column is straight as an arrow, a spewing jet of white-gold-blue fire. It is many kilometers across—I cannot even begin to estimate, but I know just by looking that it is immense—and it's coming directly from the solar disk that is Helios.

This fiercely spewing jet is pointing directly here from the system center, originating from the star, Helios. And what remains of our battle barge, War-2 is floating in pieces around us.

It occurs to me, with a sickening certainty of madness, that this spewing solar plasma jet—something that wasn't here before, not when we first arrived at these coordinates—is what blasted us into pieces.

Then a different thought comes—at such a proximity, how is it that I'm still alive?

I don't have time to ponder any of this, because I feel a different kind of tug on my waist, and this time I see it's Erita and not just rotational momentum. Her spacesuit is moving, and she is now reeling *me* in.

Oh, thank God, she's alive!

I begin to pull her in also, and in moments, with our efforts combined, we are next to each other, then grabbing each other's suits in an awkward embrace.

I stare wildly inside the glassy helmet and see Erita's familiar face, her frantic expression, and then she is tapping my forearm.

Of course, my interstellar comm system. I tap the controls for a local linkup connection, and at once Erita's voice sounds inside my helmet speakers: "Gwen! Your life support pack! Turn it on! There's only half an hour of basic, built-in life support in the suit without it!"

"Okay!" I say. "Where is it? Where?" Even as I try to move, I fumble with my hands around my suit, trying to recall where it was the last time I checked—at my back?

"Hold still," she says. "Let me try." And then she turns me around and does something at the back of my suit, where I guess my pack has been attached all along, and I forgot completely—it's a small portable brick and slipped my mind since I attached it earlier this morning. Then she presses the control at my waist.

A moment later, I hear the hiss of fresh air at my face, and the pressure normalizes. At once I feel better, and my headache and vertigo lessen.

Stupid idiot Gwen, your suit wasn't pressurized properly, no wonder you were sick!

But there's no time for pointless self-reproach.

"What happened?" I exclaim.

"*Shebet* happened," Erita retorts. "War-2 blew up. Probably as a result of the enemy attack—though I'm not entirely sure how. I'm going to need to use your secure interstellar comm linkup to see if I can call out to the others so we can at least assess the situation and ask for help. My own suit comm is local radius only, and I tried it already to call for help, with no luck. If there are any survivors, they're outside my radius. Right now, I don't see any bodies floating around either, or any undamaged fighter ships, so we might be in deep trouble."

"Do you see that big light column thing behind us?" I ask. "What the hell is that? It's coming from Helios. Did it destroy the ship?"

"Yeah. Probably." Erita says, turning her body slightly to stare at the stack of blinding light. "Magnetic solar flare, maybe. Relativistic jet. I don't know. But it's bad news for us. We're gonna need to get as far away from it as possible."

"Oh, crap," I whisper. "I think we're actually drifting *toward* it."

"*Bashtooh . . .*" Erita sputters inside her helmet.

"Is there a way to propel the suit?" I ask.

"There's an electromagnetic propulsion field generator. But it's a clip-on attachment that doesn't come standard with the suit, and we don't have it on us." Erita cusses again. "We'll just have to toss-propel each other to achieve momentum. Basic space survival training."

"Which I haven't had," I conclude sadly.

"I'll teach you, it's easy. But first, let me access your interstellar and borrow your tablet."

M oments later, Erita is cycling through screen windows on the tablet (which fortunately is space vacuum-proof), as both of us hold it and stare at the little screen, while the audio is being piped into our helmets. Good thing my tablet stayed attached to the suit!

"Mission Control! *Astroctadra* Mission Control!" Erita says loudly. "This is Tefnut on behalf of Lark! Please acknowledge!" The window icon designated as Aeson's linkup coordinates at Ishtar and War-7 does not answer.

My heart starts to pound violently in my chest.

"Aeson!" I exclaim. "Aeson, please, this is Gwen! Are you okay?"

"Mission Control at Ishtar! Phoebos, respond! We need urgent assistance!"

Then we try other windows. A vague crackle comes when we try Gordie's location, and some kind of video comes in but it's a broken blur of images. Similar crackle and static from the other locations around the four planets in alignment.

And then we try Manala, who is on the opposite side of Helios from us, on the same perpendicular plane.

Suddenly there's a full picture, and our connection goes live immediately.

There is some kind of fumble, and glimpses of space and stars tumbling, and abruptly the tablet on the other end is turned and steadied. We see a helmeted face staring at us, superimposed against a field of ship debris similar to ours.

Only the person in the helmet is not Manala—it is Hasmik.

"Gwen! Gwen-*janik!*" she exclaims. "You are alive! So terrible here!"

"Oh no, you too!" I respond. "Are you okay? Where is Manala? My brother George?"

"I don't know!" Hasmik exclaims, and her voice starts to crack. "I don't know anything! We blew up! This tablet—she told me to hold it! She was very upset about her father . . . we had to calm her down so she could sing. Then—we were in the Resonance Chamber, she finished singing with all of you, and then there were alarms and explosions outside! I put my helmet on like they told me, and Xelio gave me his things to hold while he and George were helping her with the helmet and gloves, and Consul Denu also, and then, a super big, bright explosion!"

"Same here," Erita says.

"Then I woke up here, in space, next to this thing!" Hasmik says, and she turns her tablet around to show a panorama of spacecraft debris, and another immense column of white fire spewing from Helios.

"Yeah. We got that too." Erita's voice is grim.

"The ship is gone," Hasmik continues. "Everyone is gone, and all I know is how to use the tablet and some of the suit. I think I'm going to die here. There is no one! *Atsvats! Inch petke anem?*" And Hasmik goes silent, her voice cracking.

"You're *not* alone," I say, my own voice faint with the rising cold of realization. "We are with you!"

"Yes, only eight days of travel away at high speed!" Hasmik starts to laugh softly.

"Speaking of which, how much air and life support time do we have in these suits?" I say to Erita.

"With or without the life support pack running?" she retorts. "Without, as I said earlier, the suit alone is worth half an hour. With the pack on continuously, you get three days."

"Oh no," I whisper.

It takes four days to get to our location from Atlantis. From Ishtar, about the same or longer.

"Hey!" Erita addresses Hasmik. "Did you plug in your life support pack and turn it on?"

Hasmik's face looks confounded. "Yes, I think so. They explained it, but I am not sure I remember now; my mind is so messed up—"

"Check!" Erita says roughly in a commanding officer tone. And then she explains to Hasmik where to look and how to check.

Hasmik does as she's told, and her pack is successfully enabled.

"What else have you got there?" Erita continues.

Hasmik picks up the brick-shaped thing floating on a short cord from her waist. "Xelio gave this to me to hold."

Erita makes a snort. "Lucky you. And, smart Xel. You know what that is? He gave you an electromagnetic propulsion field generator. Which means you can use it to move around, to propel yourself in any direction. Short distances, of course, and good for about three days also. But still, really lucky!"

Then Erita explains to both of us what other suit features we have. We've heard most of this already, but now we are getting training in the field.

"So these are like ropes here? Cords and cables?" Hasmik asks, pulling out a short length of cable from her suit."

"Yes, use it to attach yourself to other people or things."

"How long is it? Does it pull out all the way? Is it flexible like a bungee cord? What kind of material or fabric is it made of? Is there another?" Suddenly Hasmik has so many questions.

I recall that Hasmik works with defense fabrics in her civilian job which gives her some kind of level clearance in fact. No wonder she's curious.

It's not like we have anything else to do.

Just as I think that, my heart constricts with agony. *George! Manala! Xelio!*

"Have you tried calling on your suit's local comms?" I ask. "Maybe they are nearby, and alive?"

"I did, but there was no answer. Let me try again," Hasmik says, and her voice regains a tone of sadness.

"Have you tried cycling frequencies when you called?" Erita says.

"No . . . I don't know how."

So Erita explains.

Hasmik starts tweaking her suit comm control and cycles as instructed to search the entire radius. There is crackle and silence and random space noise on her audio, which we all get to hear.

Suddenly, another crackle, and then, voices.

"Hello! *Hello!*" Hasmik exclaims.

"Hasmik! Is that you?" Xelio's strong voice comes clearly on the linkup.

"Yes! Oh, is this Xelio Vekahat? I am so glad you are alive!" Hasmik exclaims with such joy that my own hope soars. "Is Manala with you?"

"Manala, George, myself, Consul Seval Denu, Command Pilot Uru Onophris, and several others—we are all sealed inside a partially damaged transport. Safety seal is holding, with basic life support. However, we are drifting without propulsion. Where are you?"

"Oh, I'm here!" Hasmik exclaims. "I don't know where here is but I am drifting in space."

"Shamash, this is Tefnut, with Lark," Erita cuts in. "We're in a similar predicament on the opposite side of Helios from you."

There's a brief pause, then Xelio says, "*Bashtooh*, you're alive, *daimon!* Good to hear your voice, Tefnut!"

And then he adds, "I think we did it. Or should I say, Lark, Manala, and the rest of the six did it. According to the others, the enemy grid is no longer out of reach in its dimensional bubble. The alien spheres are now physically solid, tangible, and wonderfully vulnerable in our space-time. We can blast them into oblivion. And we're presently doing just that—at all the four planet locations."

"You're serious?" Erita says with a smile. "That's great! How do you know?"

"A one-way communication from Phoebos came in on Manala's interstellar. They're having a good time flying in combat without us."

"Ah," Erita says. "But do they have a huge bi-directional solar jet frying their ships like we do?"

"Apparently, they *do* have something of the sort," Xelio replies. "There are huge plasma explosions that started issuing from the grids just before the Logos voices did their magic thing. These explosions are currently hanging suspended like fiery nebulas around Rah, Septu, Tammuz, and Ishtar—perfectly contained, of course—inside the same dimensional bubble-space that our own fiery plasma jets occupy."

"Wait, what?" Erita's voice is incredulous. "Those spewing jets are *contained?*"

I, too, stare with a frown, as I listen.

"Oh, yeah," Xel says. "These jets exploding from Helios barely had time to crack open our unfortunate battle barges before the new quantum containment shield sucked them in. Otherwise we'd all be fried and subatomic by now. Everything for countless mag-heitar around these solar jets, including us and the debris, would be incinerated."

He pauses.

"Whatever else the Logos voices might've accomplished, they *inverted* the dimensions. The enemy grids got tossed out of *their* space-time, while the energy of the explosions they caused in *our* space-time got pulled in."

Chapter 97

"Oh, that's great!" I say. "Xelio, this is Gwen! I'm so glad to hear we have one thing less to worry about right now! Because we're drifting in the direction of that solar jet, and we don't have any propulsion packs to get out of the way!"

There's a short pause.

"Ah, My Imperial Lady Gwen, it is good to hear your voice," says Xelio. "Well done on the mission objective. What happened to your propulsion pack?"

"It got separated from me somehow," Erita says gravely. "Probably ripped off during the explosion, judging by the missing hookup and tear at my waist."

"You have a tear in your suit, Erita?" I exclaim. "Oh no! I didn't know!"

"Not a big deal, just a surface layer tear," she responds calmly. "Mostly localized and self-contained. Pressurization still works, and if there's any leak, it's going to be very slow. Nothing to be done about it anyway."

"Oh, Erita!" I say anxiously.

"Relax," Erita tells me with a bright smile that I can see through her helmet.

"So what's going to happen? Is there hope for a rescue? What's the plan?" I say after a small pause, as I try to calm myself and everyone, because the alternative is a dark place.

"Well, considering that we can't seem to get anyone else on this interstellar linkup on our end," Erita says, "Shamash, you need to tell me the status of your own comms."

"Not sure if we're any better off than you right now," Xel says. "The transport we're in has no working comms. We're bouncing off Manala's suit high-security comms just to talk to you. And apparently the tablet is somewhere outside with Hasmik. So far, it seems we can receive, but not transmit to Ishtar or any of the other planetary locations. Could be temporary interference, with all the new quantum fields going up."

"Can you relay to Phoebos our location coordinates using the transport's on-board long-range beacon code?"

"Already done," Xel replies. "I transmitted a broad-range message to all stations that we're alive, and our coordinates. But that was just for *our* location here, before I knew you two also needed help. Let me do the same for you—Give me a few daydreams, now."

"Oh yeah. We have all the daydreams in the world," Erita snorts. "Go do your thing, Shamash, we'll wait."

There's a crackle, followed by silence. But then, moments later, another voice comes on the line. "This is George Lark," my brother says loudly. "Gwen! Are you there?"

"Oh my God, *George!*" I exclaim. "George, yes, I'm here— you're okay?"

"Sure am, sis, but please don't call me God. That's reserved for the future Mrs. Lark."

I chortle with silly joy, hearing my older brother's typical humor. "Oh, George, love hearing your voice—you, silly!"

"You too—mwah on the airwaves!" he responds, and I bet I can just imagine the Cheshire Cat smile on his face as he mouths the air-kiss. "You hang in there, Gee Two! I promise, help is coming," he says. And his tone grows strong and serious.

"You promise?" I smile bitterly. "You know, I *am* literally *hanging* here . . . in space."

"I know. You're my Major Tom. But—way better."

"Naturally." I grow quiet, swallowing so as not to let him hear me cry.

"Okay, while Mr. Vekahat works the beacon code," George says, "here's M'nala. You talk to her, okay?"

"Okay. . . ."

"Gwen! This is Manala!" the high, nervous voice of the Imperial Princess sounds loudly in the speakers. "I am so sorry! So sorry you are so far away! But we will be rescued somehow, I know it."

"Of course, we will, *janik!*" Hasmik's voice suddenly joins us from her lonely location.

"Hasmik!" Manala cries. "Hasmik, oh please, please do not die!"

"Manala, Hasmik, yes!" I say with rising emotion. "We are all going to be rescued, I firmly believe it! You must promise to stay strong, all of you!"

"That's right," Erita's voice joins us. "We've got to keep fighting."

Not sure how much longer we talk. Then Xelio comes back in on the line to say he's finished transmitting a second beacon emergency message on our behalf.

"Now they just need to respond and send some fast ships to both our opposite coordinates," he says.

"Yeah. We have about three days for them to get here." Erita adds.

"What time is it? In Poseidon, I mean." I ask. It's mostly a rhetorical question, because I can look it up on my suit wrist controls, or on the tablet, and because right now it hardly matters. And yet it matters tremendously for our survival, long-term. We're all on limited time here. And some of us have less time than others.

"Looks like it's only twelfth hour and twelve daydreams of Ra. Not even noon yet, in Poseidon."

"Use the water tube in your helmet to drink," Erita reminds all of us who are stuck in space, locked up in space suits and not inside a transport shuttle. "It's that little thing you can pull toward you with your tongue."

"Am I . . . drinking recycled pee?" I ask.

"There's a little extra water that comes packaged in the suit for optimum body balance," Erita says. "But at this point, oh yeah."

"Well, well, Gee Two," George's voice breaks in. "Remember how I've always told you, since we were kids, that at some point I'm going to catch you drinking pee? I rest my case."

I chortle. "Shut up, Gee One. Wait till you get thirsty."

"Speaking of—how much resources and life support does your transport have?" Erita asks.

An unfamiliar male voice now sounds on the comms. "This is Command Pilot Uru Onophris, formerly in command of War-6, now on board a damaged, 100-crew ferry-class *depet* transport. Pilot Qwas, we're unfortunately very low on all the basics including breathable air, pressurization, and climate controls. There is a small tank of water that will help replenish the resources inside our suits.

Altogether, between suits and transport, we have enough to survive four days, maybe five—which should be enough time for rescue. Normally this ship is rated for a 100 crew, but in the short-term ferry capacity, not long-term survival capacity. Nine crew in addition to the *Astroctadra* Mission members, for a total of fourteen souls, plus the one person outside, once we find her—or she finds us."

"You mean Hasmik." Erita says gravely.

"Yes, I am here! Hasmik Tigranian!" Hasmik's voice sounds, both frightened and forcefully cheerful, and her helmet shows on the tablet screen as she waves to us with her gloved hand. Of course, only Erita and I get to see her, since we have the only functional video comm equipment.

"Hasmik!" Xelio's voice breaks in. "Listen to me, Hasmik! You are going to need to find us somehow."

"I know!" Hasmik replies. "But I'm not sure how. . . ."

"Look around you, do you see any large objects? The shuttle transport we're in is a mid-range vessel, 100 personnel capacity, hard to miss."

"I'm looking . . . I see many pieces of things. Some of them may be large, but I cannot tell at this distance—"

Suddenly there's a beep inside my helmet.

I frown, trying to comprehend where it's coming from, and then, since Erita can hear it too, she interrupts. "Your tablet! Someone else is calling you!"

My heart skips a beat with hope. *Is that Aeson? It must be! Oh, please, God!*

"Hasmik, we're getting another call! Sorry—so sorry—but I need to disconnect from you briefly," I say with urgency, as I minimize her window, then swipe the blinking caller icon.

Please, let it be Aeson. . . .

It's not.

It's Nefir Mekei, calling from Earth.

"Nefir!" I exclaim. "Oh, Nefir, I am so happy to see you!"

Yeah, I bet that was the last thing he expected to hear from me.

But I don't have time for bitterness, or past grudges, when the primary goal right now is to *survive*.

"Imperial Lady Gwen," he says with some surprise, looking at me from behind a desk inside ship quarters. "You are—where are you?"

"In space! I'm in deep space! War-2 has exploded, and I'm marooned in space at our *Astroctadra* Mission coordinates, together with Pilot Erita Qwas, and no other known survivors at our location here. However, War-6 is also gone, but Princess Manala Kassiopei is alive with other survivors at their location. None of us is able to get Aeson or anyone else on the interstellar comms—"

"My Imperial Lady! I am so sorry! I had no idea of any of this!" Nefir leans closer to the screen, and his expression focuses intensely. "I'm going to contact Ishtar immediately. Please, allow me a moment—"

And just like that, Nefir disconnects the call.

I have a sudden sickening feeling. What if he's just lying, and has no plans to call Aeson? Considering our history, I wouldn't put it past him now.

"So, the *chazuf* is going to call for help," Erita says, floating next to me and watching the tablet. Erita knows all about Nefir and his actions in regard to my mother's rescue, about his betrayal of Aeson's trust and mine, and she shares our antipathy.

"Let's hope he does," I say. "At least now we know the linkup works on his end. Maybe we can get through to Aeson and the others."

Erita takes the tablet from me and starts cycling through programmed icons, starting with Aeson's. Unfortunately, there's still nothing but crackle and static coming from any of them. She even tries tapping the Imperator's pre-programmed line for good measure, but it is dead also.

He is no longer the Imperator, just Romhutat Kassiopei, my father-in-law.

And he is likely dead now, his ship in pieces, having become part of the accretion disk of Ae-Leiterra. . . .

Just as my thoughts go down that dark path, the tablet bleeps inside my helmet.

Nefir is back on the line. And this time he is holding up a tablet on his own end, and on it I see a face that I never thought to see again, that of my beloved husband.

Aeson!

So, Nefir came through.

Nefir places the tablet flat on his desk and manipulates its touch screen. Suddenly he and his desk disappear, and our main view is replaced with the contents of the tablet screen. Aeson's face, superimposed against the background of his own ship's quarters, fills the display in closeup as he stares directly into the camera—and he appears distraught at the sight of me.

"Gwen!" Aeson exclaims in a voice of such emotion that he's never shown in public. "I've been trying to contact you repeatedly, but cannot seem to establish a solid connection with two of our six coordinate points—including yours and Manala's! What happened?"

And so, I tell him. I tell him how we blew up, and how Manala's ship blew up, and that we're marooned and need help.

"I'm coming for you!" he exclaims, stirring in his seat as if ready to run. "There's a battle here, and we're fighting for our lives and all of Atlantis—even now! And yes, I'm the Commander. I'm responsible for this Fleet, and may not in all good conscience abandon my post at such a critical time, even though we're holding our own. . . . And yet—by all that's holy, I am coming for you, *im amrevu!* You must stay strong, while I take the fastest velo-cruiser, and will cut all time, and aim for three days instead of four!"

"Aeson, I love you!" I whisper. "But are you sure? Maybe you can send someone else? Someone like Quoni, again? Because you have a war to fight—"

"Not this time!" he says with a fierce gleam in his lapis-blue eyes. There's a strange sense of impossible-to-explain *rightness* that radiates from him in that moment—a cosmic inevitability of actions and choices and outcomes—all of it converging in his one immovable *decision.* "This time I will find you myself, for this is too critical, too much of a fine balance of time and circumstances to be left to someone else—I will fight the war remotely, from the velo-cruiser, on the way to you. I wish I could be in three places at once, but indeed Quoni and several others will be sent to get Manala and your brother and the rest of the survivors there. But you—I will see you soon, Gwen!"

"Okay," I say softly, as a lump starts to form in the back of my throat.

"I'll take care of her, Kass," Erita says, moving closer to peer into the tablet screen.

"Erita—*promise me* you will continue as my Shield," Aeson says with raw intensity. "Protect her! Stay alive, both of you!"

"I promise. Now hurry your ass over here."

And Aeson's screen goes blank.

Nefir appears again in the view, and we suddenly recall that he is there, facilitating this communication.

"Thank you, Nefir," I say.

"It's the least I can do, Imperial Lady Gwen."

That's true, I think. And suddenly I'm reminded of another urgent time when Nefir helped me to contact Aeson—by messaging him from Earth directly to the ark-ship in orbit, during Qualification. It now seems such a long, long time ago, an event in another life.

"Now, what were you calling about, before all this?" Erita asks Nefir coldly and hangs back, giving me the tablet.

Nefir nods, gathering himself politely and this time speaks in a measured tone. "It's about Earth. My Imperial Lady, I wanted to speak with you about the options before us to deal with the asteroid which is expected to make impact with the Earth's surface tomorrow, your time. That is, Poseidon Time, at eleventh hour and seventeen daydreams of Ra, on Red Mar-Yan 17—or its Earth equivalent which is November 18, at 18:47 UTC."

"Oh, ugh, yes . . ." I say, wincing. "Only a day left until Earth's doomsday . . . ugh. So what is being done about it?"

Nefir pauses. "There is very little that can be done. Right now, I am on AS-1999, and we are following along with the asteroid, flying with it to measure trajectory deviations under various impact scenarios, running more tests."

"Impact scenarios?"

"Yes," he says. "I am talking about the option of using this very ark-ship to strike the asteroid at high speed."

"Oh, wow," I say. "Do you mean to crash your ship into it?"

"Yes, that was the intent—to abandon the ship and take our various lifeboats, and set it on auto-pilot to ram the asteroid hard enough to set it a few degrees off course. Unfortunately, our predictive programs told us the result would be insufficient to make a difference in the trajectory. The asteroid is too mass-heavy to be moved by the power resources of this one ship. Furthermore, it will not break apart in most scenarios, and will still strike Earth—but at slightly different and potentially even more catastrophic coordinates, regardless of which direction we aimed the strike. And in scenarios where it did crumble, the individual smaller pieces were equally deadly and now, completely unpredictable."

"Oh, no. . . ."

"Yes, the Archaeon Imperator chose a perfectly destructive object from the Oort Cloud, specified a very direct route for impact, and set it on course." Nefir pauses thoughtfully. "The biggest problem is the material makeup of the asteroid's solid metal core. It has the remarkably dense composition of iron, osmium, platinum, iridium, plutonium, and radium. And, before you ask, we tried magnetic tractoring to pull it via electromagnetic forces. However, there is something else in its core that interfered with the tractor, negating the magnetic force. We are now thinking it is the material that used to be orichalcum before it was fried and made inert by the Imperial Sovereign himself."

"You mean Romhutat Kassiopei," I correct. "Because, just in case you haven't heard, Romhutat abdicated in favor of his Son earlier today. Before witnesses. Just before he Jumped into Ae-Leiterra."

"What?" Nefir's face stills into a mask of shock.

"Yes, Aeson is now Imperator. *Your* Imperator." I feel an odd stab of satisfaction saying this to Nefir.

"Ah . . ." Nefir says softly after a long pause. "In that case— you are now my Imperatris—My Sovereign Lady."

Holy crap. . . .

The realization strikes me stupidly, just then. I am now the Archaeona Imperatris of Imperial *Atlantida*.

Both of us pause, for different reasons, as we digest the bizarre new reality.

"All right," I say at last, as I float next to Erita, holding the tablet in one hand and seeing out of the corner of my eye the white column of incandescent plasma which is the solar jet, looming in the cosmic distance. "So you cannot ram the asteroid. What's the next option?"

Nefir shakes his head slowly. "There is no other option that I— and the crew experts—can think of. Maybe if we had more ships, larger ships."

"And breaking up the asteroid into pieces by laser-cutting it, is no good?"

"Not enough power or tools at our disposal to cut through that much metal in time. Also, same problem with the smaller pieces acquiring multiple unpredictable trajectories."

I sigh in frustration and think.

Giving up is unthinkable. *I do not accept it.*

There has to be some other way.

"Can you involve Earth in this, by any chance? Reveal your presence to the public and see if you can somehow use their resources, ships, weapons?"

Nefir shakes his head again. "They are doing it already, on their own. Earth is in chaos, but there are many factions, such as Earth Union, who believe in fighting up to the very end. Yes, there will be weapons fired and ships going up in orbit. None of it sufficient to assist us. Some of it might even end up being detrimental."

"Damn. . . ." I whisper.

"Yes." Nefir pauses, and his tone is sad and no longer reserved. "This is why I called. I was instructed to do all in my power to stop this situation, and wanted to update you on our efforts, as promised."

"Thank you." I sigh, trying not to breathe too deeply and waste the air inside my suit. "Please, keep trying! Do not give up on Earth!"

"I am not giving up. We will be working on scenarios and trying things, up to the last moment. I promise you this, my Sovereign Lady. I will also contact you periodically—with your permission, of course—to provide updates and to make sure you are keeping well in your own ordeal."

"Yes, please do," I say.

After Nefir ends our communication, we connect back with Hasmik, to keep her company in her horrific isolation, and to continue to try working on solutions.

As we get back on the line with Hasmik, she is in the middle of a discussion with Xelio and the others about the best way to locate them.

"The fact that you are picking us up on your local suit comms means we are within your proximity radius," Xelio is saying. "If you start losing us, turn around and propel yourself in the other direction!"

Apparently, while we were on the line with Nefir and Aeson, Hasmik figured out how to use the propulsion pack to get around, and has been moving carefully, combing the area for their location and for any other survivors or useful debris.

"Hey, I have an idea, Hasmik," Erita says. "Did you know, your suit has multiple cameras, including one on your helmet, that can give us your perspective view—here on this tablet. That way we can see what *you* are seeing as we receive your suit's camera feed through your helmet's vantage point."

"Okay," Hasmik says. "What do I do?"

Erita explains, while she also manipulates the tablet controls here.

Moments later, Hasmik "disappears," and instead we see a view of entirely different space and debris and a column of solar plasma similar to our own.

It's dizzying to think that we're looking at what could be a mirror-image view on the opposite side of Helios, directly across from ourselves, billions of miles away—and yet it looks very much like our own present surroundings, including the solar jet column and the remains of a battle barge.

"Okay, is it working now?" Hasmik's voice comes in through the speakers in our helmets, piped in from the tablet. "I can still only see both of you on my tablet, so I don't know—"

"Oh, yes," Erita replies. "Working as intended. Now we can help you, a little bit—as much as possible. Shamash—too bad you have no visuals on your end, else you would be the one to guide her."

"Yes, it is regretful," Xel's low voice comes, sounding almost tired. "Now, I've been thinking and it might be possible to use the plasma column as a reference point. Hasmik, turn and face the jet, and Tefnut will describe to me the feed and what's visible in the surroundings, including column thickness based on notches of the view grid. . . . We might be able to estimate distance. . . ."

They keep talking, and I start to space out a little—funny to say this, I know, considering I am literally "spacing"—but it does describe my current state.

Little things itch inside my suit, body parts I cannot scratch . . . I am dehydrated already despite sipping from the little tube, and at least I don't need to move my bowels.

How much time has elapsed?

I stare at the distant pieces of the great battle barge around me, and then—I start seeing *bodies*. . . .

There are people floating in space suits out there. They are motionless from this distance—or they could be just conserving strength and keeping still—same as us. I point the fact out to Erita.

Immediately she starts cycling on our local comms to try to contact them.

No response.

If there are living survivors, they're not answering.

Therefore, bodies.

"What's the likelihood we're the only survivors of War-2?" I ask. "Where are the others? What about the fighter ships?"

"My guess is, those of us who survived—on both ships—were safely contained inside the Resonance Chambers," Erita says. "As for the fighter vessels, they're built to be self-contained, so very likely most are still intact. They could've been ejected far outward in opposite directions, and we just can't see them. Given time, we might see some drifting this way."

"Could be," Xelio says from his end, billions of miles across from us. "We were lucky in that we hooked up the cables between all our suits to form a tethered human chain while still in the Resonance Chamber, which kept us together. Then the transport shuttle was within reach, so we took it."

"Unfortunately, Command Pilot Uluatl didn't connect his suit with us," Erita says, then yawns tiredly.

I hope it's just that and not the beginnings of oxygen deprivation.

Chapter 98

It's hard to have a sense of time when you're floating disembodied in deep space, with few frames of reference.

Hours pass.

We chat some, mostly conserving oxygen, watch the tablet view of Hasmik's helmet perspective as she is floating with determination toward various debris in search of the others, past many, many dead bodies, even checking them bravely for signs of life.

"If you find stuff you can use, take it!" Erita advises her. "Such as additional life support packs—don't feel, bad, these troops no longer need it. So, scavenge away!"

"Good idea about life support packs." Xelio agrees.

"This is very sad, but all right," Hasmik says softly.

I can hear her shallow breathing as she moves around, and see her gloved hands in action when she touches the suited bodies, checking their waist area for tools.

I notice, Hasmik starts unspooling the various cords and wire leads from the suits she finds, removes them all the way and attaches all of it to herself in a large loop she formed out of one cable. She proceeds to hang things on the loop at her waist, and then wraps more and more cords, connecting them by the ends into a long line. As she moves, she keeps adding to its length and winds it neatly.

We watch her hands move very *quickly* and with amazing skill, despite the cumbersome suit gloves. And then she starts to crochet the lines together, forming a kind of loose net.

Holy crap, that's some hard-core Yellow Quadrant skills!

"What are you doing, Hasmik?" I ask with wonder.

"Making a net, *janik*, making a net," she replies. "It might be useful."

"That's crazy good," Erita says with a smile. "Where did you pick up such solid Yellow skills?"

"In Yerevan, Armenia," Hasmik says with a little sound of amusement. "Boston too, but later. We knit and crochet."

"Apparently even in the vacuum of outer space!" I say.

"What's happening? What is she doing?" Xelio asks with strange tension in his voice.

We try to describe, but it's nearly impossible.

And then Hasmik keeps going, canvassing the area, picking up stuff and adding it to her arsenal.

M ore time passes.
According to the chronometers on the suits it's eighth hour of Khe, Poseidon Time. We could be eating an early *niktos* meal.

Don't think about food.

Instead, I think about Dad and Gordie. About Gracie and Laronda and Chiyoko back on Atlantis, in orbit aboard War-1.

Consul Denu comes on the line to tell us some Atlantean Court anecdotes, making us smile, and making Erita roll her eyes.

Nefir calls with another Earth-and-asteroid update. Unfortunately, no new developments, but supposedly several United Nations spacecraft are being launched from Earth's surface, carrying nukes. . . .

However, Nefir relays a message from Aeson, who is making good progress on his way here, flying at top speed. The message for me is to *stay strong and to survive.*

I drift off periodically, in a kind of shallow sleep that gives no real rest and leaves my mind racing with stress.

Hasmik has stopped moving, and she too is taking a break and has probably gone to sleep briefly while drifting alone among the debris. We don't dare turn off the tablet in case she needs us, and besides, the tablet's power source capacity is rated for several months, so we don't need to worry about conserving it.

"What time is it?" I ask a rhetorical question with a yawn.

"Hmm, looks like *bashtooh* thirteenth hour of Khe and twenty daydreams." Erita yawns back.

"Why do you call minutes daydreams anyway? And seconds heartbeats?" I ask stupidly.

"It's an old tradition—very natural, if you think about it," Erita says. "Has to do with the rhythms of our bodies, I suppose. I don't know."

"Time is weird," I say. "So many conversions, and it's all kind of meaningless. Earth time, Atlantean time. Not to mention, all the time zones. And on Earth we have this stupid thing called Daylight Savings Time in some places."

Erita chuckles. "Yes, I've heard. And it's genuinely one of the most *hoohvak* thing humans have done for themselves. Changing time to fool and accommodate themselves instead of just changing themselves to be in tune with the environment. Although—we do similar things on the Fleet ships during long space missions. Time tweaking, we call it."

"Oh, really?" I ask.

"You know, we did that on the Earth mission, multiple times. For example, you know how we arrived back on Atlantis and it was nice and early morning, ship time, somewhere around 7:30 AM, based on the ship's UTC clock?"

"It was 7:24 AM, Earth UTC, actually," I say.

I'll never forget that time of arrival in Atlantis orbit.

"Yeah, right, 7:24 AM," Erita says. "Well, it wasn't *real* Earth UTC. It was off by 8 hours and 38 minutes, which they added on to the Earth UTC, if I recall correctly. They tweaked the ark-ship time right after the Jump, to make your arrival be during daylight hours. Actual Earth UTC in that moment was somewhere in the middle of the night, or maybe late afternoon, according to the 24-hour clock."

"Wow," I say.

"Yeah, it's those little things," Erita says. "Easy to tweak, but for a good reason, I suppose. Now, why don't you get some sleep."

"Right," I say. "Sleep conserves oxygen."

And that's the kind of stupid conversations we have in those long, weird hours as we float aimlessly in deep space with nothing else to do but live.

At some point, I suppose, it's morning on Poseidon. Here, it's just another jolt into a wakeful period for me.

But then I remember.

Today is Red Mar-Yan 17.

Asteroid Day.

Immediately I feel a sickening pang in my stomach. And it has nothing to do with me being hungry, thirsty, itchy, weightless, and miserable.

Today Earth is going to suffer a catastrophic disaster that could end all life on its surface, indefinitely.

I feel a sudden urge to run, to fly, to do something, *anything*.

"Nefero eos, im amrevu," Erita says, tapping me on the shoulder, and I see from the silly expression inside her helmet that she must've just woken up.

I look around us, because it has gotten really bright, for some reason, and realize that we are now floating right *at* the immense column of solar jet plasma. We must be only a few hundred meters away, because the plasma is now a wall of light before us.

"Rawah bashtooh!" Erita exclaims. "Xel better be right about this spewing solar geyser thing being locked in another quantum dimension. Else we're done for. . . . Okay, close your eyes, Gwen, quickly, it's getting too bright. Don't stare at it. I don't know if these helmets have blackout mode on the visors—they look like older, standard issue models which require manual inserts. You would think that War-2 would have better equipment on board—ah, crap—"

Just then, we float directly into the column of blinding light.

I shut my eyes immediately, then *squeeze* them shut because the light around us is so powerful that I can see it through my closed eyelids.

"This is so horrible!" I exclaim through gritted teeth as we continue to hurtle through the endless fiery hell.

"Not as horrible as if it had been in our actual space-time—we'd be incinerated," Erita says. "Keep squeezing your eyes!"

"Hello? What is happening on your end?" Hasmik's voice comes in.

"Oh, nothing much," I say. "We're now *inside* the extradimensional solar flare jet, that's all."

"Just drifted in moments ago, and yes, we can report that it is quantum locked and safe," Erita adds.

"How long is this hell going to last?" I ask. "Not sure I can keep squeezing my eyes this long."

"Just hang in there," Erita mutters. "We'll emerge on the other side at some point. We're bound to, since we're still drifting."

"If we make it back to Atlantis alive," I say, "and if I still have my *eyeballs* intact, much less my vision, remind me never to go into space again. This *sucks!*"

About half an hour later—or what feels like hours—we indeed emerge on the other side of the light column, into perfectly soothing darkness.

We carefully open our eyes and discover that we've been partially blinded, and there are aftereffects of the infernal brightness obscuring our fields of vision.

It takes at least another half an hour of darkness for the effect to wear off and both Erita and I begin to see again. The field of debris of War-2 is thicker here, so it's a good thing we can see now, because we need to pay attention to our surroundings.

Just as we maneuver around a once elegant and now badly broken hull of what must be the remains of a *sebasaret*, in search of anything useful that might help us, we hear Hasmik's voice rise in excitement. Erita picks up the tablet, and we pause to watch.

The view from Hasmik's helmet shows us a feed of a similar floating "shipyard" of vessels and ship parts and bodies of the crew.

A transport looms ahead of her, an oval, pill-shaped vessel with some hull damage. And yet there is a faint violet glow of plasma coming from its hull, which tells us the force field is engaged, and someone could be inside.

"Is this them?" Erita asks. "Hasmik! That *depet* looks viable!"

"How can I tell?" Hasmik's gloved hands appear before us as she is propelling herself faster to approach.

"Shamash, this is Tefnut. If you are able, pulse the security force shield on your *depet* off and on. I believe Hasmik has found you."

"This is Shamash, stand by. Engaging pulse code now."

The next moment the purple-violet plasma glow around the hull of the ship on the tablet screen begins to blink. Three, then six times.

"Yes!" Hasmik exclaims. "I can see your plasma blinking!"

"Good, now let her in," Erita says.

"Stand by," Xelio's voice says. "Hasmik, move to the long side of the hull and find the smallest hatch of three in a row. As soon as you do, I'll lower the shield, and you will be able to access the airlock. The other hatches open directly on deck, and we cannot open those safely."

Hasmik does as instructed, and we watch her progress along the side of the transport's hull.

She pauses before several hatches and finds the smallest one. The force field goes off. She tries the hatch, but it remains closed.

"Hello! Xelio, I cannot open the door!"

Xel's voice comes in after a small pause. "Hang in, let me go over there and manually unlock it for you. Stand by."

Moments go by.

"Hello?" Hasmik says with a new tone of alarm, and her palms are now flat on the hatch as she tries to push it or move it somehow. "Are you there?"

"Yes, I'm here," Xel replies. "I'm working on it."

And then, long moments later, he says. "There is some kind of locking damage. I'm sorry, Hasmik, I cannot get the door open. Let me find some micro-cutting tools that will not damage the hatch. Meanwhile, stand back, because the force shield must be turned back on, or we'll lose environmental controls and pressure."

"Okay, Xelio," she says. "I'll be right outside."

"Yes! Don't go anywhere, stay close to this hatch," he replies immediately.

And so, Hasmik waits.

Over on our side of things, the tablet beeps with a call from Nefir. His face appears drawn and exhausted on the screen, and I'm guessing Nefir hasn't slept in a bed either.

"My Sovereign Lady, how are you?" he asks.

"Still here, still breathing. How is the asteroid?"

"The same. There are now *six* Earth hours remaining until impact. We are still following alongside it, with no successful solutions. Would you like to see it?" Nefir shakes his head with tired hopelessness.

"Yes, please," I say.

Suddenly, our tablet view shows us a large, generally rounded, dark rock hurtling in space. It's brightly lit on one side with the distant Sol's light, revealing a white albedo, with some crags and cliff-like surface features showing in the light. Plumes of white ice particles stream from it in places.

"As you can see, it is considerable in size. We've sent shuttles to land on it, and it has some gravity due to its dense core. It is also moving extremely fast, having been artificially accelerated along its natural course."

I stare and stare at the asteroid.

Here it is, Earth killer.

They never gave it a proper designation, if I remember correctly, only referred to it by a number, as if to minimize its threat for the public.

If you don't name it, it doesn't exist.

But some people, especially toward the last days, just before Qualification began, started calling it that.

Earth killer.

A weird idea comes to me.

"Nefir," I say. "Can you put things in orbit around it? Does it have enough gravity to do that? In other words, does it even have an orbit?"

Nefir thinks. "Theoretically, yes, but with its present velocity, it would be hard for it to retain anything. What do you have in mind?"

"Well," I say. "You know about the *astroctadra* alignment voice sequences which we just used successfully to remove large planetary objects from other dimensions into our own space-time—or push them back in there. I wonder if we can send this Earth killer to another dimension the same way. We would need six orichalcum objects to be placed around it in an *astroctadra* formation, and I can try singing—"

Half an hour later, six panels are launched from Ark-Ship AS-1999. Tractor technology is used to position them at six precise coordinates of a four-point star in three dimensions. Unfortunately, there is insufficient gravity to keep them in the asteroid's high orbit without being ripped off and flung into space at the present velocity, and too much gravity to maintain a low orbit. And a tractor field cannot maintain all of them in place since it requires line of sight and has a limited range. If only there was more than one ship with tractor capability!

And so I watch in despair as the panels are blown off or crash onto the asteroid's craggy surface.

"I am so sorry," Nefir says, returning.

"Can you send small shuttles or velo-cruisers to position them around the coordinates?"

"A fine idea!" Nefir hurries to execute this plan.

Another half an hour later, six shuttles are in place, forming a perfect *astroctadra* around the asteroid.

I focus on them and sing the now familiar sequence. My voice is strong and clear despite my being confined inside the space suit.

And nothing happens.

"I believe you need a Resonance Chamber, My Sovereign Lady," Nefir suggests.

"Then take me to the AS-1999 Resonance Chamber, please!"

Nefir transfers our interstellar linkup connection to his tablet and walks me over to the heart of the ark-ship. After some prep work, the chamber is readied, and there I am, ready to try again.

Four and a half hours until impact.

I sing, and my rich mezzo voice, piped remotely from the tablet, still manages to fill the airy expanse of the spherical interior with Logos-level power, despite my own space suit confinement and its inherent limitations. When I'm done, Nefir tells me that there is some strange quantum instability being picked up around the asteroid by the ship's sensors, but the huge rock itself is still physically tangible and fully present in our space-time.

"So, in other words, it didn't work," I say, exhaling with tension. "I realize we need six Logos voices at each of the coordinates, and probably six Resonance Chambers. Do the shuttles have Resonance Chambers?"

"They are resonant along the hull for basic flight, but no, not a true Resonance Chamber as in an interstellar class vessel such as this."

"Oh, lord!" I exclaim in angry frustration. "Do you have portable Resonance Chambers? Little ones? Anything?"

Nefir appears grave and thoughtful. "Let me investigate and get back to you. Although, I must state the sad reality, My Sovereign Lady, that even with such smaller Resonance Chambers in place at every location, there is only one of *you*."

"I *know*," I whisper with despair. "I know."

Three hours and a half until impact, and Nefir is still working on an alternative solution to the Resonance Chambers problem. He comes back to me saying that the only other full Resonance Chambers at their disposal on AS-1999, ironically, are available in nano-cameras.

"Say what?" I ask. "You mean, those teeny tiny things that look like dust motes or snow?"

"The problem with the nano-cams is that their micro chambers don't have sufficient range and output for such a monumental resonance task."

"What if you took a bunch of them and linked them up in a crazy little network? Put them inside the shuttles?"

Okay, I know, now I'm being crazy.

"The problem again is range and output," Nefir says. "They would have to be rather close to each other, and there will have to be many of them. Basically, you would need to blanket the area."

"So do it! Fill the shuttles and—"

"No, that will not suffice, because they still will not have the range to transmit *between* the shuttles themselves. The nano-cams would need to be placed directly around the asteroid's orbit."

"Then do it, please!"

Two hours and forty-five minutes until impact. A roiling sea of nano-cams is ejected by AS-1999, and they fill the asteroid's orbital area. With me, hooked up to the nano-cam network through the AS-1999 Resonance Chamber, I prepare to sing. . . .

And that's when Nefir is informed by the crew that the majority of the nano-cams are already *gone* from the asteroid's orbit—basically blown off by its high velocity—and of the remaining ones, there are just not enough in the micro-network to create a viable linkup.

"I am so terribly sorry," Nefir says tiredly.

Locked inside a space suit, on the other side of the universe, I begin to cry.

But then, I stop.

I cannot waste tears like this, not now.

Besides, I have an idea.

"Nefir," I ask. "Do you have a 3D printer on board? And can it print nano-cams?"

Nefir frowns. "Yes, we have several 3D printer units. And yes, we certainly can print nano-cams. We do need the basic materials, which is mostly orichalcum. But we can always utilize the ship's interior wall panels for raw materials. What did you have in mind?"

I take a shuddering breath. This is crazy . . . this is very, very crazy.

It's the craziest idea you've had yet, Gwen nutcase Lark who is Imperatris and Kassiopei.

"Nefir," I say slowly. "I want you to print as many nano-cams as it takes to create a really, really big network. A gazillion billion of them. Not around the asteroid. Forget the dratted asteroid. We're going to launch the nano-cams in orbit around *Earth*."

Chapter 99

"What?" Nefir frowns, and his expression is utter confusion.

"Yes," I say, starting to chortle with wild, absurd hope. "I'm going to place Earth inside a quantum trans-dimensional force field. Temporarily!"

"But—that's an immense undertaking!" he says, shaking his head. "I really don't think—"

"Nefir! Listen to me: Earth is so crazy-huge, compared to the asteroid, yes—but it is *stable*. It has a stable, dense atmosphere and so many placement options for a network of satellites! Not to mention, it's travelling through space at a leisurely speed in comparison. So run your numbers quickly to figure out the optimum orbital placement so that the little nano-cams don't burn up on entry and don't get sucked out into the outer space vacuum, and let's just do it!"

"Very well." Nefir nods. "I'll start the process at once. I don't know how many nano-units we can print in the short time we have, considering we have to seed the orbit with them and that alone will take an hour at least—"

"*Go!* Just go do it!"

And Nefir disconnects the call.

While I wait, I let the others know what is happening. Erita, who has been a witness to my interactions with Nefir, looks at me with an intensely curious expression. "My Imperial Lady—I mean, my *Sovereign* Lady—this is so unbelievable, and not sure if it's even possible, but—I believe in you . . . Shoelace Girl."

"Thank you," I say in a calm tone, trying not to *feel* anything just yet, because I have to keep up my strength for this upcoming voice command sequence that I have to perform all alone, the solitary Logos voice.

But, does it have to be *me*, alone?

When George, Manala, Xelio, and the others respond to my explanation of what's happening on Earth, and what I plan to do, there are many exclamations and discussion.

"This is definitely nuts, insanity taken to the next level, but it's better than doing nothing," George says with enthusiasm.

"Assuming they get all the network connections and nano-cam placement in time," Xelio says. "Really cutting it close. How much time until impact?"

"A little over two hours," Erita says, checking her suit chronometer.

Xelio whistles.

"You can do it, Gwen-*jan!*" Hasmik's voice comes in.

"Hasmik!" I say. "So sorry I've been dealing with this, what is happening with you?"

"I'm okay, still waiting here," she says in a resigned voice.

Xelio replies simultaneously, "I'm still working on the airlock hatch lock."

"Oh no," I say, "I thought Hasmik might be inside your ship by now!"

"The problem here is that our main hatch seal is also damaged," Xelio replies, and there's a hard edge to his voice. "When we first took this vessel, we had to seal ourselves in manually with some non-standard, *permanent* welding methods. And now, if I cut us out again and force the hatch open, we won't be able to seal the ship back up again and will lose all the life support it provides. It wouldn't help Hasmik. But it would force all the rest of us to switch back to suit support packs for primary life support while we hang out in this no-longer-pressurized, useless hull space."

"At least you'd all be together," Erita says with sarcasm.

"Yes," Xelio replies, taking her words at face value. "It would give me much joy to hold Hasmik's hand right now, if only to make her feel less alone. In fact, the tradeoff might be worth it—"

"No, don't say that," Hasmik cuts in. "I can wait. I'm okay."

"Yes, you *are*," Xel replies. There's a pause and I can hear his breath come roughly over the audio. "I wish—Hasmik—that you . . . danced with me."

A pause.

"I wish I danced with you, too," Hasmik says softly.

"So why didn't you?" Xel's raw voice continues.

Silence.

"Maybe if you ask me again, I will . . . next time."

Another, longer pause.

"Okay, we seriously need to get rescued pronto, folks," George says.

"Agreed," I say. "And we *will*."

And then I decide to bring up another oddball idea in regard to saving Earth. "Manala," I say, when the time comes for me to sing the voice sequence, will you join me? Your Logos voice would really help!"

"Oh, but how?" Manala asks. "How will I sing from here inside this suit?"

"The same way you are speaking to me now," I reply. "The same way I'll be singing! Just sing the best you can, and I will transmit us to Nefir, who will be in the AS-1999 Resonance Chamber. And the Chamber will send out our voices to the network of nano-cams."

"But won't we need to be at those specific coordinates on Earth?" Manala asks.

"Probably." I laugh bitterly. "But we're doing this crazy thing anyway, right? No one knows if it will work, but we have to try!"

"Okay," Manala says with a hint of hope in her voice.

"In fact," I add, "I think everyone should sing too! Whether or not you have a Logos voice doesn't matter, just sing, all of you, and *focus on Earth*—on saving lives, on saving its wonders!"

"My dearest Sovereign Lady Gwen," Consul Denu's voice comes on unexpectedly, "I will be deeply honored to sing with you in this important endeavor, despite all my humble vocal limitations. And I believe everyone here will strive to do the same, to the best of our abilities."

My heart feels a profound surge of emotion.

Thank you, dear Consul Denu. . . .

I hold myself steady and breathe evenly with a rising inner ocean that must be held in check, even as I hear the others voice their agreement in turn.

One hour until asteroid impact.

Nefir calls to let me know they are making good progress

on printing the nano-cams and the orbital seeding process will begin shortly, as they return even now to Earth, well ahead of the asteroid.

"Nefir," I say. "There's one more thing I want you to do. I want you to contact Earth—the United Nations, all the governments, the public. Let them know we're here and what we're doing. Yes, I know it's stupid and ridiculous and probably useless. But these people are all about to die. It's bad enough we—the Imperator, Imperial *Atlantida*—lied to them about everything, including their elites getting rescued at the last minute. At least here is something they can do to help *themselves*."

"My Sovereign Lady, what do you mean?"

I take a deep breath, forgetting again to conserve my air, like the numbskull that I am.

But this is just too important.

"I want everyone on Earth to sing with us, Nefir. I don't know how, or if it's even possible, to hook up so many audio transmissions together and to funnel all of it into your ark-ship Resonance Chamber. Maybe just get a few key connections, all the best professional and amateur singers to do it, hook them in somehow, send them the musical notes of the sequence to learn in a hurry, send them sheet music, whatever!—maybe use their phones—in short, I want Earth to try to do something about this situation and just maybe help *me* help *them*. I mean—I'm so far away from them while they—they're right there, on Earth! At worst—they will die singing."

Nefir says nothing for several long moments, then nods slowly. "To die singing, with hope, might be one of the best ways to go. I will see what can be done. Although, it might be far too late for anything."

"I understand," I say softly. "Thank you for trying."

Fifteen minutes until asteroid impact.

Nefir calls me directly from the Resonance Chamber.

"The last of the nano-cams are being seeded, My Sovereign Lady, and Earth has been notified—with some confusion and much immediate argument, but they are willing, because they are desperate. Approximately thirty global locations with the best singers have been connected into our network. They are studying the sequence notes."

"Thank you!" I say with feeling. "We are ready here on our end."

"Then you should probably begin. The asteroid will be here in minutes, and this sequence may have to be repeated. . . ."

A nd I begin to sing.
   I sing for Earth, with all my focus and all my being.

At first, my voice rises alone, in the thick silence of my helmet, with lousy acoustics and little breathable air. I sound breathy and weak, and it takes me several notes to be on tune.

Then Manala's high voice sounds on the linkup.

She joins me in her crystalline clarity, and now we sing in tandem, across billions of miles. Then, George, Xelio, Hasmik, Erita, Consul Denu, the Command Pilot of War-6 and all the living crew, carefully join us, lending their voices with practiced precision, even though they are not Logos, simply *human*.

And then I hear others in the Resonance Chamber.

Voices of others singing on the surface. Female, male, young, old.

Earth is singing with me.

T he Resonance Chamber swells with sound.
   I cannot describe it because I am in the process of making it, and I am overwhelmed with the ocean of acoustic glory around me, in which I am but a tiny single note.

I am *nothing*.

In my mind, I imagine Earth, its lapis lazuli oceans and golden landmass, its cities shining with energy grids of illumination as they once had been before the raging fires and the wars. . . . I imagine rushing rivers and forests, country fields full of crops and the frozen tundra, deserts of sand and frozen fiords, cathedrals and mosques and temples of every faith. . . . I imagine animals running free in the brush, along the prairie and plain, birds soaring through the blue skies, waters full of fish and sea life.

I sing and sing and there is no end. . . .

Until something in my heart tells me, it is done.

O ne minute until asteroid impact.
   The Resonance Chamber is now silent. Nefir changes the

screen for me, so that now I see the view of the asteroid on approach, the live feed coming from AS-1999 as it hangs at its orbit coordinates, watching the arrival.

Thirty seconds until impact.

The asteroid is a white monster, hurtling at us head-on, illuminated by Earth's yellow sun.

The asteroid enters the layers of atmosphere.

And yet, there is no heating on entry, no reaction, no wind, no stirring of clouds along the way.

The asteroid is a ghost.

Earth is a ghost.

No connection, no contact between them.

The *moment of impact* happens, and the asteroid keeps going. . . .

Through the coordinates of Ancient Atlantis it moves, where the dimensional rift was/is/might still be. Through layers of earth's crust, mantle, core, deeper, deeper.

Minutes later it emerges on the other side.

A lonely voyager, it will continue now, a perfect ghostly stranger, outward into eternity.

S ilence.
    There is no cheering. No other voices are heard from Earth, because Earth is now incorporeal, in another *time-place*. But it cannot stay there; it needs the sun's warmth and the heliosphere's mantle for life to continue to thrive, and it needs to be a part of the fabric of our space-time.

I must bring it back.

There will be no vocal assistance from the surface this time, since they are locked in another reality, another dimension, isolated by our joint efforts. What must the people, the animals, the living flora on the surface be experiencing now, imprisoned in a strange other reality?

What's it like? I wonder. Oh, to be them for a minute, to see and feel it . . . a sudden cosmic cold maybe? A neutral balance of all things suspended, energies contained—particles fixed and frozen in their quantum states? Even light itself, suspended with no outlet? Or is light photon energy slowly seeping out, passing between the trans-dimensional membrane of *here* and *there?*

Maybe one day I will get the chance to ask someone who lived through it.

But now—now, everything must be brought back.

And this time, it is up to us alone, who are on the opposite side of the universe.

I begin to sing again, a reverse sequence that may or may not work. Manala joins me, followed by my brother George, Hasmik, the others.

The Resonance Chamber fills again with the greatest flood of acoustic harmony—fewer voices this time, but no less intense.

We are done, and now comes the moment of truth. Nefir and the AS-1999 crew check their sensor readings to verify if they are once again orbiting a gravity-producing object. Shuttles are sent down to the surface and immediately they encounter atmospheric resistance and winds at re-entry.

Earth is back. . . .

Nefir smiles at me tentatively, with mixed emotions—full of possibilities and repercussions and all that he must now face when dealing with an Earth that lives on—and I can now take a breath and let it go, a shallow breath. In many ways I don't envy him and the political morass he will need to navigate. I merely ask him to let Aeson know that Earth is no longer in immediate danger.

Earth has survived—at least for the time being.

Now it's my turn.

I close my eyes and drift off to sleep—dreaming surreal nightmare images of Earth on fire, interspersed with calming images of Aeson—and Erita doesn't bother me with chit-chat. I've earned it, after such an emotional overload.

The next time I come to, it's because of frantic voices inside my helmet, coming over the linkup.

Apparently the transport in which Manala and the other survivors are locked is drifting inevitably on a crash course with a large wreck of a *sebasaret* or possibly several *ankhurats*, mangled together in an ugly deformed mass of twisted metal.

Metal that bristles with sharp edges.

If Manala's *depet* collides with the wreck, its hull would likely be cut open as though with a can opener. All of this is clearly visible through Hasmik's helmet camera perspective.

"Is there anything that can be done?" Erita muses, after she describes the disturbing visuals to Xelio.

"A couple of options," he replies in a grim voice. "We pray the weakened plasma shield can act as enough of a buffer to reduce the impact. Or we get cut open and will have to abandon ship."

"Any interior chambers which you can pressurize separately and lock yourselves inside?"

"Not in this *shebet depet.*"

Erita snorts.

"Is there something I can do from the outside?" Hasmik asks.

"Yes! You can stay back as far as possible when the impact happens," Xelio replies in frustration.

Hasmik makes a little annoyed sound. "Let me look at it," she says in contrariness, and we see her start moving toward the wreck.

Moments later, she's up close and personal with sharp, ugly metal parts. "I can tie some of these together, you know," she says. "Draw lines between them, here and here, make a net. It may slow down the crash."

"What?" Xelio exclaims. "No, stop before you get hurt!"

"Be careful, please!" I say.

And Hasmik gets to work. Good thing the ship is drifting slowly and she is moving fast.

In a nutshell, Hasmik creates a basic tick-tac-toe grid out of four extended cables, tying them to various protrusions and bits of rough metal among the wreckage, and incorporating the smaller net she made earlier and has been carrying with her all this time. The idea is, the stretched lines of the simple net will act like a spiderweb put up between the drifting vessel and the wreckage. The cables alone are not strong enough to hold back the ship, but their tension will create enough resistance to slow down the ship on impact.

Once again, it's a marvel to see Hasmik's gloved hands move skillfully as she propels herself from one point to another.

"Enough! Get out of there, Hasmik!" Erita says.

She finishes just as the vessel is about a hundred meters away from the wreckage. It heads directly into the net. Hasmik propels her suit quickly out of the way, then turns around to look at her handiwork.

In the perfect silence of deep space, we watch the *depet* sail forward and slow down as it meets the net's resistance.

The net cables start to buckle, and two of them snap and go sailing into the cosmic vacuum.

But the transport comes to an absolute crawl and now barely inches toward the sharp edges of the wreckage.

And then it stops, a meter away.

"*Shebet*, she did it!" Erita says. "Shamash, you are safely stalled in place."

That's when we hear cheers coming from Manala's interstellar linkup.

"Hasmik Tigranian," George says, with a laugh, clapping something on his end. "When this is over, we owe you dinners, drinks, and your favorite things!"

"Hard to believe this girl is a civilian," Command Pilot Uru Onophris says in appreciation. "Very well done."

Chapter 100

Time slows down to an undefined value as we all continue to endure the wait for rescue. The transport remains stalled in Hasmik's net in the wreckage "shipyard," while Hasmik herself stays nearby, floating in the area of the hatch. Meanwhile Xelio tries to do micro-surgery on the airlock mechanism.

Erita and I float in the middle of nowhere, slowly drifting away from the column of the solar jet. We sleep, wake, sip water, periodically check the tablet and try the various comm icons just in case.

I check the chronometer, and Red Mar-Yan 17 is over, and it is sometime in the early hours of Red Mar-Yan 18, Poseidon Time.

Earth is still here with us, undamaged... it occurs to me in a wild, hopeful surge of joy, as I think back on the recent events.

But then I remember, there's still an alien grid being built around Sol, and the dimensional rift may still be open.... I'm afraid to know whether the *pegasei* managed to close the rift or not, and what has happened to Romhutat.

Maybe I should sing the frequency and call Arion one last time.

I feel a painful twinge of emotion at the thought. It would only be another bittersweet goodbye.

This is now the start of our third day inside these space suits.

There is little that can be said about the time that follows, a slow, boring, grueling ordeal of taking each breath, sipping a little water, and being miserable for many hopeless hours.

We stop checking time because it makes it only that much more difficult, waiting and waiting.

Occasional pieces of debris float by, and a few bodies in suits.

I shut my eyes each time, and pray to something, anything, an unknown universal power of good.

I think of Aeson. . . .

And then, at some point, the "day" ends, and it is Red Mar-Yan 19, somewhere out there in Poseidon. Does it even matter?

Here it is only hours of eternal, unrelieved darkness, and among this homogeneity, time itself becomes a hazy memory.

At some point in what must be early morning, I am jolted out of my numb daze.

"Well, it's time to turn on our suit emergency beacons," Erita announces suddenly. "We're getting closer and closer to the end of our life support resources, and that's why I waited for so long. The interstellar long-range beacon uses a lot of energy. It would've drained us faster if we enabled it earlier. Let's hope Kass gets here soon, *today*."

Erita explains to Hasmik and me how to enable the beacons. The others, safely inside the pressurized *depet*, don't need to worry about their suits yet. Besides, the transport beacon is broadcasting for them.

"You might hold off also, Hasmik," Erita says, after some thought. "You're right next to the ship so they'll find you easily at your location. Save your suit power."

And then she adds, "You too, My Sovereign Lady Gwen. I have my beacon on and that's enough for both of us—save your power." And she turns off my beacon.

"We can take turns," I offer. "That way, we only use up half our beacon power."

"No." Inside her suit, Erita shakes her head slowly. "I promised Kass I will take care of you."

"But that's awful!" I say. "You'll run out of power early, and then what will I do without you?"

"Don't worry about it," Erita says with a smile.

"I do worry!"

A few hours later, the power level indicators on our suits start turning on. They glow red, displaying only ten percent life support power remaining. Erita, Hasmik and myself are the only ones affected, since the others, again, are inside the *depet*, pressurized. Hasmik, however, has scavenged a few additional life support packs from the dead bodies, so she is not under the same pressure we are—or so she tells us.

"Rawah bashtooh," Erita whispers, staring at the power indicators.

I feel a stab of terror in my gut. "What does that mean? How much time is left?" I ask.

"Depends. Could be an hour or two, could be less." Erita's voice sounds grim.

Oh God, we're about to die. . . .

After all this time, all these things achieved, we're going to die here. . . . Suffocate, depressurize, freeze—whichever comes first, I don't know; don't want to know or ask.

"Let me see, let me look at your suit," Erita says, noticing what must be my pathetic deer-in-the-headlights expression.

She turns me around and fumbles. I let her, helpless and stupid with sudden debilitating terror.

And then suddenly I see Erita rip out the cable connecting us together from the hookup at her waist. At the same time, I notice that her life support pack is now attached to *me,* plugged into another, secondary slot on my suit.

"Erita! No!" I cry—even as she pushes off from me, hard, and goes floating off into the darkness.

"Give Kass my love," Erita's voice comes resonant in my helmet speakers. "Tell him I Shielded you. Turning my comms off now. Live well! *Saret-i-xerera!"*

"Rawah bashtooh! Tefnut, no! *Erita!"* This time it's Xelio's voice, crying out desperately over the linkup.

But there is no answer.

I take a breath and start to bawl.

For several seconds I allow myself to sob and shudder, as my face fills with tears and snot. And then I stop—because Erita just gave her life for me and I have *no right* to compromise what little extra chances she has given me by using up my resources and incapacitating myself.

I take more controlled breaths to stifle the sobbing. And I think, desperately.

Then I make the decision I've been putting off and sing the frequency to call Arion, afraid he will never again answer.

But instantly I hear his familiar, warm voice inside my mind.

And then a burst of plasma filled with rainbow colors explodes in space before me.

Gwen Lark who is Kassiopei, Arion says. *I am glad you called me at last.*

"Arion! Oh, Arion!" I exclaim out loud. "Please help her! Help Erita! I know you helped Aeson somehow, kept him alive, so you can help her the same way! She's only been disconnected for a minute or so! Please help!"

I will help her, the quantum being tells me softly. *But you must understand that the rest is up to you. Aeson, your beloved, is on his way here, and he will arrive, but not fast enough. I and my kind can keep all of you alive in the interim. But it will not solve the true problem still before you.*

"I don't understand," I say, "but please, help Erita first!"

Look . . . out there. She is being helped already.

And as I focus my gaze, I see that in the distance another rainbow plasma cloud has burst into existence. It surrounds and has enveloped the pale speck that is the floating suit with Erita inside. . . .

"Is she alive?" I ask.

She lives.

"What happens now?" I whisper. "What happened at the rift, does it still remain open?"

The rift remains open as we wait for you.

"What?" I exclaim. "What are you waiting for? And—is Romhutat Kassiopei—are you keeping him safe also?"

We offered to keep him safe, but he made his choice. He will go with us, with she-who-wields-Starlight—as we pass into the rift.

Sacrifice.

A strange wave of bitter sorrow washes over me.

So, he's gone for real.

Aeson's father is gone. . . . I should be relieved, considering all the things he's done. And yet, I feel strange, unexpected grief.

He rejected our offer to grant him a safe passage back, in order to spare us time, so that the rift might be closed earlier—precisely within your accounting of what you know as time.

"But why?" I ask.

Because the heart of the problem is still before you, and you cannot make it right until you learn to use Starlight.

I stare with confusion at the glowing colorful cloud of aurora borealis before me, a speck of a greater cosmic nebula.

I stare deeper afield.

The stars are everywhere.

What does it mean? What am I supposed to do?

Think . . . Arion says. *But—use your heart, also.*

A nd so, I think with all my heart.

What are stars? No, I don't mean the giant spherical thermonuclear furnaces of gases and plasma that radiate energy and light and fill the cosmic expanse all around us. I know what *they* are.

I mean, what are stars, the little dots of light, pinpoint dots visible against the darkness?

Each tiny dot of light that I see, as I gaze into the deep, is ancient light. It has travelled untold distances across the universe from some giant incandescent sphere to reach the lens of my eye, over hundreds, thousands, millions of years. . . .

Each tiny photon traveling from *there* to *here*, from *then* to *now*, has spanned so much that there is no human way to comprehend it. It has crossed everything, even while its original source has long since transformed, dissipated, possibly died in a supernova, and is now only a lost memory.

And yet, it is not. It has been preserved, and taken along for the most incredible ride, as part of a seemingly infinite *string* of starlight, moving through space and time, and arriving inside my eye, becoming a tiny part of me—even if only as a single photon hitting my cornea.

The ancient star and I are now connected on a physical level.

For a split second of being, we are together, literally. So much so, as if I had reached out with my hand into the past, across billions of miles, and touched its ancient, fiery surface—as it had been, millions of years ago.

We are entangled.

And all because I looked up and chose to glance at a tiny dot of ancient light, recognizing it out of countless others. By doing so, I also changed its quantum state—and it changed mine.

The most fundamental network of connection of all, spanning everything, is *starlight*.

But the real act of connection is a *choice*. Because while each one of us might be constantly bombarded with trillions of photons and other particles from all sources—since we're all a part of a quantum cosmic soup that is the world—*entanglement* happens when we choose to acknowledge it.

To do that, I must focus on the smallest quantum level of being.

Dive deep into the fundamental world, the micro-world . . . down, down, down.

I must choose to focus on an entity—a single node on the universal network.

I must claim it.

By that example, all I have to do is reach out to *anything* around me—regardless of time and distance—by a mere act of shifting my focus, allocating a thought—and I can make contact with it.

Suddenly, just like that, I understand the fundamental Principle of the Yellow Quadrant, which rules Nets and Cords.

Universal networks and cosmic strings.

A universal system, a "Theory of Everything," based on Starlight.

I blink, filled with clarity of thought, knowing with one part of my mind that, *just in that instant alone*, I just blinked away the quantum residue of a billion ancient stars. . . .

The stream of universal data rushes through me like a great flood.

"I think I begin to understand," I say to Arion in my mind.

I am glad, he replies, shimmering with color before me. *Now act on your understanding, quickly. It is very ephemeral in your 3D reality, and will elude you easily if you let it, since it is a higher-dimensional concept. Act quickly to retain it.*

And I do.

You entangle with love. You claim with song.

It really is that simple.

And it cuts through everything, inter-dimensionally—across space and time and everything else unnamed and unnamable in 3D.

I can make *rifts* all around me, as easily as reaching out with my hand to pass my fingers through vapor.

Rifts to cross the divide in any direction. Rifts to *negate* time and distance.

Simply, focus my intent with my Logos voice of creation.

I take a deep breath of what little canned air remains in my space suit helmet. And looking out across the stars, regardless of actual direction, I think of Aeson, my *love*.

And I sing a single, pure note.

My go-to note, a middle F.

It is not particularly powerful or loud.

It could be a child's effort at song, a breathy whisper. . . .

But it is true.

I hold the note, a random sound frequency, but I imbue it with Starlight.

And then, out of nowhere before me, a Fleet ship appears, hanging in space.

There are no fancy special effects, no flashes of light or blinding supernovae to herald its coming.

The velo-cruiser simply wasn't there before, but now *is*. It stills, coming to a sudden stop from its previous state of hyper-motion, to float about a hundred meters away.

The rift which "brought" it to me is neither tangible nor recognizable, as space folds upon itself to accommodate my entanglement, and then unfurls again, closing up on itself naturally.

Aeson is here.

Inside my helmet, I chortle with joy, like a little kid.

How do I know? I just do.

After all, I brought him to me.

Starlight Sorceress.

What happens next is an emotional whirlwind. A hatch on the velo-cruiser opens, and *im amrevu*, in a space suit, comes floating out toward me, propelled by passion and a propulsion pack.

I laugh and wave awkwardly, seeing him approach, choking on old snot and tears that I cannot wipe away. Nebulous Arion pulses next to me and transmits sympathetic joy in the *pegasei* language of images.

Seconds later, Aeson has me, strong gloved hands clasping my arms, then attaching a cable to my waist, and I see the raw, awed expression on his face through his helmet.

"Gwen! My *Gwen!*" he shouts, his voice coming through on local comms, blasting my ears with the energy of his joy. "What is going on? You are okay! How did I get here?"

I laugh and laugh, as he reels me in, and we enter the velo-cruiser through the airlock hatch. "I did something, and here you are!" I say, chortling as if I'm drunk.

"Whatever you did—"

"Weird, I know!" I interrupt. "But first, we must get Erita!"

And I hastily explain what happened, how Arion and the *pegasei* are keeping her alive.

"Phoebos? *Bashtooh!* Is that you?" Xelio's incredulous voice sounds on our comms just then, and Aeson replies.

"Stay here!" he tells me meanwhile, and launches himself back outside, even as the distant rainbow cloud of *pegasei* approach, towing Erita toward us.

Xelio, Command Pilot Uru Onophris, Consul Denu, Manala, George—suddenly it seems that everyone is on the interstellar comms at once, animated voices talking at us across a billion miles on the opposite side of Helios.

"Did you get her? Did you get Erita?" Xel asks anxiously.

"Yes! I have her," Aeson replies, lifting up Erita's motionless suited body and pulling her inside.

We seal the ship, move Erita out of the airlock into the main hull space and Aeson re-pressurizes and enables Minimum Fundamental Gravity. It makes me stagger initially as I re-establish my footing after three days of zero-g.

Oh, my God, I can take my helmet off!

Just for a moment, I pause, shell-shocked. First, I pull off my gloves, slowly, feeling cool air wash over my skin. Then I remove the helmet with shaking hands, barely managing the twist, revealing my messy, dirty face and head, as I breathe deeply.

And then I turn to help Erita.

Aeson is already on it, his own gloves and helmet off, and he gives me a quick, intense glance that has a world of meaning, then gets back to carefully removing Erita's head gear.

Erita appears sickly and unconscious, her head lolling to the side, and Aeson administers CPR with a medical device as I watch, ready to assist.

The *pegasei* float in clouds around us, having rematerialized in the cabin.

She is alive, Arion tells us.

And just then Erita shudders and takes a deep breath, then opens her eyes.

Both Aeson and I exhale in relief. And then the two of us start laughing.

It's a ridiculous moment of all things coming together into a perfect resolution, when just for a moment all is well with the universe.

Aeson and I reach for each other without words, and his large warm fingers stroke my messy cheeks as he kisses me roughly, desperately, not bothered by my snot and dried tears.

"How did you—" Erita groans just then, squinting at us weakly. "*Bashtooh*, am I dead or what? Kass?"

"I am so profoundly grateful to you, *daimon*," Aeson says, letting go of me to lean back over her. "You have done everything to keep my beloved safe, and there is no amount of honor I can give that would come close to repaying your sacrifice—"

Erita shakes her head and coughs, and a slow smile comes to her exhausted face.

And then we begin to talk all at once, breathless, since there is so much to tell, including the rescue of Earth from the asteroid— Aeson stares with raised brows, hearing about it.

While Erita and I recuperate in the small bathroom facilities and gulp down water, Aeson contacts Manala's side of things, still using the interstellar linkup on my suit, which seems to be the only thing that works reliably to connect us to the other survivors.

"Any word when our rescue is coming?" Xelio asks.

"According to Quoni, they still have at least four and a half hours inside the Quantum Stream before they get to your coordinates," Aeson says, giving me a curious glance. "Then another half hour to do the global position sensor sweep for your beacon."

"How did you manage to trim so much time, Commander?" Command Pilot Onophris asks.

"Still not sure," Aeson replies, with another look at me.

"Aeson! Oh, so glad to hear your voice," Manala comes on the line suddenly.

"And I yours. How do you feel?" Aeson smiles.

Manala launches into an emotional explanation, and then says, "And so I wish we could be rescued, but first, Hasmik should be rescued, since she's been outside for so long!"

"Hasmik, they are coming soon for you," I add. "Please hang in there."

"Not soon enough," Xel says. "She is priority one right now."

"Hasmik!" I say, "How are you doing?"

There's no answer.

I frown. It occurs to me suddenly: Hasmik has been really quiet for some time now.

Aeson looks from Erita to me with a newly tense expression.

Meanwhile, over on the comms, I hear Xelio calling Hasmik's name.

"The tablet!" I say, fumbling for the reliable tablet still attached to my suit. "We can try seeing through her helmet camera!"

The tablet screen loads and the window shows nothing but empty space and stars. Hasmik is motionless and appears to be drifting somewhere.

There's no sign of the *depet* transport or the wreckage nearby, no debris floating.

Wherever she is, in whatever condition, she is all alone now.

And then I notice a lacework pattern of frost starting to build at the edges of the camera lens, indicating the likelihood that power is no longer present in the suit itself.

No power, no life support.

Hasmik!

I cry out with a new surge of despair. And then I focus all of my *self*, my core of being, on that *frost*—a tiny crystalline structure, infinitely fine, infinitely precise. . . .

Aeson and Erita stare at me with wonder and confusion, as I part my lips and sing a gentle, clear, equally crystalline note.

For an instant, the world blinks around us.

And then it reconnects.

Aeson makes a small sound of awe as he notices a velo-cruiser suddenly appear on the tablet's screen where previously it has been nothing but space and starlight.

"Whoa. That's one of our ships," Aeson remarks. "But—it can't be Quoni yet. Another velo-cruiser? Who?"

And then he comprehends.

Hasmik's helmet camera is seeing *us*—just now, we've somehow jumped across several billion miles and landed a tiny, visible distance away from her space-suit.

Chapter 101

*R*emember, this knowledge is ephemeral, Arion had told me. *You must act quickly.*

Right now, I've no idea what I just did.

How did I manage to focus sufficiently on some long-distance icicle . . . and suddenly, there we are?

Things are happening too quickly for me, but in this moment it doesn't matter how.

We're here, and Hasmik needs our help if she is still alive.

"Arion!" I exclaim again in my mind. "Please go to help her!"

Yes, it is why I am still here, the quantum being says.

And suddenly he disappears from the velo-cruiser cabin and reappears in place where Hasmik floats, so that suddenly an iridescent glow surrounds the lens of the helmet camera and space itself takes on the colors of the rainbow.

I watch this on the tablet, even as I hear Arion in my mind.

She too will survive.

"Oh, thank God!" I exclaim. "Thank you, Arion, thank you so much for helping yet again!"

This is the last time, Arion says. *She is in my embrace . . . but you must hurry and take her inside your ship and its environment.*

"Yes, of course, on my way now!" This time it's Aeson who replies, as he must also be hearing Arion's mind-speech.

Aeson quickly dons his helmet and gloves and goes out through the airlock. Erita and I watch the tablet screen and see Aeson's suited form propel forward. Moments later, he is at Hasmik's side, tethering her and bringing her in.

"On your way where? What kind of *shar-ta-haak shebet* is going on there?" Xelio's voice comes in on the local comms. "Phoebos! Where are you now? Why are you on my *local* comms and not interstellar?"

"He is getting Hasmik!" I exclaim. "Don't ask how just yet, but we are *here!*"

Aeson returns just then, carrying Hasmik's limp form through the airlock.

"Here where? At our coordinates? That's insane!" Xelio persists. "Did he use the stationary Jump to cross the system and somehow you all survived reentry? I don't understand!"

But we don't answer, too busy reviving Hasmik, who looks pale, bloodless, and frankly, dead. When her suit helmet is removed, she is cold to the touch, with frost in places on the greyish skin of her face and her matted, dark brown hair.

We implement CPR, and it takes longer to revive her than Erita. But eventually she does come back to us, breathing faintly, and opening her fluttering eyelids. Seeing us and where she is, she looks even more amazed than we are.

"Hasmik!" I exclaim.

"Gwen . . . how?" the girl barely whispers. "What day is it? How did I—"

"She is alive!" Xelio's frantic voice breaks in.

"Yes, yes, she is," Aeson responds firmly with relief.

"Hasmik," I say. "What happened to you there?"

Aeson glances over Hasmik's space suit. "I believe her suit was depressurized due to a slow leak."

Hasmik nods. "Yes, it's been leaking for some time now. There was a lot of sharp metal when I made the net—"

"Oh, but you should've said something!" I exclaim with reproach.

Hasmik shakes her head tiredly. "There was nothing you or I could do, so I said nothing."

"You saved this *depet*," Xelio says softly.

"It still doesn't explain how any of you are here," Command Pilot Onophris's voice says.

"I'm not sure I can even begin to explain," I say. "A little later. Maybe."

I take a deep breath, then smile down at Hasmik and smooth back her dark hair. "But we must thank Arion and the *pegasei* for all they've done. And now that we're here, we can go pick up the rest of you, Xelio, Manala, George—"

It is time now, Arion interrupts me suddenly. *We must go and finish it. You have achieved Starlight, Gwen Lark who is Kassiopei. Strive not to forget it. And if you do, remember—it is within reach but will require constant effort to maintain comprehension of its trans-dimensional nature for a 3D-locked entity such as your species. To regain your understanding, look at the stars, as Arlenari did, and it will return to you.*

"I will try," I say. "Carry her well. May the ancient dead finally have peace."

We will carry her. She who wields Starlight is ancient by your reckoning. But she is not dead.

"What?" I exclaim with a jolt. "Arlenari Kassiopei is *alive?*"

Arion's laughter fills my mind. *Our Tears and Blood have encased her for eons, and she travels on a Ship of Eternity.*

I am stunned. What does that even mean?

But Arion's final words now echo inside me.

At last, we go to close and silence the rift on Earth. Once we pass through the Rim of Ae-Leiterra, we may not return.

"I—understand," I say with a thickness in the back of my throat. "Goodbye, my *friend.*"

Goodbye, Gwen Lark who is Kassiopei who wields Starlight. We leave your species now, to finish what we promised. And now— They *are coming.*

Like vapor, the rainbow plasma being disappears gently, fades away like smoke, and so do the others of its kind in the cabin. Aurora borealis is no more.

"Arion. . . ." My voice ends on a whisper.

Aeson blinks. "Wait—did he say 'they' are coming?"

Just in that moment of utter befuddlement, we hear a crackle on the local comms. Voices of Xelio, George, and the others on the *depet* transport start to fade in and out . . . and then, there's an impossible, blinding flare of light without a known source, that comes from *inside* the ship.

I squeeze my eyes closed, reminded momentarily of being in the interior of the solar jet column of light.

When I open them next, the light has dimmed to a bearable radiance. But the hologram view of the velo-cruiser is suddenly enabled, showing us what is in deep space outside.

The blackness of space is filled with great four-point *stars* in three dimensions. Hundreds of them, hanging like garish holiday ornaments against the cosmic black velvet.

They are *astroctadra* shapes of blinding golden light.

Disoriented, we stare at the holo-view, but the greater urgency is *what* is now inside the velo-cruiser, with us. . . .

A disembodied golden *sun*, about a meter in diameter, takes up space in the cabin, floating in the air before us. It fluctuates and spins around its axis, sending forth waves of plasma like small armlets that grow longer with each swirl.

In heartbeats it starts to re-form, so that two longer rays extend down like legs in bilateral symmetry, and eight rays flare outward to the sides bilaterally, four on the right and four on the left, like the many-armed Hindu deity—Vishnu? Durga?

Another ray flares in the center, rising upward in a blunt disk, to form a head.

The golden being of pure light is now in humanoid form, standing up seven or eight feet tall, its/her/his head nearly touching the cabin ceiling. It has no face, no features, no mouth or eyes, only light.

Aeson takes a step, attempting to shield me, but freezes in place, as the golden being stretches forth one if its eight arms, palm facing us, in a universal "Stop" gesture, which can also be interpreted as a gesture of peace.

I breathe faintly and stare, noting with one part of my mind the strange elegance of its movement, the long slender fingers of light, blurring at the edges like moving flames.

And the being extends another of its many hands, on the other side. Slowly it moves both of the extended hands, turning palms inward and outward, and then bringing them closer to shape a ball in the air—in the same way a practitioner of Tai Chi or another spiritual discipline forms an energy ball of chi or prana.

Except in this case, there is an actual visible sphere of delicate golden translucence that starts to form in the air, pouring from the fingers of light.

The being separates its hands, and suddenly the chi ball "pops" and stretches horizontally into a string of light—like a string of putty attached to its fingertips—and it starts to vibrate.

At first, the light string merely forms rapid waves, which fluctuate. And then the waves grow shorter and shorter, and the frequency speeds up.

Suddenly, there is *sound*.

Momentarily I am reminded of the antique early recordings of howling wind on Mars, taken by various Mars probes.

The sound of the wind hisses, wails, and slithers on a lifeless rocky plain.

And then the sound starts to make sense.

"Th-h-h-h-h. . . ." it vibrates. "Th . . . th . . . th . . . th."

"Tho . . . tho . . . tho . . . th . . ."

"Tho . . . . . . th . . ."

I frown, because it is so familiar. A word at the tip of my tongue.

Thoth.

A deity in Ancient Egypt.

Holy crap!

My heart starts pounding while I raise my hand in reply, slowly, carefully mimicking it, palm outward. And then I say, "Thoth?"

And the string of light instantly vibrates and repeats my word and pronunciation, switching from a desolate hiss to my own intonation. "Thoth?" it says. "Thoth."

I nod, and say slowly, pointing, "Yes! You? You are Thoth? Can you understand me?"

Instead of an answer, three more suns burst into existence inside the ship's cabin.

I hold back a tiny shriek.

Aeson starts.

Erita and Hasmik exclaim in alarm—Hasmik still lying on the floor where we rushed to revive her.

The three newly arrived suns begin re-forming into wavelets and assume similar humanoid shapes with many appendages.

They now loom like giants around us, overshadowing everything in the cabin—four *alien gods* materialized.

Each of the three new arrivals starts to shape similar chi balls with their hands, extending them into strings, and the strings begin to vibrate with sounds of alien wilderness, until they take on a more recognizable acoustic shape.

"Se . . . . . . th . . ." one string vibrates.

"E-e-e-e . . . the-e-e . . . th . . ." sings another. "Isi . . . . . . th . . ."

"Ho . . . ru . . . . . . th . . ." sounds the third. "Horu . . . . . . th . . ."

I nod again. "I think I understand you. *Set, Isis, Horus.* Yes?"

"Yeh . . . . . . th . . ." echoes the one who arrived first, and who first uttered "Thoth."

"Are these ancient gods of Earth?" Aeson speaks up. "Who are you? Are you—truly gods? No, it's not possible. Are you our ancient enemy?"

"No-o-o . . . Yeh . . . th . . . th . . . th . . . th . . . No-o-o . . ." All four beings start to echo, the four strings vibrating in strange harmony between their palms.

Okay, this is ridiculous.

They are not really speaking English or even Atlanteo *right now, are they?* I think. What if they're just echoing us automatically, senselessly? They can't be actual gods, whatever that means, right?

Also, what if they are possibly reading our minds now, like the *pegasei?*

"Who are you?" I ask, repeating Aeson's question.

"Who-o-o-o-o are you-u-u-u-u?" Thoth's string says. And then it vibrates more cleanly, repeating. "Who are you?"

"Are you learning English now, my language?"

"Learning now . . ." Thoth repeats. And he/she/it raises a third hand, in a similar palm out "Stop" gesture.

"Okay, you mean for us to wait?"

"Wait . . ." repeats the light string.

We pause, suspended for several extremely long moments.

"Those light spheres—the hostile grid formations of light objects that are attacking our system—are they you?" Aeson asks in a hard voice, breaking the silence.

Suddenly all four beings respond in a great chorus:

"OOOH . . . THEEE . . . REEE . . . THHH . . ." they clamor. "Ooh . . . see . . . ree . . . th . . ."

I strain to understand.

"Osiris!" I repeat.

"Yesss . . ." says the string of Thoth. And suddenly it continues, in a voice that slides lower and lower into a bass register, where its stays.

"Osiris," Thoth says clearly. "Osiris is running. OSIRIS."

"Running where? Who is Osiris?" Erita asks. "So confused right now."

"OSIRIS is the process of destruction," Thoth's string replies in a suddenly clear, perfect English. "It is a program running now. It has been running for thousands of your years."

Holy crap!

"You can speak!" I exclaim.

"Yes, we learned this new language now. Your species has many new languages every time we come."

"You've been here before?"

"Yes. We come now, because of OSIRIS and because of *her*." And Thoth uses yet another hand to point at me.

Aeson shakes his head with a growing frown. "Explain!"

In reply, a different being—the one calling itself "Horus"—takes a step closer to us, so that I tense in alarm, looking high up at its blazing golden head towering over me. Horus outstretches two more of its arms, palm up, and on each palm a holographic sphere grows. It takes on recognizable features, and suddenly I'm looking at a little Earth, the size of a basketball, balanced on one palm, and a little Atlantis, proportionately sized, on the other.

Horus flicks one elegant finger on each hand, and suddenly Earth re-forms into a miniature solar system, with Earth reduced to a tiny marble, and Sol in the center, with other planets around it (none of it proportionately accurate, of course, since that would require a football field of space to account for true relative distances). The same thing happens on the other hand, where a solar system of Helios now rests, tiny marble-sized planets spinning.

"Your handiwork," Thoth says. "A long time ago, your primitive species caused great harm with your destructive irresponsibility, tearing a rift in the universal fabric. This initiated OSIRIS, an automated cosmic sequence to *cleanse* your world and your solar system of *you*."

I listen, forgetting to breathe.

"We came to you then, to reason with you, and to seek an end without such a final solution. Your ancestors made promises to us, but then persisted in their harmful ways. It is then we permitted the program to run its course."

"Are you saying the light grid objects are *not* you but some kind of automated mechanical sequence?" Aeson asks.

"Yes, the OSIRIS mechanism code generates sphere objects to cleanse within a given diameter, always with a solar engine at its center. They are energy scattering machines powered by the local star. It is also a very old, brute-force program that we no longer use but which *you* left running for over ten thousand of your years—it was active, but paused, until recently."

Aeson rubs his forehead.

"When you say 'left running,'" I ask, "do you mean—"

"Your ancestors were clever enough to hide the rift within a quantum shield, but not clever enough to understand that it was only going to be a temporary solution. All shields fail eventually—especially when stretched to their limit from one solar system to another, across galaxies and the vastness of the cosmos, through a forced wormhole. But for the time being, since OSIRIS could no longer find the rift, it simply paused itself—instead of either completing the wipe or being properly terminated by us. We alone control OSIRIS, and nothing else can stop its inevitable progress once it is started. It is why we no longer use such a merciless solution for primitive sentient civilizations."

"It is merciless and cruel," Aeson says with anger. "Do you know how many innocent lives were lost here around the Helios system?"

"We regret those lives. We also regret the persistent, short-sighted selfishness and stupidity of your species. We sent the ancient asteroid in a simple surgical strike to close the rift without terminating your entire species. Instead you shifted it enough to miss and cover your tracks—poorly."

"What right have you to judge us, with all our faults?" Aeson demands. "Did you create us?"

"No, we found you," Horus replies. "They who made you, left you as a primitive species making a mess."

"Ah, so you know who made us?" Aeson whispers abruptly. "Can you tell us what is the purpose of our species?"

"We do not know who made you. But we know your *purpose*, for we have watched your evolution, and it is the same for all sentient species starting out. It is to *support each other* as you advance into eternity. Instead of consuming each other, you must nourish. Instead of abusing the non-sentient animal species that share your worlds, you must care for, steward, and protect them."

Aeson's expression is filled with the energy of fire. "If you have seen so much, watched us for so long, maybe—just maybe, you must know. What is the origin of my bloodline, Kassiopei? Are we truly divine? Were we made as gods to rule?"

"We know you, Kassiopei," the being called "Isis" utters suddenly. "We are not gods, and neither are you. You were made as servants—strong, resilient, and virile. You were the earliest, healthiest of your kind, your DNA engineered to reinforce and maintain the genetic integrity of your then-unstable young species. You were designated as priests—to serve the spirit of all the living with the Logos voice of creation, and to *service* the early population with your body.

"Instead, you set yourselves apart, refused your duties of general commingling and began to bestow controlled favors. You claimed the Logos voice for your own, when in truth it belongs to all, and *anyone* can summon the inner resources to wield it—if the need and the focus is strong enough. Over time, you gained power and limited all interaction with your people to such an extent that your duty transformed into an elite ritual. It is how we encountered you the last time, more than twelve thousand years ago."

"Servant priests. . . . That makes terrible but perfect sense," Aeson says. "And you are not gods. What, then, are you?"

"Merely something more, something that you are not." Horus speaks. "As such, we were unto gods once, to your ancient Earth peoples—teaching them complex realities perceived as wonders—but we do not presume. Nor do we want the worship."

Aeson nods his head slowly, deep in thought.

"Which brings us to now," Thoth says, the string vibrating lower than the others, down at the bass register. "OSIRIS is currently in progress. It is running, even though stretched thin across the universe, newly restarted on Earth and in mid-stage on Atlantis."

"So can you stop it now, please?" I ask.

"Why should we?" the fourth being, called "Set," answers, and there is a kind of incredulous sarcasm in the otherwise toneless words. "What a strange mess you have made, of not one but *two* star systems. You managed to cleverly disrupt OSIRIS yet again, with a new quantum field reset—pulling the energy spheres out of their native dimension into *yours* and swapping them with their energy output—but at what cost? Your sun, Helios—it is now a *neutron star* in its early stages, barely contained and spewing itself into another dimension. . . . Higher-dimensional objects were inverted into lower ones and back again, *repeatedly*. . . . Planets and moons pulled in and out of ghostly quantum stasis. . . . Trans-dimensional higher sentient beings you call *pegasei* used to *line* a wormhole for twelve thousand years—you, homo sapiens, are awful!"

"You're not so great yourselves," Hasmik says quietly, from her place on the floor.

"Yeah," Erita says. "Your OSIRIS program is a piece of *shebet* coded by a *shibet*."

In reply, the string of Isis vibrates with what could only be laughter.

"That may be so. But truly, your species is ridiculous," Set continues in the same manner. "We have never seen anything like it before, and we have seen so many things. Yes, you are an incredibly resourceful mess, but still a mess."

"And yet," Thoth says, "we are here because despite all this spewing disaster of your making, you have done something right."

And saying this, he/it/she looks at me. "You—we *sensed* you touching the true fabric of the universe. You have reached out and grasped the delicate cosmic strings, and you used them correctly. You opened two perfect, benign, dimensional rifts in close succession, using Starlight. And for that, we give you a *chance*."

"Okay . . ." I say.

"Prove to us that this *sentience experiment* that is homo sapiens, your painfully awkward species, deserves to be allowed to continue," Thoth says. "Show us that your actions were not a fluke, and that you can move the cosmic fabric—with reverence and at will."

The greatest flood of emotion and wonder strikes at my heart—and then recedes, like a thing of translucence and foam, a gentle wave dissolving in swirls along a sandy beach. A quiet resolve forms inside me.

"You mean like this?" I ask, focusing on the tiny, spinning marble that is the planet Atlantis, floating above the palm of Horus.

My focus narrows, going subatomic, and at the same time I visualize Atlantis, the beautiful green-blue world, as it looks from orbit—and I visualize all of us inside the velo-cruiser, and all the people with Manala inside their *depet*—and I reach out with my heart across the cosmic divide, while I sing a simple, clean note.

Space-time folds, and we're there.

What happens next is both ordinary and the stuff of legend. Our two ships traverse space-time in the quantum equivalent of a blink, and we find ourselves in orbit around Atlantis (sorry, Quoni, and whoever else is about to arrive on a rescue mission and not find us there). The alien gods—if it's even right to call them *anything*—pop up alongside us.

"Is this good enough for you?" I ask. "Now, can you please turn off that awful OSIRIS, take all the associated grids everywhere, and leave us to ourselves, once and for all? I promise, no more old-style rifts, and the one on Earth should now be closed—for real, this time, thanks to the *pegasei*."

And then I add, "Oh, before you go, can you also fix that neutron star thing? I'm assuming you can. I would really prefer for Helios to *not* go supernova or whatever, when our quantum shield fails, and then have to colonize yet a third silly planet."

And crazy enough, the alien gods-not-gods listen and do what I ask.

After all, the ultimate sign of a stable, sentient civilization is the ability to create entanglement by reaching out with love, and I think I've just done that, to anyone's satisfaction.

Chapter 102

From here on, things happen pretty fast and all at once, in multiple locations, so let me see if I can make some sense of it and bring it all together.

As promised, the alien light beings reverse the crazy thermonuclear process inside Helios, so that it's no longer on the verge of blowing its core—or whatever it is that was about to happen with those two solar jets and the explosions around the *astroctadra* points. The jets recede safely, the explosions fade, sucked into some other dimensional plane, and the messy quantum shield we hastily put in place is carefully lifted.

Helios is once more just your average white-hot star doing whatever it was doing before the OSIRIS program took over and started to drain it for battery power.

As soon as the OSIRIS solar engine is terminated, the golden light spheres (in retrospect, I've come to think of them as *energy drones*) simply dissipate in place—which is a major relief for all the Atlantean SPC Fleets around Rah, Septu, Tammuz, and Ishtar. The Pilots there have been fighting a fierce battle with those same nasty energy drones for days now—ever since they became tangible in our reality and vulnerable to our weapons—and using up a lot of plasma firepower to neutralize each one at the quantum level.

But now the Fleets can come home, and everyone is amazed, perplexed, and relieved to be on their way back home to Atlantis or to their designated normal stations around the system.

We find out that the light grid that started building around Earth's Sol is also gone, as promised.

Reports from Poseidon downtown have confirmed that the Atlantis Grail Monument is no longer humming, and neither is the great golden dome of the Ra-Disk at New Deshret, which makes Pharikon Heru extremely happy. The ancient Vimana ark-ship has gone silent at last, all its pieces reposing in venerable peace instead of resonating in sympathetic song to the dimensional *wound* that was the rift on Earth, far across the universe. . . .

That's because, somewhere in the middle of the Atlantic, among its cool blue waters, on Earth, the ancient dimensional rift has been sealed. The last of the *pegasei* passed through it, supposedly together with the mysterious Arlenari Kassiopei and the man who used to be the Imperator of Atlantis. The *pegasei's* tentative, entirely unconfirmed presence on Earth itself for all millennia is now come to an end.

It is said, the area of the Bermuda Triangle no longer reports anomalies: strange colorful lights like the rainbow, flashes of ghostly brilliance, disappearances of solid objects and people, or electromagnetic disturbance. Elsewhere on Earth, will-o'-the-wisps are less prevalent, and there's a noticeable difference in the nature of the Southern and Northern Lights. On the other hand, Earth's magnetic poles are shifting rapidly, and have been for quite some time, which could explain some of it.

What matters is, the rift is sealed. Although, we will never really know what actually happened in the process—whether Romhutat burned up like a glorious meteor somewhere along the way at the flaming Rim of Ae-Leiterra, or if the quantum ocean swallowed him during the wormhole passage. Anything is possible, including the miraculous possibility that he somehow mysteriously survived the ordeal and is now headed toward an unknown cosmic destination. His complicated memory will always be with us, and with Aeson in particular, who plans to honor his late father with a black armband for his final service to all.

As for Arlenari Kassiopei, the remarkable woman who was purged from history and forgotten for eons, we have a plan to remedy this. After all, whoever she was—whoever she really *is*— she ultimately saved us by sharing her knowledge and gentle wisdom across time, and her name deserves to be properly recognized and passed on to the next generation. Arleana is so much more than an ancient children's story about a girl who played with Starlight—she could be our evolutionary future. So much to learn, so many secrets yet to be revealed in the ancient places recently uncovered, both on the Ghost Moon surface and deep inside Vimana itself. The museums, the archeologists, the antiquities experts, the historians, and Charles Lark, my own Dad, are going to have so much amazing work before them. Arlenari's legacy is a treasure trove to be explored.

For that reason, in about a month from now, at the start of Yellow Season, there will be a Naming Ceremony, in which Atlantis will officially recognize its fourth planetary moon. We're giving the Ghost Moon a proper name, and it is "Arlenari."

Now, Arlenari can take her permanent place in the Atlantean star-filled night skies along with Pegasus, Mar-Yan, and Amrevet—that is, as *permanent* as relative things can be in our constantly moving, wondrous universe. At least we're getting the weather control algorithm working again, this time with *four* gravitational tide-causing planetary bodies in the mix.

When we return to Atlantis after our ordeal, and the godlike aliens take care of OSIRIS and depart, it is good to know that the military conflict never made it as far as the planet itself.

There are a few violent skirmishes in local high orbit, with randomly forming "mini-grids" of energy drones from the Ishtar grid that traversed space-time during the *astroctadra* blast and somehow ended up here in our neighborhood.

Fortunately, War-1, under the skillful leadership of Command Pilot Manakteon Resoi, makes short work of them. The Earth Cadets—the *shirén*—are dispatched in Waves alongside native Atlantean Fleet personnel. Hundreds of Wings comprised solely of *shirén* Pilots fly bravely, various Pinions show amazing resourcefulness and courage, and veteran officers in the Fleet remark that there is raw talent and even *astra daimon* material there, no doubt.

So, yeah, it's a little weird to think about it, but my baby sister Gracie participates in her first real space battle—and so do Laronda, Blayne, Chiyoko, Logan, Brie, and so many others. They have some insane flight stories to tell, and now we'll get to hear it all the time, whenever we get together, which is as often as anyone can imagine.

As for all the remaining members of our fateful *astroctadra* mission, our international partners Anen Qur and Sheolaat Heru have now been returned safely to their respective countries, Ubasti and New Deshret—we are being informed.

And then of course, there's my family. Right after I used Starlight to show the aliens that we homo sapiens, as a species, *can* be permitted to stick around (and we found ourselves in orbit over Atlantis), I use Starlight *again*—to bring Dad and Gordie home, after making an interstellar call and visually confirming their present whereabouts on board one of War-8's *sebasarets*.

As soon as Gordie and Dad get to the Palace (accompanied by Oalla who took very good care of them during the entire mission, according to my Dad), and we all take hot showers and order a "monstrous big" *niktos* meal service from the Imperial Palace kitchen—Gordie insists—we spend a wonderful, weird, and bittersweet time being *together* as family and friends.

Right now, we are all still shellshocked—still numb from our ordeal, and amazed at just being *alive*—and yes, we are in the Imperial Crown Prince's Quarters.

The Imperial Quarters on the top floor are now legally ours to occupy. But . . . maybe not just yet.

Everyone has been invited, and everyone who can make it is here. Gracie, Laronda, Blayne, Dawn, Oalla, several other *daimon*, Consul Suval Denu. Meanwhile, Keruvat is still on his way here, on a fast ship coming from Ishtar, where Aeson left him, to handle things as the SPC next-in-command.

Quoni, Nergal, Radanthet, Culuar, and others who have gone on the rescue mission to get Manala are still afield and will need an explanation of what they did *not* find at the coordinates when they got there. They are still running sweeps of the area of the wreckage of War-6 for survivors, and additional ships have been sent to my own former coordinates to sweep the area of War-2. Even despite all this time, it is theoretically possible that someone out there is still alive, and the SPC does not leave troops behind.

Meanwhile, Erita and Hasmik are being treated for long-term space exposure at the finest medical center in Poseidon—where they will be for the rest of the day and the next, as a precaution—and Xelio is there, keeping them company, as he insisted.

According to Erita—who's been messaging back and forth with me from her medical bed all throughout—Xelio has been making "sweet eyes" at Hasmik, and Erita says she is "ready to chuck up her own *niktos* meal if this keeps getting any more sugary-sweet."

"How are you feeling?" I continue to ask her worriedly.

"Don't you worry about me," Erita messages me back. "Worry about your dear friend Hasmik in the next bed over. Our bad boy

Shamash has lost it completely. He's been smacked hard by *amrevet* disease, taken by *her* all the way to its cruel and inevitable end, which leads to vows and babies. And your girl has it too. They need a private room. *I* need a private room. Somebody, please, kill me now."

Reading her text message, I repress a silly giggle. And then I sober up again as I look around the room.

Right now, Devora and Manala mostly weep quietly on the sofa. Aeson, myself, my Dad, George, Consul Denu, and the rest of us, do what we can to make the painful time easier to bear. George has gone down to Manala's Quarters on the floor below and brought Khemji over, carrying the huge cat in his arms, this time without any mishap (and without gratuitous floor-mopping action on a harness).

But Aeson himself is not doing too well right now, even though he tries to hide it underneath his usual stoic mask of composure.

The really surreal part is—Aeson, *im amrevu*, my Imperial Husband, is now Archaeon Imperator.

He doesn't want to talk about it just yet.

There will be a Coronation Ceremony in a few days when he officially ascends the Imperial Throne of *Atlantida*. The First Priest, Shirahtet, is making all the arrangements, and the IEC is calling meetings all this coming week about the state of the government, the nation, necessary changes due to the current life-changing events, and "the course from here on." The media is having trouble processing and keeping up with all the events of the last few days, so we're keeping the TV feeds off, to retain our own sanity.

Instead, we sit around the room and talk. Heartfully, tiredly, silly with exhaustion and pain and deflated stress, breaking out in nervous laughter upon occasion at the *absurdity* of it all, and then some of us weeping a little. We talk about the godlike aliens made of golden light who came and left and changed our world—or maybe we changed theirs—these things are not mutually exclusive. We talk of battles and energy drones, of *pegasei* and those who have left us.

The elephant in the room is *me* and my role in what has happened.

No one really understands, and I'm not sure I can even begin to explain this thing—this fragile, ephemeral, higher-dimensional concept of universal Starlight. Aeson glances at me often, meeting my gaze with his own. There are few words between us, but we *know*.

I suppose there will be formal questions raised later, tech and science commissions set up to investigate. And I will have to try to explain to them—to stuffy individuals such as STA Director Rovat Bennu, ACA Director Hijep Tiofon and their ilk—what it means to work with . . .

. . . Starlight.

The evening is over at last, and everyone goes to their beds, either here at the Palace in guest quarters, or home. Dad and George get ready for bed in their own guest quarters, while Gordie takes an adjacent guest room to be with all of us, and Gracie gets to sleep in my bedroom with the *astroctadra* window.

Just before I leave them to it, I notice that Mom's urn once again stands on top of the side table in its gentle place of honor. Dad placed her back there when he returned today, and I am quietly grateful for this small, steady reminder of a sense of *home*.

When Aeson and I are finally alone in our Master bedroom— for the first time after our impossible reunion in space and all that came after—we simply come together, and there are no words, as we hold each other in silent intimacy.

At first, we are stilled in a motionless, tight embrace, as we stand listening to each other's beating hearts for a few intense minutes. I reach up with my fingers and stroke Aeson's cheeks, feeling him begin to shudder and tense up under my light touch.

"Gwen," *im amrevu* says, taking my face between his palms and holding me like a precious thing. "Who are you, my love? The things you did . . . the impossible, wonderful things that seem to go against all known laws of physics, and yet make perfect sense now. How?"

"I'll show you sometime," I say, glancing at the star-filled night outside the window. "It's just something anyone can do, really. You just need to *focus* with all your heart, become very, very small, and reach out into the fine, quantum fabric of *everything* that's around you. . . ."

"They will honor you and worship you for this," he says, suddenly thoughtful. "You deserve so much more than mere acknowledgement."

"Wow, I hope not." I smile. "I'm sure, as with all things, eventually they'll forget. I might forget too. Arion was right— Starlight is so elusive. It requires constant focus and practice just to remember it *exists*, much less how it works."

My husband shakes his head with wonder, and continues to look deep into my eyes. His own expression is filled with a complex mixture of yearning, unconditional love, and—simmering underneath it all—his own pent-up grief.

"How is it," he says, "that I have *you* in my life, *im amrevu?* Of all the rare and precious coincidences that brought us together, when I first happened to visit the Pennsylvania RQC-3 and you were there. What made me reach out and find you?"

I gaze at him with all my soul. "Maybe it was Starlight."

And then, out of nowhere, we are consumed with sudden passion. It takes us over, like a summer storm. . . .

Aeson and I pull at each other's clothing, hair, grasp each other's bodies, pull and squeeze and pant, flesh against flesh. Aeson enters me with a desperate gasp and when it's over, he collapses and cries in my arms.

I hold him to me, stroke his hair, his face, embracing my love tight as he weeps for his loss, at long last—his wordless, tortured loss of the difficult man whom he loved and who was his father.

Later, we make love again, this time without bitterness. Sweet, gentle, starry night fills the open window, and a flock of moons travels the boundless dark sky.

"Look, there's Amrevet," I say, pointing at the grand lavender moon as I lie with my cheek against Aeson's chest, feeling his warm skin and breathing his musky scent.

He chuckles softly. "They say that if you see Amrevet first thing after you make love, you will be with child—"

Oh, crap!

I realize in that moment that, while I was marooned in space these past few crazy days, I'd missed taking my weekly dose of my special contraceptive.

Yellowday is my usual day to take it, but even if I could, I was a little too busy saving Earth on Red Mar-Yan 17 to remember!

And so, I tell Aeson, and I laugh, and he laughs with joy, because, boy oh boy, are we so pregnant now!

But, just in case we're not, we then again engage in certain highly pleasurable activities to assure, without the shadow of a doubt, that we are.

And over the next few days and weeks, it is confirmed.

Gwen Kassiopei, Archaeona Imperatris, is going to have a baby.

W e don't announce it just yet—there will be plenty of time for that in the coming weeks. But I do have a good intimate talk with Devora who embraces me warmly and then tells me all she can to help with the important process. I sense that Devora, now a former Imperatris and still gently grieving her own loss, will find much joy and solace in taking an active part in all these loving interactions still to come.

But first, we have so much other business to take care of.

There is the Coronation. Not much I can say, except it is all the pomp and ceremony you might expect from a traditional *Atlantida* Court event, and I have to be there too since—I get crowned also. Aeson wears the full Imperial robe and regalia, all in Blue, and his Khepresh with the Uraeus is impressive, while all I get is a delicate coronet (for which I am highly grateful, because the weight of all that head gear is terrifying, especially in this gravity). Everyone who's anyone gets to be there, and the amount of lapis lazuli, sapphire, azure, cerulean, navy, and other blue shades is overwhelming.

Aeson is now Archaeon Imperator, and the transition to power takes a lot of his daily work hours. Aeson is planning to resign as chief commanding officer of the international Star Pilot Corps, which would be a conflict of interest for any head of state and is forbidden by the rules of international cooperation. He now needs to appoint a successor, and several of the *daimon* are in the running for this most responsible position of Commander. My gut tells me that it will be either Keruvat or Oalla, but I'm not willing to bet on it, nor do I rule out Xelio or Radanthet.

Among some of his other duties as Imperator, Aeson presides over the ceremony of honoring the dead and the fallen, and the presentation of the black armbands to three new recipients—two of them still *living*, amazingly, just as himself.

At a solemn evening ceremony with a thousand orbs of light illuminating the Hovering Gardens of the Imperial Palace, Erita Qwas and Hasmik Tigranian are honored with the presentation of black armbands (in addition to noble rank and Citizenship at another ceremony a few days earlier, when the rest of my family get theirs—which stuns them both), while Devora Kassiopei receives the black ribbon on behalf of her husband, Romhutat. Afterwards, voices join in song, and the memorial harmony rises to the sky.

And then we remember the other dead, at my request, those who perished in this year's Games. I sing for Zaap, who will be honored in a few days yet again, when we go visit the spacious verdant lands where we have established his natural preserve. It will be called Guvai and will remain untouched by human hand, allowing the wild *sesemet* to roam free. . . .

With all this business of transitioning to Imperatris, I am pleasantly surprised that my personal assistant Lolu Eetatu is invaluable. I'm ashamed to admit that I'd completely forgotten that I hired Lolu to work for me, with all the events that had come to pass, so now I call her in, and Lolu gets to work organizing my time, my life, my very existence.

It is very helpful to have her deal with some of the little things and meticulously go over the details with me, Consul Denu, and other Imperial Palace experts, on how to manage an estate, deal with foreign dignitaries, and various media.

It is also very helpful when I need to get away from it all, such as the time when we have a private family matter to take care of.

There was a digital photograph that Aeson had hanging on the wall in his office on ICS-2, a picture of a beautiful landscape with a waterfall.

Apparently, it is one of the many Kassiopei Family estates, one where he spent some of the happiest times of his early childhood.

We head there now, Aeson and myself, and my immediate family—my siblings and my Dad. We climb the rocky verdant hills, hike up to the top of the exact same spot on the picture.

The waterfall cascades down a cliff into a glorious abyss of a distant lake below, and the early light of dawn breaks into a clean white radiance over a mauve and silver sky, over tree-covered mountains in the milk-haze of distance. We stand, leaning into a crisp wind, and watch with exultation the sparkling white spray of water as it dances and falls.

Dad holds our Mom's urn to his chest, tight against his heart, and for several long moments he does nothing, merely smiles faintly and squints his eyes into the light.

And then he opens the lid of the urn, leans forward slightly, and pours the beloved ashes into the wind.

Just in that moment, a flock of small birds lifts from the trees nearby, and circles, silhouetted against the rising dayfire. In that abyss of air and mist and watery spray, the ashes mingle with the light that splinters into rainbows—and there, a lark among them, just for a moment, Margot flies. . . .

"Mom would have loved this place," Gracie whispers as I hold her hand, and hold my Dad, who watches with exalted eyes. "She wanted something like this."

"She wanted to be with us," George says, placing his hand on Gordie's shoulder and staring into the distance.

"Well," Dad says, "Now that she is *here*, I can never leave. Atlantis is home."

The next few weeks go by in a whirlwind of events, but they are mostly lighthearted ones. I start thinking about baby clothes. Aeson constantly puts his head on my tummy to listen, even before I have a bump, and so, of course, I must pat *him* on his silly head with a smile and tug a lock or two of his soft, golden hair which I love touching so much.

I wonder if the baby is going to have the Kassiopei hair and *wedjat* eyes if we *don't* perform the special ritualized ceremony before birth? There's still time to decide on that. . . . Tradition or not, the choice these days is ours.

Kind of like the Games of the Atlantis Grail.

Did I mention there are going to be big changes? Now that the public knows the true origin of these awful things—yes, Arlenari's Diary has been published and is quite a literary bestseller—the historical perspective is on our side to adjust the levels of violence and modernize the whole thing. We have a choice in how we treat our population, and citizenship should not be contingent on the outcome of a barbaric, bloody contest.

With all these bright new changes happening in every walk of life, there's also the unexpected reality of Earth having survived its apocalypse, and now we need to deal with it. Politics are coming into play. Reaching out to Earth governments that now expect a lot of answers—and a lot of assistance—is going to be quite an ordeal in itself. And then we have the *shìrén* who are faced with the sudden new option of possibly going home—that is, if they still think of Earth as home. Truth be told, many don't, but just as many do.

Laronda tells me she definitely wants to go back to Earth, but temporarily—just to see her brother Jamil and her Auntie Janice and to help them out if possible, maybe even bring them here to Atlantis. She also wants them to meet Anu. Many of my other friends express similar desires. Looks like Earth relocation, or at least tourism, is going to be a "thing."

So we're going to have liaisons going back and forth now, dealing with all of the nightmarish logistics of this. Logan Sangre is another one of those people who is planning to return. He doesn't say if it's permanent, because Logan can make an excellent liaison between two worlds.

Brie Walton is going also. I am sure some of it has to do with Logan, and a whole lot of it has to do with the fact that Brie has strong ties to Earth Union. So maybe in this instance it's a matter of Logan wanting to go back with *her*. In any case, just before they leave, I plan to see Brie and return Logan's knife to her—a love gift of sorts—which now more appropriately belongs with Brie. It has served me well as a reminder of certain things and now it can serve her.

With all these new options opening up to so many of us, my brother George still hasn't decided what he wants to do in terms of a career or profession. However, he now has his own small apartment in the city as he considers the opportunities.

"If I were in college now, my major would still be decidedly undecided," George says, lifting one brow in sarcasm, when he drops by for a visit—as he scratches Khemji behind the ear, and Manala watches with rapt curiosity. Lately, Manala has been noticeably present whenever George is here and, to be honest, George has been present here whenever Manala is around.

"Though, I suppose I could go into Philosophy," George continues. "Or Marketing. Or the philosophy of marketing. Or standup comedy featuring pot-bellied cats."

"You're a people person, Gee One," I say. "You can go into anything."

"My dear *Ter* George," Consul Denu says, with a look of appraisal. "May I suggest exploring diplomacy, starting with a position in the Assembly of the Imperial Executive Council. In fact, I do believe I can recommend you most highly for one of our openings there."

"Or I could go into veterinary medicine," George replies, as the loudly purring Khemji adjusts his position for a more thorough rub.

Speaking of jobs—my Dad gets a position working in the newly opened Earth antiquities wing of the Imperial Poseidon Museum. As an Earth historian he gets to research and lecture and even teach a few classes to the public. He also gets to observe a ridiculous level of competition and hostility among other museums.

Turns out, now that Earth is on the road to recovery, many of the institutions are being rebuilt and resurrected—including the major world museums and art centers back on our home world.

The Louvre is first. The Imperial Poseidon Museum gets an interstellar message about a certain collection it happens to have. "Would you mind kindly returning the Mona Lisa?" the director of the Louvre writes, following it up by a polite video call.

The director of the Imperial Poseidon Museum responds with polite words, declining the request.

Next, the Cairo Museum contacts the Sekar Mehet Museum in New Deshret and asks for the Gold Mask of Tutankhamen.

"We don't have the Gold Mask of Tutankhamen," the director of that institution replies archly. "And even if we did, we would not consider parting with such property under any circumstances."

"Then *who* has the Mask of Tutankhamen?" Cairo asks with indignation.

"We have no notion, and please do not ask again," the director replies.

"How can you *lose* Tutankhamen? We have every record indicating you took the Mask of Tutankhamen when you appropriated Vincent van Gogh under questionable interplanetary circumstances."

"We did not appropriate, it was a rescue operation of your valuable cultural heritage, and Atlantis certainly does not need to explain its benevolent actions to an inferior intellect such as yours."

"Only an inferior intellect would endeavor to misplace the Mask of Tutankhamen!"

"Have you tried asking those pedantic *chazufs* at the Imperial Poseidon Museum? I assure you, it is highly likely they can assist you with your *hoohvak* request because, once and for all, we at Sekar Mehet do *not* have any *shar-ta-haak* Mask of your *shebet* Tutankhamen!"

This goes on for weeks, and then of course we have the British Museum, the Vatican, the National Gallery of London, the Hermitage and the Tretiakov Gallery in Russia, the Museo del Prado, the Met, and endless others—all start clamoring for their works of art to be returned immediately.

There is some kind of Earth class action suit presented to the Atlantis international art community, and a very insistent message full of harsh language comes in to the legal departments of each venerable institution.

The message is returned in kind with some harsh language in both *Atlanteo* and English, in addition to the local language of the Earth country in question.

Then, there is an interstellar conference call, replete with lawyers, arbiters, and mediators, and much shouting is done in *Atlanteo*, Deshi, English, and many other Earth tongues. Finally, a short text arrives, signed by every director of every art institution on Earth.

"Earth to Atlantis. What would it take? Earth wants its artifacts back."

Epilogue

Day One. Or maybe, Day One Thousand and One in my Book of Everything.

I decided today is a day when I begin writing down the events of my crazy, amazing life, both on Earth and now here on my new home, Atlantis.

There is just so much to tell.

I'm writing this a few years after the main events that I'm going to describe, just because it took me all that time to get my act together, and so, bear with me here as I try to remember all the fun and the not-so-fun stuff that happened.

First, let me tell you my name. I am Gwen.

Gwen, Gwen, Gwen.

Gwen Lark who is Kassiopei who is Imperatris who is a silly numbskull on occasion.

Like, right this minute—pardon me, daydream—the kids are screaming and I really need to write this. . . .

Okay, yes, the kids. You know how once I promised Aeson we'll have half a dozen kids?

It wasn't too far off. We have *five*.

First, there's Margot Arlenari, the eldest, and she's five. Yes, Atlanteans don't exactly do middle names but hey, I'm Imperatris, so who's going to stop me?

Then there's the twins, three and a half—Romhutat Charles and Suval Gordon.

Finally, the babies, Oalla Ann who's two, and the precious bundle of newborn screaming joy, Erita Hasmik—*oh, for God's sake, Aeson, can you please go check the baby, I am trying to write this thing!*

Okay, I'm back—Aeson was telling me something, and the grown man is covered with baby food goo, so of course I got interrupted again.

Anyway, what was I saying?

Oh, yes, I am Gwen Lark who is Kassiopei who is Imperatris who is occasionally someone who dabbles in Starlight.

Oh no—I think someone is being *disruptive* again. Holy moly, what did Rommi do this time? Or was that Suvi? *Aeson? Holy crap on a stick!*

Be right back.

As you can see, this Book of Everything is going to take a while.

The End of SURVIVE: The Atlantis Grail, Book Four

Actually, the Beginning

Can't get enough of Gwen and Aeson?
Don't worry, the TAG novellas are coming!

Also, a new <u>prequel series</u> exploring the events of Ancient Atlantis, 12,500 years ago, begins in
Dawn of the Atlantis Grail
Coming soon!

About the Author

Vera Nazarian is a two-time Nebula Award® Finalist, a Dragon Award 2018 Finalist, and a member of Science Fiction and Fantasy Writers of America. She immigrated to the USA from the former USSR as a kid, sold her first story at 17, and has been published in numerous anthologies and magazines, honorably mentioned in Year's Best volumes, and translated into eight languages.

Vera made her novelist debut with the critically acclaimed *Dreams of the Compass Rose,* followed by *Lords of Rainbow.* Her novella *The Clock King and the Queen of the Hourglass* made the 2005 Locus Recommended Reading List. Her debut collection *Salt of the Air* contains the 2007 Nebula Award-nominated "The Story of Love." Recent work includes the 2008 Nebula Finalist novella *The Duke in His Castle,* science fiction collection *After the Sundial* (2010), *The Perpetual Calendar of Inspiration* (2010), three Jane Austen parodies, *Mansfield Park and Mummies* (2009), *Northanger Abbey and Angels and Dragons* (2010), and *Pride and Platypus: Mr. Darcy's Dreadful Secret* (2012), all part of her *Supernatural Jane Austen Series,* a parody of self-help and supernatural relationships advice, *Vampires are from Venus, Werewolves are from Mars: A Comprehensive Guide to Attracting Supernatural Love* (2012), *Cobweb Bride Trilogy* (2013), and the four books in the bestselling international cross-genre phenomenon series *The Atlantis Grail,* now optioned for development as a feature film and/or TV series, *Qualify* (2014), *Compete* (2015), *Win* (2017), and *Survive* (2020).

After many years in Los Angeles, Vera now lives in a small town in Vermont. She uses her Armenian sense of humor and her Russian sense of suffering to bake conflicted pirozhki and make art.

In addition to being a writer, philosopher, and award-winning artist, she is also the publisher of Norilana Books.

Official website:
veranazarian.com

The Atlantis Grail Fan Discussion Forum:
atlantisgrail.proboards.com

Astra Daimon and Shoelace Girls (Facebook fan group):
facebook.com/groups/adasg/

TAG Fandom website:
tag.fan

Acknowledgements

There are so many of you whose unwavering, loving support helped me bring this book to life. My gratitude is boundless, and I thank you with all my heart (and in alphabetical order, because in any other way lies madness)!

To my absolutely brilliant first readers, advisors, topic experts, editors, proofreaders, fandom moderators, and friends, Dorothy Kent, Elanor Dean, Elizabeth Logotheti, Heather Dryer, Jeanne Miller, Jeremy Frank, NASA, Katherine Akulicz, Marie Estock, Nancy Huett, Nydia Fernandez Burdick, Roby James, Shelley Bruce, Susan Franzblau, Susan Macdonald, Teri N. Sears, West Yarbrough McDonough, Will Toohey, with a special thanks to Dr. Michelle Thaller, NASA. Any astrophysics and science mistakes are all mine.

To the lovely and wonderful group of Vermont writers and friends, Anne Stuart, Ellen Jareckie, Lina Gimble, and Valerie Gillen.

To all the wonderful and enthusiastic members of the "Astra Daimon and Shoelace Girls" Facebook group and the official TAG Discussion Forum Members including "forum member username Dave46."

To my awesome and fabulous Wattpad friends and fans who kept reading each preview chapter and making me smile, laugh, and otherwise delight in your hilarious, stunning, amazing, and insightful responses to the story! Thank you immensely!

If I've forgotten or missed anyone, the fault is mine; please know that I love and appreciate you all.

Finally, I would like to thank all of you dear reader friends, who decided to take my hand and step into my world of the Atlantis Grail.

My deepest thanks to all for your support!

Printed in the USA
CPSIA information can be obtained
at www.ICGtesting.com
LVHW040301140524
780142LV00011B/427